NOBLE HOUSE

'I swear by the Lord God that whomsoever
produces the other half of any of these coins I
will grant him whatsoever he asks.'

Dirk Struan, June 10th, 1841

That was the promise made by the first of the
tai-pans of the Noble House, the oldest and most
important trading house in Hong Kong, and it
was to be honoured by all the tai-pans to follow.
Now it was up to Ian Dunross to fulfil the
ancient pledge.

JAMES CLAVELL

James Clavell is a half-Irish Englishman who was born in Australia and now lives mostly in Canada and the States. He was brought up in England and served as a Captain in the Royal Artillery during the war. In 1942 he was captured by the Japanese and sent to Changi. His first bestselling novel, KING RAT, is based upon his experiences there.

After the war James Clavell went into the film business and has written the screenplays of such highly successful films as *The Great Escape*. He has written, produced and directed four films, including *To Sir With Love* and *The Last Valley*. KING RAT was followed by TAI-PAN, an even greater bestseller which spent nearly a year on the American bestseller lists. After this came SHOGUN, James Clavell's record breaking epic novel set in feudal Japan which has recently been filmed for Paramount.

NOBLE HOUSE
is the fourth novel in the Asian Saga that
so far consists of:

All novels are available
in Coronet Books

NOBLE HOUSE

A novel of Hong Kong
by

JAMES CLAVELL

Coronet Books
Hodder and Stoughton

Copyright © 1981 by James Clavell

First published in Great Britain 1981 by
Hodder and Stoughton Ltd.

Coronet edition 1981
Second impression 1982

British Library C.I.P.

Clavell, James
  Noble house.
  I. Title
  823'.914[F]   PR6053.L365

  ISBN 0-340-26877-8

Printed and bound in Great Britain for
Hodder and Stoughton Paperbacks, a
division of Hodder and Stoughton Ltd.,
Mill Road, Dunton Green, Sevenoaks,
Kent (Editorial Office: 47 Bedford
Square, London, WC1 3DP) by
Richard Clay (The Chaucer Press), Ltd.,
Bungay, Suffolk. Photoset by
Rowland Phototypesetting Ltd.,
Bury St Edmunds, Suffolk.

I would like to offer this
work as a tribute to Her
Britannic Majesty, Elizabeth II,
to the people of Her Crown
Colony of Hong Kong—*and
perdition to their enemies*.

Of course this is a novel. It is peopled with imaginary persons and companies and no reference to any person or company that was, or is, part of Hong Kong or Asia is intended.

I would also like to apologize at once to all Hong Kong *yan*—all Hong Kong *persons*—for rearranging their beautiful city, for taking incidents out of context, for inventing people and places and streets and companies and incidents that, hopefully, may appear to have existed but have never existed, for this, truly, is a story. . . .

Contents

June 8, 1960

Prologue

11:45 P.M.:

His name was Ian Dunross and in the torrential rain he drove his old MG sports car cautiously around the corner into Dirk's Street that skirted the Struan Building on the waterfront of Hong Kong. The night was dark and foul. Throughout the Colony—here on Hong Kong Island, across the harbor in Kowloon and the New Territories that were part of the China Mainland—streets were almost totally deserted, everyone and everything battened down, waiting for Typhoon Mary. The number nine storm warning had been hoisted at dusk and already eighty- to a hundred-knot gusts came out of the tempest that stretched a thousand miles southward to send the rain horizontal against the roofs and hillsides where tens of thousands of squatters huddled defenseless in their shanty-towns of makeshift hovels.

Dunross slowed, blinded, the wipers unable to cope with the quantity of rain, the wind tearing at the canvas roof and side screens. Then the wind-shield cleared momentarily. At the end of Dirk's Street, directly ahead, was Connaught Road and the praya, then sea walls and the squat bulk of the Golden Ferry Terminal. Beyond in the vast, well-protected harbor, half a thousand ships were snug with all anchors out.

Ahead on the praya, he saw an abandoned street stall ripped bodily off the ground by a gust and hurled at a parked car, wrecking it. Then the car and the stall were sent skittering out of sight. His wrists were very strong and he held the wheel against the eddies that trembled his car violently. The car was old but well kept, the souped-up engine and brakes perfect. He waited, his heart beating nicely, loving the storm, then eased up onto

15

the sidewalk to park in the lee, well against the building, and got out.

He was fair-haired with blue eyes, in his early forties, lean and trim and he wore an old raincoat and cap. Rain drenched him as he hurried along the side street then ducked around the corner to hurry for the main entrance of the twenty-two-story building. Over the huge doorway was the Struan crest—the Red Lion of Scotland entwined with the Green Dragon of China. Gathering himself he strode up the broad steps and went in.

'Evening, Mr. Dunross,' the Chinese concierge said.

'The tai-pan sent for me.'

'Yes sir.' The man pressed the elevator button for him.

When the elevator stopped, Dunross walked across the small hall, knocked and went into the penthouse living room. 'Evening, tai-pan,' he said with cold formality.

Alastair Struan was leaning against the fine fireplace. He was a big, ruddy, well-kept Scotsman with a slight paunch and white hair, in his sixties, and he had ruled Struan's for eleven years. 'Drink?' He waved a hand at the Dom Pérignon in the silver bucket.

'Thank you.' Dunross had never been in the tai-pan's private quarters before. The room was spacious and well furnished, with Chinese lacquer and good carpets, old oils of their early clipper ships and steamers on the walls. The big picture windows that would normally overlook all Hong Kong, the harbor and Kowloon across the harbor were now black and rain streaked.

He poured. 'Health,' he said formally.

Alastair Struan nodded and, equally coldly, raised his glass in return. 'You're early.'

'Five minutes early is on time, tai-pan. Isn't that what Father hammered into me? Is it important that we meet at midnight?'

'Yes. It's part of our custom. Dirk's custom.'

Dunross sipped his wine, waiting in silence. The antique ship's clock ticked loudly. His excitement increased, not knowing what to expect. Over the fireplace was a marriage portrait of a young girl. This was Tess Struan who had married Culum, second tai-pan and son of their founder Dirk Struan, when she was sixteen.

16

Dunross studied it. A squall dashed the windows. 'Filthy night,' he said.

The older man just looked at him, hating him. The silence grew. Then the old clock chimed eight bells, midnight.

There was a knock on the door.

'Come in,' Alastair Struan said with relief, glad that now they could begin.

The door was opened by Lim Chu, the tai-pan's personal servant. He stepped aside to admit Phillip Chen, compradore of Struan's, then closed the door after him.

'Ah, Phillip, you're on time as usual,' Alastair Struan said, trying to sound jovial. 'Champagne?'

'Thank you, tai-pan. Yes, thank you. Good evening, Ian Struan Dunross,' Phillip Chen said to the younger man with unusual formality, his English very upper-class British. He was Eurasian, in his late sixties, spare, rather more Chinese than European, a very handsome man with gray hair and high cheekbones, fair skin, and dark, very dark Chinese eyes. 'Dreadful night, what?'

'Yes, it is indeed, Uncle Chen,' Dunross replied, using the polite Chinese form of address for Phillip, liking him and respecting him as much as he despised his cousin, Alastair.

'They say this typhoon's going to be a bastard.' Alastair Struan was pouring the champagne into fine glasses. He handed Phillip Chen a glass first, then Dunross. 'Health!'

They drank. A rain squall rattled the windows. 'Glad I'm not afloat tonight,' Alastair Struan said thoughtfully. 'So, Phillip, here you are again.'

'Yes, tai-pan. I'm honored. Yes, very honored.' He sensed the violence between the two men but dismissed it. Violence is a pattern, he thought, when a tai-pan of the Noble House hands over power.

Alastair Struan sipped again, enjoying the wine. At length he said, 'Ian, it's our custom that there be a witness to a handing over from tai-pan to tai-pan. It's always—and only—our current compradore. Phillip, how many times does this make?'

'I've been witness four times, tai-pan.'

'Phillip has known almost all of us. He knows too many of our secrets. Eh, old friend?' Phillip Chen just smiled. 'Trust him, Ian. His counsel's wise. You can trust him.'

17

As much as any tai-pan should trust anyone, Dunross thought grimly. 'Yes sir.'

Alastair Struan set down his glass. 'First: Ian Struan Dunross, I ask you formally, do you want to be tai-pan of Struan's?'

'Yes sir.'

'You swear by God that all of these proceedings will be kept secret by you and not divulged to anyone but your successor?'

'Yes sir.'

'Swear it formally.'

'I swear by God these proceedings will be secret and never divulged to anyone but my successor.'

'Here.' The tai-pan handed him a parchment, yellow with age. 'Read it aloud.'

Dunross took it. The writing was spidery, but perfectly legible. He glanced at the date—August 30, 1841—his excitement soaring. 'Is this Dirk Struan's writing?'

'Aye. Most of it—part was added by his son, Culum Struan. Of course we've photocopies in case of damage. Read it!'

'"My Legacy shall bind every tai-pan that succeedeth me and he shall read it aloud and shall swear before God in front of witnesses in the manner set forth by me, Dirk Struan, founder of Struan and Company, to accept them, and to ever keep them secret, prior to taking to himself my mantle. I require this to ensure a pleasing continuity and in anticipation of difficulties which will, in the following years, beset my successors because of the blood I have spilled, because of my debts of honor, and because of the vagaries of the ways of China to which we are wedded, which are without doubt unique on this earth. This is my Legacy:

'"First: There shall be only one tai-pan at one time and he hath total, absolute authority over the Company, power to employ or remove from employment all others, authority over all our captains and our ships and companies wherever they may be. The tai-pan is always alone, that being the joy and the hurt of it. His privacy must be guarded by all and his back protected by all. Whatsoever he orders, it shall be obeyed, and no committees or courts or inner circles shall ever be formed or allowed in the Company to curb this absolute power.

'"Second: When the tai-pan stands on the quarterdeck of any of our ships he takes precedence over the captain thereof, and

18

his battle orders or sailing orders are law. All captains will be so sworn before God, before appointment to any of our ships.

'"Third: The tai-pan alone chooses his successor who shall be selected only from an Inner Court of six men. Of these, one shall be our comprador who shall, in perpetuity, be from the House of Chen. The other five shall be worthy to be tai-pan, shall be good men and true with at least five whole years of service in the Company as China Traders, and shall be wholesome in spirit. They must be Christian and must be kinsmen to the clan Struan by birth or marriage—my line and my brother Robb's line not taking precedence, unless by fortitude or qualities over and above all others. This Inner Court may be advisors to the tai-pan if he so desires, but let it be said again, the vote of the tai-pan shall weight seven against one for each of them.

'"Fourth: If the tai-pan be lost at sea, or killed in battle, or vanished for six lunar months, before he hath his successor chosen, then the Inner Court shall elect one of their members to succeed, each having one vote, except the vote of the comprador shall count four. The tai-pan shall then be sworn in the same manner set forth before his fellows—those who voted against his election in open ballot being expelled at once, without remuneration, from the Company forever.

'"Fifth: Election to the Inner Court, or removal therefrom, shall be solely at the tai-pan's pleasure and, on his retirement which shall be at a time when it pleasures him, he shall take no more than ten parts of every hundred of all value for himself, except that all our ships shall always be excluded from any valuation . . . our ships, their captains and their crews being our lifeblood and our lifeline into future times.

'"Sixth: Each tai-pan shall approve the election of the comprador. The comprador shall acknowledge in writing prior to his election that he may be removed at any time, without need for explanations, that he will step aside should the tai-pan wish it.

'"Last: The tai-pan shall swear his successor, whom he alone chooses, in the presence of the comprador using the words set down under my hand in our family Bible, here in Hong Kong, this thirtieth day of August in the year of our Lord 1841.'"

Dunross exhaled. 'It's signed by Dirk Struan and witnessed by—I can't read the chop characters, sir, they're archaic.'

Alastair glanced at Phillip Chen who said, 'The first witness is my grandfather's foster father, Chen Sheng Arn, our first compradore. The second, my great-aunt, T'Chung Jin May-may.'

'Then the legend's true!' Dunross said.

'Some of it. Yes, some of it.' Phillip Chen added, 'Talk to my auntie Sarah. Now that you're to be tai-pan she'll tell you lots of secrets. She's eighty-four this year. She remembers my grandfather, Sir Gordon Chen, very well, and Duncan and Kate T'Chung, May-may's children by Dirk Struan. Yes. She remembers many things . . .'

Alastair Struan went over to the lacquered bureau and very carefully picked out the heavy threadbare Bible. He put on his spectacles and Dunross felt the hackles on his neck rise. 'Repeat after me: I, Ian Struan Dunross, kinsman to the Struans, Christian, sweareth before God in the presence of Alastair McKenzie Duncan Struan, eleventh tai-pan, and Phillip T'Chung Sheng Chen, fourth compradore, that I shall obey all the Legacy read out by me in their presence here in Hong Kong, that I shall further bind the Company to Hong Kong and to the China trade, that I shall maintain my main place of business here in Hong Kong while tai-pan, that, before God, I assume the promises, responsibility and the gentleman's word of honor of Dirk Struan to his eternal friend Chen-tse Jin Arn, also known as Jin-qua, or to his successors; further, that I w—'

'What promises?'

'You swear before God, blind, like all the tai-pans did before you! You'll learn soon enough what you inherit.'

'And if I won't?'

'You know the answer to that!'

The rain was battering the windows and its violence seemed to Dunross to equal the thumping in his chest as he weighed the insanity of such an open-ended commitment. But he knew he could not be tai-pan unless he did, and so he said the words and made the commitment before God, and continued to say the words read out to him.

'. . . further that I will use all powers, and any means, to keep the Company steadfast as the First House, the Noble House of Asia, that I swear before God to commit any deed necessary to vanquish, destroy and cast out from Asia the company called Brock and Sons and particularly my enemy, the founder, Tyler

Brock, his son Morgan, their heirs or any of their line excepting only Tess Brock and her issue, the wife of my son Culum, from the face of Asia. . . .' Dunross stopped again.

'When you've finished you can ask any questions you want,' Alastair Struan said. 'Finish it!'

'Very well. Lastly: I swear before God that my successor as tai-pan will also be sworn, before God, to all of this Legacy, so help me God!'

Now the silence was broken only by the rain slashing the windows. Dunross could feel the sweat on his back.

Alastair Struan put down the Bible and took off his spectacles. 'There, it's done.' Tautly he put out his hand. 'I'd like to be the first to wish you well, tai-pan. Anything I can do to help, you have.'

'And I'm honored to be second, tai-pan,' Phillip Chen said with a slight bow, equally formally.

'Thank you.' Dunross's tension was great.

'I think we all need a drink,' Alastair Struan said. 'With your permission, I'll pour,' he added to Dunross with untoward formality. 'Phillip?'

'Yes, tai-pan. I—'

'No. Ian's tai-pan now.' Alastair Struan poured the champagne and gave the first glass to Dunross.

'Thank you,' Dunross said, savoring the compliment, knowing nothing had changed. 'Here's to the Noble House,' he said, raising his glass.

The three men drank, then Alastair Struan took out an envelope. 'This is my resignation from the sixty-odd chairmanships, managing directorships and directorships that automatically go with the tai-pan position. Your appointment in my stead is equally automatic. By custom I become chairman of our London subsidiary—but you can terminate that anytime you wish.'

'It's terminated,' Dunross said at once.

'Whatever you say,' the old man muttered, but his neck was purple.

'I think you'd be more useful to Struan's as deputy chairman of the First Central Bank of Edinburgh.'

Struan looked up sharply. 'What?'

'That's one of our appointments, isn't it?'

'Yes,' Alastair Struan said. 'Why that?'

I'm going to need help. Struan's goes public next year.'

Both men stared at him, astounded. 'What!'

'We're going publ—'

'We've been a private company for 132 years!' the old man roared. 'Jesus bloody Christ I've told you a hundred times that's our strength, with no god-cursed stockholders or outsiders prying into our private affairs!' His face was flushed and he fought to control his anger. 'Don't you ever listen?'

'All the time. Very carefully,' Dunross said in an unemotional voice. 'The only way we can survive is to go public . . . that's the only way we can get the capital we need.'

'Talk to him, Phillip—get some sense into him.'

Nervously the compradore said, 'How will this affect the House of Chen?'

'Our formal compradore system is ended from tonight.' He saw Phillip Chen's face go white but he continued, 'I have a plan for you—in writing. It changes nothing, and everything. Officially you'll still be compradore, unofficially we'll operate differently. The major change is that instead of making about a million a year, in ten years your share will bring you 20, in fifteen years about 30.'

'Impossible!' Alastair Struan burst out.

'Our net worth today's about 20 million U.S. In ten years it'll be 200 million and in fifteen, with joss, it'll be 400 million—and our yearly turnover approaching a billion.'

'You've gone mad,' Struan said.

'No. The Noble House is going international—the days of being solely a Hong Kong trading company are gone forever.'

'Remember your oath, by God! We're Hong Kong based!'

'I won't forget. Next: What responsibility do I inherit from Dirk Struan?'

'It's all in the safe. Written down in a sealed envelope marked "The Legacy." Also the Hag's "Instructions to future tai-pans."'

'Where's the safe?'

'Behind the painting in the Great House. In the study.' Sourly Alastair Struan pointed to an envelope beside the clock on the mantelpiece. 'That contains the special key—and the present combination. You will of course change it. Put the figures into one of the tai-pan's private safety deposit boxes at the bank, in

22

case of accidents. Give Phillip one of the two keys.'

Phillip Chen said, 'By our rules, while you're alive, the bank is obliged to refuse me permission to open it.'

'Next: Tyler Brock and his sons—those bastards were obliterated almost a hundred years ago.'

'Aye, the legitimate male line was. But Dirk Struan was vindictive and his vengeance reaches out from his grave. There's an up-to-date list of Tyler Brock's descendants, also in the safe. It makes interesting reading, eh Phillip?'

'Yes, yes it does.'

'The Rothwells and the Tomms, Yadegar and his brood, you know about. But Tusker's on the list though he doesn't know it, Jason Plumm, Lord Depford-Smyth and, most of all, Quillan Gornt.'

'Impossible!'

'Not only is Gornt tai-pan of Rothwell-Gornt, our main enemy, but he's also a secret, direct male descendant of Morgan Brock—direct though illegitimate. He's the last of the Brocks.'

'But he's always claimed his great-grandfather was Edward Gornt, the American China Trader.'

'He comes from Edward Gornt all right. But Sir Morgan Brock was really Edward's father and Kristian Gornt his mother. She was an American from Virginia. Of course it was kept secret—society wasn't any more forgiving then than now. When Sir Morgan became tai-pan of Brock's in 1859, he fetched this illegitimate son of his out of Virginia, bought him a partnership in the old American trading firm of Rothwell and Company in Shanghai, and then he and Edward bided their time to destroy us. They almost did—certainly they caused the death of Culum Struan. But then Lochlin and Hag Struan broke Sir Morgan and smashed Brock and Sons. Edward Gornt never forgave us, his descendants never will either—I'd wager they too have a pact with their founder.'

'Does he know we know?'

'I don't know. But he's enemy. His genealogy's in the safe, with all the others. My grandfather was the one who discovered it, quite by chance, during the Boxer Rebellion in '99. The list is interesting, Ian, very. One particular person for you. The head of—'

A sudden violent gust shook the building. One of the ivory

bric-à-brac on the marble table toppled over. Nervously Phillip Chen stood it up. They all stared at the windows, watching their reflections twist nauseatingly as the gusts stretched the huge panes of glass.

'*Tai-fun!*' Phillip muttered, sweat beading him.

'Yes.' They waited breathlessly for the 'Devil Wind' to cease. These sudden squalls came haphazardly from all points of the compass, sometimes gusting to a hundred and fifty knots. In their wake was always devastation.

The violence passed. Dunross went over to the barometer, checked it and tapped it. 980.3.

'Still falling,' he said.

'Christ!'

Dunross squinted at the windows. Now the rain streaks were almost horizontal. '*Lasting Cloud* is due to dock tomorrow night.'

'Yes, but now she'll be hove to somewhere off the Philippines. Captain Moffatt's too canny to get caught,' Struan said.

'I don't agree. Moffatt likes hitting schedules. This typhoon's unscheduled. You . . . he should have been ordered.' Dunross sipped his wine thoughtfully. '*Lasting Cloud* better not get caught.'

Phillip Chen heard the undercurrent of fury. 'Why?'

'We've our new computer aboard and two million pounds worth of jet engines. Uninsured—at least the engines are.' Dunross glanced at Alastair Struan.

Defensively the old man said, 'It was that or lose the contract. The engines are consigned to Canton. You know we can't insure them, Phillip, since they're going to Red China.' Then he added irritably, 'They're, er, they're South American owned and there're no export restrictions from South America to China. Even so, no one's willing to insure them.'

After a pause Phillip Chen said, 'I thought the new computer was coming in March.'

'It was but I managed to jump it forward,' Alastair said.

'Who's carrying the paper on the engines?' Phillip Chen asked.

'We are.'

'That's a lot of risk.' Phillip Chen was very uneasy. 'Don't you agree, Ian?'

Dunross said nothing.

'It was that or lose the contract,' Alastair Struan said, even more irritably. 'We stand to double our money, Phillip. We need the money. But more than that the Chinese need the engines, they made that more than clear when I was in Canton last month. And we need China—they made that clear too.'

'Yes, but 12 million, that's . . . a lot of risk in one ship,' Phillip Chen insisted.

Dunross said, 'Anything we can do to take business away from the Soviets is to our advantage. Besides, it's done. You were saying, Alastair, there's someone on the list I should know about? The head of?'

'Marlborough Motors.'

'Ah,' Dunross said with sudden grim delight. 'I've detested those sods for years. Father and son.'

'I know.'

'So the Nikklins're descendants of Tyler Brock? Well it won't be long before we can wipe them off the list. Good. very good. Do they know they're on Dirk Struan's oblit list?'

'I don't think so.'

'That's even better.'

'I don't agree! You hate young Nikklin because he beat you.' Angrily Alastair Struan stabbed a finger at Dunross. 'It's time you gave up car racing. Leave all the hill climbs and Macao Grand Prix to the semiprofessionals. The Nikklins have more time to spend on their cars, it's their life, and now you've other races to run, more important ones.'

'Macao's amateur and those bastards cheated last year.'

'That was never proved—your engine blew up. A lot of engines blow up, Ian. That was just joss!'

'My car was tampered with.'

'And that was never proved either! For Christ's sake, you talk about bad blood? You're as stupid about some things as Devil Struan himself!'

'Oh?'

'Yes, and—'

Phillip Chen interrupted quickly, wanting an end to the violence in the room. 'If it's so important, please let me see if I can find out the truth. I've sources not available to either of you. My Chinese friends will know, should know, if either Tom or

25

young Donald Nikklin were involved. Of course,' he added delicately, 'if the tai-pan wishes to race, then that's up to the tai-pan. Isn't it, Alastair?'

The older man controlled his rage though his neck was still choleric. 'Yes, yes you're right. Still, Ian, my advice is you cease. They'll be after you even more because they detest you equally.'

'Are there others I should know about—on the list?'

After a pause, Struan said, 'No, not now.' He opened the second bottle and poured as he talked. 'Well, now it's all yours—all the fun and all the sweat. I'm glad to pass everything over to you. After you've been through the safe you'll know the best, and the worst.' He gave them each a glass and sipped his. 'By the Lord Jesus, that's as fine a wine as ever came out of France.'

'Yes,' Phillip Chen said.

Dunross thought Dom Pérignon overpriced and overrated and knew the year, '54, was not a particularly good one. But he held his peace.

Struan went over to the barometer. It read 979.2. 'We're in for a bad one. Well, never mind that. Ian, Claudia Chen has a file for you on important matters, and a complete list of our stockholdings—with names of the nominees. Any questions, have them for me before the day after tomorrow—I'm booked for London then. You'll keep Claudia on, of course.'

'Of course.' Claudia Chen was the second link from tai-pan to tai-pan after Phillip Chen. She was executive secretary to the tai-pan, a distant cousin to Phillip Chen.

'What about our bank—the Victoria Bank of Hong Kong and China?' Dunross asked, savoring the question. 'I don't know our exact holdings.'

'That's always been tai-pan knowledge only.'

Dunross turned to Phillip Chen. 'What's your holding, openly or through nominees?'

The compradore hesitated, shocked.

'In future I'm going to vote your holdings as a block with ours.' Dunross kept his eyes on the compradore's. 'I want to know now and I'll expect a formal transfer of perpetual voting power, in writing, to me and following tai-pans, tomorrow by noon, and first refusal on the shares should you ever decide to sell.'

The silence grew.

'Ian,' Phillip Chen began, 'those shares . . .' But his resolve wavered under the power of Dunross's will. '6 percent . . . a little over 6 percent. I . . . you'll have it as you wish.'

'You won't regret it.' Dunross put his attention on Alastair Struan and the older man's heart missed a beat. 'How much stock have we? How much's held by nominees?'

Alastair hesitated. 'That's tai-pan knowledge only.'

'Of course. But our compradore is to be trusted, absolutely,' Dunross said, giving the old man face, knowing how much it had hurt to be dominated in front of Alastair Struan. 'How much?'

Struan said, '15 percent.'

Dunross gasped and so did Phillip Chen and he wanted to shout, Jesus bloody Christ, we have 15 percent and Phillip another 6 percent and you haven't had the sodding intelligence to use what's got to be a major interest to get us major funding when we're almost bankrupt?

But instead he reached forward and poured the remains of the bottle into the three glasses and this gave him time to stop the pounding of his heart.

'Good,' he said with his flat unemotional voice. 'I was hoping together we'd make it better than ever.' He sipped his wine. 'I'm bringing forward the Special Meeting. To next week.'

Both men looked up sharply. Since 1880, the tai-pans of Struan's, Rothwell-Gornt and the Victoria Bank had, despite their rivalry, met annually in secret to discuss matters that affected the future of Hong Kong and Asia.

'They may not agree to bring the meeting forward,' Alastair said.

'I phoned everyone this morning. It's set for Monday next at 9 A.M. here.'

'Who's coming from the bank?'

'Deputy Chief Manager Havergill—the old man's in Japan then England on leave.' Dunross's face hardened. 'I'll have to make do.'

'Paul's all right,' Alastair said. 'He'll be the next chief.'

'Not if I can help it,' Dunross said.

'You've never liked Paul Havergill, have you, Ian?' Phillip Chen said.

'No. He's too insular, too Hong Kong, too out of date, and too pompous.'

'And he supported your father against you.'

'Yes. But that's not the reason he should go, Phillip. He should go because he's in the way of the Noble House. He's too conservative, far too generous to Asian Properties and I think he's a secret ally of Rothwell-Gornt.'

'I don't agree,' Alastair said.

'I know. But we need money to expand and I intend to get the money. So I intend to use *my* 21 percent very seriously.'

The storm outside had intensified but they did not seem to notice.

'I don't advise you to set your cap against the Victoria,' Phillip Chen said gravely.

'I agree,' Alastair Struan said.

'I won't. Provided *my* bank cooperates.' Dunross watched the rain streaks for a moment. 'By the way, I've also invited Jason Plumm to the meeting.'

'What the hell for?' Struan asked, his neck reddening again.

'Between us and his Asian Properties we—'

'Plumm's on Dirk Struan's oblit list, as you call it, and absolutely opposed to us.'

'Between the four of us we have a majority say in Hong Kong—' Dunross broke off as the phone rang loudly. They all looked at it.

Alastair Struan said sourly, 'It's your phone now, not mine.'

Dunross picked it up. 'Dunross!' He listened for a moment then said, 'No, Mr. Alastair Struan has retired, I'm tai-pan of Struan's now. Yes. Ian Dunross. What's the telex say?' Again he listened. 'Yes, thank you.'

He put down the phone. At length he broke the silence. 'It was from our office in Taipei. *Lasting Cloud* has foundered off the north coast of Formosa. They think she's gone down with all hands. . . .'

1

The police officer was leaning against one corner of the information counter watching the tall Eurasian without watching him. He wore a light tropical suit and a police tie and white shirt, and it was hot within the brightly lit terminal building, the air humid and smell laden, milling noisy Chinese as always. Men, women, children, babes. An abundance of Cantonese, some Asians, a few Europeans.

'Superintendent?'

One of the information girls was offering him a phone. 'It's for you, sir,' she said and smiled prettily, white teeth, dark hair, dark sloe eyes, lovely golden skin.

'Thanks,' he said, noticing that she was Cantonese and new, and did not mind that the reality of her smile was empty, with nothing behind it but a Cantonese obscenity. 'Yes?' he said into the phone.

'Superintendent Armstrong? This is the tower—*Yankee 2*'s just landed. On time.'

'Still Gate 16?'

'Yes. She'll be there in six minutes.'

'Thanks.' Robert Armstrong was a big man and he leaned across the counter and replaced the phone. He noticed her long legs and the curve of her rump in the sleek, just too tight, uniformed *cheong-sam* and he wondered briefly what she would be like in bed. 'What's your name?' he asked, knowing that any Chinese hated to be named to any policeman, let alone European.

'Mona Leung, sir.'

'Thank you, Mona Leung.' He nodded to her, kept his pale

31

blue eyes on her and saw a slight shiver of apprehension go through her. This pleased him. Up yours too, he thought, then turned his attention back to his prey.

The Eurasian, John Chen, was standing beside one of the exits, alone, and this surprised him. Also that he was nervous. Usually John Chen was unperturbable, but now every few moments he would glance at his watch, then up at the arrivals board, then back to his watch again.

Another minute and then we'll begin, Armstrong thought.

He began to reach into his pocket for a cigarette, then remembered that he had given up smoking two weeks ago as a birthday present to his wife, so he cursed briefly and stuck his hands deeper into his pockets.

Around the information counter harassed passengers and meeters-of-passengers rushed up and pushed and went away and came back again, loudly asking the where and when and how and why and where once more in myriad dialects. Cantonese he understood well. Shanghainese and Mandarin a little. A few Chu Chow expressions and most of their swear words. A little Taiwanese.

He left the counter now, a head taller than most of the crowd, a big, broad-shouldered man with an easy, athletic stride, seventeen years in the Hong Kong Police Force, now head of CID—Criminal Investigation Department—of Kowloon.

'Evening, John,' he said. 'How're things?'

'Oh hi, Robert,' John Chen said, instantly on guard, his English American-accented. 'Everything's great, thanks. You?'

'Fine. Your airport contact mentioned to Immigration that you were meeting a special plane. A charter—*Yankee 2*.'

'Yes—but it's not a charter. It's privately owned. By Lincoln Bartlett—the American millionaire.'

'He's aboard?' Armstrong asked, knowing he was.

'Yes.'

'With an entourage?'

'Just his Executive VP—and hatchet man.'

'Mr. Bartlett's a friend?' he asked, knowing he was not.

'A guest. We hope to do business with him.'

'Oh? Well, his plane's just landed. Why don't you come with me? We'll bypass all the red tape for you. It's the least we can do for the Noble House, isn't it?'

'Thanks for your trouble.'

'No trouble.' Armstrong led the way through a side door in the Customs barrier. Uniformed police looked up, saluting him instantly and watched John Chen thoughtfully, recognizing him at once.

'This Lincoln Bartlett,' Armstrong continued with pretended geniality, 'doesn't mean anything to me. Should it?'

'Not unless you were in business,' John Chen said, then rushed on nervously. 'He's nicknamed "Raider"—because of his successful raids and takeovers of other companies, most times much bigger than himself. Interesting man, I met him in New York last year. His conglomerate grosses almost half a billion dollars a year. He says he started in '45 with two thousand borrowed dollars. Now he's into petrochemicals, heavy engineering, electronics, missiles—lots of U.S. Government work—foam, polyurethane foam products, fertilizers—he even has one company that makes and sells skis, sports goods. His group's Par-Con Industries. You name it, he has it.'

'I thought your company owned everything already.'

John Chen smiled politely. 'Not in America,' he said, 'and it is not my company. I'm just a minor stockholder of Struan's, an employee.'

'But you're a director and you're the eldest son of Noble House Chen so you'll be next compradore.' By historic custom the compradore was a Chinese or Eurasian businessman who acted as the exclusive intermediary between the European trading house and the Chinese. All business went through his hands and a little of everything stuck there.

So much wealth and so much power, Armstrong thought, yet with a little luck we can bring you down like Humpty-Dumpty and Struan's with you. Jesus Christ, he told himself, the anticipation sickly sweet, if that happens the scandal's going to blow Hong Kong apart. 'You'll be compradore, like your father and grandfather and great-grandfather before you. Your great-grandfather was the first, wasn't he? Sir Gordon Chen, compradore to the great Dirk Struan who founded the Noble House and damn nearly founded Hong Kong.'

'No. Dirk's compradore was a man called Chen Sheng. Sir Gordon Chen was compradore to Dirk's son, Culum Struan.'

'They were half-brothers, weren't they?'

'So the legend goes.'

'Ah yes, legends—the stuff we feed on. Culum Struan, another legend of Hong Kong. But Sir Gordon, he's a legend too—you're lucky.'

Lucky? John Chen asked himself bitterly. To be descended from an illegitimate son of a Scots pirate—an opium runner, a whoring evil genius and murderer if some of the stories are true—and a Cantonese singsong girl bought out of a filthy little cathouse that still exists in a filthy little Macao alley? To have almost everyone in Hong Kong know your lineage and to be despised for it by both races? 'Not lucky,' he said, trying to be outwardly calm. His hair was gray-flecked and dark, his face Anglo-Saxon and handsome, though a little slack at the jowls, and his dark eyes only slightly Asian. He was forty-two and wore tropicals, impeccably cut as always, with Hermès shoes and Rolex watch.

'I don't agree,' Armstrong said, meaning it. 'To be compradore to Struan's, the Noble House of Asia . . . that's something. Something special.'

'Yes, that's special.' John Chen said it flat. Ever since he could think, he had been bedeviled by his heritage. He could feel eyes watching him—him, the eldest son, the next in line—he could feel the everlasting greed and the envy. It had terrified him continuously, however much he tried to conquer the terror. He had never wanted any of the power or any of the responsibility. Only yesterday he had had another grinding row with his father, worse than ever before. 'I don't want any part of Struan's!' he had shouted. 'For the hundredth time I want to get the hell out of Hong Kong, I want to go back to the States, I want to lead my own life, as I want, where I want, and how I want!'

'For the thousandth time, you'll listen to me. I sent you to Am—'

'Let me run our American interests, Father. Please. There's more than enough to do! You could let me have a couple of mill—'

'*Ayeeyah* you will listen to me! It's here, here in Hong Kong and Asia we make our money! I sent you to school in America to prepare the family for the modern world. You are prepared, it's your duty to the fam—'

'There's Richard, Father, and young Kevin—Richard's ten

34

times the businessman I am and chomping at the bit. What about Uncle Jam—?'

'You'll do as I say! Good God, you know this American Bartlett is vital to us. We need your knowl—'

'—Uncle James or Uncle Thomas. Uncle James'd be the best for you; best for the family and the bes—'

'You're my eldest son. You're the next head of the family and the next compradore!'

'I won't be, by God!'

'Then you won't get another copper cash!'

'And that won't be much of a change! We're all kept on a pittance, whatever outsiders think! What are you worth? How many millions? Fifty? Seventy? A hun—?'

'Unless you apologize at once and finish with all this nonsense, finish with it once and for all, I'll cut you off right now! Right now!'

'I apologize for making you angry but I'll never change! Never!'

'I'll give you until my birthday. Eight days. Eight days to become a dutiful son. That's my last word. Unless you become obedient by my birthday I'll chop you and your line off our tree forever! Now get out!'

John Chen's stomach twisted uneasily. He hated the interminable quarreling, his father apoplectic with rage, his wife in tears, his children petrified, his stepmother and brothers and cousins all gloating, wanting him gone, all of his sisters, most of his uncles, all their wives. Envy, greed. The hell with it and them, he thought. But Father's right about Bartlett, though not the way he thinks. No. This one is for me. This deal. Just this one then I'll be free forever.

They were almost through the long, brightly lit Customs Hall now.

'You going racing Saturday?' John Chen asked.

'Who isn't!' The week before, to the ecstasy of all, the immensely powerful Turf Club with its exclusive monopoly on horse racing—the only legal form of gambling allowed in the Colony—had put out a special bulletin: 'Though our formal season does not start this year until October 5, with the kind permission of our illustrious Governor, Sir Geoffrey Allison, the Stewards have decided to declare Saturday, August 24 a

Very Special Race Day for the enjoyment of all and as a salute to our hardworking population who are bearing the heavy weight of the second worst drought in our history with fortitude. . . .'

'I hear you've got Golden Lady running in the fifth,' Armstrong said.

'The trainer says she's got a chance. Please come by Father's box and have a drink with us. I could use some of your tips. You're a great punter.'

'Just lucky. But my ten dollars each way hardly compares with your ten thousand.'

'But that's only when we've one of our horses running. Last season was a disaster. . . . I could use a winner.'

'So could I.' Oh Christ how I need a winner, Armstrong thought. But you, Johnny Chen, it doesn't matter a twopenny tick in hell if you win or lose ten thousand or a hundred thousand. He tried to curb his soaring jealousy. Calm down, he told himself. Crooks're a fact and it's your job to catch them if you can—however rich, however powerful—and to be content with your rotten pay when every street corner's groaning with free silver. Why envy this bastard—he's for the chopper one way or another. 'Oh by the way, I sent a constable to your car to take it through the gate. It'll be waiting at the gangway for you and your guests.'

'Oh, that's great, thanks. Sorry for the trouble.'

'No trouble. It's a matter of face. Isn't it? I thought it must be pretty special for you to come yourself.' Armstrong could not resist another barb. 'As I said, nothing's too much trouble for the Noble House.'

John Chen kept his polite smile but screw you, he thought. We tolerate you because of what you are, a very important cop, filled with envy, heavily in debt, surely corrupt and you know nothing about horses. Screw you in spades. *Dew neh loh moh* on all your generations, John Chen thought, but he kept the obscenity hidden carefully, for though Armstrong was roundly hated by all Hong Kong *yan*, John Chen knew from long experience that Armstrong's ruthless, vengeful cunning was worthy of a filthy Manchu. He reached up to the half-coin he wore on a thin leather thong around his neck. His fingers trembled as they touched the metal through his shirt. He shivered involuntarily.

36

'What's the matter?' Armstrong asked.

'Nothing. Nothing at all.' Get hold of yourself, John Chen thought.

Now they were through the Customs Hall and into the Immigration area, the night dark outside. Lines of anxious, unsettled, tired people waited in front of the neat, small desks of the cold-faced, uniformed Immigration officers. These men saluted Armstrong. John Chen felt their searching eyes.

As always, his stomach turned queasy under their scrutiny even though he was safe from their probing questions. He held a proper British passport, not just a second-class Hong Kong passport, also an American Green Card—the Alien Card—that most priceless of possessions that gave him free access to work and play and live in the U.S.A., all the privileges of a born American except the right to vote. Who needs to vote, he thought, and stared back at one of the men, trying to feel brave, but still feeling naked under the man's gaze.

'Superintendent?' One of the officers was holding up a phone. 'It's for you, sir.'

He watched Armstrong walk back to take the call and he wondered what it would be like to be a policeman with so much opportunity for so much graft, and, for the millionth time, what it would be like to be all British or all Chinese, and not a Eurasian despised by both.

He watched Armstrong listening intently, then heard him say above the hubbub, 'No, just stall. I'll deal with it personally. Thanks, Tom.'

Armstrong came back. 'Sorry,' he said, then headed past the Immigration cordon, up a small corridor and into the VIP Lounge. It was neat and expansive, with bar facilities and a good view of the airport and the city and the bay. The lounge was empty except for two Immigration and Customs officers and one of Armstrong's men waiting beside Gate 16—a glass door that let out onto the floodlit tarmac. They could see the 707 coming onto her parking marks.

'Evening, Sergeant Lee,' Armstrong said. 'All set?'

'Yes sir. *Yankee 2*'s just shutting down her engines.' Sergeant Lee saluted again and opened the gate for them.

Armstrong glanced at John Chen, knowing the neck of the trap was almost closed. 'After you.'

'Thanks.' John Chen walked out onto the tarmac.

Yankee 2 towered over them, its dying jets now a muted growl. A ground crew was easing the tall, motor-driven gangway into place. Through the small cockpit windows they could see the dimly lit pilots. To one side, in the shadows, was John Chen's dark blue Silver Cloud Rolls, the uniformed Chinese chauffeur standing beside the door, a policeman nearby.

The main cabin door of the aircraft swung open and a uniformed steward came out to greet the two airport officials who were waiting on the platform. He handed one of the officials a pouch with the airplane's documents and arrival manifests, and they began to chat affably. Then they all stopped. Deferentially. And saluted politely.

The girl was tall, smart, exquisite and American.

Armstrong whistled quietly. '*Ayeeyah!*'

'Bartlett's got taste,' John Chen muttered, his heart quickening. They watched her come down the stairs, both men lost in masculine musings.

'You think she's a model?'

'She moves like one. A movie star, maybe?'

John Chen walked forward. 'Good evening. I'm John Chen of Struan's. I'm meeting Mr. Bartlett and Mr. Tchuluck.'

'Oh yes of course, Mr. Chen. This's very kind of you, sir, particularly on a Sunday. I'm pleased to meet you. I'm K. C. Tcholok. Linc says if you . . .'

'Casey Tchuluck?' John Chen gaped at her. 'Eh?'

'Yes,' she said, her smile nice, patiently passing over the mispronunciation. 'You see my initials are *K.C.*, Mr. Chen, so *Casey* became my nickname.' She turned her eyes on Armstrong. 'Evening. You're also from Struan's?' Her voice was melodious.

'Oh, er, excuse me, this, this is Superintendent Armstrong,' John Chen stuttered, still trying to recover.

'Evening,' Armstrong said, noticing that she was even more attractive close up. 'Welcome to Hong Kong.'

'Thank you. Superintendent? That's police?' Then the name clicked into place. 'Ah, Armstrong. Robert Armstrong? Chief of CID Kowloon?'

He covered his surprise. 'You're very well informed, Miss Tcholok.'

She laughed. 'Just part of my routine. When I go to a new place, particularly one like Hong Kong, it's my job to be pre-pared . . . so I just sent for your current listings.'

'We don't have published listings.'

'I know. But the Hong Kong Government puts out a government phone book which anyone can buy for a few pennies. I just sent for one of those. All police departments are listed—heads of departments, most with their home numbers—along with every other government office. I got one through your Hong Kong PR office in New York.'

'Who's head of Special Branch?' he asked, testing her.

'I don't know. I don't think that department was listed. Is it?'

'Sometimes.'

A slight frown stood in her eyes. 'You greet all private air-planes, Superintendent?'

'Only those I wish to.' He smiled at her. 'Only those with pretty, well-informed ladies aboard.'

'Something's wrong? There's trouble?'

'Oh no, just routine. Kai Tak's part of my responsibility,' Armstrong said easily. 'May I see your passport, please?'

'Of course.' Her frown deepened as she opened her handbag and handed her U.S. passport over.

Years of experience made his inspection very detailed indeed. 'Born Providence, Rhode Island, November 25, 1936, height 5 feet 8 inches, hair blond, eyes hazel.' Passport's valid with two years left to run. Twenty-six, eh? I'd've guessed younger, though there's a strangeness to her eyes if you look closely.

With apparent haphazardness he flipped carelessly through the pages. Her three-month Hong Kong visa was current and in order. A dozen immigration visa stamps, all England, France, Italy or South American. Except one. USSR, dated July this year. A seven-day visit. He recognized the Moscow frank. 'Sergeant Lee!'

'Yes sir?'

'Get it stamped for her,' he said casually, and smiled down at her. 'You're all cleared. You may stay more or less as long as you like. Towards the end of three months just go to the nearest police station and we'll extend your visa for you.'

'Thanks very much.'

'You'll be with us for a while?'

'That depends on our business deal,' Casey said after a pause. She smiled at John Chen. 'We hope to be in business for a long time.'

John Chen said, 'Yes. Er, we hope so too.' He was still nonplussed, his mind churning. It's surely not possible for Casey Tcholok to be a woman, he thought.

Behind them the steward, Sven Svensen, came bouncing down the stairs, carrying two air suitcases. 'Here you are, Casey. You're sure this's enough for tonight?'

'Yes. Sure. Thanks, Sven.'

'Linc said for you to go on. You need a hand through Customs?'

'No thanks. Mr. John Chen kindly met us. Also, Superintendent Armstrong, head of Kowloon CID.'

'Okay.' Sven studied the policeman thoughtfully for a moment. 'I'd better get back.'

'Everything all right?' she asked.

'I think so.' Sven Svensen grinned. 'Customs're just checking our stocks of booze and cigarettes.' Only four things were subject to any import license or Customs duty in the Colony—gold, liquor, tobacco and gasoline—and only one contraband—apart from narcotics—and totally forbidden: all forms of firearms and ammunition.

Casey smiled up at Armstrong. 'We've no rice aboard, Superintendent. Linc doesn't eat it.'

'Then he's in for a bad time here.'

She laughed, then turned back to Svensen. 'See you tomorrow. Thanks.'

'9 A.M. on the dot!' Svensen went back to the airplane and Casey turned to John Chen.

'Linc said for us not to wait for him. Hope that's all right,' she said.

'Eh?'

'Shall we go? We're booked into the Victoria and Albert Hotel, Kowloon.' She began to pick up her bags but a porter materialized out of the darkness and took them from her. 'Linc'll come later . . . or tomorrow.'

John Chen gawked at her. 'Mr. Bartlett's not coming?'

'No. He's going to stay in the airplane overnight if he can get permission. If not, he'll follow us by cab. In any event he'll join us tomorrow for lunch as arranged. Lunch is still on, isn't it?'

'Oh yes, but . . .' John Chen was trying to get his mind working. 'Then you'll want to cancel the 10 A.M. meeting?'

'Oh no. I'll attend that as arranged. Linc wasn't expected at that meeting. That's just financing—not policy. I'm sure you understand. Linc's very tired, Mr. Chen,' she said. 'He just got back yesterday from Europe.' She looked back at Armstrong. 'The captain asked the tower if Linc could sleep in, Superintendent. They checked with Immigration who said they'd get back to us but I presume our request'll come through channels to you. We'd certainly appreciate it if you'd approve. He's really been on the jet lag trail for too long.'

Armstrong found himself saying, 'I'll chat with him about it.'

'Oh thanks. Thanks very much,' she said, and then to John Chen, 'Sorry for all this trouble, Mr. Chen. Shall we go?' She began to head for Gate 16, the porter following, but John Chen pointed to his Rolls. 'No, this way, Miss Tchu—er, Casey.'

Her eyes widened. 'No Customs?'

'Not tonight,' Armstrong said, liking her. 'A present from Her Majesty's Government.'

'I feel like visiting royalty.'

'All part of the service.'

She got into the car. Lovely smell of leather. And luxury. Then she saw the porter hurrying through the gate into the terminal building. 'But what about my bags?'

'No need to worry about those,' John Chen said irritably. 'They'll be in your suite before you are.'

Armstrong held on to the door for a moment. 'John came with two cars. One for you and Mr. Bartlett—the other for luggage.'

'Two cars?'

'Of course. Don't forget you're in Hong Kong now.'

He watched the car drive off. Linc Bartlett's a lucky man, he thought, and wondered absently why Special Intelligence was interested in her.

'Just meet the airplane and go through her passport personally,' the director of SI had told him this morning. 'And Mr. Lincoln Bartlett's.'

'May I ask why, sir?'

'No, Robert, you may not ask why. You're no longer in this

41

branch—you're in a nice cushy job at Kowloon. A positive sinecure, what?'

'Yes sir.'

'And Robert, kindly don't balls up this operation tonight— there may be a lot of very big names involved. We go to a great deal of trouble to keep you fellows abreast of what the nasties are doing.'

'Yes sir.'

Armstrong sighed as he walked up the gangway followed by Sergeant Lee. *Dew neh loh moh* on all senior officers, particularly the director of SI.

One of the Customs officials was waiting at the top of the gangway with Svensen. 'Evening, sir,' he said. 'Everything's shipshape aboard. There's a .38 with a box of a hundred shells unopened as part of ship's stores. A Verey Light pistol. Also three hunting rifles and a twelve-bore with ammo belonging to Mr. Bartlett. They're all listed on the manifest and I inspected them. There's a locked gun cabinet in the main cabin. Captain has the key.'

'Good.'

'You need me anymore, sir?'

'No, thanks.' Armstrong took the airplane's manifest and began to check it. Lots of wine, cigarettes, tobacco, beer and spirits. Ten cases of Dom Pérignon '59, fifteen Puligny Montrachet '53, nine Château Haut Brion '53. 'No Lafite Rothschild 1916, Mr. Svensen?' he said with a small smile.

'No sir.' Svensen grinned. ''16 was a very bad year. But there's half a case of the 1923. It's on the next page.'

Armstrong flipped the page. More wines and the cigars were listed. 'Good,' he said. 'Of course all this is in bond while you're on the ground.'

'Yes sir. I'd already locked it—your man's tagged it. He said it was okay to leave a twelve-pack of beer in the cooler.'

'If the owner wants to import any of the wines, just let me know. There's no fuss and just a modest contribution to Her Majesty's bottom drawer.'

'Sir?' Svensen was perplexed.

'Eh? Oh, just an English pun. Refers to a lady's bottom drawer in a chest of drawers—where she puts away the things she needs in the future. Sorry. Your passport please.' Svensen's passport was Canadian. 'Thanks.'

'May I introduce you to Mr. Bartlett? He's waiting for you.'

Svensen led the way into the airplane. The interior was elegant and simple. Right off the small hallway was a sitting area with half a dozen deep leather chairs and a sofa. A central door closed off the rest of the airplane, aft In one of the chairs a stewardess was half asleep, her travel bags beside her. Left was the cockpit door. It was open.

The captain and first officer/copilot were in their seats, still going through their paper work.

'Excuse me, Captain. This is Superintendent Armstrong,' Svensen said, and stepped aside.

'Evening, Superintendent,' the captain said. 'I'm Captain Jannelli and this's my copilot, Bill O'Rourke.'

'Evening. May I see your passports please?'

Both pilots had massed international visas and immigration stamps. No Iron Curtain countries. Armstrong handed them to Sergeant Lee for stamping. 'Thank you, Captain. Is this your first visit to Hong Kong?'

'No sir. I was here a couple of times R and R during Korea. And I had a six-month tour with Far Eastern as first officer on their round-the-world route in '56, during the riots.'

'What riots?' O'Rourke asked.

'The whole of Kowloon blew apart. Couple hundred thousand Chinese went on a sudden rampage, rioting, burning. The cops—sorry, the police tried to settle it with patience, then the mobs started killing so the cops, police, they got out a couple of Sten guns and killed half a dozen jokers and everything calmed down very fast. Only police have guns here which is a great idea.' To Armstrong he said, 'I think your guys did a hell of a job.'

'Thank you, Captain Jannelli. Where did this flight emanate?'

'L.A.—Los Angeles. Linc's—Mr. Bartlett's head office's there.'

'Your route was Honolulu, Tokyo, Hong Kong?'

'Yes sir.'

'How long did you stop in Tokyo?'

Bill O'Rourke turned up the flight log at once. 'Two hours and seventeen minutes. Just a refueling stop, sir.'

'Just enough time to stretch your legs?'

Jannelli said, 'I was the only one who got out. I always check my gear, the landing gear, and do an exterior inspection whenever we land.'

'That's a good habit,' the policeman said politely. 'How long are you staying?'

'Don't know, that's up to Linc. Certainly overnight. We couldn't leave before 1400. Our orders're just to be ready to go anywhere at any time.'

'You've a fine aircraft, Captain. You're approved to stay here till 1400. If you want an extension, call Ground Control before that time. When you're ready, just clear Customs through that gate. And would you clear all your crew together, please.'

'Sure. Soon as we're refueled.'

'You and all your crew know the importing of any firearms into the Colony is absolutely forbidden? We're very nervous about firearms in Hong Kong.'

'So am I, Superintendent—anywhere. That's why I've the only key to the gun cabinet.'

'Good. Any problems, please check with my office.' Armstrong left and went into the anteroom, Svensen just ahead.

Jannelli watched him inspect the air hostess's passport. She was pretty, Jenny Pollard. 'Son of a bitch,' he muttered, then added quietly, 'Something stinks around here.'

'Huh?'

'Since when does CID brass check goddamn passports for chrissake? You sure we're not carrying anything curious?'

'Hell no. I always check everything. Including Sven's stores. Of course I don't go through Linc's stuff—or Casey's—but they wouldn't do anything stupid.'

'I've flown him for four years and never once. . . . Even so, something sure as hell stinks.' Jannelli wearily twisted and settled himself in his pilot's seat more comfortably. 'Jesus, I could use a massage and a week off.'

In the anteroom Armstrong was handing the passport to Sergeant Lee who stamped it. 'Thank you, Miss Pollard.'

'Thank you.'

'That's all the crew, sir,' Svensen said. 'Now Mr. Bartlett.'

'Yes, please.'

Svensen knocked on the central door and opened it without

44

waiting. 'Linc, this's Superintendent Armstrong,' he said with easy informality.

'Hi,' Linc Bartlett said, getting up from his desk. He put out his hand. 'May I offer you a drink? Beer?'

'No thanks. Perhaps a cup of coffee.'

Svensen turned for the galley at once. 'Coming up,' he said.

'Make yourself at home. Here's my passport,' Bartlett said. 'Won't be a moment.' He went back to the typewriter and continued tapping the keys with two fingers.

Armstrong studied him leisurely. Bartlett was sandy haired with gray-flecked blue eyes, a strong good-looking face. Trim. Sports shirt and jeans. He checked the passport. Born Los Angeles, October 1, 1922. He looks young for forty, he thought. Moscow franking, same as Casey Tcholok, no other Iron Curtain visits.

His eyes wandered the room. It was spacious, the whole width of the airplane. There was a short central corridor aft with two cabins off it and two toilets. And at the end a final door which he presumed was the master suite.

The cabin was fitted as if it were a communications center. Teletype, international telephone capability, built-in typewriters. An illuminated world time clock on a bulkhead. Filing cabinets, duplicator and a built-in leather-topped desk strewn with papers. Shelves of books. Tax books. A few paperbacks. The rest were war books and books on generals or by generals. Dozens of them. Wellington and Napoleon and Patton, Eisenhower's *Crusade in Europe*, Sun Tzu's *The Art of War* . . .

'Here you are, sir,' broke into Armstrong's inspection.

'Oh, thank you, Svensen.' He took the coffee cup and added a little cream.

Svensen put a fresh, opened can of chilled beer beside Bartlett, picked up the empty, then went back to the galley, closing the door after him. Bartlett sipped the beer from the can, rereading what he had written, then pressed a buzzer. Svensen came at once. 'Tell Jannelli to ask the tower to send this off.' Svensen nodded and left. Bartlett eased his shoulders and swung around in the swivel chair. 'Sorry—I had to get that right off.'

'That's all right, Mr. Bartlett. Your request to stay overnight is approved.'

'Thanks—thanks very much. Could Svensen stay as well?' Bartlett grinned. 'I'm not much of a housekeeper.'

'Very well. How long will your aircraft be here?'

'Depends on our meeting tomorrow, Superintendent. We hope to go into business with Struan's. A week, ten days.'

'Then you'll need an alternate parking place tomorrow. We've another VIP flight coming in at 1600 hours. I told Captain Jannelli to phone Ground Control before 1400 hours.'

'Thanks. Does the head of CID Kowloon usually deal with parking around here?'

Armstrong smiled. 'I like to know what's going on in my division. It's a tedious habit but ingrained. We don't often have private aircraft visiting us—or Mr. Chen meeting someone personally. We like to be accommodating if we can. Struan's owns most of the airport and John's a personal friend. He's an old friend of yours?'

'I spent time with him in New York and L.A. and liked him a lot. Say, Superintendent, this airplane's my comm—' One of the phones rang. Bartlett picked it up. 'Oh hello Charlie, what's happening in New York? . . . Jesus, that's great. How much? . . . Okay Charlie, buy the whole block. . . . Yes, the whole 200,000 shares. . . . Sure, first thing Monday morning, soon as the market opens. Send me a confirm by telex. . . .' Bartlett put the phone down and turned to Armstrong. 'Sorry. Say, Superintendent, this's my communications center and I'll be lost without it. If we park for a week, is it okay to come back and forth?'

'I'm afraid that might be dicey, Mr. Bartlett.'

'Is that yes or no or maybe?'

'Oh that's slang for difficult. Sorry, but our security at Kai Tak's very particular.'

'If you have to put on extra men, I'd be glad to pay.'

'It's a matter of security, Mr. Bartlett, not money. You'll find Hong Kong's phone system first class.' Also it will be far easier for Special Intelligence to monitor your calls, he thought.

'Well, if you can I'd appreciate it.'

Armstrong sipped the coffee. 'This's your first visit to Hong Kong?'

'Yes sir. My first time in Asia. Farthest I've gotten was Guadalcanal, in '43.'

'Army?'

'Sergeant, Engineers. Construction—we used to build anything: hangars, bridges, camps, anything. A great experience.' Bartlett sipped from the can. 'Sure I can't give you a drink?'

'No thanks.' Armstrong finished his cup, began to get up. 'Thanks for the coffee.'

'Now may I ask you a question?'

'Of course.'

'What's Dunross like? Ian Dunross. The head of Struan's?'

'*The* tai-pan?' Armstrong laughed outright. 'That depends whom you ask, Mr. Bartlett. You've never met him?'

'No, not yet. I do tomorrow. At lunch. Why do you call him *the tai-pan?*'

'*Tai-pan* means "supreme leader" in Cantonese—the person with the ultimate power. The European heads of all the old trading companies are all tai-pans to the Chinese. But even among tai-pans there's always the greatest. *The* tai-pan. Struan's is nicknamed the "Noble House" or "Noble *Hong*," *hong* meaning "company." It goes back to the beginning of the China trade and the early days of Hong Kong. Hong Kong was founded in 1841, January 26, actually. The founder of Struan and Company was a legend, still is in some ways—Dirk Struan. Some say he was a pirate, some a prince. In any event he made a fortune smuggling Indian opium into China, then converting that silver into China teas which he shipped to England in a fleet of China clippers. He became a merchant prince, earned the title of *the* tai-pan, and ever since, Struan's has always tried to be first in everything.'

'Are they?'

'Oh a couple of companies dog their heels, Rothwell-Gornt particularly, but yes, I'd say they were first. Certainly not a thing comes into Hong Kong or goes out, is eaten or buried or made without Struan's, Rothwell-Gornt, Asian Properties, Blacs—the Bank of London and China—or the Victoria Bank having a finger in the stew somewhere.'

'And Dunross himself? What's he like?'

Armstrong thought a moment, then said lightly, 'Again it depends very much whom you ask, Mr. Bartlett. I know him just a little, socially—we meet from time to time at the races. I've had two official meetings with him. He's charming, very good at

47

his job. . . . I suppose *brilliant* might sum him up.'

'He and his family own a lot of Struan's?'

'I don't know that for certain. I doubt if anyone does, outside of the family. But his stockholdings aren't the key to the tai-pan's desk. Oh no. Not of Struan's. Of that I'm very certain.' Armstrong locked his eyes on Bartlett's. 'Some say Dunross is ruthless and ready to kill. I know I wouldn't like him as an enemy.'

Bartlett sipped his beer and the little lines beside his eyes crinkled with a curious smile. 'Sometimes an enemy's more valuable than a friend.'

'Sometimes. I hope you have a profitable stay.'

At once Bartlett got up. 'Thanks. I'll see you out.' He opened the door and ushered Armstrong and Sergeant Lee through it, then followed them out of the main cabin door onto the landing steps. He took a deep breath of air. Once again he caught a strangeness on the wind, neither pleasant nor unpleasant, neither odor nor perfume—just strange, and curiously exciting. 'Superintendent, what's that smell? Casey noticed it too, the moment Sven opened the door.'

Armstrong hesitated. Then he smiled. 'That's Hong Kong's very own, Mr. Bartlett. It's money.'

2

'All gods bear witness to the foul luck I'm having tonight,' Four
Finger Wu said and spat on the deck. He was aft, on the high
poop of his oceangoing junk that was moored to one of the great
clusters of boats that sprawled over Aberdeen harbor on the
south coast of Hong Kong Island. The night was hot and humid
and he was playing mah-jong with three of his friends. They
were old and weatherbeaten like himself, all captains of junks
that they owned. Even so, they sailed in his fleet and took
orders from him. His formal name was Wu Sang Fang. He was a
short, illiterate fisherman, with few teeth and no thumb on his
left hand. His junk was old, battered and filthy. He was head of
the seaborne Wu, captain of the fleets, and his flag, the Silver
Lotus, flew on all the four seas.

When it was his turn again, he picked up another of the ivory
tiles. He glanced at it and as it did not improve his hand,
discarded it noisily and spat again. The spittle glistened on the
deck. He wore a ragged old undershirt and black coolie pants,
like his friends, and he had ten thousand dollars riding on this
single game.

'*Ayeeyah*,' Pockmark Tang said, pretending disgust though
the tile he had just picked up made him only one short of a
winning combination—the game somewhat like gin rummy.
'Fornicate all mothers except ours if I don't win!' He discarded a
tile with a flourish.

'Fornicate yours if you win and I don't!' another said and they
all laughed.

'And fornicate those foreign devils from the Golden Mountain if they don't arrive tonight,' Goodweather Poon said.

49

'They'll arrive,' Four Finger Wu told him confidently. 'Foreign devils are glued to schedules. Even so, I sent Seventh Son to the airport to make sure.' He began to pick up a tile but stopped and looked over his shoulder and watched critically as a fishing junk eased past, chugging quietly, heading up the twisting, narrow access channel between the banks of boats toward the neck of the harbor. She had only riding lights, port and starboard. Ostensibly she was just going fishing but this junk was one of his and she was out to intercept a Thai trawler with a cargo of opium. When she was safely passed, he concentrated on the game once more. It was low tide now, but there was deep water around most of the boat islands. From the shore and flats came the stench of rotting seaweed, shellfish and human waste.

Most of the sampans and junks were dark now, their multitudes sleeping. There were a few oil lamps here and there. Boats of all sizes were moored precariously to each other, seemingly without order, with tiny sea alleys between the floating villages. These were the homes of the Tanka and Haklo people—the boat dwellers—who lived their lives afloat, were born afloat and died afloat. Many of these boats never moved from these moorings but stayed locked together until they sank or fell apart, or went down in a typhoon or were burnt in one of the spectacular conflagrations that frequently swept the clusters when a careless foot or hand knocked over a lamp or dropped something inflammable into the inevitable open fires.

'Grandfather!' the youthful lookout called.

'What is it?' Wu asked.

'On the jetty, look! Seventh Son!' The boy, barely twelve, was pointing to the shore.

Wu and the others got up and peered shorewards. The young Chinese was paying off a taxi. He wore jeans and a neat T-shirt and sneakers. The taxi had stopped near the gangway of one of the huge floating restaurants that were moored to the modern jetties, a hundred yards away. There were four of these gaudy floating palaces—three, four or five stories tall—ablaze with lights, splendiferous in scarlet and green and gold with fluted Chinese roofs and gods, gargoyles and dragons.

'You've good eyes, Number Three Grandson. Good. Go and meet Seventh Son.' Instantly the child scurried off, sure-footed across the rickety planks that joined this junk to others. Four

Fingers watched his seventh son head for one of the jetties where ferry sampans that serviced the harbor were clustered. When he saw that the boatman he had sent had intercepted him, he turned his back on the shore and sat down again. 'Come on, let's finish the game,' he said grimly. 'This's my last fornicating hand. I've got to go ashore tonight.'

They played for a moment, picking up tiles and discarding them.

'*Ayeeyah!*' Pockmark Tang said with a shout as he saw the face of the tile that he had just picked up. He slammed it onto the table face upwards with a flourish and laid down his other thirteen hidden tiles that made up his winning hand. 'Look, by all the gods!'

Wu and the others gawked at the hand. 'Pisss!' he said and hawked loudly. 'Piss on all your generations, Pockmark Tang! What luck!'

'One more game? Twenty thousand, Four Finger Wu?' Tang said gleefully, convinced that tonight old devil, Chi Kung, the god of gamblers, was sitting on his shoulder.

Wu began to shake his head, but at that moment a seabird flew overhead and called plaintively. 'Forty,' he said immediately, changing his mind, interpreting the call as a sign from heaven that his luck had changed. 'Forty thousand or nothing! But it'll have to be dice because I've no time now.'

'I haven't got forty cash by all gods, but with the twenty you owe me, I'll borrow against my junk tomorrow when the bank opens and give you all my fornicating profit on our next gold or opium shipment until you're paid, *heya?*'

Goodweather Poon said sourly, 'That's too much on one game. You two fornicators've lost your minds!'

'Highest score, one throw?' Wu asked.

'*Ayeeyah*, you've gone mad, both of you,' Poon said. Nonetheless, he was as excited as the others. 'Where are the dice?'

Wu produced them. There were three. 'Throw for your fornicating future, Pockmark Tang!'

Pockmark Tang spat on his hands, said a silent prayer, then threw them with a shout.

'Oh oh oh,' he cried out in anguish. A four, a three and another four. 'Eleven!' The other men were hardly breathing.

Wu spat on the dice, cursed them, blessed them and threw. A

51

six, a two and a three. 'Eleven! Oh all gods great and small! Again—throw again!'

Excitement gathered on the deck. Pockmark Tang threw. 'Fourteen!'

Wu concentrated, the tension intoxicating, then threw the dice. '*Ayeeyah!*' he exploded, and they all exploded. A six, a four and a two.

'Eeeee,' was all Pockmark Tang could say, holding his belly, laughing with glee as the others congratulated him and commiserated with the loser.

Wu shrugged, his heart still pounding in his chest. 'Curse all seabirds that fly over my head at a time like that!'

'Ah, is that why you changed your mind, Four Finger Wu?'

'Yes—it was like a sign. How many seabirds call as they fly overhead at night?'

'That's right. I would have done the same.'

'Joss!' Then Wu beamed. 'Eeeee, but the gambling feeling's better than the Clouds and the Rain, *heya?*'

'Not at my age!'

'How old are you, Pockmark Tang?'

'Sixty—perhaps seventy. Almost as old as you are.' Haklos did not have permanent records of births, like all village land dwellers. 'I don't feel more than thirty.'

'Have you heard the Lucky Medicine Shop at Aberdeen Market's got a new shipment of Korean ginseng, some of it a hundred years old! That'll stick fire in your stalk!'

'His stalk's all right, Goodweather Poon! His third wife's with child again!' Wu grinned toothlessly and pulled out a big roll of 500-dollar notes. He began counting, his fingers nimble even though his left thumb was missing. Years ago it had been hacked off in a fight with river pirates during a smuggling expedition. He stopped momentarily as his number seven son came on deck. The young man was tall for a Chinese, twenty-six. He walked across the deck awkwardly. An incoming jet began to whine past overhead.

'Did they arrive, Seventh Son?'

'Yes, Father, yes they did.'

Four Fingers pounded the upturned keg with glee. 'Very good. Now we can begin!'

'Hey, Four Fingers,' Pockmark Tang said thoughtfully,

motioning at the dice. 'A six, a four and a two—that's twelve, which's also three, the magic three.'

'Yes, yes I saw.'

Pockmark Tang beamed and pointed northwards and a little east to where Kai Tak airport would be—behind the Aberdeen mountains, across the harbor in Kowloon, six miles away. 'Perhaps your luck has changed, *heya?*'

MONDAY

3

5:16 A.M.:

At half-dawn a jeep with two overalled mechanics aboard came around Gate 16 at the eastern end of the terminal and stopped close beside the main landing gear of *Yankee 2*. The gangway was still in place and the main door slightly ajar. The mechanics, both Chinese, got out and one began to inspect the eight-wheeled main gear while the other, equally carefully, scrutinized the nose gear. Methodically, they checked the tires and wheels and then the hydraulic couplings of the brakes, then peered into the landing bays. Both used flashlights. The mechanic at the main landing gear took out a spanner and stood on one of the wheels for a closer inspection, his head and shoulder now well into the belly of the airplane. After a moment he called out softly in Cantonese, *'Ayeeyah!* Hey, Lim, take a look at this.'

The other man strolled back and peered up, sweat staining his white overalls. 'Are they there or not? I can't see from down here.'

'Brother, put your male stalk into your mouth and flush yourself down a sewer. Of course they're here. We're rich. We'll eat rice forever! But be quiet or you'll wake the dung-stained foreign devils above! Here . . .' The man handed down a long, canvas-wrapped package which Lim took and stowed quietly and quickly in the jeep. Then another and another small one, both men sweating and very nervous, working fast but quietly.

Another package. And another . . .

And then Lim saw the police jeep whirl around the corner and simultaneously other uniformed men come pouring out of Gate 16, among them Europeans. 'We're betrayed,' he gasped as he fled in a hopeless dash for freedom. The jeep intercepted him easily and he stopped, shivering with pent-up terror. Then he spat and cursed the gods and withdrew into himself.

The other man had jumped down at once and leaped into the driving seat. Before he could turn on the ignition he was swamped and handcuffed.

'So, little oily mouth,' Sergeant Lee hissed, 'where do you think you're going?'

'Nowhere, Officer, it was him, him there, that bastard son of a whore, Officer, he swore he'd cut my throat if I didn't help him. I don't know anything, on my mother's grave!'

'You lying bastard, you never had a mother. You're going to go to jail for fifty years if you don't talk!'

'I swear, Officer, by all the gods th—'

'Piss on your lies, dungface. Who's paying you to do this job?'

Armstrong was walking slowly across the tarmac, the sick sweet taste of the kill in his mouth. 'So,' he said in English, 'what have we here, Sergeant?' It had been a long night's vigil and he was tired and unshaven and in no mood for the mechanic's whining protestations of innocence, so he said softly in perfect gutter Cantonese, 'One more tiny, insignificant word out of you, purveyor of leper dung, and I'll have my men jump on your Secret Sack.'

The man froze.

'Good. What's your name?'

'Tan Shu Ta, lord.'

'Liar! What's your friend's name?'

'Lim Ta-cheung, but he's not my friend, lord, I never met him before this morning.'

'Liar! Who paid you to do this?'

'I don't know who paid him, lord. You see he swore he'd cut—'

'Liar! Your mouth's so full of dung you must be the god of dung himself. What's in those packages?'

'I don't know. I swear on my ancestor's gr—'

'Liar!' Armstrong said it automatically, knowing that the lies were inevitable.

'John *China*man's not the same as us,' his first police teacher, an old China hand, had told him. 'Oh I don't mean cut on the cross or anything like that—he's just different. He lies through

58

his teeth all the time to a copper and when you nab a villain fair and square he'll still lie and be as slippery as a greased pole in a pile of shit. He's different. Take their names. All Chinese have four different names, one when he's born, one at puberty, one when he's an adult and one he chooses for himself, and they forget one or add another at the drop of a titfer. And their names—God stone the crows! Chinese call themselves *lao-tsi-sing*—the Ancient One Hundred Names. They've only got a basic hundred surnames in all China and of those there're twenty Yus, eight Yens, ten Wus and God knows how many Pings, Lis, Lees, Chens, Chins, Chings, Wongs and Fus and each one of them you pronounce five different ways so God knows who's who!'

'Then it's going to be difficult to identify a suspect, sir?'

'Full marks, young Armstrong! Full marks, lad. You can have fifty Lis, fifty Changs and four hundred Wongs and not one related to the other. God stone the crows! That's the problem here in Hong Kong.'

Armstrong sighed. After eighteen years Chinese names were still as confusing as ever. And on top of that everyone seemed to have a nickname by which they were generally known.

'What's your name?' he asked again and didn't bother to listen to the answer. 'Liar! Sergeant! Unwrap one of those! Let's see what we've got.'

Sergeant Lee eased aside the last covering. Inside was an M14, an automatic rifle, U.S. Army. New and well greased.

'For this, you evil son of a whore's left tit,' Armstrong grated, 'you'll howl for fifty years!'

The man was staring at the gun stupidly, aghast. Then a low moan came from him. 'Fornicate all gods I never knew they were guns.'

'Ah, but you did know!' Armstrong said. 'Sergeant, put this piece of dung in the wagon and book him for smuggling guns.'

The man was dragged away roughly. One of the young Chinese policemen was unwrapping another package. It was small and square. 'Hold it!' Armstrong ordered in English. The policeman and everyone in hearing distance froze. 'One of them may be booby-trapped. Everyone get away from the jeep!' Sweating, the man did as he was ordered. 'Sergeant, get our bomb disposal wallahs. There's no hurry now.'

59

'Yes sir.' Sergeant Lee hurried to the intercom in the police wagon.

Armstrong went under the airplane and peered into the main gear bay. He could see nothing untoward. Then he stood on one of the wheels. 'Christ!' he gasped. Five snug racks were neatly bolted to each side of the inner bulkhead. One was almost empty, the others still full. From the size and shape of the packages he judged them to be more M14s and boxes of ammo—or grenades.

'Anything up there, sir?' Inspector Thomas asked. He was a young Englishman, three years in the force.

'Take a look! But don't touch anything.'

'Christ! There's enough for a couple of riot squads!'

'Yes. But who?'

'Commies?'

'Or Nationalists—or villains. These'd—'

'What the hell's going on down there?'

Armstrong recognized Linc Bartlett's voice. His face closed and he jumped down, Thomas following him. He went to the foot of the gangway. 'I'd like to know that too, Mr. Bartlett,' he called up curtly.

Bartlett was standing at the main door of the airplane, Svensen beside him. Both men wore pajamas and robes and were sleep tousled.

'I'd like you to take a look at this.' Armstrong pointed to the rifle that was now half hidden in the jeep.

At once Bartlett came down the gangway, Svensen following. 'What?'

'Perhaps you'd be kind enough to wait in the airplane, Mr. Svensen.'

Svensen started to reply, stopped. Then he glanced at Bartlett who nodded. 'Fix some coffee, Sven, huh?'

'Sure, Linc.'

'Now what's this all about, Superintendent?'

'That!' Armstrong pointed.

'That's an M14.' Bartlett's eyes narrowed. 'So?'

'So it seems your aircraft is bringing in guns.'

'That's not possible.'

'We've just caught two men unloading. There's one of the buggers'—Armstrong stabbed a finger at the handcuffed mechanic waiting sullenly beside the jeep—'and the other's in the wagon. Perhaps you'd be kind enough to look up in the main gear bay, sir.'

'Sure. Where?'

'You'll have to stand on a wheel.'

Bartlett did as he was told. Armstrong and Inspector Thomas watched exactly where he put his hands for fingerprint identification. Bartlett stared blankly at the racks. 'I'll be goddamned! If these're more of the same, it's a goddamn arsenal!'

'Yes. Please don't touch them.'

Bartlett studied the racks, then climbed down, wide awake now. 'This isn't a simple smuggling job. Those racks are custom made.'

'Yes. You've no objection if the aircraft's searched?'

'No. Of course not.'

'Go ahead, Inspector,' Armstrong said at once. 'And do it very carefully indeed. Now, Mr. Bartlett, perhaps you'd be kind enough to explain.'

'I don't run guns, Superintendent. I don't believe my captain would—or Bill O'Rourke. Or Svensen.'

'What about Miss Tcholok?'

'Oh for chrissake!'

Armstrong said icily, 'This is a very serious matter, Mr. Bartlett. Your aircraft is impounded and without police approval until further notice neither you nor any of your crew may leave the Colony pending our inquiries. Now, what about Miss Tcholok?'

'It's impossible, it's totally impossible that Casey is involved in any way with guns, gun smuggling or any kind of smuggling. Impossible.' Bartlett was apologetic but quite unafraid. 'Nor would any of the rest of us.' His voice sharpened. 'You were tipped off, weren't you?'

'How long did you stop at Honolulu?'

'An hour or two, just to refuel, I don't remember exactly.' Bartlett thought for a moment. 'Jannelli got off but he always does. Those racks couldn't've been loaded in an hour or so.'

'Are you sure?'

'No, but I'd still bet it was done before we left the States. Though when and where and why and who I've no idea. Have you?'

'Not yet.' Armstrong was watching him keenly. 'Perhaps you'd like to go back to your office, Mr. Bartlett. We could take your statement there.'

'Sure.' Bartlett glanced at his watch. It was 5:43 A.M. 'Let's do that now, then I can make a few calls. We're not wired into your system yet. There's a local phone there?' He pointed to the terminal.

'Yes. Of course we'd prefer to question Captain Jannelli and Mr. O'Rourke before you do—if you don't mind. Where are they staying?'

'At the Victoria and Albert.'

'Sergeant Lee!'

'Yes sir.'

'Get on to HQ.'

'Yes sir.'

'We'd also like to talk to Miss Tcholok first. Again if you don't mind.'

Bartlett walked up the steps, Armstrong beside him. At length he said, 'All right. Provided you do that personally, and not before 7:45. She's been working overtime and she's got a heavy day today and I don't want her disturbed unnecessarily.'

They went into the airplane. Sven was waiting by the galley, dressed now and very perturbed. Uniformed and plainclothes police were everywhere, searching diligently.

'Sven, how about that coffee?' Bartlett led the way through the anteroom into his office-study. The central door, aft, at the end of the corridor, was open. Armstrong could see part of the master suite with its king-size bed. Inspector Thomas was going through some drawers.

'Shit!' Bartlett muttered.

'Sorry,' Armstrong said, 'but this is necessary.'

'That doesn't mean I have to like it, Superintendent. Never did like strangers peeking into my private life.'

'Yes. I agree.' The superintendent beckoned one of the plain-clothes officers. 'Sung!'

'Yes sir.'

'Take this down, will you please?'

'Just a minute, let's save some time,' Bartlett said. He turned to a bank of electronic gear and pressed two switches. A twin cassette tape deck clicked into operation. He plugged in a microphone and set it on the desk. 'There'll be two tapes, one for you, one for me. After your man's typed it up—if you want a signature I'm here.'

'Thank you.'

'Okay, let's begin.'

Armstrong was suddenly uneasy. 'Would you please tell me what you know about the illegal cargo found in the main gear bay of your aircraft, Mr. Bartlett?'

Bartlett repeated his denial of any knowledge. 'I don't believe any of my crew or any of my people are involved in any way. None of them has ever been involved with the law as far as I know. And I would know.'

'How long has Captain Jannelli been with you?'

'Four years. O'Rourke two. Svensen since I got the airplane in '58.'

'And Miss Tcholok?'

After a pause Bartlett said, 'Six—almost seven years.'

'She's a senior executive in your company?'

'Yes. Very senior.'

'That's unusual, isn't it, Mr. Bartlett?'

'Yes. But that has nothing to do with this problem.'

'You're the owner of this aircraft?'

'My company is. Par-Con Industries Incorporated.'

'Do you have any enemies—anyone who'd want to embarrass you seriously?'

Bartlett laughed. 'Does a dog have fleas? You don't get to head a half-billion-dollar company by making friendships.'

'No enemy in particular?'

'You tell me. Running guns is a special operation—this has to have been done by a professional.'

'Who knew about your flight plan to Hong Kong?'

'The visit's been scheduled for a couple of months. My board knew. And my planning staff.' Bartlett frowned. 'It was no real secret. No reason to be.' Then he added, 'Of course Struan's knew—exactly. For at least two weeks. In fact we confirmed the date on the 12th by telex, exact ETD and ETA. I wanted it sooner but Dunross said Monday the 19th'd suit him better, which is today. Maybe you should ask him.'

'I will, Mr. Bartlett. Thank you, sir. That will do for the moment.'

'I've got some questions, Superintendent, if you don't mind What's the penalty for smuggling guns?'

'Ten years without parole.'

'What's the value of this cargo?'

'Priceless, to the right buyer, because no guns—absolutely none—are available to anyone.'

'Who's the right buyer?'

'Anyone who wants to start a riot, insurrection, or commit mass murder, bank robbery, or some crime of whatever magnitude.'

'Communists?'

Armstrong smiled and shook his head. 'They don't have to shoot at us to take over the Colony, or smuggle M14s—they've got guns a-plenty of their own.'

'Nationalists? Chiang Kai-shek's men?'

'They're more than well supplied with all sorts of armaments by the U.S. Government, Mr. Bartlett. Aren't they? So they don't need to smuggle this way either.'

'A gang war maybe?'

'Good God, Mr. Bartlett, our gangs don't shoot each other. Our gangs—triads as we call them—our triads settle their differences in sensible, civilised Chinese fashion, with knives and axes and fighting irons and anonymous calls to the police.'

'I'll bet it was someone in Struan's. That's where you'll find the answer to the riddle.'

'Perhaps.' Armstrong laughed strangely, then said again, 'Perhaps. Now if you'll excuse me . . .'

'Of course.' Bartlett turned off the recorder, took out the two cassettes and handed one over.

'Thank you, Mr. Bartlett.'

'How long will this search go on?'

'That depends. Perhaps an hour. We may wish to bring in some experts. We'll try to make it as easy as possible. You'll be off the plane before lunch?'

'Yes.'

'If you want access please check with my office. The number's 88-77-33. There'll be a permanent police guard here for the time being. You'll be staying at the Vic?'

'Yes. Am I free to go into town now, do what I like?'

'Yes sir, provided you don't leave the Colony, pending our inquiries.'

Bartlett grinned. 'I've got that message already, loud and clear.'

Armstrong left. Bartlett showered and dressed and waited until all the police went away except the one who was guarding the gangway. Then he went back into his office suite and closed the door. Quite alone now he checked his watch. It was 7:37. He went over to his communications center and clicked on two micro switches and pressed the sending button.

In a moment there was a crackle of static and Casey's sleepy voice. 'Yes, Linc?'

'*Geronimo*,' he said clearly, into the mike.

There was a long pause. 'Got it,' she said. The loudspeaker went dead.

4

The Rolls came off the car ferry that linked Kowloon to Hong Kong Island and turned east along Connaught Road, joining the heavy traffic. The morning was very warm, humid and cloudless under a nice sun. Casey settled deeper into the back cushions. She glanced at her watch, her excitement growing.

'Plenty time, Missee,' the sharp-eyed chauffeur said. 'Noble House down street, tall building, ten, fifteen minutes never mind.'

'Good.'

This is the life, she told herself. One day I'll have a Rolls of my very own and a neat, polite quiet Chinese chauffeur and I'll not have to worry about the price of gas. Not ever. Maybe—at long last—this is where I'm going to get my *drop dead* money. She smiled to herself. Linc was the first one who had explained about drop dead money. He had called it *screw you* money. Enough to say screw you to anybody or anything. 'Screw you money's the most valuable in the world . . . but the most expensive,' he had said. 'If you work for me—with me but for me—I'll help you get your screw you money. But Casey, I don't know if you'll want to pay the cost.'

'What's the cost?'

'I don't know. I only know it varies, person to person—and always costs you more than you're prepared to pay.'

'Has yours?'

'Oh yes.'

Well, she thought, the price hasn't been too high yet. I make $52,000 a year, my expense account is good and my job stretches my brain. But the government takes too much and there's not enough left to be drop dead money. 'Drop dead money comes from a killing,' Linc had said. 'Not from cash flow.'

How much do I need?

She had never asked herself the question before.

$500,000? At 7 percent that'll bring $35,000 a year forever but that's taxable. What about the Mexican Government guarantee of 11 percent, less 1 for them for their trouble? Still taxable. In tax free bonds at 4 percent it's $20,000 but bonds are dangerous and you don't gamble your drop dead money.

'That's the first rule, Casey,' Linc had said. 'You never risk it. Never.' Then he had laughed that lovely laugh of his which disarmed her as always. 'You never risk your screw you money except the once or twice you decide to.'

A million? Two? Three?

Get your mind on the meeting and don't dream, she told herself. I won't, but my price is 2 million cash in the bank. Tax free. That's what I want. 2 million at 5¼ percent tax free will bring $105,000 a year. And that will give me and the family everything I want with enough to spare forever. And I could better 5¼ percent on my money.

But how to get 2 million tax free?

I don't know. But somehow I know this's the place.

The Rolls stopped suddenly as a mass of pedestrians dodged through the tightly packed lines of cars and double-decker buses and taxis and trucks and carts and lorries and bicycles and handcarts and some rickshaws. Thousands of people scurried this way and that, pouring out of or into the alleys and side roads, spilling off the pavements onto the roadway in the morning rush hour. Rivers of human ants.

Casey had researched Hong Kong well, but she was still not prepared for the impact that the incredible overcrowding had made upon her.

'I never saw anything like it, Linc,' she had said this morning when he had arrived at the hotel just before she left for the meeting. 'It was after ten when we drove here from the airport, but there were thousands of people out—including kids—and everything—restaurants, markets, shops—were still open.'

'People mean profit—why else're we here?'

'We're here to usurp the Noble House of Asia with the secret help and collusion of a Judas Iscariot, John Chen.'

Linc had laughed with her. 'Correction. We're here to make a deal with Struan's, and to look around.'

'Then the plan's changed?'

'Tactically yes. The strategy's the same.'

'Why the change, Linc?'

'Charlie called last night. We bought another 200,000 shares of Rothwell-Gornt.'

'Then the bid for Struan's is just a blind and our real target's Rothwell-Gornt?'

'We still have three targets: Struan's, Rothwell-Gornt and Asian Properties. We look around and we wait. If things look good we attack. If not, we can make 5, maybe 8 million this year on our straight deal with Struan's. That's cream.'

'You're not here for 5 or 8 million. What's the real reason?'

'Pleasure.'

The Rolls gained a few yards then stopped again, the traffic heavier now as they approached Central District. Ah Linc, she thought, your pleasure covers a multitude of piracies.

'This first visit to Hong Kong, Missee?' broke into her thoughts.

'Yes, yes it is. I arrived last night,' she said.

'Ah very good. Weather very bad never mind. Very smelly, very humid. Always humid in summer. First day very pretty, *heya?*'

First day had started with the sharp buzz of her citizens band transceiver jerking her out of sleep. And '*Geronimo.*'

It was their code word for danger—beware. She had showered and dressed quickly, not knowing where the danger was coming from. She had just put in her contact lenses when the phone rang. 'This is Superintendent Armstrong. Sorry to bother you so early, Miss Tcholok, but could I see you for a moment?'

'Certainly, Superintendent.' She had hesitated. 'Give me five minutes—I'll meet you in the restaurant?'

They had met and he had questioned her, telling her only that contraband had been found aboard the airplane.

'How long have you worked for Mr. Bartlett?'

'Directly, six years.'

'Have there ever been any police problems before? Of any sort?'

'You mean with him—or with me?'

'With him. Or with you.'

'None. What's been found aboard, Superintendent?'

'You don't seem unduly worried, Miss Tcholok.'

'Why should I be? I've done nothing illegal, neither has Linc. As to the crew, they're carefully picked professionals, so I'd doubt they have anything to do with smuggling. It's drugs, isn't it? What sort of drugs?'

'Why should it be drugs?'

'Isn't that what people smuggle in here?'

'It was a very large shipment of guns.'

'*What?*'

There had been more questions, most of which she had answered, and then Armstrong was gone. She had finished her coffee and refused, for the fourth time, the home-baked, warm hard French rolls offered by a starched and smiling boy-waiter. They reminded her of those she had had in the South of France three years ago.

Ah, Nice and Cap D'Ail and the vin de Provence. And dear Linc, she had thought, going back to the suite to wait for him to phone.

'Casey? Listen, th—'

'Ah Linc, I'm glad you called,' she had said at once, deliberately interrupting him. 'Superintendent Armstrong was here a few minutes ago—and I forgot to remind you last night to call Martin about the shares.' *Martin* was also a code word, meaning, 'I think this conversation's being overheard.'

'I'd thought about him too. That's not important now. Tell me exactly what happened.'

So she told him. He related briefly what had occurred. 'I'll fill in the rest when I get there. I'm heading for the hotel right now. How's the suite?'

'Fantastic! Yours is called Fragrant Spring, my room's adjoining, guess it's normally part of it. Seems like there are ten houseboys per suite. I called room service for coffee and it arrived on a silver tray before I'd put the phone down. The bathrooms're big enough for a cocktail party for twenty with a three-piece combo.'

'Good. Wait for me.'

She sat in one of the deep leather sofas in the luxurious sitting room and began to wait, enjoying the quality that surrounded her. Beautiful Chinese lacquered chests, a well-stocked bar in a mirrored alcove, discreet flower arrangements and a bottle of monogrammed Scotch—Lincoln Bartlett—with the compliments of the chief manager. Her bedroom suite through an interlocking door was one side, his, the master suite, the other. Both were the biggest she had ever seen, with king-size beds.

Why were guns put on our airplane and by whom?

Lost in thought she glanced out of the wall-to-wall window and faced Hong Kong Island and the dominating Peak, the tallest mountain on the island. The city, called Victoria after Queen Victoria, began at the shoreline, then rose, tier on tier, on the skirts of the sharply rising mountain, lessening as the slopes soared, but there were apartment buildings near the crest. She could see one just above the terminal of the Peak's funicular. The view from there must be fantastic, she thought absently.

The blue water was sparkling nicely, the harbor as traffic-bound as the streets of Kowloon below. Liners and freighters were anchored or tied up alongside the wharves of Kowloon or steaming out or in, their sirens sounding merrily. Over at the dockyard Hong Kong side was a Royal Navy destroyer and, nearby at anchor, a dark-gray U.S. Navy frigate. There were hundreds of junks of every size and age—fishing vessels mostly—some powered, some ponderously sailing this way and that. Crammed double-decker ferries darted in and out of the traffic like so many dragonflies, and everywhere tiny sampans, oared or powered, scurried unafraid across the ordered sea-lanes.

Where do all these people live? she asked herself, appalled. And how do they support themselves?

A room boy opened the door with his passkey, without knocking, and Linc Bartlett strode in. 'You look great, Casey,' he said, shutting the door behind him.

'So do you. This gun thing's bad, isn't it?'

'Anyone here? Any maids in the rooms?'

'We're alone, but the houseboys seem to come in and out as they please.'

'This one had his key out before I reached the door.' Linc told her what had happened at the airport. Then he dropped his voice. 'What about John Chen?'

'Nothing. He just made nervous, light conversation. He didn't want to talk shop. I don't think he'd recovered from the fact that I'd turned out to be a woman. He dropped me at the hotel and said they'd send a car at 9:15.'

'So the plan worked fine?'

'Very fine.'

'Good. Did you get it?'

'No. I said I was authorized by you to take delivery and offered the initial sight draft. But he pretended to be surprised and said he'd talk to you privately when he drives you back after the lunch. He seemed very nervous.'

'Doesn't matter. Your car'll be here in a few minutes. I'll see you at lunch.'

'Should I mention the guns to Struan's? To Dunross?'

'No. Let's wait and see who brings it up.'

'You think it might be them?'

'Easily. They knew our flight plan, and they've a motive.'

'What?'

'To discredit us.'

'But why?'

'Maybe they think they know our battle plan.'

'But then wouldn't it have been much wiser for them not to do anything—to sucker us in?'

'Maybe. But this way they've made the opening move. Day One: Knight to King Bishop 3. The attack's launched on us.'

'Yes. But by whom—and are we playing White or Black?'

His eyes hardened and lost their friendliness. 'I don't care, Casey, as long as we win.' He left.

Something's up, she told herself. Something dangerous he's not telling me about.

'Secrecy's vital, Casey,' he had said back in the early days. 'Napoleon, Caesar, Patton—any of the great generals—often hid their *real* plan from their staff. Just to keep them—and therefore enemy spies—off balance. If I withhold from you it's not mistrust, Casey. But you must never withhold from me.'

'That's not fair.'

'Life's not fair. Death's not fair. War's not fair. Big business is war. I'm playing it like it was war and that's why I'm going to win.'

'Win what?'

71

'I want Par-Con Industries bigger than General Motors and Shell combined.'

'Why?'

'For my goddamn pleasure.'

'Now tell me the real reason.'

'Ah, Casey, that's why I love you. You listen and you know.'

'Ah, Raider, I love you too.'

Then they had both laughed together for they knew they did not love the other, not in the ordinary sense of that word. They had agreed, way back in the beginning, to put aside the ordinary for the extraordinary. For seven years.

Casey looked out of the window at the harbor and the ships in the harbor.

Crush, destroy, and win. Big Business, the most exciting Monopoly game in the world. And my leader's Raider Bartlett, Mastercraftsman. But time's running out on us, Linc. This year, the seventh year, the last year ends on my birthday, November 25, my twenty-seventh birthday. . . .

Her ears heard the half knock and the passkey in the lock and she turned to say come in but the starched houseboy was already in.

'Morning, Missee. I'm Number One Houseboy Daytime Chang.' Chang was gray haired and solicitous. He beamed. 'Tidy room plees?'

'Don't any of you ever wait for someone to say come in?' she asked sharply.

Chang stared at her blankly. 'Missee?'

'Oh never mind,' she said wearily.

'Pretty day, *heya*? Which first, Master's room or Missee's?'

'Mine. Mr. Bartlett hasn't used his yet.'

Chang grinned toothily. *Ayeeyah*, did you and Master tumble together in yours, Missee, before he went out? But there were only fourteen minutes between Master's arrival and leaving and certainly he did not look flushed when he went away.

Ayeeyah, first it's supposed to be two men foreign devils sharing my suite and then one's a she—confirmed by Nighttime Ng, who of course went through her luggage and found serious proof that she was a true she—proof reconfirmed this morning with great gusto by Third Toiletmaid Fung.

Golden pubics! How vile!

And Golden Pubics is not only *not* the Master's chief wife— she is not even a second wife, and oh ko, worst of all she did not have the good manners to pretend she was so the hotel rules could be honored and everyone save face.

Chang chortled, for this hotel had always had astounding rules about ladies in men's rooms—oh gods what else is a bed for?—and now a female was living openly in barbarian sin! Oh how tempers had soared last night. Barbarians! *Dew neh loh moh* on all barbarians! But this one is surely a dragon because she stared down the Eurasian assistant manager, and the Eurasian night manager, and even old mealy-mouth, Chief Manager Big Wind himself.

'No no no,' he had wailed, so Chang had been told.

'Yes yes yes,' she had replied, insisting that she have the adjoining half of the Fragrant Spring suite.

It was then that Honorable Mong, chief porter and chief triad and therefore leader of the hotel, solved the unsolvable. 'The Fragrant Spring suite has three doors, *heya*?' he had said. 'One for each bedroom, one for the main room. Let her be shown into Fragrant Spring B which is the inferior room anyway, through its own door. But the inner door to the main sitting room and thence to the Master's quarters shall be tight locked. But let a key be left nearby. If the mealy-mouthed whore unlocks the door herself . . . what can one do? And then, if there happens to be a mix-up in bookings tomorrow or the next day and our honorable chief manager has to ask the billionaire and his strumpet from the Land of the Golden Mountain to leave, well so sorry never mind, we have bookings enough and to spare and our face to protect.'

And so it was done.

The outer door to B was unlocked and Golden Pubics invited in. That she took up the key and at once unlocked the inner door—who is to say? That the door is open now, well, certainly I would never tell any outsider, my lips are sealed. As always.

Ayeeyah, but though outer doors may be locked and be prudish, the inner ones may be flung wide and be luscious. Like her Jade Gate, he thought pensively. *Dew neh loh moh* I wonder what it would be like to storm a Jade Gate the size of hers? 'Make bed, Missee?' he asked sweetly in English.

'Go right ahead.'

Oh how truly awful the sound of their barbarian tongue is Ugh!

Daytime Chang would have hawked and cleared the spit god from his mouth, but that was against hotel rules.

'*Heya*, Daytime Chang,' Third Toiletmaid Fung said brightly as she came into the bedroom after knocking half-heartedly on the suite door long after she had opened it. 'Yes, Missee, so sorry, Missee,' in English, then again to Chang in Cantonese, 'Haven't you finished yet? Is her dung so sweet you want to dawdle in her drawers?'

'*Dew neh loh moh* in yours, Sister. Watch your tongue or your old father may give you a good drubbing.'

'The only drubbing your old mother wants, you can't help me with! Come on, let me help you make her bed quickly. There's a mah-jong game beginning in half an hour. Honorable Mong sent me for you.'

'Oh, thank you, Sister. *Heya*, did you really see her pubics?'

'Haven't I told you already? Am I a liar? They're pure golden, lighter than her head hair. She was in the bath and I was as close as we are now. And, oh yes, her nipples're pinkish, not brown.'

'Eeee! Imagine!'

'Just like a sow's.'

'How awful!'

'Yes. Did you read today's *Commercial Daily?*'

'No, Sister, not yet. Why?'

'Well their astrologer says this is a very good week for me and today the financial editor says it looks as though there's a new boom beginning.'

'*Dew neh loh moh* you don't say!'

'So I told my broker this morning to buy a thousand more Noble House, the same Golden Ferry, 40 of Second Great House and 50 Good Luck Properties. My bankers are generous but now I haven't a single brass cash left in Hong Kong I can beg or borrow!'

'Eeeee, you're plunging, Sister. I'm stretched out myself. Last week I borrowed from the bank on my shares and bought another 600 Noble House. That was Tuesday. I bought in at 25:23!'

'*Ayeeyah*, Honourable Chang, they were 29:14 at close last night.' Third Toiletmaid Fung made an automatic calculation.

'You're already 2,348 Hong Kong ahead! And they say Noble House's going to bid for Good Luck Properties. If they try, it will send their enemies' rage to boiling point. Ha! The tai-pan of Second Great House will fart dust!'

'Oh oh oh but meanwhile the shares will skyrocket! Of all three companies! Ha! *Dew neh loh moh*, where can I get more cash?'

'The races, Daytime Chang! Borrow 500 against your present winnings and put it on the daily double on Saturday or the double quinella. 4 and 5 are my lucky numbers. . . .'

They both looked up as Casey came into the bedroom. Chang switched to English. 'Yes Missee?'

'There's some laundry in the bathroom. Can you have it picked up, please?'

'Oh yes I fix. Today six o'clock come by okay never mind.' These foreign devils are so stupid, Chang thought contemptuously. What am I, an empty-headed dung heap? Of course I'll take care of the laundry if there's laundry.

'Thank you.'

They both watched fascinated as she checked her makeup in the bedroom mirror, preparing to leave.

'Her tits don't droop at all, do they, Sister?' Chang said. 'Pink nipples *heya*? Extraordinary!'

'Just like a sow's, I told you. Are your ears merely pots to piss in?'

'In your ear, Third Toiletmaid Fung.'

'Has she tipped you yet?'

'No. The Master gave too much and she nothing. Disgusting *heya*?'

'Yes. What can you do? People from the Golden Mountain are really very uncivilized, aren't they, Daytime Chang?'

5

The tai-pan came over the rise and barreled down the Peak Road in his E-Type Jaguar, going east toward Magazine Gap. On the winding road there was but a single lane each side with few places to pass and precipitous on most corners. Today the surface was dry and, knowing the way so well, Ian Dunross rode the bends fast and sweetly, hugging the mountainside, his scarlet convertible tight to the inside curve. He did a racing shift down and braked hard as he swooped a bend and came up to an ancient, slow-moving truck. He waited patiently, then, at the perfect moment, swung out onto the wrong side and was past safely before the oncoming car had rounded the blind corner ahead.

Now Dunross was clear for a short stretch and could see that the snaking road ahead was empty. He jammed his foot down and slid some corners, usurping the whole of the road, taking the straightest line, using hand and eye and foot and brake and gearshift in unison, feeling the vast power of the engine and the wheels in all of him. Ahead, suddenly, was an oncoming truck from the far corner and his freedom vanished. He geared down and braked in split-second time, hugging his side, regretting the loss of freedom, then accelerated and was away again into more treacherous bends. Now another truck, this time laden with passengers, and he waited a few yards behind, knowing there was no place to pass for a while. Then one of the passengers noticed his number plate, 1-1010, and she pointed and they all looked, chattering excitedly one to another, and one of them banged on the cabin of the truck. The driver obligingly squeezed off the road onto the tiny shoulder and flagged him on. Dunross made sure he was safe then passed, waving to them with a grin.

More corners, the speed and the waiting-to-pass and the passing and the danger pleasing him. Then he cut left into Magazine Gap Road, down the hill, the bends trickier, the traffic building up now and slower. He overtook a taxi and jumped three cars very fast and was back in line though still over the speed limit when he saw the traffic motorcycle policemen waiting ahead. He changed down and passed them going the regulation 30 mph. He waved good-naturedly. They waved back.

'You really must slow down, Ian,' his friend, Henry Foxwell, Senior Superintendent of Traffic, had said recently. 'You really should.'

'I've never had an accident—yet. Or a ticket.'

'Good God, Ian, there's not a traffic copper on the island who'd dare give you one! You, *the* tai-pan? Perish the thought. I meant for your own good. Keep that speed devil of yours bottled for Monaco, or your Macao Road Race.'

'Monaco's professional. I don't take chances, and I don't drive that fast anyway.'

'67 mph over Wongniechong isn't exactly slow, old chap. Admittedly it was 4:23 A.M. on an almost empty road. But it is a 30 mph zone.'

'There're lots of E-Types in Hong Kong.'

'Yes, I agree. Seven. Scarlet convertibles with a special number plate? With a black canvas roof, racing wheels and tires, that goes like the clappers of hell? It was last Thursday, old chap. Radar and all that. You'd been to . . . to visit friends. In Sinclair Road, I believe.'

Dunross had contained his sudden rage. 'Oh?' he said, the surface of his face smiling. 'Thursday? I seem to remember I had dinner with John Chen then. At his apartment in Sinclair Towers. But I thought I was home long before 4:23.'

'Oh I'm sure you were. I'm sure the constable got the number plate and color and everything all wrong.' Foxwell clapped him on the back in friendly style. 'Even so, slow down a little will you? It'd be so boring if you killed yourself during my term. Wait till I'm transferred back to Special Branch—or the police college, eh? Yes, I'm sure he made a mistake.'

But there was no mistake, Dunross had said to himself. You

77

know it, I know it, and John Chen would know it and so would Wei-wei.

So you fellows know about Wei-wei! That's interesting.

'Are you fellows watching me?' he had asked bluntly.

'Good God no!' Foxwell had been shocked. 'Special Intelligence was watching a villain who's got a flat at Sinclair Towers. You happened to be seen. You're very important here, you know that. I happened to pick it up through channels. You know how it is.'

'No, I don't.'

'They say one word to the wise is sufficient, old chap.'

'Yes they do. So perhaps you'd better tell your Intelligence fellows to be more intelligent in future.'

'Fortunately they're very discreet.'

'Even so I wouldn't like my movements a matter of record.'

'I'm sure they're not. Not a matter of record.'

'Good. What villain in Sinclair Towers?'

'One of our important capitalist dogs but suspected secret Commie fellows. Very boring but SI have to earn their daily bread, don't they?'

'Do I know him?'

'I imagine you know everyone.'

'Shanghainese or Cantonese?'

'What makes you think he's either?'

'Ah, then he's European?'

'He's just a villain, Ian. Sorry, it's all very hush-hush at the moment.'

'Come on, we own that block. Who? I won't tell anyone.'

'I know. Sorry old boy, but I can't. However, I've another hypothetical idea for you. Say a hypothetical married VIP had a lady friend whose uncle happened to be the undercover deputy chief of the illegal Kuomintang Secret Police for Hong Kong. Say, hypothetically, the Kuomintang wanted this VIP on their side. Certainly he could be pressured by such a lady. Couldn't he?'

'Yes,' Dunross had said easily. 'If he was stupid.' He already knew about Wei-wei Jen's uncle and had met him at a number of private parties several times in Taipei. And liked him. No problem there, he had thought, because she's not my mistress or even a lady friend, however beautiful and desirable. And tempting.

He smiled to himself as he drove in the stream of traffic down Magazine Gap Road then waited in line to circle the roundabout and head down Garden Road toward Central, half a mile below, and to the sea.

Now he could see the soaring modern office block that was Struan's. It was twenty-two stories high and fronted Connaught Road and the sea, almost opposite the Terminal of the Golden Ferries that plied between Hong Kong and Kowloon. As always, the sight pleased him.

He weaved in and out of heavy traffic where he could, crawled past the Hilton Hotel and the Cricket Ground on his left, then turned into Connaught Road, the sidewalks jammed with pedestrians. He stopped outside his front entrance.

This's the big day, he thought. The Americans have arrived.

And, with joss, Bartlett's the noose that'll strangle Quillan Gornt once and for all time. Christ, if we can pull this off!

'Morning, sir.' The uniformed doorman saluted crisply.

'Morning, Tom.' Dunross eased himself out of the low-slung car and ran up the marble steps, two at a time, toward the huge glass entrance. Another doorman drove the car off to its underground parking and still another opened the glass door for him. He caught the reflection of the Rolls drawing up. Recognizing it, he glanced back. Casey got out and he whistled involuntarily. She carried a briefcase. Her sea-green silk suit was tailored and very conservative, but even so, it hid none of the trim of her figure or the dance to her stride and the sea green enhanced the tawny gold of her hair.

She looked around, feeling his eyes. Her recognition was immediate and she measured him as he measured her and though the instant was short it seemed long enough to both of them. Long and leisurely.

She moved first and walked toward him. He met her halfway.

'Hello, Mr. Dunross.'

'Hello. We've never met, have we?'

'No. But you're easy to recognize from your photos. I didn't expect to have the pleasure of meeting you till later. I'm Cas—'

'Yes,' he said and grinned. 'I had a deranged call from John Chen last night. Welcome to Hong Kong, Miss Tcholok. It is Miss, isn't it?'

'Yes. I hope my being a woman won't upset things too much.'

'Oh yes it will, very much. But we'll try to accommodate the problem. Would you and Mr. Bartlett care to be my guests at the races on Saturday? Lunch and all that?'

'I think that would be lovely. But I have to check with Linc—may I confirm this afternoon?'

'Of course.' He looked down at her. She looked back. The doorman still held the door open.

'Well, come along, Miss Tcholok, and let battle commence.'

She glanced at him quickly. 'Why should we battle? We're here to do business.'

'Oh yes, of course. Sorry, it's just a Sam Ackroyd saying. I'll explain another time.' He ushered her in and headed for the bank of elevators. The many people already lined up and waiting immediately moved aside for them to get into the first elevator, to Casey's embarrassment.

'Thanks,' Dunross said, not noticing anything out of the ordinary. He guided her in, pressed 20, the top button, noticing absently that she wore no perfume or jewelry, just a thin gold chain around her neck.

'Why's the front door at an angle?' she asked.

'Sorry?'

'The front entrance seems to be on a slight tilt—it's not quite straight—I was wondering why.'

'You're very observant. The answer is *fung sui*. When the building was put up four years ago, somehow or other we forgot to consult our house *fung sui* man. He's like an astrologer, a man who specializes in heaven, earth, water currents, and devils, that sort of thing, and makes sure you're building on the Earth Dragon's back and not on his head.'

'What?'

'Oh yes. You see every building in the whole of China's on some part of the Earth Dragon. To be on his back's perfect, but if you're on his head it's very bad, and terrible if you're on his eyeball. Anyway, when we did get around to asking, our *fung sui* man said we were on the Dragon's back—thank God, otherwise we'd've had to move—but that devils were getting in the door and this was what was causing all the trouble. He advised me to reposition the door, and so, under his direction we changed the angle and now the devils are all deflected.'

She laughed. 'Now tell me the real reason.'

'*Fung sui*. We had very bad joss here—bad luck—rotten in fact until the door was changed.' His face hardened momentarily then the shadow passed. 'The moment we changed the angle, everything became good again.'

'You're telling me you really believe that? Devils and dragons?'

'I believe none of it. But you learn the hard way when you're in China that it's best to act a little Chinese. Never forget that though Hong Kong's British it's still China.'

'Did you learn th—'

The elevator stopped and opened on a paneled hallway and a desk and a neat, efficient Chinese receptionist. Her eyes priced Casey's clothes instantly.

Cow, Casey thought, reading her loud and clear, and smiled back as sweetly.

'Morning, tai-pan,' the receptionist said smoothly.

'Mary, this is Miss K. C. Tcholok. Please show her into Mr. Struan's office.'

'Oh but—' Mary Li tried to cover her shock. 'They're, they're waiting for a . . .' She picked up the phone but he stopped her. 'Just show her in. Now. No need to announce her.' He turned back to Casey and smiled. 'You're launched. I'll see you shortly.'

'Yes, thanks. See you.'

'Please follow me, Miss Tchuluck,' Mary Li said and started down the hall, her *cheong-sam* tight and slit high on her thighs, long silk-stockinged legs and saucy walk. Casey watched her for a moment. It must be the cut that makes their walk so blatantly sexual, she thought, amused by such obviousness. She glanced at Dunross and raised an eyebrow.

He grinned. 'See you later, Miss Tchulok.'

'Please call me Casey.'

'Perhaps I'd prefer Kamalian Ciranoush.'

She gaped at him. 'How do you know my names? I doubt if even Linc remembers.'

'Ah, it pays to have friends in high places, doesn't it?' he said with a smile. '*À bientôt.*'

'*Oui, merci,*' she replied automatically.

He strode for the elevator opposite and pressed the button. The doors opened instantly and closed after him.

Thoughtfully Casey walked after Mary Li who was waiting, ears still tuned for every nuance.

Inside the elevator Dunross took out a key and inserted it into the lock and twisted it. Now the elevator was activated. It serviced the top two floors only. He pressed the lower button. Only three other persons had similar keys: Claudia Chen, his executive secretary; his personal secretary, Sandra Yi; and his Number One Houseboy, Lim Chu.

The twenty-first floor contained his private offices, and the Inner Court boardroom. The twenty-second, the penthouse, was the tai-pan's personal suite. And he alone had the key to the last private elevator that connected the basement garage directly with the penthouse.

'Ian,' his predecessor tai-pan, Alastair Struan, had said when he handed over the keys after Phillip Chen had left them, 'your privacy's the most valuable thing you have. That too Dirk Struan laid down in his legacy and how wise he was! Never forget, the private lifts aren't for luxury or ostentation, any more than the tai-pan's suite is. They're there just to give you the measure of secrecy you'll need, perhaps even a place to hide yourself. You'll understand better after you've read the legacy and been through the tai-pan's safe. Guard that safe with all you've got. You can't be too careful, there's lots of secrets there—too many I think sometimes—and some are not so pretty.'

'I hope I won't fail,' he had said politely, detesting his cousin, his excitement huge that at long last he had the prize he had worked so hard to achieve and gambled so much for.

'You won't. Not you,' the old man had said tautly. 'You've been tested, and you've wanted the job ever since you could think. Eh?'

'Yes,' Dunross had said. 'I've tried to train for it. Yes. I'm only surprised you've given it to me.'

'You're being given the ultimate in Struan's not because of your birthright—that only made you eligible for the Inner Court—but because I think you're the best we've got to follow me, and you've been conniving and pushing and shoving for years. That's the truth, isn't it?'

'Struan's needs changing. Let's have more truth: the Noble House is in a mess. It's not all your fault, there was the war, then

Korea, then Suez—you've had bad joss for several years. It'll take years to make us safe. If Quillan Gornt—or any one of twenty enemies—knew half the truth, knew how far we're overextended, we'd be drowned in our own useless paper within the week.'

'Our paper's good—it's not useless! You're exaggerating—as usual!'

'It's worth twenty cents on the dollar because we've insufficient capital, not enough cash flow and we're absolutely in mortal danger.'

'Rubbish!'

'Is it?' Dunross's voice had sharpened for the first time. 'Rothwell-Gornt could swallow us in a month if they knew the value of our present accounts receivable, against our pressing liabilities.'

The old man had just stared at him without answering. Then he said, 'It's a temporary condition. Seasonal and temporary.'

'Rubbish! You know very well you're giving me the job because I'm the only man who can clean up the mess you leave, you, my father, and your brother.'

'Aye, I'm gambling you can. That's true enough,' Alastair had flared at him. 'Aye. You've surely got the right amount of Devil Struan in your blood to serve that master if you've a mind.'

'Thank you. I admit I'll let nothing stand in my way. And since this is a night for truth, I can tell you why you've always hated me, why my own father has also hated me.'

'Can you now?'

'Yes. It's because I survived the war and your son didn't and your nephew, Linbar, the last of your branch of the Struan's, is a nice lad but useless. Yes, I survived but my poor brothers didn't, and that's still sending my father round the bend. It's the truth, isn't it?'

'Yes,' Alastair Struan had said. 'Aye, I'm afraid it is.'

'I'm not afraid it is. I'm not afraid of anything. Granny Dunross saw to that.'

'*Heya*, tai-pan,' Claudia Chen said brightly as the elevator door opened. She was a jolly, gray-haired Eurasian woman in her mid-sixties, and she sat behind a huge desk that dominated the twenty-first-floor foyer. She had served the Noble House for forty-two years and succeeding tai-pans, exclusively, for twenty-five of them. *'Neh hoh mah?'* How're you?

'Ho ho,' he replied absently. Good. Then in English, 'Did Bartlett call?'

'No.' She frowned. 'He's not expected until lunch. Do you want me to try to reach him?'

'No, never mind. What about my call to Foster in Sydney?'

'That's not through either. Or your call to Mr. MacStruan in Edinburgh. Something's troubling you?' she asked, having instantly sensed his mood.

'What? Oh, no, nothing.' He threw off his tension and walked past her desk into his office that overlooked the harbor and sat in an easy chair beside the phone. She closed the door and sat down nearby, her notepad ready.

'I was just remembering my D Day,' he said. 'The day I took over.'

'Oh. Joss, tai-pan.'

'Yes.'

'Joss,' she repeated, 'and a long time ago.'

He laughed. 'Long time? It's forty lifetimes. It's barely three years but the whole world's changed and it's going so fast. What's the next couple of years going to be like?'

'More of the same, tai-pan. I hear you met Miss Casey Tcholok at our front door.'

'Eh, who told you that?' he asked sharply.

'Great good God, tai-pan, I can't reveal my sources. But I heard you stared at her and she stared at you. *Heya?'*

'Nonsense! Who told you about her?'

'Last night I called the hotel to see that everything was all right. The manager told me. Do you know what silly man was going to be "overbooked"? Huh, if they share a suite or a bed or don't, never mind I told him. This is 1963 and the modern age with lots of liberations, and anyway it's a fine suite with two entrances and separate rooms and most important they're our guests.' She chortled. 'I pulled a little rank. . . . *Ayeeyah*, power is a pretty toy.'

'Did you tell young Linbar or the others about K.C. being female?'

'No. No one. I knew you knew. Barbara Chen told me Master

84

John had already phoned you about Casey Tcholok. What's she like?'

'*Beddable* would be one word,' he said and grinned.

'Yes—but what else?'

Dunross thought a moment. 'She's very attractive, very well dressed—though subdued today, for our benefit I imagine. Very confident and very observant—she noticed the front door was out of whack and asked about it.' He picked up an ivory paper knife and toyed with it. 'John didn't like her at all. He said he'd bet she was one of those pathetic American women who're like California fruit: great to look at, with plenty of body, but no taste whatsoever!'

'Poor Master John, much as he likes America, he does prefer certain, er, aspects of Asia!'

Dunross laughed. 'How clever a negotiator she is we'll soon find out.' He smiled. 'I sent her in unannounced.'

'I'll wager 50 HK at least one of them knew in advance she was a she.'

'Phillip Chen of course—but that old fox wouldn't tell the others. A hundred says neither Linbar, Jacques or Andrew Gavallan knew.'

'Done,' Claudia said happily. 'You can pay me now, tai-pan. I checked very discreetly, this morning.'

'Take it out of petty cash,' he told her sourly.

'So sorry.' She held out her hand. 'A bet is a bet, tai-pan.'

Reluctantly he gave her the red one-hundred-dollar note.

'Thank you. Now, a hundred says Casey Tcholok will walk all over Master Linbar, Master Jacques and Andrew Gavallan.'

'What do you know?' he asked her suspiciously. 'Eh?'

'A hundred?'

'All right.'

'Excellent!' she said briskly, changing the subject. 'What about the dinners for Mr. Bartlett? The golf match and the trip to Taipei? Of course, you can't take a woman along on those. Shall I cancel them?'

'No. I'll talk to Bartlett—he'll understand. I did invite her to Saturday's races though, with him.'

'Oh, that's two too many. I'll cancel the Pangs, they won't mind. Do you want to sit them together at your table?'

Dunross frowned. 'She should be at my table, guest of honor, and sit him next to Penelope, guest of honor.'

'Very well. I'll call Mrs. Dunross and tell her. Oh and Barbara—Master John's wife—wants to talk with you.' Claudia sighed and smoothed a crease in her neat dark blue *cheong-sam*. 'Master John didn't come back last night—not that that's anything out of the ordinary. But it's 10:10 now and I can't find him either. It seems he wasn't at Morning Prayers.'

'Yes, I know. Since he dealt with Bartlett last night I told him to skip them.' Morning Prayers was the jocular way that insiders in Struan's referred to the daily obligatory 8:00 A.M. meeting with the tai-pan of all managing directors of all Struan's subsidiaries. 'No need for him to come today, there's nothing for him to do until lunch.' Dunross pointed out of the window at the harbor. 'He's probably on his boat. It's a great day for a sail.'

'Her temperature's very high, tai-pan, even for her.'

'Her temperature's always high, poor bugger! John's on his boat—or at Ming-li's flat. Did you try her flat?'

She sniffed. 'Your father used to say a closed mouth catches no wee beasties. Even so, I suppose I can tell you now, Ming-li's been Number Two Girl Friend for almost two months. The new favorite calls herself Fragrant Flower, and she occupies one of his "private flats" off Aberdeen Main Road.'

'Ah, conveniently near his mooring!'

'Oh very, yes. She's a flower all right, a Fallen Flower from the Good Luck Dragon Dance Hall in Wanchai. But she doesn't know where Master John is either. He didn't visit either of them though he had a date with Miss Fallen Flower, so she says, at midnight.'

'How did you find out all this?' he asked, filled with admiration.

'Power, tai-pan—and a network of relations built up over five generations. How else do we survive, *heya*?' She chuckled. 'Of course if you want a little real scandal, John Chen doesn't know she wasn't the virgin she was and the broker claimed she was when he first pillowed her.'

'Eh?'

'No. He paid the broker . . .' One of the phones rang and she picked it up and said 'Please hold one moment,' clicked on the hold button and continued happily in the same breath, '. . . 500 cash, U.S. dollars, but all her tears and all the, er, evidence, was a pretend. Poor fellow, but it serves him right, eh, tai-pan? What should a man like him at his age want virginity to nourish the yang for—he's only forty-two, *heya?*' She pressed the *on* connection. 'Tai-pan's office, good morning,' she said attentively.

He watched her. He was amused and bemused, astounded as always at her sources of information, pithy and otherwise, and her delight in knowing secrets. And passing them on. But only to clan members and special insiders.

'Just one moment please.' She clicked the hold button. 'Superintendent Armstrong would like to see you. He's downstairs with Superintendent Kwok. He's sorry to come without an appointment, but could you spare them a moment?'

'Ah, the guns. Our police're getting more efficient every day,' he said with a grim smile. 'I didn't expect them till after lunch.'

At seven this morning he had had a detailed report from Phillip Chen who had been called by one of the police sergeants who made the raid and was a relation of the Chens.

'You'd better put all our private sources on finding out the who and the why, Phillip,' he had said, very concerned.

'I already have. It's too much of a coincidence that guns should be on Bartlett's plane.'

'It could be highly embarrassing if we're found to be connected with it in any way.'

'Yes.'

He saw Claudia waiting patiently. 'Ask Armstrong to give me ten minutes. Bring them up then.'

She dealt with that, then said, 'If Superintendent Kwok's been brought in so soon, it must be more serious than we thought, *heya*, tai-pan?'

'Special Branch or Special Intelligence has to be involved at once. I'll bet the FBI and CIA have already been contacted. Brian Kwok's logical because he's an old mate of Armstrong's—and one of the best they've got.'

'Yes,' Claudia agreed proudly. 'Eeeee what a lovely husband he'd make for someone.'

'Provided she's a Chen—all that extra power, *heya?*' It was common knowledge that Brian Kwok was being groomed to be the first Chinese assistant commissioner.

'Of course such power has to be kept in the family.' The

phone rang. She answered it. 'Yes, I'll tell him, thank you.' She replaced the phone huffily. 'The governor's equerry—he called to remind you about cocktails at 6:00 P.M.—huh, as if I'd forget!'

Dunross picked up one of the phones and dialed.

'*Weyyyy?*' came the coarse voice of the *amah*, the Chinese servant. Hello?

'Chen *tai-tai*,' he said into the phone, his Cantonese perfect. 'Mrs. Chen please, this is Mr. Dunross.'

He waited. 'Ah, Barbara, good morning.'

'Oh hello, Ian. Have you heard from John yet? Sorry to bother you,' she said.

'No bother. No, not yet. But the moment I do I'll get him to call you. He might have gone down to the track early to watch Golden Lady work out. Have you tried the Turf Club?'

'Yes, but they don't remember him breakfasting there, and the workout's between 5:00 and 6:00. Damn him! He's so inconsiderate. *Ayeeyah*, men!'

'He's probably out on his boat. He's got nothing here until lunch and it's a great day for a sail. You know how he is—have you checked the mooring?'

'I can't, Ian, not without going there, there's no phone. I have a hairdressing appointment which I simply can't break—all Hong Kong will be at your party tonight—I simply can't go rushing off to Aberdeen.'

'Send one of your chauffeurs,' Dunross said dryly.

'Tang's off today and I need Wu-chat to drive me around, Ian. I simply can't send him over to Aberdeen—that could take an hour and I've a mah-jong game from two till four.'

'I'll get John to call you. It'll be around lunch.'

'I won't be back till five at the earliest. When I catch up with him he's going to get what for never mind. Oh well, thanks, sorry to bother you. 'Bye.'

''Bye.' Dunross put the phone down and sighed. 'I feel like a bloody nursemaid.'

'Talk to John's father, tai-pan,' Claudia Chen said.

'I have. Once. And that's enough. It's not all John's fault. That lady's enough to drive anyone bonkers.' He grinned. 'But I agree her temperature's gone to the moon—this time it's going to cost John an emerald ring or at least a mink coat.'

The phone rang again. Claudia picked it up. 'Hello, the tai-pan's office! Yes? Oh!' Her happiness vanished and she hardened. 'Just a moment, please.' She punched the hold button. 'It's a person to person from Hiro Toda in Yokohama.'

Dunross knew how she felt about him, knew she hated the Japanese and loathed the Noble House's connection with them. He could never forgive the Japanese either for what they had done to Asia during the war. To those they had conquered. To the defenseless. Men, women and children. The prison camps and unnecessary deaths. Soldier to soldier he had no quarrel with them. None. War was war.

His own war had been against the Germans. But Claudia's war had been here in Hong Kong. During the Japanese Occupation, because she was Eurasian, she had not been put into Stanley Prison with all European civilians. She and her sister and brother had tried to help the POWs with food and drugs and money, smuggling it into the camp. The Kampeitai, the Japanese military police, had caught her. Thereafter she could have no children.

'Shall I say you're out?' she asked.

'No.' Two years before Dunross had committed an enormous amount of capital to Toda Shipping Industries of Yokohama for two giant bulk ships to build up the Struan fleet that had been decimated in the war. He had chosen this Japanese shipyard because their product was the finest, their terms the best, they guaranteed delivery and all the things the British shipyards would not, and because he knew it was time to forget. 'Hello, Hiro,' he said, liking the man personally. 'Nice to hear from you. How's Japan?'

'Please excuse me for interrupting you, tai-pan. Japan's fine though hot and humid. No change.'

'How're my ships coming along?'

'Perfectly, tai-pan. Everything is as we arranged. I just wanted to advise you that I will be coming to Hong Kong on Saturday morning for a business trip. I will be staying for the weekend, then on to Singapore and Sydney, back in time for our closing in Hong Kong. You'll still be coming to Yokohama for both launchings?'

'Oh yes. Yes, absolutely. What time do you arrive Saturday?'

'At 11:10, Japan Air Lines.'

'I'll send a car to meet you. What about coming directly to Happy Valley to the races? You could join us for lunch, then my car will take you to the hotel. You're staying at the Victoria and Albert?'

'This time at the Hilton, Hong Kong side. Tai-pan, please excuse me, I do not wish to put you to any trouble, so sorry.'

'It's nothing. I'll have one of my people meet you. Probably Andrew Gavallan.'

'Ah, very good. Then thank you, tai-pan. I look forward to seeing you, so sorry to inconvenience you.'

Dunross put the phone down. I wonder why he called, the real reason? he asked himself. Hiro Toda, managing director of the most go-ahead shipbuilding complex in Japan, never does anything sudden or unpremeditated.

Dunross thought about the closing of their ship deal and the three payments of 2 million each that were due imminently on September 1, 11 and 15, the balance in ninety days. $12 million U.S. in all that he didn't have at the moment. Or the charterer's signed contract that was necessary to support the bank loan that he did not have, yet. 'Never mind,' he said easily, 'everything's going to be fine.'

'For them, yes,' Claudia said. 'You know I don't trust them, tai-pan. Any of them.'

'You can't fault them, Claudia. They're only trying to do economically what they failed to do militarily.'

'By pricing everyone out of the world markets.'

'They're working hard, they're making profits and they'll bury us, if we let them.' His eyes hardened too. 'But after all, Claudia, scratch an Englishman—or a Scot—and find a pirate. If we're such bloody fools to allow it we deserve to go under—isn't that what Hong Kong's all about?'

'Why help the enemy?'

'They were the enemy,' he said kindly. 'But that was only for twenty-odd years and our connections there go back a hundred. Weren't we the first traders into Japan? Didn't Hag Struan buy us the first plot offered for sale in Yokohama in 1860? Didn't she order that it be a cornerstone of Struan's policy to have the China-Japan-Hong Kong triangle?'

'Yes, tai-pan, but don't you thi—'

'No, Claudia, we've dealt with the Todas, the Kasigis, the

90

Toranagas for a hundred years, and right now Toda Shipping's very important to us.'

The phone rang again. She answered it. 'Yes, I'll phone him back.' Then to Dunross. 'It's the caterers—about your party tonight.'

'What's the problem?'

'None, tai-pan—they're moaning. After all, it's *the* tai-pan's twentieth wedding anniversary. All Hong Kong will be there and all Hong Kong better be impressed.' Again the phone rang. She picked it up. 'Ahh good! Put him through. . . . It's Bill Foster from Sydney.'

Dunross took the phone. 'Bill . . . no, you were top of the list. Have you closed on the Woolara Properties deal yet? . . . What's the holdup? . . . I don't care about that.' He glanced at his watch. 'It's just past noon your time. Call them right now and offer them fifty cents Australian more a share, the offer good till the close of business today. Get on to the bank in Sydney at once and tell them to demand full repayment of all their loans at the close of business today. . . . I couldn't care less, they're thirty days overdue already. I want control of that company now. Without it our new bulk-carrier charter deal will fall apart and we'll have to begin all over again. And catch the Qantas Flight 543 on Thursday. I'd like you here for a conference.' He put the phone down. 'Get Linbar up here as soon as the Tcholok meeting's over. Book him on Qantas 716 for Sydney on Friday morning.'

'Yes, tai-pan.' She made a note and handed him a list. 'Here're your appointments for today.'

He glanced at it. Four board meetings of some subsidiary companies this morning: Golden Ferry at 10:30, Struan's Motor Imports of Hong Kong at 11:00, Chong-Li Foods at 11:15 and Kowloon Investments at 11:30. Lunch with Lincoln Bartlett and Miss Casey Tcholok 12:40 to 2:00 P.M. More board meetings this afternoon, Peter Marlowe at 4:00 P.M., Phillip Chen at 4:20, cocktails at 6:00 with the governor, his anniversary party beginning at 8:00, a reminder to call Alastair Struan in Scotland at 11:00, and at least fifteen other people throughout Asia to phone during the day.

'Marlowe?' he asked.

'He's a writer, staying at the Vic—remember, he wrote for an

91

appointment a week ago. He's researching a book on Hong Kong.'

'Oh yes—the ex-RAF type.'

'Yes. Would you like him put off?'

'No. Keep everything as arranged, Claudia.' He took out a thin black leather memo-card case from his back pocket and gave her a dozen cards covered with his shorthand. 'Here're some cables and telexes to send off at once and notes for the various board meetings. Get me Jen in Taipei, then Havergill at the bank, then run down the list.'

'Yes, tai-pan. I hear Havergill's going to retire.'

'Marvelous. Who's taking over?'

'No one knows yet.'

'Let's hope it's Johnjohn. Put your spies to work. A hundred says I find out before you do!'

'Done!'

'Good.' Dunross held out his hand and said sweetly, 'You can pay me now. It's Johnjohn.'

'Eh?' She stared at him.

'We decided it last night—all the directors. I asked them to tell no one until eleven today.'

Reluctantly she took out the hundred-dollar note and offered it. '*Ayeeyah*, I was particularly attached to this note.'

'Thank you,' Dunross said and pocketed it. 'I'm particularly attached to that one myself.'

There was a knock on the door. 'Yes?' he said.

The door was opened by Sandra Yi, his private secretary. 'Excuse me, tai-pan, but the market's up two points and Holdbrook's on line two.' Alan Holdbrook was head of their in-house stockbroking company.

Dunross punched the line two button. 'Claudia, soon as I'm through bring in Armstrong.' She left with Sandra Yi.

'Yes, Alan?'

'Morning, tai-pan. First: There's a heavy rumor that we're going to make a bid for control of Asian Properties.'

'That's probably put out by Jason Plumm to boost his shares before their annual meeting. You know what a canny bastard he is.'

'Our stock's gone up ten cents, perhaps on the strength of it.'

'Good. Buy me 20,000 at once.'

'On margin?'

'Of course on margin.'

'All right. Second rumor: We've closed a multimillion-dollar deal with Par-Con Industries—huge expansion.'

'Pipe dreams,' Dunross said easily, wondering furiously where the leaks were. Only Phillip Chen—and in Edinburgh, Alastair Struan and old Sean MacStruan—was supposed to know about the ploy to smash Asian Properties. And the Par-Con deal was top secret to the Inner Court only.

'Third: someone's buying large parcels of our stock.'

'Who?'

'I don't know. But there's something smelly going on, tai-pan. The way our stock's been creeping up the last month . . . There's no reason that I know of, except a buyer, or buyers. Same with Rothwell-Gornt. I heard a block of 200,000 was bought offshore.'

'Find out who.'

'Christ, I wish I knew how. The market's jittery, and very nervous. A lot of Chinese money's floating around. Lots of little deals going on . . . a few shares here, a few there, but multiplied by a hundred thousand or so . . . the market might start to fall apart . . . or to soar.'

'Good. Then we'll all make a killing. Give me a call before the market closes. Thanks, Alan.' He put the phone down, feeling the sweat on his back. 'Shit,' he said aloud. 'What the hell's going on?'

In the outer office Claudia Chen was going over some papers with Sandra Yi who was her niece on her mother's side—and smart, very good to look at, twenty-seven with a mind like an abacus. Then she glanced at her watch and said in Cantonese, 'Superintendent Brian Kwok's downstairs, Little Sister, why don't you fetch him up?—in six minutes.'

'*Ayeeyah*, yes, Elder Sister!' Sandra Yi hastily checked her makeup and swished away. Claudia smiled after her and thought Sandra Yi would be perfect—a perfect choice for Brian Kwok. Happily she sat behind her desk and began to type the telexes. Everything's done that should be done, she told herself. No, something the tai-pan said . . . what was it? Ah yes! She dialed her home number.

'*Weyyyyy?*' said her *amah*, Ah Sam.

'Listen, Ah Sam,' she said in Cantonese, 'isn't Third Toilet-maid Fung at the Vic your cousin three times removed?'

'Oh yes, Mother,' Ah Sam replied, using the Chinese polite-ness of servant to mistress. 'But she's four times removed, and from the Fung-tats, not the Fung-sams which is my branch.'

'Never mind that, Ah Sam. You call her and find out all you can about two foreign devils from the Golden Mountain. They're in Fragrant Spring suite.' Patiently she spelled their names, then added delicately, 'I hear they have peculiar pillow habits.'

'*Ayeeyah*, if anyone can find out, Third Toiletmaid Fung can. Ha! What peculiars?'

'Strange peculiars, Ah Sam. You get on with it, little oily mouth.' She beamed and hung up.

The elevator doors opened and Sandra Yi ushered the two police officers in, then left reluctantly. Brian Kwok watched her go. He was thirty-nine, tall for a Chinese, just over six foot, very handsome, with blue-black hair. Both men wore civilian clothes. Claudia chatted with them politely, but the moment she saw the light on line two go out she ushered them in and closed the door.

'Sorry to come without an appointment,' Armstrong said.

'No sweat, Robert. You look tired.'

'A heavy night. It's all the villainy that goes on in Hong Kong,' Armstrong said easily. 'Nasties abound and saints get crucified.'

Dunross smiled, then glanced across at Kwok. 'How's life treating you, Brian?'

Brian Kwok smiled back. 'Very good, thanks, Ian. Stock market's up—I've a few dollars in the bank, my Porsche hasn't fallen apart yet, and ladies will be ladies.'

'Thank God for that! Are you doing the hill climb on Sunday?'

'If I can get Lulu in shape. She's missing an offside hydraulic coupling.'

'Have you tried our shop?'

'Yes. No joy, tai-pan. Are you going?'

'Depends. I've got to go to Taipei Sunday afternoon—I will if I've got time. I entered anyway. How's SI?'

Brian Kwok grinned. 'It beats working for a living.' Special Intelligence was a completely independent department within the elite, semisecret Special Branch responsible for preventing and detecting subversive activities in the Colony. It had its own secret ways, secret funding and overriding powers. And it was responsible to the governor alone.

Dunross leaned back in the chair. 'What's up?'

Armstrong said, 'I'm sure you already know. It's about the guns on Bartlett's plane.'

'Oh yes, I heard this morning,' he said. 'How can I help? Have you any idea why and where they were destined? And by whom? You caught two men?'

Armstrong sighed. 'Yes. They were genuine mechanics all right—both ex-Nationalist Air Force trained. No previous record, though they're suspected of being members of secret triads. Both have been here since the exodus of '49. By the way, can we keep all this confidential, between the three of us?'

'What about your superiors?'

'I'd like to include them in—but keep it just for your ears only.'

'Why?'

'We have reason to believe the guns were destined for someone in Struan's.'

'Who?' Dunross asked sharply.

'Confidential?'

'Yes. Who?'

'How much do you know about Lincoln Bartlett and Casey Tcholok?'

'We've a detailed dossier on him—not on her. Would you like it? I can give you a copy, provided it too is kept confidential.'

'Of course. That would be very helpful.'

Dunross pressed the intercom.

'Yes sir?' Claudia asked.

'Make a copy of the Bartlett dossier and give it to Superintendent Armstrong on his way out.' Dunross clicked the intercom off.

'We won't take much more of your time,' Armstrong said. 'Do you always dossier potential clients?'

'No. But we like to know who we're dealing with. If the Bartlett deal goes through it could mean millions to us, to him, a thousand new jobs to Hong Kong—factories here, warehouses, a very big expansion—along with equally big risks to us.

95

Everyone in business does a confidential financial statement—perhaps we're a bit more thorough. I'll bet you fifty dollars to a broken hatpin he's done one on me.'

'No criminal connections mentioned?'

Dunross was startled. 'Mafia? That sort of thing? Good God no, nothing. Besides, if the Mafia were trying to come in here they wouldn't send a mere ten M14 rifles and two thousand rounds and a box of grenades.'

'Your information's damn good,' Brian Kwok interrupted. 'Too damn good. We only unpacked the stuff an hour ago. Who's your informant?'

'You know there're no secrets in Hong Kong.'

'Can't even trust your own coppers these days.'

'The Mafia would surely send in a shipment twenty times that and they'd be handguns, American style. But the Mafia would be bound to fail here, whatever they did. They could never displace our triads. No, it can't be Mafia—only someone local. Who tipped you about the shipment, Brian?'

'Tokyo Airport Police,' Kwok said. 'One of their mechanics was doing a routine inspection—you know how thorough they are. He reported it to his superior, their police phoned us and we said to let it through.'

'In that case get hold of the FBI and the CIA—get them to check back to Honolulu—or Los Angeles.'

'You went through the flight plan too?'

'Of course. That's obvious. Why someone in Struan's?'

'Both of the villains said . . .' Armstrong took out his pad and referred to it. 'Our question was, "Where were you to take the packages?" Both answered using different words: "To 15 go-down, we were to put the packages in Bay 7 at the back."' He looked up at Dunross.

'That proves nothing. We've the biggest warehouse operation at Kai Tak—just because they take it to one of our go-downs proves nothing—other than they're smart. We've got so much merchandise going through, it'd be easy to send in an alien truck.' Dunross thought a moment. '15's right at the exit—perfect placing.' He reached for the phone. 'I'll put my security folk on it right n—'

'Would you not, please, just for the moment.'

'Why?'

'Our next question,' Armstrong continued, 'was, "Who employed you?" Of course they gave fictitious names and descriptions and denied everything but they'll be more helpful soon.' He smiled grimly. 'One of them did say, however, when one of my sergeants was twisting his ear a little, figuratively speaking of course'—he read from the pad—'"You leave me alone, I've got very important friends!" "You've no friends in the world," the sergeant said. "Maybe, but the Honorable Tsu-yan has and Noble House Chen has."'

The silence became long and heavy. They waited.

Those God-cursed guns, Dunross thought furiously. But he held his face calm and his wits sharpened. 'We've a hundred and more Chens working for us, related, unrelated—Chen's as common a name as Smith.'

'And Tsu-yan?' Brian Kwok asked.

Dunross shrugged. 'He's a director of Struan's—but he's also a director of Blacs, the Victoria Bank and forty other companies, one of the richest men in Hong Kong and a name anyone in Asia could pull out of a hat. Like Noble House Chen.'

'Do you know he's suspected of being very high up in the triad hierarchy—specifically in the Green Pang?' Brian Kwok asked.

'Every important Shanghainese's equally suspect. Jesus Christ, Brian, you know Chiang Kai-shek was supposed to have given Shanghai to the Green Pang years ago as their exclusive bailiwick if they'd support his northern campaign against the warlords. Isn't the Green Pang still, more or less, an official Nationalist secret society?'

Brian Kwok said, 'Where'd Tsu-yan make his money, Ian? His first fortune?'

'I don't know. You tell me, Brian.'

'He made it during the Korean War smuggling penicillin, drugs and petrol—mostly penicillin—across the border to the Communists. Before Korea all he owned was a loincloth and a broken-down rickshaw.'

'That's all hearsay, Brian.'

'Struan's made a fortune too.'

'Yes. But it would really be very unwise to imply we did it smuggling—publicly or privately,' Dunross said mildly. 'Very unwise indeed.'

'Didn't you?'

'Struan's began with a little smuggling 120-odd years ago, so rumor has it, but it was an honorable profession and never against British law. We're law-abiding capitalists and China Traders and have been for years.'

Brian Kwok did not smile. 'More hearsay's that a lot of his penicillin was bad. Very bad.'

'If it was, if that's the truth, then please go get him, Brian,' Dunross said coldly. 'Personally I think that's another rumor spread by jealous competitors. If it was true he'd be floating in the bay with the others who tried, or he'd be punished like Bad Powder Wong.' He was referring to a Hong Kong smuggler who had sold a vast quantity of adulterated penicillin over the border during the Korean War and invested his fortune in stocks and land in Hong Kong. Within seven years he was very very rich. Then certain triads of Hong Kong were ordered to balance the books. Every week one member of his family vanished, or died. By drowning, car accident, strangulation, poison or knife. No assailant was ever caught. The killing went on for seventeen months and three weeks and then stopped. Only he and one semi-imbecile infant grandson remained alive. They lived today, still holed up in the same vast, once luxurious penthouse apartment with one servant and one cook, in terror, guarded night and day, never going out—knowing that no guards or any amount of money could ever prevent the inexorability of his sentence published in a tiny box in a local Chinese newspaper: Bad Powder Wong will be punished, he and all his generations.

Brian Kwok said, 'We interviewed that sod once, Robert and I.'

'Oh?'

'Yes. Scary. Every door's double locked and chained, every window nailed up and boarded over with planks—just spy holes here and there. He hasn't been out since the killing started. The place stank, my God did it stink! All he does is play Chinese checkers with his grandson and watch television.'

'And wait,' Armstrong said. 'One day they'll come for both of them. His grandson must be six or seven now.'

Dunross said, 'I think you prove my point. Tsu-yan's not like him and never was. And what possible use could Tsu-yan have for a few M14s? If he wanted to, I imagine he could muster half the Nationalist army along with a battalion of tanks.'

'In Taiwan but not in Hong Kong.'

'Has Tsu-yan ever been involved with Bartlett?' Armstrong asked. 'In your negotiations?'

'Yes. He was in New York once and in Los Angeles on our behalf. Both times with John Chen. They initialed the agreement between Struan's and Par-Con Industries which is to be finalized—or abandoned—here this month, and they formally invited Bartlett to Hong Kong on my behalf.'

Armstrong glanced at his Chinese partner. Then he said, 'When was this?'

'Four months ago. It's taken that time for both sides to prepare all the details.'

'John Chen, eh?' Armstrong said. 'He certainly could be Noble House Chen.'

'You know John's not the type,' Dunross said. 'There's no reason why he should be mixed up in such a ploy. It must be just coincidence.'

'There's another curious coincidence,' Brian Kwok said. 'Tsu-yan and John Chen both know an American called Banastasio, at least both have been seen in his company. Does that name mean anything?'

'No. Who's he?'

'A big-time gambler and suspected racketeer. He's also supposed to be closely connected with one of the Cosa Nostra families. Vincenzo Banastasio.'

Dunross's eyes narrowed. 'You said, "seen in his company." Who did the seeing?'

'The FBI.'

The silence thickened a little.

Armstrong reached into his pocket for a cigarette.

Dunross pushed across the silver cigarette box. 'Here.'

'Oh, thanks. No, I won't—I wasn't thinking. I've stopped for the last couple of weeks. It's a killer.' Then he added, trying to curb the desire, 'The FBI passed the info on to us because Tsu-yan and Mr. John Chen are so prominent here. They asked us to keep an eye on them.'

Then Dunross suddenly remembered Foxwell's remark about a prominent capitalist who was a secret Communist that they were watching in Sinclair Towers. Christ, he thought, Tsu-yan's got a flat there, and so has John Chen. Surely it's impossible either'd be mixed up with Communists.

'Of course heroin's big business,' Armstrong was saying, his voice very hard.

'What does that mean, Robert?'

'The drug racket requires huge amounts of money to finance it. That kind of money can only come from banks or bankers, covertly of course. Tsu-yan's on the board of a number of banks—so's Mr. Chen.'

'Robert, you'd better go very slow on that sort of remark,' Dunross grated. 'You are drawing very dangerous conclusions without any proof whatsoever. That's actionable, I'd imagine, and I won't have it.'

'You're right, sorry. I withdraw the coincidence. Even so, the drug trade's big business, and it's here in Hong Kong in abundance, mostly for ultimate U.S. consumption. Somehow I'm going to find out who our nasties are.'

'That's commendable. And you'll have all the help you want from Struan's and me. I hate the traffic too.'

'Oh I don't hate it, tai-pan, or the traffickers. It's a fact of life. It's just another business—illegal certainly but still a business. I've been given the job of finding out who the tai-pans are. It's a matter of personal satisfaction, that's all.'

'If you want help, just ask.'

'Thank you.' Armstrong got up wearily. 'Before we go there're a couple more coincidences for you. When Tsu-yan and Noble House Chen were named this morning we thought we'd like to chat with them right away, but shortly after we ambushed the guns Tsu-yan caught the early flight to Taipei. Curious, eh?'

'He's back and forth all the time,' Dunross said, his disquiet soaring. Tsu-yan was expected at his party this evening. It would be extraordinary if he did not appear.

Armstrong nodded. 'It seems it was a last-minute decision—no reservation, no ticket, no luggage, just a few extra dollars under the counter and someone was bounced off and him on. He was carrying only a briefcase. Strange, eh?'

Brian Kwok said, 'We haven't a hope in hell of extraditing him from Taiwan.'

Dunross studied him then looked back at Armstrong, his eyes

steady and the color of sea ice. 'You said there were a couple of coincidences. What's the other?'

'We can't find John Chen.'

'What're you talking about?'

'He's not at home, or at his lady friend's, or at any of his usual haunts. We've been watching him and Tsu-yan off and on for months, ever since the FBI tipped us.'

The silence gathered. 'You've checked his boat?' Dunross asked, sure that they had.

'She's at her moorings, hasn't been out since yesterday. His boat-boy hasn't seen him either.'

'Golf course?'

'No, he's not there,' Armstrong said. 'Nor at the racetrack. He wasn't at the workout, though he was expected, his trainer said. He's gone, vanished, scarpered.'

6

There was a stunned silence in the boardroom.

'What's wrong?' Casey asked. 'The figures speak for themselves.'

The four men around the table looked at her. Andrew Gavallan, Linbar Struan, Jacques deVille and Phillip Chen, all members of the Inner Court.

Andrew Gavallan was tall and thin and forty-seven. He glanced at the sheaf of papers in front of him. *Dew neh loh moh* on all women in business, he thought irritably. 'Perhaps we should check with Mr. Bartlett,' he said uneasily, still very unsettled that they were expected to deal with a woman.

'I've already told you I have authority in all these areas,' she said, trying to be patient. 'I'm treasurer and executive vice-president of Par-Con Industries and empowered to negotiate with you. We confirmed that in writing last month.' Casey held her temper. The meeting had been very heavy going. From their initial shock that she was a woman to their inevitable, overpolite awkwardness, waiting for her to sit, waiting for her to talk, then not sitting until she had asked them to, making small talk, not wanting to get down to business, not wishing to negotiate with her as a person, a business person, at all, saying instead that their wives would be delighted to take her shopping, then gaping because she knew all the intimate details of their projected deal. It was all part of a pattern that, normally, she could deal with. But not today. Jesus, she thought, I've got to succeed. I've got to get through to them.

'It's really quite easy,' she had said initially, trying to clear their awkwardness away, using her standard opening. 'Forget that I'm a woman—judge me on my ability. Now, there are three subjects on our agenda: the polyurethane factories, our computer-leasing representation and last, general representation of our petrochemical products, fertilizers, pharmaceutical and sports goods throughout Asia. First let's sort out the polyurethane factories, the chemical mix supplies and a projected time schedule for the financing.' At once she gave them graphics and prepared documentation, verbally synopsized all the facts, figures and percentages, bank charges and interest charges, simply and very quickly, so that even the slowest brain could grasp the project. And now they were staring at her.

Andrew Gavallan broke the silence. 'That's . . . that's very impressive, my dear.'

'Actually I'm not your "dear,"' she said with a laugh. 'I'm very hard-nosed for my corporation.'

'But mademoiselle,' Jacques deVille said with a suave Gallic charm, 'your nose is perfect and not hard at all.'

'*Merci, monsieur*,' she replied at once, and added lightly in passable French, 'but please may we leave the shape of my nose for the moment and discuss the shape of this deal. It's better not to mix the two, don't you think?'

Another silence.

Linbar Struan said, 'Would you like some coffee?'

'No thanks, Mr. Struan,' Casey said, being careful to conform to their customs and not to call them by their Christian names too early. 'May we zero in on this proposal? It's the one we sent you last month. . . . I've tried to cover your problems as well as ours.'

There was another silence. Linbar Struan, thirty-four, very good-looking with sandy hair and blue eyes with a devil-may-care glint to them, persisted, 'Are you sure you wouldn't like coffee? Tea perhaps?'

'No thanks. Then you accept our proposal as it stands?'

Phillip Chen coughed and said, 'In principle we agree to want to be in business with Par-Con in several areas. The Heads of Agreement indicate that. As to the polyurethane factories . . .'

She listened to his generalizations, then once more tried to get to the specifics—the whole reason for this meeting. But the going was very hard and she could feel them squirming. This's the worst it's ever been. Perhaps it's because they're English,

103

and I've never dealt with the English before.

'Is there anything specific that needs clarifying?' she asked. 'If there's anything you don't understand . . .'

Gavallan said, 'We understand very well. You present us with figures which are lopsided. We're financing the building of the factories. You provide the machines but their cost is amortized over three years which'll mess up any cash flow and mean no profits for five years at least.'

'I'm told it is your custom in Hong Kong to amortize the full cost of a building over a three-year period,' she replied equally sharply, glad to be challenged. 'We're just proposing to follow your custom. If you want five—or ten years—you may have them, provided the same applies to the building.'

'You're not paying for the machines—they're on a lease basis and the monthly charge to the joint venture is high.'

'What's your bank prime rate today, Mr. Gavallan?'

They consulted, then told her. She used her pocket slide rule for a few seconds. 'At today's rate you'd save 17,000 HK a week per machine if you take our deal which, over the period we're talking . . .' another quick calculation, '. . . would jump your end of the profits 32 percent over the best you could do—and we're talking in millions of dollars.'

They stared at her in silence.

Andrew Gavallan cross-questioned her about the figures but she never faltered. Their dislike for her increased.

Silence.

She was sure they were fogged by her figures. What else can I say to convince them? she thought, her anxiety growing. Struan's will make a bundle if they get off their asses, we'll make a fortune and I'll get my drop dead money at long last. The foam part of the deal alone will make Struan's rich and Par-Con nearly $80,000 net a month over the next ten years and Linc said I could have a piece.

'How much do you want?' he had asked her, just before they had left the States.

'51 percent,' she had replied with a laugh, 'since you're asking.'

'3 percent.'

'Come on, Linc, I need my drop dead money.'

'Pull off the whole package and you've got a stock option of

100,000 Par-Con at four dollars below market.'

'You're on. But I want the foam company too,' she had said, holding her breath. 'I started it and I want that. 51 percent. For me.'

'In return for what?'

'Struan's.'

'Done.'

Casey waited outwardly calm. When she judged the moment correct she said innocently, 'Are we agreed then, that our proposal stands as is? We're fifty-fifty with you, what could be better than that?'

'I still say you're not providing 50 percent of the financing of the joint venture,' Andrew Gavallan replied sharply. 'You're providing the machines and materials on a lease carry-back so your risk's not equivalent to ours.'

'But that's for our tax purposes and to lessen the amount of cash outlay, gentlemen. We're financing from cash flow. The figures add up the same. The fact that we get a depreciation allowance and various rebates is neither here nor there.' Even more innocently, baiting the trap, she added, 'We finance in the States, where we've the expertise. You finance in Hong Kong where you're the experts.'

Quillan Gornt turned back from his office window. 'I repeat, we can better any arrangement you can make with Struan's, Mr. Bartlett. Any arrangement.'

'You'd go dollar for dollar?'

'Dollar for dollar.' The Englishman strolled back and sat behind his paperless desk and faced Bartlett again. They were on the top floor of the Rothwell-Gornt Building also fronting Connaught Road and the waterfront. Gornt was a thickset, hard-faced, bearded man, just under six feet, with graying black hair and graying bushy eyebrows and brown eyes. 'It's no secret our companies are very serious rivals, but I assure you we can outbid them and outmatch them, and I'd arrange our side of the financing within the week. We could have a profitable partnership, you and I. I'd suggest we set up a joint company under Hong Kong law—the taxes here're really quite reasonable—15 percent of everything earned in Hong Kong, with the rest of the world free of all taxes.' Gornt smiled. 'Better than the U.S.A.'

'Much better,' Bartlett said. He was sitting in a high-backed leather chair. 'Very much better.'

'Is that why you're interested in Hong Kong?'

'One reason.'

'What're the others?'

'There's no American outfit as big as mine here in strength yet, and there should be. This is the age of the Pacific. But you could benefit from our coming. We've a lot of expertise you don't have and a major say in areas of the U.S. market. On the other hand, Rothwell-Gornt—and Struan's—have the expertise we lack and a major say in the Asian markets.'

'How can we cement a relationship?'

'First I have to find out what Struan's are after. I started negotiating with them, and I don't like changing airplanes in mid-ocean.'

'I can tell you at once what they're after: profit for them and the hell with anyone else.' Gornt's smile was hard.

'The deal we've discussed seems very fair.'

'They're past masters at appearing to be very fair and putting up a half share, then selling out at their own choosing to skim the profit and yet retain control.'

'That wouldn't be possible with us.'

'They've been at it for almost a century and a half. They've learned a few tricks by now.'

'So've you.'

'Of course. But Struan's is very different from us. We own things and companies—they're percentagers. They've little more than a 5 percent holding in most of their subsidiaries yet they still exercise absolute control by special voting shares, or by making it mandatory in the Articles of Association that their tai-pan's also tai-pan of the subsidiary with overriding say.'

'That sounds smart.'

'It is. And they are. But we're better and straighter—and our contacts and influence in China and throughout the Pacific Rim, except for the U.S. and Canada, are stronger than theirs and growing stronger every day.'

'Why?'

'Because our company operations originated in Shanghai—

106

the greatest city in Asia—where we were dominant. Struan's has always concentrated on Hong Kong which, until recently, was almost a provincial backwater.'

'But Shanghai's a dead issue and has been since the Commies closed off the Mainland in '49. There's no foreign trade going through Shanghai today—it's all through Canton.'

'Yes. But it's the Shanghainese who left China and came south with money, brains and guts, who made Hong Kong what it is today and what it'll be tomorrow: the now and future metropolis of the whole Pacific.'

'Better than Singapore?'

'Absolutely.'

'Manila?'

'Absolutely.'

'Tokyo?'

'That will only ever be for Japanese.' Gornt's eyes sparkled, the lines on his face crinkled. 'Hong Kong is the greatest city in Asia, Mr. Bartlett. Whoever masters it will eventually master Asia. . . . Of course I'm talking about trade, financing, shipping and big business.'

'What about Red China?'

'We think Hong Kong benefits the PRC—as we call the People's Republic of China. We're the controlled "open door" for them. Hong Kong and Rothwell-Gornt represent the future.'

'Why?'

'Because since Shanghai was the business and industrial center of China, the pacesetter, Shanghainese are the go-getters of China, always have been and always will be. And now the best are with us here. You'll soon see the difference between Cantonese and Shanghainese. Shanghainese're the entrepreneurs, the industrialists, promoters and internationalists. There's not a great textile or shipping magnate or industrialist who isn't Shanghainese. Cantonese-run family businesses, Mr. Bartlett, they're loners, but Shanghainese understand partner-ships, corporate situations and above all, banking and financing.' Gornt lit another cigarette. 'That's where our strength is, why we're better than Struan's—why we'll be number one eventually.'

Linc Bartlett studied the man opposite him. From the dossier that Casey had prepared he knew that Gornt had been born in Shanghai of British parents, was forty-eight, a widower with two grown children, and that he had served as a captain in the Australian infantry '42–'45 in the Pacific. He knew too that he ruled Rothwell-Gornt very successfully as a private fief and had done so for eight years since he took over from his father.

Bartlett shifted in the deep leather chair. 'If you've got this rivalry with Struan's and you're so sure you'll be number one eventually, why wait? Why not take them now?'

Gornt was watching him, his craggy face set. 'There's nothing in the world that I'd like to do more. But I can't, not yet. I nearly did three years ago—they'd overreached themselves, the previous tai-pan's joss had run out.'

'Joss?'

'It's a Chinese word meaning luck, fate, but a bit more.' Gornt watched him thoughtfully. 'We're very superstitious out here. Joss is very important, like timing. Alastair Struan's joss ran out, or changed. He had a disastrous last year, and then, in desperation, handed over to Ian Dunross. They almost went under that time. A run had started on their stock. I went after them, but Dunross squeezed out of the run and stabilized the market.'

'How?'

'Let's say he exercised an undue amount of influence in certain banking circles.' Gornt remembered with cold fury how Havergill at the bank had suddenly, against all their private, secret agreements, not opposed Struan's request for a temporary, enormous line of credit that had given Dunross the time to recover.

Gornt remembered his blinding rage when he had called Havergill. 'What the hell did you do that for?' he had asked him. 'A hundred million as an Extraordinary Credit? You've saved their necks for chrissake! We had them. Why?' Havergill had told him that Dunross had mustered enough votes on the board and put an extreme amount of personal pressure on him. 'There was nothing I could do. . . .'

Yes, Gornt thought, looking at the American. I lost that time but I think you're the twenty-four-carat explosive key that will trigger the bomb to blow Struan's to hell out of Asia forever. 'Dunross went to the edge that time, Mr. Bartlett. He made some implacable enemies. But now we're equally strong. It's what you'd call a standoff. They can't take us and we can't take them.'

'Unless they make a mistake.'

'Or we make a mistake.' The older man blew a smoke ring and studied it. At length he glanced back at Bartlett. 'We'll win eventually. Time in Asia's a little different from time in the U.S.A.'

'That's what people tell me.'

'You don't believe it?'

'I know the same rules of survival apply here, there or where the hell ever. Only the degree changes.'

Gornt watched the smoke from his cigarette curling to the ceiling. His office was large with well-used old leather chairs and excellent oils on the walls and it was filled with the smell of polished leather and good cigars. Gornt's high-backed chair old oak and carved, with red plush fitted seat and back looked hard, functional and solid, Bartlett thought, like the man.

'We can outbid Struan's and we've time on our side, here, there, where the hell ever,' Gornt said.

Bartlett laughed.

Gornt smiled too but Bartlett noticed his eyes weren't smiling. 'Look around Hong Kong, Mr. Bartlett. Ask about us, and about them. Then make up your mind.'

'Yes, I'll do that.'

'I hear your aircraft's impounded.'

'Yes. Yes it is. The airport cops found some guns aboard.'

'I heard. Curious. Well, if you need any help to unimpound it, perhaps I can be of service.'

'You could help right now by telling me why and who.'

'I've no idea—but I'll wager someone in Struan's knows.'

'Why?'

'They knew your exact movements.'

'So did you.'

'Yes. But it was nothing to do with us.'

'Who knew we were to have this meeting, Mr. Gornt?'

'You and I. As we agreed. There was no leak from here, Mr. Bartlett. After our private meeting in New York last year, everything's been by telephone—not even a confirming telex. I sub-

109

scribe to your wisdom of caution, secrecy and dealing face to face. In private. But who on your side knows of our . . . our continuing interest?'

'No one but me.'

'Not even your lady treasurer executive vice-president?' Gornt asked with open surprise.

'No sir. When did you learn Casey was a she?'

'In New York. Come now, Mr. Bartlett, it's hardly likely we'd contemplate an association without ascertaining your credentials and those of your chief executives.'

'Good. That will save time.'

'Curious to have a woman in such a key position.'

'She's my right and left arm and the best executive I've got.'

'Then why wasn't she told of our meeting today?'

'One of the first rules of survival is to keep your options open.'

'Meaning?'

'Meaning I don't run my business by committee. Besides, I like to play off the cuff, to keep certain operations secret.' Bartlett thought a moment then added, 'It's not lack of trust. Actually, I'm making it easier for her. If anyone at Struan's finds out and asks her why I'm meeting with you now, her surprise will be genuine.'

After a pause Gornt said, 'It's rare to find anyone really trustworthy. Very rare.'

'Why would someone want M14s and grenades in Hong Kong and why would they use my plane?'

'I don't know but I'll make it my business to find out.' Gornt stubbed out his cigarette. The ashtray was porcelain—Sung dynasty. 'Do you know Tsu-yan?'

'I've met him a couple of times. Why?'

'He's a very good fellow, even though he's a director of Struan's.'

'He's Shanghainese?'

'Yes. One of the best.' Gornt looked up, his eyes very hard. 'It's possible there could be peripheral benefit to dealing with us, Mr. Bartlett. I hear Struan's is quite extended just now—Dunross's gambling heavily on his fleet, particularly on the two super bulk cargo carriers he has on order from Japan. The first's due to be paid for substantially in a week or so. Then, too, there's a strong rumor he's going to make a bid for Asian Properties. You've heard of them?'

'A big land operation, real estate, all over Hong Kong.'

'Yes. They're the biggest—even bigger than his own K.I.'

'Kowloon Investments is part of Struan's? I thought they were a separate company.'

'They are, outwardly. But Dunross is tai-pan of K.I.—they always have the same tai-pan.'

'Always?'

'Always. It's in their Heads of Agreement. But Ian's over-riding himself. The Noble House may soon become ignoble. He's very cash light at the moment.'

Bartlett thought a moment, then he asked, 'Why don't you join with another company, maybe Asian Properties, and take Struan's? That's what I'd do in the States if I wanted a company I couldn't take alone.'

'Is that what you want to do here, Mr. Bartlett?' Gornt asked at once, pretending shock. 'To "take" Struan's?'

'Is it possible?'

Gornt looked at the ceiling carefully before answering. 'Yes—but you'd have to have a partner. Perhaps you could do it with Asian Properties but I doubt it. Jason Plumm, the tai-pan, hasn't the balls. You'd need us. Only we have the perspicacity, the drive, the knowledge and the desire. Nevertheless, you'd have to risk a very great deal of money. Cash.'

'How much?'

Gornt laughed outright. 'I'll consider that. First you'll have to tell me how serious you are.'

'And if I am, would you want in?'

Gornt stared back, his eyes equally level. 'First I would have to be sure, very sure, how serious you are. It's no secret I detest Struan's generally and Ian Dunross personally, would want them obliterated. So you already know my long-term posture. I don't know yours. Yet.'

'If we could take over Struan's—would it be worth it?'

'Oh yes, Mr. Bartlett. Oh yes—yes it'd be worth it,' Gornt said jovially, then once more his voice iced. 'But I still need to know how serious you are.'

'I'll tell you when I've seen Dunross.'

'Are you going to suggest the same thought to him—that

111

together you can swallow Rothwell-Gornt?'

'My purpose here is to make Par-Con international, Mr. Gornt. Maybe up to a $30 million investment to cover a whole range of merchandising, factories and warehousing. Up to a short time ago I'd never heard of Struan's—or Rothwell-Gornt. Or your rivalry.'

'Very well, Mr. Bartlett, we'll leave it at that. Whatever you do will be interesting. Yes. It will be interesting to see if you can hold a knife.'

Bartlett stared at him, not understanding.

'That's an old Chinese cooking term, Mr. Bartlett. Do you cook?'

'No.'

'It's a hobby of mine. The Chinese say it's important to know how to hold a knife, that you can't use one until you can hold it correctly. Otherwise you'll cut yourself and be off to a very bad start indeed. Won't you?'

Bartlett grinned. 'Hold a knife, is it? I'll remember that. No, I can't cook. Never got around to learning—Casey can't cook worth a damn either.'

'The Chinese say there're three arts in which no other civilization can compare to theirs—literature, brush painting and cooking. I'm inclined to agree. Do you like good food?'

'The best meal I ever had was in a restaurant just outside Rome on the Via Flaminia, the Casale.'

'Then we've at least that in common, Mr. Bartlett. The Casale's one of my favorites too.'

'Casey took me there once—*spaghetti alla matriciana al dente* and *buscetti* with an ice-cold bottle of beer followed by the *piccata* and more beer. I'll never forget it.'

Gornt smiled. 'Perhaps you'll have dinner with me while you're here. I can offer you *alla matriciana* too—actually it'll compare favorably, it's the very same recipe.'

'I'd like that.'

'And a bottle of Valpolicella, or a great Tuscany wine.'

'Personally, I like beer with pasta. Iced American beer out of the can.'

After a pause Gornt asked, 'How long are you staying in Hong Kong?'

'As long as it takes,' Bartlett said without hesitation.

'Good. Then dinner one day next week? Tuesday or Wednesday?'

'Tuesday'd be fine, thanks. May I bring Casey?'

'Of course.' Then Gornt added, his voice flatter, 'By that time perhaps you'll be more sure of what you want to do.'

Bartlett laughed. 'And by that time you'll find out if I can hold a knife.'

'Perhaps. But just remember one thing, Mr. Bartlett. If we ever join forces to attack Struan's, once the battle is joined there will be almost no way to withdraw without getting severely mauled. Very severely mauled indeed. I'd have to be very sure. After all, you can always retire hurt to the U.S.A. to fight another day. We stay—so the risks are unequal.'

'But the spoils are unequal too. You'd gain something priceless which doesn't mean ten cents to me. You'd become the Noble House.'

'Yes,' Gornt said, his eyes lidding. He leaned forward to select another cigarette and his left foot moved behind the desk to press a hidden floor switch. 'Let's leave everything until Tues—'

The intercom clicked on. 'Excuse me, Mr. Gornt, would you like me to postpone the board meeting?' his secretary asked.

'No,' Gornt said. 'They can wait.'

'Yes sir. Miss Ramos is here. Could you spare her a few minutes?'

Gornt pretended to be surprised. 'Just a moment.' He looked up at Bartlett. 'Have we concluded?'

'Yes.' Bartlett got up at once. 'Tuesday's firm. Let's keep everything cooking till then.' He turned to go but Gornt stopped him. 'Just a moment, Mr. Bartlett,' he said, then into the intercom, 'ask her to come in.' He clicked off the switch and stood up. 'I'm glad to have had the meeting.'

The door opened and the girl came in. She was twenty-five and stunning with short black hair and sloe eyes, clearly Eurasian, casually dressed in tight, American washed jeans and a shirt. 'Hello, Quillan,' she said with a smile that warmed the room, her English slightly American accented. 'Sorry to interrupt but I've just got back from Bangkok and wanted to say hello.'

'Glad you did, Orlanda.' Gornt smiled at Bartlett who was

113

staring at her. 'This is Linc Bartlett, from America. Orlanda Ramos.'

'Hello,' Bartlett said.

'Hi . . . oh, Linc Bartlett? The American millionaire gun-runner?' she said and laughed.

'What?'

'Oh don't look so shocked, Mr. Bartlett. Everyone in Hong Kong knows—Hong Kong's just a village.'

'Seriously—how did you know?'

'I read it in my morning paper.'

'Impossible! It only happened at 5:30 this morning.'

'It was in the *Fai Pao*—the *Express*—in the Stop Press column at nine o'clock. It's a Chinese paper and the Chinese know everything that's going on here. Don't worry, the English papers won't pick it up till the afternoon editions, but you can expect the press on your doorstep around the happy hour.'

'Thanks.' The last thing I want's the goddamn press after me, Bartlett thought sourly.

'Don't worry, Mr. Bartlett, I won't ask you for an interview, even though I am a free-lance reporter for the Chinese press. I'm really very discreet,' she said. 'Am I not, Quillan?'

'Absolutely. I'll vouch for that,' Gornt said. 'Orlanda's absolutely trustworthy.'

'Of course if you want to *offer* an interview—I'll accept. Tomorrow.'

'I'll consider it.'

'I'll guarantee to make you look marvelous!'

'The Chinese really know everything here?'

'Of course,' she said at once. 'But *quai loh*—foreigners—don't read the Chinese papers, except for a handful of old China hands—like Quillan.'

'And the whole of Special Intelligence, Special Branch and the police in general,' Gornt said.

'And Ian Dunross,' she added, the tip of her tongue touching her teeth.

'He's that sharp?' Bartlett asked.

'Oh yes. He's got Devil Struan's blood in him.'

'I don't understand.'

'You will, if you stay here long enough.'

Bartlett thought about that, then frowned. 'You knew about the guns too, Mr. Gornt?'

'Only that the police had intercepted contraband arms aboard "the millionaire American's private jet which arrived last night." It was in my Chinese paper this morning too. The *Sing Pao*.' Gornt's smile was sardonic. 'That's *The Times* in Cantonese. It was in their Stop Press column too. But, unlike Orlanda, I am surprised you haven't been intercepted by members of our English press already. They're very diligent here in Hong Kong. More diligent than Orlanda gives them credit for being.'

Bartlett caught her perfume but persisted. 'I'm surprised you didn't mention it, Mr. Gornt.'

'Why should I? What do guns have to do with our possible future association?' Gornt chuckled. 'If worst comes to worst we'll visit you in jail, Orlanda and I.'

She laughed. 'Yes indeed.'

'Thanks a lot!' Again her perfume. Bartlett put aside the guns and concentrated on her. 'Ramos—that's Spanish?'

'Portuguese. From Macao. My father worked for Rothwell-Gornt in Shanghai—my mother's Shanghainese. I was brought up in Shanghai until '49, then went to the States for a few years, to high school in San Francisco.'

'Did you? L.A.'s my hometown—I went to high school in the Valley.'

'I love California,' she said. 'How d'you like Hong Kong?'

'I've just arrived.' Bartlett grinned. 'Seems I made an explosive entrance.'

She laughed. Lovely white teeth. 'Hong Kong's all right—provided you can leave every month or so. You should visit Macao for a weekend—it's old- worldly, very pretty, only forty miles away with good ferries. It's very different from Hong Kong.' She turned back to Gornt. 'Again, I'm sorry to interrupt, Quillan, just wanted to say hello. . . .' She started to leave.

'No, we're through—I was just going,' Bartlett said, interrupting her. 'Thanks again, Mr. Gornt. See you Tuesday if not before. . . . Hope to see you again, Miss Ramos.'

'Yes, that would be nice. Here's my card—if you'll grant the interview I guarantee a good press.' She held out her hand and he touched it and felt her warmth.

115

Gornt saw him to the door and then closed it and came back to his desk and took a cigarette. She lit the match for him and blew out the flame, then sat in the chair Bartlett had used.

'Nice-looking man,' she said.

'Yes. But he's American, naive, and a very cocky bastard who may need taking down a peg.'

'That's what you want me to do?'

'Perhaps. Did you read his dossier?'

'Oh yes. Very interesting.' Orlanda smiled.

'You're not to ask him for money,' Gornt said sharply.

'*Ayeeyah*, Quillan, am I that dumb?' she said as abrasively, her eyes flashing.

'Good.'

'Why would he smuggle guns into Hong Kong?'

'Why indeed, my dear? Perhaps someone was just using him.'

'That must be the answer. If I had all his money I wouldn't try something as stupid as that.'

'No,' Gornt said.

'Oh, did you like that bit about my being a free-lance reporter? I thought I did that very well.'

'Yes, but don't underestimate him. He's no fool. He's very sharp. Very.' He told her about the Casale. 'That's too much of a coincidence. He must have a dossier on me too, a detailed one. Not many know of my liking for that place.'

'Maybe I'm in it too.'

'Perhaps. Don't let him catch you out. About the free-lancing.'

'Oh, come on, Quillan, who of the tai-pans except you and Dunross read the Chinese papers—and even then you can't read all of them. I've already done a column or two . . . "by a Special Correspondent." If he grants me an interview I can write it. Don't worry.' She moved the ashtray closer for him. 'It went all right, didn't it? With Bartlett?'

'Perfectly. You're wasted. You should be in the movies.'

'Then talk to your friend about me, please, please, Quillan dear. Charlie Wang's the biggest producer in Hong Kong and owes you lots of favors. Charlie Wang has so many movies going that . . . just one chance is all I need. . . . I could become a star! Please?'

'Why not?' he asked dryly. 'But I don't think you're his type.'

'I can adapt. Didn't I act exactly as you wanted with Bartlett? Am I not dressed perfectly, American style?'

'Yes, yes you are.' Gornt looked at her, then said delicately, 'You could be perfect for him. I was thinking you could perhaps have something more permanent than an affair. . . .'

All her attention concentrated. 'What?'

'You and he could fit together like a perfect Chinese puzzle. You're good-humored, the right age, beautiful, clever, educated, marvelous at the pillow, very smart in the head, with enough of an American patina to put him at ease.' Gornt exhaled smoke and added, 'And of all the ladies I know, you could really spend his money. Yes, you two could fit perfectly . . . he'd be very good for you and you'd brighten his life considerably. Wouldn't you?'

'Oh yes,' she said at once. 'Oh yes I would.' She smiled then frowned. 'But what about the woman he has with him? They're sharing a suite at the Vic. I heard she's gorgeous. What about her, Quillan?'

Gornt smiled thinly. 'My spies say they don't sleep together though they're better than friends.'

Her face fell. 'He's not queer, is he?'

Gornt laughed. It was a good rich laugh. 'I wouldn't do that to you, Orlanda! No, I'm sure he's not. He's just got a strange arrangement with Casey.'

'What is it?'

Gornt shrugged.

After a moment she said, 'What do I do about her?'

'If Casey Tcholok's in your way, remove her. You've got claws.'

'You're . . . Sometimes I don't like you at all.'

'We're both realists, you and I. Aren't we?' He said it very flat.

She recognized the undercurrent of violence. At once she got up and leaned across the desk and kissed him lightly. 'You're a devil,' she said, placating him. 'That's for old times.'

His hand strayed to her breast and he sighed, remembering, enjoying the warmth that came through the thin material. '*Ayeeyah*, Orlanda, we had some good times, didn't we?'

She had been his mistress when she was seventeen. He was her first and he had kept her for almost five years and would have continued but she went with a youth to Macao when he was away and he had been told about it. And so he had stopped. At once. Even though they had a daughter then, he and she, one year old.

'Orlanda,' he had told her as she had begged for forgiveness, 'there's nothing to forgive. I've told you a dozen times that youth needs youth, and there'd come a day. . . Dry your tears, marry the lad—I'll give you a dowry and my blessing. . .' And throughout all her weepings he had remained firm. 'We'll be friends,' he had assured her, 'and I'll take care of you when you need it. . . .'

The next day he had turned the heat of his covert fury on the youth, an Englishman, a minor executive in Asian Properties and, within the month, he had broken him.

'It's a matter of face,' he had told her calmly.

'Oh I know. I understand but . . . what shall I do now?' she had wailed. 'He's leaving tomorrow for England and he wants me to go with him and marry him but I can't marry now, he's got no money or future or job or money. . . .'

'Dry your tears, then go shopping.'

'What?'

'Yes. Here's a present.' He had given her a first-class, return ticket to London on the same airplane that the youth was traveling tourist. And a thousand pounds in crisp, new ten-pound notes. 'Buy lots of pretty clothes, and go to the theater. You're booked into the Connaught for eleven days—just sign the bill— and your return's confirmed, so have a happy time and come back fresh and without problems!'

'Oh thank you, Quillan darling, oh thank you. . . . I'm so sorry. You forgive me?'

'There's nothing to forgive. But if you ever talk to him again, or see him privately . . . I won't be friendly to you or your family ever again.'

She thanked him profusely through her tears, cursing herself for her stupidity, begging for the wrath of heaven to descend upon whoever had betrayed her. The next day the youth had tried to speak to her at the airport and on the plane and in London but she just cursed him away. She knew where her rice bowl rested. The day she left London he committed suicide.

When Gornt heard about it, he lit a fine cigar and took her out to a dinner atop the Victoria and Albert with candelabra and fine linen and fine silver, and then, after he had had his Napoleon brandy and she her crème de menthe, he had sent her home, alone, to the apartment he still paid for. He had ordered another brandy and stayed, watching the lights of the harbor, and the Peak, feeling the glory of vengeance, the majesty of life, his face regained.

'*Ayeeyah*, we had some good times,' Gornt said again now, still desiring her, though he had not pillowed with her from the time he had heard about Macao.

'Quillan . . .' she began, his hand warming her too.

'No.'

Her eyes strayed to the inner door. 'Please. It's three years, there's never been anyone . . .'

'Thank you but no.' He held her away from him, his hands now firm on her arms but gentle. 'We've already had the best,' he said as a connoisseur would. 'I don't like second best.'

She sat back on the edge of the desk, watching him sullenly. 'You always win, don't you?'

'The day you become lovers with Bartlett I'll give you a present,' he said calmly. 'If he takes you to Macao and you stay openly with him for three days I'll give you a new Jag. If he asks you to marry him you get the apartment and everything in it, and a house in California as a wedding present.'

She gasped, then smiled gloriously. 'An XK-E, a black one, Quillan, oh that would be perfect!' Then her happiness evaporated. 'What's so important about him? Why is he so important to you?'

He just stared at her.

'Sorry,' she said, 'sorry, I shouldn't have asked.' Thoughtfully she reached for a cigarette and lit it and leaned over and gave it to him.

'Thanks,' he said, seeing the curve of her breast, enjoying it, yet a little saddened that such beauty was so transient. 'Oh, by the way, I wouldn't like Bartlett to know of our arrangement.'

'Nor would I.' She sighed and forced a smile. Then she got up and shrugged. '*Ayeeyah*, it would never have lasted with us anyway. Macao or not Macao. You would have changed— you'd have become bored, men always do.'

She checked her makeup and her shirt and blew him a kiss

and left him. He stared at the closed door then smiled and stubbed out the cigarette she had given him, never having puffed on it, not wanting the taint of her lips. He lit a fresh one and hummed a little tune.

Excellent, he thought happily. Now we'll see, Mr. Bloody Cocky Confident Yankee Bartlett, now we'll see how you handle that knife. Pasta with beer indeed!

Then Gornt caught a lingering whiff of her perfume and he was swept back momentarily into memories of their pillowing. When she was young, he reminded himself. Thank God there's no premium on youth or beauty out here, and a substitute's as close as a phone call or a hundred-dollar note.

He reached for the phone and dialed a special private number, glad that Orlanda was more Chinese than European. Chinese are such practical people.

The dial tone stopped and he heard Paul Havergill's crisp voice. 'Yes?'

'Paul, Quillan. How're things?'

'Hello, Quillan—of course you know Johnjohn's taking over the bank in November?'

'Yes. Sorry about that.'

'Damnable. I thought I was going to be confirmed but instead the board chose Johnjohn. It was official last night. It's Dunross again, his clique, and the damned stock they have. How did your meeting go?'

'Our American's chomping at the bit, just as I told you he would be.' Gornt took a deep drag of his cigarette and tried to keep the excitement out of his voice. 'How would you like a little special action before you retire?'

'What had you in mind?'

'You're leaving end of November?'

'Yes. After twenty-three years. In some ways I won't be sorry.'

Nor will I, Gornt thought contentedly. You're out of date and too bloody conservative. The only thing in your favor is that you hate Dunross. 'That's almost four months. That'd give us plenty of time. You, me and our American friend.'

'What do you have in mind?'

'You remember one of my hypothetical game plans, the one I called "Competition"?'

120

Havergill thought a moment. 'That was how to take over or eliminate an opposition bank, wasn't it? Why?'

'Say someone dusted off the plan and made a few changes and pushed the *go* button . . . two days ago. Say someone knew Dunross and the others would vote you out and wanted some revenge. "Competition" would work perfectly.'

'I don't see why. What's the point of attacking Blacs?' The Bank of London, Canton and Shanghai was the Victoria's main opposition. 'Doesn't make sense.'

'Ah, but say someone changed the target, Paul.'

'To whom?'

'I'll come by at three and explain.'

'To whom?'

'Richard.' Richard Kwang controlled the Ho-Pak Bank—one of the largest of all the many Chinese banks in Hong Kong.

'Good God! But that's . . .' There was a long pause. 'Quillan you've really begun Competition . . . to put it into effect?'

'Yes, and no one knows about it except you and me.'

'But how is that going to work against Dunross?'

'I'll explain later. Can Ian meet his commitments on his ships?'

There was a pause which Gornt noted. 'Yes,' he heard Havergill say.

'Yes, but what?'

'But I'm sure he'll be all right.'

'What other problems has Dunross got?'

'Sorry, but that wouldn't be ethical.'

'Of course.' Gornt added thinly, 'Let me put it another way: Say their boat was a little rocked. Eh?'

There was a longer pause. 'At the right moment, a smallish wave could scuttle them, or any company. Even you.'

'But not the Victoria Bank.'

'Oh no.'

'Good. See you at three.' Gornt hung up and mopped his brow again, his excitement vast. He stubbed out his cigarette, made a quick calculation, lit another cigarette, then dialed. 'Charles, Quillan. Are you busy?'

'No. What can I do for you?'

'I want a balance sheet.' A balance sheet was a private signal for the attorney to telephone eight nominees who would buy or

121

sell on the stock market on Gornt's behalf, secretly, to avoid the trading being traced back to him. All shares and all monies would pass solely through the attorney's hands so that neither the nominees nor the brokers would know for whom the transactions were being made.

'A balance sheet it will be. What sort, Quillan?'

'I want to sell short.' To sell short meant he sold shares he did not own on the presumption their value would go down. Then, before he had to buy them back—he had a maximum margin of two weeks in Hong Kong—if the stock had indeed gone down, he would pocket the difference. Of course if he gambled wrong and the stock had gone up, he would have to pay the difference.

'What shares and what numbers?'

'A hundred thousand shares of Ho-Pak . . .'

'Holy Christ . . .'

'. . . the same, as soon as the market opens tomorrow, and another 200 during the day. I'll give you further instructions then.'

There was a stunned silence. 'You did say Ho-Pak?'

'Yes.'

'It'll take time to borrow all those shares. Good God, Quillan, four hundred thousand?'

'While you're about it, get another hundred. A round half a million.'

'But . . . but Ho-Pak's as blue a blue chip as we've got. It hasn't gone down in years.'

'Yes.'

'What've you heard?'

'Rumors,' Gornt said gravely and chuckled to himself. 'Would you like an early lunch, eat at the club?'

'I'll be there.'

Gornt hung up, then dialed another private number.

'Yes?'

'It's me,' Gornt said cautiously. 'Are you alone?'

'Yes. And?'

'At our meeting, the Yankee suggested a raid.'

'*Ayeeyah!* And?'

'And Paul's in,' he said, the exaggeration coming easily. 'Absolutely secretly, of course. I've just talked to him.'

'Then I'm in. Provided I get control of Struan's ships, their

Hong Kong property operation and 40 percent of their land-holdings in Thailand and Singapore.'

'You must be joking!'

'Nothing's too much to smash them. Is it, old boy?'

Gornt heard the well-bred, mocking laugh and hated Jason Plumm for it. 'You despise him just as much as I do,' Gornt said.

'Ah, but you'll need me and my special friends. Even with Paul on or off the fence, you and the Yankee can't pull it off, not without me and mine.'

'Why else am I talking to you?'

'Listen, don't forget I'm not asking for any piece of the American's pie.'

Gornt kept his voice calm. 'What's that got to do with anything?'

'I know you. Oh yes. I know you, old boy.'

'Do you now?'

'Yes. You won't be satisfied just with destructing our "friend," you'll want the whole pie.'

'Will I now?'

'Yes. You've wanted a stake in the U.S. market too long.'

'And you.'

'No. We know where our toast's toasted. We're content to trail along behind. We're content with Asia. We don't want to be a noble anything.'

'Oh?'

'No. Then it's a deal?'

'No,' Gornt said.

'I'll drop the shipping totally. Instead I'll take Ian's Kowloon Investments, the Kai Tak operation, and 40 percent of the land-holdings in Thailand and Singapore, and I'll accept 25 percent of Par-Con and three places on the board.'

'Get stuffed!'

'The offer's good till Monday.'

'Which Monday?'

'Next Monday.'

'*Dew neh loh moh* on all your Mondays!'

'And yours! I'll make you a last offer. Kowloon Investments and their Kai Tak operation totally, 35 percent of all their land-holdings in Thailand and Singapore, and 10 percent of the Yankee pie with three seats on the board.'

123

'Is that all?'

'Yes. Again, the offer's good till next Monday. And don't think you can gobble us in the process.'

'Have you gone mad?'

'I told you—I know you. Is it a deal?'

'No.'

Again the soft, malevolent laugh. 'Till Monday—next Monday. That's time enough for you to make up your mind.'

'Will I see you at Ian's party tonight?' Gornt asked thinly.

'Have you gone bonkers! I wouldn't go if . . . Good God, Quillan, are you really going to accept? *In person?*'

'I wasn't going to—but now I think I will. I wouldn't want to miss perhaps the last great party of the Struans' last tai-pan. . . .'

7

In the boardroom it was still rough going for Casey. They would take none of the baits she offered. Her anxiety had increased and now as she waited she felt a wave of untoward fear go through her.

Phillip Chen was doodling, Linbar fiddling with his papers, Jacques de Ville watching her thoughtfully. Then Andrew Gavallan stopped writing the latest percentages she had quoted. He sighed and looked up at her. 'Clearly this should be a co-financing operation,' he said, his voice sharp. Electricity in the room soared and Casey had difficulty suppressing a cheer as he added, 'How much would Par-Con be prepared to put up, joint financing, for the whole deal?'

'18 million U.S. this year should cover it,' she answered immediately, noting happily that they all covered a gasp.

The published net worth of Struan's last year was almost 28 million, and she and Bartlett had gauged their offer on this figure.

'Make the first offer 20 million,' Linc had told her. 'You should hook 'em at 25 which'd be great. It's essential we co-finance, but the suggestion's got to come from them.'

'But look at their balance sheet, Linc. You can't tell for sure what their real net worth is. It could be 10 million either way, maybe more. We don't know how strong they really are . . . or how weak. Look at this item: "14.7 million retained in subsidiaries." What subsidiaries, where and what for? Here's another one: "7.4 million transferred to—"'

'So what, Casey? So it's 30 million instead of 25. Our projection's still valid.'

'Yes—but their accounting procedures . . . My God, Linc, if we did one percent of this in the States the SEC'd have our asses in a sling and we'd end up in jail for fifty years.'

'Yes. But it's not against *their* law, which is a major reason for going to Hong Kong.'

'20 is too much for openers.'

'I'll leave it to you, Casey. Just remember in Hong Kong we play Hong Kong rules—whatever's legal. I want in their game.'

'Why? And don't say "for my goddamn pleasure."'

Linc had laughed. 'Okay—then for *your* goddamn pleasure. Just make the Struan deal!'

The humidity in the boardroom had increased. She would have liked to reach for a tissue but she kept still, willing them onward, pretending calm.

Gavallan broke the silence. 'When would Mr. Bartlett confirm the offer of 18 million . . . if we accepted?'

'It's confirmed,' she said sweetly, passing over the insult. 'I have clearance to commit up to 20 million on this deal without consulting Linc or his board,' she said, deliberately giving them room to maneuver. Then she added innocently, 'Then it's all settled? Good.' She began to sort out her papers. 'Next: I'd—'

'Just a moment,' Gavallan said, off balance. 'I, er, 18 is . . . In any event we have to present the package to the tai-pan.'

'Oh,' she said, pretending surprise. 'I thought we were negotiating as equals, that you four gentlemen had powers equal to mine. Perhaps I'd better talk to Mr. Dunross direct in the future.'

Andrew Gavallan flushed. 'The tai-pan has final say. In everything.'

'I'm very glad to know it, Mr. Gavallan. I only have final say up to 20 million.' She beamed at them. 'Very well, put it to your tai-pan. Meanwhile, shall we set a time limit on the consideration period?'

Another silence.

'What do you suggest?' Gavallan said, feeling trapped.

'Whatever the minimum is. I don't know how fast you like to work,' Casey said.

Phillip Chen said, 'Why not table that answer until after lunch, Andrew?'

'Yes—good idea.'

'That's fine with me,' Casey said. I've done my job, she thought. I'll settle for 20 million when it could've been 30 and they're men and expect, and over twenty-one and they think I'm a sucker. But now I get my drop dead money. Dear God in heaven let this deal go through because then I'm free forever.

Free to do what?

Never mind, she told herself. I'll think about that later.

She heard herself continue the pattern: 'Shall we go through the details of how you'd like the 18 million and . . .'

'18 is hardly adequate,' Phillip Chen interrupted, the lie coming very easily. 'There are all sorts of added costs. . . .'

In perfect negotiating style Casey argued and allowed them to push her to 20 million and then, with apparent reluctance, she said, 'You gentlemen are exceptional businessmen. Very well, 20 million.' She saw their hidden smiles and laughed to herself.

'Good,' Gavallan said, very satisfied.

'Now,' she said, wanting to keep the pressure on, 'how do you want our joint venture corporate structure to be? Of course subject to your tai-pan—sorry, subject to *the* tai-pan's approval,' she said, correcting herself with just the right amount of humility.

Gavallan was watching her, irritably wishing she were a man. Then I could say, up yours, or go shit in your hat, and we'd laugh together because you know and I know you always have to check with the tai-pan in some way or another—whether it's Dunross or Bartlett or a board or your wife. Yes, and if you were a man we wouldn't have this bloody sexuality in the boardroom which doesn't belong here in the first place. Christ, if you were an old bag maybe that'd make a difference but, shit, a bird like you?

What the hell gets into American women? Why in the name of Christ don't they stay where they belong and be content with what they're great at? Stupid!

And stupid to concede financing so quickly, and even more stupid to give us an extra two million when ten would probably have been acceptable in the first place. For God's sake, you should have been more patient and you would have made a much better deal! That's the trouble with you Americans, you've—no finesse and no patience and no style and you don't understand the art of negotiation, and you, dear lady, you're much too impatient to prove yourself. So now I know how to play you.

He glanced at Linbar Struan who was watching Casey covertly, waiting for him or Phillip or Jacques to continue. When I'm tai-pan, Gavallan thought grimly, I'm going to break you, young Linbar, break you or make you. You need shoving out into the world on your own, to make you think for yourself, to rely on yourself, not on your name and your heritage. Yes, with a lot more hard work to take some of the heat out of your yang—the sooner you remarry the better.

His eyes switched to Jacques deVille who smiled back at him. Ah Jacques, he thought without rancor, you're my main opposition. You're doing what you usually do: saying little, watching everything, thinking a lot—rough, tough and mean if necessary. But what's in your mind about this deal? Have I missed something? What does your canny legal Parisian mind forecast? Ah but she stopped you in your tracks with her joke about your joke about her nose, eh?

I'd like to bed her too, he thought absently, knowing Linbar and Jacques had already decided the same. Of course—who wouldn't?

What about you, Phillip Chen?

Oh no. Not you. You like them very much younger and have it done to you strangely, if there's any truth to the rumors, *heya*?

He looked back at Casey. He could read her impatience. You don't look lesbian, he thought and groaned inwardly. Is that your other weakness? Christ, that'd be a terrible waste!

'The joint venture should be set up under Hong Kong law,' he said.

'Yes of course. There's—'

'Sims, Dawson and Dick can advise us how. I'll arrange an appointment for tomorrow or the day after.'

'No need for that, Mr. Gavallan. I already got their tentative proposals, hypothetical and confidential, of course, just in case we decided to conclude.'

'What?' They gaped at her as she took out five copies of a short-form legal contract and handed one to each of them.

'I found out they were your attorneys,' she said brightly. 'I had our people check them out and I was advised they're the best so they were fine with us. I asked them to consider our joint hypothetical needs—yours as well as ours. Is anything the matter?'

'No,' Gavallan said, suddenly furious that their own firm had not told them of Par-Con's inquiries. He began to scan the letter.

Dew neh loh moh on Casey bloody whatever her names are, Phillip Chen was thinking, enraged at the loss of face. May your golden gully wither and be ever dry and dust-filled for your foul manners and your fresh, filthy unfeminine habits!

God protect us from American women!

Ayeeyah, it is going to cost Lincoln Bartlett a pretty penny for daring to stick this . . . this creature upon us, he promised himself. How dare he!

Nevertheless, his mind was estimating the staggering value of the deal they were being offered. It has to be at least 100 million U.S., potentially, over the next few years, he told himself, his head reeling. This will give the Noble House the stability it needs.

Oh happy day, he gloated. And co-financing dollar for dollar! Unbelievable! Stupid to give us that so quickly without even a tiny concession in return. Stupid, but what can you expect from a stupid woman? *Ayeeyah*, the Pacific Rim will gorge on all the polyurethane foam products we can make—for packaging, building, bedding and insulating. One factory here, one in Taiwan, one in Singapore, one in Kuala Lumpur and a last, initially, in Jakarta. We'll make millions, tens of millions. And as to the computer-leasing agency, why at the rental these fools are offering us, 10 percent less than IBM's list price, less our 7½ percent commission—with just a little haggling we would have been delighted to agree to 5 percent—by next weekend I can sell three in Singapore, one here, one in Kuala Lumpur and one to that shipping pirate in Indonesia for a clear profit of $67,500 each, or $405,000 for six phone calls. And as to China . . .

And as to China . . .

Oh all gods great and small and very small, help this deal to go through and I will endow a new temple, a cathedral, in Tai-ping Shan, he promised, consumed with fervor. If China will drop some controls, or even ease them just a fraction, we can fertilize the paddy fields of Kwantung Province and then of all China and over the next twelve years this deal will mean tens of hundreds of millions of dollars, U.S. dollars not Hong Kong dollars!

The thought of all this profit mollified his rage considerably. 'I think this proposal can form the basis for further discussion,' he said, finishing reading. 'Don't you, Andrew?'

'Yes.' Gavallan put the letter down. 'I'll call them after lunch. When would it be convenient for Mr. Bartlett . . . and you of course . . . to meet?'

'This afternoon—the sooner the better—or anytime tomorrow but Linc won't come. I handle all the details, that's my job,' Casey said crisply. 'He sets policy—and will formally sign the final documents—after I've approved them. That's the function of the commander-in-chief, isn't it?' She beamed at them.

'I'll make an appointment and leave a message at your hotel,' Gavallan was saying.

'Perhaps we could set it up now—then that's out of the way?'

Sourly Gavallan glanced at his watch. Almost lunch, thank God. 'Jacques—how're you fixed tomorrow?'

'Morning's better than the afternoon.'

'And for John too,' Phillip Chen said.

Gavallan picked up the phone and dialed. 'Mary? Call Dawson and make an appointment for eleven tomorrow to include Mr. deVille and Mr. John Chen and Miss Casey. At their offices.' He put the phone down. 'Jacques and John Chen handle all our corporate matters. John's sophisticated on American problems and Dawson's the expert. I'll send the car for you at 10:30.'

'Thanks, but there's no need for you to trouble.'

'Just as you wish,' he said politely. 'Perhaps this is a good time to break for lunch.'

Casey said, 'We've a quarter of an hour yet. Shall we start on how you'd like our financing? Or if you wish we can send out for a sandwich and work on through.'

They stared at her, appalled. 'Work through lunch?'

'Why not? It's an old American custom.'

'Thank God it's not a custom here,' Gavallan said.

'Yes,' Phillip Chen snapped.

She felt their disapproval descend like a pall but she did not care. Shit on all of you, she thought irritably, then forced herself to put that attitude away. Listen, idiot, don't let these sons of bitches get you! She smiled sweetly. 'If you want to stop now for lunch, that's fine with me.'

'Good,' Gavallan said at once and the others breathed a sigh of relief. 'We begin lunch at 12:40. You'll probably want to powder your nose first.'

'Yes, thank you,' she said, knowing they wanted her gone so they could discuss her—and then the deal. It should be the other way around, she thought, but it won't be. No. It'll be the same as always: they'll lay bets as to who'll be the first to score. But it'll be none of them, because I don't want any of *them* at the moment, however attractive they are in their way. These men are like all the others I've met: they don't want love, they just want sex.

Except Linc.

Don't think about Linc and how much you love him and how rotten these years have been. Rotten and wonderful.

Remember your promise.

I won't think about Linc and love.

Not until my birthday which is ninety-eight days from now. The ninety-eighth day ends the seventh year and because of my darling by then I'll have my drop dead money and really be equal, and, God willing, we'll have the Noble House. Will that be my wedding present to him? Or his to me?

Or a good-bye present?

'Where's the ladies' room?' she asked, getting up, and they all stood and towered over her, except Phillip Chen whom she topped by an inch, and Gavallan directed her.

Linbar Struan opened the door for her and closed it behind her. Then he grinned. 'A thousand says you'll never make it, Jacques.'

'Another thousand,' Gavallan said. 'And ten that you won't, Linbar.'

'You're on,' Linbar replied, 'provided she's here a month.'

'You're slowing up, aren't you, old chap?' Gavallan said, then to Jacques, 'Well?'

The Frenchman smiled. 'Twenty that you, Andrew, will never charm such a lady into bed—and as to you, poor young Linbar. Fifty against your racehorse says the same.'

'I like my filly for God's sake. Noble Star's got a great chance

131

of being a winner. She's the best in our stable.'

'Fifty.'

'A hundred and I'll consider it.'

'I don't want any horse that much.' Jacques smiled at Phillip Chen. 'What do you think, Phillip?'

Phillip Chen got up. 'I think I'll go home to lunch and leave you stallions to your dreams. It's curious though that you're all betting the others won't—not that any of you could.' Again they laughed.

'Stupid to give us the extra, eh?' Gavallan said.

'The deal's fantastic,' Linbar Struan said. 'Christ, Uncle Phillip, fantastic!'

'Like her *derrière*,' deVille said as a connoisseur would. 'Eh, Phillip?'

Good-naturedly Phillip Chen nodded and walked out, but as he saw Casey disappearing into the ladies' room, he thought, *Ayeeyah*, who'd want the big lump anyway?

Inside the ladies' room, Casey looked around, appalled. It was clean but smelled of old drains and there were pails piled one on top of another and some were filled with water. The floor was tiled but water-spotted and messy. I've heard the English are not very hygienic, she thought disgustedly, but here in the Noble House? Ugh! Astonishing!

She went into one of the cubicles, its floor wet and slippery, and after she had finished she pulled the handle and nothing happened. She tried it again, and again, and still nothing happened so she cursed and lifted off the top of the cistern. The cistern was dry and rusty. Irritably she unbolted the door and went to the basin and turned on the water but none came out.

What's the matter with this place? I'll bet those bastards sent me here deliberately!

There were clean hand towels so she poured a pail of water into the basin awkwardly, spilling some, washed her hands, then dried them, furious that her shoes had got splashed. At a sudden thought, she took another pail and flushed the toilet, then used still another bucket to clean her hands again. When she left, she felt very soiled.

I suppose the goddamn pipe's broken somewhere and the plumber won't come until tomorrow. Goddamn all water systems!

Calm down, she told herself. You'll start making mistakes.

The corridor was covered with fine Chinese silk carpet, and the walls were lined with oil paintings of clipper ships and Chinese landscapes. As she approached she could hear the muted voices from the boardroom and a laugh—the kind of laugh that comes from a ribald joke or a smutty remark. She knew the moment she opened the door, the good humor and comradeship would vanish and the awkward silence would return.

She opened the door and they all got up.

'Are you having trouble with your water mains?' she asked, holding her anger down.

'No, I don't think so,' Gavallan said, startled.

'Well, there's no water. Didn't you know?'

'Of course there's no— Oh!' He stopped. 'You're staying at the V and A so . . . Didn't anyone tell you about the water shortage?'

They all began talking at once but Gavallan dominated them. 'The V and A has its own water supply—so do a couple of other hotels—but the rest of us're on four hours of water every fourth day, so you've got to use a pail. Never occurred to me you didn't know. Sorry.'

'How do you manage? *Every fourth day?*'

'Yes. For four hours, 6:00 A.M. till 8:00 A.M., then 5:00 till 7:00 in the evening. It's a frightful bore because of course it means we've got to store four days supply. Pails, or the bath, whatever you can. We're short of pails—it's our water day tomorrow. Oh my God, there was water for you, wasn't there?'

'Yes, but . . . You mean the water mains are turned off? Everywhere?' she asked incredulously.

'Yes,' Gavallan said patiently. 'Except for those four hours every fourth day. But you're all right at the V and A. As they're right on the waterfront they can refill their tanks daily from lighters—of course, they have to buy it.'

'You can't shower or bathe?'

Linbar Struan laughed. 'Everyone gets pretty grotty after three days in this heat but at least we're all in the same sewer. Still, it's survival training to make sure there's a full pail before you go.'

'I had no idea,' she said, aghast that she had used *three* pails.

133

'Our reservoirs are empty,' Gavallan explained. 'We've had almost no rain this year and last year was dry too. Bloody nuisance, but there you are. Just one of those things. Joss.'

'Then where does your water come from?'

They stared at her blankly. 'From China of course. By pipes over the border into the New Territories, or by tanker from the Pearl River. The government's just chartered a fleet of ten tankers that go up the Pearl River, by agreement with Peking. They bring us about 10 million gallons a day. It'll cost the government upwards of 25 million for this year's charter. Saturday's paper said our consumption's down to 30 million gallons a day for our 3½ million population—that includes industry. In your country, one person uses 150 gallons a day, so they say.'

'It's the same for everyone? Four hours every fourth day?'

'Even at the Great House you use a pail.' Gavallan shrugged again. 'But the tai-pan's got a place at Shek-O that has its own well. We all pile over there when we're invited, to get the slime off.'

She thought again of the three pails of water she had used. Jesus, she thought, did I use it all? I don't recall if there's any left.

'I guess I've a lot to learn,' she said.

Yes, they all thought. Yes, you bloody have.

'Tai-pan?'

'Yes, Claudia?' Dunross said into the intercom.

'The meeting with Casey's just broken for lunch. Master Andrew is on line four. Master Linbar's on his way up.'

'Cancel him till after lunch. Any luck on Tsu-yan?'

'No sir. The plane landed on time at 8:40. He's not at his office in Taipei. Or his flat. I'll keep trying, of course. Another thing, I've just had an interesting call, tai-pan. It seems that Mr. Bartlett went to Rothwell-Gornt this morning and had a private meeting with Mr. Gornt.'

'Are you sure?' he asked, ice in his stomach suddenly.

'Yes, oh very yes.'

Bastard, Dunross thought. Does Bartlett mean me to find out? 'Thanks,' he said, putting the question aside for the moment, but very glad to know. 'You've got a thousand dollars on any horse on Saturday.'

'Oh thank you, tai-pan.'

'Back to work, Claudia!' He punched the number four button. 'Yes, Andrew? What's the deal?'

Gavallan told him the important part.

'20 million in cash?' he asked with disbelief.

'In marvelous, beautiful U.S. cash!' Dunross could feel his beam down the phone. 'And when I asked when Bartlett would confirm the deal the little scrubber had the bloody cheek to say, "Oh it's confirmed now—I can commit up to 20 million on this deal without consulting him or anyone." Do you think that's possible?'

'I don't know.' Dunross felt a little weak in the knees. 'Bartlett's due any moment. I'll ask.'

'Hey, tai-pan, if this goes through . . .'

But Dunross was hardly listening as Gavallan ran on ecstatically. It's an unbelievable offer, he was telling himself.

It's too good. Where's the flaw?

Where's the flaw?

Ever since he had become tai-pan he had had to maneuver, lie, cajole and even threaten—Havergill of the bank for one—far more than ever he had expected, to stay ahead of the disasters he had inherited, and the natural and political ones that seemed to be besetting the world. Even going public had not given him the capital and time he had expected because a worldwide slump had ripped the markets to pieces. And last year in August, Typhoon Wanda had struck, leaving havoc in her wake, hundreds dead, a hundred thousand homeless, half a thousand fishing boats sunk, twenty ships sunk, one of their three thousand tonners flung ashore, their giant half-completed wharf wrecked and their entire building program smashed for six months. In the fall the Cuban crisis and more slump. This spring de Gaulle had vetoed Britain's entry into the Common Market and more slump. China and Russia quarreling and more slump. . . .

And now I've almost got 20 million U.S. but I think we're somehow involved in gun-running, Tsu-yan's apparently on the run and John Chen's God knows where!

'Christ all sodding mighty!' he said angrily.

'What?' Gavallan stopped, aghast, in midflow. 'What's up?'

'Oh nothing—nothing, Andrew,' he said. 'Nothing to do with you. Tell me about her. What's she like?'

'Good at figures, fast and confident, but impatient. And she's the best-looking bird I've seen in years, with potentially the best pair of knockers in town.' Gavallan told him about the bets. 'I think Linbar's got the inside track.'

'I'm going to fire Foster and send Linbar down to Sydney for six months, get him to sort everything out there.'

'Good idea.' Gavallan laughed. 'That'll stop his farting in church—though they say the ladies Down Under are very accommodating.'

'You think this deal will go through?'

'Yes. Phillip was ecstatic about it. But it's shitty dealing through a woman and that's the truth. Do you think we could bypass her and deal with Bartlett direct?'

'No. He was quite clear in his correspondence that K. C. Tcholok was his chief negotiator.'

'Oh well . . . into the breach and all that! What we do for the Noble House!'

'Have you found her weak spot?'

'Impatience. She wants to "belong"—to be one of the boys. I'd say her Achilles' heel is that she desperately wants acceptance in a man's world.'

'No harm in wanting that—like the Holy Grail. The meeting with Dawson's set for eleven tomorrow?'

'Yes.'

'Get Dawson to cancel it, but not until nine tomorrow morning. Tell him to make an excuse and reset it for Wednesday at noon.'

'Good idea, keep her off balance, what?'

'Tell Jacques I'll take that meeting myself.'

'Yes, tai-pan. What about John Chen? You'll want him there?'

After a pause Dunross said, 'Yes. Have you seen him yet?'

'No. He's expected for lunch—you want me to chase him?'

'No. Where's Phillip?'

'He went home. He's coming back at 2:30.'

Good, Dunross thought, and tabled John Chen until that time. 'Listen . . .' The intercom buzzed. 'Just a minute, Andrew.' He punched the hold. 'Yes, Claudia?'

'Sorry to interrupt, tai-pan, but I've got your call to Mr. Jen in Taipei on line two and Mr. Bartlett's just arrived downstairs.'

'Bring him in as soon as I'm through with Jen.' He stabbed line four again. 'Andrew, I may be a couple of minutes late. Host drinks and that sort of thing for me. I'll bring Bartlett up myself.'

'Okay.'

Dunross stabbed line two. *'Tsaw an?'* he said in Mandarin dialect—How are you?—glad to talk to Wei-wei's uncle, General Jen Tang-wa, deputy chief of the illegal Kuomintang secret police for Hong Kong.

'Shey-shey,' then in English, 'What's up, tai-pan?'

'I thought you should know . . .' Dunross told him briefly about the guns and Bartlett, that the police were involved, but not about Tsu-yan or John Chen.

'Ayeeyah! That's very curious indeed.'

'Yes. I thought so too. Very curious.'

'You're convinced it's not Bartlett?'

'Yes. There appears to be no reason. None at all. It'd be stupid to use your own plane. Bartlett's not stupid,' Dunross said. 'Who'd need that sort of armament here?'

There was a pause. 'Criminal elements.'

'Triads?'

'Not all triads are criminals.'

'No,' Dunross said.

'I'll see what I can find out. I'm sure it's nothing to do with us, Ian. Are you still coming Sunday?'

'Yes.'

'Good. I'll see what I can find out. Drinks at 6:00 P.M.?'

'How about eight o'clock? Have you seen Tsu-yan yet?'

'I thought he wasn't due until the weekend. Isn't he making up our foursome on Monday with the American?'

'Yes. I heard he caught an early flight today.' Dunross kept his voice matter-of-fact.

'He's sure to call—do you want him to phone?'

'Yes. Anytime. It's nothing important. See you Sunday at eight.'

'Yes, and thanks for the information. If I get anything I'll phone at once. 'Bye.'

Dunross put the phone down. He had been listening very carefully to the tone of Jen's voice but he had heard nothing untoward. Where the hell's Tsu-yan?

A knock.

'Come in.' He got up and went to meet Bartlett. 'Hello.' He smiled and held out his hand. 'I'm Ian Dunross.'

'Linc Bartlett.' They shook hands firmly. 'Am I too early?'

'You're dead on time. You must know I like punctuality.' Dunross laughed. 'I heard the meeting went well.'

'Good,' Bartlett replied, wondering if Dunross meant the Gornt meeting. 'Casey knows her facts and figures.'

'My fellows were most impressed—she said she could finalize things herself. Can she, Mr. Bartlett?'

'She can negotiate and settle up to 20 million. Why?'

'Nothing. Just wanted to find out your form. Please sit down—we've a few minutes yet. Lunch won't begin till 12:40. It sounds as though we may have a profitable enterprise in front of us.'

'I hope so. As soon as I've checked with Casey, perhaps you and I can get together?'

Dunross looked at his calendar. 'Tomorrow at ten. Here?'

'You're on.'

'Smoke?'

'No thanks. I quit a few years back.'

'So did I—still want a cigarette though.' Dunross leaned back in his chair. 'Before we go to lunch, Mr. Bartlett, there're a couple of minor points. I'm going to Taipei on Sunday afternoon, will be back Tuesday in time for dinner, and I'd like you to come along. There're a couple of people I'd like you to meet a golf match you might enjoy. We could chat leisurely, you could see the potential plant sites. It could be important. I've made all the arrangements, but it's not possible to take Miss Tcholok.'

Bartlett frowned, wondering if Tuesday was just a coincidence. 'According to Superintendent Armstrong I can't leave Hong Kong.'

'I'm sure that could be changed.'

'Then you know about the guns too?' Bartlett said and cursed himself for the slip. He managed to keep his eyes steady.

'Oh yes. Someone else's been bothering you about them?' Dunross asked, watching him.

'The police even chased Casey! Jesus! My airplane's seized,

we're all suspect, and I don't know a goddamn thing about any guns.'

'Well, there's no need to worry, Mr. Bartlett. Our police are very good.'

'I'm not worried, just teed off.'

'That's understandable,' Dunross said, glad the Armstrong meeting was confidential. Very glad.

Christ, he thought queasily, if John Chen and Tsu-yan are involved somehow, Bartlett's going to be very teed off indeed, and we'll lose the deal and he'll throw in with Gornt and then . . .

'How did you hear about the guns?'

'We were informed by our office at Kai Tak this morning.'

'Nothing like this ever happened before?'

'Yes.' Dunross added lightly, 'But there's no harm in smuggling or even a little gun-running—actually they're both very honorable professions—of course we do them elsewhere.'

'Where?'

'Wherever Her Majesty's Government desires.' Dunross laughed. 'We're all pirates here, Mr. Bartlett, at least we are to outsiders.' He paused. 'Presuming I can make arrangements with the police, you're on for Taipei?'

Bartlett said, 'Casey's very close-mouthed.'

'I'm not suggesting she's not to be trusted.'

'She's just not invited?'

'Certain of our customs here are a little different from yours, Mr. Bartlett. Most times she'll be welcome—but sometimes, well, it would save a lot of embarrassment if she were excluded.'

'Casey doesn't embarrass easily.'

'I wasn't thinking of her embarrassment. Sorry to be blunt but perhaps it's wiser in the long run.'

'And if I can't "conform"?'

'It will probably mean you cannot take advantage of a unique opportunity, which would be a very great pity—particularly if you intend a long-term association with Asia.'

'I'll think about that.'

'Sorry, but I have to have a yes or no now.'

'You do?'

'Yes.'

'Then go screw!'

139

Dunross grinned. 'I won't. Meanwhile, finally: yes or no.'

Bartlett broke out laughing. 'Since you put it that way, I'm on for Taipei.'

'Good. Of course I'll have my wife look after Miss Tcholok while we're away. There'll be no loss of face for her.'

'Thank you. But you needn't worry about Casey. How are you going to fix Armstrong?'

'I'm not going to *fix* him, just ask the assistant commissioner to let me be responsible for you, there and back.'

'Parole me in your custody?'

'Yes.'

'How do you know I won't just leave town? Maybe I was gun-running.'

Dunross watched him. 'Maybe you are. Maybe you'll try— but I can deliver you back dead or alive, as they say in the movies. Hong Kong and Taipei are within my fief.'

'Dead or alive, eh?'

'Hypothetically, of course.'

'How many men have you killed in your lifetime?'

The mood in the room changed and both men felt the change deeply.

It's not dangerous yet between him and me, Dunross thought, not yet.

'Twelve,' he replied, his senses poised, though the question had surprised him. 'Twelve that I'm sure of. I was a fighter pilot during the war. Spitfires. I got two single-seat fighters, a Stuka, and two bombers—they were Dornier 17s and they'd have a crew of four each. All the planes burned as they went down. Twelve that I'm sure of, Mr. Bartlett. Of course we shot up a lot of trains, convoys, troop concentrations. Why?'

'I'd heard you were a flier. I don't think I've killed anyone. I was building camps, bases in the Pacific, that sort of thing. Never shot a gun in anger.'

'But you like hunting?'

'Yes. I went on a safari in '59 in Kenya. Got an elephant and a great kudu bull and lots of game for the pot.'

Dunross said after a pause, 'I think I prefer to kill planes and trains and boats. Men, in war, are incidental. Aren't they?'

'Once the general's been put into the field by the ruler, sure. That's a fact of war.'

'Have you read Sun Tzu's *The Art of War*?'

'The best book on war I've ever read,' Bartlett said enthusiastically. 'Better'n Clausewitz or Liddell Hart, even though it was written in 500 B.C.'

'Oh?' Dunross leaned back, glad to get away from the killings. I haven't remembered the killing for years, he thought. That's not fair to those men, is it?

'Did you know Sun Tzu's book was published in French in 1782? I've a theory Napoleon had a copy.'

'It's certainly in Russian—and Mao always carried a copy that was dog-eared with use,' Dunross said.

'You've read it?'

'My father beat it into me. I had to read the original in characters—in Chinese. And then he'd question me on it, very seriously.'

A fly began to batter itself irritatingly against the window-pane. 'Your dad wanted you to be a soldier?'

'No. Sun Tzu, like Machiavelli, wrote about life more than death—and about survival more than war. . . .' Dunross glanced at the window then got up and went over to it and obliterated the fly with a controlled savagery that sent warning signals through Bartlett.

Dunross returned to his desk. 'My father thought I should know about survival and how to handle large bodies of men. He wanted me to be worthy to become tai-pan one day, though he never thought I'd amount to much.' He smiled.

'He was tai-pan too?'

'Yes. He was very good. At first.'

'What happened?'

Dunross laughed sardonically. 'Ah, skeletons so early, Mr. Bartlett? Well, briefly, we had a rather tedious, long-drawn-out difference of opinion. Eventually he handed over to Alastair Struan, my predecessor.'

'He's still alive?'

'Yes.'

'Does your British understatement mean you went to war with him?'

'Sun Tzu's very specific about going to war, Mr. Bartlett. Very bad to go to war he says, unless you need to. Quote: "Supreme excellence of generalship consists in breaking the enemy's resistance without fighting." '

'You broke him?'

'He removed himself from the field, Mr. Bartlett, like the wise man he was.'

Dunross's face had hardened. Bartlett studied him. Both men knew they were drawing battle lines in spite of themselves.

'I'm glad I came to Hong Kong,' the American said. 'I'm glad to meet you.'

'Thank you. Perhaps one day you won't be.'

Bartlett shrugged. 'Maybe. Meanwhile we've got a deal cooking—good for you, good for us.' He grinned abruptly, thinking about Gornt and the cooking knife. 'Yes. I'm glad I came to Hong Kong.'

'Would you and Casey care to be my guests this evening? I'm having a modest bash, a party, at 8:30 odd.'

'Formal?'

'Just dinner jacket—is that all right?'

'Fine. Casey said you like the tux and black tie bit.' Then Bartlett noticed the painting on the wall: an old oil of a pretty Chinese boat girl carrying a little English boy, his fair hair tied in a queue. 'That's a Quance? An Aristotle Quance?'

'Yes, yes it is,' Dunross said, barely covering his surprise.

Bartlett walked over and looked at it. 'This the original?'

'Yes. You know much about art?'

'No, but Casey told me about Quance as we were coming out here. She said he's almost like a photographer, really a historian of the early times.'

'Yes, yes he is.'

'If I remember this one's supposed to be a portrait of a girl called May-may, May-may T'Chung, and the child is one of Dirk Struan's by her?'

Dunross said nothing, just watched Bartlett's back.

Bartlett peered a little closer. 'Difficult to see the eyes. So the boy is Gordon Chen, Sir Gordon Chen to be?' He turned and looked at Dunross.

'I don't know for certain, Mr. Bartlett. That's one story.'

Bartlett watched him for a moment. The two men were well matched, Dunross slightly taller but Bartlett wider in the shoulders. Both had blue eyes, Dunross's slightly more greenish, both wideset in lived-in faces.

142

'You enjoy being tai-pan of the Noble House?' Bartlett asked.

'Yes.'

'I don't know for a fact what a tai-pan's powers are, but in Par-Con I can hire and fire anyone, and can close it down if I want.'

'Then you're a tai-pan.'

'Then I enjoy being a tai-pan too. I want in in Asia—you need an in in the States. Together we could sew up the whole Pacific Rim into a tote bag for both of us.'

Or a shroud for one of us, Dunross thought, liking Bartlett despite the fact that he knew it was dangerous to like him.

'I've got what you lack, you've got what I lack.'

'Yes,' Dunross said. 'And now what we both lack is lunch.'

They turned for the door. Bartlett was there first. But he did not open it at once. 'I know it's not your custom but since I'm going with you to Taipei, could you call me Linc and I call you Ian and we begin to figure out how much we're gonna bet on the golf match? I'm sure you know my handicap's thirteen, officially, and I know yours's ten, officially, which probably means at least one stroke off both of us for safety.'

'Why not?' Dunross said at once. 'But here we don't normally bet money, just balls.'

'I'm goddamned if I'm betting mine on a golf match.'

Dunross laughed. 'Maybe you will, one day. We usually bet half a dozen golf balls here—something like that.'

'It's a bad British custom to bet money, Ian?'

'No. How about five hundred a side, winning team take all?'

'U.S. or Hong Kong?'

'Hong Kong. Among friends it should be Hong Kong. Initially.'

Lunch was served in the directors' private dining room on the nineteenth floor. It was an L-shaped corner room, with a high ceiling and blue drapes, mottled blue Chinese carpets and large windows from which they could see Kowloon and the airplanes taking off and landing at Kai Tak and as far west as Stonecutters Island and Tsing Yi Island, and, beyond, part of the New Territories. The great, antique oak dining table which could seat twenty easily was laid with placemats and fine silver, and

Waterford's best crystal. For the six of them, there were four silent, very well-trained waiters in black trousers and white tunics embroidered with the Struan emblem.

Cocktails had been started before Bartlett and Dunross arrived. Casey was having a dry vodka martini with the others—except for Gavallan who had a double pink gin. Bartlett, without being asked, was served an ice-cold can of Anweiser, on a Georgian silver tray.

'Who told you?' Bartlett said, delighted.

'Compliments of Struan and Company,' Dunross said. 'We heard that's the way you like it.' He introduced him to Gavallan, deVille and Linbar Struan, and accepted a glass of iced Chablis, then smiled at Casey. 'How are you?'

'Fine, thanks.'

'Excuse me,' Bartlett said to the others, 'but I have to give Casey a message before I forget. Casey, will you call Johnston in Washington tomorrow?—find out who our best contact'd be at the consulate here.'

'Certainly. If I can't get him I'll ask Tim Diller.'

Anything to do with Johnston was code for: how's the deal progressing? In answer: Diller meant good, Tim Diller very good, Jones bad, George Jones very bad.

'Good idea,' Bartlett said and smiled back, then to Dunross, 'This is a beautiful room.'

'It's adequate,' Dunross said.

Casey laughed, getting the underplay. 'The meeting went very well, Mr. Dunross,' she said. 'We came up with a proposal for your consideration.'

How American to come out with it like that—no finesse! Doesn't she know business is for after lunch, not before. 'Yes. Andrew gave me the outline,' Dunross replied. 'Would you care for another drink?'

'No thanks. I think the proposal covers everything, sir. Are there any points you'd like me to clarify?'

'I'm sure there will be, in due course,' Dunross said, privately amused, as always, by the *sir* that many American women used conversationally, and often, incongruously, to waiters. 'As soon as I've studied it I'll get back to you. A beer for Mr. Bartlett,' he added, once more trying to divert business until later. Then to Jacques, '*Ça va?*'

144

'*Oui merci. A rien.*' Nothing yet.

'Not to worry,' Dunross said. Yesterday Jacques's adored daughter and her husband had had a bad car accident while on holiday in France—how bad he was still waiting to hear. 'Not to worry.'

'No.' Again the Gallic shrug, hiding the vastness of his concern.

Jacques was Dunross's first cousin and he had joined Struan's in '45. His war had been rotten. In 1940 he had sent his wife and two infants to England and had stayed in France. For the duration. Maquis and prison and condemned and escaped and Maquis again. Now he was fifty-four, a strong, quiet man but vicious when provoked, with a heavy chest and brown eyes and rough hands and many scars.

'In principle, does the deal sound okay?' Casey asked.

Dunross sighed inwardly and put his full concentration on her. 'I may have a counterproposal on a couple of minor points. Meanwhile,' he added decisively, 'you can proceed on the assumption that, in general terms, it's acceptable.'

'Oh fine,' Casey said happily.

'Great,' Bartlett said, equally pleased, and raised his can of beer. 'Here's to a successful conclusion and big profits—for you and for us.'

They drank the toast, the others reading the danger signs in Dunross, wondering what the tai-pan's counterproposal would be.

'Will it take you long to finalize, Ian?' Bartlett asked, and all of them heard the *Ian*. Linbar Struan winced openly.

To their astonishment, Dunross just said, 'No,' as though the familiarity was quite ordinary, adding, 'I doubt if the solicitors will come up with anything insurmountable.'

'We're seeing them tomorrow at eleven o'clock,' Casey said. 'Mr. deVille, John Chen and I. We've already gotten their advance go-through . . . no problems there.'

'Dawson's very good—particularly on U.S. tax law.'

'Casey, maybe we should bring out our tax guy from New York,' Bartlett said.

'Sure, Linc, soon as we're set. And Forrester.' To Dunross she said, 'He's head of our foam division.'

'Good. And that's enough shoptalk before lunch,' Dunross

said. 'House rules, Miss Casey: no shop with food, it's very bad for the digestion.' He beckoned Lim. 'We won't wait for Master John.'

Instantly waiters materialized and chairs were held out and there were typed place names in silver holders and the soup was ladled.

The menu said sherry with the soup, Chablis with the fish— or claret with the roast beef and Yorkshire pudding if you preferred it—boiled string beans and boiled potatoes and boiled carrots. Sherry trifle as dessert. Port with the cheese tray.

'How long will you be staying, Mr. Bartlett?' Gavallan asked.

'As long as it takes. But Mr. Gavallan, since it looks as though we're going to be in business together a long time, how about you dropping the "Mr." Bartlett and the "Miss" Casey and calling us Linc and Casey?'

Gavallan kept his eyes on Bartlett. He would have liked to have said, Well Mr. Bartlett, we prefer to work up to these things around here—it's one of the few ways you tell your friends from your acquaintances. For us first names are a private thing. But as the tai-pan hasn't objected to the astonishing 'Ian' there's not a thing I can do. 'Why not, Mr. Bartlett?' he said blandly. 'No need to stand on ceremony. Is there?'

Jacques deVille and Struan and Dunross chuckled inside at the "Mr. Bartlett," and the way Gavallan had neatly turned the unwanted acceptance into a put-down and a loss of face that neither of the Americans would ever understand.

'Thanks, Andrew,' Bartlett said. Then he added, 'Ian, may I bend the rules and ask one more question before lunch: Can you finalize by next Tuesday, one way or another?'

Instantly the currents in the room reversed. Lim and the other servants hesitated, shocked. All eyes went to Dunross. Bartlett thought he had gone too far and Casey was sure of it. She had been watching Dunross. His expression had not changed but his eyes had. Everyone in the room knew that the tai-pan had been called as a man will call another in a poker game. Put up or shut up. By next Tuesday.

They waited. The silence seemed to hang. And hang.

Then Dunross broke it. 'I'll let you know tomorrow,' he said, his voice calm, and the moment passed and everyone sighed inwardly and the waiters continued and everyone relaxed. Except Linbar. He could still feel the sweat on his hands because he alone of them knew the thread that went through all of the descendants of Dirk Struan—a strange, almost primeval, sudden urge to violence—and he had seen it almost surface then, almost but not quite. This time it had gone away. But the knowledge of it and its closeness terrified him.

His own line was descended from Robb Struan, Dirk Struan's half-brother and partner, so he had none of Dirk Struan's blood in his veins. He bitterly regretted it and loathed Dunross even more for making him sick with envy.

Hag Struan on you, Ian bloody Dunross, and all your generations, he thought, and shuddered involuntarily at the thought of her.

'What's up, Linbar?' Dunross asked.

'Oh nothing, tai-pan,' he said, almost jumping out of his skin. 'Nothing—just a sudden thought. Sorry.'

'What thought?'

'I was just thinking about Hag Struan.'

Dunross's spoon hesitated in midair and the others stared at him. 'That's not exactly good for your digestion.'

'No sir.'

Bartlett glanced at Linbar, then at Dunross. 'Who's Hag Struan?'

'A skeleton,' Dunross said with a dry laugh. 'We've lots of skeletons in our family.'

'Who hasn't?' Casey said.

'Hag Struan was our eternal bogeyman—still is.'

'Not now, tai-pan, surely,' Gavallan said. 'She's been dead for almost fifty years.'

'Maybe she'll die out with us, with Linbar, Kathy and me, with our generation, but I doubt it.' Dunross looked at Linbar strangely. 'Will Hag Struan get out of her coffin tonight and gobble us up?'

'I swear to God I don't like even joking about her like that, tai-pan.'

'The pox on Hag Struan,' Dunross said. 'If she was alive I'd say it to her face.'

'I think you would. Yes,' Gavallan laughed suddenly. 'That I'd like to have seen.'

'So would I.' Dunross laughed with him, then he saw Casey's

147

expression. 'Ah, just bravado, Casey. Hag Struan was a fiend from hell if you believe half the legends. She was Culum Struan's wife—he was Dirk Struan's son—our founder's son. Her maiden name was Tess, Tess Brock and she was the daughter of Dirk's hated enemy, Tyler Brock. Culum and Tess eloped in 1841, so the story goes. She was sweet sixteen and a beauty, and he heir to the Noble House. It was rather like Romeo and Juliet—except they lived and it made no difference whatsoever to the blood feud of Dirk against Tyler or the Struans versus the Brocks, it just heightened and complicated it. She was born Tess Brock in 1825 and died Hag Struan in 1917, aged ninety-two, toothless, hairless, besotten, vicious and dreadful to her very last day. Life's strange, *heya*?'

'Yes. Unbelievable sometimes,' Casey said thoughtfully. 'Why is it people change so much growing old—get so sour and bitter? Particularly women?'

Fashion, Dunross could have answered at once, and because men and women age differently. It's unfair—but an immortal fact. A woman sees the lines beginning and the sagging beginning and the skin no longer so fresh and firm but her man's still fine and sought after and then she sees the young dolly birds and she's petrified she'll lose him to them and eventually she will because he'll become bored with her carping and the self-fed agony of the self-mutilation—and too, because of his built-in uncontrollable urge toward youth. . . .

'*Ayeeyah*, there's no aphrodisiac in the world like youth,' old Chen-Chen—Phillip Chen's father—Ian's mentor would always say. 'None, young Ian, there's none. None none none. Listen to me. The yang needs the yin juices, but young juices, oh yes they should be young, the juices young to extend your life and nourish the yang—oh oh oh! Remember, the older your Male Stalk becomes the more it needs youth and change and young enthusiasm to perform exuberantly, and the more the merrier! But also remember that the Beauteous Box that nests between all their thighs, peerless though it is, delectable, delicious, unearthly, oh so sweet and oh so satisfying as it also is, beware! Ha! It's also a trap, ambush, torture chamber and your coffin!' Then the old, old man would chuckle and his belly would jump up and down and the tears would run down his face. 'Oh the gods are marvelous, are they not? They grant us heaven on earth but it's living hell when you can't get your one-eyed monk to raise his head to enter paradise. Joss, my child! That's our joss—to crave the Greedy Gully until she eats you up, but oh oh oh . . .'

It must be very difficult for women, particularly Americans, Dunross thought, this trauma of growing old, the inevitability of it happening so early, too early—worse in America than anywhere else on earth.

Why should I tell you a truth you must already know in your bones, Dunross asked himself. Or say further that American fashion demands you try to grasp an eternal youth neither God nor devil nor surgeon can give you. You can't be twenty-five when you're thirty-five nor have a thirty-five-year-old youthfulness when you're forty-five, or forty-five when you're fifty-five. Sorry, I know it's unfair but it's a fact.

Ayeeyah, he thought fervently, thank God—if there is a God—thank all gods great and small I'm a man and not a woman. I pity you, American lady with the beautiful names.

But Dunross answered simply, 'I suppose that's because life's no bed of roses and we're fed stupid pap and bad values growing up—not like the Chinese who're so sensible—Christ, how unbelievably sensible they are! In Hag Struan's case perhaps it was her rotten Brock blood. I think it was her joss—her fate or luck or unluck. She and Culum had seven children, four sons and three daughters. All her sons died violently, two of the "flux"—probably plague—here in Hong Kong, one was murdered, knifed in Shanghai, and the last was drowned off Ayr in Scotland, where our family lands are. That'd be enough to send any mother round the bend, that and the hatred and envy that surrounded Culum and her all their lives. But when you add to this all the problems of living in Asia, the passing over of the Noble House to other people's sons . . . well, you can understand.' Dunross thought a moment, then added, 'Legend has it she ruled Culum Struan all his life and tyrannized the Noble House till the day she died—and all tai-pans, all daughters-in-law, all sons-in-law and all the children as well. Even after she died. I can remember one English nanny I had, may she burn in hell forever, saying to me, "You better behave, Master Ian, or I'll conjure up Hag Struan and she'll gobble you up. . ." I can't have been more than five or six.'

'How terrible,' Casey said.

Dunross shrugged. 'Nannies do that to children.'

'Not all of them, thank God,' Gavallan said.

'I never had one who was any good at all. Or a *gan sun* who was ever bad.'

'What's a *gan sun?*' Casey asked.

'It means "near body," it's the correct name for an *amah*. In China pre-'49, children of well-to-do families and most of the old European and Eurasian families out here always had their own "near body" to look after them—in many cases they kept them all their lives. Most *gan sun* take a vow of celibacy. You can always recognize them by the long queue they wear down their back. My *gan sun's* called Ah Tat. She's a great old bird. She's still with us,' Dunross said.

Gavallan said, 'Mine was more like a mother to me than my real mother.'

'So Hag Struan's your great-grandmother?' Casey said to Linbar.

'Christ no! No, I'm—I'm not from Dirk Struan's line,' he replied and she saw sweat on his forehead that she did not understand. 'My line comes from his half-brother, Robb Struan. Robb Struan was Dirk's partner. The tai-pan's descended direct from Dirk, but even so . . . none of us're descended from the Hag.'

'You're all related?' Casey asked, feeling curious tensions in the room. She saw Linbar hesitate and glance at Dunross as she looked at him.

'Yes,' he said. 'Andrew's married to my sister, Kathy. Jacques is a cousin, and Linbar . . . Linbar carries our name.' Dunross laughed. 'There're still lots of people in Hong Kong who remember the Hag, Casey. She always wore a long black dress with a big bustle and a funny hat with a huge moth-eaten feather, everything totally out of fashion, and she'd have a black stick with a silver handle on it with her. Most times she was carried in a sort of palanquin by four bearers up and down the streets. She wasn't much more than five foot but round and tough as a coolie's foot. The Chinese were equally petrified by her. Her nickname was "Honorable Old Foreign Devil Mother with the Evil Eye and Dragon's Teeth."'

'That's right,' Gavallan said with a short laugh. 'My father and grandmother knew her. They had their own trading company here and in Shanghai, Casey, but got more or less wiped out in the Great War and joined up with Struan's in '19. My old man told me that when he was a boy he and his friends used to follow the Hag around the streets and when she got particularly angry she'd take out her false teeth and chomp them at them.' They all laughed with him as he parodied her. 'My old man swore the teeth were two feet tall and on some form of spring and they'd go crunch crunch crunch!'

'Hey Andrew, I'd forgotten that,' Linbar broke in with a grin. 'My *gan sun*, old Ah Fu, knew Hag Struan well and every time you'd mention her, Ah Fu's eyes'd turn up and she'd petition the gods to protect her from the evil eye and magic teeth. My brother Kyle and I . . .' He stopped, then began again in a different voice. 'We used to tease Ah Fu about her.'

Dunross said to Casey, 'There's a portrait of her up at the Great House—two in fact. If you're interested, I'll show them to you one day.'

'Oh thanks—I'd like that. Is there one of Dirk Struan?'

'Several. And one of Robb, his half-brother.'

'I'd love to see them.'

'Me too,' Bartlett said. 'Hell, I've never even seen a photo of my grandparents, let alone a portrait of my great-great-grandfather. I've always wanted to know about my forebears, what they were like, where they came from. I know nothing about them except my grandpa was supposed to have run a freight company in the Old West in a place called Jerrico. Must be great to know where you're from. You're lucky.' He had been sitting back listening to the undercurrents, fascinated by them, seeking clues against the time he'd have to decide: Dunross or Gornt. If it's Dunross, Andrew Gavallan's an enemy and will have to go, he told himself. Young Struan hates Dunross, the Frenchman's an enigma and Dunross himself is nitroglycerine and just as dangerous. 'Your Hag Struan sounds fantastic,' he said. 'And Dirk Struan too must have been quite a character.'

'Now that's a masterpiece of understatement!' Jacques deVille said, his dark eyes sparkling. 'He was the greatest pirate in Asia! You wait—you look at Dirk's portrait and you'll see the family resemblance! Our tai-pan's the spitting image, and *ma foi*, he's inherited all the worst parts.'

'Drop dead, Jacques,' Dunross said good-naturedly. Then to Casey, 'It's not true. Jacques is always ribbing me. I'm nothing like him at all.'

'But you're descended from him.'

'Yes. My great-grandmother was Winifred, Dirk's only legitimate daughter. She married Lechie Struan Dunross, a clansman. They had one son who was my grandfather—he was taipan after Culum. My family—the Dunrosses—are Dirk Struan's only direct descendants, as far as we know.'

'You, you said legitimate?'

Dunross smiled. 'Dirk had other sons and daughters. One son, Gordon Chen, was from a lady called Shen actually, that you know of. That's the Chen line today. There's also the T'Chung line—from Duncan T'Chung and Kate T'Chung, his son and daughter by the famous May-may T'Chung. Anyway that's the legend, they're accepted legends here though no one can prove or disprove them.' Dunross hesitated and his eyes crinkled with the depth of his smile. 'In Hong Kong and Shanghai our predecessors were, well, friendly, and the Chinese ladies beautiful, then as now. But they married their ladies rarely and the pill's only a very recent invention—so you don't always know who you might be related to. We, ah, we don't discuss this sort of thing publicly—in true British fashion we pretend it doesn't exist though we all know it does, then no one loses face. Eurasian families of Hong Kong usually took the name of their mothers, in Shanghai their fathers. We all seem to have accommodated the problem.'

'It's all very friendly,' Gavallan said.

'Sometimes,' Dunross said.

'Then John Chen's related to you?' Casey asked.

'If you go back to the garden of Eden everyone's related to everyone I suppose.' Dunross was looking at the empty place. Not like John to run off, he thought uneasily, and he's not the sort to get involved in gun smuggling, for any reason. Or be so stupid as to get caught. Tsu-yan? Well he's Shanghainese and he could easily be panicked—if he's mixed up in this. John's too easily recognized not to have been seen getting on a plane this morning so it's not that way. It has to be by boat—if he has run off. A boat where? Macao—no, that's a dead end. Ship? Too easy, he thought, if it was planned or even not planned and arranged at an hour's notice. Any day of the year there'd be thirty or forty scheduled sailings to all parts of the world, big ships and little ships, let alone a thousand junks nonscheduled, and even if on the run, a few dollars here and there and too easy to smuggle out—out or in. Men, women, children. Drugs. Anything. But no reason to smuggle inward except humans and drugs and guns and liquor and cigarettes and petrol—everything else is duty free and unrestricted.

Except gold.

Dunross smiled to himself. You import gold legally under license at thirty-five dollars an ounce for transit to Macao and what happens then is nobody's business but immensely profitable. Yes, he thought, and our Nelson Trading board meeting's this afternoon. Good. That's one business venture that never fails.

As he took some of the fish from the proffered silver tray he noticed Casey staring at him. 'Yes, Casey?'

'Oh I was just wondering how you knew my names.' She turned to Bartlett. 'The tai-pan surprised me, Linc. Before we were even introduced he called me Kamalian Ciranoush as though it were Mary Jane.'

'That's Persian?' Gavallan asked at once.

'Armenian originally.'

'Kamahly-arn Cirrrannoooossssh,' Jacques said, liking the sibilance of the names. '*Très jolie, mademoiselle. Ils ne sont pas difficile sauf pour les crfins.*'

'*Ou les* English,' Dunross said and they all laughed.

'How did you know, tai-pan?' Casey asked him, feeling more at home with *tai-pan* than with Ian. *Ian* doesn't belong, yet, she thought, swept by his past and Hag Struan and the shadows that seemed to be surrounding him.

'I asked your attorney.'

'What do you mean?'

'John Chen called me last night around midnight. You hadn't told him what K.C. stood for and I wanted to know. It was too early to talk to your office in Los Angeles—just 8 A.M., L.A. time—so I called your attorney in New York. My father used to say, when in doubt ask.'

'You got Seymour Steigler III on a Saturday?' Bartlett asked, amazed.

'Yes. At his home in White Plains.'

'But his home number's not in the book.'

'I know. I called a Chinese friend of mine in the U.N. He tracked him down for me. I told Mr. Steigler I wanted to know because of invitations—which is, of course, the truth. One should be accurate, shouldn't one?'

'Yes,' Casey said, admiring him greatly. 'Yes one should.'

'You knew Casey was . . . Casey was a woman, last night?' Gavallan asked.

'Yes. Actually I knew several months ago, though not what K.C. stood for. Why?'

'Nothing, tai-pan. Casey, you were saying about Armenia. Your family migrated to the States after the war?'

'After the First World War in 1918,' Casey said, beginning the oft-told story. 'Originally our surname was Tcholokian. When my grandparents arrived in New York they dropped the *ian* for simplicity, to help Americans. I still got Kamalian Ciranoush though. As you know, Armenia is the southern part of Caucasus—just north of Iran and Turkey and south of Russian Georgia. It used to be a free sovereign nation but now it's all absorbed by Soviet Russia or Turkey. My grandmother was Georgian—there was lots of intermarriage in the old days. My people were spread all over the Ottoman Empire, about two million, but the massacres, particularly in 1915 and '16 . . .' Casey shivered. 'It was genocide really. There's barely 500,000 of us left and now we're scattered throughout the world. Armenians were traders, artists, painters and jewelry makers, writers, warriors too. There were nearly 50,000 Armenians in the Turkish Army before they were disarmed, outcast and shot by the Turks during World War One—generals, officers and soldiers. They were an elite minority and had been for centuries.'

'Is that why the Turks hated them?' deVille asked.

'They were hardworking and clannish and very good traders and businessmen for sure—they controlled lots of business and trade. My granddad said trading's in our blood. But perhaps the main reason is that Armenians are Christian—they were the first Christian state in history under the Romans—and of course the Turks are Mohammedan. The Turks conquered Armenia in the sixteenth century and there was always a border war going on between Christian Tsarist Russia and the "Infidel" Turks. Up to 1917 Tsarist Russia was our real protector. . . . The Ottoman Turks were always a strange people, very cruel, very strange.'

'Your family got out before the trouble?'

'No. My grandparents were quite rich, and like a lot of people thought nothing could happen to them. They escaped just ahead of the soldiers, took two sons and a daughter out the back door with just what they could grab in their dash for freedom. The rest of the family never made it. My grandfather bribed his way out of Istanbul onto a fishing boat that smuggled him and my grandmother to Cyprus where, somehow, they got visas to the States. They had a little money and some jewelry—and lots of talent. Granny's still alive . . . she can still haggle with the best of them.'

'Your grandfather was a trader?' Dunross asked. 'Is that how you first got interested in business?'

'We certainly had it drummed into us as soon as we could think about being self-sufficient,' Casey said. 'My granddad started an optical company in Providence, making lenses and microscopes and an import-export company dealing mostly in carpets and perfumes, with a little gold and precious stones trading on the side. My dad designed and made jewelry. He's dead now but he had a small store of his own in Providence, and his brother, my uncle Bghos, worked with Granddad. Now, since Granddad died, my uncle runs the import-export company. It's small but stable. We grew up, my sister and I, around haggling, negotiating and the problem of profit. It was a great game and we were all equals.'

'Where . . . oh, more trifle, Casey?'

'No thanks, I'm fine.'

'Where did you take your business degree?'

'I suppose all over,' she said. 'After I got out of high school, I put myself through a two-year business course at Katharine Gibbs in Providence: shorthand, typing, simple accounting, filing, plus a few business fundamentals. But ever since I could count I worked nights and holidays and weekends with Granddad in his business. I was taught to think and plan and put the plan into effect, so most of my training's been in the field. Of course since I've gotten out of school I've kept up with specialized courses that I wanted to take—at night school

155

mostly.' Casey laughed. 'Last year I even took one at the Harvard Business School which went down like an H-bomb with some members of the faculty, though it's getting a little easier now for a woman.'

'How did you manage to become hatchetman—hatchetlady—to Par-Con Industries?' Dunross said.

'Perspicacity,' she said and they laughed with her.

Bartlett said, 'Casey's a devil for work, Ian. Her speed reading's fantastic so she can cover more ground than two normal execs. She's got a great nose for danger, she's not afraid of a decision, she's more of a deal maker than a deal breaker, and she doesn't blush easily.'

'That's my best point,' Casey said. 'Thanks, Linc.'

'But isn't it very hard on you, Casey?' Gavallan asked. 'Don't you have to concede a hell of a lot as a woman to keep up? It can't be easy for you to do a man's job.'

'I don't consider my job a man's job, Andrew,' she replied at once. 'Women have just as good brains and work capacity as men.'

There was an immediate hoot of friendly derision from Linbar and Gavallan and Dunross overrode them and said, 'I think we'll table that one for later. But again, Casey, how did you get where you are at Par-Con?'

Shall I tell you the real story, Ian lookalike to Dirk Struan, the greatest pirate in Asia, or shall I tell you the one that's become legend, she asked herself.

Then she heard Bartlett begin and she knew she could safely drift for she had heard his version a hundred times before and it was part true, part false and part what he wanted to believe had happened. How many of *your* legends are true—Hag Struan and Dirk Struan and what's your real story and how did you become tai-pan? She sipped her port, enjoying the smooth sweetness, letting her mind wander.

There's something wrong here, she was thinking now. I can feel it strongly. Something's wrong with Dunross.

What?

'I first met Casey in Los Angeles, California—about seven years ago,' Bartlett had begun. 'I'd gotten a letter from a Casey Tcholok, president of Hed-Opticals of Providence, who wanted to discuss a merger. At that time I was in construction all over the L.A. area—residential, supermarkets, a couple of good-sized office buildings, industrial, shopping centers—you name it, I'd build it. We had a turnover of 3.2 million and I'd just gone public—but I was still a million miles away from the Big Board. I'd—'

'You mean the New York Stock Exchange?'

'Yes. Anyway, Casey comes in bright as a new penny and says she wants me to merge with Hed-Opticals which she says grossed $277,600 last year, and then together we'd go after Randolf Opticals, the granddaddy of them all—53 million in sales, quoted on the Big Board, a huge slice of the lens market and lots of cash in the bank—and I said you're crazy but why Randolf? She said because first she was a stockholder in Bartlett Construction—she'd bought ten one-dollar shares—I'd capitalized at a million shares and sold 500,000 at par—and she figured it'd be dandy for Bartlett Construction to own Randolf, and second, "because this son of a bitch George Toffer who runs Randolf Opticals is a liar, a cheat, a thief, and he's trying to put me out of business."'

Bartlett grinned and paused for breath and Dunross broke in with a laugh. 'This's true, Casey?'

Casey came back quickly. 'Oh yes, I said that George Toffer was a liar, a cheat, thief and son of a bitch. He still is.' Casey smiled without humor. 'And he was certainly trying to put me out of business.'

'Why?'

'Because I had told him to go—to drop dead.'

'Why'd you do that?'

'I'd just taken over Hed-Opticals. My granddad had died the previous year and we'd flipped a coin, my uncle Bghos and I, who'd get which business. . . . I'd won Hed-Opticals. We'd had an offer from Randolf to buy us out a year or so back but we'd turned it down—we had a nice, small operation, a good work force, good technicians—a number of them Armenians— a little slice of the market. But no capital and no room to maneuver but we got by and the quality of Hed-Opticals was optimum. Just after I took over, George Toffer "happened to drop by." He fancied himself, my God how he fancied himself. He claimed he was a U.S. Army war hero but I found out he wasn't—he was that sort of guy. Anyway, he made me another

157

ridiculous offer to take Hed-Opticals off my hands . . . the poor little girl who should be in the kitchen bit, along with the "let's have dinner tonight in my suite and why don't we have a little fun because I'm here alone for a few days. . . ." I said no thanks and he was very put out. Very. But he said okay and went back to business and suggested that instead of a buy-out we subcontract some of his contracts. He made me a good offer and after haggling a bit we agreed on terms. If I performed on this one he said he'd double the deal. Over the next month we did the work better and cheaper than he could ever have done it—I delivered according to contract and he made a fantastic profit. But then he reneged on a verbal clause and deducted—stole— $20,378, and the next day five of my best customers left us for Randolf, and the next week another seven—they'd all been offered deals at less than cost. He let me sweat for a week or two then he phoned. "Hi, baby," he said, happy as a toad in a pail of mud, "I'm spending the weekend alone at Martha's Vineyard." That's a little island off the East Coast. Then he added, "Why don't you come over and we'll have some fun and discuss the future and doubling our orders." I asked for my money, and he laughed at me and told me to grow up and suggested I better reconsider his offer because at the rate I was going soon there'd be no Hed-Opticals.

'I cursed him,' Casey said. 'I can curse pretty good when I get mad and I told him what to do with himself in three languages. Within four more weeks I'd no customers left. Another month and the work force had to get other jobs. About that time I thought I'd try California. I didn't want to stay in the East.' She smiled wryly. 'It was a matter of face—if I'd known about face then. I thought I'd take a couple of weeks off to figure out what to do. Then one day I was wandering aimlessly around a state fair in Sacramento and Linc was there. He was selling shares in Bartlett Construction in a booth and I bought—'

'He what?' Dunross asked.

'Sure,' Bartlett said. 'I sold upwards of 20,000 shares that way. I covered state fairs, mail orders, supermarkets, stockbrokers, shopping centers—along with investment banks. Sure. Go on, Casey!'

'So I read his prospectus and watched him a while and thought he had a lot of get up and go. His figures and balance sheet and expansion rate were exceptional and I thought any-one who'd pitch his own stock has got to have a future. So I bought ten shares, wrote him and went to see him. End of story.'

'The hell it is, Casey,' Gavallan said.

'You tell it, Linc,' she said.

'Okay. Well, then—'

'Some port, Mr.—sorry, Linc?'

'Thanks Andrew, but, er, may I have another beer?' It arrived instantly. 'So, Casey'd come to see me. After she'd told it, almost like she's told it now, I said, "One thing, Casey, Hed-Opticals grossed less than 300,000-odd last year. What's it going to do this year?"

'"Zero," she said with that smile of hers. "I'm Hed-Opticals' total asset. In fact, I'm all there is."

'"Then what's the use of my merging with zero—I've got enough problems of my own."

'"I know how to take Randolf Opticals to the cleaners."

'"How?"

'"22 percent of Randolf's is owned by three men—all of whom despise Toffer. With 22 percent you could get control. I know how you could get their proxies, and most of all, I know the weakness of Toffer."

'"What's that?"

'"Vanity, and he's a megalomaniac, but most of all he's stupid."

'"He can't be stupid and run that company."

'"Perhaps he wasn't once, but now he is. He's ready to be taken."

'"And what do you want out of this, Casey?"

'"Toffer's head—I want to do the firing."

'"What else?"

'"If I succeed in showing you how . . . if we succeed in taking over Randolf Opticals, say within six months, I'd like . . . I'd like a one-year deal with you, to be extended to seven, at a salary you think is commensurate with my ability, as your executive vice-president in charge of acquisitions. But I'd want it as a person, not as a woman, just as an equal person to you. You're the boss of course, but I'm to be equal as a man would be equal, as an individual . . . if I deliver."'

Bartlett grinned and sipped his beer. 'I said, okay you've got a deal. I thought, what've I got to lose—me with my lousy three-quarter million and her with her nothing zero balance for Randolf Opticals in six months, now that's one helluva steal. So we shook, man to woman.' Bartlett laughed. 'First time I'd ever made a deal with a woman, just like that—and I've never regretted it.'

'Thanks, Linc,' Casey said softly, and every one of them was envious.

And what happened after you fired Toffer, Dunross was thinking with all the others. Is that when you two began?

'The takeover,' he said to Bartlett. 'It was smooth?'

'Messy, but we got blooded and the lessons I learned, we learned, paid off a thousand percent. In five months we'd control. Casey and I had conquered a company 53½ times our size. At D-hour minus one I was down to minus 4 million dollars in the bank and goddamn near in jail, but the next hour I'd control. Man, that was a battle and a half. In a month and a half we'd reorganized it and now Par-Con's Randolf Division grosses $150 millions yearly and the stock's way up. It was a classic blitzkrieg and set the pattern for Par-Con Industries.'

'And this George Toffer, Casey? How did you fire him?'

Casey took her tawny eyes off Linc and turned them on Dunross and he thought, Christ I'd like to possess you.

Casey said, 'The hour we got control I—' She stopped as the single phone rang and there was a sudden tension in the room. Everyone, even the waiters, immediately switched their total attention to the phone—except Bartlett. The color had drained out of Gavallan's face and deVille's. 'What's the matter?' Casey asked.

Dunross broke the silence. 'It's one of our house rules. No phone calls are put through during lunch unless it's an emergency—a personal emergency—for one of us.'

They watched Lim put down the coffee tray. It seemed to take him forever to walk across the room and pick up the phone. They all had wives and children and families and they all wondered what death or what disaster and please God, let the call be for someone else, remembering the last time the phone had rung, two days ago. For Jacques. Then another time last month, for Gavallan, his mother was dying. They had all had calls, over the years. All bad.

Andrew Gavallan was sure the call was for him. His wife, Kathren, Dunross's sister, was at the hospital for the results of exhaustive tests—she had been sick for weeks for no apparent reason. Jesus Christ, he thought, get hold of yourself, conscious of others watching him.

'*Weyyyy?*' Lim listened a moment. He turned and offered the phone. 'It's for you, tai-pan.'

The others breathed again and watched Dunross. His walk was tall. 'Hello? . . . Oh hel— What? . . . . No . . . no, I'll be right there. . . . No, don't do anything, I'll be right there.' They saw his shock as he replaced the phone in the dead silence. After a pause he said, 'Andrew, tell Claudia to postpone my afternoon board meetings. You and Jacques continue with Casey. That was Phillip. I'm afraid poor John Chen's been kidnapped.' He left.

8

2:35 P.M.:

Dunross got out of his car and hurried through the open door of
the vast, Chinese-style mansion that was set high on the mountain crest called Struan's Lookout. He passed a glazed servant
who closed the door after him, and went into the living room.
The living room was Victorian and gaudy and over-stuffed with
bric-à-brac and ill-matched furniture.

'Hello, Phillip,' he said. 'I'm so sorry. Poor John! Where's the
letter?'

'Here.' Phillip picked it up from the sofa as he got up. 'But first
look at that.' He pointed at a crumpled cardboard shoebox on a
marble table beside the fireplace.

As Dunross crossed the room he noticed Dianne, Phillip
Chen's wife, sitting in a high-backed chair in a far corner. 'Oh,
hello, Dianne, sorry about this,' he said again.

She shrugged impassively. 'Joss, tai-pan.' She was fifty-two,
Eurasian, Phillip Chen's second wife, an attractive, bejeweled
matron who wore a dark brown *cheong-sam*, a priceless jade
bead necklace and a four-carat diamond ring—amid many other
rings. 'Yes, joss,' she repeated.

Dunross nodded, disliking her a little more than usual. He
peered down at the contents of the box without touching them.
Among loose, crumpled newspaper he saw a fountain pen that
he recognized as John Chen's, a driving license, some keys on a
key ring, a letter addressed to John Chen, 14A Sinclair Towers,
and a small plastic bag with a piece of cloth half-stuffed into it.
With a pen that he took out of his pocket he flipped open the
cover of the driving license. John Chen.

'Open the plastic bag,' Phillip said.

'No. I might mess up any fingerprints that're on it,' Dunross said, feeling stupid but saying it anyway.

'Oh—I'd forgotten about that. Damn. Of course, fingerprints! Mine are . . . I opened it of course. Mine must be all over it—all over everything.'

'What's in it?'

'It's—' Phillip Chen came over and before Dunross could stop him pulled the cloth out of the plastic, without touching the plastic again. 'You can't have fingerprints on cloth, can you? Look!' The cloth contained most of a severed human ear, the cut clean and sharp and not jagged.

Dunross cursed softly. 'How did the box arrive?' he asked.

'It was hand delivered.' Phillip Chen shakily rewrapped the ear and put it back in the box. 'I just . . . I just opened the parcel as anyone would. It was hand delivered half an hour or so ago.'

'By whom?'

'We don't know. He was just a youth, the servant said. A youth on a motor scooter. She didn't recognize him or take any number. We get lots of parcels delivered. It was nothing out of the ordinary—except the "Mr. Phillip Chen, a matter of great importance, to open personally," on the outside of the package, which she didn't notice at once. By the time I'd opened it and read the letter . . . it was just a youth who said, "Parcel for Mr. Phillip Chen," and went away.'

'Have you called the police?'

'No, tai-pan, you said to do nothing.'

Dunross went to the phone. 'Have you got hold of John's wife yet?'

Dianne said at once, 'Why should Phillip bear bad tidings to her? She'll throw a temperament that will raise the roof tiles never mind. Call Barbara? Oh dear no, tai-pan, not . . . not until we've informed the police. They should tell her. They know how to do these things.'

Dunross's disgust increased. 'You'd better get her here quickly.' He dialed police headquarters and asked for Armstrong. He was not available. Dunross left his name then asked for Brian Kwok.

'Yes tai-pan?'

'Brian, can you come over here right away? I'm at Phillip Chen's house up on Struan's Lookout. John Chen's been kidnapped.' He told him about the contents of the box.

There was a shocked silence, then Brian Kwok said, 'I'll be there right away. Don't touch anything and don't let him talk to anyone.'

'All right.'

Dunross put the phone down. 'Now give me the letter, Phillip.' He handled it carefully, holding it by the edges. The Chinese characters were clearly written but not by a well-educated person. He read it slowly, knowing most of the characters:

> Mr. Phillip Chen, I beg to inform you that I am badly in need of 500,000 Hong Kong currency and I hereby consult you about it. You are so wealthy that this is like plucking one hair from nine oxen. Being afraid that you might refuse I therefore have no alternative but to hold your son hostage. By doing so there is not a fear of your refusal. I hope you will think it over carefully thrice and take it into serious consideration. It is up to you whether you report to the police or not. I send herewith some articles which your son uses every day as proof of the situation your son is in. Also sent is a little bit of your son's ear. You should realize the mercilessness and cruelty of my actions. If you smoothly pay the money the safety of your son will be ensured. Written by the Werewolf.

Dunross motioned at the box. 'Sorry, but do you recognize the, er . . . that?'

Phillip Chen laughed nervously and so did his wife. 'Do you, Ian? You've known John all your life. That's . . . how does one recognize something like that, *heya*?'

'Does anyone else know about this?'

'No, except the servants of course, and Shitee T'Chung and some friends who were lunching with me here. They . . . they were here when the parcel arrived. They, yes, they were here. They left just before you arrived.'

Dianne Chen shifted in her chair and said what Dunross was thinking. 'So of course it will be all over Hong Kong by evening!'

'Yes. And banner headlines by dawn.' Dunross tried to collate the multitude of questions and answers flooding his mind.

'The press'll pick up about the, er, ear and the "Werewolf" and make it a field day.'

'Yes. Yes, they will.' Phillip Chen remembered what Shitee T'Chung had said the moment they had all read the letter. 'Don't pay the ransom for at least a week, Phillip old friend, and you'll be world famous! *Ayeeyah*, fancy, a piece of his ear and Werewolf! Eeeee, you'll be world famous!'

'Perhaps it's not his ear at all and a trick,' Phillip Chen said hopefully.

'Yes.' If it is John's ear, Dunross thought, greatly perturbed, and if they've sent it on the first day before any negotiation or anything, I'll bet the poor sod's already dead. 'No point in hurting him like that,' he said. 'Of course you'll pay.'

'Of course. It's lucky we're not in Singapore, isn't it?'

'Yes.' By law in Singapore now, the moment anyone was kidnapped all bank accounts of the family were frozen to prevent payment to the kidnappers. Kidnapping had become endemic there with almost no arrests, Chinese preferring to pay quickly and quietly and say nothing to the police. 'What a bastard! Poor old John.'

Phillip said, 'Would you like some tea—or a drink? Are you hungry?'

'No thanks. I'll wait until Brian Kwok gets here then I'll be off.' Dunross looked at the box and at the keys. He had seen the key ring many times. 'The safety deposit key's missing,' he said.

'What key?' Dianne Chen asked.

'John always had a deposit box key on his ring.'

She did not move from her chair. 'And it's not there now?'

'No.'

'Perhaps you're mistaken. That he always had it on the ring.'

Dunross looked at her and then at Phillip Chen. They both stared back at him. Well, he thought, if the crooks didn't take it, now Phillip or Dianne have, and if I were them I'd do the same. God knows what might be in such a box. 'Perhaps I'm mistaken,' he said levelly.

'Tea, tai-pan?' Dianne asked, and he saw the shadow of a smile in the back of her eyes.

'Yes, I think I will,' he said, knowing they had taken the key.

She got up and ordered tea loudly and sat down again. 'Eeee, I wish they'd hurry up . . . the police.'

Phillip was looking out of the window at the parched garden. 'I wish it would rain.'

'I wonder how much it'll cost to get John back?' she muttered.

After a pause, Dunross said, 'Does it matter?'

'Of course it matters,' Dianne said at once. 'Really, tai-pan!'

'Oh yes,' Phillip Chen echoed. '$500,000! *Ayeeyah*, $500,000—that's a fortune. Damn triads! Well, if they ask five I can settle for $150,000. Thank God they didn't ask a million!' His eyebrows soared and his face became more ashen. '*Dew neh loh moh* on all kidnappers. They should get the chop—all of them.'

'Yes,' Dianne said. 'Filthy triads. The police should be more clever! More sharp and more clever and protect us better.'

'Now that's not fair,' Dunross said sharply. 'There hasn't been a major kidnapping in Hong Kong for years and it happens every month in Singapore! Crime's fantastically low here—our police do a grand job—grand.'

'Huh,' Dianne sniffed. 'They're all corrupt. Why else be a policeman if it's not to get rich? I don't trust any of them. . . . We know, oh yes we know. As to kidnapping, huh, the last one was six years ago. It was my third cousin, Fu San Sung—the family had to pay $600,000 to get him back safely. . . . It nearly bankrupted them.'

'Ha!' Phillip Chen scoffed. 'Bankrupt Hummingbird Sung? Impossible!' Hummingbird Sung was a very wealthy Shanghainese shipowner in his fifties with a sharp nose—long for a Chinese. He was nicknamed Hummingbird Sung because he was always darting from dance hall to dance hall, from flower to flower, in Singapore, Bangkok and Taipei, Hong Kong, dipping his manhood into a myriad of ladies' honey pots, the rumor being it wasn't his manhood because he enjoyed mutual cunnilingus.

'The police got most of the money back if I remember rightly, and sent the criminals to jail for twenty years.'

'Yes, tai-pan, they did. But it took them months and months. And I wouldn't mind betting one or two of the police knew more than they said.'

'Absolute nonsense!' Dunross said. 'You've no cause to believe anything like that! None.'

'Quite right!' Phillip Chen said irritably. 'They caught them, Dianne.' She looked at him. At once he changed his tone. 'Of

166

course, dear, some police may be corrupt but we're very lucky here, very lucky. I suppose I wouldn't mind so much about, about John—it's only a matter of ransom and as a family we've been very lucky so far—I wouldn't mind except for . . . for that.' He motioned at the box disgustedly. 'Terrible! And totally uncivilized.'

'Yes,' Dunross said, and wondered if it wasn't John Chen's ear, whose was it—where do you get an ear from? He almost laughed at the ridiculousness of his questions. Then he put his mind back to pondering if the kidnapping was somehow tied in with Tsu-yan and the guns and Bartlett. It's not like a Chinese to mutilate a victim. No, and certainly not so soon. Kidnapping's an ancient Chinese art and the rules have always been clear: pay and keep silent and no problem, delay and talk and many problems.

He stared out of the window at the gardens and at the vast northern panorama of city and seascape below. Ships and junks and sampans dotted the azure sea. There was a fine sky above and no promise of rain weather, the summer monsoon steady from the southwest and he wondered absently what the clippers had looked like as they sailed before the wind or beat up against the winds in his ancestors' time. Dirk Struan had always had a secret lookout atop the mountain above. There the man could see south and east and west and the great Sheung Sz Mun Channel which approached Hong Kong from the south—the only path inward bound for ships from home, from England. From Struan's Lookout, the man could secretly spot the incoming mail ship and secretly signal below. Then the tai-pan would dispatch a fast cutter to get the mails first, to have a few hours' leeway over his rivals, the few hours perhaps meaning the trading difference between fortune and bankruptcy—so vast the time from home. Not like today with instant communication, Dunross thought. We're lucky—we don't have to wait almost two years for a reply like Dirk did. Christ, what a man he must have been.

I must not fail with Bartlett. I must have those 20 million.

'The deal looks very good, tai-pan,' Phillip Chen said as though reading his mind.

'Yes. Yes it is.'

'If they really put up cash we'll all make a fortune and it'll be *h'eung yau* for the Noble House,' he added with a beam.

Dunross's smile was again sardonic. *H'eung yau* meant 'fragrant grease' and normally referred to the money, the payoff, the squeeze, that was paid by all Chinese restaurants, most businesses, all gambling games, all dance halls, all ladies of easy virtue, to triads, some form of triad, throughout the world.

'I still find it staggering that *h'eung yau*'s paid wherever a Chinese is in business.'

'Really, tai-pan,' Dianne said as though he were a child. 'How can any business exist without protection? You expect to pay, naturally, so you pay never mind. Everyone gives *h'eung yau*— some form of *h'eung yau*.' Her jade beads clicked as she shifted in her chair, her eyes dark, dark in the whiteness of her face—so highly prized among Chinese. 'But the Bartlett deal, tai-pan, do you think the Bartlett deal will go through?'

Dunross watched her. Ah Dianne, he told himself, you know every important detail that Phillip knows about his business and my business, and a lot Phillip would weep with fury if he knew you knew. So you know Struan's could be in very great trouble if there's no Bartlett deal, but if the deal is consummated then our stock will skyrocket and we'll be rich again—and so will you be, if you can get in early enough, to buy early enough.

Yes.

And I know you Hong Kong Chinese ladies like poor Phillip doesn't, because I'm not even a little part Chinese. I know you Hong Kong Chinese ladies are the roughest women on earth when it comes to money—or perhaps the most practical. And you, Dianne, I also know you are ecstatic now, however much you'll pretend otherwise. Because John Chen's not your son. With him eliminated, your own two sons will be direct in line and your eldest, Kevin, heir apparent. So you'll pray like you've never prayed before that John's gone forever. You're delighted. John's kidnapped and probably murdered, but what about the Bartlett deal?

'Ladies are so practical,' he said.

'How so, tai-pan?' she asked, her eyes narrowing.

'They keep things in perspective.'

'Sometimes I don't understand you at all, tai-pan,' she replied, an edge to her voice. 'What more can we do now about John Chen? Nothing. We've done everything we can. When the ransom note arrives we negotiate and we pay and everything's as it was. But the Bartlett deal is important, very important, very very important whatever happens, *heya? Moh ching, moh meng.*' No money, no life.'

'Quite. It is very important, tai-pan.' Phillip caught sight of the box and shuddered. 'I think under the circumstances, tai-pan, if you'll excuse us this evening . . . I don't th—'

'No, Phillip,' his wife said firmly. 'No. We must go. It's a matter of face for the whole House. We'll go as planned. As difficult as it will be for us—we will go as planned.'

'Well, if you say so.'

'Yes.' Oh very yes she was thinking, replanning her whole ensemble to enhance the dramatic effect of their entrance. We'll go tonight and we'll be the talk of Hong Kong. We'll take Kevin of course. Perhaps he's heir now. *Ayeeyah!* Who should my son marry? I've got to think of the future now. Twenty-two's a perfect age and I have to think of his new future. Yes, a wife. Who? I'd better choose the right girl at once and quickly if he's heir, before some young filly with a fire between her legs and a rapacious mother does it for me. *Ayeeyah*, she thought, her temperature rising, gods forbid such a thing! 'Yes,' she said, and touched her eyes with her handkerchief as though a tear were there, 'there's nothing more to be done for poor John but wait—and continue to work and plan and maneuver for the good of the Noble House.' She looked up at Dunross, her eyes glittering. 'The Bartlett deal would solve everything, wouldn't it?'

'Yes.' And you're both right, Dunross thought. There's nothing more to be done at the moment. Chinese are very wise and very practical.

So put your mind on important things—he told himself. Important things—like do you gamble? Think. What better place or time than here and now could you find to begin the plan you've been toying with ever since you met Bartlett?

None.

'Listen,' he said, deciding irrevocably, then looked around at the door that led to the servants' quarters, making sure that they were alone. He lowered his voice to a conspiratorial whisper and Phillip and his wife leaned forward to hear better. 'I had a private meeting with Bartlett before lunch. We've made the deal. I'll need some minor changes, but we close the contract

169

formally on Tuesday of next week. The 20 million's guaranteed and a further 20 million next year.'

Phillip Chen's beam was huge. 'Congratulations.'

'Not so loud, Phillip,' his wife hissed, equally pleased. 'Those turtle mouth slaves in the kitchen have ears that can reach to Java. Oh but that's tremendous news, tai-pan.'

'We'll keep this in the family,' Dunross said softly. 'This afternoon I'm instructing our brokers to start buying Struan's stock secretly—every spare penny we've got. You do the same, in small lots and spread the orders over different brokers and nominees—the usual.'

'Yes. Oh yes.'

'I bought 40 thousand this morning personally.'

'How much will the stock go up?' Dianne Chen asked.

'Double!'

'How soon?'

'Thirty days.'

'Eeeee,' she chortled. 'Think of that.'

'Yes,' Dunross said agreeably. Think of that! Yes. And you two will only tell your very close relations, of which there are many, and they will only tell their very close relations, of which there are a multitude, and you'll all buy and buy because this is an inside-inside, gilt-edged tip and hardly any gamble at all which will further fuel the stock rise. The fact that it's only family will surely leak and more will jump in, then more, and then the formal announcement of the Par-Con deal will add fire and then, next week, I'll announce the takeover bid for Asian Properties and then all Hong Kong will buy. Our stock will skyrocket. Then, at the right moment, I dump Asian Properties and go after the real target.

'How many shares, tai-pan?' Phillip Chen asked—his mind swamped by his own calculations of the possible profits.

'Maximum. But it has to be family only. Our stocks'll lead the boom.'

Dianne gasped. 'There's going to be a boom?'

'Yes. We'll lead it. The time's ripe, everyone in Hong Kong's ready. We'll supply the means, we'll be the leader, and with a judicious shove here and there, there'll be a stampede.'

There was a great silence. Dunross watched the avarice on her face.

Her fingers clicked the jade beads. He saw Phillip staring into the distance and he knew that part of his compradore's mind was on the various notes that he, Phillip, had countersigned for Struan's that were due in thirteen to thirty days: $12 million U.S. to Toda Shipping Industries of Yokohama for the two super bulk cargo freighters, $6,800,000 to the Orlin International Merchant Bank, and $750,000 to Tsu-yan, who had covered another problem for him. But most of Phillip's mind would be on Bartlett's 20 million and the stock rise—the doubling that he had arbitrarily forecast.

Double?

No way—no not at all, not a chance in hell . . .

Unless there's a boom. Unless there's a boom!

Dunross felt his heart quicken. 'If there's a boom . . . Christ, Phillip, we can do it!'

'Yes—yes, I agree, Hong Kong's ripe. Ah yes.' Phillip Chen's eyes sparkled and his fingers drummed. 'How many shares, tai-pan?'

'Every bl—'

Excitedly Dianne overrode Dunross, 'Phillip, last week my astrologer said this was going to be an important month for us! A boom! That's what he must have meant.'

'That's right, I remember you telling me, Dianne. Oh oh oh! How many shares, tai-pan?' he asked again.

'Every bloody penny! We'll make this the big one. But family only until Friday. Absolutely until Friday. Then, after the market closes I'll leak the Bartlett deal. . . .'

'*Eeeeee*,' Dianne hissed.

'Yes. Over the weekend I'll say "no comment"—you make sure you're not available, Phillip—and come Monday morning, everyone'll be chomping at the bit. I'll still say "no comment," but Monday we buy openly. Then, just after close of business Monday, I'll announce the whole deal's confirmed. Then, come Tuesday . . .'

'The boom's on!'

'Yes.'

'Oh happy day,' Dianne croaked delightedly. 'And every *amah*, houseboy, coolie, businessman, will decide their joss is perfect and out will come their savings and everything gets fed, all stocks will rocket. What a pity there won't be an editorial

171

tomorrow . . . even better, an astrologer in one of the papers . . . say Hundred Year Fong . . . or . . .' Her eyes almost crossed with excitement. 'What about *the* astrologer, Phillip?'

He stared at her, shocked. 'Old Blind Tung?'

'Why not? Some *h'eung yau* in his palm . . . or the promise of a few shares of whatever stock you name. *Heya?*'

'Well, I—'

'Leave that one to me. Old Blind Tung owes me a favor or two, I've sent him enough clients! Yes. And he won't be far wrong announcing heavenly portents that herald the greatest boom in Hong Kong's history, will he?'

9

5:25 P.M.:

The police pathologist, Dr. Meng, adjusted the focus of the microscope and studied the sliver of flesh that he had cut from the ear. Brian Kwok watched him impatiently. The doctor was a small pedantic little Cantonese with thick-lensed glasses perched on his forehead. At length he looked up and his glasses fell conveniently on to his nose. 'Well, Brian, it could have been sliced from a living person and not a corpse . . . possibly. Possibly within the last eight or ten hours. The bruising . . . here, look at the back'—Dr. Meng motioned delicately at the discoloration at the back and at the top—'. . . that certainly indicates to me that the person was alive at the time.'

'Why bruising, Dr. Meng? What caused it? The slash?'

'It could have been caused by someone holding the specimen tightly,' Dr. Meng said cautiously, 'while it was being removed.'

'By what—knife, razor, zip knife, or Chinese chopper—cooking chopper?'

'By a sharp instrument.'

Brian Kwok sighed. 'Would that kill someone? The shock? Someone like John Chen?'

Dr. Meng steepled his fingers. 'It could, possibly. Possibly not. Does he have a history of a weak heart?'

'His father said he hadn't—I haven't checked with his own doctor yet— the bugger's on holiday but John's never given any indication of being anything but healthy.'

'This mutilation probably shouldn't kill a healthy man but he'd be very uncomfortable for a week or two.' The doctor beamed. 'Very uncomfortable indeed.'

'Jesus!' Brian said. 'Isn't there anything you can give me that'll help?'

'I'm a forensic pathologist, Brian, not a seer.'

'Can you tell if the ear's Eurasian—or pure Chinese?'

'No. No, with this specimen that'd be almost impossible. But it's certainly not Anglo-Saxon, or Indian or Negroid.' Dr. Meng took off his glasses and stared myopically up at the tall superintendent. 'This could possibly cause quite a ripple in the House of Chen, *heya*?'

'Yes. And the Noble House.' Brian Kwok thought a moment. 'In your opinion, this Werewolf, this maniac, would you say he's Chinese?'

'The writing could have been a civilized person's, yes— equally it could have been done by a *quai loh* pretending to be a civilized person. But if he or she was a civilized person that doesn't necessarily mean that the same person who did the act wrote the letter.'

'I know that. What are the odds that John Chen's dead?'

'From the mutilation?'

'From the fact that the Werewolf, or more probably Were-wolves, sent the ear even before starting negotiations.'

The little man smiled and said dryly, 'You mean old Sun Tzu's "kill one to terrorize ten thousand"? I don't know. I don't speculate on such imponderables. I only estimate odds on horses, Brian, or the stock market. What about John Chen's Golden Lady on Saturday?'

'She's got a great chance. Definitely. And Struan's Noble Star—Gornt's Pilot Fish and even more, Richard Kwang's Butterscotch Lass. She'll be the favorite, I'll bet. But Golden Lady's a real goer. She'll start about three to one. She's a flier and the going'll be good for her. Dry. She's useless in the wet.'

'Ah, any sign of rain?'

'Possible. They say there's a storm coming. Even a sprinkle could make all the difference.'

'Then it better not rain till Sunday, *heya*?'

'It won't rain this month—not unless we're enormously lucky.'

'Well if it rains it rains and if it doesn't it doesn't never mind! Winter's coming—then this cursed humidity will go away.' Dr. Meng glanced at the wall clock. It was 5:35 P.M. 'How about a quick one before we go home?'

'No thanks. I've still got a few things to do. Bloody nuisance this.'

'Tomorrow I'll see what clues I can come up with from the cloth, or the wrapping paper or the other things. Perhaps fingerprinting will help you,' the doctor added.

'I wouldn't bet on that. This whole operation is very smelly. Very smelly indeed.'

Dr. Meng nodded and his voice lost its gentleness. 'Anything to do with the Noble House and their puppet House of Chen's smelly. Isn't it?'

Brian Kwok switched to *sei yap*, one of the main dialects of the Kwantung Province, spoken by many Hong Kong Cantonese. 'Eh, Brother, don't you mean any and all capitalist running dogs are smelly, of which the Noble House and the House of Chen are chief and dung heavy?' he said banteringly.

'Ah, Brother, don't you know yet, deep in your head, that the winds of change are whirling throughout the world? And China under the immortal guidance of Chairman Mao, and Mao Thought, is the lead—'

'Keep your proselytizing to yourself,' Brian Kwok said coldly, switching back to English. 'Most of the thoughts of Mao are out of the writings of Sun Tzu, Confucius, Marx, Lao Tsu and others. I know he's a poet— a great one—but he's usurped China and there's no freedom there now. None.'

'Freedom?' the little man said defiantly. 'What's freedom for a few years when, under the guidance of Chairman Mao, China's once more China and has taken back her rightful place in the world. Now China is feared by all filthy capitalists! Even by revisionist Russia.'

'Yes. I agree. For that I thank him. Meanwhile if you don't like it here go home to Canton and sweat your balls off in your Communist paradise and *dew neh loh moh* on all Communists— and their fellow travelers!'

'You should go there, see for yourself. It's propaganda that communism's bad for China. Don't you read the newspapers? No one's starving now.'

'What about the twenty-odd million who were murdered after the takeover? What about all the brainwashing?'

'More propaganda! Just because you've been to English and

175

Canadian public schools and talk like a capitalist swine doesn't mean you're one of them. Remember your heritage.'

'I do. I remember it very well.'

'Your father was mistaken to send you away!' It was common knowledge that Brian Kwok had been born in Canton and, at the age of six, sent to school in Hong Kong. He was such a good student that in '37, when he was twelve, he had won a scholarship to a fine public school in England and had gone there, and then in '39, with the beginning of World War II, the whole school was evacuated to Canada. In '42, at eighteen, he had graduated top of his class, senior prefect, and had joined the Royal Canadian Mounted Police in their plainclothes branch in Vancouver's huge Chinatown. He spoke Cantonese, Mandarin, *sei yap*, and had served with distinction. In '45 he had requested a transfer to the Royal Hong Kong Police. With the reluctant approval of the RCMP, who had wanted him to stay on, he had returned. 'You're wasted working for them, Brian,' Dr. Meng continued. 'You should serve the masses and work for the Party!'

'The Party murdered my father and my mother and most of my family in '43!'

'There was never proof of that! Never. It was hearsay. Perhaps the Kuomintang devils did it—there was chaos then in Canton. I was there, I know! Perhaps the Japanese swine were responsible—or triads—who knows? How can you be certain?'

'I'm certain, by God.'

'Was there a witness? No! You told me that yourself!' Meng's voice rasped and he peered up at him myopically. '*Ayeeyah*, you're Chinese, use your education for China, for the masses, not for the capitalist overlord.'

'Up yours!'

Dr. Meng laughed and his glasses fell on to the top of his nose. 'You wait, Superintendent Kar-shun Kwok. One day your eyes will open. One day you will see the beauty of it all.'

'Meanwhile get me some bloody answers!' Brian Kwok strode out of the laboratory and went up the corridor to the elevator, his shirt sticking to his back. I wish it would rain, he thought.

He got into the elevator. Other policemen greeted him and he them. At the third floor he got out and walked along the corridor to his office. Armstrong was waiting for him, idly reading a Chinese newspaper. 'Hi, Robert,' he said, pleased to see him. 'What's new?'

'Nothing. How about you?'

Brian Kwok told him what Dr. Meng had said.

'That little bugger and his "could possiblys"! The only thing he's ever emphatic about's a corpse—and even then he'll have to check a couple of times.'

'Yes—or about Chairman Mao.'

'Oh, he was on that broken record again?'

'Yes.' Brian Kwok grinned. 'I told him to go back to China.'

'He'll never leave.'

'I know.' Brian stared at the pile of papers in his in tray and sighed. Then he said, 'It's not like a local to cut off an ear so soon.'

'No, not if it's a proper kidnapping.'

'What?'

'It could be a grudge and the kidnapping a cover,' Armstrong said, his well-used face hardening. 'I agree with you and Dunross. I think they did him in.'

'But why?'

'Perhaps John was trying to escape, started a fight, and they or he panicked and before they or he knew what was happening, they or he'd knifed him, or bonked him with a blunt instrument.' Armstrong sighed and stretched to ease the knot in his shoulders. 'In any event, old chap, our Great White Father wants this solved quickly. He honored me with a call to say the governor had phoned personally to express his concern.'

Brian Kwok cursed softly. 'Foul news travels quickly! Nothing in the press yet?'

'No, but it's all over Hong Kong and we'll have a red hot wind fanning our tails by morning. Mr. Bloody Werewolf Esquire—assisted by the pox-ridden, black-hearted, uncooperative Hong Kong press—will, I fear, cause us nothing but grief until we catch the bastard, or bastards.'

'But catch him we will, oh yes, catch him we will!'

'Yes. How about a beer—or better, a very large gin and tonic? I could use one.'

'Good idea. Your stomach off again?'

'Yes. Mary says it's all the good thoughts I keep bottled up.'

They laughed together and headed for the door and were in the corridor when the phone rang.

'Leave the bloody thing, don't answer it, it's only trouble,' Armstrong said, knowing neither he nor Brian would ever leave it.

Brian Kwok picked up the phone and froze.

It was Roger Crosse, senior superintendent, director of Special Intelligence. 'Yes sir?'

'Brian, would you please come up right away.'

'Yes sir.'

'Is Armstrong with you?'

'Yes sir.'

'Bring him too.' The phone clicked off.

'Yes sir.' He replaced the receiver and felt the sweat on his back. 'God wants us, on the double.'

Armstrong's heart jumped a beat. 'Eh? Me?' He caught up with Brian who was heading for the elevator. 'What the hell does he want me for? I'm not in SI now.'

'Ours not to reason why, ours just to shit when he murmurs.' Brian Kwok pressed the *up* button. 'What's up?'

'Got to be important. The Mainland perhaps?'

'Chou En-lai's ousted Mao and the moderates're in power?'

'Dreamer! Mao'll die in office—the Godhead of China.'

'The only good thing you can say about Mao is that he's Chinese first and Commie second. God-cursed Commies!'

'Hey, Brian, maybe the Soviets are hotting up the border again. Another incident?'

'Could be. Yes. War's coming—yes, war's coming between Russia and China. Mao's right in that too.'

'The Soviets aren't that stupid.'

'Don't bet on it, old chum. I've said it before and I've said it again, the Soviets are the world enemy. There'll be war—you'll soon owe me a thousand dollars, Robert.'

'I don't think I want to pay that bet. The killing'll be hideous.'

'Yes. But it'll still happen. Again Mao's right in that. It'll be hideous all right—but not catastrophic.' Irritably Brian Kwok punched the elevator button again. He looked up suddenly. 'You don't think the invasion from Taiwan's launched at long last?'

'That old chestnut? That old pipe dream? Come off it, Brian!

Chiang Kai-shek'll never get off Taiwan.'

'If he doesn't the whole world's in the manure pile. If Mao gets thirty years to consolidate . . . Christ, you've no idea. A billion automatons? Chiang was so right to go after the Commie bastards—they're the real enemy of China. They're the plague of China. Christ, if they get time to Pavlov all the kids.'

Armstrong said mildly, 'Anyone'd think you're a running dog Nationalist. Simmer down, lad, everything's lousy in the world which is now and ever shall be rormal—but you, capitalist dog, you can go racing Saturday, hill climbing Sunday and there're lots of birds ready to be plucked. Eh?'

'Sorry.' They got into the elevator. 'That little bastard Meng caught me off balance,' Brian said, stabbing the top-floor button.

Armstrong switched to Cantonese. *'Thy mother on your sorry, Brother.'*

'And thine was stuffed by a vagrant monkey with one testicle in a pail of pig's nightsoil.'

Armstrong beamed. 'That's not bad, Brian,' he said in English. 'Not bad at all.'

The elevator stopped. They walked along the drab corridor. At the door they prepared themselves. Brian knocked gently.

'Come in.'

Roger Crosse was in his fifties, a thin tall man with pale blue eyes and fair thinning hair and small, long-fingered hands. His desk was meticulous, like his civilian clothes—his office spartan. He motioned to chairs. They sat. He continued to read a file. At length he closed it carefully and set it in front of him. The cover was drab, interoffice and ordinary. 'An American millionaire arrives with smuggled guns, an ex-drug-peddling, very suspect Shanghainese millionaire flees to Taiwan, and now a VIP kidnapping with, God help us, Werewolves and a mutilated ear. All in nineteen-odd hours. Where's the connection?'

Armstrong broke the silence. 'Should there be one, sir?'

'Shouldn't there?'

'Sorry sir, I don't know. Yet.'

'That's very boring, Robert, very boring indeed.'

'Yes sir.'

'Tedious in fact, particularly as the powers that be have already begun to breathe heavily down my neck. And when that happens . . .' He smiled at them and both suppressed a shudder. 'Of course, Robert, I did warn you yesterday that important names might be involved.'

'Yes sir.'

'Now Brian, we're grooming you for high office. Don't you think you could take your mind off horse racing, car racing and almost anything in skirts and apply some of your undoubted talents to solving this modest conundrum.'

'Yes sir.'

'Please do. Very quickly. You're assigned to the case with Robert because it might require your expertise—for the next few days. I want this out of the way very very quickly indeed because we've a slight problem. One of our American friends in the consulate called me last night. Privately.' He motioned at the file. 'This is the result. With his tip we intercepted the original in the bleak hours—of course this's a copy, the original was naturally returned and the . . .' he hesitated, choosing the correct word, '. . . the courier, an amateur by the way, left undisturbed. It's a report, a sort of newsletter with different headings. They're all rather interesting. Yes. One's headed, "The KGB in Asia." It claims that they've a deep-cover spy ring I've never even heard of before, code name "Sevrin," with high-level hostiles in key positions in government, police, business—at the tai-pan level—throughout Southeast Asia, *particularly here in Hong Kong.*'

The air hissed out of Brian Kwok's mouth.

'Quite,' Crosse said agreeably. 'If it's true.'

'You think it is, sir?' Armstrong said.

'Really, Robert, perhaps you're in need of early retirement on medical grounds: softening of the brain. If I wasn't perturbed do you think I'd endure the unhappy pleasure of having to petition the assistance of the CID Kowloon?'

'No sir, sorry sir.'

Crosse turned the file to face them and opened it to the title page. Both men gasped. It read, *'Confidential to Ian Dunross only. By hand, report 3/1963. One copy only.'*

'Yes,' he continued. 'Yes. This's the first time we've actual proof Struan's have their own intelligence system.' He smiled at them and their flesh crawled. 'I'd certainly like to know how tradesmen manage to be privy to all sorts of very intimate information we're supposed to know ages before them.'

'Yes sir.'

'The report's obviously one of a series. Oh yes, and this one's signed on behalf of Struan's Research Committee 16, by a certain A. M. Grant—dated in London three days ago.'

Brian Kwok gasped again. 'Grant? Would that be the Alan Medford Grant, the associate of the Institute for Strategic Planning in London?'

'Full marks, Brian, ten out of ten. Yes. Mr. AMG himself. Mr. VIP, Mr. Advisor to Her Majesty's Government for undercover affairs who really knows onions from leeks. You know him, Brian?'

Brian Kwok said, 'I met him a couple of times in England last year, sir, when I was on the Senior Officers Course at the General Staff College. He gave a paper on advanced strategic considerations for the Far East. Brilliant. Quite brilliant.'

'Fortunately he's English and on our side. Even so . . .' Crosse sighed again. 'I certainly hope he's mistaken this time or we're in the mire deeper than even I imagined. It seems few of our secrets are secrets anymore. Tiring. Very. And as to this,' he touched the file again, 'I'm really quite shocked.'

'Has the original been delivered, sir?' Armstrong asked.

'Yes. To Dunross personally at 4:18 this afternoon.' His voice became even more silky. 'Fortunately, thank God, my relations with our cousins across the water are first class. Like yours, Robert—unlike yours, Brian. You never did like America, did you, Brian?'

'No sir.'

'Why, may I ask?'

'They talk too much, sir, you can't trust them with any secrets—they're loud, and I find them stupid.'

Crosse smiled with his mouth. 'That's no reason not to have good relations with them, Brian. Perhaps you're the stupid one.'

'Yes sir.'

'They're not all stupid, oh dear no.' The director closed the file but left it facing them. Both men stared at it, mesmerized.

'Did the Americans say how they found out about the file, sir?' Armstrong asked without thinking.

'Robert, I really do believe your sinecure in Kowloon has

181

addled your brain. Shall I recommend you for a medical retirement?'

The big man winced. 'No sir, thank you sir.'

'Would we reveal our sources to them?'

'No sir.'

'Would they have told me if I'd been so crass as to ask them?'

'No sir.'

'This whole business is very tedious and filled with loss of face. Mine. Don't you agree, Robert?'

'Yes sir.'

'Good, that's something.' Crosse leaned back in his chair, rocking it. His eyes ground into them. Both men were wondering who the tipster was, and why.

Can't be the CIA, Brian Kwok was thinking. They'd have done the intercept themselves, they don't need SI to do their dirty work for them. Those crazy bastards'll do anything, tread on any toes, he thought disgustedly. If not them, who?

Who?

Must be someone who's in Intelligence but who can't, or couldn't do the intercept, who's on good terms, safe terms with Crosse. A consular official? Possible. Johnny Mishauer, Naval Intelligence? Out of his channel. Who? There's not many . . . Ah, the FBI man, Crosse's protégé! Ed Langan. Now, how would Langan know about this file? Information from London? Possible, but the FBI doesn't have an office there. If the tip came from London, probably MI-5 or 6 would know it first and they'd've arranged to get the material at the source and would have telexed it to us, and given us hell for being inept in our own backyard. Did the courier's aircraft land at Lebanon? There's an FBI man there I seem to recall. If not from London or Lebanon, the information must have come from the aircraft itself. Ah, an accompanying friendly informer who saw the file, or the cover? Crew? *Ayeeyah!* Was the aircraft TWA or Pan Am? The FBI has all sorts of links, close links—with all sorts of ordinary businesses, rightly so. Oh yes. Is there a Sunday flight? Yes. Pan Am, ETA 2030. Too late for a night delivery by the time you've got to the hotel. Perfect.

'Strange that the courier came Pan Am and not BOAC—it's a much better flight,' he said, pleased with the oblique way his mind worked.

'Yes. I thought the same,' Crosse said as evenly. 'Terribly un-British of him. Of course, Pan Am does land on time whereas you never know with poor old BOAC these days—' He nodded at Brian agreeably. 'Full marks again. Go to the head of the class.'

'Thank you sir.'

'What else do you deduce?'

After a pause Brian Kwok said, 'In return for the tip, you agreed to provide Langan with an exact copy of the file.'

'And?'

'And you regret having honored that.'

Crosse sighed. 'Why?'

'I'll know only after I've read the file.'

'Brian, you really are surpassing yourself this afternoon. Good.' Absently the director fingered the file and both men knew he was titillating them, deliberately, but neither knew why. 'There are one or two very curious coincidences in other sections of this. Names like Vincenzo Banastasio . . . meeting places like Sinclair Towers . . . Does Nelson Trading mean anything to either of you?'

They both shook their heads.

'All very curious. Commies to the right of us, commies to the left . . .' His eyes became even stonier. 'It seems we even have a nasty in our own ranks, possibly at superintendent level.'

'Impossible!' Armstrong said involuntarily.

'How long were you with us in SI, dear boy?'

Armstrong almost flinched. 'Two tours, almost five years sir.'

'The spy Sorge was impossible—Kim Philby was impossible —dear God, Philby!' The sudden defection to Soviet Russia in January this year by this Englishman, this onetime top agent of MI-6—British military intelligence for overseas espionage and counterespionage—had sent shock waves throughout the Western world, particularly as, until recently, Philby had been at the British Embassy in Washington, responsible for liaison with U.S. Defense, State, and the CIA on all security matters at the highest level. 'How in the name of all that's holy he could have been a Soviet agent for all those years and remain un-detected is impossible, isn't it, Robert?'

'Yes sir.'

'And yet he was, and privy to our innermost secrets for years.

Certainly from '42 to '58. And where did he start spying? God save us, at Cambridge in 1931. Recruited into the Party by the other arch-traitor, Burgess, also of Cambridge, and his friend Maclean, may they both roast in hell for all eternity.' Some years ago these two highly placed Foreign Office diplomats—both of whom had also been in Intelligence during the war—had abruptly fled to Russia only seconds ahead of British counter-espionage agents and the ensuing scandal had rocked Britain and the whole of NATO. 'Whom else did they recruit?'

'I don't know, sir,' Armstrong said carefully. 'But you can bet that now they're all VIPs in government, the Foreign Office, education, the press, particularly the press—and, like Philby, all burrowed very bloody deep.'

'With people nothing's impossible. Nothing. People are really very dreadful.' Crosse sighed and straightened the file slightly. 'Yes. But it's a privilege to be in SI isn't it, Robert?'

'Yes sir.'

'You have to be invited in, don't you? You can't volunteer, can you?'

'No sir.'

'I never did ask why you didn't stay with us, did I?'

'No sir.'

'Well?'

Armstrong groaned inwardly and took a deep breath. 'It's because I like being a policeman, sir, not a cloak-and-dagger man. I like being in CID. I like pitting your wits against the villain, the chase and the capture and then the proving it in court, according to rules—to the law, sir.'

'Ah but in SI we don't, eh? We're not concerned with courts or laws or anything, only results?'

'SI and SB have different rules, sir,' Armstrong said carefully. 'Without them the Colony'd be up the creek without a paddle.'

'Yes. Yes it would. People are dreadful and fanatics multiply like maggots in a corpse. You were a good undercover man. Now it seems to me it's time to repay all the hours and months of careful training you've had at Her Majesty's expense.'

Armstrong's heart missed twice but he said nothing, just held his breath and thanked God that even Crosse couldn't transfer him out of CID against his will. He had hated his tours in SI—in the beginning it had been exciting and to be chosen was a great vote of confidence, but quickly it had palled—the sudden swoop on the villain in the dark hours, hearings *in camera*, no worry about exact proof, just results and a quick, secret deportation order signed by the governor, then off to the border at once, or onto a junk to Taiwan, with no appeal and no return. Ever.

'It's not the British way, Brian,' he had always said to his friend. 'I'm for a fair, open trial.'

'What's it matter? Be practical, Robert. You know the bastards're all guilty—that they're the enemy, Commie enemy agents who twist our rules to stay here, to destroy us and our society—aided and abetted by a few bastard lawyers who'd do anything for thirty pieces of silver, or less. The same in Canada. Christ, we had the hell of a time in the RCMP, our own lawyers and politicians were the enemy—and recent Canadians— curiously always British—all socialist trades unionists who were always in the forefront of any agitation. What does it matter so long as you get rid of the parasites?'

'It matters, that's what I think. And they're not all Commie villains here. There's a lot of Nationalist villains who want to—'

'The Nationalists want Commies out of Hong Kong, that's all.'

'Balls! Chiang Kai-shek wanted to grab the Colony after the war. It was only the British navy that stopped him after the Americans gave us away. He still wants sovereignty over us. In that he's no different from Mao Tse-tung!'

'If SI doesn't have the same freedom as the enemy, how are we going to keep us out of the creek?'

'Brian, lad, I just said *I* don't like being in SI. You're going to enjoy it. I just want to be a copper, not a bloody Bond!'

Yes, Armstrong thought grimly, just a copper, in CID until I retire to good old England. Christ, I've enough trouble now with the god-cursed Werewolves. He looked back at Crosse and kept his face carefully noncommittal and waited.

Crosse watched him then tapped the file. 'According to this we're very much deeper in the mire than even I imagined. Very distressing. Yes.' He looked up. 'This report refers to previous ones sent to Dunross. I'd certainly like to see them as soon as possible. Quickly and quietly.'

Armstrong glanced at Brian Kwok. 'How about Claudia Chen?'

'No. No chance. None.'

'Then what do you suggest, Brian?' Crosse asked. 'I imagine my American friend will have the same idea . . . and if he's been misguided enough to pass on the file, a copy of the file, to the director of the CIA here . . . I really would be very depressed if they were there first again.'

Brian Kwok thought a moment. 'We could send a specialized team into the tai-pan's executive offices and his penthouse, but it'd take time—we just don't know where to look—and it would have to be at night. That one could be hairy, sir. The other reports—if they exist—might be in a safe up at the Great House, or at his place at Shek-O—even at his, er, at his private flat at Sinclair Towers or another one we don't even know about.'

'Distressing,' Crosse agreed. 'Our intelligence is getting appallingly lax even in our own bailiwick. Pity. If we were Chinese we'd know everything, wouldn't we, Brian?'

'No sir, sorry sir.'

'Well, if you don't know where to look you'll have to ask.'

'Sir?'

'Ask. Dunross's always seemed to be cooperative in the past. After all he is a friend of yours. Ask to see them.'

'And if he says, no, or that they were destroyed?'

'You use your talented head. You cajole him a little, you use a little art, you warm to him, Brian. And you barter.'

'Do we have something current to barter with, sir?'

'Nelson Trading.'

'Sir?'

'Part's in the report. Plus a modest little piece of information I'll be delighted to give you later.'

'Yes sir, thank you sir.'

'Robert, what have you done to find John Chen and the Werewolf or Werewolves?'

'The whole of CID's been alerted, sir. We got the number of his car at once and that's on a 1098. We've interviewed his wife Mrs. Barbara Chen, among others—she was in hysterics most of the time, but lucid, very lucid under the flood.'

'Oh?'

'Yes sir. She's . . . Well, you understand.'

'Yes.'

'She said it wasn't unusual for her husband to stay out late—she said he had many late business conferences and sometimes he'd go early to the track or to his boat. I'm fairly certain she knew he was a man about town. Retracing his movements last night's been fairly easy up to 2:00 A.M. He dropped Casey Tcholok at the Old Vic at about 10:30—'

'Did he see Bartlett last night?'

'No sir, Bartlett was in his aircraft at Kai Tak all the time.'

'Did John Chen talk to him?'

'Not unless there's some way for the airplane to link up with our phone system. We had it under surveillance until the pickup this morning.'

'Go on.'

'After dropping Miss Tcholok—I discovered it was his father's Rolls, by the way—he took the car ferry to the Hong Kong side where he went to a private Chinese club off Queen's Road and dismissed the car and chauffeur. . . .' Armstrong took out his pad and referred to it '. . . It was the Tong Lau Club. There he met a friend and business colleague, Wo Sang Chi, and they began to play mah-jong. About midnight the game broke up. Then, with Wo Sang Chi and the two other players, both friends, Ta Pan Fat, a journalist, and Po Cha Sik, a stockbroker, they caught a taxi.'

Robert Armstrong heard himself reporting the facts, falling into the familiar police pattern and this pleased him and took his mind off the file and all the secret knowledge he possessed, and the problem of the money that he needed so quickly. I wish to God I could just be a policeman, he thought, detesting Special Intelligence and the need for it. 'Ta Pan Fat left the taxi first at his home on Queen's Road, then Wo Sang Chi left on the same road shortly afterwards. John Chen and Po Cha Sik—we think he's got triad connections, he's being checked out now very carefully—went to the Ting Ma Garage on Sunning Road, Causeway Bay, to collect John Chen's car, a 1960 Jaguar.' Again he referred to his notebook, wanting to be accurate, finding the Chinese names confusing as always, even after so many years. 'A garage apprentice, Tong Ta Wey, confirms this. Then John Chen drove his friend Po Cha Sik to his home at 17 Village Street in Happy Valley where the latter left the car. Meanwhile Wo

Sang Chi, John Chen's business colleague, who, curiously, heads Struan's haulage company which has the monopoly of cartage to and from Kai Tak, had gone to the Sap Wah Restaurant on Fleming Road. He states that after being there for thirty minutes, John Chen joined him and they left the restaurant in Chen's car, intending to pick up some dancing girls in the street and take them to supper—'

'He wouldn't even go to the dance hall and buy the girls out?' Crosse asked thoughtfully. 'What's the going rate, Brian?'

'Sixty dollars Hong Kong, sir, at that time of night.'

'I know Phillip Chen's got the reputation of being a miser, but is John Chen the same?'

'At that time of night, sir,' Brian Kwok said helpfully, 'lots of girls start leaving the clubs if they haven't arranged a partner yet—most of the clubs close around 1:00 A.M.—Sunday's not a good pay night, sir. It's quite usual to cruise, there's certainly no point in wasting sixty, perhaps two or three times sixty dollars, because the decent girls are in twos or threes and you usually take two or three to dinner first. No point wasting all that money, is there, sir?'

'Do you cruise, Brian?'

'No sir. No need—no sir.'

Crosse sighed and turned back to Armstrong. 'Go on, Robert.'

'Well sir, they failed to pick up any girls and went to the Copacabana Night Club in the Sap Chuk Hotel in Gloucester Road for supper, getting there about one o'clock. About 1:45 A.M. they left and Wo Sang Chi said he saw John Chen get into his car, but he did not see him drive off—then he walked home, as he lived nearby. He said John Chen was not drunk or bad-tempered, anything like that, but seemed in good spirits, though earlier at the club, the Tong Lau Club, he'd appeared irritable and cut the mah-jong game short. There it ends. John Chen's not known to have been seen again by any of his friends—or family.'

'Did he tell Wo Sang Chi where he was going?'

'No. Wo Sang Chi told us he presumed he was going home—but then he said, "He might have gone to visit his girl friend." We asked him who, but he said he didn't know. After pressing him he said he seemed to remember a name, Fragrant Flower,

188

but no address or phone number—that's all.'

'Fragrant Flower? That could cover a multitude of ladies of the night.'

'Yes sir.'

Crosse was lost in thought for a moment. 'Why would Dunross want John Chen eliminated?'

The two police officers gaped at their superior.

'Put that in your abacus brain, Brian.'

'Yes sir, but there's no reason. John Chen's no threat to Dunross, wouldn't possibly be—even if he became compradore. In the Noble House the tai-pan holds all the power.'

'Does he?'

'Yes. By definition.' Brian Kwok hesitated, thrown off balance again. 'Well yes sir—I . . . in the Noble House, yes.'

Crosse turned his attention to Armstrong. 'Well?'

'No reason I can think of, sir. Yet.'

'Well think about it.'

Crosse lit a cigarette and Armstrong felt the smoke hunger pangs heavily. I'll never keep my vow, he thought. Bloody bastard Crosse-that-we-all-have-to-carry! What the hell's in his mind? He saw Crosse offer him a packet of Senior Service, the brand he always used to smoke—don't fool yourself, he thought, the brand you still smoke. 'No thank you sir,' he heard himself say, shafts of pain in his stomach and through all of him.

'You're not smoking, Robert?'

'No sir, I've stopped . . . I'm just trying to stop.'

'Admirable! Why should Bartlett want John Chen eliminated?'

Again both police officers gawked at him. Then Armstrong said throatily, 'Do you know why, sir?'

'If I knew, why should I ask you? That's for you to find out. There's a connection somewhere. Too many coincidences, too neat, too pat—and too smelly. Yes it smells of KGB involvement to me, and when that happens in my domain I must confess I get irritable.'

'Yes sir.'

'Well, so far so good. Put surveillance on Mrs. Phillip Chen—she could easily be implicated somewhere. The stakes for her are certainly high enough. Tail Phillip Chen for a day or two as well.'

'That's already done, sir. Both of them. On Phillip Chen, not that I suspect him but just because I think they'll both do the usual—be uncooperative, keep mum, negotiate secretly, pay off secretly and breathe a sigh of relief once it's over.'

'Quite. Why is it these fellows—however well educated—think they're so much smarter than we are and won't help us do the work we're paid to do?'

Brian Kwok felt the steely eyes grinding into him and the sweat trickled down his back. Control yourself, he thought. This bastard's only a foreign devil, an uncivilized, manure-eating, dung-ladened, motherless, *dew neh loh moh* saturated, monkey-descended foreign devil. 'It's an old Chinese custom which I'm sure you know, sir,' he said politely, 'to distrust all police, all government officials—they've four thousand years of experience, sir.'

'I agree with the hypothesis, but with one exception. The British. We have proved beyond all doubt we're to be trusted, we can govern, and, by and large, our bureaucracy's incorruptible.'

'Yes sir.'

Crosse watched him for a moment, puffing his cigarette. Then he said, 'Robert, do you know what John Chen and Miss Tcholok said or talked about?'

'No sir. We haven't been able to interview her yet—she's been at Struan's all day. Could it be important?'

'Are you going to Dunross's party tonight?'

'No sir.'

'Brian?'

'Yes sir.'

'Good. Robert, I'm sure Dunross won't mind if I bring you with me, call for me at 8:00 P.M. All Hong Kong that counts will be there—you can keep your ears to the grindstone and your nose everywhere.' He smiled at his own joke and did not mind that neither smiled with him. 'Read the report now. I'll be back shortly. And Brian, please don't fail tonight. It really would be very boring.'

'Yes sir.'

Crosse left.

When they were alone Brian Kwok mopped his brow. 'That bugger petrifies me.'

'Yes. Same for me, old chum, always has.'

'Would he really order a team into Struan's?' Brian Kwok asked incredulously. 'Into the inner kernel of the Noble House?'

'Of course. He'd even lead it himself. This's your first tour with SI, old lad, so you don't know him like I do. That bugger'd lead a team of assassins into hell if he thought it important enough. Bet you he got the file himself. Christ, he's been over the border twice that I know of to chat to a friendly agent. He went alone, imagine that!'

Brian gasped. 'Does the governor know?'

'I wouldn't think so. He'd have a hemorrhage, and if MI-6 ever heard, he'd be roasted and Crosse'd get sent to the Tower of London. He knows too many secrets to take that chance—but he's Crosse and not a thing you can do about it.'

'Who was the agent?'

'Our guy in Canton.'

'Wu Fong Fong?'

'No, a new one—at least he was new in my time. In the army.'

'Captain Ta Quo Sa?'

Armstrong shrugged. 'I forget.'

Kwok smiled. 'Quite right.'

'Crosse still went over the border. He's a law unto himself.'

'Christ, you can't even go to Macao because you were in SI a couple of years ago and he goes over the border. He's bonkers to take that risk.'

'Yes.' Armstrong began to mimic Crosse. 'And how is it tradesmen know things before we do, dear boy? Bloody simple,' he said, answering himself, and his voice lost its banter. 'They spend money. They spend lots of bloody money, whereas we've sweet f.a. to spend. He knows it and I know it and the whole world knows it. Christ, how does the FBI, CIA, KGB or Korean CIA work? They spend money! Christ, it's too easy to get Alan Medford Grant on your team—Dunross hired him. Ten thousand pounds retainer, that'd buy lots of reports, that's more than enough, perhaps it was less. How much are we paid? Two thousand quid a year for three hundred and sixty-six, twenty-five-hour days and a copper on the beat gets four hundred quid. Look at the red tape we'd have to go through to get a secret ten thousand quid to pay to one man to buy info. Where'd the FBI, CIA and god-cursed KGB be without unlimited funds?

Christ,' he added sourly, 'it'd take us six months to get the money, if we could get it, whereas Dunross and fifty others can take it out of petty cash.' The big man sat in his chair slouched and loose-limbed, dark shadows under his eyes that were red rimmed, his cheekbones etched by the overhead light. He glanced at the file on the desk in front of him but did not touch it yet, just wondered at the evil news it must contain. 'It's easy for the Dunrosses of the world,' he said.

Brian Kwok nodded and wiped his hands and put his handkerchief away. 'They say Dunross's got a secret fund—the tai-pan's fund—started by Dirk Struan in the beginning with the loot he got when he burned and sacked Foochow, a fund that only the current tai-pan can use for just this sort of thing, for *h'eung yau* and payoffs, anything—maybe even a little murder. They say it runs into millions.'

'I'd heard that rumor too. Yes. I wish to Christ . . . oh well.' Armstrong reached for the file, hesitated, then got up and went for the phone. 'First things first,' he told his Chinese friend with a sardonic smile. 'First we'd better breathe on a few VIPs.' He dialed Police HQ in Kowloon. 'Armstrong—give me Sergeant Tang-po please.'

'Good evening, sir. Yes sir?' Sergeant Tang-po's voice was warm and friendly.

'Evening,' he said sweetly using the contraction of Sergeant Major as was customary. 'I need information. I need information on who the guns were destined for. I need information on who the kidnappers of John Chen are. I want John Chen—or his body—back in three days. And I want this Werewolf—or Werewolves, in the dock very quickly.'

There was a slight pause. 'Yes sir.'

'Please spread the word. The Great White Father is very angry indeed. And when he gets even just a little angry superintendents get posted to other commands, and so do inspectors—even sergeants, even staff sergeants class one. Some even get demoted to police constable and sent to the border. Some might even get discharged or deported or go to prison. Eh?'

There was an even longer pause. 'Yes sir.'

'And when he's very angry indeed wise men flee, if they can, before anticorruption falls on the guilty—and even on innocents.'

Another pause. 'Yes sir. I'll spread the word, sir, at once. Yes, at once.'

'Thank you, 'Major. The Great White Father is really very angry indeed. And oh, yes.' His voice became even thinner. 'Perhaps you'd ask your brother sergeants to help. They'll surely understand, too, my modest problem is theirs as well.' He switched to Cantonese. '*When the Dragons belch, all Hong Kong defecates. Heya?*'

A longer pause. 'I'll take care of it, sir.'

'Thank you.' Armstrong replaced the receiver.

Brian Kwok grinned. 'That's going to cause a few sphincter muscles to oscillate.'

The Englishman nodded and sat down again but his face did not lose its hardness. 'I don't like to pull that too often—actually that's only the second time I've ever done it—but I've no option. He made that clear, so did the Old Man. You better do the same with your sources.'

'Of course. "When the Dragons belch . . ." You were punning on the legendary Five Dragons?'

'Yes.'

Now Brian Kwok's handsome face settled into a mold—cold black eyes in his golden skin, his square chin almost beardless. 'Tang-po's one of them?'

'I don't know, not for certain. I've always thought he was, though I've nothing to go on. No, I'm not certain, Brian. Is he?'

'I don't know.'

'Well, it doesn't matter if he is or isn't. The word'll get to one of them, which is all I'm concerned about. Personally I'm pretty certain the Five Dragons exist, that they're five Chinese sergeants, perhaps even station sergeants, who run all the illegal street gambling of Hong Kong—and probably, possibly, some protection rackets, a few dance halls and girls.'

'I'd say the Five Dragons're real, Robert—perhaps there are more, perhaps less, but all street gambling's run by police.'

'*Probably* run by Chinese members of our Royal Police Force, lad,' Armstrong said, correcting him. 'We've still no proof, none—and we've been chasing that will o' the wisp for years. I doubt if we'll ever be able to prove it.' He grinned. 'Maybe you will when you're made assistant commissioner.'

'Come off it, for God's sake, Robert.'

'Christ, you're only thirty-nine, you've done the special bigwig Staff College course and you're a super already. A hundred to ten says you'll end up with that rank.'

'Done.'

'I should have made it a hundred thousand,' Armstrong said, pretending sourness. 'Then you wouldn't have taken it.'

'Try me.'

'I won't. I can't afford to lose that amount of tootie—you might get killed or something, this year or next, or resign—but if you don't you're in for the big slot before you retire, presuming you want to go the distance.'

'Both of us.'

'Not me—I'm too mad dog English.' Armstrong clapped him on the back happily. 'That'll be a great day. But you won't close down the Dragons either—even if you'll be able to prove it, which I doubt.'

'No?'

'No. I don't care about the gambling. All Chinese want to gamble and if some Chinese police sergeants run illegal street gambling it'll be mostly clean and mostly fair though bloody illegal. If they don't run it, triads will, and then the splinter groups of rotten little bastards we so carefully keep apart will join together again into one big *tong* and then we'll really have a real problem. You know me, lad, I'm not one to rock any boats, that's why I won't make assistant commissioner. I like the status quo. The Dragons run the gambling so we keep the triads splintered—and just so long as the police always stick together and are absolutely the strongest triad in Hong Kong, we'll always have peace in the streets, a well-ordered population and almost no crime, violent crime.'

Brian Kwok studied him. 'You really believe that, don't you?'

'Yes. In a funny sort of way, right now the Dragons are one of our strongest supports. Let's face it, Brian, only Chinese can govern Chinese. The status quo's good for them too—violent crime's bad for them. So we get help when we need it—sometimes, probably—help that we foreign devils couldn't get any other way. I'm not in favor of their corruption or of breaking the law, not at all—or bribery or all the other shitty things we have to do, or informers, but what police force in the world could operate without dirty hands sometimes and snotty little bastard informers? So the evil the Dragons represent fills a need here, I think. Hong Kong's China and China's a special case. Just so long as it's just illegal gambling I don't care never mind. Me, if it was left up to me I'd make gambling legal tonight but I'd break anyone for any protection racket, any dance hall protection or girls or whatever. I can't stand pimps as you know. Gambling's different. How can you stop a Chinese gambling? You can't. So make it legal and everyone's happy. How many years have the Hong Kong police been advising that and every year we're turned down. Twenty that I know of. But oh no and why? Macao! Simple as that. Dear old Portuguese Macao feeds off illegal gambling and gold smuggling and that's what keeps them alive and we can't afford, we, the UK, we can't afford to have our old ally go down the spout.'

'Robert Armstrong for prime minister!'

'Up yours! But it's true. The take on illegal gambling's our only slush fund—a lot of it goes to pay our ring of informers. Where else can we get quick money? From our grateful government? Don't make me laugh! From a few extra tax dollars from the grateful population we protect? Ha!'

'Perhaps. Perhaps not, Robert. But it's certainly going to backfire one day. The payoffs—the loose and uncounted money that "happens" to be in a station drawer? Isn't it?'

'Yes, but not on me 'cause I'm not in on it, or a taker, and the vast majority aren't either. British *or Chinese*. Meanwhile, how do we three hundred and twenty-seven poor foreign devil police officers control eight odd thousand civilized junior officers and coppers, and another three and a half million civilized little bastards who hate our guts never mind.'

Brian Kwok laughed. It was an infectious laugh and Armstrong laughed with him and added, 'Up yours again for getting me going.'

'Likewise. Meanwhile, are you going to read that first or am I?'

Armstrong looked down at the file he held in his hand. It was thin and contained twelve closely typewritten pages and seemed to be more of a newsletter with topics under different headings. The contents page read: Part One: The Political and Business Forecast of the United Kingdom. Part Two: The KGB in Asia. Part Three: Gold. Part Four: Recent CIA Developments.

Wearily Armstrong put his feet on the desk and eased himself more comfortably in his chair. Then he changed his mind and passed the file over. 'Here, you can read it. You read faster than I do anyway. I'm tired of reading about disaster.'

Brian Kwok took it, his impatience barely contained, his heart thumping heavily. He opened it and began to read.

Armstrong watched him. He saw his friend's face change immediately and lose color. That troubled him greatly. Brian Kwok was not easily shocked. He saw him read through to the end without comment, then flick back to check a paragraph here and there. He closed the file slowly.

'It's that bad,' Armstrong said.

'It's worse. Some of it—well, if it wasn't signed by A. Medford Grant, I'd say he was off his rocker. He claims the CIA have a serious connection with the Mafia, that they're plotting and have plotted to knock off Castro, they're into Vietnam in strength, into drugs and Christ knows what else—here—read it for yourself.'

'What about the mole?'

'We've a mole all right.' Brian reopened the file and found the paragraph. 'Listen: "There's no doubt that presently there is a high-level Communist agent in the Hong Kong police. Top-secret documents brought to our side by General Hans Richter—second-in-command of the East German Department of Internal Security—when he defected to us in March of this year clearly state the agent's code name is 'Our Friend,' that he has been in situ for at least ten, probably fifteen years. His contact is probably a KGB officer in Hong Kong posing as a visiting friendly businessman from the Iron Curtain countries, possibly as a banker or journalist, or posing as a seaman off one of the Soviet freighters visiting or being repaired in Hong Kong. Among other documented information we now know 'Our Friend' has provided the enemy with are: All restricted radio channels, all restricted private phone numbers of the governor, chief of police and top echelon of the Hong Kong Government, along with very private dossiers on most of them . . .'"

'Dossiers?' Armstrong interrupted. 'Are they included?'

'No.'

'Shit! Go on, Brian.'

'"... most of them; the classified police battle plans against a

196

Communist-provoked insurrection, or a recurrence of the Kowloon riots; copies of all private dossiers of all police officers above the rank of inspector; the names of the six chief Nationalist undercover agents of the Kuomintang operating in Hong Kong under the present authority of General Jen Tang-wa (Appendix A); a detailed list of Hong Kong's Special Intelligence agents in Kwantung under the general authority of Senior Agent Wu Fong Fong (Appendix B).'''

'Jesus!' Armstrong gasped. 'We'd better get old Fong Fong and his lads out right smartly.'

'Yes.'

'Is Wu Tat-sing on the list?'

Kwok checked the appendix. 'Yes. Listen, this section ends: ". . . It is the conclusion of your committee that until this traitor is eliminated, the internal security of Hong Kong is at risk. Why this information has not yet been passed on to the police themselves we do not yet know. We presume this ties in with the current political Soviet infiltration of UK administration on all levels which enables the Philbys to exist, and permits such information as this to be buried, or toned down, or misrepresented (which was the material for Study 4/1962). We would suggest this report—or portions of it—should be leaked at once to the governor or the commissioner of police, Hong Kong, *if you consider them trustworthy*."' Brian Kwok looked up, his mind rocking. 'There's a couple of other pieces here, Christ, the political situation in the UK and then there's Sevrin. . . . Read it.' He shook his head helplessly. 'Christ, if this's true . . . we're in it up to our necks. God in Heaven!'

Armstrong swore softly. 'Who? Who could the spy be? Got to be high up. Who?'

After a great silence, Brian said, 'The only one . . . the only one who could know all of this's Crosse himself.'

'Oh come on for chrissake!'

'Think about it, Robert. He knew Philby. Didn't he go to Cambridge also? Both have similar backgrounds, they're the same age group, both were in Intelligence during the war—like Burgess and Maclean. If Philby could get away with it for all those years, why not Crosse?'

'Impossible!'

'Who else but him? Hasn't he been in MI-6 all his life? Didn't

197

he do a tour here in the early fifties and wasn't he brought back here to set up our SI as a separate branch of SB five years ago? Hasn't he been director ever since?'

'That proves nothing.'

'Oh?'

There was a long silence. Armstrong was watching his friend closely. He knew him too well not to know when he was serious. 'What've you got?' he asked uneasily.

'Say Crosse is homosexual.'

'You're plain bonkers,' Armstrong exploded. 'He's married and . . . and he may be an evil son of a bitch but there's never been a smell of anything like that, never.'

'Yes, but he's got no children, his wife's almost permanently in England and when she's here they have separate rooms.'

'How do you know?'

'The *amah* would know, so if I wanted to know it'd be easy to find out.'

'That proves nothing. Lots of people have separate rooms. You're wrong about Crosse.'

'Say I could give you proof?'

'What proof?'

'Where does he always go for part of his leave? The Cameron Highlands in Malaya. Say he had a friend there, a young Malayan, a known deviate.'

'I'd need photos and we both know photos can be easily doctored,' Armstrong said harshly. 'I'd need tape recordings and we both know those can be doctored too. The youth himself? That proves nothing—it's the oldest trick in the book to produce false testimony and false witnesses. There's never been a hint . . . and even if he's AC-DC, that proves nothing—not all deviates are traitors.'

'No. But all deviates lay themselves open to blackmail. And if he is, he'd be highly suspect. Highly suspect. Right?'

Armstrong looked around uneasily. 'I don't even like talking about it here, he could have this place tapped.'

'And if he has?'

'If he has and if it's true he can fry us so quickly your head would spin. He can fry us anyway.'

'Perhaps—but if he is the one then he'll know we're on to him and if he's not he'll laugh at us and I'm out of SI. In any event,

Robert, he can't fry every Chinese in the force.'

Armstrong stared at him. 'What's that supposed to mean?'

'Perhaps there's a file on him. Perhaps every Chinese above the rank of corporal's read it.'

'What?'

'Come on, Robert, you know Chinese are great joiners. Perhaps there's a file, per—'

'You mean you're all organized into a brotherhood? A *tong*, a secret society? A triad within the force?'

'I said perhaps. This is all surmise, Robert. I said perhaps and maybe.'

'Who's the High Dragon? You?'

'I never said there was such a grouping. I said perhaps.'

'Are there other files? On me, for instance?'

'Perhaps.'

'And?'

'And if there was, Robert,' Brian Kwok said gently, 'it'd say you were a fine policeman, uncorrupted, that you had gambled heavily on the stock market and gambled wrong and needed twenty-odd thousand to clean up some pressing debts—and a few other things.'

'What other things?'

'This is China, old chum. We know almost everything that goes on with *quai loh* here. We have to, to survive, don't we?'

Armstrong looked at him strangely. 'Why didn't you tell me before?'

'I haven't told you anything now. Nothing. I said perhaps and I repeat perhaps. But if this's all true . . .' He passed over the file and wiped the sweat off his upper lip. 'Read it yourself. If it's true we're up the creek without a paddle and we'll need to work very quickly. What I said was all surmise. But not about Crosse. Listen Robert, I'll bet you a thousand . . . a thousand to one, he's the mole.'

10

Dunross finished reading the blue-covered file for the third time. He had read it as soon as it had arrived—as always—then again on the way to the Governor's Palace. He closed the blue cover and set it onto his lap for a moment, his mind possessed. Now he was in his study on the second floor of the Great House that sat on a knoll on the upper levels of the Peak, the leaded bay windows overlooking floodlit gardens, and then far below, the city and the immensity of the harbor.

The ancient grandfather clock chimed a quarter to eight.

Fifteen minutes to go, he thought. Then our guests arrive and the party begins and we all take part in a new charade. Or perhaps we just continue the same one.

The room had high ceilings and old oak paneling, dark green velvet curtains and Chinese silk rugs. It was a man's room, comfortable, old, a little worn and very cherished. He heard the muted voices of the servants below. A car came up the hill and passed by.

The phone rang. 'Yes? Oh hello, Claudia.'

'I haven't reached Tsu-yan yet, tai-pan. He wasn't in his office. Has he called?'

'No. No not yet. You keep trying.'

'Yes. See you in a little while. 'Bye.'

He was sitting in a deep, high-winged chair and wore a dinner jacket, his tie not yet tied. Absently he stared out of the windows, the view ever pleasing. But tonight he was filled with foreboding, thinking about Sevrin and the traitor and all the other evil things the report had foretold.

What to do?

'Laugh,' he said out loud. 'And fight.'

He got up and went with his easy stride to the oil painting of Dirk Struan that was on the wall over the mantelpiece. Its frame was heavy and carved gilt and old, the gilt chipped off here and there, and it was secretly hinged on one side. He moved it away from the wall and opened the safe the painting covered. In the safe were many papers, some neatly tied with scarlet ribbons, some ancient, some new, a few small boxes, a neat, well-oiled, loaded Mauser in a clip attached to one of the sides, a box of ammunition, a vast old Bible with the Struan arms etched into the fine leather and seven blue-covered files similar to the one he had in his hand.

Thoughtfully he slid the file alongside the others in sequence. He stared at them a moment, began to close the safe but changed his mind as his eyes fell on the ancient Bible. His fingers caressed it, then he lifted it out and opened it. Affixed to the thick flyleaf with old sealing wax were halves of two old Chinese bronze coins, crudely broken. Clearly, once upon a time, there had been four such half-coins for there was still the imprint of the missing two and the remains of the same red sealing wax attached to the ancient paper. The handwriting heading the page was beautiful copperplate: 'I swear by the Lord God that whomsoever produces the other half of any of these coins, I will grant him whatsoever he asks.' It was signed Dirk Struan, June 10, 1841, and below his signature was Culum Struan's and all the other tai-pans and the last name was Ian Dunross.

Alongside the first space where once a coin had been was written: 'Wu Fang Choi, paid in part, August 16, Year of our Lord 1841,' and signed again by Dirk Struan and cosigned below by Culum Struan and dated 18 June 1845 'paid in full.' Alongside the second: 'Sun Chen-yat, paid in full, October 10, 1911,' and signed boldly, Hag Struan.

Ah, Dunross told himself, bemused, what lovely arrogance— to be so secure to be able to sign the book thus and not Tess Struan, for future generations to see.

How many more generations? he asked himself. How many more tai-pans will have to sign blindly and swear the Holy Oath to do the bidding of a man dead almost a century and a half?

Thoughtfully he ran his finger over the jagged edges of the

two remaining half-coins. After a moment he closed the Bible firmly, put it into its place again, touched it once for luck and locked the safe. He swung the painting back into its place and stared up at the portrait, standing now with his hands deep in his pockets in front of the mantelpiece, the heavy old oak carved with the Struan arms, chipped and broken here and there, an old Chinese fire screen in front of the huge fireplace.

This oil of Dirk Struan was his favorite and he had taken it out of the long gallery when he became tai-pan and had hung it here in the place of honor—instead of the portrait of Hag Struan that had been over the mantelpiece in the tai-pan's study ever since there was a Great House. Both had been painted by Aristotle Quance. In this one, Dirk Struan was standing in front of a crimson curtain, broad-shouldered and arrogant, his high-cut coat black and his waistcoat and cravat and ruffled shirt white and high-cut. Heavy eyebrows and strong nose and clean-shaven, with reddish hair and mutton-chop sideburns, lips curled and sensual and you could feel the eyes boring into you, their green enhanced by the black and white and crimson.

Dunross half-smiled, not afraid, not envious, more calmed than anything by his ancestor's gaze—knowing he was possessed, partially possessed by him. He raised his glass of champagne to the painting in half-mocking jest as he had done many times before: 'Health!'

The eyes stared back at him.

What would you do, Dirk—Dirk o' the will o' the wisp, he thought.

'You'd probably just say find the traitors and kill them,' he mused aloud, 'and you'd probably be right.'

The problem of the traitor in the police did not shatter him as much as the information about the Sevrin spy ring, its U.S. connections and the astonishing, secret gains made by the Communists in Britain. Where the hell does Grant get all his info? he asked himself for the hundredth time.

He remembered their first meeting. Alan Medford Grant was a short, elflike, balding man with large eyes and large teeth, in his neat pin-striped suit and bowler hat and he liked him immediately.

'Don't you worry, Mr. Dunross,' Grant had said when Dunross had hired him in 1960, the moment he became tai-pan.

'I assure you there'll be no conflict of interest with Her Majesty's Government if I chair your research committee on the non-exclusive basis we've discussed. I've already cleared it with them in fact. I'll only give you—confidentially of course, for you personally of course, and absolutely not for publication—I'll only give you classified material that does not, in my opinion, jeopardize the national interest. After all, our interests are the same there, aren't they?'

'I think so.'

'May I ask how you heard of me?'

'We have friends in high places, Mr. Grant. In certain circles your name is quite famous. Perhaps even a foreign secretary would recommend you,' he had added delicately.

'Ah yes.'

'Our arrangement is satisfactory?'

'Yes—one year initially, extended to five if everything goes well. After five?'

'Another five,' Dunross said. 'If we achieve the results I want, your retainer will be doubled.'

'Ah. That's very generous. But may I ask why you're being so generous—perhaps *extravagant* would be the word—with me and this projected committee?'

'Sun Tzu said: "What enables a wise sovereign or good general to strike and to conquer and to achieve things beyond the reach of normal men is foreknowledge. Foreknowledge comes only through spies. Nothing is of more importance to the state than the quality of its spies. *It is ten thousand times cheaper to pay the best spies lavishly than even a tiny army poorly.*"'

Alan Medford Grant beamed. 'Quite right! My 8,500 pounds a year is lavish indeed, Mr. Dunross. Oh yes. Yes indeed.'

'Can you think of a better investment for me?'

'Not if I perform correctly, if I and the ones I choose are the best to be had. Even so, 30-odd thousand pounds a year in salaries—a fund of up to 100,000 pounds to draw on for . . . for informants and information, all secret monies . . . well, I hope you will be satisfied with your investment.'

'If you're the best I'll recoup a thousandfold. I expect to recoup a thousandfold,' he had said, meaning it.

'I'll do everything in my power of course. Now, specifically what sort of information do you want?'

'Anything and everything, commercial, political, that'd help Struan's plan ahead, with accent on the Pacific Rim, on Russian, American and Japanese thinking. We'd probably know more about Chinese attitudes ourselves. Please give me more rather than less. Actually anything could be valuable because I want to take Struan's out of the China trade—more specifically I want the company international and want to diversify out of our present dependence on China trade.'

'Very well. First: I would not like to trust our reports to the mails.'

'I'll arrange a personal courier.'

'Thank you. Second: I must have free range to select, appoint and remove the other members of the committee—and spend the money as I see fit?'

'Agreed.'

'Five members will be sufficient.'

'How much do you want to pay them?'

'5,000 pounds a year for a nonexclusive retainer each would be excellent. I can get top men for that. Yes. I'll appoint associate members for special studies as I need them. As, er, as most of our contacts will be abroad, many in Switzerland, could funds be available there?'

'Say I deposit the full amount we've agreed quarterly in a numbered Swiss account. You can draw funds as you need them—your signature or mine only. You account to me solely, quarterly in arrears. If you want to erect a code that's fine with me.'

'Excellent. I won't be able to name anyone—I can't account to whom I give money.'

After a pause Dunross had said, 'All right.'

'Thank you. We understand one another, I think. Can you give me an example of what you want?'

'For example, I don't want to get caught like my predecessor was over Suez.'

'Oh! You mean the 1956 fiasco when Eisenhower betrayed us again and caused the failure of the British-French-Israeli attack on Egypt—because Nasser had nationalized the canal?'

'Yes. That cost us a fortune—it wrecked our Middle East interests, almost ruined us. If the previous tai-pan'd known about a possible closure of Suez we could have made a fortune

204

booking cargo space—increasing our fleet . . . or if we'd had an advanced insight into American thinking, particularly that Eisenhower would side again with Soviet Russia against us, we could certainly have cut our losses.'

The little man had said sadly, 'You know he threatened to freeze all British, French and Israeli assets in the States instantly if we did not at once withdraw from Egypt when we were a few hours from victory? I think all our present problems in the Middle East stem from that U.S. decision. Yes. Inadvertently the U.S. approved international piracy for the first time and set a pattern for future piracies. Nationalization. What a joke! *Theft* is a better word—or piracy. Yes. Eisenhower was ill-advised. And very ill-advised to go along with the fatuous political Yalta agreement of an ailing Roosevelt, the incompetent Attlee to allow Stalin to gorge most of Europe, when it was militarily clear to even the most stupid politician or hidebound general that *it was contrary to our absolute national interest, ours and the United States', to hold back.* I think Roosevelt hated us really, and our British Empire.'

The little man steepled his fingers and beamed. 'I'm afraid there's one big disadvantage in employing me, Mr. Dunross. I'm entirely pro-British, anti-Communist, and particularly anti-KGB which is the main instrument of Soviet foreign policy, which is openly and forever committed to our destruction, so some of my more peppery forecasts you can discount, if you wish. I'm entirely against a left-wing dominated Labour Party and I will constantly remind anyone who will listen that the anthem of the Labour Party's "The Red Flag."' Alan Medford Grant smiled in his pixy way. 'It's best you know where you stand in the beginning. I'm royalist, loyalist and believe in the British parliamentary way. I'll never knowingly give you false information though my evaluations will be slanted. May I ask what your politics are?'

'We have none in Hong Kong, Mr. Grant. We don't vote, there are no elections—we're a colony, particularly a free-port colony, not a democracy. The Crown rules—actually the governor rules despotically for the Crown. He has a legislative council but it's a rubber-stamp council and the historic policy is *laissez-faire*. Wisely he leaves things alone. He listens to the business community, makes social changes very cautiously and leaves everyone to make money or not make money, to build, expand, go broke, to go or to come, to dream or to stay awake, to live or to die as best you can. And the maximum tax is 15 percent but only on money earned in Hong Kong. We don't have politics here, don't want politics here—neither does China want us to have any here. They're for the status quo too. My personal politics? I'm royalist, I'm for freedom, for freebooting and free trade. I'm a Scotsman, I'm for Struan's, I'm for *laissez-faire* in Hong Kong and freedom throughout the world.'

'I think we understand one another. Good. I've never worked for an individual before—only the government. This will be a new experience for me. I hope I will satisfy you.' Grant paused and thought a moment. 'Like Suez in '56?' The lines beside the little man's eyes crinkled. 'Very well, plan that the Panama Canal will be lost to America.'

'That's ridiculous!'

'Oh don't look so shocked, Mr. Dunross! It's too easy. Give it ten or fifteen years of enemy spadework and lots of liberal talk in America, ably assisted by do-gooders who believe in the benevolence of human nature, add to all this a modest amount of calculated Panamanian agitation, students and so on—preferably, ah, always students—artfully and secretly assisted by a few highly trained, patient, professional agitators and oh so secret KGB expertise, finance and a long-range plan—ergo, in due course the canal could be out of U.S. hands into the enemy's.'

'They'd never stand for it.'

'You're right, Mr. Dunross, but they will sit for it. What could be a better garrotte in time of hostilities, or even crisis, against your main, openly stated capitalistic enemy than to be able to inhibit the Panama Canal or rock it a little? One ship sunk in any one of a hundred spots, or a lock wrecked, could dam up the canal for years.'

Dunross remembered how he had poured two more drinks before answering, and then he had said, 'You're seriously suggesting we should make contingency plans against that.'

'Yes,' the little man said with his extraordinary innocence. 'I'm very serious about my job, Mr. Dunross. My job, the one I've chosen for me, is to seek out, to uncover and evaluate enemy moves. I'm not anti-Russian or anti-Chinese or anti-East

206

German or anti any of that bloc—on the absolute contrary I want desperately to help them. I'm convinced that we're in a state of war, that the enemy of all the people is the Communist Party member, whether British, Soviet, Chinese, Hungarian, American, Irish . . . even Martian . . . and all are linked in one way or another; that the KGB, like it or not, is in the center of their web.' He sipped the drink Dunross had just refilled for him. 'This is marvelous whiskey, Mr. Dunross.'

'It's Loch Vey—it comes from a small distillery near our homelands in Ayr. It's a Struan company.'

'Marvelous!' Another appreciative sip of the whiskey and Dunross reminded himself to send Alan Medford Grant a case for Christmas—if the initial reports proved interesting.

'I'm not a fanatic, Mr. Dunross, nor a rabble-rouser. Just a sort of reporter and forecaster. Some people collect stamps, I collect secrets. . . .'

The lights of a car rounding the half-hidden curve of the road below distracted Dunross momentarily. He wandered over to the window and watched the car until it had gone, enjoying the sound of the highly tuned engine. Then he sat in a high-winged chair and let his mind drift again. Yes, Mr. Grant, you certainly collect secrets, he thought, staggered as usual by the scope of the little man's knowledge.

Sevrin—Christ almighty! If that's true . . .

How accurate are you this time? How far do I trust you this time—how far do I gamble?

In previous reports Grant had given two projections that, so far, could be proved. A year in advance, Grant had predicted that de Gaulle would veto Britain's effort to join the EEC, that the French general's posture would be increasingly anti-British, anti-American and pro-Soviet, and that de Gaulle would, prompted by outside influences and encouraged by one of his closest advisors—an immensely secret, covert KGB mole—mount a long-term attack on the U.S. economy by speculation in gold. Dunross had dismissed this as farfetched and so had lost a potential fortune.

Recently, six months in advance, Grant had forecast the missile crisis in Cuba, that Kennedy would slam down the gauntlet, blockade Cuba and exert the necessary pressure and not buckle under the strain of brinkmanship, that Khrushchev would back off under pressure. Gambling that Grant was correct this time—though a Cuban missile crisis had seemed highly unlikely at the time forecast—Dunross had made Struan's half a million pounds by buying Hawaiian sugar futures, another 600,000 on the stock market, plus 600,000 for the tai-pan's secret fund—and cemented a long-range plan to invest in Hawaiian sugar plantations as soon as he could find the financial tool. And you've got it now, he told himself gleefully. Par-Con.

'You've almost got it,' he muttered, correcting himself.

How far do I trust this report? Thus far AMG's committee's been a gigantic investment for all his meanderings, he thought. Yes. But it's almost like having your own astrologer. A few accurate forecasts don't mean they'll all be. Hitler had his own forecaster. So did Julius Caesar. Be wise, be cautious, he reminded himself.

What to do? It's now or never.

Sevrin. Alan Medford Grant had written: 'Documents brought to us and substantiated by the French spy Marie d'Orleans caught by the Sûreté June 16 indicate that the KGB Department V (Disinformation—FAR EAST) have in situ a hitherto unknown, deep-cover espionage network throughout the Far East, code name *Sevrin*. The purpose of Sevrin is clearly stated in the stolen Head Document:

'Aim: To cripple revisionist China—formally acknowledged by the Central Committee of the USSR as the main enemy, second only to capitalist U.S.A.

'Procedure: The permanent obliteration of Hong Kong as the bastion of capitalism in the Far East and China's pre-eminent source of all foreign currency, foreign assistance and all technical and manufactured assistance of every kind.

'Method: Long-term infiltration of the press and media, the government, police, business and education with friendly aliens controlled by Center—but only in accordance with most special procedures throughout Asia.

'Initiation date: Immediate.

'Duration of operation: Provisionally thirty years.

'Target date: 1980–83.

'Classification: *Red One*.

'Funding: Maximum.

'Approval: L.B. March 14, 1950.

208

'It's interesting to note,' Grant had continued, 'that the document is signed in 1950 by L.B.—presumed to be Lavrenti Beria—when Soviet Russia was openly allied with Communist China, and that, even in those days, China was secretly considered their Number Two enemy. (Our previous report 3/1962, Russia versus China refers.)

'China, historically, is the great prize that always was—and ever will be—sought by imperialistic and hegemonic Russia. Possession of China, or its mutilation into balkanized subject states, is the perpetual keystone of Russian foreign policy. First is, of course, the obliteration of Western Europe, for then, Russia believes, China can be swallowed at will.

'The documents reveal that the Hong Kong cell of Sevrin consists of a resident controller, code name Arthur, and six agents. We know nothing about Arthur, other than that he has been a KGB agent since recruitment in England in the thirties (it's not known if he was born in England, or if his parents are English, but he would be in his late forties or early fifties). His mission is, of course, a long-term, deep-cover operation.

'Supporting top-secret intelligence documents stolen from the Czechoslovak STB (State Secret Security) dated April 6, 1959, translate in part, ". . . between 1946 and 1959 six key, deep-cover agents have been recruited through information supplied by the controller, Arthur: one each in the Hong Kong Colonial Office (code name Charles), Treasury (code name Mason), Naval Base (John), the Bank of London and China (Vincent), the Hong Kong Telephone Company (William), and Struan and Company (Frederick). According to normal procedures only the controller knows the true identity of the others. Seven safe houses have been established. Among them are Sinclair Towers in Hong Kong Island and the Nine Dragons Hotel in Kowloon. Sevrin's New York contact has the code name Guillio. He is very important to us because of his Mafia and CIA connections."'

Grant had continued, 'Guillio is believed to be Vincenzo Banastasio, a substantial racketeer and the present don of the Sallapione family. This is being checked through our U.S. sources. We don't know if the deep-cover enemy agent in the police (covered in detail in another section) is part of Sevrin or not but presume he is.

'In our opinion, China will be forced to seek ever-increasing amounts of trade with the West to counterbalance imperialist Soviet hegemony and to fill the void and chaos created by the sudden withdrawal in 1960 of all Soviet funding and technicians. China's armed forces badly need modernizing. Harvests have been bad. Therefore all forms of strategic materials and military hardware will find a ready market for many years to come, and food, basic foodstuffs. The long-range purchase of American rice futures is recommended.

'I have the honor to be, sir, your obedient servant, AMG, London, August 15, 1963.'

Jets and tanks and nuts and bolts and rockets and engines and trucks and petrol and tires and electronics and food, Dunross thought, his mind soaring. A limitless spectrum of trade goods, easy to obtain, easy to ship, and nothing on earth like a war for profit if you can trade. But China's not buying now, whatever they need, whatever Grant says.

Who could Arthur be?

Who in Struan's? Jesus Christ! John Chen and Tsu-yan and smuggled guns and now a KGB agent within. Who? What about . . .

There was a gentle knock on the door.

'Come in,' he said, recognizing his wife's knock.

'Ian, it's almost eight,' Penelope, his wife said, 'I thought I'd better tell you. You know how you are.'

'Yes.'

'How did it go today? Awful about John Chen, isn't it? I suppose you read the papers? Are you coming down?'

'Yes. Champagne?'

'Thanks.'

He poured for her and replenished his glass. 'Oh by the way, Penn, I invited a fellow I met this afternoon, an ex-RAF type. He seemed a decent fellow—Peter Marlowe.'

'Fighters?'

'Yes. But Hurricanes—not Spits. Is that a new dress?'

'Yes.'

'You look pretty,' he said.

'Thank you but I'm not. I feel so old, but thank you.' She sat in the other winged chair, her perfume as delicate as her features. 'Peter Marlowe, you said?'

'Yes. Poor bugger got caught in Java in '42. He was a POW for three and a half years.'

'Oh, poor man. He was shot down?'

'No, the Japanese plastered the 'drome before he could scramble. Perhaps he was lucky. The Zeros got two on the ground and the last two just after they were airborne—the pilots flamed in. Seems those four Hurricanes were the last of the Few—the last of the whole air defense of the Far East. What a balls-up that was!'

'Terrible.'

'Yes. Thank God our war was in Europe.' Dunross watched her. 'He said he was a year in Java, then the Japanese sent him to Singapore on a work party.'

'To Changi?' she asked, her voice different.

'Yes.'

'Oh!'

'He was there for two and a half years.' Changi in Malay meant 'clinging vine,' and Changi was the name of the jail in Singapore that was used by the Japanese in World War II for one of their infamous prisoner-of-war camps.

She thought a moment, then smiled a little nervously. 'Did he know Robin there?' Robin Grey was her brother, her only living relative: her parents had been killed in an air raid in London in 1943, just before she and Dunross were married.

'Marlowe said yes, he seemed to remember him, but clearly he didn't want to talk about those days so I let it drop.'

'I can imagine. Did you tell him Robin was my brother?'

'No.'

'When's Robin due back here?'

'I don't know exactly. In a few days. This afternoon the governor told me the delegation's in Peking now.' A British Parliamentary Trade Delegation drawn from MPs of the three parties—Conservative, Liberal and Labour—had been invited out from London by Peking to discuss all manner of trade. The delegation had arrived in Hong Kong two weeks ago and had gone directly on to Canton where all trade negotiations were conducted. It was very rare for anyone to get an invitation, let alone a parliamentary delegation—and even rarer to be invited on to Peking. Robin Grey was one of the members—representative of the Labour Party. 'Penn darling, don't you think we

211

should acknowledge Robin, give a reception for him? After all, we haven't seen him for years, this's the first time he's been to Asia since the war—isn't it time you buried the hatchet and made peace?'

'He's not invited to my house. Any of my houses.'

'Isn't it time you relaxed a little, let bygones be bygones?'

'No, I know him, you don't. Robin has his life and we have ours, that's what he and I agreed years ago. No, I've no wish to see him ever again. He's awful, dangerous, foul-mouthed and a bloody bore.'

Dunross laughed. 'I agree he's obnoxious and I detest his politics—but he's only one of a half dozen MPs. This delegation's important. I should do something to entertain them, Penn.'

'Please do, Ian. But preferably not here—or else tell me in good time so I can have the vapors and see that the children do the same. It's a matter of face and that's the end of it.' Penelope tossed her head and shook off her mood. 'God! Let's not let him spoil this evening! What's this Marlowe doing in Hong Kong?'

'He's a writer. Wants to do a book on Hong Kong, he said. He lives in America now. His wife's coming too. Oh, by the way, I also invited the Americans, Linc Bartlett and Casey Tcholok.'

'Oh!' Penelope Dunross laughed. 'Oh well, four or forty extra won't make any difference at all—I won't know most of them anyway, and Claudia's organized everything with her usual efficiency.' She arched an eyebrow. 'So! A gun-runner amongst the pirates! That won't even cause a ripple.'

'Is he?'

'Everyone says so. Did you see the piece in this afternoon's *Mirror*, Ian? Ah Tat's convinced the American is bad joss—she informed the whole staff, the children and me—so that makes it official. Ah Tat told Adryon that her astrologer insisted she tell you to watch out for bad influence from the East. Ah Tat's sure that means the Yanks. Hasn't she bent your ear yet?'

'Not yet.'

'God, I wish I could chatter Cantonese like you and the children. I'd tell that old harpy to keep her superstitions and opinions to herself—she's a bad influence.'

'She'd give her life for the children.'

'I know she's your *gan sun* and almost brought you up and

thinks she's God's gift to the Dunross clan. But as far as I'm concerned she's a cantankerous, loathsome old bitch and I hate her.' Penelope smiled sweetly. 'I hear the American girl's pretty.'

'Attractive—not pretty. She's giving Andrew a bad time.'

'I can imagine. A lady talking business! What are we coming to in this great world of ours? Is she any good?'

'Too soon to tell. But she's very smart. She's—she'll make things awkward certainly.'

'Have you seen Adryon tonight?'

'No—what's up?' he asked, instantly recognizing the tone of voice.

'She's been into my wardrobe again—half my best nylons are gone, the rest are scattered, my scarves are all jumbled up, my new blouse's missing and my new belt's disappeared. She's even whipped my best Hermès . . . that child's the end!'

'Nineteen's hardly a child,' he said wearily.

'She's the end! The number of times I've told her!'

'I'll talk to her again.'

'That won't do a bit of good.'

'I know.'

She laughed with him. 'She's such a pill.'

'Here.' He handed her a slim box. 'Happy twentieth!'

'Oh thank you, Ian. Yours is downstairs. You'll . . .' She stopped and opened the box. It contained a carved jade bracelet, the jade inset into silver filigree, very fine, very old—a collector's piece. 'Oh how lovely, thank you, Ian.' She put it on her wrist over the thin gold chain she was wearing and he heard neither real pleasure nor real disappointment under her voice, his ears tuned to her. 'It's beautiful,' she said and leaned forward and brushed her lips against his cheek. 'Thank you, darling. Where did you get it? Taiwan?'

'No, here on Cat Street. At Wong Chun Kit's, he ga—'

The door flew open and a girl barreled in. She was tall and slim and oh so fair and she said in a breathless rush, 'I hope it's all right I invited a date tonight and I just had the call that he's coming and he'll be late but I thought it'd be okay. He's cool. And very trick.'

'For the love of God, Adryon,' Dunross said mildly, 'how many times do I have to ask you to knock before you charge in

213

here and would you kindly talk English? What the hell's *trick*?'

'Good, great, cool, trick. Sorry, Father, but you really are rather square because cool and trick are very in, even in Hong Kong. See you soon, have to dash, after the party I'm going out—I'll be late so don't—'

'Wait a min—'

'That's my blouse, my new blouse,' Penelope burst out. 'Adryon, you take it off this minute! I've told you fifty times to stay the hell out of my wardrobe.'

'Oh, Mother,' Adryon said as sharply, 'you don't need it, can't I borrow it for this evening?' Her tone changed. 'Please? Pretty please? Father, talk to her.' She switched to perfect *amah* Cantonese, 'Honorable Father . . . please help your Number One Daughter to achieve the unachievable or I shall weep weep *oh ko* . . .' Then back into English in the same breath, 'Mother . . . you don't need it and I'll look after it, truly. Please?'

'No.'

'Come on, pretty please, I'll look after it, I promise.'

'No.'

'Mother!'

'Well if you pr—'

'Oh thanks.' The girl beamed and turned and rushed out and the door slammed behind her.

'Jesus bloody Christ,' Dunross said sourly, 'why the hell does a door always happen to slam behind her!'

'Well at least it's not deliberate now.' Penelope sighed. 'I don't think I could go through that siege again.'

'Nor me. Thank God Glenna's reasonable.'

'It's purely temporary, Ian. She takes after her father, that one, like Adryon.'

'Huh! I don't have a filthy temper,' he said sharply. 'And since we're on the subject I hope to God Adryon has found someone decent to date instead of the usual shower! Who is this she's bringing?'

'I don't know, Ian. This is the first I've heard of it too.'

'They're always bloody awful! Her taste in men's appalling. . . . Remember that melon-headed berk with the neolithic arms that she was "madly in love with"? Christ Jesus, she was barely fifteen an—'

'She was almost sixteen.'

'What was his name? Ah yes, Byron. Byron for chrissake!'

'You really shouldn't have threatened to blow his head off, Ian. It was just puppy love.'

'It was gorilla bloody love, by God,' Dunross said even more sourly. 'He was a bloody gorilla. . . . You remember that other one, the one before bloody Byron—the psychiatric bastard . . . what was his name?'

'Victor. Yes, Victor Hopper. He was the one . . . oh yes, I remember, he was the one who asked if it was all right if he slept with Adryon.'

'He *what*?'

'Oh yes.' She smiled up at him so innocently. 'I didn't tell you at the time . . . thought I'd better not.'

'He *what*?'

'Don't get yourself all worked up, Ian. That's at least four years ago. I told him no, not at the moment, Adryon's only fourteen, but yes, certainly, when she was twenty-one. That was another that died on the vine.'

'Jesus Christ! *He asked* you if he co—'

'At least he asked, Ian! That was something. It's all so very ordinary.' She got up and poured more champagne into his glass, and some for herself. 'You've only got another ten years or so of purgatory, then there'll be the grandchildren. Happy anniversary and the best of British to you!' She laughed and touched his glass and drank and smiled at him.

'You're right again,' he said and smiled back, liking her very much. So many years, good years. I've been lucky, he thought. Yes. I was blessed that first day. It was at his RAF station at Biggin Hill, a warm, sunny August morning in 1940 during the Battle of Britain and she was a WAAF and newly posted there. It was his eighth day at war, his third mission that day and first kill. His Spitfire was latticed with bullet holes, parts of his wing gone, his tail section tattooed. By all the rules of joss, he should be dead but he wasn't and the Messerschmitt was and her pilo was and he was home and safe and blood raging, drunk with fear and shame and relief that he had come back and the youth he had seen in the other cockpit, the enemy, had burned screaming as he spiraled.

'Hello, sir,' Penelope Grey had said. 'Welcome home sir. Here.' She had given him a cup of hot sweet tea and she had said nothing else though she should have begun debriefing him at once—she was in Signals. She said nothing but smiled and gave him time to come out of the skies of death into life again. He had not thanked her, just drank the tea and it was the best he had ever had.

'I got a Messerschmitt,' he had said when he could talk, his voice trembling like his knees. He could not remember unsnapping his harness or getting out of his cockpit or climbing into the truck with the other survivors. 'It was a 109.'

'Yes sir, Squadron Leader Miller has already confirmed the kill and he says to please get ready, you're to scramble any minute again. You're to take Poppa Mike Kilo this time. Thank you for the kill, sir, that's one less of those devils . . . oh how I wish I could go up with you to help you all kill those monsters. . . .'

But they weren't monsters, he thought, at least the first pilot and first plane that he had killed had not been—just a youth like himself, perhaps the same age, who had burned screaming, died screaming, a flaming falling leaf, and this afternoon or tomorrow or soon it would be his turn—too many of them, the enemy, too few of us.

'Did Tommy get back, Tom Lane?'

'No sir, sorry sir. He . . . the squadron leader said Flight Lieutenant Lane was jumped over Dover.'

'I'm petrified of burning, going down,' he had said.

'Oh you won't, sir, not you. They won't shoot you down. *I know*. You won't, sir, no, not you. They'll never get you, never never never,' she had said, pale blue eyes, fair hair and fair face, not quite eighteen but strong, very strong and very confident.

He had believed her and her faith had carried him through four more months of missions—sometimes five missions each day—and more kills and though she was wrong and later he was blown out of the sky, he lived and burned only a little. And then, when he came out of the hospital, grounded forever, they had married.

'Doesn't seem like twenty years,' he said, holding in his happiness.

'Plus two before,' she said, holding in her happiness.

'Plus two be—'

The door opened. Penelope sighed as Ah Tat stalked into the

216

room, talking Cantonese fifty to the dozen, '*Ayeeyah*, my Son, but aren't you ready yet, our honored guests will be here any moment and your tie's not tied and that motherless foreigner from North Kwantung brought unnecessarily into our house to cook tonight . . . that smelly offspring of a one-dollar strumpet from North Kwantung where all the best thieves and worst whores come from who fancies himself a cook . . . ha! . . . This man and his equally despicable foreign staff is befouling our kitchen and stealing our peace. *Oh ko*,' the tiny wizened old woman continued without a breath as her clawlike fingers reached up automatically and deftly tied his tie, 'and that's not all! Number Two Daughter . . . Number Two Daughter just won't put on the dress that Honorable First Wife has chosen for her and her rage is flying to Java! Eeeee, this family! Here, my Son,' she took the telex envelope out of her pocket and handed it to Dunross, 'here's another barbarian message bringing more congratulations for this happy day that your poor old Mother had to carry up the stairs herself on her poor old legs because the other good-for-nothing servants are good for nothing and bone idle. . . .' She paused momentarily for breath.

'Thank you, Mother,' he said politely.

'In your Honorable Father's day, the servants worked and knew what to do and your old Mother didn't have to endure dirty strangers in our Great House!' She walked out muttering more curses on the caterers. 'Now don't you be late, my Son, otherwise . . .' She was still talking after she'd closed the door.

'What's up with *her*?' Penelope asked wearily.

'She's rattling on about the caterers, doesn't like strangers—you know what she's like.' He opened the envelope. In it was the folded telex.

'What was she saying about Glenna?' his wife asked, having recognized *yee-chat*, Second Daughter, though her Cantonese was minimal.

'Just that she was having a fit about the dress you picked for her.'

'What's wrong with it?'

'Ah Tat didn't say. Look, Penn, perhaps Glenna should just go to bed—it's almost past her bedtime now and sh—'

'Dreamer! No chance till hell freezes over. Even Hag Struan

217

wouldn't keep Glenna from her first grown-up as she calls it! You did agree, Ian, *you* agreed, I didn't, you did!'

'Yes, but don't you th—'

'No. She's quite old enough. After all she's thirteen going on thirty.' Penelope calmly finished her champagne. 'Even so I shall now deal with that young lady never mind.' She got up. Then she saw his face. He was staring at the telex.

'What's the matter?'

'One of our people's been killed. In London. Grant. Alan Medford Grant.'

'Oh. I don't know him, do I?'

'I think you met him once in Ayrshire. He was a small, pixyish man. He was at one of our parties at Castle Avisyard—it was on our last leave.'

She frowned. 'Don't remember.' She took the offered telex. It read: 'Regret to inform you A. M. Grant was killed in motorcycle accident this morning. Details will follow when I have them. Sorry. Regards, Kiernan.' 'Who's Kiernan?'

'His assistant.'

'Grant's . . . he was a friend?'

'In a way.'

'He's important to you?'

'Yes.'

'Oh, sorry.'

Dunross forced himself to shrug and keep his voice level. But in his mind he was cursing obscenely. 'Just one of those things. Joss.'

She wanted to commiserate with him, recognizing at once the depth of his shock. She knew he was greatly perturbed, trying to hide it—and she wanted to know immediately the who and the why of this unknown man. But she held her peace.

That's my job, she reminded herself. Not to ask questions, to be calm and to be there—to pick up the pieces, but only when I'm allowed to. 'Are you coming down?'

'In a moment.'

'Don't be long, Ian.'

'Yes.'

'Thanks again for my bracelet,' she said, liking it very much and he said, 'It's nothing,' but she knew he had not really heard her. He was already at the phone asking for long distance. She

218

walked out and closed the door quietly and stood miserably in the long corridor that led to the east and west wings, her heart thumping. Curse all telexes and all telephones and curse Struan's and curse Hong Kong and curse all parties and all hangers-on and oh how I wish we could leave forever and forget Hong Kong and forget work and the Noble House and Big Business and the Pacific Rim and the stock market and all curs—

'Motherrrrr!'

She heard Glenna's voice screeching from the depths of her room around the far corner in the east wing and at once all her senses concentrated. There was frustrated rage in Glenna's voice, but no danger, so she did not hurry, just called back, 'I'm coming . . . what is it, Glenna?'

'Where are *youuuuu?*'

'I'm coming, darling,' she called out, her mind now on important things. Glenna will look pretty in that dress, she thought. Oh I know, she told herself happily, I'll lend her my little rope of pearls. That'll make it perfect.

Her pace quickened.

Across the harbor in Kowloon, Sergeant Tang-po, CID, climbed the rickety stairs and went into the room. The inner core of his secret triad was already there. 'Get this through that bone some of you carry between your ears: the Dragons want Noble House Chen found and these pox-dripping, dung-eating Werewolves caught so fast even gods will blink!'

'Yes, Lord,' his underlings chorused, shocked at the quality of his voice.

They were in Tang-po's safe house, a small, drab three-room apartment behind a drab front door on the fifth floor of an equally drab apartment building over very modest shops in a dirty alley just three blocks from their police headquarters of Tsim Sha Tsui District that faced the harbor and the Peak on the tip of Kowloon Peninsula. There were nine of them: one sergeant, two corporals, the rest constables—all plainclothes detectives of the CID, all Cantonese, all handpicked and sworn with blood oaths to loyalty and secrecy. They were Tang-po's secret *tong* or Brotherhood, which protected all street gambling in Tsim Sha Tsui District.

'Look everywhere, talk to everyone. We have three days,' Tang-po said. He was a strongly built man of fifty-five with slightly graying hair and heavy eyebrows and his rank was the highest he could have and not be an officer. 'This is the order of me—all my Brother Dragons—and the High One himself. Apart from that,' he added sourly, 'Big Mountain of Dung has promised to demote and post us to the border or other places, all of us, if we fail, and that's the first time he's ever threatened that. All gods piss from a great height on all foreign devils, particularly those motherless fornicators who won't accept their rightful squeeze and behave like civilized persons!'

'Amen!' Sergeant Lee said with great fervor. He was a sometime Catholic because in his youth he had gone to a Catholic school.

'Big Mountain of Dung made it quite clear this afternoon: results, or off to the border where there's not a pot to piss in and no squeeze within twenty miles. *Ayeeyah*, all gods protect us from failure!'

'Yes,' Corporal Ho said for all of them, making a note in his book. He was a sharp-featured man who was studying at night school to become an accountant, and it was he who kept the Brotherhood's books and minutes of their meetings.

'Elder Brother,' Sergeant Lee began politely, 'is there a fixed reward we can offer our informers? Is there a minimum or a maximum?'

'Yes,' Tang-po told them, then added carefully, 'The High Dragon has said 100,000 HK if within three days . . .' The room was suddenly silent at the vastness of the reward. '. . . half for finding Noble House Chen, half for finding the kidnappers. And a bonus of 10,000 to the Brother whose informer produces either—and promotion.'

'One 10,000 for Chen and one ten for the kidnappers?' the corporal asked. O gods grant me the prize, he prayed, as they all were praying. 'Is that right, Elder Brother?'

'*Dew neh loh moh* that's what I said,' Tang-po replied sharply, puffing his cigarette. 'Are your ears filled with pus?'

'Oh no, sorry Honorable Sir. Please excuse me.'

All their minds were on the prize. Sergeant Lee was thinking, Eeee, 10,000 and—and promotion if in three days! Ah, if within three days then it will be in time for Race Day and then . . . O all gods great and small bless me this once and a second time on Saturday's double quinella.

Tang-po was referring to his notes. 'Now to other business. Through the cooperation of Daytime Chang and the Honorable Song, the Brotherhood can use their showers daily at the V and A between 8:00 A.M. and 9:00 A.M., not 7:00 A.M. to 8:00 A.M. as before. Wives and concubines on a roster basis. Corporal Ho, you rearrange the roster.'

'Hey, Honored Lord,' one of the young detectives called out, 'did you hear about Golden Pubics?'

'Eh?'

The youth related what Daytime Chang had told him this morning when he went to the hotel kitchens for breakfast. They all guffawed.

'*Ayeeyah*, imagine that! Like gold, *heya?*'

'Have you ever pillowed a foreign devil, Honorable Lord?'

'No never. No. *Ayeeyah*, the very thought . . . ugh!'

'I'd like one,' Lee said with a laugh, 'just to see what was what!'

They laughed with him and one called out, 'A Jade Gate's a Jade Gate but they say some foreign devils are lopsided!'

'I heard they were cleft sideways!'

'Honored Sir, there was another thing,' the young detective said when the laughter had died down. 'Daytime Chang told me to tell you Golden Pubics has a miniature transmitter-receiver—best he'd ever seen, better than anything we've got, even in Special Branch. She carries it around with her.'

Tang-po stared at him. 'That's curious. Now why should a foreign devil woman want a thing like that?'

Lee said, 'Something to do with the guns?'

'I don't know, Younger Brother. Women with transceivers? Interesting. It wasn't in her luggage when our people went through it last night, so it must've been in her handbag. Good, very good. Corporal Ho, after our meeting leave a gift for Daytime Chang—a couple of reds.' A red note was 100 HK. 'I'd certainly like to know who those guns were for,' he added thoughtfully. 'Make sure all our informers know I'm very interested in that too.'

'Is Noble House Chen tied into the guns and these two foreign devils?' Lee asked.

221

'I think so, Younger Brother. I think so. Yes. Another curiosity—to send an ear is not civilized—not so soon. Not civilized at all.'

'Ah, then you think the Werewolves're foreign devils? Or fornicating half-persons? Or Portuguese?'

'I don't know,' Tang-po said sourly. 'But it happened in our district, so it's a matter of face for all of us. Big Mountain of Dung is very enraged. His face is in the mangle too.'

'Eeee,' Lee said, 'that fornicator has such a very filthy temper.'

'Yes. Perhaps the information about the transceiver will appease him. I think I'll ask all my Brothers to put surveillance on Golden Pubics and her gun-running friend just in case. Now, there was something else . . .' Again Tang-po referred to his notes. 'Ah yes, why is our contribution from the Happy Hostess Night Club down 30 percent?'

'A new ownership's just taken over, Honored Sir,' Sergeant Lee, in whose area the dance hall was, said. 'One Eye Pok sold out to a Shanghainese fornicator called Wang—Happy Wang. Happy Wang says the Fragrant Grease's too high, business is bad, very bad.'

'*Dew neh loh moh* on all Shanghainese. Is it?'

'It's down, but not much.'

'That's right, Honored Sir,' Corporal Ho said. 'I was there at midnight to collect the fornicating week's advance—the stinking fornicating place was about half full.'

'Any foreign devils there?'

'Two or three, Honored Lord. No one of importance.'

'Give Honorable Happy Wang a message from me: He has three weeks to improve his business. Then we'll reconsider. Corporal Ho, tell some of the girls at the Great New Oriental to recommend the Happy Hostess for a month or so—they've plenty of foreign devil customers . . . and tell Wang that there's a nuclear aircraft carrier—the *Corregidor*—coming in the day after tomorrow for R and R . . .' He used the English letters, everyone understanding rest and recreation from the Korean War days. 'I'll ask my Brother Dragon in Wanchai and the dock area if Happy Wang can send some visiting cards over there. A thousand or so Golden Country barbarians will certainly be a help! They're here for eight days.'

222

'Honored Sir, I'll do that tonight,' Corporal Ho promised.

'My friend in marine police told me that there are going to be lots of visiting warships soon—the American Seventh Fleet is being increased.' Tang-po frowned. 'Doubled, so he says. The talk from the Mainland is that American soldiers are going to go into Vietnam in strength—they already run an airline there—at least,' he added, 'their triad CIA does.'

'Eeee, that's good for business! We'll have to repair their ships. And entertain their men. Good! Very good for us.'

'Yes. Very good. But very stupid for them. Honorable Chou En-lai's sent them warnings, politely, for months that China doesn't want them there! Why won't they listen? Vietnam's our outer barbarian sphere! Stupid to pick that foul jungle and those detestable barbarians to fight against. If China couldn't subdue those outer barbarians for centuries, how can they?' Tang-po laughed and lit another cigarette. 'Where's old One Eye Pok gone?'

'That old fox's permanent visa came through and he was off on the next airplane to San Francisco—him, his wife and eight kids.'

Tang-po turned to his accountant. 'Did he owe us any money?'

'Oh no Honored Sir. He was fully paid up-to-date, Sergeant Lee saw to that.'

'How much did it cost that old fornicator? To get the visa?'

'His exit was smoothed by a gift of 3,000 HK to Corporal Sek Pun So in Emigration on our recommendation—our percentage was paid—we also assisted him to find the right diamond merchant to convert his wealth into the best blue whites available.' Ho referred to his books. 'Our 2 percent commission came to 8,960 HK.'

'Good old One Eye!' Tang-po said, pleased for him 'He's done very well for himself. What was his "unique services" job for his visa?'

Sergeant Lee said, 'A cook in a restaurant in Chinatown—the Good Eating Place it's called. *Oh ko*, I've tasted his home cooking and old One Eye is very bad indeed.'

'He'll hire another to take his place while he goes into real estate, or gambling and a nightclub,' someone said. 'Eeee, what joss!'

'But what did his U.S. visa cost him?'

'Ah, the golden gift to Paradise!' Ho sighed. 'I heard he paid 5,000 U.S. to jump to the head of the list.'

'*Ayeeyah*, that's more than usual! Why?'

'It seems there's also a promise of a U.S. passport as soon as the five years are up and not too much harassment about his English—old One Eye doesn't talk English as you know. . .'

'Those fornicators from the Golden Country—they squeeze but they aren't organized. They've no style, none at all,' Tang-po said scornfully. 'One or two visas here and there—when everyone here knows you can buy one if you're at the right time with the right squeeze. So why don't they do it properly in a civilized way? Twenty visas a week—even forty—they're all mad these foreign devils!'

'*Dew neh loh moh* but you're right,' Sergeant Lee said, his mind boggled at the potential amount of squeeze he could make if he were a vice-consul in the U.S. Consulate of Hong Kong in the Visa Department. 'Eeeeee!'

'We should have a civilized person in that position, then we'd soon be set up like Mandarins and policing San Francisco!' Tang-po said, and they all guffawed with him. Then he added disgustedly, 'At least they should have a man there, not one who likes a Steaming Stalk in his Ghastly Gulley, or his in another's!'

They laughed even more. 'Hey,' one of them called out, 'I heard his partner's young Foreign Devil Stinknose Pork Belly in the Public Works—you know, the one who's selling building permits that shouldn't be!'

'That's old news, Chan, very old. They've both moved on to unwiser pastures. The latest rumor is our vice-consul devil's connected with a youth. . . .' Tang-po added delicately, 'Son of a prominent accountant who's also a prominent Communist.'

'Eeeee, that's not good,' Sergeant Lee said, knowing at once who the man was.

'No,' Tang-po agreed. 'Particularly as I heard yesterday the youth has a secret flat around the corner. In my district! And my district has the least crime of any.'

'That's right,' they all said proudly.

'Should he be spoken to, Elder Brother?' Lee asked.

224

'No, just put under special surveillance. I want to know all about these two. Everything. Even if they belch.' Tang-po sighed. He gave Sergeant Lee the address and made the work assignments. 'Since you're all here, I've decided to bring pay-day forward from tomorrow.' He opened the large bag that contained bank notes. Each man received the equivalent of his police pay plus authorized expenses.

300 HK a month salary with no expenses was not enough for a constable to feed even a small family and have a small flat, not even a two-room apartment with one tap and no sanitation, and to send one child to school; or enough to be able to send a little back to the home village in the Kwantung to needy fathers and grandmothers and mothers and uncles and grandfathers, many of whom, years upon years ago, had given their life's saving to help launch him on the broken road to Hong Kong.

Tang-po had been one of these. He was very proud that he had survived the journey as a six-year-old, alone, and had found his relations and then, when he was eighteen, had joined the police—thirty-six years ago. He had served the Queen well, the police force impeccably, the Japanese enemy during their occupation not at all and now was in charge of a key division in the Colony of Hong Kong. Respected, rich, with one son in college in San Francisco, another owning half a restaurant in Vancouver, Canada, his family in Kwantung supported—and, most important, his Division of Tsim Sha Tsui with fewer un-solved robberies, fewer unsolved woundings and maimings and triad wars than any other district—and only three murders in four years and all solved and the culprits caught and sentenced, and one of those a foreign devil seaman who'd killed another over a dance-hall girl. And almost no petty theft and never a tourist foreign devil harassed by beggars or sneak thieves and this the largest tourist area with upward of also 300,000 civilized persons to police and protect from evildoers and from themselves.

Ayeeyah, yes, Tang-po told himself. If it wasn't for us those bone-headed fornicating peasants'd be at each other's throats, raging, looting, killing, and then the inevitable mob cry would go up: Kill the foreign devils! And they would try and then we would be back in the riots again. Fornicate disgustingly all wrongdoers and unpeaceful persons!

'Now,' he said affably, 'we'll meet in three days. I've ordered a ten-course feast from Great Food Chang's. Until then, let everyone put an eye to the orifice of the gods and get me the answers. I want the Werewolves—and I want John Chen back. Sergeant Lee, you stay a moment. Corporal Ho, write up the minutes and let me have the accounts tomorrow at five.'

'Yes, Honored Lord.'

They all trooped out. Tang-po lit another cigarette. So did Sergeant Lee. Tang-po coughed.

'You should quit smoking, Elder Brother.'

'So should you!' Tang-po shrugged. 'Joss! If I'm to go, I'm to go. Joss. Even so, for peace I've told my Chief Wife I've stopped. She nags and nags and nags.'

'Show me one that doesn't and she'll turn out to be a he with a ghastly gulley.'

They laughed together.

'That's the truth. *Heya*, last week she insisted I see a doctor and you know what that motherless fornicator said? He said, you'd better give up smoking, old friend, or you'll be nothing but a few cinders in a burial jar before you're twenty moons older and then I guarantee your Chief Wife'll be spending all your money on loose boys and your concubine'll be tasting another's fruits!'

'The swine! Oh the swine!'

'Yes. He really frightened me—I felt his words right down in my secret sack! But maybe he was speaking the truth.'

He took out a handkerchief, blew his nose, his breath wheezing, cleared his throat noisily and spat into the spittoon. 'Listen, Younger Brother, our High Dragon says the time has come to organize Smuggler Yuen, White Powder Lee and his cousin Four Finger Wu.'

Sergeant Lee stared at him in shock. These three men were believed to be the High Tigers of the opium trade in Hong Kong. Importers and exporters. For local use and also, rumor had it, for export to the Golden Country where the great money was. Opium brought in secretly and converted into morphine and then into heroin. 'Bad, very bad. We've never touched that trade before.'

'Yes,' Tang-po said delicately.

'That'd be very dangerous. Narcotics Branch are very serious

226

against it. Big Mountain of Dung himself is very seriously interested in catching those three—very fornicating serious.'

Tang-po stared at the ceiling. Then he said, 'The High Dragon explained it this way: A ton of opium in the Golden Triangle costs 67,000 U.S. Changed into fornicating morphine and then into fornicating heroin and the pure heroin diluted to 5 percent, the usual strength on the streets of the Golden Country, delivered there you have almost 680 million worth in American dollars. From one ton of opium.' Tang-po coughed and lit another cigarette.

The sweat began on Lee's back. 'How many tons could go through those three fornicators?'

'We don't know. But he's been told about 380 tons a year are grown in the whole Golden Triangle—Yunnan, Burma, Laos and Thailand. Much of it comes here. They'd handle 50 tons, he said. He's certain of 50 tons.'

'*Oh ko!*'

'Yes.' Tang-po was sweating too. 'Our High Dragon says we should invest in the trade now. It's going to grow and grow. He has a plan to get Marine with us. . . .'

'*Dew neh loh moh*, you can't trust those seagoing bastards.'

'That's what I said, but he said we need the seagoing bastards and we can trust a selected few, who else can snatch and intercept a token 20 percent—even 50 percent to appease Mountain of Dung himself at prearranged moments?' Tang-po spat deftly again. 'If we could get Marine, Narcotics Branch, and the Gang of Three, our present *h'eung yau* would be like an infant's piddle in the harbor.'

There was a serious silence in the room.

'We would have to recruit new members and that's always dangerous.'

'Yes.'

Lee helped himself to the teapot and poured some jasmine tea, sweat running down his back now, the smoke-ladened air sultry and overbearing. He waited.

'What do you think, Younger Brother?'

These two men were not related but used the Chinese politeness between themselves because they had trusted each other for more than fifteen years. Lee had saved his superior's life in the riots of 1956. He was thirty-five now and his heroism in the riots had earned him a police medal. He was married and had three children. He had served sixteen years in the force and his whole pay was 843 HK a month. He took the tram to work. Without supplementing his income through the Brotherhood, like all of them, he would have had to walk or bicycle, most days. The tram took two hours.

'I think the idea is very bad,' he said. 'Drugs, any drugs, that's fornicating bad—yes, very bad. Opium, that's bad though it's good for old people—the white powder, cocaine, that's bad, but not as bad as the death squirts. It'd be bad joss to deal in the death squirts.'

'I told him the same.'

'Are you going to obey him?'

'What's good for one Brother should be good for all,' Tang-po said thoughtfully, avoiding an answer.

Again Lee waited. He did not know how a Dragon was elected, or exactly how many there were, or who the High Dragon was. He only knew that his Dragon was Tang-po who was a wise and cautious man who had their interests at heart.

'He also said one or two of our foreign devil superiors are getting itchy piles about their fornicating slice of the gambling money.'

Lee spat disgustedly. 'What do those fornicators do for their share? Nothing. Just close their fornicating eyes. Except the Snake.'

'Ah him! He should be stuffed down the sewer, that fornicator. Soon those who he pays off above him won't be able to hide his stink anymore. And his stench'll spread over all of us.'

'He's due to retire in a couple of years,' Lee said darkly. 'Perhaps he'll finger his rear to all those high-ups until he leaves and there won't be a thing they can do. His friends are very high, so they say.'

'Meanwhile?' Tang-po asked.

Lee sighed. 'My advice, Elder Brother, is to be cautious, not to do it if you can avoid it. If you can't . . .' he shrugged. 'Joss. Is it decided?'

'No, not yet. It was mentioned at our weekly meeting. For consideration.'

'Has an approach been made to the Gang of Three?'

'I understand White Powder Lee made the approach,

Younger Brother. It seems the three are going to join together.'

Lee gasped. 'With blood oaths?'

'It seems so.'

'They're going to work together? Those devils?'

'So they said. I'll bet old Four Finger Wu will be the Highest Tiger.'

'*Ayeeyah*, that one? They say he's murdered fifty men himself,' Lee said darkly. He shivered at the danger. 'They must have three hundred fighters in their pay. It'd be better for all of us if those three were dead—or behind bars.'

'Yes. But meanwhile White Powder Lee says they're ready to expand, and for a little cooperation from us they can *guarantee* a giant return.' Tang-po mopped his brow and coughed and lit another cigarette. 'Listen, Little Brother,' he said softly. 'He swears they've been offered a very large source of American money, cash money and bank money, and a very large retail outlet for their goods there, based in this place called Manhattan.'

Lee felt the sweat on his forehead. 'A retail outlet there . . . *ayeeyah*, that means millions. They will guarantee?'

'Yes. With very little for us to do. Except close our eyes and make sure Marine and Narcotics Branch seize only the correct shipments and close their eyes when they're supposed to. Isn't it written in the Ancient Books: If you don't squeeze, lightning will strike you?'

Again a silence. 'When does the decision . . . when's it going to be decided?'

'Next week. If it's decided yes, well, the flow of trade will take months to organize, perhaps a year.' Tang-po glanced at the clock and got up. 'Time for our shower. Nighttime Song has arranged dinner for us afterwards.'

'Eeeee, very good.' Uneasily Lee turned out the single overhead light. 'And if the decision is no?'

Tang-po stubbed out his cigarette and coughed. 'If no . . .' He shrugged. 'We only have one life, gods notwithstanding, so it is our duty to think of our families. One of my relations is a captain with Four Finger Wu. . . .'

11

8:30 P.M.:

'Hello, Brian,' Dunross said. 'Welcome.'

'Evening, tai-pan—congratulations—great night for a party,' Brian Kwok said. A liveried waiter appeared out of nowhere and he accepted a glass of champagne in fine crystal. 'Thanks for inviting me.'

'You're very welcome.' Dunross was standing beside the door of the ballroom in the Great House, tall and debonair, Penelope a few paces away greeting other guests. The half-full ballroom was open to crowded floodlit terraces and gardens where the majority of brightly dressed ladies and dinner-jacketed men stood in groups or sat at round tables. A cool breeze had come with nightfall.

'Penelope darling,' Dunross called out, 'you remember Superintendent Brian Kwok.'

'Oh of course,' she said, threading her way over to them with her happy smile, not remembering at all. 'How're you?'

'Fine thanks—congratulations!'

'Thank you—make yourself at home. Dinner's at nine fifteen, Claudia has the seating lists if you've lost your card. Oh excuse me a moment. . . .' She turned away to intercept some other guests, her eyes trying to watch everywhere to see that everything was going well and that no one stood alone—knowing in her secret heart that if there was a disaster there was nothing for her to do, that others would make everything well again.

'You're very lucky, Ian,' Brian Kwok said. 'She gets younger every year.'

'Yes.'

'So. Here's to twenty more years! Health!' They touched

230

glasses. They had been friends since the early fifties when they had met at the first racing hill climb and had been friendly rivals ever since—and founding members of the Hong Kong Sports Car and Rally Club.

'But you, Brian, no special girl friend? You arrive alone?'

'I'm playing the field.' Brian Kwok dropped his voice. 'Actually I'm staying single permanently.'

'Dreamer! This's your year—you're the catch of Hong Kong. Even Claudia's got her eyes on you. You're a dead duck, old chap.'

'Oh Christ!' Brian dropped the banter for a moment. 'Say, tai-pan, could I have a couple of private minutes this evening?'

'John Chen?' Dunross asked at once.

'No. We've got every man looking, but nothing yet. It's something else.'

'Business?'

'Yes.'

'How private?'

'Private.'

'All right,' Dunross said, 'I'll find you after dinner. What ab—'

A burst of laughter caused them to look around. Casey was standing in the center of an admiring group of men—Linbar Struan and Andrew Gavallan and Jacques deVille among them—just outside one of the tall French doors that led to the terrace.

'Eeeee,' Brian Kwok muttered.

'Quite,' Dunross said and grinned.

She was dressed in a floor-length sheath of emerald silk, molded just enough and sheer just enough.

'Christ, is she or isn't she?'

'What?'

'Wearing anything underneath?'

'Seek and ye shall find.'

'I'd like to. She's stunning.'

'I thought so too,' Dunross said agreeably, 'though I'd say 100 percent of the other ladies don't.'

'Her breasts are perfect, you can see that.'

'Actually you can't. Just. It's all in your mind.'

'I'll bet there isn't a pair in Hong Kong to touch them.'

'Fifty dollars to a copper cash says you're wrong—provided we include Eurasians.'

'How can we prove who wins?'

'We can't. Actually I'm an ankle man myself.'

'What?'

'Old Uncle Chen-Chen used to say, "First look at the ankles, my son, then you tell her breeding, how she'll behave, how she'll ride, how she'll . . . like any filly. But remember, all crows under heaven are black!"'

Brian Kwok grinned with him then waved at someone in friendly style. Across the room a tall man with a lived-in face was waving back. Beside him was an extraordinarily beautiful woman, tall, fair, with gray eyes. She waved happily too.

'Now there's an English beauty at her best!'

'Who? Oh, Fleur Marlowe? Yes, yes she is. I didn't know you knew the Marlowes, tai-pan.'

'Likewise! I met him this afternoon, Brian. You've known him long?'

'Oh a couple of months-odd. He's persona grata with us.'

'Oh?'

'Yes. We're showing him the ropes.'

'Oh? Why?'

'Some months ago he wrote to the commissioner, said he was coming to Hong Kong to research a novel and asked for our cooperation. Seems the Old Man happened to have read his first novel and had seen some of his films. Of course we checked him out and he appears all right.' Brian Kwok's eyes went back to Casey. 'The Old Man thought we could do with an improved image so he sent word down that, within limits, Peter was approved and to show him around.' He glanced back at Dunross and smiled thinly. 'Ours not to reason why!'

'What was his book?'

'Called *Changi*, about his POW days. The Old Man's brother died there, so I suppose it hit home.'

'Have your read it?'

'Not me—I've too many mountains to climb! I did skim a few pages. Peter says it's fiction but I don't believe him.' Brian Kwok laughed. 'He can drink beer though. Robert had him on a couple of his Hundred Pinters and he held his end up.' A Hundred Pinter was a police stag party to which the officers contributed a barrel of a hundred pints of beer. When the beer was gone, the party ended.

Brian Kwok's eyes were feasting on Casey, and Dunross wondered for the millionth time why Asians favored Anglo-Saxons and Anglo-Saxons favored Asians.

'Why the smile, tai-pan?'

'No reason. But Casey's not bad at all, is she?'

'Fifty dollars says she's *bat jam gai, heya?*'

Dunross thought a moment, weighing the bet carefully. *Bat jam gai* meant, literally, white chicken meat. This was the way Cantonese referred to ladies who shaved off their pubic hair. 'Taken! You're wrong, Brian, she's *see yau gai,*' which meant soya chicken, 'or in her case red, tender and nicely spicy. I have it on the highest authority!'

Brian laughed. 'Introduce me.'

'Introduce yourself. You're over twenty-one.'

'I'll let you win the hill climb on Sunday!'

'Dreamer! Off you go and a thousand says you won't.'

'What odds'll you give me?'

'You must be joking!'

'No harm in asking. Christ, I'd like to carry the book on that one. Where's the lucky Mr. Bartlett?'

'I think he's in the garden—I told Adryon to chaperone him. Excuse me a moment. . . .' Dunross turned away to greet someone Brian Kwok did not recognize.

Upward of 150 guests had already arrived and been greeted personally. Dinner was for 217, each carefully seated according to face and custom at round tables that were already set and candlelit on the lawns. Candles and candelabra in the halls, liveried waiters offering champagne in cut glass crystal, or smoked salmon and caviar from silver trays and tureens.

A small band was playing on the dais and Brian Kwok saw a few uniforms among the dinner jackets, American and British, army, navy and air force. It was no surprise that Europeans were dominant. This party was strictly for the British inner circle that ruled Central District and were the power bloc of the Colony, their Caucasian friends, and a few very special Eurasians, Chinese and Indians. Brian Kwok recognized most of the guests: Paul Havergill of the Victoria Bank of Hong Kong, old Sir Samuel Samuels, multi-millionaire, tai-pan of twenty real estate, banking, ferry and stockbroking companies; Christian Toxe, editor of the *China Guardian*, talking to Richard Kwang, chairman of the Ho-Pak Bank; multimillionaire ship-owner V. K. Lam talking to Phillip and Dianne Chen, their son Kevin with them; the American Zeb Cooper, inheritor of the oldest American trading company, Cooper-Tillman, having his ear bent by Sir Dunstan Barre, tai-pan of Hong Kong and Lan Tao Farms. He noticed Ed Langan, the FBI man, among the guests and this surprised him. He had not known that Langan or the man he was talking to, Stanley Rosemont, a deputy director of the China-watching CIA contingent, were friends of Dunross. He let his eyes drift over the chattering group of men, and the mostly separate groups of their wives.

They're all here, he thought, all the tai-pans except Gornt and Plumm, all the pirates, all here in incestuous hatred to pay homage to *the* tai-pan.

Which one is the spy, the traitor, controller of Sevrin, *Arthur?*

He's got to be European.

I'll bet he's here. And I'll catch him. Yes. I'll catch him, soon, now that I know about him. We'll catch him and catch them all, he thought grimly. And we'll catch these crooks with their hands in their tills, we'll stamp out their piracies for the common good.

'Champagne, Honored Sir,' the waiter asked in Cantonese with a toothy smile.

Brian accepted a full glass. 'Thank you.'

The waiter bowed to hide his lips. 'The tai-pan had a blue-covered file among his papers when he came in tonight,' he whispered quickly.

'Is there a safe, a secret hiding place here?' Brian asked equally cautiously in the same dialect.

'The servants say in his office on the next floor,' the man said. His name was Wine Waiter Feng, and he was one of SI's under-cover network of intelligence agents. His cover as a waiter for the company that catered all Hong Kong's best and most exclu-sive parties gave him great value. 'Perhaps it's behind the painting, I heard. . . .' He stopped suddenly and switched to pidgin English. 'Champ-igy-nee Missee?' he asked toothily, offering the tray to the tiny old Eurasian lady who was coming up to them. 'Wery wery first class.'

'Don't you Missee me, you impertinent young puppy,' she rapped haughtily in Cantonese.

'Yes, Honored Great-Aunt, sorry, Honored Great-Aunt.' He beamed and fled.

'So, young Brian Kwok,' the old lady said, peering up at him. She was eighty-eight, Sarah Chen, Phillip Chen's aunt, a tiny birdlike person with pale white skin and Asian eyes that darted this way and that. And though she appeared frail her back was upright and her spirit very strong. 'I'm glad to see you. Where's John Chen? Where's my poor grand-nephew?'

'I don't know, Great Lady,' he said politely.

'When are you going to get my Number One Grand-nephew back?'

'Soon. We're doing everything we can.'

'Good. And don't you interfere with young Phillip if he wants to pay John's ransom privately. You see to it.'

'Yes. I'll do what I can. Is John's wife here?'

'Eh? Who? Speak up, boy!'

'Is Barbara Chen here?'

'No. She came earlier but as soon as *that* woman arrived she "got a headache" and left. Huh, I don't blame her at all!' Her old rheumy eyes were watching Dianne Chen across the room. 'Huh, that woman! Did you see her entrance?'

'No, Great Lady.'

'Huh, Like Dame Nellie Melba herself. She swept in, handkerchief to her eyes, her eldest son Kevin in tow—I don't like that boy—and my poor nephew Phillip like a second-class cook boy in the rear. Huh! The only time Dianne Chen ever wept was in the crash of '56 when her stocks went down and she lost a fortune and wet her drawers. Ha! Look at her now, preening herself! Pretending to be upset when everyone knows she's acting as though she's already Dowager Empress! I could pinch her cheeks! Disgusting!' She looked back at Brian Kwok. 'You find my grand-nephew John—I don't want that woman or her brat *loh-pan* of our house.'

'But he can be *tai-pan*?'

They laughed together. Very few Europeans knew that though *tai-pan* meant great leader, in the old days in China a *tai-pan* was the colloquial title of a man in charge of a whorehouse or public toilet. So no Chinese would ever call himself *tai-pan*, only *loh-pan*—which also meant great leader or head leader. Chinese and Eurasians were greatly amused that Europeans enjoyed calling themselves *tai-pan*, stupidly passing over the correct title.

'Yes. If he's the right *pan*,' the old woman said and they chuckled. 'You find my John Chen, young Brian Kwok!'

'Yes. Yes, we'll find him.'

'Good. Now, what do you think of Golden Lady's chances on Saturday?'

'Good, if the going's dry. At three to one she's worth a bundle. Watch Noble Star—she's got a chance too.'

'Good. After dinner come and find me. I want to talk to you.'

'Yes, Great Lady.' He smiled and watched her go off and knew that all she wanted was to try to act the marriage broker for some great-niece. *Ayeeyah*, I'll have to do something about that soon, he thought.

His eyes strayed back to Casey. He was delighted by the disapproving looks from all the women—and the cautious covert admiration from all their escorts. Then Casey glanced up and saw him watching her across the room and she stared back at him briefly with equally frank appraisal.

Dew neh loh moh, he thought uneasily, feeling somehow undressed. I'd like to possess that one. Then he noticed Roger Crosse with Armstrong beside him. He put his mind together and headed for them.

'Evening, sir.'

'Evening, Brian. You're looking very distinguished.'

'Thank you, sir.' He knew better than to volunteer anything pleasant in return. 'I'm seeing the tai-pan after dinner.'

'Good. As soon as you've seen him, find me.'

'Yes sir.'

'So you think the American girl stunning?'

'Yes sir.' Brian sighed inwardly. He had forgotten that Crosse could lip-read English, French and some Arabic—he spoke no Chinese dialects—and that his eyesight was exceptional.

'Actually she's rather obvious,' Crosse said.

'Yes sir.' He saw Crosse concentrating on her lips and knew that he was overhearing her conversation from across the room and he was furious with himself that he had not developed the talent.

'She seems to have a passion for computers.' Crosse turned his eyes back on them. 'Curious, what?'

'Yes sir.'

'What did Wine Waiter Feng say?'

Brian told him.

'Good. I'll see Feng gets a bonus. I didn't expect to see Langan and Rosemont here.'

'It could be a coincidence, sir,' Brian Kwok volunteered. 'They're both keen punters. They've both been to the tai-pan's box.'

'I don't trust coincidences,' Crosse said. 'As far as Langan's concerned, of course you know nothing, either of you.'

'Yes sir.'

'Good. Perhaps you'd both better be about our business.'

'Yes sir.' Thankfully the two men turned to leave but stopped as there was a sudden hush. All eyes went to the doorway. Quillan Gornt stood there, black-browed, black-bearded, conscious that he had been noticed. The other guests hastily picked up their conversations and kept their eyes averted but their ears concentrated.

Crosse whistled softly. 'Now why is he here?'

'Fifty to one says he's up to no good,' Brian Kwok said, equally astounded.

They watched Gornt come into the ballroom and put out his hand to Dunross and Penelope beside him. Claudia Chen who was nearby was in shock, wondering how she could reorganize Dunross's table at such short notice because of course Gornt would have to be seated there.

'I hope you don't mind my changing my mind at the last moment,' Gornt was saying, his mouth smiling.

'Not at all,' Dunross replied, his mouth smiling.

'Good evening, Penelope. I felt I had to give you my congratulations personally.'

'Oh, thank you,' she said. Her smile was intact but her heart was beating very fast now. 'I, I was sorry to hear about your wife.'

'Thank you.' Emelda Gornt had been arthritic and confined to a wheelchair for some years. Early in the year she had caught pneumonia and had died. 'She was very unlucky,' Gornt said. He looked at Dunross. 'Bad joss about John Chen too.'

237

'Very.'

'I suppose you read the afternoon *Gazette?*'

Dunross nodded and Penelope said, 'Enough to frighten everyone out of their wits.' All the afternoon papers had had huge headlines and dwelt at length on the mutilated ear and the Werewolves. There was a slight pause. She rushed to fill it. 'Your children are well?'

'Yes. Annagrey's going to the University of California in September—Michael is here on his summer holiday. They're all in very good shape I'm glad to say. And yours?'

'They're fine. I do wish Adryon would go to university though. Dear me, children are very difficult these days, aren't they?'

'I think they always were.' Gornt smiled thinly. 'My father was always pointing out how difficult I was.' He looked at Dunross again.

'Yes. How is your father?'

'Hale and hearty I'm glad to say. The English climate suits him, he says. He's coming out for Christmas.' Gornt accepted a proffered glass of champagne. The waiter quailed under his look, and fled. He raised his glass. 'A happy life and many congratulations.'

Dunross toasted him in return, still astonished that Gornt had arrived. It was only for politeness and for face that Gornt and other enemies had been sent formal invitations. A polite refusal was all that was expected—and Gornt had already refused.

Why's he here?

He's come to gloat, Dunross thought. Like his bloody father. That must be the reason. But why? What devilment has he done to us? Bartlett? Is it through Bartlett?

'This's a lovely room, beautiful proportions,' Gornt was saying. 'And a lovely house. I've always envied this house.'

Yes, you bastard, I know, Dunross thought furiously, remembering the last time any of the Gornts had been in the Great House. Ten years ago, in 1953, when Ian's father, Colin Dunross, was still *the* tai-pan. It was during Struan's Christmas party, traditionally the biggest of the season, and Quillan Gornt had arrived with his father, William, then tai-pan of Rothwell-Gornt, again unexpectedly. After dinner there had been a bitter, public clash between the two tai-pans in the billiard room where a dozen or so of the men had gathered for a game. That was when Struan's had just been blocked by the Gornts and their Shanghainese friends in their attempt to take over South Orient Airways, which, because of the Communist conquest of the Mainland, had just become available. This feeder airline monopolized all air traffic in and out of Shanghai from Hong Kong, Singapore, Taipei, Tokyo and Bangkok, and if merged with Air Struan, their fledgling airline, Struan's would have virtual feeder monopoly in the Far East based out of Hong Kong. Both men had accused the other of underhand practices—both accusations were true.

Yes, Ian Dunross told himself, both men went to the brink that time. William Gornt had tried every way to become established in Hong Kong after Rothwell-Gornt's huge losses in Shanghai. And when Colin Dunross knew Struan's could not prevail, he had snatched South Orient out of William Gornt's grasp by throwing his weight to a safe Cantonese group.

'And so you did, Colin Dunross, so you did. You fell into the trap and you'll never stop us now,' William Gornt had gloated. 'We're here to stay. We'll hound you out of Asia, you and your god-cursed Noble House. South Orient's just the beginning. We've won!'

'The hell you have! The Yan-Wong-Sun group's associated with us. We have a contract.'

'It's hereby canceled.' William Gornt had motioned to Quillan, his eldest son and heir apparent, who took out the copy of an agreement. 'This contract's between the Yan-Wong-Sun group who're nominees of the Tso-Wa-Feng group,' he said happily, 'who're nominees of Ta-Weng-Sap who sells control of South Orient to Rothwell-Gornt for one dollar more than the original cost!' Quillan Gornt had laid it on the billiard table with a flourish. 'South Orient's ours!'

'I don't believe it!'

'You can. Happy Christmas!' William Gornt had given a great, scorn-filled laugh, and walked out. Quillan had replaced his billiard cue, laughing too. Ian Dunross had been near the door.

'One day I'll own this house,' Quillan Gornt had hissed at him, then turned and called out to the others, 'If any of you want jobs, come to us. Soon you'll all be out of work. Your Noble House won't be noble much longer.' Andrew Gavallan had been there, Jacques deVille, Alastair Struan, Lechie and David MacStruan, Phillip Chen, even John Chen.

Dunross remembered how his father had raged that night, and blamed treachery and nominees and bad joss, knowing all the time that he himself had warned him, many times, and that his warnings had been shoved aside. Christ, how we lost face! All Hong Kong laughed at us that time—the Noble House peed on from a great height by the Gornts and their Shanghainese interlopers.

Yes. But that night finalized Colin Dunross's downfall. That was the night I decided that he had to go before the Noble House was lost forever. I used Alastair Struan. I helped him to shove my father aside. Alastair Struan had to become tai-pan. Until I was wise enough and strong enough to shove him aside.

Am I wise enough now?

I don't know, Dunross thought, concentrating on Quillan Gornt now, listening to his pleasantries, hearing himself react with equal charm, while his mind said, I haven't forgotten South Orient, or that we had to merge our airline with yours at a fire-sale price and lose control of the new line renamed All Asia Airways. Nothing's forgotten. We lost that time but this time we'll win. We'll win everything by God.

Casey was watching both men with fascination. She had noticed Quillan Gornt from the first moment, recognizing him from the photographs of the dossier. She had sensed his strength and masculinity even from across the room and had been uneasily excited by him. As she watched, she could almost touch the tension between the two men squaring off—two bulls in challenge.

Andrew Gavallan had told her at once who Gornt was. She had volunteered nothing, just asked Gavallan and Linbar Struan why they were so shocked at Gornt's arrival. And then, as they were alone now, the four of them—Casey, Gavallan, deVille and Linbar Struan—they told her about the 'Happy Christmas' and 'One day I'll own this house.'

240

'What did the tai-pan . . . what did Ian do?' she asked.

Gavallan said, 'He just looked at Gornt. You knew if he had a gun or a knife or a cudgel he'd've used it, you just knew it, and as he hadn't a weapon you knew any moment he was going to use his hands or teeth. . . . He just stood rock still and looked at Gornt and Gornt went back a pace, out of range—literally. But that bugger Gornt's got *cojones*. He sort of gathered himself together and stared back at Ian for a moment. Then, without saying a word he went around him slowly, very cautiously, his eyes never leaving Ian, and he left.'

'What's that bastard doing here tonight?' Linbar muttered.

Gavallan said, 'It's got to be important.'

'Which one?' Linbar asked. 'Which important?'

Casey looked at him and at the edge of her peripheral vision she saw Jacques deVille shake his head warningly and at once the shades came down on Linbar and on Gavallan. Even so she asked, 'What *is* Gornt doing here?'

'I don't know,' Gavallan told her, and she believed him.

'Have they met since that Christmas?'

'Oh yes, many times, all the time,' Gavallan told her. 'Socially of course. Then, too, they're on the boards of companies, committees, councils together.' Uneasily he added, 'But . . . well I'm sure they're both just waiting.'

She saw their eyes wander back to the two enemies and her eyes followed. Her heart was beating strongly. They saw Penelope move away to talk to Claudia Chen. In a moment, Dunross glanced across at them. She knew he was signaling Gavallan in some way. Then his eyes were on her. Gornt followed his glance. Now both men were looking at her. She felt their magnetism. It intoxicated her. A devil in her pushed her feet toward them. She was glad now that she had dressed as she had, more provocatively than she had planned, but Linc had told her this was a night to be less businesslike.

As she walked she felt the brush of the silk, and her nipples hardened. She felt their eyes flow over her, undressing her, and this time, strangely, she did not mind. Her walk became imperceptibly more feline.

'Hello, tai-pan,' she said with pretended innocence. 'You wanted me to join you?'

'Yes,' he replied at once. 'I believe you two know each other.'

241

She shook her head and smiled at both of them, not noticing the trap. 'No. We've never met. But of course I know who Mr. Gornt is. Andrew told me.'

'Ah, then let me introduce you formally. Mr. Quillan Gornt, tai-pan of Rothwell-Gornt. Miss Tcholok-Ciranoush Tcholok—from America.'

She held out her hand, knowing the danger of getting between the two men, half her mind warmed by the danger the other half shouting, Jesus, what're you doing here.

'I've heard a lot about you, Mr. Gornt,' she said, pleased that her voice was controlled, pleased by the touch of his hand—different from Dunross's, rougher and not as strong. 'I believe the rivalry of your firms goes back generations.'

'Only three. It was my grandfather who first felt the not so tender mercies of the Struans,' Gornt said easily. 'One day I'd enjoy telling you our side of the legends.'

'Perhaps you two should smoke a pipe of peace,' she said. 'Surely Asia's wide enough for both of you.'

'The whole world isn't,' Dunross said affably.

'No,' Gornt agreed, and if she had not heard the real story she would have presumed from their tone and manner they were just friendly rivals.

'In the States we've many huge companies—and they live together peacefully. In competition.'

'This isn't America,' Gornt said calmly. 'How long will you be here, Miss Tcholok?'

'That depends on Linc—Linc Bartlett—I'm with Par-Con Industries.'

'Yes, yes I know. Didn't he tell you we're having dinner on Tuesday?'

The danger signals poured through her. 'Tuesday?'

'Yes. We arranged it this morning. At our meeting. Didn't he mention it?'

'No,' she said, momentarily in shock. Both men were watching her intently and she wished she could back off and come back in five minutes when she had thought this through. Jesus, she thought and fought to retain her poise as all the implications swamped her. 'No,' she said again, 'Linc didn't mention any meeting. What did you arrange?'

Gornt glanced at Dunross who still listened expressionlessly.

'Just to have dinner next Tuesday. Mr. Bartlett and yourself—if you're free.'

'That would be nice—thank you.'

'Where's your Mr. Bartlett now?' he asked.

'In—in the garden, I think.'

Dunross said, 'Last time I saw him he was on the terrace. Adryon was with him. Why?'

Gornt took out a gold cigarette case and offered it to her.

'No thank you,' she said. 'I don't smoke.'

'Does it bother you if I do?'

She shook her head.

Gornt lit a cigarette and looked at Dunross. 'I'd just like to say hello to him, before I leave,' he said pleasantly. 'I hope you don't mind my coming for just a few minutes—if you'll excuse me I won't stay for dinner. I have some pressing business to attend to . . . you understand.'

'Of course.' Dunross added, 'Sorry you can't stay.'

Neither man showed anything in his face. Except the eyes. It was in their eyes. Hatred. Fury. The depth shocked her. 'Ask Ian Dunross to show you the Long Gallery,' Gornt was saying to her. 'I hear there're some fine portraits there. I've never been in the Long Gallery—only the billiard room.' A chill went down her spine as he looked again at Dunross who watched him back.

'This meeting this morning,' Casey said, thinking clearly now, judging it wise to bring everything out in front of Dunross at once. 'When was it arranged?'

'About three weeks ago,' Gornt said. 'I thought you were his chief executive, I'm surprised he didn't mention it to you.'

'Linc's our tai-pan, Mr. Gornt. I work for him. He doesn't have to tell me everything,' she said, calmer now. 'Should he have told me, Mr. Gornt? I mean, was it important?'

'It could be. Yes. I confirmed, formally, that we can better any offer Struan's can make. Any offer.' Gornt glanced back at the tai-pan. His voice hardened a fraction. 'Ian, I wanted to tell you, personally, that we're in the same marketplace.'

'Is that why you came?'

'One reason.'

'The other?'

'Pleasure.'

'How long have you known Mr. Bartlett?'

'Six months or so. Why?'

Dunross shrugged, then looked at Casey and she could read nothing from his voice or face or manner other than friendliness. 'You didn't know of any Rothwell-Gornt negotiations?'

Truthfully she shook her head, awed by Bartlett's skilful long-range planning. 'No. Are negotiations in progress, Mr. Gornt?'

'I would say yes.' Gornt smiled.

'Then we shall see, won't we?' Dunross said. 'We shall see who makes the best deal. Thank you for telling me personally, though there was no need. I knew, of course, that you'd be interested too. There's no need to belabor that.'

'Actually there's a very good reason,' Gornt said sharply. 'Neither Mr. Bartlett nor this lady may realize how vital Par-Con is to you. I felt obliged to make the point personally to them. And to you. And of course to offer my congratulations.'

'Why vital, Mr. Gornt?' Casey asked, committed now.

'Without your Par-Con deal and the cash flow it will generate, Struan's will go under, could easily go under in a few months.'

Dunross laughed and those few who listened covertly shuddered and moved their own conversations up a decibel, aghast at the thought of Struan's failing, at the same time thinking, What deal? Par-Con? Should we sell or buy? Struan's or Rothwell-Gornt?

'No chance of that,' Dunross said. 'Not a chance in hell!'

'I think there's a very good chance.' Gornt's tone changed. 'In any event, as you say, we shall see.'

'Yes, we will—meanwhile . . .' Dunross stopped as he saw Claudia approaching uneasily.

'Excuse me, tai-pan,' she said, 'your personal call to London's on the line.'

'Oh thank you.' Dunross turned and beckoned Penelope. She came over at once. 'Penelope, would you entertain Quillan and Miss Tcholok for a moment. I've got a phone call—Quillan's not staying for dinner—he has pressing business.' He waved cheerily and left them. Casey noticed the animal grace to his walk.

'You're not staying for dinner?' Penelope was saying, her relief evident though she tried to cover it.

'No. I'm sorry to inconvenience you—arriving so abruptly,

after declining your kind invitation. Unfortunately I can't stay.'

'Oh. Then . . . would you excuse me a moment, I'll be back in a second.'

'There's no need to worry about us,' Gornt said gently. 'We can look after ourselves. Again, sorry to be a nuisance—you're looking marvelous, Penelope. You never change.' She thanked him and he willed her away. Gratefully she went over to Claudia Chen who was waiting nearby.

'You're a curious man,' Casey said. 'One moment war, the next great charm.'

'We have rules, we English, in peace and war. Just because you loathe someone, that's no reason to curse him, spit in his eye or abuse his lady.' Gornt smiled down at her. 'Shall we find your Mr. Bartlett? Then I really should go.'

'Why did you do that? To the tai-pan? The battle challenge—the "vital" bit. That was the formal gauntlet, wasn't it? In public.'

'Life's a game,' he said. 'All life's a game and we English play it with different rules from you Americans. Yes. And life's to be enjoyed. Ciranoush—what a lovely name you have. May I use it?'

'Yes,' she said after a pause. 'But why the challenge now?'

'Now was the time. I didn't exaggerate about your importance to Struan's. Shall we go and find your Mr. Bartlett?'

That's the third time he's said *your* Mr. Bartlett, she thought. Is that to probe, or to needle? 'Sure, why not?' She turned for the garden, conscious of the looks, overt and covert, of the other guests, feeling the danger pleasantly. 'Do you always make dramatic entrances like this?'

Gornt laughed. 'No. Sorry if I was abrupt, Ciranoush—if I distressed you.'

'You mean about your private meeting with Linc? You didn't. It was very shrewd of Linc to approach the opposition without my knowledge. That gave me a freedom of action that otherwise I'd not have had this morning.'

'Ah, then you're not irritated that he didn't trust you in this?'

'It has nothing to do with trust. I often withhold information from Linc, until the time's ripe, to protect him. He was obviously doing the same for me. Linc and I understand one another. At least I think I understand him.'

'Then tell me how to finalize a deal.'

'First I have to know what you want. Apart from Dunross's head.'

'I don't want his head, or death or anything like that—just an early demise of their Noble House. Once Struan's is obliterated we become the Noble House.' His face hardened. 'Then all sorts of ghosts can sleep.'

'Tell me about them.'

'Now's not the time, Ciranoush, oh no. Too many hostile ears. That'd be for your ears only.' They were out in the garden now, the gentle breeze grand, a fine night sky overhead, star filled. Linc Bartlett was not on this terrace so they went down the wide stone steps through other guests to the lower one, toward the paths that threaded the lawns. Then they were intercepted.

'Hello, Quillan, this's a pleasant surprise.'

'Hello, Paul. Miss Tcholok, may I introduce you to Paul Havergill? Paul's presently in charge of the Victoria Bank.'

'I'm afraid that's very temporary, Miss Tcholok, and only because our chief manager's on sick leave. I'm retiring in a few months.'

'To our regret,' Gornt said, then introduced Casey to the rest of this group: Lady Joanna Temple-Smith, a tall, stretched-faced woman in her fifties, and Richard Kwang and his wife Mai-ling. 'Richard Kwang's chairman of the Ho-Pak, one of our finest Chinese banks.'

'In banking we're all friendly competitors, Miss, er, Miss, except of course for Blacs,' Havergill said.

'Sir?' Casey said.

'Blacs? Oh that's a nickname for the Bank of London, Canton and Shanghai. They may be bigger than we are, a month or so older, but we're the best bank here, Miss, er . . .'

'Blacs're my bankers,' Gornt said to Casey. 'They do me very well. They're first-class bankers.'

'Second-class, Quillan.'

Gornt turned back to Casey. 'We've a saying here that Blacs consists of gentlemen trying to be bankers, and those at the Victoria are bankers trying to be gentlemen.'

Casey laughed. The others smiled politely.

'You're all just friendly competition, Mr. Kwang?' she asked.

'Oh yes. We wouldn't dare oppose Blacs or the Victoria,' Richard Kwang said amiably. He was short and stocky and middle-aged with gray-flecked black hair and an easy smile, his English perfect. 'I hear Par-Con's going to invest in Hong Kong, Miss Tchelek.'

'We're here to look around, Mr. Kwang. Nothing's firm yet.' She passed over his mispronunciation.

Gornt lowered his voice. 'Just between ourselves, I've formally told both Bartlett and Miss Tcholok that I will better any offer Struan's might make. Blacs are supporting me one hundred percent. And I've friendly bankers elsewhere. I'm hoping Par-Con will consider all possibilities before making any commitment.'

'I imagine that would be very wise,' Havergill said. 'Of course Struan's does have the inside track.'

'Blacs and most of Hong Kong would hardly agree with you,' Gornt said.

'I hope it won't come to a clash, Quillan,' Havergill said. 'Struan's is our major customer.'

Richard Kwang said, 'Either way, Miss Tchelek, it would be good to have such a great American company as Par-Con here. Good for you, good for us. Let's hope that a deal can be found that suits Par-Con. If Mr. Bartlett would like any assistance . . .' The banker produced his business card. She took it, opened her silk handbag and offered hers with equal dexterity, having come prepared for the immediate card exchanging that is good manners and obligatory in Asia. The Chinese banker glanced at it, then his eyes narrowed.

'Sorry I haven't had it translated into characters yet,' she said. 'Our bankers in the States are First Central New York and the California Merchant Bank and Trust Company.' Casey mentioned them proudly, sure the combined assets of those banking giants were in excess of 15 billions. 'I'd be gl—' She stopped, startled at the sudden chill surrounding her. 'Is something wrong?'

'Yes and no,' Gornt said after a moment. 'It's just that the First Central New York Bank's not at all popular here.'

'Why?'

Havergill said disdainfully, 'They turned out to be a shower— that's, er, English for a bad lot, Miss, er, Miss. The First Central

247

New York did some business here before the war, then expanded in the mid-forties while we at the Victoria and other British institutions were picking ourselves off the floor. In '49 when Chairman Mao threw Chiang Kai-shek off the Mainland to Taiwan, Mao's troops were massed on our border just a few miles north in the New Territories. It was touch and go whether or not the hordes would spill over and overrun the Colony. A lot of people cut and ran, none of us of course, but all the Chinese who could got out. Without any warning, the First Central New York called in all their loans, paid off their depositors, closed their doors and fled—all in the space of one week.'

'I didn't know,' Casey said, aghast.

'They were a bunch of yellow bastards, my dear, if you'll excuse the expression,' Lady Joanna said with open contempt. 'Of course, they were the *only* bank that scarpered—ran away. But then they were . . . well, what can you expect, my dear?'

'Probably better, Lady Joanna,' Casey said, furious with the VP in charge of their account for not warning them. 'Perhaps there were mitigating circumstances. Mr. Havergill. Were the loans substantial?'

'At that time, very, I'm afraid. Yes. That bank ruined quite a lot of important businesses and people, caused an enormous amount of grief and loss of face. Still,' he said with a smile, 'we all benefited by their leaving. A couple of years ago they had the effrontery to apply to the financial secretary for a new charter!'

Richard Kwang added jovially, 'That's one charter that'll never be renewed! You see, Miss Tchelek, all foreign banks operate on a renewable yearly charter. Certainly we can do very well without that one, or for that matter any other American bank. They're such . . . well, you'll find the Victoria, Blacs or the Ho-Pak, perhaps all three Miss K.C., can fulfill all Par-Con's needs perfectly. If you and Mr. Bartlett would like to chat . . .'

'I'd be glad to visit with you, Mr. Kwang. Say tomorrow? Initially I handle most of our banking needs. Maybe sometime in the morning?'

'Yes, yes of course. You'll find us competitive,' Richard Kwang said without a flicker. 'At ten?'

'Great. We're at the V and A, Kowloon. If ten's not good for you just let me know,' she said. 'I'm pleased to meet you personally too, Mr. Havergill. I presume our appointment for tomorrow is still in order?'

'Of course. At four, isn't it? I look forward to chatting at length with Mr. Bartlett . . . and you, of course, my dear.' He was a tall, lean man and she noticed his eyes rise from her cleavage. She dismissed her immediate dislike. I may need him, she thought, and his bank.

'Thank you,' she said with the right amount of deference and turned her charm on Lady Joanna. 'What a pretty dress, Lady Joanna,' she said, loathing it and the row of small pearls that circled the woman's scrawny neck.

'Oh, thank you, my dear. Is yours from Paris too?'

'Indirectly. It's a Balmain but I got it in New York.' She smiled down at Richard Kwang's wife, a solid, well-preserved Cantonese lady with an elaborate coiffure, very pale skin and narrow eyes. She was wearing an immense imperial jade pendant and a seven-carat diamond ring. 'Pleased to meet you, Mrs. Kwang,' she said, awed by the wealth that the jewelry represented. 'We were looking for Linc Bartlett. Have you seen him?'

'Not for a while,' Havergill volunteered. 'I think he went into the east wing. Believe there's a bar there. He was with Adryon—Dunross's daughter.'

'Adryon's turned out to be such a pretty girl,' Lady Joanna said. 'They make such a nice couple together. Charming man, Mr. Bartlett. He's not married, is he, dear?'

'No,' Casey said, equally pleasantly, adding Lady Joanna Temple-Smith to her private list of loathsome people. 'Linc's not married.'

'He'll be gobbled up soon, mark my words. I really believe Adryon's quite smitten. Perhaps you'd like to come to tea on Thursday, my dear? I'd love you to meet some of the girls. That's the day of our Over Thirty Club.'

'Thank you,' Casey said. 'I don't qualify—but I'd love to come anyway.'

'Oh I'm sorry, dear! I presumed . . . I'll send a car for you. Quillan, are you staying for dinner?'

'No, can't. Got pressing business.'

'Pity.' Lady Joanna smiled and showed her bad teeth.

'If you'll excuse us—just want to find Bartlett and then I have to leave. See you Saturday.' Gornt took Casey's arm and guided her away.

They watched them leave. 'She's quite attractive in a common sort of way, isn't she?' Lady Joanna said. 'Chuluk. That's Middle European, isn't it?'

'Possibly. It could be Mideastern, Joanna, you know, Turkish, something like that, possibly the Balkans. . . .' Havergill stopped. 'Oh, I see what you mean. No, I don't think so. She certainly doesn't look Jewish.'

'One really can't tell these days, can one? She might have had her nose fixed—they do marvelous things these days, don't they?'

'Never occurred to me to look. Hum! Do you think so?'

Richard Kwang passed Casey's card over to his wife who read it instantly and got the same message instantly. 'Paul, her card says treasurer and executive VP of the holding company . . . that's quite impressive, isn't it? Par-Con's a big company.'

'Oh my dear fellow, but they're American. They do extraordinary things in America. Surely it's just a title—that's all.'

'Giving his mistress face?' Joanna asked.

12

9:00 P.M.:

The billiard cue struck the white ball and it shot across the green table and slashed the red into a far pocket and stopped perfectly behind another red.

Adryon clapped gleefully. 'Oh Linc, that was super! I was sure you were just boasting. Oh do it again!'

Linc Bartlett grinned. 'For one dollar that red around the table and into that pocket and the white here.' He marked the spot with a flick of chalk.

'Done!'

He leaned over the table and sighted and the white stopped within a millimeter of his mark, the red sunk with marvelous inevitability.

'*Ayeeyah!* I haven't got a dollar with me. Damn! Can I owe it to you?'

'A lady—however beautiful—has to pay her gambling debts at once.'

'I know. Father says the same. Can I pay you tomorrow?'

He watched her, enjoying her, pleased that his skill pleased her. She was wearing a knee-length black skirt and the lovely silk blouse. Her legs were long, very long, and perfect. 'Nope!' He pretended ill humor and then they laughed together in the huge room, the vast lights low over the full-size billiard table, the rest of the room dark and intimate but for the shaft of light from the open door.

'You play incredibly well,' she said.

'Don't tell anyone but I made my living in the Army playing pool.'

'In Europe?'

251

'No. Pacific.'

'My father was a fighter pilot. He got six planes before he was shot down and grounded.'

'I guess that made him an ace, didn't it?'

'Were you part of those awful landings against the Japs?'

'No. I was in construction. We came in when everything was secured.'

'Oh.'

'We built bases, airfields in Guadalcanal, and islands all over the Pacific. My war was easy—nothing like your dad's.' As he went over to the cue rack, he was sorry for the first time that he had not been in the Marines. Her expression when he had said construction made him feel unmanned. 'We should go look for your boyfriend. Maybe he's here by now.'

'Oh he's not important! He's not a real boyfriend, I just met him a week or so ago at a friend's party. Martin's a journalist on the *China Guardian*. He's not a lover.'

'Are all young English ladies so open about their lovers?'

'It's the pill. It's released us from masculine servitude forever. Now we're equal.'

'Are you?'

'I am.'

'Then you're lucky.'

'Yes, I know I'm very lucky.' She watched him. 'How old are you, Linc?'

'Old.' He snapped the cue into its rack. It was the first time in his life that he had not wanted to tell his age. Goddamn, he thought, curiously unsettled. What's your problem?

None. There's no problem. Is there?

'I'm nineteen,' she was saying.

'When's your birthday?'

'October 27—I'm a Scorpio. When's yours?'

'October 1.'

'Oh it's not! Tell me honestly!'

'Cross my heart and hope to die.'

She clapped her hands with delight. 'Oh that's marvelous! Father's the tenth. That's marvelous—a good omen '

'Why?'

'You'll see.' Happily she opened her handbag and found a crumpled cigarette package and a battered gold lighter He took the lighter and flicked it for her but it did not light. A second and a third time but nothing.

'Bloody thing,' she said. 'Bloody thing's never worked properly, but Father gave it to me. I love it. Of course I dropped it a couple of times.'

He peered at it, blew the wick and fiddled a moment. 'You shouldn't smoke anyway.'

'That's what Father always says.'

'He's right.'

'Yes. But I like smoking for the time being. How old are you, Linc?'

'Forty.'

'Oh!' He saw the surprise. 'Then you're the same age as Father! Well, almost. He's forty-one.'

'Both were great years,' Linc said dryly, and he thought, Whichever way you figure it, Adryon, I really am old enough to be your father.

Another frown creased her brow. 'It's funny, you don't seem the same age at all.' Then she added in a rush, 'In two years I'll be twenty-one and that's practically over the hill, I just can't imagine being twenty-five let alone thirty and as to forty . . God, I think I'd rather be pushing up daisies.'

'Twenty-one's old—yes ma'am, mighty old,' he said. And he thought, It's a long time since you spent time with such a young one. Watch yourself. This one's dynamite. He flicked the lighter and it lit. 'What d'you know!'

'Thanks,' she said and puffed her cigarette alight. 'You don't smoke?' she asked.

'No, not now. Used to but Casey sent me illustrated pamphlets on cancer and smoking every hour on the hour until I got the message. Didn't bother me a bit to stop—once I'd decided. It sure as hell improved my golf and tennis and . . .' he smiled. 'And all forms of sports.'

'Casey is gorgeous. Is she really your executive vice-president?'

'Yes.'

'She's going to . . . it'll be very difficult for her here. The men won't like dealing with her at all.'

'Same in the States. But they're getting used to it. We built Par-Con in six years. Casey can work with the best of them.

She's a winner.'

'Is she your mistress?'

He sipped his beer. 'Are all young English ladies so blunt?'

'No.' She laughed. 'I was just curious. Everyone says . . . everyone presumes she is.'

'That a fact?'

'Yes. You're the talk of Hong Kong society, and tonight will cap everything. You both made rather a grand entrance, what with your private jet, the smuggled guns and Casey being the last European to see John Chen, so the papers said. I liked your interview.'

'Eh, those bas—those press guys were waiting on the doorstep this afternoon. I tried to keep it short and sharp.'

'Par-Con's really worth half a billion dollars?'

'No. About 300 million—but it'll be a billion-dollar company soon. Yes, it'll be soon now.'

He saw her looking at him with those frank, gray-green eyes of hers, so adult yet so young. 'You're a very interesting man, Mr. Linc Bartlett. I like talking to you. I like you too. Didn't at first. I screamed bloody murder when Father told me I had to chaperone you, introduce you around for a while. I haven't done a very good job, have I?'

'It's been *super*.'

'Oh come on.' She grinned too. 'I've totally monopolized you.'

'Not true. I met Christian Toxe the editor, Richard Kwang and those two Americans from the consulate. Lannan, wasn't it?'

'Langan, Edward Langan. He's nice. I didn't catch the other one's name—I don't know them really, they've just been racing with us. Christian's nice and his wife's super. She's Chinese so she's not here tonight.'

Bartlett frowned. 'Because she's Chinese?'

'Oh, she was invited but she wouldn't come. It's face. To save her husband's face. The nobs don't approve of mixed marriages.'

'Marrying the natives?'

'Something like that.' She shrugged. 'You'll see. I'd better introduce you to some more guests or I'll get hell!'

'How about to Havergill the banker? What about him?'

'Father thinks Havergill's a berk.'

254

'Then by God he's a twenty-two-carat berk from here on in!'

'Good,' she said and they laughed together.

'Linc?'

They looked around at the two figures silhouetted in the shaft of light from the doorway. He recognized Casey's voice and shape at once but not the man. It was not possible from where they were to see against the light.

'Hi, Casey! How's it going?'

He took Adryon's arm casually and propelled her toward the silhouette. 'I've been teaching Adryon the finer points of pool.'

Adryon laughed. 'That's the understatement of the year, Casey. He's super at it, isn't he?'

'Yes. Oh Linc, Quillan Gornt wanted to say hi before he left.'

Abruptly Adryon jerked to a stop and the color left her face. Linc stopped, startled. 'What's wrong?' he asked her.

'Evening, Mr. Bartlett,' Gornt said, moving toward them into the light. 'Hello, Adryon.'

'What're you doing here?' she said in a tiny voice.

'I just came for a few minutes,' Gornt said.

'Have you seen Father?'

'Yes.'

'Then get out. Get out and leave this house alone.' Adryon said it in the same small voice.

Bartlett stared at her. 'What the hell's up?'

Gornt said calmly, 'It's a long story. It can wait until tomorrow—or next week. I just wanted to confirm our dinner on Tuesday—and if you're free over the weekend, perhaps you two would like to come out on my boat for the day. Sunday if the weather's good.'

'Thanks, I think so, but may we confirm tomorrow?' Bartlett asked, still nonplussed by Adryon.

'Adryon,' Gornt said gently, 'Annagrey's leaving next week, she asked me to ask you to give her a call.' Adryon did not answer, just stared at him, and Gornt added to the other two, 'Annagrey's my daughter. They're good friends—they've both gone to the same schools most of their lives. She's off to university in California.'

'Oh—then if there's anything we could do for her . . .' Casey said.

'That's very kind of you,' he said. 'You'll meet her Tuesday.

255

Perhaps we can talk about it then. I'll say g—'

The door at the far end of the billiard room swung open and Dunross stood there.

Gornt smiled and turned his attention back to them. 'Good night, Mr. Bartlett—Ciranoush. See you both on Tuesday. Good night, Adryon.' He bowed slightly to them and walked the length of the room and stopped. 'Good night, Ian,' he said politely. 'Thank you for your hospitality.'

''Night,' Dunross said, as politely, and stood aside, a slight smile twisting his lips.

He watched Gornt walk out of the front door and then turned his attention back to the billiard room. 'Almost time for dinner,' he said, his voice calm. And warm. 'You must all be starving. I am.'

'What . . . what did he want?' Adryon said shakily.

Dunross came up to her with a smile, gentling her. 'Nothing. Nothing important, my pet. Quillan's mellowing in his old age.'

'You're sure?'

'Sure.' He put his arm around her and gave her a little hug. 'No need to worry your pretty head.'

'Has he gone?'

'Yes.'

Bartlett started to say something but stopped instantly as he caught Dunross's eye over Adryon's head.

'Yes. Everything's grand, my darling,' Dunross was saying as he gave her another little hug, and Bartlett saw Adryon gather herself within the warmth. 'Nothing to worry about.'

'Linc was showing me how he played pool and then . . . It was just so sudden. He was like an apparition.'

'You could have knocked me down with a feather too when he appeared like the Bad Fairy.' Dunross laughed, then added to Bartlett and Casey, 'Quillan goes in for dramatics.' Then to Bartlett alone, 'We'll chat about that after dinner, you and I.'

'Sure,' Bartlett said, noticing the eyes weren't smiling.

The dinner gong sounded. 'Ah, thank God!' Dunross said. 'Come along, everyone, food at long last. Casey, you're at my table.' He kept his arm around Adryon, loving her, and guided her out into the light.

Casey and Bartlett followed.

*   *   *

256

Gornt got into the driver's seat of the black Silver Cloud Rolls that he had parked just outside the Great House. The night was good, though the humidity had increased again. He was very pleased with himself. And now for dinner and Jason Plumm, he thought. Once that bugger's committed, Ian Dunross's as good as finished and I own this house and Struan's and the whole kit and caboodle!

It couldn't have been better: first Casey and Ian almost at once, and everything laid out in front of him and in front of her. Then Havergill and Richard Kwang together. Then Bartlett in the billiard room and then Ian himself again.

Perfect!

Now Ian's called, Bartlett's called, Casey, Havergill, Richard Kwang and so's Plumm. Ha! If they only knew.

Everything's perfect. Except for Adryon. Pity about her, pity that children have to inherit the feuds of the fathers. But that's life. Joss. Pity she won't go out into the world and leave Hong Kong, like Annagrey—at least until Ian Dunross and I have settled our differences, finally. Better she's not here to see him smashed—nor Penelope too. Joss if they're here, joss if they're not. I'd like him here when I take possession of his box at the races, the permanent seat on all boards, all the sinecures, the legislature—oh yes. Soon they'll all be mine. Along with the envy of all Asia.

He laughed. Yes. And about time. Then all the ghosts will sleep. God curse all ghosts!

He switched on the ignition and started the engine, enjoying the luxury of real leather and fine wood, the smell rich and exclusive. Then he put the car into gear and swung down the driveway, past the carpark where all the other cars were, down to the huge wrought-iron main gates with the Struan arms entwined. He stopped for passing traffic and caught sight of the Great House in his rear mirror. Tall, vast, the windows ablaze, welcoming.

Soon I really will own you, he thought. I'll throw parties there that Asia's never seen before and never will again. I suppose I should have a hostess.

What about the American girl?

He chuckled. 'Ah, Ciranoush, what a lovely name,' he said out loud with the same, perfect amount of husky charm that he had used previously. That one's a pushover, he told himself confidently. You just use old world charm and great wine, light but excellent food and patience—along with the very best of upper-class English, masculine sophistication and no swear words and she'll fall where and when you want her to. And then, if you choose the correct moment, you can use gutter English and a little judicious roughness, and you'll unlock all her pent-up passion like no man ever has done.

If I read her correctly she needs an expert pillowing rather badly. So either Bartlett's inadequate or they're really not lovers as the confidential report suggested. Interesting.

But do you want her? As a toy—perhaps. As a tool—of course. As a hostess no, much too pushy.

Now the road was clear so he pulled out and went down to the junction and turned left and soon he was on Peak Road going downhill toward Magazine Gap where Plumm's penthouse apartment was. After dinner with him he was going to a meeting, then to Wanchai, to one of his private apartments and the welcoming embrace of Mona Leung. His pulse quickened at the thought of her violent lovemaking, her barely hidden hatred for him and all *quai loh* that was ever in perpetual conflict with her love of luxury, the apartment that was on loan to her and the modest amount of money he gave her monthly.

'Never give 'em enough money,' his father William had told him early on. 'Clothes, jewelry, holidays—that's fine. But not too much money. Control them with dollar bills. And never think they love you for you. They don't. It's only your money, only your money and always will be. Just under the surface they'll despise you, always will. That's fair enough if you think about it—we're not Chinese and never will be.'

'There's never an exception?'

'I don't think so. Not for a *quai loh*, my son. I don't think so. Never has been with me and I've known a few. Oh she'll give you her body, her children, even her life, but she'll always despise you. She has to, she's Chinese and we're *quai loh!*'

Ayeeyah, Gornt thought. That advice's proved itself time and time again. And saved me so much anguish. It'll be good to see the Old Man, he told himself. This year I'll give him a fine Christmas present: Struan's.

He was driving carefully down the left side of the winding

road hugging the mountainside, the night good, the surface fine and traffic light. Normally he would have been chauffeur-driven but tonight he wanted no witnesses to his meeting with Plumm.

No, he thought. Nor any witnesses when I meet Four Finger Wu. What the hell does that pirate want? Nothing good. Bound to be dangerous. Yes. But during the Korean War Wu did you a very large favor and perhaps now is the time he wants the favor repaid. There's always a reckoning sooner or later, and that's fair and that's Chinese law. You get a present, you give one back a little more valuable. You have a favor done . . .

In 1950 when the Chinese Communist armies in Korea were battering and bleeding their way south from the Yalu with monstrous losses, they were desperately short of all strategic supplies and very willing to pay mightily those who could slip through the blockade with the supplies they needed. At that time, Rothwell-Gornt was also in desperate straits because of their huge losses at Shanghai the previous year thanks to the conquest by Mao. So in December of 1950, he and his father had borrowed heavily and secretly bought a huge shipment of penicillin, morphine, sulfanalamides and other medical supplies in the Philippines, avoiding the obligatory export license. These they smuggled onto a hired ocean-going junk with one of their trusted crews and sent it to Wampoa, a bleak island in the Pearl River near Canton. Payment was to be in gold on delivery, but en route, in the secret backwaters of the Pearl River Estuary, their junk had been intercepted by river pirates favoring Chiang Kai-shek's Nationalists and a ransom demanded. They had no money to ransom the cargo, and if the Nationalists found out that Rothwell-Gornt was dealing with their hated Communist enemy, their own future in Asia was lost forever.

Through his compradore Gornt had arranged a meeting in Aberdeen Harbor with Four Finger Wu, supposedly one of the biggest smugglers in the Pearl River Estuary.

'Where ship now?' Four Finger Wu had asked in execrable pidgin English.

Gornt had told him as best he could, conversing in pidgin, not being able to speak Haklo, Wu's dialect.

'Perhaps, perhaps not!' Four Finger Wu smiled 'I phone three day. *Nee choh wah* password. Three day, *heya*?'

On the third day he phoned. 'Bad, good, don' know. Meet two day Aberdeen. Begin Hour of Monkey.' That hour was ten o'clock at night. Chinese split the day into twelve two-hour segments, each with a name, always in the same sequence, beginning at 4:00 A.M. with the Cock, then at 6:00 A.M. with the Dog, and so on; Boar, Rat, Ox, Tiger, Rabbit, Dragon, Snake, Monkey, Horse and Sheep.

At the Hour of the Monkey on Wu's junk at Aberdeen two days later, he had been given the full payment for his shipment in gold *plus an extra 40 percent*. A staggering 500 percent profit.

Four Finger Wu had grinned. 'Make better trade than *quai loh*, never mind. 28,000 taels of gold.' A tael was a little more than an ounce. 'Next time me ship. Yes?'

'Yes.'

'You buy, me ship, me sell, 40 percent mine, sale price.'

'Yes.' Gornt had thankfully tried to press a much larger percentage on him this time but Wu had refused.

'40 percent only, sale price.' But Gornt had understood that now he was in the smuggler's debt.

The gold was in five-tael smuggler bars. It was valued at the official rate of $35 U.S. an ounce. But on the black market, smuggled into Indonesia, India or back into China, it was worth two or three times as much . . . sometimes more. On this one shipment again with Wu's help, Rothwell-Gornt had made a million and a half U.S. and were on the road to recovery.

After that there had been three more shipments, immensely profitable to both sides. Then the war had ceased and so had their relationship.

Never a word since then, Gornt thought. Until the phone call this afternoon.

'Ah, old friend, can see? Tonight?' Four Finger Wu had said. 'Can do? Anytime—I wait. Same place as old days. Yes?'

So now the favor's to be returned. Good.

Gornt switched on the radio. Chopin. He was driving the winding road automatically, his mind on the meetings ahead, the engine almost silent. He slowed for an advancing truck, then swung out and accelerated on the short straight to overtake a slow-moving taxi. Going quite fast now he braked sharply in good time nearing the blind corner, then something seemed to snap in the innards of the engine, his foot sank to the floorboards, his stomach turned over and he went into the hairpin too fast.

In panic he jammed his foot on the brake again and again but nothing happened, his hands whirling the wheel around. He took the first corner badly, swerving drunkenly as he came out of it onto the wrong side of the road. Fortunately there was nothing coming at him but he overcorrected and lurched for the mountainside, his stomach twisting with nausea, overcorrected again, going very fast now and the next corner leapt at him. Here the grade was steeper, the road more winding and narrow. Again he cornered badly but once through he had a split second to grab the hand brake and this slowed him only a little, the new corner was on him, and he came out of it way out of his lane, oncoming headlights blinding him.

The taxi skittered in panic to the shoulder and almost went over the side, its horn blaring but he was passed by a fraction of an inch, lurching petrified for the correct side, and then went on down the hill out of control. A moment of straight road and he managed to jerk the gear lever into low as he hurtled into another blind corner, the engine howling now. The sudden slowing would have pitched him through the windshield but for his seat belt, his hands almost frozen to the wheel.

He got around this corner but again he was out too far and he missed the oncoming car by a millimeter, skidded back to his side once more, swerved, overcorrecting, slowing a little now but there was no letup in the grade or twisting road ahead. He was still going too fast into the new hairpin and coming out of the first part he was too far over. The heavily laden truck grinding up the hill was helpless.

Panic-stricken he tore the wheel left and just managed to get around the truck with a glancing blow. He tried to jerk the gear lever into reverse but it wouldn't go, the cogs shrieking in protest. Then, aghast, he saw slow traffic ahead in his lane, oncoming traffic in the other and the road vanish around the next bend. He was lost so he turned left into the mountainside, trying to ricochet and stop that way.

There was a howl of protesting metal, the back side window shattered and he bounced away. The oncoming car lurched for the far shoulder, its horn blaring. He closed his eyes and braced for the head-on collision but somehow it didn't happen and he was past and just had enough strength to jerk the wheel hard over again and went into the mountainside. He hit with a glancing blow. The front left fender ripped away. The car ploughed into the shrub and earth, then slammed into a rock outcrop, reared up throwing Gornt aside, but as the car fell back the near-side wheel went into the storm drain and held, and just before smashing into the paralyzed little Mini ahead, it stopped.

Gornt weakly pulled himself up. The car was still half upright. Sweat was pouring off him and his heart was pounding. He found it hard to breathe or to think. Traffic both ways was stopped, snarled. He heard some horns hooting impatiently below and above, then hurried footsteps.

'You all right, old chap?' the stranger asked.

'Yes, yes I think so. My, my brakes went.' Gornt wiped the sweat off his forehead, trying to get his brain to work. He felt his chest, then moved his feet and there was no pain. 'I . . . the brakes went . . . I was turning a corner and . . . then everything . . .'

'Brakes, eh? Not like a Rolls. I thought you were pretending to be Stirling Moss. You were very lucky. I thought you'd had it twenty times. If I were you I'd switch off the engine.'

'What?' Then Gornt realized the engine was still gently purring and the radio playing so he turned the ignition off and, after a moment, pulled the keys out.

'Nice car,' the stranger said, 'but it's a right proper mess now. Always liked this model. '62, isn't it?'

'Yes. Yes it is.'

'You want me to call the police?'

Gornt made the effort and thought a moment, his pulse still pounding in his ears. Weakly he unsnapped the seat belt. 'No. There's a police station just back up the hill. If you'd give me a lift to there?'

'Delighted, old chap.' The stranger was short and rotund. He looked around at the other cars and taxis and trucks that were stopped in both directions, their Chinese drivers and Chinese passengers gawking at them from their windows. 'Bloody people,' he muttered sourly. 'You could be dying in the street and you'd be lucky if they stepped over you.' He opened the door and helped Gornt out.

'Thanks.' Gornt felt his knees shaking. For a moment he

could not dominate his knees and he leaned against the car.

'You sure you're all right?'

'Oh yes. It's . . . that frightened me to death!' He looked at the damage, the nose buried into earth and shrub, a huge score down the right side, the car jammed well into the inside curve. 'What a bloody mess!'

'Yes, but it hasn't telescoped a sausage! You were bloody lucky you were in a good car, old chap.' The stranger let the door swing and it closed with a muted click. 'Great workmanship. Well, you can leave it here. No one's likely to steal it.' The stranger laughed, leading the way to his own car which was parked, its blinker lights on, just behind. 'Hop in, won't take a jiffy.'

It was then Gornt remembered the mocking half-smile on Dunross's face that he had taken for bravado as he left. His mind cleared. Would there have been time for Dunross to tamper . . . with his knowledge of engines . . . surely he wouldn't . . .?

'Son of a bitch,' he muttered, aghast.

'Not to worry, old chap,' the stranger said, as he eased past the wreck, making the turn. 'The police'll make all the arrangements for you.'

Gornt's face closed. 'Yes. Yes they will.'

13

10:25 P.M.:

'Grand dinner, Ian, better than last year's,' Sir Dunstan Barre said expansively from across the table.

'Thank you.' Dunross raised his glass politely and took a sip of the fine cognac from the brandy snifter.

Barre gulped his port then refilled his glass, more florid than usual. 'Ate too much, as usual, by God! Eh Phillip? Phillip!'

'Yes . . . oh yes . . . much better . . .' Phillip Chen muttered.

'Are you all right, old chap?'

'Oh yes . . . it's just . . . oh yes.'

Dunross frowned, then let his eyes rove the other tables, hardly listening to them.

There were just the three of them now at this round table that had seated twelve comfortably. At the other tables spread across the terraces and lawns, men were lounging over their cognac, port and cigars, or standing in clusters, all the ladies now inside the house. He saw Bartlett standing over near the buffet tables that an hour ago had been groaning under the weight of roast legs of lamb, salads, sides of rare beef, vast hot steak-and-kidney pies, roast potatoes and vegetables of various kinds, and the pastries and cakes and ice cream sculptures. A small army of servants was cleaning away the debris. Bartlett was in deep conversation with Chief Superintendent Roger Crosse and the American Ed Langan. In a little while I'll deal with him, he told himself grimly—but first Brian Kwok. He looked around. Brian Kwok was not at his table, the one that Adryon had hosted, or at any of the others, so he sat back patiently, sipped his cognac and let himself drift.

Secret files, MI-6, Special Intelligence, Bartlett, Casey, Gornt, no Tsu-yan and now Alan Medford Grant very dead. His phone call before dinner to Kiernan, Alan Medford Grant's assistant in London, had been a shocker. 'It was sometime this morning, Mr. Dunross,' Kiernan had said. 'It was raining, very slippery and he was a motorcycle enthusiast as you know. He was coming up to town as usual. As far as we know now there were no witnesses. The fellow who found him on the country road near Esher and the A3 highway, just said he was driving along in the rain and then there in front of him was the bike on its side and a man sprawled in a heap on the edge of the road. He said as far as he could tell, AMG was dead when he reached him. He called the police and they've begun inquiries but . . . well, what can I say? He's a great loss to all of us.'

'Yes. Did he have any family?'

'Not that I know of, sir. Of course I informed MI-6 at once.'

'Oh?'

'Yes sir.'

'Why?'

There was heavy static on the line. 'He'd left instructions with me, sir. If anything happened to him I was to call two numbers at once and cable you, which I did. Neither number meant anything to me. The first turned out to be the private number of a high-up official in MI-6—he arrived within half an hour with some of his people and they went through AMG's desk and private papers. They took most of them when they left. When he saw the copy of the last report, the one we'd just sent you, he just about hit the roof, and when he asked for copies of all the others and I told him, following AMG's instructions, I always destroyed the office copy once we'd heard you had received yours, he just about had a hemorrhage. It seems AMG didn't really have Her Majesty's Government's permission to work for you.'

'But I have Grant's assurance in writing he'd got clearance from HMG in advance.'

'Yes sir. You've done nothing illegal but this MI-6 fellow just about went bonkers.'

'Who was he? What was his name?'

'I was told, *told*, sir, not to mention any names. He was very pompous and mumbled something about the Official Secrets Act.'

'You said two numbers?'

'Yes sir. The other was in Switzerland. A woman answered and after I'd told her, she just said, oh, so sorry, and hung up. She was foreign, sir. One interesting thing, in AMG's final instructions he had said not to tell either number about the other but, as this gentlemen from MI-6 was, to put it lightly, incensed, I told him. He called at once but got a busy line and it was busy for a very long time and then the exchange said it had been temporarily disconnected. He was bloody furious, sir.'

'Can you carry on AMG's reports?'

'No sir. I was just feeder—I collated information that he got. I just wrote the reports for him, answered the phone when he was away, paid office bills. He spent a good part of the time on the Continent but he never said where he'd been, or volunteered anything. He was . . . well, he played his cards close to his nose. I don't know who gave him anything—I don't even know his office number in Whitehall. As I said, he was very secretive. . .'

Dunross sighed and sipped his brandy. Bloody shame, he thought. Was it an accident—or was he murdered? And when do MI-6 fall on my neck? The numbered account in Switzerland? That's not illegal either, and no one's business but mine and his.

What to do? There must be a substitute somewhere.

Was it an accident? Or was he killed?

'Sorry?' he asked, not catching what Barre had said.

'I was just saying it was bloody funny when Casey didn't want to go and you threw her out.' The big man laughed. 'You've got balls, old boy.'

At the end of the dinner just before the port and cognac and cigars had arrived, Penelope had got up from her table where Linc Bartlett was deep in conversation with Havergill and the ladies had left with her, and then Adryon at her table, and then, all over the terraces, ladies had begun trickling away after her. Lady Joanna, who was sitting on Dunross's right, had said, 'Come on, girls, time to powder.'

Obediently the other women got up with her and the men politely pretended not to be relieved with their exodus.

'Come along, dear,' Joanna had said to Casey, who had remained seated.

'Oh I'm fine, thanks.'

'I'm sure you are but, er, come along anyway.'

Then Casey had seen everyone staring. 'What's the matter?'

'Nothing, dear,' Lady Joanna had said. 'It's custom that ladies leave the men alone for a while with the port and cigars. So come along.'

Casey had stared at her blankly. 'You mean we're sent off while the men discuss affairs of state and the price of tea in China?'

'It's just good manners, dear. When in Rome . . .' Lady Joanna had watched her, a slight, contemptuous smile on her lips, enjoying the embarrassed silence and the shocked looks of most of the men. All eyes went back to the American girl.

'You can't be serious. That custom went out before the Civil War,' Casey said.

'In America I'm sure it did.' Joanna smiled her twisted smile. 'Here it's different, this is part of England. It's a matter of manners. Do come along, dear.'

'I will—dear,' Casey said as sweetly. 'Later.'

Joanna had sighed and shrugged and raised an eyebrow at Dunross and smiled crookedly and gone off with the other ladies. There was a stunned silence at the table.

'Tai-pan, you don't mind if I stay, do you?' Casey had said with a laugh.

'Yes, I'm sorry but I do,' he had told her gently. 'It's just a custom, nothing important. It's really so the ladies can get first crack at the loo and the pails of water.'

Her smile faded and her chin began to jut. 'And if I prefer not to go?'

'It's just our custom, Ciranoush. In America it's custom to call someone you've just met by his first name, it's not here. Even so . . .' Dunross stared back calmly, but just as inflexibly. 'There's no loss of face in it.'

'I think there is.'

'Sorry about that—I can assure you there isn't.'

The others had waited, watching him and watching her, enjoying the confrontation, at the same time appalled by her. Except Ed Langan who was totally embarrassed for her. 'Hell, Casey,' he said, trying to make a joke of it, 'you can't fight City Hall.'

'I've been trying all my life,' she had said sharply—clearly furious. Then, abruptly, she had smiled gloriously. Her fingers drummed momentarily on the tablecloth and she got up. 'If you gentlemen will excuse me . . .' she had said sweetly and sailed away, an astonished silence in her wake.

'I hardly threw her out,' Dunross said.

'It was bloody funny, even so,' Barre said. 'I wonder what changed her mind? Eh Phillip?'

'What?' Phillip Chen asked absently.

'For a moment I thought she was going to belt poor old Ian, didn't you? But something she thought of changed her mind. What?'

Dunross smiled. 'I'll bet it's no good. That one's as touchy as a pocketful of scorpions.'

'Great knockers, though,' Barre said.

They laughed. Phillip Chen didn't. Dunross's concern for him increased. He had tried to cheer him up all evening but nothing had drawn the curtain away. All through dinner Phillip had been dulled and monosyllabic. Barre got up with a belch. 'Think I'll take a leak while there's space.' He lurched off into the garden.

'Don't pee on the camellias,' Ian called after him absently, then forced himself to concentrate. 'Phillip, not to worry,' he said, now that they were alone. 'They'll find John soon.'

'Yes, I'm sure they will,' Phillip Chen said dully, his mind not so much swamped by the kidnapping as appalled by what he had discovered in his son's safety deposit box this afternoon. He had opened it with the key that he had taken from the shoebox.

'Go on, Phillip, take it, don't be a fool,' his wife Dianne had hissed. 'Take it—if we don't the tai-pan will!'

'Yes, yes I know.' Thank all gods I did, he thought, still in shock, remembering what he had found when he'd rifled through the contents. Manila envelopes of various sizes, mostly itemized, a diary and phone book. In the envelope marked 'debts' betting slips for 97,000 HK for current debts to illegal, off-course gamblers in HK. A note in favor of Miser Sing, a notorious moneylender, for 30,000 HK at 3 percent per month interest; a long overdue sight demand note from the Ho-Pak Bank for $20,000 U.S. and a letter from Richard Kwang dated last week saying unless John Chen made some arrangements soon he would have to talk to his father. Then there were letters which documented a growing friendship between his son and an American gambler, Vincenzo Banastasio, who assured John Chen that his debts were not pressing: '. . . take your time, John, your credit's the best, anytime this year's fine . . .' and, attached, was the photocopy of a perfectly legal, notorized promissory note binding his son, his heirs or assignees, to pay Banastasio, on demand, $485,000 U.S., plus interest.

Stupid, stupid, he had raged, knowing his son had not more than a fifth of those assets, so he himself would have to pay the debt eventually.

Then a thick envelope marked 'Par-Con' had caught his attention.

This contained a Par-Con employment contract signed by K. C. Tcholok, three months ago, hiring John Chen as a private consultant to Par-Con for '. . . $100,000 down ($50,000 of which is hereby acknowledged as already paid) and, once a satisfactory deal is signed between Par-Con and Struan's, Rothwell-Gornt or any other Hong Kong company of Par-Con's choosing, a further one million dollars spread over a five-year period in equal installments; and within thirty days of the signing of the above said contract, a debt to Mr. Vincenzo Banastasio of 85 Orchard Road, Las Vegas, Nevada, of $485,000 paid off, the first year's installment of $200,000, along with the balance of $50,000 . . .'

'In return for what,' Phillip Chen had gasped helplessly in the bank vault.

But the long contract spelled out nothing further except that John Chen was to be a 'private consultant in Asia.' There were no notes or papers attached to it.

Hastily he had rechecked the envelope in case he had missed anything but it was empty. A quick leafing through the other envelopes produced nothing. Then he happened to notice a thin airmail envelope half stuck to another. It was marked 'Par-Con II.' It contained photocopies of handwritten notes from his son to Linc Bartlett.

The first was dated six months ago and confirmed that he, John Chen, would and could supply Par-Con with the most intimate knowledge of the innermost workings of the whole Struan complex of companies, '. . . of course this has to be kept totally secret, but for example, Mr. Bartlett, you can see from the enclosed Struan balance sheets for 1954 through 1961 (when Struan's went public) what I advise is perfectly feasible. If you look at the chart of Struan's corporate structure, and the list of some of the important stockholders of Struan's and their secret holdings, including my father's, you should have no trouble in any takeover bid Par-Con cares to mount. Add to these photo-copies the other thing I told you about—I swear to God that you can believe me—I guarantee success. I'm putting my life on the line, that should be collateral enough, but if you'll advance me fifty of the first hundred now, I'll agree to let you have posses-sion on arrival—on your undertaking to return it to me once your deal's set—or for use against Struan's. I guarantee to use it against Struan's. In the end Dunross has to do anything you want. Please reply to the usual box and destroy this as we have agreed.'

'Possession of what?' Phillip Chen had muttered, beside him-self with anxiety. His hands were shaking now as he read the second letter. It was dated three weeks ago. 'Dear Mr. Bartlett. This will confirm your arrival dates. Everything's prepared. I look forward to seeing you again and meeting Mr. K. C. Tcholok. Thanks for the fifty cash which arrived safely—all future monies are to go to a numbered account in Zurich—I'll give you the bank details when you arrive. Thank you also for agreeing to our unwritten understanding that if I can assist you in the way I've claimed I can, then I'm in for 3 percent of the action of the new Par-Con (Asia) Trading Company.

'I enclose a few more things of interest: note the date that Struan's demand notes (countersigned by my father) become due to pay Toda Shipping for their new super container ships— September 1, 11 and 15. There's not enough money in Struan's till to meet them.

'Next: to answer Mr. Tcholok's question about my father's position in any takeover or proxy fight. He can be neutralized. Enclosed photocopies are a sample of many that I have. These show a very close relationship with White Powder Lee and his cousin, Wu Sang Fang who's also known as Four Finger Wu, from the early fifties, and secret ownership with them—even today—of a property company, two shipping companies and Bangkok trading interests. Though outwardly, now, both pose

270

as respectable businessmen, property developers and shipping millionaires, it's common knowledge they have been successful pirates and smugglers for years—and there's a very strong rumor in Chinese circles that they are the High Dragons of the opium trade. If my father's connection with them was made public it would take his face away forever, would sever the very close links he has with Struan's, and all the other *hongs* that exist today, and most important, would destroy forever his chance for a knighthood, the one thing he wants above all. Just the threat of doing this would be enough to neutralize him—even make him an ally. Of course I realize these papers and the others I have need further documentation to stick in a court of law but I have this already in abundance in a safe place. . . .'

Phillip Chen remembered how, panic-stricken, he had searched frantically for the further documentation, his mind shrieking that it was impossible for his son to have so much secret knowledge, impossible for him to have Struan's balance sheets of the prepublic days, impossible to know about Four Finger Wu and those secret things.

Oh gods that's almost everything I know—even Dianne doesn't know half of that! What else does John know—what else has he told the American?

Beside himself with anxiety he had searched every envelope but there was nothing more.

'He must have another box somewhere—or safe,' he had muttered aloud, hardly able to think.

Furious he had scooped everything into his briefcase, hoping that a more careful examination would answer his questions—and slammed the box shut and locked it. At a sudden thought, he had reopened it. He had pulled the slim tray out and turned it upside down. Taped to the underside were two keys. One was a safety deposit box key with the number carefully filed off. He stared at the other, paralyzed. He recognized it at once. It was the key to his own safe in his house on the crest. He would have bet his life that the only key in existence was the one that he always wore around his neck, that had never been out of his possession—ever since his father had given it to him on his deathbed sixteen years ago.

'*Oh ko,*' he said aloud, once more consumed with rage.

Dunross said, 'You all right? How about a brandy?'

'No, no thank you,' Phillip Chen said shakily, back in the present now. With an effort he pulled his mind together and stared at the tai-pan, knowing he should tell him everything. But he dare not. He dare not until he knew the extent of the secrets stolen. Even then he dare not. Apart from many trans- actions the authorities could easily misconstrue, and others that could be highly embarrassing and lead to all sorts of court cases, civil if not criminal—stupid English law, he thought furiously, stupid to have one law for everyone, stupid not to have one law for the rich and another for the poor, why else work and slave and gamble and scheme to be rich—apart from all this he would still have to admit to Dunross that he had been documenting Struan secrets for years, that his father had done so before him—balance sheets, stockholdings and other secret, very very private personal family things, smugglings and payoffs—and he knew it would be no good saying I did it just for protection, to protect the House, because the tai-pan would rightly say, yes but it was to protect the House of Chen and not the Noble House, and he would rightly turn on him, turn his full wrath on him and his brood, and in the holocaust of a fight against Struan's he was bound to lose—Dirk Struan's will had provided for that—and everything that almost a century and a half had built up would vanish.

Thank all gods that everything was not in the safe, he thought fervently. Thank all gods the other things are buried deep.

Then, suddenly, some words from his son's first letter ripped to the forefront of his mind, '. . . Add to these photocopies *the other thing* I told you about . . .'

He paled and staggered to his feet. 'If you'll excuse me, tai-pan . . . I, er, I'll say good night. I'll just fetch Dianne and I . . . I'll . . . thank you, good night.' He hurried off toward the house.

Dunross stared after him, shocked.

'Oh, Casey,' Penelope was saying, 'may I introduce Kathren Gavallan—Kathren's Ian's sister.'

'Hi!' Casey smiled at her, liking her at once. They were in one of the antechambers on the ground floor among other ladies who were talking or fixing their makeup or standing in line, waiting their turn to visit the adjoining powder room. The room was large, comfortable and mirrored. 'You both have the same eyes—I'd recognize the resemblance anywhere,' she said. 'He's quite a man, isn't he?'

'We think so,' Kathren replied with a ready smile. She was thirty-eight, attractive, her Scots accent pleasing, her flowered silk dress long and cool. 'This water shortage's a bore, isn't it?'

'Yes. Must be very difficult with children.'

'No, *chérie*, the children, they just love it,' Susanne deVille called out. She was in her late forties, chic, her French accent slight. 'How can you insist they bathe every night?'

'My two are the same.' Kathren smiled. 'It bothers us parents, but it doesn't seem to bother them. It's a bore though, trying to run a house.'

Penelope said, 'God, I hate it! This summer's been ghastly. You're lucky tonight, usually we'd be dripping!' She was checking her makeup in the mirror. 'I can't wait till next month. Kathren, did I tell you we're going home for a couple of weeks' leave—at least I am. Ian's promised to come too but you never know with him.'

'He needs a holiday,' Kathren said and Casey noticed shadows in her eyes and care rings under her makeup. 'Are you going to Ayr?'

'Yes, and London for a week.'

'Lucky you. How long are you staying in Hong Kong, Casey?'

'I don't know. It all depends on what Par-Con does.'

'Yes. Andrew said you had a meeting all day with them.'

'I don't think they went much for having to talk business with a woman.'

'That is the understatement,' Susanne deVille said with a laugh, lifting her skirts to pull down her blouse. 'Of course my Jacques is half French, so he understands that women are in the business. But the English . . .' Her eyebrows soared.

'The tai-pan didn't seem to mind,' Casey said, 'but then I haven't had any real dealings with him yet.'

'But you have with Quillan Gornt,' Kathren said, and Casey, very much on guard even in the privacy of the ladies' room, heard the undercurrent in her voice.

'No,' she replied. 'I haven't—not before tonight—but my boss has.'

Just before dinner she had had time to tell Bartlett the story of Gornt's father and Colin Dunross.

'Jesus! No wonder Adryon went cross-eyed!' Bartlett had said. 'And in the billiard room too.' He had thought a moment then he had shrugged. 'But all that means is that this puts more pressure on Dunross.'

'Maybe. But their enmity goes deeper than anything I've experienced, Linc. It could easily backfire.'

'I don't see how—yet. Gornt was just opening up a flank like a good general should. If we hadn't had John Chen's advance information, what Gornt said could've been vital to us. Gornt's got no way of knowing we're ahead of him. So he's stepping up the tempo. We haven't even got our big guns out yet and they're both wooing us already.'

'Have you decided yet which one to go with?'

'No. What's your hunch?'

'I haven't got one. Yet. They're both formidable. Linc, do you think John Chen was kidnapped because he was feeding us information?'

'I don't know. Why?'

'Before Gornt arrived I was intercepted by Superintendent Armstrong. He questioned me about what John Chen had said last night, what we'd talked about, exactly what was said. I told him everything I could remember—except I never mentioned I was to take delivery of "it." Since I still don't know what "it" is.'

'It's nothing illegal, Casey.'

'I don't like not knowing. Not now. It's getting . . . I'm getting out of my depth, the guns, this brutal kidnapping and the police so insistent.'

'It's nothing illegal. Leave it at that. Did Armstrong say there was a connection?'

'He volunteered nothing. He's a strong, silent English gentleman police officer and as smart and well trained as anything I've seen in the movies. I'm sure he was sure I was hiding something.' She hesitated. 'Linc, what's John Chen got that's so important to us?'

She remembered how he had studied her, his eyes deep and blue and quizzical and laughing.

'A coin,' he had said calmly.

'What?' she had asked, astounded.

'Yes. Actually half a coin.'

'But Linc, what's a coi—'

'That's all I'm telling you now, Casey, but you tell me, does Armstrong figure there's some connection between Chen's kidnapping and the guns?'

'I don't know.' She had shrugged. 'I don't think so, Linc. I couldn't even give you odds. He's too cagey that one.' Again she had hesitated. 'Linc, have you made a deal, any deal with Gornt?'

'No. Nothing firm. Gornt just wants Struan out and wants to join with us to smash them. I said we'd discuss it Tuesday. Over dinner.'

'What're you going to tell the tai-pan after dinner?'

'Depends on his questions. He'll know it's good strategy to probe enemy defenses.'

Casey had begun to wonder who's the enemy, feeling very alien even here among all the other ladies. She had felt only hostility except from these two, Penelope and Kathren Gavallan—and a woman she had met earlier in the line for the toilet.

'Hello,' the woman had said softly. 'I hear you're a stranger here too.'

'Yes, yes I am,' Casey had said, awed by her beauty.

'I'm Fleur Marlowe. Peter Marlowe's my husband. He's a writer. I think you look super!'

'Thanks. So do you. Have you just arrived too?'

'No. We've been here for three months and two days but this is the first really English party we've been to,' Fleur said, her English not as clipped as the others. 'Most of the time we're with Chinese or by ourselves. We've a flat in the Old V and A annex. God,' she added, looking at the toilet door ahead, 'I wish she'd hurry up—my back teeth are floating.'

'We're staying at the V and A too.'

'Yes, I know. You two are rather famous.' Fleur Marlowe laughed.

'Infamous! I didn't know they had apartments there.'

'They're not, really. Just two tiny bedrooms and a sitting room. The kitchen's a cupboard. Still, it's home. We've got a bath, running water, and the loos flush.' Fleur Marlowe had big gray eyes that tilted pleasingly and long fair hair and Casey

275

thought she was about her age.

'Your husband's a journalist?'

'Author. Just one book. He mostly writes and directs films in Hollywood. That's what pays the rent.'

'Why're you with Chinese?'

'Oh, Peter's interested in them.' Fleur Marlowe had smiled and whispered conspiratorially, looking around at the rest of the women. 'They're rather overpowering, aren't they?—more English than the English. The old school tie and all that balls.'

Casey frowned. 'But you're English too.'

'Yes and no. I'm English but I come from Vancouver, B.C. We live in the States, Peter and I and the kids, in good old Hollywood, California. I really don't know what I am, half of one, half of the other.'

'We live in L.A. too, Linc and I.'

'I think he's smashing. You're lucky.'

'How old are your kids?'

'Four and eight—thank God we're not water rationed yet.'

'How do you like Hong Kong?'

'It's fascinating, Casey. Peter's researching a book here so it's marvelous for him. My God, if half the legends are true . . . the Struans and Dunrosses and all the others, and your Quillan Gornt.'

'He's not mine. I just met him this evening.'

'You created a minor earthquake by walking across the room with him.' Fleur laughed. 'If you're going to stay here, talk to Peter, he'll fill you in on all sorts of scandals.' She nodded at Dianne Chen who was powdering her nose at one of the mirrors. 'That's John Chen's stepmother, Phillip Chen's wife. She's wife number two—his first wife died. She's Eurasian and hated by almost everyone, but she's one of the kindest persons I've ever known.'

'Why's she hated?'

'They're jealous, most of them. After all, she's the wife of the compradore of the Noble House. We met her early on and she was terrific to me. It's . . . it's difficult living in Hong Kong for a woman, particularly an outsider. Don't really know why but she treated me like family. She's been grand.'

'She's Eurasian? She looks Chinese.'

'Sometimes it's hard to tell. Her maiden name's T'Chung, so

Peter says, her mother's Sung. The T'Chungs come from one of Dirk Struan's mistresses and the Sung line's equally illegitimate from the famous painter, Aristotle Quance. Have you heard of him?'

'Oh yes.'

'Lots of, er, our best Hong Kong families are, well, old Aristotle spawned four branches . . .'

At that moment the toilet door opened and a woman came out and Fleur said, 'Thank God!'

While Casey was waiting her turn she had listened to the conversations of the others with half an ear. It was always the same: clothes, the heat, the water shortages, complaints about *amahs* and other servants, how expensive everything was or the children or schools. Then it was her turn and afterward, when she came out, Fleur Marlowe had vanished and Penelope had come up to her. 'Oh I just heard about your not wanting to leave. Don't pay any attention to Joanna,' Penelope had said quietly. 'She's a pill and always has been.'

'It was my fault—I'm not used to your customs yet.'

'It's all very silly but in the long run it's much easier to let the men have their way. Personally I'm glad to leave. I must say I find most of their conversation boring.'

'Yes, it is, sometimes. But it's the principle. We should be treated as equals.'

'We'll never be equal, dear. Not here. This is the Crown Colony of Hong Kong.'

'That's what everyone tells me. How long are we expected to stay away?'

'Oh, half an hour or so. There's no set time. Have you known Quillan Gornt long?'

'Tonight was the first time I'd met him,' Casey said.

'He's—he's not welcome in this house,' Penelope said.

'Yes, I know. I was told about the Christmas party.'

'What were you told?'

She related what she knew.

There was a sharp silence. Then Penelope said, 'It's not good for strangers to be involved in family squabbles, is it?'

'No.' Casey added, 'But then all families squabble. We're here, Linc and I, to start a business—we're hoping to start a business with one of your big companies. We're outsiders here,

277

we know that—that's why we're looking for a partner.'

'Well, dear, I'm sure you'll make up your mind. Be patient and be cautious. Don't you agree, Kathren?' she asked her sister-in-law.

'Yes, Penelope. Yes I do.' Kathren looked at Casey with the same level gaze that Dunross had. 'I hope you choose correctly, Casey. Everyone here's pretty vengeful.'

'Why?'

'One reason's because we're such a closely knit society, very interrelated, and everyone knows everyone else—and almost all their secrets. Another's because hatreds here go back generations and have been nurtured for generations. When you hate you hate with all your heart. Another's because this is a piratical society with very few curbs so you can get away with all sorts of vengeances. Oh yes. Another's because here the stakes are high—if you make a pile of gold you can keep it legally even if it's made outside the law. Hong Kong's a place of transit—no one ever comes here to stay, even Chinese, just to make money and leave. It's the most different place on earth.'

'But the Struans and Dunrosses and Gornts have been here for generations,' Casey said.

'Yes, but individually they came here for one reason only: money. Money's our god here. And as soon as you have it, you vanish, European, American—and certainly the Chinese.'

'You exaggerate, Kathy dear,' Penelope said.

'Yes. It's still the truth. Another reason's that we live on the edge of catastrophe all the time: fire, flood, plague, landslide, riots. Half our population is Communist, half Nationalist, and they hate each other in a way no European can ever understand. And China—China can swallow us any moment. So you live for today and to hell with everything, grab what you can because tomorrow, who knows? Don't get in the way! People are rougher here because everything really is precarious, and nothing lasts in Hong Kong.'

'Except the Peak,' Penelope said. 'And the Chinese.'

'Even the Chinese want to get rich quickly to get out quickly—they more than most. You wait, Casey, you'll see. Hong Kong will work its magic on you—or evil, depending how you see it. For business it's the most exciting place on earth and soon you'll feel you're at the center of the earth. It's wild and exciting for a

278

man; my God, it's marvelous for a man but for us it's awful and every woman, every wife, hates Hong Kong with a passion, however much they pretend otherwise.'

'Come on, Kathren,' Penelope began, 'again you exaggerate.'

'No. No I don't. We're all threatened here, Penny, you know it! We women fight a losing battle . . .' Kathren stopped and forced a weary smile. 'Sorry, I was getting quite worked up. Penn, I think I'll find Andrew and if he wants to stay I'll slip off if you don't mind.'

'Are you feeling all right, Kathy?'

'Oh yes, just tired. The young one's a bit of a trial but next year he'll be off to boarding school.'

'How was your checkup?'

'Fine.' Kathy smiled wearily at Casey. 'When you've the inclination give me a call. I'm in the book. Don't choose Gornt. That'd be fatal. 'Bye, darling,' she added to Penelope and left.

'She's such a dear,' Penelope said. 'But she does work herself into a tizzy.'

'Do you feel threatened?'

'I'm very content with my children and my husband.'

'She asked whether you feel threatened, Penelope.' Susanne deVille deftly powdered her nose and studied her reflection. 'Do you?'

'No. I'm overwhelmed at times. But . . but I'm not threatened any more than you are.'

'Ah, *chérie*, but I am Parisienne, how can I be threatened? You've been to Paris, m'selle?'

'Yes,' Casey said. 'It's beautiful.'

'It is the world,' Susanne said with Gallic modesty. 'Ugh, I look at least thirty-six.'

'Nonsense, Susanne.' Penelope glanced at her watch. 'I think we can start going back now. Excuse me a second. . . .'

Susanne watched her go then turned her attention back to Casey. 'Jacques and I came out to Hong Kong in 1946.'

'You're family too?'

'Jacques's father married a Dunross in the First World War—an aunt of the tai-pan's.' She leaned forward to the mirror and touched a fleck of powder away. 'In Struan's it is important to be family.'

Casey saw the shrewd Gallic eyes watching her in the mirror.

'Of course, I agree with you that it is nonsense for the ladies to leave after dinner, for clearly, when we have gone, the heat she has left too, no?'

Casey smiled. 'I think so. Why did Kathren say "threatened"? Threatened by what?'

'By youth, of course, by youth! Here there are tens of thousands of chic, sensible, lovely young *Chinoise* with long black hair and pretty, saucy *derrières* and golden skins who really understand men and treat sex for what it is: food, and often, barter. It is the gauche English puritan who has twisted the minds of their ladies, poor creatures. Thank God I was born French! Poor Kathy!'

'Oh,' Casey said, understanding at once. 'She's found out that Andrew's having an affair?'

Susanne smiled and did not answer, just stared at her reflection. Then she said, 'My Jacques . . . of course he has affairs, of course all the men have affairs, and so do we if we're sensible. But we French, we understand that such transgressions should not interfere with a good marriage. We put correctly the amount of importance on to it, *non*?' Her dark brown eyes changed a little. '*Oui!*'

'That's tough, isn't it? Tough for a woman to live with?'

'Everything is tough for a woman, *chérie*, because men are such *crétins*.' Susanne deVille smoothed a crease away then touched perfume behind her ears and between her breasts. 'You will fail here if you try to play the game according to masculine rules and not according to *feminine* rules. You have a rare chance here, mademoiselle, if you are woman enough. And if you remember that the Gornts are all poisonous. Watch your Linc Bartlett, Ciranoush, already there are ladies here who would like to possess him, and humble you.'

14

Upstairs on the second floor the man came cautiously out of the shadows of the long balcony and slipped through the open French windows into the deeper darkness of Dunross's study. He hesitated, listening, his black clothes making him almost invisible. The distant sounds of the party drifted into the room making the silence and the waiting more heavy. He switched on a small flashlight.

The circle of light fell on the picture over the mantelpiece. He went closer. Dirk Struan seemed to be watching him, the slight smile taunting. Now the light moved to the edges of the frame. His hand reached out delicately and he tried it, first one side and then the other. Silently the picture moved away from the wall.

The man sighed.

He peered at the lock closely then took out a small bunch of skeleton keys. He selected one and tried it but it would not turn. Another. Another failure. Another and another, then there was a slight click and the key almost turned, almost but not quite. The rest of the keys failed too.

Irritably he tried the almost-key again but it would not work the lock.

Expertly his fingers traced the edges of the safe but he could find no secret catch or switch. Again he tried the almost-key, this way and that, gently or firmly, but it would not turn.

Again he hesitated. After a moment he pushed the painting carefully back into place, the eyes mocking him now, and went to the desk. There were two phones on it. He picked up the phone that he knew had no other extensions within the house and dialed.

The ringing tone went on monotonously, then stopped. 'Yes?' a man's voice said in English.

'Mr. Lop-sing please,' he said softly, beginning the code.

'There's no Lop-*ting* here. Sorry, you have a wrong number.'

The code response was what he wanted to hear. He continued, 'I want to leave a message.'

'Sorry, you have a wrong number. Look in your phone book.'

Again the correct response, the final one. 'This is Lim,' he whispered, using his cover name. 'Arthur please. Urgent.'

'Just a moment.'

He heard the phone being passed and the dry cough he recognized at once. 'Yes, Lim? Did you find the safe?'

'Yes,' he said. 'It's behind the painting over the fireplace but none of the keys fit. I'll need special equip—' He stopped suddenly. Voices were approaching. He hung up gently. A quick, nervous check that everything was in place and he switched off the flashlight and hurried for the balcony that ran the length of the north face. The moonlight illuminated him for an instant. It was Wine Waiter Feng. Then he vanished, his black waiter's clothes melding perfectly with the darkness.

The door opened. Dunross came in followed by Brian Kwok. He switched on the lights. At once the room became warm and friendly. 'We won't be disturbed here,' he said. 'Make yourself at home.'

'Thanks.' This was the first time Brian Kwok had been invited upstairs.

Both men were carrying brandy snifters and they went over to the cool of the windows, the slight breeze moving the gossamer curtains, and sat in the high-backed easy chairs facing one another. Brian Kwok was looking at the painting, its own light perfectly placed. 'Smashing portrait.'

'Yes.' Dunross glanced over and froze. The painting was imperceptibly out of place. No one else would have noticed it.

'Something's the matter, Ian?'

'No. No, nothing,' Dunross said, recovering his senses that had instinctively reached out, probing the room for an alien presence. Now he turned his full attention back to the Chinese superintendent, but he wondered deeply who had touched the painting and why. 'What's on your mind?'

'Two things. First, your freighter, *Eastern Cloud*.'

Dunross was startled. 'Oh?' This was one of Struan's many coastal tramps that plied the trade routes of Asia. *Eastern Cloud* was a ten thousand tonner on the highly lucrative Hong Kong, Bangkok, Singapore, Calcutta, Madras, Bombay route, with the occasional stop at Rangoon in Burma—all manner of Hong Kong manufactured goods outward bound, and all manner of Indian, Malayan, Thai and Burmese raw materials, silks, gems, teak, jute, foodstuffs, inbound. Six months ago she had been impounded by Indian authorities in Calcutta after a sudden customs search had discovered 36,000 taels of smugglers' gold in one of the bunkers. A little over one ton.

'The gold's one thing, your Excellency, that's nothing to do with us,' Dunross had said to the consul general of India in Hong Kong, 'but to impound our ship's something else!'

'Ah, very so sorry, Mr. Dunross sah. The law is the law and the smuggling of gold into India very serious indeed sah and the law says any ship with smuggled goods aboard may be impounded and sold.'

'Yes, *may* be. Perhaps, Excellency, in this instance you could prevail on the authorities . . .' But all of his entreaties had been shuttled aside and attempted high-level intercessions over the months, here, in India, even in London, had not helped. Indian and Hong Kong police inquiries had produced no evidence against any member of his crew but, even so, *Eastern Cloud* was still tied up in Calcutta harbor.

'What about *Eastern Cloud?*' he asked.

'We think we can persuade the Indian authorities to let her go.'

'In return for what?' Dunross asked suspiciously.

Brian Kwok laughed. 'Nothing. We don't know who the smugglers are, but we know who did the informing.'

'Who?'

'Seven odd months ago you changed your crewing policy. Up to that time Struan's had used exclusively Cantonese crew on their ships, then, for some reason you decided to employ Shanghainese. Right?'

'Yes.' Dunross remembered that Tsu-yan, also Shanghainese, had suggested it, saying that it would do Struan's a lot of good to extend help to some of their northern refugees. 'After all, tai-pan, they're just as good mariners,' Tsu-yan had said, 'and their wages are very competitive.'

'So Struan's signed on a Shanghainese crew into *Eastern Cloud*—this was the first I believe—and the Cantonese crew that wasn't hired lost all face so they complained to their triad Red Rod leader wh—'

'Come off it for God's sake, our crews aren't triads!'

'I've said many times the Chinese are great joiners, Ian. All right, let's call the triad with Red Rod rank their union representative—though I know you don't have unions either—but this bugger said in no uncertain terms, *oh ko* we really have lost face because of those northern louts, I'll fix the bastards, and he tipped an Indian informer here who, for a large part of the reward, agreed of course in advance, passed on the info to the Indian consulate.'

'What?'

Brian Kwok beamed. 'Yes. The reward was split twenty-eighty between the Indian and the Cantonese crew of the *Eastern Cloud* that should have been—Cantonese face was regained and the despised Shanghainese northern trash put into a stinking Indian pokey and their face lost instead.'

'Oh Christ!'

'Yes.'

'You have proof?'

'Oh yes! But let's just say that our Indian friend is helping us with future inquiries, in return for, er, services rendered, so we'd prefer not to name him. Your "union shop steward"? Ah, one of his names was Big Mouth Tuk and he was a stoker on *Eastern Cloud* for three odd years. *Was* because, alas, we won't see him again. We caught him in full 14K regalia last week—in very senior Red Rod regalia—courtesy of a friendly Shanghainese informer, the brother of one of your crew that languished in said stinky Indian pokey.'

'He's been deported?'

'Oh yes, quick as a wink. We really don't approve of triads. They are criminal gangs nowadays and into all sorts of vile occupations. He was off to Taiwan where I believe he won't be welcome at all—seeing as how the northern Shanghainese Green Pang triad society and the southern Cantonese 14K triad society are still fighting for control of Hong Kong. Big Mouth Tuk was a 426 all right—'

'What's a 426?'

'Oh, thought you might know. All officials of triads are known by numbers as well as symbolic titles—the numbers always divisible by the mystical number three. A leader's a 489, which also adds up to twenty-one, which adds up to three, and twenty-one's also a multiple of three, representing creation, times seven, death, signifying rebirth. A second rank's a White Fan, 438, a Red Rod's a 426. The lowest's a 49.'

'That's not divisible by three, for God's sake!'

'Yes. But four times nine is thirty-six, the number of the secret blood oaths.' Brian Kwok shrugged. 'You know how potty we Chinese are over numbers and numerology. He was a Red Rod, a 426, Ian. We caught him. So triads exist, or existed, on one of your ships at least. Didn't they?'

'So it seems.' Dunross was cursing himself for not prethinking that of course Shanghainese and Cantonese face would be involved so of course there'd be trouble. And now he knew he was in another trap. Now he had seven ships with Shanghainese crews against fifty-odd Cantonese.

'Christ, I can't fire the Shanghainese crews I've already hired and if I don't there'll be more of the same and loss of face on both sides. What's the solution to that one?' he asked.

'Assign certain routes exclusively to the Shanghainese, but only after consulting with their 426 Red Rod . . . sorry, with their shop stewards, and of course their Cantonese counterparts—*only* after consulting with a well-known soothsayer who suggested to you it would be fantastic joss to both sides to do this. How about Old Blind Tung?'

'Old Blind Tung?' Dunross laughed. 'Perfect! Brian you're a genius! One good turn deserves another. For your ears only?'

'All right.'

'Guaranteed?'

'Yes.'

'Buy Struan's first thing tomorrow morning.'

'How many shares?'

'As many as you can afford.'

'How long do I hold them?'

'How are your *cojones?*'

Brian whistled tonelessly. 'Thanks.' He thought a moment,

285

then forced his mind once more onto the matters in hand. 'Back to *Eastern Cloud*. Now we come to one of the interesting bits, Ian. 36,000 taels of gold is legally worth $1,514,520 U.S. But melted down into the smugglers' five-tael bars and secretly delivered on shore in Calcutta, that shipment'd be worth two, perhaps three times that amount to private buyers—say 4.5 million U.S., right?'

'I don't know exactly.'

'Oh, but I do. The lost profit's over 3 million—the lost investment about one and a half.'

'So?'

'So we all know Shanghainese are as secretive and cliquey as Cantonese, or Chu Chow or Fukenese or any other tiny groupings of Chinese. So of course the Shanghainese crew were the smugglers—have to be, Ian, though we can't prove it, yet. So you can bet your bottom dollar that Shanghainese also smuggled the gold out of Macao to Hong Kong and onto *Eastern Cloud*, that Shanghainese money bought the gold originally in Macao, and that therefore certainly part of that money was Green Pang funds.'

'That doesn't follow.'

'Have you heard from Tsu-yan yet?'

Dunross watched him. 'No. Have you?'

'Not yet but we're making inquiries.' Brian watched him back. 'My first point is that the Green Pang has been mauled and criminals loathe losing their hard-earned money, so Struan's can expect lots of trouble unless you nip the trouble in the bud as I've suggested.'

'Not all Green Pang are criminals.'

'That's a matter of opinion, Ian. Second point, for your ear only: We're sure Tsu-yan's in the gold-smuggling racket. My third and last point is that if a certain company doesn't want its ships impounded for smuggling gold, it could easily lessen the risk by reducing its gold imports into Macao.'

'Come again?' Dunross said, pleasantly surprised to hear that he had managed to keep his voice sounding calm, wondering how much Special Intelligence knew and how much they were guessing.

Brian Kwok sighed and continued to lay out the information that Roger Crosse had given him. 'Nelson Trading.'

With a great effort, Dunross kept his face impassive. 'Nelson Trading?'

'Yes. Nelson Trading Company Limited of London. As you know, Nelson Trading has the Hong Kong Government's exclusive license for the purchase of gold bullion on the international market for Hong Kong's jewelers, and, vastly more important, the equally exclusive monopoly for transshipment of gold bullion *in bond*, through Hong Kong to Macao—along with a minor second company, Saul Feinheimer Bullion Company, also of London. Nelson Trading and Feinheimer's have several things in common. Several directors for example, the same solicitors for example.'

'Oh?'

'Yes. I believe you're also on the board.'

'I'm on the board of almost seventy companies,' Dunross said.

'True and not all of those are wholly or even partially owned by Struan's. Of course, some could be wholly owned through nominees, secretly, couldn't they?'

'Yes, of course.'

'It's fortunate in Hong Kong we don't have to list directors—or holdings, isn't it?'

'What's your point, Brian?'

'Another coincidence: Nelson Trading's registered head offices in the city of London are in the same building as your British subsidiary, Struan London Limited.'

'That's a big building, Brian, one of the best locations in the city. There must be a hundred companies there.'

'Many thousands if you include all the companies registered with solicitors there—all the holding companies that hold other companies with nominee directors that hide all sorts of skeletons.'

'So?' Dunross was thinking quite clearly now, pondering where Brian had got all this information, wondering too where in the hell all this was leading. Nelson Trading had been a secret, wholly owned subsidiary through nominees ever since it was formed in 1953 specifically for the Macao gold trade—Macao being the only country in Asia where gold importation was legal.

'By the way, Ian, have you met that Portuguese genius from

287

Macao, Signore Lando Mata?'

'Yes. Yes I have. Charming man.'

'Yes he is—and so well connected. The rumor is that some fifteen years ago he persuaded the Macao authorities to create a monopoly for the importation of gold, then to sell the monopoly to him, and a couple of friends, for a modest yearly tax: about one U.S. dollar an ounce. He's the same fellow, Ian, who first got the Macao authorities to legalize gambling . . . and curiously, to grant him and a couple of friends the same monopoly. All very cosy, what?'

Dunross did not answer, just stared back at the smile and at the eyes that did not smile.

'So everything went smoothly for a few years,' Brian continued, 'then in '54 he was approached by some Hong Kong gold enthusiasts—our Hong Kong gold law was changed in '54—who offered a now legal improvement on the scheme: their company buys the gold bullion legally in the world bullion markets on behalf of this Macao syndicate at the legal $35 an ounce and brings it to Hong Kong openly by plane or by ship. On arrival, our own Hong Kong customs fellows legally guard and supervise the transshipment from Kai Tak or the dock to the Macao ferry or the Catalina flying boat. When the ferry or flying boat arrives in Macao it's met by Portuguese Customs officials and the bullion, all in regulation four-hundred-ounce bars, is transshipped under guard to cars, taxis actually, and taken to the bank. It's a grotty, ugly little building that does no ordinary banking, has no known customers—except the syndicate— never opens its doors—except for the gold—and doesn't like visitors at all. Guess who owns it? Mr. Mata and his syndicate. Once inside their bank the gold vanishes!' Brian Kwok beamed like a magician doing his greatest trick. 'Fifty-three tons this year so far. Forty-eight tons last year! Same the year before and the year before that and so on.'

'That's a lot of gold,' Dunross said helpfully.

'Yes it is. Very strangely the Macao authorities or the Hong Kong ones don't seem to care that what goes in never seems to come out. You with me still?'

'Yes.'

'Of course, what really happens is that once inside the bank the gold's melted down from the regulation four-hundred-ounce bars into little pieces, into two, or the more usual five-tael bars which are much more easily carried, and smuggled. Now we come to the only illegal part of the whole marvelous chain: getting the gold out of Macao and smuggling it into Hong Kong. Of course, it's not illegal to remove it from Macao, only to smuggle it into Hong Kong. But you know and I know that it's relatively easy to smuggle anything into Hong Kong. And the incredible beauty of it all is that once in Hong Kong, *however the gold gets there*—it's perfectly legal for *anyone* to own it and no questions asked. Unlike say in the States or Britain where no citizen is ever allowed to own any gold bullion privately. Once legally owned, it can be legally exported.'

'Where's all this leading to, Brian?' Dunross sipped his brandy.

Brian Kwok swilled the ancient, aromatic spirit in the huge glass and let the silence gather. At length he said, 'We'd like some help.'

'We? You mean Special Intelligence?' Dunross was startled.

'Yes.'

'Who in SI? You?'

Brian Kwok hesitated. 'Mr. Crosse himself.'

'What help?'

'He'd like to read all your Alan Medford Grant reports.'

'Come again?' Dunross said to give himself time to think, not expecting this at all.

Brian Kwok took out a photocopy of the first and last page of the intercepted report and offered it. 'A copy of this has just come into our possession.' Dunross glanced at the pages. Clearly they were genuine. 'We'd like a quick look at all the others.'

'I don't follow you.'

'I didn't bring the whole report, just for convenience, but if you want it you can have it tomorrow,' Brian said and his eyes didn't waver. 'We'd appreciate it—Mr. Crosse said he'd appreciate the help.'

The enormity of the implications of the request paralyzed Dunross for a moment.

'This report—and the others if they still exist—are private,' he heard himself say carefully. 'At least all the information in them is private to me personally, and to the Government. Surely you can get everything you want through your own intelligence channels.'

'Yes. Meanwhile, Superintendent Crosse'd really appreciate it, Ian, if you'd let us have a quick look.'

Dunross took a sip of his brandy, his mind in shock. He knew he could easily deny that the others existed and burn them or hide them or just leave them where they were, but he did not wish to avoid helping Special Intelligence. It was his duty to assist them. Special Intelligence was a vital part of Special Branch and the Colony's security and he was convinced that, without them, the Colony and their whole position in Asia would be untenable. And without a marvelous counterintelligence, if a twentieth of AMG's reports were true, all their days were numbered.

Christ Jesus, in the wrong hands . . .

His chest felt tight as he tried to reason out his dilemma. Part of that last report had leapt into his mind: about the traitor in the police. Then he remembered that Kiernan had told him that his back copies were the only ones in existence. How much was private to him and how much was known to British Intelligence? Why the secrecy? Why didn't Grant get permission? Christ, say I was wrong about some things being farfetched! In the wrong hands, in enemy hands, much of the information would be lethal.

With an effort he calmed his mind and concentrated. 'I'll consider what you said and talk to you tomorrow. First thing.'

'Sorry, Ian. I was told to in—to impress upon you the urgency.'

'Were you going to say *insist?*'

'Yes. Sorry. We wish to ask for your assistance. This is a formal request for your cooperation.'

'And *Eastern Cloud* and Nelson Trading are barter?'

'*Eastern Cloud*'s a gift. The information was also a gift. Nelson Trading is no concern of ours, except for passing interest. Everything said was confidential. To my knowledge, we have no records.'

Dunross studied his friend, the high cheekbones and wide, heavy-lidded eyes, straight and unblinking, the face good-looking and well proportioned with thick black eyebrows.

'Did you read this report, Brian?'

'Yes.'

'Then you'll understand my dilemma,' he said, testing him.

'Ah, you mean the bit about a police traitor?'

'What was that?'

'You're right to be cautious. Yes, very correct. You're referring to the bit about a hostile being possibly at superintendent level?'

'Yes. Do you know who he is?'

'No. Not yet.'

'Do you suspect anyone?'

'Yes. He's under surveillance now. There's no need to worry about that, Ian, the back copies'll just be seen by me and Mr. Crosse. They'll have top classification never mind.'

'Just a moment, Brian—I haven't said they exist,' Dunross told him, pretending irritation, and at once he noticed a flash in the eyes that could have been anger or could have been disappointment. The face had remained impassive. 'Put yourself in my position, a layman,' he said, his senses fine-honed, continuing the same line, 'I'd be pretty bloody foolish to keep such info around, wouldn't I? Much wiser to destroy it—once the pertinent bits have been acted on. Wouldn't I?'

'Yes.'

'Let's leave it at that for tonight. Until say ten in the morning.'

Brian Kwok hesitated. Then his face hardened. 'We're not playing parlor games, Ian. It's not for a few tons of gold, or some stock market shenanigans or a few gray area deals with the PRC however many millions're involved. This game's deadly and the millions involved are people and unborn generations and the Communist plague. Sevrin's bad news. The KGB's very bad news—and even our friends in the CIA and KMT can be equally vicious if need be. You'd better put a heavy guard on your files here tonight.'

Dunross stared at his friend impassively. 'Then your official position is that this report's accurate?'

'Crosse thinks it could be. Might be wise for us to have a man here just in case, don't you think?'

'Please yourself, Brian.'

'Should we put a man out at Shek-O?'

'Please yourself, Brian.'

'You're not being very cooperative, are you?'

'You're wrong, old chum. I'm taking your points very seriously,' Dunross said sharply. 'When did you get the copy and how?'

Brian Kwok hesitated. 'I don't know, and if I knew I don't know if I should tell you.'

Dunross got up. 'Come on then, let's go and find Crosse.'

'But why do the Gornts and the Rothwells hate the Struans and Dunrosses so much, Peter?' Casey asked. She and Bartlett were strolling the beautiful gardens in the cool of the evening with Peter Marlowe and his wife, Fleur.

'I don't know all the reasons yet,' the Englishman said. He was a tall man of thirty-nine with fair hair, a patrician accent and a strange intensity behind his blue-gray eyes. 'The rumor is that it goes back to the Brocks—that there's some connection, some family connection between the Gornt family and the Brock family. Perhaps to old Tyler Brock himself. You've heard of him?'

'Sure,' Bartlett said. 'How did it start, the feud?'

'When Dirk Struan was a boy he'd been an apprentice seaman on one of Tyler Brock's armed merchantmen. Life at sea was pretty brutal then, life anywhere really, but my God in those days at sea . . . Anyway, Tyler Brock flogged young Struan unmercifully for an imagined slight, then left him for dead somewhere on the China coast. Dirk Struan was fourteen then, and he swore before God and the Devil that when he was a man he'd smash the House of Brock and Sons and come after Tyler with a cat-o'-nine-tails. As far as I know he never did though there's a story he beat Tyler's eldest son to death with a Chinese fighting iron.'

'What's that?' Casey asked uneasily.

'It's like a mace, Casey, three or four short links of iron with a spiked ball on one end and a handle on the other.'

'He killed him for revenge on his father?' she said, shocked.

'That's another bit I don't know yet, but I'll bet he had a good reason.' Peter Marlowe smiled strangely. 'Dirk Struan, old Tyler and all the other men who made the British Empire, conquered India, opened up China. Christ, they were giants! Did I mention Tyler was one-eyed? One of his eyes was torn out by a whipping

292

halyard in a storm in the 1830s when he was racing his three-masted clipper, the *White Witch*, after Struan with a full cargo of opium aboard. Struan was a day ahead in his clipper, *China Cloud*, in the race from the British opium fields of India to the market of China. They say Tyler just poured brandy into the socket and cursed his sailors aloft to put on more canvas.' Peter Marlowe hesitated, then he continued, 'Dirk was killed in a typhoon in Happy Valley in 1841 and Tyler died penniless, bankrupt, in '63.'

'Why penniless, Peter?' Casey asked.

'The legend is that Tess, his eldest daughter—Hag Struan to be—had plotted her father's downfall for years—you know she married Culum, Dirk's only son? Well, Hag Struan secretly plotted with the Victoria Bank, which Tyler had started in the 1840s and with Cooper-Tillman, Tyler's partners in the States. They trapped him and brought down the great house of Brock and Sons in one gigantic crash. He lost everything—his shipping line, opium hulks, property, warehouses, stocks, everything. He was wiped out.'

'What happened to him?'

'I don't know, no one does for certain, but the story is that that same night, October thirty-first, 1863, old Tyler went to Aberdeen—that's a harbor on the other side of Hong Kong—with his grandson, Tom, who was then twenty-five, and six sailors, and they pirated an oceangoing lorcha—that's a ship with a Chinese hull but European rigged—and put out to sea. He was mad with rage, so they say, and he hauled up the Brock pennant to the masthead and he had pistols in his belt and a bloody cutlass in his hand—they'd killed four men to pirate the ship. At the neck of the harbor a cutter came after him and he blew it out of the water—in those days almost all boats were armed with cannon because of pirates—these seas have always been infested with pirates since time immemorial. So old Tyler put to sea, a good wind blowing from the east and a storm coming. At the mouth of Aberdeen he started bellowing out curses. He cursed Hag Struan and cursed the island, and cursed the Victoria Bank that had betrayed him, and the Coopers of Cooper-Tillman, but most of all he cursed the tai-pan who'd been dead more than twenty years. And old Tyler Brock swore revenge. They say he screamed out that he was going north to plunder and he was going to start again. He was going to build his House again and then, ''. . . and then I be back by God . . . I be back and I be venged and then I be Noble House by God. . . . I be back. . . .'''

Bartlett and Casey felt a chill go down their backs as Peter Marlowe coarsened his voice. Then he continued, 'Tyler went north and was never heard of again, no trace of him or the lorcha or his crew, ever. Even so, his presence is still here—like Dirk Struan's. You'd better remember, in any dealing with the Noble House you've got to deal with those two as well, or their ghosts. The night Ian Dunross took over as tai-pan, Struan's lost their freighter flagship, *Lasting Cloud*, in a typhoon. It was a gigantic financial disaster. She foundered off Formosa—Taiwan—and was lost with all hands except one seaman, a young English deckhand. He'd been on the bridge and he swore that they'd been lured onto the rocks by false lights and that he heard a maniac laughing as they went down.'

Casey shivered involuntarily.

Bartlett noticed it and slipped his arm casually through hers and she smiled at him.

He said, 'Peter, people here talk about people who've been dead a hundred years as though they're in the next room.'

'Old Chinese habit,' Peter Marlowe replied at once. 'Chinese believe the past controls the future and explains the present. Of course Hong Kong's only a hundred and twenty years old so a man of eighty today'd . . . Take Phillip Chen, the present compradore, for example. He's sixty-five now—his grandfather was the famous Sir Gordon Chen, Dirk Struan's illegitimate son who died in 1907 at the age of eighty-six. So Phillip Chen would have been nine then. A sharp boy of nine'd remember all sorts of stories his revered grandfather would have told him about *his* father, the tai-pan, and May-may, his famous mistress. The story is that old Sir Gordon Chen was one hell of a character, truly an ancestor. He had two official wives, eight concubines of various ages, and left the sprawling Chen family rich, powerful and into everything. Ask Dunross to show you his portraits— I've only seen copies but, my, he was a handsome man. There're dozens of people alive here today who knew him—one of the original great founders. And my God, Hag Struan died only forty-six years ago. Look over there. . . .' He nodded at a wizened little man, thin as a bamboo and just as strong, talking volubly to a young woman. 'That's Vincent McGore, tai-pan of the fifth great *hong*, International Asian Trading. He worked for Sir Gordon for years and then the Noble House.' He grinned suddenly. 'Legend says he was Hag Struan's lover when he was eighteen and just off the cattle boat from some Middle Eastern port—he's not really Scots at all.'

'Come off it, Peter,' Fleur said. 'You just made that up!'

'Do you mind,' he said, but his grin never left him. 'She was only seventy-five at the time.'

They all laughed.

'That's the truth?' Casey asked. 'For real?'

'Who knows what's truth and what's fiction, Casey? That's what I was told.'

'I don't believe it,' Fleur said confidently. 'Peter makes up stories.'

'Where'd you find out all this, Peter?' Bartlett asked.

'I read some of it. There are copies of newspapers that go back to 1870 in the Law Court library. Then there's the *History of the Law Courts of Hong Kong*. It's as seamy a great book as you'll ever want if you're interested in Hong Kong. Christ, the things they used to get up to, so-called judges and colonial secretaries, governors and policemen, and the tai-pans, the highborn and the lowborn. Graft, murder, corruption, adultery, piracy, bribery . . . it's all there!

'And I asked questions. There are dozens of old China hands who love to reminisce about the old days and who know a huge amount about Asia and Shanghai. Then there are lots of people who hate, or are jealous and can't wait to pour a little poison on a good reputation or a bad one. Of course, you sift, you try to sift the true from the false and that's very hard, if not impossible.'

For a moment Casey was lost in thought. Then she said, 'Peter, what was Changi like? Really like?'

His face did not change but his eyes did. 'Changi was genesis, the place of beginning again.' His tone made them all chilled and she saw Fleur slip her hand into his and in a moment he came back. 'I'm fine, darling,' he said. Silently, somewhat embarrassed, they walked out of the path onto the lower terrace, Casey knowing she had intruded. 'We should have a drink. Eh, Casey?' Peter Marlowe said kindly and made it all right again.

'Yes. Thank you, Peter.'

'Linc,' Peter Marlowe said, 'there's a marvelous strain of violence that passes from generation to generation in these buccaneers—because that's what they are. This is a very special place—it breeds very special people.' After a pause, he added thoughtfully, 'I understand you may be going into business here. If I were you I'd be very, very careful.'

15

11:05 P.M.:

Dunross, with Brian Kwok in tow, was heading for Roger Crosse, chief of Special Intelligence, who was on the terrace chatting amiably with Armstrong and the three Americans, Ed Langan, Commander John Mishauer the uniformed naval officer, and Stanley Rosemont, a tall man in his fifties. Dunross did not know that Langan was FBI, or that Mishauer was U.S. Naval Intelligence, only that they were at the consulate. But he did know that Rosemont was CIA though not his seniority. Ladies were still drifting back to their tables, or chattering away on the terraces and in the garden. Men were lounging over drinks, and the party was mellow like the night. Some couples were dancing in the ballroom to sweet and slow music. Adryon was among them, and he saw Penelope stoically coping with Havergill. He noticed Casey and Bartlett in deep conversation with Peter and Fleur Marlowe, and he would have dearly loved to be overhearing what was being said. That fellow Marlowe could easily become a bloody nuisance, he thought in passing. He knows too many secrets already and if he was to read our book . . . No way, he thought. Not till hell freezes! That's one book he'll never read. How Alastair could be so stupid!

Some years ago Alastair Struan had commissioned a well-known writer to write the history of Struan's to celebrate their 125 years of trading and had passed over old ledgers and trunks of old papers to him unread and unsifted. Within the year the writer had produced an inflammatory tapestry that documented many happenings and transactions that were thought to have been buried forever. In shock they had thanked the writer and paid him off with a handsome bonus and the book, the only two copies, put in the tai-pan's safe.

Dunross had considered destroying them. But then, he thought, life is life, joss is joss and provided only we read them, there's no harm.

'Hello, Roger,' he said, grimly amused. 'Can we join you?'

'Of course, tai-pan.' Crosse greeted him warmly, as did the others. 'Make yourself at home.'

The Americans smiled politely at the joke. They chatted for a moment about inconsequential things and Saturday's races and then Langan, Rosemont and Commander Mishauer, sensing that the others wanted to converse privately, politely excused themselves. When they were alone, Brian Kwok summarized exactly what Dunross had told him.

'We will certainly appreciate your help, Ian,' Crosse said, his pale eyes penetrating. 'Brian's right about it possibly being quite dicey—if of course AMG's other reports exist. Even if they don't, some nasties might want to investigate.'

'Just exactly how and when did you get the copy of my latest one?'

'Why?'

'Did you get it yourselves—or from a third party?'

'Why?'

Dunross's voice hardened. 'Because it's important.'

'Why?'

The tai-pan stared at him and the three men felt the power of his personality. But Crosse was equally willful.

'I can partially answer your question, Ian,' he said coolly. 'If I do, will you answer mine?'

'Yes.'

'We acquired a copy of your report this morning. An intelligence agent—I presume in England—tipped a friendly amateur here that a courier was en route to you with something that'd interest us. This Hong Kong contact asked us if we'd be interested in having a look at it—for a fee of course.' Crosse was so convincing that the other two policemen who remembered the real story were doubly impressed. 'This morning, the photocopy was delivered to my home by a Chinese I'd never met before. He was paid—of course you understand in these things you don't ask for a name. Now, why?'

'When this morning?'

298

'At 6:04 if you want an exact time. But why is this important to you?'

'Because Alan Medford Gr—'

'Oh, Father, sorry to interrupt,' Adryon said, rushing up breathlessly, a tall, good-looking young man in tow, his crumpled sacklike dinner jacket and twisted tie and scruffy brown-black shoes out of place in all this elegance. 'Sorry to interrupt but can I do something about the music?'

Dunross was looking at the young man. He knew Martin Haply and his reputation. The English-trained Canadian journalist was twenty-five, and had been in the Colony for two years and was now the scourge of the business community. His biting sarcasm and penetrating exposés of personalities and of business practices that were legitimate in Hong Kong but nowhere else in the Western world were a constant irritation.

'The music, Father,' Adryon repeated, running on, 'it's ghastly. Mother said I had to ask you. Can I tell them to play something different, please?'

'All right, but don't turn my party into a happening.'

She laughed and he turned his attention back to Martin Haply. 'Evening.'

'Evening, tai-pan,' the young man said with a confident, challenging grin. 'Adryon invited me. I hope it was all right to come after dinner?'

'Of course. Have fun,' Dunross said, and he added dryly, 'there are a lot of your friends here.'

Haply laughed. 'I missed dinner because I was on the scent of a dilly.'

'Oh?'

'Yes. Seems that certain interests in conjunction with a certain great bank have been spreading nasty rumors about a certain Chinese bank's solvency.'

'You mean the Ho-Pak?'

'It's all nonsense though. The rumors. Just more Hong Kong shenanigans.'

'Oh?' All day Dunross had heard rumors about Richard Kwang's Ho-Pak Bank being overextended. 'Are you sure?'

'Have a column on it in tomorrow's *Guardian*. Talking about the Ho-Pak though,' Martin Haply added breezily, 'did you hear that upwards of a hundred people took all their money out of the Aberdeen branch this afternoon? Could be the beginning of a run and—'

'Sorry, Father . . . come on Martin, can't you see Father's busy?' She leaned up and kissed Dunross lightly and his hand automatically went around her and hugged her.

'Have fun, darling.' He watched her rush off, Haply following. Cocky son of a bitch, Dunross thought absently, wanting tomorrow's column now, knowing Haply to be painstaking, unbribable and very good at his job. Could Richard be overextended?

'You were saying, Ian? Alan Medford Grant?' broke into his thoughts.

'Oh, sorry, yes.' Dunross sat back at the table, compartmentalizing those problems. 'AMG's dead,' he said quietly.

The three policemen gaped at him. 'What?'

'I got a cable at one minute to eight this evening, and talked to his assistant in London at 9:11.' Dunross watched them. 'I wanted to know your "when" because it's obvious there'd be plenty of time for your KGB spy—if he exists—to have called London and had poor old AMG murdered. Wouldn't there?'

'Yes.' Crosse's face was solemn. 'What time did he die?'

Dunross told him the whole of his conversation with Kiernan but he withheld the part about the call to Switzerland. Some intuition warned him not to tell. 'Now, the question is: was it accident, coincidence or murder?'

'I don't know,' Crosse said. 'But I don't believe in coincidences.'

'Nor do I.'

'Christ,' Armstrong said through his teeth, 'if AMG hadn't had clearance . . . Christ only knows what's in those reports, Christ and you, Ian. If you've got the only existing copies this makes them potentially more explosive than ever.'

'If they exist,' Dunross said.

'Do they?'

'I'll tell you tomorrow. At 10 o'clock.' Dunross got up. 'Will you excuse me, please,' he said politely with his easy charm. 'I must see to my other guests now. Oh, one last thing. What about *Eastern Cloud*?'

Roger Crosse said, 'She'll be released tomorrow.'

'One way or the other?'

Crosse appeared shocked. 'Good Lord, tai-pan, we weren't bartering! Brian, didn't you say we were just trying to help out?'

'Yes sir.'

'Friends should always help out friends, shouldn't they, tai-pan?'

'Yes. Absolutely. Thank you.'

They watched him walk away until he was lost.

'Do they or don't they?' Brian Kwok muttered.

'Exist? I'd say yes,' Armstrong said.

'Of course they exist,' Crosse said irritably. 'But where?' He thought a moment, then added more irritably and both men's hearts skipped a beat, 'Brian, while you were with Ian, Wine Waiter Feng told me none of his keys would fit.'

'Oh, that's bad, sir,' Brian Kwok said cautiously.

'Yes. The safe here won't be easy.'

Armstrong said, 'Perhaps we should look at Shek-O, sir, just in case.'

'Would you keep such documents there—if they exist?'

'I don't know, sir. Dunross's unpredictable. I'd say they were in his penthouse at Struan's, that'd be the safest place.'

'Have you been there?'

'No sir.'

'Brian?'

'No sir.'

'Neither have I.' Crosse shook his head. 'Bloody nuisance!'

Brian Kwok said thoughtfully, 'We'd only be able to send in a team at night, sir. There's a private lift to that floor but you need a special key. Also there's supposed to be another lift from the garage basement, nonstop.'

'There's been one hell of a slipup in London,' Crosse said. 'I can't understand why those bloody fools weren't on the job. Nor why AMG didn't ask for clearance.'

'Perhaps he didn't want insiders to know he was dealing with an outsider.'

'If there was one outsider, there could have been others.' Crosse sighed, and, lost in thought, lit a cigarette. Armstrong felt the smoke hunger pangs. He took a swallow of his brandy but that did not ease the ache.

'Did Langan pass on his copy, sir?'

'Yes, to Rosemont here and in the diplomatic bag to his FBI

301

HQ in Washington.'

'Christ,' Brian Kwok said sourly, 'then it'll be all over Hong Kong by morning.'

'Rosemont assured me it would not.' Crosse's smile was humorless. 'However, we'd better be prepared.'

'Perhaps Ian'd be more cooperative if he knew, sir.'

'No, much better to keep that to ourselves. He's up to something though.'

Armstrong said, 'What about getting Superintendent Foxwell to talk to him, sir, they're old friends?'

'If Brian couldn't persuade him, no one can.'

'The governor, sir?'

Crosse shook his head. 'No reason to involve him. Brian, you take care of Shek-O.'

'Find and open his safe, sir?'

'No. Just take a team out there and make sure no one else moves in. Robert, go to HQ, get on to London. Call Pensely at MI-5 and Sinders at MI-6. Find out exact times on AMG, everything you can, check the tai-pan's story. Check everything—perhaps other copies exist. Next, send back a team of three agents here to watch this place tonight, particularly to guard Dunross, without his knowledge of course. I'll meet the senior man at the junction of Peak Road and Culum's Way in an hour, that'll give you enough time. Send another team to watch Struan's building. Put one man in the garage—just in case. Leave me your car, Robert. I'll see you in my office in an hour and a half. Off you both go.'

The two men sought out their host and made their apologies and gave their thanks and went to Brian Kwok's car. Going down Peak Road in the old Porsche, Armstrong said what they both had been thinking ever since Dunross had told them. 'If Crosse's the spy he'd have had plenty of time to phone London, or to pass the word to Sevrin, the KGB or who the hell ever.'

'Yes.'

'We left his office at 6:10—that'd be 11:00 A.M. London time—so it couldn't've been us, not enough time.' Armstrong shifted to ease the ache in his back. 'Shit, I'd like a cigarette.'

'There's a packet in the glove compartment, old chum.'

'Tomorrow—I'll smoke tomorrow. Just like AA, like a bloody addict!' Armstrong laughed but there was no humor in it. He glanced across at his friend. 'Find out quietly who else's read the AMG file today—apart from Crosse—quick as you can.'

'My thought too.'

'If he's the only one who read it . . . well, it's another piece of evidence. It's not proof but we'd be getting there.' He stifled a nervous yawn, feeling very tired. 'If it's him we really are up shit's creek.'

Brian was driving very fast and very well. 'Did he say when he gave the copy to Langan?'

'Yes. At noon. They had lunch.'

'The leak could be from them, from the consulate—that place's like a sieve.'

'It's possible but my nose says no. Rosemont's all right, Brian—and Langan. They're professionals.'

'I don't trust them.'

'You don't trust anyone. They've both asked their HQs to check the Bartlett and Casey Moscow frankings.'

'Good. I think I'll send a telex to a friend in Ottawa. They might have something on file on them also. That Casey's a bird amongst birds, isn't she though? Was she wearing anything underneath that sheath?'

'Ten dollars to a penny you never find out.'

'Done.'

As they turned a corner, Armstrong looked at the city below and the harbor, the American cruiser lit all over tied up at the dockyard, Hong Kong side. 'In the old days we'd have had half a dozen warships here of our own,' he said sadly. 'Good old Royal Navy!' He had been in destroyers during the war, lieutenant R.N. Sunk twice, once at Dunkirk, the second time on D-Day plus three, off Cherbourg.

'Yes. Pity about the Navy, but, well, time marches on.'

'Not for the better, Brian. Pity the whole bloody Empire's up the spout! It was better when it wasn't. The whole bloody world was better off! Bloody war! Bloody Germans, bloody Japs . . .'

'Yes. Talking about Navy, how was Mishauer?'

'The U.S. Naval Intelligence fellow? He was okay,' Armstrong said wearily. 'He talked a lot of shop. He whispered to the Old Man that the U.S.'re going to double their Seventh Fleet. It's so supersecret he didn't even want to trust the phone. There's going to be a big land expansion in Vietnam.'

'Bloody fools—they'll get chewed up like the French. Don't they read the papers, let alone intelligence reports?'

'Mishauer whispered also their nuclear carrier's coming in the day after tomorrow for an eight-day R and R visit. Another top secret. He asked us to double up on security—and wet-nurse all Yankees ashore.'

'More bloody trouble.'

'Yes.' Armstrong added thinly, 'Particularly as the Old Man mentioned a Soviet freighter "limped in" for repairs on the evening tide.'

'Oh Christ!' Brian corrected an involuntary swerve.

'That's what I thought. Mishauer almost had a coronary and Rosemont swore for two minutes flat. The Old Man assured them of course none of the Russian seamen'll be allowed ashore without special permission, as usual, and we'll tail them all, as usual, but a couple'll manage to need a doctor or whatever, suddenly, and mayhaps escape the net.'

'Yes.' After a pause Brian Kwok said, 'I hope we get those AMG files, Robert. Sevrin is a knife in the guts of China.'

'Yes.'

They drove in silence a while.

'We're losing our war, aren't we?' Armstrong said.

'Yes.'

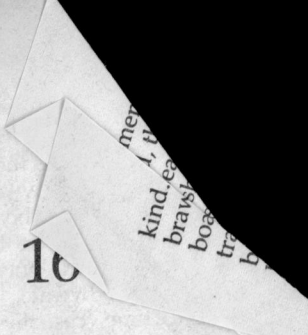

11:25 P.M.:

The Soviet freighter, *Sovetsky Ivanov*, was tied up alongside the vast Wampoa Dockyard that was built on reclaimed land on the eastern side of Kowloon. Floodlights washed her. She was a twenty-thousand tonner that plied the Asian trade routes out of Vladivostok, far to the north. Atop her bridge were many aerials and modern radar equipment. Russian seamen lounged at the foot of the fore and the aft gangways. Nearby, a uniformed policeman, a youthful Chinese, in neat regulation khaki drills, short pants, high socks, black belt and shoes, was at each gangway. A shore-going seaman had his pass checked by his shipmates and then by the constable, and then, as he walked toward the dockyard gates, two Chinese in civilian clothes came out of the shadows and began to dog his footsteps—openly.

Another seaman went down the aft gangway. He was checked through and then, soon, more silent Chinese plain-clothes police began to follow him.

Unnoticed, a rowing boat eased silently from the blind side of the ship's stern and ducked into the shadows of the wharf. It slid quietly along the high wall toward a flight of dank sea steps half a hundred yards away. There were two men in the boat and the rowlocks were muffled. At the foot of the sea steps the boat stopped. Both men began listening intently.

At the forward gangway a third seaman going ashore reeled raucously down the slippery steps. At the foot he was inter-cepted and his pass checked and an argument began. He was refused permission by the shore guard and he was clearly drunk, so, cursing loudly, he let fly at one of them, but this man sidestepped and gave him a haymaker which was returned in

...'s attention zeroed on the one-sided ...hickset man who sat in the aft of the rowing ...steps, across the floodlit wharf and railway ...ed into the alleyways of the dockyard without ...urely the rowing boat began to return the way it ...d in a moment, the brawl ceased. The helpless ...arried back aboard, not unkindly.

...the dockyard's byways, the tousled man sauntered ...om time to time, casually and expertly, he glanced ... to ensure he was not being followed. He wore dark ...als and neat rubber-soled shoes. His ship's papers ...umented him as Igor Voranski, seaman first class, Soviet ...erchant Marine.

He avoided the dock gates and the policeman who watched them and followed the wall for a hundred yards or so to a side door. The door opened onto an alley in the Tai-wan Shan resettlement area—a maze of corrugated iron, plywood and cardboard hovels. His pace quickened. Soon he was out of the area and into brightly lighted streets of shops and stalls and crowds that eventually led him to Chatham Road. There he hailed a taxi.

'Mong Kok, quick as you can,' he said in English. 'Yaumati Ferry.'

The driver stared at him insolently. 'Eh?'

'*Ayeeyah!*' Voranski replied at once and added in harsh, perfect Cantonese, 'Mong Kok! Are you deaf! Have you been sniffing the White Powder? Do you take me for a foreign devil tourist from the Golden Mountain—me who is clearly a Hong Kong person who has lived here twenty years? *Ayeeyah!* Yaumati Ferry on the other side of Kowloon. Do you need directions? Are you from Outer Mongolia? Are you a stranger, eh?'

The driver sullenly pulled the flag down and sped off, heading south and then west. The man in the back of the car watched the street behind. He could see no trailing car but he still did not relax.

They're too clever here, he thought. Be cautious!

At Yaumati Ferry station he paid off the taxi and gave the man barely the correct tip then went into the crowds and slid out of them and hailed another taxi. 'Golden Ferry.'

turns...
stiles he ...ed sleepily, ya...
men's room an... he paid o...
phone booth and w... ... ferries.
followed he was more re... gat...

He put in a coin and dialed. ... no...

'Yes?' a man's voice answered in ...

'Mr. Lop-sing please.'

'I don't know that name. There's no Mr. Lo... ... here. You have a wrong number.'

'I want to leave a message.'

'Sorry, you have a wrong number. Look in your phone book!'

Voranski relaxed, his heart slowing a little. 'I want to speak to Arthur,' he said, his English perfect.

'Sorry, he's not here yet.'

'He was told to be there, to wait my call,' he said curtly. 'Why is there a change?'

'Who is this please?'

'Brown,' he snapped, using his cover name.

He was somewhat mollified as he heard the other voice instantly take on just deference. 'Ah, Mr. Brown, welcome back to Hong Kong. Arthur's phoned to tell me to expect your call. He asked me to welcome you and to say everything's prepared for the meeting tomorrow.'

'When do you expect him?'

'Any moment, sir.'

Voranski cursed silently for he was obliged to report back to the ship by phone within the hour. He did not like divergences in any plan.

'Very well,' he said. 'Tell him to call me at 32.' This was the code name for their safe apartment in Sinclair Towers. 'Has the American arrived yet?'

'Yes.'

'Good. He was accompanied?'

'Yes.'

'Good. And?'

'Arthur told me nothing more.'

307

't her yet?'
…rthur?'
…don't know.'
'Has contact been made yet with eith…
'Sorry, I don't know. Arthur did…get to 32, if necessary?'
'And the tai-pan? What abo…want us to meet you there?'
'Everything's arranged.'…
'Good. How long wou…
'Ten to fifteen …
'I'll decide …t,' Arthur thought you might like a little com-
'Oh M…
pany …er such a voyage. Her name's Koh, Maureen Koh.'

'That was thoughtful of him—very thoughtful.'

'Her phone number's beside the phone at 32. Just ring and she'll arrive within half an hour. Arthur wanted to know if your superior was with you tonight—if he'd need companionship also.'

'No. He'll join us as planned tomorrow. But tomorrow evening he will expect hospitality. Good night.' Voranski hung up arrogantly, conscious of his KGB seniority. At that instant the booth door swung open and the Chinese barged in and another blocked the outside. 'What the—'

The words died as he did. The stiletto was long and thin. It came out easily. The Chinese let the body fall. He stared down at the inert heap for a moment then cleaned the knife on the corpse and slid it back into its sheath in his sleeve. He grinned at the heavyset Chinese who still blocked the glass windows in the upper part of the booth as though he was the next customer, then put a coin in and dialed.

On the third ring a polite voice said, 'Tsim Sha Tsui Police Station, good evening.'

The man smiled sardonically and said rudely in Shanghainese, 'You speak Shanghainese?'

A hesitation, a click, and now another voice in Shanghainese said, 'This is Sergeant Tang-po. What is it, caller?'

'A Soviet pig slipped through your mother-fornicating net tonight as easily as a bullock shits, but now he's joined his ancestors. Do we of the 14K have to do all your manure-infected work for you?'

16

The Soviet freighter, *Sovetsky Ivanov*, was tied up alongside in the vast Wampoa Dockyard that was built on reclaimed land on the eastern side of Kowloon. Floodlights washed her. She was a twenty-thousand tonner that plied the Asian trade routes out of Vladivostok, far to the north. Atop her bridge were many aerials and modern radar equipment. Russian seamen lounged at the foot of the fore and the aft gangways. Nearby, a uniformed policeman, a youthful Chinese, in neat regulation khaki drills, short pants, high socks, black belt and shoes, was at each gangway. A shore-going seaman had his pass checked by his shipmates and then by the constable, and then, as he walked toward the dockyard gates, two Chinese in civilian clothes came out of the shadows and began to dog his footsteps—openly.

Another seaman went down the aft gangway. He was checked through and then, soon, more silent Chinese plainclothes police began to follow him.

Unnoticed, a rowing boat eased silently from the blind side of the ship's stern and ducked into the shadows of the wharf. It slid quietly along the high wall toward a flight of dank sea steps half a hundred yards away. There were two men in the boat and the rowlocks were muffled. At the foot of the sea steps the boat stopped. Both men began listening intently.

At the forward gangway a third seaman going ashore reeled raucously down the slippery steps. At the foot he was intercepted and his pass checked and an argument began. He was refused permission by the shore guard and he was clearly drunk, so, cursing loudly, he let fly at one of them, but this man sidestepped and gave him a haymaker which was returned in

305

kind. Both policemen's attention zeroed on the one-sided brawl. The tousled, thickset man who sat in the aft of the rowing boat ran up the sea steps, across the floodlit wharf and railway tracks, and vanished into the alleyways of the dockyard without being seen. Leisurely the rowing boat began to return the way it had come, and in a moment, the brawl ceased. The helpless drunk was carried back aboard, not unkindly.

Deep in the dockyard's byways, the tousled man sauntered now. From time to time, casually and expertly, he glanced behind to ensure he was not being followed. He wore dark tropicals and neat rubber-soled shoes. His ship's papers documented him as Igor Voranski, seaman first class, Soviet Merchant Marine.

He avoided the dock gates and the policeman who watched them and followed the wall for a hundred yards or so to a side door. The door opened onto an alley in the Tai-wan Shan resettlement area—a maze of corrugated iron, plywood and cardboard hovels. His pace quickened. Soon he was out of the area and into brightly lighted streets of shops and stalls and crowds that eventually led him to Chatham Road. There he hailed a taxi.

'Mong Kok, quick as you can,' he said in English. 'Yaumati Ferry.'

The driver stared at him insolently. 'Eh?'

'*Ayeeyah!*' Voranski replied at once and added in harsh, perfect Cantonese, 'Mong Kok! Are you deaf! Have you been sniffing the White Powder? Do you take me for a foreign devil tourist from the Golden Mountain—me who is clearly a Hong Kong person who has lived here twenty years? *Ayeeyah!* Yaumati Ferry on the other side of Kowloon. Do you need directions? Are you from Outer Mongolia? Are you a stranger, eh?'

The driver sullenly pulled the flag down and sped off, heading south and then west. The man in the back of the car watched the street behind. He could see no trailing car but he still did not relax.

They're too clever here, he thought. Be cautious!

At Yaumati Ferry station he paid off the taxi and gave the man barely the correct tip then went into the crowds and slid out of them and hailed another taxi. 'Golden Ferry.'

The driver nodded sleepily, yawned and headed south.

At the ferry terminal he paid off the driver almost before he had stopped and joined the crowds that were hurrying for the turnstiles of the Hong Kong ferries. But once through the turnstiles he did not go to the ferry gate but instead went to the men's room and then, out once more, he opened the door of a phone booth and went in. Very sure now that he had not been followed he was more relaxed.

He put in a coin and dialed.

'Yes?' a man's voice answered in English.

'Mr. Lop-sing please.'

'I don't know that name. There's no Mr. Lop-*ting* here. You have a wrong number.'

'I want to leave a message.'

'Sorry, you have a wrong number. Look in your phone book!'

Voranski relaxed, his heart slowing a little. 'I want to speak to Arthur,' he said, his English perfect.

'Sorry, he's not here yet.'

'He was told to be there, to wait my call,' he said curtly. 'Why is there a change?'

'Who is this please?'

'Brown,' he snapped, using his cover name.

He was somewhat mollified as he heard the other voice instantly take on just deference. 'Ah, Mr. Brown, welcome back to Hong Kong. Arthur's phoned to tell me to expect your call. He asked me to welcome you and to say everything's prepared for the meeting tomorrow.'

'When do you expect him?'

'Any moment, sir.'

Voranski cursed silently for he was obliged to report back to the ship by phone within the hour. He did not like divergences in any plan.

'Very well,' he said. 'Tell him to call me at 32.' This was the code name for their safe apartment in Sinclair Towers. 'Has the American arrived yet?'

'Yes.'

'Good. He was accompanied?'

'Yes.'

'Good. And?'

'Arthur told me nothing more.'

307

'Have you met her yet?'

'No.'

'Has Arthur?'

'I don't know.'

'Has contact been made yet with either of them?'

'Sorry, I don't know. Arthur didn't tell me.'

'And the tai-pan? What about him?'

'Everything's arranged.'

'Good. How long would it take you to get to 32, if necessary?'

'Ten to fifteen minutes. Did you want us to meet you there?'

'I'll decide that later.'

'Oh Mr. Brown, Arthur thought you might like a little company after such a voyage. Her name's Koh, Maureen Koh.'

'That was thoughtful of him—very thoughtful.'

'Her phone number's beside the phone at 32. Just ring and she'll arrive within half an hour. Arthur wanted to know if your superior was with you tonight—if he'd need companionship also.'

'No. He'll join us as planned tomorrow. But tomorrow evening he will expect hospitality. Good night.' Voranski hung up arrogantly, conscious of his KGB seniority. At that instant the booth door swung open and the Chinese barged in and another blocked the outside. 'What the—'

The words died as he did. The stiletto was long and thin. It came out easily. The Chinese let the body fall. He stared down at the inert heap for a moment then cleaned the knife on the corpse and slid it back into its sheath in his sleeve. He grinned at the heavyset Chinese who still blocked the glass windows in the upper part of the booth as though he was the next customer, then put a coin in and dialed.

On the third ring a polite voice said, 'Tsim Sha Tsui Police Station, good evening.'

The man smiled sardonically and said rudely in Shanghainese, 'You speak Shanghainese?'

A hesitation, a click, and now another voice in Shanghainese said, 'This is Sergeant Tang-po. What is it, caller?'

'A Soviet pig slipped through your mother-fornicating net tonight as easily as a bullock shits, but now he's joined his ancestors. Do we of the 14K have to do all your manure-infected work for you?'

'What Sovie—'

'Hold your mouth and listen! His turtle-dung corpse's in a phone booth at Golden Ferry, Kowloonside. Just tell your mother-fornicating superiors to keep their eyes on enemies of China and not up their fornicating stink holes!'

At once he hung up and eased out of the box. He turned back momentarily and spat on the body, then shut the door and he and his companion joined the streams of passengers heading for the Hong Kong ferry.

They did not notice the man trailing them. He was a short, tubby American dressed like all the other tourists with the inevitable camera around his neck. Now he was leaning against the starboard gunnel melding into the crowd perfectly, pointing his camera this way and that as the ferry scuttled toward Hong Kong Island. But unlike other tourists his film was very special, so was his lens, and his camera.

'Hello, friend,' another tourist said with a beam, wandering up to him. 'You having yourself a time?'

'Sure,' the man said. 'Hong Kong's a great place, huh?'

'You can say that again.' He turned and looked at the view. 'Beats the hell outta Minneapolis.'

The first man turned also but kept his peripheral vision locked onto the two Chinese, then dropped his voice. 'We got problems.'

The other tourist blanched. 'Did we lose him? He didn't double back, Tom, I'm certain. I covered both exits. I thought you had him pegged in the booth.'

'You bet your ass he was pegged. Look back there, center row—the Chinese joker with the white shirt and the one next to him. Those two sons of bitches knocked him off.'

'Jesus!' Marty Povitz, one of the team of CIA agents assigned to cover the *Sovetsky Ivanov*, carefully looked at the two Chinese. 'Kuomintang? Nationalists? Or Commies?'

'Shit, I don't know. But the stiff's still in a phone booth back there. Where's Rosemont?'

'He's g—' Povitz stopped then raised his voice and became affable and tourist again as passengers began to crowd nearer the exit. 'Lookit there,' he said, pointing to the crest of the Peak. The apartment buildings were tall and well lit and so were the houses that dotted the slopes, one particularly, one very high, the highest private mansion in Hong Kong. It was floodlit and sparkled like a jewel. 'Say, whoever lives there's just about on top of the world, huh?'

Tom Connochie, the senior of the two, sighed. 'Gotta be a tai-pan's house.' Thoughtfully he lit a cigarette and let the match spiral into the black waters. Then, openly chatting tourist-style, he took a shot of the house and casually finished the roll of film, taking several more of the two Chinese. He reloaded his camera and, unobserved, passed the roll of exposed film to his partner. Hardly using his lips, he said, 'Call Rosemont up there, soon as we dock—tell him we got problems—then go get these processed tonight. I'll phone you when these two've bedded down.'

'You crazy?' Povitz said. 'You're not tailing them alone.'

'Have to, Marty, the film might be important. We're not risking that.'

'No.'

'Goddamnit, Marty, I'm tai-pan of this operation.'

'Orders say two g—'

'Screw orders!' Connochie hissed. 'Just call Rosemont and don't foul up the film.' Then he raised his voice and said breezily, 'Great night for a sail, huh?'

'Sure.'

He nodded at the sparkle of light on the crest of the Peak, then focused on it through his super-powered telescopic lens viewfinder. 'You live up there, you got it made, huh?'

Dunross and Bartlett were facing each other in the Long Gallery at the head of the staircase. Alone.

'Have you made a deal with Gornt?' Dunross asked.

'No,' Bartlett said. 'Not yet.' He was as crisp and tough as Dunross and his dinner jacket fitted as elegantly.

'Neither you nor Casey?' Dunross asked.

'No.'

'But you have examined possibilities?'

'We're in business to make money, Ian—as are you!'

'Yes. But there're ethics involved.'

'Hong Kong ethics?'

'May I ask how long you have been dealing with Gornt?'

'About six months. Are you agreeing to our proposal today?'

Dunross tried to put away his tiredness. He had not wanted to seek out Bartlett tonight but it had been necessary. He felt the eyes from all the portraits on the walls watching him. 'You said Tuesday. I'll tell you Tuesday.'

'Then until then, if I want to deal with Gornt or anyone else, that's my right. If you accept our offer now, it's a deal. I'm told you're the best, the Noble House, so I'd rather deal with you than him—provided I get top dollar with all the necessary safeguards. I'm cash heavy, you're not. You're Asian heavy, I'm not. So we should deal.'

Yes, Bartlett told himself, covering his foreboding, though delighted that his diversion this morning with Gornt had produced the confrontation so quickly and brought his opponent to bay—at the moment, Ian, you're just that, an opponent, until we finalize, if we finalize.

Is now the time to blitzkrieg?

He had been studying Dunross all evening, fascinated by him and the undercurrents and everything about Hong Kong—so totally alien to anything he had ever experienced before. New jungle, new rules, new dangers. Sure, he thought grimly, with both Dunross and Gornt as dangerous as a swamp full of rattlers and no yardstick to judge them by. I've got to be cautious like never before.

He felt his tension strongly, conscious of the eyes that watched from the walls. How far dare I push you, Ian? How far do I gamble? The profit potential's huge, the prize huge, but one mistake and you'll eat us up, Casey and me. You're a man after my own heart but even so still an opponent and governed by ghosts. Oh yes, I think Peter Marlowe was right in that, though not in everything.

Jesus! Ghosts and the extent of the hatreds! Dunross, Gornt, Penelope, young Struan, Adryon . . . Adryon so brave after her initial fright.

He looked back at the cold blue eyes watching him. What would I do now, Ian, if I were you, you with your wild-ass heritage standing there so outwardly confident?

I don't know. But I know me and I know what Sun Tzu said about battlefields: only bring your opponent to battle at a time and a place of your own choosing. Well it's chosen and it's here and now.

311

'Tell me, Ian, before we decide, how are you going to pay off your three September notes to Toda Shipping?'

Dunross was shocked. 'I beg your pardon?'

'You haven't got a charterer yet and your bank won't pay without one, so it's up to you, isn't it?'

'The bank . . . there's no problem.'

'But I understand you've already overextended your line of credit 20 percent. Doesn't that mean you'll have to find a new line of credit?'

'I'll have one if I need it,' Dunross said, his voice edgy, and Bartlett knew he had gotten under his guard.

'12 million to Toda's a lot of cash when you add it to your other indebtedness.'

'What other indebtedness?'

'The installment of $6,800,000 U.S. due September 8 on your Orlin International Banking loan of 30 million unsecured; you've 4.2 million in consolidated corporate losses so far this year against a written-up paper profit of seven and a half last year; and 12 million from the loss of *Eastern Cloud* and all those contraband engines.'

The color was out of Dunross's face. 'You seem to be particularly well informed.'

'I am. Sun Tzu said that you've got to be well informed about your allies.'

The small vein in Dunross's forehead was pulsating. 'You mean enemies.'

'Allies sometimes become enemies, Ian.'

'Yes. Sun Tzu also hammered about spies. Your spy can only be one of seven men.'

Bartlett replied as harshly, 'Why should I have a spy? That information's available from banks—all you've got to do is dig a little. Toda's bank's the Yokohama National of Japan—and they're tied in with Orlin in a lot of deals—so're we, Stateside.'

'Whoever your spy is, he's wrong. Orlin will extend. They always have.'

'Don't bet on it this time. I know those bastards and if they smell a killing, they'll have your ass so fast you'll never know what happened.'

'A killing of Struan's?' Dunross laughed sardonically.

312

'There's no way Orlin or any god-cursed bank could—or would want us wrecked.'

'Maybe Gornt's got a deal cooking with them.'

'Christ Jesus. . . .' Dunross held on to his temper with an effort. 'Has he or hasn't he?'

'Ask him.'

'I will. Meanwhile if you know anything, tell me now!'

'You've got enemies every which way.'

'So have you.'

'Yes. Does that make us good or bad partners?' Bartlett stared back at Dunross. Then his eyes fell on a portrait at the far end of the gallery. Ian Dunross was staring down at him from the wall, the likeness marvelous; part of a three-masted clipper in the background.

'Is that . . . Jesus, that's gotta be Dirk, Dirk Struan!'

Dunross turned and looked at the painting. 'Yes.'

Bartlett walked over and studied it. Now that he looked closer he could see that the sea captain was not Dunross, but even so, there was a curious similarity. 'Jacques was right,' he said.

'No.'

'He's right.' He turned and studied Dunross as though the man was a picture, comparing them back and forth. At length he said, 'It's the eyes and the line of the jaw. And the taunting look in the eyes which says, "You'd better believe I can kick the shit out of you anytime I want to."'

The mouth smiled at him. 'Does it now?'

'Yes.'

'There's no problem on a line of credit, new or old.'

'I think there is.'

'The Victoria's our bank—we're big stockholders.'

'How big?'

'We've alternative sources of credit if need be. But we'll get everything we want from the Vic. They're cash heavy too.'

'Your Richard Kwang doesn't think so.'

Dunross looked back from the portrait sharply. 'Why?'

'He didn't say, Ian. He didn't say anything, but Casey knows bankers and she read the bottom line and that's what she thinks he thinks. I don't think she's much taken by Havergill either.'

After a pause, Dunross said, 'What else does she think?'

'That maybe we should go with Gornt.'

'Be my guest.'

'I may. What about Taipei?' Bartlett asked, wanting to keep Dunross off balance.

'What about it?'

'I'm still invited?'

'Yes, yes of course. That reminds me, you're released into my custody by kind permission of the assistant commissioner of police. Armstrong will be so informed tomorrow. You'll have to sign a piece of paper that you guarantee you'll return when I do.'

'Thanks for arranging it. Casey is still not invited?'

'I thought we settled that this morning.'

'Just asking. What about my airplane?'

Dunross frowned, off balance. 'I suppose it's still impounded. Did you want to use it for the Taipei trip?'

'It'd be convenient, wouldn't it, then we could leave to suit ourselves.'

'I'll see what I can do.' Dunross watched him. 'And your offer's firm until Tuesday?'

'Firm, just as Casey said. Until close of business Tuesday.'

'Midnight Tuesday,' Dunross countered.

'Do you always barter whatever the hell someone says?'

'Don't you?'

'Okay, midnight Tuesday. Then one minute into Wednesday all debts and friendships are canceled.' Bartlett needed to keep the pressure on Dunross, needed the counteroffer now and not Tuesday so he could use it with or against Gornt. 'The guy from Blacs, the chairman, what was his name?'

'Compton Southerby.'

'Yes, Southerby. I was talking to him after dinner. He said they were all the way in back of Gornt. He implied Gornt also has a lot of Eurodollars on call if he ever needed them.' Again Bartlett saw the piece of information slam home. 'So I still don't know how you're going to pay Toda Shipping,' he said.

Dunross didn't answer at once. He was still trying to find a way out of the maze. Each time he came back to the beginning: the spy must be Gavallan, deVille, Linbar Struan, Phillip Chen, Alastair Struan, David MacStruan, or his father, Colin Dunross. Some of Bartlett's information the banks would know—but not their corporate losses this year. That figure had been too accu-

314

rate. That was the shocker. And the '. . . written-up paper profit.'

He was looking at the American, wondering how much more inside knowledge the man had, feeling the trap closing on him with no way to maneuver, yet knowing he could not concede too much or he would lose everything.

What to do?

He glanced at Dirk Struan on the wall and saw the twisted half-smile and the look that said to him, Gamble laddie, where are thy balls?

Very well.

'Don't worry about Struan's. If you decide to join us, I want a two-year deal—20 million next year too,' he said, going for broke. 'I'd like 7 on signing the contract.'

Bartlett kept the joy off his face. 'Okay on the two-year deal. As to the cash flow, Casey offered 2 million down and then one and a half per month on the first of each month. Gavallan said that would be acceptable.'

'It's not. I'd like 7 down, the rest spread monthly.'

'If I agree to that I want title to your new Toda ships as a guarantee this year.'

'What the hell do you want guarantees for?' Dunross snapped. 'The whole point of the deal is that we'd be partners, partners in an immense expansion into Asia.'

'Yes. But our 7 million cash covers your September payments to Toda Shipping, takes you off the Orlin hook and we get nothing in return.'

'Why should I give you any concession? I can discount your contract immediately and get an advance of 18 of the 20 million you provide with no trouble at all.'

Yes, you can, Bartlett thought—once the contract's signed. But before that you've got nothing. 'I'll agree to change the down payment, Ian. But in return for what?' Casually he glanced at a painting opposite him, but he did not see it for all of his senses were concentrating on Dunross, knowing they were getting down to the short strokes. Title to the huge Toda bulk-cargo ships would cover all of Par-Con's risk whatever Dunross did.

'Don't forget,' he added, 'your 21 percent of the Victoria Bank stock is already in hock, signed over as collateral against your

315

indebtedness to them. If you fail on the Toda payment or the Orlin, your old pal Havergill'll jerk the floor out. I would.'

Dunross knew he was beaten. If Bartlett knew the exact amount of their secret bank holdings, Chen's secret holdings, together with their open holdings, there was no telling what other power the American had over him. 'All right,' he said. 'I'll give you title to my ships for three months, provided first, you guarantee to keep it secret between the two of us; second, that our contracts are signed within seven days from today; third, that you agree to the cash flow I've suggested. Last, you guarantee not to leak one word of this until I make the announcement.'

'When do you want to do that?'

'Sometime between Friday and Monday.'

'I'd want to know in advance,' Bartlett said.

'Of course. Twenty-four hours.'

'I want title to the ships for six months, contracts within ten days.'

'No.'

'Then no deal,' Bartlett said.

'Very well,' Dunross said immediately. 'Then let's return to the party.' He turned at once and calmly headed for the stairs.

Bartlett was startled with the abrupt ending of the negotiations. 'Wait,' he said, his heart skipping a beat.

Dunross stopped at the balustrade and faced him, one hand casually on the banister.

Grimly Bartlett tried to gauge Dunross, his stomach twisting uneasily. He read finality in the eyes. 'All right, title till January first, that's four months-odd, secret to you, me and Casey, contracts next Tuesday—that gives me time to get my tax people here—the cash flow as you laid it out subject to . . . when's our meeting tomorrow?'

'It was at ten. Can we make it eleven?'

'Sure. Then it's a deal, subject to confirmation tomorrow at eleven.'

'No. You've no need for more time. I might have but you haven't.' Again the thin smile. 'Yes or no?'

Bartlett hesitated, all his instincts saying close now, stick out your hand and close, you've everything you wanted. Yes—but what about Casey? 'This's Casey's deal. She can commit up to

20 million. You mind shaking with her?'

'A tai-pan deals with a tai-pan on a closing, it's an old Chinese custom. Is she tai-pan of Par-Con?'

'No,' Bartlett said evenly. 'I am.'

'Good.' Dunross came back and put out his hand, calling him, playing with him, reading his mind. 'Then it's a deal?'

Bartlett looked at the hand then into the cold blue eyes, his heart pounding heavily. 'It's a deal—but I want her to close it with you.'

Dunross let his hand fall. 'I repeat, who's tai-pan of Par-Con?'

Bartlett looked back levelly. 'A promise is a promise, Ian. It's important to her, and I promised she had the ball up to 20 million.'

He saw Dunross begin to turn away, so he said firmly, 'Ian, if I have to choose between the deal and Casey, my promise to Casey, then that's no contest. None. I'd consider it a fav—' He stopped. Both their heads jerked around as there was a slight, involuntary noise from an eavesdropper in the shadows at the far end of the gallery where there was a group of high-backed settees and tall winged chairs. Instantly, Dunross spun on his heel and, catlike, hurtled silently to the attack. Bartlett's reactions were almost as fast. He, too, went quickly in support.

Dunross stopped at the green velvet settee. He sighed. It was no eavesdropper but his thirteen-year-old daughter, Glenna, fast asleep, curled up, all legs and arms like a young filly, angelic in her crumpled party dress, his wife's thin rope of pearls around her neck.

Bartlett's heart slowed and he whispered, 'Jesus, for a moment . . . Hey, she's as cute as a button!'

'Do you have any children?'

'Boy and two girls. Brett's sixteen, Jenny's fourteen and Mary is thirteen. Unfortunately I don't see them very often.' Bartlett, gaining his breath again, continued quietly, 'They're on the East Coast now. Afraid I'm not very popular. Their mother . . . we, we were divorced seven years ago. She's remarried now but . . .' Bartlett shrugged, then looked down at the child. 'She's a doll! You're lucky.'

Dunross leaned over and gently picked up his child. She hardly stirred, just nestled closer to him, contentedly. He looked at the American thoughtfully. Then he said, 'Bring

317

Casey back here in ten minutes. I'll do what you ask—as much as I disapprove of it—because you wish to honor your promise.' He walked away, surefooted, and disappeared into the east wing where Glenna's bedroom was.

After a pause, Bartlett glanced up at the portrait of Dirk Struan. The smile mocked him. 'Go screw yourself,' he muttered, feeling that Dunross had outsmarted him somehow. Then he grinned. 'Eh, what the hell! Your boy's doing all right, Dirk old buddy!'

He went for the stairs. Then he noticed an unlit portrait in a half-hidden alcove. He stopped. The oil painting was of an old gray-bearded sea captain with one eye, hook-nosed and arrogant, his face scarred, a cutlass on the table beside him.

Bartlett gasped as he saw that the canvas was slashed and counterslashed, with a short knife buried in the man's heart, impaling the painting to the wall.

Casey was staring at the knife. She tried to hide her shock. She was alone in the gallery, waiting uneasily. Dance music wafted up from below—rhythm and blues music. A short wind tugged the curtains and moved a strand of her hair. A mosquito droned.

'That's Tyler Brock.'

Casey spun around, startled. Dunross was watching her. 'Oh, I didn't hear you come back,' she said.

'Sorry,' he said. 'I didn't mean to make you jump.'

'Oh, that's all right.'

She looked back at the painting. 'Peter Marlowe was telling us about him.'

'He knows a lot about Hong Kong, but not everything, and not all his information's accurate. Some of it's quite wrong.'

After a moment she said, 'It's . . . it's a bit melodramatic, isn't it, leaving the knife like that?'

'Hag Struan did it. She ordered it left that way.'

'Why?'

'It pleased her. She was tai-pan.'

'Seriously, why?'

'I was serious.' Dunross shrugged. 'She hated her father and wanted us all to be reminded about our heritage.'

Casey frowned, then motioned at a portrait on the opposite wall. 'That's her?'

'Yes. It was done just after she was married.' The girl in the painting was slim, about seventeen, pale blue eyes, fair hair. She wore a low-cut ball gown—tiny waist, budding bosom—an ornate green necklace encircling her throat.

They stood there looking at the picture for a moment. There was no name on the little brass plaque on the bottom of the ornate gilt frame, just the years, 1825–1917. Casey said, 'It's an ordinary face, pretty but ordinary, except for the lips. They're thin and tight and disapproving—and tough. The artist captured a lot of strength there. It's a Quance?'

'No. We don't know who painted it. It was supposed to be her favorite portrait. There's a Quance of her in the Struan penthouse, painted about the same time. It's quite different, yet very much the same.'

'Did she ever have a portrait done in later life?'

'Three. She destroyed them all, the moment they were finished.'

'Are there any photos of her?'

'Not to my knowledge. She hated cameras—wouldn't have one in the house.' Dunross laughed and she saw the tiredness in him. 'Once a reporter for the *China Guardian* took her picture, just before the Great War. Within an hour she sent an armed crew from one of our merchantmen into their offices with orders to burn the place if she didn't get the negative and all copies back, and if the editor didn't promise to "cease and desist from harassing her." He promised.'

'Surely you can't do that and get away with it?'

'No, you can't—unless you're tai-pan of the Noble House. Besides, everyone knew that Hag Struan didn't want her picture taken and this cocky young bastard had broken the rule. She was like the Chinese. She believed every time your picture's taken you lose part of your soul.'

Casey peered at the necklace. 'Is that jade?' she asked.

'Emeralds.'

She gasped. 'That must have been worth a fortune.'

'Dirk Struan willed the necklace to her—it was never to leave Asia—it was to belong to the wife of each tai-pan of the Noble House, an heirloom to be passed on from lady to lady.' He

319

smiled oddly. 'Hag Struan kept the necklace all her life, and, when she died, she ordered it burned with her.'

'Jesus! Was it?'

'Yes.'

'What a waste!'

Dunross looked back at the portrait. 'No,' he said, his voice different. 'She kept Struan's the Noble House of Asia for almost seventy-five years. She was *the* tai-pan, the real tai-pan, though others had the title. Hag Struan fought off enemies and catastrophes and kept faith with Dirk's legacy and smashed the Brocks and did whatever was necessary. So what's a pretty bauble that probably cost nothing in the first place? It was probably pirated from the treasury of some Mandarin who stole it from someone else, whose peasants paid for it with sweat.'

Casey watched him staring at the face, almost past it into another dimension. 'I only hope I can do as well,' he muttered absently, and it seemed to Casey he was saying it to *her*, to the girl in the picture.

Her eyes strayed beyond Dunross to the portrait of Dirk Struan and she saw again the marvelous likeness. There was a strong family resemblance in all the ten large portraits—nine men and the girl—that hung on the walls amid landscapes of all sizes of Hong Kong and Shanghai and Tiensin and many seascapes of the elegant Struan clipper ships and some of their merchantmen. Below the portrait of each tai-pan was a small brass plaque with his name and the years of his life: 'Dirk Dunross, 4th Tai-pan 1852–1894, lost at sea in the India Ocean with all hands in *Sunset Cloud*' . . . 'Sir Lochlin Struan, 3rd Tai-pan, 1841–1915' . . . 'Alastair Struan, 9th Tai-pan, 1900–' . . . 'Dirk Struan, 1798–1841' . . . 'Ross Lechie Struan, 7th Tai-pan, 1887–1915, Captain Royal Scots Regiment, killed in action at Ypres' . . .

'So much history,' she said, judging it time to break his thought pattern.

'Yes. Yes it is,' he said, looking at her now.

'You're the 10th tai-pan?'

'Yes.'

'Have you had your portrait done yet?'

'No.'

'You'll have to, won't you?'

'Yes, yes in due course. There's no hurry.'

'How do you become tai-pan, Ian?'

'You have to be chosen by the previous one. It's his decision.'

'Have you chosen who'll follow you?'

'No,' he said, but Casey thought that he had. Why should he tell me, she asked herself. And why are you asking him so many questions?

She looked away from him. A small portrait caught her attention. 'Who's that?' she asked, disquieted. The man was misshapen, a hunchbacked dwarf, his eyes curious and his smile sardonic. 'Was he a tai-pan too?'

'No. That's Stride Orlov, he was Dirk's chief captain. After *the tai-pan* was killed in the great typhoon and Culum took over, Stride Orlov became master of our clipper fleet. Legend has it he was a great seaman.'

After a pause she said, 'Sorry but there's something about him that gives me the creeps.' There were pistols in Orlov's belt and a clipper ship in the background. 'It's a frightening face,' she said.

'He had that effect on everyone—except *the tai-pan* and Hag Struan—even Culum was supposed to have hated him.' Dunross turned and studied her and she felt his probing. It made her feel warm and at the same time unsettled.

'Why did *she* like him?' she asked.

'The story is that right after the great typhoon when everyone in Hong Kong was picking up the pieces, Culum included, Devil Tyler started to take over the Noble House. He gave orders, assumed control, treated Culum and Tess like children . . . he sent Tess aboard his ship, the *White Witch*, and told Culum to be aboard by sunset or else. As far as Tyler was concerned the Noble House was now Brock-Struan and he was *the* tai-pan! Somehow or other—no one knows why or how Culum got the courage—my God, Culum was only twenty then and Tess barely sixteen—but Culum ordered Orlov to go aboard the *White Witch* and *fetch* his wife ashore. Orlov went alone, at once—Tyler was still ashore at the time. Orlov brought her back and in his wake left one man dead and another half a dozen with broken heads or limbs.' Dunross was looking at her and she recognized the same half-mocking, half-violent, half-devilish smile that was on *the tai-pan*'s face. 'Ever afterwards, Tess—Hag

Struan to be—loved him, so they say. Orlov served our fleet well until he vanished. He was a fine man, and a great seaman, for all his ugliness.'

'He vanished? He was lost at sea?'

'No. Hag Struan said he went ashore one day in Singapore and never returned. He was always threatening to leave and go home to Norway. So perhaps he went home. Perhaps he was knifed. Who knows, Asia's a violent place, though Hag Struan swore no man could kill Stride Orlov and that it must have been a woman. Perhaps Tyler ambushed him. Who knows?'

Inexorably her eyes went back to Tyler Brock. She was fascinated by the face and the implications of the knife. 'Why did she do that to her father's image?'

'One day I'll tell you but not tonight, except to say that she hammered the knife into the wall with my grandfather's cricket bat and cursed before God and the devil anyone who took *her* knife out of *her* wall.' He smiled at Casey and again she noticed an extraordinary tiredness in him and was glad because her own tiredness was creeping up on her and she did not want to make any mistakes now. He put out his hand. 'We have to shake on a deal.'

'No,' Casey said calmly, glad to begin. 'Sorry, I have to cancel out.'

His smile evaporated. 'What?'

'Yes. Linc told me the changes you want. It's a two-year deal—that ups our ante so I can't approve it.'

'Oh?'

'No.' She continued in the same flat but pleasant tone, 'Sorry, 20 million's my limit so you'll have to close with Linc. He's waiting in the bar.'

Understanding flashed over his face for an instant—and relief, she thought—and then he was calm again. 'Is he now?' he said softly, watching her.

'Yes.' She felt a wave of heat go through her, her cheeks began to burn and she wondered if the color showed.

'So we can't shake, you and I. It has to be Linc Bartlett?'

With an effort she kept her eyes unwavering. 'A tai-pan should deal with a tai-pan.'

'That's a basic rule, even in America?' His voice was soft and gentle.

'Yes.'

'Is this your idea or his?'

'Does it matter?'

'Very much.'

'If I say it's Linc's, he loses face, and if I say it's mine, he still loses face, though in a different way.'

Dunross shook his head slightly and smiled. The warmth of it increased her inner warmth. Although she was very much in charge of herself, she felt herself responding to his unadulterated masculinity.

'We're all bound by face, aren't we, in some way or another,' he said.

She did not answer, just glanced away to give herself time. Her eyes saw the portrait of the girl. How could such a pretty girl become known as the *Hag*, she wondered. It must be hateful to become old in face and body when you're young at heart and still strong and tough—so unfair for a woman. Will I be known one day as Hag Tcholok? Or 'that old dyke Tcholok' if I'm still alone, unmarried, in the business world, the man's world, still working for the same things they work for—identity, power and money—and hated for being as good or better than they are at it? I don't care so long as we win, Linc and I. So play the part you've chosen tonight, she told herself, and thank the French lady for her advice. 'Remember, child,' her father had drummed into her, 'remember that advice, good advice, comes from unexpected places at unexpected times.' Yes, Casey thought happily, but for Susanne's reminder about how a lady should operate in this man's world, Ian, perhaps I wouldn't have given you that face-saving formula. But don't be mistaken, Ian Struan Dunross. This is my deal, and in this I'm tai-pan of Par-Con.

Casey felt an untoward glow as another current went through her. Never before had she articulated her actual position in Par-Con to herself. Yes, she thought, very satisfied, that's what I am.

She looked at the girl in the portrait critically and she saw, now, how wrong she had been before and how very special the girl was. Wasn't she *the tai-pan*, in embryo, even then?

'You're very generous,' Dunross said, breaking into her thoughts.

'No,' she replied at once, prepared, and glanced back at him,

323

and she was thinking, If you want the truth, tai-pan, I'm not generous at all. I'm merely being demure and sweet and gentle because it makes you feel more at home. But she said none of this to him, only dropped her eyes and murmured with the right amount of softness, 'It's you who're generous.'

He took her hand and bowed over it and kissed it with old-fashioned gallantry.

She was startled and tried to cover it. No one had ever done that to her before. In spite of her resolve she was moved.

'Ah Ciranoush,' he said with mock gravity, 'any time you need a champion, send for me.' Then he grinned suddenly. 'I'll probably make a bog of it but never mind.'

She laughed, all tension gone now, liking him very much. 'You've got yourself a deal.'

Casually he put his arm around her waist and gently propelled her toward the stairs. The contact with him felt good—too good, she thought. This one's no child. Be cautious.

17

11:58 P.M.:

Phillip Chen's Rolls screeched to a halt in the driveway of his house. He got out of the backseat, flushed with rage, Dianne nervously in tow. The night was dark, the lights of the city and ships and high rises blazing far below. 'Bolt the gates, then you come inside too,' he snapped to his equally nervous chauffeur, then hurried for the front door.

'Hurry up, Dianne,' he said, irritably shoving his key into the lock.

'Phillip, what on earth's the matter with you? Why can't you tell me? Wh—'

'Shut up!' he shouted, his temper snapping, and she jerked to a halt, shocked. 'Just shut up and do what you're told!' He ripped the front door open. 'Get the servants here!'

'But Phi—'

'*Ah sun! Ah Tak!*'

The two tousled, sleepy *amahs* appeared hastily out of the kitchen and gaped at him, shocked at his untoward rage. 'Yes Father? Yes Mother?' they chorused in Cantonese. 'What in the name of all gods ha—'

'Hold your tongues!' Phillip Chen roared, his neck red and now his face more red. 'Go into that room and stay there until I tell you all to come out!' He pulled the door open. It was their dining room and the windows faced the road north. 'All of you stay there until I tell you to come out and if any one of you moves or looks out of the windows before I come back I'll . . . I'll have some friends put weights on you and get you all thrown into the harbor!'

The two *amahs* began wailing but everyone hurriedly obeyed

him and he slammed the door shut.

'Stop it both of you!' Dianne Chen screeched at the *amahs*, then reached over and pinched one sharply on the cheek. This stopped the old woman's wailing and she gasped, her eyes rolling, 'What's got into everyone? What's got into Father? Oh oh oh, his rage's gone to Java . . . oh oh oh. . . .'

'Shut up, Ah Tak!' Dianne fanned herself, seething, beside herself with fury. What in the name of all gods *has* got into him? Doesn't he trust me—me, his only true wife and the love of his life? In all my life . . . And to rush off like that from the tai-pan's party when everything was going so fine—us the talk of Hong Kong and everyone admiring my darling Kevin, fawning on him, now surely the new heir of the House of Chen, for everyone agrees John Chen would certainly have died of shock when his ear was cut off. Anyone would! I certainly would.

She shivered, feeling her own ear being cut again and being kidnapped as in her dream this afternoon when she had awoken in a cold sweat from her nap.

'*Ayeeyah*,' she muttered to no one in particular. 'Has he gone mad?'

'Yes, Mother,' her chauffeur said confidently, 'I think he has. It's the result of the kidnapping. I've never seen Father like this in all my yea—'

'Who asked you?' Dianne shrieked. 'It's all your fault anyway! If you'd brought my poor John home instead of leaving him to his mealy-mouthed whores this would never have happened!'

Again the two *amahs* began whimpering at her fury and she turned her spleen on them for a moment, adding, 'And as to you two, while I think of it, the quality of service in this house's enough to give anyone loose bowels. Have you asked me if I need a physic or aspirins? Or tea? Or a cold towel?'

'Mother,' one of them said placatingly, hopefully pointing at the lacquered sideboard, 'I can't make tea but would you like some brandy?'

'*Wat?* Ah, very good. Yes, yes, Ah Tak.'

At once the old woman bustled over to the sideboard and opened it, brought out some cognac that she knew her mistress liked, poured it into a glass. 'Poor Mother, to have Father in such a rage! Terrible! What's possessed him and why doesn't he want us to look out of the window?'

Because he doesn't want you turtle-dung thieves to see him dig up his secret safe in the garden, Dianne was thinking. Or even me. She smiled grimly to herself, sipping the fine smooth liquor, calmer in the knowledge that she knew where the iron box was buried. It was only right that she should have protected him by secretly watching him bury it, in case, God forbid, the gods took him from this earth before he could tell her where the secret hiding place was. It had been her duty to break her promise not to watch him that night during the Japanese Occupation when he had wisely scooped up all their valuables and hidden them.

She did not know what was in the box now. She did not care. It had been opened and closed many times, all in secret as far as he was concerned. She did not care so long as she knew where her husband was, where all his deposit boxes of various kinds were, their keys, just in case.

After all, she told herself confidently, if he dies, without me the House of Chen will crumble. 'Stop sniveling, Ah Sun!' She got up and closed the long drapes. Outside, the night was dark and she could see nothing of the garden, only the driveway, the tall iron gates and the road beyond.

'More drink, Mother?' the old *amah* asked.

'Thank you, little oily mouth,' she replied affectionately, the warmth of the spirit soothing her anger away. 'And then you can massage my neck. I've got a headache. You two sit down, hold your tongues and don't make a sound till Father gets back!'

Phillip Chen was hurrying down the garden path, a flashlight in one hand, a shovel in the other. The path curled downward through well-tended gardens that meandered into a grove of trees and shrubs. He stopped a moment, getting his bearings, then found the place he sought. He hesitated and glanced back, even though he knew he was well hidden from the house now. Reassured that he could not be watched he switched on the flashlight. The circle of light wandered over the undergrowth and stopped at the foot of a tree. The spot appeared to be untouched. Carefully he pushed aside the natural mulch. When he saw the earth below had been disturbed he cursed obscenely.

'Oh the swine . . . my own son!' Collecting himself with difficulty he began to dig. The earth was soft.

Ever since he had left the party he had been trying to remember exactly when he had last dug up the box. Now he was sure it had been in the spring when he needed the deeds to a row of slum dwellings in Wanchai that he had sold for fifty times cost to Donald McBride for one of his great new developments.

'Where was John then?' he muttered. 'Was he in the house?'

As he dug he tried to recall but he could not. He knew that he would never have dug up the box when it was dangerous or when there were strangers in the house and that he would always have been circumspect. But John? Never would I have thought . . . John must have followed me somehow.

The shovel struck the metal. Carefully he cleaned off the earth and pulled the protective cloth away from the box and heavy lock and opened it. The hinges of the lid were well greased. His fingers shaking, he held the flashlight over the open box. All his papers and deeds and private balance sheets seemed to be in order and undisturbed, but he knew they must all have been taken out and read—and copied or memorized. Some of the information in his son's safety deposit box could only have come from here.

All the jewel boxes, big and small, were there. Nervously he reached out for the one he sought and opened it. The half-coin had vanished and the document explaining about the coin had vanished.

Tears of rage seeped down his cheeks. He felt his heart pounding and smelled the damp earth and knew if his son was there he would happily have strangled him with his own hands.

'Oh my son my son . . . all gods curse you to hell!'

His knees were weak. Shakily he sat on a rock and tried to collect his wits. He could hear his father on his deathbed cautioning him: 'Never lose the coin my son—it's our key to ultimate survival and power over the Noble House.'

That was in 1937 and the first time he had learned the innermost secrets of the House of Chen: that he who became compradore became the ranking leader in Hong Kong of the Hung Mun—the great secret triad society of China that, under Sun Yat-sen had become the 14K, originally formed to spearhead China's revolt against their hated Manchu overlords; that the compradore was the main, legitimate link between the Chinese hierarchy on the Island and the inheritors of the 14K on the Mainland; that because of Chen-tse Jin Arn, known as Jin-qua, the legendary chief merchant of the co-*hong* that had possessed the Emperor's monopoly on all foreign trade, the House of Chen was perpetually interlinked with the Noble House by ownership and by blood.

'Listen carefully, my son,' the dying man had whispered. 'The tai-pan, Great-grandfather Dirk Struan, was Jin-qua's creation, as was the Noble House. Jin-qua nurtured it, formed it *and* Dirk Struan. The tai-pan had two concubines. The first was Kai-sung, one of Jin-qua's daughters by a fifth wife. Their son was Gordon Chen, my father, your grandfather. The tai-pan's second concubine was T'Chung Jin May-may, his mistress for six years whom he married in secret just before the great typhoon that killed them both. She was twenty-three then, a brilliant, favored granddaughter of Jin-qua, sold to the tai-pan when she was seventeen to teach him civilized ways without his knowing he was being taught. From them came Duncan and Kate who took the surname *T'Chung* and were brought up in my father's house. Father married off Kate to a Shanghai China Trader called Peter Gavallan—Andrew Gavallan is also a cousin though he doesn't know it. . . . So many stories to tell and now so little time to tell them. Never mind, all the family trees are in the safe. There are so many. We're all related, the Wu, Kwang, Sung, Kau, Kwok, Ng—all the old families. Use the knowledge carefully. Here's the key to the safe.

'Another secret, Phillip, my son. Our line comes from my father's second wife. Father married her when he was fifty-three and she sixteen. She was the daughter of John Yuan, the illegitimate son of the great American Trader Jeff Cooper, and a Eurasian lady, Isobel Yau. Isobel Yau was the oh-so-secret Eurasian daughter of Robb Struan, the tai-pan's half-brother and cofounder of the Noble House, so we have blood from both sides of the Struans. Alastair Struan is a cousin and Colin Dunross is a cousin—the MacStruans are not, their history's in Grandfather's diaries. My son, the English and the Scots barbarians came to China and they never married those whom they adored and most times abandoned when they returned to the gray island of mist and rain and overcast. My God how I hate the English weather and loathe the past!

'Yes, Phillip, we're Eurasian, not of one side or the other. I've never been able to come to terms with it. It is our curse and our cross but it is up to all of us to make it a blessing. I pass our House on to you rich and strong like Jin-qua wished—do so to your son and make sure he does it to his. Jin-qua birthed us in a way, gave us wealth, secret knowledge, continuity and power—and he gave us one of the coins. Here, Phillip, read about the coin.'

The calligraphy of the ancient scroll was exquisite: 'On this eighth day of the sixth month of the year 1841 by barbarian count, I, Chen-tse Jin Arn of Canton, Chief Merchant of the co-*hong*, have this day loaned to Green-Eyed Devil the tai-pan of the Noble House, chief pirate of all foreign devils who have made war on the Heavenly Kingdom and have stolen our island Hong Kong, forty lacs of silver . . . one million sterling in their specie . . . and have, with this bullion, saved him from being swallowed by One-Eye, his arch-enemy and rival. In return, the tai-pan grants us special trade advantages for the next twenty years, promises that one of the House of Chen will forever be compradore to the Noble House, and swears that he or his descendants will honor all debts and the debt of the coins. There are four of them. The coins are broken into halves. I have given the tai-pan four halves. Whenever one of the other halves is presented to him, or to a following tai-pan, he has sworn whatever favor is asked will be granted . . . *whether within their law, or ours, or outside it.*

'One coin I keep; one I give to the warlord Wu Fang Choi, my cousin; one will be given to my grandson Gordon Chen; and the last recipient I keep secret. Remember, he who reads this in the future, do not use the coin lightly, for the tai-pan of the Noble House must grant anything—*but only once.* And remember that though the Green-Eyed Devil himself will honor his promise and so will his descendants, he is still a mad-dog barbarian, cunning as a filthy Manchu because of *our* training, and as dangerous always as a nest of vipers.'

Phillip Chen shuddered involuntarily, remembering the violence that was always ready to explode in Ian Dunross. He's a descendant of Green-Eyed Devil all right, he thought. Yes, him and his father.

330

Goddamn John! What possessed him? What devilment has he planned with Linc Bartlett? Has Bartlett got the coin now? Or does John still have it with him and now perhaps the kidnappers have it.

While his tired brain swept over the possibilities, his fingers checked the jewel boxes, one by one. Nothing was missing. The big one he left till last. There was a tightness in his throat as he opened it but the necklace was still there. A great sigh of relief went through him. The beauty of the emeralds in the flashlight gave him enormous pleasure and took away some of his anxiety. How stupid of Hag Struan to order them to be burned with her body. What an arrogant, awful, unholy waste that would have been! How wise of Father to intercept the coffin before the fire and remove them.

Reluctantly he put the necklace away and began to close up the safe. What to do about the coin? I almost used it the time the tai-pan took away our bank stock—and most of our power. Yes. But I decided to give him time to prove himself and this is the third year and nothing is yet proved, and though the American deal seems grand it is not yet signed. And now the coin is gone.

He groaned aloud, distraught, his back aching like his head. Below was all the city, ships tied up at Glessing's Point and others in the roads. Kowloon was equally brilliant and he could see the jetliner taking off from Kai Tak, another turning to make a landing, another whining high overhead, its lights blinking.

What to do? he asked himself exhaustedly. Does Bartlett have the coin? Or John? Or the Werewolves?

In the wrong hands it could destroy us all.

TUESDAY

18

Gornt said, 'Of course Dunross could have buggered my brakes, Jason!'

'Oh come on, for God's sake! Climbing under your car during a party with two hundred guests around? Ian's not that stupid.'

They were in Jason Plumm's penthouse above Happy Valley, the midnight air good though the humidity had increased again. Plumm got up and threw his cigar butt away, took a fresh one and lit it. The tai-pan of Asian Properties, the third largest *hong*, was taller than Gornt, in his late fifties, thin-faced and elegant, his smoking jacket red velvet. 'Even Ian bloody Dunross's not that much of a bloody berk.'

'You're wrong. For all his Scots cunning, he's an animal of sudden action, unpremeditated action, that's his failing. I think he did it.'

Plumm steepled his fingers thoughtfully. 'What did the police say?'

'All I told them was that my brakes had failed. There was no need to involve those nosy buggers, at least not yet. But Rolls brakes just *don't* go wrong by themselves for God's sake. Well, never mind. Tomorrow I'll make sure Tom Nikklin gets me an answer, an absolute answer, if there is one. Time enough for the police then.'

'I agree.' Plumm smiled thinly. 'We don't need police to wash our various linens however droll—do we?'

'No.' Both men laughed.

'You were very lucky. The Peak's no road to lose your brakes on. Must have been very unpleasant.'

'For a moment it was, Jason, but then it was no problem, once

I was over the initial shock.' Gornt stretched the truth and sipped his whiskey and soda. They had eaten an elegant dinner on the terrace overlooking Happy Valley, the racecourse and city and sea beyond, just the two of them—Plumm's wife was in England on vacation and their children grown up and no longer in Hong Kong. Now they were sitting over cigars in great easy chairs in Plumm's book-lined study, the room luxurious though subdued, in perfect taste like the rest of the ten-room penthouse. 'Tom Nikklin'll find out if my car was tampered with if anyone can,' he said with finality.

'Yes.' Plumm sipped a glass of iced Perrier water. 'Are you going to wind up young Nikklin again about Macao?'

'Me? You must be joking!'

'No. I'm not, actually,' Plumm said with his mocking well-bred chuckle. 'Didn't Dunross's engine blow up during the race three years ago and he bloody nearly killed himself?'

'Racing cars are always going wrong.'

'Yes, yes they do frequently, though they're not always helped by the opposition.' Plumm smiled.

Gornt kept his smile but inside he was not smiling. 'Meaning?'

'Nothing, dear boy. Just rumors.' The older man leaned over and poured more whiskey for Gornt, then used the soda syphon. 'Rumor has it that a certain Chinese mechanic, for a small fee, put . . . put, as we say, a small spanner in the works.'

'I doubt if that'd be true.'

'I doubt if it could be proved. One way or another. It's disgusting, but some people will do anything for quite a small amount of money.'

'Yes. Fortunately we're in the big-money market.'

'My whole point, dear boy. Now.' Plumm tapped the ash off his cigar. 'What's the scheme?'

'It's very simple: provided Bartlett does not actually sign a deal with Struan's in the next ten days we can pluck the Noble House like a dead duck.'

'Lots of people have thought that before and Struan's is still the Noble House.'

'Yes. But at the moment, they're vulnerable.'

'How?'

'The Toda Shipping notes, and the Orlin installment.'

'Not true. Struan's credit is excellent—oh, they're stretched, but no more than anyone else. They'll just increase their line of credit—or Ian will go to Richard Kwang—or Blacs.'

'Say Blacs won't help—they won't—and say Richard Kwang's neutralized. That leaves only the Victoria.'

'Then Dunross'll ask the bank for more credit and we'll have to give it to him. Paul Havergill will put it to a vote of the board. We all know we can't outvote the Struan's block so we'll go along with it and save face, pretending we're very happy to oblige, as usual.'

'Yes. But this time I'm happy to say Richard Kwang will vote against Struan's. That will tie up the board, the credit request will be delayed—he won't be able to make his payments, so Dunross goes under.'

'For God's sake, Richard Kwang's not even on the board! Have you gone bonkers?'

Gornt puffed his cigar. 'No, you've forgotten my game plan. The one called Competition. It was started a couple of days ago.'

'Against Richard?'

'Yes.'

'Poor old Richard!'

'Yes. He'll be our deciding vote. And Dunross'll never expect an attack from there.'

Plumm stared at him. 'Richard and Dunross are great friends.'

'But Richard's in trouble. The run's started on the Ho-Pak. He'll do anything to save himself.'

'I see. How much Ho-Pak stock did you sell short?'

'Lots.'

'Are you sure Richard hasn't got the resources to stave off the run—that he can't pull in extra funds?'

'If he does, we can always abort, you and I.'

'Yes, yes we can.' Jason Plumm watched his cigar smoke spiral. 'But just because Dunross won't meet those payments doesn't mean he's finished.'

'I agree. But after the Ho-Pak "disaster," the news that Struan's have defaulted will send his stock plummeting. The market'll be very nervous, there'll be all the signs of a crash looming which we fuel by selling short. There's no board meeting scheduled for a couple of weeks unless Paul Havergill calls a special meeting. And he won't. Why should he? He wants their chunk of stock back more than anything else in the world. So everything will be fixed beforehand. He'll set the ground rules for rescuing Richard Kwang, and voting as Paul decides will be one of them. So the board lets Ian stew for a few days, then offers to extend credit and restore confidence—in return for Struan's piece of the bank stock—it's pledged against the credit anyway.'

'Dunross'll never agree—neither he nor Phillip Chen, nor Tsu-yan.'

'It's that or Struan's goes under—provided you hold tight and you've voting control. Once the bank gets his block of stock away from him . . . if you control the board, and therefore the Victoria Bank, then he's finished.'

'Yes. But say he gets a new line of credit?'

'Then he's only badly mauled, maybe permanently weakened, Jason, but we make a killing either way. It's all a matter of timing, you know that.'

'And Bartlett?'

'Bartlett and Par-Con are mine. He'll never go with Struan's sinking ship. I'll see to that.'

After a pause Plumm said, 'It's possible. Yes, it's possible.'

'Are you in then?'

'After Struan's, how are you going to gobble up Par-Con?'

'I'm not. But *we* could—possibly.' Gornt stubbed out his cigar. 'Par-Con's a long-term effort and a whole different set of problems. First Struan's. Well?'

'If I get Struan's Hong Kong property division—35 percent of their landholdings in Thailand and Singapore and we're fifty-fifty on their Kai Tak operation?'

'Yes, everything except Kai Tak—I need that to round off All Asia Airways, I'm sure you'll understand, old boy. But you've a seat on the board of the new company, ten percent of the stock at par, seats on Struan's of course, and all their subsidiaries.'

'15 percent. And chairmanship of Struan's, alternate years with you?'

'Agreed, but I'm first.' Gornt lit a cigarette. Why not? he thought expansively. By this time next year Struan's will be dismembered so your chairmanship is really academic, Jason old boy. 'So everything's agreed? We'll put it in a joint memo if you like, one copy for each of us.'

Plumm shook his head and smiled. 'Don't need a memo, perish the thought! Here.' He held out his hand. 'I agree!'

The two men shook hands firmly. 'Down with the Noble House!' They both laughed, very content with the deal they had made. Acquisition of Struan's landholdings would make Asian Properties the largest land company in Hong Kong. Gornt would acquire almost a total monopoly of all Hong Kong's air cargo, sea freighting and factoring—and preeminence in Asia.

Good, Gornt thought. Now for Four Finger Wu. 'If you'll call me a taxi I'll be off.'

'Take my car, my chauffeur will—'

'Thanks but no, I'd rather take a taxi. Really, Jason, thanks anyway.'

So Plumm phoned down to the concierge of the twenty-story apartment building which was owned and operated by his Asian Properties. While they waited, they toasted each other and the destruction of Struan's and the profits they were going to make. A phone rang in the adjoining room.

'Excuse me a moment, old chap.' Plumm went through the door and half-closed it behind him. This was his private bedroom which he used sometimes when he was working late. It was a small, very neat room, soundproofed, fitted up like a ship's cabin with a built-in bunk, hi fi speakers that piped in the music, a small self-contained hot plate and refrigerator. And, on one side, was a huge bank of elaborate, shortwave, ham radio transceiver equipment which had been Jason Plumm's abiding hobby since his childhood.

He picked up the phone. 'Yes?'

'Mr. Lop-sing please?' the woman's voice said.

'There's no Mr. Lop-*ting* here,' he said easily. 'Sorry, you have a wrong number.'

'I want to leave a message.'

'You have a wrong number. Look in your phone book.'

'An urgent message for Arthur: Center radioed that the meeting's postponed until the day after tomorrow. Standby for urgent instructions at 0600.' The line went dead. Again a dial tone.

Plumm frowned and he put the phone back on its cradle.

*   *   *

Four Finger Wu stood at the gunnel of his junk with Good-weather Poon watching Gornt get into the sampan that he had sent for him.

'He hasn't changed much in all this time, has he?' Wu said absently, his narrowed eyes glittering.

'Foreign devils all look alike to me, never mind. How many years is it? Ten?' Poon asked, scratching his piles.

'No, it's nearer twelve now. Good times then, *heya*,' Wu said. 'Lots of profit. Very good, slipping upstream toward Canton, evading the foreign devils and their lackeys, Chairman Mao's people welcoming us. Yes. Our own people in charge and not a foreign devil anywhere—nor a fat official wanting his hand touched with fragrant grease. You could visit all your family and friends then and no trouble, *heya*? Not like now, *heya*?'

'The Reds're getting tough, very clever and very tough—worse than the Mandarins.'

Wu turned as his seventh son came on deck. Now the young man wore a neat white shirt and gray trousers and good shoes. 'Be careful,' he called out brusquely. 'You're sure you know what to do?'

'Yes, Father.'

'Good,' Four Fingers said, hiding his pride. 'I don't want any mistakes.'

He watched him head awkwardly for the haphazard gangway of planks that joined this junk to the next and thence across other junks to a makeshift landing eight boats away.

'Does Seventh Son know anything yet?' Poon asked softly.

'No, no not yet,' Wu said sourly. 'Those dogmeat fools to be caught with my guns! Without the guns, all our work will be for nothing.'

'Evening, Mr. Gornt. I'm Paul Choy—my uncle Wu sent me to show you the way,' the young man said in perfect English, repeating the lie that was now almost the real truth to him.

Gornt stopped, startled, then continued up the rickety stairs, his sea legs better than the young man's. 'Evening,' he said. 'You're American? Or did you just go to school there, Mr. Choy?'

'Both.' Paul Choy smiled. 'You know how it is. Watch your

head on the ropes—and it's slippery as hell.' He turned and began to lead the way back. His real name was Wu Fang Choi and he was his father's seventh son by his third wife, but, when he was born, his father Four Finger Wu had sought a Hong Kong birth certificate for him, an unusual act for a boat dweller, put his mother's maiden name on the birth certificate, added Paul and got one of his cousins to pose as the real father.

'Listen, my son,' Four Finger Wu had said, as soon as Paul could understand, 'when speaking Haklo aboard my ship, you can call me Father—but never in front of a foreign devil, even in Haklo. All other times I'm "Uncle," just one of many uncles. Understand?'

'Yes. But why, Father? Have I done something wrong? I'm sorry if I've offended you.'

'You haven't. You're a good boy and you work hard. It's just better for the family for you to have another name.'

'But why, Father?'

'When it's time you will be told.' Then, when he was twelve and trained and had proved his value, his father had sent him to the States. 'Now you're to learn the ways of the foreign devil. You must begin to speak like one, sleep like one, become one outwardly but never forget who you are, who your people are, or that all foreign devils are inferior, hardly human beings, and certainly not fornicating civilized.'

Paul Choy laughed to himself. If Americans only knew—from tai-pan to meathead—and British, Iranians, Germans, Russians, every race and color, if they all really knew what even the lousiest coolie thought of them, they'd hemorrhage, he told himself for the millionth time. It's not that all the races of China despise foreigners, it's just that foreigners're just beneath any consideration. Of course we're wrong, he told himself. Foreigners are human and some are civilized—in their way— and far ahead of us technically. But we *are* better. . . .

'Why the smile?' Gornt asked, ducking under ropes, avoiding rubbish that scattered all the decks.

'Oh, I was just thinking how crazy life is. This time last month I was surfing at Malibu Colony, California. Boy, Aberdeen's something else, isn't it?'

'You mean the smell?'

'Sure.'

'Yes it is.'

'It's not much better at high tide. No one but me seems to smell the stench!'

'When were you last here?'

'Couple of years back—for ten days—after I graduated, B.A. in business, but I never seem to get used to it.' Choy laughed. 'New England it ain't!'

'Where did you go to school?'

'Seattle first. Then undergraduate school, University of Washington at Seattle. Then I got a master's at Harvard, Harvard Business School.'

Gornt stopped. 'Harvard?'

'Sure. I got an assist, a scholarship.'

'That's very good. When did you graduate?'

'June last year. It was like getting out of prison! Boy, they really put your ass on the block if you don't keep up your grades. Two years of hell! After I got out I headed for California with a buddy, doing odd jobs here and there to make enough to keep surfing, have ourselves a time after sweating out so much school. Then . . .' Choy grinned. '. . . then a couple of months back Uncle Wu caught up with me and said it's time you went to work so here I am! After all, he paid for my education. My parents died years ago.'

'Were you top of your class at Harvard?'

'Third.'

'That's very good.'

'Thank you. It's not far now, ours is the end junk.'

They negotiated a precarious gangway, Gornt watched suspiciously by silent boat dwellers as they crossed from floating home to floating home, the families dozing or cooking or eating or playing mah-jong, some still repairing fishing nets, some children night fishing.

'This bit's slippery, Mr. Gornt.' He jumped on to the tacky deck. 'We made it! Home sweet home!' He tousled the hair of the sleepy little boy who was the lookout and said in Haklo, which he knew Gornt did not understand, 'Keep awake, Little Brother, or the devils will get us.'

'Yes, yes I will,' the boy piped, his suspicious eyes on Gornt.

Paul Choy led the way below. The old junk smelled of tar and teak, rotting fish and sea salt and a thousand storms. Below

342

decks the midship gangway opened on the normal single large cabin for'ard that went the breadth of the ship and the length to the bow. An open charcoal fire burned in a careless brick fireplace with a sooty kettle singing over it. Smoke curled upward and found its way to the outside through a rough flue cut in the deck. A few old rattan chairs, tables and tiers of rough bunks lined one side.

Four Finger Wu was alone and he waved at one of the chairs and beamed. '*Heya*, good see,' he said in halting, hardly understandable English. 'Whiskey?'

'Thanks,' Gornt said. 'Good to see you too.'

Paul Choy poured the good Scotch into two semiclean glasses.

'You want water, Mr. Gornt?' he asked.

'No, straight's fine. Not too much please.'

'Sure.'

Wu accepted his glass and toasted Gornt. 'Good see you, *heya?*'

'Yes. Health!'

They watched Gornt sip his whiskey.

'Good,' Gornt said. 'Very good whiskey.'

Wu beamed again and motioned at Paul. 'Him sister son.'

'Yes.'

'Good school—Golden Country.'

'Yes. Yes, he told me. You should be very proud.'

'*Wat?*'

Paul Choy translated for the old man. 'Ah thank, thank you. He talk good, *heya?*'

'Yes.' Gornt smiled. 'Very good.'

'Ah, good never mind. Smoke?'

'Thank you.' They watched Gornt take a cigarette. Then Wu took one and Paul Choy lit both of them. Another silence.

'Good with old frien'?'

'Yes. And you?'

'Good.' Another silence. 'Him sister son,' the old seaman said again and saw Gornt nod and say nothing, waiting. It pleased him that Gornt just sat there, waiting patiently for him to come to the point as a civilized person should.

Some of these pink devils are learning at long last. Yes, but some have learned too fornicating well—*the* tai-pan for in-

343

stance, him with those cold, ugly blue fish-eyes that most foreign devils have, that stare at you like a dead shark—the one who can even speak a little Haklo dialect. Yes, the tai-pan's too cunning and too civilized, but then he's had generations before him and his ancestors had the Evil Eye before him. Yes, but old Devil Green Eyes, the first of his line, who made a pact with my ancestor the great sea warlord, Wu Fang Choi and his son, Wu Kwok, and kept it, and saw that his sons kept it—and their sons. So this present tai-pan must be considered an old friend even though he's the most deadly of the line.

The old man suppressed a shudder and hawked and spat to scare away the evil spit god that lurked in all men's throats. He studied Gornt. Eeeee, he told himself, it must be vile to have to look at that pink face in every mirror—all that face hair like a monkey and a pallid white toad's belly skin elsewhere! Ugh!

He put a smile on his face to cover his embarrassment and tried to read Gornt's face, what was beneath it, but he could not. Never mind, he told himself gleefully, that's why all the time and money's been spent to prepare Number Seven Son—he'll know.

'Maybe ask favor?' he said tentatively.

The beams of the ship creaked pleasantly as she wallowed at her moorings.

'Yes. What favor, old friend?'

'Sister son—time go work—give job?' He saw astonishment on Gornt's face and this annoyed him but he hid it. ''Splain,' he said in English then added to Paul Choy in guttural Haklo, 'Explain to this Eater of Turtle Shit what I want. Just as I told you.'

'My uncle apologizes that he can't speak direct to you so he's asked me to explain, Mr. Gornt,' Paul Choy said politely. 'He wants to ask if you'd give me a job—as a sort of trainee—in your airplane and shipping division.'

Gornt sipped his whiskey. 'Why those, Mr. Choy?'

'My uncle has substantial shipping interests, as you know, and he wants me to modernize his operation. I can give you chapter and verse on my background, if you'd consider me, sir—my second year at Harvard was directed to those areas— my major interest was transportation of all types. I'd been accepted in the International Division of the Bank of Ohio before my uncle jer—pulled me back.' Paul Choy hesitated. 'Anyway that's what he asks.'

'What dialects do you speak, other than Haklo?'

'Mandarin.'

'How many characters can you write?'

'About four thousand.'

'Can you take shorthand?'

'Speedwriting only, sir. ı can type about eighty words a minute but not clean.'

'*Wat*?' Wu asked.

Gornt watched Paul Choy as the young man translated what had been said for his uncle, weighing him—and Four Finger Wu. Then he said, 'What sort of trainee do you want to be?'

'He wants me to learn all there is to know about running shipping and airlines, the broking and freighting business also, the practical operation, and of course to be a profitable cog for you in your machine. Maybe my Yankee expertise, theoretical expertise, could help you somehow. I'm twenty-six. I've a master's. I'm into all the new computer theory. Of course I can program one. At Harvard I backgrounded in conglomerates, cash flows.'

'And if you don't perform, or there's, how would you put it, a personality conflict?'

The young man said firmly, 'There won't be, Mr. Gornt—leastways I'll work my can off to prevent that.'

'*Wat*? What did he say? Exactly?' Four Fingers asked sharply in Haklo, noticing a change in inflection, his eyes and ears highly tuned.

His son explained, exactly.

'Good,' Wu said, his voice a rasp. 'Tell him exactly, if you don't do all your tasks to his satisfaction you'll be cast out of the family and my wrath will waste your days.'

Paul Choy hesitated, hiding his shock, all his American training screaming to tell his father to go screw, that he was a Harvard graduate, that he was an American and had an American passport that *he'd* earned, whatever goddamn sampan or goddamn family he came from. But he kept his eyes averted and his anger off his face.

Don't be ungrateful, he ordered himself. You're not

345

American, truly American. You're Chinese, and the head of your family has the right to rule. But for him you could be running a floating cathouse here in Aberdeen.

Paul Choy sighed. He knew that he was more fortunate than his eleven brothers. Four were junk captains here in Aberdeen, one lived in Bangkok and plied the Mekong River, one had a ferryboat in Singapore, another ran an import/export shipwright business in Indonesia, two had been lost at sea, one brother was in England—doing what, he didn't know—and the last, the eldest, ruled the dozen feeder sampans in Aberdeen Harbor that were floating kitchens—and also three pleasure boats and eight ladies of the night.

After a pause Gornt asked, 'What did he say? Exactly?'

Paul Choy hesitated, then decided to tell him, exactly.

'Thank you for being honest with me, Mr. Choy. That was wise. You're a very impressive young man,' Gornt said. 'I understand perfectly.' Now for the first time since Wu had asked the original question he turned his eyes to the old seaman and smiled. 'Of course. Glad to give nephew job.'

Wu beamed and Paul Choy tried to keep the relief off his face.

'I won't let you down, Mr. Gornt.'

'Yes, I know you won't.'

Wu motioned at the bottle. 'Whiskey?'

'No thank you. This is fine,' Gornt said.

'When start job?'

Gornt looked at Paul Choy. 'When would you like to start?'

'Tomorrow? Whenever's good for you, sir.'

'Tomorrow. Wednesday.'

'Gee thanks. Eight o'clock?'

'Nine, eight thereafter. A six-day week of course. You'll have long hours and I'll push you. It'll be up to you how much you can learn and how fast I can increase your responsibilities.'

'Thanks, Mr. Gornt.' Happily Paul Choy translated for his father. Wu sipped his whiskey without hurrying. 'What money?' he asked.

Gornt hesitated. He knew it had to be just the right sum, not too much, not too little, to give Paul Choy face and his uncle face. '1,000 HK a month for the first three months, then I'll review.'

The young man kept his gloom off his face. That was hardly

200 U.S. but he translated it into Haklo.

'Maybe 2,000?' Wu said, hiding his pleasure. A thousand was the perfect figure but he was bargaining merely to give the foreign devil face and his son face.

'If he's to be trained, many valuable managers will have to take time away from their other duties,' Gornt said politely. 'It's expensive to train anyone.'

'Much money Golden Mountain,' Wu said firmly. 'Two?'

'1,000 first month, 1,250 next two months?'

Wu frowned and added, 'Month three, 1,500?'

'Very well. Months three and four at 1,500. And I'll review his salary after four months. And Paul Choy guarantees work for Rothwell-Gornt for at least two years.'

'*Wat?*'

Paul Choy translated again. Shit, he was thinking, how'm I going to vacation in the States on 50 bucks a week, even 60. Shit! And where the hell'm I gonna live? On a goddamn sampan? Then he heard Gornt say something and his brain twisted.

'Sir?'

'I said because you've been so honest with me, we'll give you free accommodation in one of our company houses—The Gables. That's where we put all our managerial trainees who come out from England. If you're going to be part of a foreign devil *hong* then you'd better mix with its future leaders.'

'Yes sir!' Paul Choy could not stop the beam. 'Yes sir, thank you sir.'

Four Finger Wu asked something in Haklo.

'He wants to know where's the house, sir?'

'It's on the Peak. It's really very nice, Mr. Choy. I'm sure you'll be more than satisfied.'

'You can bet your . . . yes sir.'

'Tomorrow night be prepared to move in.'

'Yes sir.'

After Wu had understood what Gornt had said, he nodded his agreement. 'All agree. Two year then see. Maybe more, *heya?*'

'Yes.'

'Good. Thank old frien'.' Then in Haklo, 'Now ask him what you wanted to know . . . about the bank.'

Gornt was getting up to go but Paul Choy said, 'There's

something else my uncle wanted to ask you, sir, if you can spare the time.'

'Of course.' Gornt settled back in his chair and Paul Choy noticed that the man seemed sharper now, more on guard.

'My uncle'd like to ask your opinion about the run on the Aberdeen branch of the Ho-Pak Bank today.'

Gornt stared back at him, his eyes steady. 'What about it?'

'There're all sorts of rumors,' Paul Choy said. 'My uncle's got a lot of money there, so've most of his friends. A run on that bank'd be real bad news.'

'I think it would be a good idea to get his money out,' Gornt said, delighted with the unexpected opportunity to feed the flames.

'Jesus,' Paul Choy muttered, aghast. He had been gauging Gornt very carefully and he had noticed sudden tension and now equally sudden pleasure which surprised him. He pondered a moment, then decided to change tactics and probe. 'He wanted to know if you were selling short.'

Gornt said wryly, 'He or you, Mr. Choy?'

'Both of us, sir. He's got quite a portfolio of stocks which he wants me to manage eventually,' the young man said, which was a complete exaggeration. 'I was explaining the mechanics of modern banking and the stock market to him—how it ticks and how Hong Kong's different from Stateside. He gets the message very fast, sir.' Another exaggeration. Paul Choy had found it impossible to break through his father's prejudices. 'He asks if he should sell short?'

'Yes. I think he should. There have been lots of rumors that Ho-Pak's overextended—borrowing short and cheap, lending long and expensive, mostly on property, the classic way any bank would get into serious difficulties. For safety he should get all his money out and sell short.'

'Next question, sir: Will Blacs, or the Victoria Bank do a bail-out?'

With an effort Gornt kept his face impassive. The old junk dipped slightly as waves from another chugging past lapped her sides. 'Why should other banks do that?'

I'm trapped, Gornt was thinking, aghast. I can't tell the truth to them—there is no telling who else will get the information. At the same time, I daren't *not* tell the old bastard and his god-cursed whelp. He's asking for the return of *the* favor and I have to pay, that's a matter of face.

Paul Choy leaned forward in his chair, his excitement showing. 'My theory's that if there's a real run on the Ho-Pak the others won't let it crash—not like the East India and Canton Bank disaster last year because it'd create shock waves that the market, the big operators in the market, wouldn't like. Everyone's waiting for a boom, and I bet the biggies here won't let a catastrophe wreck that chance. Since Blacs and the Victoria're the top bananas it figures they'd be the ones to do a bail-out.'

'What's your point, Mr. Choy?'

'If someone knew in advance when Ho-Pak stock'd bottom out and either bank, or both, were launching a bail-out operation, that person could make a fortune.'

Gornt was trying to decide what to do but he was tired now and not as sharp as he should be. That accident must have taken more out of me than I thought, he told himself. Was it Dunross? Was that bastard trying to even the score, repay me for *the* Christmas night or the Pacific Orient victory or fifty other victories—perhaps even the old Macao score.

Gornt felt a sudden glow as he remembered the white hot thrill he had felt watching the road race, knowing that any moment the tai-pan's engine would seize up—watching the cars howl past lap after lap, and then Dunross, the leader, not coming in his turn—then waiting and hoping and then the news that he had spun out at Melco Hairpin in a metal-screaming crash when his engine went. Waiting again, his stomach churning. Then the news that the whole racing car had exploded in a ball of fire but Dunross had scrambled out unscathed. He was both very sorry and very glad.

He didn't want Dunross dead. He wanted him alive and destroyed, alive to realize it.

He chuckled to himself. Oh it wasn't me who pressed the button that put that ploy into operation. Of course I did nudge young Donald Nikklin a little and suggest all sorts of ways and means that a little *h'eung yau* in the right hands . . .

His eyes saw Paul Choy and the old seaman waiting, watching him, and all of his good humor vanished. He pushed away his vagrant thoughts and concentrated.

'Yes, you're right of course, Mr. Choy. But your premise is

wrong. Of course this is all theoretical, the Ho-Pak hasn't failed yet. Perhaps it won't. But there's no reason why any bank should do what you suggest, it never has in the past. Each bank stands or falls on its own merits, that's the joy of our free enterprise system. Such a scheme as you propose would set a dangerous precedent. It would certainly be impossible to prop up every bank that was mismanaged. Neither bank needs the Ho-Pak, Mr. Choy. Both have more than enough customers of their own. Neither has ever acquired other banking interests here and I doubt whether either would ever need to.'

Horseshit, Paul Choy was thinking. A bank's committed to growth like any other business and Blacs and the Victoria are the most rapacious of all—except Struan's and Rothwell-Gornt. Shit, and Asian Properties and all the other *hongs*.

'I'm sure you're right, sir. But my uncle Wu'd appreciate it if you heard anything, one way or another.'

He turned to his father and said in Haklo, 'I'm finished now, Honored Uncle. This barbarian agrees the bank may be in trouble.'

Wu's face lost color. 'Eh? How bad?'

'I'll be the first in line tomorrow. You should take all your money out quickly.'

'*Ayeeyah!* By all the gods!' Wu said, his voice raw, 'I'll personally slit Banker Kwang's throat if I lose a single fornicating cash piece, even though he's my nephew!'

Paul Choy stared at him. 'He is?'

'Banks are just fornicating inventions of foreign devils to steal honest people's wealth,' Wu raged. 'I'll get back every copper cash or his blood will flow! Tell me what he said about the bank!'

'Please be patient, Honored Uncle. It is polite, according to barbarian custom, not to keep this barbarian waiting.'

Wu bottled his rage and said to Gornt in his execrable pidgin, 'Bank bad, *heya?* Thank tell true. Bank bad custom, *heya?*'

'Sometimes,' Gornt said cautiously.

Four Finger Wu unknotted his bony fists and forced calmness. 'Thank for favor . . . yes . . . also want like sister son say *heya?*'

'Sorry, I don't understand. What does your uncle mean, Mr. Choy?'

After chatting with his father a moment for appearances, the young man said, 'My uncle would consider it a real favor if he could hear privately, in advance, of any raid, takeover attempt or bail-out—of course it'd be kept completely confidential.'

Wu nodded, only his mouth smiling now. 'Yes. Favor.' He put out his hand and shook with Gornt in friendly style, knowing that barbarians liked the custom though he found it uncivilized and distasteful, and contrary to correct manners from time immemorial. But he wanted his son trained quickly and it had to be with Second Great Company and he needed Gornt's information. He understood the importance of advance knowledge. Eeeee, he thought, without my friends in the Marine Police forces of Asia my fleets would be powerless.

'Go ashore with him, Nephew. See him into a taxi then wait for me. Fetch Two Hatchet Tok and wait for me, there, by the taxi stand.'

He thanked Gornt again, then followed them to the deck and watched them go. His ferry sampan was waiting and he saw them get into it and head for the shore.

It was a good night and he tasted the wind. There was moisture on it. Rain? At once he studied the stars and the night sky, all his years of experience concentrating. Rain would come only with storm. Storm could mean typhoon. It was late in the season for summer rains but rains could come late and be sudden and very heavy and typhoon as late as November, as early as May, and if the gods willed, any season of the year.

We could use rain, he thought. But not typhoon.

He shuddered. Now we're almost into Ninth Month.

Ninth Month had bad memories for him. Over the years of his life, typhoon had savaged him nineteen times in that month, seven times since his father had died in 1937 and he had become Head of the House of the Seaborne Wu and Captain of the Fleets.

Of these seven times the first was that year. Winds of 115 knots tore out of the north/northwest and sank one whole fleet of a hundred junks in the Pearl River Estuary. Over a thousand drowned that time—his eldest son with all his family. In '49 when he had ordered all his Pearl River-based armada to flee the Communist Mainland and settle permanently into Hong Kong waters, he had been caught at sea and sunk along with ninety junks and three hundred sampans. He and his family were saved but he had lost 817 of his people. Those winds came out of the east. Twelve years ago from the east/northeast again and seventy junks lost. Ten years ago Typhoon Susan with her eighty-knot gales from the northeast, veering to east/southeast, had decimated his Taiwan-based fleet and cost another five hundred lives there, and another two hundred as far south as Singapore and another son with all his family. Typhoon Gloria in '57, one-hundred-knot gales, another multitude drowned. Last year Typhoon Wanda came and wrecked Aberdeen and most of the Haklo sea villages in the New Territories. Those winds came from the north/northwest and backed to northwest then veered south.

Wu knew the winds well and the number of the days well. September second, eighth, second again, eighteenth, twenty-second, tenth, and Typhoon Wanda first day. Yes, he thought, and those numbers add up to sixty-three, which is divisible by the magic number three, which then makes twenty-one which is three again. Will typhoon come on the third day of the Ninth Month this year? It never has before, never in all memory, but will it this year? Sixty-three is also nine. Will it come on the ninth day?

He tasted the wind again. There was more moisture in it. Rain was coming. The wind had freshened slightly. It came from north/northeast now.

The old seaman hawked and spat. Joss! If it's the third or ninth or second it's joss never mind. The only certain thing is that typhoon will come from some quarter or other and it will come in the Ninth Month—or this month which is equally bad.

He was watching the sampan now and he could see his son sitting amid-ships, alongside the barbarian, and he wondered how far he could trust him. The lad's smart and knows the foreign devil ways very well, he thought, filled with pride. Yes, but how far has he been converted to their evils? I'll soon find out never mind. Once the lad's part of the chain he'll be obedient. Or dead. In the past the House of Wu always traded in opium with or for the Noble House, and sometimes for ourselves. Once opium was honorable.

It still is for some. Me, Smuggler Mo, White Powder Lee, ah, what about them? Should we join into a Brotherhood, or not?

But the White Powders? Are they so different? Aren't they

just stronger opium—like spirit is to beer?

What's the trading difference between the White Powders and salt? None. Except that now stupid foreign devil law says one's contraband and the other isn't! *Ayeeyah*, up to twenty-odd years ago when the barbarians lost their fornicating war to the fiends from the Eastern Sea, the government monopolized the trade here.

Wasn't Hong Kong trade with China built on opium, greased only by opium grown in barbarian India?

But now that they've destroyed their own producing fields, they're trying to pretend the trade never happened, that it's immoral and a terrible crime worth twenty years in prison!

Ayeeyah, how can a civilized person understand a barbarian? Disgustedly he went below.

Eeeee, he thought wearily. This had been a difficult day. First John Chen vanishes. Then those two Cantonese dogmeat fornicators are caught at the airport and my shipment of guns is stolen by the fornicating police. Then this afternoon the tai-pan's letter arrived by hand: 'Greetings Honored Old Friend. On reflection I suggest you put Number Seven Son with the enemy—better for him, better for us. Ask Black Beard to see you tonight. Telephone me afterwards.' It was signed with the tai-pan's chop and 'Old Friend.'

'Old Friend' to a Chinese was a particular person or company who had done you an extreme favor in the past, or someone in business who had proved trustworthy and profitable over the years. Sometimes the years went over generations.

Yes, Wu thought, this tai-pan's an old friend. It was he who had suggested the birth certificate and the new name for his Seventh Son, who suggested sending him to the Golden Country and had smoothed the waters there and the waters into the great university, and had watched over him there without his knowledge—the subterfuge solving his dilemma of how to have one of his sons trained in America without the taint of the opium connection.

What fools barbarians are! Yes, but even so, this tai-pan is not. He's truly an old friend—and so is the Noble House.

Wu remembered all the profits he and his family had made secretly over the generations, with or without the help of the Noble House, in peace and war, trading where barbarian ships could not: contraband, gold, gasoline, opium, rubber, machinery, medical drugs, anything and everything in short supply. Even people, helping them escape from the Mainland or to the Mainland, their passage money considerable. With and without but mostly with the assistance of the Noble House, with this tai-pan and before him Old Hawk Nose, his old cousin, and before him, Mad Dog, his father, and before him the cousin's father, the Wu clan had prospered.

Now Four Finger Wu had 6 percent of the Noble House, purchased over the years and hidden with their help in a maze of nominees but still in his sole control, the largest share of their gold transmittal business, along with heavy investments here, in Macao, Singapore and Indonesia and in property, shipping, banking.

Banking, he thought grimly. I'll cut my nephew's throat after I've fed him his Secret Sack if I lose one copper cash!

He was below now and he went into the seamy, littered main cabin where he and his wife slept. She was in the big straw-filled bunk and she turned over in half-sleep. 'Are you finished now? Are you coming to bed?'

'No. Go to sleep,' he said kindly. 'I've work to do.'

Obediently she did as she was told. She was his *tai-tai*, his chief wife, and they had been married for forty-seven years.

He took off his clothes and changed. He put on a clean white shirt and clean socks and shoes, and the creases of his gray trousers were sharp. He closed the cabin door quietly behind him and came nimbly on deck feeling very uncomfortable and tied in by the clothes. 'I'll be back before dawn, Fourth Grandson,' he said.

'Yes, Grandfather.'

'You stay awake now!'

'Yes, Grandfather.'

He cuffed the boy gently then went across the gangways and stopped at the third junk.

'Goodweather Poon?' he called out.

'Yes . . . yes?' the sleepy voice said. The old man was curled up on old sacking, dozing.

'Assemble all the captains. I'll be back within two hours.'

Poon was immediately alert. 'We sail?' he asked.

'No. I'll be back in two hours. Assemble the captains!'

354

Wu continued on his way and was bowed into his personal ferry sampan. He peered at the shore. His son was standing beside his big black Rolls with the good luck number plate—the single number *8*—that he had purchased for 150,000 HK in the government auction, his uniformed chauffeur and his body-guard, Two Hatchet Tok, waiting deferentially beside him. As always he felt pleasure seeing his great machine and this over-rode his growing concern. Of course, he was not the only dweller in the sea villages who owned a Rolls. But, by custom, his was always the largest and the newest. 8, *baat*, was the luckiest number because it rhymed with *faat* which meant 'ex-panding prosperity.'

He felt the wind shift a point and his anxiety increased. Eeeee, this has been a bad day but tomorrow will be worse.

Has that lump of dogmeat John Chen escaped to the Golden Country or is he truly kidnapped? Without that piece of dung I'm still the tai-pan's running dog. I'm tired of being a running dog. The 100,000 reward for John Chen is money well invested. I'd pay twelve times that for John Chen and his fornicating coin. Thank all gods I put spies in Noble House Chen's household.

He stabbed his hand shoreward. 'Be quick, old man,' he ordered the boatman, his face grim. 'I've a lot to do before dawn!'

19

The day was hot and very humid, the sky sultry, clouds beginning a buildup. Since the opening this morning there had been no letup in the milling, noisy, sweating crowds inside and outside the small Aberdeen branch of the Ho-Pak Bank.

'I've no more money to pay out, Honorable Sung,' the frightened teller whispered, sweat marking her neat *cheong-sam*.

'How much do you need?'

'$7,457 for customer Tok-sing but there must be fifty more people waiting.'

'Go back to your window,' the equally nervous manager replied. 'Delay. Pretend to check the account further—Head Office swore another consignment left their office an hour ago . . . perhaps the traffic . . . Go back to your window, Miss Pang.' Hastily he shut the door of his office after her and, sweating, once more got on the phone. 'The Honorable Richard Kwang please. Hurry. . . .'

Since the bank had opened promptly at ten o'clock, four or five hundred people had squirmed their way up to one of the three windows and demanded their money in full and their savings in full and then, blessing their joss, had shoved and pushed their way out into the world again.

Those with safety deposit boxes had demanded access. One by one, accompanied by an official, they had gone below to the vault, ecstatic or faint with relief. There the official had used his key and the client his key and then the official had left. Alone in the musty air the sweating client had blessed the gods that his joss had allowed him to be one of the lucky ones. Then his shaking hands had scooped the securities or cash or bullion or jewels and all the other secret things into a briefcase or suitcase or paper bag—or stuffed them into bulging pockets, already full with bank notes. Then, suddenly frightened to have so much wealth, so open and vulnerable, all the wealth of their individual world, their happiness had evaporated and they had slunk away to let another take their place, equally nervous, and, initially, equally ecstatic.

The line had started to form long before dawn. Four Finger Wu's people took the first thirty places. This news had rushed around the harbor, so others had joined instantly, then others, then everyone with any account whatsoever as the news spread, swelling the throng. By ten, the nervous, anxious gathering was of riot proportions. Now a few uniformed police were strolling among them, silent and watchful, their presence calming. More came as the day grew, their numbers quietly and carefully orchestrated by East Aberdeen police station. By noon a couple of Black Maria police vans were in one of the nearby alleys with a specially trained riot platoon in support. And European officers.

Most of the crowd were simple fisherfolk and locals, Haklos and Cantonese. Perhaps one in ten was born in Hong Kong. The rest were recent migrants from the People's Republic of China, the Middle Kingdom, as they called their land. They had poured into the Hong Kong sanctuary fleeing the Communists or fleeing the Nationalists, or famine, or just simple poverty as their forebears had done for more than a century. Ninety-eight of every hundred of Hong Kong's population were Chinese and this proportion had been the same ever since the Colony began.

Each person who came out of the bank told anyone who asked that they had been paid in full. Even so, the others who waited were sick with apprehension. All were remembering the crash of last year, and a lifetime in their home villages of other crashes and failures, frauds, rapacious money lenders, embezzlements and corruptions and how easy it was for a life's savings to evaporate through no fault of your own, whatever the government, Communist, Nationalist or warlord. For four thousand years it had always been the same.

And all loathed their dependence on banks—but they had to put their cash somewhere safe, life being what it was and robbers as plentiful as fleas. *Dew neh loh moh* on all banks, most were thinking, they're inventions of the devil—of the foreign devils! Yes. Before foreign devils came to the Middle Kingdom there was no paper money, just real money, silver or gold or copper—mostly silver and copper—that they could feel and hide, that would never evaporate. Not like filthy paper. Rats can eat paper, and men. Paper money's another invention of the foreign devil. Before they came to the Middle Kingdom life was good. Now? *Dew neh loh moh* on all foreign devils!

At eight o'clock this morning, the anxious bank manager had called Richard Kwang. 'But Honored Lord, there must be five hundred people already and the queue goes from here all along the waterfront.'

'Never mind, Honorable Sung! Pay those who want their cash. Don't worry! Just talk to them, they're mostly just superstitious fisherfolk. Talk them out of withdrawing. But those who insist—pay! The Ho-Pak's as strong as Blacs or the Victoria! It's a malicious lie that we're overstretched! Pay! Check their savings books carefully and don't hurry with each client. Be methodical.'

So the bank manager and the tellers had tried to persuade their clients that there was really no need for any anxiety, that false rumors were being spread by malicious people.

'Of course you can have your money, but don't you think . . .'

'*Ayeeyah*, give her the money,' the next in line said irritably, 'she wants her money, I want mine, and there's my wife's brother behind me who wants his and my auntie's somewhere outside. *Ayeeyah*, I haven't got all day! I've got to put to sea. With this wind there'll be a storm in a few days and I have to make a catch. . . .'

And the bank had begun to pay out. In full.

Like all banks, the Ho-Pak used its deposits to service loans to others—all sorts of loans. In Hong Kong there were few regulations and few laws. Some banks lent as much as 80 percent of their cash assets because they were sure their clients would never require back all their money at the same time.

Except today at Aberdeen. But, fortunately, this was only one of eighteen branches throughout the Colony. The Ho-Pak was not yet threatened.

Three times during the day the manager had had to call for

358

extra cash from Head Office in Central. And twice for advice.

At one minute past ten this morning Four Finger Wu was grimly sitting beside the manager's desk with Paul Choy, and Two Hatchet Tok standing behind him.

'You want to close all your Ho-Pak accounts?' Mr. Sung gasped shakily.

'Yes. Now,' Wu said and Paul Choy nodded.

The manager said weakly, 'But we haven't en—'

Wu hissed, 'I want all my money now. Cash or bullion. Now! Don't you understand?'

Mr. Sung winced. He dialed Richard Kwang and explained quickly. 'Yes, yes, Lord.' He offered the phone. 'Honorable Kwang wants to speak to you, Honorable Wu.'

But no amount of persuasion would sway the old seaman. 'No. *Now.* My money, and the money of my people *now.* And also from those other accounts, the, er, those special ones wherever they are.'

'But there isn't that amount of cash in that branch, Honored Uncle,' Richard Kwang said soothingly. 'I'd be glad to give you a cashier's check.'

Wu exploded. 'I don't want checks, I want money! Don't you understand? Money!' He did not understand what a cashier's check was so the frightened Mr. Sung began to explain. Paul Choy brightened. 'That'll be all right, Honored Uncle,' he said. 'A cashier's check's . . .'

The old man roared, 'How can a piece of paper be like cash money? I want money, my money now!'

'Please let me talk to the Honorable Kwang, Great Uncle,' Paul Choy said placatingly, understanding the dilemma. 'Perhaps I can help.'

Wu nodded sourly. 'All right, talk, but get my cash money.'

Paul Choy introduced himself on the telephone and said, 'Perhaps it'd be easier in English, sir.' He talked a few moments then nodded, satisfied. 'Just a moment, sir.' Then in Haklo, 'Great Uncle,' he said, explaining, 'the Honorable Kwang will give you payment in full in government securities, gold or silver at his Head Office, and a piece of paper which you can take to Blacs, or the Victoria for the remainder. But, if I may suggest, because you've no safe to put all that bullion in, perhaps you'll accept Honorable Kwang's cashier's check—with which I can open accounts at either bank for you. Immediately.'

'*Banks!* Banks are foreign devil lobster-pot traps for civilized lobsters!'

It had taken Paul Choy half an hour to convince him. Then they had gone to the Ho-Pak's Head Office but Wu had left Two Hatchet Tok with the quaking Mr. Sung. 'You stay here, Tok. If I don't get my money you will take it out of this branch!'

'Yes, Lord.'

So they had gone to Central and by noon Four Finger Wu had new accounts, half at Blacs, half at the Victoria. Paul Choy had been staggered by the number of separate accounts that had had to be closed and opened afresh. And the amount of cash.

Twenty-odd million HK.

In spite of all his pleading and explaining the old seaman had refused to invest some of his money in selling Ho-Pak short, saying that that was a game for *quai loh* thieves. So Paul had slipped away and gone to every stockbroker he could find, trying to sell short on his own account. 'But, my dear fellow, you've no credit. Of course, if you'll give me your uncle's chop, or assurance in writing, of course. . . .'

He discovered that stockbroking firms were European, almost exclusively, the vast majority British. Not one was Chinese. All the seats on the stock exchange were European held, again the vast majority British. 'That just doesn't seem right, Mr. Smith,' Paul Choy said.

'Oh, I'm afraid our locals, Mr., Mr. . . . Mr. Chee was it?'

'Choy, Paul Choy.'

'Ah yes. I'm afraid all our locals aren't really interested in complicated, modern practices like broking and stock markets—of course you know our locals are all immigrants? When we came here Hong Kong was just a barren rock.'

'Yes. But I'm interested, Mr. Smith. In the States a stockbr—'

'Ah yes, America! I'm sure they do things differently in America, Mr. Chee. Now if you'll excuse me . . . good afternoon.'

Seething, Paul Choy had gone from broker to broker but it was always the same. No one would back him without his father's chop.

Now he sat on a bench in Memorial Square near the Law Courts and the Struan's highrise and Rothwell-Gornt's, and looked out at the harbor, and thought. Then he went to the Law Court library and talked his way past the pedantic librarian. 'I'm from Sims, Dawson and Dick,' he said airily. 'I'm their new attorney from the States. They want some quick information on stock markets and stockbroking.'

'Government regulations, sir?' the elderly Eurasian asked helpfully.

'Yes.'

'There aren't any, sir.'

'Eh?'

'Well, practically none.' The librarian went to the shelves. The requisite section was just a few paragraphs in a giant tome.

Paul Choy gaped at him. 'This's all of it?'

'Yes sir.'

Paul Choy's head reeled. 'But then it's wide open, the market's wide open!'

The librarian was gently amused. 'Yes, compared to London, or New York. As to stockbroking, well, anyone can set up as a broker, sir, provided someone wants them to sell shares and there's someone who wants them to buy and both are prepared to pay commission. The problem is that the, er, the existing firms control the market completely.'

'How do you bust this monopoly?'

'Oh I wouldn't want to, sir. We're really for the status quo in Hong Kong.'

'How do you break in then? Get a piece of the action?'

'I doubt if you could, sir. The, the British control everything very carefully,' he said delicately.

'That doesn't seem right.'

The elderly man shook his head and smiled gently. He steepled his fingers, liking the young Chinese he saw in front of him, envying him his purity—and his American education. 'I presume you want to play the market on your own account?' he asked softly.

'Yeah . . .' Paul Choy tried to cover his mistake and stuttered, 'At least . . . Dawson said for me—'

'Come now, Mr. Choy, you're not from Sims, Dawson and Dick,' he said, chiding him politely. 'If they'd hired an American—an unheard-of innovation—oh I would have heard of it along with a hundred others, long before you even arrived here. You must be Mr. Paul Choy, the great Wu Sang Fang's nephew, who has just come back from Harvard in America.'

Paul Choy gaped at him. 'How'd you know?'

'This is Hong Kong, Mr. Choy. It's a very tiny place. We have to know what's going on. That's how we survive. You do want to play the market?'

'Yes. Mr. . . . ?'

'Manuel Pereira. I'm Portuguese from Macao.' The librarian took out a fountain pen and wrote in beautiful copybook writing an introduction on the back of one of his visiting cards. 'Here. Ishwar Soorjani's an old friend. His place of business is just off the Nathan Road in Kowloon. He's a Parsee from India and deals in money and foreign exchange and buys and sells stocks from time to time. He might help you—but remember if he loans money, or credit, it will be expensive so you should not make any mistakes.'

'Gee thanks, Mr. Pereira.' Paul Choy stuck out his hand. Surprised, Pereira took it. Paul Choy shook warmly then began to rush off but stopped. 'Say, Mr. Pereira . . . the stock market. Is there a long shot? Anything? Any way to get a piece of the action?'

Manuel Pereira had silver-gray hair and long, beautiful hands, and pronounced Chinese features. He considered the youth in front of him. Then he said softly, 'There's nothing to prevent you from forming a company to set up your own stock market, a Chinese stock market. That's quite within Hong Kong law—or lack of it.' The old eyes glittered. 'All you need is money, contacts, knowledge and telephones. . . .'

'My money please,' the old *amah* whispered hoarsely. 'Here's my savings book.' Her face was flushed from the heat within the Ho-Pak branch at Aberdeen. It was ten minutes to three now and she had been waiting since dawn. Sweat streaked her old white blouse and black pants. A long graying ratty queue hung down her back. '*Ayeeyah*, don't shove,' she called out to those behind her. 'You'll get your turn soon!'

Wearily the young teller took the book and glanced again at the clock. *Ayeeyah!* Thank all gods we close at three, she thought, and wondered anxiously through her grinding headache how they were going to close the doors with so many irritable people crammed in front of the grilles, pressed forward by those outside.

The amount in the savings book was 323.42 HK. Following Mr. Sung's instructions to take time and be accurate she went to the files trying to shut her ears to the stream of impatient, muttered obscenities that had gone on for hours. She made sure the amount was correct, then checked the clock again as she came back to her high stool and unlocked her cash drawer and opened it. There was not enough money in her till so she locked the drawer again and went to the manager's office. An undercurrent of rage went through the waiting people. She was a short clumsy woman. Eyes followed her, then went anxiously to the clock and back to her again.

She knocked on his door and closed it after her. 'I can't pay Old Ah Tam,' she said helplessly. 'I've only 100 HK, I've delayed as much . . .'

Manager Sung wiped the sweat off his upper lip. 'It's almost three so make her your last customer, Miss Cho.' He took her through a side door to the vault. The safe door was ponderous. She gasped as she saw the empty shelves. At this time of the day usually the shelves were filled with neat stacks of notes and paper tubes of silver, the notes clipped together in their hundreds and thousands and tens of thousands. Sorting the money after closing was the job she liked best, that and touching the sensuous bundles of new, crisp, fresh bills.

'Oh this is terrible, Honorable Sung,' she said near to tears. Her thick glasses were misted and her hair askew.

'It's just temporary, just temporary, Miss Cho. Remember what the Honorable Haply wrote in today's *Guardian!*' He cleared the last shelf, committing his final reserves, cursing the consignment that had not yet arrived. 'Here.' He gave her 15,000 for show, made her sign for it, and took 15 for each of the other two tellers. Now the vault was empty.

When he came into the main room there was a sudden electric, exciting hush at the apparently large amount of money, cash money.

He gave the money to the other two tellers, then vanished into his office again.

Miss Cho was stacking the money neatly in her drawer, all

eyes watching her and the other tellers. One packet of 1,000 she left on the desk. She broke the seal and methodically counted out 320, and three ones and the change, recounted it and slid it across the counter. The old woman stuffed it into a paper bag, and the next in line irritably shoved forward and thrust his savings book into Miss Cho's face. 'Here, by all the gods. I want seven thous—'

At that moment, the three o'clock bell went and Mr. Sung appeared instantly and said in a loud voice, 'Sorry, we have to close now. All tellers close your—' The rest of his words were drowned by the angry roar.

'By all gods I've waited since dawn . . .'

'*Dew neh loh moh* but I've been here eight hours. . . .'

'*Ayeeyah*, just pay me, you've enough . . .'

'Oh please please please please . . .'

Normally the bank would just have shut its doors and served those within but this time, obediently, the three frightened tellers locked their tills in the uproar, put up their CLOSED signs and backed away from the outstretched hands.

Suddenly the crowd within the bank became a mob.

Those in front were shoved against the counter as others fought to get into the bank. A girl shrieked as she was slammed against the counter. Hands reached out for the grilles that were more for decoration than protection. Everyone was enraged now. One old seaman who had been next in line reached over to try to jerk the till drawer open. The old *amah* was jammed in the seething mass of a hundred or more people and she fought to get to one side, her money clasped tightly in her scrawny hands. A young woman lost her footing and was trampled on. She tried to get up but the milling legs defied her so, in desperation, she bit into one leg and got enough respite to scramble up, stockings ripped, *cheong-sam* torn and now in panic. Her panic whipped the mob further then someone shouted, 'Kill the motherless whore's son . . .' and the shout was taken up, 'Killlllllll!'

There was a split second of hesitation, then, as one, they surged forward.

'*Stop!*'

The word blasted through the atmosphere in English and then in Haklo and then in Cantonese and then in English again.

The silence was sudden and vast.

The uniformed chief inspector stood before them, unarmed and calm, an electric megaphone in his hand. He had come through the back door into an inner office and now he was looking at them.

'It's three o'clock,' he said softly in Haklo. 'The law says banks close at three o'clock. This bank is now closed. Please turn around and go home! Quietly!'

Another silence, angrier this time, then the beginning of a violent swell and one man muttered sullenly, 'What about my fornicating money . . .?' and others almost took up the shout but the police officer moved fast, very fast, directly at the man, fearlessly lifted the countertop and went straight at him into the mob. The mob backed off.

'Tomorrow,' the police officer said gently, towering over him. 'You'll get all your money tomorrow.' The man dropped his eyes, hating the cold blue fish-eyes and the nearness of a foreign devil. Sullenly he moved back a pace.

The policeman looked at the rest of them, into their eyes. 'You at the back,' he ordered, instantly selecting the man with un-erring care, his voice commanding yet with the same quiet confidence, 'Turn around and make way for the others.'

Obediently the man did as he was ordered. The mob became a crowd again. A moment's hesitation then another turned and began to push for the door. '*Dew neh loh moh* I haven't got all day, hurry up,' he said sourly.

They all began to leave, muttering, furious—but individually, not as a mob. Sung and the tellers wiped the sweat off their brows, then sat trembling behind the safety of the counter.

The chief inspector helped the old *amah* up. A fleck of blood was at the corner of her mouth. 'Are you all right, Old Lady?' he asked in Haklo.

She stared at him without understanding. He repeated it in Cantonese.

'Ah, yes . . . yes,' she said hoarsely, still clasping her paper bag tight against her chest. 'Thank you, Honored Lord.' She scuttled away into the crowd and vanished. The room emptied. The Englishman went out to the sidewalk after the last person and stood in the doorway, whistling tonelessly as he watched them stream away.

'Sergeant!'

'Yes sir.'

'You can dismiss the men now. Have a detail here at nine tomorrow. Put up barriers and let the buggers into the bank just three at a time. Yourself and four men'll be more than enough.'

'Yes sir.' The sergeant saluted. The chief inspector turned back into the bank. He locked the front door and smiled at Manager Sung. 'Rather humid this afternoon, isn't it?' he said in English to give Sung face—all educated Chinese in Hong Kong prided themselves on speaking the international language.

'Yes sir,' Sung replied nervously. Normally he liked him and admired this chief inspector greatly. Yes, he thought. But this was the first time he had actually seen a *quai loh* with the Evil Eye, daring a mob, standing alone like a malevolent god in front of the mob, daring it to move, to give him the opportunity to spit fire and brimstone.

Sung shuddered again. 'Thank you, Chief Inspector.'

'Let's go into your office and I can take a statement.'

'Yes, please.' Sung puffed himself up in front of his staff, taking command again. 'The rest of you make up your books and tidy up.'

He led the way into his office and sat down and beamed. 'Tea, Chief Inspector?'

'No thank you.' Chief Inspector Donald C. C. Smyth was about five foot ten and well built, with fair hair and blue eyes and a taut sunburned face. He pulled out a sheaf of papers and put them on the desk. 'These are the accounts of my men. At nine tomorrow, you will close their accounts and pay them. They'll come to the back door.'

'Yes of course. I would be honored. But I will lose face if so many valuable accounts leave me. The bank is as sound as it was yesterday, Chief Inspector.'

'Of course. Meanwhile tomorrow at nine. In cash please.' He handed him some more papers. And four savings books. 'I'll take a cashier's check for all of these. Now.'

'But Chief Inspector, today was extraordinary. There's no problem with the Ho-Pak. Surely you could . . .'

'Now.' Smyth smiled sweetly. 'Withdrawal slips are all signed and ready.'

Sung glanced at them. All were Chinese names that he knew were nominees of nominees of this man whose nickname was the Snake. The accounts totaled nearly 850,000 HK. And that's just in this branch alone, he thought, very impressed with the Snake's acumen. What about the Victoria and Blacs and all the other branches in Aberdeen?

'Very well,' he said wearily. 'But I'll be very sorry to see so many accounts leave the bank.'

Smyth smiled again. 'The whole of the Ho-Pak's not broke yet, is it?'

'Oh no, Chief Inspector,' Sung said, shocked. 'We have published assets worth a billion HK and cash reserves of many tens of millions. It's just these simple people, a temporary problem of confidence. Did you see Mr. Haply's column in the *Guardian*?'

'Yes.'

'Ah.' Sung's face darkened. 'Malicious rumors spread by jealous tai-pans and other banks! If Haply claims that, of course it's true.'

'Of course! Meanwhile I am a little busy this afternoon.'

'Yes. Of course. I'll do it at once. I, er, I see in the paper you've caught one of those evil Werewolves.'

'We've a triad suspect, Mr. Sung, just a suspect.'

Sung shuddered. 'Devils! But you'll catch them all . . . devils, sending an ear! They must be foreigners. I'll wager they're foreigners never mind. Here, sir, I've made the checks . . .'

There was a knock on the door. A corporal came in and saluted. 'Excuse me, sir, a bank truck's outside. They say they're from Ho-Pak's Head Office.'

'*Ayeeyah*,' Sung said, greatly relieved, 'and about time. They promised the delivery at two. It's more money.'

'How much?' Smyth asked.

'Half a million,' the corporal volunteered at once, handing over the manifest. He was a short, bright man with dancing eyes.

'Good,' Smyth said. 'Well, Mr. Sung, that'll take the pressure off you, won't it?'

'Yes. Yes it will.' Sung saw the two men looking at him and he said at once, expansively, 'If it wasn't for you, and your men . . . With your permission I'd like to call Mr. Richard Kwang now. I feel sure he would be honored, as I would be, to make a modest contribution to your police benevolent fund as a token of our thanks.'

'That's very thoughtful, but it's not necessary, Mr. Sung.'

'But I will lose terrible face if you won't accept, Chief Inspector.'

'You're very kind,' Smyth said, knowing truly that without his presence in the bank and that of his men outside, Sung and the tellers and many others would be dead. 'Thank you, but that's not necessary.' He accepted the cashier's checks and left.

Mr. Sung pleaded with the corporal who, at length, sent for his superior. Sergeant Mok declined also. 'Twenty thousand times,' he said.

But Mr. Sung insisted. Wisely. And Richard Kwang was equally delighted and equally honored to approve the unsolicited gift. 20,000 HK. In immediate cash. 'With the bank's great appreciation, Sergeant Mok.'

'Thank you, Honorable Manager Sung,' Mok said politely, pocketing it, pleased to be in the Snake's division and totally impressed that 20,000 was the exact fair market figure the Snake had considered their afternoon's work was worth. 'I hope your great bank stays solvent and you weather this storm with your usual cleverness. Tomorrow will be orderly, of course. We will be here at nine A.M. promptly for our cash. . . .'

The old *amah* still sat on the bench on the harbor wall, catching her breath. Her ribs hurt but then they always hurt, she thought wearily. Joss. Her name was Ah Tam and she began to get up but a youth sauntered up to her and said, 'Sit down, Old Woman, I want to talk to you.' He was short and squat and twenty-one, his face pitted with smallpox scars. 'What's in that bag?'

'What? What bag?'

'The paper bag you clutch to your stinking old rags.'

'This? Nothing, Honored Lord. It's just my poor shopping that—'

He sat on the bench beside her and leaned closer and hissed, 'Shut up, Old Hag! I saw you come out of the fornicating bank. How much have you got there?'

The old woman held on to the bag desperately, her eyes closed in terror and she gasped, 'It's all my savings, Hon—'

He pulled the bag out of her grasp and opened it. '*Ayeeyah!*'

The notes were old and he counted them. '$323!' he said scornfully. 'Who are you *amah* to—a beggar? You haven't been very clever in this life.'

'Oh yes, you're right, Lord!' she said, her little black eyes watching him now.

'My *h'eung yau*'s 20 percent,' he said and began to count the notes.

'But Honored Sir,' she said, her voice whining now, '20 is too high, but I'd be honored if you'd accept 5 with a poor old woman's thanks.'

'15.'

'6!'

'10 and that's my final offer. I haven't got all day!'

'But sir, you are young and strong, clearly a 489. The strong must protect the old and weak.'

'True, true.' He thought a moment, wanting to be fair. 'Very well, 7 percent.'

'Oh how generous you are, sir. Thank you, thank you.' Happily she watched him count 22 dollars, then reach into his jeans pocket and count 61 cents. 'Here.' He gave her the change and the remainder of her money back.

She thanked him profusely, delighted with the bargain she had made. By all the gods, she thought ecstatically, 7 percent instead of, well, at least 15 would be fair. 'Have you also money in the Ho-Pak, Honored Lord?' she asked politely.

'Of course,' the youth said importantly as though it were true. 'My Brotherhood's account has been there for years. We have . . .' he doubled the amount he first thought of, '. . . we have over 25,000 in this branch alone.'

'Eeeee,' the old woman crooned. 'To be so rich! The moment I saw you I knew you were 14K . . . and surely an Honorable 489.'

'I'm better than that,' the youth said proudly at once, filled with bravado. 'I'm . . .' But he stopped, remembering their leader's admonition to be cautious, and so did not say, I'm Kin Sop-ming, Smallpox Kin, and I'm one of the famous Werewolves and there are four of us. 'Run along, old woman,' he said, tiring of her. 'I've more important things to do than talk with you.'

She got up and bowed and then her old eyes spotted the man who had been in the line in front of her. The man was Cantonese, like her. He was a rotund shopkeeper she knew who had a poultry street stall in one of Aberdeen's teeming marketplaces. 'Yes,' she said hoarsely, 'but if you want another customer I see an easy one. He was in the queue before me. Over $8,000 he withdrew.'

'Oh, where? Where is he?' the youth asked at once.

'For a 15 percent share?'

'7—and that's final. 7!'

'All right. 7. Look, over there!' she whispered. 'The fat man, plump as a Mandarin, in the white shirt—the one who's sweating like he's just enjoyed the Clouds and the Rain!'

'I see him.' The youth got up and walked quickly away to intercept the man. He caught up with him at the corner. The man froze and bartered for a while, paid 16 percent and hurried off, blessing his own acumen. The youth sauntered back to her.

'Here, Old Woman,' he said. 'The fornicator had $8,162. 16 percent is . . .'

'$1305.92 and my 7 percent of that is $91.41,' she said at once.

He paid her exactly and she agreed to come tomorrow to spot for him.

'What's your name?' he asked.

'Ah Su, Lord,' she said, giving a false name. 'And yours?'

'Mo Wu-fang,' he said, using a friend's name.

'Until tomorrow,' she said happily. Thanking him again she waddled off, delighted with her day's profit.

His profit had been good too. Now he had over 3,000 in his pockets where this morning he had had only enough for the bus. And it was all windfall for he had come to Aberdeen from Glessing's Point to post another ransom note to Noble House Chen.

'It's for safety,' his father, their leader, had said. 'To put out a false scent for the fornicating police.'

'But it will bring no money,' he had said to him and to the others disgustedly. 'How can we produce the fornicating son if he's dead and buried? Would you pay off without some proof that he was alive? Of course not! It was a mistake to hit him with the shovel.'

'But the fellow was trying to escape!' his brother said.

'True, Younger Brother. But the first blow didn't kill him, only bent his head a little. You should have left it at that!'

'I would have but the evil spirits got into me so I hit him again. I only hit him four times! Eeeee, but these highborn fellows have soft skulls!'

'Yes, you're right,' his father had said. He was short and balding with many gold teeth, his name Kin Min-ta, Baldhead Kin. '*Dew neh loh moh* but it's done so there's no point in remembering it. Joss. It was his own fault for trying to escape! Have you seen the early edition of *The Times?*'

'No—not yet, Father,' he had replied.

'Here, let me read it to you: "The Chief of all the Police said today that they have arrested a triad who they suspect is one of the Werewolves, the dangerous gang of criminals who kidnapped John Chen. The authorities expect to have the case solved any moment."'

They all laughed, he, his younger brother, his father and the last member, his very good friend, Dog-eared Chen—Pun Po Chen—for they knew it was all lies. Not one of them was a triad or had triad connections, and none had ever been caught for any crime before, though they had formed their own Brotherhood and his father had, from time to time, run a small gambling syndicate in North Point. It was his father who had proposed the first kidnapping. Eeee, that was very clever, he thought, remembering. And when John Chen had, unfortunately, had himself killed because he stupidly tried to escape, his father had also suggested cutting off the ear and sending it. 'We will turn his bad joss into our good. "Kill one to terrify ten thousand!" Sending the ear will terrify all Hong Kong, make us famous and make us rich!'

Yes, he thought, sitting in the sun at Aberdeen. But we haven't made our riches yet. Didn't I tell Father this morning: 'I don't mind going all the way to post the letter, Father, that's sensible and what Humphrey Bogart would order. But I still don't think it will bring us any ransom.'

'Never mind and listen! I've a new plan worthy of Al Capone himself. We wait a few days. Then we phone Noble House Chen. If we don't get immediate cash, then we snatch the compradore himself! Great Miser Chen himself!'

They had all stared at him in awe.

'Yes, and if you don't think he'll pay up quickly after seeing his son's ear—of course we'll tell him it was his son's ear . . .

371

perhaps we'll even dig up the body and show him, *heya?*'

Smallpox Kin beamed, recalling how they had all chortled. Oh how they had chortled, holding their bellies, almost rolling on the floor of the tenement apartment.

'Now to business. Dog-eared Chen, we need your advice again.'

Dog-eared Chen was a distant cousin of John Chen and worked for him as a manager of one of the multitudinous Chen companies. 'Your information about the son was perfect. Perhaps you can supply us with the father's movements too?'

'Of course, Honored Leader, that's easy,' Dog-eared Chen had said. 'He's a man of habit—and easily frightened. So is his *tai-tai—ayeeyah*, that mealy-mouthed whore knows which side of the bed she sleeps in! She'll pay up very quickly to get him back. Yes, I'm sure he'll be very cooperative now. But we'll have to ask double what we would settle for because he's an accomplished negotiator. I've worked for the fornicating House of Chen all my working life so I know what a miser he is.'

'Excellent. Now, by all the gods, how and when should we kidnap Noble House Chen himself?'

20

Sir Dunstan Barre was ushered into Richard Kwang's office with the deference he considered his due. The Ho-Pak Building was small and unpretentious, off Ice House Street in Central, and the office was like most Chinese offices, small, cluttered and drab, a place for working and not for show. Most times two or three people would share a single office, running two or three separate businesses there, using the same telephone and same secretary for all. And why not, a wise man would say? A third of the overhead means more profit for the same amount of labor.

But Richard Kwang did not share his office. He knew it did not please his *quai loh* customers—and the few that he had were important to his bank and to him for face and for the highly sought after peripheral benefits they could bring. Like the possible, oh so important election as a voting member to the super-exclusive Turf Club, or membership of the Hong Kong Golf Club or Cricket Club—or even *the* Club itself—or any of the other minor though equally exclusive clubs that were tightly controlled by the British tai-pans of great *hongs* where all the really big business was conducted.

'Hello, Dunstan,' he said affably. 'How are things going?'

'Fine. And you?'

'Very good. My horse had a great workout this morning.'

'Yes. I was at the track myself.'

'Oh, I didn't see you!'

'Just popped in for a minute or two. My gelding's got a temperature—we may have to scratch him on Saturday. But Butterscotch Lass was really flying this morning.'

'She almost pipped the track record. She'll definitely be trying on Saturday.'

Barre chuckled. 'I'll check with you just before race time and you can tell me the inside story then! You can never trust trainers and jockeys, can you—yours or mine or anyone's!'

They chatted inconsequentially, then Barre came to the point.

Richard Kwang tried to cover his shock. 'Close all your corporate accounts?'

'Yes, old boy. Today. Sorry and all that but my board thinks it wise for the moment, until you weath—'

'But surely you don't think we're in trouble?' Richard Kwang laughed. 'Didn't you see Haply's article in the *Guardian*? ". . . malicious lies spread by certain tai-pans and a certain big bank. . . ."'

'Oh yes, I saw that. More of his poppycock, I'd say. Ridiculous! Spread rumors? Why should anyone do that? Huh, I talked to both Paul Havergill and Southerby this morning and they said Haply better watch out this time if he implies it's them or he'll get a libel suit. That young man deserves a horsewhipping! However . . . I'd like a cashier's check now—sorry, but you know how boards are.'

'Yes, yes I do.' Richard Kwang kept his smile on the surface of his face but he hated the big florid man even more than usual. He knew that the board was a rubber stamp for Barre's decisions. 'We've no problems. We're a billion-dollar bank. As to the Aberdeen branch, they're just a lot of superstitious locals.'

'Yes, I know.' Barre watched him. 'I heard you had a few problems at your Mong Kok branch this afternoon too, also at Tsim Sha Tsui . . . at Sha Tin in the New Territories, even, God help us, on Lan Tao.' Lan Tao Island was half a dozen miles east of Hong Kong, the biggest island in the whole archipelago of almost three hundred islands that made up the Colony—but almost unpopulated because it was waterless.

'A few customers withdrew their savings,' Richard Kwang said with a scoff. 'There's no trouble.'

But there was trouble. He knew it and he was afraid everyone knew it. At first it was just at Aberdeen. Then, during the day, his other managers had begun to call with ever-increasing anxiety. He had eighteen branches throughout the Colony. At four of them, withdrawals were untoward and heavy. At Mong Kok, a bustling hive within the teaming city of Kowloon, a line had formed in early afternoon. Everyone had wanted all their money. It was nothing like the frightening proportions at Aberdeen, but enough to show a clear indication of failing confidence. Richard Kwang could understand that the sea villages would hear about Four Finger Wu's withdrawals quickly, and would rush to follow his lead—but what about Mong Kok? Why there? And why Lan Tao? Why at Tsim Sha Tsui, his most profitable branch, which was almost beside the busy Golden Ferry Terminal where 150,000 persons passed by daily, to and from Hong Kong?

It must be a plot!

Is my enemy and arch-rival Smiler Ching behind it? Is it those fornicators, those jealous fornicators at Blacs or the Victoria?

Is Thin Tube of Dung Havergill masterminding the attack? Or is it Compton Southerby of Blacs— he's always hated me. These filthy *quai loh!* But why should they attack me? Of course I'm a much better banker than them and they're jealous but my business is with civilized people and hardly touches them. Why? Or has it leaked somehow that against my better judgment, over my objections, my partners who control the bank have been insisting that I borrow short and cheap and lend long and high on property deals, and now, through their stupidity, we are temporarily overextended and cannot sustain a run?

Richard Kwang wanted to shout and scream and tear his hair out. His secret partners were Lando Mata and Tightfist Tung, major shareholders of Macao's gambling and gold syndicate, along with Smuggler Mo, who had helped him form and finance the Ho-Pak ten years ago. 'Did you see Old Blind Tung's predictions this morning?' he asked, the smile still on his face.

'No. What'd he say?'

Richard Kwang found the paper and passed it over. 'All the portents show we're ready for a boom. The lucky eight is everywhere in the heavens and we're in the eighth month, my birthday is the eighth of the eighth month. . . .'

Barre read the column. In spite of his disbelief in soothsayers, he had been too long in Asia to dismiss them totally. His heart quickened. Old Blind Tung had a vast reputation in Hong Kong. 'If you believe him we're in for the biggest boom in the history of the world,' he said.

'He's usually much more cautious. *Ayeeyah*, that would be good, *heya?*'

'Better than good. Meanwhile Richard old boy, let's finish our business, shall we?'

'Certainly. It's all a typhoon in an oyster shell, Dunstan. We're stronger than ever—our stock's hardly a point off.' When the market had opened, there had been a mass of small offerings to sell, which if not reacted to at once would have sent their stock plummeting. Richard Kwang had instantly ordered his brokers to buy and to keep buying. This had stabilized the stock. During the day, to maintain the position, he had had to buy almost five million shares, an unheard-of number to be traded in one day. None of his experts could pinpoint who was selling big. There was no reason for a lack of confidence, other than Four Finger Wu's withdrawals. All gods curse that old devil and his fornicating, too smart Harvard-trained nephew! 'Why not le—'

The phone rang. ''Scuse me,' then curtly into the phone, 'I said no interruptions!'

'It's Mr. Haply from the *Guardian*, he says it's important,' his secretary, his niece Mary Yok said. 'And the tai-pan's secretary called. The Nelson Trading board meeting's brought forward to this afternoon at five o'clock. Mr. Mata called to say he would be there too.'

Richard Kwang's heart skipped three beats. Why? he asked himself, aghast. *Dew neh loh moh* it was supposed to be postponed to next week. *Oh ko* why? Then quickly he put aside that question to consider Haply. He decided that to answer now in front of Barre was too dangerous. 'I'll call him back in a few minutes.' He smiled at the red-faced man in front of him. 'Leave everything for a day or two, Dunstan, we've no problems.'

'Can't, old boy. Sorry. There was a special meeting, have to settle it today. The board insisted.'

'We've been generous in the past—you've forty million of our money unsecured now—we're joint venturing another seventy million with you on your new building program.'

'Yes, indeed you are, Richard, and your profit will be substantial. But they're another matter and those loans were negotiated in good faith months ago and will be settled in good faith when they're due. We've never defaulted on a payment to the Ho-Pak or anyone else.' Barre passed the newspaper back and with it signed documents imprinted with his corporate seal. 'The accounts are consolidated so one check will suffice.'

The amount was a little over nine and a half million.

Richard Kwang signed the cashier's check and smiled Sir Dunstan Barre out, then, when it was safe, cursed everyone in sight and went back into his office, slamming the door behind him. He kicked his desk then picked up the phone and shouted at his niece to get Haply and almost broke the phone as he slammed it back on its cradle.

'*Dew neh loh moh* on all filthy *quai loh*,' he shrieked to the ceiling and felt much better. That lump of dogmeat! I wonder . . . oh, I wonder if I could prevail on the Snake to forbid any lines at all tomorrow? Perhaps he and his men could break a few arms.

Gloomily Richard Kwang let his mind drift. It had been a rotten day. It had begun badly at the track. He was sure his trainer—or jockey—was feeding Butterscotch Lass pep pills to make her run faster to shorten her odds—she'd be favorite now—then Saturday they'd stop the pills and back an outsider and clean up without his being in on the profit-making. Dirty dog bones, all of them! Liars! Do they think I own a racehorse to lose money?

The banker hawked and spat into the spittoon.

Maggot-mouthed Barre and dog bone Uncle Wu! Those withdrawals will take most of my cash. Never mind, with Lando Mata, Smuggler Mo, Tightfist Tung and the tai-pan I'm quite safe. Oh I'll have to shout and scream and curse and weep but nothing can really touch me or the Ho-Pak. I'm too important to them.

Yes, it had been a rotten day. The only bright spot had been his meeting this morning with Casey. He had enjoyed looking at her, enjoyed her clean-smelling, smart, crisp Americanness of the great outdoors. They had fenced pleasantly about financing and he felt sure he could get all or certainly part of their business. Clearly the pickings would be huge. She's so naive, he thought. Her knowledge of banking and finance's impressive but of the Asian world, nil! She's so naive to be so open with their plans. Thank all gods for Americans.

'I love America, Miss Casey. Yes. Twice a year I go there, to eat good steaks and go to Vegas—and to do business of course.'

Eeeee, he thought happily, the whores of the Golden Country are the best and most available *quai loh* in the world, and *quai lohs*'re so cheap compared to Hong Kong girls! Oh oh oh! I get such a good feeling pillowing them, with their great deodorized armpits, their great tits and thighs and rears. But in Vegas it's the best. Remember the golden-haired beauty that towered over me but lying down she . . .

His private phone rang. He picked it up, irritated as always that he had had to install it. But he had had no option. When his previous secretary of many years had left to get married, his wife had planted her favorite niece firmly in her place, of course to spy on me, he thought sourly. Eeeee, what can a man do?

'Yes?' he asked, wondering what his wife wanted now.

'You didn't call me all day. . . . I've been waiting for hours!'

His heart leapt at the unexpected sound of the girl's voice. He dismissed the petulance, her Cantonese sweet like her Jade Gate. 'Listen, Little Treasure,' he said, his voice placating. 'Your poor Father's been very busy today. I've—'

'You just don't want your poor Daughter anymore. I'll have to throw myself in the harbor or find another person to cherish me oh oh oh. . . .'

His blood pressure soared at the sound of her tears. 'Listen, Little Oily Mouth, I'll see you this evening at ten. We'll have an eight-course feast at Wanchai at my fav—'

'Ten's too late and I don't want a feast I want a steak and I want to go to the penthouse at the V and A and drink champagne!'

His spirit groaned at the danger of being seen and reported secretly to his *tai-tai*. Oh oh oh! But, in front of his friends and his enemies and all Hong Kong he would gain enormous face to escort his new mistress there, the young exotic rising star in TV's firmament, Venus Poon.

'At ten I'll call f—'

'Ten's too late. Nine.'

Rapidly he tried to sort out all his meetings tonight to see how he could accommodate her. 'Listen, Little Treasure, I'll se—'

'Ten's too late. Nine. I think I will die now that you don't care anymore.'

'Listen. Your Father has three meetings and I th—'

'Oh my head hurts to think you don't want me anymore oh oh oh. This abject person will have to slit her wrists, or. . . .' He heard the change in her voice and his stomach twisted at the threat, 'Or answer the phone calls of others, lesser than her revered Father of course, but just as rich nonetheless and m—'

'All right, Little Treasure. At nine!'

'Oh you do *love* me, don't you!' Though she was speaking Cantonese Venus Poon used the English word and his heart flipped. English was the language of love for modern Chinese, there were no romantic words in their own language. 'Tell me!' she said imperiously. 'Tell me you *love* me!'

He told her, abjectly, then hung up. The mealy-mouthed little whore, he thought irritably. But then, at nineteen she's a right to be demanding and petulant and difficult if you're almost sixty and she makes you feel twenty and the Imperial Yang blissful. Eeeee, but Venus Poon's the best I've ever had. Expensive but, eeee, she's got muscles in her Golden Gully that only the legendary Emperor Kung wrote about!

He felt his yang stir and scratched pleasantly. I'll give that little baggage what for tonight. I'll buy an extra specially large device, ah yes, a ring with bells on it. Oh oh oh! That'll make her wriggle!

Yes, but meanwhile think about tomorrow. How to prepare for tomorrow?

Call your High Dragon friend, Sergeant Tang-po at Tsim Sha Tsui and enlist his help to see that his branch and all branches in Kowloon are well policed. Phone Blacs and Cousin Tung of the huge Tung Po Bank and Cousin Smiler Ching and Havergill to arrange extra cash against the Ho-Pak's securities and holdings. Ah yes, phone your very good friend Joe Jacobson, VP of the Chicago Federal and International Merchant Bank—his bank's got assets of four billion and he owes you lots of favors. Lots. There're lots of *quai loh* who're deeply in your debt, and civilized people. Call them all!

Abruptly Richard Kwang came out of his reverie as he remembered the tai-pan's summons. His soul twisted. Nelson Trading's deposits in bullion and cash were huge. *Oh ko* if Nels—

The phone jangled irritably. 'Uncle, Mr. Haply's on the line.'

'Hello, Mr. Haply, how nice to talk to you. Sorry I was engaged before.'

'That's all right, Mr. Kwang. I just wanted to check a couple of facts if I may. First, the riot at Aberdeen. The police w—'

'Hardly a riot, Mr. Haply. A few noisy, impatient people, that's all,' he said, despising Haply's Canadian-American accent, and the need to be polite.

'I'm looking at some photos right now, Mr. Kwang, the ones that're in this afternoon's *Times*—it looks like a riot all right.'

The banker squirmed in his chair and fought to keep his voice calm. 'Oh—oh well I wasn't there so . . . I'll have to talk to Mr. Sung.'

'I did, Mr. Kwang. At 3:30. Spent half an hour with him. He said if it hadn't been for the police they'd've torn the place apart.' There was a hesitation. 'You're right to play it down, but, say, I'm trying to help, and I can't without the facts, so if you'll level with me . . . How many folks wanted their money out at Lan Tao?'

Richard Kwang said, '18,' halving the real figure.

'Our guy said 36. 82 at Sha Tin. How about Mong Kok?'

'A cupful.'

'My guy said 48, and there was a good 100 left at closing. How about Tsim Sha Tsui?'

'I haven't got the figures yet, Mr. Haply,' Richard Kwang said smoothly, consumed with anxiety, hating the staccato questioning.

'All the evening editions're heavy with the Ho-Pak run. Some're even using the word.'

'*Oh ko. . . .*'

'Yeah. I'd say you'd better get ready for a real hot day tomorrow, Mr. Kwang. I'd say your opposition's very well organized. Everything's too pat to be a coincidence.'

'I certainly appreciate your interest.' Then Richard Kwang added delicately, 'If there's anything I can do . . .'

Again the irritating laugh. 'Have any of your big depositors pulled out today?'

Richard Kwang hesitated a fraction of a moment and he heard Haply jump into the breach. 'Of course I know about Four Finger Wu. I meant the big British *hongs*.'

'No, Mr. Haply, not yet.'

'There's a strong rumor that Hong Kong and Lan Tao Farms's going to change banks.'

Richard Kwang felt that barb in his Secret Sack. 'Let's hope it's not true, Mr. Haply. Who're the tai-pans and what big bank or banks? Is it the Victoria or Blacs?'

'Perhaps it's Chinese. Sorry, I can't divulge a news source. But you'd better get organized—it sure as hell looks as though the big guys are after you.'

21

'They don't sleep together, tai-pan,' Claudia Chen said.

'Eh?' Dunross looked up absently from the stack of papers he was going through.

'No. At least they didn't last night.'

'Who?'

'Bartlett and your Cirrannousshee.'

Dunross stopped working. 'Oh?'

'Yes. Separate rooms, separate beds, breakfast together in the main room—both neat and tidy and dressed in modest robes which is interesting because neither wears anything in bed.'

'They don't?'

'No, at least they didn't last night.'

Dunross grinned and she was glad that her news pleased him. It was his first real smile of the day. Since she had arrived at 8:00 A.M. he had been working like a man possessed, rushing out for meetings, hurrying back again: the police, Phillip Chen, the governor, twice to the bank, once to the penthouse to meet whom she did not know. No time for lunch and, so the doorman had told her, the tai-pan had arrived with the dawn.

She had seen the weight on his spirit today, the weight that sooner or later bowed all tai-pans—and sometimes broke them. She had seen Ian's father withered away by the enormous shipping losses of the war years, the catastrophic loss of Hong Kong, of his sons and nephews—bad joss piling on bad joss. It was the loss of Mainland China that had finally crushed him. She had seen how Suez had broken Alastair Struan, how that tai-pan had never recovered from that debacle and how bad joss had piled on bad joss for him until the Gornt-mounted run on their stock had shattered him.

It must be a terrible strain, she thought. All our people to worry about and our House, all our enemies, all the unexpected catastrophes of nature and of man that seem to be ever present—and all the sins and piracies and devil's work of the past that are waiting to burst forth from our own Pandora's box as they do from time to time. It's a pity the tai-pans aren't Chinese, she thought. Then the sins of the past would be so much gossamer.

'What makes you sure, Claudia?'

'No sleep things for either—pajamas or filmy things.' She beamed.

'How do you know?'

'Please, tai-pan, I can't divulge my sources!'

'What else do you know?'

'Ah!' she said, then blandly changed the conversation. 'The Nelson Trading board meeting's in half an hour. You wanted to be reminded. Can I have a few minutes beforehand?'

'Yes. In a quarter of an hour. Now,' he said with a finality she knew too well. 'What else do you know?'

She sighed, then importantly consulted her notepad. 'She's never been married. Oh, lots of suitors but none have lasted, tai-pan. In fact, according to rumors, none have . . .'

Dunross's eyebrows shot up. 'You mean she's a virgin?'

'Of that we're not sure—only that she has no reputation for staying out late, or overnight, with a gentleman. No. The only gentleman she goes out socially with is Mr. Bartlett and that's infrequently. Except on business trips. He, by the way, tai-pan, he's quite a gadabout—*swinger* was the term used. No one lady bu—'

'Used by whom?'

'Ah! Mr. Handsome Bartlett doesn't have one special girl friend, tai-pan. Nothing steady as they say. He was divorced in 1956, the same year that your Cirrrannnousshee joined his firm.'

'She's not my Ciranoush,' he said.

Claudia beamed more broadly. 'She's twenty-six She's Sagittarius.'

'You got someone to snitch her passport—or got someone to take a peek?'

'Very good gracious no, tai-pan.' Claudia pretended to be

shocked. 'I don't spy on people. I just ask questions. But 100 says she and Mr. Bartlett have been lovers at some time or another.'

'That's no bet, I'd be astounded if they weren't. He's certainly in love with her—and she with him. You saw how they danced together. That's no bet at all.'

The lines around her eyes crinkled. 'Then what odds will you give me they've never been lovers?'

'Eh? What d'you know?' he asked suspiciously.

'Odds, tai-pan?'

He watched her. Then he said, 'A thousand to . . . I'll give you ten to one.'

'Done! A hundred. Thank you tai-pan. Now, about the Nels—'

'Where'd you get all this information? Eh?'

She extracted a telex from the papers she was carrying. The rest she put into his in-tray. 'You telexed our people in New York the night before last for information on her and to recheck Bartlett's dossier. This's just arrived.'

He took it and scanned it. His reading was very fast and his memory almost photographic. The telex gave the information Claudia had related in bald terms without her embroidered interpretation and added that K. C. Tcholok had no known police record, $46,000 in a savings account at the San Fernando Savings and Loan, and $8,700 in her checking account at the Los Angeles and California Bank.

'It's shocking how easy it is in the States to find out how much you've got in the bank, isn't it, Claudia?'

'Shocking. I'd never use one, tai-pan.'

He grinned. 'Except to borrow from! Claudia, just give me the telex next time.'

'Yes, tai-pan. But isn't my way of telling certain things more exciting?'

'Yes. But where's it say about the nakedness? You made that up!'

'Oh no, that's from my own source here. Third Toiletma—' Claudia stopped just too late to avoid falling into his trap.

His smile was seraphic. 'So! A spy in the V and A! Third Toiletmaid! Who? Which one, Claudia?'

To give him face she pretended to be annoyed. '*Ayeeyah!* A

384

spymaster may reveal nothing, *heya?*' Her smile was kindly. 'Here's a list of your calls. I've put off as many as I can till tomorrow—I'll buzz you in good time for the meeting.'

He nodded but she saw that his smile had vanished and now he was lost in thought again. She went out and he did not hear the door close. He was thinking about spymasters and AMG and his meeting with Brian Kwok and Roger Crosse this morning at ten, and the one coming at six o'clock.

The meeting this morning had been short, sharp and angry. 'First, is there anything new on AMG?' he had asked.

Roger Crosse had replied at once. 'It was, apparently, an accident. No suspicious marks on the body. No one was seen nearby, no car marks, impact marks or skid marks—other than the motorcycle's. Now, the files, Ian—oh by the way we know now you've got the only copies existent.'

'Sorry but I can't do what you asked.'

'Why?' There had been a sour edge to the policeman's voice.

'I'm still not admitting one way or the other that they exist but y—'

'Oh for chrissake, Ian, don't be ridiculous! Of course the copies exist. Do you take us for bloody fools? If they didn't, you'd've come out with it last night and that would have been that. I strongly advise you to let us copy them.'

'And I strongly advise you to have a tighter hold on your temper.'

'If you think I've lost my temper, Ian, then you know very little about me. I formally ask you to produce those documents. If you refuse I'll invoke my powers under the Official Secrets Act at six o'clock this evening and tai-pan or not, of the Noble House or not, friend or not, by one minute past six you'll be under arrest. You'll be held incommunicado and we'll go through all your papers, safes, deposit boxes until we've found them! Now kindly produce the files!'

Dunross remembered the taut face and the iced eyes staring at him, his real friend Brian Kwok in shock. 'No.'

Crosse had sighed. The threat in the sound had sent a tremor through him. 'For the last time, why?'

'Because, in the wrong hands, I think they'd be damaging to Her Maj—'

'Good sweet Christ, I'm head of Special Intelligence!'

'I know.'

'Then kindly do as I ask.'

'Sorry. I spent most of the night trying to work out a safe way to giv—'

Roger Crosse had got up. 'I'll be back at six o'clock for the files. Don't burn them, Ian. I'll know if you try and I'm afraid you'll be stopped. Six o'clock.'

Last night while the house slept, Dunross had gone to his study and reread the files. Rereading them now with the new knowledge of AMG's death and possible murder, the involvement of MI-5 and -6, probably the KGB, and Crosse's astounding anxiety; and then the added thought that perhaps some of the material might not yet be available to the Secret Service, together with the possibility that many of the pieces he had dismissed as too farfetched were not—now all the reports took on new importance. Some of them blew his mind.

To hand them over was too risky. To keep them now, impossible.

In the quiet of the night Dunross had considered destroying them. Finally he concluded it was his duty not to. For a moment he had considered leaving them openly on his desk, the French windows wide to the terrace darkness, and going back to sleep. If Crosse was so concerned about the papers then he and his men would be watching now. To lock them in the safe was unsafe. The safe had been touched once. It would be touched again. No safe was proof against an absolute, concerted professional attack.

There in the darkness, his feet perched comfortably, he had felt the excitement welling, the beautiful, intoxicating lovely warmth of danger surrounding him, physical danger. Of enemies nearby. Of being perched on the knife edge between life and void. The only thing that detracted from his pleasure was the knowledge that Struan's was betrayed from within, the same question always grinding: Is the Sevrin spy the same as he who gave their secrets to Bartlett? One of seven? Alastair, Phillip, Andrew, Jacques, Linbar, David MacStruan in Toronto, or his father. All unthinkable.

His mind had examined each one. Clinically, without passion. All had the opportunity, all the same motive: jealousy, and hatred, in varying degrees. But not one would sell the Noble

House to an outsider. Not one. Even so, one of them did.

Who?

The hours passed.

Who? Sevrin, what to do about the files, was AMG murdered, how much of the files're true?

Who?

The night was cool now and the terrace had beckoned him. He stood under the stars. The breeze and the night welcomed him. He had always loved the night. Flying alone above the clouds at night, so much better than the day, the stars so near, eyes always watching for the enemy bomber or enemy night fighter, thumb ready on the trigger . . . ah, life was so simple then, kill or be killed.

He stood there for a while, then, refreshed, he went back and locked the files away and sat in his great chair facing the French windows, on guard, working out his options, choosing one. Then, satisfied, he had dozed an hour or so and awoke, as usual, just before dawn.

His dressing room was off his study which was next door to their master bedroom. He had dressed casually and left silently. The road was clear. Sixteen seconds were clipped from his record. In his penthouse he bathed and shaved and changed into a tropical suit, then went to his office on the floor below. It was very humid today with a curious look to the sky. A tropical storm's coming, he had thought. Perhaps we'll be lucky and it won't pass us by like all the others and it'll bring rain. He turned away from his windows and concentrated on running the Noble House.

There was a pile of overnight telexes to deal with on all manner of negotiations and enterprises, problems and business opportunities throughout the Colony and the great outside. From all points of the compass. As far north as the Yukon where Struan's had an oil-prospecting joint venture with the Canadian timber and mining giant, McLean-Woodley. Singapore and Malaya and as far south as Tasmania for fruit and minerals to carry to Japan. West to Britain, east to New York, the tentacles of the new international Noble House that Dunross dreamed about were beginning to reach out, still weak, still tentative, and without the sustenance he knew was vital to their growth.

Never mind. Soon they'll be strong. The Par-Con deal will

make our web like steel, with Hong Kong the center of the earth and us the nucleus of the center. Thank God for the telex and telephones.

'Mr. Bartlett please.'

'Hello?'

'Ian Dunross, good morning, sorry to disturb you so early, could we postpone our meeting till 6:30?'

'Yes. Is there a problem?'

'No. Just business. I've a lot to catch up with.'

'Anything on John Chen?'

'Not yet, no. Sorry. I'll keep you posted though. Give my regards to Casey.'

'I will. Say, that was some party last night. Your daughter's a charmer!'

'Thanks. I'll come to the hotel at 6:30. Of course Casey's invited. See you then. 'Bye!'

Ah Casey! he thought.

Casey and Bartlett. Casey and Gornt. Gornt and Four Finger Wu.

Early this morning he had heard from Four Finger Wu about his meeting with Gornt. A pleasant current had swept through him on hearing that his enemy had almost died. The Peak Road's no place to lose your brakes, he thought.

Pity the bastard didn't die. That would have saved me lots of anguish. Then he dismissed Gornt and rethought Four Finger Wu.

Between the old seaman's pidgin and his Haklo they could converse quite well. Wu had told him everything he could. Gornt's comment on the Ho-Pak, advising Wu to withdraw his money, was surprising. And cause for concern. That and Haply's article.

Does that bugger Gornt know something I don't?

He had gone to the bank. 'Paul, what's going on?'

'About what?'

'The Ho-Pak.'

'Oh. The run? Very bad for our banking image, I must say. Poor Richard! We're fairly certain he's got all the reserves he needs to weather his storm but we don't know the extent of his commitments. Of course I called him the moment I read Haply's ridiculous article. I must tell you, Ian, I also called Christian

388

Toxe and told him in no uncertain terms he should control his reporters and that he'd better cease and desist or else.'

'I was told there was a queue at Tsim Sha Tsui.'

'Oh? I hadn't heard that. I'll check. Even so, surely the Ching Prosperity and the Lo Fat banks will support him. My God, he's built up the Ho-Pak into a major banking institution. If he went broke God knows what'll happen. We even had some withdrawals at Aberdeen ourselves. No, Ian, let's hope it'll all blow over. Talking about that, do you think we'll get some rain? It feels dicey today, don't you think? The news said there might be a storm coming through. Do you think it'll rain?'

'I don't know. Let's hope so. But not on Saturday!'

'My God yes! If the races were rained out that would be terrible. We can't have that. Oh, by the way, Ian, it was a lovely party last night. I enjoyed meeting Bartlett and his girl friend. How're your negotiations with Bartlett proceeding?'

'First class! Listen, Paul . . .'

Dunross smiled to himself, remembering how he had dropped his voice even though in Havergill's office . . . Havergill's office which overlooked the whole of Central Distrct was book-lined and very carefully soundproofed. 'I've closed my deal. It's two years initially. We sign the papers within seven days. They're putting up 20 million cash in each of the years, succeeding ones to be negotiated.'

'Congratulations, my dear fellow. Heartiest congratulations! And the down payment?'

'Seven.'

'That's marvelous! That covers everything nicely. It'll be marvelous to have the Toda specter away from the balance sheet—and with another million for Orlin, well, perhaps they'll give you more time, then at long last you can forget all the bad years and look forward to a very profitable future.'

'Yes.'

'Have you got your ships chartered yet?'

'No. But I'll have charterers in time to service our loan.'

'I noticed your stock's jumped two points.'

'It's on the way now. It's going to double, within thirty days.'

'Oh? What makes you think so?'

'The boom.'

'Eh?'

389

'All the signs point that way, Paul. Confidence's up. Our Par-Con deal will lead the boom. It's long overdue.'

'That would be marvelous! When do you make the initial announcement about Par-Con?'

'Friday, after the market closes.'

'Excellent. My thought entirely. By Monday everyone will be on the bandwagon!'

'But let's keep everything in the family until then.'

'Of course. Oh, did you hear Quillan almost killed himself last night. It was just after your party. His brakes failed on the Peak Road.'

'Yes I heard. He should have killed himself—that would have sent Second Great Company's stock skyrocketing with happiness!'

'Come now, Ian! A boom eh? You really think so?'

'Enough to want to buy heavily. How about a million credit—to buy Struan's?'

'Personal—or for the House?'

'Personal.'

'We would hold the stock?'

'Of course.'

'And if the stock goes down?'

'It won't.'

'Say it dies, Ian?'

'What do you suggest?'

'Well, it's all in the family so why don't we say if it goes two points below market at today's closing, we can sell and debit your account with the loss?'

'Three. Struan's is going to double.'

'Yes. Meanwhile, let's say two until you sign the Par-Con deal. The House is rather a lot over on its revolving credit already. Let's say two, eh?'

'All right.'

I'm safe at two, Dunross thought again, reassuring himself. I think.

Before he had left the bank he had gone by Johnjohn's office. Bruce Johnjohn, second deputy chief manager and heir apparent to Havergill, was a stocky, gentle man with a humming-bird's vitality. Dunross had given him the same news. Johnjohn had been equally pleased. But he had advised caution on projecting a boom and, contrary to Havergill, was greatly concerned with the Ho-Pak run.

'I don't like it at all, Ian. It's very smelly.'

'Yes. What about Haply's article?'

'Oh, it's all nonsense. We don't go in for those sort of shenanigans. Blacs? Equally foolish. Why should we want to eliminate a major Chinese bank, even if we could. The Ching Bank might be the culprit. Perhaps. Perhaps old Smiler Ching would—he and Richard have been rivals for years. It could be a combination of half a dozen banks, Ching included. It might even be that Richard's depositors are really scared. I've heard all sorts of rumors for three months or so. They're in deep with dozens of dubious property schemes. Anyway, if he goes under it'll affect us all. Be bloody careful, Ian!'

'I'll be glad when you're upstairs, Bruce.'

'Don't sell Paul short—he's very clever and he's been awfully good for Hong Kong and the bank. But we're in for some hairy times in Asia, Ian. I must say I think you're very wise to try to diversify into South America—it's a huge market and untapped by us. Have you considered South Africa?'

'What about it?'

'Let's have lunch next week. Wednesday? Good. I've an idea for you.'

'Oh? What?'

'It'll wait, old chum. You heard about Gornt?'

'Yes.'

'Very unusual for a Rolls, what?'

'Yes.'

'He's very sure he can take Par-Con away from you.'

'He won't.'

'Have you seen Phillip today?'

'Phillip Chen? No, why?'

'Nothing.'

'Why?'

'Bumped into him at the track. He seemed . . . well, he looked awful and very distraught. He's taking John's . . . he's taking the kidnapping very badly.'

'Wouldn't you?'

'Yes. Yes I would. But I didn't think he and his Number One Son were that close.'

Dunross thought about Adryon and Glenna and his son Duncan who was fifteen and on holiday on a friend's sheep station in Australia. What would I do if one of them were kidnapped? What would I do if a mutilated ear came through the mails at me like that?

I'd go mad.

I'd go mad with rage. I'd forget everything else and I'd hunt down the kidnappers and then, and then my vengeance would last a thousand years. I'd . . .

There was a knock on the door. 'Yes? Oh hello, Kathy,' he said, happy as always to see his younger sister.

'Sorry to interrupt, Ian dear,' Kathy Gavallan said in a rush from the door to his office, 'but Claudia said you had a few minutes before your next appointment. Is it all right?'

''Course it's all right,' he said with a laugh, and put aside the memo he was working on.

'Oh good, thanks.' She closed the door and sat in the high chair that was near the window.

He stretched to ease the ache in his back and grinned at her. 'Hey, I like your hat.' It was pale straw with a yellow band that matched her cool-looking silk dress. 'What's up?'

'I've got multiple sclerosis.'

He stared at her blankly. 'What?'

'That's what the tests say. The doctor told me yesterday but yesterday I couldn't tell you or . . . Today he checked the tests with another specialist and there's no mistake.' Her voice was calm and her face calm and she sat upright in the chair, looking prettier than he had ever seen her. 'I had to tell someone. Sorry to say it so suddenly. I thought you could help me make a plan, not today, but when you've time, perhaps over the weekend. . . .' She saw his expression and she laughed nervously. 'It's not as bad as that. I think.'

Dunross sat back in his big leather chair and fought to get his shocked mind working. 'Multiple . . . that's dicey, isn't it?'

'Yes. Yes it is. Apparently it's something that attacks your nervous system that they can't cure yet. They don't know what it is or where or how you . . . how you get it.'

'We'll get other specialists. No, even better, you go to England with Penn. There'd be specialists there or in Europe. There's got to be some form of cure, Kathy, got to be!'

'There isn't, dear. But England is a good idea. I'm . . . Dr. Tooley said he'd like me to see a Harley Street specialist for treatment. I'd love to go with Penn. I'm not too advanced and there's nothing to be too concerned about, if I'm careful.'

'Meaning?'

'Meaning that if I take care of myself, take their medication, nap in the afternoon to stop getting tired, I'll still be able to take care of Andrew and the house and the children and play a little tennis and golf occasionally, but only one round in the mornings. You see, they can arrest the disease but they can't repair the damage already done so far. He said if I don't take care of myself and rest—it's rest mostly he said—if I don't rest, it will start up again and then each time you go down a plateau. Yes. And then you can never get back up again. Do you see, dear?'

He stared at her, keeping his agony for her bottled. His heart was grinding in his chest and he had eight plans for her and he thought Oh Christ poor Kathy! 'Yes. Well, thank God you can rest all you want,' he said, keeping his voice calm like hers. 'Do you mind if I talk to Tooley?'

'I think that would be all right. There's no need to be alarmed, Ian. He said I'd be all right if I took care of myself, and I told him I'd be ever so good so he needn't have any worries on that score.' Kathy was surprised that her voice was calm and her hands and fingers rested in her lap so easily, betraying none of the horror she felt within. She could almost feel the disease bugs or microbes or viruses seeping through her system, feeding on her nerves, eating them away oh so slowly, second by second hour by hour until there would be more tingling and more numbness in her fingers and toes, then her wrists and ankles and legs and and and and and oh Jesus Christ God almighty . . .

She took a little tissue out of her purse and gently dabbed beside her nose and forehead. 'It's awfully humid today, isn't it?'

'Yes. Kathy, why is it so sudden?'

'Well it isn't dear, not really. They just couldn't diagnose it. That's what all the tests were for.' It had begun as a slight dizziness and headaches about six months ago. She'd noticed it most when she was playing golf. She would be standing over her ball, steadying herself, but her eyes would go dizzy and she could not focus and the ball would split and become two and three and two again and they would never stay still. Andrew had laughed and told her to see an optician. But it wasn't glasses, and aspirins did not help, nor stronger pills. Then dear old Tooley, their family doctor forever, had sent her to Matilda Hospital on the Peak for tests and more tests and brain scans in case there was a tumor but they had shown nothing, nor had all the other tests. Only the awful spinal tap gave a clue. Other tests confirmed it. Yesterday. Oh sweet Jesus, was it only yesterday they condemned me to the wheelchair, at length to become a helpless slobbering thing?

'You've told Andrew?'

'No dear,' she said, pulled once more back from the brink. 'I haven't told him yet. I couldn't, not yet. Poor dear Andrew does get into a tizzy so easily. I'll tell him tonight. I couldn't tell him before I told you. I had to tell you first. We always used to tell you everything first, didn't we? Lechie, Scotty and I? You always used to know first. . . .' She was remembering when they were all young, all the lovely happy times here in Hong Kong and in Ayr at Castle Avisyard, at their lovely old rambling house on the crest of the hill amid the heather, overlooking the sea—Christmas and Easter and the long summer holidays, she and Ian—and Lechie, the oldest, and Scott, her twin brother—such happy days when Father wasn't there, all of them terrified of their father except Ian who was always their spokesman, always their protector, who always took the punishments—no supper tonight, and write five hundred times I will not argue anymore, a child's place is to be seen and not heard—who took all the beatings and never complained. Oh poor Lechie and Scotty . . .

'Oh Ian,' she said, her tears welling suddenly, 'I'm so sorry.' Then she felt his arms wrap around her and she felt safe at last and the nightmare softened. But she knew it would never go away. Not now. Never. Nor would her brothers come back, except in her dreams, nor would her darling Johnny. 'It's all right, Ian,' she said through her tears. 'It's not for me, not me really. I was just thinking about Lechie and Scotty and home at Ayr when we were small, and my Johnny, and I was oh ever so sad for all of them. . . .'

Lechie was the first to die. Second Lieutenant, Highland Light Infantry. He was lost in 1940 in France. Nothing was ever found of him. One moment he had been there beside the road, and then he was gone, the air filled with acrid smoke from the barrage that the Nazi panzers had laid down on the little stone bridge over the stream on the way to Dunkirk. For all the war years they had all lived in the hope that Lechie was now a POW in some good prison camp—not one of those terrible ones. And after the war, the months of searching but never a sign, never a witness, not even the littlest sign and then they, the family, and at length Father had laid Lechie's ghost to rest.

Scott had been sixteen in '39 and he'd gone to Canada for safety, there to finish schooling, and then, already a pilot, the day he was eighteen, in spite of Father's howling protests, he had joined the Canadian Air Force, wanting blood vengeance for Lechie. And he had got his wings at once and joined a bomber squadron and had come over well in time for D Day. Gleefully he had blown many a town to pieces and many a city to pieces until February 14, 1945, now Squadron Leader, DFC and Bar; coming home from the supreme holocaust of Dresden, his Lancaster had been jumped by a Messerschmitt and though his copilot had brought the crippled plane to rest in England, Scotty was dead in the left seat.

Kathy had been at his funeral and Ian had been there—in uniform, come home on leave from Chungking where he had been attached to Chiang Kai-shek's air force after he was shot down and grounded. She had wept on Ian's shoulder, wept for Lechie and wept for Scotty and wept for her Johnny. She was a widow then. Flight Lieutenant John Selkirk, DFC, another happy god of war, inviolate, invincible, had been blown out of the sky, torched out of the sky, the debris burning on the way to earth.

Johnny had had no funeral. There was nothing to bury. Like Lechie. Just a telegram came. One for each of them.

Oh Johnny my darling my darling my darling . . .

'What an awful waste, Ian dear, all of them. And for what?'

'I don't know, little Kathy,' he said, still holding her. 'I don't know. And I don't know why I made it and why they didn't.'

'Oh I'm ever so glad you did!' She gave him a little hug and gathered herself. Somehow she put away her sadness for all of them. Then she dried her tears, took out a small mirror and looked at herself. 'God, I look a mess! Sorry.' His private bathroom was concealed behind a bookcase and she went there and repaired her makeup.

When she came back he was still staring out of the window. 'Andrew's out of the office at the moment but the moment he comes back I'll tell him,' he said.

'Oh no dear, that's my job. I must do that. I must. That's only fair.' She smiled up at him and touched him. 'I love you, Ian.'

'I love you, Kathy.'

22

4:55 P.M.:

The cardboard box that the Werewolves had sent to Phillip Chen was on Roger Crosse's desk. Beside the box was the ransom note, key ring, driver's license, pen, even the crumpled pieces of torn newspaper that had been used for packing. The little plastic bag was there, and the mottled rag. Only its contents were missing.

Everything had been tagged.

Roger Crosse was alone in the room and he stared at the objects, fascinated. He picked up a piece of newspaper. Each had been carefully smoothed out, most were tagged with a date and the name of the Chinese newspaper it had come from. He turned it over, seeking hidden information, a hidden clue, something that might have been missed. Finding nothing, he put it back neatly and leaned on his hands, lost in thought.

Alan Medford Grant's report was also on his desk, near the intercom. It was very quiet in the room. Small windows overlooked Wanchai and part of the harbor toward Glessing's Point.

His phone jangled. 'Yes?'

'Mr. Rosemont, CIA, and Mr. Langan, FBI, sir.'

'Good.' Roger Crosse replaced his phone. He unlocked his top desk drawer and carefully put the AMG file on top of the decoded telex and relocked it. The middle drawer contained a high-quality tape recorder. He checked it and touched a hidden switch. Silently the reels began to turn. The intercom on his desk contained a powerful microphone. Satisfied, he relocked his drawer. Another hidden desk switch slid a bolt open on the door soundlessly. He got up and opened the door.

'Hello, you two, please come in,' he said affably. He closed

397

the door behind the two Americans and shook hands with them. Unnoticed, he slid the bolt home again. 'Take a seat. Tea?'

'No thanks,' the CIA man said.

'What can I do for you?'

Both men were carrying manila envelopes. Rosemont opened his and took out a sheaf of good quality eight-by-ten photos, clipped into two sections. 'Here,' he said, passing over the top section.

They were various shots of Voranski running across the wharf, on the streets of Kowloon, getting into and out of taxis, phoning, and many more of his Chinese assassins. One photograph showed the two Chinese leaving the phone booth with a clear glimpse of the crumpled body in the background.

Only Crosse's superb discipline kept him from showing astonishment, then blinding rage. 'Good, very good,' he said gently, putting them on the desk, very conscious of the ones Rosemont had retained in his hand. 'So?'

Rosemont and Ed Langan frowned. 'You were tailing him too?'

'Of course,' Crosse said, lying with his marvelous sincerity. 'My dear fellow, this is Hong Kong. But I do wish you'd let us do our job and not interfere.'

'Rog, we, er, we don't want to interfere, just want to backstop you.'

'Perhaps we don't need backstopping.' There was a sharpness to his voice now.

'Sure.' Rosemont took out a cigarette and lit it. He was tall and thin with gray crew-cut hair and good features. His hands were strong, like all of him. 'We know where the two killers're holed up. We think we know,' he said. 'One of our guys thinks he's pegged them.'

'How many men have you got watching the ship?'

'Ten. Our guys didn't notice any of yours tailing this one. The diversion almost spooked us too.'

'Very dicey,' Crosse said agreeably, wondering what diversion.

'Our guys never got to go through his pockets—we know he made two calls from the booth. . . .' Rosemont noted Crosse's eyes narrow slightly. That's curious, he thought. Crosse didn't know that. If he doesn't know that, maybe his operators weren't tailing the target either. Maybe he's lying and the Commie was loose in Hong Kong until he was knifed. 'We radioed a mug shot back home—we'll get a call back fast. Who was he?'

'His papers said Igor Voranski, seaman first class, Soviet merchant marine.'

'You have a file on him, Rog?'

'It's rather unusual for you two to call together, isn't it? I mean, in the movies, we're always led to believe the FBI and CIA are always at odds.'

Ed Langan smiled. 'Sure we are—like you and MI-5—like the KGB, GRU and fifty other Soviet operations. But sometimes our cases cross—we're internal U.S., Stan's external, but we're both out for the same thing: security. We thought . . . we're asking if we could all cooperate. This could be a big one, and we're . . . Stan and I're out of our depth.'

'That's right,' Rosemont said, not believing it.

'All right,' Crosse said, needing their information. 'But you first.'

Rosemont sighed. 'Okay, Rog. We've had a buzz for some time there's something hotting up in Hong Kong—we don't know what—but it sure as hell's got tie-ins to the States. I figure the AMG file's the link. Lookit: take Banastasio—he's Mafia. Big-time. Narcotics, the lot. Now take Bartlett and the guns. Guns—'

'Is Bartlett tied into Banastasio?'

'We're not sure. We're checking. We are sure the guns were put aboard in L.A.—Los Angeles—where the airplane's based. Guns! Guns, narcotics and our growing interest in Vietnam. Where do narcotics come from? The Golden Triangle. Vietnam, Laos and the Yunnan Province of China. Now we're into Vietnam and—'

'Yes, and you're ill-advised to be there, old chum—I've pointed that out fifty times.'

'We don't make policy, Rog, any more than you do. Next: Our nuclear carrier's here and the goddamn *Sovetsky Ivanov* arrives last night. That's too convenient, maybe the leak came from here. Then Ed tips you off and we get AMG's wild-assed letters from London and now there's Sevrin! Turns out the KGB've plants all over Asia and you've a high-placed hostile somewheres.'

'That's not yet proved.'

'Right. But I know about AMG. He's nobody's fool. If he says Sevrin's in place and you've a mole, you've a mole. Sure we've got hostiles in the CIA too, so've the KGB. I'm sure Ed has in the FBI—'

'That's doubtful,' Ed Langan interrupted sharply. 'Our guys are hand-picked and trained. You get your firemen from all over.'

'Sure,' Rosemont said, then added to Crosse, 'Back to narcotics. Red China's our big enemy and—'

'Again, you're wrong, Stanley. The PRC's not the big enemy anywhere. Russia is.'

'China's Commie. Commies're the enemy. Now, it'd be real smart to flood the States with cheap narcotics and Red China . . . okay the People's Republic of China can open the dam gates.'

'But they haven't. Our Narcotics Branch's the best in Asia— they've never come up with anything to support your misguided official theory that they're behind the trade. Nothing. The PRC are as anti-drug traffic as the rest of us.'

'Have it your way,' Rosemont said. 'Rog, you got a file on this agent? He's KGB, isn't he?'

Crosse lit a cigarette. 'Voranski was here last year. That time he went under the cover name of Sergei Kudryov, again seaman first class, again off the same ship—they're not very inventive, are they?' Neither of the two men smiled. 'His real name's Major Yuri Bakyan, First Directorate, KGB, Department 6.'

Rosemont sighed heavily.

The FBI man glanced at him. 'Then you're right. It all ties in.'

'Maybe.' The tall man thought a moment. 'Rog, what about his contacts from last year?'

'He acted like a tourist, staying at the Nine Dragons in Kowloon. . . .'

'That's in AMG's report, that hotel's mentioned,' Langan said.

'Yes. We've been covering it for a year or so. We've found nothing. Bakyan—Voranski—did ordinary tourist activities. We had him on twenty-four-hour surveillance. He stayed a couple of weeks, then, just before the ship sailed, sneaked back aboard.'

'Girl friend?'

'No. Not a regular one. He used to hang out at the Good Luck Dance Hall in Wanchai. Quite a cocksman, apparently, but he asked no questions and met no one out of the ordinary.'

'He ever visit Sinclair Towers?'

'No.'

'Pity,' Langan said, 'that'd've been dandy. Tsu-yan's got a place there. Tsu-yan knows Banastasio, John Chen knows Banastasio, and we're back to guns, narcotics, AMG and Sevrin.'

'Yeah,' Rosemont said, then added, 'Have you caught up with Tsu-yan yet?'

'No. He got to Taipei safely, then vanished.'

'You think he's holed up there?'

'I would imagine so,' Crosse said. But inside he believed him dead, already eliminated by Nationalist, Communist, Mafia or triad. I wonder if he could have been a double agent—or the supreme devil of all intelligence services, a triple agent?

'You'll find him—or we will—or the Taiwan boys will.'

'Roger, did Voranski lead you anywhere?' Langan asked.

'No. Nowhere, even though we've had tabs on him for years. He's been attached to the Soviet Trade Commission in Bangkok, he spent time in Hanoi, and Seoul, but no covert activities we know of. Once the cheeky bugger even applied for a British passport and almost got one. Luckily our fellows vet all applications and spotted flaws in his cover. I'm sorry he's dead—you know how hard it is to identify nasties. Waste of a lot of time and effort.' Crosse paused and lit a cigarette. 'His major's rank is quite senior which suggests something very smelly. Perhaps he was just another of their specials who was ordered to cruise Asia and get into deep cover for twenty or thirty years.'

'Those bastards have had their game plan set for so long it stinks!' Rosemont sighed. 'What're you going to do with the corpse?'

Crosse smiled. 'I got one of my Russian-speaking fellows to call the captain of the ship—Gregor Suslev. He's a Party member, of course, but fairly harmless. Has a sporadic girl friend with a flat in Mong Kok—a bar girl who gets a modest allowance from him and entertains him when he's here. He goes to the races, theater, Macao gambling a couple of times, speaks good English. Suslev's under surveillance. I don't want any of your hotshots ponging on one of our known hostiles.'

'So Suslev's regular here then?'

'Yes, he's been playing these waters for years, based out of Vladivostok—he's an ex-submarine commander by the way. He wanders around the fringe here, mostly under the weather.'

'What do you mean?'

'Drunk, but not badly so. Cavorts with a few of our British pinkos like Sam and Molly Finn.'

'The ones who're always writing letters to the papers?'

'Yes. They're more of a nuisance than a security risk. Anyway, under instructions, my Russian-speaking fellow told Captain Suslev we were frightfully sorry but it seemed that one of his seamen had had a heart attack in a phone booth at Golden Ferry Terminal. Suslev was suitably shocked and quite reasonable. In Voranski's pocket there "happened" to be an accurate, verbatim report of the assassin's phone conversation. We put it in Russian as a further sign of our displeasure. They're all professionals aboard that ship, and sophisticated enough to know we don't remove their agents without very great cause and provocation. They know we just watch the ones we know about and, if we're really very irritated, we deport them.' Crosse looked across at Rosemont, his eyes hard though his voice stayed matter-of-fact. 'We find our methods more effective than the knife, garrotte, poison or bullet.'

The CIA man nodded. 'But who would want to kill him?'

Crosse glanced at the photos again. He did not recognize the two Chinese, but their faces were clear and the body in the background unbelievable evidence. 'We'll find them. Whoever they are. The one who phoned our police station claimed they were 14K. But he only spoke Shanghainese with a Ningpo dialect, so that's unlikely. Probably he was a triad of some sort. He could be Green Pang. He was certainly a trained professional —the knife was used perfectly, with great precision—one moment alive, the next dead and no sound. Could be one of your CIA's trainees in Chiang Kai-shek's intelligence agency. Or perhaps the Korean CIA, more of your trainees—they're anti-Soviet too, aren't they? Possibly PRC agents, but that's improbable. Their agents don't usually go in for *quai loh* murder, and certainly not in Hong Kong.'

Rosemont nodded and let the censure pass. He gave Crosse the remaining photos, wanting the Englishman's cooperation and needing it. 'These're shots of the house they went into. And the street sign. Our guy couldn't read characters but it translates, "Street of the First Season, Number 14." It's a rotten little alley in back of the bus depot in North Point.'

Crosse began to examine them with equal care. Rosemont glanced at his watch, then got up and went to the single window that faced part of the harbor. 'Look!' he said proudly.

The other two went over to him. The great nuclear carrier was just rounding North Point heading for the navy yard, Hong Kong side. She was dressed overall, all her obligatory flags stiff in the breeze, crowds of white-clothed sailors on her vast deck, with neat lines of her vicious fighter jet airplanes. Almost 84,000 tons. No smokestack, just a vast, ominous bridge complex, with an eleven-hundred-foot angled runway that could retrieve and launch jets simultaneously. The first of a generation.

'That's some ship,' Crosse said enviously. This was the first time the colossus had entered Hong Kong since her commissioning in 1960. 'Pretty,' he said, hating the fact she was American and not British. 'What's her top speed?'

'I don't know—that's classified along with most everything else.' Rosemont turned to watch him. 'Can't you send that goddamn Soviet spy ship to hell out of port?'

'Yes, and we could blow it up, but that would be equally foolish. Stanley, relax, you have to be a little civilized about these things. Repairing their ships—and some of them really do need it—is a good source of revenue, and intelligence, and they pay their bills promptly. Our ways have been tried and tested over the years.'

Yes, Rosemont was thinking without rancor, but your ways don't work anymore. The British Empire's no more, the British raj no more and we've a different enemy now, smarter rougher dedicated totalitarian fanatic, with no Queensberry rules and a worldwide plan that's lavishly funded by whatever it takes. You British've no dough now, no clout, no navy, no army, no air force, and your goddamn government's filled with socialist and enemy pus, and *we* think they sold you out. You've been screwed from within, your security's the pits from Klaus Fuchs and Philby on down. Jesus, we won both goddamn wars for you, paid for most of it and both times you've screwed up the peace. And if it wasn't for *our* Strategic Air Command, our missiles, our nuclear strike force, our navy, our army, our air force, our taxpayers, our dough, you'd all be dead or in god-damn Siberia. Meanwhile, like it or not I got to deal with you. We need Hong Kong as a window and right now your cops to guard the carrier.

'Rog, thanks for the extra men,' he said. 'We sure appreciate it.'

'We wouldn't want any trouble while she's here either. Pretty ship. I envy you having her.'

'Her captain'll have the ship and crew under tight wraps—the shore parties'll all be briefed, and warned, and we'll cooperate a hundred percent.'

'I'll see you get a copy of the list of bars I've suggested your sailors stay out of—some're known Communist hangouts, and some are frequented by our lads off H.M.S. *Dart*.' Crosse smiled. 'There'll still be the odd brawl.'

'Sure. Rog, this Voranski killing's too much of a coincidence. Can I send a Shanghai speaker to assist the interrogation?'

'I'll let you know if we need help.'

'Can we have our copies of the tai-pan's other AMG reports now? Then we can get out of your hair.'

Crosse stared back at him, twisting uneasily, even though he was prepared for the question. 'I'll have to get approval from Whitehall.'

Rosemont was surprised. 'Our top man in England's been on to your Great White Father and it's approved. You should have had it an hour ago.'

'Oh?'

'Sure. Hell, we'd no idea AMG was on the tai-pan's payroll let alone passing classified stuff for chrissake! The wires've been red hot since Ed got the top copy of AMG's last will and testament. We got an all-points from Washington on getting copies of the other reports and we're trying to trace the call to Switzerland but—'

'Say again?'

'Kiernan's call. The second call he made.'

'I don't follow you.'

Rosemont explained.

Crosse frowned. 'My people didn't tell me about that. Nor did Dunross. Now why should Dunross lie—or avoid telling me that?' He related to them exactly what Dunross had told him. 'There was no reason for him to hide that, was there?'

'No. All right, Rog. Is the tai-pan kosher?'

Crosse laughed. 'If you mean is he a one hundred percent British Royalist freebooter whose allegiance is to his House, himself and the Queen—not necessarily in that order—the answer's an emphatic yes.'

'Then if we can have our copies now, Rog, we'll be on our way.'

'When I've got Whitehall's approval.'

'If you'll check your decoding room—it's a Priority 1-4a. It says to let us have copies on receipt.'

1-4a's were very rare. They called for immediate clearance and immediate action.

Crosse hesitated, wanting to avoid the trap he was in. He dared not tell them he did not yet have possession of the AMG reports. He picked up the phone and dialed. 'This is Mr. Crosse. Is there anything for me from Source? A 1-4a?'

'No sir. Other than the one we sent up an hour ago—that you signed for,' the SI woman said.

'Thank you.' Crosse put the phone down. 'Nothing yet,' he said.

'Shit,' Rosemont muttered, then added, 'They swore they'd already beamed it out and you'd have it before we got here. It's got to be here any second. If you don't mind we'll wait.'

'I've an appointment in Central shortly. Perhaps later this evening?'

Both men shook their heads. Langan said, 'We'll wait. We've been ordered to send 'em back instantly by hand with a twenty-four-hour guard. An army transport's due now at Kai Tak to carry the courier—we can't even copy them here.'

'Aren't you overreacting?'

'You could answer that. What's in them?'

Crosse toyed with his lighter. It had Cambridge University emblazoned on it. He had owned it since his undergraduate days. 'Is it true what AMG said about the CIA and the Mafia?'

Rosemont stared back at him. 'I don't know. You guys used all sort of crooks during World War Two. We learned from you to take advantage of what we've got—that was your first rule. Besides,' Rosemont added with utter conviction, 'this war's our war and whatever it takes we're going to win.'

'Yes, yes we must,' Langan echoed, equally sure. 'Because if we lose this one, the whole world's gone and we'll never get another chance.'

On the closed-in bridge of the *Sovetsky Ivanov* three men had binoculars trained on the nuclear carrier. One of the men was a civilian and he wore a throat mike that fed into a tape recorder. He was giving an expert, technical running commentary of what he saw. From time to time the other two would add a comment. Both wore light naval uniform. One was Captain Gregor Suslev, the other his first officer.

The carrier was coming up the roads nicely, tugs in attendance, but no tug ropes. Ferries and freighters tooted a jaunty welcome. A marine band played on her aft deck. White-clad sailors waved at passing ships. The day was very humid and the afternoon sun cast long shadows.

'The captain's expert,' the first officer said.

'Yes. But with all that radar even a child could handle her,' Captain Suslev replied. He was a heavy-shouldered, bearded man, his Slavic brown eyes deepset in a friendly face. 'Those sweepers aloft look like the new GEs for very long-range radar. Are they, Vassili?'

The technical expert broke off his transmission momentarily. 'Yes, Comrade Captain. But look aft! They've four F5 interceptors parked on the right flight deck.'

Suslev whistled tonelessly. 'They're not supposed to be in service till next year.'

'No,' the civilian said.

'Report that separately as soon as she docks. That news alone pays for our voyage.'

'Yes.'

Suslev fine-tuned his focus now as the ship turned slightly. He could see the airplanes' bomb racks. 'How many more F5s does she carry in her guts, and how many atomic warheads for them?'

They all watched the carrier for a moment.

'Perhaps we'll get lucky this time, Comrade Captain,' the first officer said.

'Let's hope so. Then Voranski's death won't be so expensive.'

'The Americans are fools to bring her here—don't they know every agent in Asia'll be tempted by her?'

'It's lucky for us they are. It makes our job so much easier.' Once more Suslev concentrated on the F5s that looked like soldier hornets among other hornets.

Around him the bridge was massed with advanced surveillance equipment. One radar was sweeping the harbor. A gray-haired impassive sailor watched the screen, the carrier a large clear blip among the myriad of blips.

Suslev's binoculars moved to the carrier's ominous bridge complex, then wandered the length of the ship. In spite of himself he shivered at her size and power. 'They say she's never refueled—not since she was launched in 1960.'

Behind him the door to the radio room that adjoined the bridge opened and a radio operator came up to him and saluted, offering the cable. 'Urgent from Center, Comrade Captain.'

Suslev took the cable and signed for it. It was a meaningless jumble of words. A last look at the carrier and he let the binoculars rest on his chest and strode off the bridge. His sea cabin was just aft on the same deck. The door was guarded, like both entrances to the bridge.

He relocked his cabin door behind him and opened the small, concealed safe. His cipher book was secreted in a false wall. He sat at his desk. Quickly he decoded the message. He read it carefully, then stared into space for a moment.

He read it a second time, then replaced the cipher book, closed the safe and burned the original of the cable in an ashtray. He picked up his phone. 'Bridge? Send Comrade Metkin to my cabin!' While he waited he stood by the porthole lost in thought. His cabin was untidy. Photographs of a heavyset woman, smiling self-consciously, were on his desk in a frame. Another of a good-looking youth in naval uniform, and a girl in her teens. Books, a tennis racket and a newspaper on the half-made bunk.

A knock. He unlocked the door. The sailor who had been staring at the radar screen stood there.

'Come in, Dimitri.' Suslev motioned at the decoded cable and relocked the door after him.

The sailor was short and squat, with graying hair and a good face. He was, officially, political commissar and therefore senior officer on the ship. He picked up the decoded message. It read: 'Priority One. Gregor Suslev. You will assume Voranski's duties and responsibilities at once. London reports optimum CIA and MI-6 interest in information contained in blue-covered files leaked to Ian Dunross of Struan's by the British Intelligence coordinator, AMG. Order Arthur to obtain copies immediately. If Dunross has destroyed the copies, cable feasibility plan to detain him for chemical debriefing in depth.' The sailor's face closed. He looked across at Captain Suslev. 'AMG? Alan Medford Grant?'

'Yes.'

'May that one burn in hell for a thousand years.'

'He will, if there's any justice in this world or the next.' Suslev smiled grimly. He went to a sideboard and took out a half-full vodka bottle and two glasses. 'Listen, Dimitri, if I fail or don't return, you take command.' He held up the key. 'Unlock the safe. There're instructions about decoding and everything else.'

'Let me go tonight in your place. You're more impor—'

'No. Thank you, old friend.' Suslev clapped him warmly on the shoulders. 'In case of an accident you assume command and carry out your mission. That's what we've been trained for.' He touched glasses with him. 'Don't worry. Everything will be fine,' he said, glad he could do as he wished and very content with his job and his position in life. He was, secretly, deputy controller in Asia for the KGB's First Directorate, Department 6, that was responsible for all covert activities in China, North Korea and Vietnam; a senior lecturer in Vladivostok University's Department of Foreign Affairs, 2A–Counterintelligence; a colonel in the KGB; and, most important of all, a senior Party member in the Far East. 'Center's given the order. You must guard our tails here. Eh?'

'Of course. You needn't worry about that, Gregor. I can do everything. But I worry about you,' Metkin said. They had sailed together for several years and he respected Suslev very much though he did not know from where his overriding authority came. Sometimes he was tempted to try to find out. You're getting on, he told himself. You retire next year and you may need powerful friends and the only way to have the help of powerful friends is to know their skeletons. But Suslev or no Suslev your well-earned retirement will be honorable, quiet and at home in the Crimea. Metkin's heart beat faster at the thought of all that lovely countryside and grand climate on the Black Sea, dreaming the rest of his life away with his wife and sometimes seeing his son, an up-and-coming KGB officer presently in Washington, no longer at risk and in danger from within or without.

Oh God protect my son from betrayal or making a mistake, he prayed fervently, then at once felt a wave of nausea, as always, in case his superiors knew that he was a secret believer and that his parents, peasants, had brought him up in the Church. If they knew there would be no retirement in the Crimea, only some icy backwater and no real home ever again.

'Voranski,' he said, as always cautiously hiding his hatred of the man. 'He was a top operator, eh? Where did he slip?'

'He was betrayed, that was his problem,' Suslev said darkly. 'We will find his murderers and they will pay. If my name is on the next knife . . .' The big man shrugged, then poured more vodka with a sudden laugh. 'So what, eh? It's in the name of the cause, the Party and Mother Russia!'

They touched glasses and drained them.

'When're you going ashore?'

Suslev bit on the raw liquor. Then, thankfully, he felt the great good warmth begin inside and his anxieties and terrors seemed less real. He motioned out of the porthole. 'As soon as she's moored and safe,' he said with his rolling laugh. 'Ah, but she's a pretty ship, eh?'

'We've got nothing to touch that bastard, Captain, have we? Or those fighters. Nothing.'

Suslev smiled as he poured again. 'No, comrade. But if the enemy has no real will to resist they can have a hundred of those carriers and it doesn't matter.'

'Yes, but Americans're erratic, one general can go off at half-cock, and they can smash us off the face of the earth.'

'I agree, now they can, but they won't. They've no balls.' Suslev drank again. 'And soon? Just a little more time and we'll stick their noses up their asses!' He sighed. 'It will be good when we begin.'

'It'll be terrible.'

'No, a short, almost bloodless war against America and then the rest'll collapse like the pus-infected corpse it is.'

'Bloodless? What about their atom bombs? Hydrogen bombs?'

'They'll never use atomics or missiles against us, they're too scared, even now, of *ours!* Because they're *sure* we'll use them.'

'Will we?'

'I don't know. Some commanders would. I don't know. We'll certainly use them back. But first? I don't know. The threat will always be enough. I'm sure we'll never need a fighting war.' He lit a corner of the decoded message and put it in the ashtray. 'Another twenty years of détente—ah what Russian genius invented that—we'll have a navy bigger and better than theirs, an air force bigger and better than theirs. We've got more tanks now and more soldiers, but without ships and airplanes we must wait. Twenty years is not long to wait for Mother Russia to rule the earth.'

'And China? What about China?'

Suslev gulped the vodka and refilled both glasses again. The bottle was empty now and he tossed it onto his bunk. His eyes saw the burning paper in the ashtray twist and crackle, dying. 'Perhaps China's the one place to use our atomics,' he said matter-of-factly. 'There's nothing there we need. Nothing. That'd solve our China problem once and for all. How many men of military age did they have at last estimate?'

'116 million between the ages of eighteen and twenty-five.'

'Think of that! 116 million yellow devils sharing 5,000 miles of our frontiers . . . and then foreigners call us paranoiac about China!' He sipped the vodka, this time making it last. 'Atomics'd solve our China problem once and for all. Quick, simple and permanent.'

The other man nodded. 'And this Dunross? The papers of AMG?'

'We'll get them from him. After all, Dimitri, one of our people is family, another, one of his partners, another's in Special Intelligence, there's Arthur and Sevrin everywhere he turns, and then we've a dozen decadents to call on in his parliament, some in his government.' They both began laughing.

'And if he's destroyed the papers?'

Suslev shrugged. 'They say he's got a photographic memory.'

'You'd do the interrogation here?'

'It'd be dangerous to do an in-depth chemic quickly. I've never done one. Have you?'

'No.'

The captain frowned. 'When you report tonight, get Center to ready an expert in case we need one—Koranski from Vladivostok if he's available.'

Dimitri nodded, lost in thought. This morning's *Guardian*, lying half-crumpled on the captain's bunk, caught his eye. He went over and picked it up, his eyes alight. 'Gregor—if we have to detain Dunross, why not blame them, then you've all the time you'll need?' The screaming headline read, SUSPECTS IN WEREWOLVES KIDNAP CASE. 'If Dunross doesn't return . . . perhaps our man'd become tai-pan! Eh?'

Suslev began to chuckle. 'Dimitri, you're a genius.'

Rosemont glanced at his watch. He had waited long enough. 'Rog, can I use your phone?'

'Certainly,' Crosse said.

The CIA man stubbed out his cigarette and dialed the central CIA exchange in the consulate.

'This is Rosemont—give me 2022.' That was the CIA communications center.

'2022. Chapman—who's this?'

'Rosemont. Hi, Phil, anything new?'

'No, excepting Marty Povitz reports a lot of activity on the bridge of the *Ivanov*, high-powered binoculars. Three guys, Stan. One's a civilian, others're the captain and the first officer. One of their short-rage radar sweep's working overtime. You want us to notify the *Corregidor*'s captain?'

'Hell no, no need to make his tail wriggle more than needs be. Say, Phil, we get a confirm on our 40-41?'

'Sure, Stan. It came in at . . . stand by one . . . it came in at 1603 local.'

'Thanks, Phil, see you.'

Rosemont lit another cigarette. Sourly Langan, a nonsmoker, watched him but said nothing as Crosse was smoking too.

'Rog, what are you pulling?' Rosemont asked harshly, to Langan's shock. 'You got your Priority 1-4a at 1603, same time as we did. Why the stall?'

'I find it presently convenient,' Crosse replied, his voice pleasant.

Rosemont flushed, so did Langan. 'Well I don't and we've instructions, official instructions, to pick up our copies right now.'

'So sorry, Stanley.'

Rosemont's neck was now very red but he kept his temper. 'You're not going to obey the 1-4a?'

'Not at the moment.'

Rosemont got up and headed for the door. 'Okay, Rog, but they'll throw the book at you.' He ripped the bolt back, jerked the door open and left. Langan was on his feet, his face also set.

'What's the reason, Roger?' he asked.

Crosse stared back at him calmly. 'Reason for what?'

Ed Langan began to get angry but stopped, suddenly appalled. 'Jesus, Roger, you haven't got them yet? Is that it?'

'Come now, Ed,' Crosse said easily, 'you of all people should know we're efficient.'

'That's no answer, Roger. Have you or haven't you?' The FBI man's level eyes stayed on Crosse, and did not phase Crosse at all. Then he walked out, closing the door after him. At once Crosse touched the hidden switch. The bolt slid home. Another hidden switch turned off his tape recorder. He picked up his phone and dialed. 'Brian? Have you heard from Dunross?'

'No sir.'

'Meet me downstairs at once. With Armstrong.'

'Yes sir.'

Crosse hung up. He took out the formal arrest document that was headed DETAINMENT ORDER UNDER THE OFFICIAL SECRETS ACT. Quickly he filled in 'Ian Struan Dunross' and signed both copies. The top copy he kept, the other he locked in his drawer. His eyes roamed his office, checking it. Satisfied, he delicately positioned a sliver of paper in the crack of his drawer so that he alone would know if anyone had opened it or tampered with it. He walked out. Heavy security locks slid home after him.

23

5:45 P.M.:

Dunross was in the Struan boardroom with the other directors of Nelson Trading, looking at Richard Kwang. 'No, Richard. Sorry, I can't wait till after closing tomorrow.'

'It'll make no difference to you, tai-pan. It will to me.' Richard Kwang was sweating. The others watched him—Phillip Chen, Lando Mata and Zeppelin Tung.

'I disagree, Richard,' Lando Mata said sharply. 'Madonna, you don't seem to realize the seriousness of the run!'

'Yes,' Zeppelin Tung said, his face shaking with suppressed rage.

Dunross sighed. If it wasn't for his presence he knew they would all be raving and screaming at each other, the obscenities flying back and forth as they do at any formal negotiation between Chinese, let alone one as serious as this. But it was a Noble House law that all board meetings were to be conducted in English, and English inhibited Chinese swearing and also unsettled Chinese which was of course the whole idea. 'The matter has to be dealt with now, Richard.'

'I agree.' Lando Mata was a handsome, sharp-featured Portuguese in his fifties, his mother's Chinese blood clear in his dark eyes and dark hair and golden complexion. His long fine fingers drummed continuously on the conference table and he knew Richard Kwang would never dare disclose that he, Tightfist Tung and Smuggler Mo controlled the bank. Our bank's one enterprise, he thought angrily, but our bullion's something else. 'We can't have our bullion, or our cash, in jeopardy!'

'Never,' Zeppelin Tung said nervously. 'My father wanted me to make that clear too. He wants his gold!'

'*Madre de Dios*, we've almost fifty tons of gold in your vaults.'

'Actually it's over fifty tons,' Zeppelin Tung said, the sweat beading his forehead. 'My old man gave me the figures—it's 1,792,668 ounces in 298,778 five-tael bars.' The air in the large room was warm and humid, the windows open. Zeppelin Tung was a well-dressed, heavyset man of forty with small narrow eyes, the eldest son of Tightfist Tung, and his accent was upper-class British. His nickname came from a movie that Tightfist had seen the day of his birth. 'Richard, isn't that right?'

Richard Kwang shifted the agenda paper in front of him which listed the quantity of gold and Nelson Trading's current balance. If he had to give up the bullion and cash tonight it would severely hurt the bank's liquidity and, when the news leaked, as of course it would, that would rock their whole edifice.

'What're you going to do, you dumbhead dog bone!' his wife had screamed at him just before he had left his office.

'Delay, delay and hope th—'

'No! Pretend to be sick! If you're sick you can't give them our money. You can't go to the meeting! Rush home and we'll pretend—'

'I can't, the tai-pan called personally. And so did that dog bone Mata! I daren't not go! Oh oh oh!'

'Then find out who's hounding us and pay him off! Where's your head? Who have you offended? You must have offended one of those dirty *quai lohs*. Find the man and pay him off or we'll lose the bank, lose our membership in the Turf Club, lose the horses, lose the Rolls and lose face forever! *Ayeeyah!* If the bank goes you'll never be Sir Richard Kwang, not that being Lady Kwang matters to me oh no! Do something! Find the . . .'

Richard Kwang felt the sweat running down his back but he kept his composure and tried to find a way out of the maze. 'The gold's as safe as it could be and so's your cash. We've been Nelson Trading's bankers since the beginning, we've never had a sniff of trouble. We gambled heavily with you in the beginning—'

'Come now, Richard,' Mata said, keeping his loathing hidden. 'You don't gamble on gold. Certainly not on *our* gold.' The gold belonged to the Great Good Luck Company of Macao which had also owned the gambling monopoly for almost thirty years. The present worth of the company was in excess of two billion U.S. Tightfist Tung owned 30 percent, personally, Lando

Mata 40 percent personally—and the descendants of Smuggler Mo, who had died last year, the other 30 percent.

And between us, Mata was thinking, we own 50 percent of the Ho-Pak which you, you stupid lump of dog turd, have somehow put into jeopardy. 'So sorry, Richard, but I vote Nelson Trading changes its bank—at least temporarily. Tightfist Tung is really very upset . . . and I have the Chin family's proxy.'

'But Lando,' Richard Kwang began, 'there's nothing to worry about.' His finger stabbed at the half-opened newspaper, the *China Guardian*, that lay on the table. 'Haply's new article says again that we're sound—that it's all a storm in an oyster shell, all started by malicious ban—'

'That's possible. But Chinese believe rumors, and the run's a fact,' Mata said sharply.

'My old man believes rumors,' Zeppelin Tung said fervently. 'He also believes Four Finger Wu. Four Fingers phoned him this afternoon telling him he'd taken out all his money and suggested he do the same, and within the hour we, Lando and I, we were in our Catalina and heading here and you know how I hate flying. Richard, you know jolly well if the old man wants something done *now*, it's done *now*.'

Yes, Richard Kwang thought disgustedly, that filthy old miser would climb out of his grave for fifty cents cash. 'I suggest we wait a day or so . . .'

Dunross was letting them talk for face. He had already decided what to do. Nelson Trading was a wholly owned subsidiary of Struan's so the other directors really had little say. But even though Nelson Trading had the Hong Kong Government's exclusive gold-importing license, without the Great Good Luck Company's gold business—which meant without Tightfist Tung and Lando Mata's favor—Nelson Trading's profits would be almost zero.

Nelson Trading got a commission of one dollar an ounce on every ounce imported for the company, delivered to the jetty at Macao, a further one dollar an ounce on exports from Hong Kong. As a further consideration for suggesting the overall Hong Kong scheme to the company, Nelson Trading had been granted 10 percent of the real profit. This year the Japanese Government had arbitrarily fixed their official rate of gold at 55 dollars an ounce—a profit of 15 dollars an ounce. On the black market it would be more. In India it would be almost 98 dollars.

Dunross glanced at his watch. In a few minutes Crosse would arrive.

'We've assets over a billion, Lando,' Richard Kwang repeated.

'Good,' Dunross said crisply jumping in, finalizing the meeting. 'Then, Richard, it really makes no difference one way or another. There's no point in waiting. I've made certain arrangements. Our transfer truck will be at your side door at eight o'clock precisely.'

'But—'

'Why so late, tai-pan?' Mata asked. 'It's not six o'clock yet.'

'It'll be dark then, Lando. I wouldn't want to shift 50 tons of gold in daylight. There might be a few villains around. You never know. Eh?'

'My God, you think . . . triads?' Zeppelin Tung was shocked. 'I'll phone my father. He'll have some extra guards.'

'Yes,' Mata said, 'call at once.'

'No need for that,' Dunross told him. 'The police suggested that we don't make too much of a show. They said they'll be there in depth.'

Mata hesitated. 'Well if you say so, tai-pan. You're responsible.'

'Of course,' Dunross said politely.

'How do we know the Victoria's safe?'

'If the Victoria fails we might as well not be in China.' Dunross picked up the phone and dialed Johnjohn's private number at the bank. 'Bruce? Ian. We'll need the vault—8:30 on the dot.'

'Very well. Our security people will be there to assist. Use the side door—the one on Dirk's Street.'

'Yes.'

'Have the police been informed?'

'Yes.'

'Good. By the way, Ian, about . . . is Richard still with you?'

'Yes.'

'Give me a call when you can—I'm at home this evening. I've been checking and things don't look very good at all for him. My Chinese banking friends are all very nervous—even the Mok-tung had a mini-run out at Aberdeen, so did we. Of course we'll advance Richard all the money he needs against his securities,

416

bankable securities, but if I were you I'd get any cash you control out. Get Blacs to deal with your check first at clearing tonight.'

All bank clearing of checks and bank loans was done in the basement of the Bank of London, Canton and Shanghai at midnight, five days a week.

'Thanks, Bruce. See you later.' Then to the others. 'That's all taken care of. Of course the transfer should be kept quiet. Richard, I'll need a cashier's check for Nelson Trading balance.'

'And I'll have one for my father's balance!' Zeppelin echoed.

Richard Kwang said, 'I'll send the checks over first thing in the morning.'

'Tonight,' Mata said, 'then they can clear tonight.' His eyes lidded even more. 'And, of course, another for my personal balance.'

'There isn't enough cash to cover those three checks—no bank could have that amount,' Richard Kwang exploded. 'Not even the Bank of England.'

'Of course. Please call whomever you wish to pledge some of your securities. Or Havergill, or Southerby.' Mata's fingers stopped drumming. 'They're expecting your call.'

'What?'

'Yes. I talked to both of them this afternoon.'

Richard Kwang said nothing. He had to find a way to avoid giving the money over tonight. If not tonight, he would gain a day's interest and by tomorrow perhaps it would not be necessary to pay. *Dew neh loh moh* on all filthy *quai loh* and half *quai loh*, who're worse! His smile was as sweet as Mata's. 'Well, as you wish. If you'll both meet me at the bank in an hour . . .'

'Even better,' Dunross said. 'Phillip will go with you now. You can give him all the checks. Is that all right with you, Phillip?'

'Oh, oh yes, yes, tai-pan.'

'Good, thank you. Then if you'll take them right over to Blacs, they'll clear at midnight. Richard, that gives you plenty of time. Doesn't it?'

'Oh yes, tai-pan,' Richard Kwang said, brightening. He had just thought of a brilliant answer. A pretended heart attack! I'll do it in the car going back to the bank and then . . .

Then he saw the coldness in Dunross's eyes and his stomach twisted and he changed his mind. Why should they have so much of my money? he thought as he got up. 'You don't need me for anything more at the moment? Good, come along, Phillip.' They walked out. There was a vast silence.

'Poor Phillip, he looks ghastly,' Mata said.

'Yes. It's no wonder.'

'Dirty triads,' Zeppelin Tung said with a shudder. 'The Werewolves must be foreigners to send his ear like that!' Another shudder. 'I hope they don't come to Macao. There's a strong rumor Phillip's dealing with them already, negotiating with the Werewolves in Macao.'

'There's no truth to that,' Dunross said.

'He wouldn't tell you if he was, tai-pan. I'd keep that secret from everyone too.' Zeppelin Tung stared gloomily at the phone. '*Dew neh loh moh* on all filthy kidnappers.'

'Is the Ho-Pak finished?' Mata asked.

'Unless Richard Kwang can stay liquid, yes. This afternoon Dunstan closed all his accounts.'

'Ah, so once again a rumor's correct!'

'Afraid so!' Dunross was sorry for Richard Kwang and the Ho-Pak but tomorrow he would sell short. 'His stock's going to plummet.'

'How will that affect the boom you've forecast?'

'Have I?'

'You're buying Struan's heavily, so I hear.' Mata smiled thinly. 'So has Phillip, and his *tai-tai*, and her family.'

'Anyone's wise to buy our stock, Lando, at any time. It's very underpriced.'

Zeppelin Tung was listening very carefully. His heart quickened. He too had heard rumors about the Noble House Chens buying today. 'Did you see Old Blind Tung's column today? About the coming boom? He was very serious.'

'Yes,' Dunross said gravely. When he had read it this morning he had chortled, and his opinion of Dianne Chen's influence had soared. In spite of himself Dunross had reread it and had wondered briefly if the soothsayer had really been forecasting his own opinion.

'Is Old Blind Tung a relation, Zep?' he asked.

'No, tai-pan, no, not that I know of. *Dew neh loh moh* but it's hot today. I'll be glad to get back to Macao—the weather's much better in Macao. Are you in the motor race this year, tai-pan?'

418

'Yes, I hope so.'

'Good! Damn the Ho-Pak! Richard will give us our checks, won't he? My old man will bust a blood vessel if one penny cash is missing.'

'Yes,' Dunross said, then noticed a strangeness in Mata's eyes. 'What's up?'

'Nothing.' Mata glanced at Zeppelin. 'Zep, it's really important we have your father's approval quickly. Why don't you and Claudia track him down.'

'Good idea.' Obediently the Chinese got to his feet and walked out, closing the door. Dunross turned his attention to Mata. 'And?'

Mata hesitated. Then he said quietly, 'Ian, I'm considering taking all my funds out of Macao and Hong Kong and putting them in New York.'

Dunross stared at him perturbed. 'If you did that you'd rattle our whole system. If you withdraw, Tightfist will too, and the Chins, Four Fingers . . . and all the others.'

'Which is more important, tai-pan, the system or your own money?'

'I wouldn't want the system shaken like that.'

'You've closed with Par-Con?'

Dunross watched him. 'Verbally yes. Contracts in seven days. Withdrawing will hurt us all, Lando. Badly. What's bad for us will be very bad for you and very very bad for Macao.'

'I'll consider what you say. So Par-Con's coming into Hong Kong. Very good—and if American Superfoods' takeover of the H.K. General Stores goes through, that'll add another boost to the market. Perhaps Old Blind Tung wasn't exaggerating again. Perhaps we'll be lucky. Has he ever been wrong before?'

'I don't know. Personally I don't think he has a private connection with the Almighty, though a lot of people do.'

'A boom would be very good, very good indeed. Perfect timing. Yes,' Mata added strangely, 'we could add a little fuel to the greatest boom in our history. Eh?'

'Would you assist?'

'Ten million U.S., between myself and the Chins—Tightfist won't be interested, I know. You suggest where and when.'

'Half a million into Struan's last thing Thursday, the rest spread over Rothwell-Gornt, Asian Properties, Hong Kong

Wharf, Hong Kong Power, Golden Ferries, Kowloon Investments and H.K. General Stores.'

'Why Thursday? Why not tomorrow?'

'The Ho-Pak will bring the market down. If we buy a quantity Thursday just before closing, we'll make a fortune.'

'When do you announce the Par-Con deal?'

Dunross hesitated. Then he said, 'Friday, after the market closes.'

'Good. I'm with you, Ian. Fifteen million. Fifteen instead of ten. You'll sell Ho-Pak short tomorrow?'

'Of course, Lando. Do you know who's behind the run on the Ho-Pak?'

'No. But Richard is overextended, and he hasn't been too wise. People talk, Chinese always distrust any bank, and they react to rumors. I think the bank will crash.'

'Christ!'

'Joss.' Mata's fingers stopped drumming. 'I want to triple our gold imports.'

Dunross stared at him. 'Why? You're up to capacity now. If you push them too fast they'll make mistakes and your seizure rate will go up. At the moment you've balanced everything perfectly.'

'Yes, but Four Fingers and others assure us they can make substantial bulk shipments safely.'

'No need to push them—or your market. No need at all.'

'Ian, listen to me a moment. There's trouble in Indonesia, trouble in China, India, Tibet, Malaya, Singapore, ferment in the Philippines and now the Americans are going into Southeast Asia which will be marvelous for us and dreadful for them. Inflation will soar and then, as usual, every sensible businessman in Asia, particularly Chinese businessmen, will want to get out of paper money and into gold. We should be ready to service that demand.'

'What've you heard, Lando?'

'Lots of curious things, tai-pan. For example, that certain top U.S. generals want a full-scale confrontation with the Communists. Vietnam's chosen.'

'But the Americans'll never win there. China can't let them, any more than they could in Korea. Any history book will tell them China *always* crosses her borders to protect her buffer zones when any invader approaches.'

'Even so, the confrontation will take place.'

Dunross studied Lando Mata whose enormous wealth and longtime involvement in the honorable profession of trading, as he described it, gave him vast entrée into the most secretive of places. 'What else have you heard, Lando?'

'The CIA has had its budget doubled.'

'This has to be classified. No one could know that.'

'Yes. But I know. Their security's appalling. Ian, the CIA's into everything in Southeast Asia. I believe some of their misguided zealots are even trying to wheedle into the opium trade in the Golden Triangle for the benefit of their friendly Mekong hill tribes—to encourage them to fight the Viet Cong.'

'Christ!'

'Yes. Our brethren in Taiwan are furious. And there's growing abundance of U.S. Government money pouring into airfields, harbors, roads. In Okinawa, Taiwan and particularly in South Vietnam. Certain highly connected political families are helping to supply the cement and steel on very favorable terms.'

'Who?'

'Who makes cement? Perhaps in . . . say in New England?'

'Good sweet Christ, are you sure?'

Mata smiled humorlessly. 'I even heard that part of a very large government loan to South Vietnam was expended on a nonexistent airfield that's still impenetrable jungle. Oh yes, Ian, the pickings are already huge. So please order triple shipments from tomorrow. We institute our new hydrofoil services next month—that'll cut the time to Macao from three hours to seventy-five minutes.'

'Wouldn't the Catalina still be safer?'

'No. I don't think so. The hydrofoils can carry much more gold and can outrun anything in these waters—we'll have constant radar communications, the best, so we can outrun any pirates.'

After a pause, Dunross said, 'So much gold could attract all sorts of villains. Perhaps even international crooks.'

Mata smiled his thin smile. 'Let them come. They'll never leave. We've long arms in Asia.' His fingers began drumming again. 'Ian, we're old friends, I would like some advice.'

'Glad to—anything.'

'Do you believe in change?'

'Business change?'

'Yes.'

'It depends, Lando,' Dunross answered at once. 'The Noble House's changed little in almost a century and a half, in other ways it's changed vastly.' He watched the older man, and he waited.

At length Mata said, 'In a few weeks the Macao Government is obliged to put the gambling concession up for bids again. . .' Instantly Dunross's attention zeroed. All big business in Macao was conducted on monopoly lines, the monopoly going to the person or company that offered the most taxes per year for the privilege. '. . . This's the fifth year. Every five years our department asks for closed bids. The auction's open to anyone but, in practice, we scrutinize very particularly those who are invited to bid.' The silence hung a moment, then Mata continued. 'My old associate, Smuggler Mo's already dead. His offspring're mostly profligate or more interested in the Western world, gambling in southern France or playing golf, than in the health and future of the syndicate. For the Mo it's the age-old destiny: one-in-ten-thousand coolie strikes gold, harbors money, invests in land, saves money, becomes rich, buys young concubines who use him up quickly. Second generation discontented, spend money, mortgage land to buy face and ladies' favors. Third generation sell land, go bankrupt for some favors. Fourth generation coolie.' His voice was calm, even gentle. 'My old friend's dead and I've no feeling for his sons, or their sons. They're rich, hugely rich because of me, and they'll find their own level, good, bad or very bad. As to Tightfist . . .' Again his fingers stopped. 'Tightfist's dying.'

Dunross was startled. 'But I saw him only a week or so ago and he looked healthy, frail as always, but full of his usual piss and vinegar.'

'He's dying, Ian. I know because I was his interpreter with the Portuguese specialists. He didn't want to trust any of his sons— that's what he told me. It took me months to get him to go to see them but both doctors were quite sure: cancer of the colon. His system's riddled with it. They gave him a month, two months . . . this was a week ago.' Mata smiled. 'Old Tightfist just swore at them, told them they were wrong and fools and that he'd never pay for a wrong diagnosis.' The lithe Portuguese laughed without humor. 'He's worth over 600 million U.S. but he'll never pay that doctor bill, or do anything but continue to drink foul-smelling, foul-tasting Chinese herbal brews and smoke his occasional opium pipe. He just won't accept a Western, a *quai loh* diagnosis—you know him. You know him very well, eh?'

'Yes.' When Dunross was on his school holidays his father would send him to work for certain old friends. Tightfist Tung had been one of them and Dunross remembered the hideous summer he had spent sweating in the filthy basement of the syndicate bank in Macao, trying to please his mentor and not to weep with rage at the thought of what he had to endure while all his friends were out playing. But now he was glad for that summer. Tightfist had taught him much about money—the value of it, how to make it, hold on to it, about usury, greed and the normal Chinese lending rate, in good times, of 2 percent a month.

'Take twice as much collateral as you need but if he has none then look at the eyes of the borrower!' Tightfist would scream at him. 'No collateral, then of course charge a bigger interest. Now think, can you trust him? Can he repay the money? Is he a worker or a drone? Look at him, fool, *he's* your collateral! How much of my hard-earned money does he want? Is he a hard worker? If he is, what's 2 percent a month to him—or 4? Nothing. But it's my money that'll make the fornicator rich if it's his joss to be rich. The man himself's all the collateral you ever need! Lend a rich man's son anything if he's borrowing against his heritage and you have the father's chop—it'll all be thrown away on singsong girls but never mind, it's his money not yours! How do you become rich? You save! You save money, buy land with one third, lend one third and keep one third in cash. Lend only to civilized persons and never trust a *quai loh* . . .' he would cackle.

Dunross remembered well the old man with his stony eyes, hardly any teeth—an illiterate who could read but three characters and could write but three characters, those of his name—who had a mind like a computer, who knew to the nearest copper cash who owed him what and when it was due. No one had ever defaulted on one of his loans. It wasn't worth the incessant hounding.

That summer he had been thirteen and Lando Mata had

befriended him. Then, as now, Mata was almost a wraith, a mysterious presence who moved in and out of Macao's government spheres as he wished, always in the background, hardly seen, barely known, a strange man who came and went at whim, gathered what he liked, harvesting unbelievable riches as and when it pleased him. Even today there were but a handful of people who knew his name, let alone the man himself. Even Dunross had never been to his villa on the Street of the Broken Fountain, the low sprawling building hidden behind the iron gates and the huge stone encircling walls, or knew anything about him really—where he came from, who his parents were or how he had managed to acquire those two monopolies of limitless wealth.

'I'm sorry to hear about old Tightfist,' Dunross said. 'He was always a rough old bastard, but no rougher to me than to any of his own sons.'

'Yes. He's dying. Joss. And I've no feeling for any of his heirs. Like the Chins, they'll be rich, all of them. Even Zeppelin,' Lando Mata said with a sneer. 'Even Zeppelin'll get 50 to 75 million U.S.'

'Christ, when you think of all the money gambling makes . . .'

Mata's eyes lidded. 'Should I make a change?'

'If you want to leave a monument, yes. At the moment the syndicate only allows Chinese gambling games: fan-tan, dominoes and dice. If the new group was modern, far-seeing, and they modernized . . . if they built a grand new casino, with tables for roulette, vingt-et-un, chemin der fer, even American craps you'd have all Asia flocking to Macao.'

'What're the chances of Hong Kong legalizing gambling?'

'None—you know better than I do that without gambling and gold Macao'd drift into the sea and it's a cornerstone of British and Hong Kong business policy never to let that happen. We have our horse racing—you've the tables. But with modern ownership, new hotels, new games, new hydrofoils you'd have so much revenue you'd have to open your own bank.'

Lando Mata took out a slip of paper, glanced at it, then handed it over. 'Here are four groups of three names of people who might be allowed to bid. I'd like your opinion.'

Dunross did not look at the list. 'You'd like me to choose the group of three you've already decided on?'

Mata laughed. 'Ah, Ian, you know too much about me! Yes, I've chosen the group that should be successful, if their bid is substantial enough.'

'Do any of the groups know now that you might take them as partners?'

'No.'

'What about Tightfist—and the Chins? They won't lose their monopoly lightly.'

'If Tightfist dies before the auction, a new syndicate will come to pass. If not, the change will be made but differently.'

Dunross glanced at the list. And gasped. All the names were well-known Hong Kong and Macao Chinese, all substantial people, some with curious pasts. 'Well, they're certainly all famous, Lando.'

'Yes. To earn such great wealth, to run a gambling empire needs men of vision.'

Dunross smiled with him. 'I agree. Then why is it I'm not on the list?'

'Resign from Noble House within the month and you can form your own syndicate. I guarantee your bid will be successful. I take 40 percent.'

'Sorry, that's not possible, Lando.'

'You could have a personal fortune of 500 million to a billion dollars within ten years.'

Dunross shrugged. 'What's money?'

'*Moh ching moh meng!*' No money no life.

'Yes, but there's not enough money in the world to make me resign. Still, I'll make a deal with you. Struan's'll run the gambling for you, through nominees.'

'Sorry, no. It has to be all or nothing.'

'We could do it better and cheaper than anyone, with more flair.'

'If you resign. All or none, tai-pan.'

Dunross's head hurt at the thought of so much money, but he heard Lando Mata's finality. 'Fair enough. Sorry, I'm not available,' he said.

'I'm sure you'd, you personally, would be welcomed as a . . . as a consultant.'

'If I choose the correct group?'

'Perhaps.' The Portuguese smiled. 'Well?'

Dunross was wondering whether or not he could risk such an association. To be part of the Macao gambling syndicate was not like being a steward of the Turf Club. 'I'll think about that and let you know.'

'Good, Ian. Give me your opinion within the next two days, eh?'

'All right. Will you tell me what the successful bid is—if you decide to change?'

'An associate or consultant should have that knowledge. Now a last item and I must go. I don't think you'll ever see your friend Tsu-yan again.'

Dunross stared at him. 'What?'

'He called me from Taipei, yesterday morning, in quite a state. He asked if I'd send the Catalina for him, to pick him up privately. It was urgent he said, he'd explain when he saw me. He'd come straight to my home, the moment he arrived.' Mata shrugged and examined his perfectly manicured nails. 'Tsu-yan's an old friend, I've accommodated old friends before, so I authorized the flight. He never appeared, Ian. Oh he came with the flying boat—my chauffeur was on the jetty to meet him.' Mata looked up. 'It's all rather unbelievable. Tsu-yan was dressed in filthy coolie rags with a straw hat. He mumbled something about seeing me later that night and jumped into the first taxi and took off as though all the devils from hell were at his heels. My driver was stunned.'

'There's no mistake? You're sure it was he?'

'Oh yes, Tsu-yan's well known—fortunately my driver's Portuguese and can take some initiative. He charged in pursuit. He says Tsu-yan's taxi headed north. Near the Barrier Gate the taxi stopped and then Tsu-yan fled on foot, as fast as he could run, through the Barrier Gate into China. My man watched him run all the way up to the soldiers on the PRC's side and then he vanished into the guardhouse.'

Dunross stared at Mata in disbelief. Tsu-yan was one of the best-known capitalists and anti-Communists in Hong Kong and Taiwan. Before the fall of the Mainland he had been almost a minor warlord in the Shanghai area. 'Tsu-yan'd never be welcome in the PRC,' he said. 'Never! He must be top of their shit list.'

Mata hesitated. 'Unless he was working for them.'

'It's not possible.'

'Anything's possible in China.'

Twenty stories below, Roger Crosse and Brian Kwok were getting out of the police car, followed by Robert Armstrong. A plainclothes SI man met them. 'Dunross's still in his office, sir.'

'Good.' Robert Armstrong stayed at the entrance and the other two went for the elevator. On the twentieth floor they got out.

'Ah good evening, sir,' Claudia said and smiled at Brian Kwok. Zeppelin Tung was waiting by the phone. He stared at the policemen in sudden shock, obviously recognizing them.

Roger Crosse said, 'Mr. Dunross's expecting me.'

'Yes sir.' She pressed the boardroom button and, in a moment, spoke into her phone. 'Mr. Crosse's here, tai-pan.'

Dunross said, 'Give me a minute, then show him in, Claudia.' He replaced his phone and turned to Mata. 'Crosse's here. If I miss you at the bank tonight, I'll catch up with you tomorrow morning.'

'Yes. I'm . . . please call me, Ian. Yes. I want a few minutes with you privately. Tonight or tomorrow.'

'At nine tonight,' Dunross said at once. 'Or anytime tomorrow.'

'Call me at nine. Or tomorrow. Thank you.' Mata walked across the room and opened a hardly noticeable door that was camouflaged as part of the bookshelves. This opened onto a private corridor which led to the floor below. He closed the door behind him.

Dunross stared after him thoughtfully. I wonder what's on his mind? He put the agenda papers in a drawer and locked it, then leaned back at the head of the table trying to collect his wits, his eyes on the door, his heart beating a little quicker. The phone rang and he jumped.

'Yes?'

'Father,' Adryon said in her usual rush, 'sorry to interrupt but Mother wanted to know what time you'd be in for dinner.'

'I'll be late. Ask her to go ahead. I'll get something on the run. What time did you get in last night?' he asked, remembering

427

that he had heard her car return just before dawn.

'Early,' she said, and he was going to give her both barrels but he heard unhappiness under her voice.

'What's up, pet?' he asked.

'Nothing.'

'What's up?'

'Nothing really. I had a grand day, had lunch with your Linc Bartlett—we went shopping but that twit Martin stood me up.'

'What?'

'Yes. I waited a bloody hour for him. We had a date to go to the V and A for tea but he never showed up. Rotten twit!'

Dunross beamed. 'You just can't rely on some people, can you, Adryon? Fancy! Standing you up! What cheek!' he told her, suitably grave, delighted that Haply was going to get what for.

'He's a creep! A twenty-four-carat creep!'

The door opened. Crosse and Brian Kwok came in. He nodded to them, beckoned them. Claudia shut the door after them.

'Got to go, darling. Hey pet, love you! 'Bye!' He put the phone down. 'Evening,' he said, no longer perturbed.

'The files please, Ian.'

'Certainly, but first we've got to see the governor.'

'First I want those files.' Crosse pulled out the warrant as Dunross picked up the phone and dialed. He waited only a moment. 'Evening, sir. Superintendent Crosse's here . . . yes sir.' He held out the phone. 'For you.'

Crosse hesitated, hard-faced, then took it. 'Superintendent Crosse,' he said into the phone. He listened a moment. 'Yes sir. Very well, sir.' He replaced the phone. 'Now, what the hell shenanigans are you up to?'

'None. Just being careful.'

Crosse held up the warrant. 'If I don't get the files, I've clearance from London to serve this on you at six P.M. today, governor or no.'

Dunross stared back at him, just as hard. 'Please go ahead.'

'You're served, Ian Struan Dunross! Sorry, but you're under arrest!'

Dunross's jaw jutted a little. 'All right. But first by God we *will* see the governor!'

428

24

The tai-pan and Roger Crosse were walking across the white pebbles toward the front door of the Governor's Palace. Brian Kwok waited beside the police car. The front door opened and the young equerry in Royal Navy uniform greeted them politely, then ushered them into an exquisite antechamber.

His Excellency Sir Geoffrey Allison, D.S.O., O.B.E., was a sandy-haired man in his late fifties, neat, soft-spoken and very tough. He sat at an antique desk and watched them. 'Evening,' he said easily and waved them to seats. His equerry closed the door, leaving them. 'It seems we have a problem, Roger. Ian has some rather private property that he legally owns and is reluctant to give you—that you want.'

'Legally want, sir. I've London's authority under the Official Secrets Act.'

'Yes, I know that, Roger. I talked to the minister an hour ago. He said, and I agree, we can hardly arrest Ian and go through the Noble House like a dose of salts. That really wouldn't be very proper, or very sensible, however serious we are in obtaining the AMG files. And, equally, it wouldn't be very proper or sensible to acquire them with cloaks and daggers—that sort of thing. Would it?'

Crosse said, 'With Ian's cooperation none of that would be necessary. I've pointed out to him that Her Majesty's Government was completely involved. He just doesn't seem to get the message, sir. He should cooperate.'

'I quite agree. The minister said the same. Of course when Ian came here this morning he did explain his reasons for being so, so cautious . . . quite proper reasons if I may say so! The minister agrees too.' The gray eyes became piercing. 'Just exactly who is the deep-cover Communist agent in my police? Who are the Sevrin plants?'

There was a vast silence. 'I don't know, sir.'

'Then would you be kind enough to find out very quickly. Ian was kind enough to let me read the AMG report you rightly intercepted.' The governor's face mottled, quoting from it, '". . . this information should be leaked privately to the police commissioner or governor *should they be considered loyal* . . ."' Bless my soul! What's going on in the world?'

'I don't know, sir.'

'Well, you're supposed to, Roger. Yes.' The governor watched them. 'Now. What about the mole? What sort of man would he be?'

'You, me, Dunross, Havergill, Armstrong—anyone,' Crosse said at once. 'But with one characteristic: I think this one's so deep that he's probably almost forgotten who he really is, or where his real political interest and loyalty lie. He'd be very special—like all of Sevrin.' The thin-faced man stared at Dunross. 'They must be special—SI's checks and balances are really very good, and the CIA's, but we've never had a whiff of Sevrin before, not a jot or a tittle.'

Dunross said, 'How're you going to catch him?'

'How're you going to catch your plant in Struan's?'

'I've no idea.' Would the Sevrin spy be the same as the one who betrayed our secrets to Bartlett? Dunross was asking himself uneasily. 'If he's top echelon, he's one of seven—all unthinkable.'

'There you have it,' Crosse said. 'All unthinkable, but one's a spy. If we get one, we can probably break the others out of him if he knows them.' Both the other men felt icy at the calm viciousness in his voice. 'But to get the one, someone has to make a slip, or we have to get a little luck.'

The governor thought a moment. Then he said, 'Ian assures me there's nothing in the previous reports that names anyone— or gives any clues. So the other reports wouldn't help us immediately.'

'They could, sir, in other areas, sir.'

'I know.' The words were quietly spoken but they said Shut up, sit down and wait till I've finished. Sir Geoffrey let the

430

silence hang for a while. 'So our problem seems to be simply a matter of asking Ian for his cooperation. I repeat, I agree that his caution is justified.' His face tightened. 'Philby, Burgess and Maclean taught us all a fine lesson. I must confess every time I make a call to London I wonder if I'm talking to another bloody traitor.' He blew his nose in a handkerchief. 'Well, enough of that. Ian, kindly tell Roger the circumstances in which you'll hand over the AMG copies.'

'I'll hand them, personally, to the head or deputy head of MI-6 or MI-5, provided I have His Excellency's guarantee in writing that the man I give them to is who he purports to be.'

'The minister agrees to this, sir?'

'If you agree, Roger.' Again it was said politely but the undercurrent said You'd better agree, Roger.

'Very well, sir. Has Mr. Sinders agreed to the plan?'

'He will be here on Friday, BOAC willing.'

'Yes sir.' Roger Crosse glanced at Dunross. 'I'd better keep the files then until then. You can give me a sealed pa—'

Dunross shook his head. 'They're safe until I deliver them.'

Crosse shook his head. 'No. If we know, others'd know. The others're not so clean-handed as we are. We must know where they are—we'd better have a guard around the clock.'

Sir Geoffrey nodded. 'That's fair enough, Ian?'

Dunross thought a moment. 'Very well. I've put them in a vault at the Victoria Bank.' Crosse's neck became pink as Dunross produced a key and laid it on the desk. The numbers were carefully defaced. 'There's about a thousand safety deposit boxes. I alone know the number. This's the only key. If you'll keep it, Sir Geoffrey. Then . . . well, that's about the best I can do to avoid risks.'

'Roger?'

'Yes sir. If you agree.'

'They're certainly safe there. Certainly not possible to break open all of them. Good, then that's all settled. Ian, the warrant's canceled. You do promise, Ian, to deliver them to Sinders the moment he arrives?' Again the eyes became piercing. 'I have really gone to a lot of trouble over this.'

'Yes sir.'

'Good. Then that's settled. Nothing yet on poor John Chen, Roger?'

'No sir, we're trying everything.'

'Terrible business. Ian, what's all this about the Ho-Pak? Are they really in trouble?'

'Yes sir.'

'Will they go under?'

'I don't know. The word seems to be they will.'

'Damnable! I don't like that at all. Very bad for our image. And the Par-Con deal?'

'It looks good. I hope to have a favorable report for you next week, sir.'

'Excellent. We could use some big American firms here.' He smiled. 'I understand the girl's a stunner! By the way, the Parliamentary Trade Delegation's due from Peking tomorrow. I'll entertain them Thursday—you'll come of course.'

'Yes sir. Will the dinner be stag?'

'Yes, good idea.'

'I'll invite them to the races Saturday—the overflow can go into the bank's box, sir.'

'Good. Thank you, Ian. Roger, if you'll spare me a moment.'

Dunross got up and shook hands and left. Though he had come with Crosse in the police car, his own Rolls was waiting for him. Brian Kwok intercepted him. 'What's the poop, Ian?'

'I was asked to let your boss tell you,' he said.

'Fair enough. Is he going to be long?'

'I don't know. Everything's all right, Brian. No need to worry. I think I dealt with the dilemma correctly.'

'Hope so. Sorry—bloody business.'

'Yes.' Dunross got into the back of the Silver Cloud. 'Golden Ferry,' he said crisply.

Sir Geoffrey was pouring the fine sherry into two exquisite, eggshell porcelain cups. 'This AMG business is quite frightening, Roger,' he said. 'I'm afraid I'm still not inured to treachery, betrayal and the rotten lengths the enemy will go to—even after all this time.' Sir Geoffrey had been in the Diplomatic Corps all of his working life, except for the war years when he was a staff officer in the British Army. He spoke Russian, Mandarin, French and Italian. 'Dreadful.'

'Yes sir.' Crosse watched him. 'You're sure you can trust Ian?'

'On Friday you won't need London's clearance to proceed. You have an Order in Council. On Friday we take possession.'

'Yes sir.' Crosse accepted the porcelain cup, its fragility bothering him. 'Thank you, sir.'

'I suggest you have two men in the bank vaults at all times, one SI, one CID for safety, and a plainclothes guard on the tai-pan—quietly, of course.'

'I'll arrange about the bank before I leave. I've already put him under blanket surveillance.'

'You've already done it?'

'On him? Yes sir. I presumed he'd manipulate the situation to suit his purposes. Ian's a very tricky fellow. After all, the tai-pan of the Noble House is never a fool.'

'No. Health!' They touched glasses delicately. The ring of the pottery was beautiful. 'This tai-pan's the best I've dealt with.'

'Did Ian mention if he'd reread all the files recently, sir? Last night, for instance?'

Sir Geoffrey frowned, rethinking their conversation this morning. 'I don't think so. Wait a minute, he did say . . . exactly he said, "When I first read the reports I thought some of AMG's ideas were too farfetched. But now—and now that he's dead, I've changed my mind . . ." That could imply he's reread them recently. Why?'

Crosse was examining the paper-thin porcelain cup against the light. 'I've often heard he's got a remarkable memory. If the files in the vaults are untouchable . . . well, I wouldn't want the KGB tempted to snatch him.'

'Good God, you don't think they'd be that stupid, do you? The tai-pan?'

'It depends what importance they put on the reports, sir,' Crosse said dispassionately. 'Perhaps our surveillance should be relatively open—that should scare them off if they happen to have that in mind. Would you mention it to him, sir?'

'Certainly.' Sir Geoffrey made a note on his pad. 'Good idea. Damnable business. Could the Werewolves . . . could there be a link between the smuggled guns and the John Chen kidnapping?'

'I don't know, sir. Yet. I've put Armstrong and Brian Kwok on to the case. If there's a connection they'll find it.' He watched the dying sunlight on the pale, powder blue translucence of the porcelain that seemed to enhance the golden sheen of the dry La Ina sherry. 'Interesting, the play of colors.'

'Yes. They're T'ang Ying—named after the director of the Emperor's factory in 1736. Emperor Ch'en Leung actually.' Sir Geoffrey looked up at Crosse. 'A deep-cover spy in my police, in my Colonial Office, my Treasury Department, the naval base, the Victoria, telephone company, and even the Noble House. They could paralyze us and create untold mischief between us and the PRC.'

'Yes sir.' Crosse peered at the cup. 'Seems impossible that it should be so thin. I've never seen such a cup before.'

'You're a collector?'

'No sir. Afraid I don't know anything about them.'

'These're my favorites, Roger, quite rare. They're called *t'o t'ai*—without body. They're so thin that the glazes, inside and out, seem to touch.'

'I'm almost afraid to hold it.'

'Oh, they're quite strong. Delicate of course but strong. Who could be Arthur?'

Crosse sighed. 'There's no clue in this report. None. I've read it fifty times. There must be something in the others, whatever Dunross thinks.'

'Possibly.'

The delicate cup seemed to fascinate Crosse. 'Porcelain's a clay, isn't it?'

'Yes. But this type is actually made from a mixture of two clays, Roger, kaolin—after the hilly district of Kingtehchen where it's found—and *pan tun tse*, the so-called little white blocks. Chinese call these the flesh and the bones of porcelain.' Sir Geoffrey walked over to the ornate leather-topped table that served as a bar and brought back the decanter. It was about eight inches high and quite translucent, almost transparent. 'The blue's remarkable too. When the body's quite dry, cobalt in powder form's blown onto the porcelain with a bamboo pipe. Actually the color's thousands of individual tiny specks of blue. Then it's glazed and fired—at about 1300 degrees.' He put it back on the bar, the touch of the workmanship and the sight of it pleasing him.

'Remarkable.'

There was always an Imperial Edict against their export. We

quai loh were only entitled to articles made out of *hua shih*, slippery stone, or *tun ni*—brick mud.' He looked at his cup again, as a connoisseur. 'The genius who made this probably earned 100 dollars a year.'

'Perhaps he was overpaid,' Crosse said and the two men smiled with one another.

'Perhaps.'

'I'll find Arthur, sir, and the others. You can depend on it.'

'I'm afraid I have to, Roger. Both the minister and I agree. He will have to inform the Prime Minister—and the Chiefs of Staff.'

'Then the information has to go through all sorts of hands and tongues and the enemy'll be bound to find out that we may be on to them.'

'Yes. So we'll have to work fast. I bought you four days' grace, Roger. The minister won't pass anything on for that time.'

'Bought, sir?'

'Figuratively speaking. In life one acquires and gives IOUs—even in the Diplomatic Corps.'

'Yes sir. Thank you.'

'Nothing on Bartlett and Miss Casey?'

'No sir. Rosemont and Langan have asked for up-to-date dossiers. There seems to be some connection between Bartlett and Banastasio—we're not sure yet what it is. Both he and Miss Tcholok were in Moscow last month.'

'Ah!' Sir Geoffrey replenished the cups. 'What did you do about that poor fellow Voranski?'

'I sent the body back to his ship, sir.' Crosse told him the gist of his meeting with Rosemont and Langan and about the photographs.

'That's a stroke of luck! Our cousins are getting quite smart,' the governor said. 'You'd better find those assassins before the KGB do—or the CIA, eh?'

'I have teams around the house now. As soon as they appear we'll grab them. We'll hold them incommunicado of course. I've tightened security all around the *Ivanov*. No one else'll slip through the net. I promise you. No one.'

'Good. The police commissioner said he'd ordered CID to be more alert too.' Sir Geoffrey thought a moment. 'I'll send a minute to the secretary about your not complying with the 1-4a.

435

American liaison in London's sure to be very upset, but in the circumstances, how could you obey?'

'If I might suggest, it might be better to ask him not to mention we haven't got the files yet, sir. That information might also get into the wrong hands. Leave well alone, as long as we can.'

'Yes, I agree.' The governor sipped his sherry. 'There's lots of wisdom in laissez-faire, isn't there?'

'Yes sir.'

Sir Geoffrey glanced at his watch. 'I'll phone him in a few minutes, catch him before lunch. Good. But there's one problem I can't leave alone: the *Ivanov*. This morning I heard from our unofficial intermediary that Peking views that ship's presence here with the greatest concern.' The quite unofficial spokesman for the PRC in Hong Kong and the ranking Communist appointment was believed to be, presently, one of the deputy chairmen of the Bank of China, China's central bank through which passed all foreign exchange and all the billion U.S. dollars earned by supplying consumer goods and almost all Hong Kong's food and water. Britain had always maintained, bluntly, that Hong Kong was British soil, a Crown Colony. In all of Hong Kong's history, since 1841, Britain had never allowed any *official* Chinese representative to reside in the Colony. None.

'He went out of his way to jiggle me about the *Ivanov*,' Sir Geoffrey continued, 'and he wanted to register Peking's extreme displeasure that a Soviet spy ship was here. He even suggested I might think it wise to expel it. . . . After all, he said, we hear one of the Soviet KGB spies posing as a seaman had actually got himself killed on our soil. I thanked him for his interest and told him I'd advise my superiors—in due course.' Sir Geoffrey sipped some sherry. 'Curiously, he didn't appear irritated that the nuclear carrier was here.'

'That's strange!' Crosse was equally surprised.

'Does that indicate another policy shift—a distinct significant foreign-policy change, a desire for peace with the U.S.? I can't believe that. Everything indicates pathological hatred of the U.S.A.'

The governor sighed and refilled the cups. 'If it leaked that Sevrin's in existence, that we're undermined here . . . God almighty, they'd go into convulsions, and rightly so!'

'We'll find the traitors, sir, don't worry. We'll find them!'

'Will we? I wonder.' Sir Geoffrey sat down at the window seat and stared out at the manicured lawns and English garden, shrubs, flower beds surrounded by the high white wall, the sunset good. His wife was cutting flowers, wandering among the beds at the far end of the gardens, followed by a sour-faced, disapproving Chinese gardener. Sir Geoffrey watched her a moment. They had been married thirty years and had three children, all married now, and they were content and at peace with each other. 'Always traitors,' he said sadly. 'The Soviets are past masters in their use. So easy for the Sevrin traitors to agitate, to spread a little poison here and there, so easy to get China upset, poor China who's xenophobic anyway! Oh how easy it is to rock our boat here! Worst of all, who's *your* spy? The police spy? He must be at least a chief inspector to have access to that information.'

'I've no idea. If I had, he'd've been neutralized long since.'

'What are you going to do about General Jen and his Nationalist under-cover agents?'

'I'm going to leave them alone—they've been pegged for months. Much better to leave known enemy agents in situ than to have to ferret out their replacements.'

'I agree—they'd certainly all be replaced. Theirs, and ours. Sad, so sad! We do it and they do it. So sad and so stupid—this world's such a paradise, could be such a paradise.'

A bee hummed in the bay windows then flew back to the garden again as Sir Geoffrey eased the curtain aside. 'The minister asked me to make sure our visiting MPs—our trade delegation to China that returns tomorrow—to make sure their security was optimum, judicious, though totally discreet.'

'Yes sir. I understand.'

'It appears that one or two of them might be future cabinet ministers if the Labour Party get in. It'd be good for the Colony to create a fine impression on them.'

'Do you think they've a chance next time? The Labour Party?'

'I don't comment on those sort of questions, Roger.' The governor's voice was flat, and reproving. 'I'm not concerned with party politics—I represent Her Majesty the Queen—but personally I really do wish some of their extremists would go away and leave us to our own devices for clearly much of their left wing socialist philosophy is alien to our English way of life.' Sir Geoffrey hardened. 'It's quite obvious some of them do assist the enemy, willingly—or as dupes. Since we're on the subject, are any of our guests security risks?'

'It depends what you mean, sir. Two are left-wing trade unionists back-benchers, fire-eaters—Robin Grey and Lochin Donald McLean. McLean openly flaunts his admiration for the Communist Party. He's fairly high on our S-list. All the other Socialists are moderates. The Conservative members are moderate, middle-class, all ex-service. One's rather imperialist, the Liberal Party representative, Hugh Guthrie.'

'And the fire-eaters? They're ex-service?'

'McLean was a miner, at least his father was. Most of his life's been as a shop steward and unionist in the Scottish coalfields. Robin Grey was army, a captain, infantry.'

Sir Geoffrey looked up. 'You don't usually associate ex-captains with being fire-eating trades unionists, do you?'

'No sir.' Crosse sipped his sherry, appreciating it, savoring his knowledge more. 'Nor with being related to a tai-pan.'

'Eh?'

'Robin Grey's sister is Penelope Dunross.'

'Good God!' Sir Geoffrey stared at him, astounded. 'Are you sure?'

'Yes sir.'

'But why hasn't, why hasn't Ian mentioned it before?'

'I don't know, sir. Perhaps he's ashamed of him. Mr. Grey is certainly the complete opposite of Mrs. Dunross.'

'But . . . Bless my soul, you're sure?'

'Yes sir. Actually, it was Brian Kwok who spotted the connection. Just by chance. The MPs had to furnish the usual personal information to the PRC to get their visas, date of birth, profession, next of kin, etcetera. Brian was doing a routine check to make sure all the visas were in order to avoid any problem at the border. Brian happened to notice Mr. Grey had put "sister, Penelope Grey" as his next of kin, with an address, Castle Avisyard in Ayr. Brian remembered that that was the Dunross family home address.' Crosse pulled out his silver cigarette case. 'Do you mind if I smoke, sir?'

'No, please go ahead.'

'Thank you. That was a month or so ago. I thought it important enough for him to follow up the information. It took us relatively little time to establish that Mrs. Dunross really was his sister and next of kin. As far as we know now, Mrs. Dunross quarreled with her brother just after the war. Captain Grey was a POW in Changi, caught in Singapore in 1942. He got home in the later part of 1945—by the way their parents were killed in the London blitz of '43. At that time she was already married to Dunross—they'd married in 1943, sir, just after he was shot down—she was a WAAF. We know brother and sister met when Grey was released. As far as we can tell now, they've never met again. Of course it's none of our affair anyway, but the quarrel must have been—'

Crosse stopped as there was a discreet knock and Sir Geoffrey called out testily, 'Yes?'

The door opened. 'Excuse me, sir,' his aide said politely, 'Lady Allison asked me to tell you that the water's just gone on.'

'Oh, marvelous! Thank you.' The door closed. At once Crosse got up but the governor waved him back to his seat. 'No, please finish, Roger. A few minutes won't matter, though I must confess I can hardly wait. Would you like to shower before you go?'

'Thank you, sir, but we've our own water tanks at police HQ.'

'Oh yes. I forgot. Go on. You were saying—the quarrel?'

'The quarrel must have been pretty serious because it seems to have been final. A close friend of Grey told one of our people a few days ago that as far as he knew, Robin Grey had no living relatives. They really must hate each other.'

Sir Geoffrey stared at his cup, not seeing it. Suddenly he was remembering his own rotten childhood and how he had hated his father, hated him so much that for thirty years he had never called him, or written to him, and, when he was dying last year, had not bothered to go to him, to make peace with the man who had given him life. 'People are terrible to each other,' he muttered sadly. 'I know. Yes. Family quarrels are too easy. And then, when it's too late, you regret it, yes, you really regret it. People are terrible to each other . . .'

Crosse watched and waited, letting him ramble, letting him reveal himself, cautious not to make the slightest movement to distract him, wanting to know the man's secrets, and skeletons.

439

Like Alan Medford Grant, Crosse collected secrets. Goddamn that bastard and his god-cursed files! God curse Dunross and his devilry! How in the name of Christ can I get those files before Sinders?

Sir Geoffrey was staring into space. Then the water gurgled delightedly in the pipes somewhere in the walls and he came back into himself. He saw Crosse watching him. 'Hmmm, thinking aloud! Bad habit for a governor, eh?'

Crosse smiled and did not fall into the trap. 'Sir?'

'Well. As you said, it's really none of our business.' The governor finished his drink with finality and Crosse knew that he was dismissed. He got up. 'Thank you, sir.'

When he was alone the governor sighed. He thought a moment then picked up the special phone and gave the operator the minister's private number in London.

'This is Geoffrey Allison. Is he in please?'

'Hello, Geoffrey!'

'Hello, sir. I've just seen Roger. He assures me that the hiding place and Dunross will be completely guarded. Is Mr. Sinders en route?'

'He'll be there on Friday. I presume there have been no repercussions from that seaman's unfortunate accident?'

'No sir. Everything seems to be under control.'

'The P.M. was most concerned.'

'Yes sir.' The governor added, 'About the 1-4a . . . perhaps we shouldn't mention anything to our friends, yet.'

'I've already heard from them. They were distressingly irritated. So were our fellows. All right, Geoffrey. Fortunately it's a long weekend this week so I'll inform them Monday and draft his reprimand then.'

'Thank you sir.'

'Geoffrey, that American senator you have with you at the moment. I think he should be guided.'

The governor frowned. *Guided* was a code word between them, meaning 'watched very carefully.' Senator Wilf Tillman, a presidential hopeful, was visiting Hong Kong en route to Saigon for a well-publicized fact-finding mission.

'I'll take care of it as soon as I'm off the phone. Was there anything else, sir?' he asked, impatient now to bathe.

'No, just give me a private minute on what the senator's

program has been.' *Program* was another code which meant to furnish the Colonial Office with detailed information. 'When you've time.'

'I'll have it on your desk Friday.'

'Thank you Geoffrey. We'll chat at the usual time tomorrow.' The line went dead.

The governor replaced the phone thoughtfully. Their conversation would have been electronically scrambled and, at either end, unscrambled. Even so, they were guarded. They knew the enemy had the most advanced and sophisticated eavesdropping equipment in the world. For any really classified conversation or meeting he would go to the permanently guarded, concrete, cell-like room in the basement that was meticulously rechecked by security experts for possible electronic bugs every week.

Bloody nuisance, Sir Geoffrey thought. Bloody nuisance all this cloak-and-dagger stuff! Roger? Unthinkable, even so, once there was Philby.

25

6:20 P.M.:

Captain Gregor Suslev waved jauntily to the police at the dock-yard gates in Kowloon, his two plainclothes detectives fifty yards in tow. He was dressed in well-cut civilians and he stood by the curb a moment watching the traffic, then hailed a passing taxi. The taxi took off and a small gray Jaguar with Sergeant Lee, CID, and another plainclothes CID man driving, followed smartly.

The taxi went along Chatham Road in the usual heavy traffic, southward, skirting the railway line, then turned west along Salisbury Road on the southmost tip of Kowloon, passing the railway terminus, near the Golden Ferry Terminal. There it stopped. Suslev paid it off and ran up the steps of the Victoria and Albert Hotel. Sergeant Lee followed him as the other detective parked the police Jag.

Suslev walked with an easy stride and he stood for a moment in the immense, crowded foyer with its high ceilings, lovely and ornate, and old-fashioned electric fans overhead, and looked for an empty table among the multitude of tables. The whole room was alive with the clink of ice in cocktail glasses and conversation. Mostly Europeans. A few Chinese couples. Suslev wandered through the people, found a table, loudly ordered a double vodka, sat and began to read his paper. Then the girl was standing near him.

'Hello,' she said.

'Ginny, *doragaya!*' he said with a great beam and hugged her, lifting her off her little feet to the shocked disapproval of every woman in the place and the covert envy of every man. 'It's been a long time, *golubchik.*'

442

'*Ayeeyha,*' she said with a toss of her head, her short hair dancing, and sat down, conscious of the stares, enjoying them, hating them. 'You late. Wat for you keep me wait? A lady no like wait in Victoria by herself, *heya?*'

'You're right, *golubchik!*' Suslev pulled out a slim package and gave it to her with another beam. 'Here, all the way from Vladivostok!'

'Oh! How thank you?' Ginny Fu was twenty-eight and most nights she worked at the Happy Drinkers Bar in an alley off Mong Kok, half a mile or so to the north. Some nights she went to the Good Luck Ballroom. Most days she would pinch-hit for her friends behind the counter of tiny shops within shops when they were with a client. White teeth and jet eyes and jet hair and golden skin, her gaudy *cheong-sam* slit high on her long, stockinged thighs. She looked at the present excitedly. 'Oh thank, Gregor, thank very much!' She put it in her large purse and grinned at him. Then her eyes went to the waiter who was strolling up with Suslev's vodka, along with the smug, open contempt reserved by all Chinese for all young Chinese women who sat with *quai loh.* They must of course be third-class whores—who else would sit with a *quai loh* in a public place, particularly in the foyer of the Vic? He set down the drink with practiced insolence and stared back at her.

'*Dew neh loh moh* on all your pig-swill ancestors,' she hissed in gutter Cantonese. 'My husband here is a 489 in the police and if I say the word he'll have those insignificant peanuts you call your balls crushed off your loathsome body an hour after you leave work tonight!'

The waiter blanched. 'Eh?'

'Hot tea! Bring me fornicating hot tea and if you spit in it I'll get my husband to put a knot in that straw you call your stalk!'

The waiter fled.

'What did you say to him?' Suslev asked, understanding only a few words of Cantonese, though his English was very good.

Ginny Fu smiled sweetly. 'I just ask him bring tea.' She knew the waiter would automatically spit in her tea now, or more probably, for safety, get a friend to do it for him, so she would not drink it and thus cause him to lose even more face. Dirty dog bone! 'Next time no like meet here, lotsa nasty peoples,' she said imperiously, looking around, then crinkled her nose at a group

443

of middle-aged Englishwomen who were staring at her. 'Too much body stinky,' she added loudly, tossing her hair again, and chortled to herself seeing them flush and look away. 'This gift, Gregy. Thank so very!'

'Nothing,' Suslev said. He knew she would not open the gift now—or in front of him—which was very good, sensible Chinese manners. Then, if she did not like the gift or was disappointed or cursed aloud that what was given was the wrong size, or wrong color, or at the miserliness of the giver or bad taste or whatever, then he could not lose face and she could not lose face.

'Very sensible!'

'Wat?'

'Nothing.'

'You looks good.'

'You too.' It was three months since his last visit and though his mistress in Vladivostok was a Eurasian with a White Russian mother and Chinese father, he enjoyed Ginny Fu.

'Gregy,' she said, then dropped her voice, her smile saucy. 'Finish drink. We begin holiday! I got vodka . . . I got other things!'

He smiled back at her. 'That you have, *golubchik!*'

'How many day you got?'

'At least three but . . .'

'Oh!' She tried to hide her disappointment.

'. . . I'm back and forth to my ship. We've tonight, most of it, and tomorrow and all tomorrow night. And the stars will shine!'

'Three month long time, Gregy.'

'I'll be back soon.'

'Yes.' Ginny Fu put away her disappointment and became pragmatic again. 'Finish drink and we begin!' She saw the waiter hurrying with her tea. Her eyes ground into the man as he put it down. 'Huh! Clearly it's cold and not fresh!' she said disgustedly. 'Who am I! A dirty lump of foreign devil dogmeat? No, I'm a civilized person from the Four Provinces who, because her rich father gambled away all his money, was sold by him into concubinage to become Number Two Wife for this chief of police of the foreign devils! So go piss in your hat!' She got up.

The waiter backed off a foot.

'What's up?' Suslev asked.

'Don't pay for teas, Gregy. Not hot!' she said imperiously. 'No give tip!'

Nonetheless Suslev paid and she took his arm and they walked out together, eyes following them. Her head was high, but inside she hated the looks from all the Chinese, even the young, starched bellboy who opened the door—the image of her youngest brother whose life and schooling she paid for.

Dunross was coming up the steps. He waited for them to pass by, an amused glint in his eyes, then he was bowed in politely by the beaming bellboy. He headed through the throng for the house phone. Many noticed him at once and eyes followed him. He walked around a group of tourists, camera bedecked, and noticed Jacques deVille and his wife Susanne at a corner table. Both were set-faced, staring at their drinks. He shook his head, wearily amused. Poor old Jacques has been caught again and she's twisting his infidelity in its well-worn wound. Joss! He could almost hear old Chen-chen laugh. 'Man's life is to suffer, young Ian! Yes, it's the eternal yin warring on our oh so vulnerable yang. . . .'

Normally Dunross would have pretended not to notice them, leaving them to their privacy, but some instinct told him otherwise.

'Hello, Jacques—Susanne. How're things?'

'Oh hello, hello, tai-pan.' Jacques deVille got up politely. 'Would you care to join us?'

'No thanks, can't.' Then he saw the depth of his friend's agony and he remembered the car accident in France. Jacques's daughter Avril and her husband! 'What's happened? Exactly!' Dunross said it as a leader would say it, requiring an instant answer.

Jacques hesitated. Then he said, 'Exactly, tai-pan: I heard from Avril. She phoned from Cannes just as I was leaving the office. She, she said, "Daddy . . . Daddy, Borge's dead. . . . Can you hear me? I've been trying to reach you for two days . . . it was head-on, and the, the other man was . . . My Borge's dead . . . can you hear me. . . ?"' Jacques's voice was flat. 'Then the line went dead. We know she's in the hospital at Cannes. I thought it best for Susanne to go at once. Her, her flight's delayed so . . . so we're just waiting here. They're trying to get a call through to Cannes but I don't hope for much.'

'Christ, I'm so sorry,' Dunross said, trying to dismiss the twinge that had rushed through him as his mind had substituted Adryon for Avril. Avril was just twenty and Borge Escary a fine young man. They had been married just a year and a half and this was their first holiday after the birth of a son. 'What time's the flight?'

'Eight o'clock now.'

'Susanne, would you like us to look after the baby? Jacques, why not get on the flight—I'll take care of everything here.'

'No,' Jacques said. 'Thanks but no. It's best that Susanne go. She'll bring Avril home.'

'Yes,' Susanne said, and Dunross noticed that she seemed to have sagged. 'We have the *amahs* . . . it's best just me, tai-pan. *Merci*, but no, this way is best.' A spill of tears went down her cheeks. 'It's not fair, is it? Borge was so nice a boy!'

'Yes. Susanne, I'll get Penn to go over daily so don't worry, we'll make sure the babe's fine and Jacques too.' Dunross weighed them both. He was confident that Jacques was well in control. Good, he thought. Then he said as an order, 'Jacques, when Susanne's safely on the flight go back to the office. Telex our man in Marseilles. Get him to arrange a suite at the Capitol, to meet her with a car and ten thousand dollars worth of francs. Tell him from me he's to be at her beck and call as long as she's there. He's to call me tomorrow with a complete report on Avril, the accident, who was driving and who the other driver was.'

'Yes, tai-pan.'

'You sure you're all right?'

Jacques forced a smile. '*Oui. Merci, mon ami.*

'*Rien.* I'm so sorry, Susanne—call collect if we can do anything.' He walked away. Our man in Marseilles is good, he thought. He'll take care of everything. And Jacques's a man of iron. Have I covered everything? Yes, I think so. It's dealt with for the moment.

God protect Adryon and Glenna and Duncan and Penn, he thought. And Kathy, and all the others. And me—until the Noble House is inviolate. He glanced at his watch. It was exactly 6:30. He picked up a house phone. 'Mr. Bartlett, please.' A moment, then he heard Casey's voice.

'Hello?'

'Ah, hello, Ciranoush,' Dunross said. 'Would you tell him I'm in the lobby.'

'Oh hello, sure! Would you like to come up? We're—'

'Why don't you come down? I thought, if you're not too busy I'd take you on my next appointment—it might be interesting for you. We could eat afterwards, if you're free.'

'I'd love that. Let me check.'

He heard her repeat what he had said and he wondered, very much, about his bet with Claudia. Impossible that those two aren't lovers, he thought, or haven't been lovers, living so close together. Wouldn't be natural!

'We'll be right down, tai-pan!' He heard the smile in her voice as he hung up.

The Most High Headwaiter was hovering beside him now, waiting for the rare honor of seating the tai-pan. He had been summoned by the Second Headwaiter the moment the news had arrived that Dunross had been seen approaching the front door. His name was Afternoon Pok and he was gray-haired, majestic, and ruled this shift with a bamboo whip.

'Ah Honored Lord, this is a pleasure,' the old man said in Cantonese with a deferential bow. 'Have you eaten rice today?' This was the polite way of saying good-day or good evening or how are you in Chinese.

'Yes, thank you, Elder Brother,' Dunross replied. He had known Afternoon Pok most of his life. As long as he could remember, Afternoon Pok had been the headwaiter in the foyer from noon till six, and many times when Dunross was young, sent on an errand here, sore from a whipping or cuffing, the old man would seat him in a corner table, slip him a pastry, tap him kindly on the head and never give him a bill. 'You're looking prosperous!'

'Thank you, tai-pan. Oh, you are looking very healthy too! But you've still only one son! Don't you think it's time your revered Chief Wife found you a second wife?'

They smiled together. 'Please follow me,' the old man said importantly and led the way to the choice table that had miraculously appeared in a spacious, favored place acquired by four energetic waiters who had squeezed other guests and the tables out of the way. Now they stood, almost at attention, all beaming.

447

'Your usual, sir?' the wine waiter asked. 'I've a bottle of the '52.'

'Perfect,' Dunross said, knowing this would be the La Doucette that he enjoyed so much. He would have preferred tea but it was a matter of face to accept the wine. The bottle was already there, in an ice bucket. 'I'm expecting Mr. Bartlett and Miss Tcholok.' Another waiter went at once to wait for them at the elevator.

'If there's anything you need, please call me.' Afternoon Pok bowed and walked off, every waiter in the foyer nervously conscious of him. Dunross sat down and noticed Peter and Fleur Marlowe trying to control two pretty, boisterous girls of four and eight and he sighed and thanked God his daughters were past that age. As he sipped the wine approvingly, he saw old Willie Tusk look over at him and wave. He waved back.

When he was a boy he used to come over from Hong Kong three or four times a week with business orders for Tusk from old Sir Ross Struan, Alastair's father—or, more likely, they were orders from his own father who, for years, had run the foreign division of the Noble House. Occasionally Tusk would service the Noble House in areas of his expertise—anything to do with getting anything out of Thailand, Burma or Malaya and shipping it anywhere, with just a little *h'eung yau* and his standard trading fee of 7½ percent.

'What's the half percent for, Uncle Tusk?' he remembered asking one day, peering up at the man he now towered over.

'That's what I call my dollymoney, young Ian.'

'What's dollymoney?'

'That's a little extra for your pocket to give away to dollies, to ladies of your choice.'

'But why do you give money to ladies?'

'Well that's a long story, laddie.'

Dunross smiled to himself. Yes, a very long story. That part of his education had had various teachers, some good, some very good and some bad. Old Uncle Chen-chen had arranged for his first mistress when he was fourteen.

'Oh do you really mean it, Uncle Chen-chen?'

'Yes, but you're not to tell anyone or your father will have my guts for garters! Huh,' the lovely old man had continued, 'your father should have arranged it, or asked me to arrange it but never mind. Now wh—'

'But when do I, when do I . . . oh are you sure? I mean how, how much do I pay and when, Uncle Chen-chen? When? I mean before or, or after or when? That's what I don't know.'

'You don't know lots! You still don't know when to talk and when not to talk! How can I instruct you if you talk? Have I all day?'

'No sir.'

'*Eeeee*,' old Chen-chen had said with that huge smile of his, 'eeeee, but how lucky you are! Your first time in a Gorgeous Gorge! It will be the first time, won't it? Tell the truth!'

'Er . . . well er er well . . . er, yes.'

'Good!'

It wasn't till years after that Dunross had discovered that some of the most famous houses in Hong Kong and Macao had secretly bid for the privilege of servicing the first pillow time of a future tai-pan and the great-great-grandson of Green-Eyed Devil himself. Apart from the face the house would gain for generations from being the one chosen by the compradore of the Noble House, it would also be enormous joss for the lady herself. First Time Essence of even the meanest personage was an elixir of marvelous value—just as, in Chinese lore, for the elderly man, the yin juices of the virgin were equally prized and sought after to rejuvenate the yang.

'Good sweet Christ, Uncle Chen-chen!' he had exploded. 'It's true? You actually sold me? You mean to tell me you sold me to a bloody house! Me?'

'Of course.' The old man had peered up at him, and chuckled and chuckled, bedridden now in the great house of the Chens on the ridge of Struan's Lookout, almost blind now and near death but sweetly unresisting and content. 'Who told you, who, eh? Eh, young Ian?'

It was Tusk, a widower, a great frequenter of Kowloon's dance halls and bars and houses who had been told it as a legend by one of the mama-sans who had heard that it was a custom in the Noble House that the compradore had to arrange the first pillow time for the progeny of Green-Eyed Devil Struan. 'Yes, old boy,' Tusk had told him. 'Dirk Struan said to Sir Gordon Chen, old Chen-chen's father, he'd put his Evil Eye on the House of Chen if they didn't choose correctly.'

'Balls,' Dunross had said to Tusk, who had continued, pained, that he was just passing on a legend which was now part of Hong Kong's folklore and, balls or not Ian old chum, your first bang-ditty-bang-bang was worth thousands Hong Kong to that old rake!

'I think that's pretty bloody awful, Uncle Chen-chen!'

'But why? It was a most profitable auction. It cost you nothing but gave you enormous pleasure. It cost me nothing but gave me 20,000 HK. The girl's house gained vast face and so did the girl. It cost her nothing but gave her years of a huge clientele who would want to share the specialness of your Number One choice!'

Elegant Jade had been the only name he knew her by. She had been twenty-two and very practiced, a professional since she had been sold to the house by her parents when she was twelve. Her house was called the House of a Thousand Pleasures. Elegant Jade was sweet and gentle—when it pleased her and a total dragon when it pleased her. He had been madly in love with her and their affair had lasted over two summer holidays from boarding school in England, which was the contract time that Chen-chen had arranged. The moment he had returned on the first day of the third summer he had hurried to the house, but she had vanished.

Even today Dunross could remember how distraught he had been, how he had tried to find her. But the girl had left no trace in her wake.

'What happened to her, Uncle Chen-chen? Really happened?'

The old man sighed, lying back in his huge bed, tired now. 'It was time for her to go. It is always too easy for a young man to give too much to a girl, too much time, too much thought. It was time for her to go . . . after her you could choose for yourself and you needed to put your mind on the House and not on her. . . . Oh don't try to hide your desire, I understand, oh, how I understand! Don't worry, she was well paid, my son, you had no child by her . . .'

'Where is she now?'

'She went to Taiwan. I made sure she had enough money to begin her own house, she said that's what she wanted to do and . . . and part of my arrangement was that I bought her out of her

450

contract. That cost me, was it 5 . . . or 10,000. . . . I can't remember. . . . Please excuse me, I'm tired now. I must sleep a little. Please come back tomorrow, my son. . . .'

Dunross sipped his wine, remembering. That was the only time that old Chen-chen ever called me my son, he thought. What a grand old man! If only I could be so wise, so kind and so wise, and worthy of him.

Chen-chen had died a week later. His funeral was the greatest Hong Kong had ever seen, with a thousand professional wailers and drums following the coffin to its burial place. The white-clad women had been paid to follow the coffin, wailing loudly to the Heavens, petitioning the gods to grease the way of this great man's spirit to the Void or rebirth or to whatever happens to the spirit of the dead. Chen-chen was a nominal Christian so he had had two services for safety, one Christian, the other Budd-hist. . .

'Hello, tai-pan!'

Casey was there with Linc Bartlett beside her. Both were smiling though both were looking a little tired.

He greeted them and Casey ordered a Scotch and soda and Linc a beer.

'How's your day been?' Casey asked.

'Up and down,' he said after a pause. 'How was yours?'

'Busy, but we're getting there,' she said. 'Your attorney, Dawson, canceled our date this morning—that's on again for tomorrow at noon. The rest of my day was on the phone and the telex to the States, getting things organized. Service is good here, this is a great hotel. We're all set to complete our side of the agreement.'

'Good. I think I'll attend the meeting with Dawson,' Dunross said. 'That'll expedite matters. I'll get him to come over to our offices. I'll send a car for you at 11:10.'

'No need for that, tai-pan. I know my way on the ferry,' she said. 'I went back and forth this afternoon. Best five cents American I've ever spent. How'd you keep the fares so low?'

'We carried forty-seven million passengers last year.' Dunross glanced at Bartlett. 'Will you be at the meeting tomorrow?'

'Not unless you want me for something special,' he said easily. 'Casey handles the legals initially. She knows what we want, and we've got Seymour Steigler III coming in on Pan Am's flight Thursday—he's our head counsel and tax attorney. He'll keep everything smooth with your attorneys so we can close in seven days, easy.'

'Excellent.' A smiling obsequious waiter brought their drinks and topped up Dunross's glass. When they were alone again Casey said quietly, 'Tai-pan, your ships. You want them as a separate agreement? If the attorneys draw it up it won't be private. How do we keep it private?'

'I'll draw up the document and put our chop on it. That'll make it legal and binding. Then the agreement stays secret between the three of us, eh?'

'What's a chop, Ian?' Bartlett asked.

'It's the equivalent of a seal.' Dunross took out a slim, oblong bamboo container, perhaps two inches long and half an inch square, and slid back the tight-fitting top. He took out the chop, which fitted the scarlet silk-lined box, and showed it to them. It was made of ivory. Some Chinese characters were carved in relief on the bottom. 'This is my personal chop—it's hand-carved so almost impossible to forge. You stick this end in the ink . . .' The ink was red and almost solid, neatly in its compartment in one end of the box. '. . . and imprint the paper. Quite often in Hong Kong you don't sign papers, you just chop them. Most aren't legal without a chop. The company seal's the same as this, only a little bigger.'

'What do the characters mean?' Casey asked.

'They're a pun on my name, and ancestor. Literally they mean "illustrious, razor sharp, throughout the noble green seas." The pun's on Green-Eyed Devil, as Dirk was called, the Noble House, and a dirk or knife.' Dunross smiled and put it away. 'It has other meanings—the surface one's "tai-pan of the Noble House." In Chinese . . .' He glanced around at the sound of a bicycle bell. The young bellhop was walking through the crowds carrying a small paging board aloft on a pole that bore the scrawled name of the person wanted. The page was not for them so he continued, 'With Chinese writing, there are always various levels of meanings. That's what makes it complex, and interesting.'

Casey was fanning herself with a menu. It was warm in the foyer though the ceiling fans were creating a gentle breeze. She took out a tissue and pressed it beside her nose. 'Is it always this humid?' she asked.

Dunross smiled. 'It's relatively dry today. Sometimes it's ninety degrees and ninety-five humidity for weeks on end. Autumn and spring are the best times to be here. July, August, September are hot and wet. Actually, though, they're forecasting rain. We might even get a typhoon. I heard on the wireless there's a tropical depression gathering southeast of us. Yes. If we're lucky it'll rain. There's no water rationing in the V and A yet, is there?'

'No,' Bartlett said, 'but after seeing the pails in your house last night, I don't think I'll ever take water for granted again.'

'Nor me,' Casey said. 'It must be terribly hard.'

'Oh, you get used to it. By the way my suggestion about the document is satisfactory?' Dunross asked Bartlett, wanting it settled and irritated with himself that he was trapped into having to ask. He was grimly amused to notice that Bartlett hesitated a fraction of a second and glanced imperceptibly at Casey before saying, 'Sure.'

'Ian,' Bartlett continued, 'I've got Forrester—the head of our foam division—coming in on the same flight. I thought we might as well get the show on the road. There's no reason to wait until we have papers, is there?'

'No.' Dunross thought a moment and decided to test his theory. 'How expert is he?'

'Expert.'

Casey added, 'Charlie Forrester knows everything there is to know about polyurethane foam—manufacturing, distribution and sales.'

'Good.' Dunross turned to Bartlett and said innocently, 'Would you like to bring him to Taipei?' He saw a flash behind the American's eyes and knew that he had been correct. Squirm, you bastard, he thought, you haven't told her yet! I haven't forgotten the rough time you gave me last night, with all your secret information. Squirm out of this one with face! 'While we're golfing or whatever, I'll put Forrester with my experts— he can check out possible sites and set that in motion.'

'Good idea,' Bartlett said, not squirming at all, and Dunross's opinion of him went up.

'Taipei? Taipei in Taiwan?' Casey asked excitedly. 'We're

going to Taipei? When?'

'Sunday afternoon,' Bartlett said, his voice calm. 'We're going for a couple of days, Ian an—'

'Perfect, Linc,' she said with a smile. 'While you're golfing, I can check things out with Charlie. Let me play next time around. What's your handicap, tai-pan?'

'Ten,' Dunross answered, 'and since Linc Bartlett knows I'm sure you do too.'

She laughed. 'I'd forgotten that vital statistic. Mine's fourteen on a very good day.'

'Give or take a stroke or two?'

'Sure. Women cheat in golf as much as men.'

'Oh?'

'Yes. But unlike men they cheat to lower their handicap. A handicap's a status symbol, right? The lower the score, the more the status! Women don't usually bet more than a few dollars so a low handicap's not that vital except for face. But men? I've seen them hit one deliberately into the rough to pick up two extra strokes if they were on a dynamite round that would drop their handicap a notch. Of course that was only if they weren't playing that particular round for money. What's the stake between your pairs?'

'500 HK.'

She whistled. 'A hole?'

'Hell, no,' Bartlett said. 'The game.'

'Even so, I think I'd better kibtz this one.'

Dunross said, 'What's that mean?'

'To watch. If I'm not careful, Linc will put my end of Par-Con on the line.' Her smiled warmed both of them, and then, because Dunross had deliberately dropped Bartlett into the trap, he decided to extract him.

'That's a fine idea, Casey,' he said, watching her carefully. 'But on second thought, perhaps it would be better for you and Forrester to check out Hong Kong before Taipei—this will be our biggest market. And if your lawyer arrives Thursday you might wish to spend time with him here.' He looked at Bartlett direct, the picture of innocence. 'If you want to cancel our trip, that's all right too, you've plenty of time to go to Taipei. But I must go.'

'No,' Bartlett said. 'Casey, you cover this end. Seymour will need all the help you can give him. I'll make a preliminary tour this time and we can do it together later.'

She sipped her drink and kept her face clear. So I'm not invited, huh? she thought with a flash of irritation. 'You're off Sunday?'

'Yes,' Dunross said, sure that the finesse had worked, detecting no change in her. 'Sunday afternoon I may be doing a hill climb in the morning, so that's the earliest I can make it.'

'Hill climb? Mountain climbing, tai-pan?'

'Oh no. Just with a motorcar—in the New Territories. You're both welcome if you're interested.' He added to Bartlett, 'We could go direct to the airport. If I can clear your aircraft, I will. I'll ask about that tomorrow.'

'Linc,' Casey said, 'what about Armstrong and the police? You're grounded here.'

'I arranged that today,' Dunross said, 'he's parolled into my custody.'

She laughed. 'Fantastic! Just don't jump bail!'

'I won't.'

'You're off Sunday, tai-pan? Back when?'

'Tuesday, in time for dinner.'

'Tuesday's when we sign?'

'Yes.'

'Linc, isn't that cutting it tight?'

'No. I'll be in constant touch. The deal's set. All we need is to put it on paper.'

'Whatever you say, Linc. Everything will be ready for signature when you two get back. Tai-pan, I'm to deal with Andrew if there's any problem?'

'Yes. Or Jacques.' Dunross glanced at the far corner. Now their table was occupied by others. Never mind, he told himself. Everything was done that could be done. 'The phone service is good to Taipei so there's no need to worry. Now, are you free for dinner?'

'We certainly are,' Bartlett said.

'What sort of food would you like?'

'How about Chinese?'

'Sorry, but you've got to be more specific,' Dunross said. 'That's like saying you want European cooking—which could run the gamut from Italian to boiled English.'

'Linc, shouldn't we leave it to the tai-pan?' Casey said, and added, 'Tai-pan, I have to confess, I like sweet and sour, egg rolls, chop suey and fried rice. I'm not much on anything far out.'

'Nor am I,' Bartlett agreed. 'No snake, dog or anything exotic.'

'Snake's very good in season,' Dunross said. 'Especially the bile—mixed with tea. It's very invigorating, a great pick-me-up! And little young chow dog stewed in oyster sauce is just perfect.'

'You've tried it? You've tried dog?' She was shocked.

'I was told it was chicken. It tasted a lot like chicken. But never eat dog and drink whiskey at the same time, Casey. They say it turns the meat into lumps of iron that'll give you a very hard time indeed. . . .'

He was listening to himself make jokes and inconsequential small talk while he was watching Jacques and Susanne getting into a taxi. His heart went out to them and to Kathy and to all the others and he wanted to get on the plane himself, to rush there and bring Avril back safely—such a nice girl, part of his family. . . .

How in the name of Christ do you live as a man, rule the Noble House and stay sane? How do you help the family and make deals and live with all the rest of it?

'That's the joy and the hurt of being tai-pan,' Dirk Struan had said to him in his dreams, many times.

Yes, but there's very little joy.

You're wrong and Dirk's right and you're being far too serious, he told himself. The only serious problems are Par-Con, the boom, Kathy, AMG's papers, Crosse, John Chen, Toda Shipping, and the fact that you turned down Lando Mata's offer, not necessarily in that order. So much money.

What is it I want out of life? Money? Power? Or all China?

He saw Casey and Bartlett watching him. Since these two've arrived, he thought, I've had nothing but trouble. He looked back at them. She was certainly worth looking at with her tight pants and clinging blouse. 'Leave it to me,' he said, deciding that tonight he would like some Cantonese food.

They heard the page bell and saw the paging board and the name was 'Miss K. C. Shuluk.' Dunross beckoned the youth.

'He'll show you to the phone, Casey.'

'Thanks.' She got up. Eyes followed the long, elegant legs and her sensuous walk—the women jealous, hating her.

'You're a son of a bitch,' Bartlett said calmly.

'Oh?'

'Yes.' He grinned and that took the curse off everything. '20 to 1 says Taipei was a probe—but I'm not calling you on it, Ian. No. I was rough last night—had to be, so maybe I deserved a roasting. But don't do that a second time with Casey or I'll hand you your head.'

'Will you now?'

'Yes. She's off limits.' Bartlett's eyes went back to Casey. He saw her pass the Marlowe table, stop a second and greet them and their children, then go on again. 'She knows she wasn't invited.'

Dunross was perturbed. 'Are you sure? I thought . . . I didn't cover properly? The moment I realized you hadn't told her yet . . . Sorry, thought I'd covered.'

'Hell, you were perfect! But five'll still get you ten she knows she wasn't invited.' Bartlett smiled again, and, once more, Dunross wondered what was under the smile. I'll have to watch this bugger more closely, he thought. So Casey's off limits, is she? I wonder what he really meant by that?

Dunross had chosen the foyer deliberately, wanting to be seen with the now famous—or infamous Bartlett and his lady. He knew it would fuel rumors of their impending deal and that would further agitate the stock market and put the punters off balance. If the Ho-Pak crashed, provided it did not bring other banks down with it, the boom could still happen. If Bartlett and Casey would bend a little, he thought, and if I could really trust them, I could make a killing of killings. So many ifs. Too many. I'm out of control of this battle at the moment. Bartlett and Casey have all the momentum. How far will they cooperate?

Then something Superintendent Armstrong and Brian Kwok had said triggered a vagrant thought and his anxiety increased.

'What do you think of that fellow Banastasio?' he asked, keeping his voice matter-of-fact.

'Vincenzo?' Bartlett said at once. 'Interesting guy. Why?'

'Just wondering,' Dunross said, outwardly calm but inwardly shocked that he had been right. 'Have you known him long?'

'Three or four years. Casey an' I have gone to the track with him a few times—to Del Mar. He's a big-time gambler there and in Vegas. He'll bet 50,000 on a race—so he told us. He and John Chen are quite friendly. Is he a friend of yours?'

'No. I've never met him but I heard John mention him once or twice,' he said, 'and Tsu-yan.'

'How is Tsu-yan? He's another gambler. When I saw him in L.A., he couldn't wait to get to Vegas. He was at the track the last time we were there with John Chen. Nothing yet on John or the kidnappers?'

'No.'

'Rotten luck.'

Dunross was hardly listening. The dossier he had prepared on Bartlett had given no indication of any Mafia connections— but Banastasio linked everything. The guns, John Chen, Tsu-yan and Bartlett.

Mafia meant dirty money and narcotics, with a constant search for legitimate fronts for the laundering of money. Tsu-yan used to deal heavily in medical supplies during Korea—and now, so the story went, he was heavily into gold smuggling in Taipei, Indonesia and Malaya with Four Finger Wu. Could Banastasio be shipping guns to . . . to whom? Had poor John Chen stumbled onto something and was he kidnapped for that reason?

Does that mean part of Par-Con's money is Mafia money—is Par-Con Mafia-dominated or controlled by Mafia?

'I seem to remember John saying Banastasio was one of your major stockholders,' he said, stabbing into the dark again.

'Vincenzo's got a big chunk of stock. But he's not an officer or director. Why?'

Dunross saw that now Bartlett's eyes were concentrated and he could almost feel the mind waves reaching out, wondering about this line of questioning. So he ended it. 'It's curious how small the world really is, isn't it?'

Casey picked up the phone, inwardly seething. 'Operator, this is Miss Tcholok. You've a call for me?'

'Ah one moment plees.'

So I'm not invited to Taipei, she was thinking furiously. Why didn't the tai-pan just come out and say it and not twist things around and why didn't Linc tell me about it too? Jesus, is he under the tai-pan's spell like I was last night? Why the secret? What else are they cooking?

Taipei, eh? Well I've heard it's a man's place so if all they're after's a dirty weekend it's fine with me. But not if it's business. Why didn't Linc say? What's there to hide?

Casey's fury began to grow, then she remembered what the Frenchwoman had said about beautiful *Chinoise* so readily available and her fury turned to an untoward anxiety for Linc.

Goddamn men!

Goddamn men and the world they've made exclusively to fit themselves. And it's worse here than anywhere I've ever been.

Goddamn the English! They're all so smooth and smart and their manners great and they say please and thank you and get up when you come in and hold your chair for you but, just under the surface, they're just as rotten as any others. They're worse. They're hypocrites, that's what they are! Well I'll get even. One day we'll play golf, Mr. Tai-pan Dunross and you'd better be good because I can play down to ten on a good day—I learned about golf in a man's world early—so I'll rub your nose in it. Yes. Or maybe a game of pool—or billiards. Sure, and I know what reverse English is too.

Casey thought of her father with a sudden shaft of joy, and how he had taught her the rudiments of both games. But it was Linc who taught her how to stab low on the left side with the cue to give the ball a twist to the right to swerve around the eight ball—showed her when, foolishly, she had challenged him to a game. He had slaughtered her before he gave her any lessons.

'Casey, you'd better make sure you know all a man's weak points before you battle with him. I wiped the board with you to prove a point. I don't play games for pleasure—just to win. I'm not playing games with you. I want you, nothing else matters. Let's forget the deal we made and get married and . . .'

That was just a few months after she had started working for Linc Bartlett. She was just twenty and already in love with him. But she still wanted revenge on the other man more, and independent wealth more and to find herself more, so she had said, 'No, Linc, we agreed seven years. We agreed up front, as equals. I'll help you get rich and I'll get mine on the way to your

459

millions, and neither of us owes the other anything. You can fire me anytime for any reason, and I can leave for any reason. We're equals. I won't deny that I love you with all my heart but I still won't change our deal. But if you're still willing to ask me to marry you when I reach my twenty-seventh birthday, then I will. I'll marry you, live with you, leave you—whatever you want. But not now. Yes. I love you but if we become lovers now I'll . . . I'll never be able to . . . I just can't, Linc, not now. There's too much I have to find out about myself.'

Casey sighed. What a twisted crazy deal it is. Has all the power and dealing and wheeling—and all the years and tears and loneliness been worth it?

I just don't know. I just don't know. And Par-Con? Can I ever reach my goal: Par-Con *and* Linc, or will I have to choose between them?

'Ciranoush?' came through the earpiece.

'Oh! Hello, Mr. Gornt!' She felt a surge of warmth. 'This is a pleasant surprise,' she added, collecting her wits.

'I hope I'm not disturbing you?'

'Not at all. What can I do for you?'

'I wondered if you are able to confirm this Sunday yet, if you and Mr. Bartlett are available? I want to plan my boat party and I'd like the two of you as my honored guests.'

'I'm sorry, Mr. Gornt, but Linc can't make it. He's all tied up.'

She heard the hesitation and then the covered pleasure in his voice. 'Would you care to come without him? I was thinking of having a few business friends. I'm sure you'd find it interesting.'

It might be very good for Par-Con if I went, she thought. Besides, if Linc and the tai-pan are going to Taipei without me, why can't I go boating without them? 'I'd love to,' she said, warmth in her voice, 'if you're sure I won't be in the way.'

'Of course not. We'll pick you up at the wharf, just opposite the hotel, near the Golden Ferry. Ten o'clock—casual. Do you swim?'

'Sure.'

'Good—the water's refreshing. Water-ski?'

'Love it!'

'Very good!'

'Can I bring anything? Food or wine or anything?'

'No. I think we'll have everything aboard. We'll go to one of the outer islands and picnic, water-ski—be back just after sunset.'

'Mr. Gornt, I'd like to keep this excursion to ourselves. I'm told Confucius said, "A closed mouth catches no flies."'

'Confucius said many things. He once likened a lady to a moonbeam.'

She hesitated, the danger signals up. But then she heard herself say lightly, 'Should I bring a chaperone?'

'Perhaps you should,' he said and she heard his smile.

'How about Dunross?'

'He'd hardly be a chaperone—merely the destruction of what could perhaps be a perfect day.'

'I look forward to Sunday, Mr. Gornt.'

'Thank you.' The phone clicked off instantly.

You arrogant bastard! she almost said aloud. How much are you taking for granted? Just thank you and click and no goodbye.

I'm Linc's and not up for grabs.

Then why did you play the coquette on the phone and at the party? she asked herself. And why did you want that bastard to keep your Sunday date quiet?

Women like secrets too, she told herself grimly. Women like a lot of things men like.

26

The coolie was in the dingy gold vaults of the Ho-Pak Bank. He was a small, old man who wore a tattered grimy undershirt and ragged shorts. As the two porters lifted the canvas sack onto his bent back, he adjusted the forehead halter and leaned against it, taking the strain with his neck muscles, his hands grasping the two worn straps. Now that he had the full weight, he felt his overtaxed heart pumping against the load, his joints shrieking for relief.

The sack weighed just over ninety pounds—almost more than his own weight. The tally clerks had just sealed it. It contained exactly 250 of the little gold smuggler bars, each of five taels—a little over six ounces—just one of which would have kept him and his family secure for months. But the old man had no thought of trying to steal even one of them. All of his being was concentrated on how to dominate the agony, how to keep his feet moving, how to do his share of the work, to get his pay at the end of his shift, and then to rest.

'Hurry up,' the foreman said sourly, 'we've still more than twenty fornicating tons to load. Next!'

The old man did not reply. To do so would take more of his precious energy. He had to guard his strength zealously tonight if he was to finish. With an effort he set his feet into motion, his calves knotted and varicosed and scarred from so many years of labor.

Another coolie took his place as he shuffled slowly out of the dank concrete room, the shelves ladened with a seemingly never-ending supply of meticulous stacks of little gold bars that waited under the watchful eyes of the two neat bank clerks— waited to be loaded into the next canvas sack, to be counted and

462

recounted, then sealed with a flourish.

On the narrow stairway the old man faltered. He regained his balance with difficulty, then lifted a foot to climb another step—only twenty-eight more now—and then another and he had just made the landing when his calves gave out. He tottered against the wall, leaning against it to ease the weight, his heart grinding, both hands grasping the straps, knowing he could never resettle the load if he stepped out of the harness, terrified lest the foreman or a subforeman would pass by. Through the spectrum of pain he heard footsteps coming toward him and he fought the sack higher onto his back and into motion once more. He almost toppled over.

'Hey, Nine Carat Chu, are you all right?' the other coolie asked in Shantung dialect, steadying the sack for him.

'Yes . . . yes . . .' He gasped with relief, thankful it was his friend from his village far to the north and the leader of his gang of ten. 'Fornicate all gods, I . . . I just slipped. . . .'

The other man peered at him in the coarse light from the single bare light overhead. He saw the tortured, rheumy old eyes and the stretched muscles. 'I'll take this one, you rest a moment,' he said. Skillfully he eased off the weight and swung the sack to the floorboards. 'I'll tell that motherless foreigner who thinks he's got brains enough to be a foreman that you've gone to relieve yourself.' He reached into his ragged, torn pants pocket and handed the old man one of his small, screwed-up pieces of cigarette foil. 'Take it. I'll deduct it from your pay tonight.'

The old man mumbled his thanks. He was all pain now, barely thinking. The other man swung the sack onto his back, grunting with the effort, leaned against the head band, then, his calves knotted, slowly went back up the stairs, pleased with the deal he had made.

The old man slunk off the landing into a dusty alcove and squatted down. His fingers trembled as he smoothed out the cigarette foil with its pinch of white powder. He lit a match and held it carefully under the foil to heat it. The powder began to blacken and smoke. Carefully he held the smoking powder under his nostrils and inhaled deeply, again and again, until every grain had vanished into the smoke that he pulled oh so gratefully into his lungs.

463

He leaned back against the wall. Soon the pain vanished and left euphoria. It was all-pervading. He felt young again and strong again and now he knew that he would finish his shift perfectly and this Saturday, when he went to the races, he would win the double quinella. Yes, this would be his lucky week and he would put most of his winnings down on a piece of property, yes, a small piece of property at first but with the boom my property will go up and up and up and then I'll sell that piece and make a fortune and buy more and more and then I'll be an ancestor, my grandchildren flocking around my knees . . .

He got up and stood tall then went back down the stairs again and stood in line, waiting his turn impatiently. '*Dew neh loh moh* hurry up,' he said in his lilting Shantung dialect. 'I haven't all night! I've another job at midnight.'

The other job was on a construction site in Central, not far from the Ho-Pak and he knew he was blessed to have two bonus jobs in one night on top of his regular day job as a construction laborer. He knew, too, that it was the expensive white powder that had transformed him and taken his fatigue and pain away. Of course, he knew the white powder was dangerous. But he was sensible and cautious and only took it when he was at the limit of strength. That he took it most days now, twice a day most days now, did not worry him. Joss, he told himself with a shrug, taking the new canvas sack on his back.

Once he had been a farmer and the eldest son of landowning farmers in the northern province of Shantung, in the fertile, shifting delta of the Yellow River where, for centuries, they had grown fruit and grain and soybeans, peanuts, tobacco and all the vegetables they could eat.

Ah, our lovely fields, he thought happily, climbing the stairs now, oblivious of his pounding heart, our lovely fields rich with growing crops. So beautiful! Yes. But then the Bad Times began thirty years ago. The Devils from the Eastern Sea came with their guns and their tanks and raped our earth, and then, after warlord Mao Tse-tung and warlord Chiang Kai-shek beat them off, they fought among themselves and again the land was laid waste. So we fled the famine, me and my young wife and my two sons and came to this place, Fragrant Harbor, to live among strangers, southern barbarians and foreign devils. We walked all the way. We survived. I carried my sons most of the way and now my sons are sixteen and fourteen and we have two daughters and they all eat rice once a day and this year will be my lucky year. Yes. I'll win the quinella or the daily double and one day we'll go home to my village and I'll take our lands back and plant them again and Chairman Mao will welcome us home and let us take our lands back and we'll live so happily, so rich and so happy. . . .

He was out of the building now, in the night, standing beside the truck. Other hands lifted the sack and stacked it with all the other sacks of gold, more clerks checking and rechecking the numbers. There were two trucks in the side street. One was already filled and waiting under its guards. A single unarmed policeman was watching idly as the traffic passed. The night was warm.

The old man turned to go. Then he noticed the three Europeans, two men and a woman, approaching. They stopped near the far truck, watching him. His mouth dropped open.

'*Dew neh loh moh!* Look at that whore—the monster with the straw hair,' he said to no one in particular.

'Unbelievable!' another replied.

'Yes,' he said.

'It's revolting the way their whores dress in public, isn't it?' a wizened old loader said disgustedly. 'Flaunting their loins with those tight trousers. You can see every fornicating wrinkle in her lower lips.'

'I'll bet you could put your whole fist and whole arm in it and never reach bottom!' another said with a laugh.

'Who'd want to?' Nine Carat Chu asked and hawked loudly and spat and let his mind drift pleasantly to Saturday as he went below again.

'I wish they wouldn't spit like that. It's disgusting!' Casey said queasily.

'It's an old Chinese custom,' Dunross said. 'They believe there's an evil god-spirit in your throat which you've got to get rid of constantly or it will choke you. Of course spitting's against the law but that's meaningless to them.'

'What'd that old man say?' Casey asked, watching him plod back into the side door of the bank, now over her anger and very glad to be going to dinner with them both.

'I don't know—I didn't understand his dialect.'

'I'll bet it wasn't a compliment.'

Dunross laughed. 'You'd win that one, Casey. They don't think much of us at all.'

'That old man must be eighty if he's a day and he's carried his load as though it was a feather. How'd they stay so fit?'

Dunross shrugged and said nothing. He knew.

Another coolie heaved his burden into the truck, stared at her, hawked, spat and plodded away again. 'Up yours too,' Casey muttered and then parodied an awful hawk and a twenty-foot spit and they laughed with her. The Chinese just stared.

'Ian, what's this all about? What're we here for?' Bartlett asked.

'I thought you might like to see fifty tons of gold.'

Casey gasped. 'Those sacks're filled with gold?'

'Yes. Come along.' Dunross led the way down the dingy stairs into the gold vault. The bank officials greeted him politely and the unarmed guards and loaders stared. Both Americans felt disquieted under the stares. But their disquiet was swamped by the gold. Neat stacks of gold bars on the steel shelves that surrounded them—ten to a layer, each stack ten layers high.

'Can I pick one up?' Casey asked.

'Help yourself,' Dunross told them, watching them, trying to test the extent of their greed. I'm gambling for high stakes, he thought again. I have to know the measure of these two.

Casey had never touched so much gold in her life. Nor had Bartlett. Their fingers trembled. She caressed one of the little bars, her eyes wide, before she lifted it. 'It's so heavy for its size,' she muttered.

'These're called smuggler bars because they're easy to hide and to transport,' Dunross said, choosing his words deliberately. 'Smugglers wear a sort of canvas waistcoat with little pockets in it that hold the bars snugly. They say a good courier can carry as much as eighty pounds a trip—that's almost 1,300 ounces. Of course they have to be fit and well trained.'

Bartlett was hefting two in each hand, fascinated by them. 'How many make up eighty pounds?'

'About two hundred, give or take a little.'

466

Casey looked at him, her hazel eyes bigger than usual. 'Are these yours, tai-pan?'

'Good God, no! They belong to a Macao company. They're shifting it from here to the Victoria Bank. Americans or English aren't allowed by law to own even one of these. But I thought you might be interested because it's not often you see fifty tons all in one place.'

'I never realized what *real* money was like before,' Casey said. 'Now I can understand why my dad's and uncle's eyes used to light up when they talked about gold.'

Dunross was watching her. He could see no greed in her. Just wonder.

'Do banks make many shipments like this?' Bartlett asked, his voice throaty.

'Yes, all the time,' Dunross said and he wondered if Bartlett had taken the bait and was considering a Mafioso-style hijack with his friend Banastasio. 'We've a very large shipment coming in in about three weeks,' he said, increasing the lure.

'What's fifty tons worth?' Bartlett asked.

Dunross smiled to himself remembering Zeppelin Tung with his exactitude of figures. As if it mattered! '63 million dollars legally, give or take a few thousand.'

'And you're moving it just with a bunch of old men, two trucks that're not even armored and no guards?'

'Of course. That's no problem in Hong Kong, which's one of the reasons our police are so sensitive about guns here. If they've the only guns in the Colony, well, what can the crooks and nasties do except curse?'

'But where're the police? I didn't see but one and he wasn't armed.'

'Oh, they're around, I suppose,' Dunross said, deliberately underplaying it.

Casey peered at the gold bar, enjoying the touch of the metal. 'It feels so cool and so permanent. Tai-pan, if it's 63 million legal, what's it worth on the black market?'

Dunross noticed tiny beads of perspiration now on her upper lip. 'However much someone's prepared to pay. At the moment, I hear the best market's India. They'd pay about $80 to $90 an ounce, U.S., delivered into India.'

Bartlett smiled crookedly and reluctantly put his four bars

back onto their pile. 'That's a lot of profit.'

They watched in silence as another canvas bag was sealed, the bars checked and rechecked by both clerks. Again the two loaders lifted the sack onto a bent back and the man plodded out.

'What're those?' Casey asked, pointing to some much bigger bars that were in another part of the vault.

'They're the regulation four-hundred-ounce bars,' Dunross said. 'They weigh around twenty-five pounds apiece.' The bar was stamped with a hammer and sickle and 99,999. 'This's Russian. It's 99.99 percent pure. South African gold is usually 99.98 percent pure so the Russian's sought after. Of course both're easy to buy in the London gold market.' He let them look awhile longer, then said, 'Shall we go now?'

On the street there was still only one policeman and the sloppy, unarmed bank guards, the two truck drivers smoking in their cabins. Traffic eased past from time to time. A few pedestrians.

Dunross was glad to get out of the close confinement of the vault. He had hated cellars and dungeons ever since his father had locked him in a cupboard when he was very small, for a crime he could not now remember. But he remembered old Ah Tat, his *amah*, rescuing him and standing up for him—him staring up at his father, trying to hold back the terror tears that would not be held back.

'It's good to be out in the air again,' Casey said. She used a tissue. Inexorably her eyes were dragged to the sacks in the nearly full truck. 'That's real money,' she muttered, almost to herself. A small shudder racked her and Dunross knew at once that he had found her jugular.

'I could use a bottle of beer,' Bartlett said. 'So much money makes me thirsty.'

'I could use a Scotch and soda!' she said, and the spell was broken.

'We'll stroll over to the Victoria and see the delivery begin, then we'll eat—' Dunross stopped. He saw the two men chatting near the trucks, partially in shadow. He stiffened slightly.

The two men saw him. Martin Haply of the *China Guardian* and Peter Marlowe.

'Oh, hello, tai-pan,' young Martin Haply said, coming up to

him with his confident grin. 'I didn't expect to see you here. Evening, Miss Casey, Mr. Bartlett. Tai-pan, would you care to comment on the Ho-Pak matter?'

'What Ho-Pak matter?'

'The run on the bank, sir.'

'I didn't know there was one.'

'Did you happen to read my column about the various branches and the rumo—'

'My dear Haply,' Dunross said with his easy charm, 'you know I don't seek interviews or give them lightly . . . and never on street corners.'

'Yes sir.' Haply nodded at the sacks. 'Transferring all this gold out's kinda rough for the Ho-Pak, isn't it? That'll put the kiss of death on the bank when all this leaks.'

Dunross sighed. 'Forget the Ho-Pak, Mr. Haply. Can I have a word in private?' He took the young man's elbow and guided him away with velvet firmness. When they were alone, half covered by one of the trucks, he let go of the arm. His voice dropped. Involuntarily, Haply flinched and moved back half a pace. 'Since you are going out with my daughter, I just want you to know that I'm very fond of her and among gentlemen there are certain rules. I'm presuming you're a gentleman. If you're not, God help you. You'll answer to me personally, immediately and without mercy.' Dunross turned and went back to the others, full of sudden bonhomie. 'Evening, Marlowe, how're things?'

'Fine, thank you, tai-pan.' The tall man nodded at the trucks. 'Astonishing, all this wealth!'

'Where did you hear about the transfer?'

'A journalist friend mentioned it about an hour ago He said that some fifty tons of gold were being moved from here to the Victoria. I thought it'd be interesting to see how it was done. Hope it's not . . . hope I'm not treading on any corns.'

'Not at all.' Dunross turned to Casey and Bartlett. 'There, you see, I told you Hong Kong was just like a village—you can never keep any secrets here for long. But all this'—he waved at the sacks—'this is all lead—fool's gold. The real shipment was completed an hour ago. It wasn't fifty tons, only a few thousand ounces. The majority of the Ho-Pak's bullion's still intact.' He smiled at Haply who was not smiling but listening, his face set.

469

'This's all fake after all?' Casey gasped.

Peter Marlowe laughed. 'I must confess I did think this whole operation was a bit haphazard!'

'Well, good night you two,' Dunross said breezily to Marlowe and Martin Haply. He took Casey's arm momentarily. 'Come on, it's time for dinner.' They started down the street, Bartlett beside them.

'But tai-pan, the ones we saw,' Casey said, 'the one I picked up, that was fake? I'd've bet my life, wouldn't you have, Linc?'

'Yes,' Bartlett agreed. 'But the diversion was wise. That's what I'd've done.'

They turned the corner, heading along toward the huge Victoria Bank building, the air warm and sticky.

Casey laughed nervously. 'That golden metal was getting to me—and it was fake all the time!'

'Actually it was all real,' Dunross said quietly and she stopped. 'Sorry to confuse you, Casey. I only said that for Haply and Marlowe's benefit, to pour suspicion on their source. They could hardly prove it one way or another. I was asked to make the arrangements for the transfer little more than an hour ago—which I did, obviously, with great caution.' His heart quickened. He wondered how many other people knew about the AMG papers and the vault and the box number in the vault.

Bartlett watched him. 'I bought what you said, so I guess they did,' he said, but he was thinking, Why did you bring us to see the gold? That's what I'd like to know.

'It's curious, tai-pan,' Casey said with a little nervous laugh. 'I knew, I just knew the gold was real to begin with. Then I believed you when you said it was fake, and now I believe you back again. Is it that easy to fake?'

'Yes and no. You only know for certain if you put acid on it—you've got to put it to the acid test. That's the only real test for gold. Isn't it?' he added to Bartlett and saw the half-smile and he wondered if the American understood.

'Guess that's right, Ian. For gold—or for people.'

Dunross smiled back. Good, he thought grimly, we understand each other perfectly.

*   *   *

470

It was quite late now. Golden Ferries had stopped running and Casey and Linc Bartlett were in a small private hire-launch chugging across the harbor, the night grand, a good sea smell on the wind, the sea calm. They were sitting on one of the thwarts facing Hong Kong, arm in arm. Dinner had been the best they had ever eaten, the conversation filled with lots of laughter, Dunross charming. They'd ended with cognac atop the Hilton. Both were feeling marvelously at peace with the world and with themselves.

Casey felt the light pressure of his arm and she leaned against him slightly. 'It's romantic, isn't it, Linc? Look at the Peak, and all the lights. Unbelievable. It's the most beautiful and exciting place I've ever been.'

'Better than the south of France?'

'That was so different.' They had had a holiday on the Côte d'Azur two years ago. It was the first time they had holidayed together. And the last. It had been too much of a strain on both of them to stay apart. 'Ian's fantastic, isn't he?'

'Yes. And so are you.'

'Thank you, kind sir, and so are you.' They laughed, happy together.

At the wharf, Kowloon side, Linc paid the boat off and they strolled to the hotel, arm in arm. A few waiters were still on duty in the lobby.

'Evening, sir, evening, missee,' the old elevator man said sibilantly, and, on their floor, Nighttime Chang scurried ahead of them to open the door of the suite. Automatically Linc gave him a dollar and they were bowed in. Nighttime Chang closed the door.

She bolted it.

'Drink?' he asked.

'No thanks. It'd spoil that brandy.'

She saw him looking at her. They were standing in the center of the living room, the huge picture window displaying all of Hong Kong behind him, his bedroom to the right, hers to the left. She could feel the vein in her neck pulsing, her loins seemed liquid and he looked so handsome to her.

'Well, it's . . . thanks for a lovely evening, Linc. I'll . . . I'll see you tomorrow,' she said. But she did not move.

'It's three months to your birthday, Casey.'

'Thirteen weeks and six days.'

'Why don't we finesse them and get married now. Tomorrow?'

'You've . . . you've been so wonderful to me, Linc, so good to be patient and put up with my . . . my craziness.' She smiled at him. It was a tentative smile. 'It's not long now. Let's do it as we agreed. Please?'

He stood there and watched her, wanting her. Then he said, 'Sure.' At his door he stopped. 'Casey, you're right about this place. It is romantic and exciting. It's got to me too. Maybe, maybe you'd better get another room.'

His door closed.

That night she cried herself to sleep.

WEDNESDAY

27

5:45 A.M.:

The two racehorses came out of the turn into the final stretch going very fast. It was false dawn, the sky still dark to the west, and the Happy Valley Racecourse was spotted with people at the morning workout.

Dunross was up on Buccaneer, the big bay gelding, and he was neck and neck with Noble Star, ridden by his chief jockey, Tom Leung. Noble Star was on the rails and both horses were going well with plenty of reserve. Then Dunross saw the winning post ahead and he had that sudden urge to jam in his heels and best the other horse. The other jockey sensed the challenge and looked across at him. But both riders knew they were there just to exercise and not to race, there to confuse the opposition, so Dunross bottled his almost blinding desire.

Both horses had their ears down now. Their flanks were wet with sweat. Both felt the bit in between their teeth. And now, well into the stretch, they pounded toward the winning post excitedly, the inner training sand track not as fast as the encircling grass, making them work harder. Both riders stood high in the stirrups, leaning forward, reins tight.

Noble Star was carrying less weight. She began to pull away. Dunross automatically used his heels and cursed Buccaneer. The pace quickened. The gap began to close. His exhilaration soared. This gallop was barely half a lap so he thought he would be safe. No opposing trainer could get an accurate timing on them so he kicked harder and the race was on. Both horses knew. Their strides lengthened. Noble Star had her nose ahead and then, feeling Buccaneer coming up fast, she took the bit, laid to and charged forward on her own account and drew away and beat Dunross by half a length.

Now the riders slackened speed and, standing easily, continued around the lovely course—a patch of green surrounded by massed buildings and tiers of high rises that dotted the mountainsides. When Dunross had cantered up the final stretch again, he broke off the exercising, reined in beside where the winner's circle would normally be and dismounted. He slapped the filly affectionately on the neck, threw the reins to a stable hand. The man swung into the saddle and continued her exercise.

Dunross eased his shoulders, his heart beating nicely, the taste of blood in his mouth. He felt very good, his stretched muscles aching pleasantly. He had ridden all of his life. Horse racing was still officially all amateur in Hong Kong. When he was young he had raced two seasons and he would have continued, but he had been warned off the course by his father, then tai-pan and chief steward, and again by Alastair Struan when he took over both jobs, and ordered to quit racing on pain of instant dismissal. So he had stopped racing though he continued to exercise the Struan stable at his whim. And he raced in the dawn when the mood was on him.

It was the getting up when most of the world slept, to gallop in half light—the exercise and excitement, the speed, and the danger that cleared his head.

Dunross spat the sweet sick taste of not winning out of his mouth. That's better, he thought. I could have taken Noble Star today, but I'd've done it in the turn, not in the stretch.

Other horses were exercising on the sand track, more joining the circuit or leaving it. Knots of owners and trainers and jockeys were conferring, *ma-foos*—stable hands—walking horses in their blankets. He saw Butterscotch Lass, Richard Kwang's great mare, canter past, a white star on her forehead, neat fetlocks, her jockey riding her tightly, looking very good. Over on the far side Pilot Fish, Gornt's prize stallion, broke into a controlled gallop, chasing another of the Struan string, Impatience, a new, young, untried filly, recently acquired in the first balloting of this season. Dunross watched her critically and thought she lacked stamina. Give her a season or two and then we'll see, he thought. Then Pilot Fish ripped past her and she skittered in momentary fright, then charged in pursuit until her jockey pulled her in, teaching her to gallop at his whim and not at hers.

'So, tai-pan!' his trainer said. He was a leather-faced, iron-hard Russian émigré in his late sixties with graying hair and this was his third season with Struan's.

'So, Alexi?'

'So the devil got into you and you gave him your heel and did you see Noble Star surge ahead?'

'She's a trier. Noble Star's a trier, everyone knows that,' Dunross replied calmly.

'Yes, but I'd've preferred only you and I to be reminded of it today and not'—the small man jerked a calloused thumb at the onlookers and grinned—'. . . and not every *viblyadok* in Asia.'

Dunross grinned back. 'You notice too much.'

'I'm paid to notice too much.'

Alexi Travkin could outride, outdrink, outwork and outstay a man half his age. He was a loner among the other trainers. Over the years he had told various stories about his past—like most of those who had been caught in the great turmoils of Russia and her revolutions, China and her revolutions, and now drifted the byways of Asia seeking a peace they could never find.

Alexi Ivanovitch Travkin had come out of Russia to Harbin in Manchuria in 1919, then worked his way south to the International Settlement of Shanghai. There he began to ride winners. Because he was very good and knew more about horses than most men know about themselves, he soon became a trainer. When the exodus happened again in '49 he fled south, this time to Hong Kong where he stayed a few years then drifted south again to Australia and the circuits there. But Asia beckoned him so he returned. Dunross was trainerless at that time and offered him the stable of the Noble House.

'I'll take it, tai-pan,' he had said at once.

'We haven't discussed money,' Dunross had said.

'You're a gentleman, so am I. You'll pay me the best for face—and because I'm the best.'

'Are you?'

'Why else do you offer me the post? You don't like to lose either.'

Last season had been good for both of them. The first not so good. Both knew this coming season would be the real test.

Noble Star was walking past, settling down nicely.

'What about Saturday?' Dunross asked.

'She'll be trying.'

'And Butterscotch Lass?'

'She'll be trying. So will Pilot Fish. So will all the others—in all eight races. This's a very special meeting. We'll have to watch our entries very carefully.'

Dunross nodded. He caught sight of Gornt talking with Sir Dunstan Barre by the winner's circle. 'I'll be very peed off if I lose to Pilot Fish.'

Alexi laughed. Then added wryly, 'In that case perhaps you'd better ride Noble Star yourself, tai-pan. Then you can shove Pilot Fish into the rails in the turn if he looks like a threat, or put the whip across his jockey's eyes. Eh?' The old man looked up at him. 'Isn't that what you'd've done with Noble Star today if it'd been a race?'

Dunross smiled back. 'As it wasn't a race you'll never know—will you?'

A *ma-foo* came up and saluted Travkin, handing him a note. 'Message, sir. Mr. Choi'd like you to look at Chardistan's bindings when you've a moment.'

'I'll be there shortly. Tell him to put extra bran in Buccaneer's feed today and tomorrow.' Travkin glanced back at Dunross, who was watching Noble Star closely. He frowned. 'You're not considering riding Saturday?'

'Not at the moment.'

'I wouldn't advise it.'

Dunross laughed. 'I know. See you tomorrow, Alexi. Tomorrow I'll work Impatience.' He clapped him in friendly style and left.

Alexi Travkin stared after him; his eyes strayed to the horses that were in his charge, and their opposition that he could see. He knew this Saturday would be vicious and that Noble Star would have to be guarded. He smiled to himself, pleased to be in a game where the stakes were very high.

He opened the note that was in his hand. It was short and in Russian: 'Greetings from Kurgan, Highness. I have news of Nestorova . . .' Alexi gasped. The color drained from his face. By the blood of Christ, he wanted to shout. No one in Asia knows my home was in Kurgan, in the flatlands on the banks of the River Tobol, nor that my father was Prince of Kurgan and Tobol, nor that my darling Nestorova, my child-wife of a thousand lifetimes ago, swallowed up in the revolution while I was with my regiment . . . I swear to God I've never mentioned her name to anyone, not even to myself. . . .

In shock he reread the note. Is this more of their devilment, the Soviets—the enemy of all the Russians? Or is it a friend? Oh Christ Jesus let it be a friend.

After 'Nestorova' the note had ended, 'Please meet me at the Green Dragon Restaurant, in the alley just off 189 Nathan Road, the back room at three this afternoon.' There was no signature.

Across the paddock, near the winning post, Richard Kwang was walking toward his trainer when he saw his sixth cousin, Smiler Ching, chairman of the huge Ching Prosperity Bank, in the stands, his binoculars trained on Pilot Fish.

'Hello, Sixth Cousin,' he said affably in Cantonese, 'have you eaten rice today?'

The sly old man was instantly on guard. 'You won't get any money out of me,' he said coarsely, his lips sliding back from protruding teeth that gave him a perpetual smiling grimace.

'Why not?' Richard Kwang said equally rudely. 'I've got 17 fornicating millions on loan to you an—'

'Yes but that's on ninety-day call and well invested. We've always paid the 40 percent interest,' the old man snarled.

'You miserable old dog bone, I helped you when you needed money! Now it's time to repay!'

'Repay what? What?' Smiler Ching spat. 'I've repaid you a fortune over the years. I've taken the risks and you've reaped the profit. This whole disaster couldn't happen at a worse time! I've every copper cash out—every one! I'm not like some bankers. My money's always put to good use.'

The good use was narcotics, so legend went. Of course Richard Kwang had never asked, and no one knew for certain, but everyone believed that Smiler Ching's bank was secretly one of the main clearinghouses for the trade, the vast majority of which emanated from Bangkok. 'Listen, Cousin, think of the family,' Richard Kwang began. 'It's only a temporary problem. The fornicating foreign devils are attacking us. When that happens civilized people have to stick together!'

'I agree. But you're the cause of the run on the Ho-Pak. You are. It's on you—not on my bank. You've offended the fornicators somehow! They're after you—don't you read the papers? Yes, and you've got all your cash out on some very bad deals so I hear. You, Cousin, you've put your own head into the cangue. Get money out of that evil son of a Malayan whore half-caste partner of yours. He's got billions—or out of Tightfist. . . .' The old man suddenly cackled. 'I'll give you 10 for every 1 that old fornicator loans you!'

'If I go down the toilet the Ching Prosperity Bank won't be far behind.'

'Don't threaten me!' the old man said angrily. His lips had a flick of saliva permanently in the corners and then they worked over his teeth once and fell apart again in his grimace. 'If you go down it won't be my fault—why wish your rotten joss on family? I've done nothing to hurt you—why try and pass your bad joss on to me? If today . . . *ayeeyah*, if today your bad joss spills over and those dog bone depositors start a run on me I won't last the day!'

Richard Kwang momentarily felt better that the Ching empire was equally threatened. Good, very good. I could use all his business—particularly the Bangkok connection. Then he saw the big clock over the Totalisator and groaned. It was just past six now and at ten, banks would open and the stock market would open and though arrangements had been made with Blacs, the Victoria and the Bombay and Eastern Bank of Kowloon to pledge securities that should cover everything and to spare, he was still nervous. And enraged. He had had to make some very tough deals that he had no wish to honor. 'Come on, Cousin, just 50 million for ten days—I'll extend the 17 million for two years and add another 20 in thirty days.'

'50 million for three days at 10 percent interest a day, your present loan to be collateral and I'll also take deed to your property in Central as further collateral!'

'Go fornicate in your mother's ear! That property's worth four times that.'

Smiler Ching shrugged and turned his binoculars back on Pilot Fish. 'Is the big black going to beat Butterscotch Lass too?'

Richard Kwang looked at Gornt's horse sourly. 'Not unless

480

my weevil-mouthed trainer and jockey join together to pull her or dope her!'

'Filthy thieves! You can't trust one of them! My horse's never come in the money once. Never. Not even third. Disgusting!'

'50 million for one week—2 percent a day?'

'5. Plus the Central pro—'

'Never!'

'I'll take a 50 percent share of the property.'

'6 percent,' Richard Kwang said.

Smiler Ching estimated his risk. And his potential profit. The profit was huge if. If the Ho-Pak didn't fail. But even if it did, the loan would be well covered by the property. Yes, the profit would be huge, provided there wasn't a real run on himself. Perhaps I could gamble and pledge some future shipments and raise the 50 million.

'15 percent and that's final,' he said knowing that he would withdraw or change by noon once he saw how the market was, and the run was—and he would continue to sell Ho-Pak short to great profit. 'And also you can throw in Butterscotch Lass.'

Richard Kwang swore obscenely and they bargained back and forth then agreed that the 50 million was on call at two o'clock. In cash. He would also pledge Smiler Ching 39 percent of the Central property as added collateral, and a quarter share in his mare. Butterscotch Lass was the clincher.

'What about Saturday?'

'Eh?' Richard Kwang said, loathing the grimace and buck teeth.

'Our horse's in the fifth race, *heya?* Listen, Sixth Cousin, perhaps we'd better make an accommodation with Pilot Fish's jockey. We pull our horse—she'll be favorite—and back Pilot Fish and Noble Star for safety!'

'Good idea. We'll decide Saturday morning.'

'Better to eliminate Golden Lady too, eh?'

'John Chen's trainer suggested that.'

'Eeeee, that fool, to get himself kidnapped. I'll expect you to give me the real information on who's going to win. I want the winner too!' Smiler hawked and spat.

'All gods defecate, don't we all! Those filthy trainers and jockeys! Disgusting the way they puppet us owners. Who pays their salaries, *heya?'*

'The Turf Club, the owners, but most the punters who aren't in the know. I hear you were at the Old Vic last night for foreign devil food.'

Richard Kwang beamed. His dinner with Venus Poon had been an enormous success. She had worn the new knee-length Christian Dior he had bought for her, black clinging silk and gossamer underneath. When he had seen her get out of his Rolls and come up the steps of the Old Vic his heart had turned over and his Secret Sack had jiggled.

She had been all smiles at the effect her entrance had on the entire foyer, her chunky gold bracelets glittering, and had insisted on walking up the grand staircase instead of using the elevator. His chest had been tight with suppressed glee and terror. They had walked through the formal, well-groomed diners, European and Chinese, many in evening dress—husbands and wives, tourists and locals, men at business dinners, lovers and would-be lovers of all ages and nationalities. He was wearing a new, Savile Row dark suit of the most expensive lightweight cashmere wool. As they moved toward the choice table that had cost him a red—100 dollars—he had waved to many friends, and groaned inwardly four times as he saw four of his Chinese intimates with their wives, bouffant and over-jeweled. The wives had stared at him glassily.

Richard Kwang shuddered. Wives really are dragons and all the same, he thought. Oh oh oh! And your lies sound false to them even before you've spoken to them. He had not gone home yet to face Mai-ling who would have already been told by at least three very good friends about Venus Poon. He would let her rant and scream and weep and tear her hair for a while to release her devil wind and would say that enemies had filled her head with bile—how can she listen to such evil women?—and then he would meekly tell her about the full-length mink that he had ordered three weeks ago, that he was to collect today in time for her to wear to the races Saturday. Then there would be peace in the house—until the next time.

He chortled at his acumen in ordering the mink. That he had ordered it for Venus Poon and had, this morning, just an hour ago in the warmth of her embrace, promised it to her tonight so she would wear it to the races on Saturday did not bother him at all. It's much too good for the strumpet anyway, he was thinking. That coat cost 40,000 HK. I'll get her another one. Ah, perhaps I could find a secondhand one. . . .

He saw Smiler Ching leering at him. 'What?'

'Venus Poon, *heya*?'

'I'm thinking of going into film production and making her a star,' he said grandly, proud of the cover story he had invented as part of his excuse to his wife.

Smiler Ching was impressed. 'Eeee, but that's a risky business, *heya*?'

'Yes, but there are ways to . . . to insure your risk.' He winked knowingly.

'*Ayeeyah*, you mean a nudie film? Oh! Let me know when you set the production, I might take a point or two. Venus Poon naked! *Ayeeyah*, all Asia'd pay to see that! What's she like at the pillow?'

'Perfect! Now that I've educated her. She was a virgin when I fir—'

'What joss!' Smiler Ching said, then added, 'How many times did you scale the Rámparts?'

'Last night? Three times—each time stronger than before!' Richard Kwang leaned forward. 'Her Flower Heart's the best I've ever seen. Yes. And her triangle! Lovely silken hair and her inner lips pink and delicate. Eeeee, and her Jade Gate . . . her Jade Gate's really heart-shaped and her "one square inch" is a perfect oval, pink, fragrant, and the Pearl on the Step also pink. . . .' Richard Kwang felt himself beginning to sweat as he remembered how she had spread herself on the sofa and handed him a big magnifying glass. 'Here,' she had said proudly. 'Examine the goddess your bald-headed monk's about to worship.' And he had. Meticulously.

'The best pillow partner I've ever had,' Richard Kwang continued expansively, stretching the truth. 'I was thinking about buying her a large diamond ring. Poor Little Mealy Mouth wept this morning when I left the apartment I'd given her. She was swearing suicide because she's so *in love* with me.' He used the English word.

'Eeeee, you're a lucky man!' Smiler Ching spoke no English except the words of love. He felt eyes on his back and he glanced around. In the next section of the stands, fifty yards away, slightly above him, was the foreign devil policeman Big Mountain of Dung, the hated chief of the CID Kowloon. The cold fish-eyes were staring at him, binoculars hanging from the man's neck. *Ayeeyah*, Ching muttered to himself, his mind darting over the various checks and traps and balances that guarded his main source of revenue.

'Eh? What? What's the matter with you, Smiler Ching?'

'Nothing. I want to piss, that's all. Send the papers over at two o'clock if you want my money.' Sourly he turned away to go to the toilet, wondering if the police were aware of the imminent arrival of the foreign devil from the Golden Mountain, a High Tiger of the White Powders with the outlandish name of Vincenzo Banastasio.

He hawked and spat loudly. Joss if they do, joss if they don't. They can't touch me, I'm only a banker.

Robert Armstrong had noted that Smiler Ching was talking to Banker Kwang and knew surely that the pair of them were up to no good. The police were well aware of the whispers about Ching and his Prosperity Bank and the narcotics trade but so far had no real evidence implicating him or his bank, not even enough circumstantial evidence to merit SB detention, interrogation and summary deportation.

Well, he'll slip sometime, Robert Armstrong thought calmly, and turned his binoculars back on to Pilot Fish, then to Noble Star, then to Butterscotch Lass, and then to Golden Lady, John Chen's mare. Which one's got the form?

He yawned and stretched wearily. It had been another long night and he had not yet been to bed. Just as he was leaving Kowloon Police HQ last night there had been a flurry of excitement as another anonymous caller phoned to say that John Chen had been seen out in the New Territories, in the tiny fishing village of Sha Tau Kwok which bisected the eastern tip of the border.

He had rushed out there with a team and searched the village, hovel by hovel. His search had had to be done very cautiously for the whole border area was extremely sensitive, particularly at the village where there was one of the three border checkpoints. The villagers were a hardy, tough, uncompromising bellicose lot that wanted to be left alone. Particularly by foreign devil police. The search had proved to be just another false alarm though they had uncovered two illegal stills, a small heroin factory that converted raw opium into morphine and thence into heroin, and had broken up six illegal gambling dens.

When Armstrong had got back to Kowloon HQ there was another call about John Chen, this time Hong Kong side in Wanchai, down near Glessing's Point in the dock area. Apparently John Chen had been seen being bundled into a tenement house, a dirty bandage over his right ear. This time the caller had given his name and driver's license number so that he could claim the reward of 50,000 HK, offered by Struan's and Noble House Chen. Again Armstrong had brought units to surround the area and had led the meticulous search. It was already five o'clock in the morning by the time he called off the operation and dismissed his men.

'Brian, it's me for bed,' he said. 'Waste of another *fang-pi* night.'

Brian Kwok yawned too. 'Yes. But while we're this side, how about breakfast at the Para and then, then let's go and look at the morning workouts?'

At once most of Robert Armstrong's tiredness fell away. 'Great idea!'

The Para Restaurant in Wanchai Road near Happy Valley Racecourse was always open. The food was excellent, cheap and it was a well-known meeting place for triads and their girls. When the two policemen strode into the large, noisy, bustling, plate-clattering room a sudden silence fell. The proprietor, One Foot Ko, limped over to them and beamed them to the best table in the place.

'*Dew neh loh moh* on you too, Old Friend,' Armstrong said grimly and added some choice obscenities in gutter Cantonese, staring back pointedly at the nearest group of gaping young thugs who nervously turned away.

One Foot Ko laughed and showed his bad teeth. 'Ah, Lords, you honor my poor establishment. *Dim sum?*'

'Why not?' *Dim sum*—small chow or small foods—were bite-sized dough envelopes packed with minced shrimps or vegetables or various meats then steamed or deep-fried and eaten with a touch of soya, or saucers of chicken and other meats in various sauces or pastries of all kinds.

'Your Worships are going to the track?'

Brian Kwok nodded, sipping his jasmine tea, his eyes roving the diners, making many of them very nervous. 'Who's going to win the fifth?' he asked.

The restaurateur hesitated, knowing he'd better tell the truth. He said carefully in Cantonese, 'They say that neither Golden Lady, Noble Star, Pilot Fish nor Butterscotch Lass has . . . has yet been touted as having an edge.' He saw the cold black-brown eyes come to rest on him and he tried not to shudder. 'By all the gods, that's what they say.'

'Good. I'll come here Saturday morning. Or I'll send my sergeant. Then you can whisper in his ear if some foul play's contemplated. Yes. And if it turns out one of those are doped or cut and I don't know about it on Saturday morning . . . perhaps your soups will addle for fifty years.'

One Foot smiled nervously. 'Yes, Lord. Let me see to your food no—'

'Before you go, what's the latest gossip on John Chen?'

'None. Oh very none, Honored Lord,' the man said, a little perspiration on his upper lip. 'Fragrant Harbor's as clean of information on him as a virgin's treasure. Nothing, Lord. Not a dog's fart of a real rumor though everyone's looking. I hear there's an extra great reward.'

'What? How much?'

'100,000 extra dollars if within three days.'

Both policemen whistled. 'Offered by whom?' Armstrong asked.

One Foot shrugged, his eyes hard. 'No one knows, Sire. They say by one of the Dragons—or all the Dragons. 100,000 and promotion if within three days—if he's recovered alive. Please, now let me see about your food.'

They watched him go. 'Why did you lean on One Foot?' Armstrong asked.

'I'm tired of his mealy-mouthed hypocrisy—and all these rotten little thugs. The cat-o'-nine-tails'd solve our triad problems.'

Armstrong called for a beer. 'When I leaned on Sergeant Tang-po I didn't think I'd get such action so fast. 100,000's a lot of money! This can't be just a simple kidnapping. Jesus Christ that's a lot of reward! There's got to be something special about John.'

'Yes. If it's true.'

But they had arrived at no conclusions and when they came to the track, Brian Kwok had gone to check in with HQ and now Armstrong had his binoculars trained on the mare. Butterscotch Lass was leaving the track to walk back up the hill to the stables. *She looks in great fettle*, he thought. *They all do. Shit, which one?*

'Robert?'

'Oh hello, Peter.'

Peter Marlowe smiled at him. 'Are you up early or going to bed late?'

'Late.'

'Did you notice the way Noble Star charged without her jockey doing a thing?'

'You've sharp eyes.'

Peter Marlowe smiled and shook his head. He pointed at a group of men around one of the horses. 'Donald McBride told me.'

'Ah!' McBride was an immensely popular racing steward, a Eurasian property developer who had come to Hong Kong from Shanghai in '49. 'Has he given you the winner? He'll know if anyone does.'

'No, but he invited me to his box on Saturday. Are you racing?'

'Do you mind! I'll see *you* in the members' box—*I* don't cavort with the nobs!'

They both watched the horses for a while. 'Golden Lady looks good.'

'They all do.'

'Nothing on John Chen yet?'

'Nothing.' Armstrong caught sight of Dunross in his binoculars, talking to some stewards. Not far away was the SI guard that Crosse had assigned to him. *Roll on Friday*, the policeman thought. *The sooner we see those AMG files the better.* He felt slightly sick and he could not decide if it was apprehension about the papers, or Sevrin, or if it was just fatigue. He began to reach for a cigarette—stopped. *You don't need a smoke*, he ordered himself. 'You should give up smoking, Peter. It's very bad for you.'

487

'Yes. Yes I should. How's it going with you?'

'No trouble. Which reminds me, Peter, the Old Man approved your trip around the border road. Day after tomorrow, Friday, 6:00 A.M. on the dot at Kowloon HQ. That all right?'

Peter Marlowe's heart leaped. At long last he could look into Mainland China, into the unknown. In all the borderland of the New Territories there was only one accessible lookout that tourists could use to see into China, but the hill was so far away you could not see much at all. Even with binoculars. 'How terrific!' he said, elated. At Armstrong's suggestion he had written to the commissioner and applied for this permission. The border road meandered from shore to shore. It was forbidden to all traffic and all persons—except locals in certain areas. It ran a wide stretch of no-man's-land between the Colony and China. Once a day it was patrolled under very controlled circumstances. The Hong Kong Government had no wish to rock any PRC boats.

'One condition, Peter: You don't mention it or talk about it for a year or so.'

'My word on it.'

Armstrong suppressed another yawn. 'You'll be the only Yank who's ever gone along it, perhaps ever will.'

'Terrific! Thanks.'

'Why did you become a citizen?'

After a pause Peter Marlowe said, 'I'm a writer. All my income comes from there, almost all of it. Now people are beginning to read what I write. Perhaps I'd like the right to criticize.'

'Have you ever been to any Iron Curtain countries?'

'Oh yes. I went to Moscow in July for the film festival. One of the films I wrote was the American entry. Why?'

'Nothing,' Armstrong said, remembering Bartlett's and Casey's Moscow franks. He smiled. 'No reason.'

'One good turn deserves another. I heard a buzz about Bartlett's guns.'

'Oh?' Armstrong was instantly attentive. Peter Marlowe was very rare in Hong Kong inasmuch as he crossed social strata and was accepted as a friend by many normally hostile groups.

'It's just talk probably but some friends have a theory—'

'Chinese friends?'

'Yes. They think the guns were a sample shipment, bound for one of our piratical Chinese citizens—at least, one with a history of smuggling—for shipment to one of the guerilla bands operating in South Vietnam, called Viet Cong.'

Armstrong grunted. 'That's farfetched, Peter, Hong Kong's not the place to transit guns.'

'Yes. But this shipment was special, the first, and it was asked for in a hurry and was to be delivered in a hurry. You've heard of Delta Force?'

'No,' Armstrong said, staggered that Peter Marlowe had already heard of what Rosemont, CIA, had assured them in great secrecy was a very classified operation.

'I understand it's a group of specially trained U.S. combat soldiers, Robert, a special force who're operating in Vietnam in small units under the control of the American Technical Group, which's a cover name for the CIA. It seems they're succeeding so well that the Viet Cong need modern weapons fast and in great quantity and are prepared to pay handsomely. So these were rushed here on Bartlett's plane.'

'Is he involved?'

'My friends doubt it,' he said after a pause. 'Anyway, the guns're U.S. Army issue, Robert, right? Well, once this shipment was approved, delivery in quantity was going to be easy.'

'Oh, how?'

'The U.S. is going to supply the arms.'

'What?'

'Sure.' Peter Marlowe's face settled. 'It's really very simple: Say these Viet Cong guerrillas were provided *in advance* with all exact U.S. shipment dates, exact destinations, quantities and types of arms—small arms to rockets—when they arrived in Vietnam?'

'Christ!'

'Yes. You know Asia. A little *h'eung yau* here and there and constant hijacking'd be simple.'

'It'd be like them having their own stockpile!' Armstrong said, appalled. 'How're the guns going to be paid for? A bank here?'

Peter Marlowe looked at him. 'Bulk opium. Delivered here. One of our banks here supplies the financing.'

The police officer sighed. The beauty of it fell into place.

489

'Flawless,' he said.

'Yes. Some rotten bastard traitor in the States just passes over schedules. That gives the enemy all the guns and ammunition they need to kill off our own soldiers. The enemy pays for the guns with a poison that costs them nothing—I imagine it's about the only salable commodity they've got in bulk and can easily acquire. The opium's delivered here by the Chinese smuggler and converted to heroin because this's where the expertise is. The traitors in the States make a deal with the Mafia who sell the heroin at enormous profit to more kids and so subvert and destroy the most important bloody asset we have: youth.'

'As I said, flawless. What some buggers'll do for money!' Armstrong sighed again and eased his shoulders. He thought a moment. The theory tied in everything very neatly. 'Does the name Banastasio mean anything?'

'Sounds Italian.' Peter Marlowe kept his face guileless. His informants were two Portuguese Eurasian journalists who detested the police. When he had asked them if he could pass on the theory, da Vega had said, 'Of course, but the police'll never believe it. Don't quote us and don't mention any names, not Four Finger Wu, Smuggler Pa, the Ching Prosperity, or Banastasio or anyone.'

After a pause, Armstrong said, 'What else have you heard?'

'Lots, but that's enough for today—it's my turn to get the kids up, cook breakfast and get them toddling off to school.' Peter Marlowe lit a cigarette and again Armstrong achingly felt the smoke in his own lungs. 'Except one thing, Robert. I was asked by a friendly member of the press to tell you he'd heard there's to be a big narcotics meeting soon in Macao.'

The blue eyes narrowed. 'When?'

'I don't know.'

'What sort of meeting?'

'Principals. "Suppliers, importers, exporters, distributors" was the way he put it.'

'Where in Macao?'

'He didn't say.'

'Names?'

'None. He did add that the meeting'll include a visiting VIP from the States.'

'Bartlett?'

'Christ, Robert, I don't know and he didn't say that. Linc Bartlett seems a jolly nice fellow, and straight as an arrow. I think it's all gossip and jealousy, trying to implicate him.'

Armstrong smiled his jaundiced smile. 'I'm just a suspicious copper. Villains exist in very high places, as well as in the boghole. Peter, old fellow, give your friendly journalist a message. If he wants to give me information, phone me direct.'

'He's frightened of you. So am I!'

'In my hat you are.' Armstrong smiled back at him, liking him, very glad for the information and that Peter Marlowe was a safe go-between who could keep his mouth shut. 'Peter, ask him where in Macao and when and who and—' At a sudden thought, Armstrong said, stabbing into the unknown, 'Peter, if you were to choose the best place in the Colony to smuggle in and out, where'd you pick?'

'Aberdeen or Mirs Bay. Any fool knows that—they're just the places that've always been used first, ever since there was a Hong Kong.'

Armstrong sighed. 'I agree.' Aberdeen, he thought. What Aberdeen smuggler? Any one of two hundred. Four Finger Wu'd be first choice. Four Fingers with his big black Rolls and lucky 8 number plate, that bloody thug Two Hatchet Tok and that young nephew of his, the one with the Yankee passport, the one from Yale, was it Yale? Four Fingers would be first choice. Then Goodweather Poon, Smuggler Pa, Ta Sap-fok, Fisherman Pok . . . Christ, the list's endless, just of the ones we know about. In Mirs Bay, northeast beside the New Territories? The Pa Brothers, Big Mouth Fang and a thousand others . . .

'Well,' he said, very very glad now for the information—something tweaking him about Four Finger Wu though there had never been any rumor that he was in the heroin trade. 'One good turn deserves another: Tell your journalist friend our visiting members of Parliament, the trade delegation, come in today from Peking . . . What's up?'

'Nothing,' Peter Marlowe said, trying to keep his face clear. 'You were saying?'

Armstrong watched him keenly, then added, 'The delegation arrives on the afternoon train from Canton. They'll be at the border, transferring trains at 4:32—we just heard of the change of plan last night so perhaps your friend could get an exclusive interview. Seems they've made very good progress.'

'Thanks. On my friend's behalf. Yes thanks. I'll pass it on at once. Well, I must be off. . . .'

Brian Kwok came hurrying toward them. 'Hello, Peter.' He was breathing quite hard. 'Robert, sorry but Crosse wants to see us right now.'

'Bloody hell!' Armstrong said wearily. 'I told you it'd be better to wait before checking in. That bugger never sleeps.' He rubbed his face to clear his tiredness away, his eyes red-rimmed. 'You get the car, Brian, and I'll meet you at the front entrance.'

'Good.' Brian Kwok hurried away. Perturbed, Armstrong watched him go.

Peter Marlowe said as a joke, 'The Town Hall's on fire?'

'In our business the Town Hall's always on fire, lad, some-where.' The policeman studied Peter Marlowe. 'Before I leave, Peter, I'd like to know what's so important about the trade delegation to you.'

After a pause the man with the curious eyes said, 'I used to know one of them during the war. Lieutenant Robin Grey. He was provost marshal of Changi for the last two years.' His voice was flat now, more flat and more icy than Armstrong had imagined possible. 'I hated him and he hated me. I hope I don't meet him, that's all.'

Across the winner's circle Gornt had his binoculars trained on Armstrong as he walked after Brian Kwok. Then, thoughtfully, he turned them back on Peter Marlowe who was wandering toward a group of trainers and jockeys.

'Nosy bugger!' Gornt said.

'Eh? Who? Oh Marlowe?' Sir Dunstan Barre chuckled. 'He's not nosy, just wants to know everything about Hong Kong. It's your murky past that fascinates him, old boy, yours and the tai-pan's.'

'You've no skeletons, Dunstan?' Gornt asked softly. 'You're saying you and your family're lily white?'

'God forbid!' Barre was hastily affable, wanting to turn Gornt's sudden venom into honey. 'Good God no! Scratch an

Englishman find a pirate. We're all suspect! That's life, what?'

Gornt said nothing. He despised Barre but needed him. 'I'm having a bash on my yacht on Sunday, Dunstan. Would you care to come—you'll find it interesting.'

'Oh? Who's the honored guest?'

'I thought of making it stag only—no wives, eh?'

'Ah! Count me in,' Barre said at once, brightening. 'I could bring a lady friend?'

'Bring two if you like, old chap, the more the merrier. It'll be a small, select, safe group. Plumm, he's a good sort and his girl friend's lots of fun.' Gornt saw Marlowe change direction as he was called over to a group of stewards dominated by Donald McBride. Then, at a sudden thought, he added, 'I think I'll invite Marlowe too.'

'Why if you think he's nosy?'

'He might be interested in the real stories about the Struans, our founding pirates and the present-day ones.' Gornt smiled with the front of his face and Barre wondered what devilment Gornt was planning.

The red-faced man mopped his brow. 'Christ, I wish it would rain. Did you know Marlowe was in the Hurricanes—he got three of the bloody Boche in the Battle of Britain before he got sent out to Singapore and that bloody mess. I'll never forgive those bloody Japs for what they did to our lads there, here or in China.'

'Nor will I,' Gornt agreed darkly. 'Did you know my old man was in Nanking in '37, during the rape of Nanking?'

'No, Christ, how did he get out?'

'Some of our people hid him for a few days—we'd had associates there for generations. Then he pretended to the Japs that he was a friendly correspondent for the London *Times* and talked his way back to Shanghai. He still has nightmares about it.'

'Talking about nightmares, old chap, were you trying to give Ian one last night by going to his party?'

'You think he got even by taking care of my car?'

'Eh?' Barre was appalled. 'Good God! You mean your car was tampered with?'

'The master cylinder was ruptured by a blow of some kind. The mechanic said it could've been done by a rock thrown up against it.'

Barre stared at him and shook his head. 'Ian's not a fool. He's wild, yes, but he's no fool. That'd be attempted murder.'

'It wouldn't be the first time.'

'If I were you I'd not say that sort of thing publicly, old chap.'

'You're not public, old chap. Are you?'

'No. Of cour—'

'Good.' Gornt turned his dark eyes on him. 'This is going to be a time when friends should stick together.'

'Oh?' Barre was instantly on guard.

'Yes. The market's very nervous. This Ho-Pak mess could foul up a lot of all our plans.'

'My Hong Kong and Lan Tao Farms's as solid as the Peak.'

'You are, provided your Swiss bankers continue to grant you your new line of credit.'

Barre's florid face whitened. 'Eh?'

'Without their loan you can't take over Hong Kong Docks and Wharves, Royal Insurance of Hong Kong and Malaya, expand into Singapore or complete a lot of other tricky little deals you've on your agenda—you and your newfound friend, Mason Loft, the whiz kid of Threadneedle Street. Right?'

Barre watched him, cold sweat running down his back, shocked that Gornt was privy to his secrets. 'Where'd you hear about those?'

Gornt laughed. 'I've friends in high places, old chap. Don't worry, your Achilles' heel's safe with me.'

'We're . . . we're in no danger.'

'Of course not.' Gornt turned his binoculars back on his horse. 'Oh by the way, Dunstan, I might need your vote at the next meeting of the bank.'

'On what?'

'I don't know yet.' Gornt looked down at him. 'I just need to know that I can count on you.'

'Yes. Yes of course.' Barre was wondering nervously what Gornt had in mind and where the leak was. 'Always happy to oblige, old chap.'

'Thank you. You're selling Ho-Pak short?'

'Of course. I got all my money out yesterday, thank God. Why?'

'I heard Dunross's Par-Con deal won't go through. I'm considering selling him short too.'

'Oh? The deal's not on? Why?'

Gornt smiled sardonically. 'Because, Dunstan—'

'Hello, Quillan, Dunstan, sorry to interrupt,' Donald McBride said, bustling up to them, two men in tow. 'May I introduce Mr. Charles Biltzmann, vice-president of American Superfoods. He'll be heading up the new General Stores-Superfoods merger and based in the Colony from now on. Mr. Gornt and Sir Dunstan Barre.'

The tall, sandy-haired American wore a gray suit and tie and rimless glasses. He stuck out his hand affably. 'Glad to meet you. This's a nice little track you've got here.'

Gornt shook hands without enthusiasm. Next to Biltzmann was Richard Hamilton Pugmire, the present tai-pan of H.K. General Stores, a steward of the Turf Club, a short arrogant man in his late forties who carried his smallness as a constant challenge. 'Hello, you two! Well, who's the winner of the fifth?'

Gornt towered over him. 'I'll tell you after the race.'

'Oh come on, Quillan, you know it'll be fixed before the horses even parade.'

'If you can prove that I'm sure we'd all like to know. I certainly would, wouldn't you, Donald?'

'I'm sure Richard was just joking,' Donald McBride replied. He was in his sixties, his Eurasian features pleasing, and the warmth of his smile pervaded him. He added to Biltzmann, 'There're always these rumors about race fixing but we do what we can and when we catch anyone—off with his head! At least off the course he goes.'

'Hell, races get fixed in the States too but I guess here where it's all amateur and wide open, it's got to be easier,' Biltzmann said breezily. 'That stallion you have, Quillan. He's Australian, partial pedigree, isn't he?'

'Yes,' Gornt said abruptly, detesting his familiarity.

'Don here was explaining some of the rules of your racing. I'd sure like to be part of your racing fraternity—hope I can get to be a voting member too.'

The Turf Club was very exclusive and very tightly controlled. There were two hundred voting members and four thousand nonvoting members. Only voting members could get into the members' box. Only voting members could own horses. Only voting members could propose two persons a year to be nonvoting members—the stewards' decision, approval or non-approval being final, their voting secret. And only voting members could become a steward.

'Yes,' Biltzmann repeated, 'that'd be just great.'

'I'm sure that could be arranged,' McBride said with a smile. 'The club's always looking for new blood—and new horses.'

'Do you plan to stay in Hong Kong, Mr. Biltzmann?' Gornt asked.

'Call me Chuck. I'm here for the duration,' the American replied. 'I suppose I'm Superfoods of Asia's new tai-pan. Sounds great, doesn't it?'

'Marvelous!' Barre said, witheringly.

Biltzmann continued happily, not yet tuned to English sarcasm, 'I'm the fall guy for our board in New York. As the man from Missouri said, the buck stops here.' He smiled but no one smiled with him. 'I'll be here at least a couple of years and I'm looking forward to every minute. We're getting ready to settle in right now. My bride arrives tomorrow an—'

'You're just married, Mr. Biltzmann?'

'Oh no, that's just a, an American expression. We've been married twenty years. Soon as our new place's fixed the way she wants it, we'd be happy for you to come to dinner. Maybe a barbecue? We got the steaks organized, all prime, T-bones and New Yorks, being flown over once a month. And Idaho potatoes,' he added proudly.

'I'm glad about the potatoes,' Gornt said and the others settled back, waiting, knowing that he despised American cooking—particularly charcoaled steaks and hamburgers and 'gooped-up baked potatoes', as he called them. 'When does the merger finalize?'

'End of the month. Our bid's accepted. Everything's agreed. I certainly hope our American know-how'll fit into this great little island.'

'I presume you'll build a mansion?'

'No sir. Dickie here,' Biltzmann continued, and everyone winced, 'Dickie's got us the penthouse of the company's apartment building on Blore Street, so we're in fat city.'

'That's convenient,' Gornt said. The others bit back their laughter. The oldest and most famous of the Colony's Houses of Easy Virtue had always been on Blore Street at Number One.

Number One, Blore Street, had been started by one of Mrs. Fotheringill's 'young ladies', Nellie Blore, in the 1860s, with money reportedly given her by Culum Struan, and was still operating under its original rules—European or Australian ladies only and no foreign gentlemen or natives allowed.

'Very convenient,' Gornt said again. 'But I wonder if you'd qualify.'

'Sir?'

'Nothing. I'm sure Blore Street is most apt.'

'Great view, but the plumbing's no good,' Biltzmann said. 'My bride'll soon fix that.'

'She's a plumber too?' Gornt asked.

The American laughed. 'Hell no, but she's mighty handy around the house.'

'If you'll excuse me I have to see my trainer.' Gornt nodded to the others and turned away with, 'Donald, have you a moment? It's about Saturday.'

'Of course, see you in a moment, Mr. Biltzmann.'

'Sure. But call me Chuck. Have a nice day.'

McBride fell into step beside Gornt. When they were alone Gornt said, 'You're surely not seriously suggesting he should be a voting member?'

'Well, yes.' McBride looked uncomfortable. 'It's the first time a big American company's made a bid to come into Hong Kong. He'd be quite important to us.'

'That's no reason to let him in here, is it? Make him a non-voting member. Then he can get into the stands. And if you want to invite him to your box, that's your affair. But a voting member? Good God, he'll probably have "Superfoods" as his racing colors!'

'He's just new and out of his depth, Quillan. I'm sure he'll learn. He's decent enough even though he does make a few gaffes. He's quite well off an—'

'Since when has money been an open sesame to the Turf Club? Good God, Donald, if that was the case, every upstart Chinese property gambler or stock market gambler who'd made a killing on our market'd swamp us. We wouldn't have room to fart.'

'I don't agree. Perhaps the answer's to increase the voting membership.'

'No. Absolutely not. Of course you stewards will do what you like. But I suggest you reconsider.' Gornt was a voting member but not a steward. The two hundred voting members elected the twelve stewards annually by secret ballot. Each year Gornt's name was put on the open list of nominees for steward and each year he failed to get enough votes. Most stewards were re-elected by the membership automatically until they retired, though from time to time there was lobbying.

'Very well,' McBride said, 'when his name's proposed I'll mention your opposition.'

Gornt smiled thinly. 'That'll be tantamount to getting him elected.'

McBride chuckled. 'I don't think so, Quillan, not this time. Pug asked me to introduce him around. I must admit he gets off on the wrong foot every time. I introduced him to Paul Havergill and Biltzmann immediately started comparing banking procedures here with those in the States, and not very pleasantly either. And with the tai-pan . . .' McBride's graying eyebrows soared. '. . . he said he was sure glad to meet him as he wanted to learn about Hag Struan and Dirk Struan and all the other pirates and opium smugglers in his past!' He sighed. 'Ian and Paul'll certainly blackball him for you, so I don't think you've much to worry about. I really don't understand why Pug sold out to them anyway.'

'Because he's not his father. Since old Sir Thomas died General Stores've been slipping. Still, Pug makes 6 million U.S. personally and has a five-year unbreakable contract—so he has all the pleasure and none of the headaches and the family's taken care of. He wants to retire to England, Ascot and all that.'

'Ah! That's a very good deal for old Pug!' McBride became more serious. 'Quillan, the fifth race—the interest's enormous. I'm worried there'll be interference. We're going to increase surveillance on all the horses. There're rumors th—'

'About doping?'

'Yes.'

'There're always rumors and someone will always try. I think the stewards do a very good job.'

'The stewards agreed last night that we'd institute a new rule: in future we'll have an obligatory chemical analysis before and after each race, as they do at the major tracks in England or America.'

'In time for Saturday? How're you going to arrange that?'

'Dr. Meng, the police pathologist, has agreed to be responsible—until we have an expert arranged.'

'Good idea,' Gornt said.

McBride sighed. 'Yes, but the Mighty Dragon's no match for the Local Serpent.' He turned and left.

Gornt hesitated, then went to his trainer who stood beside Pilot Fish talking with the jockey, another Australian, Bluey White. Bluey White was ostensibly a manager of one of Gornt's shipping divisions—the title given to him to preserve his amateur status.

'G'day, Mr. Gornt,' they said. The jockey touched his forelock.

'Morning.' Gornt looked at them a moment and then he said quietly, 'Bluey, if you win, you've a 5,000 bonus. If you finish behind Noble Star, you're fired.'

The tough little man whitened. 'Yes, guv!'

'You'd better get changed now,' Gornt said, dismissing him.

'I'll win,' Bluey White said as he left.

The trainer said uneasily, 'Pilot Fish's in very good fettle, Mr. Gornt. He'll be try—'

'If Noble Star wins you're fired. If Noble Star finishes ahead of Pilot Fish you're fired.'

'My oath, Mr. Gornt.' The man wiped the sudden sweat off his mouth. 'I don't fix who ge—'

'I'm not suggesting you do anything. I'm just telling you what's going to happen to you.' Gornt nodded pleasantly and strode off. He went to the club restaurant, which overlooked the course, and ordered his favorite breakfast, eggs Benedict with his own special hollandaise that they kept for his exclusive use, and Javanese coffee that he also supplied.

On his third cup of coffee the waiter came over. 'Excuse me, sir, you're wanted on the telephone.'

He went to the phone. 'Gornt.'

'Hello, Mr. Gornt, this's Paul Choy . . . Mr. Wu's nephew. . . . I hope I'm not disturbing you.'

Gornt covered his surprise. 'You're calling rather early, Mr. Choy.'

'Yes sir, but I wanted to be in early the first day,' the young man said in a rush, 'so I was the only one here a couple of minutes ago when the phone rang. It was Mr. Bartlett, Linc Bartlett, you know, the guy with the smuggled guns, the millionaire.'

Gornt was startled. 'Bartlett?'

'Yes sir. He said he wanted to get hold of you, implied it was kinda urgent, said he'd tried your home. I put two and two together and came up with you might be at the workout and I'd better get off my butt. I hope I'm not disturbing you?'

'No. What did he say?' Gornt asked.

'Just that he wanted to talk to you, and were you in town? I said I didn't know, but I'd check around and leave a message and give him a call back.'

'Where was he calling from?'

'The Vic and Albert. Kowloon side 662233, extension 773—that's his office extension, not his suite.'

Gornt was very impressed. 'A closed mouth catches no flies, Mr. Choy.'

'Jesus, Mr. Gornt, that's one thing you never need worry about,' Paul Choy said fervently. 'My old Uncle Wu wopped that into us all like there was no tomorrow.'

'Good. Thanks, Mr. Choy. I'll see you shortly.'

'Yes sir.'

Gornt hung up, thought a moment, then dialed the hotel. '773 please.'

'Linc Bartlett.'

'Good morning Mr. Bartlett, this's Mr. Gornt. What can I do for you?'

'Hey, thanks for returning my call. I've had disturbing news which sort of ties in with what we were discussing.'

'Oh?'

'Yes. Does Toda Shipping mean anything to you?'

Gornt's interest soared. 'Toda Shipping's a huge Japanese conglomerate, shipyards, steel mills, heavy engineering. Struan's have a two-ship deal with them, bulk vessels I believe. Why?'

'It seems Toda have some notes due from Struan's, $6 million in three installments—on the first, eleventh, and fifteenth of next month—and another $6 million in 90 days. Then there's

500

another 6.8 million due on the eighth to Orlin International Bank—you know them?'

With a great effort Gornt kept his voice matter-of-fact. 'I've, I've heard of them,' he said, astounded that the American would have such details of the debts. 'So?' he asked.

'So I heard Struan's have only 1.3 million in cash, with no cash reserves and not enough cash flow to make payment. They're not expecting a significant block of income until they get 17 million as their share of one of Kowloon Investments' property deals, not due until November, and they're 20 percent overextended at the Victoria Bank.'

'That's . . . that's very intimate knowledge,' Gornt gasped, his heart thumping in his chest, his collar feeling tight. He knew about the 20 percent overdraft—Plumm had told him—all the directors of the bank would know. But not the details of their cash, or their cash flow.

'Why're you telling me this, Mr. Bartlett?'

'How liquid are you?'

'I've already told you, I'm twenty times stronger than Struan's,' he said automatically, the lie coming easily, his mind churning the marvelous opportunities all this information unlocked. 'Why?'

'If I go through with the Struan deal he'll be using my cash down payment to get off the Toda and Orlin hooks—if his bank doesn't extend his credit.'

'Yes.'

'Will the Vic support him?'

'They always have. Why?'

'If they don't, then he's in big trouble.'

'Struan's are substantial stockholders. The bank is obliged to support them.'

'But he's overdrawn there and Havergill hates him. Between Chen's stock, Struan's and their nominees, they've 21 percent. . . .'

Gornt almost dropped the phone. 'Where the hell did you get that information? No outsider could possibly know that!'

'That's right,' he heard the American say calmly, 'but that's a fact. Could you muster the other 79 percent?'

'What?'

'If I had a partner who could put the bank against him just this once and he couldn't get credit elsewhere . . . bluntly: it's a matter of timing. Dunross's mortally overextended and that means he's vulnerable. If his bank won't give him credit, he's got to sell something—or get a new line of credit. In either case he's wide open for an attack and ripe for a takeover at the fire-sale price.'

Gornt mopped his brow, his brain reeling. 'Where the hell did you get all this information?'

'Later, not now.'

'When?'

'When we're down to the short strokes.'

'How . . . how sure are you your figures are correct?'

'Very. We've his balance sheets for the last seven years.'

In spite of his resolve Gornt gasped. 'That's impossible!' Want to bet?'

Gornt was really shaken now and he tried to get his mind working. Be cautious, he admonished himself. For chrissake control yourself. 'If . . . if you've all that, if you know that and get one last thing . . . their interlocking corporate structure, if you knew that we could do anything we want with Struan's.'

'We've got that too. You want in?'

Gornt heard himself say calmly, not feeling calm at all, 'Of course. When could we meet? Lunch?'

'How about now? But not here, and not at your office. This has to be kept very quiet.'

Gornt's heart hurt in his chest. There was a rotten taste in his mouth and he wondered very much how far he could trust Bartlett. 'I'll . . . I'll send a car for you. We could chat in the car.'

'Good idea, but why don't I meet you Hong Kong side. The Golden Ferry Terminal in an hour.'

'Excellent. My car's a Jag—license's 8888. I'll be by the taxi rank.'

He hung up and stared at the phone a moment, then went back to his table.

'Not bad news I hope, Mr. Gornt?'

'Er, no, no not at all. Thank you.'

'Some more of your special coffee? It's freshly made.'

'No, no thank you. I'd like a half bottle of the Taittinger Blanc de Blancs. The '55.' He sat back feeling very strange. His enemy was almost in his grasp—if the American's facts were true and if

502

the American was to be trusted and not in some devious plot with Dunross.

The wine came but he hardly tasted it. His whole being was concentrated, sifting, preparing.

Gornt saw the tall American come through the crowds and, for a moment he envied him his lean, trim figure and the easy, careless dress—jeans, open-neck shirt, sports coat—and his obvious confidence. He saw the elaborate camera, smiled sardonically, then looked for Casey. When it was obvious Bartlett was alone he was disappointed. But this disappointment did not touch the glorious anticipation that had possessed him ever since he had put the phone down.

Gornt leaned over and opened the side door. 'Welcome Hong Kong side, Mr. Bartlett,' he said with forced joviality, starting the engine. He drove off along Gloucester Road toward Glessing's Point and the Yacht Club. 'Your inside information's astonishing.'

'Without spies you can't operate, can you?'

'You can, but then that's amateur. How's Miss Casey? I thought she'd be with you.'

'She's not in this. Not yet.'

'Oh?'

'No. No, she's not in on the initial attack. She's more valuable if she knows nothing.'

'She knows nothing of this? Not even your call to me?'

'No. Nothing at all.'

After a pause he said, 'I thought she was your executive VP . . . your right arm you called her.'

'She is, but I'm boss of Par-Con, Mr. Gornt.'

Gornt saw the level eyes and, for the first time, felt that that was true and that his original estimation was wrong. 'I've never doubted it,' he said, waiting, his senses honed, waiting him out.

Then Bartlett said, 'Is there somewhere we can park—I've got something I want to show you.'

'Certainly.' Gornt was driving along the sea front on Gloucester Road in the usual heavy traffic. In a moment he found a parking place near Causeway Bay typhoon shelter with its massed, floating islands of boats of all sizes.

'Here.' Bartlett handed him a typed folder. It was a detailed copy of Struan's balance sheet for the year before the company went public. Gornt's eyes raced over the figures. 'Christ,' he muttered. 'So *Lasting Cloud*'s cost them 12 million?'

'It almost broke them. Seems they had all sorts of wild-assed cargo aboard. Jet engines for China, uninsured.'

'Of course they'd be uninsured—how the hell can you insure contraband?' Gornt was trying to take in all the complicated figures. His mind was dazed. 'If I'd known half of this I'd've got them the last time. Can I keep it?'

'When we've made a deal I'll give you a copy.' Bartlett took the folder back and gave him a paper. 'Try this one for size.' It showed, graphically, Struan's stockholdings in Kowloon Investments and detailed how, through nominee companies, the tai-pan of Struan's exercised complete control over the huge insurance-property-wharfing company that was supposedly a completely separate company and quoted as such on the stock exchange.

'Marvelous,' Gornt said with a sigh, awed by the beauty of it. 'Struan's have only a tiny proportion of the stock publicly held but retain 100 percent control, and perpetual secrecy.'

'In the States whoever figured this out'd be in jail.'

'Thank God Hong Kong laws aren't the same, and that this's all perfectly legal, if a trifle devious.' The two men laughed.

Bartlett pocketed the paper. 'I've got similar details of the rest of their holdings.'

'Bluntly, what have you in mind, Mr. Bartlett?'

'A joint attack on Struan's, starting today. A blitzkrieg. We go 50–50 on all spoils. You get the Great House on the Peak, the prestige, his yacht—and 100 percent of the box at the Turf Club including his stewardship.'

Gornt glanced at him keenly. Bartlett smiled. 'We know that's kind of special to you. But everything else right down the middle.'

'Except their Kai Tak operations. I need that for my airline.'

'All right. But then I want Kowloon Investments.'

'No,' Gornt said, immediately on guard. 'We should split that 50–50, and everything 50–50.'

'No. You need Kai Tak, I need Kowloon Investments. It'll be a great nucleus for Par-Con's jump into Asia.'

'Why?'

'Because all great fortunes in Hong Kong are based on property. K. I. will give me a perfect base.'

'For further raids?'

'Sure,' Bartlett said easily. 'Your friend Jason Plumm's next on the list. We could swallow his Asian Properties easy. 50–50. Right?'

Gornt said nothing for a long time. 'And after him?'

'Hong Kong and Lan Tao Farms.'

Again Gornt's heart leapt. He had always hated Dunstan Barre and that hatred was tripled last year when Barre had been given a knighthood in the Queen's Birthday Honors List—an honor maneuvered, Gornt was sure, with judicious contributions to the Conservative Party fund. 'And how would you swallow him?'

'There's always a time when any army, any country, any company's vulnerable. Every general or company president has to take chances, sometime, to stay ahead. You've got to, to stay ahead. There's always some enemy snapping at your heels, wanting yours, wanting your place in the sun, wanting your territory. You've got to be careful when you're vulnerable.'

'Are you vulnerable now?'

'No. I was two years ago but not now. Now I've the muscle I need—we need. If you're in.'

A flock of seabirds were dipping and weaving and cawing overhead. 'What do you want me to do?'

'You're the pathfinder, the spearhead. I defend the rear. Once you've punched a hole through his defense, I'll deliver the knockout. We sell Struan's short—I guess you've already taken a position on the Ho-Pak?'

'I've sold short, yes. Modestly.' Gornt told the lie easily.

'Good. In the States you could get their own accountants to leak the cash flow facts to the right mouth. That'd soon be all over town. Could the same ploy work here?'

'Probably. But you'd never get their accountants to do that.'

'Not for the right fee?'

'No. But rumors could be started.' Gornt smiled grimly. 'It's very bad of Dunross to hide his inept position from his shareholders. Yes. That's possible. And then?'

'You sell Struan's short, as soon as the market opens. Big.'

Gornt lit a cigarette. 'I sell short, and what do you do?'

'Nothing openly. That's our ace in the hole.'

'Perhaps it really is, and I'm being set up,' Gornt said.

'What if I cover all losses? Would that be proof enough I'm with you?'

'What?'

'I pay all losses and take half the profit for today, tomorrow and Friday. If we haven't got him on the run by Friday afternoon you buy back in, just before closing, and we've failed. If it looks like we've got him, we sell heavily, to the limit, just before closing. That'll sweat him out over the weekend. Monday I jerk the rug and our blitzkrieg's on. It's infallible.'

'Yes. If you're to be trusted.'

'I'll put $2 million in any Swiss bank you name by ten o'clock today. That's 10 million HK which sure as hell's enough to cover any shorting losses you might have. $2 million with no strings, no paper, no promissory note, just your word it's to cover any losses, that if we win we split profits and the rest of the deal as it's been laid out—50–50 except Kowloon Investments for me, Struan's at Kai Tak Airport for you, and for Casey and me, voting membership at the Turf Club. We'll put it to paper Tuesday—after he's crashed.'

'You'll put up 2 million U.S., and it's my decision as to when I buy to cover any losses?' Gornt was incredulous.

'Yes. 2 million's the extent of my gamble. So how can you get hurt? You can't. And because he knows how you feel about him, if you mount the attack he won't be suspicious, won't be prepared for a flanking blitz from me.'

'This all depends on whether your figures are correct—the amounts and the dates.'

'Check them out. There must be a way you can do that—enough to convince yourself.'

'Why the sudden change, Mr. Bartlett? You said you'd wait till Tuesday—perhaps later.'

'We've done some checking and I don't like the figures I've come up with. We owe Dunross nothing. We'd be crazy to go with him when he's so weak. As it is, what I'm offering you is a great gamble, great odds: the Noble House against 2 lousy million. If we win that'd be parlayed into hundreds of millions.'

'And if we fail?'

Bartlett shrugged. 'Maybe I'll go home. Maybe we'll work out a Rothwell-Gornt-Par-Con deal. You win sometimes and you lose a lot more times. But this raid's too good not to try it. Without you it'd never work. I've seen enough of Hong Kong to know it has its own special rules. I've no time to learn them. Why should I—when I've got you.'

'Or Dunross?'

Bartlett laughed and Gornt read no guile in him. 'You're not stretched, you're not vulnerable, he is—that's his bad luck. What d'you say? Is the raid on?'

'I'd say you're very persuasive. Who gave you the information—and the document?'

'Tuesday I'll tell you. When Struan's have crashed.'

'Ah, there's a payoff to Mister X?'

'There's always a payoff. It'll come off the top, but no more than 5 percent—any more comes out of my share.'

'Two o'clock Friday, Mr. Bartlett? That's when I decide to buy back in and perhaps lose your 2 million—or we confer and continue the surge?'

'Friday at two.'

'If we continue over the weekend you'll cover any further risk with further funds?'

'No. You won't need any more. 2 million's tops. By Friday afternoon either his stock will be way down and we'll have him running scared, or not. This's no long-term, well-organized raid. It's a once, er, a onetime attempt to fool's mate an opponent.' Bartlett grinned happily. 'I risk 2 lousy million for a game that will go down in history books. In less than a week we knock off the Noble House of Asia!'

Gornt nodded, torn. How far can I trust you, Mr. Bloody Raider, you with the key to Devil Dunross? He glanced out of the window and watched a child skulling a boat among the junks, the sea as safe and familiar to her as dry land. 'I'll think about what you said.'

'How long?'

'Till eleven.'

'Sorry, this's a raid, not a business deal. It's now—or not at all!'

'Why?'

'There's a lot to do, Mr. Gornt. I want this settled now or not at all.'

Gornt glanced at his watch. There was plenty of time. A call to the right Chinese newspaper and whatever he told them would be on the stands in an hour. He smiled grimly to himself. His own ace in the hole was Havergill. Everything dovetailed perfectly.

A seabird cawed and flew inland, riding thermals toward the Peak. He watched it. Then his eyes noticed the Great House on the crest, white against the green of the slopes.

'It's a deal,' he said and stuck out his hand.

Bartlett shook. 'Great. This is strictly between us?'

'Yes.'

'Where d'you want the 2 million?'

'The Bank of Switzerland and Zurich, in Zurich, account number 181819.' Gornt reached into his pocket, noticing his fingers were trembling. 'I'll write it down for you.'

'No need. The account's in your name?'

'Good God, no! Canberra Limited.'

'Canberra Limited's 2 million richer! And in three days with any luck, you'll be tai-pan of the Noble House. How about that!' Bartlett opened the door and got out. 'See you.'

'Wait,' Gornt said, startled, 'I'll drop you wh—'

'No thanks. I've got to get to a phone. Then at 9:15 I've an interview with your friend Orlanda, Miss Ramos—thought there was no harm in it. After that maybe I'll take a few pictures.' He waved cheerily and walked off.

Gornt wiped the sweat off his hands. Before leaving the club he had phoned Orlanda to phone Bartlett and make the date. That's very good, he thought, still in shock. She'll keep an eye on him once they're lovers, and they will be, Casey or not. Orlanda has too much to gain.

He watched Bartlett, envying him. In a few moments the American had vanished into the crowds of Wanchai.

Suddenly he was very tired. It's all too pat, too fine, too easy, he told himself. And yet . . . and yet! Shakily he lit a cigarette. Where did Bartlett get those papers?

Inexorably his eyes went back to the Great House on the Peak. He was possessed by it and by a hatred so vast that it swept his mind back to his ancestors, to Sir Morgan Brock

508

whom the Struans broke, to Gorth Brock whom Dirk Struan murdered, to Tyler Brock whom his daughter betrayed. Without wishing it, he renewed the oath of vengeance that he had sworn to his father, that his father had sworn to his—back to Sir Morgan Brock who, penniless, destroyed by his sister, Hag Struan, paralyzed, a shell of a man, had begged for vengeance on behalf of all the Brock ghosts on the Noble House and all the descendants of the most evil man who had ever lived.

Oh gods give me strength, Quillan Gornt prayed. Let the American be telling the truth. I will have vengeance.

28

10:50 A.M.:

The sun bore down on Aberdeen through a slight overcast. The air was sultry, ninety-two degrees Fahrenheit with ninety percent humidity. It was low tide. The smell of rotting kelp and offal and exposed mudflats added to the oppressive weight of the day.

There were five hundred or more sullen impatient people jamming against one another, trying to surge through the bottleneck of barriers ahead that the police had erected outside this branch of Ho-Pak. The barriers allowed only one person through at a time. Men and women of all ages, some with infants, were constantly jostling each other, no one waiting a turn, everyone trying to inch forward to get to the head of the line.

'Look at the bloody fools,' Chief Inspector Donald C. C. Smyth said sourly. 'If they'd stretch out and not crowd they'd all get through quicker, and we could leave one copper here to keep order and the rest of us could go to lunch instead of getting the riot squad ready. Do it!'

'Yes sir,' Sergeant Mok said politely. *Ayeeyah*, he was thinking as he walked over to the squad car, the poor fool still doesn't understand that we Chinese are not stupid foreign devils—or devils from the Eastern Sea—who'll line up patiently for hours. Oh no, we civilized persons understand life and it's every man for himself. He clicked on the police transmitter. 'Sergeant Mok! The chief inspector wants a riot squad here on the double. Park just behind the fish market but keep in contact!'

'Yes sir.'

Mok sighed and lit a cigarette. More barriers had been erected across the street, outside Blacs and the Victoria Aberdeen

510

branches, and more at the Ching Prosperity Bank around the corner. His khaki uniform was ironed sharp on the creases and there were big sweat rings under his arms. He was very concerned. This crowd was very dangerous and he did not want a repetition of yesterday. If the bank shut its doors before three he was sure the crowd would tear the place apart. He knew that if he still had any money in there, he would be the first to tear the door open to get *his* money. *Ayeeyah*, he thought, very thankful for the Snake's authority that had unlocked all their money this morning to the last penny.

'Piss on all banks!' Mok muttered to no one. 'All gods, let the Ho-Pak pay all customers today! Let it fail tomorrow! Tomorrow's my day off so let it fail tomorrow.' He stubbed out his cigarette.

'Sergeant Major?'

'Yes?'

'Look over there!' the eager young plainclothes detective said, hurrying up to him. He wore spectacles and was in his early twenties. 'By the Victoria Bank. The old woman. The old *amah*.'

'Where? Oh yes, I see her.' Mok watched her for a while but detected nothing untoward. Then he saw her scuttle through the crowd and whisper to a young tough, wearing jeans, who was leaning against a railing. She pointed to an old man who had just come out of the bank. At once the young tough sauntered after him and the old *amah* squeezed and squirmed and cursed her way back to the head of the barrier where she could see those who entered and those who came out.

'That's the third time, sir,' the young detective said.'The old *amah* points out someone who's just come out of the bank to the tough, then off he goes. In a few minutes he comes back again. That's the third time. I'm sure I saw him slip her something once. I think it was money.'

'Good! Very good, Spectacles Wu. It's bound to be a triad shakedown. The old hag's probably his mother. You follow the young bastard and I'll intercept him the other way. Keep out of sight!'

Sergeant Mok slipped around the corner, down a busy alley lined with stalls and street hawkers and open shops, moving carefully through the crowds. He turned into another alley just in time to catch a glimpse of some money being passed over by the old man. He waited until Wu had blocked the other end of the alley, then he walked ponderously forward.

'What's going on here?'

'What? Eh? Nothing, nothing at all,' the old man said nervously, sweat running down his face. 'What's the matter? I've done nothing!'

'Why did you give this young man money, *heya*? I saw you give him money!' The young thug stared back at Mok insolently, unafraid, knowing he was Smallpox Kin, one of the Werewolves who had all Hong Kong petrified. 'Is he accosting you? Trying to squeeze you? He looks like a triad!'

'Oh! I . . . I . . . I owed him 500 dollars. I've just got it out of the bank and I paid him.' The old man was clearly terrified but he blustered on, 'He's my cousin.' A crowd began to collect. Someone hawked and spat.

'Why're you sweating so much?'

'All gods fornicate all pigs! It's hot! Everyone's sweating. Everyone!'

'That's fornicating right,' someone called out.

Mok turned his attention on the youth who waited truculently. 'What's your name?'

'Sixth Son Wong!'

'Liar! Turn out your pockets!'

'Me, I've done nothing! I know the law. You can't search people without a warran—'

Mok's iron fist snapped out and twisted the youth's arm and he squealed. The crowd laughed. They fell silent as Spectacles Wu came out of nowhere to search him. Mok held Smallpox Kin in a vise. Another uneasy undercurrent swept through the onlookers as they saw the rolls of money, and change. 'Where'd you get all this?' Mok snarled.

'It's mine. I'm . . . I'm a moneylender and I'm collecting forn—'

'Where's your place of business?'

'It's . . . it's in Third Alley, off Aberdeen Road.'

'Come on, we'll go and look.'

Mok released the young man who, unafraid, still stared back angrily. 'First give me my money!' He turned to the crowd and appealed to them. 'You saw him take it! I'm an honest moneylender! These're servants of the foreign devils and you all know them! Foreign devil law forbids honest citizens being searched!'

'Give him back his fornicating money!' someone shouted.

'If he's a moneylender . . .'

The crowd began to argue back and forth and then Smallpox Kin saw a small opening in the crowd and he darted for it. The crowd let him pass and he fled up the alley, vanishing into the traffic, but when Spectacles Wu charged in pursuit they closed up and jostled him and became a little uglier. Mok called him back. In the momentary mêlée the old man had disappeared. Wearily Mok said, 'Let the motherless turd go! He was just a triad—another triad turd who preys on law-abiding people.'

'What're you going to do with his fornicating money?' someone called out from the back of the crowd.

'I'm going to give it to an old woman's rest home,' Mok shouted back equally rudely. 'Go defecate in your grand-mother's ear!'

Someone laughed and the crowd began to break up and then they all went about their business. In a moment Mok and Spectacles Wu were standing like stones in a river, the passers-by eddying round them. Once back on the main street, Mok wiped his brow. *'Dew neh loh moh!'*

'Yes. Why're they like that, Sergeant Major?' the young detective asked. 'We're only trying to help them. Why didn't the old man just admit that triad bastard was squeezing him?'

'You don't learn about mobs of people in schoolbooks,' Mok said kindly, knowing the anxiety of the youth to succeed. Spectacles Wu was new, one of the recent university graduates to join the force. He was not one of Mok's private unit. 'Be patient. Neither of them wanted anything to do with us because we're police and they all still believe we'll never help them, only ourselves. It's been the same in China since the first policeman.'

'But this is Hong Kong,' the youth said proudly. 'We're different. We're British police.'

'Yes.' Mok felt a sudden chill. He did not wish to disillusion the youth. I used to be loyal too, loyal to the Queen and to the *quai loh* flag. I learned differently. When I needed help and protection and security I got none. Never once. The British used to be rich and powerful but they lost the war to those Eastern Sea Devils. The war took all their face away and humbled them and put the great tai-pans into Stanley Prison like common thieves—even the tai-pans of the Noble House and Great Bank and even the great high governor himself—put them away like common criminals, into Stanley with all their women and all the children and treated them like turds!

And then after the war, even though they had humbled the Eastern Devils, they never regained their power, or their face.

Now in Hong Kong and in all Asia, now it's not the same and never will be as before. Now every year the British get poorer and poorer and less powerful and how can they protect me and my family from evildoers if they're not rich and powerful? They pay me nothing and treat me like dogmeat! Now my only protection is money, money in gold so that we can flee if need be—or money in land or houses if we do not need to flee. How can I educate my sons in England or America without money? Will the grateful Government pay? Not a fornicating brass cash, and yet I'm supposed to risk my life and keep the streets clean of fornicating triads and pickpockets and rioting lumps of leper turd!

Mok shivered. The only safety for my family is in my own hands as always. Oh how wise the teachings of our ancestors are! Was the police commissioner loyal to me when I needed money, even steerage money, for my son to go to school in America? No. But the Snake was. He loaned me 10,000 dollars at only 10 percent interest so my son went like a Mandarin by Pan American aircraft, with three years of school money, and now he's a qualified architect with a Green Card and next month he'll have an American passport and then he can come back and no one will be able to touch him. He can help protect my generation and will protect his own and his son's and his son's sons!

Yes, the Snake gave me the money, long since paid back with full interest out of money he helped me earn. I shall be loyal to the Snake—until he turns. One day he'll turn, all *quai loh* do, all snakes do, but now I'm a High Dragon and neither gods nor devils nor the Snake himself can hurt my family or my bank accounts in Switzerland and Canada.

'Come along, we'd better go back, young Spectacles Wu,' he said kindly and when he got back to the barriers he told Chief Inspector Smyth what had happened.

'Put the money in our kitty, 'Major,' Smyth said. 'Order a grand banquet for our lads tonight.'

'Yes sir.'

'It was Detective Constable Wu? The one who wants to join SI?'

'Yes sir. Spectacles is very keen.'

Smyth sent for Wu, commended him. 'Now, where's that old *amah?*'

Wu pointed her out. They saw her looking at the corner the thug had gone around, waiting impatiently. After a minute she squirmed out of the swarm and hobbled away, muttering obscenities.

'Wu,' Smyth ordered, 'follow her. Don't let yourself be seen. She'll lead you to the rotten little bugger who fled. Be careful, and when she goes to ground, phone the 'major.'

'Yes sir.'

'Do *not* take any risks—perhaps we can catch the whole gang, there's bound to be a gang.'

'Yes sir.'

'Off you go.' They watched him following her. 'That lad's going to be good. But not for us, 'Major, eh?'

'No sir.'

'I think I'll recommend him to SI. Perhaps—'

Suddenly there was an ominous silence, then shouts and an angry roar. The two policemen rushed back around the corner. In their absence the crowd had shoved aside parts of the barricade, overpowering the four policemen, and now were surging into the bank. Manager Sung and his assistant were vainly trying to close the doors against the shouting, cursing throng. The barricades began to buckle.

'Get the riot squad!'

Mok raced for the squad car. Fearlessly Smyth rushed to the head of the line with his bullhorn. The tumult drowned his order to stop fighting. More reinforcements came running from across the street. Quickly and efficiently they charged to Smyth's support, but the mob was gathering strength. Sung and his tellers slammed the door shut but it was forced open again. Then a brick came out of the crowd and smashed one of the plate-glass windows. There was a roar of approval. The people in front were trying to get out of the way and those at the back were trying to get to the door. More bricks were hurtled at the building, then pieces of wood grabbed from a building site nearby. Another stone went through the glass and it totally shattered. Roaring, the mob surged forward. A girl fell and was crushed.

'Come on,' Smyth shouted, 'give me a hand!' He grabbed one of the barriers and, with four other policemen, used it as a shield and shoved it against the front of the mob, forcing them back. Above the uproar he shouted for them to use their shoulders and they fought the frenzied crowd. Other policemen followed his lead. More bricks went into the bank and then the shout went up, 'Kill the fornicating bank thieves, kill them, they've stolen our money . . .'

'Kill the fornicators . . .'

'I want my money . . .'

'Kill the foreign devils . . .'

Smyth saw the mood of those near him change and his heart stopped as they took up the shout and forgot the bank and their hands reached out for him. He had seen that look before and knew he was a dead man. That other time was during the riots of '56 when 200,000 Chinese suddenly went on a senseless rampage in Kowloon. He would have been killed then if he had not had a Sten gun. He had killed four men and blasted a path to safety. Now he had no gun and he was fighting for his life. His hat was ripped away, someone grabbed his Sam Browne belt and a fist went into his groin, another into his face and talons clawed at his eyes. Fearlessly, Mok and others charged into the milling mass to rescue him. Someone hacked at Mok with a brick, another with a piece of wood that tore a great gash in his cheek. Smyth was engulfed, his hands and arms desperately trying to protect his head. Then the riot squad's Black Maria, siren screaming, skidded around the corner. The ten-man team fell on the crowd roughly and pulled Smyth away. Blood seeped from his mouth, his left arm dangled uselessly.

'You all right, sir?'

'Yes, for chrissake get those sodding barriers up! Get those bastards away from the bank—fire hoses!'

But the fire hoses weren't necessary. At the first violent charge of the riot squad the front of the mob had wilted and now the rest had retreated to a safe distance and stood there watching sullenly, some of them still shouting obscenities. Smyth grabbed the bullhorn. In Cantonese he said, 'If anyone comes within twenty yards, he'll be arrested and deported!' He tried to catch his breath. 'If anyone wants to visit the Ho-Pak, line up a hundred yards away.'

The scowling crowd hesitated, then as Mok and the riot squad came forward fast, they retreated hastily and began to move away, treading on each other.

'I think my bloody shoulder's dislocated,' Smyth said and cursed obscenely.

'What do we do about those bastards, sir?' Mok asked, in great pain, breathing hard, his cheek raw and bleeding, his uniform ripped.

Smyth held his arm to take the growing pain away and looked across the street at the sullen gawking crowd. 'Keep the riot squad here. Get another from West Aberdeen, inform Central. Where's my bloody hat? If I catch the bas—'

'Sir!' one of his men called out. He was kneeling beside the girl who had been trampled on. She was a bar girl or a dance hall girl: she had that sad, sweet or so hard, young-old look. Blood was dribbling from her mouth, her breathing coming in hacking gasps.

'Christ, get an ambulance!'

As Smyth watched helplessly, the girl choked in her own blood and died.

Christian Toxe, editor of the *Guardian*, was scribbling notes, the phone jammed against his ear. 'What was her name, Dan?' he asked over the hubbub of the newsroom.

'I'm not sure. One savings book said Su Tzee-Ian,' Dan Yap the reporter on the other end of the phone at Aberdeen told him. 'There was $4,360 in it—the other was in the name . . . Hang on a second, the ambulance's just leaving now. Can you hear all right, Chris, the traffic's heavy here.'

'Yes. Go on. The second savings book?'

'The second book was in the name of Tak H'eung fah. Exactly 3,000 in that one.'

Tak H'eung fah seemed to touch a memory. 'Do any of the names mean anything?' Toxe asked. He was a tall rumpled man in his untidy cubbyhole of an office.

'No. Except one means Wisteria Su and the other Fragrant Flower Tak. She was pretty, Chris. Might have been Eurasian. . . .'

Toxe felt a sudden ice shaft in his stomach as he remembered his own three daughters, six and seven and eight, and his lovely Chinese wife. He tried to push that perpetual cross back into the recess of his mind, the secret worry of was it right to mix East and West, and what does the future hold for them, my darlings, in this lousy rotten bigoted world?

With an effort he concentrated again. 'That's quite a lot of money for a dance hall girl, isn't it?'

'Yes. I'd say she had a patron. One interesting bit: in her purse was a crumpled envelope dated a couple of weeks ago with a mushy love letter in it. It was addressed to . . . hang on . . . to Tak H'eung fah, apartment 14, Fifth Alley, Tsung-pan Street in Aberdeen. It was soppy, swearing eternal love. Educated writing though.'

'English?' Toxe asked surprised, writing swiftly.

'No. Characters. There was something about the writing— could be a *quai loh*.'

'Did you get a copy?'

'The police wouldn't le—'

'Get a photocopy. Beg borrow or steal a photocopy in time for the afternoon edition. A week's bonus if you do it.'

'Cash this afternoon?'

'All right.'

'You have it.'

'Any signature?'

'"Your only love." The *love* was in English.'

'Mr. Toxe! Mrs. Publisher's on line two!' The English secretary called out through the open door, her desk just outside the glass partition.

'Oh Christ, I'll . . . I'll call her back. Tell her I've got a big story breaking.' Then into the phone again, 'Dan, keep on this story—keep close to the police, go with them to the dead girl's flat—if it's her flat. Find out who owns it—who her people are, where they live. Call me back!' Toxe hung up and called out to his assistant editor, 'Hey, Mac!'

The lean, dour, gray-haired man got up from his desk and wandered in. 'Aye?'

'I think we should put out an extra. Headline . . .' He scrawled on a piece of paper, 'Mob Kills Fragrant Flower!'

'How about "Mob Murders Fragrant Flower"?'

'Or, "First Death at Aberdeen"?'

'"Mob Murders" is better.'

'That's it then. Martin!' Toxe called out. Martin Haply looked up from his desk and came over. Toxe ran his fingers through his hair as he told them both what Dan Yap had related. 'Martin, do a follow-up: "The beautiful young girl was crushed by the feet of the mob—but who were the real killers? Is it an incompetent government who refuses to regulate our outdated banking system? Are the killers those who started the rumors? Is the run on the Ho-Pak as simple as it sounds . . ." etcetera.'

'Got it.' Haply grinned and went back to his desk in the main office. He gulped a cold cup of coffee out of a plastic cup and started to type, his desk piled high with reference books, Chinese newspapers and stock market reports. Teletypes chattered in the background. A few silent copy boys and trainees delivered or picked up copy.

'Hey, Martin! What's the latest from the stock market?'

Martin Haply dialed a number without looking at the phone, then called back to the editor. 'Ho-Pak's down to 24.60, four points from yesterday. Struan's are down a point though there's been some heavy buying. Hong Kong Lan Tao up three points—the story's just been confirmed. Dunstan Barre took their money out yesterday.'

'They did? Then you were right again! Shit!'

'Victoria's off half a point—all banks are edgy and no buyers. There's a rumor a line's forming outside Blacs and the Victoria's head office in Central.' Both men gasped.

'Send someone to check the Vic!' Mac hurried out. Jesus Christ, Toxe thought, his stomach churning, Jesus Christ if a run starts on the Vic the whole sodding island'll collapse and my sodding savings with it.

He leaned back in his old chair and put his feet on the desk, loving his job, loving the pressure and immediacy.

'Do you want me to call her?' his secretary asked. She was round and unflappable.

'Who? Oh shit, Peg, I'd forgotten. Yes—call the Dragon.'

The Dragon was the wife of the publisher, Mong Pa-tok, the present head of the sprawling Mong family who owned this paper and three Chinese newspapers and five magazines, whose antecedents went back to the earliest days. The Mongs were supposed to have descended from the first editor-owner-publisher of the paper, Morley Skinner. The story was that Dirk Struan had given Skinner control of the paper in return for helping him against Tyler Brock and his son Gorth by hushing up the killing of Gorth in Macao. It was said Dirk Struan had provoked the duel. Both men had used fighting irons. Once, some years ago, Toxe had heard old Sarah Chen in her cups relate that when the Brocks came to collect Gorth's body they did not recognize him. The old woman had added that her father, Sir Gordon Chen, had had to mobilize most of China-town to prevent the Brocks from setting afire the Struan ware-houses. Tyler Brock had set Tai-ping Shan alight instead. Only the great typhoon that came that night stopped the whole city from going up in flames—the same holocaust that had de-stroyed Dirk Struan's Great House and him and his secret Chinese wife, May-may.

'She's on line two.'

'Eh? Oh! All right, Peg.' Toxe sighed.

'Ah Mr. Toxe, I was waiting your call, *heya*?'

'What can I do for you, or Mr. Mong?'

'Your pieces on the Ho-Pak Bank, yesterday and today, that the adverse rumors about the Ho-Pak are untrue and started by tai-pans and another big bank. I see more today.'

'Yes. Haply's quite sure.'

'My husband and I hear this not true. No tai-pans or banks are putting out rumors or have put out rumors. Perhaps wise to drop this attack.'

'It's not an attack, Mrs. Mong, just an attitude. You know how susceptible Chinese are to rumors. The Ho-Pak's as strong as any bank in the Colony. We feel sure the rumors were started by a bi—'

'Not by tai-pans and not big bank. My husband and I not like this attitude never mind. Please to change,' she said and he heard the granite in her voice.

'That's editorial policy and I have control over editorial policy,' he said grimly.

'*We* are publisher. It is *our* newspaper. *We* tell you to stop so you will stop.'

'You're ordering me to stop?'

'Of course it is order.'

'Very well. As you order it, it's stopped.'

'Good!' The phone went dead. Christian Toxe snapped his pencil and threw it against the wall and began to curse. His secretary sighed and discreetly closed the door and when he was done Toxe opened the door. 'Peg, how about some coffee? Mac! Martin!'

Toxe sat back at his desk. The chair creaked. He mopped the sweat off his cheeks and lit a cigarette and inhaled deeply.

'Yes, Chris?' Haply asked.

'Martin, cancel the piece I asked for and do another on Hong Kong banking and the need to have some form of banking insurance. . . .'

Both men gaped at him.

'Our publisher doesn't like the rumors approach.'

Martin Haply flushed. 'Well screw him! You heard the guys yourself at the tai-pan's party!'

'That proves nothing. You've no proof. We're stopping that approach. It's not proven so I can't take a stand.'

'But, lo—'

Toxe's neck went purple. *'It's bloody well stopped,'* he roared. *'Understand?'*

Haply began to say something but changed his mind. Choked with rage he turned on his heel and left. He walked across the big room and jerked the front door open and slammed it behind him.

Christian Toxe exhaled. 'He's got a lousy bloody temper that lad!'

He stubbed his cigarette out and lit another. 'Christ, I'm smoking too much!' Still seething, his brown eyes watched the older man. 'Someone must have called her, Mac. Now what would you like as a return favor if you were Mrs. Dragon Mong?'

Suddenly Mac beamed. 'Na a voting membership of the Turf Club!'

'Go to the head of the class!'

Singh, the Indian reporter, came in with a foot of teletype. 'You might need this for extra, Chris.'

It was a series of Reuters reports from the Middle East. 'Teheran 0832 hours: High-level diplomatic sources in Iran report sudden extensive Soviet military maneuvers have begun close to their north border near the oil-rich border area of Azerbaijan where more rioting took place. Washington is reported to have asked permission to send observers to the area.'

The next paragraph was: 'Tel Aviv 0600 hours: The Knesset confirmed late last night that another huge irrigation project had been funded to further divert the waters of the River Jordan into the southern Negev Desert. There was immediate adverse and hostile reaction from Jordan, Egypt and Syria.'

'Negev? Isn't Israel's brand spanking new atomic plant in the Negev?' Toxe asked.

'Aye. Now there's another splendid addition to the peace conference tables. Would the water be for that?'

'I don't know Mac, but this's certainly going to parch a few Jordanian and Palestinian throats. Water water everywhere but not a drop to shower in. I wish to Christ it would rain. Singh, tidy up these reports and we'll put them on the back page. They won't sell a single bloody paper. Do a follow-up piece on the Werewolves for the front page: "The police have a vast dragnet out but the vicious kidnappers of Mr. John Chen continue to elude them. According to sources close to the family of his father, compradore of Struan's, no ransom note has yet been received but one is expected imminently. The *China Guardian* asks all its readers to assist in the capture of these fiends . . ." That sort of thing.'

At Aberdeen Spectacles Wu saw the old woman come out of the tenement building, a shopping basket in her hand, and join the noisy crowds in the narrow alley. He followed cautiously feeling very pleased with himself. While he had waited for her to reappear he had struck up a conversation with a street hawker whose permanent place of business was a patch of broken pavement opposite. The hawker sold tea and small bowls of hot congee—rice gruel. Wu had ordered a bowl, and during his meal, the hawker had told him about the old woman, Ah Tam, who had been in the neighborhood since last year. She'd come to the Colony from a village near Canton with the huge waves of immigrants who had flooded over the border last summer. She didn't have any family of her own and the people she worked for had no sons around twenty, though he had seen her with a young man early this morning. 'She says her village was Ning-tok. . . .'

It was then that Wu had felt a glow at his stroke of luck. Ning-tok was the same village his own parents had come from and he spoke that dialect.

Now he was twenty paces behind her and he watched her haggle brilliantly for vegetables, selecting only the very best onions and greens, all just a few hours fresh from the fields in the New Territories. She bought very little so he knew that the family she worked for was poor. Then she was standing in front of the poultry stall with its layers of barely alive, scrawny chickens crammed helplessly into cages, their legs tied. The rotund stall owner bartered with her, both sides enjoying the foul language, insults, choosing this bird, then that, then another, prodding them, discarding them, until the bargain was made. Because she was a good, salty trader, the man allowed his profit to be shaved. Then he strangled the bird deftly without thought, tossing the carcass to his five-year-old daughter, who squatted in a pile of feathers and offal, for plucking and cleaning.

'Hey, Mr. Poultryman,' Wu called out, 'I'd like a bird at the same price. That one!' He pointed at a good choice and paid no attention to the man's grumbling. 'Elder Sister,' he said to her politely, 'clearly you have saved me a great deal of cash. Would you like to have a cup of tea while we wait for our birds to be cleaned?'

'Ah thank you, yes, these old bones are tired. We'll go there!' Her gnarled finger pointed to a stall opposite. 'Then we can watch to make sure we get what we paid for.' The poultry man muttered an obscenity and they laughed.

She shoved her way across the street, sat down on a bench, ordered tea and a cake and was soon telling Wu how she hated Hong Kong and living among strangers. It was easy for him to butter her up by using the odd word of Ning-tok patois; then pretending to be equally surprised when she switched to that dialect and told him she came from the same village and oh how wonderful it was to find a neighbor after all these months among foreigners! She told him that she had worked for the same family in Ning-tok ever since she was seven. But, sadly, three years ago her mistress—the child that she had brought up, now an old lady like herself—had died. 'I stayed in the house but it had fallen on hard times. Then last year the famine was bad. Many in the village decided to come to this place. Chairman Mao's people didn't mind, in fact they encouraged us—"Useless Mouths" as they called us. Somehow we got split up and I managed to get over the border and found my way to this place here, penniless, hungry, with no family, no friends, nowhere to turn. At length I got a job and now I work as a cook-*amah* for the family Ch'ung who're street cleaners. The dog bones pay me nothing but my keep and my food and chief wife Ch'ung's a maggot-mouthed hag but soon I'll be rid of all of them! You said your father came here with his family ten years ago?'

'Yes. We owned a field near the bamboo glade beside the river. His name was Wu Cho-tam an—'

'Ah, yes I think I remember the family. Yes, I think so. Yes, and I know the field. My family was Wu Ting-top and their family owned the pharmacy at the crossroads for more than a hundred years.'

'Ah, Honorable Pharmacy Wu? Oh yes of course!' Spectacles Wu did remember the family well. Pharmacy Wu had always been a Maoist sympathizer. Once he had had to flee the Nationalists. In this village of a thousand souls he had been well liked and trusted and he had kept life in the village as calm and as protected from outsiders as he could.

'So, you're one of Wu Cho-tam's sons, Younger Brother!' Ah Tam was saying. 'Eeeee, in the early days it was so wonderful in Ning-tok but for the last years . . . terrible.'

'Yes. We were lucky. Our field was fertile and we tilled the soil like always but after a few years outsiders came and accused all the landowners—as if we were exploiters! We only tilled our own field. Even so, from time to time some landowners were taken away, some shot, so one night ten years ago my father fled with all of us. Now my father is dead but I live with my mother not far away.'

'There were many fleeings and famines in the early days. I hear that now it is better. Did you hear too? Outsiders came, wasn't it? They would come and they would leave. The village is not so bad again, Younger Brother, oh no! Outsiders leave us alone. Yes, they left my mistress and us alone because Father was important and one of chairman Mao's supporters from the beginning. My mistress's name was Fang-ling, she's dead now. There's no collective near us so life is like it's always been, though we all have to study Chairman Mao's Red Book. The village isn't so bad, all my friends are there. . . . Hong Kong is a foul place and my village is home. Life without family is nothing. But now . . .' Then the old woman dropped her voice and chortled, carried away with pleasure. 'But now the gods have favored me. In a month or two I'm going home, home forever. I'll have enough money to retire on and I'll buy the small house at the end of my street and perhaps a little field and . . .'

'Retire?' Wu said, leading her on. 'Who has that sort of money, Elder Sister? You said you were paid nothing th—'

'Ah,' the old woman replied, puffed up. 'I've an important friend.'

'What sort of friend?'

'A very important business friend who needs my help! Because I've been so useful he's promised to give me a huge amount of money—'

'You're making this all up, Elder Sister,' he scoffed. 'Am I a foolish stranger wh—'

'I tell you my friend's so important he can hold the whole island in thrall!'

'There are no such persons!'

'Oh yes there are!' She dropped her voice and whispered hoarsely, 'What about the Werewolves!'

Spectacles Wu gaped at her. 'What?'

She chortled again, delighted with the impact of her confidence. 'Yes.'

The young man took hold of his blown mind and put the pieces quickly back together; if this were true he would get the reward and the promotion and maybe an invitation to join Special Intelligence. 'You're making this up!'

'Would I lie to someone from my own village? My friend's one of them I tell you. He's also a 489 and his Brotherhood's going to be the richest in all Hong Kong.'

'Eeeee, how lucky you are, Elder Sister! And when you see him again please ask if perhaps he can use someone like me. I'm a street fighter by trade though my triad's poor and the leader stupid and a stranger. Is he from Ning-tok?'

525

'No. He's . . . he's my nephew,' she said, and the young man knew it was a lie. 'I'm seeing him later. Yes, he's coming later. He owes me some money.'

'Eeeee, that's good, but don't put it in a bank and certainly not in the Ho-Pak or y—'

'Ho-Pak?' she said suspiciously, her little eyes narrowing suddenly in the creases of her face. 'Why do you mention the Ho-Pak? What has the Ho-Pak to do with me?'

'Nothing, Elder Sister,' Wu said, cursing himself for the slip, knowing her guard was now up. 'I saw the queues this morning, that's all.'

She nodded, not convinced, then saw that her chicken was packaged and ready so she thanked him for the tea and cake and scuttled off, muttering to herself. Most carefully he followed her. From time to time she would look back but she did not see him. Reassured, she went home.

The CIA man got out of his car and walked quickly into police headquarters. The uniformed sergeant at the information desk greeted him. 'Afternoon, Mr. Rosemont.'

'I've an appointment with Mr. Crosse.'

'Yes sir. He's expecting you.'

Sourly Rosemont went to the elevator. The whole goddamn-piss-poor island makes me want to shit, and the goddamn British along with it.

'Hello, Stanley,' Armstrong said. 'What're you doing here?'

'Oh hi, Robert. Gotta meeting with your chief.'

'I've already had that displeasure once today. At 7:01 precisely.' The elevator opened. Rosemont went in and Armstrong followed.

'I hope you've got some good news for Crosse,' Armstrong said with a yawn. 'He's really in a foul mood.'

'Oh? You in this meeting too?'

'Afraid so.'

Rosemont flushed. 'Shit, I asked for a private meeting.'

'I'm private.'

'You sure are, Robert. And Brian, and everyone else. But some bastard isn't.'

Armstrong's humor vanished. 'Oh?'

'No.' Rosemont said nothing more. He knew he had hurt the Englishman but he didn't care. It's the truth, he thought bitterly. The sooner these goddamn limeys open their goddamn eyes the better.

The elevator stopped. They walked down the corridor and were ushered into Crosse's room by Brian Kwok. Rosemont felt the bolts slide home behind him and he thought how goddamn foolish and useless and unnecessary; the man's a knucklehead.

'I asked for a private meeting, Rog.'

'It's private. Robert's very private, Brian is. What can I do for you, Stanley?' Crosse was politely cool.

'Okay, Rog, today I got a long list for you: first, you're personally 100 percent in the creek with me, my whole department, up to the director in Washington himself. I'm told to tell you—among other things—your mole's surpassed himself this time.'

'Oh?'

Rosamont's voice was grating now. 'For starters, we just heard from one of our sources in Canton that Fong-fong and all your lads were hit last night. Their cover's gone—they're blown.' Armstrong and Brian Kwok looked shocked. Crosse was staring back at him and he read nothing in his face. 'Got to be your mole, Rog. Got to be fingered from the tai-pan's AMG papers.'

Crosse looked across at Brian Kwok. 'Use the emergency wireless code. Check it!'

As Brian Kwok hurried out, Rosemont said again, 'They're blown, the poor bastards.'

'We'll check it anyway. Next?'

Rosemont smiled mirthlessly. 'Next: Almost everything that was in the tai-pan's AMG papers's spread around the intelligence community in London—on the wrong side.'

'God curse all traitors,' Armstrong muttered.

'Yeah, that's what I thought, Robert. Next, another little gem—AMG was no accident.'

'What?'

'No one knows the who, but we all know the why. The bike was hit by an auto. No make, no serial number, no witnesses, no nothing yet, but he was hit—and of course, fingered from here.'

'Then why haven't I been informed by Source? Why's the information coming from you?' Crosse asked.

Rosemont's voice sharpened. 'I just got off the phone to London. It's just past 5:00 A.M. there so maybe your people plan to let you know when they get to the office after a nice leisurely bacon and eggs and a goddamn cup of tea!'

Armstrong shot a quick glance at Crosse and winced at the look on his face.

'Your . . . your point's well taken, Stanley,' Crosse said. 'Next?'

'The photos we gave you of the guys who knocked off Voranski . . . what happened?'

'We had their place covered. The two men never reappeared, so I raided the place in the early hours. We went through that whole tenement, room by room, but found no one who looked anything like the photographs. We searched for a couple of hours and there were no secret doors or anything like that. They weren't there. Perhaps your fellow made a mistake. . . .'

'Not this time. Marty Povitz was sure. We had the place staked out soon as we deciphered the address but there was a time when it wasn't all covered, front and back. I think they were tipped, again by your mole.' Rosemont took out a copy of a telex and passed it over. Crosse read it, reddened and passed it over to Armstrong.

Decoded from Director, Washington, to Rosemont, Deputy Director Station Hong Kong: Sinders MI-6 brings orders from Source, London, that you are to go with him Friday to witness the handover of the papers and get an immediate photocopy.

'You'll get your copy in today's mail, Rog,' the American said.

'I can keep this?' Crosse asked.

'Sure. By the way, we have a tail on Dunross too. W—'

Crosse said angrily, 'Would you kindly not interfere with our jurisdiction!'

'I told you you were in Shitsville, Rog!' Tautly Rosemont placed another cable on the table.

Rosemont, Hong Kong. You will hand this cable to Chief of SI personally. Until further orders Rosemont is authorized to proceed independently to assist in the uncovering of the hostile in any way he chooses. He is, however, required to stay within the law and keep you advised personally of what he is doing. Source 8–98/3.

Rosemont saw Crosse bite back an explosion. 'What else've you authorized?' Crosse asked.

'Nothing. Yet. Next: We'll be at the bank on Fri—'

'You know where Dunross's put the files?'

'It's all over town—among the community. I told you your mole's been working overtime.' Abruptly Rosemont flared, 'Come on for chrissake, Rog, you know if you tell a hot item to someone in London, it's all over town! We've all got security problems but yours're worse!' With an effort the American simmered down. 'You could've leveled with me about the Dunross screw-up—it would've saved us all a lot of heartache and a lotta face.'

Crosse lit a cigarette. 'Perhaps. Perhaps not. I was trying to maintain security.'

'Remember me? I'm on our side!'

'Are you?'

'You bet your ass!' Rosemont said it very angrily. 'And if it was up to me I'd have every safety deposit box open before sundown—and the hell with the consequences.'

'Thank God you can't do that.'

'For chrissake we're at war and God only knows what's in those other files. Maybe they'll finger your goddamn mole and then we can get the bastard and give him his!'

'Yes,' Crosse said, his voice a whiplash, 'or maybe there's nothing in the papers at all!'

'What do you mean?'

'Dunross agreed to hand the files over to Sinders on Friday. What if there's nothing in them? Or what if he burned the pages and gives us just the covers? What the hell do we do then?'

Rosemont gaped at him. 'Jesus—is that a possibility?'

'Of course it's a possibility! Dunross's clever. Perhaps they're not there at all, or the vault ones are false or nonexistent. We don't know he put them there, he just says he put them there. Jesus Christ, there're fifty possibilities. You're so smart, you CIA fellows, you tell me which deposit box and I'll open it myself.'

529

'Get the key from the governor. Give me and some of my boys private access for five hours an—'

'Out of the question!' Crosse snarled, suddenly red-faced, and Armstrong felt the violence strongly. Poor Stanley, you're the target today. He suppressed a shudder, remembering the times he had had to face Crosse. He had soon learned that it was easier to tell the man the truth, to tell everything at once. If Crosse ever really went after him in an interrogation, he knew beyond doubt he would be broken. Thank God he's never yet had reason to try, he thought thankfully, then turned his eyes on Rosemont who was flushed with rage. I wonder who Rosemont's informants are, and how he knows for certain that Fong-fong and his team have been obliterated.

'Out of the question,' Crosse said again.

'Then what the hell do we do? Sit on our goddamn lard till Friday?'

'Yes. We wait. We've been ordered to wait. Even if Dunross has torn out pages, or sections, or disposed of whole files, we can't put him in prison—or force him to remember or tell us anything.'

'If the director or Source decides he should be leaned on, there're ways. That's what the enemy'd do.'

Crosse and Armstrong stared at Rosemont. At length Armstrong said coldly, 'But that doesn't make it right.'

'That doesn't make it wrong either. Next: For your ears only, Rog.'

At once Armstrong got up but Crosse motioned him to stay. 'Robert's my ears.' Armstrong hid the laughter that permeated him at so ridiculous a statement.

'No. Sorry, Rog, orders—your brass and mine.'

Armstrong saw Crosse hesitate perfectly. 'Robert, wait outside. When I buzz come back in. Check on Brian.'

'Yes sir.' Armstrong went out and closed the door, sorry that he would not be present for the kill.

'Well?'

The American lit another cigarette. 'Top secret. At 0400 today the whole Ninety-second Airborne dropped into Azerbaijan supported by large units of Delta Force and they've fanned out all along the Iran-Soviet border.' Crosse's eyes widened. 'This was at the direct request of the Shah, in response to massive

530

Soviet military preparations just over the border and the usual Soviet-sponsored riots all over Iran. Jesus, Rog, can't you get some air conditioning in here?' Rosemont mopped his brow. 'There's a security blanket all over Iran now. At 0600 support units landed at Teheran airport. Our Seventh Fleet's heading for the Gulf, the Sixth—that's the Mediterranean—is already at battle stations off Israel, the Second, Atlantic, is heading for the Baltic, NORAD's alerted, NATO's alerted, and all Poseidons are one step from Red.'

'Jesus Christ, what the hell's going on?'

'Khrushchev is making another real play for Iran—always an optimum Soviet target right? He figures he has the advantage. It's right on his own border where his own lines of communication're short and ours huge. Yesterday the Shah's security people uncovered a "democratic socialist" insurrection scheduled to explode in the next few days in Azerbaijan. So the Pentagon's reacting like mashed cats. If Iran gòes so does the whole Persian Gulf, then Saudi Arabia and that wraps up Europe's oil and that wraps up Europe.'

'The Shah's been in trouble before. Isn't this more of your overreacting?'

The American hardened. 'Khrushchev backed down over Cuba—first goddamn time there's been a Soviet backoff—because JFK wasn't bluffing and the only thing Commies understand is force. *Big-massive-honest-to-god-damn force!* The Big K better back off this time too or we'll hand him his head.'

'You'll risk blowing up the whole bloody world ov, r some illiterate, rioting, fanatic nutheads who've probably got some right on their side anyway?'

'I'm not into politics, Rog, only into winning. Iran oil, Persian Gulf oil, Saudi oil're the West's jugular. We're not gonna let the enemy get it.'

'If they want it they'll take it.'

'Not this time, they won't. We're calling the operation Dry Run. The idea's to go in heavy, frighten 'em off and get out fast, quietly, so no one's the wiser except the enemy, and particularly no goddamn liberal fellow-traveler congressman or journalist. The Pentagon figures the Soviets don't believe we could possibly respond so fast, so massively from so far away, so they'll

531

go into shock and run for cover and close everything down—until next time.'

The silence thickened.

Crosse's fingers drummed. 'What am I supposed to do? Why're you telling me this?'

'Because the brass ordered me to. They want all allied chief SIs to know because if the stuff hits the fan there'll be sympathy riots all over, as usual, well-coordinated rent-a-mob riots, and you'll have to be prepared. AMG's papers said that Sevrin had been activated here—maybe there's a tie-in. Besides, you here in Hong Kong are vital to us. You're the back door to China, the back door to Vladivostok and the whole of east Russia—and our best shortcut to their Pacific naval and atomic-sub bases.' Rosemont took out another cigarette, his fingers shaking. 'Listen, Rog,' he said, controlling his grumbling anger, 'let's forget all the interoffice shit, huh? Maybe we can help each other.'

'What atomic subs?' Crosse said with a deliberate sneer, baiting him. 'They haven't got atomic subs yet an—'

'Jesus Christ!' Rosemont flared. 'You guys've got your heads up your asses and you won't listen. You spout détente and try to muzzle us and they're laughing their goddamn heads off. They got nuclear subs and missile sites and naval bases all over the Sea of Okhotsk!' Rosemont got up and went to the huge map of China and Asia that dominated one wall and stabbed the Kamchatka peninsula, north of Japan. '. . . Petropavlovsk, Vladivostok . . . they've giant operations all along this whole Siberian coast, here at Komsomolsk at the mouth of the Amur and on Sakhalin. But Petropavlovsk's the big one. In ten years, that'll be the greatest war-port in Asia with support airfields, atomic-protected subpens and atomic-safe fighter strips and missile silos. And from there they threaten all Asia—Japan, Korea, China, the Philippines—not forgetting Hawaii and our West Coast.'

'U.S. forces are preponderant and always will be. You're overreacting again.'

Rosemont's face closed. 'People call me a hawk. I'm not. Just a realist. They're on a war footing. Our Midas III's have pinpointed all kinds of crap, our . . .' He stopped and almost kicked himself for letting his mouth run on. 'Well, we know a lot of what they're doing right now, and they're not making goddamn ploughshares.'

'I think you're wrong. They don't want war any more than we do.'

'You want proof? You'll get it tomorrow, soon as I've clearance!' the American said, stung. 'If it's proved, can we cooperate better?'

'I thought we were cooperating well now.'

'Will you?'

'Whatever you want. Does Source want me to react in any specific way?'

'No, just to be prepared. I guess this'll all filter down through channels today.'

'Yes.' Crosse was suddenly gentle. 'What's really bothering you, Stanley?'

Rosemont's hostility left him. 'We lost one of our best setups in East Berlin, last night, a lot of good guys. A buddy of mine got his crossing back to us, and we're sure it's tied into AMG.'

'Oh, sorry about that. It wasn't Tom Owen, was it?'

'No. He left Berlin last month. It was Frank O'Connell.'

'Don't think I ever met him. Sad.'

'Listen, Rog, this mole thing's the shits.' He got up and went to the map. He stared at it a long time. 'You know about Iman?'

'Sorry?'

Rosemont's stubby finger stabbed a point on the map. The city was inland, 180 miles north of Vladivostok at a rail junction. 'It's an industrial center, railways, lots of factories.'

'So?' Crosse asked.

'You know about the airfield there?'

'What airfield?'

'It's underground, whole goddamn thing, just out of town, built into a gigantic maze of natural caves. It's got to be one of the wonders of the world. It's atomic capable, Rog. The whole base was constructed by Japanese and Nazi slave labor in '45, '6 and '7. A hundred thousand men they say. It's all underground, Rog, with space for 2,500 airplanes, air crews and support personnel. It's bombproof—even atomic proof—with eighty runways that lead out onto a gigantic airstrip that circles eighteen low hills. It took one of our guys nine hours to drive around it. That was back in '46—so what's it like now?'

'Improved—if it exists.'

'It's operational now. A few guys, intelligence, ours and yours, even a few of the better newspaper guys, knew about it even in '46. So why the silence now? That base alone's a massive threat to all of us and no one screams a shit. Even China, and she sure as hell's got to know about Iman.'

'I can't answer that.'

'I can. I think that info's being buried, deliberately, along with a lot of other things.' The American got up and stretched. 'Jesus, the whole world's falling apart and I got a backache. You know a good chiropractor?'

'Have you tried Doc Thomas on Pedder Street? I use him all the time.'

'I can't stand him. He makes you wait in line—won't give you an appointment. Thank God for chiropractors! Trying to get my son to be one instead of an M.D.'

The phone rang and Crosse answered it.

'Yes Brian?' Rosemont watched Crosse as he listened. 'Just a minute, Brian. Stanley, are we through now?'

'Sure. Just a couple of open, routine things.'

'Right. Brian, come in with Robert as soon as you come up.' Crosse put the phone down. 'We couldn't establish contact with Fong-fong. You're probably correct. They'll be MPD'd or MPC'd in forty-eight hours.'

'I don't understand.'

'Missing Presumed Dead or Missing Presumed Captured.'

'Rough. Sorry to bring bad news.'

'Joss.'

'With Dry Run and AMG, how about pulling Dunross into protective custody?'

'Out of the question.'

'You have the Official Secrets Act.'

'Out of the question.'

'I'm going to recommend it. By the way, Ed Langan's FBI boys tied Banastasio in with Bartlett. He's a big shareholder in Par-Con. They say he supplied the dough for the last merger that put Par-Con into the big time.'

'Anything on the Moscow visas for Bartlett and Tcholok?'

'Best we can find is that they went as tourists Maybe they did, maybe it was a cover.'

'Anything on the guns?' This morning Armstrong had told Crosse of Peter Marlowe's theory and he had ordered an immediate watch on Four Finger Wu and offered a large reward for information.

'The FBI're sure they were put aboard in L.A. It'd be easy—Par-Con's hangar's got no security. They also checked on the serial numbers you gave us. They were all out of a batch that had gotten "mislaid" en route from the factory to Camp Poendleton—that's the Marine depot in southern California. Could be we've stumbled onto a big arms-smuggling racket. Over seven hundred M14s have gotten mislaid in the last six months. Talking about that . . .' He stopped at the discreet knock. He saw Crosse touch the switch. The door opened and Brian Kwok and Armstrong came back in. Crosse motioned them to sit. 'Talking about that, you remember the CARE case?'

'The suspected corruption here in Hong Kong?'

'That's the one. We might have a lead for you.'

'Good. Robert, you were handling that at one time, weren't you?'

'Yes sir.' Robert Armstrong sighed. Three months ago one of the vice-consuls at the U.S. Consulate had asked the CID to investigate the handling of the charity to see whether some light-fingered administrators were involved in a little take-away for personal profit. The digging and interviewing was still proceeding. 'What've you got, Stanley?'

Rosemont searched in his pockets then pulled out a typed note. It contained three names and an address: Thomas K. K. Lim (Foreigner Lim), Mr. Tak Chou-lan (Big Hands Tak), Mr. Lo Tup-lin (Bucktooth Lo), Room 720, Princes Building, Central. 'Thomas K. K. Lim is American, well heeled and well connected in Washington, Vietnam and South America. He's in business with the other two jokers at that address. We got a tip that he's mixed up in a couple of shady deals with AID and that Big Hands Tak is heavy in CARE. It's not in our bailiwick so it's over to you.' Rosemont shrugged and stretched again. 'Maybe it's something. The whole world's on fire but we still gotta deal with crooks! Crazy! I'll keep in touch. Sorry about Fong-fong and your people.'

He left.

Crosse told Armstrong and Brian Kwok briefly what he had

been told about Operation Dry Run.

Brian Kwok said sourly, 'One day one of those Yankee madmen're going to make a mistake. It's stupid putting atomics into hair-trigger situations.'

Crosse looked at them and their guards came up. 'I want that mole. I want him before the CIA uncover him. If they get him first . . .' The thin-faced man was clearly very angry. 'Brian, go and see Dunross. Tell him AMG was no accident and not to go out without our people nearby. In any circumstances. Say I would prefer him to give us the papers early, confidentially. Then he has nothing to fear.'

'Yes sir.' Brian Kwok knew that Dunross would do exactly as he wanted but he kept his mouth shut.

'Our normal riot planning will cover any by-product of the Iran problem and from Dry Run. However, you'd better alert CID an—' He stopped. Robert Armstrong was frowning at the piece of paper Rosemont had given him. 'What is it, Robert?'

'Didn't Tsu-yan have an office at Princes Building?'

'Brian?'

'We've followed him there several times, sir. He visited a business acquaintance. . . .' Brian Kwok searched his memory. '. . . Shipping. Name of Ng, Vee Cee Ng, nicknamed Photographer Ng. Room 721. We checked him out but everything was above board. Vee Cee Ng run Asian and China Shipping and about fifty other small allied businesses. Why?'

'This address's 720. Tsu-yan could tie in with John Chen, the guns, Banastasio, Bartlett—even the Werewolves,' Armstrong said.

Crosse took the paper. After a pause he said, 'Robert, take a team and check 720 and 721 right now.'

'It's not in my area, sir.'

'How right you are!' Crosse said at once, heavy with sarcasm. 'Yes. I know. You're CID Kowloon, Robert, not Central. However, *I* authorize the raid. Go and do it. Now.'

'Yes sir.' Armstrong left, red-faced.

The silence gathered.

Brian Kwok waited, staring stoically at the desk top. Crosse selected a cigarette with care, lit it, then leaned back in his chair. 'Brian. I think Robert's the mole.'

29

Robert Armstrong and a uniformed police sergeant got out of the squad car and headed through the crowds into the vast maw of the Princes Arcade with its jewelry and curio shops, camera shops and radio shops stuffed with the latest electronic miracles, that was on the ground floor of the old-fashioned, high-rise office building in Central. They eased their way toward a bank of elevators, joining the swarm of waiting people. Eventually he and the sergeant squeezed into an elevator. The air was heavy and fetid and nervous. The Chinese passengers watched them obliquely and uncomfortably.

On the seventh floor Armstrong and the sergeant got out. The corridor was dingy and narrow with nondescript office doors on either side. He stood for a moment looking at the board. Room 720 was billed as 'Ping-sing Wah Developments,' 721 as 'Asian and China Shipping.' He walked ponderously down the corridor, Sergeant Yat alongside.

As they turned the corner a middle-aged Chinese wearing a white shirt and dark trousers was coming out of room 720. He saw them, blanched, and ducked back in. When Armstrong got to the door he expected it to be locked but it wasn't and he jerked it open just in time to see the man in the white shirt disappearing out of the back door, another man almost jamming him in equal haste to flee. The back door slammed closed.

Armstrong sighed. There were two rumpled secretaries in the sleazy, untidy office suite of three cramped rooms, and they were gawking at him, one with her chopsticks poised in midair over a bowl of chicken and noodles. The noodles slid off her chopsticks and fell back into the soup.

'Afternoon,' Armstrong said.

The two women gaped at him, then looked at the sergeant and back to him again.

'Where are Mr. Lim, Mr. Tak and Mr. Lo, please?'

One of the girls shrugged and the other, unconcerned, began to eat again. Noisily. The office suite was untidy and unkempt. There were two phones, papers strewn around, plastic cups, dirty plates and bowls and used chopsticks. A teapot and tea cups. Full garbage cans.

Armstrong took out the search warrant and showed it to them.

The girls stared at him.

Irritably Armstrong harshened his voice. 'You speak English?'

Both girls jumped. 'Yes sir,' they chorused.

'Good. Give your names to the sergeant and answer his questions. Th—' At that moment the back door opened again and the two men were herded back into the room by two hard-faced uniformed policemen who had been waiting in ambush. 'Ah, good. Well done. Thank you, Corporal. Now, where were you two going?'

At once the two men began protesting their innocence in voluble Cantonese.

'*Shut up!*' Armstrong snarled. They stopped. 'Give me your names!' They stared at him. In Cantonese he said, 'Give me your names and you'd better not lie or I will become very fornicating angry.'

'He's Tak Chou-lan,' the one with the pronounced buck teeth said, pointing at the other.

'What's your name?'

'Er, Lo Tup-sop, Lord. But I haven't done anyt—'

'Lo Tup-sop? Not Lo Tup-lin?'

'Oh no, Lord Superintendent, that's my brother.'

'Where is he?'

The buck-toothed man shrugged. 'I don't know. Please what's go—'

'Where were you going in such a hurry, Bucktooth Lo?'

'I'd forgotten an appointment, Lord. Oh it was very important. It's urgent and I will lose a fortune, sir, if I don't go immediately. May I now please go, Honored Lo—'

538

'No! Here's my search warrant. We're going to search and take away any papers th—'

At once both men began to protest strenuously. Again Armstrong cut them short. 'Do you want to be taken to the border right now?' Both men blanched and shook their heads. 'Good. Now, where's Thomas K. K. Lim?' Neither answered so Armstrong stabbed his finger at the younger of the two men. 'You, Mr. Bucktooth Lo! Where's Thomas K. K. Lim?'

'In South America, Lord,' Lo said nervously.

'Where?'

'I don't know, sir, he just shares the office. That's his fornicating desk.' Bucktooth Lo waved a nervous hand at the far corner. There was a messy desk and a filing cabinet and a phone there. 'I've done nothing wrong, Lord. Foreigner Lim's a stranger from the Golden Mountain. Fourth Cousin Tak here just rents him space, Lord. Foreigner Lim just comes and goes as it pleases him and is nothing to do with me. Is he a foul criminal? If there's anything wrong I don't know anything about it!'

'Then what do you know about the thieving of funds from the CARE program?'

'Eh?' Both men gaped at him.

'Informers have given us proof you're all thieving charity money that belongs to starving women and children!'

At once both began protesting their innocence.

'Enough! The judge will decide! You will go to headquarters and give statements.' Then he switched back into English once more. 'Sergeant, take them back to headquarters. Corporal, let's st—'

'Honored sir,' Bucktooth Lo began in halting, nervous English, 'if I may to talk, in office, plees?' He pointed at the inner, equally untidy and cluttered office.

'All right.'

Armstrong followed Lo, towering over him. The man closed the door nervously and began talking Cantonese quickly and very quietly. 'I don't know anything about anything criminal, Lord. If something's amiss it's those other two fornicators, I'm just an honest businessman who wants to make money and send his children to university in America an—'

'Yes. Of course. What did you want to say to me privately

539

before you go down to police headquarters?'

The man smiled nervously and went to the desk and began to unlock a drawer. 'If anyone's guilty it's not me, Lord. I don't know anything about anything.' He opened the drawer. It was filled with used, red, 100-dollar notes. They were clipped into thousands. 'If you'll let me go, Lord . . .' He grinned up at him, fingering the notes.

Armstrong's foot lashed out and the drawer slammed and caught Lo's fingertips and he let out a howl of pain. He tore the drawer open with his good hand. 'Oh oh oh my fornic—'

Armstrong shoved his face close to the petrified Chinese. 'Listen, you dogmeat turd, it's against the law to try to bribe a policeman and if you claim your fingers're police brutality I'll personally grind your fornicating Secret Sack to mincemeat!'

He leaned back against the desk, his heart pounding, sickness in his throat, enraged at the temptation and sight of all that money. How easy it would be to take it and pay his debts and have more than enough over to gamble on the market and at the races, and then to leave Hong Kong before it was too late.

So easy. So much more easy to take than to resist—this time or all the other thousand times. There must be 30, 40,000 in that drawer alone. And if there's one drawer full there must be others and if I lean on this bastard he'll cough up ten times this amount.

Roughly he reached out and grabbed the man's hand. Again the man cried out. One fingertip was mashed and Armstrong thought Lo would lose a couple of fingernails and have plenty of pain but that was all. He was angry with himself that he had lost his temper but he was tired and knew it was not just tiredness. 'What do you know about Tsu-yan?'

'*Wat*? Me? Nothing. Tsu-yan who?'

Armstrong grabbed him and shook him. 'Tsu-yan! The gun-runner Tsu-yan!'

'Nothing, Lord!'

'Liar! The Tsu-yan who visits Mr. Ng next door!'

'Tsu-yan? Oh him? Gun-runner? I didn't know he's a gun-runner! I always thought he was a businessman. He's another Northerner like Photographer Ng—'

'Who?'

'Photographer Ng, Lord. Vee Cee Ng from next door. He and

540

this Tsu-yan never come in here or talk to us. . . . Oh I need a doctor . . . oh my han—'

'Where's Tsu-yan now?'

'I don't know, Lord . . . oh my fornicating hand, oh oh oh. . . . I swear by all the gods I don't know him. . . . oh oh oh. . . .'

Irritably Armstrong shoved him in a chair and jerked open the door. The three policemen and two secretaries stared at him silently. 'Sergeant, take this bugger to HQ and charge him with trying to bribe a policeman. Look at this. . . .' He beckoned him in and pointed at the drawer.

Sergeant Yat's eyes widened. *'Dew neh loh moh!'*

'Count it and get both men to sign the amount as correct and take it to HQ with them and turn it in.'

'Yes sir.'

'Corporal, you start going through the files. I'm going next door. I'll be back shortly.'

'Yes sir.'

Armstrong strode out. He knew that this money would be counted quickly, and any other money in the offices—if this drawer was full others would be—then the amount to be turned in would be quickly negotiated by the principals, Sergeant Yat and Lo and Tak, and the rest split among them. Lo and Tak would believe him to be in for a major share and his own men would consider him mad not to be. Never mind. He didn't care. The money was stolen, and Sergeant Yat and his men were all good policemen and their pay totally inadequate for their responsibilities. A little *h'eung yau* wouldn't do them any harm, it would be a godsend.

Won't it?

In China you have to be pragmatic, he told himself grimly as he knocked on the door of 721 and went in. A good-looking secretary looked up from her lunch—a bowl of pure white rice and slivers of roast pork and jet green broccoli steaming nicely.

'Afternoon.' Armstrong flashed his ID card. 'I'd like to see Mr. Vee Cee Ng, please.'

'Sorry, sir,' the girl said, her English good and her eyes blank. 'He's out. Out for lunch.'

'Where?'

'At his club, I think. He—he won't be back today until five.'

'Which club?'

She told him. He had never heard of it but that meant nothing as there were hundreds of private Chinese lunching or dining or mah-jong clubs.

'What's your name?'

'Virginia Tong. Sir,' she added as an afterthought.

'Do you mind if I look around?' He saw her eyes flash nervously. 'Here's my search warrant.'

She took it and read it and he thought, full marks, young lady. 'Do you think you could wait, wait till five o'clock?' she asked.

'I'll take a short look now.'

She shrugged and got up and opened the inner office. It was small and empty but for untidy desks, phones, filing cabinets, shipping posters and sailing schedules. Two inner doors led off it and a back door. He opened one door on the 720 side but it was a dank, evil-smelling toilet and dirty washbasin. The back door was bolted. He slid the bolts back and went onto the dingy back-stairs landing that served as a makeshift fire escape and alternate means of exit. He rebolted it, watched all the time by Virginia Tong. The last door, on the far side, was locked.

'Would you open it please?'

'Mr. Vee Cee has the only key, sir.'

Armstrong sighed. 'I do have a search warrant, Miss Tong and the right to kick the door in, if necessary.'

She stared back at him so he shrugged and stood away from the door and readied to kick it in. Truly.

'Just . . . just a moment, sir,' she stammered. 'I . . . I'll see if there . . . if he left his key before he went out.'

'Good. Thank you.' Armstrong watched her open a desk drawer and pretend to search, then another drawer and another and then, sensing his impatience, she found a key under a money box. 'Ah, here it is!' she said as though a miracle had happened. He noticed she was perspiring now. Good, he thought. She unlocked the door and stood back. This door opened directly onto another. Armstrong opened it and whistled involuntarily. The room beyond was large, luxurious, thick-carpeted with elegant suede leather sofas and rosewood furniture and fine paintings. He wandered in. Virginia Tong watched from the doorway. The fine antique rosewood, tooled

542

leather desk was bare and clean and polished, a bowl of flowers on it, and some framed photographs, all of a beaming Chinese leading in a garlanded racehorse, and one of the same Chinese in dinner jacket shaking hands with the governor, Dunross nearby.

'That's Mr. Ng?'

'Yes sir.'

Top-quality hi-fi and record player were to one side, and a tall cocktail cabinet. Another doorway let off this room. He pushed the half-opened door aside. An elegant, very feminine bedroom with a huge, unmade king-sized bed, mirror-lined ceiling and a decorator's bathroom off it, with perfumes, aftershave lotions, gleaming modern fittings and many buckets of water.

'Interesting,' he said and looked at her.

She said nothing, just waited.

Armstrong saw that she had nylon-clad legs and was very trim with well-groomed nails and hair. I'll bet she's a dragon, and expensive. He turned away from her and looked around thoughtfully. Clearly this self-contained apartment had been made out of the adjoining suite. Well, he told himself with a touch of envy, if you're rich and you want a private, secret flat for an afternoon's nooky behind your office there's no law against that. None. And none against having an attractive secretary. Lucky bastard. I wouldn't mind having one of these places myself.

Absently he opened a desk drawer. It was empty. All the drawers were empty. Then he went through the bedroom drawers but found nothing of interest. One cupboard contained a fine camera and some portable lighting equipment and cleaning equipment but nothing suspicious.

He came back into the main room satisfied that he had missed nothing. She was still watching him, and though she tried to hide it, he could sense a nervousness.

That's understandable, he told himself. If I were her and my boss was out and some rotten *quai loh* came prying I'd be nervous too. No harm in having a private place like this. Lots of rich people have them in Hong Kong. His eye was caught by the rosewood cocktail cabinet. The key in the lock beckoned him. He opened it. Nothing out of the ordinary. Then his sharp, well-trained eyes noticed the untoward width of the doors. A moment's inspection and he opened the false doors. His mouth dropped open.

The side walls of the cabinet were covered with dozens of photographs of Jade Gates in all their glory. Each photograph was neatly framed and tagged with a typed name and a date. Involuntarily he let out a bellow of embarrassed laughter, then glanced around. Virginia Tong had vanished. Quickly he scanned the names. Hers was third from the last.

Another paroxysm of laughter was barely contained. The policeman shook his head helplessly. What some buggers'll do for fun—and I suppose some ladies for money! I thought I'd seen it all but this . . . Photographer Ng, eh? So that's where the nickname came from.

Now over his initial shock, he studied the photographs. Each of them had been taken with the same lens from the same distance.

Good God, he thought after a minute, astounded, there's really quite a lot of difference between . . . I mean if you can forget what you're looking at and just look, well, there's a fantastic amount of difference in the shape and size of the whole, the position and protuberance of the Pearl on the Step, the quality and quantity of pubicity and . . . *ayeeyah* there's one piece *bat jam gai*. He looked at the name. Mona Leung—now where have I heard that name before? That's curious—Chinese usually consider lack of pubicity unlucky. Now why . . . oh my God! He peered at the next name tag to make sure. There was no mistake. Venus Poon. *Ayeeyah*, he thought elatedly, so that's hers, that's what she really looks like, the darling of the telly who daily projects such sweet, virginal innocence so beautifully!

He concentrated on her, his senses bemused. I suppose if you compare hers with, say, say Virginia Tong's, well she does have a certain delicacy. Yes, but if you want my considered opinion I'd still rather have had the mystery and not seen these at all. None of them.

Idly his eyes went from name to name. 'Bloody hell,' he said, recognizing one: Elizabeth Mithy. She was once a secretary at Struan's, one of the band of wanderers from the small towns in Australia and New Zealand, girls who aimlessly found their way to Hong Kong for a few weeks, to stay for months, perhaps years, to fill minor jobs until they married or vanished forever. I'll be damned. Liz Mithy!

Armstrong was trying to be dispassionate but he could not help comparing Caucasian with Chinese and he found no difference. Thank God for that, he told himself, and chuckled. Even so he was glad the photographs were black and white and not in color.

'Well,' he said out loud, still very embarrassed, 'there's no law against taking photos that I know of, and sticking them in your own cabinet. The young ladies must've cooperated. . . .' He grunted, amused and at the same time disgusted. Damned if I'll ever understand the Chinese! 'Liz Mithy, eh?' he muttered. He had known her slightly when she was in the Colony, knew that she was quite wild, but what could have possessed her to pose for Ng? If her old man knew, he'd hemorrhage. Thank God we don't have children, Mary and I.

Be honest, you bleed for sons and daughters but you can't have them, at least Mary can't, so the doctors say—so you can't.

With an effort Armstrong buried that everlasting curse again and relocked the cabinet and walked out, closing the doors after him.

In the outer office Virginia Tong was polishing her nails, clearly furious.

'Can you get Mr. Ng on the phone, please?'

'No, not until four,' she said sullenly without looking at him.

'Then please call Mr. Tsu-yan instead,' Armstrong told her, stabbing in the dark.

Without looking up the number, she dialed, waited impatiently, chatted gutturally for a moment in Cantonese and slammed the phone down. 'He's away. He's out of town and his office doesn't know where he is.'

'When did you last see him?'

'Three or four days ago.' Irritably she opened her appointments calendar and checked it. 'It was Friday.'

'Can I look at that please?'

She hesitated, shrugged and passed it over, then went back to polishing her nails.

Quickly he scanned the weeks and the months. Lots of names he knew: Richard Kwang, Jason Plumm, Dunross—Dunross several times—Thomas K. K. Lim—the mysterious American

Chinese from next door—Johnjohn from the Victoria Bank, Donald McBride, Mata several times. Now who's Mata? he asked himself, never having heard the name before. He was about to give the calendar back to her when he flipped forward. 'Saturday 10:00 A.M.—V. Banastasio.' His heart twisted. This coming Saturday.

He said nothing, just put the appointment calendar back on her desk, and leaned back against one of the files, lost in thought. She paid no attention to him. The door opened.

'Excuse me, sir, phone for you!' Sergeant Yat said. He was looking much happier so Armstrong knew the negotiation must have been fruitful. He would have liked to know how much, exactly, but then, face would be involved and he would have to take action, one way or another.

'All right, Sergeant, stay here till I get back,' he said, wanting to make sure no secret phone calls were made. Virginia Tong did not look up as he left.

In the other office Bucktooth Lo was still moaning, nursing his hand, and the other man, Big Hands Tak, was pretending to be nonchalant, going through some papers, loudly berating his secretary for her inefficiency. As he came in both men started loudly protesting their continued innocence and Lo groaned with increasing vigor.

'Quiet! Why did you jam your fingers in the drawer?' Armstrong asked and added without waiting for a reply, 'People who try to bribe honest policemen deserve to be deported at once.' In the aghast silence he picked up the phone. 'Armstrong.'

'Hello, Robert, this is Don, Don Smyth at East Aberdeen . . .'

'Oh, hello!' Armstrong was startled, not expecting to hear from the Snake, but he kept his voice polite though he loathed him and loathed what he was suspected of doing within his jurisdiction. It was one thing for constables and the lower ranks of Chinese police to supplement their income from illicit gambling. It was another for a British officer to sell influence, and to squeeze like an old-fashioned Mandarin. But though almost everyone believed Smyth was on the make, there was no proof, he had never been caught, and had never been investigated. Rumor had it that he was protected by certain VIP individuals who were deeply involved with him as well as in their own graft. 'What's up?' he asked.

'Had a bit of luck. I think. You're heading up the John Chen kidnapping, aren't you?'

'That's right.' Armstrong's interest soared. Smyth's graft had nothing to do with the quality of his police work—East Aberdeen had the lowest crime rate in the Colony. 'Yes. What've you got?'

Smyth told him about the old *amah* and what had happened with Sergeant Mok and Spectacles Wu, then added, 'He's a bright young chap, that, Robert. I'd recommend him for SI if you want to pass it on. Wu followed the old bird back to her fairly filthy lair, then called us. He obeys orders too, which is rare these days. On a hunch I told him to wait around and if she came out, to follow her. What do you think?'

'A twenty-four-carat lead!'

'What's your pleasure? Wait, or pull her in for real questioning?'

'Wait. I'll bet the Werewolf never comes back but it's worth waiting until tomorrow. Keep the place under surveillance and keep me posted.'

'Good. Oh very good!'

Armstrong heard Smyth chortle down the phone and he could not think why he was so happy. Then he remembered the huge reward that the High Dragons had offered. 'How's your arm?'

'It's my shoulder. Bloody thing's dislocated and I lost my favorite sodding hat. Apart from that everything's fine. Sergeant Mok's going through all our mug shots now and I've got one of my lads doing an Identi-Kit on him—I think I even saw the sod myself. His face is quite pockmarked. If we've got him on file we'll have him nailed by sundown.'

'Excellent. How's it going down there?'

'Everything under control but it's bad. The Ho-Pak's still paying out but too slowly—everyone knows they're stalling. I hear it's the same all over the Colony. They're finished, Robert. The queue'll go on till every last cent's out. There's another run on the Vic here and no letup in the crowds. . . .'

Armstrong gasped. 'The Vic?'

'Yes, they're handing out cash by the bagful and taking nothing in. Triads are swarming . . . the pickings must be huge. We

547

arrested eight pickpockets and busted up twenty-odd fights. I'd say it's very bad.'

'Surely the Vic's okay?'

'Not in Aberdeen it isn't, old lad. Me, I'm liquid. I've closed all my accounts. I took every cent out. I'm all right. If I were you I'd do the same.'

Armstrong felt queasy. His life's savings were in the Victoria. 'The Vic's got to be all right. All the government funds're in it.'

'Right you are. But nothing in their constitution says your money's protected too. Well, I've got to get back to work.'

'Yes. Thanks for the info. Sorry about your shoulder.'

'I thought I was going to have my bloody head bashed in. The sods'd just started the old "kill the *quai loh*" bit. I thought I was a goner.'

Armstrong shivered in spite of himself. Ever since the '56 riots it was a recurring nightmare of his that he was back in that insane, screaming mob again. It was in Kowloon. The mob had just overturned the car with the Swiss consul and his wife in it and set it afire. He and other policemen had charged through the mob to rescue them. When they got to the car the man was already dead and the young wife afire. By the time they'd dragged her out, all her clothes had burned off her and her skin came away like a pelt. And all around, men, women and young people were raving, '*Kill the quai loh . . .*'

He shivered again, his nostrils still smelling burned flesh. 'Christ, what a bastard!'

'Yes, but all in the day's work. I'll keep you posted. If that bloody Werewolf comes back to Aberdeen he'll be in a net tighter than a gnat's arsehole.'

30

Phillip Chen stopped flipping through his mail, his face suddenly ashen. The envelope was marked, 'Mr. Phillip Chen to open personally.'

'What is it?' his wife asked.

'It's from them.' Shakily he showed it to her. 'The Werewolves.'

'Oh!' They were at their lunch table that was set haphazardly in a corner of the living room of the house far up on the crest of Struan's Lookout. Nervously she put down her coffee cup. 'Open it, Phillip. But, but better use your handkerchief in . . . in case of fingerprints,' she added uneasily.

'Yes, yes of course, Dianne, how stupid of me!' Phillip Chen was looking very old. His coat was over his chair and his shirt damp. There was a slight breeze from the open window behind him but it was hot and humid and a brooding afternoon haze had settled over the Island. Carefully he used an ivory paper knife and unfolded the paper. 'Yes, it's . . . it's from the Werewolves. It's . . . it's about the ransom.'

'Read it out.'

'All right: "To Phillip Chen, compradore of the Noble House, greetings. I beg to inform you now how the ransom money is to be paid. 500,000 to you is as meaningless as a pig's scream in a slaughterhouse but to us poor farmers would be a heritage for our star—"'

'Liars!' Dianne hissed, her lovely gold and jade necklace glittering in a shaft of muted sunlight. 'As if farmers would kidnap John or mutilate him like that. Dirty stinky foreign triads! Go on, Phillip.'

549

'''. . . would be a heritage for our starving grandchildren. That you have already consulted the police is to us like pissing in the ocean. But now you will not consult. No. Now you will keep secret or the safety of your son will be endangered and he will not return and everything bad will be your own fault. Beware, our eyes are everywhere. If you try to betray us, the worst will happen and everything will be your own fault. Tonight at six o'clock I will phone you. Tell no one, not even your wife. Meanw—'''

'Dirty triads! Dirty whores' sons to try to spread trouble between husband and wife,' Dianne said angrily.

'''. . . meanwhile prepare the ransom money in used 100-dollar notes. . . .'''' Irritably Phillip Chen glanced at his watch. 'I don't have much time to get to the bank. I'll have—'

'Finish the letter!'

'All right, be patient, my dear,' he said placatingly, his over-taxed heart skipping a beat as he recognized the edge to her voice. 'Where was I? Ah yes, ''. . . notes. If you obey my instructions faithfully, you may have your son back to-night. . . .'' Oh God I hope so,' he said, breaking off momentarily, then continued, '''Do not consult the police or try to trap us. Our eyes are watching you even now. Written by the Were-wolf.''' He took off his glasses. His eyes were red-rimmed and tired. Sweat was on his brow. '''Watching you even now?'' Could one of the servants . . . or the chauffeur be in their pay?'

'No, no of course not. They've all been with us for years.'

He wiped the sweat off, feeling dreadful, wanting John back, wanting him safe, wanting to strangle him. 'That means nothing. I'd . . . I'd better call the police.'

'Forget them! Forget them until we know what you have to do. Go to the bank. Get 200,000 only—you should be able to settle for that. If you get more you might be tempted to give it all to them if tonight . . . if they really mean what they say.'

'Yes . . . very wise. If we could settle for that . . .' He hesitated. 'What about the tai-pan? Do you think I should tell the tai-pan, Dianne? He, he might be able to help.'

'Huh!' she said scornfully. 'What help can he give us? We're dealing with dog-bone triads not foreign devil crooks. If we need help we have to stay with our own.' Her eyes began boring into him. 'And now you'd better tell me what's really the matter, why you were so angry the night before last and why you've been like a spiteful cat with a thorn in its rump ever since and not attending to business!'

'I've been attending to business,' he said defensively.

'How many shares have you bought? Eh? Struan shares? Have you taken advantage of what the tai-pan told us about the coming boom? Do you remember what Old Blind Tung forecast?'

'Of course, of course I remember!' he stuttered. 'I've, I've secretly doubled our holdings and have equally secret orders out with various brokers for half as much again.'

Dianne Chen's abacus mind glowed at the thought of that vast profit, and all the private profit she would be making on all the shares she had bought on her own behalf, pledging her entire portfolio. But she kept her face cold and her voice icy. 'And how much did you pay?'

'They averaged out at 28.90.'

'Huh! According to today's paper Noble House opened at 28.80,' she said with a disapproving sniff, furious that he had paid five cents a share less than she had. 'You should have been at the market this morning instead of moping around here, sleeping your life away.'

'I wasn't feeling very well, dear.'

'It all goes back to the night before last. What sent you into that unbelievable rage? *Heya?*'

'It was nothing.' He got up, hoping to flee. 'Noth—'

'Sit down! *Nothing* that you shouted at me, me your faithful wife in front of the servants? *Nothing* that I was ordered into my own dining room like a common whore? *Heya?*' Her voice began rising and she let herself go, knowing instinctively that this was the perfect time, now that they were alone in the house, knowing that he was defenseless and she could press her advantage. 'You think it's nothing that you abuse me, me who has given you the best years of her life, working and slaving and guarding you for twenty-three years? Me, Dianne Mai-wei T'Chung who has the blood of the great Dirk Struan in her veins, who came to you virgin, with property in Wanchai, North Point and even on Lan Tao, with stocks and shares and the best schooling in England? Me who never complains about your snoring and whoring or about the brat you sired out of that dance-hall girl

551

you've sent to school in America!'

'Eh?'

'Oh I know all about you and her and all the others and all the other nasty things you do, and that you never loved me but just wanted my property and a perfect decoration to your drab life. . . .'

Phillip Chen was trying to close his ears but he could not. His heart was pounding. He hated rows and hated the shriek to her voice that, somehow, was perfectly tuned to set his teeth on edge, his brain oscillating and his bowels in turmoil. He tried to interrupt her but she overrode him, battering him, accusing him of all sorts of dalliances and mistakes and private matters that he was shocked she knew about.

'. . . and what about your club?'

'Eh, what club?'

'The private Chinese lunch club with forty-three members called the 74 in a block off Pedder Street that contains a gourmet chef from Shanghai, teen-age hostesses and bedrooms and saunas and devices that dirty old men need to raise their Steam-less Stalks? Eh?'

'It's nothing like that at all,' Phillip Chen spluttered, aghast that she knew. 'It's a pl—'

'Don't lie to me! You put up 87,000 good U.S. greenbacks as the down payment with Shitee T'Chung and those two mealy-mouthed friends of yours and even now pay 4,000 HK-a-month fees. Fees for what? You'd better . . . Where do you think you're going?'

Meekly he sat down again. 'I—I was—I want to go to the bathroom.'

'Huh! Whenever we have a discussion you want the bath-room! You're just ashamed of the way you treat me and guilty. . . .' Then, seeing him about to explode back at her, she switched abruptly, her voice crooningly gentle. 'Poor Phillip! Poor boy! Why were you so angry? Who's hurt you?'

So he told her, and once he began the telling he felt better and his anguish and fear and fury started to melt away. Women are clever and cunning in these things, he told himself confidently, rushing on. He told her about opening John's safety deposit in the bank, about the letters to Linc Bartlett and about finding a duplicate key to his own safe in their bedroom. 'I brought all the letters back,' he said, almost in tears, 'they're upstairs, you can read them for yourself. My own son! He's betrayed us!'

'My God, Phillip,' she gasped, 'if the tai-pan found out you and Father Chen-chen were keeping . . . if he knew he'd ruin us!'

'Yes, yes I know! That's why I've been so upset! By the rules of Dirk's legacy he has the right and the means. We'd be ruined. But, but that's not all. John knew where our secret safe was in the garden an—'

'*Wat?*'

'Yes, and he dug it up.' He told her about the coin.

'*Ayeeyah!*' She stared at him in absolute shock, half her mind filled with terror, the other half with ecstasy, for now, whether John came back or not, he had destroyed himself. John would never inherit now! My Kevin's Number One Son now and future compradore to the Noble House! Then her fears drowned her excitement and she muttered, aghast, 'If there's still a House of Chen.'

'What? What did you say?'

'Nothing, never mind. Wait a moment, Phillip, let me think. Oh the rotten boy! How could John do this to us, we who have cherished him all his life! You . . . you'd better go to the bank. Get 300,000 out—in case you need to barter more. We must get John back at all costs. Would he keep the coin with him, on him, or would it be in his other safety deposit box?'

'It'd be in the box—or hidden at his flat in Sinclair Towers.'

Her face closed. 'How can we search that place with *her* in residence? That wife of his? That strumpet Barbara! If she suspects we're after something . . .' Her mind caught a vagrant thread. 'Phillip, does it mean, *whoever* presents the coin gets whatever they want?'

'Yes.'

'Eeeeee! What power!'

'Yes.'

Now her mind was working cleanly. 'Phillip,' she said, in control again, everything else forgotten, 'we need all the help we can get. Phone your cousin Four Fingers . . .' He looked at her, startled, then began to smile. '. . . arrange with him to have some of his street fighters follow you secretly to protect you when you pay over the ransom, then to follow the Werewolf to his lair and to rescue John whatever the cost. Whatever you do don't tell him about the coin—just that you want help to rescue poor John. That's it. We must get poor John back at all costs.'

'Yes,' he replied, much happier now. 'Four Fingers is the perfect choice. He owes us a favor or two. I know where I can reach him this afternoon.'

'Good. Off you go to the bank, but give me the key to the safe. I'll cancel my hairdressing appointment and I'll read John's papers at once.'

'Very good.' He got up immediately. 'The key's upstairs,' he said, lying, and hurried out, not wanting her prying into the safe. There were a number of things there he did not want her to know about. I'd better hide them somewhere else, he thought uneasily, just in case. His euphoria evaporated and his over-whelming anxiety returned. Oh my poor son, he told himself near tears. Whatever possessed you? I was a good father to you and you'll always be my heir and I've loved you like I loved your mother. Poor Jennifer, poor little thing, dying birthing my first-born son. O all gods: let me get my poor son back again, safe again, whatever he's done, let us extract ourselves from all this madness, and I'll endow a new temple for all of you equally!

The safe was behind the brass bedstead. He pulled it away from the wall, opened the safe and took out all of John's papers, then his very private deeds, letters and promissory notes which he stuffed into his coat pocket and went downstairs again.

'Here are John's letters,' he said. 'I thought I'd save you the trouble of moving the bed.'

She noticed the bulge in his coat pocket but said nothing.

'I'll be back by 5:30 P.M. sharp.'

'Good. Drive carefully,' she said absently, her whole being concentrated on a single problem—how to get the coin for Kevin and herself. Secretly.

The phone rang. Phillip Chen stopped at the front door as she picked it up. '*Weyyyy?*' Her eyes glazed. 'Oh hello, tai-pan, how're you today?' Phillip Chen blanched.

'Just fine thank you,' Dunross said. 'Is Phillip there?'

'Yes, yes just a minute.' She could hear many voices behind Dunross's voice and she thought she heard an undercurrent of covered urgency which increased her dread. 'Phillip, it's for you,' she said, trying to keep the nervousness out of her voice.

'The tai-pan!' She held up the phone, motioning him silently to keep the earpiece a little away from his ear so she could hear too.

'Yes, tai-pan?'

'Hello, Phillip. What're your plans this afternoon?'

'Nothing particular. I was just leaving to go to the bank, why?'

'Before you do that, drop by the exchange. The market's gone mad. The run on the Ho-Pak's Colony-wide now and the stock's teetering even though Richard's supporting it for all he's worth. Any moment it'll crash. The run's spilling over to lots of other banks, I hear—the Ching Prosperity, even the Vic . . .' Phillip Chen and his wife glanced at each other, perturbed. 'I heard the Vic's got problems at Aberdeen and at Central. Everything's down, all our blue chips: the V and A, Kowloon Investments, Hong Kong Power, Rothwell-Gornt, Asian Properties, H.K.L.F., Zong Securities, Solomon Textiles, us . . . everyone.'

'How many points are we off?'

'From this morning? Three points.'

Phillip Chen gasped and almost dropped the phone. 'What?'

'Yes,' Dunross agreed pleasantly. 'Someone's started rumors about us. It's all over the market that we're in trouble, that we can't pay Toda Shipping next week—nor the Orlin installment. I think now we're being sold short.'

31

Gornt was sitting beside his stockbroker, Joseph Stern, in the exchange watching the big board delightedly. It was warm and very humid in the large room that was packed and noisy, phones ringing, sweating brokers, Chinese clerks and runners. Normally the exchange was calm and leisurely. Today it was not. Everyone was tense and concentrating. And uneasy. Many had their coats off.

Gornt's own stock was off a point but that did not bother him a bit. Struan's was down 3.50 now and Ho-Pak tottering. Time's running out for Struan's, he thought, everything's primed, everything's begun. Bartlett's money had been put into his Swiss bank within the hour, no strings—just 2 million transferred from an unknown account to his. Seven phone calls began the rumors. Another call to Japan confirmed the accuracy of the Struan payment dates. Yes, he thought, the attack's begun.

His attention went to the Ho-Pak listing on the board as some more sell offerings were written up by a broker. There were no immediate buyers.

Since he had secretly started selling Ho-Pak short on Monday just before the market closed at three o'clock—long before the run had started in earnest—he was millions ahead. On Monday the stock had sold at 28.60, and now, even with all the support Richard Kwang was giving it, it was down to 24.30—off more points than the stock had moved ever since the bank was formed eleven years ago.

4.30 times 500,000 makes 2,150,000, Gornt was thinking happily, all in honest-to-God HK currency if I wanted to buy back right now which isn't bad for forty-eight hours of labor. But I won't buy back in yet, oh dear no. Not yet. I'm sure now that the stock will crash, if not today, tomorrow, Thursday. If not then, Friday—Monday at the latest, for no bank in the world can sustain such a run. Then, when the crash comes I'll buy back in at a few cents on the dollar and make twenty times half a million.

'Sell 200,000,' he said, beginning to sell short openly now— the other shares hidden carefully among his secret nominees.

'Good God, Mr. Gornt,' his stockbroker gasped. 'The Ho-Pak'll have to put up almost 5 million to cover. That'll rock the whole market.'

'Yes,' he said jovially.

'We'll have a hell of a time borrowing the stock.'

'Then do it.'

Reluctantly his stockbroker began to leave but one of the phones rang. 'Yes? Oh hello, Daytime Chang,' he said in passable Cantonese. 'What can I do for you?'

'I hope you can save all my money, Honorable Middleman. What is Noble House selling for?'

'25.30.'

There was a screech of dismay. 'Woe woe woe, there's barely half a dog-bone hour of trading left, woe woe woe! Please sell! Please sell all Noble House companies at once, Noble House, Good Luck Properties and Golden Ferry, also . . . what's Second Great Company selling at?'

'23.30.'

'Ayeeyah, one point off from this morning? All gods bear witness to foul joss! Sell. Please to sell everything at once!'

'But Daytime Chang, the market's really quite sound an—'

'At once! Haven't you heard the rumors? Noble House will crash! Eeeee, sell, waste not a minute! Hold a moment, my associate Fung-tat wants to talk to you too.'

'Yes, Third Toiletmaid Fung?'

'Just like Daytime Chang, Honorable Middleman! Sell! Before I'm lost! Sell and call us back with prices oh oh oh! Please hurry!'

He put the phone down. This was the fifth panic call he had had from old customers and he did not like it at all. Stupid to panic, he thought, checking his stock. Between the two of them, Daytime Chang and Third Toiletmaid Fung had invested over 40,000 HK in various stocks. If he sold now they would be ahead, well ahead, but for the Struan losses today which would shave off most of their profit.

Joseph Stern was head of the firm of Stern and Jones that had been in Hong Kong for fifty years. They had become stock-brokers only since the war. Before that they were money-lenders, dealers in foreign exchange and ship's chandlers. He was a small, dark-haired man, mostly bald, in his sixties, and many people thought he had Chinese blood in him a few generations back.

He walked to the front of the board and stopped beside the column that listed Golden Ferry. He wrote down the combined Chang and Fung holdings in the sell column. It was a minor offering.

'I'll buy at 30 cents off listing,' a broker said.

'There's no run on Golden Ferry,' he said sharply.

'No, but it's a Struan company. Yes or no?'

'You know very well Golden Ferry's profits are up this quarter.'

'Tough titty! Christ, isn't it bloody hot? Don't you think we could afford air conditioning in the exchange? Is it yes or no, old chap?'

Joseph Stern thought a moment. He did not want to fuel the nervousness. Only yesterday Golden Ferry had soared a dollar because all the business world knew their annual meeting was next week, it had been a good year and it was rumored there was going to be stock split. But he knew the first rule of all exchanges: yesterday has nothing to do with today. The client had said, Sell.

'20 cents off market?' he asked.

'30. Last offer. What the hell do you care, you still get paid. Is it 30 off?'

'All right.' Stern worked his way down the board, selling most of their stocks without trouble though each time he had to concede on price. With difficulty he borrowed the Ho-Pak stock. Now he stopped at the column listing the bank. There were many sell orders. Most of them were small figures. He wrote 200,000 at the bottom of the list in the sell column. A shock wave went through the room. He paid no attention, just looked at Forsythe, who was Richard Kwang's broker. Today he was the only buyer of Ho-Pak.

'Is Quillan trying to wreck the Ho-Pak?' a broker asked.

'It's already under siege. Do you want to buy the shares?'

'Not on your bloody life! Are you selling Struan short too?'

'No. No I'm not.'

'Christ, I don't like this at all.'

'Keep calm, Harry,' someone else said. 'The market's come alive for once, that's all that counts.'

'Great day, what?' another broker said to him. 'Is the crash on? I'm totally liquid myself, sold out this morning. Is it going to be a crash?'

'I don't know.'

'Shocking about Struan's, isn't it?'

'Do you believe all the rumors?'

'No, of course not, but one word to the wise is sufficient they say, what?'

'I don't believe it.'

'Struan's off 3½ points in one day, old boy, a lot of people believe it,' another broker said. 'I sold out my Struan's this morning. Will Richard sustain the run?'

'That's in the hands of . . .' Joseph Stern was going to say God but he knew that Richard Kwang's future was in the hands of his depositors and that they had already decided. 'Joss,' he said sadly.

'Yes. Thank God we get our commissions either way, feast or famine, jolly good, what?'

'Jolly good,' Stern echoed, privately loathing, the smug, self-satisfied upper-class English accent of the exclusive British public schools, schools that, because he was Jewish, he had never been able to attend. He saw Forsythe put the phone down and look at the board. Once more he tapped his offering. Forsythe beckoned him. He walked through the throng, eyes watching him.

'Are you buying?' he asked.

'In due course, Joseph, old boy!' Forsythe added softly. 'Between you and me, can't you get Quillan off our backs? I've reason to believe he's in cahoots with that berk Southerby.'

'Is that a public accusation?'

'Oh come on, it's a private opinion, for chrissake! Haven't you read Haply's column? Tai-pans and a big bank spreading rumors? You know Richard's sound. Richard's as sound as . . . as the Rothschilds! You know Richard's got over a billion in res—'

'I saw the crash of '29, old chap. There were trillions in reserve then but even so everyone went broke. It's a matter of cash, credit and liquidity. And confidence. You'll buy our offering, yes or no?'

'Probably.'

'How long can you keep this up?'

Forsythe looked at him. 'Forever. I'm just a stockbroker. I just follow orders. Buy or sell I make a quarter of one percent.'

'If the client pays.'

'He has to. We have his stock, eh? We have rules. But while I think of it, go to hell.'

Stern laughed. 'I'm British, I'm going to heaven, didn't you know?' Uneasily, he walked back to his desk. 'I think he'll buy before the market closes.'

It was a quarter to three. 'Good,' Gornt said. 'Now I wa—' He stopped. They both looked back as there was an undercurrent. Dunross was escorting Casey and Linc Bartlett to the desk of Alan Holdbrook—Struan's in-house broker—on the other side of the hall.

'I thought he'd left for the day,' Gornt said with a sneer.

'The tai-pan never runs away from trouble. It's not in his nature.' Stern watched them thoughtfully. 'They look pretty friendly. Perhaps the rumors are all wrong and Ian'll make the Par-Con deal and make the payments.'

'He can't. That deal's going to fall through,' Gornt said. 'Bartlett's no fool. Bartlett'd be mad to throw in with that tottering empire.'

'I didn't even know until a few hours ago that Struan's were indebted to the Orlin Bank. Or that the Toda payments were due in a week or so. Or the even more nonsensical rumor that the Vic won't support the Noble House. Lot of nonsense. I called Havergill and that's what he said.'

'What else would he say?'

After a pause, Stern said, 'Curious that all that news surfaced today.'

'Very. Sell 200,000 Struan's.'

Stern's eyes widened and he plucked at his bushy eyebrows. 'Mr. Gornt, don't you think th—'

'No. Please do as I ask.'

'I think you're wrong this time. The tai-pan's too clever. He'll get all the support he needs. You'll get burned.'

'Times change. People change. If Struan's have extended themselves and can't pay . . . Well, my dear fellow, this's Hong Kong and I hope the buggers go to the wall. Make it 300,000.'

'Sell at what figure, Mr. Gornt?'

'At market.'

'It'll take time to borrow the shares. I'll have to sell in much smaller lots. I'll hav—'

'Are you suggesting my credit's not good enough or you can't perform normal stockbroking functions?'

'No. No of course not,' Stern replied, not wanting to offend his biggest customer.

'Good, then sell Struan's short. Now.'

Gornt watched him walk away. His heart was beating nicely.

Stern went to Sir Luis Basilio of the old stockbroking firm of Basilio and Sons, who had a great block of Struan's personally, as well as many substantial clients with more. He borrowed the stock then walked to the board and wrote the huge offering in the sell column. The chalk scraped loudly. Gradually the room fell silent. Eyes switched to Dunross and Alan Holdbrook and the Americans, then to Gornt and back to Dunross again. Gornt saw Linc Bartlett and Casey watching him and he was glad she was there. Casey was wearing a yellow silk skirt and blouse, very Californian, a green scarf tying her golden hair back. Why is she so sexual, Gornt asked himself absently. A strange invitation seemed to surround her. Why? Is it because no man yet has ever satisfied her?

He smiled at her, nodding slightly. She half-smiled back and he thought he noticed a shadow there. His greeting to Bartlett was polite and returned equally politely. His eyes held Dunross and the two men stared at each other.

The silence mounted. Someone coughed nervously. Everyone was conscious of the immensity of the offering and the implications of it.

Stern tapped his offering again. Holdbrook leaned forward and consulted with Dunross who half shrugged and shook his head, then began talking quietly to Bartlett and Casey.

Joseph Stern waited. Then someone offered to buy a portion and they haggled back and forth. Soon, 50,000 shares had changed hands and the new market price was 24.90. He changed the 300,000 to 250,000 and again waited. He sold a few more but the bulk remained. Then, as there were no takers, he came back to his seat. He was sweating.

'If that number stays there overnight it'll do Struan's no good at all.'

'Yes.' Gornt still watched Casey. She was listening intently to Dunross. He sat back and thought a moment. 'Sell another 100,000 Ho-Pak—and 200,000 Struan's.'

'Good God, Mr. Gornt, if Struan's gets brought down the whole market'll totter, even your own company'll lose.'

'There'll be an adjustment, lots of adjustments, certainly.'

'There'll be a bloodbath. If Struan's goes, so will other companies, thousands of investors'll be wiped out an—'

'I really don't need a lecture on Hong Kong economics, Mr. Stern,' Gornt said coldly. 'If you don't want to follow instructions I'll take my business elsewhere.'

Stern flushed. 'I'll . . . I'll have to round up the shares first. That number . . . to get that sum . . .'

'Then I suggest you hurry up! I want that on the board today!' Gornt watched him go, enjoying the moment immensely. Cocky bastard, he was thinking. Stockbrokers are just parasites, every one of them. He felt quite safe. Bartlett's money was in his account. He could buy back Ho-Pak and Struan's even now and be millions ahead. Contentedly his eyes strayed back to Casey. She was watching him. He could read nothing in her expression.

Joseph Stern was weaving through the brokers. Again he stopped at the Basilio desk. Sir Luis Basilio looked away from the board and smiled up at him. 'So, Joseph? You want to borrow more Noble House shares?'

'Yes, please.'

'For Quillan?' Sir Luis asked. He was a fine old man, small, elegant, very thin, and in his seventies—this year's chairman of the committee that ran the exchange.

'Yes.'

'Come, sit down, let's talk a moment, old friend. How many do you want now?'

'200,000.'

Sir Luis frowned. '300,000 on the board—another 2? Is this an all-out attack?'

'He . . . he didn't say that but I think it is.'

'It's a great pity those two can't make peace with one another.'

'Yes.'

The older man thought a moment, then said even more quietly, 'I'm considering suspending dealing in Ho-Pak shares, and, since lunch, Noble House shares. I'm very worried. At this precise moment a Ho-Pak crash, coupled with a Noble House crash, could wreck the whole market. Madonna, it's unthinkable for the Noble House to crash, it would pull down hundreds of us, perhaps all Hong Kong, unthinkable!'

'Perhaps the Noble House needs overhauling. Can I borrow 200,000 shares?'

'First answer me this, yes or no, and if yes when: Should we suspend the Ho-Pak? Should we suspend Struan's? I've polled all the other members of the committee except you. They're divided almost equally.'

'Neither has ever been suspended. It would be bad to suspend either. This's a free society—in its best sense, I think. You should let it work itself out, let them sort themselves out, the Struans, and the Gornts and all the rest, let the best get to the top and the worst . . .' Stern shook his head wearily. 'Ah but it's easy for me to say that, Luis, I'm not a big investor in either.'

'Where's your money?'

'Diamonds. All Jews need small things, things you can carry and things you can hide, things you can convert easily.'

'There's no need for you to be afraid here, Joseph. How many years has your family been here and prospered? Look at Solomon—surely he and his family are the richest in all Asia.'

'For Jews fear is a way of life. And being hated.'

Again the old man sighed. 'Ah this world, this lovely world, how lovely it should be.' A phone rang and he picked it up delicately, his hands tiny, his Portuguese sounding sweet and liquid to Stern though he understood none of it. He only caught 'Señor Mata' said deferentially several times but the name meant nothing to him. In a moment Sir Luis replaced the receiver very thoughtfully. 'The financial secretary called just after lunch, greatly perturbed. There's a deputation from Parliament here and a bank crash would look extremely bad for all of us,' he said. He smiled a pixyish smile. 'I suggested he introduce legislation for the governor's signature to govern banks like they had in England and the poor fellow almost had a fit. I really mustn't pull his leg so much.' Stern smiled with him. 'As if we need government interference here!' The eyes sharpened. 'So Joseph, do you vote to let well alone—or suspend either or both of the stocks, if so when?'

Stern glanced at the clock. If he went to the board now he would have plenty of time to write up both sell offerings and still be able to challenge Forsythe. It was a good feeling to know that he held the fate of both houses in his hands, if only temporarily. 'Perhaps it would be very good, perhaps bad. What's the voting so far?'

'I said, almost equal.' There was another burst of excitement and both men looked up. Some more Struan shares were changing hands. The new market price dropped to 24.70. Now Phillip Chen was leaning over Holdbrook's desk.

'Poor Phillip, he doesn't look well at all,' Sir Luis said compassionately.

'No. Pity about John. I liked him. What about the Werewolves? Do you think the papers are overplaying it?'

'No. No, I don't.' The old eyes twinkled. 'No more than you, Joseph.'

'What?'

'You've decided to pass. You want to let today's time run out, don't you? That's what you want, isn't it?'

'What better solution could there be?'

'If I wasn't so old I'd agree with you. But being so old and not knowing about tomorrow, or if I shall live to see tomorrow, I prefer my drama today. Very well. I'll discount your vote this time and now the committee's deadlocked so I will decide, as I'm allowed to do. You can borrow 200,000 Noble House shares until Friday, Friday at two. Then I may ask for them back—I have to think of my own House, eh?' The sharp but kindly eyes in the lined face urged Stern to his feet. 'What are you going to do now, my friend?'

Joseph Stern smiled sadly. 'I'm a stockbroker.'

He went to the board and wrote in the Ho-Pak sell column with a firm hand. Then in the new silence he went to the Struan column and wrote the figure clearly, conscious that he was on center stage now. He could feel the hate and the envy. More than 500,000 Noble House shares were now on offer, more than at any one time in the history of the exchange. He waited, wanting the clock to run out. There was a flurry of interest as Soorjani, the Parsee, bought some blocks of shares but it was well known he was nominee for many of the Struan and Dunross family and supporters. And though he bought 150,000, it made little difference to the enormity of Gornt's offering. The quiet was hurting. One minute to go now.

'*We buy!*' The tai-pan's voice shattered the silence.

'All my shares?' Stern asked hoarsely, his heart racing.

'Yes. Yours and all the rest. At market!'

Gornt was on his feet. 'With what?' he asked sardonically. 'That's almost 9 million cash.'

Dunross was on his feet too, a taunting half-smile on his face. 'The Noble House is good for that—and millions more. Has anyone ever doubted it?'

'I doubt it—and I sell short tomorrow!'

At that moment the finish bell sounded shrilly, the tension broke and there was a roar of approval.

'Christ what a day. . . .'

'Good old tai-pan. . . .'

'Couldn't stand much more of that . . .'

'Is Gornt going to beat him this time . . . ?'

'Maybe those rumors are all nonsense . . .'

'Christ I made a bloody fortune in commissions . . .'

'I think Ian's running scared. . . .'

'Don't forget he's got five days to pay for the shares . . .'

'He can't buy like that tomorrow . . .'

'Christ, tomorrow! What's going to happen tomorrow . . .'

Casey shifted in her seat, her heart thumping. She pried her eyes off Gornt and Dunross and looked back at Bartlett, who sat staring at the board, whistling tonelessly. She was awed—awed and a little frightened.

Just before coming here to meet Dunross, Linc Bartlett had told her his plan, about his call to Gornt and all about the meeting with him. 'Now you know it all, Casey,' he had said softly, grinning at her. 'Now they're both set up and we control the battlefield, all for 2 million. Both're at each other's throats, both going for the jugular, each ready to cannibalize the other. Now we wait. Monday's D Day. If Gornt wins, we win. If Dunross wins, we win. Either way we become the Noble House.'

32

3:03 P.M.:

Alexi Travkin who trained the racehorses of the Noble House went up the busy alley off Nathan Road in Kowloon and into the Green Dragon Restaurant. He wore a small .38 under his left arm and his walk was light for a man of his age.

The restaurant was small, ordinary and drab, with no table-cloths on the dozen or so tables. At one of them, four Chinese were noisily eating soup and noodles, and, as he came in, a bored waiter by the cash register looked up from his racing form and began to get up with a menu. Travkin shook his head and walked through the archway that led to the back.

The little room contained four tables. It was empty but for one man.

'*Zdrastvuytye,*' Suslev said lazily, his light clothes well cut.

'*Zdrastvuytye,*' Travkin replied, his Slavic eyes narrowing even more. Then he continued in Russian, 'Who're you?'

'A friend, Highness.'

'Please don't call me that, I'm not a highness. Who're you?'

'Still a friend. Once you were a prince. Will you join me?' Suslev politely motioned to a chair. There was an opened bottle of vodka on his table and two glasses. 'Your father Nicoli Petrovitch was a prince too, like his father and back for generations, Prince of Kurgan and even Tobol.'

'You talk in ciphers, friend,' Travkin said, outwardly calm, and sat opposite him. The feel of the .38 took away some of his apprehension. 'From your accent you're Muscovite—and Georgian.'

Suslev laughed. 'Your ear is very good, Prince Kurgan. Yes I'm Muscovite but I was born in Georgia. My name's unimportant but I'm a friend wh—'

'Of me, Russia or the Soviets?'

'Of all three. Vodka?' Suslev asked, lifting the bottle.

'Why not?' Travkin watched the other man pour the two glasses, then without hesitation he picked up the wrong glass, the one farthest from him, and lifted it. 'Health!'

Without hesitation Suslev picked up the other, touched glasses, drained it and poured again. 'Health!'

'You're the man who wrote to me?'

'I have news of your wife.'

'I have no wife. What do you want from me, *friend?*' The way Travkin used the word it was an insult. He saw the flash of anger as Suslev looked up from his glass and he readied.

'I excuse your rudeness this once, Alexi Ivanovitch,' Suslev said with dignity. 'You've no cause to be rude to me. None. Have I insulted you?'

'Who are you?'

'Your wife's name is Nestorova Mikail and her father was Prince Anotoli Zergeyev whose lands straddle Karaganda, which is not so far away from your own family lands east of the Urals. He was a Kazaki, wasn't he, a great prince of the Kazaki, whom some people called Cossacks?'

Travkin kept his gnarled hands still and his face impassive, but he could not keep the blood from draining from his face. He reached out and poured two more glasses, the bottle still half full. He sipped the spirit. 'This's good vodka, not like the piss in Hong Kong. Where did you get it?'

'Vladivostok.'

'Ah. Once I was there. It's a flat dirty town but the vodka's good. Now, what's your real name and what do you want?'

'You know Ian Dunross well?'

Travkin was startled. 'I train his horses . . . I've . . . this is my third year, why?'

'Would you like to see the Princess Nestor—'

'Good sweet Christ Jesus whoever you are, I told you I have no wife. Now, for the last time, what do you want from me?'

Suslev filled his glass and his voice was even more kindly. 'Alexi Ivanovitch Travkin, your wife the princess today is sixty-three. She lives in Yakutsk on th—'

'On the Lena? In Siberia?' Travkin felt his heart about to explode. 'What *gulag* is that, you turd?'

Through the archway in the other room, which was empty now, the waiter looked up momentarily, then yawned and went on reading.

'It's not a *gulag*, why should it be a *gulag*?' Suslev said, his voice hardening. 'The princess went there of her own accord. She's lived there since she left Kurgan. Her . . .' Suslev's hand went into his pocket and he brought out his wallet. 'This is her *dacha* in Yakutsk,' he said, putting down a photograph. 'It belonged to her family, I believe.' The cottage was snowbound, within a nice glade of trees, the fences well kept, and it was pretty with good smoke coming out of the chimney. A tiny bundled-up figure waved gaily at the camera—too far away for the face to be seen clearly.'

'And that's my wife?' Travkin said, his voice raw.

'Yes.'

'I don't believe you!'

Suslev put down a new snapshot. A portrait. The lady was white-haired and in her fifties or sixties and though the cares of a whole world marked her, her face was still elegant, still patrician. The warmth of her smile reached out and broke him.

'You . . . you KGB turd,' he said hoarsely, sure that he recognized her. 'You filthy rotten mother-eating . . .'

'To have found her?' Suslev said angrily. 'To have seen that she was looked after and left in peace and not troubled and not sent to . . . to the correction places she and your whole class deserved?' Irritably he poured himself another drink. 'I'm Russian and proud of it—you're émigré and you left. My father and his were *owned* by one of your class. My father died at the barricades in 1916, and my mother—and before they died they were starving. They . . .' With an effort he stopped. Then he said in a different voice, 'I agree there's much to forgive and much to forget on both sides, and that's all past now but I tell you we Soviets, we're not all animals—not all of us. We're not like Bloody Beria and the murdering archfiend Stalin. . . . Not everyone.' He found his pack of cigarettes. 'Do you smoke?'

'No. Are you KGB or GRU?' KGB stood for the Committee for State Security; GRU for the Chief Intelligence Directorate of the General Staff. This was not the first time Travkin had been approached by one of them. Before, he had always been able to slough them off with his drab, unimportant cover story. But now he was trapped. This one knew too much about him, too much truth. Who are you, bastard? And what do you really want? he thought as he watched Suslev light a cigarette.

'Your wife knows you're alive.'

'Impossible. She's dead. She was murdered by mobs when our pal—when our house in Kurgan was sacked, put to the torch, torn apart—the prettiest, most unarmed mansion within a hundred miles.'

'The masses had the right t—'

'Those weren't my people and they were led by imported Trotskyites who afterwards murdered my peasants by the thousands—until they themselves were all purged by more of their own vermin.'

'Perhaps, perhaps not,' Suslev said coldly. 'Even so, Prince of Kurgan and Tobol, she escaped with one old servant and fled east thinking she could find you, could escape after you through Siberia to Manchuria. The servant came originally from Austria. Pavchen was her name.'

The breath seemed to have vanished from Travkin's lungs. 'More lies,' he heard himself say, no longer believing it, his spirit ripped apart by her lovely smile. 'My wife's dead. She'd never go so far north.'

'Ah but she did. Her escape train was diverted northwards. It was autumn. Already the first snows had come so she decided to wait the winter out in Yakutsk. She had to . . .' Suslev put down another snapshot. '. . . she was with child. This is your son and his family. It was taken last year.' The man was good-looking, in his forties, wearing a Soviet major's air force uniform, self-consciously smiling at the camera, his arm around a fine woman in her thirties with three happy children, a babe, a beaming girl of six or seven missing front teeth, a boy of about ten trying to be serious. 'Your wife called him Pietor Ivanovitch after your grandfather.'

Travkin did not touch the photo. He just stared at it, his face chalky. Then he pried his eyes away and poured a drink for himself, and as an afterthought, one for Suslev. 'It's . . . it's all a brilliant reconstruction,' he said, trying to sound convincing. 'Brilliant.'

'The child's name is Victoria, the girl is Nichola after your grandmother. The boy is Alexi. Major Ivanovitch is a bomber pilot.'

Travkin said nothing. His eyes went back to the portrait of the beautiful old lady and he was near tears but his voice was still controlled. 'She knows I'm alive, eh?'

'Yes.'

'For how long?'

'Three months. About three months ago. One of our people told her.'

'Who're they?'

'Do you want to see her?'

'Why only three months—why not a year—three years?'

'It was only six months ago we discovered who you were.'

'How did you do that?'

'Did you expect to remain anonymous forever?'

'If she knows I'm alive and one of your people told her then she'd've written. . . . Yes. They would have asked her to do that if . . .' Travkin's voice was strange. He felt out of himself, in a nightmare, as he tried to think clearly. 'She would have written a letter.'

'She has. I will give it to you within the next few days. Do you want to see her?'

Travkin forced his agony down. He motioned at the family portrait. 'And . . . and he knows I'm alive too?'

'No. None of them do. That was not at our suggestion, Alexi Ivanovitch. It was your wife's idea. For safety—to protect him, she thought. As if we would wreak vengeance for the sins of the fathers on the sons! She waited out two winters in Yakutsk. By that time peace had come to Russia so she stayed. By that time she presumed you dead, though she hoped you were alive. The boy was brought up believing you dead, and knew nothing of you. He still doesn't. As you can see, he's a credit to you both. He was head of his local school, then went to university as all gifted children do nowadays. . . . Do you know, Alexi Ivanovitch, in my day I was the first of my whole province ever to get to a university, the very first ever from a *peasant* family. We're fair in Russia today.'

'How many corpses have you made to become what you are now?'

'A few,' Suslev said darkly, 'all of them criminals or enemies of Russia.'

'Tell me about them.'

'I will. One day.'

'Did you fight the last war—or were you a commissar?'

'Sixteenth Tank Corp, Forty-fifth Army. I was at Sebastopol . . . and at Berlin. Tank commander. Do you want to see your wife?'

'More than my whole life is worth, if this really is my wife and if she's alive.'

'She is. I can arrange it.'

'Where?'

'Vladivostok.'

'No, here in Hong Kong.'

'Sorry, that's impossible.'

'Of course.' Travkin laughed without mirth. 'Of course, *friend*. Drink?' He poured the last of the vodka, splitting it equally. 'Health!'

Suslev stared at him. Then he looked down at the portrait and the snapshot of the air force major and his family and picked them up, lost in thought. The silence grew. He scratched his beard. Then he said decisively, 'All right. Here in Hong Kong,' and Travkin's heart leapt.

'In return for what?'

Suslev stubbed his cigarette out. 'Information. And cooperation.'

'What?'

'I want to know everything you know about the tai-pan of the Noble House, everything you did in China, who you know, who you met.'

'And the cooperation?'

'I will tell you later.'

'And in return you'll bring my wife to Hong Kong?'

'Yes.'

'When?'

'By Christmas.'

'How can I trust you?'

'You can't. But if you cooperate she will be here at Christmas.' Travkin was watching the two photos Suslev toyed with in his fingers, then he saw the look in his eyes and his stomach twisted. 'Either way, you must be honest with me. With or without your wife, Prince Kurgan, we always have your son and your grandchildren hostage.'

Travkin sipped his drink, making it last. 'Now I believe you are what you are. Where do you want to start?'

'The tai-pan. But first I want to piss.' Suslev got up and asked the waiter where the toilet was and went out through the kitchen.

Now that Travkin was alone despair gripped him. He picked up the snapshot of the cottage that was still on the table and peered at it. Tears filled his eyes. He brushed them away and felt the gun that nestled beneath his shoulder but that did not help him now. With all his inner strength he resolved to be wise and not believe, but in his heart he knew he had seen her picture and that he would do anything, risk anything to see her.

For years he had tried to avoid these hunters, knowing that he was always pursued. He had been the leader of the Whites in his area across the Trans-Siberian Railroad and he had killed many Reds. At length he had wearied of the killing and in 1919 had left for Shanghai and a new home until the Japanese armies came, escaping them to join Chinese guerrillas, fighting his way south and west to Chungking, there to join other marauders, English, French, Australian, Chinese—anyone who would pay—until the Japanese unconditionally surrendered, and so back to Shanghai again, soon to flee once more. Always fleeing, he thought.

By the blood of Christ, my darling, I know you're dead. I know it. I was told by someone who saw the mob sack our palace, saw them swarm over you. . . .

But now?

Are you really alive?

Travkin looked at the kitchen door with hatred, knowing he would forever be haunted until he was certain about her. Who is that shit eater? he thought. How did they find me?

Grimly he waited and waited and then in sudden panic went to find him. The toilet was empty. He rushed into the street but it was filled with other people. The man had vanished.

There was a vile taste in Travkin's mouth now and he was sick with apprehension. In the name of God, what does he want with the tai-pan?

33

'Hello, Ian,' Penelope said. 'You're home early! How was your day?'

'Fine, fine,' Dunross said absently. Apart from all the disasters, just before he left the office he had had a call from Brian Kwok saying, among other things, that AMG was probably murdered and warned him to take serious precautions.

'Oh, it was one of those, was it?' she said at once. 'How about a drink? Yes. How about champagne?'

'Good idea.' Then he noticed her smile and smiled back and felt much better. 'Penn, you're a mind reader!' He tossed his briefcase onto a sideboard and followed her into one of the sitting rooms of the Great House. The champagne was already in an ice bucket, opened, with two glasses partially filled and another waiting for him in the ice.

'Kathy's upstairs. She's reading Glenna a bedtime story,' Penelope said, pouring for him. 'She . . . she's just told me about . . . about the, about the disease.'

'Oh.' He accepted the glass. 'Thanks. How's Andrew taking it? He didn't mention anything today.'

'She's going to tell him tonight. The champagne was to give her some courage.' Penelope looked up at him, anguished. 'She's going to be all right, isn't she, Ian?'

'I think so. I had a long talk with Doc Tooley. He was encouraging, gave me the names of the top three experts in England and another three in America. I've cabled for appointments with the three in England and Doc Ferguson's air-mailing them case histories—they'll be there when you arrive.'

573

She sipped her wine. A light breeze made the sultry day much better. The french doors were open to the garden. It was near six o'clock. 'Do you think we should go at once? Will a few days make any difference?'

'I don't think so.'

'But we should go?'

'If it were you, Penn, we'd've been on the first plane the very first moment.'

'Yes. If I'd told you.'

'You would have told me.'

'Yes. I suppose I would. I've made reservations for to-morrow. Kathy thought it a good idea too. The BOAC flight.'

He was startled. 'Claudia never mentioned it.'

She smiled. 'I made them myself. I'm really quite capable. I've reservations for Glenna, me and Kathy. We could take the case histories with us. I thought Kathy should go without any of her children. They'll be perfectly all right with the *amahs*.'

'Yes, that's much the best. Doc Tooley was adamant about her taking it easy. That's the main thing he said, lots of rest.' Dunross smiled at her. 'Thanks, Penn.'

She was staring at the beads of condensation on the outside of the bottle and the ice bucket. 'Bloody awful, isn't it?'

'Worse, Penn. There's no cure. He thinks . . . he thinks the medication will arrest it.' He finished his glass and poured for both of them. 'Any messages?'

'Oh, sorry! Yes, they're on the sideboard. There was a long-distance call from Marseilles a moment ago.'

'Susanne?'

'No. A Mr. Deland.'

'He's our agent there.'

'Rotten about young Borge.'

'Yes.' Dunross skimmed the messages. Johnjohn at the bank, Holdbrook, Phillip Chen, and the inevitable catchall 'please call Claudia'. He sighed. It was only half an hour since he left the office and he was going to call her anyway. No rest for the wicked, he thought, and smiled to himself.

He had enjoyed besting Gornt at the exchange. That he did not have the money at the moment to pay did not worry him. There's five days of grace, he thought. Everything's covered—with joss. Ah yes, joss!

574

Since his stockbroker had called him in panic at a few minutes past ten about the rumors sweeping the exchange and how their stock was shifting, he had been bolstering his defenses against the sudden, unexpected attack. With Phillip Chen, Holdbrook, Gavallan and deVille he had marshaled all the major stockholders they could reach and told them that the rumors Struan's couldn't meet their obligations were nonsense and suggested they refuse to lend Gornt any big blocks of Struan stock but to keep him dangling, letting him have a few shares here and there. He told the selected few in the strictest confidence that the Par-Con deal was signed, sealed and about to be chopped, and that this was a marvelous opportunity to smash Rothwell-Gornt once and for all.

'If Gornt sells short, let him. We pretend to be vulnerable but support the stock. Then Friday we announce, our stock'll soar and he'll lose his shirt, tie and trousers,' he had told them all. 'We get back our airline along with his, and with his ships and ours together, we'll dominate all air and surface inbound and outbound trade in Asia.'

If we could really smash Gornt, he thought fervently, we'd be safe for generations. And we could, given joss, Par-Con and more joss. Christ, but it's going to be very dicey!

He had exuded confidence all day, not feeling confident at all. Many of his big stockholders had called nervously but he had quieted them. Both Tightfist Tung and Four Finger Wu owned major blocks of stock through devious nominees. He had phoned both this afternoon to get their agreement not to loan or sell their major holdings for the next week or so. Both had agreed but it had not been easy with either of them.

All in all, Dunross thought, I've fought off the initial onslaught. Tomorrow will tell the real story—or Friday: is Bartlett enemy, friend or Judas?

He felt his anger rising but he pushed it back. Be calm, he told himself, think calmly. I will but it's bloody curious that everything Bartlett said the night of the party—all those very secret things he had so readily and suddenly produced to shatter my defenses—miraculously went through the market today like a typhoon. Who's the spy? Who gave him the info? Is he the Sevrin spy too? Well, never mind for the moment, everything's covered. I think.

Dunross went to the phone and asked the operator to get Mr. Deland, person to person, and to call him back.

'Would Susanne be there yet?' Penelope asked.

'I think so. If her plane's on time. It's about eleven, Marseilles time, so it shouldn't be an emergency. Bloody shame about Borge! I liked him.'

'What's Avril going to do?'

'She's going to be all right. Avril's going to come home to bring up the child and soon she'll meet a Prince Charming, a new one, and her son'll join Struan's and meanwhile she'll be protected and cherished.'

'Do you believe that, Ian—about the Prince Charming?'

'Yes,' he said firmly. 'I believe everything will be all right. It's going to be all right, Penn, for her, for Kathy, for . . . for everyone.'

'You can't carry everyone, Ian.'

'I know. But no one, no one in the family will ever need for anything while I'm alive and that's going to be forever.'

His wife looked at him and remembered the first time she had seen him, a godlike youth sitting in his shattered fighter that should have crashed but somehow miraculously hadn't. Ian, just sitting there, then getting out, holding the terror down, she seeing in his eyes for the first time what death was like but him dominating it and coming back and just accepting the cup of tea saying, 'Oh, jolly good, thanks. You're new, aren't you?' in his lovely patrician accent that was so far from her own background.

Such a long time ago, a thousand years ago, another lifetime, she thought. Such wonderful ghastly terrible beautiful agonizing days: will he die today or come back today? Will I die today, in the morning bombing or in the evening one? Where's Dad and Mum and is the phone just bombed out of service as usual or has the rotten little terraced house in Streatham vanished along with all the other thousands like it?

One day it had and then she had no past. Just Ian and his arms and strength and confidence, and she terrified that he would go like all the others. That was the worst part, she told herself. The waiting and anticipating and knowing how mortal the Few were and we all are. My God how quickly we had to grow up!

'I hope it is forever, darling,' she said in her cool, flat voice, wanting to hide the immensity of her love. 'Yes. I want you to be immortal!'

He grinned at her, loving her. 'I'm immortal, Penn, never mind. After I'm dead I'll still be watching over you and Glenna and Duncan and Adryon and all the rest.'

She watched him. 'Like Dirk Struan does?'

'No,' he said serious now. 'He's a presence I'll never match. He's perpetual—I'm temporary.' His eyes were watching hers. 'You're rather serious tonight, aren't you?'

They laughed.

She said, 'I was just thinking how triansient life is, how violent, unexpected, how cruel. First John Chen and now Borge, Kathy . . .' A little shiver went through her, ever petrified she would lose him. 'Who's next?'

'Any one of us. Meanwhile be Chinese. Remember under heaven all crows are black. Life is good. Gods make mistakes and go to sleep so we do the best we can and never trust a *quai loh!*'

She laughed, at peace again. 'There are times, Ian Struan Dunross, when I quite like you. Do you th—' The phone rang and she stopped and thought, God curse that bloody phone. If I was omnipotent I'd outlaw all phones after 6:00 P.M. but then poor Ian'd go mad, and the bloody Noble House'd crumble and that's poor Ian's life. I'm second, so are the children and that's as it should be. Isn't it?

'Oh hello, Lando,' Dunross was saying, 'what's new?'

'Hope I'm not disturbing you, tai-pan.'

'Not at all,' he replied, all his energy concentrated. 'I've just got in. What can I do for you?'

'Sorry, but I'm withdrawing the 15 million support I promised for tomorrow. Temporarily. The market makes me nervous.'

'Nothing to worry about,' Dunross said, his stomach churning. 'Gornt's up to his tricks. That's all.'

'I'm really very worried. It's not just Gornt. It's the Ho-Pak and the way the whole market's reacting,' Mata said. 'With the bank run seeping over to the Ching Prosperity and even the Vic . . . all the signs are very bad so I want to wait and see.'

'Tomorrow's the day, Lando. Tomorrow. I was counting on you.'

'Have you tripled our next gold consignment as I asked?'

'Yes, I did that personally. I've Zurich's telexed confirms in the usual code.'

'Excellent, excellent!'

'I'll need your letter of credit tomorrow.'

'Of course. If you'll send a messenger to my home now I'll give you my check for the full amount.'

'Personal check?' Dunross held on to his astonishment. 'On which bank, Lando?'

'The Victoria.'

'Christ, that's a lot of money to remove just now.'

'I'm not removing it, I'm just paying for some gold. I'd rather have some of my funds in gold outside Hong Kong for the next week or so, and this's an ideal moment to do it. You can get them to telex it first thing tomorrow. First thing. Yes. I'm not withdrawing funds, Ian, just paying for gold. If I were you I'd try to get liquid too.'

Again his stomach fell over. 'What have you heard?' he asked, his voice controlled.

'You know me, I'm just more cautious than you, tai-pan. The cost of my money comes very high.'

'No more than mine.'

'Yes. We'll consult tomorrow, then we'll see. But don't count on our 15 million. Sorry.'

'You've heard something. I know you too well. What is it? *Chi pao pu chu huo.*' Literally, Paper cannot wrap up a fire, meaning a secret cannot be kept forever.

There was a long pause, then Mata said in a lower voice, 'Confidentially, Ian, old Tightfist's selling heavily. He's getting ready to unload *all* his holdings. That old devil may be dying but his nose is as sensitive to the loss of a brass cash as ever and I've never known him to be wrong.'

'All his holdings?' Dunross asked sharply. 'When did you talk to him?'

'We've been in contact all day. Why?'

'I reached him after lunch and he promised he wouldn't sell or loan any Struan's. Has he changed his mind?'

'No. I'm sure he hasn't. He can't. He hasn't any Struan stock.'

'He has 400,000 shares!'

'He *did* have, tai-pan, though actually the number was nearer

578

600,000—Sir Luis had very few shares of his own, he's one of Tightfist's many nominees. He's unloaded all 600,000 shares. Today.'

Dunross bit back an obscenity. 'Oh?'

'Listen, my young friend, this is all in the strictest confidence but you should be prepared: Tightfist ordered Sir Luis to sell or loan all his Noble House stock the moment the rumors started this morning. 100,000 were spread throughout the brokers and sold immediately, the remainder. . . . the half million shares you bought from Gornt were Tightfist's. The moment it was evident there was a major assault on the House and Gornt was selling short, Tightfist told Sir Luis to go ahead and loan it all, except for a token 1,000 shares, which he's kept. For face. Yours. When the exchange closed, Tightfist was very pleased. On the day he's almost 2 million ahead.'

Dunross was standing rock still. He heard that his voice was matter-of-fact and level and controlled and that pleased him, but he was in shock. If Tightfist had sold, the Chins would sell and a dozen other friends would follow his lead and that meant chaos. 'The old bugger!' he said, bearing him no grudge. It was his own fault, he had not reached Tightfist in time. 'Lando, what about your 300,000 shares—plus?'

He heard the Portuguese hesitate and his stomach twisted again. 'I've still got them. I bought at 16 when you first went public so I'm not worried yet. Perhaps Alastair Struan was right when he advised against going public—the Noble House's only vulnerable because of that.'

'Our growth rate's five times Gornt's and without going public we could never have weathered the disasters I inherited. We're supported by the Victoria. We've still got our bank stock and a majority vote on the board so they have to support us. We're really very strong and once this temporary situation's over we'll be the biggest conglomerate in Asia.'

'Perhaps. But perhaps you'd have been wiser to accept our proposal instead of leaving yourself constantly open to the risk of takeovers or market disasters.'

'I couldn't then. I can't now. Nothing's changed.' Dunross smiled grimly. Lando Mata, Tightfist Tung and Gambler Chin collectively had offered him 20 percent of their gold and gambling syndicate revenue for 50 percent of Struan's—if he kept it as a wholly private-owned company.

'Come, tai-pan, be sensible! Tightfist and I will give you 100 million cash today for 50 percent ownership. U.S. dollars. Your position as tai-pan will not be touched, you will head the new syndicate and manage our gold and gambling monopolies, secretly or openly—with 10 percent of all profit as a personal fee.'

'Who appoints the next tai-pan?'

'You do—in consultation.'

'There, you see! It's impossible. A 50 percent control gives you power over Struan's and that I'm not allowed to give. That would negate Dirk's legacy, make my oath invalid and give away absolute control. Sorry, it's not possible.'

'Because of an oath to an unknown, unknowable god in which you don't believe—on behalf of a murdering pirate who's been dead over a hundred years?'

'For whatever reason the answer is, thank you, no.'

'You could easily lose the whole company.'

'No. Between the Struans and the Dunrosses we have 60 percent voting control and I alone vote all the stock. What I'd lose is everything material we own, and cease to be the Noble House, and that by the Lord God is not going to happen either.'

There was a long silence. Then Mata said, his voice friendly as always, 'Our offer is good for two weeks. If joss is against you and you fail, the offer to head the new syndicate stands. I shall sell or lend my stock at 21.'

'Below 20—not at 21.'

'It will go that low?'

'No. Just a habit I have. 20 is better than 21.'

'Yes. Good. Then let us see what tomorrow brings. I wish you good joss. Good night, tai-pan.'

Dunross put down the phone and sipped the last of his champagne. He was up the creek without a paddle. That old bugger Tightfist, he thought again, admiring his cleverness—to agree so reluctantly not to sell or barter any Struan shares, knowing that only 1,000 remained, knowing the revenue from almost 600,000 was already safe—that old bastard's a great negotiator. It's so very clever of both Lando and Tightfist to make the new offer now. 100 million! Jesus Christ, that'd stop

Gornt farting in church! I could use that to smash him to pieces, and in short order take over Asian Properties and put Dunstan into an early retirement. Then I could pass the House over to Jacques or Andrew in great shape and . . .

And then what? What would I do then? Retire to the moors and shoot grouse? Throw vast parties in London? Or go into Parliament and sleep on the Back Bench while the bloody Socialists give the country to the Communists? Christ, I'd be bored to bloody death! I'd . . .

'What?' He was startled. 'Oh sorry, Penn, what did you say?'

'I just said that all sounded like bad news!'

'Yes. Yes it was.' Then Dunross grinned and all his anxiety dropped away. 'It's joss! I'm tai-pan,' he said happily. 'You've got to expect it.' He picked up the bottle. It was empty. 'I think we deserve another . . . No, pet, I'll get it.' He went to the concealed refrigerator that was set into a vast old Chinese scarlet, lacquered sideboard.

'How do you cope, Ian?' she asked. 'I mean, it always seems to be something bad, ever since you took over—and there's always some disaster, every phone call, you work all the time, never take a holiday . . . ever since we came back to Hong Kong. First your father and then Alastair and then . . . Isn't it ever going to stop pouring cats and dogs?'

'Of course not—that's the job.'

'Is it worth it?'

He concentrated on the cork, knowing there was no future in this conversation. 'Of course.'

To you it is, Ian, she thought. But not to me. After a moment she said, 'Then it's all right for me to go?'

'Yes, yes of course. I'll watch Adryon and don't worry about Duncan. You just have a great time and hurry back.'

'Are you going to do the hill climb Sunday?'

'Yes. Then I'm going to Taipei, back Tuesday. I'm taking Bartlett.'

She thought about Taipei and wondered if there was a girl there, a special girl, a Chinese girl, half her age, with lovely soft skin and warmth, not much warmer than herself or softer or trimmer but half her age, with a ready smile, without the years of survival bowing her—the rotten growing-up years, the good and terrible war years, and childbearing years and child-rearing years and the exhausting reality of marriage, even to a good man.

I wonder I wonder I wonder. If I were a man . . . there're so many beauties here, so anxious to please, so readily available. If you believe a tenth of what the others say.

She watched him pour the fine wine, the bubbles and froth good, his face strong and craggy and greatly pleasing, and she wondered, Does any woman possess any man for more than a few years?

'What?' he asked.

'Nothing,' she said, loving him. She touched his glass. 'Be careful on the hill climb.'

'Of course.'

'How do you cope with being tai-pan, Ian?'

'How do you cope with running a home, bringing up the kids, getting up at all hours, year after year, keeping the peace, and all the other things you've had to do? I couldn't do that. Never could. I'd've given up the ghost long ago. It's part training and part what you're born to do.'

'A woman's place is in the home?'

'I don't know about others, Penn, but so long as you're in my home all's good in my world.' He popped the cork neatly.

'Thank you, dear,' she said and smiled. Then she frowned. 'But I'm afraid I don't have much option and never had. Of course it's different now and the next generation's lucky, they're going to change things, turn things around and give men their comeuppance once and for all.'

'Oh?' he said, most of his mind back on Lando Mata and tomorrow and how to get the 100 million without conceding control.

'Oh yes. The girls of the next generation aren't going to put up with the boring "a woman's place is by the sink". God how I hate housework, how every woman hates housework. Our daughters are going to change all that! Adryon for one. My God I'd hate to be her husband.'

'Every generation thinks they're going to change the world,' Dunross said, pouring. 'This's great champagne. Remember how we did? Remember how we used to bitch, still do, about our parents' attitudes?'

'True. But our daughters have the pill and that's a whole new kettle of fish an—'

'Eh?' Dunross stared at her, shocked. 'You mean Adryon's on the pill? Jesus Christ how long . . . do you mean sh—'

'Calm down, Ian, and listen. That little pill's unlocked womanhood from fear forever—men too, in a way. I think very few people realize what an enormous social revolution it's going to create. Now women can all make love without fear of having a child, they can use their bodies as men use their bodies, for gratification, for pleasure, and without shame.' She looked at him keenly. 'As to Adryon, she's had access to the pill since she was seventeen.'

'What?'

'Of course. Would you prefer her to have a child?'

'Jesus Christ, Penn, of course not,' Dunross spluttered, 'but Jesus Christ who? You . . . you mean she's having an affair, had affairs or. . . .'

'I sent her to Dr. Tooley. I thought it best she should see him.'

'You what?'

'Yes. When she was seventeen, she asked me what to do, said most of her friends were on the pill. As there are various types I wanted her to have expert advice. Dr. Too— What are you so red about, Ian? Adryon's nineteen now, twenty next month, it's all very ordinary.'

'It isn't by God. It just isn't!'

'Och laddie but it is,' she said, aping the broad Scots accent of Granny Dunross whom he had adored, 'and my whole point is that the lassies of today know what they're aboot and dinna ye dare mention it to Adryon that I've told ye or I'll take my stick to your britches!'

He stared at her.

'Health!' Smugly she raised her glass. 'Did you see the *Guardian* Extra this afternoon?'

'Don't change the subject, Penn. Don't you think I should talk to her?'

'Absolutely not. No. It's a . . . it's a very private matter. It's really her body and her life and whatever you say, Ian, she has the right to do with her life what she pleases and really nothing you say will make any difference. It'll all be very embarrassing for both of you. There's face involved,' she added and was pleased with her cleverness. 'Oh of course Adryon'll listen and take your views to heart but you really must be adult and

583

modern for your own sake, as well as hers.'

Suddenly an uncontrollable wave of heat went through his face.

'What is it?' she asked.

'I was thinking about . . . I was just thinking.'

'About who was, is or could be her lover?'

'Yes.'

Penelope Dunross sighed. 'For your own sanity, Ian, don't! She's very sensible, over nineteen . . . well, quite sensible. Come to think of it I haven't seen her all day. The little rotter rushed out with my new scarf before I could catch her. You remember the blouse I lent her? I found it scrumpled up on her bathroom floor! I shall be very glad to see her off on her own and in her own apartment.'

'She's too young for God's sake!'

'I don't agree, dear. As I was saying, there's really nothing you can do about progress, and the pill is a marvelous fantastic unbelievable leap forward. You really must be more sensible. Please?'

'It's . . . Christ, it's a bit sudden, that's all.'

She laughed outright. 'If we were talking about Glenna I could unders—Oh for God's sake, Ian, I'm only joking! It never really occurred to me that you wouldn't have presumed Adryon was a very healthy, well-adjusted though foul-tempered, infuriating, very frustrated young lady, most of whose frustrations spring from trying to please us with our old-fashioned ideas.'

'You're right.' He tried to sound convincing but he wasn't and he said sourly, 'You're right even so . . . you're right.'

'Laddie, dinna ye think ye'd better visit our Shrieking Tree?' she asked with a smile. It was an ancient clan custom in the old country that somewhere near the dwelling of the oldest woman of the laird's family would be the Shrieking Tree. When Ian was young, Granny Dunross was the oldest, and her cottage was in a glade in the hills behind Kilmarnock and Ayrshire where the Struan lands were. The tree was a great oak. It was the tree that you went out to when the Deevil—as old Granny Dunross called it—when the Deevil was with you, and alone, you shrieked whatever curses you liked. '. . . and then, lassie,' the lovely old woman had told her the first night, '. . . and then, lassie, there would be peace in the home and never a body has need to really curse a husband or wife or lover or child. Aye, just a wee tree and the tree can bear all the curse words that the Deevil himself invented. . . .'

Penelope was remembering how old Granny Dunross had taken her into her heart and into the clan from the first moment. That was just after she and Ian were married and visiting for the second time, Ian on sick leave, still on crutches, his legs badly burned but healing, the rest of him untouched in the flaming crash-landing but for his mad, all-consuming anger at being grounded forever, she so pleased secretly, thanking God for the reprieve.

'But whisht, lassie,' Granny Dunross had added with a chuckle that night when the winter winds were whining off the moors, sleet outside, and they all warm and toasty in front of the great fire, safe from the bombing, well fed and never a care except that Ian should get well quickly, '. . . there was a time when this Dunross was six and, och aye, he had a terrible temper even then and his father Colin was off in those heathen foreign parts as always, so this Dunross would come to Ayr on holiday from boarding school. Aye, and sometimes he would come to see me and I'd tell him tales o' the clan and his grandfather and great-grandfather but this time nothing would take away the deevil that possessed him. It was a night like this and I sent him out, the poor wee bairn, aye I sent him out to the Shrieking Tree. . . .' The old woman had chuckled and chuckled and sipped whiskey and continued, 'Aye and the young deevil went out, cock of the walk, the gale under his kilt, and he cursed the tree. Och aye, surely the wee beasties in the forest fled before his wrath and then he came back. "Have you given it a good drubbing," I asked him. "Aye," he said in his wee voice. "Aye, Grandma, I gave it a good drubbing, the very best ever."

'"Good," I said. "And now you're at peace!"

'"Well, not really, Grandmother, but I am tired." And then, lassie, at that moment, there was an almighty crash and the whole house shook and I thought it was the end of the world but the wee little bairn ran out to see what had happened and a lightning bolt had blasted the Shrieking Tree to pieces. 'Och aye, Granny,' he said in his piping little voice when he came back, his eyes wide, "that really was the very best I ever did. Can I do it again?"'

Ian had laughed. 'That's all a story, I don't remember that at all. You're making it up, Granny!'

'Whisht on you! You were five or six and the next day we went into the glade and picked the new tree, the one you'll see tomorrow, lassie, and blessed it in the clan's name and I told young Ian to be a mite more careful next time!'

They had laughed together and then, later that night, she had woken up to find Ian gone and his crutches gone. She had watched and waited. When he came back he was soaked but tired and at peace. She pretended sleep until he was in bed again. Then she turned to him and gave him all the warmth she had.

'Remember, lassie,' Granny Dunross had said to her privately the day they left, 'if ye want to keep your marriage sweet, make sure this Dunross always has a Shrieking Tree nearby. Dinna be afeared. Pick one, always pick one wherever you go. This Dunross needs a Shrieking Tree close by though he'll never admit it and will never use it but rarely. He's like the Dirk. He's too strong. . . .'

So wherever they had gone they had had one. Penelope had insisted. Once, in Chungking, where Dunross had been sent to be an Allied liaison officer after he was well again, she had made a bamboo their Shrieking Tree. Here in Hong Kong it was a huge jacaranda that dominated the whole garden. 'Don't you think you should pay her a wee visit?' The tree was always a her for him and a him for her. Everyone should have a Shrieking Tree, Penelope thought. Everyone.

'Thanks,' he said. 'I'm okay now.'

'How did Granny Dunross have so much wisdom and stay so marvelous after so much tragedy in her life?'

'I don't know. Perhaps they built them stronger in those days.'

'I miss her.' Granny Dunross was eighty-five when she died. She was Agnes Struan when she married her cousin Dirk Dunross—Dirk McCloud Dunross, whom his mother Winifred, Dirk Struan's only daughter, had named after her father in remembrance. Dirk Dunross had been fourth tai-pan and he had been lost at sea in *Sunset Cloud* driving her homeward. He was only forty-two when he was lost, she thirty-one. She never married again. They had had three sons and one daughter. Two of her sons were killed in World War I, the eldest at Gallipoli at twenty-one, the other gassed at Ypres in Flanders, nineteen. Her daughter Anne had married Gaston deVille, Jacques's father. Anne had died in the London bombing where all the deVilles had fled except Jacques who had stayed in France and fought the Nazis with the Maquis. Colin, the last of her sons, Ian's father, also had three sons and a daughter, Kathren. Two sons also were killed in World War II. Kathren's first husband, Ian's squadron leader, was killed in the Battle of Britain. 'So many deaths, violent deaths,' Penelope said sadly. 'To see them all born and all die . . . terrible. Poor Granny! Yet when she died she seemed to go so peacefully with that lovely smile of hers.'

'Perhaps it was joss. But the others, that was joss too. They only did what they had to, Penn. After all, our family history's ordinary in that. We're British. War's been a way of life for centuries. Look at your family—one of your uncles was lost at sea in the navy in the Great War, another in the last at El Alamein, your parents killed in the blitz . . . all very ordinary.' His voice hardened. 'It's not easy to explain to any outsider, is it?'

'No. We all had to grow up so quickly, didn't we, Ian?' He nodded and after a moment she said, 'You'd better dress for dinner, dear, you'll be late.'

'Come on, Penn, for God's sake, you take an hour longer than me. We'll put in a quick appearance and leave directly after chow. Wh—' The phone rang and he picked it up. 'Yes? Oh hello, Mr. Deland.'

'Good evening, tai-pan. I wish to report about Mme. deVille's daughter and son-in-law, M. Escary.'

'Yes, please go ahead.'

'I am sad to have the dishonor of bringing such bad tidings. The accident was a, how do you say, sideswipe on the upper Corniche just outside Eze. The driver of the other car was drunk. It was at two in the morning about, and when the police arrived, M. Escary was already dead and his wife unconscious. The doctor says she will mend, very well, but he is afraid that her, her internal organs, her childbearing organs may have permanent hurt. She may require an operation. He—'

587

'Does she know this?'

'No, m'sieu, not yet, but Mme. deVille was told, the doctor told her. I met her as you ordered and have taken care of everything. I have asked for a specialist in these things from Paris to consult with the Nice Hospital and he arrives this afternoon.'

'Is there any other damage?'

'Externally, *non*. A broken wrist, a few cuts, nothing. But . . . the poor lady is distraught. It was glad . . . I was glad that her mother came, that helped, has helped. She stays at the Métropole in a suite and I met her airplane. Of course I will be in the constant touch.'

'Who was driving?'

'Mme. Escary.'

'And the other driver?'

There was a hesitation. 'His name is Charles Sessonne. He's a baker in Eze and he was coming home after cards and an evening with some friends. The police have . . . Mme. Escary swears his car was on the wrong side of the road. He cannot remember. Of course he is very sorry and the police have charged him with drunk driving an—'

'Is this the first time?'

'*Non. Non*, once before he was stopped and fined.'

'What'll happen under French law?'

'There will be a court and then . . . I do not know, m'sieu. There were no other witnesses. Perhaps a fine, perhaps jail; I do not know. Perhaps he will remember he was on the right side, who knows? I'm sorry.'

Dunross thought a moment. 'Where does this man live?'

'Rue de Verte 14, Eze.'

Dunross remembered the village well, not far from Monte Carlo, high above, and the whole of the Côte d'Azur below and you could see beyond Monte Carlo into Italy, and beyond Cap Ferrat to Nice. 'Thank you, Mr. Deland. I've telexed you 10,000 U.S. for Mme. deVille's expenses and anything else. Whatever's necessary please do it. Call me at once if there's anything . . . yes and ask the specialist to call me immediately after he's examined Mme. Escary. Have you talked with Mr. Jacques deVille?'

'No, tai-pan. You did not instruct this. Should I phone?'

'No. I'll call him. Thank you again.' Dunross hung up and told Penelope everything, except about the internal injuries.

'How awful! How . . . how senseless!'

Dunross was looking out at the sunset. It was at his suggestion the young couple had gone to Nice and Monte Carlo where he and Penelope had had so much fun, and marvelous food, marvelous wine and a little gambling. Joss, he thought, then added, Christ all bloody mighty!

He dialed Jacques deVille's house but he was not there. He left a message for him to return the call. 'I'll see him at the dinner tonight,' he said, the champagne now tasteless. 'Well, we'd better get changed.'

'I'm not going, dear.'

'Oh but . . .'

'I've lots to do to get ready for tomorrow. You can make an excuse for me—of course you have to go. I'll be ever so busy. There's Glenna's school things—and Duncan gets back on Monday and his school things have to be sorted. You'll have to put him on the aircraft, make sure he has his passport . . . You can easily make an excuse for me tonight as I'm leaving.'

He smiled faintly. 'Of course, Penn, but what's the real reason?'

'It's going to be a big do. Robin's bound to be there.'

'They're not back till tomorrow!'

'No, it was in the *Guardian*'s Extra. They arrived this afternoon. The whole delegation. They're sure to be invited.' The banquet was being given by a multimillionaire property developer, Sir Shi-teh T'Chung, partially to celebrate the knighthood he had received in the last Honors List, but mostly to launch his latest charity drive for the new wing of the new Elizabeth Hospital. 'I've really no wish to go, and so long as you're there, everything'll be all right. I really want an early night too. Please.'

'All right. I'll deal with these calls, then I'll be off. I'll see you though before I go.' Dunross walked upstairs and went into his study. Lim was waiting there, on guard. He wore a white tunic and black pants and soft shoes. 'Evening, Lim,' Dunross said in Cantonese.

'Good evening, tai-pan.' Quietly the old man motioned him to the window. Dunross could see two men, Chinese, loitering

589

across the street outside the high wall that surrounded the Great House, near the tall, open iron gates. 'They've been there some time, tai-pan.'

Dunross watched them a moment, disquieted. His own guard had just been dismissed and Brian Kwok, who was also a guest at Sir Shi-teh's tonight, would come by shortly and go with him, acting as a substitute. 'If they don't go away by dusk call Superintendent Crosse's office.' He wrote the number down, then added in Cantonese, his voice abruptly hard, 'While I think of it, Lim, if I want any foreign devil car interfered with, *I* will order it.' He saw the old eyes staring back at him impassively. Lim Chu had been with the family since he was seven, like his father before him, and *his* father, the first of his line, who in the very old days, before Hong Kong had existed, had been Number One Boy and looked after the Struan mansion in Macao.

'I don't understand, tai'pan.'

'You cannot wrap fire in paper. The police are clever and old Black Beard's a great supporter of police. Experts can examine brakes and deduce all sorts of information.'

'I know nothing of police.' The old man shrugged then beamed. 'Tai-pan, I do not climb trees to find a fish. Nor do you. May I mention that in the night I could not sleep and I came here. There was a shadow on the veranda balcony. The moment I opened the study door the shadow slid down the drainpipe and vanished into the shrubs.' The old man took out a torn piece of cloth. 'This was on the drainpipe.' The cloth was nondescript.

Dunross studied it, perturbed. He glanced at Dirk Struan's oil painting over the fireplace. It was perfectly in position. He moved it away and saw that the hair he had delicately balanced on a hinge of the safe was untouched. Satisfied, he replaced the picture, then checked the locks on the French windows. The two men were still loitering. For the first time Dunross was very glad that he had an SI guard.

34

It was hot and humid in Phillip Chen's study and he was sitting beside the phone staring at it nervously. The door swung open and he jumped. Dianne sailed in.

'There's no point in waiting anymore, Phillip,' she said irritably. 'You'd better go and change. That devil Werewolf won't call tonight. Something must have happened. Do come along!' She wore an evening *cheong-sam* in the latest, most expensive fashion, her hair bouffant, and she was bejeweled like a Christmas tree. 'Yes. Something must have happened. Perhaps the police . . . huh, it's too much to expect they caught him. More likely that *fang pi* devil's playing with us. You'd better change or we'll be late. If you hurr—'

'I really don't want to go,' he snapped back at her. 'Shitee T'Chung's a bore and now that he's Sir Shitee he's a double one.' Years ago Shi-teh had adulterated down to become the nickname *Shitee* to his intimate friends. 'Anyway, it's hardly eight o'clock and dinner's not till 9:30 and he's always late, his banquets are always at least an hour late. For God's sake, you go!'

'*Ayeeyah* you've got to come. It's a matter of face,' she replied, equally ill-tempered. 'My God, after today at the stock market . . . if we don't go we'll lose terrible face and it's sure to push the stock down further! All Hong Kong will laugh at us. They can't wait. They'll say we're so ashamed the House can't pay its bills that we won't show our face in public. Huh! And as for Shitee's new wife, Constance, that mealy-mouthed whore can't wait to see me humbled!' She was near screeching. Her losses on the day exceeded 100,000 of her own secret private dollars. When

591

Phillip had called her from the stock market just after three to relate what had happened she had almost fainted. '*Oh ko* you have to come or we'll be ruined!'

Miserably her husband nodded. He knew what gossips and rumormongers would be at the banquet. All day he had been inundated with questions, moans and panic. 'I suppose you're right.' He was down almost a million dollars on the day and if the run continued and Gornt won he knew he would be wiped out. Oh oh oh why did I trust Dunross and buy so heavily? he was thinking, so angry that he wanted to kick someone. He looked up at his wife. His heart sank as he recognized the signs of her awesome displeasure at the world in general, and him in particular. He quaked inside. 'All right,' he said meekly. 'I won't be a moment.'

When he got to the door the phone rang. Once more his heart twisted and he felt sick. There had been four calls since around six. Each had been a business call bewailing the fate of the stock, and were the rumors true and *oh ko*, Phillip, I'd better sell—each time worse than the last. '*Weyyyy?*' he asked angrily.

There was a short pause, then an equally rude voice said in crude Cantonese, 'You're in a foul temper whoever you are! Where are your fornicating manners?'

'Who's this? Eh, who's calling?' he asked in Cantonese.

'This is the Werewolf. The Chief Werewolf, by all the gods! Who're you?'

'Oh!' The blood drained from Phillip Chen's face. In panic he beckoned his wife. She rushed forward and bent to listen too, everything else forgotten except the safety of the House. 'This . . . this is Honorable Chen,' he said cautiously. 'Please, what's . . . what's your name?'

'Are your ears filled with wax? I said I was the Werewolf. Am I so stupid to give you my name?'

'I'm . . . I'm sorry but how do I know you're . . . you're telling me the truth?'

'How do I know who you are? Perhaps you're a dung-eating policeman. Who are you?'

'I'm Noble House Chen. I swear it!'

'Good. Then I wrote you a letter saying I'd call about 6:00 P.M. today. Didn't you get the letter?'

'Yes, yes I got the letter,' Phillip Chen said, trying to control a relief that was mixed with rage and frustration and terror. 'Let me talk to my Number One Son, please.'

'That's not possible, no, not possible! Can a frog think of eating a swan? Your son's in another part of the Island . . . actually, he's in the New Territories, not near a telephone but quite safe, Noble House Chen, oh yes, quite safe. He lacks for nothing. Do you have the ransom money?'

'Yes . . . at least I could only raise 100,000. Th—'

'All gods bear witness to my fornicating patience!' the man said angrily. 'You know very well we asked for 500,000! 5 or 10 it's still like one hair on ten oxen to you!'

'Lies!' Phillip Chen shrieked. 'That's all lies and rumors spread by my enemies! I'm not that rich. . . . Didn't you hear about the stock market today?' Phillip Chen groped for a chair, his heart pounding, and sat down still holding the phone so she could listen too.

'*Ayeeyah*, stock market! We poor farmers don't deal on the stock market! Do you want his other ear?'

Phillip Chen blanched. 'No. But we must negotiate. Five is too much. One and a half I can manage.'

'If I settle for one and a half I will be the laughingstock of all China! Are you accusing me of displaying a lamb's head but selling dogmeat? One and a half for the Number One Son of Noble House Chen? Impossible! It's face! Surely you can see that.'

Phillip Chen hesitated. 'Well,' he said reasonably, 'you have a point. First I want to know when I get my son back.'

'As soon as the ransom's paid! I promise on the bones of my ancestors! Within a few hours of getting the money he'll be put on the main Sha Tin Road.'

'Ah, he's in Sha Tin now?'

'*Ayeeyah*, you can't trap me, Noble House Chen. I smell dung in this conversation. Are the fornicating police listening? Is the dog acting fierce because his master's listening? Have you called the police?'

'No, I swear it. I haven't called the police and I'm not trying to trap you, but please, I need assurances, reasonable assurances.' Phillip Chen was beaded with sweat. 'You're quite safe, you have my oath, I haven't called the police. Why should I? If I call them how can we negotiate?'

There was another long hesitation, then the man said, somewhat mollified, 'I agree. But we have your son so any trouble that happens is your fault and not ours. All right, I'll be reasonable too. I will accept 400,000, but it must be tonight!'

'That's impossible! You ask me to fish in the sea to catch a tiger! I didn't get your letter till after the banks were closed but I've got 100,000 cash, in small bills. . . .' Dianne nudged him and held up two fingers. 'Listen, Honorable Werewolf, perhaps I can borrow more tonight. Perhaps . . . listen, I will give you two tonight. I'm sure I can raise that within the hour. 200,000!'

'May all gods smite me dead if I sell out for such a fornicating pittance. 350,000!'

'200,000 within the hour!'

'His other ear within two days or 300,000 tonight!'

Phillip Chen wailed and pleaded and flattered and cursed and they negotiated back and forth. Both men were adept. Soon both were caught up in the battle of wits, each using all his powers, the kidnapper using threats, Phillip Chen using guile, flattery and promises. At length, Phillip said, 'You are too good for me, too good a negotiator. I will pay 200,000 tonight and a further 100,000 within four months.'

'Within one month!'

'Three!' Phillip Chen was aghast at the flow of obscenities that followed and he wondered if he had misjudged his adversary.

'Two!'

Dianne nudged him again, nodding agreement. 'Very well,' he said, 'I agree. Another 100,000 in two months.'

'Good!' the man sounded satisfied, then he added, 'I will consider what you say and call you back.'

'But wait a moment, Honorable Werewolf. When wil—'

'Within the hour.'

'Bu—' The line went dead. Phillip Chen cursed, then mopped his brow again. 'I thought I had him. God curse the motherless dog turd!'

'Yes.' Dianne was elated. 'You did very well, Phillip! Only two now and another hundred in two months! Perfect! Anything can happen in two months. Perhaps the dirty police will catch them and then we won't have to pay the hundred!' Happily she took out a tissue and blotted the perspiration off her upper lip. Then her smile faded. 'What about Shitee

T'Chung? We've got to go but you'll have to wait.'

'Ah, I have it! Take Kevin, I'll come later. There'll be plenty of space for me whenever I get there. I'll . . . I'll wait for him to call back.'

'Excellent! How clever you are! We've got to get our coin back. Oh very good! Perhaps our joss has changed and the boom will happen like Old Blind Tung forecast. Kevin's so concerned for you, Phillip. The poor boy's so upset that you have all these troubles. He's very concerned for your health.' She hurried out, thanking the gods, knowing she would be back long before John Chen returned safely. Perfect, she was thinking, Kevin can wear his new white sharkskin dinner jacket. It's time he began to live up to his new position. 'Kevinnnnn!'

The door closed. Phillip Chen sighed. When he had gathered his strength, he went to the sideboard and poured himself a brandy. After Dianne and Kevin had left, he poured himself another. At a quarter to nine the phone rang again.

'Noble House Chen?'

'Yes . . . yes, Honorable Werewolf?'

'We accept. But it has to be tonight!'

Phillip Chen sighed. 'Very well. Now wh—'

'You can get all the money?'

'Yes.'

'The notes will be hundreds as I asked?'

'Yes. I have 100,000 and can get another hundred from a friend . . .'

'You have rich friends,' the man said suspiciously. 'Mandarins.'

'He's a bookmaker,' Phillip Chen said quickly, cursing himself for his slip. 'When you hung up I . . . I made the arrangements. Fortunately this happened to be one of his big nights.'

'All right. Listen, take a taxi—'

'Oh but I have a car an—'

'I know you have a fornicating car and I know the license number,' the man said rudely, 'and we know all about you and if you try to betray us to the police you will never see your son again and you will be next on our list! Understand?'

'Yes . . . yes, of course, Honorable Werewolf,' Phillip Chen said placatingly. 'I'm to take a taxi—where to?'

'The triangle garden at Kowloon Tong. There's a road called

Essex Road. There's a wall fence there and a hole in the wall. An arrow drawn on the pavement of the road has its arrowhead pointing at the hole. You put your hand in this hole and you'll get a letter. You read it then our street fighters will approach you and say '*Tin koon chi fook*' and you hand the bag over.'

'Oh! Isn't it possible I can hand it to the wrong man?'

'You won't. You understand the password and everything?'

'Yes . . . yes.'

'How long will it take you to get there?'

'I can come at once. I'll . . . I can get the other money on the way, I can come at once.'

'Then come immediately. Come alone, you cannot come with anyone else. You will be watched the moment you leave the door.'

Phillip Chen mopped his brow. 'And my son? When do I ge—'

'Obey instructions! Beware and come alone.'

Again the phone went dead. His fingers were shaking as he picked up the glass and drained the brandy. He felt a warm afterglow but it took away none of his apprehension. When he had collected himself, he dialed a very private number. 'I want to speak to Four Finger Wu,' he said in Wu's dialect.

'One moment please.' There were some muffled Haklo voices, and then, 'Is this Mr. Chen, Mr. Phillip Chen?' the voice asked in American English.

'Oh!' he said, startled, then added cautiously, 'Who's this?'

'This's Paul Choy, Mr. Chen. Mr. Wu's nephew. My uncle had to go out but he left instructions for me to wait until you called. He's made some arrangements for you. This is Mr. Chen?'

'Yes, yes, it is.'

'Ah, great. Have you heard from the kidnappers?'

'Yes, yes I have.' Phillip Chen was uneasy talking to a stranger but now he had no option. He told Paul Choy the instructions he had been given.

'Just a moment, sir.'

He heard a hand being put over the phone and again muffled, indistinct talking in Haklo dialect for a moment. 'Everything's set, sir. We'll send a cab to your house—you're phoning from Struan's Lookout?'

'Yes—yes, I'm home.'

'The driver'll be one of our guys. There'll be more of my uncle's, er, people scattered over Kowloon Tong so not to worry, you'll be covered every foot of the way. Just hand over the money and, er, and they'll take care of everything. My uncle's chief lieut—er, his aide, says not to worry, they'll have the whole area swarming . . . Mr. Chen?'

'Yes, I'm still here. Thank you.'

'The cab'll be there in twenty minutes.'

Paul Choy put down the phone. 'Noble House Chen says thank you, Honorable Father,' he told Four Finger Wu placatingly in their dialect, quaking under the stony eyes. Sweat was beading his face. He tried unsuccessfully to hide the fear of the others. It was hot and stuffy in the crowded main cabin of this ancient junk that was tied up in a permanent berth to an equally ancient dock in one of Aberdeen's multitude of estuaries. 'Can I go with your fighters, too?'

'Do you send a rabbit against a dragon?' Four Finger Wu snarled. 'Are you trained as a street fighter? Am I a fool like you? Treacherous like you?' He jerked a horny thumb at Goodweather Poon. 'Lead the fighters!' The man hurried out The others followed.

Now the two of them were alone in the cabin.

The old man was sitting on an upturned keg. He lit another cigarette, inhaled deeply, coughed and spat loudly on the deck floor. Paul Choy watched him, the sweat running down his back, more from fear than from the heat. Around them were some old desks, filing cabinets, rickety chairs and two phones, and this was Four Fingers's office and communications center. It was mostly from here that he sent messages to his fleets. Much of his business was regular freighting but wherever the Silver Lotus flag flew, his order to his captains was: Anything, shipped anywhere, at any time—at the right price.

The tough old man coughed again and glared at him under shaggy eyebrows. 'They teach you curious ways in the Golden Mountain, *heya*?'

Paul Choy held his tongue and waited, his heart thumping, and wished he had never come back to Hong Kong, that he was still Stateside, or even better in Honolulu surfing in the Great Waves or lying on the beach with his girl friend. His spirit twisted at the thought of her.

'They teach you to bite the hand that feeds you, *heya?*'

'No, Honored Father, sorr—'

'They teach that my money is yours, my wealth yours and my chop yours to use as you wish, *heya?*'

'No, Honored Lord. I'm sorry to displease you,' Paul Choy muttered, wilting under the weight of his fear.

This morning, early, when Gornt had jauntily come into the office from the meeting with Bartlett, it was still before the secretaries were due so Paul Choy had asked if he could help him. Gornt had told him to get several people on the phone. Others he had dialed himself on his private line. Paul Choy had thought nothing of it at the time until he happened to overhear part of what was, obviously, inside information about Struan's being whispered confidentially over the phone. Remembering the Bartlett call earlier, deducing that Gornt and Bartlett had had a meeting—a successful one judging by Gornt's good humor— and realizing Gornt was relating the same confidences over and over, his curiosity peaked. Later, he happened to hear Gornt saying to his solicitor, '. . . selling short . . . No, don't worry, nothing's going to happen till I'm covered, not till about eleven. . . . Certainly. I'll send the order, chopped, as soon as . . .'

The next call he was asked to make was long distance to the manager of the Bank of Switzerland and Zurich that, discreetly, he listened to. '. . . I'm expecting a large draft of U.S. dollars this morning, before eleven. Phone me the instant, the very instant it's in my account . . .'

So, bemused, he had put the various pieces of the equation together and come up with a theory: If Bartlett has arranged a sudden secret partnership with Gornt, Struan's known enemy, to launch one of his raids, if Bartlett also takes part of the risk, or most of it—by secretly putting large sums in one of Gornt's numbered Swiss accounts to cover any sell-short losses—and lastly, if he's talked Gornt into being the front guy while he sits on the fence, the stuff is going to hit the fan in the exchange and Struan's stock has got to go down.

This precipitated an immediate business decision: Jump in

quickly and sell Struan's short before the big guys and we'll make a bundle.

He remembered how he had almost groaned aloud because he had no money, no credit, no shares and no means to borrow any. Then he recalled what one of his instructors at Harvard Business School had kept drumming into them: A faint heart never laid a lovely lady. So he'd gone into a private office and phoned his newfound friend, Ishwar Soorjani, the money-lender and dealer in foreign exchange whom he had met through the old Eurasian at the library. 'Say, Ishwar, your brother's head of Soorjani Stockbrokers, isn't he?'

'No, Young Master. Arjan is my very first cousin. Why?'

'If I wanted to sell a stock short would you back me?'

'Certainly, as I told you before, buying or selling I support you to the holster, if you have reasonable cash to cover any losses . . . or the equivalent. No cash or equivalent so sorry.'

'Say I had some red-hot information?'

'The road to hell and debtor's prison is flooded to drowning with red-hot information, Young Master. I advise against red-hot informations.'

'Boy,' Paul Choy said unhappily, 'I could make us a few 100,000 before three.'

'Oh? Would you care to whisper the illustrious name of the stock?'

'Would you back me for . . . for 20,000 U.S.?'

'Ah, so sorry, Young Master, I'm a moneylender not a money giver. My ancestors forbid it!'

'20,000 HK?'

'Not even 10 dollars in your Rebel Dixie redbacks.'

'Gee, Ishwar, you're not much help.'

'Why not ask your illustrious uncle? His chop . . . and I would instantly go to half a million HK.'

Paul Choy knew that among his father's cash and assets transferred from the Ho-Pak to the Victoria had been many stock certificates and a list of securities held by various stock-brokers. One was for 150,000 Struan shares. Jesus, he thought, if I'm right the old man might get dumped. If Gornt presses the raid the old man could get caught.

'Good idea, Ishwar. I'll call you back!' At once he had phoned his father but he could not reach him. He left messages wher-

599

ever he could and began to wait. His anxiety grew. Just before ten he heard Gornt's secretary answer the phone. 'Yes? . . . Oh, one moment please. . . . Mr. Gornt? A person-to-person call from Zurich. . . . You're through.'

Once more he had tried to reach his father, wanting to give him the urgent news. Then Gornt had sent for him. 'Mr Choy, would you please run this over to my solicitor at once.' He handed over the sealed envelope. 'Give it to him personally.'

'Yes sir.'

So he had left the office. At every phone he had stopped and tried to reach his father. Then he had delivered the note, personally, watching the solicitor's face carefully. He saw glee. 'Is there a reply, sir?' he asked politely.

'Just say everything will be done as ordered.' It was a few minutes past ten.

Outside the office door and going down the elevator Paul Choy had weighed the pluses and the minuses. His stomach twisting uneasily, he stopped at the nearest phone. 'Ishwar? Say, I've an urgent order from my uncle. He wants to sell his Struan stock. 150,000 shares.'

'Ah, wise wise, there are terrible rumors speeding around.'

'I suggested you and Soorjani's should do it for him. 150,000 shares. He asks can you do it instantly? Can you do that?'

'Like a bird on the wing. For the Esteemed Four Fingers we will go forth like Rothschilds! Where are the shares?'

'In the vault.'

'I will need his chop at once.'

'I'm going to get it now but he said to sell at once. He said to sell in small blocks so as not to shock the market. He wants the very best price. You'll sell at once?'

'Yes, never fear, at once. And we will get the best price!'

'Good. And most important, he said to keep this secret.'

'Verily, Young Master, you may trust us implicitly. And the stock that you yourself wished to sell short?'

'Oh that . . . well that'll have to wait . . . until I've credit *heya?*'

'Wise very wise.'

Paul Choy shivered. His heart was pounding now in the silence and he watched his father's cigarette, not the angry face, knowing those cold black eyes were boring into him, deciding his fate. He remembered how he had almost shouted with excitement when the stock began to fall almost immediately, monitoring it moment by moment, then ordering Soorjani to buy back just before close and feeling light-headed and in euphoria. At once he had phoned his girl, spending nearly 30 of his valuable U.S. dollars telling her how fantastic his day had been and how much he missed her. She said how much she missed him too and when was he coming back to Honolulu? Her name was Mika Kasunari and she was *sansei*, third-generation American of Japanese descent. Her parents hated him because he was Chinese, as he knew his father would hate her because she was Japanese except they were both American, both of them, and they had met and fallen in love at school.

'Very soon, honey,' he had promised her ecstatically, 'guaranteed by Christmas! After today my uncle'll surely give me a bonus. . . .'

The work that Gornt gave him for the rest of the day he breezed through. Late in the afternoon Goodweather Poon had phoned to say his father would see him in Aberdeen at 7:30 P.M. Before he went there he had collected Soorjani's check made out to his father. 615,000 HK less brokerage.

Elated, he had come to Aberdeen and given him the check, and when he told him what he had done he was aghast at the extent of his father's rage. The tirade had been interrupted by Phillip Chen's phone call.

'I'm deeply sorry I've offended you, Hon—'

'So my chop is yours, my wealth is yours *heya*?' Four Finger Wu shouted suddenly.

'No, Honored Father,' he gasped, 'but the information was so good and I wanted to protect your stock as well as make money for you.'

'But not for you *heya*?'

'No, Honored Father. It was for you. To make you money, and help repay all the money you invested in me . . . they were your shares and it's your money. I tried to ca—'

'That's no fornicating excuse! You come with me!'

Shakily Paul Choy got up and followed the old man onto the deck. Four Finger Wu cursed his bodyguard away and pointed a stubby finger at the befouled muddy waters in the harbor. 'If you weren't my son,' he hissed, 'if you weren't my son you'd be feeding the fish there, your feet in a chain, this very moment.'

'Yes, Father.'

'If you ever again use my name, my chop, my anything without my approval you're a dead man.'

'Yes, Father,' Paul Choy muttered, petrified, realizing that his father had the means, the will and the authority to put that threat into effect without fear of retaliation. 'Sorry, Father. I swear I'll never do that again.'

'Good. If you'd lost one bronze cash you'd be there now. It's only because you fornicating won that you're alive now.'

'Yes, Father.'

Four Finger Wu glared at his son and continued to hide his delight at the huge windfall. 615,000 HK less a few dollars. Unbelievable! All with a few phone calls and inside knowledge, he was thinking. That's as miraculous as having ten tons of opium leap ashore over the heads of the Customs boat! The boy's paid for his education twenty times over and he's here hardly three weeks. How clever . . . but also how dangerous!

He shivered at the thought of other minions making decisions themselves. *Dew neh loh moh* then I would be in their power and surely in jail for their mistakes and not my own. And yet, he told himself helplessly, this is the way barbarians act in business. Number Seven Son is trained as a barbarian. All gods bear witness, I did not wish to create a viper!

He looked at his son, not understanding him, hating his direct way of speaking, the barbarian way and not in innuendo and obliquely like a civilized person.

And yet . . . and yet better than 600,000 HK in one day. If I had talked to him beforehand I would never have agreed and I would have lost all that profit! *Ayeeyah!* Yes, my stock would be down all that fortune in one day . . . oh oh oh!

He groped for a box and sat down, his heart thumping at that awful thought.

His eyes were watching his son. What to do about him? he asked himself. He could feel the weight of the check in his pocket. It seemed unbelievable that his son could make that amount of money for him in a few hours, without moving the stock from its hiding place.

'Explain to me why that black-faced foreign devil with the foul name owes me so much money!'

Paul Choy explained the mechanics patiently, desperate to please.

The old man thought about that. 'Then tomorrow I should do the same and make the same?'

'No, Honored Father. You take your gains and keep them. Today was almost a certainty. It was a sudden attack, a raid. We do not know how the Noble House will react tomorrow, or if Gornt really intends to continue the raid. He can buy back in and be way ahead too. It would be dangerous to follow Gornt tomorrow, very dangerous.'

Four Finger Wu threw his cigarette away. 'Then what should I do tomorrow?'

'Wait. The foreign devil market's nervous and in the hands of foreign devils. I counsel you to wait and see what happens with the Ho-Pak and the Victoria. May I use your name to ask the foreign devil Gornt about the Ho-Pak?'

'What?'

Patiently Paul Choy refreshed his father's memory about the bank run and possible stock manipulation.

'Ah, yes, I understand,' the old man said loftily. Paul Choy said nothing, knowing he did not. 'Then we . . . then I just wait?'

'Yes, Honored Father.'

Four Fingers pulled out the check distastefully. 'And this fornicating piece of paper? What about this?'

'Convert it into gold, Honored Father. The price hardly varies at all. I could talk to Ishwar Soorjani, if you wish. He deals in foreign exchange.'

'And where would I keep the gold?' It was one thing to smuggle other people's gold but quite another to have to worry about your own.

Paul Choy explained that physical possession of the gold was not necessary to own it.

'But I don't trust banks,' the old man said angrily. 'If it's my gold it's my gold and not a bank's!'

'Yes, Father. But this would be a Swiss bank, not in Hong Kong, and completely safe.'

'You guarantee it with your life?'

'Yes, Father.'

'Good.' The old man took out a pen and signed his name on

the back with instructions to Soorjani to convert it at once into gold. He gave it to his son. 'On your head, my son. And we wait tomorrow? We don't make money tomorrow?'

'There might be an opportunity for further profit but I could not guarantee it. I might know around noon.'

'Call me here at noon.'

'Yes, Father. Of course if we had our own exchange we could manipulate a hundred stocks . . .' Paul Choy let the idea hang in the air.

'What?'

Carefully the young man began to explain how easy it would be for them to form their own exchange, a Chinese-dominated exchange, and the limitless opportunities for profit their own exchange would give. He talked for an hour, gaining confidence with the minutes, explaining as simply as he could.

'If it's so easy, my son, why hasn't Tightfist Tung done it—or Big Noise Sung—or Moneybags Ng—or that half-barbarian gold-smuggler from Macao—or Banker Kwang or dozens of others, *heya*?'

'Perhaps they've never had the idea, or courage. Perhaps they want to work within the foreign devil system—the Turf Club, Cricket Club, knighthoods, and all that English foolishness. Perhaps they are afraid to go against the tide or they haven't got the knowledge. We have the knowledge and expertise. Yes. And I've a friend in the Golden Mountain, a good friend, who was at school with me who co—'

'What friend?'

'He's Shanghainese and a dragon in stocks, a broker in New York now. Together, with the cash support, we could do it. I know we could.'

'*Ayeeyah!* With a northern barbarian?' Four Finger Wu scoffed. 'How could you trust him?'

'I think you could trust him, Honored Father—of course you'd set boundaries against weeds like a good market gardener does.'

'But all business power in Hong Kong is in the hands of foreign devils. Civilized persons couldn't support an opposition exchange.'

'You may be right, Honored Father,' Paul Choy agreed cautiously, keeping his excitement off his face and out of his voice.

'But all Chinese love to gamble. Yet at the moment there's not one civilized person stockbroker! Why do foreign devils keep us out? Because we'd outplay them. For us the stock market's the greatest profession in the world. Once our people in Hong Kong see our market is wide open to civilized persons and *their* companies, they'll flock to us. Foreign devils will be forced to open up their own exchange to us as well. We're better gamblers than they are. After all, Honorable Father'—he waved his hand at the shore, at the tall high rises and the boats and junks and floating restaurants—'this could be all yours! It's in stocks and shares and the stock market that the modern man *owns* the might of his world.'

Four Fingers smoked leisurely. 'How much would your stock market cost, Number Seven Son?'

'A year of time. An initial investment of . . . I don't know exactly.' The young man's heart was grinding. He could sense his father's avarice. The implications of forming a Chinese stock exchange in this unregulated capitalistic society were so far-reaching to him that he felt faint. It would be so easy given time and . . . and how much? 'I could give you an estimate within a week.'

Four Fingers turned his shrewd old eyes on his son and he could read his son's excitement, and his greed. Is it for money, or for power? he asked himself.

It's for both, he decided. The young fool doesn't know that they're both the same. He thought about Phillip Chen's power and the power of the Noble House and the power of the half-coin that John Chen had stolen. Phillip Chen and his wife are fools too, he told himself. They should remember that there are always ears on the other side of walls and once a jealous mother knows a secret it is a secret no longer. Nor can secrets be kept in hotels, among foreign devils, who always presume servants cannot speak the barbarian tongue, nor have long ears and sharp eyes.

Ah sons, he mused. Sons are certainly the wealth of a father—but sometimes also cause the death of the father.

A man's a fool to trust a son. Completely. *Heya?*

'Very well, my son,' he said easily. 'Give me your plan, written down, and the amount. And I will decide.'

* * *

Phillip Chen got out of the taxi at the grass triangle in Kowloon Tong, the attaché case clutched to his chest. The driver turned the meter off and looked at him. The meter read 17.80 HK. If it had been left up to Phillip he would not have taken the same taxi all the way from Struan's Lookout, which meant using the taxi ferry, the meter running all the time. No. He would have crossed the harbor by the Golden Ferry for 15 cents, and got another taxi in Kowloon and saved at least 8 dollars. Terrible waste of money, he thought.

Carefully he counted out 18 dollars. As an afterthought he added a thirty-cent tip, feeling generous. The man drove off and left him standing near the grassy triangle.

Kowloon Tong was just another suburb of Kowloon, a multitudinous nest of buildings, slums, alleys, people and traffic. He found Essex Road, that skirted the garden, and walked around the road. The attaché case seemed to be getting heavier and he felt sure everyone knew it contained 200,000 HK. His nervousness increased. In an area like this you could buy the death of a man for a few hundred if you knew whom to ask—and for this amount, you could hire an army. His eyes were on the broken pavement. When he had gone almost all the way around the triangle he saw the arrow on the pavement pointing at the wall. His heart was weighty in his chest, hurting him. It was quite dark here, with few streetlights. The hole was formed by some bricks that had fallen away. He could see what looked like a crumpled-up newspaper within the hole. He hastily took it out, made sure there was nothing else left, then went over to a seat under a lamp and sat down. When his heart had slowed and his breathing become more calm he opened the newspaper. In it was an envelope. The envelope was flat and some of his anxiety left him. He had been petrified that he was going to get the other ear.

The note said: 'Walk to Waterloo Road. Go north toward the army camp, staying on the west side of the road. Beware, we are watching you now.'

A shiver went through him and he looked around. No one seemed to be watching him. Neither friend nor foe. But he could feel eyes. His attaché case became even more leaden.

All gods protect me, he prayed fervently, trying to gather his courage to continue. Where the devil are Four Finger Wu's men?

Waterloo Road was nearby, a busy main thoroughfare. He paid the crowds no attention, just plodded north feeling naked, seeing no one in particular. The shops were all open, restaurants bustling, alleyways more crowded. In the nearby embankment a goods train whistled mournfully, going north, mixing with the blaring horns that all traffic used indiscriminately. The night was bleak, the sky overcast and very humid.

Wearily he walked half a mile, crossing side streets and alleys. In a knot of people he stopped to let a truck pass, then went across the mouth of another narrow alleyway, moving this way and that as oncomers jostled him. Suddenly two young men were in front of him, barring his path, and one hissed, '*Tin koon chi fook!*'

'Eh?'

Both wore caps pulled down low, both wore dark glasses, their faces similar. '*Tin koon chi fook!*' Smallpox Kin repeated malevolently. '*Dew neh loh moh* give me the bag!'

'Oh!' Blankly Phillip Chen handed it to him. Smallpox Kin grabbed it. 'Don't look around, and keep on walking north!'

'All right, but please keep your prom—' Phillip Chen stopped. The two youths were gone. It seemed that they had only been in front of him a split second. Still in shock he forced his feet into motion, trying to etch the little he had seen of their faces on his memory. Then an oncoming woman shoved him rudely and he swore, their faces fading. Then someone grabbed him roughly.

'Where's the fornicating bag?'

'What?' he gasped, staring down at the evil-looking thug who was Goodweather Poon.

'Your bag—where's it gone?'

'Two young men . . .' Helplessly he pointed backward. The man cursed and hurried past, weaving in and out of the crowd, put his fingers to his lips and whistled shrilly. Few people paid any attention to him. Other toughs began to converge, then Goodweather Poon caught sight of the two youths with the attaché case as they turned off the well-lit main road into an alley. He broke into a run, others following him.

Smallpox Kin and his younger brother went into the crowds without hurrying, the alley unlit except for the bare bulbs of the dingy stalls and stores. They grinned, one to another. Com-

607

pletely confident now, they took off their glasses and caps and stuffed them into their pockets. Both were very similar—almost twins—and now they melted even more into the raucous shoppers.

'*Deh neh loh moh* that old bastard looked frightened to death!' Smallpox Kin chortled. 'In one step we have reached heaven!'

'Yes. And next week when we snatch him he'll pay up as easily as an old dog farts!'

They laughed and stopped a moment in the light of a stall and peeked into the bag. When they both saw the bundle of notes both sighed. '*Ayeeyah*, truly we've reached heaven with one step, Elder Brother. Pity the son is dead and buried.'

Smallpox Kin shrugged as they went on, turning into a smaller alley, then another, surefooted in the darkening maze. 'Honorable Father's right. We have turned ill luck into good. It wasn't your fault that bastard's head was soft! Not at all! When we dig him up and leave him on the Sha Tin Road with the note on his fornicating chest. . . .' He stopped a moment and they stepped aside in the bustling, jostling crowds to allow a laden, broken-down truck to squeeze past. As they waited he happened to glance back. At the far end of this alley he saw three men change direction, seeing him, then begin to hurry toward him.

'*Dew neh loh moh* we're betrayed,' he gasped then shoved his way forward and took to his heels, his brother close behind.

The two youths were very fast. Terror lent cunning to their feet as they rushed through the cursing crowd, maneuvering around the inevitable potholes and small stalls, the darkness helping them. Smallpox Kin led the charge. He ducked between some stalls and fled down the narrow unlit passageway, the attaché case clutched tightly. 'Go home a different way, Young Brother,' he gasped.

At the next corner he rushed left and his brother went directly on. Their three pursuers split up as well, two following him. It was almost impossible to see now in the darkness and the alleys twisted and turned and never a dead end. His chest was heaving but he was well ahead of his pursuers. He fled into a shortcut and at once turned into a bedraggled store that, like all the rest, served as a dwelling. Careless of the family huddled around a screeching television he rushed through them and out the back door, then doubled back to the end of the alley. He peered around the corner with great caution. A few people watched him curiously but continued on their way without stopping, wanting no part of what clearly was trouble.

Then, hoping he was safe, he slid into the crowds and walked away quietly, his head down. His breath was still labored and his head was filled with obscenities and he swore vengeance on Phillip Chen for betraying them. All gods bear witness, he thought furiously, when we kidnap him next week, before we let him go I'll slice off his nose! How dare he betray us to the police! Hey, wait a moment, were those police?

He thought about that as he wandered along the stream, cautiously doubling back from time to time, just in case. But now he was sure he was not followed. He let his mind consider the money and he beamed. Let's see, what will I do with my 50,000! I'll put 40 down on an apartment and rent it out at once. *Ayeeyah*, I'm a property owner! I'll buy a Rolex and a revolver and a new throwing knife. I'll give my wife a bracelet or two, and a couple to White Rose at the Thousand Pleasure Whorehouse. Tonight we'll have a feast. . . .

Happily he continued on his way. At a street stall he bought a small cheap suitcase and, in an alley, secretly transferred the money into it. Farther down the street in another side alley he sold Phillip Chen's good leather attaché case to a hawker for a handsome sum after haggling for five minutes. Now, very pleased with himself, he caught a bus for Kowloon City where his father had rented a small apartment in an assumed name as one of their havens, far away from their real home in Wanchai near Glessing's Point. He did not notice Goodweather Poon board the bus, nor the other two men, nor the taxi that followed the bus.

Kowloon City was a festering mass of slums and open drains and squalid dwellings. Smallpox Kin knew he was safe here. No police ever came, except in great strength. When China had leased the New Territories for ninety-nine years in 1898 it had maintained suzerainty over Kowloon City in perpetuity. In theory the ten square acres were Chinese territory. The British authorities left the area alone provided it remained quiet. It was a seething mass of opium dens, illegal gambling schools, triad headquarters, and a sanctuary for the criminal. From time to time the police would sweep through. The next day Kowloon City would become as it had always been.

The stairs to the fifth-floor apartment in the tenement building were rickety and messy, the plaster cracked and mildewed. He was tired now. He knocked on the door, in their secret code. The door opened.

'Hello, Father, hello, Dog-eared Chen,' he said happily. 'Here's the cash!' Then he saw his younger brother. 'Oh good, you escaped too?'

'Of course! Dung-eating police in civilian clothes! We ought to kill one or two for their impertinence.' Kin Pak waved a .38. 'We ought to have vengeance!'

'Perhaps you're right, now that we've got the first money,' Father Kin said.

'I don't think we should kill any police, that would send them mad,' Dog-eared Chen said shakily.

'*Dew neh loh moh* on all police!' young Kin Pak said and pocketed the gun.

Smallpox Kin shrugged. 'We've got the cash th—'

At that moment the door burst open. Goodweather Poon and three of his men were in the room, knives out. Everyone froze. Abruptly Father Kin slid a knife out of his sleeve and ducked left but before he could throw it Goodweather Poon's knife was flailing through the air and thwanged into his throat. He clawed at it as he fell backward. Neither Dog-eared Chen nor the brothers had moved. They watched him die. The body twitched, the muscles spasmed for a moment, then was still.

'Where's Number One Son Chen?' Goodweather Poon said, a second knife in his hand.

'We don't know any Num—'

Two of the men fell on Smallpox Kin, slammed his hands outstretched on the table and held them there. Goodweather Poon leaned forward and sliced off his index finger. Smallpox Kin went gray. The other two were paralyzed with fear.

'Where's Number One Son Chen?'

Smallpox Kin was staring blankly at his severed finger and the blood that was pulsing onto the table. He cried out as Goodweather Poon lunged again. 'Don't don't,' he begged, 'he's dead . . . dead and we've buried him I swear it!'

'Where?'

'Near the Sha . . . the Sha Tin Road. Listen,' he screeched desperately, 'we'll split the money with you. We'll—' He froze as Goodweather Poon put the tip of his knife into his mouth.

'Just answer questions, you fornicating whore's turd, or I'll slit your tongue. Where's Number One Son's things? The things he had on him?'

'We, we sent everything to Noble House Chen, everything except the money he had. I swear it.' He whimpered at the pain. Suddenly the two men put pressure on one of his elbows and he cried out, 'All gods bear witness it's the truth!' He screamed as the joint went, and fainted. Across the room Dog-eared Chen groaned with fear. He started to cry out but one of the men smashed him in the face, his head crashed against the wall and he collapsed, unconscious.

Now all their eyes went to Kin Pak. 'It's true,' Kin Pak gasped in terror at the suddenness of everything. 'Everything he told you. It's true!'

Goodweather Poon cursed him. Then he said, 'Did you search Noble House Chen before you buried him?'

'Yes, Lord, at least I didn't, he . . .' Shakily he pointed at his father's body. 'He did.'

'You were there?'

The youth hesitated. Instantly Poon darted at him, moving with incredible speed for such an old man. His knife nicked Kin Pak's cheek a deliberate fraction below his eyes and stayed there. 'Liar!'

'I was there,' the youth choked out, 'I was going to tell you, Lord, I was, there. I won't lie to you I swear it!'

'The next time you lie it will be your left eye. You were there, *heya?*'

'Yes . . . yes, Lord!'

'Was he there?' he said pointing at Smallpox Kin.

'No, Lord.'

'Him?'

'Yes. Dog-eared was there!'

'Did you search the body?'

'Yes, Lord, yes I helped our father.'

'All his pockets, everything?'

'Yes yes everything.'

'Any papers? Notebook, diary? Jewelry?'

The youth hesitated, frantic, trying to think, the knife never moving away from his face. 'Nothing, Lord, that I remember. We sent all his things to Noble House Chen, except, except the money. We kept the money. And his watch—I'd forgotten his watch! It's, it's that one!' He pointed at the watch on his father's outstretched wrist.

Goodweather Poon swore again. Four Finger Wu had told him to recapture John Chen, to get any of his possessions the kidnappers still had, particularly any coins or parts of coins, and then, equally anonymously, to dispose of the kidnappers. I'd better phone him in a moment, he thought. I'd better get further instructions. I don't want to make a mistake.

'What did you do with the money?'

'We spent it, Lord. There were only a few hundred dollars and some change. It's gone.'

One of the men said, 'I think he's lying!'

'I'm not, Lord, I swear it!' Kin Pak almost burst into tears. 'I'm not. Pl—'

'Shut up! Shall I cut this one's throat?' the man said genially, motioning at Smallpox Kin who was still unconscious, sprawled across the table, the pool of blood thickening.

'No, no, not yet. Hold him there.' Goodweather Poon scratched his piles while he thought a moment. 'We'll go and dig up Number One Son Chen. Yes that's what we'll do. Now, Little Turd, who killed him?'

At once Kin Pak pointed at his father's body. 'He did. It was terrible. He's our father and he hit him with a shovel . . . he hit him with a shovel when he tried to escape the night . . . the night we got him.' The youth shuddered, his face chalky, his fear of the knife under his eye consuming him. 'It, it wasn't my fault, Lord.'

'What's your name?'

'Soo Tak-gai, Lord,' he said instantly, using their prearranged emergency names.

'Him?' The finger pointed at his brother.

'Soo Tak-tong.'

'Him?'

'Wu-tip Sup.'

'And him?'

The youth looked at his father's body. 'He was Goldtooth

Soo, Lord. He was very bad, but we . . . we, we had to obey. We had to obey him, he was our, our father.'

'Where did you take Number One Son Chen before you killed him?'

'To Sha Tin, Lord, but I didn't kill him. We snatched him Hong Kong side then put him in the back of a car we stole and went to Sha Tin. There's an old shack our father rented, just outside the village . . . he planned everything. We had to obey him.'

Poon grunted and nodded at his men. 'We'll search here first.' At once they released Smallpox Kin, the unconscious youth who slumped to the floor, leaving a trail of blood. 'You, bind up his finger!' Hastily Kin Pak grabbed an old dishcloth and, near vomiting, began to tie a rough tourniquet around the stump.

Poon sighed, not knowing what to do first. After a moment he opened the suitcase. All their eyes went to the mountain of notes. They all felt the greed. Poon shifted the knife into his other hand and closed the suitcase. He left it in the center of the table and started to search the dingy apartment. There was just a table, a few chairs and an old iron bedstead with a soiled mattress. Paper was peeling off the walls, the windows mostly boarded up and glassless. He turned the mattress over, then searched it but it concealed nothing. He went into the filthy, almost empty kitchen and switched on the light. Then into the foul-smelling toilet. Smallpox Kin whimpered, coming around.

In a drawer Goodweather Poon found some papers, ink and writing brushes. 'What's this for?' he asked, holding up one of the papers. On it was written in bold characters: 'This Number One Son Chen had the stupidity to try to escape us. No one can escape the Werewolves! Let all Hong Kong beware. Our eyes are everywhere!' 'What's this for, *heya?*'

Kin Pak looked up from the floor, desperate to please. 'We couldn't return him alive to Noble House Chen so our father ordered that . . . that tonight we were to dig Number One Son up and put that on his chest and put him beside the Sha Tin Road.'

Goodweather Poon looked at him. 'When you start to dig you'd better find him quickly, the first time,' he said malevolently. 'Yes. Or your eyes, Little Turd, won't be anywhere.

613

35

Orlanda Ramos came up the wide staircase of the vast *Floating Dragon* restaurant at Aberdeen and moved through the noisy, chattering guests at Sir Shi-teh T'Chung's banquet looking for Linc Bartlett—and Casey.

The two hours that she had spent with Linc this morning for the newspaper interview had been revealing, particularly about Casey. Her instincts had told her the sooner she brought the enemy to battle the better. It had been easy to have them both invited tonight—Shi-teh was an old associate of Gornt and an old friend. Gornt had been pleased with her idea.

They were on the top deck. There was a nice smell of the sea coming through the large windows, the night good though humid, overcast, and all around were the lights of the high rises and the township of Aberdeen. Out in the harbor, nearby, were the brooding islands of junks, partially lit, where 150,000 boat people lived their lives.

The room they were in, scarlet and gold and green, stretched half the length and the whole breadth of the boat, off the central staircase. Ornate wood and plaster gargoyles and unicorns and dragons were everywhere throughout the three soaring decks of the restaurant ablaze with lights and packed with diners. Below decks, the cramped kitchens held twenty-eight cooks, an army of helpers, a dozen huge cauldrons—steam, sweat and smoke. Eighty-two waiters serviced the *Floating Dragon*. There were seats for four hundred on each of the first two decks and two hundred on the third. Sir Shi-teh had taken over the whole top deck and now it was well filled with his guests, standing in impatient groups amid the round tables that seated twelve.

Orlanda felt fine tonight and very confident. She had again dressed meticulously for Bartlett. This morning when she had had the interview with him she had worn casual American clothes and little makeup, and the loose, silk blouse that she had selected so carefully did not flaunt her bralessness, merely suggested it. This daring new fashion pleased her greatly, making her even more aware of her femininity. Tonight she wore delicate white silk. She knew her figure was perfect, that she was envied for her open, unconscious sensuality.

That's what Quillan did for me, she thought, her lovely head high and the curious half-smile lighting her face—one of the many things. He made me understand sensuality.

Havergill and his wife were in front of her and she saw their eyes on her breasts. She laughed to herself, well aware that, even discreetly, she would be the only woman in the room who had dared to be so modern, to emulate the fashion that had begun the year before in Swinging London.

'Evening, Mr. Havergill, Mrs. Havergill,' she said politely, moving around them in the crush. She knew him well. Many times he had been invited onto Gornt's yacht. Sometimes Gornt's yacht would steam out from the Yacht Club, Hong Kong side, with just her and Quillan and his men friends aboard and go over to Kowloon, to the sea-washed steps beside the Golden Ferry where the girls would be waiting, dressed in sun clothes or boating clothes.

In her early days with Quillan she too had had to wait Kowloon side, honoring the golden rule in the Colony that discretion was all important and when you live Hong Kong side you play Kowloon side, live Kowloon side, play Hong Kong side.

In the days when Quillan's wife was bedridden and Orlanda was openly, though still most discreetly, Quillan's mistress, Quillan would take her with him to Japan and Singapore and Taiwan but never Bangkok. In those days Paul Havergill was Paul or more likely, Horny—Horny Hav-a-girl, as he was known to most of his intimates. But even then, whenever she would meet him in public, like tonight, it would always be Mr. Havergill. He's not a bad man, she told herself, remembering that though most of his girls never liked him, they fawned on him for he was reasonably generous and could always arrange a sudden loan at low interest for a friend through one of his banking associates, but never at the Vic.

Wise, she thought, amused, and a matter of face. Ah, but I could write such a book about them all if I wanted to. I never will—I don't think I ever will. Why should I, there's no reason. Even after Macao I've always kept the secrets. That's another thing Quillan taught me—discretion.

Macao. What a waste! I can hardly remember what that young man looked like now, only that he was awful at the pillow and, because of him, my life was destroyed. The fool was only a sudden, passing fancy, the very first. It was only loneliness because Quillan was away a month and everyone away, and it was lust for youth—just the youth-filled body that had attracted me and proved to be so useless. Fool! What a fool I was!

Her heart began fluttering at the thought of all those nightmares: being caught, being sent to England, having to fight the youth off, desperate to please Quillan, then coming back and Quillan so cool and never pillowing with him again. And then the greater nightmare of adjusting to a life without him.

Terrifying days. That awful unquenchable desire. Being alone. Being excluded. All the tears and the misery then trying to begin again but cautiously, always hoping he would relent if I was patient. Never anyone in Hong Kong, always alone in Hong Kong, but when the urge was too much, going away and trying but never satisfied. Oh Quillan, what a lover you were!

Not long ago his wife had died and then, when the time was right, Orlanda had gone to see him. To seduce him back to her. That night she had thought that she had succeeded but he had only been toying with her. 'Put your clothes on, Orlanda. I was just curious about your body, I wanted to see if it was still as exquisite as it was in *my* day. I'm delighted to tell you it is—you're still perfection. But, so sorry, I don't desire you.' And all her frantic weepings and pleadings made no difference. He just listened and smoked a cigarette then stubbed it out. 'Orlanda, please don't ever come here again uninvited,' he had said so quietly. 'You chose Macao.'

And he was right, I did, I took his face away. Why does he still support me? she asked herself, her eyes wandering the guests, seeking Bartlett. Do you have to lose something before you find its true value? Is that what life is?

'Orlanda!'

She stopped, startled, as someone stepped in her way. Her eyes focused. It was Richard Hamilton Pugmire. He was slightly shorter than she was. 'May I introduce Charles Biltzmann from America,' he was saying with a leer, his nearness making her skin crawl. 'Charles's going to be, the, er, the new tai-pan of General Stores. Chuck, this's Orlanda Ramos!'

'Pleased to meet you, ma'am!'

'How are you?' she said politely, instantly disliking him. 'I'm sorry—'

'Call me Chuck. It's Orlanda? Say, that's a mighty pretty name, mighty pretty dress!' Biltzmann produced his visiting card with a flourish. 'Old Chinese custom!'

She accepted it but did not reciprocate. 'Thank you. Sorry, Mr. Biltzmann, would you excuse me? I have to join my friends an—' Before she could prevent it, Pugmire took her arm, led her aside a pace and whispered throatily, 'How about dinner? You look fantas—'

She jerked her arm away trying not to be obvious. 'Go away, Pug.'

'Listen, Orlan—'

'I've told you politely fifty times to leave me alone! Now *dew neh loh moh* on you and all your line!' she said and Pugmire flushed. She had always detested him, even in the old days. He was always looking at her behind Quillan's back, leching, and when she had been discarded, Pugmire had pestered her and tried every way to get her into bed—still did. 'If you ever call or talk to me again I'll tell all Hong Kong about you and your peculiar habits.' She nodded politely to Biltzmann, let his card drop unnoticed and walked off. After a moment, Pugmire went back to the American.

'What a body!' Biltzmann said, his eyes still following her.

'She's—she's one of our well-known whores,' Pugmire said with a sneer. 'I wish to Christ they'd hurry up with the food. I'm starving.'

'She's a tramp?' Biltzmann gaped at him.

'You can never tell here.' Pugmire added, keeping his voice down, 'I'm surprised Shitee T'Chung invited her. Still, I don't suppose he gives a shit now that his knighthood's dubbed and paid for Years ago, Orlanda used to be a girlfriend of a friend

617

but she was up to her old tricks of selling it on the side. He caught her at it and gave her the Big E.'

'The Big E?'

'The Elbow—the shove.'

Biltzmann could not take his eyes off her. 'Jesus,' he muttered, 'I don't know about the Big E but I'd sure as hell like to give her the Big One.'

'That's just a matter of money but I can assure you, old chap, she's not worth it. Orlanda's dreadful in the sack, I know, and nowadays you can never tell who's been there before, eh?' Pugmire laughed at the American's expression. 'Never fancied her myself after the first time, but if you dip your wick there you'd better use precautions.'

Dunross had just arrived and he was listening with half an ear to Richard Kwang who was talking grandly about the deals he had made to stave off the run, and how foul certain people were to spread such rumors.

'I quite agree, Richard,' Dunross said, wanting to join the visiting MPs, who were at the far end of the room. 'There really are a lot of bastards around. If you'll excuse me . . .'

'Of course, tai-pan.' Richard Kwang dropped his voice but could not prevent some of his anxiety showing. 'I might need a hand.'

'Anything, of course, except money.'

'You could talk to Johnjohn at the Vic for me. He'd—'

'He won't, you know that, Richard. Your only chance is one of your Chinese friends. What about Smiler Ching?'

'Huh, that old crook—wouldn't ask him for any of his dirty money!' Richard Kwang said with a sneer. Smiler Ching had reneged on their deal and had refused to lend him money—or credit. 'That old crook deserves prison! There's a run on him too, but that's what he deserves! I think it's all started by the Communists, they're trying to ruin us all. The Bank of China! Did you hear about the queues at the Vic in Central? There're more at Blacs. Old Big Belly Tok's Bank of East Asia and Japan's gone under. They won't open their doors tomorrow.'

'Christ, are you sure?'

'He called me tonight asking for 20 million. *Dew neh loh moh*, tai-pan, unless we all get help Hong Kong's going under.

618

We've . . .' Then he saw Venus Poon in the doorway on the arm of Four Finger Wu and his heart skipped eight beats. This evening she had been furious when he did not arrive with the mink coat that he had promised her. She had wept and shouted and her *amah* had wailed and they would not accept his excuse that his furrier had let him down and they both had gone on and on until he promised without fail that before the races he would bring her the gift that he had promised.

'Are you taking me to Shi-teh's?'

'My wife changed her mind and now she's going, so I can't, but afterwards we'll go—'

'Afterwards I'll be tired! First no present and now I can't go to the party! Where's the aquamarine pendant you promised me last month? Where did my mink go? On your wife's back I'll bet! *Ayeeyah*, my hairdresser and her hairdresser are friends so I'll find out if it did. Oh woe woe woe you don't really love your Daughter anymore. I'll have to kill myself or accept Four Finger Wu's invitation.'

'Wat?'

Richard Kwang remembered how he had almost had a hemorrhage then and there, and he had ranted and raved and screamed that her apartment cost him a fortune and her clothes cost thousands a week and she had ranted and raved and screamed back. 'And what about the run on the bank? Are you solvent? What about my savings? Are they safe *heya?*'

'*Ayeeyah* you miserable whore, what savings? The savings I am going to put there for you? Huh! Of course they're safe, safe as the Bank of England!'

'Woe woe woe I'm penniless now. Your poor destitute Daughter! I'll have to sell myself or commit suicide. Yes, that's it! Poison . . . that's it! I think I'll take an overdose of . . . of aspirins. *Ah Poo! Bring me an overdose of aspirins!*'

So he had begged and pleaded and eventually she had relented and allowed him to take away the aspirins and he had promised to rush back to the apartment the very moment the banquet was over and now his eyes were almost staring out of his head because there, at the doorway, was Venus Poon on the arm of Four Finger Wu, both resplendent, he puffed with pride, and she demure and innocent, wearing the dress he'd just paid for.

'What's up, Richard?' Dunross asked, concerned.

Richard Kwang tried to speak, couldn't, just tottered away toward his wife who tore her baleful eyes off Venus Poon and put them back on him.

'Hello, dear,' he said, his backbone jelly.

'Hello, dear,' Mai-ling Kwang replied sweetly. 'Who's that whore?'

'Which one?'

'That one.'

'Isn't that the . . . what's her name . . . the TV starlet?'

'Isn't her name Itch-in-her-drawers Poon, the VD starlet?'

He pretended to laugh with her but he wanted to tear all his hair out. The fact that his latest mistress had come with someone else would not be lost on all Hong Kong. Everyone would interpret it as an infallible sign that he was in absolute financial trouble and that she had, wisely, left the sinking junk for a safer haven. And coming with his uncle, Four Finger Wu, was even worse. That would confirm that all Wu's wealth had been removed from the Ho-Pak, and therefore most probably Lando Mata and the gold syndicate had done the same. All the civilized population that counted were sure that Wu was the syndicate's prime smuggler now that Smuggler Mo was dead. Woe woe woe! Troubles never come singly.

'Eh?' he asked wearily. 'What did you say?'

'I said, is the tai-pan going to approach the Victoria for us?'

He switched into Cantonese as Europeans were nearby. 'Regretfully that son of a whore's in trouble himself. No, he won't help us. We're in great trouble which is not our fault. The day has been terrible, except for one thing: we made a fine profit today. I sold all our Noble House stock.'

'Excellent. At what price?'

'We made 2.70 a share. It's all in gold now in Zurich. I'm putting it all in our joint account,' he added carefully, twisting the truth, all the while trying to figure out a ploy to get his wife out of the room so he could go over to Four Finger Wu and Venus Poon to pretend to everyone that everything was fine.

'Good. Very good. That's better.' Mai-ling was toying with her huge aquamarine pendant. Suddenly Richard Kwang's testicles chilled. This was the pendant he had promised to

Venus Poon. Oh woe woe woe . . .

'Are you feeling all right?' Mai-ling asked.

'I, er, I must have eaten some bad fish. I think I need to go to the bathroom.'

'You'd better go now. I suppose we'll eat soon. Shitee's always so late!' She noticed him take a nervous sidelong look at Venus Poon and Uncle Wu and her eyes turned baleful again. 'That whore's really quite fascinating. I'm going to watch her until you get back.'

'Why don't we go together?' He took her arm and guided her down the stairs to the door that led to the bathrooms, greeting friends here and there, trying to exude confidence. The moment she was launched into the ladies' room he rushed back up, walked over to Zeppelin Tung who was near them. He chatted a moment, then pretended to see Four Fingers. 'Oh hello, Honored Uncle,' he said expansively. 'Thank you for bringing her here. Hello, little oily mouth.'

'What?' the old man said suspiciously. 'I brought her for me not for you.'

'Yes, and don't you oily mouth me,' Venus Poon hissed and deliberately took the old man's arm and Richard Kwang almost spat blood. 'I talked to my hairdresser tonight! My mink on her back! And isn't that my aquamarine pendant too, the one she's wearing right now! To think I almost committed suicide tonight because I thought I'd displeased my Honored Father . . . and all the time it was lies lies lies. Oh I almost want to commit suicide again.'

'Eh, don't do that yet, Little Mealy Mouth,' Four Finger Wu whispered anxiously, having already negotiated a deal in excess of Smiler Ching's offer. 'Go away, Nephew, you're giving her indigestion. She won't be able to perform!'

Richard Kwang forced a glazed smile, muttered a few pleasantries and went off shakily. He headed for the staircase to wait for his wife, and someone said, 'I see a certain filly's left the paddock for more manured grass!'

'What nonsense!' he replied at once. 'Of course I asked the old fool to bring her since my wife is here. Why else would she be with him? Is that old fool hung like a bullock? Or even a bantam cock? No. *Ayeeyah*, not even Venus Poon with all the technique I taught her can get up what has no thread! It's good for his face to

621

pretend otherwise, *heya?* Of course, and she wanted to see her Old Father and to be seen too!'

'Eeeee, that's clever, Banker Kwang!' the man said, and turned away and whispered it to another, who said caustically, 'Huh, you'd swallow a bucket of shit if someone said it was stewed beef with black bean sauce! Don't you know old Four Finger's Stalk's nurtured by the most expensive salves and ointments and ginseng that money can buy? Why only last month his Number Six Concubine gave birth to a son! Eeeee, don't worry about him. Before he's through tonight, Venus Poon's in for a drubbing that'll make her Golden Gully cry out for mercy in eight dialects. . . .'

'Are you staying for dinner, tai-pan?' Brian Kwok asked, intercepting him. 'When and if it arrives.'

'Yes. Why?'

'Sorry I've got to go back to work. But there'll be someone else to chaperone you home.'

'For God's sake, Brian, aren't you overreacting?' Dunross said as quietly.

Brian Kwok kept his voice down. 'I don't think so. I've just phoned Crosse to see what happened about those two loiterers outside your house. The moment our fellows arrived they took to their heels.'

'Perhaps they were just thugs who don't like police.'

Brian Kwok shook his head. 'Crosse asked again that you give us the AMG papers right now.'

'Friday.'

'He told me to tell you there's a Soviet spy ship in port. There's already been one killing—one of their agents, knifed.'

Dunross was shocked. 'What's that got to do with me?'

'You know that better than we do. You know what's in those reports. Must be quite serious or you wouldn't be so difficult— or careful—yourself. Crosse said . . . Never mind him! Ian, look, we're old friends. I'm really very worried.' Brian Kwok switched to Cantonese. 'Even the wise can fall into thorns— poisoned thorns.'

'In two days the police Mandarin arrives. Two days is not long.'

'True. But in two days the spy may hurt us very much. Why tempt the gods? It is my ask.'

'No. Sorry.'

Brian Kwok hardened. In English he said, 'Our American friends have asked us to take you into protective custody.'

'What nonsense!'

'Not such nonsense, Ian. It's very well known you've a photographic memory. The sooner you turn the papers over the better. Even afterwards you should be careful. Why not tell me where they are and we'll take care of everything?'

Dunross was equally set-faced. 'Everything's taken care of now, Brian. Everything stays as planned.'

The tall Chinese sighed. Then he shrugged. 'Very well. Sorry, but don't say you weren't warned. Are Gavallan and Jacques staying for dinner too?'

'No, I don't think so. I asked them just to put in an appearance. Why?'

'They could've gone home with you. Please don't go anywhere alone for a while, don't try to lose your guard. For the time being, if you have any, er, private dates call me.'

'Me, a private date? Here in Hong Kong? Really, what a suggestion!'

'Does the name Jen mean anything?'

Dunross's eyes became stony. 'You buggers can be too nosy.'

'And you don't seem to realize you're in a very dirty game without Queensberry rules.'

'I've got that message, by God.'

''Night, tai-pan.'

''Night, Brian.' Dunross went over to the MPs who were in a group in one corner talking with Jacques deVille. There were only four of them now, the rest were resting after their long journey. Jacques deVille introduced him. Sir Charles Pennyworth, Conservative; Hugh Guthrie, Liberal; Julian Broadhurst and Robin Grey, both Labour. 'Hello, Robin,' he said.

'Hello, Ian. It's been a long time.'

'Yes.'

'If you'll excuse me, I'll be off,' deVille said, his face careworn. 'My wife's away and we've a young grandchild staying with us.'

'Did you talk to Susanne in France?' Dunross asked.

'Yes, tai-pan. She's . . . she'll be all right. Thank you for calling Deland. See you tomorrow. Good night, gentlemen.' He walked off.

Dunross glanced back at Robin Grey. 'You haven't changed at all.'

'Nor have you,' Grey said, then turned to Pennyworth. 'Ian and I met in London some years ago, Sir Charles. It was just after the war. I'd just become a shop steward.' He was a lean man with thin lips, thin graying hair and sharp features.

'Yes, it was some years ago,' Dunross said politely, continuing the pattern that Penelope and her brother had agreed to so many years ago—that neither side was blood kin to the other. 'So, Robin, are you staying long?'

'Just a few days,' Grey said. His smile was as thin as his lips. 'I've never been in this workers' paradise before so I want to visit a few unions, see how the other ninety-nine percent live.'

Sir Charles Pennyworth, leader of the delegation, laughed. He was a florid, well-covered man, an ex-colonel of the London Scottish Regiment, D.S.O. and Bar. 'Don't think they go much on unions here, Robin. Do they, tai-pan?'

'Our labor force does very well without them,' Dunross said.

'Sweated labor, tai-pan,' Grey said at once. 'According to some of your own statistics, government statistics.'

'Not our statistics, Robin, merely your statisticians,' Dunross said. 'Our people are the highest paid in Asia after the Japanese and this is a free society.'

'Free? Come off it!' Grey jeered. 'You mean free to exploit the workers. Well, never mind, when Labour gets in at the next election we'll change all that.'

'Come now, Robin,' Sir Charles said. 'Labour hasn't a prayer at the next election.'

Grey smiled. 'Don't bet on it, Sir Charles. The people of England want change. We didn't all go to war to keep up the rotten old ways. Labour's for social change—and getting the workers a fair share of the profits they create.'

Dunross said, 'I've always thought it rather unfair that Socialists talk about the "workers" as though they do all the work and we do none. We're workers too. We work as hard if not harder with longer hours an—'

'Ah, but you're a tai-pan and you live in a great big house that was handed down, along with your power. All that capital came from some poor fellow's sweat, and I won't even mention the opium trade that started it all. It's fair that capital should be spread around, fair that everyone should have the same start. The rich should be taxed more. There should be a capital tax. The sooner the great fortunes are broken up the better for all Englishmen, eh, Julian?'

Julian Broadhurst was a tall, distinguished man in his mid-forties, a strong supporter of the Fabian Society, which was the intellectual brains trust of the socialist movement. 'Well, Robin,' he said with his lazy, almost diffident voice, 'I certainly don't advocate as you do that we take to the barricades but I do think, Mr. Dunross, that here in Hong Kong you could do with a Trades Union Council, a minimum wage scale, elected legislature, proper unions and safeguards, socialized medicine, workman's compensation and all the modern British innovations.'

'Totally wrong, Mr. Broadhurst. China would never agree to a change in our colonial status, they would never allow any form of city-state on her border. As to the rest, who pays for them?' Dunross asked. 'Our unfettered system here's out-performing Britain twenty times and—'

'You pay for it out of all your profits, Ian,' Robin Grey said with a laugh. 'You pay a fair tax, not 15 percent. You pay the same as we do in Britain and—'

'God forbid!' Dunross said, hard put to keep his temper. 'You're taxing yourself out of business and out of c—'

'Profit?' The last MP, the Liberal, Hugh Guthrie interrupted caustically. 'The last bloody Labour Government wiped out our profits years ago, with bloody stupid profligate spending, ridiculous nationalization, giving the Empire away piecemeal with fatuous stupid abandon, disrupting the Commonwealth and shoving poor old England's face in the bloody mud. Bloody ridiculous! Attlee and all that shower!'

Robin Grey said placatingly, 'Come on, Hugh, the Labour Government did what the people wanted, what the masses wanted.'

'Nonsense! The enemy wanted it. The Communists! In barely eighteen years you gave away the greatest empire the world's ever seen, made us a second-class power and allowed the sodding Soviet enemy to eat up most of Europe. Bloody ridiculous!'

'I agree wholeheartedly that communism's dreadful. But as to "giving" away our empire, it was the wind of change, Hugh,' Broadhurst said, calming him. 'Colonialism had run its course. You really must take the long-term view.'

'I do. I think we're up the creek without a paddle. Churchill's right, always was.'

'The people didn't think so,' Grey said grimly. 'That's why he was voted out. The armed service vote did that, they'd had enough of him. As to the Empire, sorry Hugh old chap, but it was just an excuse to exploit natives who didn't know any better.' Robin Grey saw their faces and read them. He was used to the hatred that surrounded him. He hated them more and always had. After the war he had wanted to stay in the Regular Army but he had been rejected—captains were two a penny then with decorations and distinguished war service, while he spent the war a POW at Changi. So, filled with anger and resentment, he had joined Crawley's, a huge car manufacturer, as a mechanic. Quickly he had become a shop steward and union organizer, then into the lower ranks of the Trades Union General Council. Five years ago, he had become a Labour MP where he was now, a cutting, angry, hostile backbencher and protégé of the late left-wing Socialist Aneurin Bevan. 'Yes, we got rid of Churchill and when we get in next year we'll sweep out a lot more of the old tired ways and upper-class infections back where they belong. We'll nationalize every industry an—'

'Really, Robin,' Sir Charles said, 'this is a banquet not a soapbox in Hyde Park. We all agreed to cut out politics while we were on the trip.'

'You're right, Sir Charles. It was just that the tai-pan of the Noble House asked me.' Grey turned to Dunross. 'How is the Noble House?'

'Fine. Very fine.'

'According to this afternoon's paper there's a run on your stock?'

'One of our competitors is playing silly buggers, that's all.'

'And the bank runs? They're not serious either?'

'They're serious.' Dunross was choosing his words carefully. He knew the anti-Hong Kong lobby in Parliament was strong and many members of all three parties were against its colonial status, against its nonvoting status and freewheeling nature—

and most of all envious of its almost tax-free basis. Never mind, he thought. Since 1841 we've survived hostile Parliaments, fire, typhoon, pestilence, plague, embargo, depression, occupation and the periodic convulsions that China goes through, and somehow we always will.

'The run's on the Ho-Pak, one of our Chinese banks,' Dunross said.

'It's the largest, isn't it?' Grey said.

'No. But it's large. We're all hoping it'll weather the problem.'

'If it goes broke, what about all the depositors' money?'

'Unfortunately they lose it,' Dunross said, backed into a corner.

'You need English banking laws.'

'No, we've found our system operates very well. How did you find China?' Dunross asked.

Before Sir Charles could answer, Grey said, 'Our majority view is that they're dangerous, hostile, should be locked up and the Hong Kong border sealed. They're openly committed to becoming a world irritant and their brand of communism is merely an excuse for dictatorship and exploitation of their masses.'

Dunross and the other Hong Kong *yan* blanched as Sir Charles said sharply, 'Come now, Robin, that's only your view and the Comm—the, er, and McLean's. I found just the opposite. I think China's very sincere in trying to deal with the problems of China, which are hideous, monumental and I think insoluble.'

'Thank God there's going to be big trouble there,' Grey said with a sneer. 'Even the Russians knew it, why else would they get out?'

'Because they're enemies, they share a common five thousand miles of border,' Dunross said trying to hold in his anger. 'They've always distrusted each other. Because China's invader has always come out of the West, and Russia's always out of the East. Possession of China's always been Russia's obsession and preoccupation.'

'Come now, Mr. Dunross,' Broadhurst began. 'You exaggerate, surely.'

'It's to Russia's advantage to have China weak and divided, and Hong Kong disrupted. Russia *requires* China weak as a

627

cornerstone of its foreign policy.'

'At least Russia's civilized,' Grey said. 'Red China's fanatic, dangerous and heathen and should be cut off, particularly from here.'

'Ridiculous!' Dunross said tightly. 'China has the oldest civilization on earth. China desperately wants to be friends with the West. China's Chinese first and Communist second.'

'Hong Kong and you "traders" are keeping the Communists in power.'

'Rubbish! Mao Tse-tung and Chou En-lai don't need us or the Soviets to stay in Peking!'

Hugh Guthrie said, 'As far as I'm concerned Red China and Soviet Russia're equally dangerous.'

'There's no comparison!' Grey said. 'In Moscow they eat with knives and forks and understand food! In China we had nothing but rotten food, rotten hotels and lots of double-talk.'

'I really don't understand you at all, old boy,' Sir Charles said irritably. 'You fought like hell to get on this committee, you're supposed to be interested in Asian affairs and you've done nothing but complain.'

'Being critical's not complaining, Sir Charles. Bluntly, I'm for giving Red China no help at all. None. And when I get back I'm offering a motion to change Hong Kong's status entirely: to embargo everything from and to Communist China, to hold immediate and proper elections here, introduce proper taxes, proper unionism and proper British social justice!'

Dunross's chin jutted. 'Then you'll destroy our position in Asia!'

'Of all the tai-pans, yes, the people no! Russia was right about China.'

'I'm talking about the Free World! Christ almighty, it should be clear to everyone—Soviet Russia's committed to hegemony, to world domination and our destruction. China isn't,' Dunross said.

'You're wrong, Ian. You can't see the wood for the trees,' Grey said.

'Listen! If Russia . . .'

Broadhurst interrupted smoothly. 'Russia's just trying to solve her own problems, Mr. Dunross, one of them's the U.S. containment policy. They just want to be left alone and not surrounded by highly emotional Americans with their overfed hands on nuclear triggers.'

'Balls! The Yanks're the only friends we've got,' Hugh Guthrie said angrily. 'As to the Soviets, what about the Cold War? Berlin? Hungary? Cuba, Egypt . . . they're swallowing us piecemeal.'

Sir Charles Pennyworth sighed. 'Life's strange and memories are so short. In '45, May second it was, in the evening, we joined up with the Russians at Wismar in northern Germany. I'd never been so proud or happy in my life, yes, proud. We sang and drank and cheered and toasted each other. Then my division and all of us in Europe, all the Allies had been held back for weeks to let the Russkies sweep into Germany all through the Balkans, Czechoslovakia and Poland and all the other places. At the time I didn't think much about it, I was so thankful that the war was almost over at long last and so proud of our Russian allies, but you know, looking back, now I know we were betrayed, we soldiers were betrayed—Russian soldiers included. We got buggered. I don't really know how it happened, still don't, but I truly believe we were betrayed, Julian, by our own leaders, your bloody Socialists, along with Eisenhower, Roosevelt and his misguided advisors. I swear to God I still don't know how it happened but we lost the war, we won but we lost.'

'Come now, Charles, you're quite wrong. We all won,' Broadhurst said. 'The people of the world won when Nazi Germany was sma—' He stopped, startled, as he saw the look on Grey's face. 'What's the matter, Robin?'

Grey was staring at the other side of the room. 'Ian! That man over there talking to the Chinese . . . do you know him? The tall bugger in the blazer.'

Equally astonished, Dunross glanced at the other side of the room. 'The sandy-haired fellow? You mean Marlowe, Pete—'

'Peter bloody Marlowe!' Grey muttered. 'What's . . . what's he doing in Hong Kong?'

'He's just visiting. From the States. He's a writer. I believe he's writing or researching a book on Hong Kong.'

'Writer, eh? Curious. Is he a friend of yours?'

'I met him a few days ago. Why?'

'That's his wife—the girl next to him?'

'Yes. That's Fleur Marlowe, why?'

Grey did not answer. There was a fleck of saliva at the corner of his lips.

'What's his connection with you, Robin?' Broadhurst asked, strangely perturbed.

With an effort Grey tore his eyes off Marlowe. 'We were in Changi together, Julian, the Jap POW camp. I was provost marshal for the last couple of years, in charge of camp discipline.' He wiped the sweat off his top lip. 'Marlowe was one of the black marketeers there.'

'Marlowe?' Dunross was astounded.

'Oh yes, Flight Lieutenant Marlowe, the great English gentleman,' Grey said, his voice raw with bitterness. 'Yes. He and his pal, an American called King, Corporal King, were the main ones. Then there was a fellow called Timsen, an Aussie. . . . But the American was the biggest, he was the King all right. A Texan. He had colonels on his payroll, English gentlemen all—colonels, majors, captains. Marlowe was his interpreter with the Jap and Korean guards . . . we mostly had Korean guards. They were the worst. . . .' Grey coughed. 'Christ, it's such a short time ago. Marlowe and the King lived off the fat of the land—those two buggers ate at least one egg a day, while the rest of us starved. You can't imagine how . . .' Again Grey wiped the sweat off his lip without noticing it.

'How long were you a POW?' Sir Charles asked compassionately.

'Three and a half years.'

'Terrible,' Hugh Guthrie said. 'My cousin bought it on the Burma railroad. Terrible!'

'It was all terrible,' Grey said. 'But it wasn't so terrible for those who sold out. On the Road or at Changi!' He looked at Sir Charles and his eyes were strange and bloodshot. 'It's the Marlowes of the world who betrayed us, the ordinary people without privileges of birth.' His voice became even more bitter. 'No offense but now you're all getting your comeuppance and about time. Christ, I need a drink. Excuse me a moment.' He stalked off, heading for the bar that was set up to one side.

'Extraordinary,' Sir Charles said.

Guthrie said with a slight, nervous laugh, 'For a moment I thought he was going for Marlowe.'

They all watched him, then Broadhurst noticed Dunross frowning after Grey, his face set and cold. 'Don't pay any attention to him, Mr. Dunross. I'm afraid Grey's very tiresome and a rather vulgar bore. He's . . . well he's not at all representative of the Labour echelon, thank God. You'd like our new leader, Harold Wilson, you'd approve of him. Next time you're in London I'd be glad to introduce you if you've time.'

'Thank you. Actually I was thinking about Marlowe. It's hard to believe he "sold out" or betrayed anyone.'

'You never know about people, do you?'

Grey got a whiskey and soda and turned and went across the room. 'Well, if it isn't Flight Lieutenant Marlowe!'

Peter Marlowe turned, startled. His smile vanished and the two men stared at one another. Fleur Marlowe froze.

'Hello, Grey,' Marlowe said, his voice flat. 'I heard you were in Hong Kong. In fact, I read your interview in the afternoon paper.' He turned to his wife. 'Darling, this is Robin Grey, MP.' He introduced him to the Chinese, one of whom was Sir Shi-teh T'Chung.

'Ah, Mr. Grey, it's an honor to have you here,' Shi-teh said with an Oxford English accent. He was tall, dark, good-looking, slightly Chinese and mostly European. 'We hope your stay in Hong Kong will be good. If there's anything I can do, just say the word!'

'Ta,' Grey said carelessly. They all noticed his rudeness. 'So, Marlowe! You haven't changed much.'

'Nor have you. You've done well for yourself.' Marlowe added to the others, 'We were in the war together. I haven't seen Grey since '45.'

'We were POWs, Marlowe and I,' Grey said, then added, 'We're on opposite sides of the political blanket.' He stopped and stepped out of the way to allow Orlanda Ramos to pass. She greeted Shi-teh with a smile and continued on. Grey watched her briefly, then turned back. 'Marlowe old chap, are you still in trade?' It was a private English insult. 'Trade' to someone like Marlowe who came from a long line of English officers meant everything common and lower class.

631

'I'm a writer,' Marlowe said. His eyes went to his wife and his eyes smiled at her.

'I thought you'd still be in the RAF, regular officer like your illustrious forebears.'

'I was invalided out, malaria and all that. Rather boring,' Marlowe said, deliberately lengthening his patrician accent knowing that it would infuriate Grey. 'And you're in Parliament? How very clever of you. You represent Streatham East? Wasn't that where you were born?'

Grey flushed. 'Yes, yes it was . . .'

Shi-teh covered his embarrassment at the undercurrents between them. 'I must, er, see about dinner.' He hurried off. The other Chinese excused themselves and turned away.

Fleur Marlowe fanned herself. 'Perhaps we should find our table, Peter,' she said.

'A good idea, Mrs. Marlowe,' Grey said. He was in as tight control as Peter Marlowe. 'How's the King?'

'I don't know. I haven't seen him since Changi.' Marlowe looked down on Grey.

'But you're in touch with him?'

'No. No, actually I'm not.'

'You don't know where he is?'

'No.'

'That's strange, seeing how close you two were.' Grey ripped his eyes away and glanced at Fleur Marlowe and thought she was the prettiest woman he had ever seen. So pretty and fine and English and fair, just like his ex-wife Trina who went off with an American barely a month after he was reported missing in action. Barely a month. 'Did you know we were enemies in Changi, Mrs. Marlowe?' he said with a gentleness that she found frightening.

'Peter's never discussed Changi with me, Mr. Grey. Or anyone that I know of.'

'Curious. It was an awesome experience, Mrs. Marlowe. I've forgotten none of it. I . . . well, sorry to interrupt . . .' He glanced up at Marlowe. He began to say something but changed his mind and turned away.

'Oh, Peter, what an awful man!' Fleur said. 'He gave me the creeps.'

'Nothing to bother about, my darling.'

'Why were you enemies?'

'Not now, my pet, later.' Marlowe smiled at her, loving her. 'Grey's nothing to us.'

36

Linc Bartlett saw Orlanda before she saw him and she took his breath away. He couldn't help comparing her with Casey who was beside him talking to Andrew Gavallan. Orlanda was wearing white silk, floor-length, backless with a halter neck that, discreetly somehow, seemed to offer her golden body. Casey wore her green that he had seen many times, her tawny hair cascading.

'Would you both like to come to Shi-teh's tonight?' Orlanda had asked him this morning. 'It could be important for you and your Casey to be there.'

'Why?'

'Because almost all business that counts in Hong Kong is done at this type of function, Mr. Bartlett. It could be very important for you to become involved with people like Shi-teh—and in the Turf Club, Cricket Club, even *the* Club itself, though that'd be impossible.'

'Because I'm American?'

'Because someone has to die to create an opening—an English or Scotsman.' She had laughed. 'The waiting list's as long as Queen's Road! It's men only, very stuffy, old leather chairs, old men sleeping off their three-hour and ten-gin lunches, *The Times* and all that.'

'Hell, that sounds exciting!'

She had laughed again. Her teeth were white and he could see no blemish in her. They had talked over breakfast and he had found her more than easy to talk to. And to be with. Her perfume was enticing. Casey rarely wore perfume—she said that she'd found it just another distraction to the businessmen she had to deal with. With Orlanda, breakfast had been coffee

634

and toast and eggs and crisp bacon, American style, at a brand-new hotel she suggested, called the Mandarin. Casey didn't eat breakfast. Just coffee and toast sometimes, or croissants.

The interview had passed easily and the time too fast. He had never been in the company of a woman with such open and confident femininity. Casey was always so strong, efficient and cool and not feminine. By choice, her choice and my agreement, he reminded himself.

'That's Orlanda?' Casey was looking at him, one eyebrow arched.

'Yes,' he replied, trying unsuccessfully to read her. 'What do you think?'

'I think she's dynamite.'

'Which way?'

Casey laughed. She turned to Gavallan who was trying to concentrate and be polite but whose mind was taken up with Kathy. After Kathy had told him this evening, he had not wanted to leave her but she had insisted, saying that it was important for him to be there. 'Do you know her, Andrew?'

'Who?'

'The girl in white.'

'Where? Oh! Oh yes, but only by reputation.'

'Is it good or bad?'

'That, er, depends on your point of view, Casey. She's, she's Portuguese, Eurasian, of course. Orlanda was Gornt's friend for quite a few years.'

'You mean his mistress?'

'Yes, I suppose that's the word,' he told her politely, disliking Casey's directness intensely. 'But it was all very discreet.'

'Gornt's got taste. Did you know she was his steady, Linc?'

'She told me this morning. I met her at Gornt's a couple of days ago. He said they were still friends.'

'Gornt's not to be trusted,' Gavallan said.

Casey said, 'He's got heavy backers, in and outside Hong Kong, I was told. Far as I know he's not stretched at the moment, as you are. You must have heard he wants us to deal with him, not you.'

'We're not stretched,' Gavallan said. He looked at Bartlett. 'We do have a deal?'

'We sign Tuesday. If you're ready,' Bartlett said.

'We're ready now.'

'Ian wants us to keep it quiet till Saturday and that's fine with us,' Casey said. 'Isn't it, Linc?'

'Sure.' Bartlett glanced back at Orlanda. Casey followed his eyes.

She had noticed her the first moment the girl had hesitated in the doorway. 'Who's she talking to, Andrew?' The man was interesting-looking, lithe, elegant and in his fifties.

'That's Lando Mata. He's also Portuguese, from Macao.' Gavallan wondered achingly if Dunross would manage to persuade Mata to come to their rescue with all his millions. What would I do if I was tai-pan? he asked himself wearily. Would I buy tomorrow, or make a deal with Mata and Tightfist tonight? With their money, the Noble House would be safe for generations, though out of our control. No point in worrying now. Wait till you're tai-pan. Then he saw Mata smiling at Orlanda and then both of them looked over and began to thread their way toward them. His eyes watched her firm breasts, free under the silk. Taut nipples. Good God, he thought, awed, even Venus Poon wouldn't dare do that. When they came up he introduced them and stood back, odd man out, wanting to watch them.

'Hello,' Orlanda said warmly to Casey. 'Linc told me so much about you and how important you are to him.'

'And I've heard about you too,' Casey said as warmly. But not enough. You're much more lovely than Linc indicated, she thought. Very much more. So you're Orlanda Ramos. Beautiful and soft-spoken and feminine and a bitch piranha who has set her sights on my Linc. Jesus, what do I do now?

She heard herself making small talk but her mind was still thinking Orlanda Ramos through. On the one hand it would be good for Linc to have an affair, she thought. It would take the heat out of him. Last night was as lousy for him as it was for me. He was right about me moving out. But once this one's magic surrounds him could I extract him? Would she be just another girl like the others that were nothing to me and after a week or so, nothing to him either?

Not this one, Casey decided with finality. I've got two choices. I either stick to thirteen weeks and four days and do battle, or don't and do battle.

She smiled. 'Orlanda, your dress is fantastic.'

'Thanks. May I call you Casey?'

Both women knew the war had begun.

Bartlett was delighted that Casey obviously liked Orlanda. Gavallan watched, fascinated by the four of them. There was a strange warmth among them all. Particularly between Bartlett and Orlanda.

He turned his attention to Mata and Casey. Mata was suave, filled with old-world charm, concentrating on Casey, playing her like a fish. I wonder how far he'll get with this one. Curious that Casey doesn't seem to mind Orlanda at all. Surely she's noticed that her boyfriend's smitten? Perhaps she hasn't. Or perhaps she couldn't care less and she and Bartlett are just business partners and nothing else. Perhaps she's a dyke after all. Or maybe she's just frigid like a lot of them. How sad!

'How do you like Hong Kong, Miss Casey?' Mata asked, wondering what she would be like in bed.

'Afraid I haven't seen much of it yet though I did go out to the New Territories on the hotel tour and peek into China.'

'Would you like to go? I mean really go into China? Say to Canton? I could arrange for you to be invited.'

She was shocked. 'But we're forbidden to go into China . . . our passports aren't valid.'

'Oh, you wouldn't have to use your passport. The PRC doesn't bother with passports. So few *quai loh* go into China there's no problem. They give you a written visa and they stamp that.'

'But our State Department . . . I don't think I'd risk it right now.'

Bartlett nodded. 'We're not even supposed to go into the Communist store here. The department store.'

'Yes, your government really is very strange,' Mata said. 'As if going into a store is subversive! Did you hear the rumor about the Hilton?'

'What about it?'

'The story is that they bought a marvelous collection of Chinese antiques for the new hotel, of course all locally.' Mata smiled. 'It seems that now the U.S. has decided they can't use any of it, even here in Hong Kong. It's all in storage. At least that's the story.'

'It figures. If you can't make it in the States, you join the government,' Bartlett said sourly.

'Casey, you should decide for yourself,' Mata said. 'Visit the store. It's called China Arts and Crafts on Queen's Road. The prices are very reasonable and the Communists really don't have horns and barbed tails.'

'It's nothing like what I expected,' Bartlett said. 'Casey, you'd freak out at some of the things.'

'You've been?' she asked, surprised.

'Sure.'

'I took Mr. Bartlett this morning,' Orlanda explained. 'We happened to be passing. I'd be glad to go shopping with you if you wish.'

'Thanks, I'd like that,' Casey said as nicely, all her danger signals up. 'But we were told in L.A. the CIA monitors Americans who go in and out because they're sure it's a Communist meeting place.'

'It looked like an ordinary store to me, Casey,' Bartlett said. 'I didn't see anything except a few posters of Mao. You can't bargain though. All prices're written out. Some of the biggest bargains you ever did see. Pity we can't take them back home.' There was a total embargo on all goods of Chinese origin into the States, even antiques that had been in Hong Kong a hundred years.

'That's no problem,' Mata said at once, wondering how much he would make as a middleman. 'If there's anything you want I'd be happy to purchase it.'

'But we still can't get it into the States, Mr. Mata,' Casey said.

'Oh that's easy too. I do it for American friends all the time. I just send their purchases to a company I have in Singapore and Manila. For a tiny fee they send it to you in the States with a certificate of origin, Malaya or the Philippines, whichever you'd prefer.'

'But that'd be cheating. Smuggling.'

Mata, Gavallan and Orlanda laughed outright and Gavallan said, 'Trade's the grease of the world. Embargoed goods from the U.S. or Taiwan find their way to the PRC, PRC goods go to Taiwan and the U.S.—if they're sought after. Of course they do!'

'I know,' Casey said, 'but I don't think that's right.'

'Soviet Russia's committed to your destruction but you still trade with her,' Gavallan said to Bartlett.

'We don't ourselves,' Casey said. 'Not Par-Con, though we've been approached to sell computers. Much as we like profits they're a no-no. The government does, but only on very carefully controlled goods. Wheat, things like that.'

'Wherever there's a willing buyer of anything, there'll always be a seller,' Gavallan said, irritated by her. He glanced out of the windows and wished he was back in Shanghai. 'Take Vietnam, your Algiers.'

'Sir?' Casey said.

Gavallan glanced back at her. 'I mean that Vietnam will bleed your economy to death as it did to France and as Algiers also did to France.'

'We'll never go into Vietnam,' Bartlett said confidently. 'Why should we? Vietnam's nothing to do with us.'

'I agree,' Mata said, 'but nevertheless the States is having a growing involvement there. In fact, Mr. Bartlett, I think you're being sucked into the abyss.'

'In what way?' Casey asked.

'I think the Soviets have deliberately enticed you into Vietnam. You'll send in troops but they won't. You'll be fighting Viets and the jungle, and the Soviets will be the winners. Your CIA's already there in strength. They're running an airline. Even now airfields are being constructed with U.S. money, U.S. arms are pouring in. You've soldiers fighting there already.'

'I don't believe it,' Casey said.

'You can. They're called Special Forces, sometimes Delta Force. So sorry but Vietnam's going to be a big problem for your government unless it's very smart.'

Bartlett said confidently, 'Thank God it is. JFK handled Cuba. He'll handle Vietnam too. He made the Big K back off there and he can do it again. We won that time. The Soviets took their missiles out.'

Gavallan was grimly amused. 'You should talk to Ian about Cuba, old chap, that really gets him going. He says, and I agree, you lost. The Soviets sucked you into another trap. A fool's mate. He believes they built their sites almost openly—wanting you to detect them and you did and then there was a lot of saber-rattling, the whole world's frightened to death, and in exchange for the Soviet agreement to take the missiles out of Cuba your President tore up your Monroe Doctrine, the cornerstone of your whole security system.'

'What?'

'Certainly. Didn't JFK give Khrushchev a written promise not to invade Cuba, not to permit an invasion from American territory—or from any other place in the Western Hemisphere? *Written*, by God! So now, a hostile European power, Soviet Russia, totally against your Monroe Doctrine, is openly established ninety miles off your coast, the borders of which are guaranteed in writing by your own President and ratified by your own Congress. The Big K pulled off a colossal coup never duplicated in your whole history. And all for nothing!' Gavallan's voice harshened. 'Now Cuba's nicely safe, thank you very much, where it'll grow, expand and eventually infect all South America. Safe for Soviet subs, ships, aircraft. . . . Christ almight that's certainly a marvelous victory!'

Casey looked at Bartlett, shocked. 'But surely, Linc, surely that's not right.'

Bartlett was as shocked. 'I guess . . . if you think about it, Casey, I guess. . . . It sure as hell cost them nothing.'

'Ian's convinced of it,' Gavallan said. 'Talk to him. As to Vietnam, no one here thinks President Kennedy can handle that either, much as we admire him personally. Asia's not like Europe, or the Americas. They think differently here, act differently and have different values.'

There was a sudden silence. Bartlett broke it. 'You think there'll be war then?'

Gavallan glanced at him. 'Nothing for you to worry about. Par-Con should do very well. You've heavy industry, computers, polyurethane foam, government contracts into aerospace, petrochemicals, sonics, wireless equipment . . . With your goods and our expertise if there's a war, well, the sky's the limit.'

'I don't think I'd like to profit that way,' Casey said, irritated by him. 'That's a lousy way to earn a buck.'

Gavallan turned on her. 'A lot of things on this earth are lousy, and wrong and unfair. . . .' He was going to give her both barrels, infuriated with the way she kept interrupting his conversation with Bartlett but he decided that now was not the time, nor the place, so he said pleasantly, 'But of course you're right. No one wants to profit from death. If you'll excuse me I'll be going. . . . You know everyone has place cards? Dinner'll start any moment. Matter of face.'

He walked off.

Casey said, 'I don't think he likes me at all.'

They laughed at the way she said it. 'What you said was right, Casey,' Orlanda told her. 'You were right. War is terrible.'

'You were here during it?' Casey asked innocently.

'Yes, but in Macao. I'm Portuguese. My mother told me it wasn't too bad there. The Japanese didn't trouble Macao because Portugal was neutral.' Orlanda added sweetly, 'Of course I'm only twenty-five now so I hardly remember any of it. I was not quite seven when the war ended. Macao's nice, Casey. So different from Hong Kong. You and Linc might like to go there. It's worth seeing. I'd love to be your guide.'

I'll bet, Casey thought, feeling her twenty-six was old against Orlanda who had the skin of a seventeen-year-old. 'That'd be great. But Lando, what's with Andrew? Why was he so teed off? Because I'm a woman VP and all that?'

'I doubt that. I'm sure you exaggerate,' Mata said. 'It's just that he's not very pro-American and it drives him mad that the British Empire's no more, that the U.S. is arbiter of the world's fate and making obvious mistakes, he thinks. Most British people agree with him, I'm afraid! It's part jealousy of course. But you must be patient with Andrew. After all, your government did give away Hong Kong in '45 to Chiang—only the British navy stopped that. America did side with Soviet Russia against them over Suez, did support the Jews against them in Palestine—there are dozens of examples. It's also true lots of us here think your present hostility to China's ill-advised.'

'But they're as Communist as Russia. They went to war against us when we were only trying to protect freedom in South Korea. We weren't going to attack them.'

'But historically, China's always crossed the Yalu when any foreign invader approached that border. *Always*. Your Mac-Arthur was supposed to be a historian,' Mata said patiently, wondering if she was as naive in bed, 'he should have known. He—or your President—forced China into a path it did not want to take. I'm absolutely sure of that.'

'But we weren't invaders. North Korea invaded the South. We just wanted to help a people be free. We'd nothing to gain from South Korea. We spend billions trying to help people stay free. Look what China did to Tibet—to India last year. Seems to me we're always the fall guy and all we want is to protect freedom.' She stopped as a murmur of relief went through the room and people began heading for their tables. Waiters bearing silver-domed platters were trooping in. 'Thank God! I'm starving!'

'Me too,' Bartlett said.

'Shitee's early tonight,' Mata said with a laugh. 'Orlanda, you should have warned them it's an old custom always to have a snack before any of Shitee's banquets.'

Orlanda just smiled her lovely smile and Casey said, 'Orlanda warned Linc, who told me, but I figured I could last.' She looked at her enemy who was almost half a head shorter, about five foot three. For the first time in her life she felt big and oafish. Be honest, she reminded herself, ever since you walked out of the hotel into the streets and saw all the Chinese girls and women with their tiny hands and feet and bodies and smallness, all dark-eyed and dark-haired, you've felt huge and alien. Yes. Now I can understand why they all gape at us so much. And as for the ordinary tourist, loud, overweight, waddling along . . .

Even so, Orlanda Ramos, as pretty as you are and as clever as you think you are, you're not the girl for Linc Bartlett. So you can blow it all out of your ass! 'Next time, Orlanda,' she said so nicely, 'I'll remember to be very cautious about what you recommend.'

'I recommend we eat, Casey. I'm hungry too.'

Mata said, 'I do believe we're all at the same table. I must confess I arranged it.' Happily he led the way, more than ever excited by the challenge of getting Casey into bed. The moment he had seen her he had decided. Part of it was her beauty and tallness and beautiful breasts, such a welcome contrast to the smallness and sameness of the normal Asian girl. Part was because of the clues Orlanda had given him. But the biggest part had been his sudden thought that by breaking the Bartlett-Casey connection he might wreck Par-Con's probe into Asia. Far better to keep Americans and their hypocritical, impractical morality and meddling out of our area as long as we can, he had

642

told himself. And if Dunross doesn't have the Par-Con deal, then he will have to sell me the control I want. Then, at long last, *I* become *the tai-pan* of the Noble House, all the Dunrosses and Struans notwithstanding.

Madonna, life is really very good. Curious that this woman could be the key to the best lock in Asia, he thought. Then he added contentedly, Clearly she can be bought. It's only a matter of how much.

37

Dinner was twelve courses. Braised abalone with green sprouts, chicken livers and sliced partridge sauce, shark's fin soup, barbecued chicken, Chinese greens and peapods and broccoli and fifty other vegetables with crab meat, the skin of roast Peking duck with plum sauce and sliced spring onions and paper-thin pancakes, double-boiled mushrooms and fish maw, smoked pomfret fish with salad, rice Yangchow style, home sweet home noodles—then happiness dessert, sweetened lotus seeds and lily in rice gruel. And tea continuously.

Mata and Orlanda helped Casey and Bartlett. Fleur and Peter Marlowe were the only other Europeans at their table. The Chinese presented their visting cards and received others in exchange. 'Oh you can eat with chopsticks!' All the Chinese were openly astonished, then slid comfortably back into Cantonese, the bejeweled women clearly discussing Casey and Bartlett and the Marlowes. Their comments were slightly guarded only because of Lando Mata and Orlanda.

'What're they saying, Orlanda?' Bartlett asked quietly amid the noisy exuberance, particularly of the Chinese.

'They're just wondering about you and Miss Casey,' she said as cautiously, not translating the lewd remarks about the size of Casey's chest, the wondering where her clothes came from, how much they cost, why she didn't wear any jewelry, and what it must be like to be so tall. They were saying little about Bartlett other than wondering out loud if he was really Mafia as one of the Chinese papers had suggested.

Orlanda was sure he wasn't. But she was sure also that she would have to be very circumspect in front of Casey, neither too forward nor too slow, and never to touch him. And to be sweet to her, to try to throw her off her stride.

Fresh plates for each course were laid with a clatter, the used ones whisked away. Waiters hurried to the dumbwaiters in the central section by the staircase to dispose of the old and grab steaming platters of the new.

The kitchens, three decks below, were an inferno with the huge four-feet-wide iron woks fired with gas that was piped aboard. Some woks for steaming, some for quick frying, some for deep frying, some for stewing, and many for the pure white rice. An open, wood-fired barbecue. An army of helpers for the twenty-eight cooks were preparing the meats and vegetables, plucking chickens, killing fresh fish and lobsters and crabs and cleaning them, doing the thousand tasks that Chinese food requires—as each dish is cooked freshly for each customer.

The restaurant opened at 10:00 A.M. and the kitchen closed at 10:45 P.M.—sometimes later when a special party was arranged. There could be dancing and a floor show if the host was rich enough. Tonight, though there was no late shift or floor show or dancing, they all knew that their share of the tip from Shitee T'Chung's banquet would be very good. Shitee T'Chung was an expansive host, though most of them believed that much of the charity money he collected went into his stomach or those of his guests or onto the backs of his lady friends. He also had the reputation of being ruthless to his detractors, a miser to his family, and vengeful to his enemies.

Never mind, the head chef thought. A man needs soft lips and hard teeth in this world and everyone knows which will last the longer. 'Hurry up!' he shouted. 'Can I wait all manure-infested night? Prawns! Bring the prawns!' A sweating helper in ragged pants and ancient, sweaty undershirt rushed up with a bamboo platter of the fresh caught and freshly peeled prawns. The chef cast them into the vast wok, added a handful of monosodium glutamate, whisked them twice and scooped them out, put a handful of steaming peapods on two platters and divided up the pink, glistening succulent prawns on top equally.

'All gods urinate on all prawns!' he said sourly, his stomach ulcer paining him, his feet and calves leaden from his ten-hour shift. 'Send those upstairs before they spoil! *Dew neh loh moh* hurry . . . that's my last order. It's time to go home!'

645

Other cooks were shouting last orders and cursing as they cooked. They were all impatient to be gone. 'Hurry it up!' Then one young helper carrying a pot of used fat stumbled and the fat sprayed onto one of the gas fires, caught with a whoosh and there was sudden pandemonium. A cook screamed as the fire surrounded him and he beat at it, his face and hair singed. Someone threw a bucket of water on the fire and spread it violently. Flames soared to the rafters, billowing smoke. Shouting, shoving cooks moving out of the fire were causing a bottleneck. The acrid, black, oil smoke began to fill the air.

The man nearest the single narrow staircase to the first deck grabbed one of the two fire extinguishers and slammed the plunger down and pointed the nozzle at the fire. Nothing happened. He did it again then someone else grabbed it from him with a curse, tried unsuccessfully to make it work, and cast it aside. The other extinguisher was also a dud. The staff had never bothered to test them.

'All gods defecate on these motherless foreign devil inventions!' a cook wailed and prepared to flee if the fire approached him. A frightened coolie choking on the smoke at the other end of the kitchen backed away from a shaft of flame into some jars and toppled them. Some contained thousand-year-old eggs and others sesame oil. The oil flooded the floor and caught fire. The coolie vanished in the sudden sheet of flame. Now the fire owned half the kitchen.

It was well past eleven o'clock and most diners had already left. The top deck of the *Floating Dragon* was still partially filled. Most of the Chinese, Four Finger Wu and Venus Poon among them, were walking out or had already left as the last course had already been served long since and it was polite Chinese custom to leave as soon as the last dish was finished, table by table. Only the Europeans were lingering over Cognac or port, and cigars.

Throughout the boat, tables of mah-jong were being set up by Chinese, and the clitter-clatter of ivory tiles banging on the tables began to dominate.

'Do you play mah-jong, Mr. Bartlett?' Mata asked.

'No. Please call me Linc.'

'You should learn—it's better than bridge. Do you play bridge, Casey?'

Linc Bartlett laughed. 'She's a wiz, Lando. Don't play her for money.'

'Perhaps we can have a game sometime. You play, don't you, Orlanda?' Mata said, remembering Gornt was an accomplished player.

'Yes, a little,' Orlanda said softly and Casey thought grimly, I'll bet the bitch's a wiz too.

'I'd love a game,' Casey said sweetly.

'Good,' Mata said. 'One day next week . . . oh, hello, tai-pan!'

Dunross greeted them all with his smile. 'How did you enjoy the food?'

'It was fantastic!' Casey said, happy to see him and greatly aware of how handsome he looked in his tuxedo. 'Would you like to join us?'

'Thanks bu—'

'Good night, tai-pan,' Dianne Chen said, coming up to him, her son Kevin—a short, heavyset youth with dark curly hair and full lips—in tow.

Dunross introduced them. 'Where's Phillip?'

'He was going to come but he phoned to say he was delayed. Well, good night . . .' Dianne smiled and so did Kevin and they headed for the door, Casey and Orlanda wide-eyed at Dianne's jewelry.

'Well, I must be off too,' Dunross said.

'How was your table?'

'Rather trying,' Dunross said with his infectious laugh. He had eaten with the MPs—with Gornt, Shi-teh and his wife at the Number One Table—and there had been sporadic angry outbursts above the clatter of the plates. 'Robin Grey's rather outspoken, and ill-informed, and some of us were having at him. For once Gornt and I were on the same side. I must confess our table got served first so poor old Shi-teh and his wife could flee. He took off like a dose of salts fifteen minutes ago.'

They all laughed with him. Dunross was watching Marlowe. He wondered if Marlowe knew that Grey was his brother-in-law. 'Grey seems to know you quite well, Mr. Marlowe.'

'He has a good memory, tai-pan, though his manners are off.'

'I don't know about that, but if he has his way in Parliament God help Hong Kong. Well, I just wanted to say hello to all of

647

you.' He smiled at Bartlett and Casey. 'How about lunch to-morrow?'

'Fine,' Casey said. 'How about coming to the V and A?' She noticed Gornt get up to leave on the opposite side of the room and she wondered again who would win. 'Just before dinner Andrew was say—'

Then, with all of them, she heard faint screams. There was a sudden hush, everyone listening.

'Fire!'

'Christ, look!' They all stared at the dumbwaiter. Smoke was pouring out. Then a small tongue of flame.

A split second of disbelief, then everyone jumped up. Those nearest the main staircase rushed for the doorway, crowding it, as others took up the shout. Bartlett leapt to his feet and dragged Casey with him. Mata and some of the guests began to run for the bottleneck.

'Hold it!' Dunross roared above the noise. Everyone stopped. 'There's plenty of time. Don't hurry!' he ordered. 'There's no need to run, take your time! There's no danger yet!' His admonition helped those who were overly frightened. They started easing out of the crammed doorway. But below, on the staircase, the shouts and hysteria had increased.

Not everyone had run at the first cry of danger. Gornt hadn't moved. He puffed his cigar, all his senses concentrated. Havergill and his wife had walked over to the windows to look out. Others joined them. They could see crowds milling around the main entrance two decks below. 'I don't think we need to worry, my dear,' Havergill said. 'Once the main lot are out we can follow at leisure.'

Lady Joanna, beside them, said, 'Did you see Biltzmann rush off? What a berk!' She looked around and saw Bartlett and Casey across the room, waiting beside Dunross. 'Oh, I'd've thought they'd've fled too.'

Havergill said, 'Oh come on, Joanna, not all Yankees are cowards!'

A sudden shaft of flame and thick black smoke poured out of the dumbwaiter. The shouting to hurry up began again.

On the far side of the room nearer the fire, Bartlett said hastily, 'Ian, is there another exit?'

'I don't know,' Dunross said. 'Take a look outside. I'll hold the fort here.' Bartlett took off quickly for the exit door to the half deck and Dunross turned to the rest of them. 'Nothing to worry about,' he said, calming them and gauging them quickly. Fleur Marlowe was white but in control, Casey stared in shock at the people jamming the doorway, Orlanda petrified, near breaking. 'Orlanda! It's all right,' he said, 'there's no danger . . .'

On the other side of the room Gornt got up and went nearer to the door. He could see the crush and knew that the stairs below would be jammed. Shrieks and some screams added to the fear here but Sir Charles Pennyworth was beside the doorway trying to get an orderly withdrawal down the stairs. More smoke billowed out and Gornt thought, Christ almighty, a bloody fire, half a hundred people and one exit. Then he noticed the unattended bar. He went to it and, outwardly calm, poured himself a whiskey and soda, but the sweat was running down his back.

Below on the crowded second-deck landing Lando Mata stumbled and brought a whole group down, Dianne Chen and Kevin with them, creating a blockage in this, the only escape route. Men and women shrieked impotently, crushed against the floor as others fell or stumbled over them in a headlong dash for safety. Above on the staircase, Pugmire held onto the banister and just managed to keep his feet, using his great strength to shove his back against the people and prevent more from falling. Julian Broadhurst was beside him, frightened too but equally controlled, using his height and weight with Pugmire. Together they held the breach momentarily, but gradually all the weight of those behind overcame them. Pugmire felt his grip slipping. Ten steps below, Mata fought to his feet, trampled on a few people in his haste, then shoved on downstairs, his coat half torn from him. Dianne Chen clawed her way to her feet, dragging Kevin with her. In the shoving, milling mass of humanity she did not notice a woman grab her diamond pendant neatly and pocket it, then jostle away down the stairs. Smoke billowing up from the lower deck added to the horror. Pugmire's hold was broken. He was half-shoved into the wall by the human flood and Broadhurst missed his footing. Another small avalanche of people began. Now the stairs on both levels were clogged.

Four Finger Wu with Venus Poon had been on the first landing when the shout had gone up and he had darted down the last staircase and shoved his way out onto the drawbridge that led to the wharf, Venus Poon a few terrorized steps behind him. Safe on the wharf, he turned and looked back, his heart pounding, his breathing heavy. Men and women were stumbling out of the huge ornate doorway onto the jetty, some flames coming out of portholes near the waterline. A policeman who had been patrolling nearby ran up, watched aghast for a moment, then took to his heels for the nearest telephone. Wu was still trying to catch his breath when he saw Richard Kwang and his wife rush out pell-mell. He began to laugh and felt much better. Venus Poon thought the people looked very funny too. Onlookers were collecting in safety, no one doing anything to help, just gawking—which is only right, Wu thought in passing. One must never interfere with the decisions of the gods. The gods have their own rules and they decide a human's joss. It's my joss to escape and to enjoy this whore tonight. All gods help me to maintain my Imperial Iron until she screams for mercy.

'Come along, Little Mealy Mouth,' Four Fingers said with a cackle, 'we can safely leave them to their joss. Time's wasting.'

'No, Father,' she said quickly. 'Any moment the TV cameras and press will arrive—we must think of our image, *heya*?'

'Image? It's the pillow and the Gorgeous G—'

'Later!' she said imperiously and he bit back the curse he was going to add. 'Don't you want to be hailed as a hero?' she said sharply. 'Perhaps even a knighthood like Shitee, *heya*?' Quickly she dirtied her hands and her face and carefully ripped one of the straps above her breast and went near to the gangway where she could see and be seen. Four Fingers watched her blankly. A *quai loh* honor like Shitee? he thought astounded. Eeeeee, why not! He followed her warily, taking great care not to get too close to any danger.

They saw a tongue of flame sweep out of the chimney on the top deck and frightened people looking down from the three decks of windows. People were collecting on the wharf. Others were stumbling out to safety in hysterics, many coughing from the smoke that was beginning to possess the whole restaurant. There was another shouting crush in the doorway, a few went down and some scuttled from under the milling feet, those behind shrieking at those in front to hurry, and again Four

Fingers and other onlookers laughed.

On the top deck Bartlett leaned over the railings and looked down at the hull and the jetty below. He could see crowds on the wharf and milling, hysterical people fighting out of the entrance. There was no other staircase, ladder or escape possibility on either side. His heart was hammering but he was not afraid. There's no real danger, yet, he thought. We can jump into the water below. Easy. It's what, thirty, forty feet—no sweat if you don't belly flop. He ran back along the deck that used up half the length of the boat. Black smoke, sparks and a little flame surged out of the funnels.

He opened the top-deck door and closed it quickly in order not to create any added draft. The smoke was much worse and the flames coming out of the dumbwaiter were continuous now. The smoke smell on the air was acrid and carried the stench of burning meat. Almost everyone was crowded around the far doorway. Gornt was standing apart by himself watching them, sipping a drink. Bartlett thought, Jesus, there's one cold-blooded bastard! He skirted the dumbwaiter carefully, his eyes smarting from the smoke, and almost knocked over Christian Toxe who was hunched over the telephone shouting into it above the noise, '. . . I don't give a shit, get a photographer out here right now, and *then* phone the fire department!' Angrily Toxe slammed down the phone and muttering, 'Stupid bastards,' went back to his wife, a matronly Chinese woman who stared at him blankly. Bartlett hurried toward Dunross. The tai-pan stood motionless beside Peter and Fleur Marlowe, Orlanda and Casey, whistling tonelessly.

'Nothing, Ian,' he said quietly, noticing his voice sounded strange, 'not a goddamn thing. No ladders, nothing. But we can jump, easy, if necessary.'

'Yes. We're lucky being on this deck. The others may not be so lucky.' Dunross watched the smoke and fire spurting from the dumbwaiter that was near the exit door. 'We'll have to decide pretty soon which way to go,' he said gently. 'That fire could cut us off from the outside. If we go out we may never get back in and we'll have to jump. If we stay in, we can only use the stairs.'

'Jesus,' Casey muttered. She was trying to calm her racing heart and the feeling of claustrophobia that was welling up. Her skin felt clammy and her eyes were darting from the exit to the doorway and back again. Bartlett put an arm around her. 'It's no sweat, we can jump anytime.'

'Yes, sure, Linc.' Casey was holding on grimly.

'You can swim, Casey?' Dunross asked.

'Yes. I . . . was caught in a fire once. Ever since then I've been frightened to death of them.' It was a few years before when her little house in the Hollywood Hills of Los Angeles was in the path of one of the sudden summer conflagrations and she had been bottled in, the winding canyon road already burning below. She had turned on all the water sprinklers and begun to hose the roof. The clawing heat of the fire had reached out at her. Then the fire had crested, jumping from the top of one valley to the opposite side to begin burning down both sides towards the valley floor, whipped by hundred-mile-an-hour gusts self-generated by the fire. The roaring flames obliterated trees and houses, came closer and there was no way out. In terror, she kept the hose on her roof. Cats and dogs from the homes above fled past her and one wild-eyed Alsatian cowered in the lee of her house. The heat and the smoke and the terror surrounded her and it went on and on but this part of the fire stopped fifty feet from her boundary. For no reason. Above, all the houses on her street had gone. Most of the canyon. A swath almost half a mile wide and two long burned for three days in the hills that bisected the city of Los Angeles.

'I'm all right, Linc,' she said shakily. 'I . . . I think I'd rather be outside than here. Let's get the hell out of here. A swim'd be great.'

'I can't swim!' Orlanda was trembling. Then her control snapped and she got up to rush for the stairs.

Bartlett grabbed her. 'Everything's going to be all right. Jesus, you'll never make it that way. Listen to the poor bastards down there, they're in real trouble. Stay put, huh? The stairs're no good.' She hung onto him, petrified.

'You'll be all right,' Casey said compassionately.

'Yes,' Dunross said, his eyes on the fire and billowing smoke.

Marlowe said, 'We, er, we're really in very good shape, tai-pan, aren't we? Yes. The fire's got to be from the kitchens. They'll get it under control. Fleur, pet, there'll be no need to go over the side.'

'It's no sweat,' Bartlett assured him. 'There's plenty of sampans to pick us up!'

'Oh yes, but she can't swim either.'

Fleur put her hand on her husband's arm. 'You always said I should learn, Peter.'

Dunross wasn't listening. He was consumed with fear and trying to dominate it. His nostrils were filled with the stench of burning meat that he knew oh so well and he was near vomiting. He was back in his burning Spitfire, shot out of the sky by a Messerschmitt 109 over the Channel, the cliffs of Dover too far away, and he knew the fire would consume him before he could tear the jammed and damaged cockpit canopy free and bail out, the horror-smell of scorching flesh, his own, surrounding him. In terror he smashed his fist impotently against the Perspex, his other beating at the flames around his feet and knees, choking from the acrid smoke in his lungs, half blinded. Then there was a sudden frantic roar as the cowl ripped away, an inferno of flames surged up and surrounded him and somehow he was out and falling away from the flames, not knowing if his face was gone, the skin of his hands and feet, his boots and flying overalls still smoking. Then the shuddering nauseating jerk as his chute opened, then the dark silhouette of the enemy plane hurtled toward him out of the sun and he saw the machine guns sparking and a tracer blew part of his calf away. He remembered none of the rest except the smell of burning flesh that was the same then as now.

'What do you think, tai-pan?'

'What?'

'Shall we stay or leave?' Marlowe repeated.

'We'll stay, for the moment,' Dunross said and they all wondered how he could sound so calm and look so calm. 'When the stairs clear we can walk out. No reason to get wet if we don't have to.'

Casey smiled at him hesitantly. 'These fires happen often?'

'Not here, but they do in Hong Kong, I'm afraid. Our Chinese friends don't care much about fire regulations . . .'

It was still only a few minutes since the first violent gust of fire had swirled up in the kitchen but now the fire had a full hold there and, through the access of the dumbwaiter, a strong hold on the central sections of the three decks above. The fire in the

653

kitchen blocked half the room from the only staircase. Twenty terrified men were trapped on the wrong side. The rest of the staff had fled long since to join the heaving mass of people on the deck above. There were half a dozen portholes but these were small and rusted up. In panic one of the cooks rushed at the flaming barrier, screamed as the flames engulfed him, almost made it through but slipped and kept on screaming for a long while. A petrified moan burst from the others. There was no other escape possibility.

The head chef was trapped too. He was a portly man and he had been in many kitchen fires so he was not panicked. His mind ranged all the other fires, desperately seeking a clue. Then he remembered.

'Hurry,' he shouted, 'get bags of rice flour . . . rice . . . hurry!'

The others stared at him without moving, their terror numbing them, so he lashed out and smashed some of them into the storeroom, grabbed a fifty-pound sack himself and tore the top off. 'Fornicate all fires hurry but wait till I tell you,' he gasped, the smoke choking and almost blinding him. One of the portholes shattered and the sudden draft whooshed the flames at them. Terrified they grabbed a sack each, coughing as the smoke billowed.

'Now!' the head chef roared and hurled the sack at the flaming corridor between the stoves. The sack burst open and the clouds of flour doused some of the flames. Other sacks followed in the same area and more flames were swallowed. Another barrage of flour went over the flaming benches, snuffing them out. The passage was momentarily clear. At once the head chef led the charge through the remaining flames and they all followed him pell-mell, leaping over the two charred bodies, and gained the stairs at the far side before the flames gushed back and closed the path. The men fought their way up the narrow staircase and into the partial air of the landing, joining the milling mob that pushed and shoved and screamed and coughed their way through the black smoke into the open.

Tears streamed from most faces. The smoke was very heavy now in the lower levels. Then the wall behind the first landing where the shaft of the dumbwaiter was began to twist and blacken. Abruptly it burst open, scattering gargoyles, and flames gushed out. Those on the stairs below shoved forward in panic and those on the landing reeled back. Then, seeing they were so close to safety, the first ranks darted forward, skirting the inferno, jumping the stairs two at a time. Hugh Guthrie, one of the MPs, saw a woman fall. He held onto the banister and stopped to help her but those behind toppled him and he fell with others. He picked himself up, cursing, and fought a path clear for just enough time to drag the woman up before he was engulfed again and shoved down the last few stairs to gain the entrance safely.

Half the landing between the lower deck and the second deck was still free of flames though the fire had an unassailable hold and was fueling itself. The crowds were thinning now though more than a hundred still clogged the upper staircases and doorways. Those above were milling and cursing, not being able to see ahead.

'What's the holdup for chrissake. . . .'

'Are the stairs still clear . . .?'

'For chrissake get on with it. . . .'

'It's getting bloody hot up here . . .'

'What a sodding carve-up. . . .'

Grey was one of those trapped on the second-deck staircase. He could see the flames gushing out of the wall ahead and knew the nearby wall would go any moment. He could not decide whether to retreat or to advance. Then he saw a child cowering against the steps under the banister. He managed to pull the little boy into his arms then pressed on, cursing those in front, darted around the fire, the way to safety below still jammed.

On the top deck Gornt and others were listening to the pandemonium below. There were only thirty or so people still here. He finished his drink, set the glass down and walked over to the group surrounding Dunross—Orlanda was still sitting, twisting her handkerchief in her hands, Fleur and Peter Marlowe still outwardly calm, and Dunross, as always, in control. Good, he thought, blessing his own heritage and training. It was part of British tradition that in danger, however petrified you are, you lose face by showing it. Then, too, he reminded himself, most of us have been bombed most of our lives, shot at, sunk, slammed into POW jails or been in the Services. Gornt's sister had been in the Women's Royal Naval Service—his mother an air raid warden, his father in the army, his uncle

655

killed at Monte Cassino, and he himself had served with the Australians in New Guinea after escaping from Shanghai, and had fought his way into and through Burma to Singapore.

'Ian,' he said, keeping his voice suitably nonchalant, 'it sounds as though the fire's on the first landing now. I suggest a swim.'

Dunross glanced back at the fire near the exit door. 'Some of the ladies don't swim. Let's give it a couple of minutes.'

'Very well. I think those who don't mind jumping should go on deck. That particular fire's really very boring.'

Casey said, 'I don't find it very boring at all.'

They all laughed. 'It's just an expression,' Peter Marlowe explained.

An explosion below decks rocked the boat slightly. The momentary silence was eerie.

In the kitchen the fire had spread to the storage rooms and was surrounding the four remaining hundred-gallon drums of oil. The one that had blown up had torn a gaping hole in the floor and buckled the side of the boat. Burning embers and burning oil and some seawater poured into the scuppers. The force of the explosion had ruptured some of the great timbers of the flat-bottomed hull and water was seeping through the seams. Hordes of rats scrambled out of the way seeking an escape route.

Another of the thick metal drums blew up and ripped a vast hole in the side of the boat just below the waterline, scattering fire in all directions. The people on the wharf gasped and some reeled back though there was no danger. Others laughed nervously. Still another drum exploded and another shaft of flames sprayed everywhere. The ceiling supports and joists were seriously weakened and, oil soaked, began to burn. Above on the first deck, the feet of the frenzied escapees pounded dangerously.

Just above the first landing Grey still had the child in his arms. He held onto the banister with one hand, frightened, shoving people behind and in front of him. He waited his turn, then shielding the child as best he could, ducked around the flames on the landing and darted down the stairs, the way mostly clear. The carpet by the threshold was beginning to smoke and one heavyset man stumbled, the whole floor shaky.

'Come on,' Grey shouted desperately to those behind. He made the threshold, others close behind and in front. Just as he reached the drawbridge the last two drums exploded, the whole floor behind him disappeared and he and the child and others were hurled forward like so much chaff.

Hugh Guthrie rushed out of the onlookers and pulled them to safety. 'You all right, old chap?' he gasped.

Grey was half stunned, gasping for breath, his clothes smoldering, and Guthrie helped beat them out. 'Yes . . . yes I think so . . .' he said half out of himself.

Guthrie gently lifted the unconscious child and peered at him. 'Poor little bastard!'

'Is he dead?'

'I don't think so. Here . . .' Guthrie gave the little Chinese boy to an onlooker and both men charged back to the gateway to help the others who were still numbed by the explosion and helpless. 'Christ all bloody mighty,' he gasped as he saw that now the whole entrance was impassable. Above the uproar, they heard the wail of approaching sirens.

The fire on the top deck near the exit was building nastily. Frightened, coughing people were streaming back into the room, forced back up the stairs by the fire that now owned the lower deck. Pandemonium and the stench of fear were heavy on the air.

'Ian, we'd better get the hell out of here,' Bartlett said.

'Yes. Quillan, would you please lead the way and take charge of the deck,' Dunross said. 'I'll hold this end.'

Gornt turned and roared. *'Everyone this way!* You'll be safe on deck . . . one at a time. . . .' He opened the door and positioned himself by it and tried to bring order to the hasty retreat—a few Chinese, the remainder mostly British. Once in the open everyone was much less frightened and grateful to be away from the smoke.

Bartlett, waiting in the room, felt excitement but still no fear for he knew he could smash any one of the windows and get Casey and himself out and into the sea. People stumbled past. Flames from the dumbwaiter increased and there was a dull explosion below.

'How you doing, Casey?'

'Okay.'

'Out you go!'

'When you go.'

'Sure.' Bartlett grinned at her. The room was thinning. He helped Lady Joanna through the doorway, then Havergill, who was limping, and his wife.

Casey saw that Orlanda was still frozen to her chair. Poor girl, she thought compassionately, remembering her own absolute terror in her own fire. She went over to her. 'Come on,' she said gently and helped her up. The girl's knees were trembling. Casey kept her arm around her.

'I . . . I've lost . . . my purse,' Orlanda muttered.

'No, here it is.' Casey picked it up from the chair and kept her arm around her as she half-pushed her past the flames into the open. The deck was crowded but once outside Casey felt enormously better.

'Everything's fine,' Casey said encouragingly. She guided her to the railing. Orlanda held on tightly. Casey turned back to look for Bartlett and saw both him and Gornt watching her from inside the room. Bartlett waved at her and she waved back, wishing he were outside with her.

Peter Marlowe herded his wife onto the deck and came up to her. 'You all right, Casey?'

'Sure. How you doing, Fleur?'

'Fine. Fine. It's . . . it's rather pleasant outside, isn't it?' Fleur Marlowe said, feeling faint and awful, petrified at the idea of jumping from this great height. 'Do you think it's going to rain?'

'The sooner the better.' Casey looked over the side. In the murky waters, thirty feet below, sampans were beginning to collect. All boatmen knew that those on the top would have to jump soon. From their vantage they could see that the fire possessed most of the first and second decks. A few people were trapped there, then one man hurled a chair through one of the windows, broke the glass away, scrambled through and fell into the sea. A sampan darted forward and threw him a line. Others who were trapped followed. One woman never came up.

The night was dark though the flames lit everything nearby, casting eerie shadows. The crowds on the wharf parted as the screaming fire engines pulled up. Immediately Chinese firemen and British officers dragged out the hoses. Another detachment joined up to the nearby fire hydrant and the first jet of water played onto the fire and there was a cheer. In seconds six hoses were in operation and two masked firemen with asbestos clothing and breathing equipment strapped to their backs rushed the entrance and began to drag those who were lying unconscious out of danger. Another huge explosion sprayed them with burning embers. One of the firemen doused everyone with water then directed the hose back on the entrance again.

The top deck was empty now except for Bartlett, Dunross and Gornt. They felt the deck sway under them and almost lost their footing. 'Jesus Christ,' Bartlett gasped, 'we going to sink?'

'Those explosions could've blown her bottom out,' Gornt said urgently. 'Come on!' He went through the door quickly, Bartlett followed.

Now Dunross was alone. The smoke was very bad, the heat and stench revolting him. He made a conscious effort not to flee, dominating his terror. At a sudden thought he ran back across the room to the doorway of the main staircase to make sure there was no one there. Then he saw the inert figure of a man on the staircase. Flames were everywhere. He felt his own fear surging again but once more he held it down, darted forward and began to drag the man back up the stairs. The Chinese was heavy and he did not know if the man was alive or dead. The heat was scorching and again he smelt burning flesh and felt his bile rising. Then Bartlett was beside him and together they half-dragged, half-carried the man across the room out onto the deck.

'Thanks,' Dunross gasped.

Quillan Gornt came over to them, bent down and turned the man over. The face was partially burned. 'You could have saved yourself the heroics. He's dead.'

'Who is he?' Bartlett said.

Gornt shrugged. 'I don't know. Do you know him, Ian?'

Dunross was staring at the body. 'Yes. It's Zep . . . Zeppelin Tung.'

'Tightfist's son?' Gornt was surprised. 'My God, he's put on weight. I'd never have recognized him.' He got to his feet. 'We'd better get everyone ready to jump. This boat's a graveyard.' He saw Casey standing by the railing. 'Are you all right?' he asked going over to her.

'Yes, thanks. You?'

'Oh yes.'

Orlanda was still beside her, staring blankly at the water below. People were milling around the deck. 'I'd better help get them organized,' Gornt said. 'I'll be back in a second.' He walked off.

Another explosion jarred the boat again. The list began to increase. Several people climbed over the side and jumped. Sampans went in to rescue them.

Christian Toxe had his arm around his Chinese wife and he was staring sourly overboard.

'You're going to have to jump, Christian,' Dunross said.

'Into Aberdeen Harbor? You must be bloody joking old chap! If you don't bounce off all the bloody effluvia you'll catch the bloody plague.'

'It's that or a red-hot tail,' someone called out with a laugh.

At the end of the deck Sir Charles Pennyworth was holding onto the railing as he worked his way down the boat encouraging everyone. 'Come on, young lady,' he said to Orlanda, 'it's an easy jump.'

She shook her head, petrified. 'No . . . no not yet . . . I can't swim.'

Fleur Marlowe put an arm around her. 'Don't worry. I can't swim either. I'm staying too.'

Bartlett said, 'Peter, you can hold her hand, she'll be safe. All you have to do, Fleur, is hold your breath!'

'She's not going to jump,' Marlow said quietly. 'At least, not till the last second.'

'It's safe.'

'Yes, but it's not safe for her. She's *enceinte*.'

'What?'

'Fleur's with child. About three months.'

'Oh Jesus.'

Flames roared skyward out of one of the flues. Inside the top deck restaurant tables were afire and the great carved temple screens at the far end were burning merrily. There was a great gust of sparks as the inner central staircase collapsed. 'Jesus, this whole boat's a firetrap. What about the folk below?' Casey asked.

'They're all out long ago,' Dunross said, not believing it. Now that he was in the open he felt fine. His successful domination of his fear made him light-headed. 'The view here is quite splendid, don't you think?'

Pennyworth called out jovially, 'We're in luck! The ship's listing this way so when she goes down we'll be safe enough. Unless she capsizes. Just like old times,' he added. 'I was sunk three times in the Med.'

'So was I,' Marlowe said, 'but it was in the Bangka Strait off Sumatra.'

'I didn't know that, Peter,' Fleur said.

'It was nothing.'

'How deep's the water here?' Bartlett asked.

'It must be twenty feet or more,' Dunross said.

'That'll be en—' There was a *whoopwhoopwhoop* of sirens as the police launch came bustling through the narrow byways between the islands of boats, its searchlight darting here and there. When it was almost alongside the *Floating Dragon*, the megaphone sounded loudly, first in Chinese. 'All sampans clear the area, clear the area . . .' Then in English, 'Those on the top deck prepare to abandon ship! The hull's holed, prepare to abandon ship!'

Christian Toxe muttered sourly to no one, 'Buggered if I'm going to ruin my only dinner jacket.'

His wife tugged at his arm. 'You never liked it anyway, Chris.'

'I like it now, old girl.' He tried to smile. 'You can't bloody swim either.'

She shrugged. 'I'll bet you fifty dollar you and me we swim like a one hundred percent eel.'

'Mrs. Toxe, you have a bet. But it's only fitting we're the last to go. After all, I want an eyewitness account.' He reached into his pocket and found his cigarettes, gave her one, trying to feel brave, frightened for her safety. He searched for a match, couldn't find one. She reached into her purse and rummaged around. Eventually she found her lighter. It lit on the third go. Both were oblivious of the flames that were ten feet behind them.

Dunross said, 'You smoke too much, Christian.'

The deck twisted sickeningly. The boat began to settle. Water was pouring through the great hole in her side. Firemen used their hoses with great bravery but they had little effect on the conflagration. A murmur went through the crowd as the whole boat shuddered. Two of the mooring guys snapped.

Pennyworth was leaning against the gunnel, helping others to jump clear. Quite a few were jumping now. Lady Joanna fell awkwardly. Paul Havergill helped his wife over the side. When he saw she had surfaced he leaped too. The police launch was still blaring in Cantonese to clear the area. Sailors threw life jackets over the side as others launched a cutter. Then, led by a young marine inspector, half a dozen sailors dived over the side to help those in trouble, men, women and a few children. A sampan darted in to help Lady Joanna, Havergill and his wife. Gratefully they clambered aboard the rickety craft. Others from the top deck plunged into the water.

The *Floating Dragon* was listing badly. Someone slipped on the top deck and knocked Pennyworth off balance. He half-jumped, half-fell backward before he could catch himself and fell like a stone. His head smashed into the stern of the sampan, snapping his neck, and he slithered into the water and sank. In the pandemonium no one noticed him.

Casey was hanging onto the railings with Bartlett, Dunross, Gornt, Orlanda and the Marlowes. Nearby, Toxe was puffing away, trying to summon his courage. His wife stubbed her cigarette out carefully. Flames were surging from the air vents, skylights and exit door, then the ship grounded heavily and lurched as another of her anchoring cables snapped. Gornt's hold was torn away and he crashed headfirst into the railing, stunning himself. Toxe and his wife lost their balance and went over the side, badly. Peter Marlowe held onto his wife and just managed to prevent her being smashed into a bulkhead as Bartlett and Casey half-tumbled, half-stumbled past and fell in a heap at the railing, Bartlett protecting her as best he could, her high heels dangerous.

Below, in the water, sailors were helping people to the rescue boat. One saw Toxe and his wife rise to the surface for an instant fifteen yards away, both gasping and spluttering, before they choked, and, flailing, went down again. At once he dived for them and after a seeming eternity, grabbed her clothing and shoved her, half-drowned to the surface. The young lieutenant swam over to where he had seen Toxe and dived but missed him in the darkness. He came up for air and dived once more into the blackness, groping helplessly. When his lungs were bursting, his outstretched fingers touched some clothing and he grabbed and kicked for the surface. Toxe clung on in panic, retching and choking from all the seawater he had swallowed. The young man broke his hold, turned Toxe over and hauled him to the cutter.

Above them, the boat was tilted dangerously and Dunross picked himself up. He saw Gornt inert in a heap and he stumbled over to him. He tried to lift him, couldn't.

'I'm . . . I'm all right,' Gornt gasped, coming around, then he shook his head like a dog. 'Christ, thanks . . .' He looked up and saw it was Dunross. 'Thanks,' he said, smiled grimly as he got up shakily. 'I'm still selling tomorrow and by next week you'll have had it.'

Dunross laughed. 'Jolly good luck! The idea of burning to death or drowning with you fills me with equal dismay.'

Ten yards away, Bartlett was lifting Casey up. The angle of the deck was bad now, the fire worse. 'The whole goddamn tub could capsize any second.'

'What about them?' she asked quietly, nodding at Fleur and Orlanda.

He thought a second, then said decisvely, 'You go first, wait below!'

'Got it!' At once she gave him her small purse. He stuffed it into a pocket and hurried away as she kicked off her shoes, unzipped her long dress and stepped out of it. At once she gathered up the light silk material into a rope, tied it around her waist, swung neatly over the railing and stood there poised on the edge a moment, gauged her impact point carefully, leapt out into a perfect swan dive. Gornt and Dunross watched her go, their immediate danger forgotten.

Bartlett was beside Orlanda now. He saw Casey break the surface cleanly and before Orlanda could do anything he lifted her over the railing and said, 'Hold your breath, honey,' and dropped her carefully. They all watched her fall. She plummeted down feet first and went into the water a few yards from Casey who had already anticipated the spot and had swum down below the surface. She caught Orlanda easily, kicked for the surface, and Orlanda was breathing almost before she realized she was off the deck. Casey held her safely and swam strongly for the cutter, in perfect control.

Gornt and Dunross cheered lustily. The boat lurched again and they almost lost their footing as Bartlett stumbled over to the Marlowes.

'Peter, how's your swimming?' Bartlett asked.

'Average.'

'Trust me with her? I was a lifeguard, beach bum, for years.'

Before Marlowe could say no, Bartlett lifted Fleur into his arms and stepped over the railing onto the ledge and poised himself a second. 'Just hold your breath!' She put one arm around his neck and held her nose then he stepped into space, Fleur tightly and safely in his arms. He plunged into the sea cleanly, protecting her from the shock with his own legs and body, and kicked smoothly for the surface. Her head was hardly under a few seconds and she was not even spluttering though her heart was racing. In seconds she was at the cutter. She hung onto the side and they looked back.

When Peter Marlowe saw she was safe his heart began again. 'Oh, jolly good,' he muttered.

'Did you see Casey go?' Dunross asked. 'Fantastic!'

'What? Oh, no, tai-pan.'

'Just bra and pants with stockings attached and no ironworks and a dream dive. Christ, what a figure!'

'Oh those're pantyhose,' Marlow said absently, looking at the water below, gathering his courage. 'They've just come out in the States, they're all the rage . . .'

Dunross was hardly listening. 'Christ Agnes, what a figure.'

'Ah yes,' Gornt echoed. 'And what *cojones*.'

The boat shrieked as the last of its mooring guys snapped. The deck toppled nauseatingly.

As one, the last three men went overboard. Dunross and Gornt dived, Peter Marlowe jumped. The dives were good but both men knew they were not as good as Casey's.

38

11:30 P.M.:

On the other side of the island the old taxi was grinding up the narrow street high above West Point in Mid Levels, Suslev sprawled drunkenly in the backseat. The night was dark and he was singing a sad Russian ballad to the sweating driver, his tie askew, coat off, his shirt streaked with sweat. The overcast had thickened and lowered, the humidity was worse, the air stifling.

'*Matyeryebyets!*' he muttered, cursing the heat, then smiled, the twisted obscenity pleasing him. He looked out the window. The city and harbor lights far below were misted by wisps of clouds, Kowloon mostly obscured. 'It'll rain soon, comrade,' he said to the driver, his English slurred, not caring if the man understood or not.

The ancient taxi was wheezing. The engine coughed suddenly and that reminded him of Arthur's cough and their coming meeting. His excitement quickened.

The taxi had picked him up at the Golden Ferry Terminal, then climbed to Mid Levels on the Peak, turned west, skirting Government House where the governor lived, and the Botanical Gardens. Passing the palace, Suslev had wondered absently when the Hammer and Sickle would fly atop the empty flagpole. Soon, he had thought contentedly. With Arthur's help and Sevrin's—very soon. Just a few more years.

He peered at his watch. He would be a little late but that did not worry him. Arthur was always late, never less then ten minutes, never more than twenty. Dangerous to be a man of habit in our profession, he thought. But dangerous or not, Arthur's an enormous asset and Sevrin, his creation, a brilliant, vital tool in our KGB armament, buried so deep, waiting so patiently, like all the other Sevrins throughout the world. Only ninety-odd thousands of us KGB officers and yet we almost rule the world. We've already changed it, changed it permanently, already we own half . . . and in such a short time, only since 1917.

So few of us, so many of *them*. But now our tentacles reach out into every corner. Our armies of assistants—informers, fools, parasites, traitors, the twisted self-deluders and misshapen, misbegotten believers we so deliberately recruit are in every land, feeding off one another like the vermin they all are, fueled by their own selfish wants and fears, all expendable sooner or later. And everywhere one of us, one of the elite, the KGB officers, in the center of each web, controlling guiding eliminating. Webs within webs up to the Presidium of all the Soviets and now so tightly woven into the fabric of Mother Russia as to be indestructible. We *are* modern Russia, he thought proudly. We're Lenin's spearhead. Without us and our techniques and our orchestrated use of terror there would be no Soviet Russia, no Soviet Empire, no driving force to keep the rulers of the Party all powerful—and nowhere on earth would there be a Communist State. Yes, we're the elite.

His smile deepened.

It was hot and sultry inside the taxi even though the windows were open as it curled upward through this residential area with its ribbons of great gardenless apartment blocks that sat on small pads chewed out of the mountainside. A bead of sweat trickled down his cheek and he wiped it off, his whole body feeling clammy.

I'd love a shower, he thought, letting his mind wander. A shower with cool sweet Georgian water, not this saline filth they put through Hong Kong's pipes. I'd love to be in the *dacha* near Tiflis, oh that would be grand! Yes, back in the *dacha* with Father and Mother and I'd swim in the stream running through our land and dry off in the sun, a great Georgian wine cooling in the stream and the mountains nearby. That's Eden if there ever was an Eden. Mountains and pastures, grapes and harvest and the air so clean.

He chuckled as he remembered the fabrication about his past he had told Travkin. That parasite! Just another fool, another tool to be used and, when blunt, discarded.

His father had been a Communist since the very early days—

first in the Cheka, secretly, and then, since its inception in 1917, in the KGB. Now in his late seventies, still tall and upright and in honored retirement, he lived like an old-fashioned prince with servants and horses and bodyguards. Suslev was sure that he would inherit the same *dacha*, the same land, the same honor in due course. So would his son, a fledgling in the KGB, if his service continued to be excellent. His own work merited it, his record was impressive and he was only fifty-two.

Yes, he told himself confidently, in thirteen years I'm due for retirement. Thirteen great more years, helping the attack move forward, never easing up whatever the enemy does.

And who is the enemy, the real enemy?

All those who disobey us, all those who refuse our eminence —Russians most of all.

He laughed out loud.

The weary sour-faced young driver glanced up briefly at the rear mirror then went back to his driving, hoping his passenger was drunk enough to misread the meter and give him a great tip. He pulled up at the address he had been given.

Rose Court on Kotewall Road was a modern fourteen-story apartment block. Below were three floors of garage space and around it a small ribbon of concrete and below that, down a slight concrete embankment, was Sinclair Road and Sinclair Towers and more apartment blocks that nestled into the mountainside. This was a choice area to live. The view was grand, the apartments were below the clouds that frequently shrouded the upper reaches of the Peak where the walls would sweat, linens would mildew and everything would seem to be perpetually damp.

The meter read 8.70 HK. Suslev peered at a bunch of notes, gave the driver 100 instead of a 10 and got out heavily. A Chinese woman was fanning herself impatiently. He lurched toward the apartment intercom. She told the driver to wait for her husband and looked after Suslev disgustedly.

His feet were unsteady. He found the button he sought and pressed it: Ernest Clinker, Esq., Manager.

'Yes?'

'Ernie, it's me, Gregor,' he said thickly with a belch. 'Are you in?'

The cockney voice laughed. 'Not on your nelly! 'Course I'm

in, mate! You're late! You sound as though you've been on a pub crawl! Beer's up, vodka's up, and me'n Mabel's here to greet you!'

Suslev headed for the elevator. He pressed the *down* button. On the lowest level he got out into the open garage and went to the far side. The apartment door was already open and a ruddy-faced, ugly little man in his sixties held out his hand. 'Stone the bloody crows,' Clinker said, a grin showing cheap false teeth, 'you're a bit under the weather, ain'cher?' Suslev gave him a bear hug which was returned and they went inside.

The apartment was two tiny bedrooms, living room, kitchen, bathroom. The rooms were poorly furnished but pleasant, and the only real luxury a small tape deck that was playing opera loudly.

'Beer or vodka?'

Suslev beamed and belched. 'First a piss, then vodka, then . . . then another and then . . . then bed.' He belched hugely, lurching for the toilet.

'Right you are, Cap'n me old sport! Hey, Mabel, say hello to the Cap'n!' The sleepy old bulldog on her well-chewed mat opened one eye briefly, barked once and was almost instantly wheezily asleep again. Clinker beamed and went to the table and poured a stiff vodka and a glass of water. No ice. He drank some Guinness then called out, 'How long you staying, Gregor?'

'Just tonight, *tovarich*. Perhaps tomorrow night. To-morrow . . . tomorrow I've got to be back aboard But tomorrow night . . . perhaps, eh?'

'What about Ginny? She throw you out again . . . ?'

In the nondescript van that was parked down the road, Roger Crosse, Brian Kwok and the police radio technician were listening to this conversation through a loudspeaker, the quality of the bug good with little static, the van packed with radio surveillance equipment. They heard Clinker chuckle and say again, 'She threw you out, eh?'

'All evening we jig-jig and she . . . she says go stay with Ernie and leave me . . . leave me sleep!'

'You're a lucky bugger. She's a princess that one. Bring her over tomorrer.'

'Yes . . . yes I . . . will. Yes she's the best.'

668

They heard Suslev pour a bucket of water into the toilet and come back.

'Here, old chum!'

'Thank you.' The sound of thirsty drinking. 'I . . . I think . . . I think I want to lie down for . . . lie down. A few minutes . . .'

'A few hours more like! Don't you fret, I'll cook breakfast. Here, wanta 'nother drink. . . .'

The policemen in the van were listening carefully. Crosse had ordered the bug put into Clinker's apartment two years ago. Periodically it was monitored, always when Suslev was there. Suslev, always under loose surveillance, had met Clinker in a bar. Both men were submariners and they had struck up a friendship. Clinker had invited him to stay and from time to time Suslev did. At once Crosse had instituted a security check on Clinker but nothing untoward had been discovered. For twenty years Clinker had been a sailor with the Royal Navy. After the war he had drifted from job to job in the Merchant Marine, throughout Asia to Hong Kong, where he had settled when he retired. He was a quiet, easygoing man who lived alone and had been Rose Court's caretaker-janitor for five years now. Suslev and Clinker were a matched pair who drank a lot, caroused a lot and swapped stories. None of their hours of talk had produced anything considered valuable.

'He's had his usual tankful, Brian,' Crosse said.

'Yes sir.' Brian Kwok was bored and tried not to show it.

In the small living room Clinker gave Suslev his shoulder. 'Come on, it's you for a kip.' He stepped over the glass and helped Suslev into the small bedroom. Suslev lay down heavily and sighed.

Clinker closed the drapes then went over to another small tape deck and turned it on. In a moment heavy breathing and the beginnings of a snore came from the tape. Suslev got up soundlessly, his pretended drunkenness gone. Clinker was already on his hands and knees. He pulled away a mat and opened the trapdoor. Noiselessly, Suslev went down into it. Clinker grinned, slapped him on the back and closed the well-greased door after him. The trapdoor steps led to a rough tunnel that quickly joined the large, dry, subterranean culvert storm drain. Suslev picked his way carefully, using the flashlight that was in a bracket at the bottom of the steps. In a moment he heard a car grinding over Sinclair Road just above his head. A few more steps and he was below Sinclair Towers. Another trapdoor led to a janitor's closet. This let out onto some disused back stairs. He began to climb.

Roger Crosse was still listening to the heavy breathing, mixed with opera. The van was cramped and close, their shirts sweaty. Crosse was smoking. 'Sounds like he's bedded down for the night,' he said. They could hear Clinker humming and his movements as he cleared up the broken glass. A red warning light on the radio panel started winking. The operator clicked on the sender. 'Patrol car 1423, yes?'

'Headquarters for Superintendent Crosse. Urgent.'

'This's Crosse.'

'Duty Office, sir. A report's just come in that the *Floating Dragon* restaurant's on fire . . .' Brian Kwok gasped. '. . . Fire engines're already there, and the constable said that as many as twenty may be dead or drowned. It seems the boat caught fire from the kitchen, sir. There were several explosions. They blew out most of the hull and . . . Just a moment sir, there's another report coming in from Marine.'

They waited. Brian Kwok broke the silence. 'Dunross?'

'The party was on the top deck?' Crosse asked.

'Yes sir.'

'He's much too smart to get burned to death—or drowned,' Crosse said softly. 'Was the fire an accident, or deliberate?'

Brian Kwok did not answer.

The HQ voice came in again. 'Marine reports that the boat's capsized. They say it's a proper carve-up and it looks like a few got sucked under.'

'Was our agent with our VIP?'

'No sir, he was waiting on the wharf near his car. There was no time to get to him.'

'What about the people caught on the top deck?'

'Hang on a moment, I'll ask. . . .'

Again a silence. Brian Kwok wiped the sweat off.

'. . . They say, twenty or thirty up there jumped, sir. Unfortunately most of them abandoned ship a bit late, just before the boat capsized, Marine doesn't know how many were swamped.'

'Stand by.' Crosse thought a moment. Then he spoke into the

mike again. 'I'm sending Superintendent Kwok there at once in this transport. Send a team of frogmen to meet him. Ask the navy to assist, Priority One. I'll be at home if I'm needed.' He clicked off the mike. Then to Brian Kwok, 'I'll walk from here. Call me the moment you know about Dunross. If he's dead we'll visit the bank vaults at once and to hell with the consequences. Fast as you can now!'

He got out. The van took off up the hill. Aberdeen was over the spine of mountains and due south. He glanced at Rose Court a moment, then down across the street below to Sinclair Towers. One of his teams was still watching the entrance, waiting patiently for Tsu-yan's return. Where is that bastard? he asked himself irritably.

Very concerned, he walked off down the hill. Rain began to splatter him. His footsteps quickened.

Suslev took an ice-cold beer from the modern refrigerator and opened it. He drank gratefully. 32 Sinclair Towers was spacious, rich, clean and well furnished, with three bedrooms and a large living room. It was on the eleventh floor. There were three apartments to each floor around two cramped elevators and exit steps. Mr. and Mrs. John Chen owned 31. 33 belonged to a Mr. K. V. Lee. Arthur had told Suslev that K. V. Lee was a cover name for Ian Dunross who, following the pattern of his predecessors, had sole access to three or four private apartments spread around the Colony. Suslev had never met either John Chen or Dunross though he had seen them at the races and elsewhere many times.

If we have to interview the tai-pan what could be more convenient? he thought grimly. And with Travkin as an alternate bait. . . .

A sudden squall whipped the curtains that were drawn over open windows and he heard the rain. He shut the windows carefully and looked out. Great drops were streaking the windows. Streets and rooftops were already wet. Lightning went across the sky. The rumble of thunder followed. Already the temperature had dropped a few degrees. This'll be a good storm, he told himself gratefully, pleased to be out of Ginny Fu's tiny, sleazy fifth-floor walkup in Mong Kok, and equally happy not to be at Clinker's.

Arthur had arranged everything: Clinker, Ginny Fu, this safe house, the tunnel, certainly as well as he himself could have done in Vladivostok. Clinker was a submariner and cockney and everything he was supposed to be except that he had always detested the officer class. Arthur had said it had been easy to subvert Clinker to the cause, using the man's built-in suspicions, hatreds and secretiveness. 'Ugly Ernie knows only a little about you, Gregor—of course that you're Russian and captain of the *Ivanov*. As to the tunnel, I told him you're having an affair with a married woman in Sinclair Towers, the wife of one of the Establishment tai-pans. I told him the tape-recorded snores and secrecy are because the rotten Peelers are after you and they've sneaked in and bugged his flat.'

'Peelers?'

'That's the cockney nickname for police. It came from Sir Robert Peel, Prime Minister of England, who founded the first police force. Cockneys've always hated Peelers and Ugly Ernie would delight in outwitting them. Just be pro-*Royal* Navy and he's your dog until death. . . .'

Suslev smiled. Clinker's not a bad man, he thought, just a bore.

He sipped his beer as he wandered back into the living room. The afternoon paper was there. It was the *Guardian* Extra, the headlines screaming, MOB MURDERS FRAGRANT FLOWER, and a good photograph of the riot. He sat in an armchair and read quickly.

Then his sharp ears heard the elevator stop. He went to the table beside the door and slid the loaded automatic with its silencer from under it. He pocketed the gun and peered through the spy hole.

The doorbell was muted. He opened it and smiled. 'Come in, old friend.' He embraced Jacques deVille warmly. 'It's been a long time.'

'Yes, yes it has, comrade,' deVille said as warmly. The last time he had seen Suslev was in Singapore, five years before, at a secret meeting arranged by Arthur just after deVille had been induced to join Sevrin. He and Suslev had met just as secretly the first time in the great port of Brest in France in June '41, just days before Nazi Germany invaded Soviet Russia when the two countries were outwardly still allies. At that time deVille was in the Maquis and Suslev second-in-command and secret political commissar of a Soviet submarine that was ostensibly in for a refit from patrol in the Atlantic. It was then that deVille was asked if he would like to carry on the *real war*, the war against the capitalist enemy as a secret agent after the fascists had been destroyed.

He had agreed with all his heart.

It had been easy for Suslev to subvert him. Because of deVille's potential after the war, the KGB had secretly had him betrayed to the Gestapo, then rescued from a Gestapo prison death by Communist guerrillas. The guerrillas had given him false proof that he had been betrayed by one of his own men for money. DeVille was thirty-two then and, like many, infatuated with socialism and with some of the teachings of Marx and Lenin. He had never joined the French Communist Party but now, because of Sevrin, he was an honorary captain in the KGB Soviet Security Force.

'You seem tired, Frederick,' Suslev said, using deVille's cover name. 'Tell me what's wrong.'

'Just a family problem.'

'Tell me.'

Suslev listened intently to deVille's sad story about his son-in-law and daughter. Since their meeting in 1941 Suslev had been deVille's controller. In 1947 he had ordered him out to Hong Kong to join Struan's. Before the war deVille and his father had owned a highly successful import-export business with close ties to Struan's—as well as family ties—so the change had been easy and welcome. DeVille's secret assignment was to become a member of the Inner Court and, at length, tai-pan.

'Where's your daughter now?' he asked compassionately.

DeVille told him.

'And the driver of the other car?' Suslev committed the name and address to memory. 'I'll see that he's dealt with.'

'No,' deVille said at once. 'It . . . it was an accident. We cannot punish a man for an accident.'

'He was drunk. There is no excuse for drunk driving. In any event you are important to us. We take care of our own. I will deal with him.'

DeVille knew there was no point in arguing. A gust of rain

673

battered the windows. '*Merde*, but the rain's good. The temperature must be down five degrees. Will it last?'

'The storm front's reported to be big.'

DeVille watched globules running down the pane, wondering why he had been summoned. 'How are things with you?'

'Very good. Drink?' Suslev went to the mirrored bar. 'There's good vodka.'

'Vodka's fine, please. But a short one.'

'If Dunross retired are you the next tai-pan?'

'I would think it's between four of us: Gavallan, David MacStruan, myself and Linbar Struan.'

'In that order?'

'I don't know. Except Linbar's probably last. Thanks.' DeVille accepted his drink. They toasted each other. 'I'd bet on Gavallan.'

'Who's this MacStruan?

'A distant cousin. He's done his five years as a China Trader. At the moment he's heading up our expansion into Canada—we're trying to diversify and get into wood fibers, copper, all the Canadian minerals, mostly out of British Columbia.'

'How good is he?'

'Very good. Very tough. A very dirty fighter. Forty-one, ex-lieutenant, Paratroopers. His left hand was almost ripped off over Burma by a tangle in the shrouds of his parachute. He just tied a tourniquet around it and carried on fighting. That earned him a Military Cross. If I was tai-pan I'd choose him.' DeVille shrugged. 'By our company law only the tai-pan can appoint his successor. He can do it anytime, even in his will if he wants. Whatever way it's done it's binding on the Noble House.'

Suslev watched him. 'Has Dunross made a will?'

'Ian's very efficient.'

A silence gathered.

'Another vodka?'

'*Non, merci*, I'll stay with this one. Is Arthur joining us?'

'Yes. How could we tip the scales for you?'

DeVille hesitated, then shrugged.

Suslev poured himself another drink. 'It would be easy to discredit this MacStruan and the others. Yes. Easy to eliminate them.' Suslev turned and looked at him. 'Even Dunross '

'No. That's not the solution.'

'Is there another one?'

'Being patient.' DeVille smiled but his eyes were very tired and shadows lurked there. 'I would not like to be the cause of . . . of his removal or that of the others.'

Suslev laughed. 'It's not necessary to kill to eliminate! Are we barbarians? Of course not.' He was watching his protégé closely. DeVille needs toughening, he was thinking. 'Tell me about the American, Bartlett, and the Struan-Par-Con deal.'

DeVille told him all he knew. 'Bartlett's money will give us everything we need.'

'Can this Gornt effect a takeover?'

'Yes and no. And possibly. He's tough and he truly hates us. It's a long-term rival—'

'Yes, I know.' Suslev was surprised deVille kept repeating information he already had been given. It's a bad sign, he thought, and glanced at his watch. 'Our friend's twenty-five minutes late. That's unusual.' Both men were too seasoned to worry. Meetings such as this could never be completely firm because no one could ever control the unexpected happening.

'Did you hear about the fire in Aberdeen?' deVille asked at the sudden thought.

'What fire?'

'There was a bulletin over the wireless just before I came up.' DeVille and his wife had apartment 20 on the sixth floor. 'The *Floating Dragon* restaurant at Aberdeen burned down. Perhaps Arthur was there.'

'Did you see him?' Suslev was suddenly concerned.

'No. But I could easily have missed him. I left well before dinner.'

Suslev sipped his vodka thoughtfully. 'Has he told you yet who the others are in Sevrin?'

'No. I asked him, judiciously, as you ordered, but he nev—'

'Order? I don't order you, *tovarich*, I just suggest.'

'Of course. All he said was, "We'll all meet in due course."'

'We'll both know soon. He's perfectly correct to be cautious.' Suslev had wanted to test deVille and test Arthur. It was one of the most basic rules in the KGB that you can never be too cautious about your spies however important they are. He remembered his instructor hammering into them another direct quote from Sun Tzu's *The Art of War*, which was obligatory

675

reading for all Soviet military: 'There are five classes of spies—local spies, inward spies, converted spies, doomed spies and surviving spies. When all five categories are working in concert, the state will be secure and the army inviolate. Local spies are those who are local inhabitants. Inward spies are officials of the enemy. Converted spies are the enemies' spies you have converted. Doomed spies are those fed false information and reported to the enemy who will torture this false information from them and so be deceived. Surviving spies are those who bring back news from the enemy camp. Remember, in the whole army, none should be more liberally rewarded. But if a secret piece of news is divulged by a spy before the time is ripe, he or she must be put to death, together with the person to whom the secret is told.'

If the other AMG reports are like the one already discovered, Suslev thought dispassionately, then Dunross is doomed.

He was watching deVille, measuring him, liking him, glad that again he had passed the test—and Arthur. The last paragraph of *The Art of War*—so important a book to the Soviet elite that many knew the slim volume by heart—sprang to his mind: 'It is only the enlightened ruler and wise general who will use the highest intelligence of the army for the purposes of spying. Spies are the most important element in war because upon them depends an army's ability to move.'

That's what the KGB does, he thought contentedly. We try for the best talent in all the Soviets. We *are* the elite. We *need* spies of all five categories. We need these men, Jacques and Arthur and all the others.

Yes, we need them very much.

'Arthur's never given any clue who the others are. Nothing,' deVille was saying, 'only that there are seven of us.'

'We must be patient,' Suslev said, relieved that Arthur was correctly cautious too, for part of the plan was that the seven should never know each other, should never know that Suslev was Sevrin's controller and Arthur's superior. Suslev knew the identities of all the Sevrin moles. With Arthur he had approved all of them over the years, continually testing them all, honing their loyalties, eliminating some, substituting others. You always test, and the moment a spy wavers that's the time to neutralize or eliminate him—before he neutralizes or eliminates you. Even Ginny Fu, he thought, though she's not a spy and knows nothing. You can never be sure of anyone except yourself—that's what our Soviet system teaches. Yes. It's time I took her on the trip I've always promised. A short voyage next week. To Vladivostok. Once she's there she can be cleansed and rehabilitated and made useful, never to return here.

He sipped his vodka, rolling the fiery liquid around his tongue. 'We'll give Arthur half an hour. Please,' he said, motioning to a chair.

DeVille moved the newspaper out of the way and sat in the armchair. 'Did you read about the bank runs?'

Suslev beamed. 'Yes, *tovarich*. Marvelous.'

'Is it a KGB operation?'

'Not to my knowledge,' Suslev said jovially. 'If it is there's promotion for someone.' It was a key Leninistic policy to pay particular attention to Western banks that were at the core of Western strength, to infiltrate them to the highest level, to encourage and assist others to foment disaster against Western currencies but at the same time to borrow capital from them to the utter maximum, whatever the interest, the longer the loan the better, making sure that no Soviet ever defaulted on any repayment, *whatever the cost*. 'The crash of the Ho-Pak will certainly bring down others. The papers say there might even be a run on the Victoria, eh?'

DeVille shivered in spite of himself and Suslev noticed it. His concern deepened. '*Merde*, but that would wreck Hong Kong,' deVille said. 'Oh, I know the sooner the better but . . . but being buried so deep, sometimes you forget who you really are.'

'That's nothing to worry about. It happens to all of us. You're in turmoil because of your daughter. What father wouldn't be? It will pass.'

'When can we do something? I'm tired, so tired of waiting.'

'Soon. Listen,' Suslev said to encourage him. 'In January I was at a top echelon meeting in Moscow. Banking was high on our list. At our last count we're indebted to the capitalists nearly 30 billions in loans—most of that to America.'

DeVille gasped. 'Madonna, I had no idea you'd been so successful.'

Suslev's smile broadened. 'That's just Soviet Russia! Our satellites are in for another 6.3 billions. East Germany's just got another 1.3 billion to purchase capitalist rolling mills, computer technology and a lot of things we need.' He laughed, drained his glass and poured another, the liquor oiling his tongue. 'I really don't understand them, the capitalists. They delude themselves. We're openly committed to consume them but they give us the means to do it. They're astonishing. If we have time, twenty years—at the most twenty—by that time our debt will be 60, 70 billions and as far as they're concerned we'll still be a triple-A risk, never having defaulted on a payment ever . . . in war, peace or depression.' He let out a sudden burst of laughter. 'What was it the Swiss banker said? "Lend a little and you have a debtor—lend a lot and you have a partner!" 70 billions, Jacques old friend, and we own them. 70 and we can twist their policies to suit ourselves and then at any moment of our own choosing the final ploy: "So sorry, Mr. Capitalist Zionist Banker, we regret we're broke! Oh very sorry but we can no longer repay the loans, not even the interest on the loans. Very sorry but from this moment all our present currency's valueless. Our new currency's a red ruble, one red ruble's worth a hundred of your capitalist dollars. . . ."'

Suslev laughed, feeling very happy. '. . . and however rich the banks are collectively they'll never be able to write off 70 billions. Never. 70 plus by that time with all the Eastern Bloc billions! And if the sudden announcement's timed to one of their inevitable capitalistic recessions as it will be . . . they'll be up to their Hebrew bankers' noses in their own panic shit, begging us to save their rotten skins.' He added contemptuously, 'The stupid bastards deserve to lose! Why should we fight them when their own greed and stupidity's destroying them. Eh?'

DeVille nodded uneasily. Suslev frightened him. I must get getting old, he thought. In the early days it was so easy to believe in the cause of the masses. The cries of the downtrodden were so loud and clear then. But now? Now they're not so clear. I'm still committed, deeply committed. I regret nothing. France will be better Communist.

Will it?

I don't know anymore, not for certain, not as I used to. It's a pity for all people that there must be some 'ism' or other, he told himself, trying to cover his anguish. Better if there were no 'isms', just my beloved Côte d'Azur basking in the sun.

'I tell you, old friend, Stalin and Beria were geniuses,' Suslev was saying. 'They're the greatest Russians that have ever been.'

DeVille just managed to keep the shock off his face. He was remembering the horror of the German occupation, the humbling of France, all the villages and hamlets and vineyards, remembering that Hitler would never have dared attack Poland and start it all without Stalin's nonaggression pact to protect his back. Without Stalin there would have been no war, no holocaust and we would all be better off. 'Twenty million Russians? Countless millions of others,' he said.

'A modest cost.' Suslev poured again, his zeal and the vodka taking him. 'Because of Stalin and Beria we have all Eastern Europe from the Baltic to the Balkans—Estonia, Lithuania, Latvia, Czechoslovakia, Hungary, Rumania, Bulgaria, all Poland, Prussia, half of Germany, Outer Mongolia.' Suslev belched happily. 'North Korea, and footholds everywhere else. Their Operation Lion smashed the British Empire. Because of their support the United Nations was birthed to give us our greatest weapon in our arsenal of many weapons. And then there's Israel.' He began to laugh. 'My father was one of the controllers of that program.'

DeVille felt the hackles of his neck rise. 'What?'

'Israel was a Stalin-Beria coup of monumental proportions! Who helped it, overt and covert, come into being? Who gave it immediate recognition? *We did*, and why?' Suslev belched again, 'To cement into the guts of Arabia a perpetual cancer that will suppurate and destroy both sides and, along with them, bring down the industrial might of the West. Jew against Mohammedan against Christian. Those fanatics'll never live at peace with one another even though they could, easily. They will never bury their differences even if it costs them their stupid lives.' He laughed and stared at his glass blearily, swirling the liquid around. DeVille watched him, hating him, wanting to give him the lie back, afraid to, knowing himself totally in Suslev's power. Once, some years ago, he had balked over sending some routine Struan figures to a box number in Berlin. Within a day, a stranger had phoned him at home. Such a call had never happened before. It was friendly. But he knew.

DeVille suppressed a shudder and kept his face clear as

679

Suslev glanced up at him.

'Don't you agree, *tovarich?*' the KGB man said, beaming. 'I swear I'll never understand the capitalists. They make enemies of a hundred million Arabs who have all the world's real oil reserves one day they will need so desperately. And soon we'll have Iran and the Gulf and the Strait of Hormuz. Then we'll have a hand on the West's tap, then they're ours and no need for war—just execution.' Suslev drained his vodka and poured another.

DeVille watched him, loathing him now, wondering frantically about his own role. Is it for this that I have been an almost perfect mole, for sixteen years keeping myself prepared and ready, with no suspicion against me? Even Susanne suspects nothing and everyone believes I'm anti-Communist, pro-Struan's which is the arch-capitalistic creation in all Asia. Dirk Struan's thoughts permeate us. Profit. Profit for the tai-pan and the Noble House and then Hong Kong in that order and the hell with everyone except the Crown, England and China. And even if I don't become tai-pan, I can still make Sevrin the wrecker of China that Suslev and Arthur want it to be. But do I want to now? Now that, for the first time, I've really seen into this . . . this monster and all their hypocrisy?

'Stalin,' he said, almost wincing under Suslev's gaze. 'Did . . . you ever meet him?'

'I was near him once. Ten feet away. He was tiny but you could feel his power. That was in 1953 at a party Beria gave for some senior KGB officers. My father was invited and I was allowed to go with him.' Suslev took another vodka, hardly seeing him, swept by the past and by his family's involvement in the movement. 'Stalin was there, Beria, Malenkov . . . Did you know Stalin's real name was Iosif Vissarionovich Dzhugashvili? He was the son of a shoemaker, in Tiflis, my home, destined for the priesthood but expelled from the seminary there. Strange strange strange!'

They touched glasses.

'No need for you to be so solemn, comrade,' he said, misreading deVille. 'Whatever your personal loss. You're part of the future, part of the march to victory!' Suslev drained his glass. 'Stalin must have died a happy man. We should be so lucky, eh?'

'And Beria?'

'Beria tried to take power too late. He failed. We in the KGB are like Japanese in that we too agree the only sin is failure. But Stalin . . . There's a story my father tells that when at Yalta, for no concession, Roosevelt agreed to give Stalin Manchuria *and the Kuriles* which guaranteed us dominance over China and Japan and all Asian waters, Stalin had a hemorrhage choking back his laughter and almost died!'

After a pause, de Ville said, 'And Solzhenitsyn and the *gulags?*'

'We're at war, my friend, there are traitors within. Without terror how can the few rule the many? Stalin knew that. He was a truly great man. Even his death served us. It was brilliant of Khrushchev to use him to "humanize" the USSR.'

'That was just another ploy?' deVille asked, shaken.

'That would be a state secret.' Suslev swallowed a belch. 'It doesn't matter, Stalin will be returned to his glory soon. Now, what about Ottawa?'

'Oh. I've been in contact with Jean-Charles an—' The phone rang abruptly. A single ring. Their eyes went to it, their breathing almost stopped. After twenty-odd seconds there was a second single ring. Both men relaxed slightly. Another twenty-odd seconds and the third ring became continuous. One ring meant 'Danger leave immediately'; two, that the meeting was canceled; three that whoever was calling would be there shortly; three becoming continuous, that it was safe to talk. Suslev picked up the phone. He heard breathing, then Arthur asked in his curious accent, 'Is Mr. Lop-sing there?'

'There's no Lop-*ting* here, you have a wrong number,' Suslev said in a different voice, concentrating with an effort.

They went through the code carefully, Suslev further reassured by Arthur's slight, dry cough. Then Arthur said, 'I cannot meet tonight. Would Friday at three be convenient?' Friday meant Thursday—tomorrow—Wednesday meant Tuesday, and so on. The three was a code for a meeting place: the Happy Valley Racecourse at the dawn workout.

Tomorrow at dawn!

'Yes.'

The phone clicked off. Only the dial tone remained.

THURSDAY

39

4:50 A.M.:

About an hour before dawn in the pouring rain Goodweather Poon looked down at the half-naked body of John Chen and cursed. He had been through his clothes carefully and sifted through endless pounds of mud from the grave that the two youths, Kin Pak and Dog-eared Chen, had dug. But he had found nothing—no coins or parts of coins or jewelry, nothing. And Four Finger Wu had said earlier, 'You find that half-coin, Goodweather Poon!' Then the old man had given him further instructions and Goodweather Poon was very pleased because that relieved him of any responsibility and he could then make no mistake.

He had ordered Dog-eared Chen and Kin Pak to carry the body downstairs and had threatened Smallpox Kin, who nursed his mutilated hand, that if the youth moaned once more he would slice out his tongue. They had left Father Kin's body in the alley. Then Goodweather Poon had sought out the King of the Beggars of Kowloon City who was a distant cousin of Four Finger Wu. All beggars were members of the Beggars' Guild and there was one king in Hong Kong, one in Kowloon and one in Kowloon City. In olden days begging was a lucrative profession, but now, owing to stiff prison sentences and fines and plenty of well-paying jobs, it was not.

'You see, Honored Beggar King, this acquaintance of ours has just died,' Goodweather Poon explained patiently to the distinguished old man. 'He has no relations, so he's been put out in Flowersellers' Alley. My High Dragon would certainly appreciate a little help. Perhaps you could arrange a quiet burial?' He negotiated politely then paid the agreed price and went off to their taxi and car that waited outside the city limits, happy that now the body would vanish forever without a trace. Kin Pak was already in the taxi's front seat. He got in beside him. 'Guide us to John Chen,' he ordered. 'And be quick!'

'Take the Sha Tin Road,' Kin Pak said importantly to the driver. Dog-eared Chen was cowering in the backseat with more of Goodweather Poon's fighters. Smallpox Kin and the others followed in the car.

The two vehicles went northwest into the New Territories on the Sha Tin-Tai Po road that curled through villages and re-settlement areas and shantytowns of squatters, through the mountain pass, skirting the railway that headed north for the border, past rich market gardens heavy with the smell of dung. Just before the fishing village of Sha Tin with the sea on their right, they turned left off the main road onto a side road, the surface broken and puddled. In a glade of trees they stopped and got out.

It was warm in the rain, the land sweet-smelling. Kin Pak took the shovel and led the way into the undergrowth. Good-weather Poon held the flashlight as Kin Pak, Dog-eared Chen and Smallpox Kin searched. It was difficult in the darkness for them to find the exact place. Twice they had begun to dig, before Kin Pak remembered their father had marked the spot with a crescent rock. Cursing and soaked, at length they found the rock and began to dig. The earth was parched under the surface. Soon they had unearthed the corpse which was wrapped in a blanket. The smell was heavy. Though Goodweather Poon had made them strip the body and had searched diligently, nothing was to be found.

'You sent everything else to Noble House Chen?' he asked again, rain on his face, his clothes soaking.

'Yes,' the young Kin Pak said truculently. 'How many forni-cating times do I have to tell you?' He was very weary, his clothes sodden, and he was sure he was going to die.

'All of you take your manure-infested clothes off. Shoes socks everything. I want to go through your pockets.'

They obeyed. Kin Pak wore a string around his neck with a cheap circle of jade on it. Almost everyone in China wore a piece of jade for good luck, because everyone knew if an evil god caused you to stumble, the spirit of jade would get between you and the evil and take the brunt of the fall from you and shatter, saving you from shattering. And if it didn't, then the Jade God was regretfully sleeping and that was your joss never mind.

Goodweather Poon found nothing in Kin Pak's pockets. He threw the clothes back at him. By now he was soaked too and very irritable. 'You can dress, and dress the corpse again. And hurry it up!'

Dog-eared Chen had almost 400 HK and a jade bracelet of good quality. One of the men took the jade and Poon pocketed the money and turned on Smallpox Kin. All their eyes popped as they saw the big roll of notes he found in the youth's pants pocket.

Goodweather Poon shielded it carefully from the rain. 'Where in the name of Heavenly Whore did you get all this?'

He told them about shaking down the lucky ones outside the Ho-Pak and they laughed and complimented him on his sagacity. 'Very good, very clever,' Poon said. 'You're a good businessman. Put your clothes on. What was the old woman's name?'

'She called herself Ah Tam.' Smallpox Kin wiped the rain out of his eyes, his toes twisting into the mud, his mutilated hand on fire now and aching very much. 'I'll take you to her if you want.'

'Hey, I need the fornicating light here!' Kin Pak called out. He was on his hands and knees, fighting John Chen's clothes into place. 'Can't someone give me a hand?'

'Help him!'

Dog-eared Chen and Smallpox Kin hurried to help as Goodweather Poon directed the circle of light back to the corpse. The body was swollen and puffy, the rain washing the dirt away. The back of John Chen's head was blood-matted and crushed but his face was recognizable.

'*Ayeeyah,*' one of his men said, 'let's get on with it. I feel evil spirits lurking hereabouts.'

'Just his trousers and shirt'll do,' Goodweather Poon said sourly. He waited until the body was partially dressed. Then he turned his eyes on them. 'Now which one of you motherless whores helped the old man kill this poor fornicator?'

Kin Pak said, 'I already t—' He stopped as he saw the other two point at him and say in unison, 'He did,' and back away from him.

'I suspected it all along!' Goodweather Poon was pleased that he had at last got to the bottom of the mystery. He pointed his stubby forefinger at Kin Pak. 'Get in the trench and lie down.'

'We have an easy plan how to kidnap Noble House Chen himself that'll bring us all twice, three times what this fornicator brought. I'll tell you how, *heya?*' Kin Pak said.

Goodweather Poon hesitated a moment at this new thought. Then he remembered Four Fingers's instructions. 'Put your face in the dirt in the trench!'

Kin Pak looked at the inflexible eyes and knew he was dead. He shrugged. Joss. 'I piss on all your generations,' he said and got into the grave and lay down.

He put his head on his arms in the dirt and began to shut out the light of his life. From nothing into nothing, always part of the Kin family, of all its generations, living forever in its perpetual stream, from generation to generation, down through history into the everlasting future.

Goodweather Poon took up one of the shovels and because of the youth's courage he dispatched him instantly by putting the sharp edge of the blade between his vertebrae and shoving downward. Kin Pak died without knowing it.

'Fill up the grave!'

Dog-eared Chen was petrified but he rushed to obey. Goodweather Poon laughed and tripped him and gave him a savage kick for his cowardice. The man half-fell into the trench. At once the shovel in Poon's hands whirled in an arc and crunched into the back of Dog-eared Chen's head and he collapsed with a sigh on top of Kin Pak. The others laughed and said, 'Eeeee, you used that like a foreign devil cricket bat! Good. Is he dead?'

Goodweather Poon did not answer, just looked at the last Werewolf, Smallpox Kin. All their eyes went to him. He stood rigid in the rain. It was then that Goodweather Poon noticed the string tight around his neck. He took up the flashlight and went over to him and saw that the other end was dangling down his back. Weighing it down was a broken half-coin, a hole bored carefully into it. It was a copper cash and seemed ancient.

'All gods fart in Tsao Tsao's face! Where did you get this?' he asked, beginning to beam.

'My father gave it to me.'

'Where did he get it, little turd?'

'He didn't tell me.'

'Could he have got it from Number One Son Chen?'

Another shrug. 'I don't know. I wasn't here when they killed him. I'm innocent on my mother's head!'

With a sudden movement Goodweather Poon ripped the necklace off. 'Take him to the car,' he said to two of his fighters. 'Watch him very carefully. We'll take him back with us. Yes, we'll take him back. The rest of you fill up the grave and camouflage it carefully.' Then he ordered the last two of his men to pick up the blanket containing John Chen and to follow him. They did so awkwardly in the darkness.

He trudged off toward the Sha Tin Road, skirting the puddles. Nearby was a broken-down bus shelter. When the road was clear he motioned to his men and they quickly unwrapped the blanket and propped the body in a corner. Then he took out the sign that the Werewolves had made previously and stuck it carefully on the body.

'Why're you doing that, Goodweather Poon, *heya*? Why're you do—'

'Because Four Fingers told me to! How do I know? Keep your fornicating mouth sh—'

Headlights from an approaching car rounding the bend washed them suddenly. They froze and turned their faces away, pretending to be waiting passengers. Once the car was safely past they took to their heels. Dawn was streaking the sky, the rain lessening.

The phone jangled and Armstrong came out of sleep heavily. In the half-darkness he groped for the receiver and picked it up. His wife stirred uneasily and awoke.

'Divisional Sergeant Major Tang-po, sir, sorry to wake you, sir, but we've found John Chen. The Were—'

Armstrong was instantly awake. 'Alive?'

'*Dew neh loh moh* no sir, his body was found near Sha Tin at a bus stop, a bus shelter, sir, and those fornicating Werewolves've left a note on his chest, sir: "This Number One Son Chen had the stupidity to try to escape us. No one can escape the Werewolves! Let all Hong Kong beware. Our eyes are elsewhere!" He w—'

Armstrong listened, appalled, while the excited man told how police at Sha Tin had been summoned by an early-morning bus passenger. At once they had cordoned off the area and phoned CID Kowloon. 'What should we do, sir?'

'Send a car for me at once.'

Armstrong hung up and rubbed the tiredness out of his eyes. He wore a sarong and it looked well on his muscular body.

'Trouble?' Mary stifled a yawn and stretched. She was just forty, two years younger than he, brown-haired, taut, her face friendly though lined.

He told her, watching her.

'Oh.' The color had left her face. 'How terrible. Oh, how terrible. Poor John!'

'I'll make the tea,' Armstrong said.

'No, no I'll do that.' She got out of bed, her body firm. 'Will you have time?'

'Just a cuppa. Listen to the rain . . . about bloody time!' Thoughtfully Armstrong went off to the bathroom and shaved and dressed quickly as only a policeman or doctor can. Two gulps of the hot sweet tea and just before the toast the doorbell rang. 'I'll call you later. How about curry tonight? We can go to Singh's.'

'Yes,' she said. 'Yes, if you'd like.'

The door closed behind him.

Mary Armstrong stared at the door. Tomorrow is our fifteenth anniversary, she thought. I wonder if he'll remember. Probably not. In fourteen times, he's been out on a case eight, once I was in hospital and the rest . . . the rest, were all right, I suppose.

She went to the window and pulled the curtains back. Torrents of rain streaked the windows in the half-light, but now it was cool and pleasant. The apartment had two bedrooms and it was their furniture though the apartment belonged to the government and went with the job.

Christ, what a job!

Rotten for a policeman's wife. You spend your life waiting for him to come home, waiting for some rotten villain to knife him, or shoot him or hurt him—most nights you sleep alone or you're being woken up at all rotten hours with some more rotten disasters and off he goes again. Overworked and underpaid. Or you go to the Police Club and sit around with other wives while the men get smashed and you swap lies with the wives and drink too many pink gins. At least they have children.

Children! Oh God . . . I wish we had children.

But then, most of the wives complain about how tired they are, how exhausting children are, and about *amahs* and school and the expense . . . and everything. What the hell does this life mean? What a rotten waste! What a perfectly rotten—

The phone rang. '*Shut up!*' she shrieked at it, then laughed nervously. 'Mary Mary quite contrary where did your temper go?' she chided herself and picked the phone up. 'Hello?'

'Mary, Brian Kwok, sorry to wake you but is Rob—'

'Oh hello, dear. No, sorry, he's just left. Something about the Werewolves.'

'Yes, I just heard, that's what I was calling about. He's gone to Sha Tin?'

'Yes. Are you going too?'

'No. I'm with the Old Man.'

'Poor you.' She heard him laugh. They chatted for a moment then he rang off.

She sighed and poured herself another cup of tea, added milk and sugar and thought about John Chen. Once upon a time she had been madly in love with him. They had been lovers for more than two years and he had been her first. This was in the Japanese Internment Camp in Stanley Prison on the south part of the island.

In 1940 she had passed the Civil Service exam in England with honors and after a few months had been sent out to Hong Kong, around the Cape. She had arrived late in '41, just nineteen, and just in time to be interned with all European civilians, there to stay until 1945.

I was twenty-two when I got out and the last two years, we were lovers, John and I. Poor John, nagged constantly by his rotten father, and his sick mother, with no way to escape them and almost no privacy in the camp, cooped up with families, children, babes, husbands, wives, hatred, hunger, envy and little laughter all those years. Loving him made the camp bearable. . . .

I don't want to think about those rotten times.

Or the rotten time after the camp when he married his father's choice, a rotten little harpy but someone with money and influence and Hong Kong family connections. I had none. I should have gone home but I didn't want home—what was there to go home to? So I stayed and worked in the Colonial Office and had a good time, good enough. And then I met Robert.

Ah, Robert. You were a good man and good to me and we had fun and I was a good wife to you, still try to be. But I can't have children and you . . . we both want children and one day a few years ago, you found out about John Chen. You never asked me about him but I know you know and ever since then you've hated him. It all happened long before I met you and you knew about the camp but not about my lover. Remember how before we got married I said, Do you want to know about my past, my darling? And you said, No, old girl.

You used to call me old girl all the time. Now you don't call me anything. Just Mary sometimes.

Poor Robert! How I must have disappointed you!

Poor John! How you disappointed me, once upon a time so fine, now so very dead.

I wish I was dead too.

She began to cry.

40

'It's going to continue to rain, Alexi,' Dunross said, the track already sodden, heavy overcast and the day gloomy.

'I agree, tai-pan. If it rains even part of tomorrow too, the going will be foul on Saturday.'

'Jacques? What do you think?'

'I agree,' deVille said. 'Thank God for the rain but *merde* it would be a pity if the races were canceled.'

Dunross nodded.

They were standing on the grass near the winner's circle at the Happy Valley Racecourse, the three men dressed in raincoats and hats. There was a bad weal across Dunross's face, and bruises, but his eyes were steady and clear and he stood with his easy confidence, watching the cloud cover, the rain still falling but not as strongly as in the night, other trainers and owners and bystanders scattered around the paddock and stands, equally pensive. A few horses were exercising, among them Noble Star, Buccaneer Lass with a stable jockey up and Gornt's Pilot Fish. All of the horses were being exercised gingerly with their tight reins: the track and the approach to the track were very slippery. But Pilot Fish was prancing, enjoying the rain.

'This morning's weather report said the storm was huge.' Travkin's sloe eyes were red-rimmed with tiredness and he watched Dunross. 'If the rain stops tomorrow, the going'll still be soft on Saturday.'

'Does that help or hurt Noble Star's chances, Alexi?' Jacques asked.

'As God wills, Jacques. She's never run in the wet.' It was hard for Travkin to concentrate. Last evening the phone had

693

rung and it was the KGB stranger again and the man had rudely cut through his questions of why he had vanished so suddenly. 'It's not your privilege to question, Prince Kurgan. Just tell me everything you know about Dunross. Now. Everything. His habits, rumors about him, everything.'

Travkin had obeyed. He knew that he was in a vise, knew that the stranger who must be KGB would be taping what he said to check the truth of what he related, the slightest variation of the truth perhaps a death knell for his wife or son or his son's wife or son's children—if they truly existed.

Do they? he asked himself again, agonized.

'What's the matter, Alexi?'

'Nothing, tai-pan,' Travkin replied, feeling unclean. 'I was thinking of what you went through last night.' The news of the fire at Aberdeen had flooded the airwaves, particularly Venus Poon's harrowing eyewitness account which had been the focus of the reports. 'Terrible about the others, wasn't it?'

'Yes.' So far the known death count was fifteen burned and drowned, including two children. 'It'll take days to find out really how many were lost.'

'Terrible,' Jacques said. 'When I heard about it . . . if Susanne had been here we would have been caught in it. She . . . Curious how life is sometimes.'

'Bloody firetrap! Never occurred to me before,' Dunross said. 'We've all eaten there dozens of times—I'm going to talk to the governor this morning about all those floating restaurants.'

'But you're all right, you yourself?' Travkin asked.

'Oh yes. No problem.' Dunross smiled grimly. 'Not unless we all get the croup from swimming in that cesspit.'

When the *Floating Dragon* had suddenly capsized, Dunross, Gornt and Peter Marlowe had been in the water right below. The megaphone on the police launch had shouted a frantic warning and they had all kicked out desperately. Dunross was a strong swimmer and he and Gornt had just got clear though the surge of water sucked them backward. As his head went under he saw the half-full cutter pulled into the maelstrom and capsized and Marlowe in trouble. He let himself go with the boiling torrent as the ship settled onto her side and lunged for Marlowe. His fingers found his shirt and held on and they swirled together for a moment, drawn a few fathoms down, smashing against the deck. The blow almost stunned him but he held onto Marlowe and when the drag lessened he kicked for the surface. Their heads came out of the water together. Marlowe gasped his thanks and struck out for Fleur who was hanging onto the side of the overturned cutter with others. Around them was chaos, people gasping and drowning and being rescued by sailors and by the strong. Dunross saw Casey diving for someone. Gornt was nowhere to be seen. Bartlett came up with Christian Toxe and kicked for a life belt. He made sure that Toxe had hold of the life ring securely before he shouted to Dunross, 'I think Gornt got sucked down and there was a woman . . .' and at once dived again.

Dunross looked around. The *Floating Dragon* was almost on her side now. He felt a slight underwater explosion and water boiled around him for a moment. Casey came up for air, filled her lungs and slid under the surface again. Dunross dived too. It was almost impossible to see but he groped his way down along the top deck that was now almost vertical in the water. He swam around the wreck, searching, and stayed below as long as he could, then surfaced carefully for there were many swimmers still thrashing around. Toxe was choking out seawater, precariously hanging onto the life ring. Dunross swam over and paddled him toward a sailor, knowing Toxe could not swim.

'Hang on, Christian . . . you're okay now.'

Desperately Toxe tried to talk through his retching. 'My . . . my wife's . . . she's down th . . . down there . . . down . . .'

The sailor swam over. 'I've got him, sir, you all right?'

'Yes . . . yes . . . he says his wife was sucked down.'

'Christ! I didn't see anyone . . . I'll get some help!' The sailor turned and shouted at the police launch for assistance. At once several sailors dived overboard and began the search. Dunross looked for Gornt and could not see him. Casey came up panting and held onto the upturned cutter to catch her breath.

'You all right?'

'Yes . . . yes . . . thank God you're okay . . .' she gasped, her chest heaving. 'There's a woman down there, Chinese I think, I saw her sucked down.'

'Have you seen Gornt?'

'No. . . . Maybe he's . . .' She motioned at the launch. People were clambering up the gangway, others huddling on the deck.

Bartlett surfaced for an instant and dived again. Casey took another great breath and slid into the depths. Dunross went after her slightly to the right.

They searched, the three of them, until everyone else was safe on the launch or in sampans. They never found the woman.

When Dunross had got home Penelope was deep asleep. She awoke momentarily. 'Ian?'

'Yes. Go back to sleep, darling.'

'Did you have a nice time?' she asked, not really awake.

'Yes, go back to sleep.'

This morning, an hour ago, he had not wakened her when he left the Great House.

'You heard that Gornt made it, Alexi?' he said.

'Yes, yes I did, tai-pan. As God wills.'

'Meaning?'

'After yesterday's stock market it would have been very convenient if he hadn't made it.'

Dunross grinned and eased an ache in his back. 'Ah, but then I would have been very put out, very put out indeed, for I'd not have had the pleasure of smashing Rothwell-Gornt myself, eh?'

After a pause deVille said, 'It's astonishing more didn't die.' They watched Pilot Fish as the stallion cantered past looking very good. DeVille's eyes ranged the course.

'Is it true that Bartlett saved Peter Marlowe's wife?' Travkin asked.

'He jumped with her. Yes. Both Linc and Casey did a great job. Wonderful.'

'Will you excuse me, tai-pan?' Jacques deVille nodded at the stands. 'There's Jason Plumm—I'm supposed to be playing bridge with him tonight.'

'See you at Prayers, Jacques.' Dunross smiled at him and deVille walked off. He sighed, sad for his friend. 'I'm off to the office, Alexi. Call me at six.'

'Tai-pan . . .'

'What?'

Travkin hesitated. Then he said simply, 'I just want you to know I . . . I admire you greatly.'

Dunross was nonplussed at the suddenness and at the open, curious melancholy that emanated from the other man. 'Thanks,' he said warmly and clapped him on the shoulder. He had never touched him as a friend before. 'You're not so bad yourself.'

Travkin watched him walk off, his chest hurting him, tears of shame adding to the rain. He wiped his face with the back of his hand and went back to watching Noble Star, trying to concentrate.

In the periphery of his vision he saw someone and he turned, startled. The KGB man was in a corner of the stands, another man joining him now. The man was old and gnarled and well known as a punter in Hong Kong. Travkin searched his mind for the name. Clinker. That's it! Clinker!

He watched them blankly for a moment. Jason Plumm was in the stands just behind the KGB man and he saw Plumm get up to return Jacques deVille's wave and walk down the steps to meet him. Just then the KGB man glanced in his direction and he turned carefully, trying not to be sudden again. The KGB man had lifted binoculars to his eyes and Travkin did not know if he had been noticed or not. His skin crawled at the thought of those high-powered binoculars focused on him. Perhaps the man can lip-read, he thought, aghast. Christ Jesus and Mother of God, thank God I didn't blurt out the truth to the tai-pan.

His heart was grinding nastily and he felt sick. A flicker of lightning went across the eastern sky. Rain was puddling the concrete and the open, lower sections of the stands. He tried to calm himself and looked around helplessly not knowing what to do, wanting very much to find out who the KGB man was. Absently he noticed Pilot Fish was finishing his workout in fine form. Beyond him Richard Kwang was talking intently to a group of other Chinese he did not know. Linbar Struan and Andrew Gavallan were leaning on the rails with the American Rosemont and others from the consulate he knew by sight. They were watching the horses, oblivious of the rain. Near the changing rooms, under cover, Donald McBride was talking to other stewards, Sir Shi-teh T'Chung, Pugmire and Roger Crosse among them. He saw McBride glance over to Dunross, wave and beckon him to join them. Brian Kwok was waiting for Roger Crosse on the outskirts of the stewards. Travkin knew both of them but not that they were in SI.

Involuntarily his feet began to move toward them. The foul taste of bile rose into his mouth. He dominated his urge to rush up to them and blurt out the truth. Instead he called over his chief *ma-foo*. 'Send our string home. All of them. Make sure they're dry before they're fed.'

'Yes sir.'

Unhappily Travkin trudged for the changing rooms. From the corner of his eye he saw that the KGB man had his binoculars trained on him. Rain trickled down his neck and mixed with the fear-sweat.

'Ah, Ian, we were thinking that if it rains tomorrow, we'd better cancel the meet. Say at 6:00 P.M. tomorrow,' McBride said. 'Don't you agree?'

'No, actually I don't. I suggest we make a final decision at ten Saturday morning.'

'Isn't that a little late, old boy?' Pugmire asked.

'Not if the stewards alert the wireless and television fellows. It'll add to the excitement. Particularly if you release that news today.'

'Good idea,' Crosse said

'Then that's settled,' Dunross said. 'Was there anything else?'

'Don't you think . . . it's a matter of the turf,' McBride said. 'We don't want to ruin it.'

'I quite agree, Donald. We'll make a final decision Saturday at ten. All in favor?' There were no dissenters. 'Good! Nothing else? Sorry, but I've got a meeting in half an hour.'

Shi-teh said uncomfortably, 'O, tai-pan, I was terribly sorry about last night . . . terrible.'

'Yes. Shitee, when we meet the governor in Council at noon we should suggest he imposes new, very severe fire regulations on Aberdeen.'

'Agreed,' Crosse said. 'It's a miracle more weren't lost.'

'You mean close the restaurants down, old boy?' Pugmire was shocked. His company had an interest in two of them. 'That'll hurt the tourist business badly. You can't put in more exits. . . . You'd have to start from scratch!'

Dunross glanced back at Shi-teh. 'Why don't you suggest to the governor that he order all kitchens be put at once on barges that can be moored alongside their mother ship? He could order that fire trucks be kept nearby until the changes have been made. The cost'd be modest, it would be easy to operate and the fire hazard would be solved once and for all.'

They all stared at him. Shi-teh beamed. 'Ian, you're a genius!'

'No. I'm only sorry we didn't think of it before. Never occurred to me. Rotten about Zep . . . and Christian's wife, isn't it? Have they found her body yet?'

'I don't think so.'

'God knows how many others went. Did the MPs get out, Pug?'

'Yes, old chap. Except Sir Charles Pennyworth. Poor sod got his head bashed in on a sampan when he fell.'

Dunross was shocked. 'I liked him! What bloody bad joss!'

'There were a couple of the others near me at one stage. That bloody radical bastard, what's his name? Grey, ah yes, Grey that's it. And the other one, the other bloody Socialist berk, Broadhurst. Both behaved rather well I thought.'

'I hear your Superfoods got out too, Pug. Wasn't our "Call me Chuck" first ashore?'

Pugmire shrugged uneasily. 'I really don't know.' Then he beamed. 'I . . . er . . . I hear Casey and Bartlett did a very good job, what? Perhaps they should have a medal.'

'Why don't you suggest it?' Dunross said, anxious to leave. 'If there's nothing else . . .'

Crosse said, 'Ian, if I were you I'd get a shot. There must be bugs in that bay that haven't been invented yet.'

They all laughed with him.

'Actually I've done better than that. After we got out of the water I grabbed Linc Bartlett and Casey and we fled to Doc Tooley.' Dunross smiled faintly. 'When we told him we'd been swimming in Aberdeen Harbor he almost had a hemorrhage. He said, 'Drink this,' and like bloody berks we did and before we knew what was happening we were retching our hearts out. If I'd had any strength I'd've belted him but we were all on our hands and knees fighting for the loo not knowing which end was first. Then Casey started laughing between heaves and then we were rolling on the bloody floor!' He added with pretended sadness, 'Then, before we knew what was happening, Old Sawbones was shoving pills down our throats by the barrel and Bartlett said, "For chrissake, Doc, how about a suppository and then you've a hole in one!"' They laughed again.

'Is it true about Casey? That she stripped and dived like an Olympic star?' Pugmire asked.

'Better! Stark bollock naked, old boy,' Dunross exaggerated airily. 'Like Venus de Milo! Probably the best . . . everything . . . I've ever seen.'

'Oh?' Their eyes popped.

'Yes.'

'My God, but swimming in Aberdeen Harbor! That sewer!' McBride said, eyebrows soaring. 'If you all live it'll be a miracle!'

'Doc Tooley said the very least'll be gastroenteritis, dysentery or the plague.' Dunross rolled his eyes. 'Well, here today gone tomorrow. Anything else?'

'Tai-pan,' Shi-teh said, 'I . . . hope you don't mind but I've . . . I'd like to start a fund for the victims' families.'

'Good idea! The Turf Club should contribute too. Donald, would you canvass the other stewards today and get their approval? How about 100,000?'

'That's a bit generous, isn't it?' Pugmire said.

Dunross's chin jutted. 'No. Then let's make it 150,000 instead. The Noble House will contribute the same.' Pugmire flushed. No one said anything. 'Meeting adjourned? Good. Morning.' Dunross raised his hat politely and walked off.

'Excuse me a moment.' Crosse motioned Brian Kwok to follow him. 'Ian!'

'Yes, Roger?'

When Crosse came up to Dunross he said quietly, 'Ian, we've a report that Sinders is confirmed on the BOAC flight tomorrow. We'll go straight to the bank from the airport if that's convenient.'

'The governor will be there too?'

'I'll ask him. We should be there about six.'

'If the plane's on time.' Dunross smiled.

'Did you get *Eastern Cloud*'s formal release yet?'

'Yes, thanks. It was telexed yesterday from Delhi. I ordered her back here at once and she sailed on the tide. Brian, you remember the bet you wanted—the one about Casey. About her knockers—fifty dollars to a copper cash they're the best in Hong Kong?'

Brian Kwok reddened, conscious of Crosse's bleak stare. 'Er, yes, why?'

'I don't know about the best, but like the judgment of Paris, you'd have one helluva problem if it—they—were put to the test!'

'Then it's true, she was starkers?'

'She was Lady Godiva to the rescue.' Dunross nodded to both of them pleasantly and walked off with, 'See you tomorrow.'

They watched him go. At the exit an SI agent was waiting to follow him.

Crosse said, 'He's got something cooking.'

'I agree, sir.'

Crosse tore his eyes off Dunross and looked at Brian Kwok. 'Do you usually bet on a lady's mammary glands?'

'No sir, sorry sir.'

'Good. Fortunately women aren't the only source of beauty, are they?'

'No sir.'

'There're hounds, paintings, music, even a killing. Eh?'

'Yes sir.'

'Wait here please.' Crosse went back to the other stewards.

Brian Kwok sighed. He was bored and tired. The team of frogmen had met him at Aberdeen and though he had found out almost at once that Dunross was safe and had already gone home, he had had to wait most of the night helping to organize the search for bodies. It had been a ghoulish task. Then when he was about to go home Crosse had called him to be at Happy Valley at dawn so there had been no point in going to bed. Instead he had gone to the Para Restaurant and glowered at the triads and One Foot Ko.

Now he was watching Dunross. What's that bugger got in the reaches of his mind? he asked himself, a twinge of envy soaring through him. What couldn't I do with his power and his money!

He saw Dunross change direction for the nearby stand, then noticed Adryon sitting beside Martin Haply, both staring at the horses, oblivious of Dunross. *Dew neh loh moh*, he thought, surprised. Curious that they'd be together. Christ, what a beauty! Thank God I'm not father to that one. I'd go out of my mind.

Crosse and the others had also noticed Adryon and Martin Haply with astonishment. 'What's that bastard doing with the tai-pan's daughter?' Pugmire asked, his voice sour.

701

'No good, that's certain,' someone said.

'Blasted fellow creates nothing but trouble!' Pugmire muttered and the others nodded agreement. 'Can't understand why Toxe keeps him on!'

'Bloody man's a Socialist that's why! He should be blackballed too.'

'Oh come off it, Pug. Toxe's all right—so're some Socialists,' Shi-teh said. 'But he should fire Haply, and we'd all be better off!' They had all been subject to Haply's attacks. A few weeks ago he had written a series of scathing exposés of some of Shi-teh's trading deals within his huge conglomeration of companies and implied that all sorts of dubious contributions were being made to various VIPs in the Hong Kong Government for favors.

'I agree,' Pugmire said, hating him too. Haply, with his accuracy, had reported the private details of Pugmire's forthcoming merger with Superfoods and had made it abundantly clear Pugmire benefited far more than his shareholders in General Stores who were barely consulted on the terms of the merger. 'Rotten bastard! I'd certainly like to know where he gets his information.'

'Curious Haply should be with her,' Crosse said, watching their lips, waiting for them to speak. 'The only major company he hasn't gone after yet is Struan's.'

'You think it's Struan's turn and Haply's pumping Adryon?' one of the others asked. 'Wouldn't that be smashing!'

Excitedly they watched Dunross go into the stands, the two young people still not having noticed him.

'Maybe he'll whip him like he did the other bastard,' Pugmire said gleefully.

'Eh?' Shi-teh said. 'Who? What was that?'

'Oh, I thought you knew. About two years ago one of the Vic's junior execs straight out from England started pursuing Adryon. She was sixteen, perhaps seventeen—he was twenty-two, as big as a house, bigger than Ian, his name was Byron. He thought he was Lord Byron on the rampage and he mounted a campaign. The poor girl was bowled over. Ian warned him a last time. The creep kept calling, so Ian invited him out to his gym at Shek-O, put on gloves—he knew the bugger fancied himself as a boxer—and proceeded to pulp him.' The others laughed

702

'Within the week the bank had sent him packing.'

'Did you see it?' Shi-teh asked.

'Of course not. They were alone for God's sake, but the bloody fool was really in a bad way. I wouldn't like to go against the tai-pan—not when his temper's up.'

Shi-teh looked back at Dunross. 'Perhaps he'll do the same to that little rotter,' he said happily.

They watched. Hopefully. Crosse wandered off with Brian Kwok, going closer.

Dunross was running up the steps in the stands now with his easy strength and he stopped beside them. 'Hello, darling, you're up early,' he said.

'Oh hello, Dad,' Adryon said, startled. 'I didn't se— What happened to your face?'

'I ran into the back end of a bus. Morning, Haply.'

'Morning, sir.' Haply got up and sat down again.

'A bus?' she said, then suddenly, 'Did you prang the Jag? Oh, did you get a ticket?' she asked hopefully, having had three this year herself.

'No. You're up early aren't you?' he said, sitting beside her.

'Actually we're late. We've been up all night.'

'Oh?' He held on to forty-eight immediate questions and said instead, 'You must be tired.'

'No. No, actually I'm not.'

'What's this all about, a celebration?'

'No. Actually it's poor Martin.' She put a gentle hand on the youth's shoulder. With an effort Dunross kept his smile as gentle as her hand. He turned his attention to the young Canadian. 'What's the problem?'

Haply hesitated, then told him what had happened at the paper when the publisher had called and Christian Toxe, his editor, had canceled his rumor series. 'That bastard's sold us out. He's allowed the publisher to censor us. I know I'm right. I know I'm right.'

'How?' Dunross asked, thinking, What a callous little bastard you are!

'Sorry, I can't reveal my source.'

'He really can't, Dad, that's an infringement of freedom of the press,' Adryon said defensively.

Haply was bunching his fists, then absently he put his hand

on Adryon's knee. She covered it with one of her own. 'The Ho-Pak's being shoved into the ground for nothing.'

'Why?'

'I don't know. But Gor—but tai-pans are behind the raid and it doesn't make sense.'

'Gornt's behind it?' Dunross frowned at this new thought.

'I didn't say Gornt, sir. No I didn't say that.'

'He didn't, Father,' Adryon said. 'What should Martin do? Should he resign or just swallow his pride an—'

'I just can't, Adryon,' Martin Haply said.

'Let Father talk, he'll know.'

Dunross saw her turn her lovely eyes back on him and he felt a glow at her confident innocence that he had never felt before. 'Two things: First you go back at once. Christian will need all the help he can get. Second, y—'

'Help?'

'Haven't you heard about his wife?'

'What about her?'

'Don't you know she's dead?'

They stared at him blankly.

Quickly he told them about Aberdeen. Both of them were shocked and Haply stuttered, 'Jesus, we . . . we didn't listen to a radio or anything . . . we were just dancing and talking. . . .' He jumped up and started to leave then came back. 'I . . . I'd better go at once. Jesus!'

Adryon was on her feet. 'I'll drop you.'

Dunross said, 'Haply, would you ask Christian to emphasize in bold type that anyone who got dunked or went swimming should see their doctors right smartly—very important.'

'Got it!'

Adryon said anxiously, 'Father, did you see Doc Too—'

'Oh yes,' Dunross said. 'Cleansed inside and out. Off you go!'

'What was the second thing, tai-pan?' Haply asked.

'Second was that you should remember it's the publisher's money, therefore his newspaper and he can do what he likes. But publishers can be persuaded. I wonder, for instance, who got to him or her and why he and she agreed to call Christian. . . . if you're so sure your story's true.'

Haply beamed suddenly. 'Come on, honey,' he said and shouted thanks. They ran off hand-in-hand.

Dunross stayed sitting in the stands for the moment. He sighed deeply, then got up and went away.

Roger Crosse was with Brian Kwok under cover near the jockey's changing rooms and he had been lip-reading the tai-pan's conversation. He watched him leave, the SI guard following him. 'No need to waste any more time here, Brian. Come along.' He headed for the far exit. 'I wonder if Robert found anything at Sha Tin.'

'Those bloody Werewolves are going to have a field day. All Hong Kong'll be frightened to death. I'll bet we . . .' Brian Kwok stopped suddenly. 'Sir! Look!' He nodded at the stands, noticing Suslev and Clinker among the scattered groups who watched out of the rain. 'I wouldn't've thought he'd be up yet!'

Crosse's eyes narrowed. 'Yes. That's curious. Yes.' He hesitated, then changed direction, watching their lips carefully. 'Since he's honored us we might as well have a little chat. Ah . . . they've seen us. Clinker really doesn't like us at all.' Leisurely he led the way into the stands.

The big Russian put a smile on his face and slid out a thin flask and took a sip. He offered it to Clinker.

'No thanks, mate, I just drink beer.' Clinker's cold eyes were on the approaching policemen. 'Proper niffy around here, ain't it?' he said loudly.

'Morning, Clinker,' Crosse said, equally coldly. Then he smiled at Suslev. 'Morning, Captain. Filthy day, what?'

'We're alive, *tovarich*, alive, so how can a day be filthy, eh?' Suslev was filled with outward bonhomie, continuing his cover as a hail-fellow-well-met. 'Will there be racing Saturday Superintendent?'

'Probably. The final decision'll be made Saturday morning. How long will you be in port?'

'Not long, Superintendent. The repairs to the rudder go slowly.'

'Not too slowly I hope. We all get very nervous if our VIP harbor guests don't get very rapid service.' Crosse's voice was crisp. 'I'll talk to the harbor master.'

'Thank you, that's . . . that's very thoughtful of you. And it was thoughtful of your department . . .' Suslev hesitated, then turned to Clinker. 'Old friend, do you mind?'

'Not on your nelly,' Clinker said. 'Narks make me nervous.'

Brian Kwok looked at him. Clinker looked back unafraid. 'I'll be in me car.' He wandered off.

Suslev's voice hardened. 'It was thoughtful of your department to send back the body of our poor comrade Voranski. Have you found the murderers?'

'Unfortunately no. They could be hired assassins—from any point of the compass. Of course if he hadn't slipped ashore mysteriously he'd still be a useful operative of the . . . of whatever department he served.'

'He was just a seaman and a good man. I thought Hong Kong was safe.'

'Did you pass on the assassins' photographs and information about their phone call to your KGB superiors?'

'I'm not KGB, piss on KGB! Yes, the information was passed on . . . by my superior,' Suslev said irritably. 'You know how it is, Superintendent, for God's sake. But Voranski was a good man and his murderers must be caught.'

'We'll find them soon enough,' Crosse said easily. 'Did you know Voranski was in reality Major Yuri Bakyan, First Directorate, Department 6, KGB?'

They saw shock on Suslev's face. 'He was . . . he was just a friend to me and he came with us from time to time.'

'Who arranges that, Captain?' Crosse said.

Suslev looked at Brian Kwok who stared back at him with unconcealed distaste. 'Why're you so angry? What have I done to you?'

'Why's the Russian empire so greedy, particularly when it comes to Chinese soil?'

'Politics!' Suslev said sourly then added to Crosse, 'I don't interfere in politics.'

'You buggers interfere all the time! What's your KGB rank?'

'I don't have one.'

Crosse said, 'A little cooperation could go a long way. Who arranges your crews, Captain Suslev?'

Suslev glanced at him. Then he said, 'A word in private, eh?'

'Certainly,' Crosse said. 'Wait here, Brian.'

Suslev turned his back on Brian Kwok and led the way down the exit stairs onto the grass. Crosse followed. 'What do you think of Noble Star's chances?' Suslev asked genially.

'Good. But she's never raced in the wet.'

'Pilot Fish?'

'Look at him—you can see for yourself. He loves the wet. He'll be the favorite. You plan to be here Saturday?'

Suslev leaned on the railings. And smiled. 'Why not?'

Crosse laughed softly. 'Why not indeed?' He was sure they were quite alone now. 'You're a good actor, Gregor, very good.'

'So're you, comrade.'

'You're taking a hell of a risk, aren't you?' Crosse said, his lips hardly moving now as he talked.

'Yes, but then all life's a risk. Center told me to take over until Voranski's replacement arrives—there are too many important contacts and decisions to be made on this trip. Not the least, Sevrin. And anyway, as you know, Arthur wanted it this way.'

'Sometimes I wonder if he's wise.'

'He's wise.' The lines around Suslev's eyes crinkled with his smile. 'Oh yes. Very wise. I'm pleased to see you. Center's very very pleased with your year's work. I've much to tell you.'

'Who's the bastard who leaked Sevrin to AMG?'

'I don't know. It was a defector. As soon as we know, he's a dead man.'

'Someone's betrayed a group of my people to the PRC. The leak had to come from the AMG file. You read my copy. Who else on your ship did? Someone's infiltrated your operation here!'

Suslev blanched. 'I'll activate a security check immediately. It could have come from London, or Washington.'

'I doubt it. Not in time. I think it came from here. And then there's Voranski. You're infiltrated.'

'If the PRC . . . yes, it will be done. But who? I'd bet my life there's no spy aboard.'

Crosse was equally grim. 'There's always someone who can be subverted.'

'You have an escape plan?'

'Several.'

'I'm ordered to assist in any way. Do you want a berth on the *Ivanov*?'

Crosse hesitated. 'I'll wait until I've read the AMG files. It would be a pity after such a long time . . .'

'I agree.'

'It's easy for you to agree. If you're caught you just get

deported and asked politely, please don't come back. Me? I wouldn't want to be caught alive.'

'Of course.' Suslev lit a cigarette. 'You won't get caught, Roger. You're much too clever. You have something for me?'

'Look down there, along the rails. The tall man.'

Casually Suslev put his binoculars to his eyes. He took his time about centering the man indicated, then looked away.

'That's Stanley Rosemont, CIA. You know they're tailing you?'

'Oh yes. I can lose them if I wish to.'

'The man next to him's Ed Langan, FBI. The bearded fellow's Mishauer, American Naval Intelligence.'

'Mishauer? That sounds familiar. Do you have files on them?'

'Not yet but there's a deviate in the consulate who's having a jolly affair with the son of one of our prominent Chinese solicitors. By the time you're back on your next trip he'll be happy to oblige your slightest wish.'

Suslev smiled grimly. 'Good.' Again, casually, he glanced at Rosemont and the others, cementing their faces into his memory. 'What's his job?'

'Deputy chief of station. CIA for fifteen years. OSS and all that. They've a dozen more cover businesses here and safe houses everywhere. I've sent a list in microdots to 32.'

'Good. Center wants increased surveillance of all CIA movements.'

'No problem. They're careless but their funding's big and growing.'

'Vietnam?'

'Of course Vietnam.'

Suslev chuckled. 'Those poor fools don't know what they've been sucked into. They still think they can fight a jungle war with Korean or World War Two tactics.'

'They're not all fools,' Crosse said. 'Rosemont's good, very good. By the way, they know about the Iman Air Base.'

Suslev cursed softly and leaned on one hand, casually keeping it near his mouth to prevent any lip-reading.

'. . . Iman and almost all about Petropavlovsk, the new sub base at Korsakov on Sakhalin. . . .'

Suslev cursed again. 'How do they do it?'

'Traitors.' Crosse smiled thinly.

'Why are you a double agent, Roger?'

'Why do you ask me that every time we meet?'

Suslev sighed. He had specific orders not to probe Crosse and to help him every way he could. And although he was KGB controller of all Far Eastern espionage activities, it was only last year that even he had been allowed into the secret of Crosse's identity. Crosse, in KGB files, had the highest secret classification, an importance on the level of a Philby. But even Philby didn't know that Crosse had been working for the KGB for the last seven years.

'I ask because I'm curious,' he said.

'Aren't your orders not to be curious, comrade?'

Suslev laughed. 'Neither of us obeys orders all the time, no? Center enjoyed your last report so much I've been told to tell you your Swiss account will be credited with an extra bonus of $50,000 on the fifteenth of next month.'

'Good. Thank you. But it's not a bonus, it's a payment for value received.'

'What does SI know about the visiting delegation of Parliament?'

Crosse told him what he had told the governor. 'Why the question?'

'Routine check. Three are potentially very influential— Guthrie, Broadhurst, and Grey.' Suslev offered a cigarette. 'We're maneuvering Grey and Broadhurst into our World Peace Council. Their anti-Chinese sentiments help us. Roger, would you please put a tail on Guthrie. Perhaps he has some bad habits. If he was compromised, perhaps photographed with a Wanchai girl, it might be useful later, eh?'

Crosse nodded. 'I'll see what can be done.'

'Can you find the scum who murdered poor Voranski?'

'Eventually.' Crosse watched him. 'He must have been marked for some time. And that's ominous for all of us.'

'Were they Kuomintang? Or Mao's bandits?'

'I don't know.' Crosse smiled sardonically. 'Russia isn't very popular with any Chinese.'

'Their leaders are traitors to communism. We should smash them before they get too strong.'

'Is that policy?'

'Since Genghis Khan.' Suslev laughed. 'But now . . . now we

have to be a little patient. You needn't be.' He jerked a thumb backward at Brian Kwok. 'Why not discredit that *matyeryebyets*? I don't like him at all.'

'Young Brian's very good. I need good people. Inform Center that Sinders, of MI-6, arrives tomorrow from London to take delivery of the AMG papers. Both MI-6 and the CIA suspect AMG was murdered. Was he?'

'I don't know. He should have been, years ago. How will you get a copy?'

'I don't know. I'm fairly certain Sinders'll let me read them before he goes back.'

'And if he doesn't?'

Crosse shrugged. 'We'll get to look at them one way or another.'

'Dunross?'

'Only as a last resort. He's too valuable where he is and I'd rather have him where I can see him. What about Travkin?'

'Your information was invaluable. Everything checked.' Suslev told him the substance of their meeting, adding, 'Now he'll be our dog forever. He'll do anything we want. Anything. I think he'd kill Dunross if necessary.'

'Good. How much of what you told him was true?'

Suslev smiled. 'Not much.'

'Is his wife alive?'

'Oh yes, *tovarich*, she's alive.'

'But not in her own *dacha*?'

'Now she is.'

'And before?'

Suslev shrugged. 'I told him what I was told to tell him.'

Crosse lit a cigarette. 'What do you know about Iran?'

Again Suslev looked at him sharply. 'Quite a lot. It's one of our eight remaining great targets and there's a big operation going on right now.'

'The Ninety-second U.S. Airborne's on the Soviet-Iranian border right now!'

Suslev gaped at him. 'What?'

Crosse related all that Rosemont had told him about Dry Run and when he came to the part about the U.S. forces having nuclear arms Suslev whitened palpably. 'Mother of God! Those god-cursed Americans'll make a mistake one day and then we'll never be able to extricate ourselves! They're fools to deploy such weapons.'

'Can you combat them?'

'Of course not, not yet,' Suslev said irritably. 'The core of our strategy's never to have a direct clash until America's totally isolated and there's no doubt about final victory. A direct clash would be suicide now. I'll get on to Center at once.'

'Impress on them the Americans consider it just a dry run. Get Center to take your forces away and cool everything. Do it at once or there will be trouble. Don't give the U.S. forces any provocation. In a few days the Americans will go away. Don't leak the invasion to your inward spies in Washington. Let it come first from your people in the CIA.'

'The Ninety-second's really there? That seems impossible.'

'You'd better get your armies more airborne, more mobile with more firepower.'

Suslev grunted. 'The energies and resources of three hundred million Russians are channeled to solve that problem, *tovarıch*. If we have twenty years . . . just twenty more years.'

'Then?'

'In the eighties we rule the world.'

'I'll be dead long since.'

'Not you. You'll rule whatever province or country you want. England?'

'Sorry, the weather there's dreadful. Except for one or two days a year, most years, when it's the most beautiful place on earth.'

'Ah, you should see my home in Georgia and the country around Tiflis.' Suslev's eyes were sparkling. 'That's Eden.'

Crosse was watching everywhere as they talked. He knew they could not be overheard. Brian Kwok was sitting in the stand waiting, half-asleep. Rosemont and the others were studying him covertly. Down by the winner's circle Jacques deVille was strolling casually with Jason Plumm.

'Have you talked to Jason yet?'

'Of course, while we were in the stands.'

'Good.'

'What did he say about deVille?'

'That he doubted, too, if Jacques'd ever be chosen as tai-pan. After my meeting last night I agree—he's obviously too weak,

711

or his resolve's softened.' Suslev added, 'It often happens with deep-cover assets who have nothing active to do but wait. That's the hardest of all jobs.'

'Yes.'

'He's a good man but I'm afraid he won't achieve his assignment.'

'What do you plan for him?'

'I haven't decided.'

'Convert him from an inward spy to a doomed spy?'

'Only if you or the others of Sevrin are threatened.' For the benefit of any watchers Suslev tipped the flask to his lips and offered it to Crosse who shook his head. Both knew the flask contained only water. Suslev dropped his voice. 'I have an idea. We're increasing our effort in Canada. Clearly the French Separatist Movement is a tremendous opportunity for us. If Quebec was to split from Canada it would send the whole North American continent reeling into a completely new power structure. I was thinking that it would be perfect if deVille took over Struan's in Canada. Eh?'

Crosse smiled. 'Very good. Very very good. I like Jacques too. It would be a pity to waste him. Yes, that would be very clever.'

'It's even better than that, Roger. He has some very important French-Canadian friends from his Paris days just after the war, all openly separatist, all left-wing inclined. A few of them are becoming a prominent national political force in Canada.'

'You'd get him to drop his deep cover?'

'No. Jacques could give the separatist issue a push without jeopardizing himself. As head of an important branch of Struan's . . . and if one of his special friends became foreign minister or prime minister, eh?'

'Is that possible?'

'It's possible.'

Crosse whistled. 'If Canada swung away from the U.S. that would be a coup of coups.'

'Yes.'

After a pause, Crosse said, 'Once upon a time a Chinese sage was asked by a friend to bless his newly born son. His benediction was, "Let's pray he lives in interesting times." Well, Gregor Petrovitch Suslev whose real name is Petr Oleg Mzytryk, we certainly live in interesting times. Don't we?'

712

Suslev was staring at him in shock. 'Who told you my name?'

'Your superiors.' Crosse watched him, his eyes suddenly pitiless. 'You know me, I know you. That's fair, isn't it?'

'Of . . . of course. I . . .' The man's laugh was forced. 'I haven't used that name for so long I'd . . . I'd almost forgotten it.' He looked back at the eyes, fighting for control. 'What's the matter? Why are you so edgy, eh?'

'AMG. I think we should close this meeting for now. Our cover's that I tried to subvert you but you refused. Let's meet tomorrow at seven.' Seven was the code number for the apartment next to Ginny Fu's in Mong Kok. 'Late. Eleven o'clock.'

'Ten is better.'

Crosse motioned carefully toward Rosemont and the others. 'Before you go I need something for them.

'All right. Tomorrow I'll ha—'

'It must be now.' Crosse hardened. 'Something special—in case I can't get a look at Sinders's copy, I'll have to barter with them!'

'You divulge to no one the source. No one.'

'All right.'

'Never?'

'Never.'

Suslev thought a moment, weighing possibilities. 'Tonight one of our agents takes delivery of some top-secret material from the carrier. Eh?'

The Englishman's face lit up. 'Perfect! Is that why you came?'

'One reason.'

'When and where's the drop?'

Suslev told him, then added, 'But I still want copies of everything.'

'Of course. Good, that'll do just fine. Rosemont will be really in my debt. How long's your asset been aboard?'

'Two years, at least that's when he was first subverted.'

'Does he give you good stuff?'

'Anything off that whore's valuable.'

'What's his fee?'

'For this? $2,000. He's not expensive, none of our assets are, except you.'

Crosse smiled equally mirthlessly. 'Ah, but I'm the best you have in Asia and I've proved my quality fifty times. Up to now

713

I've been doing it practically for love, old chap.'

'Your costs, old chap, are the highest we have! We buy the entire NATO battle plan, codes, everything, yearly for less then $8,000.'

'Those amateur bastards are ruining our business. It is a business, isn't it?'

'Not to us.'

'Balls! You KGB folk are more than well rewarded. *Dachas*, places in Tiflis, special stores to shop in. Mistresses. But I have to tell you, squeezing money out of your company gets worse yearly. I'll expect a rather large increase for Dry Run and for the AMG matter when it's concluded.'

'Talk to them direct. I've no jurisdiction over money.'

'Liar.'

Suslev laughed. 'It's good—and safe—dealing with a professional. *Prosit!*' He raised his flask and drained it.

Crosse said abruptly, 'Please leave angrily. I can feel binoculars!'

At once Suslev began cursing him in Russian, softly but vehemently, then shook a fist in the policeman's face and walked off.

Crosse stared after him.

On the Sha Tin Road Robert Armstrong was looking down at the corpse of John Chen as raincoated police rewrapped it in its blanket, then carried it through the gawking crowds to the waiting ambulance. Fingerprint experts and others were all around, searching for clues. The rain was falling more heavily now and there was a great deal of mud everywhere.

'Everything's messed up, sir,' Sergeant Lee said sourly. 'There're footprints but they could be anyone's.'

Armstrong nodded and used a handkerchief to dry his face. Many onlookers were behind the crude barriers that had been erected around the area. Passing traffic on the narrow road was slowed and almost jammed, everyone honking irritably. 'Keep the men sweeping within a hundred-yard area. Get someone out to the nearest village, someone might have seen something.' He left Lee and went over to the police car. He got in, closing the door, and picked up the communicator. 'This is Armstrong. Give me Chief Inspector Donald Smyth at East

Aberdeen, please.' He began to wait, feeling dreadful.

The driver was young and smart and still dry. 'The rain's wonderful, isn't it, sir?'

Armstrong looked across sourly. The young man blanched. 'Do you smoke?'

'Yes sir.' The young man took out his pack and offered it. Armstrong took the pack. 'Why don't you join the others? They need a nice smart fellow like yourself to help. Find some clues. Eh?'

'Yes sir.' The young man fled into the rain.

Carefully Armstrong took out a cigarette. He contemplated it. Grimly he put it back and the pack into a side pocket. Hunching down into his seat, he muttered, 'Sod all cigarettes, sod the rain, sod that smart arse and most of all sod the sodding Were-wolves!'

In time the intercom came on crackling, 'Chief Inspector Donald Smyth.'

'Morning. I'm out at Sha Tin,' Armstrong began, and told him what had happened and about finding the body. 'We're covering the area but in this rain I don't expect to find anything. When the papers hear about the corpse and the message we'll be swamped. I think we'd better pick up the old *amah* right now. She's the only lead we have. Do your fellows still have her under surveillance?'

'Oh yes.'

'Good. Wait for me, then we'll move in. I want to search her place. Have a team stand by.'

'How long will you be?'

Armstrong said, 'It'll take me a couple of hours to get there. Traffic's sodded up from here all the way back to the ferry.'

'It is here too. All over Aberdeen. But it's not just the rain, old lad. There's about a thousand ghouls gawking at the wreck, then there're more bloody mobs already at the Ho-Pak, the Victoria . . . in fact every bloody bank in the vicinity, and I hear there's already about five hundred collecting outside the Vic in Central.'

'Christ! My whole miserable bloody life savings're there.'

'I told you yesterday to get liquid, old boy!' Armstrong heard the Snake's laugh. 'And by the way, if you've any spare cash, sell Struan's short—I hear the Noble House is going to crash.'

41

8:29 A.M.:

Claudia picked up a mass of notes and letters and replies from Dunross's out-tray and began to leaf through them. Rain and low clouds obscured the view but the temperature was down and very comfortable after the heavy humidity of the last weeks. The antique clock set into a silver gimbal on the mantel chimed 8:30.

One of the phones jangled. She watched it but made no attempt to answer it. It rang on and on then ceased. Sandra Yi, Dunross's secretary, came in with a new batch of documents and mail and refilled the in-tray. 'The draft of the Par-Con contract's on top, Elder Sister. Here's his appointments list for today, at least the ones I know about. Superintendent Kwok called ten minutes ago.' She blushed under Claudia's gaze, her *cheong-sam* slit high and tight, her neck collar fashionably high. 'He called for the tai-pan, not me, Elder Sister. Would the tai-pan please return his call.'

'But I hope you talked to Honorable Young Stallion at length, Younger Sister, and swooned and sighed marvelously?' Claudia replied in Cantonese, then switched to English without noticing it, still leafing through all the notes as she talked, stacking them into two different piles. 'After all, he really should be gobbled up safely in the family before some Mealy Mouth from another clan catches him.'

'Oh yes. I've also lit five candles in five different temples.'

'I hope in your time and not company's time.'

'Oh very yes.' They laughed. 'But we do have a date—tomorrow for dinner.'

'Excellent! Be demure, dress conservatively, but go without a bra—like Orlanda.'

716

'Oh, then it was true! Oh oh do you think I should?' Sandra Yi was shocked.

'For your Brian, yes.' Claudia chuckled. 'He has a nose that one!'

'My fortune-teller said this was going to be a wonderful year for me. Terrible about the fire wasn't it?'

'Yes.' Claudia checked the appointments list. Linbar in a few minutes, Sir Luis Basilio at 8:45. 'When Sir Luis arrives p—'

'Sir Luis's waiting in my office now. He knows he's early—I've given him coffee and the morning papers.' Sandra Yi's face became apprehensive. 'What's going to happen at ten?'

'The stock market opens,' Claudia told her crisply and handed her the larger stack. 'You deal with this lot, Sandra. Oh and here, he's canceled a couple of board meetings and lunch but I'll deal with those.' Both looked up as Dunross came in.

'Morning,' he said. His face was graver than before, the bruises enhancing his ruggedness.

Sandra Yi said prettily, 'Everyone's so happy you weren't hurt, tai-pan.'

'Thank you.'

She left. He noticed her walk, then Claudia's look. Some of his gravity left him. 'Nothing like a pretty bird. Is there?'

Claudia laughed. 'While you were out your private phone rang twice.' This was his unlisted phone that, by rule, he alone picked up, the number given only to family and a handful of special people.

'Oh, thank you. Cancel everything between now and noon except Linbar, old Sir Luis Basilio and the bank. Make sure everything's VIP for Penn and Miss Kathy. Gavallan's taking her to the airport. First get Tightfist Tung on the phone. Also Lando Mata—ask if I can see him today, preferably at 10:20 at the Coffee Place. You saw my note about Zep?'

'Yes, terrible. I'll take care of everything. The governor's aide called: will you be at the noon meeting?'

'Yes.' Dunross picked up a phone and dialed as Claudia left, closing the door behind her.

'Penn? You wanted me?'

'Oh Ian, yes, but I didn't phone, is that what you mean?'

'I thought it was you on the private line.'

'No, but oh I'm ever so pleased you called. I heard about the

717

fire on the early news and I . . . I wasn't sure if I'd dreamed it or not that you'd come back last night. I . . . I was quite worried, sorry. Ah Tat said you'd left early but I don't trust that old hag—she wanders sometimes. Sorry. Was it awful?'

'No. Not bad actually.' He told her about it briefly. Now that he knew everything was all right with her he wanted to get off the phone. 'I'll give you a blow-by-blow when I pick you up for the airport. I checked on the flight and it'll leave on time . . .' His intercom buzzed. 'Hang on a moment, Penn . . . Yes, Claudia?'

'Superintendent Kwok on line two. He says it's important.'

'All right. Sorry, Penn, got to go. I'll pick you up in good time for your flight. 'Bye, darling. . . . Anything else, Claudia?'

'Bill Foster's plane from Sydney's delayed another hour. Mr. Havergill and Johnjohn will see you at 9:30. I called to confirm. I hear they've been at the bank since six this morning.'

Dunross's uneasiness grew. He had been trying to talk to Havergill since 3:00 P.M. yesterday but the deputy chairman had not been available and last night was not the time. 'That's not good. There was a crowd already outside the bank when I came in at 7:30.'

'The Vic won't fail, will it?'

He heard the anxiety in her voice. 'If they do we're all up the spout.' He stabbed line two. 'Hi, Brian, what's up?' Brian Kwok told him about John Chen.

'Jesus Christ, poor John! After giving them the ransom money last night I thought . . what bastards! He's been dead some days?'

'Yes. At least three.'

'The bastards! Have you told Phillip or Dianne?'

'No, not yet. I wanted to tell you first.'

'You want me to call them? Phillip's at home now. After the payoff last night I told him to miss the eight o'clock morning meeting. I'll call him now.'

'No, Ian, that's my job. Sorry to bring bad news but I thought you should know about John.'

'Yes . . . yes, old chum, thanks. Listen, I've a do at the governor's around seven but that'll be through by 10:30. Would you like a drink or a late snack?'

'Yes. Good idea. How about the Quance Bar at the Mandarin?'

'10:45?'

'Good. By the way, I've left word for your *tai-tai* to go straight through Emigration. Sorry to bring bad news. 'Bye.'

Dunross put down the phone, got up and stared out of the window. The intercom buzzed but he did not hear it. 'Poor bugger!' he muttered. 'What a bloody waste!'

There was a discreet knock, then the door opened a fraction. Claudia said, 'Excuse me, tai-pan, Lando Mata on line two.'

Dunross sat on the edge of his desk. 'Hello Lando, can we meet at 10:20?'

'Yes, yes of course. I heard about Zeppelin. Awful! I just got out with my own life! Damned fire! Still, we got out, eh? Joss!'

'Have you been in touch with Tightfist yet?'

'Yes. He's arriving on the next ferry.'

'Good. Lando, I may need you to back me today.'

'But Ian, we went through that last night. I thought I ma—'

'Yes. But I want your backing today.' Dunross's voice had hardened.

There was a long pause. 'I'll . . . I'll talk to Tightfist.'

'I'll talk to Tightfist too. Meanwhile I'd like to know I have your backing now.'

'You've reconsidered our offer?'

'Do I have your backing, Lando? Or not?'

Another pause. Mata's voice was more serious. 'I'll . . . I'll tell you when I see you at 10:20. Sorry, Ian, but I really must talk to Tightfist first. See you for coffee. 'Bye!'

The phone clicked off. Dunross replaced his receiver gently and muttered sweetly, *'Dew neh loh moh*, Lando old friend.'

He thought a moment then dialed. 'Mr. Bartlett please.'

'No answer his phone. You want message?' the operator said.

'Please transfer me to Miss K. C. Tcholok.'

'Wat?'

'Casey . . . Miss Casey!'

The call tone rang and Casey answered sleepily, 'Hello?'

'Oh sorry, I'll call you back later. . . .'

'Oh, Ian? No . . . no, that's all right, I should . . . should have been up hours ago . . .' He heard her stifle a yawn. '. . . Jesus, I'm tired. I didn't dream that fire did I?'

'No. Ciranoush, I just wanted to make sure you were both all right. How're you feeling?'

'Not so hot. I think I must have stretched a few muscles don't know if it was the laughing or throwing up. You all right?'

'Yes. So far. You haven't a temperature or anything? That's what Doc Tooley said to watch out for.'

'Don't think so. I haven't seen Linc yet. Did you talk to him?'

'No—there's no reply. Listen, I wanted to ask you two to cocktails, at six.'

'That's lovely with me.' Another yawn. 'I'm glad you're okay.'

'I'll call you back later to . . .'

Again the intercom. 'The governor's on line two, tai-pan. I told him you'd be at the morning meeting.'

'All right. Listen, Ciranoush, cocktails at six, if not cocktails maybe late supper. I'll call later to confirm.'

'Sure, Ian. And Ian, thanks for calling.'

'Nothing. 'Bye.' Dunross stabbed line two. 'Morning, sir.'

'Sorry to disturb you, Ian, but I need to talk to you about that awful fire,' Sir Geoffrey said. 'It's a miracle that more weren't lost, the minister's hopping mad about poor Sir Charles Pennyworth's death and quite furious that our security procedures allowed that to happen. The Cabinet have been informed so we can expect high-level repercussions.'

Dunross told him his idea about the kitchens for Aberdeen, pretending it was Shi-teh T'Chung's.

'Excellent. Shitee's clever! That's a start. Meanwhile Robin Grey and Julian Broadhurst and the other MPs have already phoned for a meeting to protest about our inadequate fire regulations. My aide said Grey was quite incensed.' Sir Geoffrey sighed. 'Rightly so, perhaps. In any event that gentleman's going to stir things up nastily, if he can. I hear he's scheduled a press conference for tomorrow with Broadhurst. Now that poor Sir Charles's dead Broadhurst becomes the senior member and God only knows what'll happen if those two get on their high horse about China.'

'Ask the minister to muzzle them, sir.'

'I did and he said, "Good God, Geoffrey, muzzle an MP? That'd be worse than trying to set fire to Parliament itself." It's all really very trying. My thought was that you might be able to cool Mr. Grey down. I'll seat him next to you tonight.'

'I don't think that's a good idea at all, sir. The man's a lunatic.'

'I quite agree, Ian, but I really would appreciate it if you tried. You're the only one I'd trust. Quillan would hit him. Quillan's already phoned in a formal refusal purely because of Grey. Perhaps you could invite the fellow to the races on Saturday also?'

Dunross remembered Peter Marlowe. 'Why not invite Grey and the others to your box and I'll take him over part of the time.' Thank God Penn won't be here, he thought.

'Very well. Next: Roger asked me to meet you at the bank at six o'clock tomorrow.'

Dunross let the silence hang.

'Ian?'

'Yes sir?'

'At six. Sinders should be there by then.'

'Do you know him, sir? Personally?'

'Yes. Why?'

'I just wanted to be sure.' Dunross heard the governor's silence. His tension increased.

'Good. At six. Next: Did you hear about poor John Chen?'

'Yes sir, just a few minutes ago. Rotten luck.'

'I agree. Poor fellow! This Werewolf mess couldn't've come at a worse time. It will surely become a *cause célèbre* for all opponents of Hong Kong. Damned nuisance, apart from the tragedy so far. Dear me, well, at least we live in interesting times with nothing but problems.'

'Yes sir. Is the Victoria in trouble?' Dunross asked the question casually but he was listening intently and he heard the slightest hesitation before Sir Geoffrey said lightly, 'Good Lord no! My dear fellow, what an astonishing idea! Well, thank you, Ian, everything else can wait till our meeting at noon.'

'Yes sir.' Dunross put the phone down and mopped his brow. That hesitation was bloody ominous, he told himself. If anyone'd know how bad things are it'd be Sir Geoffrey.

A rain squall battered the windows. So much to do. His eyes went to the clock. Linbar due now, then Sir Luis. He already decided what he wanted from the head of the stock exchange, what he must have from him. He had not mentioned it at the meeting of the Inner Court this morning. The others had soured him. All of them—Jacques, Gavallan, Linbar—were convinced the Victoria would support Struan's to the limit. 'And if they don't?' he had asked.

'We've the Par-Con deal. It's inconceivable the Victoria won't help!'

'If they don't?'

'Perhaps after last night Gornt won't continue to sell.'

'He'll sell. What do we do?'

'Unless we can stop him or put off the Toda and Orlin payments we're in very great trouble.'

We can't put off the payments, he thought again. Without the bank or Mata or Tightfist—even the Par-Con deal won't stop Quillan. Quillan knows he's got all day today and all Friday to sell and sell and sell and I can't buy ev—

'Master Linbar, tai-pan.'

'Show him in, please.' He glanced at the clock. The younger man came in and closed the door. 'You're almost two minutes late.'

'Oh? Sorry.'

'I don't seem to be able to get through to you about punctuality. It's impossible to run sixty-three companies without executive punctuality. If it happens one more time you lose your yearly bonus.'

Linbar flushed. 'Sorry.'

'I want you to take over our Sydney operations from Bill Foster.'

Linbar Struan brightened. 'Yes certainly. I'd like that. I've wanted an operation of my own for some time.'

'Good. I'd like you to be on the Qantas flight tomorrow an—'

'Tomorrow? Impossible!' Linbar burst out, his happiness evaporating. 'It'll take me a couple of weeks to get ev—'

Dunross's voice became so gentle but so lashing that Linbar Struan blanched. 'I realize that, Linbar. But I want you to go there tomorrow. Stay two weeks and then come back and report to me. Understand?'

'Yes, I understand. But . . . but what about Saturday? What about the races? I want to watch Noble Star run.'

Dunross just looked at him. 'I want you in Australia. Tomorrow. Foster's failed to get possession of Woolara Properties. Without Woolara we've no charterer for our ships. Without the charterer our present banking arrangements are null and void. You've two weeks to correct that fiasco and report back.'

'And if I don't?' Linbar said, enraged.

'For chrissake don't waste time! You know the answer to that. If you fail you'll no longer be in the Inner Court. And if you're not on that plane tomorrow you're out of Struan's as long as I'm tai-pan.'

Linbar Struan started to say something but changed his mind.

'Good,' Dunross said. 'If you succeed with Woolara your salary's doubled.'

Linbar Struan just stared back at him. 'Anything else? Sir?'

'No. Good morning, Linbar.'

Linbar nodded and strode out. When the door was closed Dunross allowed himself the shadow of a smile. 'Cocky young bastard,' he muttered and got up and went to the window again, feeling closed in, wanting to be out in a speedboat or, better, in his car, racing the corners just too fast, pushing the car and himself just a little harder each lap to cleanse his head. Absently he straightened a picture and watched the raindrops, deep in thought, saddened by John Chen.

A globulet fell a wet obstacle course and vanished to be replaced by another and another. There was still no view and the rain pelted down.

His private phone jangled into life.

'Yes, Penn?' he said.

A strange voice said, 'Mr. Dunross?'

'Yes. Who's this?' he asked, startled, unable to place the man's voice or his accent.

'My name is Kirk, Jamie Kirk, Mr. Dunross. I'm, er, I'm a friend of Mr.˙Grant, Mr. Alan Medford Grant. . . .' Dunross almost dropped the phone. '. . . Hello? Mr. Dunross?'

'Yes, please go on.' Dunross was over his shock now. AMG was one of the few who had been given this number and he had known it was to be used only in emergencies and never passed on except for a very special reason. 'What can I do for you?'

'I'm, er, from London; Scotland actually. Alan told me to call you as soon as I got to Hong Kong. He, er, gave me your number. I hope I'm not disturbing you?'

'No, not at all, Mr. Kirk.'

'Alan gave me a package for you, and he also wanted me to

723

talk to you. My, er, my wife and I are in Hong Kong for three days so I, er, I wondered if we could meet.'

'Of course. Where are you staying?' he asked calmly, though his heart was racing.

'At the Nine Dragons in Kowloon, room 455.'

'When did you last see Alan, Mr. Kirk?'

'When we left London. That was, er, two weeks ago now. Yes, two weeks to the day. We've, er, we've been to Singapore and Indonesia. Why?'

'Would after lunch be convenient? Sorry but I'm jammed till 3:20. I could see you then if that would be satisfactory.'

'3:20 will be fine.'

'I'll send a car for you an—'

'Oh there's, er, there's no need for that. We can find our way to your office.'

'It's no trouble. A car will call for you at 2:30.'

Dunross replaced the phone, lost in thought.

The clock chimed 8:45. A knock. Claudia opened the door. 'Sir Luis Basilio, tai-pan.'

Johnjohn at the Victoria Bank was shouting into the phone. '. . . I don't give a sod what you bastards in London think, I'm telling you we've got the beginnings of a run here and it looks very smelly indeed. I . . . What? Speak up, man! We've got a rotten connection. . . . What? . . . I couldn't care less that it's 1:30 in the morning—where the hell were you anyway—I've been trying to get you for four hours! . . . What? . . . Whose birthday? Christ almighty . . .' His sandy eyebrows soared and he held onto his temper. 'Listen, just get down to the City and the Mint very first bloody thing and tell them . . . Hello? . . . Oh for chrissake!' He started jiggling the plunger up and down. 'Hello!' Then he slammed the receiver onto its cradle, cursed for a moment, then prodded the intercom button. 'Miss Mills, I was cut off, please get him back quickly as you can.'

'Certainly,' the cool, very English voice said. 'Mr. Dunross's here.'

Johnjohn glanced at his watch and whitened. It was 9:33. 'Oh Christ! Hold . . . yes, hold the call. I'll . . .' Hurriedly he put the phone down, rushed to the door, composed himself and opened it with forced nonchalance. 'My dear Ian, so sorry to keep you waiting. How're things?'

'Fine. And with you?'

'Marvelous!'

'Marvelous? That's interesting. There must be six or seven hundred impatient customers queuing up outside already and you're half an hour to opening time. There's even a few outside Blacs.'

'More than a few . . .' Johnjohn just caught himself in time. 'Nothing to worry about, Ian. Would you like coffee or shall we go straight up to Paul's office.'

'Paul's office.'

'Good.' Johnjohn led the way along the thickly carpeted corridor. 'No, there's no problem at all, just a few superstitious Chinese—you know how they are, rumors and all that. Rotten about the fire. I hear Casey stripped and dived to the rescue. Were you at the track this morning? The rain's grand, isn't it?'

Dunross's unease increased. 'Yes. I hear there's queues outside almost every bank in the Colony. Except the Bank of China.'

Johnjohn's laugh sounded hollow. 'Our Communist friends wouldn't take kindly to a run on them at all. They'd send in the troops!'

'So the run's on?'

'On the Ho-Pak, yes. On us? No. In any event we're nowhere near as extended as Richard Kwang. I understand he really has made some very dangerous loans. I'm afraid the Ching Prosperity's not in good shape either. Still, Smiler Ching deserves to take a drubbing after all his fiddling over the years in such dubious enterprises.'

'Drugs?'

'I really couldn't say, Ian. Not officially. But the rumor's strong.'

'But you say the run won't spread to you?'

'Not really. If it does . . . well I'm sure everything will be quite all right.' Johnjohn went on down the wide paneled corridor, everything rich, solid and safe. He nodded at the elderly English secretary, went past her and opened the door marked PAUL HAVERGILL, DEPUTY CHAIRMAN. The office was large, oak paneled, the desk huge and clear of papers. The windows faced the square.

'Ian, my dear fellow.' Havergill got up and extended his hand. 'So sorry I couldn't see you yesterday, and the party last night was hardly the place for business, eh? How're you feeling?'

'All right. I think. So far. You?'

'I've got the trots slightly but Constance's fine, thank God. Soon as we got home I gave us both a good dollop of good old Dr. Colicos's Remedy.' It was an elixir invented during the Crimean War by Dr. Colicos to cure stomach disorders when tens of thousands of British soldiers were dying of typhoid and cholera and dysentery. The formula was still a guarded secret

'Terrific stuff! Dr. Tooley gave us some too.'

'Damnable about the others, what? Toxe's wife, eh?'

Johnjohn said gravely, 'I heard they found her body under some pilings this morning. If I hadn't had a pink ticket Mary and I'd've been there too.' A pink ticket meant that you had your wife's permission to be out in the evening without her, out playing cards with friends, or at the Club, or on the town with visiting guests or wherever—but with her benevolent permission.

'Oh?' Havergill smiled. 'Who was the lucky lady?'

'I was playing bridge with McBride at the Club.'

Havergill laughed. 'Well, discretion's the better part of valor and we have the reputation of the bank to think of.'

Dunross felt the tension in the room between the two men. He smiled politely, waiting.

'What can I do for you Ian?' Havergill asked.

'I want an extra 100 million credit for thirty days.'

There was a dead silence. Both men stared at him. Dunross thought he saw the flicker of a smile rush behind Havergill's eyes. 'Impossible!' he heard him say.

'Gornt's mounting an attack on us, that's clear to anyone. You both know we're solid, safe and in good shape. I need your open, massive backing, then he won't dare proceed and I won't actually need the money. But I do need the commitment. Now.'

Another silence. Johnjohn waited and watched. Havergill lit a cigarette. 'What's the situation with the Par-Con deal, Ian?'

Dunross told them. 'Tuesday we sign.'

'Can you trust the American?'

'We've made a deal.'

Another silence. Uneasily, Johnjohn broke it. 'It's a very good deal, Ian.'

'Yes. With your open backing, Gornt and Blacs will withdraw their attack.'

'But 100 million?' Havergill said. 'That's beyond possibility.'

'I said I won't need the full amount.'

'That's surmise, my dear fellow. We could become involved in a very big power play against our wish. I've heard rumors Quillan has outside financing, German backing. We couldn't risk getting into a fight with a consortium of German banks. You are already over the limit of your revolving credit. And there's the 500,000 shares you bought today which have to be paid for on Monday. Sorry no.'

'Put it to the board.' Dunross knew that he had enough votes to carry it over Havergill's opposition.

Another silence. 'Very well. I'll certainly do that—at the next board meeting.'

'No. That's not for three weeks. Please call an emergency meeting.'

'Sorry no.'

'Why?'

'I don't have to explain my reasons to you, Ian,' Havergill said crisply. 'Struan's doesn't own or control this institution, though you do have a large interest in us, as we have in you, and you are our valued customer. I'll be glad to put it up at the next board meeting. Calling emergency meetings is within my control. Solely.'

'I agree. So is this granting of the credit. You don't need a meeting. You could do that now.'

'I will be glad to put the request to the board at the next meeting. Was there anything else?'

Dunross controlled his urge to wipe the barely concealed smugness off his enemy's face. 'I need the credit to support my stock. Now.'

'Of course, and Bruce and I really do understand that the Par-Con down payment will give you the financing to complete your ship transactions and make a partial Orlin payment.' Havergill puffed his cigarette. 'By the way, I understand Orlin won't renew—you'll have to pay them off totally within thirty days as per the contract.'

Dunross flushed. 'Where did you hear that?'

'From the chairman, of course. I called him last night to ask if the—'

'You what?'

'Of course. My dear chap,' Havergill said, now openly enjoying Dunross's and Johnjohn's shock. 'We have every right to inquire. After all, we're Struan's bankers and we need to know. Our equity's also at risk if you are to fail, isn't it?'

'And you'll help that happen?'

Havergill stubbed out his cigarette with vast enjoyment. 'It's not to our interest for any big business to fail in the Colony, let alone the Noble House. Oh dear no! You needn't worry. At the right time we'll step in and buy your shares. We'll never allow the Noble House to fail.'

'When's the right time?'

'When the shares are at a value we consider correct.'

'What's that?'

'I'd have to look into it, Ian.'

Dunross knew he was beaten but he showed none of it. 'You'll allow the stock to go down until they're at giveaway prices and then you'll buy control.'

'Struan's is a public company now, however the various companies interlock,' Havergill said. 'Perhaps it would have been wise to follow Alastair's advice, and mine—we did point out the risks you'd take as a public company. And perhaps you should have consulted us before buying that massive quantity of shares. Clearly Quillan thinks he has you and you really are stretched a bit, old boy. Well, never fear, Ian, we will not allow the Noble House to fail.'

Dunross laughed. He got up. 'The Colony will be a much better place with you out of it.'

'Oh?' Havergill snapped. 'My term of office lasts until November 23. You may be out of the Colony before me!'

'Don't you think . . .' Johnjohn began, aghast at Havergill's fury, but stopped as the deputy chairman turned to him.

'Your term of office begins November 24. Provided the annual general meeting confirms the appointment. Until that time I run the Victoria.'

Dunross laughed again. 'Don't be too sure of that.' He walked out.

Angrily Johnjohn broke the silence. 'You could easily call an emergency meeting. You could eas—'

'The matter is closed! Do you understand? Closed!' Furiously Havergill lit another cigarette. 'We've got problems of our own that have to be solved first. But if that bastard squeezes out of the vise this time I shall be very surprised. He's in a dangerous position, very dangerous. We know nothing about this damned American and his girlfriend. We do know Ian's recalcitrant, arrogant and out of his depth. He's the wrong man for the job.'

'That's not t—'

'We're a profit-making institution, not a charity, and the Dunrosses and Struans have had too much say in our affairs for too many years. If we can get control *we* become the Noble House of Asia—we do! We get his block of our stock back. We fire all the directors and put in new management at once, we double our money and I'd leave a lasting legacy to the bank forever. That's what we're here for—to make money for *our* bank and for *our* shareholders! I've always considered your friend Dunross a very high risk and now he's going to the wall. And if I can help hang him I will!'

The doctor was counting Fleur Marlowe's pulse beats against his old-fashioned, gold fob watch. One hundred and three. Too many, he thought sadly. Her wrist was delicate. He laid it back on the bedcovers, his sensitive fingers aware of the fever. Peter Marlowe came out of the small bathroom of their apartment.

'Not good, eh?' Tooley said gruffly.

Peter Marlowe's smile was weary. 'Rather tedious actually. Just cramps and not much coming out, just a little liquid.' His eyes rested on his wife who lay wanly in the small double bed. 'How're you, pet?'

'Fine,' she said. 'Fine thank you, Peter.'

The doctor reached for his old-fashioned bag and put his stethoscope away. 'Was, er, was there any blood, Mr. Marlowe?'

Peter Marlowe shook his head and sat tiredly. Neither he nor his wife had slept much. Their cramps had begun at 4:00 A.M.

and had continued since then with ever-increasing strain. 'No, at least not yet,' he said. 'It feels rather like an ordinary bout of dysentery—cramps, a lot of palaver and very little to show for it.'

'Ordinary? You've had dysentery? When? What kind of dysentery?'

'I think it was enteric. I, I was a POW in Changi in '45— actually between '42 and '45, partially in Java but mostly in Changi.'

'Oh. Oh I see. Sorry about that.' Dr. Tooley remembered all the horror stories that came out of Asia after the war about the treatment of British and American troops by the Japanese Army. 'I always felt betrayed in a curious way,' the doctor said sadly. 'The Japanese'd always been our ally . . . they're an island nation, so're we. Good fighters. I was a doctor with the Chindits. Went in with Wingate twice.' Wingate was an eccentric British general who had devised a completely unorthodox battle plan to send highly mobile columns of marauding British soldiers, code name Chindits, from India into the jungles of Burma deep behind Japanese lines, supplying them by airdrop. 'I was lucky—the whole Chindit operation was rather dicey,' he said. As he talked he was watching Fleur, weighing clues, sending his experience into her, trying to detect the disease now, trying to isolate the enemy among a myriad of possibilities before it harmed the fetus. 'Bloody planes kept missing our drops.'

'I met a couple of your fellows at Changi.' The younger man searched his memory. 'In '43 or '44, I can't remember when exactly. Or any names. They'd been sent down to Changi after they were captured.'

'That'd be '43.' The doctor was somber. 'One whole column got caught and ambushed early on. Those jungles are unbelievable if you've never been in one. We didn't know what the devil we were doing most of the time. Afraid not many of the lads survived to get to Changi.' Dr. Tooley was a fine old man with a big nose and sparse hair and warm hands, and he smiled down at Fleur. 'So, young lady,' he said with his kind, gruff voice. 'You've a slight fev—'

'Oh . . . sorry, Doctor,' she said quickly, interrupting him, suddenly white, 'I, I think . . .' She got out of bed and hurried awkwardly for the bathroom. The door closed behind her. There was a fleck of blood on the back of her nightdress.

'Is she all right?' Marlowe asked, his face stark.

'Temperature's a hundred and three, heartbeat's up. It could just be gastroenteritis. . . .' The doctor looked at him.

'Could it be hepatitis?'

'No. Not this quickly. The incubation period's six weeks to two months. I'm afraid that specter's hanging over everyone's head. Sorry.' A rain squall battered the windows. He glanced at them and frowned, remembering he had not told Dunross and the Americans about the danger of hepatitis. Perhaps it'll be better just to wait and see and be patient. Joss, he thought. 'Two months, to be safe. You've both had all your shots so there shouldn't be any problem about typhoid.'

'And the baby?'

'If the cramps get worse she may miscarry, Mr. Marlowe,' the doctor said softly. 'Sorry, but it's best to know. Either way it won't be easy for her—God only knows what viruses and bacteria're at Aberdeen. The place's a public sewer and has been for a century. Shocking, but nothing we can do about it.' He rummaged in his pocket for his prescription pad. 'You can't change the Chinese or habits of centuries. Sorry.'

'Joss,' Peter Marlowe said, feeling rotten. 'Will everyone get sick? There must have been forty or fifty of us thrashing around in the water—impossible not to drink some of that muck.'

The Doctor hesitated. 'Of fifty, perhaps five'll be very sick, five'll be untouched and the rest'll be in between. Hong Kong *yan*—that's Hong Kongites—they should be less affected than visitors. But, as you say, a lot of it's joss.' He found his pad. 'I'll give you a prescription for a rather newfangled intestinal antibiotic but continue with good old Dr. Colicos's Remedy—that will settle your tummies. Watch her very carefully. Do you have a thermometer?'

'Oh yes. With . . .' A spasm went through Peter Marlowe, shook him and went away. 'Traveling with young kids you have to have a survival kit.' Both men were trying not to watch the bathroom door. They could half-hear her as pain waxed and waned.

'How old are your children?' Dr. Tooley asked absently, keeping the concern from his voice as he wrote. When he had

731

come in he had noticed the happy chaos of the tiny second bedroom off the small drab living room—barely big enough for its two-tiered bunk, the toys scattered. 'Mine are grown up now. I've three daughters.'

'What? Oh, ours are four and eight. They're . . . they're both girls.'

'Do you have an *amah?*'

'Oh yes. Yes. With all the rain this morning she took the kids to school. They go across the harbor and pick up a *bo-pi.*' A *bo-pi* was an unlicensed taxi that was quite illegal but almost everyone used them from time to time. 'The school's off Garden Road. Most days they insist on toddling off themselves. They're perfectly safe.'

'Oh yes. Yes of course.'

Their ears were fine-tuned now to her torment. Each muted strain went through both men.

'Well, don't worry,' the doctor said hesitantly. 'I'll have the drugs sent up—there's a pharmacy in the hotel. I'll have it put on your bill. I'll come back this evening at six, as near to six as I can. If there's any problem . . .' He offered a prescription blank gently. 'My phone number's on this. Don't hesitate to call, eh?'

'Thanks. Now about your bill . . .'

'No need to worry about that, Mr. Marlowe. The first order of business is to get you well.' Dr. Tooley was concentrating on the door. He was afraid to leave. 'Were you army?'

'No. Air force.'

'Ah! My brother was one of the Few. He pranged in . . .' He stopped. Fleur Marlowe was calling out hesitantly through the door, 'Doctor . . . cou . . . could you . . . please . . .'

Tooley went to the door. 'Yes, Mrs. Marlowe? Are you all right?'

'Cou . . . could you please . . .'

He opened the door and closed it after him.

The sour sweet stench in the tiny bathroom was heavy but he paid it no attention.

'I . . . it . . .' Another spasm twisted her.

'Now don't worry,' he said, calming her, and put one hand on her back and the other on her stomach, helping to support her tormented abdominal muscles. His hands massaged gently and with great knowledge. 'There, there! Just let yourself go, I won't

732

let you fall.' He felt the knotting under his fingers and willed his warmth and strength into her. 'You're just about my daughter's age, my youngest. I've three and the eldest has two children. . . . There, just let yourself relax, just think the pains away, soon you'll feel nice and warm . . .' In time the cramps passed.

'I . . . God, sorr . . . sorry.' The young woman groped for the toilet roll but another cramp took her and another. It was awkward for him in the small room but he tended her and kept his strong hands supporting her as best he could. An ache leapt into his back.

'I'm . . . I'm all right now,' she said. 'Thank you.'

He knew she was not. The sweat had soaked her. He sponged off her face and dried it for her. Then he helped her stand, taking her weight, gentling her all the time. He cleaned her. The paper showed traces of blood and the bowl traces of blood mucus among the discolored water but she was not hemorrhaging yet and he sighed with relief. 'You're going to be fine,' he said. 'Here, hold on a second. Don't be afraid!' He guided her hands to the sink. Quickly he folded a dry towel lengthwise and wrapped it tightly around her stomach, tucking the ends in to hold it. 'This's the best for gippy tummy, the very best. It supports your tum and keeps it warm. My grandfather was a doctor too, in the Indian Army, and he swore this was the best.' He looked at her keenly. 'You're a fine brave young lady. You're going to be fine. Ready?'

'Yes. Sorr—sorry about . . .'

He opened the door. Peter Marlowe rushed to help. They put her to bed.

She lay there exhausted, a thread of damp hair on her forehead. Dr. Tooley brushed it away and stared down at her thoughtfully. 'I think, young lady, that we'll put you into a nursing home for a day or two.'

'Oh but . . . but . . .'

'Nothing to worry about. But we'd better give the baby-to-be every chance, eh? And with two small children here to fret over. Two days of rest will be enough.' His gruff voice touched both of them, calming them. 'I'll make the arrangements and be back in a quarter of an hour.' He looked at Peter Marlowe under his great bushy eyebrows. 'The nursing home's in Kowloon so it'll save any long journey to the Island. A lot of us use it and it's good, clean and equipped for any emergency. Perhaps you'd pack a small bag for her?' He wrote the address and phone number. 'So, young lady, I'll be back in a few minutes. It'll be best, then you won't have to worry about the children. I know what a trial that can be if you're sick.' He smiled at both of them. 'Don't worry about a thing, Mr. Marlowe, eh? I'll talk to your houseboy and ask him to help make things shipshape here. And don't worry about the money.' The deep lines around his eyes deepened even more. 'We're very philanthropic here in Hong Kong with our young guests.'

He went out. Peter Marlowe sat on the bed. Disconsolate.

'I hope the kids got to school all right,' she said.

'Oh yes. Ah Sop's fine.'

'How will you manage?'

'Easy. I'll be like Old Mother Hubbard. It'll only be a day or two.'

She moved wearily, leaning on a hand and watching the rain, and beyond it, the flat gray of the hotel across the narrow street that she hated so much because it cut off the sky. 'I . . . I hope it's not going . . . going to cost too much,' she said, her voice weightless.

'Don't worry about it, Fleur. We'll be all right. The Writers Guild'll pay.'

'Will they? I bet they won't, Peter, not in time. Blast! We . . . we're so tight on our budget already.'

'I can always borrow against next year's drop dead check. Don—'

'Oh no! No we won't do that, Peter. We mustn't. We agreed. Other . . . otherwise you're trapped ag . . . again.'

'Something'll turn up,' he said confidently. 'Next month we've got a Friday the thirteenth and that's always been lucky for us.' His novel was published on a thirteenth and went on to the best-seller list on a thirteenth. When he and his wife were at bottom, three years ago, on another thirteenth he had made a fine screenwriting deal that had carried them again. His first directing assignment had been confirmed on a thirteenth. And last April, Friday the thirteenth, one of the studios in Hollywood had bought the film rights to his novel for $157,000. The agent had taken 10 percent and then Peter Marlowe had spread the remainder over five years—in advance. Five years of family drop dead money. 25,000 per year every January. Enough, with care, for school and medical expenses and mortgage and car and other payments—five glorious years of freedom from all the usual worries. And freedom to turn down a directing-screen-writing job to come to Hong Kong for a year, unpaid, but free to look for the second book. Oh Christ, Peter Marlowe thought, suddenly petrified. What the hell am I looking for anyway? What the hell am I doing here? 'Christ,' he said miserably, 'if I hadn't insisted on us going to that party this would never have happened.'

'Joss.' She smiled faintly. 'Joss, Peter. Remember what you're . . . you're always saying to me. Joss. It's joss, just joss, Peter. Oh Christ I feel awful.'

42

Orlanda Ramos opened the door of her apartment and put her sodden umbrella into a stand. 'Come in, Linc,' she said radiantly. *'Minha casa é vossa casa.* My house is yours.'

Linc smiled. 'You're sure?'

She laughed and said lightly, 'Ah! That remains to be seen. It's just an old Portuguese custom . . . to offer one's house.' She was taking off her shiny, very fashionable raincoat. In the corridor he was doing the same to a soaked, well-used raincoat.

'Here, let me hang it up,' she said. 'Oh, don't mind about the wet, my *amah* will mop it up. Come on in.'

He noticed how neat and tidy the living room was, feminine, in very good taste and welcoming. She shut the door behind him and hung his coat on a peg. He went over to the French windows that led out onto a small balcony. Her apartment was on the eighth floor of Rose Court in Kotewall Road.

'Is the rain always this heavy?' he asked.

'In a real typhoon it's much worse. Perhaps twelve to eighteen inches in a day. Then there are mud slides and the resettlement areas get washed away.'

He was looking down through the overcast. Most of the view was blocked by high rises, ribbon-built on the winding roads that were cut into the mountainside. From time to time he could see glimpses of Central and the shoreline far below. 'It's like being in an airplane, Orlanda. On a balmy night it must be terrific.'

'Yes. Yes it is. I love it. You can see all of Kowloon. Before Sinclair Towers was built—that's the block straight ahead—we had the best view in Hong Kong. Did you know Struan's own

736

Sinclair Towers? I think Ian Dunross helped have it built to spite Quillan. Quillan has the penthouse apartment here . . . at least he did.'

'It spoiled his view?'

'Ruined it.'

'That's an expensive attack.'

'No. Both blocks are immensely profitable. Quillan told me everything in Hong Kong's amortized over three years. Everything. Property's the thing to own. You could make . . .' She laughed. 'You could improve your fortune if you wanted to.'

'If I stay, where should I live?'

'Here in Mid Levels. Farther up the Peak you're always very damp, the walls sweat and everything mildews.' She took off her headscarf and shook her hair free, then sat on the arm of a chair, looking at his back, waiting patiently.

'How long have you been here?' he asked.

'Five, almost six years. Since the block was built.'

He turned and leaned against the window. 'It's great,' he said. 'And so are you.'

'Thank you, kind sir. Would you like coffee?'

'Please.' Linc Bartlett ran his fingers through his hair, peering at an oil painting. 'This a Quance?'

'Yes. Yes it is. Quillan gave it to me. Espresso?'

'Yes. Black, please. Wish I knew more about paintings . . .' He was going to add, Casey does, but he stopped himself and watched her open one of the doors. The kitchen was large, modern and very well equipped. 'That's like something out of *House and Garden*!'

'This was all Quillan's idea. He loves food and loves cooking. This's all his design, the rest . . . the rest is mine though he taught me good from kitsch.'

'You sorry you broke up with him?'

'Yes and no. It's joss, karma. He . . . that was joss. The time had come.' Her quietness touched him. 'It could never have lasted. Never. Not here.' He saw a sadness go over her momentarily but she brushed it aside and busied herself with the sparkling espresso maker. All the shelves were spotless, 'Quillan was a stickler for tidiness, thank God it rubbed off on me. My *amah*, Ah Fat, she drives me insane.'

'Does she live here?'

737

'Oh yes, yes of course, but she's shopping now—her room's at the end of the corridor. Look around if you like. I won't be a minute.'

Filled with curiosity he wandered off. A good dining room with a round table to seat eight. Her bedroom was white and pink, light and airy with soft pink drapes hung from the ceiling that fell around the huge bed making it into a vast four-poster. There were flowers in a delicate arrangement. A modern bathroom, tiled and perfect, with matching towels. A second bedroom with books and phone and hi-fi and smaller bed, again everything neat and tasteful.

Casey's outclassed, he told himself, remembering the easy, careless untidiness of her little house in the Los Angeles canyon, red brick, piles of books everywhere, barbecue, phones, duplicators and electric typewriters. Troubled at his thought and the way he automatically seemed to be comparing them, he strolled back to the kitchen, bypassing the *amah's* room, his walk soundless. Orlanda was concentrating on the coffee maker, unaware that now he was watching her. He enjoyed watching her.

This morning he had phoned her early, very concerned, waking her, wanting to remind her to see a doctor, just in case. In the mêlée last night, by the time he and Casey and Dunross had got ashore she had already gone home.

'Oh, thank you, Linc, how thoughtful of you to phone! No, I'm fine,' she had said in a happy rush. 'At least I am now. Are you all right? Is Casey all right? Oh I can't thank you enough, I was petrified . . . You saved my life, you and Casey . . .'

They had chatted happily on the phone and she had promised to see her doctor anyway, and then he had asked if she'd like breakfast. At once she had said yes and he had gone Hong Kong side, enjoying the downpour, the temperature nice. Breakfast atop the Mandarin, eggs Benedict and toast and coffee, feeling grand, Orlanda sparkling and so appreciative of him and of Casey.

'I thought I was dead. I knew I'd drown, Linc, but I was too frightened to scream. If you hadn't done it all so quickly I'd never . . . The moment I was under, dear Casey was there and I was alive again and safe before I knew it. . . .'

It was the best breakfast he had ever had. She had ministered to him, small things, passing him toast and pouring coffee without having to ask for it, picking up his serviette when it fell, entertaining and being entertained, assured and feminine, making him feel masculine and strong. And she reached out once and put her hand on his arm, long fingers and exquisite nails, and the feel of that touch still lingered. Then he had escorted her home and inveigled an invitation up to her apartment and now he was here, watching her concentrate in the kitchen, silk skirt and Russian-style rain boots, loose blouse that was tight to her tiny waist, letting his eyes flow over her.

Jesus, he thought, I'd better be careful.

'Oh, I didn't see you, Linc. You walk quietly for a man of your height!'

'Sorry.'

'Don't be sorry, Linc!' The steam hissed to a crescendo. Jet droplets began to fill the cups. 'A twist of lemon?'

'Thanks. You?'

'No. I prefer cappuccino.' She heated the milk, the sound fine and the smell of the coffee grand, then carried the tray to the breakfast area. Silver spoons and good porcelain, both of them aware of the currents in the room but pretending there were none.

Bartlett sipped his coffee. 'It's wonderful, Orlanda! The best I've ever had. But it's different.'

'It's the dash of chocolate.'

'You like cooking?'

'Oh yes! Very much. Quillan said I was a good pupil. I love keeping house and organizing parties, and Quillan always . . .' A small frown was on her face now. She looked at him directly. 'I seem to be always mentioning him. Sorry but it's still . . . it's still automatic. He was the first man in my life—the only man—so he's a part of me that's indelible.'

'You don't have to explain, Orlanda, I und—'

'I know, but I'd like to. I've no real friends, I've never talked about him to anyone, never wanted to, but somehow . . . somehow well, I like being with you and . . .' A sudden, vast smile went across her. 'Of course! I'd forgotten! Now I'm your responsibility!' She laughed and clapped her tiny hands.

'What do you mean?'

'According to Chinese custom you've interfered with joss or

fate. Oh yes. You interfered with the gods. *You* saved my life because without you I'd surely have died—probably would have died—but that would have been up to the gods. But because you interfered you took over *their* responsibility, so now you have to look after me forever! That's good wise Chinese custom!' Her eyes were dancing and he had never seen whites as white or dark brown pupils so limpid, or a face so pleasing. 'Forever!'

'You're on!' He laughed with her, the strength of her joy surrounding him.

'Oh good!' she said, then became a little serious and touched him on the arm. 'I was only joking, Linc. You're so gallant—I'm not used to such gallantry. I formally release you—my Chinese half releases you.'

'Perhaps I don't want to be released.' At once he saw her eyes widen. His chest was feeling tight, his heart quickening. Her perfume tantalized him. Abruptly the force between them surged. His hand reached out and touched her hair, so silky and fine and sensuous. First touch. Caressing her. A little shiver and then they were kissing. He felt her lips and, in a moment, welcoming, just a little moist, without lipstick, the taste so clean and good.

Their passion grew. His hand moved to her breast and the heat came through the silk. Again she shivered and weakly tried to back off but he held her firmly, his heart racing, fondling her, then her hands went to his chest and stayed a while, touching him, then pressed against him and she broke the kiss but stayed close, gathering her breath, her heart racing, as intoxicated as he was.

'Linc . . . you . . .'

'You feel so good,' he said softly, holding her close. He bent to kiss her again but she avoided his kiss.

'Wait, Linc. First . . .'

He kissed her neck and tried again, sensing her want.

'Linc, wait . . . first . . .'

'First kiss, then wait!'

She laughed. The tension broke. He cursed himself for making the mistake, his desire strong, whipped by hers. Now the moment had passed and they were fencing again. His anger began to flood but before it possessed him she reached up and kissed him perfectly. At once his anger vanished. Only warmth remained.

'You're too strong for me, Linc,' she said, her voice throaty, arms around his neck but cautiously. 'Too strong and too attractive and too nice and truly, truly I do owe you a life.' Her hand caressed his neck and he felt it in his loins as she looked up at him, all her defenses settled, strong yet inviolate. Perhaps, he thought.

'First talk,' she said, moving away, 'then perhaps we will kiss again.'

'Good.' At once he went to her but, both of them in good humour now, she put her fingers on his lips, preventing him.

'Mr. Bartlett! Are all Americans like you?'

'No,' he said immediately but she would not take the bait.

'Yes, I know.' Her voice was serious. 'I know. That's what I wanted to talk to you about. Coffee?'

'Sure,' he said, waiting, wondering how to proceed, gauging her, wanting her, not sure of this jungle, fascinated by it and by her.

Carefully she poured the coffee. It tasted as good as the first. He was in control though the ache remained.

'Let's go into the living room,' she said. 'I'll bring your cup.'

He got up and kept a hand around her waist. She did not object and he felt that she liked his touch too. He sat in one of the deep armchairs. 'Sit here,' he said, patting the arm. 'Please.'

'Later. First I want to talk.' She smiled a little shyly and sat on the sofa opposite. It was dark blue velvet and matched the Chinese rug on shiny parquet floors. 'Linc, I've only known you a few days and I . . . I'm not a good-time girl.' Orlanda reddened as she said it and carried on in a rush over what he was going to say. 'Sorry but I'm not. Quillan was the first and only one and I don't want an affair. I don't want a frantic or friendly tumble and a shy or aching good-bye. I've learned to live without love, I just cannot go through that all again. I did love Quillan, I don't now. I was seventeen when we . . . when we began and now I'm twenty-five. We've been apart for almost three years. Everything's been finished for three years and I don't love him anymore. I don't love anyone and I'm sorry, I'm sorry but I'm not a good-time girl.'

'I never thought you were,' he said and knew in his heart it

741

was a lie and cursed his luck. 'Hell, what do you think I am?'

'I think you're a fine man,' she said at once, sincerely, 'but in Asia a girl, any girl, finds out very quickly that men want to pillow and that's really all they want. Sorry, Linc, casual pillowing's not my thing. Perhaps it will be one day but not now. Yes I'm Eurasian but I'm not . . . you know what I'm saying?'

'Sure,' he said and added before he could stop himself, 'you're saying you're off limits.'

Her smile vanished and she stared at him. His heart twisted at her sadness. 'Yes,' she said, slowly getting up, near tears. 'Yes, I suppose I am.'

'Jesus, Orlanda.' He went over to her and held her. 'I didn't mean it that way. I didn't mean it rotten.'

'Linc, I'm not trying to tease or play games or be diffic—'

'I understand. Hell, I'm not a child and I'm not pushing or . . . I'm not either.'

'Oh, oh I'm so glad. For a moment . . .' She looked up and her innocence melted him. 'You're not mad at me, Linc? I mean I . . . I didn't ask you up, you really insisted on coming.'

'I know,' he said, holding her in his arms, and he was thinking, It's the truth, and also the truth that I want you now and I don't know what you are, who you are but I want you. But what do I want from you? What do I really want? Do I want magic? Or just a lay? Are you the magic I've been seeking forever or just another broad? How do you stack against Casey? Do I measure loyalty against the silk of your skin? Remember how Casey said once, 'Love consists of many things, Linc, only one part of love's sex. Only one. Think of all the other parts. Judge a woman by her love, yes, but understand what a woman is.' But her warmth was going through him, her face against his chest and once more he felt himself stirring. He kissed her neck not wanting to withhold his passion.

'What are you, Orlanda?'

'I'm . . . I can only tell you what I'm not,' she said in her tiny voice. 'I'm not a tease. I don't want you to think that I'm trying to tease you. I like you, like you very much but I'm not a . . . I'm not a one-night stand.'

'I know. Jesus, what put that into your head?' He saw her eyes were glistening. 'No need for tears. None. Okay?'

'Yes.' She moved away and opened her purse and took out a

742

tissue and used it. '*Ayeeyah*, I'm acting like a teen-ager or a vestal virgin. Sorry, but it was rather sudden and I wasn't prepared for . . . I felt myself going.' She took a deep breath. 'Abject apologies.'

He laughed. 'Refused.'

'Thank God!' She watched him. 'Actually, Linc, I can usually handle the strong, the meek, and the cunning—even the very cunning—without too much trouble. I guess I've known every kind of pass it's possible for a girl to have and I've always figured I've an automatic game plan to counter them almost before they begin. But with you . . .' She hesitated, then added, 'Sorry, but almost every man I meet, well, it's always the same.'

'That's wrong?'

'No, but it's trying to walk into a room or a restaurant and feel those leering eyes. I wonder how men would handle it. You're young and handsome. What would you do if women did it to you everywhere you went. Say when you walked through the lobby of the V and A this morning you saw every woman of every age, from false-toothed old grannies, bewigged harpies, the fat, the ugly, the coarse, all of them, all openly leering at you, undressing you mentally, openly trying to get close, trying to stroke your behind, openly ogling your chest or crotch, most of them with bad breath, most of them sweating and foul-smelling, and you know they're imagining you in their bed, enthusiastically and happily doing the most intimate things to them.'

'I wouldn't like it at all. Casey said the same thing in different words when she first joined me. I know what you mean, Orlanda. At least I can imagine it. But that's the way the world's made.'

'Yes, and sometimes it's awful. Oh I don't want to be a man, Linc, I'm very happy to be a woman, but it's really quite awful sometimes. To know you're thought of as just a receptacle that can be bought, and that after it all you're to say thank you very much to the corpulent old lecher with the bad breath and accept your twenty-dollar bill and sneak off like a thief in the night.'

He frowned. 'How did we get on this kick?'

She laughed. 'You kissed me.'

He grinned, glad they were happy together. 'That's right. So maybe I deserved the lecture. I'm guilty as charged. Now, about that kiss you promised me. . . .' But he did not move. He was feeling his way, probing. Everything's changed now, he thought. Sure I wanted to—what did she call it? To pillow. Sure. Still do, more than before. But now we're changed. Now we're in a different game. I don't know if I want in. The rules've changed. Before it was simple. Now maybe it's more simple. 'You're pretty. Did I mention you were pretty?' he said, avoiding the issue that she wanted out in the open.

'I was going to talk about that kiss. You see, Linc, the truth is I just wasn't prepared for the way, to be honest, the way I, I was swamped, I guess that's the word.'

He let the word linger. 'Is that good or bad?'

'Both.' Her eyes crinkled with her smile. 'Yes, swamped with my own desire. You're something else, Mr. Bartlett, and that's also very bad, or very good. I, I enjoyed your kiss.'

'So did I.' Again he grinned at her. 'You can call me Linc.'

After a pause she said, 'I've never felt so wanting and swamped, and because of that very frightened.'

'No need to be frightened,' he said. But he was wondering what to do. His instincts said leave. His instincts said stay. Wisdom told him to say nothing and wait. He could hear his heart beating and the rain hammering the windows. Better to go, he thought. 'Orlanda, guess it's ab—'

'Do you have time to talk? Just a little?' she asked, sensing his indecision.

'Sure. Sure, of course.'

Her fingers brushed her hair from her face. 'I wanted to tell you about me. Quillan was my father's boss in Shanghai and I seem to have known him all my life. He helped pay for my education, particularly in the States and he was always very kind to me and my family—I've four sisters and a brother and I'm the oldest and they're all in Portugal now. When I came back to Shanghai from San Francisco after I'd graduated, I was seventeen, almost eighteen . . . Well he's an attractive man, to me he is, though very cruel sometimes. Very.'

'How?'

'He believes in personal vengeance, that vengeance is a man's right, if he's a man. Quillan's very much a man. He was always good to me, still is.' She studied him. 'Quillan still gives me an allowance, still pays for this apartment.'

'You don't have to tell me anything.'

'I know. But I'd like to—if you want to listen. Then you can decide.'

He studied her. 'All right.'

'You see, part of it's because I'm Eurasian. Most Europeans despise us, openly or secretly, particularly the British here—Linc, just hear me out. Most Europeans despise Eurasians. All Chinese do. So we're always on the defensive, almost always suspect, almost always presumed to be illegitimate, and certainly an easy lay. God how I loathe that Americanism! How rotten and vulgar and cheap it really is. And revealing about the American male—though, strangely, it was in the States that I gained my self-respect and got over my Eurasian guilt. Quillan taught me lots and formed me in lots of ways. I'm beholden to him. But I don't love him. That's what I wanted to say. Would you like more coffee?'

'Sure, thanks.'

'I'll make some fresh.' She got up, her walk unconsciously sensuous and again he cursed his luck.

'Why'd you bust up with him?'

Gravely she told him about Macao. 'I allowed myself to be persuaded into the fellow's bed and I slept there though nothing happened, nothing—the poor man was drunk and useless. The next day I pretended that he'd been fine.' Her voice was outwardly calm and matter-of-fact but he could feel the anguish. 'Nothing happened but someone told Quillan. Rightly, he was furious. I have no defense. It was . . . Quillan had been away. I know that's no excuse but I'd learned to enjoy pillowing and . . .' A shadow went over her. She shrugged. 'Joss. Karma.' In the same small voice she told him about Quillan's revenge. 'That's his way, Linc. But he was right to be furious with me, I was wrong.' The steam hissed and the coffee began to drip. Her hands were finding clean cups and fresh home-baked cookies and new starched linen as she talked but their minds were concentrating on the man-woman triangle.

'I still see him once in a while. Just to talk. We're just friends now and he's good to me and I do what I want, see who I want.' She turned the steam off and looked up at him. 'We . . . we had a child four years ago. I wanted it, he didn't. He said I could have the child but I should have it in England. She's in Portugal now with my parents—my father's retired and she lives with

745

them.' A tear rolled down her cheek.

'Was that his idea, to keep the child there?'

'Yes. But he is right. Once a year I go there. My parents . . . my mother wanted the child, begged to have it. Quillan's generous to them too.' The tears were rolling down her face now but there was no sound to her crying. 'So now you know it all, Linc. I've never told anyone but you and now you know I'm, I wasn't a faithful mistress and I'm, I'm not a good mother and . . .'

He went to her and held her very close and he felt her melt against him, trying to hold back the sobs, holding on, taking his warmth and his strength. He gentled her, holding her, the length of her against him, warm, tender, everything fitting.

When she was whole again she reached up on tiptoe and kissed him lightly but with great tenderness and looked at him.

He returned the kiss equally.

They looked at each other searchingly, then kissed again. Their passion grew and it seemed forever but it was not and both heard the key in the lock at the same time. They broke away, trying to catch their breath, listening to their hearts and hearing the coarse voice of the *amah* from the hall. *'Weyyyyy?'*

Weakly Orlanda brushed her hair straighter, half-shrugged to him in apology. 'I'm in the kitchen,' she called out in Shanghainese. 'Please go to your room until I call you.'

'Oh? Oh the foreign devil's still here is he? What about my shopping? I did some shopping!'

'Leave it by the door!'

'Oh, oh very well, Young Mistress,' the *amah* called back and went off grumbling. The door banged loudly behind her.

'They always slam doors?' Linc asked, his heart still thumping.

'Yes, yes it seems so.' Her hand went back to his shoulder, the nails caressing his neck. 'Sorry.'

'Nothing to be sorry about. How about dinner?'

She hesitated. 'If you bring Casey.'

'No. Just you.'

'Linc, I think it's best no,' she told him. 'We're not in danger now. Let's just say good-bye now.'

'Dinner. Eight. I'll call for you. You pick the restaurant. Shanghai food.'

She shook her head. 'No. It's too heady already. Sorry.'

'I'll call for you at eight.' Bartlett kissed her lightly, then went to the door. She took down his raincoat and held it for him. 'Thanks,' he said gently. 'No danger. Orlanda. Everything's going to come up roses. See you at eight. Okay?'

'It's best not.'

'Maybe.' He smiled down at her strangely. 'That'd be joss—karma. We must remember the gods, huh?' She did not answer. 'I'll be here at eight.'

She closed the door behind him, went slowly to the chair and sat, deep in thought, wondering if she had scared him off, petrified that she had. Wondering if he really would be back at eight and if he did, how to keep him off, how to puppet him until he was mad with desire, mad enough to marry her.

Her stomach twisted uneasily. I have to be fast, she thought. Casey holds him in thrall, she's wrapped her coils around him and my only way is good cooking and home and loving, loving loving loving and everything that Casey is not. But no pillow. That's the way Casey's trapped him. I have to do the same.

Then he'll be mine.

Orlanda felt weak. Everything had gone perfectly, she decided. Then again she remembered what Gornt had said. 'It's the law of the ages that every man has to be trapped into marriage, trapped by his own lust or possessiveness or avarice or money or fear or laziness or whatever but trapped. And no man ever willingly marries his mistress.'

Yes. Quillan's right again, she thought. But he's wrong about me. I'm not going to settle for half the prize. I'm going to try for all of it. I'm going to have not only the Jag and this apartment and all it contains but a house in California and, most of all, American wealth, away from Asia, where I'll no longer be Eurasian but a woman like any other, beautiful, carefree and loving.

Oh I'll make him the best wife a man could ever have. I'll minister to his every need, whatever he wants I'll do for him. I felt his strength and I'll be good for him, wonderful for him.

'He's gone?' Ah Fat wandered noiselessly into the room, automatically tidying as she talked the Shanghai dialect. 'Good, very good. Shall I make some tea? You must be tired. So tea, *heya?*'

'No. Yes, yes make some, Ah Fat.'

'Make some tea! Work work work!' The old woman shuffled to the kitchen. She wore black baggy pants and white smock and her hair was in a single long braid that hung down her back. She had looked after Orlanda ever since she was born. 'I took a good look at him downstairs, when you and he arrived. For an uncivilized person he's quite presentable,' she said speculatively.

'Oh? I didn't see you. Where were you?'

'Down by the stairs,' Ah Fat cackled. 'Eeeee, I took good care to hide but I wanted to look at him. Huh! You send your poor old slave out into the wet with my poor old bones when what does it matter if I'm here or not? Who's going to get you sweetmeats and tea or drinks in bed when you've finished your labors, *heya?*'

'Oh shut up! Shut up!'

'Don't shut up your poor old Mother! She knows how to look after you! Ah yes, Little Empress, but it was quite clear on both of you the yang and the yin were ready to join battle. You two looked as happy as cats in a barrel of fish! But there was no need for me to leave!'

'Foreign devils are different, Ah Fat. I wanted him here alone. Foreign devils are shy. Now make the tea and keep quiet or I'll send you out again!'

'Is he going to be the new Master?' Ah Fat called out hopefully. 'It's about time you had a Master, not good for a person not to have a Steaming Stalk at the Jade Gate. Your Gate'll shrivel up and become as dry as dust from the little use it gets! Oh, I forgot to tell you two pieces of news. The Werewolves are supposed to be Macao foreigners; they'll strike again before the new moon. That's what the rumor is. Everyone swears it's the truth. And the other's that, well, Old Cougher Tok at the fish stall says this foreign devil from Golden Mountain's got more gold than Eunuch Tung!' Tung was a legendary eunuch at the Imperial Court in the Forbidden City of Peking whose lust for gold was so immense that all China could not satisfy it; he was hated so much that the next emperor heaped his ill-gotten gains on him until the weight of the gold crushed him to death. 'You're not getting younger, Little Mother! We should be serious. Is he going to be the one?'

'I hope so,' Orlanda said slowly.

Oh yes, she thought fervently, faint with anxiety, knowing that Linc Bartlett was the single most important opportunity of her life. Abruptly she was petrified again that she had overplayed her game and that he would not come back. She burst into tears.

Eight floors below, Bartlett crossed the small foyer and went outside to join the half a dozen people waiting impatiently for a taxi. The torrent was steady now and it gushed off the concrete overhang to join the flood that swirled in a small river down Kotewall Road, overflowing the gutters, the storm drains long since choked, carrying with it stones and mud and vegetation that came off the high banks and slopes above. Cars and trucks grinding cautiously up or down the steep road splashed through the whirlpools and eddies, windshield wipers clicking, windows fogged.

Across the road the land rose steeply and Bartlett saw the multitude of rivulets cascading down the high concrete embankments that held the earth in. Weeds grew out of cracks. Part of a sodden clump fell away to join more debris and stones and mud. One side of the embankment was a walled garage and, up the slope, a half-hidden ornate Chinese mansion with a green tiled roof and dragons on its gables. Beside it was scaffolding of a building site and excavations for a high rise. Beside that was another apartment block that vanished into the overcast.

So much building, Bartlett told himself critically. Maybe we should get into construction here. Too many people chasing too little land means profit, huge profit. And amortized over three years—Jesus!

A taxi swirled up, careless of the puddles. Passengers got out and others, grumbling, got in. A Chinese couple came out of the entrance, shoved past him and the others to the head of the line—a loud chattering matron with a huge umbrella, an expensive raincoat over her *cheong-sam*, her husband meek and mild alongside her. Screw you, baby, Bartlett thought, you're not going to take my turn. He moved into a better position. His watch read 10:35.

* * *

What next, he asked himself. Don't let Orlanda distract you! Struan's or Gornt!

Today's skirmish day, tomorrow—Friday—tomorrow's the ballbreaker, the weekend's for regrouping, Monday's the final assault and by 3:00 P.M. we should have a victor.

Whom do I want to win? Dunross or Gornt?

That Gornt's a lucky man—was a lucky man, he thought, bemused. Jesus, Orlanda's something else. Would I have quit her if I'd been him? Sure. Sure I would. Well maybe not— nothing happened. But I'd've married her the moment I could and not sent *our* child packing to Portugal—that Gornt's a no-good son of a bitch. Or goddamn clever. Which?

She laid it out nice and clean—just like Casey did but different though the result's the same. Now everything's complicated, or simple. Which?

Do I want to marry her? No.

Do I want to let her drop? No.

Do I want to bed her? Sure. So mount a campaign, maneuver her into bed without commitments. Don't play the game of life according to female rules, all's fair in war and war. What's love anyway? It's like Casey said, sex's only part of it.

Casey. What about her? Not long to wait for Casey now. And then, is it bed or marriage bells or good-bye or what? God-damned if I want to get married again. The one time turned out lousy. That's strange, I haven't thought about *her* in a long time.

When Bartlett had returned from the Pacific in '45 he had met her in San Diego and married within a week, full of love and ambition and had hurled himself into beginning a construction business in southern California. The time was ripe in California, all forms of building booming. The first child had arrived within ten months and the second a year later and a third ten months after that, and all the while working Saturdays and Sundays, enjoying the work and being young and strong and succeeding hugely, but drifting apart. Then the quarreling began and the whining and the 'you never spend any time with us anymore and screw the business I don't care about the business I want to go to France and Rome and why don't you come home early have you a girl friend I know you have a girl friend. . . .'

But there was no girl friend, just work. Then one day the attorney's letter. Just through the mail.

Shit, Bartlett thought angrily, it still hurting. But then I'm only one of millions and it's happened before and it'll happen again. Even so *your* letter or *your* phone call hurts. It hurts and it costs you. It costs you plenty and the attorneys get most, get a good part and they cleverly fan the fire between you for their own goddamn gain. Sure. You're their meal ticket, we all are! From the cradle to the goddamn grave, attorneys kite trouble and feed off your blood. Shit. Attorneys're the real plague of the good old U.S. of A. I've only met four good ones in all my life, but the rest? They parasite all of us. Not one of us's safe!

Yes. That bastard Stone! He made a killing out of me, turned her into a goddamn fiend, put her and the kids against me forever and nearly broke me and the business. I hope the bastard rots for all eternity!

With an effort Bartlett took his mind off that gaping sore and looked at the rain and remembered that it was only money and that he was free, free and that made him feel marvelous.

Jesus! I'm free and there's Casey and Orlanda.

Orlanda.

Jesus, he thought, the ache still in his loins, I was really going back there. So was Orlanda. Goddamn, it's bad enough with Casey but now I've two of them.

He had not been with a girl for a couple of months. The last time was in London, a casual meeting and casual dinner then into bed. She was staying at the same hotel, divorced and no trouble. What was it Orlanda said? A friendly tumble and a shy good-bye? Yes. That's it. But that one wasn't shy.

He stood in line happily, feeling greatly alive and watching the torrents, the smell of the rain on the earth grand, the road messed with stones and mud, the flood swirling over a long wide crack in the tarmac to dance into the air like rapids of a stream.

The rain's going to bring lots of trouble, he thought. And Orlanda's lots of trouble, old buddy. Sure. Even so, there must be a way to bed her. What is it about her that blows your mind? Part's her face, part's her figure, part's the look in her eye, part's . . . Jesus, face it, she's all woman and all trouble. Better forget Orlanda. Be wise, be wise, old buddy. As Casey said, that broad's dynamite!

43

10:50 A.M.:

It had been raining now for almost twelve hours and the surface of the Colony was soaked though the empty reservoirs were barely touched. The parched earth welcomed the wet. Most of the rain ran off the baked surface to flood the lower levels, turning dirt roads into morasses, and building sites into lakes. Some of the water went deep. In the resettlement areas that dotted the mountainsides the downpour was a disaster.

Shantytowns of rickety hovels built of any scraps, cardboard, planks, corrugated iron, fencing, canvas, sidings, three-ply walls and roofs for the well-to-do, all leaning against one another, attached to one another, on top of one another, layer on layer, up and down the mountainside—all with dirt floors and dark alleys that were now awash and mucked and puddled and potholed and dangerous. Rain pouring through roofs soaking bedding, clothes and the other remnants of a lifetime, people packed on people surrounded by people who stoically shrugged and waited for the rain to stop. Tin alleys wandered higgledy-piggledy with no plan except to squeeze another space for another family of refugees and illegal aliens but not really aliens for this was China and, once past the border, any Chinese became legal settlers to stay as long as they wanted by ancient Hong Kong Government approval.

The strength of the Colony had always been its cheap, abundant and strife-free labor force. The Colony provided a permanent sanctuary and asked only peaceful labor in return at whatever the going rate of the day was. Hong Kong never sought immigrants but the people of China always came. They came by day and by night, by ship, by foot, by stretcher. They came across the border whenever famine or a convulsion racked China, families of men, women and children came to stay, to be absorbed, in time to go back home because China was always home, even after ten generations.

But refugees were not always welcome. Last year the Colony was almost swamped by a human flood. For some still unknown reason and without warning, the PRC border guards relaxed the tight control of their side and within a week thousands were pouring across daily. Mostly they came by night, over and through the token, single six-strand fence that separated the New Territories from the Kwantung, the neighboring province. The police were powerless to stem the tide. The army had to be called out. In one night in May almost six thousand of the illegal horde were arrested, fed and the next day sent back over the border—but more thousands had escaped the border net to become legal. The catastrophe went on night after night, day after day. Tens of thousands of newcomers. Soon mobs of angry sympathetic Chinese were at the border trying to disrupt the deportations. The deportations were necessary because the Colony was becoming buried in illegals and it was impossible to feed, house and absorb such a sudden, vast increase in new population. Already there were the four-plus million to worry about, all but a tiny percent illegals at one time.

Then, as suddenly as it had begun, the human gusher ceased and the border closed. Again for no apparent reason.

In the six-week period almost 70,000 had been arrested and returned. Between 100,000 and 200,000 escaped the net to stay, no one knew for certain how many. Spectacles Wu's grandparents and four uncles and their families were some of these, seventeen souls in all, and since they had arrived they had been living in a resettlement area high above Aberdeen. Spectacles Wu had arranged everything for them. This was more of the land that the Noble House Chen family had owned since the beginning that, until recently, had been without value. Now it had value. The Chens rented it, foot by foot, to any who wished to pay. Spectacles Wu had gratefully rented twenty feet by twelve feet at 1.00 HK per foot per month and, over the months, had helped the family scavenge the makings for two dwellings that, until this rain, were dry. There was one water tap per hundred families, no sewers, no electric light, but the city of these squatters thrived and was mostly well ordered. Already one uncle had a small plastic flower factory in a hovel he had rented at 1.50 HK per foot per month lower down the slopes, another had rented a stall in the market area selling tangy rice cakes and rice gruel in their Ning-tok village style. All seventeen were working—now eighteen mouths to feed with a newborn babe, born last week. Even the two-year-olds were given simple tasks, sorting plastic petals for the plastic flowers the young and old made that gave many of the hill dwellers money to buy food and money to gamble with.

Yes, Spectacles Wu thought fervently, all gods help me to get some of the reward money for the capture of the Werewolves in time for Saturday's races to put on Pilot Fish, the black stallion who, according to all the portents, is definitely going to win.

He stifled a yawn as he plodded on barefoot down one of the narrow twisting alleys in the resettlement area, his six-year-old niece beside him. She was barefoot too. The rain kept misting his thick glasses. Both picked their way cautiously, not wanting to step on any broken glass or rusting debris that was ever present. Sometimes the mud was ankle-deep. Both wore their trousers well rolled up and she had a vast straw coolie hat that dwarfed her. His hat was ordinary and secondhand like his clothes and not police regulation. These were the only clothes he possessed except for the shoes he carried in a plastic bag under his raincoat to protect them. Stepping over a foul pothole he almost lost his footing. 'Fornicate all hazards,' he cursed, glad that he did not live here and that the rented room he shared with his mother near the East Aberdeen police station was dry and not subject to quirks of the weather gods like those here. And thank all gods I don't have to make this journey every day. My clothes would be ruined and then my whole future would be in jeopardy because Special Intelligence admires neatness and punctuality. Oh gods let this be my great day!

Tiredness wafted over him. His head was hunched down and he felt the rain trickling down his neck. He had been on duty all night. When he was leaving the station early this morning he had been told that there was to be a raid on the old *amah*, Ah Tam, the one connected with the Werewolves, whom he had found and tracked to her lair. So he had said that he would hurry with his visit to his grandfather who had been taken ill and was near death and hurry back in good time.

He glanced at his watch. There was still time enough to walk the mile to the station. Reassured, he went on again, eased past a pile of garbage into a bigger alley that skirted the storm drain. The storm drain was five feet deep and served normally for sewer, laundry or sink, depending on the amount of water therein. Now it was overflowing, the swirling runoff adding to the misery of those below.

'Be careful, Fifth Niece,' he said.

'Yes. Oh yes, Sixth Uncle. Can I come all the way?' the little girl asked happily.

'Only to the candy stall. Now be careful! Look, there's another piece of glass!'

'Is Honorable Grandfather going to die?'

'That's up to the gods. The time of dying is up to the gods, not to us, so why should we worry, *heya?*'

'Yes,' she agreed importantly. 'Yes, gods are gods.'

All gods cherish Honorable Grandfather and make the rest of his life sweet, he prayed, then added carefully, for safety, 'Hail Mary Mother and Joseph, bless old Grandfather.' Who knows whether the Christian God or even the real gods exist? he thought. Better to try to placate them all, if you can. It costs nothing. Perhaps they'll help. Perhaps they're sleeping or out to lunch but never mind. Life is life, gods are gods, money is money, laws must be obeyed and today I must be very sharp.

Last night he had been out with Divisional Sergeant Mok and the Snake. This was the first time he had been taken with them on one of their special raids. They had raided three gambling joints but had, curiously, left five much more prosperous ones untouched even though they were on the same floor of the same tenement and he could hear the click of mah-jong tiles and the cries of the fan-tan croupiers.

Dew neh loh moh I wish I could get part of the squeeze, he told himself then added, Get thee behind me, Satan! I want much more to be in Special Intelligence because then I will have a safe, important job for life, I will know all manner of secrets, the secrets will protect me, and then, when I retire, the secrets will make me rich.

They turned a corner and reached the candy stall. He bartered with the old toothless woman for a minute or two, then paid her two copper cash and she gave the little girl a sweet rice cake and a good pinch of the bits of oh so chewy and tangy bittersweet sun-dried orange peel in a twist of newspaper.

'Thank you, Sixth Uncle,' the little girl said, beaming up at him from under her hat.

'I hope you enjoy them, Fifth Niece,' he replied, loving her, glad that she was pretty. If the gods favor us she will grow up to be very pretty, he thought contentedly, then we can sell her maidenhead for a vast amount of money, and her later services profitably for the good of the family.

Spectacles Wu was very proud that he had been able to do so much for this part of his family in their hour of need. Everyone safe and fed and now my percentage of Ninth Uncle's plastic flower factory, negotiated so patiently, will, with joss, pay my rent in a year or two, and I can eat good Ning-tok rice gruel three times a week free which helps eke out my money so that I needn't take the squeeze that is so easy to obtain but would ruin my future.

No. All gods bear witness! I will not take the squeeze while there's a chance for SI but it's not sensible to pay us so little. Me, 320 HK a month, after two years of service. *Ayeeyah*, barbarians are impossible to understand!

'You run along now and I'll be back tomorrow,' he said. 'Be careful as you go.'

'Oh yes!'

He bent down and she hugged him. He hugged her back and left. She headed up the hill, part of the rice cake already in her mouth, the cloying tacky sweetness oh so delicious.

The rain was monotonous and heavy. Flooding from the storm drain carried debris against the shacks in its path but she climbed the path carefully, skirting it, fascinated by the rushing water. The overflow was deep in parts and here where the way was steeper, almost like rapids. Without warning a jagged five-gallon can came swirling down the drain and hurled itself at her, narrowly missing her, to smash through a cardboard wall.

She stood stock-still, frightened.

'Get on, there's nothing to steal here!' a furious householder called out at her. 'Go home! You shouldn't be here. Go home!'

'Yes . . . yes,' she said and began to hurry, the climb more difficult now. At that moment the earth just below her gave way and the slide began. Hundreds of tons of sludge and rock and earth surged downward burying everything in its path. It went on for fifty yards or more in seconds, tearing the flimsy structure apart, scattering men, women and children, burying some, maiming others, cutting an oozing swath where once was village.

Then it stopped. As suddenly as it began.

On all the mountainside there was a great silence broken only by the sound of rain. Abruptly the silence ceased. Shouts and cries for help began. Men and women and children rushed out of untouched hovels, blessing the gods for their own safety, adding to the pandemonium and wails for help. Friends helped friends, neighbors helped neighbors, mothers searched for children, children for parents, but the great majority nearby just stood there in the rain and blessed their joss that this slide had passed them by.

The little girl was still teetering on the brink of the chasm where the earth had fallen away. She stared down into it with disbelief. Eleven feet below her now were fangs of rocks and sludge and death where seconds ago was solid ground. The lip was crumbling and small avalanches of mud and stones cascaded into the abyss, aided by the flooding from the storm drain. She felt her feet slipping so she took a tentative step backward but more of the earth gave way so she stopped, petrified, the remains of the rice cake still firmly in her hands. Her toes dug into the soft earth to try to keep her balance.

'Don't move,' an old man called out.

'Get away from the edge,' another shouted and the rest watched and waited and held their breath to see what the gods would decide.

Then a ten-foot slice of the lip collapsed and toppled into the maw carrying the little girl with it. She was buried just a little. Up to her knees. She made sure her rice cake was safe then burst into tears.

44

Superintendent Armstrong's police car eased its way through the milling angry crowds that had spilled over into the road outside the Ho-Pak Bank, heading for the East Aberdeen police station. Mobs were clogging the streets outside all the other banks in the area, big and small—even the Victoria which was across the street from the Ho-Pak—everyone impatiently waiting to get in to get their money out.

Everywhere the mood was volatile and dangerous, the downpour adding to the tension. Barricades erected to channel people into and out of the banks were manned in strength by equally anxious and irritable police—twenty per thousand, unarmed but for truncheons.

'Thank God for the rain,' Armstrong muttered.

'Sir?' the driver asked, the irritating screech of ill-adjusted windshield wipers drowning his voice.

Armstrong repeated it louder and added, 'If it was hot and humid, this whole bloody place'd be up in arms. The rain's a godsend.'

'Yes sir. Yes it is.'

In time the police car stopped outside the station. He hurried in. Chief Inspector Donald C. C. Smyth was waiting for him. His left arm was in a sling.

'Sorry to be so long,' Armstrong said, 'Bloody's traffic's jammed for bloody miles.'

'Never mind. Sorry but I'm a bit shorthanded, old chap. West Aberdeen's cooperating and so is Central, but they've problems too. Bloody banks! We'll have to do with one copper in the back—he's already in position in case we flush one of the

758

villains—and us up front with Spectacles Wu.' Smyth told Armstrong his plan.

'Good.'

'Shall we go now? I don't want to be away too long.'

'Of course. It looks pretty dicey outside.'

'I hope the bloody rain lasts until the bloody banks close their doors or pay out the last penny. Did you go liquid yourself?'

'You must be joking! My pittance makes no difference!' Armstrong stretched, his back aching. 'Ah Tam in the flat?'

'As far as we know. The family she works for is called Ch'ung. He's a dustman. One of the villains might be there too so we'll have to get in quickly. I've the commissioner's authority to carry a revolver. Do you want one too?'

'No. No thanks. Let's go, shall we?'

Smyth was shorter than Armstrong but well built and his uniform suited him. Awkwardly, because of his arm, he picked up his raincoat and began to lead the way, then stopped. 'Bugger, I forgot! Sorry, SI, Brian Kwok called, would you call him? Want to use my office?'

'Thanks. Is there any coffee? I could use a cuppa.'

'Coming up.'

The office was neat, efficient and drab, though Armstrong noticed the expensive chairs and desk and radio accoutrements. 'Gifts from grateful customers,' Smyth said airily. 'I'll leave you for a couple of minutes.'

Armstrong nodded and dialed. 'Yes, Brian?'

'Oh hello, Robert! How's it going? The Old Man says you should bring her to HQ and not investigate her at East Aberdeen.'

'All right. We're just about to leave. HQ eh? What's the reason?'

'He didn't tell me, but he's in a good mood today. It seems we've a 16/2 tonight.'

Armstrong's interest peaked. A 16/2 in SI terms meant they had broken an enemy cover and were going to take the spy or spies into custody. 'Anything to do with our problem?' he asked cautiously, meaning Sevrin.

'Perhaps.' There was a pause. 'Remember what I was saying about our mole? I'm more convinced than ever I'm right.' Brian

759

Kwok switched to Cantonese, using oblique phrases and innuendoes in case he was overheard. Armstrong listened with growing concern as his best friend told him what had happened at the track, the long private meeting between Crosse and Suslev.

'But that means nothing. Crosse knows the bugger. Even I've drunk with him once or twice, feeling him out.'

'Perhaps. But if Crosse's our mole it'd be just like him to do an exchange in public. *Heya?*'

Armstrong felt sick with apprehension. 'Now's not the time, old chum,' he said. 'Soon as I get to HQ we should have a chat. Maybe lunch and talk.'

Another pause. 'The Old Man wants you to report to him as soon as you bring the *amah* in.'

'All right. See you soon.'

Armstrong put down the phone. Smyth came back in. Thoughtfully he handed him a coffee. 'Bad news?'

'Nothing but bloody trouble,' Armstrong said sourly. 'Always bloody trouble.' He sipped his coffee. The cup was excellent porcelain and the coffee fresh, expensive and delicious. 'That's good coffee! Very good. Crosse wants me to bring her to HQ direct, not here.'

Smyth's eyebrows soared. 'Christ, what's so important about an old hag *amah?*' he asked sharply. 'She's in my jurisdic—'

'Christ I don't know! I don't give the f—' The bigger man stopped his explosion. 'Sorry, I haven't been getting much sleep the last few days. I don't give the orders. Crosse said to bring her to HQ. No explanation. He can override anyone. SI overrides everyone, you know how it is!'

'Arrogant bastard!' Smyth finished his coffee. 'Thank God I'm not in SI. I'd hate to deal with that bugger every day.'

'I'm not in SI and he still gives me trouble.'

'Was it about our mole?'

Armstrong glanced up at him. 'What mole?'

Smyth laughed, 'Come on for chrissake! There's a rumor among the Dragons that our fearless leaders have been advised to find the bugger very quickly. It seems that the minister's even roasting the governor! London's so pissed off they're sending out the head of MI-6—presume you know Sinders arrives tomorrow on the BOAC flight.'

Armstrong sighed. 'Where the hell do they get all their information?'

'Telephone operators, *amahs*, street cleaners—who cares. But you can bet, old lad, at least one of them knows everything. You know Sinders?'

'No, never met him.' Armstrong sipped his coffee, enjoying the excellence, the rich, nutty flavor that was giving him new strength. 'If they know everything, who's the mole?'

After a pause, Smyth said, 'That sort of info'd be expensive. Shall I ask the price?'

'Yes. Please.' The big man put his cup down. 'The mole doesn't bother you, does he?'

'No, not at all. I'm doing my job thank you very much and it's not my job to worry about moles or to try to catch them. The moment you catch and snatch the bugger there'll be another bugger subverted or put into place and we'll do the same to them, whoever the *them* are. Meanwhile if it wasn't for this bloody Ho-Pak mess this station'd still be the best run and my East Aberdeen area the quietest in the Colony and that's all I'm concerned about.' Smyth offered a cigarette from an expensive gold case. 'Smoke?'

'No thanks, I quit.'

'Good for you. No, so long as I'm left alone until I retire in four years all's well in the world.' He lit the cigarette with a gold lighter and Armstrong hated him a little more. 'By the way, I think you're foolish not to take the envelope that's left in your desk monthly.'

'Do you now?' Armstrong's face hardened.

'Yes. You don't have to do anything for it. Nothing at all. Guaranteed.'

'But once you've taken one you're up the creek without a paddle.'

'No. This's China and not the same.' Smyth's blue eyes hardened too. 'But then you know that better than me.'

'One of your "friends" asked you to give me the message?'

Smyth shrugged. 'I heard another rumor. Your share of the Dragons' reward for finding John Chen comes to 40,000 HK an—'

'I didn't find him!' Armstrong's voice grated.

'Even so, that'll be in an envelope in your desk this evening.

So I hear, old chap. Just a rumor, of course.'

Armstrong's mind was sifting this information. 40,000 HK covered exactly and beautifully his most pressing, long overdue debt that he had to clear by Monday, losses on the stock market that, 'Well really, old boy, you should pay up. It has been over a year and we do have rules. Though I'm not pressing I really must have the matter settled. . . .'

Smyth's right again, he thought without bitterness, the bastards know everything and it'd be so easy to find out what debts I have. So am I going to take it or not?

'Only forty?' he asked with a twisted smile.

'I imagine that's enough to cover your most pressing problem,' Smyth said with the same hard eyes. 'Isn't it?'

Armstrong was not angry that the Snake knew so much about his private life. I know just as much about his, though not how much he has or where it's stacked away. But it'd be easy to find out, easy to break him if I wanted to. Very easy. 'Thanks for the coffee. Best I've had in years. Shall we go?'

Awkwardly, Smyth put on his regulation raincoat over his well-cut uniform, adjusted the sling for his arm and put his cap to the usual jaunty angle and led the way. As they went, Armstrong made Wu repeat what had happened and what had been said by the youth who claimed to be one of the Werewolves and later by the old *amah*. 'Very good, Wu,' Armstrong said when the young man had finished. 'An excellent piece of surveillance and investigation. Excellent. Chief Inspector Smyth tells me you want to get into SI.'

'Yes sir.'

'Why?'

'It's important, an important Branch of SB, sir. I've always been interested in security and how to keep our enemies out and the Colony safe and I feel it would be very interesting and important. I'd like to help if I could, sir.'

Momentarily their ears focused on the distant wail of fire engines that came from the hillside above.

'Some stupid bastard's kicked over another stove,' Smyth said sourly. 'Christ, thank God for the rain!'

'Yes,' Armstrong said, then added to Wu, 'If this turns out as you've reported, I'll put in a word with SB or SI.'

Spectacles Wu could not stop the beam. 'Yes sir, thank you,

sir. Ah Tam is really from my village. Yes sir.'

They turned into the alley. Crowds of shoppers and stall keepers and shopkeepers under umbrellas or under the canvas overhangs watched them sullenly and suspiciously, Smyth the most well known and feared *quai loh* in Aberdeen.

'That's the one, sir,' Wu whispered. By prearrangement Smyth casually stopped at a stall, this side of the doorway, ostensibly to look at some vegetables, the owner at once in shock. Armstrong and Wu walked past the entrance then turned abruptly and the three of them converged. They went up the stairs quickly as two uniformed policemen who had been trailing from a safe distance materialized to bottle up the front. Once the narrow passageway was secure one of them hurried up an even smaller alley and around the back to make sure the plainclothes detective was still in position guarding the single exit there, then he rushed back to reinforce the undermanned barricades in front of the Victoria.

The inside of the tenement was as dingy and filthy as the outside with mess and debris on every landing. Smyth was leading and he stopped on the third landing, unbuttoned his revolver holster and stepped aside. Without hesitation Armstrong leaned against the flimsy door, burst the lock and went in quickly. Smyth followed at once, Spectacles Wu nervously staying to guard the entrance. The room was drab with old sofas and old chairs and old grimy curtains, the sweet-rank smell of opium and cooking oil in the air. A heavy-set, middle-aged matron gaped at them and dropped her newspaper. Both men went for the inner doors. Smyth pulled one open to find a scruffy bedroom, the next revealed a messy toilet and bathroom, a third another bedroom crammed with unmade bunks for four. Armstrong had the last door open. It led into a cluttered, filthy, tiny kitchen, where Ah Tam bent over a pile of washing in the grimy sink. She stared at him blankly. Behind her was another door. At once he shoved past and jerked it open. It was empty too, more of a closet than a room, window-less with a vent cut in the wall and just enough space to fit the small string mattressless bunk and a broken-down chest of drawers.

He came back into the living room, Ah Tam shuffling after him, his breathing good and his heart settling down. It had taken them only seconds and Smyth took out the papers and said sweetly, 'Sorry to interrupt, madam, but we've a search warrant.'

'*Wat?*'

'Translate for us, Wu,' Smyth ordered and at once the young constable repeated what had been said and, as previously arranged, began to act as though he was the interpreter for two dullard *quai loh* policemen who did not speak Cantonese.

The woman's mouth dropped open. 'Search!' she shrieked. 'Search what? We obey the law here! My husband works for the government and has important friends and if you're looking for the gambling school it's nothing to do with us but it's on the fourth floor at the back and we know nothing about the smelly whores in 16 who set up shop and work till all hours making the rest of us civ—'

'Enough,' Wu said sharply, 'we are police on important matters! These Lords of the police are important! You're the wife of Ch'ung the dustman?'

'Yes,' she replied sullenly. 'What do you want with us? We've done noth—'

'Enough!' Armstrong interrupted in English with deliberate arrogance. 'Is that Ah Tam?'

'You! You're Ah Tam?'

'Eh, me? *Wat?*' The old *amah* tugged at her apron nervously, not recognizing Wu.

'So you're Ah Tam! You're under arrest.'

Ah Tam went white and the middled-aged woman cursed and said in a rush. 'Ah! So it's you they're after! Huh, we know nothing about her except we picked her off the street a few months ago and gave her a home and sal—'

'Wu, tell her to shut up!'

He told her impolitely. She obeyed even more sullenly. 'These Lords want to know is there anyone else here?'

'Of course there isn't. Are they blind? Haven't they raped my house like assassins and seen for themselves?' the shrew said truculently. 'I know nothing about nothing.'

'Ah Tam! These Lords want to know where your room is.'

The *amah* found her voice and began to bluster, 'What do you want with me, Honorable Policeman? I've done nothing, I'm not an illegal, I've papers since last year. I've done nothing, I'm a law-abiding civilized person who's worked all her li—'

'Where's your room?'

The younger woman pointed. 'There,' she said in her screeching, irritating voice, 'where else would her room be? Of course it's there off the kitchen! Are these foreign devils senseless? Where else do maids live? And you, you old maggot! Getting honest people into trouble! What's she done? If it's stolen vegetables it's nothing to do with me!'

'Quiet or we shall take you to our headquarters and surely the judge will want you kept in custody! Quiet!'

The woman started to curse but bit it back.

Armstrong said, 'Now, what . . .' Then he noticed that several curious Chinese were peering into the room from the landing. He stared back, took a sudden pace toward them. They vanished. He closed the door, hiding his amusement. 'Now, ask both of them what they know about the Werewolves.'

The woman gaped at Wu. Ah Tam went a little grayer. 'Eh, me? Werewolves? Nothing! Why should I know about those foul kidnappers? What have they to do with me? Nothing at all!'

'What about you, Ah Tam?'

'Me? Nothing at all,' she said querulously, 'I'm a respectable *amah* who does her work and nothing else!'

Wu translated their answers. Both men noticed that his translation was accurate, fast and easy. Both were patient and they continued to play the game they had played so many times before. 'Tell her she'd better tell the truth quickly.' Armstrong glowered down at her. He bore her no ill feeling, neither did Smyth. They just wanted the truth. The truth might lead to the identity of the Werewolves and the sooner those villains were hung for murder the easier it would be to control Hong Kong and the sooner law-abiding citizens, including themselves, could go about their own business or hobbies—making money or racing or whoring. Yes, Armstrong thought, sorry for the old woman. Twenty dollars to a broken hatpin the shrew knows nothing but Ah Tam knows more than she'll ever tell us.

'I want the truth. Tell her!' he said.

'Truth? What truth, Honorable Lord? How could this poor old body be anyth—'

Armstrong put up his hand dramatically. 'Enough!' This was another prearranged signal. At once Spectacles Wu switched to

Ning-tok dialect which he knew neither of them understood. 'Elder Sister, I suggest you talk quickly and openly. We know everything already!'

Ah Tam gaped at him. She had only two twisted teeth in a lower gum. 'Eh, Younger Brother?' she replied in the same dialect, caught off guard. 'What do you want with me?'

'The truth! I know all about you!'

She peered at him without recognition. 'What truth? I've never seen you before in my life!'

'Don't you remember me? In the poultry market? You helped me buy a chicken and then we had tea. Yesterday. Don't you remember? You told me about the Werewolves, how they were going to give you a huge reward . . .'

All three saw the momentary flash behind her eyes. 'Werewolves?' she began querulously. 'Impossible! It was someone else! You accuse me falsely. Tell the Noble Lords I've never seen y—'

'Quiet you old baggage!' Wu said sharply and cursed her roundly. 'You worked for Wu Ting-top and your mistress's name was Fan-ling and she died three years ago and they owned the pharmacy at the crossroads! I know the place well myself!'

'Lies . . . lies . . .'

'She says it's all lies, sir.'

'Good. Tell her we'll take her to the station. She'll talk there.'

Ah Tam began shaking. 'Torture? You'll torture an old woman? Oh oh oh . . .'

'When does this Werewolf come back? This afternoon?'

'Oh oh oh . . . I don't know . . . he said he would see me but the thief never came back. I lent him five dollars to get home an—'

'Where was his home?'

'Eh? Who? Oh him, he . . . he said he was a relation of a relation and . . . I don't remember. I think he said North Point . . . I don't remember anything . . .'

Armstrong and Smyth waited and probed and soon it was apparent that the old woman knew little though she ducked and twisted the probing, her lies becoming ever more flowery.

'We'll take her in anyway,' Armstrong said.

Smyth nodded. 'Can you handle it till I can send a couple of

766

men? I really think I ought to be getting back.'

'Certainly. Thanks.'

He left. Armstrong told Wu to order the two women to sit down and be silent while he searched. They obeyed, frightened. He went into the kitchen and closed the door. At once Ah Tam pulled at her long ratty queue. 'Young Brother,' she whispered slyly, knowing her mistress did not understand Ning-tok, 'I'm guilty of nothing. I just met that young devil like I met you. I did nothing. People of the same village stick together, *heya*? A handsome man like you needs money—for girls or his wife. Are you married, Honorable Younger Brother?'

'No, Elder Sister,' Wu said politely, leading her on as he had been told to do.

Armstrong was standing in the doorway of Ah Tam's tiny bedroom and he wondered for the millionth time why it was that Chinese treated their servants so badly, why servants would work in such miserable and foul conditions, why they would sleep and live and give loyal service for a lifetime in return for a pittance, little respect and no love.

He remembered asking his teacher. The old policeman had said, 'I don't know, laddie, but I think it's because they become *family*. Usually it's a job for life. Usually their own family becomes part also. The servant *belongs*, and the *how chew*, the *good points* of the job are many. It goes without saying all servants cream off a proportion of all housekeeping money, all food, all drink, all cleaning materials, all everything, however rich or poor, of course with the employers' full knowledge and approval provided it's kept to the customary level—how else can he pay them so little if they can't make extra on the side?'

Maybe that's the answer, Armstrong thought. It's true that before a Chinese takes a job, any job, he or she will have considered the *how chew* of the job very carefully indeed, the value of the *how chew* always being the deciding factor.

The room stank and he tried to close his nose to the smell. Sprays of rainwater were coming through the vent, the sound of the rain still pelting down, the whole wall mildewed and water-stained from a thousand storms. He searched methodically and carefully, all his senses tuned. There was little space to hide anything. The bed and bedding were relatively clean though there were many bedbugs in the corners of the bunk. Nothing under the bed but a chipped and stinking chamber pot and an empty suitcase. A few old bags and a tote bag produced nothing. The chest of drawers contained a few clothes, some cheap jewelry, a poor quality jade bracelet. Hidden under some clothes was an embroidered handbag of much better quality. In it were some old letters. A news cutting. And two photographs

His heart seemed to stop.

After a moment he went into the better light of the kitchen and peered at the photographs again but he had not been mistaken. He read the news cutting, his mind reeling. There was a date on the cutting and a date on one of the photographs.

In the honeycombed basement of Police Headquarters, Ah Tam sat on a hard, backless chair in the center of a large soundproofed room that was brightly lit and painted white, white walls and white ceiling and white floors and a single, flush white door that was almost part of the wall. Even the chair was white. She was alone, petrified, and she was talking freely now.

'Now what do you know about the barbarian in the background of the photograph?' Wu's flat, metallic Ning-tok voice asked from a hidden speaker.

'I've told and told and there isn't . . . I don't know, Lord,' she whimpered. 'I want to go home. . . . I've told you, I barely saw the foreign devil . . . he only visited us this once that I know of, Lord. . . . I don't remember, it was years ago, oh can I go now I've told you everything, everything. . . .'

Armstrong was watching her through the one-sided mirror in the darkened observation room, Wu beside him. Both men were set-faced and ill-at-ease. Sweat beaded Wu's forehead even though the room was pleasantly air conditioned. A tape recorder turned noiselessly. There were microphones and a bank of electronic equipment behind them.

'I think she's told us everything we need,' Armstrong said, sorry for her.

'Yes sir.' Wu kept his nervousness out of his voice. This was the first time that he had ever been part of an SI interrogation He was frightened and excited and his head ached.

'Ask her again where she got the purse.'

Wu did as he was ordered. His voice was calm and authoritative.

'But I've told you again and again,' the old woman whimpered. 'Please can I g—'

'Tell us again and then you can go.'

'All right . . . all right . . . I'll tell you again. . . . It belonged to my Mistress who gave it to me on her deathbed, she gave it to me, I swear it and—'

'The last time you said it was given to you the day before she died. Now which is the truth?'

Anxiously Ah Tam plucked at her ratty queue. 'I . . . I don't remember, Lord. It was on her . . . it was when she died . . . I don't remember.' The old woman's mouth worked and no sound came out and then said in a querulous rush, 'I took it and hid it after she died and there were those old photos . . . I've no picture of my Mistress so I took them too and there was one tael of silver too and this paid for part of my journey to Hong Kong during the famine. I took it because none of her rotten sons or daughters or family who hated her and hated me would give me anything so I took it when no one was . . . she gave it to me before she died and I just hid it it's mine, she gave it to me. . . .'

They listened while the old woman went on and on and they let her talk herself out. The wall clock read 1:45. They had been questioning her for half an hour. 'That's enough for now, Wu. We'll repeat it in three hours just for safety but I think she's told us everything.' Wearily Armstrong picked up a phone, dialed. 'Armstrong—you can take her back to her cell now,' he said into the phone. 'Make sure she's comfortable and well looked after and have the doctor reexamine her.' It was normal SI procedure to give prisoners an examination before and after each interrogation. The doctor had said that Ah Tam had the heart and the blood pressure of a twenty-year-old.

In a moment they saw the white, almost hidden door open. A uniformed SI policewoman beckoned Ah Tam kindly. Ah Tam hobbled out. Armstrong dipped the lights, switched the tape recorder to rewind. Wu mopped his brow.

'You did very well, Wu. You learn quickly.'

'Thank you, sir.'

The high-pitched whine of the tape recorder grew. Armstrong watched it silently, still in shock. The sound ceased and the big man took the reel out of the machine. 'We always mark the date, exact time and exact duration of the interrogation and use a code name for the suspect. For safety and secrecy.' He looked up a number in a book, marked the tape, then began to make out a form. 'We cross-check with this form. We sign it as interrogators and put Ah Tam's code down here—V-11-3. This's top secret and filed in the safe.' His eyes became very hard. Wu almost quailed. 'I repeat: You'd better believe that a closed mouth catches no flies and that everything in SI, everything that you have been party to today is top secret.'

'Yes sir. Yes, you can count on me, sir.'

'You'd better also remember that SI's a law unto itself, the governor and the minister in London. Only. Good old English law and fair play and normal police codes do *not* apply to SB or SI—habeas corpus, open trials, and appeal. In an SI case there's no trial, no appeal and it's a deportation order to the PRC or Taiwan, whichever's worse. Understand?'

'Yes sir. I want to be part of SI, sir, so you can believe me. I'm not one to slake my thirst on poison,' Wu assured him, sick with hope.

'Good. For the next few days you're confined to this HQ.'

Wu's mouth dropped open. 'But sir, my . . . yes sir.'

Armstrong led the way out and locked the door after him. He gave the key and the form to an SI agent who was on guard at the main desk. 'I'll keep the reel for the moment. I've signed the receipt.'

'Yes sir.'

'You'll take care of Constable Wu? He's our guest for a couple of days. Start getting his particulars—he's been very very very helpful. I'm recommending him for SI.'

'Yes sir.'

He left them and went to the elevator and got out on his floor, a sick-sweet-sour taste of apprehension in his mouth. SI interrogations were anathema to him. He hated them though they were fast, efficient and always obtained results. He preferred to have an old-fashioned battle of wits, to use patience and not these new, modern psychological tools. 'It's all bloody dangerous if you ask me,' he muttered, walking along his corridor, the faint musty smell of headquarters in his nostrils, hating Crosse and SI and everything it stood for, hating the knowledge he had unearthed. His door was open. 'Oh hi, Brian,' he said, closing it, his face grim. Brian Kwok had his feet up on the desk and was idly reading one of the Communist Chinese morning papers, the windows rain-streaked behind him. 'What's new?'

'There's quite a big piece on Iran,' his friend said, engrossed in what he was reading. 'It says "capitalist CIA overlords in conjunction with the tyrant Shah have put down a people's revolutionary war in Azerbaijan, thousands have been killed" and so on. I don't believe all that but it looks as though the CIA and the Ninety-second Airborne have defused that area and the Yanks have done right for once.'

'Lot of bloody good that'll do!'

Brian Kwok looked up. His smile faded. 'What's up?'

'I feel rotten.' Armstrong hesitated. 'I sent for a couple of beers, then we'll have lunch. How about a curry? All right?'

'Fine, but if you're feeling rotten let's skip lunch.'

'No, it's not that sort of rotten. I . . . I just hate doing white interrogations . . . gives me the creeps.'

Brian Kwok stared at him. 'You did the old *amah* there? What the hell for?'

'It was Crosse's order. He's a bastard!'

Brian Kwok put his paper down. 'Yes he is, and I'm sure I'm right about him,' he said softly.

'Not now, Brian, over lunch maybe but not now. Christ, I need a drink! Bloody Crosse, and bloody SI! I'm not SI and yet he acts like I'm one of his.'

'Oh? But you're coming on the 16/2 this evening. I thought you'd been seconded.'

'He didn't mention it. What's on?'

'If he didn't mention it, I'd better not.'

'Of course.' It was normal SI procedure, for security, to minimize the spread of information so that even highly trustworthy agents working on the same case might not be given all the facts. 'I'm bloody not going to be seconded,' Armstrong said grimly, knowing that if Crosse ordered it there was nothing he could do to prevent it. 'Is the intercept to do with Sevrin?'

'I don't know. I hope so.' Brian Kwok studied him then smiled. 'Cheer up, Robert, I've some good news for you,' he said and Armstrong noticed again how handsome his friend

771

was, strong white teeth, golden skin, firm jaw, dancing eyes with that devil-may-care confidence about him.

'You're a good-looking sod,' he said. 'What good news? You leaned on friend One Foot at the Para Restaurant and he's given you the first four winners for Saturday?'

'Dreamer! No, it's about those files you snatched yesterday at Bucktooth Lo's and passed over to Anti-Corruption. Remember? From Photographer Ng?'

'Oh? Oh yes.'

'It seems our fair-weather American-Chinese guest, Thomas K. K. Lim, who's "somewhere in Brazil," is quite a character. His files were golden. Very golden indeed! And in English, so our Anti-Corruption fellows went through them like a dose of salts. You came up with treasure!'

'He's connected with Tsu-yan?' Armstrong asked, his mind diverted immediately.

'Yes. And a lot of other people. Very important people, ve—'

'Banastasio?'

Brian Kwok smiled with his mouth. 'Vincenzo Banastasio himself. That ties John Chen, the guns, Tsu-yan, Banastasio and Peter Marlowe's theory nicely.'

'Bartlett?'

'Not yet. But Marlowe knows someone who knows too much that we don't know. I think we should investigate him. Will you?'

'Oh yes. What else about the papers?'

'Thomas K. K. Lim's a Catholic, a third-generation American-Chinese who's a magpie. He collects all sorts of inflammatory correspondence, letters, notes, memos, etcetera.' Brian Kwok smiled his humorless smile again. 'Our Yankee friends are worse than we thought.'

'For instance?'

'For instance, a certain well-known, well-connected New England family's involved with certain generals, U.S. and Vietnamese in building several very large, very unnecessary U.S.A.F. bases in Vietnam—very profitably—for them.'

'Hallelujah! Names?'

'Names, ranks and serial numbers. If the principals knew friend Thomas had it documented, it would send a shudder of horror down the Hallowed Halls of Fame, the Pentagon and various expensive smoke-filled rooms.'

Armstrong grunted. 'He's the middle man?'

'Entrepreneur he calls himself. Oh he's on very good terms with lots of notables. American, Italian, Vietnamese, Chinese, both sides of the fence. The papers document the whole fraud. Another scheme's to channel millions of U.S. funds into another phony Vietnam aid program. 8 million to be exact—one is already paid over to them. Friend Lim even discussed how the one million *h'eung yau*'s to be diverted to Switzerland.'

'Could we make it stick?'

'Oh yes, if we catch Thomas K. K. Lim and if we wanted to make it stick. I asked Crosse but he just shrugged and said it wasn't our affair, that if Yanks wanted to cheat their government, that's up to them.' Brian Kwok smiled but his eyes didn't. 'It's powerful info, Robert. If even part became common knowledge it'd create one helluva stink right up to the top.'

'Is he going to pass it on to Rosemont? Leak it?'

'I don't know. I don't think so. In one way he's right. It's nothing to do with us. Bloody stupid to put it all down! Stupid! They deserve to get chopped! When you've a minute read the papers, they're juicy.'

'Any connection between Lim and those other villains? Bucktooth Lo and the other man? Are they stealing CARE funds?'

'Oh yes, must be, but all their files're in Chinese so it'll take longer to pin them.' Brian Kwok added strangely, 'Curious that Crosse sniffed that one out, almost as though he knew there'd be a connection.' He dropped his voice. 'I know I'm right about him.'

The silence gathered. Armstrong's mouth felt parched and tasted bad. He pried his eyes off the rain and looked at Brian Kwok.

'What've you got?'

'You know that vice-consul in the U.S. Consulate—the homo, the one who's selling visas?'

'What about him?'

'Last month Crosse had dinner with him. In *his* flat.'

Armstrong rubbed his face nervously. 'That proves nothing. Listen tomorrow, tomorrow we get the files. Tomorrow Sind—'

'Perhaps *we* won't get to read them.'

'Personally I don't give a shit. That's SI business and I'm CID and that's wh—'

A knock stopped him. The door opened. A Chinese waiter came in with a tray and two tankards of cold beer and beamed toothily. 'Afternoon, sah,' he said, offering one to Brian Kwok. He gave the other to Armstrong and went out.

'Good luck,' Armstrong said, hating himself. He drank deeply then went to his safe to lock the tape away.

Brian Kwok studied him. 'You sure you're all right, old chum?'

'Yes, yes of course.'

'What did the old woman say?'

'In the beginning she told lots of lies, lots of them. And then the truth. All of it. I'll tell you over lunch, Brian. You know how it is—you catch the lies eventually, if you're patient. I'm fed up with lies.' Armstrong finished his beer. 'Christ, I needed that.'

'Do you want mine too? Here.'

'No, no thanks, but it's me for a whiskey and soda before curry and maybe another one. Drink up and let's get the show on the road.'

Brian Kwok put his half-empty tankard down. 'That's enough for me.' He lit a cigarette. 'How's the nonsmoking going?'

'Rough.' Armstrong watched him inhale deeply. 'Anything on Voranski? Or the assassins?'

'They vanished into thin air. We've got their photos so we'll catch them, unless they're over the border.'

'Or in Taiwan.'

After a pause, Brian Kwok nodded. 'Or Macao or North Korea, Vietnam or wherever. The minister's hopping mad with Crosse over Voranski, so's MI-6, so's the CIA. The CIA top echelon in London have been chewing the minister's tail so he's passing it on. We'd better get those buggers before Rosemont or we'll lose all face. Rosemont's under fire too to come up with their heads. I hear he's got every man out looking, thinking it's to do with Sevrin, and the carrier. He's petrified there's going to be an incident involving the nuclear carrier.' Brian Kwok added, his voice hardening, 'Bloody stupid to offend the PRC by bringing her here. That monster's an open invitation to every agent in Asia.'

'If I was Soviet I'd try to infiltrate her. SI's probably trying right now. Crosse'd love to have a plant aboard. Why not?' The big man watched the smoke curling. 'If I was Nationalist perhaps I'd plant a few mines and blame the PRC—or vice versa and blame Chiang Kai-shek.'

'That's what the CIA'd do to get everyone hopping mad at China.'

'Come off it, Brian!'

Brian Kwok took a last sip then got up. 'That's enough for me. Come on.'

'Just a moment.' Armstrong dialed. 'This's Armstrong, set up another session at 1700 hours for V-11-3. I'll want . . .' He stopped, seeing his friend's eyes flutter, then glaze and he caught him easily as he fell and let him slump back in the chair. Out of himself, almost watching himself, he put the phone back on its cradle. Now there was nothing for him to do but wait.

I've done my job, he thought.

The door opened. Crosse came in. Behind him were three plainclothed SI agents, all British, all senior agents, all taut-faced and tense. Quickly one of the men put a thick black hood over Brian Kwok's head, picked him up easily and went out, the others following.

Now that it was done Robert Armstrong felt nothing, no remorse or shock or anger. Nothing. His head told him that there was no mistake though his head still told him equally that his friend of almost twenty years could not possibly be a Communist mole. But he was. The proof was irrefutable. The evidence he had been found proved conclusively that Brian Kwok was the son of Fang-ling Wu, Ah Tam's old employer, when according to his birth certificate and personal records his mother and father were supposed to have been surnamed Kwok and murdered by Communists in Canton in '43. One of the photographs had showed Brian Kwok standing beside a tiny Chinese lady in front of a pharmacy at a crossroads in a village. The quality was poor but more than good enough to read the characters of the shop sign and to recognize a face, his face. In the background was an ancient car. Behind it stood a European, his face half turned away. Spectacles Wu had identified the store as the pharmacy at the crossroads in Ning-tok, the property of the Tok-ling Wu family. Ah Tam had identified the woman as her mistress.

'And the man? Who's the man standing beside her?'

'Oh that's her son, Lord. I've told you. He's Second Son Chu-toy. Now he lives with the foreign devils across the sea in the north, the north of the Land of the Golden Mountains,' the old woman had whimpered from the white room.

'You're lying again.'

'Oh no, Lord, he's her son, Chu-toy. He's her Second Son and he was born in Ning-tok and I helped deliver him with my own hands. He was Mother's second born who went away as a child. . . .'

'He went away? He went where?'

'To . . . to the Rain Country, then to the Golden Mountains. Now he has a restaurant and two sons. . . . He's a businessman there and he came to see Father. . . . Father was dying then and he came as a dutiful son should come but then he went away and Mother wept and wept. . . .'

'How often did he visit his parents?'

'Oh, it was only once, Lord, only that once. Now he lives so far away, in such a far place, such a far place but he came as a dutiful son should and then he left. It was just by chance I saw him, Lord. Mother had sent me to visit some relations in the next village but I was lonely and I came back early and saw him. . . . It was just before he left. The young Master left in a foreign devil car. . . .'

'Where did he get the motorcar? It was his?'

'I don't know, Lord. There was no car in Ning-tok. Even the village committee did not possess one, even Father who was the pharmacist in our village. Poor Father who died in such pain. He was a member of the committee. . . . They left us alone, Chairman Mao's people, the Outsiders . . . Yes they did because though Father was an intellectual and pharmacist he was always a secret Mao supporter through I never knew, Lord, I swear I never knew. Chairman Mao's people left us alone, Lord.'

'What was his name, the son of your Mistress? The man in the photo?' he had repeated, trying to shake her.

'Chu-toy Wu, Lord, he was her second born. . . . I remember when he was sent from Ning-tok to . . . to this foul place, this

Fragrant Harbor. He was five or six and he was sent to an uncle here and—'

'What was the uncle's name?'

'I don't know, Lord, I was never told, I only remember Mother weeping and weeping when Father sent him away to school. . . . Can I go home please now, I'm tired, please. . . .'

'When you tell us what we want to know. If you tell us the truth.'

'Oh I tell you the truth, anything anything. . . .'

'He was sent to school in Hong Kong? Where?'

'I don't know, Lord, my Mistress never said, only to school and then she put him out of her mind and so did I, oh yes, it was better, because he was gone forever, you know always second sons must leave. . . .'

'When did Chu-toy Wu return to Ning-tok?'

'It was some years ago when Father was dying. He only returned that once, it was only once, Lord, don't you remember me saying, I remember saying that. Yes it was the once of the photo. Mother insisted on the photo and wept and begged him to have one taken with her. . . . Surely she felt the hand of death on her now that Father had gone and she was truly alone . . . Oh she wept and wept so Chu-toy let her have her way as a dutiful son should and my Mistress was so pleased. . . .'

'And the barbarian in the photo, who is he?' The man was half turned around, in the background, not easy to recognize if you did not know him, standing beside the car that was parked beside the pharmacy. He was a tall man, European, crumpled clothes and nondescript.

'I don't know, Lord. He was the driver and he drove Chu-toy away but the committee of the village and Chu-toy himself bowed many times to him and it was said he was very important. He was the first foreign devil I had ever seen, Lord. . . .'

'And the people in the other photograph? Who're they?' This photograph was ancient, almost sepia and showed a self-conscious couple in ill-fitting wedding clothes staring bleakly at the camera.

'Oh of course they're Father and Mother, Lord. Don't you remember me saying that? I told you many times. That's Mother

777

and Father. His name was Ting-top Wu and his *tai-tai* my Mistress was Fang-ling. . . .'

'And the cutting?'

'I don't know, Lord, it was just stuck to the photo so I left it there. Mother had stuck it there so I left it. What should I want with foreign devil nonsense or writing. . . .'

Robert Armstrong sighed. The yellowed clipping was from a Chinese newspaper of Hong Kong, dated July 16, 1937, that told of three Chinese youths who had done so well in their term examinations that they had been granted scholarships by the Hong Kong Government to an English public school. Kar-shun Kwok was the first named. Kar-shun was Brian Kwok's formal Chinese name.

'You did very well, Robert,' Crosse said, watching him.

'Did I?' he replied through the fog of his misery.

'Yes, very well. You came to me at once with the evidence, you've followed instructions perfectly and now our mole is safely asleep.' Crosse lit a cigarette and sat at the desk. 'I'm glad you drank the right beer. Did he suspect anything?'

'No. No I don't think so.' Armstrong tried to get a hold on himself. 'Would you excuse me, sir, please. I feel filthy. I've . . . I've got to get a shower. Sorry.'

'Sit down a minute, please. Yes, you must be tired. Very tiring, these sort of things.'

Christ, Armstrong wanted to shout in anguish, it's all impossible! Impossible for Brian to be a deep-cover agent but it all fits. Why else would he have a completely different name, different birth certificate? Why else such a carefully constructed cover story—that his parents were killed in Canton during the war, murdered by Communists? Why else would he risk sneaking secretly back to Ning-tok, risking everything so carefully constructed over thirty years unless his own father was really dying? And if those facts are true then others automatically follow: That he must have been in continual contact with the Mainland to know about his father's approaching death, that as a superintendent of H.K. Police he must be totally persona grata with the PRC to be allowed in secretly and allowed out secretly again. And if he was persona grata then he must be one of them, groomed over the years, nurtured over the years. 'Christ,' he muttered, 'he'd've become assistant commissioner easily, perhaps even commissioner . . .!'

'What do you suggest, now, Robert?' Crosse asked, his voice soft.

Armstrong tore his mind into the present, his training overcoming his anguish. 'Check backwards. We'll find the link. Yes. His father was a tiny Commie cog but a Ning-tok cog nonetheless, so the Hong Kong relation he was sent to would be also. They'd've kept a tight rein on Brian in England, in Canada, here, wherever—so easy to do that, so easy to feed a hatred for *quai lohs*, so easy for a Chinese to hide such a hatred. Aren't they the most patient and secretive people on earth? Yes, you check back and eventually you find the link and find the truth.'

'Robert, you're right again. But first you begin his interrogation.'

Armstrong felt a chill of horror rush into his stomach. 'Yes,' he said.

'I'm delighted to tell you that that's your honor.'

'No.'

'You'll oversee the interrogation. No Chinese in this, just senior British agents. Except Wu, Spectacles Wu. Yes, he'll be a help—just him, he's good that fellow.'

'I can't . . . I won't.'

Crosse sighed and opened the large manila envelope he had brought with him. 'What do you think of this?'

Shakily Armstrong took the photograph. It was an eight-by-ten blowup of a tiny section of the Ning-tok photograph, the European's head that was part of the background beside the car. The man's face was half turned and blurred, the grain from the magnification dense. 'I . . . I'd say he saw the camera and turned or was turning to avoid being photographed.'

'My thought too. Do you recognize him?'

Armstrong peered at the face, trying to clear his head. 'No.'

'Voranski? Our dead Soviet friend?'

'Perhaps. No, no I don't think so.'

'How about Dunross, Ian Dunross?'

More shaken, Armstrong took it to the light. 'Possible but . . . improbable. If . . . if it's Dunross then . . . you think he's the Sevrin plant? Impossible.'

'Improbable, not impossible. He's very good friends with Brian.' Crosse took the photo back and looked at it. 'Whoever he is he's familiar, what you can see of him, but I can't place the man or where I've seen him. Yet. Well, never mind. Brian will remember. Yes.' His voice became silky. 'Oh, don't worry, Robert, I'll set Brian up for you but you're the one for the coup de grâce. I want to know who this fellow is very quickly, in fact I want to know everything Brian knows very, very quickly.'

'No. Get someone els—'

'Oh Robert, don't be so bloody boring! Chu-toy Wu, alias Brian Kar-shun Kwok, is an enemy mole who's eluded us for years, that's all.' Crosse's voice cut into Armstrong. 'By the way, you're on the 16/2 tonight at 6:30 and you're also seconded to SI. I've already talked to the commissioner.'

'No, and I can't iterrog—'

'Oh but my dear fellow you can and you will. You're the only one who can, Brian's far too clever to be caught like an amateur. Of course I'm as astounded he's the mole as you are, as the governor was!'

'Please. I don—'

'He betrayed Fong-fong, another friend of yours, eh? He must have leaked the AMG papers. It must be he who's furnished all our dossiers to the enemy and all the other information. God knows what knowledge he's had access to on the General Staff Course and all the other courses.' Crosse puffed his cigarette, his face ordinary. 'In SI he has the highest security clearances and I certainly agree he was being groomed for high office—I was even going to make him my number two! So we'd better find out very quickly everything about him. Curious, we were looking for a Soviet mole and it turns out we have a PRC one instead.' He stubbed out the cigarette. 'I've ordered a Classification One interrogation on him to begin at once.'

The color drained out of Armstrong's face and he stared at Crosse, hating him openly. 'You're a bastard, a fucking rotten bastard.'

Crosse laughed gently. 'True.'

'Are you a fag too?'

'Perhaps. Perhaps only occasionally and only when it pleases me. Perhaps.' Crosse watched him calmly. 'Come now, Robert, do you really think I could be blackmailed? Me? Blackmailed? Really, Robert, don't you understand life? I hear homosexuality is quite normal, even in high places.'

'Is it?'

'Nowadays, yes, quite normal, almost fashionable, for some. Oh yes, yes it is, my dear fellow, and it's practiced, from time to time, by a most catholic grouping of VIPs everywhere. Even in Moscow.' Crosse lit another cigarette. 'Of course, one should be discreet, selective and preferably uncommitted, but a penchant for the peculiar could have all sorts of advantages in our profession. Couldn't it?'

'So you justify any sort of evil, any sort of shit, murder, cheating, lying in the name of the bloody SI—is that it?'

'Robert, I justify nothing, I know you're distraught but I think that's enough of that.'

'You can't force me into SI. I'll resign.'

Crosse laughed scornfully. 'But my dear fellow, what about all your debts? What about the 40,000 by Monday?' He got up, his eyes granite. His voice was hardly changed but now there was a vicious edge to it. 'We're both over twenty-one, Robert. Break him, and do it very quickly.'

45

3:00 P.M.:

The closing bell of the Stock Exchange rang but the sound was drowned in the fetid pandemonium of massed brokers desperately trying to complete their final transactions.

For Struan's, the day had been disastrous. Huge amounts of stock had been shoved onto the market to be bought tentatively, then hurled back again as rumors fed on more rumors and more stock was offered. The share price plummeted from 24.70 to 17.50 and there were still 300,000 shares on offer in the sell column. All bank shares were down, the market was reeling. Everyone expected the Ho-Pak to fail tomorrow—only Sir Luis Basilio suspending trading in bank shares at noon had saved the bank from going under then.

'Jesus Christ, what a stinker!' someone said. 'Screwed by the sodding bell.'

'Look at the tai-pan!' another burst out. 'Christ almighty, you'd think it was just another day and not the death knell of the Noble House!'

'He's got balls has our Ian, no doubt about that. Look at that smile on him. Christ, his stock goes from 24.70 to 17.50 in one day when it's never been below 25 since the poor bugger went public and it's as though nothing's happened. Tomorrow Gornt has to get control!'

'I agree—or the bank.'

'The Vic? No, they've troubles of their own,' another said, joining the excited, sweating group.

'Holy mackerel, you really think Gornt will do it? Gornt tai-pan of the new Noble House?'

'Can't imagine it!' another shouted over the din.

'Better get used to it, old boy. But I agree, you'd never know Ian's world's crashing about his testicles . . .'

'About bloody time!' someone else called out.

'Oh come on, the tai-pan's a good fellow, Gornt's an arrogant bastard.'

'They're both bastards!' another said.

'Oh I don't know. But I agree Ian's cold all right. Ian's as cold as charity and that's pretty chilly. . . .'

'But not as cold as poor old Willy, he's dead poor bastard!'

'Willy? Willy who?' someone asked amid the laughter. 'Eh?'

'Oh for chrissake, Charlie, it's just a ditty, a poem! Willy rhymes with chilly, that's all. How did you do on the day?'

'I made a pile in commissions.'

'I made a pile too.'

'Fantastic. I unloaded 100 percent of all my own shares. I'm liquid now, thank God! It'll be tough on some of my clients but easy come easy go and they can afford it!'

'I'm still holding 58,000 Struan's and no takers. . . .'

'*Jesusschriiist!*'

'What's up?'

'The Ho-Pak's finished! They've closed their doors.'

'*What!*'

'Every last bloody branch!'

'Christ almighty are you sure?'

'Of course I'm sure and they say the Vic won't open tomorrow either, that the governor'll declare tomorrow a bank holiday! I have it on the highest authority, old boy!'

'Good sweet Christ, *the Vic's closing?*'

'Oh Christ we're all ruined. . . .'

'Listen, I've just talked to Johnjohn. The run's spread to them but he says they'll be all right—not to worry. . . .'

'Thank God!'

'He says there was a riot at Aberdeen half an hour ago when the Ho-Pak branch there failed but Richard Kwang's just put out a press release. He's "temporarily closed" all their branches except Head Office in Central. There's no need to worry, he's got plenty of money and . . .'

'Lying bastard!'

'. . . and anyone with Ho-Pak funds has to go there with their passbook and they'll get paid.'

'What about their shares? When they liquidate how much do you think they'll pay? Ten cents on the dollar?'

'God knows! But thousands are going to lose their knickers in this crash!'

'Hey, tai-pan! Are you going to let your stock plummet or are you going to buy?'

'The Noble House's strong as it ever was, old boy,' Dunross said easily. 'My advice to you is to buy!'

'How long can you wait, tai-pan?'

'We'll weather this slight problem, don't worry.' Dunross continued to push through the crowd, heading for the exit, Linc Bartlett and Casey following, questions being fired at him. Most of them he dismissed with a pleasantry, a few he answered, then Gornt was in front of him and the two of them were in the middle of a great silence.

'Ah, Quillan, how did you do on the day?' he asked politely.

'Very good, thank you, Ian, very good. My partners and I are 3 or 4 million ahead.'

'You have partners?'

'Of course. One doesn't mount an attack on Struan's lightly—of course one must have very substantial financial backing.' Gornt smiled. 'Fortunately, Struan's're roundly detested by lots of good people and have been for a century or more. I'm delighted to tell you I've just acquired another 300,000 shares for sale first thing. That should just about bring your house atumbling down.'

'We're not Humpty-Dumpty. We're the Noble House.'

'Until tomorrow. Yes. Or perhaps the next day. Monday at the latest.' Gornt looked back at Bartlett. 'Tuesday for dinner is still on?'

'Yes.'

Dunross smiled. 'Quillan, a man can get burned selling short in such a volatile market.' He turned to Bartlett and Casey and said pleasantly, 'Don't you agree?'

'It sure as hell isn't like our New York exchange.' Bartlett replied to a general laugh. 'What's happening here today'd blow our whole economy to hell. Eh Casey?'

'Yes,' Casey replied uneasily, feeling Gornt's scrutiny. 'Hello,' she said, glancing at him.

'We're honored to have you here,' Gornt said with great

charm. 'May I compliment you on your courage last night—both of you.'

'I did nothing special,' Bartlett said.

'Nor did I,' Casey said uncomfortably, very aware she was the only woman in the room and now the center of so much attention. 'If it hadn't been for Linc and Ian . . . for the tai-pan and you and the others, I'd've panicked.'

'Ah, but you didn't. Your dive was perfection,' Gornt said, to cheers.

She said nothing but she was warmed by that thought, not for the first time. Somehow life had been different since she had taken off her clothes without thinking. Gavallan had called this morning to ask how she was. So had others. At the exchange she had felt the looks strongly. There had been lots of compliments. Many from strangers. She felt that Dunross and Gornt and Bartlett remembered because she had not failed them. Or herself. Yes, she thought, you gained great face before all the men. And increased the jealousy of all their women. Curious.

'Are you selling short, Mr. Bartlett?' Gornt was saying.

'Not personally,' Bartlett told him with a small smile. 'Not yet.'

'You should,' Gornt said agreeably. 'There's a great deal of money to be made in a falling market, as I'm sure you know. A great deal of money will change hands with control of Struan's.' He put his eyes back onto Casey, excited by her courage and her body and by the thought that she would be coming sailing on Sunday alone. 'And you, Ciranoush, are you in the market?' he asked.

Casey heard her name and the way he said it. A thrill took her. Beware, she cautioned herself. This man's dangerous. Yes. And so is Dunross and so is Linc.

Which?

I think I want all three of them, she thought, heat rushing into her.

The day had been exciting and grand from the first moment when Dunross had phoned her so solicitously. Then getting up, feeling no ill effects from the fire or the emetics of Dr. Tooley. Then working away happily all morning on all the cables and telexes and phone calls to the States, tidying business problems of Par-Con's far-flung conglomerate, cementing a merger that had been on their agenda for months, selling off another company very profitably to acquire one that would further enhance Par-Con's stab into Asia—whomever they were in business with. Then, unexpectedly, being invited for lunch by Linc. . . . Dear handsome confident attractive Linc, she thought, remembering the lunch they had had atop the Victoria and Albert in the great, green dining room overlooking the harbor, Linc so attentive, Hong Kong Island and the sea roads obscured by the driving rain. Half a grapefruit, a small salad, Perrier, all perfectly served, just what she wanted. Then coffee.

'How about going to the Stock Exchange, Casey? Say 2:30?' he had said. 'Ian invited us.'

'I've still got lots to do, Linc, an—'

'But that place is something else and the things those guys get away with's unbelievable. Insider trading's a way of life here and quite legal. Jesus, it's fantastic—wonderful—a great system! What they do here legally every day'd get you twenty years in the States.'

'That doesn't make it right, Linc.'

'No, but this is Hong Kong and their rules please them and it is their country and they support themselves and their government only creams off 15 percent tax,' he had said. 'I tell you, Casey, if you want drop dead money it's here for the taking.'

'Let's hope! You go, Linc, I've really got a pile of stuff to get through.'

'It can wait. Today might be the clincher. We should be in at the kill.'

'Gornt's going to win?'

'Sure, unless Ian gets massive financing. I hear the Victoria won't support him. And the Orlin won't renew his loan, just as I forecast!'

'Gornt told you?'

'Just before lunch—but everyone knows everything in this place. Never known anything like it.'

'Then maybe Ian knows you put up the 2 million to start Gornt off.'

'Maybe. It doesn't matter, so long as they don't know Par-Con's on the way to become the new Noble House. How 'bout Tai-pan Bartlett?'

Casey remembered his sudden grin and the warmth flooding

out at her and she felt it now, standing on the floor of the Stock Exchange, watching him, crowds of men around her, only three important—Quillan, Ian and Linc—the most vital and exciting of all the men she had ever met. She smiled back at them equally, then said to Gornt, 'No, I'm not in the market, not personally. I don't like gambling—the cost of my money comes too high.'

Someone muttered, 'What a rotten thing to say!'

Gornt paid no attention and kept his eyes on her. 'Wise, very wise. Of course, sometimes there's a sure thing, sometimes you can make a killing.' He looked at Dunross who was watching with his curious smile. 'Figuratively, of course.'

'Of course. Well, Quillan, see you tomorrow.'

'Hey, Mr. Bartlett,' someone called out, 'have you made a deal with Struan's or not?'

'Yes,' another said, 'and what does Raider Bartlett think of a raid Hong Kong style?'

Another silence fell. Bartlett shrugged. 'A raid is a raid wherever,' he said carefully, 'and I'd say this one's mounted and launched. But you never know you've won until you've won and all the votes are counted. I agree with Mr. Dunross. You can get burned.' He grinned again, his eyes dancing. 'I also agree with Mr. Gornt. Sometimes you can make a killing, figuratively.'

There was another burst of laughter. Dunross used it to push through to the door. Bartlett and Casey followed. At his chauffeured Rolls below, Dunross said, 'Come on, get in—sorry, I've got to hurry, but the car'll take you home.'

'No, that's all right, we'll take a cab. . . .'

'No, get in. In this rain you'll have to wait half an hour.'

'The ferry'll do fine, tai-pan,' Casey said. 'He can drop us there.' They got in and drove off, the traffic snarled.

'What're you going to do about Gornt?' Bartlett asked.

Dunross laughed and Casey and Bartlett tried to gauge the strength of it. 'I'm going to wait,' he said. 'It's an old Chinese custom: Patience. Everything comes to he who waits. Thanks for keeping mum about our deal. You handled that rather well.'

'You'll announce tomorrow after the market closes, as planned?' Bartlett asked.

'I'd like to leave my options open. I know this market, you

don't. Perhaps tomorrow.' Dunross looked at them both clearly. 'Perhaps not until Tuesday when we've actually signed. I presume we still have a deal? Until Tuesday at midnight?'

'Sure,' Casey said.

'Can the announcement time be left to me? I'll tell you before-hand but I may need the timing to . . . . to maneuver.'

'Certainly.'

'Thank you. Of course, if we're down the pipe then, it's no deal. I understand quite clearly.'

'Gornt can get control?' Casey asked. Both of them saw the change in the Scotsman's eyes. The smile was still there but it was only on the surface.

'No, not actually, but of course with enough stock he can force his way immediately onto the board and appoint other directors. Once on the board he will be party to most of our secrets and he'll disrupt and destroy.' Dunross glanced back at Casey. 'His purpose is to destroy.'

'Because of the past?'

'Partially.' Dunross smiled, but this time they saw a deep-seated tiredness within it. 'The stakes are high, face is involved, huge face, and this's Hong Kong. Here the strong survive and the weak perish but en route the government doesn't steal from you, or protect you. If you don't want to be free and don't like our rules, or lack of them, don't come. You've come for profit, *heya?*' He watched Bartlett. 'And profit you will have, one way or another.'

'Yes,' Bartlett agreed blandly, and Casey wondered how much Dunross knew about the arrangement with Gornt. The thought disquieted her.

'Profit's our motive, yes,' she said. 'But not to destroy.'

'That's wise,' he said. 'It's better to create than to destroy. Oh, by the way, Jacques asked if you'd both like to dine with him tonight, 8:30-ish. I can't, I've an official do with the governor but I might see you for a drink later.'

'Thanks, but I can't tonight,' Bartlett said easily, not feeling easy at the sudden thought of Orlanda. 'How about you, Casey?'

'No, no thanks. I've a stack to get through, tai-pan, maybe we could take a rain check?' she asked him happily and thought that he was wise to be close-mouthed and Linc Bartlett equally wise to cool it with Struan's for a while. Yes, she told herself, her mind diverted, and it'll be lovely to have dinner with Linc, just the two of us, like lunch. Maybe we can even take in a movie.

Dunross went into his office.

'Oh . . . oh hello, tai-pan,' Claudia said. 'Mr. and Mrs. Kirk are in the downstairs reception room. Bill Foster's resignation's in your in-tray.'

'Good. Claudia, make sure I see Linbar before he goes.' He was watching her carefully and though she was consummate at hiding her feelings, he could sense her fear. He sensed it in the whole building. Everyone pretended otherwise but confidence was tottering. 'Without confidence in the general,' Sun Tzu had written, 'no battle can be won by however many troops and with however many weapons.'

Uneasily Dunross rethought his plan and position. He knew he had very few moves, that the only true defense was attack and he could not attack without massive funds. This morning when he had met Lando Mata, he had got only a reluctant perhaps. '. . . I told you I have to consult with Tightfist Tung first. I've left messages but I just can't get hold of him.'

'He's in Macao?'

'Yes, yes I think so. He said he was arriving today but I don't know on which ferry. I really don't know, tai-pan. If he's not on the last inbound, I'll go back to Maco and see him at once—if he's available. I'll call you this evening, the moment I've talked to him. By the way, have you reconsidered either of our offers?'

'Yes. I can't sell you control of Struan's. And I can't leave Struan's and run the gambling in Maco.'

'With our money you'll smash Gornt, you co—'

'I can't pass over control.'

'Perhaps we could combine both offers. We support you against Gornt in return for control of Struan's and you run our gambling syndicate, secretly if you wish. Yes, it could be secret. . . .'

Dunross shifted in his easy chair, certain that Lando Mata and Tightfist were using the trap that he was in to further their own interests. Just like Bartlett and Casey, he thought without anger. Now that's an interesting woman. Beautiful, courageous and loyal—to Bartlett. I wonder if she knows he breakfasted with Orlanda this morning, then visited her flat. I wonder if they know I know about the 2 million from Switzerland. Bartlett's smart, very smart, and making all the correct moves, but he's wide open to attack because he's predictable and his jugular's an Asian girl. Perhaps Orlanda, perhaps not, but certainly a youth-filled Golden Skin. Quillan was clever to bait the trap with her. Yes. Orlanda's a perfect bait, he thought, then put his mind back to Lando Mata and his millions. To get those millions I'd have to break my Holy Oath and that I will not do.

'What calls do I have, Claudia?' he asked, a sudden ice shaft in his stomach. Mata and Tightfist had been his ace, the only one left.

She hesitated, glanced at the list. 'Hiro Toda called from Tokyo, person to person. Please return the call when you've a moment. Alastair Struan the same from Edinburgh. . . . David MacStruan from Toronto . . . your father from Ayr . . . old Sir Ross Struan from Nice . . .'

'Uncle Trussler from London,' he said, interrupting her, 'Uncle Kelly from Dublin . . . Cousin Cooper from Atlanta, cous—'

'From New York,' Claudia said.

'From New York. Bad news travels fast,' he told her calmly.

'Yes. Then there was . . .' Her eyes filled with tears. 'What're we going to do?'

'Absolutely not cry,' he said, knowing that a large proportion of her savings was in Struan stock.

'Yes! Oh yes.' She sniffed and used a handkerchief, sad for him but thanking the gods she had had the foresight to sell at the top of the market and not buy when the Head of the House of Chen had whispered for all the clan to buy heavily. '*Ayeeyah*, tai-pan, sorry, so sorry, please excuse me . . . yes. But it's very bad, isn't it?'

'Och aye, lassie,' he said, aping a broad Scots accent, 'but only when you're deaded. Isn't that what the old tai-pan used to say?' The old tai-pan was Sir Ross Struan, Alastair's father, the first tai-pan he could remember. 'Go on with the calls.'

'Cousin Kern from Houston and Cousin Deeks from Sydney. That's the last of the family.'

'That's all of them.' Dunross exhaled. Control of the Noble

House rested with those families. Each had blocks of shares that had been handed down to them, though by House law he alone voted all the stock—while he was tai-pan. The family holdings of the Dunrosses, descended from Dirk Struan's daughter Winifred, were 10 percent; the Struans from Robb Struan, Dirk's half-brother, 5 percent; the Trusslers and Kellys from Culum and Hag Struan's youngest daughter, each 5 percent; the Coopers, Kerns and Derbys, descended from the American trader, Jeff Cooper of Cooper-Tillman, Dirk's lifetime friend who had married Hag Struan's eldest daughter, each 5 percent; the MacStruans, believed illegitimate from Dirk, 2½ percent; and the Chens 7½ percent. The bulk of the stock, 50 percent, the personal property and legacy of Hag Struan, was left in perpetual trust, to be voted by the tai-pan 'whoever he or she may be, and the profit therefrom shall be divided yearly 50 percent to the tai-pan, the remainder in proportion to family holdings—but only if the tai-pan so decides,' she had written in her firm, bold hand. 'If he decides to withhold profit from my shares from the family for any reason he may, then that increment shall go into the tai-pan's private fund for whatever use he deems fit. But let all following tai-pans beware: the Noble House shall pass from safe Hand to safe Hand and the clans from safe Harbor to safe Harbor as *the tai-pan* himself decreed or I shall add my curse, before God, to *his*, on him or her who fails us. . . .'

Dunross felt a chill go through him as he remembered the first time he had read her will—as dominating as the legacy of Dirk Struan. Why are we so possessed by these two? he asked himself again. Why can't we be done with the past, why should we be at the beck and call of ghosts, not very good ghosts at that?

I'm not, he told himself firmly. I'm only trying to measure up to their standards.

He looked back at Claudia, matronly, tough and very together but now scared, scared for the first time. He had known her all his life and she had served old Sir Ross, then his father, then Alastair, and now himself with a fanatical loyalty, as had Phillip Chen.

Ah Phillip, poor Phillip.

'Did Phillip call?' he asked.

'Yes, tai-pan. And Dianne. She called four times.'

'Who else?'

'A dozen or more. The more important ones are Johnjohn at the bank, General Jen from Taiwan, Gavallan *père* from Paris, Four Finger Wu, Pug—'

'Four Fingers?' Dunross's hope peaked. 'When did he call?'

She referred to her list. '2:56.'

I wonder if the old pirate has changed his mind, Dunross thought, his excitement growing.

Yesterday afternoon late he had gone to Aberdeen to see Wu to seek his help but, as with Lando Mata, he had got only vague promises.

'Listen, Old Friend,' he had told him in halting Haklo, 'I've never sought a favor from you before.'

'A long line of your tai-pan ancestors have sought plenty favors and made great profits from my ancestors,' the old man had answered, his cunning eyes darting. 'Favors? Fornicate all dogs, tai-pan, I have not that amount of money. 20 millions? How could a poor old fisherman like me have that cash?'

'More came out of the Ho-Pak yesterday, old friend.'

'*Ayeeyah*, fornicate all those who whisper wrong informations! Perhaps I withdrew my money safely but it all has gone, gone to pay for goods, goods I owed money for.'

'I hope not for the White Powder,' he had told him grimly. 'The White Powder is terrible joss. Rumor has it you are interested in it. I advise against it as a friend. My ancestors, Old Green-Eyed Devil and Hag Struan of the Evil Eye and Dragon's Teeth, they both put a curse on those who deal in the White Powder, not on opium but on all White Powders and those who deal in them,' he had said stretching the truth, knowing how superstitious the old man was. 'I advise against the Killing Powder. Surely your gold business is more than profitable?'

'I know nothing of White Powder.' The old man had forced a smile, showing his gums and a few twisted teeth. 'And I don't fear curses, even from them!'

'Good,' Dunross had said, knowing it to be a lie. 'Meanwhile help me to get credit. 50 million for three days is all I want!'

'I will ask among my friends, tai-pan. Perhaps they can help, perhaps we can help together. But don't expect water from an empty well. At what interest?'

'High interest, if it's tomorrow.'

'Not possible, tai-pan.'

'Persuade Tightfist, you're an associate and old friend.'

'Tightfist is the only fornicating friend of Tightfist,' the old man had said sullenly and nothing Dunross could say would change the old man's attitudes.

He reached for the phone. 'What other calls were there, Claudia?' he asked as he dialed.

'Johnjohn at the bank, Phillip and Dianne . . . oh I told you about them. . . . Superintendent Crosse, then every major stockholder we have and every managing director of every subsidiary, most of the Turf Club . . . Travkin, your trainer, it's endless. . . .'

'Just a moment, Claudia.' Dunross held onto his anxiety and said into the phone, in Haklo, 'This is the tai-pan. Is my Old Friend there?'

'Sure, sure, Mr. Dunross,' the American voice said politely in English. 'Thanks for returning the call. He'll be right with you, sir.'

'Mr. Choy, Mr. Paul Choy?'

'Yes sir.'

'Your uncle told me all about you. Welcome to Hong Kong.'

'I . . . here he is sir.'

'Thank you.' Dunross concentrated. He had been asking himself why Paul Choy was with Four Fingers now and not busily engaged in worming his way into Gornt's affairs and why Crosse called and why Johnjohn.

'Tai-pan?'

'Yes, Old Friend. You wanted to speak to me?'

'Yes. Can . . . can we meet this evening?'

Dunross wanted to shout, Have you changed your mind? But good manners forbade it and Chinese did not like phones, always preferring to meet face-to-face. 'Of course. About eight bells, in the middle watch,' he said casually. Near midnight. 'As near as I can,' he added, remembering he was to meet Brian Kwok at 10:45 P.M.

'Good. My wharf. There will be a sampan waiting.'

Dunross replaced the phone, his heart thumping. 'First Crosse, Claudia, then bring in the Kirks. Then we'll go through the list. Set up a conference call with my father, Alastair and Sir Ross, make it for five, that's nine their time and ten in Nice. I'll call David and the others in the States this evening. No need to wake them in the middle of the night.'

'Yes, tai-pan.' Claudia was already dialing. She got Crosse, handed him the phone and left, closing the door after her.

'Yes, Roger?'

'How many times have you been into China?'

The unexpected question startled Dunross for a moment. 'That's all a matter of record,' he said. 'It's easy for you to check.'

'Yes, Ian, but could you recall now? Please.'

'Four times to Canton, to the fair, every year for the last four years. And once to Peking with a trade commission, last year.'

'Did you ever manage to get outside Canton—or Peking?'

'Why?'

'Did you?'

Dunross hesitated. The Noble House had many associations of long standing in China, and many old and trusted friends. Some were now committed Communists. Some were outwardly communists but inwardly totally Chinese and therefore far-seeing, secretive, cautious and nonpolitical. These men ranged in importance up to one in the Presidium. And all of these men, being Chinese, knew that history repeated itself, that eras could change so quickly and the Emperor of this morning could become the running dog of this afternoon, that dynasty followed dynasty at the whim of the gods, that the first of any dynasty inevitably mounted the Dragon throne with bloodstained hands, that an escape route was always to be sought after—and that certain barbarians were Old Friends and to be trusted.

But he knew most all of that the Chinese were a practical people. China needed goods and help. Without goods and help they were defenseless against their historic and only real enemy, Russia.

So many times, because of the special trust in which the Noble House was held, Dunross had been approached officially and unofficially, but always secretly. He had many private potential deals simmering for all kinds of machinery and goods in short supply, including the fleet of jet airliners. Oftentimes he had gone where others could not go. Once he had gone to a meeting in Hangchow, the most beautiful part of China. This was to greet other members of the 49 Club privately, to be wined and dined as honored guests of China. The 49 Club consisted of those companies that had continued to trade with the PRC after 1949, mostly British firms. Britain had recognized Mao Tse-tung's government as the government of China shortly after Chaing Kai-shek abandoned the Mainland and fled to Taiwan. Even so, relations between the two governments had always been strained. But, by definition, relations between *Old Friends* were not, unless an Old Friend betrayed a confidence, or cheated.

'Oh I went on a few side trips,' Dunross said airily, not wanting to lie to the chief of SI. 'Nothing to write home about. Why?'

'Could you tell me where, please.'

'If you're more specific, Roger, certainly,' he replied, his voice hardening. 'We're traders and not politicians and not spies and the Noble House has a special position in Asia. We've been here quite a few years and it's because of traders the Union Jack flies over . . . used to fly over half the earth. What had you in mind, old chap?'

There was a long pause. 'Nothing, nothing in particular. Very well, Ian, I'll wait till we've had the pleasure of reading the papers, then I'll be specific. Thanks, so sorry to trouble you. 'Bye.'

Dunross stared at the phone, troubled. What does Crosse want to know? he asked himself. Many of the deals he had made and would be making certainly would not conform to official government policy in London, or, even more, in Washington. His short-term and long-term attitude toward China clearly was opposed to theirs. What they would consider contraband he did not.

Well, as long as I'm tai-pan, he told himself firmly, come hell or typhoon, our links with China will remain our links with China and that's the end of that. Most politicians in London and Washington just won't realize Chinese are Chinese first and Communist second. And Hong Kong's vital to the peace of Asia.

'Mr. and Mrs. Jamie Kirk, sir.'

Jamie Kirk was a pedantic little man with a pink face and pink hands and a pleasing Scots accent. His wife was tall, big and American.

'Oh so pleased to m—' Kirk began.

'Yes we are, Mr. Dunross,' his wife boomed good-naturedly over him. 'Get to the point, Jamie, honey, Mr. Dunross's a very busy man and we've shopping to do. My husband's got a package for you, sir.'

'Yes, it's from Alan Medford G—'

'He knows it's from Alan Medford Grant, honey,' she said happily, talking over him again. 'Give him the package.'

'Oh. Oh yes and there's a—'

'A letter from him too,' she said. 'Mr. Dunross's very busy so give them to him and we can go shopping.'

'Oh. Yes, well . . .' Kirk handed Dunross the package. It was about fourteen inches by nine and an inch thick. Brown, non-descript and heavily taped. The envelope was sealed with red sealing wax. Dunross recognized the seal. 'Alan said to—'

'To give it to you personally and give you his best wishes,' she said with another laugh. She got up. 'You're so slow, sweet-ness. Well, thank you, Mr. Dunross, come along, hon—'

She stopped, startled as Dunross held up an imperious hand and said with polite though absolute authority, 'What shopping do you want to do, Mrs. Kirk?'

'Eh? Oh. Oh some clothes, er, I want some clothes made and honey needs some shirts an—'

Dunross held up his hand again and punched a button and Claudia was there. 'Take Mrs. Kirk to Sandra Lee at once. She's to take her at once to Lee Foo Tap downstairs and by the Lord God tell him to give Mrs. Kirk the best possible price or I'll have him deported! Mr. Kirk will join her there in a moment!' He took Mrs. Kirk by the arm and before she knew it she was con-tentedly out of the room, Claudia solicitously listening to what she wanted to buy.

Kirk sighed in the silence. It was a deep, long-suffering sigh. 'I wish I could do that,' he said gloomily, then beamed. 'Och aye, tai-pan, you're everything Alan said you were.'

'Oh? I didn't do anything. Your wife wanted to go shopping didn't she?'

'Yes but . . .' After a pause Kirk added, 'Alan said that you should, er, you should read the letter while I'm here. I . . . I didn't tell her that. Do you think I should have?'

'No,' Dunross said kindly. 'Look, Mr. Kirk, I'm sorry to tell you bad news but I'm afraid AMG was killed in a motorcycle accident last Monday.'

Kirk's mouth dropped. 'What?'

'Sorry to have to tell you but I thought you'd better know.'

Kirk stared at the rain streaks, lost in thought. 'How terrible,' he said at length. 'Bloody motorbikes, they're death traps. He was run down?'

'No. He was just found in the road, beside the bike. Sorry.'

'Terrible! Poor old Alan. Dear oh dear! I'm glad you didn't mention it in front of Frances, she's, she was fond of him too. I, er, I . . . perhaps you'd better read this letter then . . . Frances wasn't a great friend so I don't . . . poor old Alan!' He stared down at his hands. The nails were bitten and disfigured. 'Poor old Alan!'

To give Kirk time, Dunross opened the letter. It read: 'My dear Mr. Dunross: This will introduce an old schoolfriend, Jamie Kirk, and his wife Frances. The package he brings, please open in private. I wanted it safely in your hands and Jamie agreed to stop over in Hong Kong. He's to be trusted, as much as one can trust anyone these days. And, please, don't mind about Frances, she's a good sort really, good to my old friend and quite well off from previous husbands which gives Jamie the freedom he requires to sit and to think—a rare, very rare privilege these days. By the way, they're not in my line of work though they know I'm an amateur historian with private means.' Dunross would have smiled but for the fact that he was reading a letter from a dead man. The letter concluded, 'Jamie's a geologist, a marine geologist, one of the best in the world. Ask him about his work, the last years, preferably not with Frances there—not that she's not party to everything he knows but she does carry on a bit. He has some interesting theories that could perhaps benefit the Noble House and your contingency planning. Kindest regards, AMG.'

Dunross looked up. 'AMG says you're old school friends?'

'Oh yes. Yes, we were at school together. Charterhouse actually. Then I went on to Cambridge, he to Oxford. Yes. We've, er, kept in contact over the years, haphazardly, of course. Yes. Have you, er, known him long?'

'About three years. I liked him too. Perhaps you don't want to talk now?'

'Oh. Oh no, that's all right. I'm . . . it's a shock of course but well, life must go on. Old Alan . . . he's a funny sort of laddie isn't he, with all his papers and books and pipe and ash and carpet slippers.' Kirk sadly steepled his fingers. 'I suppose I should say he *was*. It doesn't seem right yet to talk about him in the past tense . . . but I suppose we should. Yes. He always wore carpet slippers. I dinna think I've ever been to his chambers when he wasn't wearing carpet slippers.'

'You mean his flat? I've never been there. We always met in my London office though he did come to Ayr once.' Dunross searched his memory. 'I don't remember him wearing carpet slippers there.'

'Ah, yes, he told me about Ayr, Mr. Dunross. Yes, he told me. It was, er, a high point in his life. You're . . . you're very lucky to have such an estate.'

'Castle Avisyard's not mine, Mr. Kirk, though it's been in the family for more than a hundred years. Dirk Struan bought it for his wife and family—a country seat so to speak.' As always, Dunross felt a sudden glow at the thought of all that loveliness, gentle rolling hills, lakes, moors, forests, glades, six thousand acres or more, good shooting, good hunting and Scotland at its best. 'It's tradition that the current tai-pan's always laird of Avisyard—while he's tai-pan. But, of course, all the families, particularly children of the various families, know it well. Summer holidays . . . Christmas at Avisyard's a wonderful tradition. Whole sheep and sides of beef, haggis at New Year, whiskey and huge roaring fires, the pipes sounding. It's a bonnie place. And a working farm, cattle, milk, butter—and not forgetting the Loch Vey distillery! I wish I could spend more time there— my wife just left today to get things ready for the Christmas vacation. Do you know that part of the world?'

'A wee bit. Mostly I know the Highlands. I know the Highlands better. My family came from Inverness.'

'Ah, then you must visit us when we're in Ayr, Mr. Kirk. AMG says in his letter you're a geologist, one of the best in the world?'

'Oh. Oh he's too kind—was too kind. My, er, my speciality's marine. Yes. With particular emph—' He stopped abruptly.

'What's the matter?'

'Oh, er, nothing, nothing really, but do you think Frances will be all right?'

'Absolutely. Would you like me to tell her about AMG?'

'No. No I can do that later. No, I . . . I, on second thoughts I think I'm going to pretend he's not dead, Mr. Dunross. You need not have told me, then I won't have to spoil her holiday. Yes. That's best, don't you think?' Kirk brightened a little. 'Then we can discover the bad news when we get home.'

'Whatever you wish. You were saying? With particular emphasis on?'

'Oh yes . . . petrology, which is, of course, the broad study of rocks including their interpretation and description. Within petrology my field has been narrowed down more recently to sedimentary rocks. I've, er, I've been on a research project for the last few years as a consultant on Paleozoic sedimentaries, porous ones. Yes. The study concentrated on the eastern coastal shelf of Scotland. AMG thought you might like to hear about it.'

'Of course.' Dunross curbed his impatience. His eyes were looking at the package on his desk. He wanted to open it and call Johnjohn and do a dozen other pressing things. There was so much to do and he did not yet understand the AMG connection between the Noble House and Kirk. 'It sounds very interesting,' he said. 'What was the study for?'

'Eh?' Kirk stared at him, startled. 'Hydrocarbons.' At Dunross's blank look he added hastily, 'Hydrocarbons are only found in porous sedimentary rocks of the Paleozoic era. Oil, Mr. Dunross, crude oil.'

'Oh! You were exploring for oil?'

'Oh no! It was a research project to determine the possibility of hydrocarbons being present offshore. Off Scotland. I'm happy to say I think they'll be there abundantly. Not close in but out in the North Sea.' The small man's pink face became pinker and he mopped his brow. 'Yes. Yes, I think there'll be quite a number of good fields out there.'

Dunross was perplexed, still not seeing the connection. 'Well, I know a little about offshore drilling in the Middle East and the Texas Gulf but out in the North Sea? Good God, Mr. Kirk, that sea's the worst in the world, probably the most fickle in the world, almost always in storm with mountainous seas. How could you drill there? How could you make the rigs safe, how would you supply the rigs, how could you possibly get the oil in bulk ashore, even if you found it? And if you got it ashore, my God, the cost'd be prohibitive.'

'Oh quite right, Mr. Dunross,' Kirk agreed. 'Everything you say's quite right, but then it's not my job to be commercial, just to find our elusive, supremely valuable hydrocarbons.' He added proudly, 'This is the first time we've ever thought they could exist there. Of course, it's still only a theory, my theory—you never know for certain until you drill—but part of my expertise's in seismic interpretation, that's the study of waves resulting from induced explosions, and my approach to the latest findings was a wee bitty unorthodox. . . .'

Dunross listened now with only the surface of his brain, still trying to puzzle out why AMG should consider this important. He allowed Kirk to continue for a while then politely brought him back. 'You've convinced me, Mr. Kirk. I congratulate you. How long are you staying in Hong Kong?'

'Oh. Oh just till Monday. Then, er, then we're going to New Guinea.'

Dunross concentrated, very concerned. 'Where in New Guinea?'

'To a place called Sukanapura, on the north coast, that's in the new Indonesian part. I've been . . .' Kirk smiled. 'Sorry, of course you'd know President Sukarno took over Dutch New Guinea in May.'

'Stolen might be another way of putting it. If it hadn't been for more ill-advised U.S. pressure, Dutch New Guinea'd still be Dutch and far better off, I think. I don't believe it'd be a good idea at all for you and Mrs. Kirk to go there for a while. It's very dicey, the political situation's very unstable and President Sukarno's hostile. The insurrection in Sarawak is Indonesian-sponsored and supported—he's very antagonistic to the West, to all Malaysia, and pro his Marxists. Besides Sukanapura is a hot, rotten, spooky port with lots of disease on top of all the other troubles.'

'Oh you don't have to worry, I have a Scots constitution, and we're invited by the government.'

'My point is that, presently, there's very little government influence.'

'Ah, but there're some very interesting sedimentaries they

want me to look at. You don't have to worry, Mr. Dunross, we're geologists, not political. Everything's arranged—this was the whole purpose of our trip—no need to worry. Well, I should be going.'

'There's . . . I'm having a small cocktail party on Saturday from 7:30 to 9:00 P.M.,' he said. 'Perhaps you and your wife would like to come? Then we can talk further about New Guinea.'

'Oh, oh that's awfully kind of you. I, er, we'd love to. Where wo—'

'I'll send a car for you. Now, perhaps you'd like to join Mrs. Kirk—I won't mention AMG if you're sure that's what you want.'

'Oh! Oh yes. Poor Alan. For a moment, discussing sedimentaries, I'd forgotten about him. Curious, isn't it, how soon one can forget.'

Dunross sent him off with another assistant and closed the door. Carefully he broke the seals of AMG's package. Inside there was an envelope and an inner package. The envelope was addressed: 'Ian Dunross, private and confidential.' Unlike the other letter, which was neatly handwritten, this was typed: 'Dear Mr. Dunross, This comes in haste to you through my old friend Jamie. I've just had some very disquieting news. There is another very serious security leak somewhere in our system, British or American, and it's quite clear our adversaries are stepping up their clandestine attacks. Some of this might even spill over onto me, even to you, hence my anxiety. To you because it could be the existence of our highly classified series of papers has been discovered. Should anything untoward happen to me please call 871-65-65 in Geneva. Ask for Mrs. Riko Gresserhoff. To her, my name is Hans Gresserhoff. Her real name is Riko Anjin. She speaks German, Japanese and English—a little French—and if I'm owed any money please assign it to her. There are certain papers she will give you, some for transmission. Please deliver them personally when convenient. As I said, it's rare to find someone to trust. I trust you. You're the only one on earth who knows about her and her real name. Remember, it is vital that neither this letter nor my previous papers go out of your hands to *anyone*.

'First, to explain about Kirk: Within ten years or so I believe the Arab nations will bury their differences and use the real power they have, not against Israel direct but against the Western world—forcing us into an intolerable position: Do we abandon Israel . . . or do we starve? They use their oil as a weapon of war.

'If they ever manage to work together, a handful of sheiks and feudal kings in Saudi Arabia, Iran, the Persian Gulf States, Iraq, Libya, can, at their whim, cut off Western and Japanese supplies of the one raw material that is indispensable. They have an even more sophisticated opportunity: to raise the price to unprecedented heights and hold our economies to ransom. Oil is the ultimate weapon for Arabia. Unbeatable so long as we're dependent on their oil. Hence my immediate interest in Kirk's theory.

'Nowadays it costs about eight cents American to get one barrel of oil to the surface of an Arabian desert. From the North Sea it would cost seven dollars to bring one barrel ashore, in bulk, to Scotland. If Arabian oil jumped from its present three dollars a barrel on the world market to nine . . . I'm sure you get the point immediately. At once North Sea becomes immensely possible, and a British national treasure.

'Jamie says the fields are to the north and east of Scotland. The port of Aberdeen would be the logical place to bring it ashore. A wise man would start looking at wharfing, real estate, airfields, in Aberdeen. Don't worry about bad weather, helicopters will be the connecting links to the rigs. Expensive yes, but viable. Further, if you will accept my forecast that Labour will win the next election because of the Profumo scandal . . .'

The case had filled the newspapers. Six months before, in March, the Secretary of State for War, John Profumo, had formally denied that he had ever had an affair with a notorious call girl, Christine Keeler, one of several girls who had suddenly sprung to international prominence with their procurer, Stephen Ward—up to that time just a well-known osteopath in London's high society. Unsubstantiated rumors began to circulate that the girl had also been having an affair with one of the Soviet attachés, a well-known KGB agent, Commander Yevgeny Ivanov, who had been recalled to Russia the previous December. In the uproar that followed, Profumo resigned, and Stephen Ward committed suicide.

'It is curious that the affair was revealed to the press at the perfect time for the Soviets,' Grant continued. 'I have no proof, yet, but it's not just a coincidence in my opinion. Remember it is Soviet doctrine to fragment countries—North Korea and South, East Germany and West, and so on—then to let their indoctrinated underlings do their work for them. So I think the pro-Soviet Socialists will help fragment Britain into England, Scotland, Wales and south and north Ireland (watch Eire and Northern Ireland which is a ready-made arena for Soviet merrymaking).

'Now for my suggested Contingency Plan One for the Noble House: To be circumspect about England and to concentrate on Scotland as a base. *North Sea oil would make Scotland abundantly self-sufficient.* The population is small, hardy and nationalistic. As an entity, Scotland would be practical now, and defensible—with an abundant exportable oil supply. A strong Scotland could perhaps help tip the scales and help a tottering England . . . our poor country, Mr. Dunross! I fear greatly for England.

'Perhaps this is another of my farfetched theories. But reconsider Scotland, Aberdeen, in the light of a new North Sea.'

'Ridiculous!' Dunross exploded and he stopped reading for a moment, his mind swept, then cautioned himself, don't go off at half cock! AMG's farfetched sometimes, given to exaggeration, he's a right-wing imperialist who sees fifteen Reds under every bed. But what he says could be possible. If it's possible, then it must be considered. If there were a vast worldwide oil shortage and we were prepared, we could make a fortune, he told himself, his excitement growing. It'd be easy to buy into Aberdeen now, easy to begin a calculated retreat from London without hurting anything—Edinburgh has all the modern amenities of banking, communications, ports, airfields, that we'd need to operate efficiently. Scotland for the Scots, with abundant oil for export? Completely viable, but not separate, somehow within a strong Britain. But if the city of London Parliament and Threadneedle Street become left-wing choked . . .

The hair on the nape of his neck twisted at the thought of Britain being buried under a shroud of left-wing socialism. What about Robin Grey? Or Julian Broadhurst? he asked himself, chilled. Certainly they'd nationalize everything, they'd grab North Sea oil, if any, and put Hong Kong on the block—they've already said they would.

With an effort he tabled that thought for later, turned the page and read on. 'Next, I think I've identified three of your Sevrin moles. The information was expensive—I may need extra money before Christmas—and I am not certain of the accuracy (I'm trying to cross-check at once, realizing the importance to you). The moles are believed to be: Jason Plumm of a company called Asian Properties; Lionel Tuke in the telephone company; and Jacques deVille in Struan's . . .'

'Impossible!' Dunross burst out loud. 'AMG's gone mad! Plumm's as impossible as Jacques, totally absolutely impossible. There's no way they co—'

His private phone began ringing. Automatically he picked it up. 'Yes?'

'This is the overseas operator calling Mr. Dunross.'

'Who's calling him please?' he snapped.

'Will Mr. Dunross accept a collect call from Sydney, Australia, from a Mr. Duncan Dunross?'

The tai-pan's heart missed a beat. 'Of course! Hello, Duncan . . . Duncan?'

'Father?'

'Hello, my son, are you all right?'

'Oh yes, sir, absolutely!' he heard his son say and his anxiety fled. 'I'm sorry to call you during the working day, Father, but my Monday flight's overbooked an—'

'Dammit, you have a confirmed booking, laddie. I'll get p—'

'No, Father, thank you, that's perfectly all right. Now I'm on an earlier one. I'm on Singapore Airlines Flight 6 which arrives Hong Kong at noon. Don't bother to meet me, I'll get a taxi an—'

'Look for the car, Duncan. Lee Choy will be there. But come to the office before you go home, eh?'

'All right. I've validated my tickets and everything.'

Dunross heard the pride in his son's voice and it warmed him. 'Good. Well done. By the way, cousin Linbar will be arriving tomorrow on Qantas at 8:00 P.M. your time. He'll be staying at the house too.' Struan's had had a company house in Sydney since 1900 and a permanent office there since the eighties. Hag Struan had gone into partnership with an immensely wealthy wheat farmer named Bill Scragger and their company had flourished until the crash of 1929. 'Did you have a good holiday?'

'Oh smashing! Smashing, yes, I want to come back next year. I met a smashing girl, Father.'

'Oh?' Half of Dunross wanted to smile, the other half was still locked into the nightmare possibility that Jacques was a traitor, and if traitor and part of Sevrin, was he the one who supplied some of their innermost secrets to Linc Bartlett? No, Jacques couldn't have. He couldn't possibly have known about our bank holdings. Who knows about those? Who wou—

'Father?'

'Yes, Duncan?'

He heard the hesitancy, then his son said in a run, trying to sound manly, 'Is it all right for a fellow to have a girl friend a little older than himself?'

Dunross smiled gently and started to dismiss the thought as his son was only just fifteen, but then he remembered Elegant Jade when he himself was not quite fifteen, surely more of a man than Duncan. Not necessarily, he thought honestly. Duncan's tall and growing and just as much a man. And didn't I love her to madness that year and the next year and didn't I almost die the next year when she vanished? 'Well,' he said as an equal, 'it really depends on who the girl is, how old the man is and how old the girl is.'

'Oh.' There was a long pause. 'She's eighteen.'

Dunross was greatly relieved. That means she's old enough to know better, he thought. 'I'd say that would be perfect,' he told Duncan in the same voice, 'particularly if the fellow was about sixteen, tall, strong and knew the facts of life.'

'Oh. Oh I didn't . . . oh! I wouldn't . . .'

'I wasn't being critical, laddie, just answering your question. A man has to be careful in this world, and girl friends should be chosen carefully. Where did you meet her?'

'She was on the station. Her name's Sheila.'

Dunross suppressed a smile. Girls in Australia were referred to as sheilas just as in England they were called birds. 'That's a nice name,' he said. 'Sheila what?'

'Sheila Scragger. She's a niece of old Mr. Tom and she's on a visit from England. She's training to be a nurse at Guy's Hospital. She was ever so super to me and Paldoon's super too. I really can't thank you enough for arranging such a super holiday.' Paldoon, the Scragger ranch, or station as it was called in Australia, was the only property they had managed to save from the crash. Paldoon was five hundred miles southwest of Sydney near the Murray River in Australia's rice lands, sixty thousand acres—thirty thousand head of sheep, two thousand acres of wheat and a thousand head of cattle—and the greatest place for a youth to holiday, working all day from dawn to dusk, mustering the sheep or cattle on horseback, galloping twenty miles in any direction and still on your own property.

'Give Tom Scragger my regards and make sure you send him a bottle of whiskey before you leave.'

'Oh I sent him a case, is that all right?'

Dunross laughed. 'Well laddie, a bottle would have done just as well, but a case is perfect. Call me if there's any change in your flight. You did very well to get it organized yourself, very good. Oh by the way, Mama and Glenna went to London today, with Aunt Kathy, so you'll have to go back to school alone an—'

'Oh jolly good, Father,' his son said happily. 'After all, I'm a man now and almost at university!'

'Yes, yes you are.' A small sweet sadness touched Dunross as he sat in his high chair, AMG's letter in his hand but forgotten. 'Are you all right for money?'

'Oh yes. I hardly spent anything on the station except for a beer or two. Father, don't tell Mother about my girl.'

'All right. Or Adryon,' he said and at once his chest tightened at the thought of Martin Haply together with Adryon and how they went off hand-in-hand. 'You should tell Adryon yourself.'

'Oh super, I'd forgotten her. How is she?'

'She's in good shape,' Dunross said, ordering himself to be adult, wise, and not to worry and it was all quite normal for boys and girls to be boys and girls. Yes, but Christ it's difficult if you're the father. 'Well, Duncan, see you Monday! Thanks for calling.'

'Oh yes, and Father, Sheila drove me up to Sydney. She . . . she's staying the weekend with friends and going to see me off! Tonight we're going to a movie, *Lawrence of Arabia*, have you seen it?'

'Yes, it's just come to Hong Kong, you'll enjoy that.'

'Oh super! Well, good-bye, Father, have to run . . . love you!'

'Love you,' he said but the connection was already dead.

How lucky I am with my family, my wife and kids, Dunross thought, and at once added, Please God let nothing happen to them!

With an effort he looked back at the letter. It's impossible for Jason Plumm or Jacques to be Communist spies, he told himself. Nothing they've ever said or done would indicate that. Lionel Tuke? No, not him either. I only know him casually. He's an ugly, unpopular fellow who keeps to himself but he's on the cricket team, a member of the Turf Club and he's been out here since the thirties. Wasn't he even interned at Stanley between '42 and '45? Maybe him, but the other two? Impossible!

I'm sorry AMG's dead. I'd call him right now about Jacques and . . .

First finish the letter, then consider the parts, he ordered himself. Be correct, be efficient. Good God! Duncan and an eighteen-year-old sheila! Thank God it wasn't Tom Scragger's youngest. How old is Priscilla now? Fourteen, pretty, built much older. Girls seem to mature early Down Under.

He exhaled. I wonder if I should do for Duncan what Chen-chen did for me.

The letter continued, '. . . As I've said, I'm not completely sure but my source is usually impeccable.

'I'm sorry to say the espionage war has hotted up since we uncovered and caught the spies Blake, Vassal—the Admiralty cipher clerk—and Philby, Burgess and Maclean all defected. They've all been seen in Moscow by the way. Expect spying to increase radically in Asia. (We were able to peg First Secretary Skripov of the Soviet Embassy in Canberra, Australia, and order him out of the country in February. This broke his Australian ring which was, I believe, tied to your Sevrin and further involved in Borneo and Indonesia.)

'The free world is abundantly infiltrated now. MI-5 and MI-6 are tainted. Even the CIA. While we've been naive and trusting, our opponents realized early that the future balance would depend on economic power as well as military power, and so they set out to acquire—steal—our industrial secrets.

'Curiously our free-world media fail dismally to point out that all Soviet advances are based originally on one of our stolen inventions or techniques, that without our grain they starve,

807

and without our vast and ever-growing financial assistance and credits to buy grains and technology they cannot fuel and refuel their whole military-industrial infrastructure which keeps their empire and people enthralled.

'I recommend you use your contacts in China to cement them to you further. The Soviets increasingly view China as their number one enemy. Equally strangely, they no longer seem to have that paranoiac fear of the U.S. which is, without doubt, now the strongest military and economic power in the world. China, which is economically and militarily weak, except in numbers of available soldiers, really presents no military threat to them. Even so China petrifies them.

'One reason is the five thousand miles of border they share. Another is national guilt over the vast areas of historic Chinese territory Soviet Russia has swallowed over the centuries; another is the knowledge that the Chinese are a patient people with long memories. One day the Chinese will take back their lands. They have always taken back their lands when it was militarily feasible to do so. I've pointed out many times that the cornerstone of Soviet (Imperialist) politics is to isolate and fragment China to keep her weak. Their great bugaboo is a tripartite alliance between China, Japan and the U.S. Your Noble House should work to promote that. (Also a Common Market between the U.S., Mexico and Canada, totally essential, in my opinion, to a stable American continent.) Where else but through Hong Kong—and therefore your hands—will all the inward wealth to China go?

'Last, back to Sevrin: I have taken a major risk and approached our most priceless asset in the inner core of the KGB's ultra-secret Department 5. I have just heard back today that the identity of *Arthur*, Sevrin's leader, is Classification One, beyond even his grasp. The only clue he could give me was that the man was English and one of his initials is *R*. Not much to go on I'm afraid.

'I look forward to seeing you. Remember, my papers must never pass into the hands of anyone else. Regards, AMG.'

Dunross committed the Geneva phone number to memory, encoded it in his address book and lit a match. He watched the airmail paper curl and begin to burn.

R. Robert Ralph Richard Robin Rod Roy Rex Rupert Red

Rodney and always back to Roger. And Robert. Robert Armstrong or Roger Crosse or—or who?

Holy Christ, Dunross thought, feeling weak.

'Geneva 871-65-65, station to station,' he said into his private phone. Tiredness engulfed him. His sleep last night had been disturbed, his dreams dragging him back to war, back to his flaming cockpit, the smell of burning in his nostrils, then waking, chilled, listening to the rain, soon to get up silently, Penn sleeping soundly, the Great House quiet except for old Ah Tat who, as always, had his tea made. Then to the track and chased all day, his enemies closing in and nothing but bad news. Poor old John Chen, he thought, then made the effort to push his weariness away. Perhaps I can kip for an hour between five and six. I'll need all my wits tonight.

The operator made the connections and he heard the number ringing.

'*Ja?*' the gentle voice said.

'*Hier ist* Herr Dunross *im* Hong Kong. Frau Gresserhoff *bitte,*' he said in good German.

'Oh!' There was a long pause. '*Ich bin* Frau Gresserhoff. Tai-pan?'

'*Ah so desu! Ohayo gozaimasu. Anata wa Anjin Riko-san?*' he asked, his Japanese accent excellent. Good morning. Your name is also Riko Anjin?

'*Hai. Hai, dozo. Ah, nihongo wa jotzu desu.*' Yes. Oh you speak Japanese very well.

'*Iye, sukoshi, gomen nasai.*' No, sorry, only a little. As part of his training, he had spent two years in their Tokyo office. 'Ah, so sorry,' he continued in Japanese, 'but I'm calling about Mr. Gresserhoff. Have you heard?'

'Yes.' He could hear the sadness. 'Yes. I heard on Monday.'

'I've just received a letter from him. He said you have some, some things for me?' he asked cautiously.

'Yes, tai-pan. Yes I have.'

'Would it be possible for you to bring them here? So sorry, but I cannot come to you.'

'Yes. Yes of course,' she said hesitantly, her Japanese soft and pleasing. 'When should I come?'

'As soon as possible. If you go to our office on Avenue Bern in a couple of hours, say at noon, there will be tickets and money for you. I believe there's a Swissair connection that leaves this afternoon—if that were possible.'

Again the hesitation. He waited patiently. AMG's letter writhed in the ashtray as it burned. 'Yes,' she said. 'That would be possible.'

'I'll make all the arrangements for you. Would you like someone to travel with you?'

'No, no thank you,' she said, her voice so quiet that he had to cup one hand over his ear to hear better. 'Please excuse me for causing all this trouble. I can make the arrangements.'

'Truly, it's no trouble,' he said, pleased that his Japanese was flowing and colloquial. 'Please go to my office at noon. . . . By the way, the weather here is warm and wet. Ah, so sorry, please excuse me for asking but is your passport Swiss or Japanese, and under what name would you travel?'

An even longer pause. 'I would . . . I think I should . . . It would be Swiss, my travel name should be Riko Gresserhoff.'

'Thank you Mrs. Gresserhoff. I look forward to seeing you. *Kiyoskette*,' he ended. Have a safe journey.

Thoughtfully he put the phone back onto its cradle. The last of AMG's letter twisted and died with a thread of smoke. Carefully he crumbled the ashes into powder.

Now what about Jacques?

46

5:45 P.M.:

Jacques deVille plodded up the marble stairs of the Mandarin Hotel to the mezzanine floor, packed with people having late tea.

He took off his raincoat and went through the crowds, feeling very old. He had just talked to his wife, Susanne, in Nice. The specialist from Paris had made another examination of Avril and thought that her internal injuries might not be as bad as first thought.

'He says we have to be patient,' Susanne had told him in her gushing Parisienne French. 'But Mother of God, how can we be? The poor child's distraught and losing her mind. She keeps saying, "But I was the driver, it was me, Mumma, me, but for me my Borge would be alive, but for me. . . ." I fear for her, *chéri!*'

'Does she know yet that her . . . about her inside?'

'No, not yet. The doctor says not to tell her until he's sure.' Susanne had begun to cry.

In agony he had calmed her as best he could and said he would call her back in an hour. For a while he had considered what he should do, then he had made arrangements and had left his office and come here.

The public phone booth near the newsstand was occupied so he bought an afternoon paper and glanced at the headlines. Twenty killed in resettlement mud slides above Aberdeen . . . Rain to continue . . . Will Saturday's Great Race be canceled? . . . JFK warns Soviets not to interfere in Vietnam . . . Atom Test Ban Treaty signed in Moscow by Dean Rusk, Andrei Gromyko and Sir Alec Douglas-Home, rejected by France and

811

China . . . Malaysian Communists step up offensive . . . Kennedy's second son, born prematurely, dies . . . Manhunt for the British Great Train Robbers continues . . . Profumo scandal damages Conservative Party . . .

'Excuse me, sir, are you waiting for the phone?' an American woman asked from behind him.

'Oh, oh yes, thank you, sorry! I didn't see that it was empty.' He went into the booth, closed the door, put in the coin and dialed. The ringing tone began. He felt his anxiety rising.

'Yes?'

'Mr. Lop-sing please,' he said, not sure of the voice yet.

'There's no Mr. Lop-*ting* here. Sorry, you have a wrong number.'

'I want to leave a message,' he said, relieved to recognize Suslev's voice.

'You have a wrong number. Look in your phone book.'

When the code was completed correctly, he began, 'Sorry to c—'

'What is your number?' interrupted him harshly.

Jacques gave it at once.

'Is it a phone booth?'

'Yes.' Immediately the phone clicked off. As he hung up he felt a sudden sweat on his hands. Suslev's number was only to be used in an emergency but this was an emergency. He stared at the phone.

'Excuse me, sir,' the American woman called out through the glass doors. 'Can I use the phone? I won't be a moment.'

'Oh! Oh I'm—I won't be a second,' Jacques said, momentarily flustered. He saw that three Chinese were waiting impatiently behind her now. They stared at him balefully. 'I'm . . . I'll just be a second.' He reclosed the door, sweat on his back. He waited and waited and waited and then the phone rang. 'Hello?'

'What's the emergency?'

'I . . . I just heard from Nice.' Carefully Jacques told Suslev about his conversation with his wife without mentioning names. 'I'm going there at once on the evening flight—and I thought I'd better tell you personally so the—'

'No, this evening's too soon. Book tomorrow, on the evening flight.'

Jacques felt his world collapse. 'But I talked to the tai-pan a few minutes ago and he said it was all right for me to go tonight. I'm booked. I can be back in three days, she really sounded awful on the phone. Don't you th—'

'No!' Suslev told him more sharply. 'I will call you tonight as arranged. This could all have waited till then. Don't use this number again unless there's a real emergency!'

Jacques opened his mouth to answer hotly but the phone was already dead. He had heard the anger. But this is an emergency, he told himself, enraged, beginning to redial. Susanne needs me there and so does Avril. And the tai-pan was all for it.

'Good idea, Jacques,' Dunross had said at once. 'Take all the time you need. Andrew can cover for you.'

And now . . . *Merde*, what do I do? Suslev's not my keeper! Isn't he?

DeVille stopped dialing, his sweat chilling, and hung up.

'Are you finished, sir?' the American woman called out with her insistent smile. She was in her fifties, her hair fashionably blue. 'There's a line waiting.'

'Oh . . . oh yes, sorry.' He fought the door open.

'You forgot your paper, sir,' she said politely.

'Oh, oh thank you.' Jacques deVille reached back for it and came out in misery. At once all the Chinese, three men and a woman, surged forward, elbowing him and the American lady out of the way. A heavyset matron got to the door first and slammed it shut behind her, the others crowding to be next.

'Hey . . . it was my turn,' the American woman began angrily but they paid no attention to her except to curse her and her antecedents openly and with great vulgarity.

Suslev was standing in the sleazy Kowloon apartment that was one of Arthur's safe houses, his heart still thumping from the suddenness of the call. There was a damp, musky, soiled smell of ancient cooking in the room and he stared down at the phone, furious with Jacques deVille. Stupid motherless turd. Jacques is becoming a liability. Tonight I'll tell Arthur what should be done with him. The sooner the better! Yes, and the sooner you calm down yourself the better, he cautioned himself. Angry people make mistakes. Put away your anger!

813

With an effort, he did just that and went out onto the dim, paint-peeled landing, locking the door behind him. Another key unlocked Ginny Fu's door next to his.

'You want vodka?' she asked with her saucy smile.

'Yes.' He grinned back, pleased to look at her. She was sitting cross-legged on the old sofa and wore only a smile. They had been kissing when his phone had rung the first time. There were two phones in her apartment. Hers and the other one, the secret one in the cupboard that only he used and answered. Arthur had told him it was safe, bootlegged, unlisted and impossible to bug. Even so, Suslev only used the other apartment and its phone for emergencies.

Matyeryebyets, Jacques, he thought, still edgy from the sudden shrilling of his private phone.

'Drink, *tovarich*,' Ginny said, offering the glass. 'Then drink me, *heya*?'

He grinned back, took the vodka and ran an appreciative hand over her cute little rump. 'Ginny, *golubushka*, you're a good girl.'

'You bet! I best girl for you.' She reached up and fondled his earlobe. 'We jig-jig *heya*?'

'Why not?' He drank the fiery liquid sparingly, wanting it to last. Her tiny nimble fingers were undoing his shirt. He stopped her for a moment and kissed her, she welcoming his kiss and returning it equally. 'Wait till clothes off, *heya*?' she chuckled.

'Next week I go, eh?' he said, holding her in his bear hug. 'How about you coming too, eh? The holiday I've always promised you?'

'Oh? Oh truly?' Her smile was immense. 'Wen? Wen? You no tease?'

'You can come with me. We'll stop in Manila, our first stop's Manila, then north and back here in a month.'

'Oh a real month . . . oh Gregy!' She hugged him with all her might. 'I make best ship's captain girl all China!'

'Yes, yes you will.'

'Wen go . . . wen we go?'

'Next week. I'll tell you when.'

'Good. Tomorrow I go get passport th—'

'No, no passport, Ginny. They'll never give it to you. Those *viblyadoks*'ll stop you. They won't ever let you come with me . . .

oh no, *golubushka*, those dirty police will never let you come with me.'

'Then wat I do, *heya?*'

'I'll smuggle you aboard in a chest!' His laugh was rich. 'Or perhaps on a magic carpet. Eh?'

She peered up at him, her dark eyes wide and brimming and anxious. 'True you take me? True? One month on your ship, *heya?*'

'At least a month. But don't tell anyone. The police watch me all the time and if they know, you won't be able to come with me. Understand?'

'All gods bear witness not tell a weevil, not even my mother,' Ginny swore vehemently, then hugged him again with the vastness of her happiness. 'Eeeee, I get huge face as captain's lady!' Another hug and then she let her fingers stray and he jerked involuntarily. She laughed and began to undress him again. 'I give you best time, best.'

She used her fingers and her lips expertly, probing and touching and withdrawing and moving against him, concentrating on her task until he cried out and became one with the gods in the Clouds and the Rain. Her hands and lips stayed on him, not leaving while the last tiny fraction of pleasure remained. Then she ceased and curled against him and listened to the deepness of his breathing, very contented that she had done her job well. She, herself, she had not experienced the Clouds and the Rain though she had pretended to several times, to increase his pleasure. Only twice in all the times that they had pillowed had she reached the zenith and both times she had been very drunk and not really sure if she had or if she had not. It was only with Third Nighttime Sandwich Cook Tok at the Victoria and Albert that she would zenith every time. All gods bless my joss, she thought happily. With one month holiday and the extra money Gregor will give me, and, with joss, one more year with him, we'll have enough money to open our own restaurant and I can have sons and grandsons and become one with the gods. Oh how lucky I am!

She was tired now for she had had to work hard, so she curled more comfortably against him, closed her eyes, liking him, thankful to the gods that they had helped her to overcome her distaste for his size and his white, toadlike skin and his rancid

815

body smell. Thank all gods, she thought happily as she wafted into sleep.

Suslev was not sleeping. He was just drifting, his mind and his body at peace. The day had been good and a little very bad. After meeting with Crosse at the racetrack he had returned to his ship, appalled that there could be a security leak from the *Ivanov*. He had encoded Crosse's information about Operation Dry Run and all the other things and sent it off in the privacy of his cabin. Incoming messages told him that Voranski would not be replaced until the next visit of the *Sovetsky Ivanov*, that the special psychochemical expert, Koronski, was available to arrive from Bangkok at twelve hours' notice, and that he, Suslev, was to assume direction of Sevrin and liaise with Arthur direct. 'Do not fail to obtain copies of the AMG files.'

He remembered how a chill had gone through him at that 'do not fail.' So few failures, so many successes, but only the failures remembered. Where was the security leak aboard? Who read the AMG file apart from me? Only Dimitri Metkin, my second-in-command. It could not be him. The leak must be from elsewhere.

How far to trust Crosse?

Not far, but that man's clearly the most priceless asset we have in the capitalistic camp of Asia and must be protected at all costs.

The feel of Ginny against him was pleasing. She was breathing softly, a tiny jerk from time to time, her breast rising and falling. His eyes went through the doorway to the old-fashioned clock that stood in a niche of one of the untidy kitchen shelves among all the half-used bottles and tins and containers. The kitchen was in an alcove off the living room. Here in the only bedroom, the bed was huge and almost filled the room. He had bought it for her when he had begun with her two, almost three years ago. It was a good bed, clean, soft but not too soft, a welcome change from his bunk aboard.

And Ginny, she was welcome too. Pliant, easygoing, no trouble. Her blue-black hair was cut short and straight across her high forehead, the way he liked it—such a contast to Vertinskaya, his mistress in Vladivostok, her with her sloe, hazel eyes, long wavy dark brown hair and the temper of a wildcat, her mother a true Princess Zergeyev and her father an insignificant half-caste Chinese shopkeeper who had bought the mother at an auction when she was thirteen. She had been on one of the cattle trucks of children fleeing Russia after the holocaust of '17.

Liberation, not holocaust, he told himself happily. Ah, but it's good to bed the daughter of a Princess Zergeyev when you're the grandson of a peasant off Zergeyev lands.

Thinking of the Zergeyevs reminded him of Alexi Travkin. He smiled to himself. Poor Travkin, such a fool! Would they really release the Princess Nestorova, his wife, to Hong Kong at Christmas? I doubt it. Perhaps they will and then poor Travkin will die of shock to see that little old hag of the snows, toothless, wrinkled and arthritic. Better to spare him that agony, he thought compassionately. Travkin's Russian and not a bad man.

Again he looked at the clock. Now it read 6:20. He smiled to himself. Nothing to do for a few hours but sleep and eat and think and plan. Then the oh so careful meeting with the English MP and, late tonight, seeing Arthur again. He chuckled. It amused him very much to know secrets Arthur did not know. But then Arthur holds back secrets too, he thought without anger. Perhaps he already knows about the MPs. He's smart, very smart, and doesn't trust me either.

That's the great law: Never trust another—man, woman or child—if you want to stay alive and safe and out of enemy clutches.

I'm safe because I *know* people, know how to keep a closed mouth and know how to further State policy as part of my own life plan.

So many wonderful plans to effect. So many exciting coups to precipitate and be part of. And then there's Sevrin . . .

Again he chuckled and Ginny stirred. 'Go to sleep, little princess,' he whispered soothingly as to a child. 'Go to sleep.'

Obediently she did not truly waken, just brushed her hair out of her eyes and snuggled more comfortably.

Suslev let his eyes close, her body sweet against him. He let his arm rest across her loins. The rain had lessened during the afternoon. Now he noticed it had stopped. He yawned as he went to sleep, knowing the storm had not yet ended its work.

47

Robert Armstrong drained his beer. 'Another,' he called out blearily, feigning drunkenness. He was in the Good Luck Girl-friend, a crowded, noisy Wanchai bar on the waterfront, filled with American sailors from the nuclear carrier. Chinese hostesses plied the customers with drink and accepted banter and touch and watered drinks in return at high cost. Occasionally one of them would order a real whiskey and show it to her partner to prove that this was a good bar and they were not being cheated.

Above the bar were rooms but it was not wise for sailors to go to them. Not all of the girls were clean or careful, not from choice just from ignorance. And, late at night, you could be rolled though only the very drunk were robbed. After all, there was no need: sailors were ready to spend everything they had.

'You want jig-jig?' the overpainted child asked him.

Dew neh loh moh on all your ancestors, he wanted to tell her. You should be home in bed with some schoolbooks. But he did not say it. That would do no good. In all probability her parents had gratefully arranged this job for her so that all the family could survive just a little. 'You want drink?' he said instead, hiding that he could speak Cantonese.

'Scottish, Scottish,' the child called out imperiously.

'Why not get tea and I'll give you the money anyway,' he said sourly.

'Fornicate all gods and the mothers of gods I not a cheater!' Haughtily the child offered the grimy glass the waiter had slapped down. It did contain cheap but real whiskey. She drained it without a grimace. 'Waiter! Another Scottish and another beer! You drink, I drink, then we jig-jig.'

Armstrong looked at her. 'What's your name?'

'Lily. Lily Chop. Twenty-five dollars short time.'

'How old are you?'

'Old. How old are you?'

'Nineteen.'

'Huh, coppers always lie!'

'How'd you know I'm a copper?'

'Boss tell me. Only twenty dollar, *heya?*'

'Who's the boss? Which one's he?'

'She. Behind the bar. She mama-*san.*'

Armstrong peered through the smoke. The woman was lean and scrawny and in her fifties, sweating and working hard, keeping up a running vulgar banter with the sailors as she filled the orders. 'How'd she know I was a copper?'

Again Lily shrugged. 'Listen, she tell me keep you happy or I out in street. We go upstairs now, *heya?* On house, no twenty dollar.' The child got up. He could see her fear now.'

'Sit down,' he ordered.

She sat, even more afraid. 'If I not pleeze she throw m—'

'You please me.' Armstrong sighed. It was an old ploy. If you went, you paid, if you didn't go, you paid and the boss always sent a young one. He passed over fifty dollars. 'Here. Go and give it to the mama-*san* with my thanks. Tell her I can't jig-jig now because I've got my monthly! Honorable Red's with me.'

Lily gawked at him then cackled like an old woman. 'Eeeee, fornicate all gods that's a good one!' She went off, hard put to walk on her high heels, her brassy *cheong-sam* slit very· high, showing her thin, very thin legs and buttocks.

Armstrong finished his beer, paid his bill and got to his feet. At once his table was claimed and he pushed through the sweating, shouting sailors for the door.

'You welcome anytime,' the mama-*san* called out as he passed her.

'Sure,' he called back without malice.

The rain was just a thin drizzle now and the day growing dark. On the street were many more raucous sailors, all of them American—British sailors had been ordered out of this area for the first few days by their captains. His skin felt wet and hot under his raincoat. In a moment he left Gloucester Road and the waterfront and strolled through the crowds up O'Brien Road, splashing through the puddles, the city smelling good and clean and washed. At the corner he turned into Lochart Road and at length found the alley he sought. It was busy, as usual, with street stalls and shops and scrawny dogs, chickens packed into cages, dried fried ducks and meats hanging from hooks, vegetables and fruits. Just inside the mouth of the alley was a small stall with stools under a canvas overhang to keep off the drizzle. He nodded at the owner, chose a shadowed corner, ordered a bowl of Singapore noodles—fine, lightly fried vermicelli-like noodles, dry, with chili and spices and chopped shrimps and fresh vegetables—and began to wait.

Brian Kwok.

Always back to Brian Kwok.

And always back to the 40,000 in used notes that he had found in his desk drawer, the one he always kept locked.

Concentrate, he told himself, or you'll slip. You'll make a mistake. You can't afford a mistake!

He was weary and felt an overpowering dirtiness that soap and hot water would not cleanse away. With an effort he forced his eyes to seek his prey, his ears to hear the street sounds, and his nose to enjoy the food.

He had just finished the bowl when he saw the American sailor. The man was thin and wore glasses and he towered over the Chinese pedestrians even though he walked with a slight stoop. His arm was around a street girl. She held an umbrella over them and was tugging at him.

'No, not this way, baby,' she pleaded. 'My room other way . . . unnerstan'?'

'Sure, honey, but first we go this way then we'll go your way. Huh? Come on, darlin'.'

Armstrong hunched deeper into the shadows. He watched them approach, wondering if this was the one. The man's accent was Southern and sweet-sounding and he was in his late twenties. As he strolled along the busy street he looked this way and that, seeking his bearings. Then Armstrong saw him spot the tailor's shop on one corner of the alley that was called Pop-ting's Handmade Suits, and, opposite it, a small, open-faced restaurant lit with bare bulbs and with a crudely written sign nailed to a post: WELCOME TO AMERICAN SAILORS. The bold column of Chinese characters over the door read: 'A Thousand

820

Years' Health to Mao Tse-tung Restaurant.'

'C'mon, honey,' the sailor said, brightening. 'Let's have a beer here.'

'No good place, baby, better come my bar, *heya*? Bett—'

'Goddamnit we're having a beer here.' He went into the open shop and sat at one of the plastic tables, bulky in his raincoat. Sullenly she followed. 'Beer. Two beers! San Miguel, huh? You savvy huh?'

From where he sat, Armstrong could see them both clearly. One of the tables was filled with four coolies who noisily sucked noodles and soup into their mouths. They glanced at the sailor and the girl briefly. One made an obscene remark and the others laughed. The girl blushed, turning her back to them. The sailor hummed as he looked around carefully, sipping his beer, then stood up. 'I gotta use the can.' Unerringly he went to the back through the flyblown string curtain, the counterman watching him sourly. Armstrong sighed and relaxed. The trap was sprung.

In a moment the sailor returned. 'C'mon,' he said, 'let's get outta here.' He drained his glass, paid, and they went off arm in arm again the way they had come.

'You want more S'pore noodles?' the stall keeper asked Armstrong rudely, his hostile eyes just slits in his high-boned face.

'No thanks. Just another beer.'

'No beer.'

'Fornicate you and all your line,' Armstrong hissed in perfect gutter Cantonese. 'Am I a fool from the Golden Mountain? No, I'm a guest in your fornicating restaurant. Get me a fornicating beer or I'll have my men slit your Secret Sack and feed those peanuts you call your treasure to the nearest dog!'

The man said nothing. Sullenly he went to the next street stall and got a San Miguel and brought it back and set it on the counter, opening it. The other diners were still gaping at Armstrong. Abruptly he hawked loudly and spat and put his cold blue eyes on the man nearest him. He saw him shiver and look away. Uneasily the others went back to their bowls too, uncomfortable to be in the presence of a barbarian policeman who had the bad manners to swear so colloquially in their tongue.

821

Armstrong eased more comfortably on the stool, then let his eyes range the road and the alley, waiting patiently.

He did not have long to wait before he saw the small, squat, chunky European coming up the alley, keeping to the side, stopping and peering into the storefront of a cheap shoe shop behind the street stalls that crowded the narrow roadway.

Ah, he's a professional, Armstrong thought, very pleased, knowing the man was using the glass as a mirror to case the restaurant. The man took his time. He wore a shapeless plastic raincoat and hat and appeared nondescript. His body was hidden for a moment as a coolie swayed past him with huge bundles on either end of the bamboo pole on his shoulders. Armstrong noticed his knotted calves, varicose-veined, as he watched the feet of the other man. They moved and he walked out of the alley, covered by the coolie, and did not stop, just continued up the road.

He's very good, the policeman thought admiringly, still having him in sight. This bugger's done this before. Must be KGB to be this smart. Well, it won't be long now, my fine fellow, before you're hooked, he told himself without rancor, as a fisherman would seeing a fat trout teasing the bait.

The man was shop-watching again. Come along, little fish.

The man was acting just like a trout. He made several passes and went away and came back but always very carefully and without attracting attention. At last he went into the open-faced restaurant and sat down and ordered a beer. Armstrong sighed again, happy now.

It seemed to take the man an interminable time before he, too, got up, asked where the toilet was, walked through the few diners and went under the bead curtain. In time he reappeared and went for his table. At once the four coolie diners fell on him from behind, pinioning his arms and holding him helpless, while another strapped a stiff collar around his neck. Other diners, real customers, and not undercover SI police, gaped, one dropped his chopsticks, a couple fled and the others froze.

Armstrong got up from his stool leisurely and walked over. He saw the tough-looking Chinese behind the counter take off his apron. 'Shut up, you bastard,' the fellow said in Russian to the man who cursed and struggled impotently. 'Evening, Superintendent,' he added to Armstrong with a sly grin. His name was Malcolm Sun, he was a senior agent, SI, and ranking Chinese on this 16/2. It was he who had organized the intercept and had paid off the cook who usually worked this shift and had taken his place.

'Evening, Malcolm. You did very well.' Armstrong turned his attention to the enemy agent. 'What's your name?' he asked pleasantly.

'Who you? Let me go . . . let go!' the man said in heavily accented English.

'All yours, Malcolm,' Armstrong said.

At once, Sun said in Russian, 'Listen you mother-eater, we know you're off the *Ivanov*, we know you're a courier and you've just picked up a drop from the American off the nuclear carrier. We've already got the bastard in custody and you'd bet—'

'Lies! You've made a mistake,' the man blustered in Russian. 'I know nothing of any American. Let me go!'

'What's your name?'

'You've made a mistake. Let me go!' A crowd of gaping, gawking onlookers was now surrounding the store.

Malcolm Sun turned to Armstrong. 'He's a ripe one, sir. Doesn't understand very good Russian. I'm afraid we'll have to take him in,' he said with a twisted smile.

'Sergeant, get the Black Maria.'

'Yes sir.' Another agent went off quickly as Armstrong went closer. The Russian was gray-haired, a squat man with small, angry eyes. He was held perfectly with no chance of escape and no chance to put a hand into a pocket or into his mouth to destroy evidence, or himself.

Armstrong searched him expertly. No manual or roll of film. 'Where did you put it?' he asked.

'I no understand!'

The man's hatred did not bother Armstrong. He bore him no malice, the man was just a target who had been trapped. I wonder who shopped this poor bugger who's frightened to death, rightly, who's now ruined with the KGB and with his own people forever and might as well be a dead man. I wonder why it's our coup and not old Rosemont's and his CIA boys? How is it we're the ones who knew about the drop and not the Yanks? How is it Crosse got to know about this? All Crosse had told him was the where and the how and that the drop was going to be made by a sailor from the carrier and intercepted by someone off the *Ivanov*.

'You're in charge, Robert, and please, don't make a balls up.'

'I won't. But please get someone else for Brian K—'

'For the last time, Robert, you're doing the Kwok interrogation and you're seconded to SI until I release you. And if you bitch once more I'll have you out of the force, out of Hong Kong, out of your pension and I hardly need remind you SI's reach is very long. I doubt if you'd work again, unless you go criminal, and then God help you. Is that finally clear?'

'Yes sir.'

'Good. Brian will be ready for you at six tomorrow morning.'

Armstrong shivered. How impossibly lucky we were to catch him! If Spectacles Wu hadn't come from Ning-tok—if the old *amah* hadn't talked to the Werewolf—if the run on the bank—Christ, so many ifs. But then that's how you catch a big fish. Pure, bloody, unadulterated luck most times. Jesus Christ, Brian Kwok! You poor bugger!

He shivered again.

'You all right, sir?' Malcolm Sun asked.

'Yes.' Armstrong looked back at the Russian. 'Were did you put the film, the roll of film?'

The man stared back at him defiantly. 'Don't understand!'

Armstrong sighed. 'You do, too well.' The big black van came through the gawking crowd and stopped. More SIs got out. 'Put him in and don't let go of him,' Armstrong said to those holding him. The crowd watched and chattered and jeered as the man was frog-marched into the van. Armstrong and Sun got in after him and closed the door.

'Off you go, driver,' Armstrong ordered.

'Yes sir.' The driver let in his clutch easing through the crowds and joined the snarled traffic heading for Central HQ.

'All right, Malcolm. You can begin.'

The Chinese agent took out a razor-sharp knife. The Soviet man blanched.

'What's your name?' Armstrong asked, sitting on a bench opposite him.

Malcolm Sun repeated the question in Russian.

'D . . . Dimitri Metkin,' the man muttered, still held viselike by the four men and unable to move a finger or a toe. 'Seaman, first class.'

'Liar,' Armstrong said easily. 'Go ahead, Malcolm.'

Malcolm Sun put the knife under the man's left eye and the man almost fainted. 'That comes later, spy,' Sun said in Russian with a chilling smile. Expertly, with a deliberate malevolent viciousness, Sun rapidly sliced the raincoat away. Armstrong searched it very carefully as Sun used the knife deftly to cut away the man's seaman's jersey and the rest of his clothes until he was naked. The knife had not cut or even nicked him once. A careful search and re-search revealed nothing. Nor his shoes, the heels or the soles.

'Unless it's a microdot transfer and we've missed it so far, it must be in him,' Armstrong said.

At once the men holding the Russian bent him over and Sun got out the surgical gloves and surgical salve and probed deeply. The man flinched and moaned and tears of pain seeped from his eyes.

'*Dew neh loh moh*,' Sun said happily. His fingers drew out a small tube of cellophane wrapping.

'Don't let go of him!' Armstrong rapped.

When he was sure the man was secure he peered at the cylindrical package. Inside he could see the double-edged circles of a film cartridge. 'Looks like a Minolta,' he said absently.

Using some tissues he wrapped the cellophane carefully and sat down opposite the man again. 'Mr. Metkin, you're charged under the Official Secrets Act for taking part in an espionage act against Her Majesty's Government and her allies. Anything you say will be taken down and used in evidence against you. Now, sir,' he continued gently, 'you're caught. We're all Special Intelligence and not subject to normal laws, any more than your own KGB is. We don't want to hurt you but we can hold you forever if we want, in solitary if we want. We would like a little cooperation. Just the answers to a few questions. If you refuse we will extract the information we require. We use a lot of your KGB techniques and we can, sometimes, go a little better.' He saw a flash of terror behind the man's eyes but something told him this man would be hard to crack.

'What's you real name? Your official KGB name?'

The man stared at him.

'What's your KGB rank?'

The man still stared.

Armstrong sighed. 'I can let my Chinese friends have at you, old chum, if you prefer. They really don't like you at all. Your Soviet armies ran all over Malcolm Sun's village in Manchuria and wiped it out and his family. Sorry, but I really must have your official KGB name, your rank on the *Sovetski Ivanov* and official position.'

Another hostile silence.

Armstrong shrugged. 'Go ahead, Malcolm.'

Sun reached up and jerked the ugly-looking crowbar from its clip and as the four men turned Metkin roughly onto his stomach and spread-eagled him, Sun inserted the tip. The man screamed. 'Wait . . . wait . . .' he gasped in guttural English, 'wait . . . I'm Dimitri . . .' Another scream. 'Nicoli Leonov, major, political commissaaaar . . .'

'That's enough, Malcolm,' Armstrong said, astonished by the importance of their catch.

'But sir . . .'

'That's enough,' Armstrong said harshly, deliberately protective as Sun was deliberately hostile and angrily slammed the crowbar back into its clips. 'Pull him up,' he ordered, sorry for the man, the indignity of it. But he had never known the trick to fail to produce a real name and rank, if done at once. It was a trick because they would never probe deeply and the first scream was always from panic and not from pain. Unless the enemy agent broke at once they would always stop and then, at headquarters, put him through a proper monitored interrogation. Torture wasn't necessary though some zealots used it against orders. This is a dangerous profession, he thought grimly. KGB methods are rougher, and Chinese have a different attitude to life and death, victor and vanquished, pain and pleasure—and the value of a scream.

'Don't take it badly, Major Leonov,' he said kindly when the others had pulled him up and sat him back on the bench, still holding him tightly. 'We don't want to harm you—or let you harm yourself.'

Metkin spat at him and began to curse, tears of terror and rage and frustration running down his face. Armstrong nodded at

Malcolm Sun who took out the prepared pad and held it firmly over Metkin's nose and mouth.

The heavy, sick-sweet stench of chloroform filled the stuffy atmosphere. Metkin struggled impotently for a moment, then subsided. Armstrong checked his eyes and his pulse to make sure he was not feigning unconsciousness. 'You can let him go now,' he told them. 'You all did very well. I'll see a commendation goes on all your records. Malcolm, we'd better take good care of him. He might suicide.'

'Yes.' Sun sat back with the others in the swaying van. It was grinding along in the heavy traffic irritatingly, stopping and starting. Later he said what was in all their minds. 'Dimitri Metkin, alias Nicoli Leonov, major, KGB, off the *Ivanov*, and her political commissar. What's a big fish like that doing on a small job like this?'

48

7:05 P.M.:

Linc Bartlett chose his tie carefully. He was wearing a pale blue shirt and light tan suit and the tie was tan with a red stripe. A beer was open on the chest of drawers, the can pearled from the cold. All day he had debated with himself whether he should call for Orlanda or not call for her, whether he should tell Casey or not tell Casey.

The day had been fine for him. First, breakfast with Orlanda and then out to Kai Tak to check his airplane and make sure he could use it, for the flight with Dunross to Taipei. Lunch with Casey, then the excitement of the exchange. After the exchange had closed he and Casey had caught the ferry to Kowloon. Canvas storm shades lashed against the rain shut out the view and made the deck claustrophobic and the crossing not pleasant. But it was pleasant with Casey, his awareness of her heightened by the knowledge of Orlanda, and the dilemma.

'Ian's had it, hasn't he, Linc?'

'I'd think so, sure. But he's smart, the battle's not over yet, only the first attack.'

'How can he get back? His stock's at bargain prices.'

'Compared to last week, sure, but we don't know his earning ratio. This exchange's like a yo-yo—you said so yourself—and dangerous. Ian was right in that.'

'I'll bet he knows about the 2 million you put up with Gornt.'

'Maybe. It's nothing he wouldn't do if he had the chance. You meeting Seymour and Charlie Forrester?'

'Yes. The Pan Am flight's on time and I've a limo coming. I'll leave soon as we get back. You think they'll want dinner?'

'No. They'll be jet-lagged to hell.' He had grinned. 'I hope.'

Both Seymour Steigler III, their attorney, and Charlie Forrester, the head of their foam division, were socially very hard going. 'What time's their flight in?'

'4:50. We'll be back around six.'

At six they had had a meeting with Seymour Steigler—Forrester was unwell and had gone straight to bed.

Their attorney was a New Yorker, a handsome man with wavy black-gray hair and dark eyes and dark rings under his eyes. 'Casey filled me in on the details, Linc,' he said. 'Looks like we're in great shape.'

By prior arrangement, Bartlett and Casey had laid out the whole deal to their attorney, excluding the secret arrangement with Dunross about his ships.

'There's a couple of clauses I'd want in, to protect us, Linc,' Steigler said.

'All right. But I don't want the deal renegotiated. We want a wrap by Tuesday, just as we've laid it out.'

'What about Rothwell-Gornt? Best I should feel them out, huh? We can kite Struan's.'

'No,' Casey had said. 'You leave Gornt and Dunross alone, Seymour.' They had not told Steigler about Bartlett's private deal with Gornt either. 'Hong Kong's more complicated than we thought. Best leave it as it is.'

'That's right,' Bartlett said. 'Leave Gornt and Dunross to Casey and me. You just deal with their attorneys.'

'What're they like?'

'English. Very proper,' Casey said. 'I met with John Dawson at noon—he's their senior partner. Dunross was supposed to be there but he sent Jacques deVille instead. He's one of Struan's directors, deals with all their corporate affairs, and some financing. Jacques is very good but Dunross runs everything and decides everything. That's the bottom line.'

'How about getting this, er, Dawson on the phone right now? I'll meet with him over breakfast, say here at eight.'

Bartlett and Casey had laughed. 'No way, Seymour!' she had said. 'It'll be a leisurely in by ten and a two-hour lunch. They eat and drink like there's no tomorrow, and everything's the "old boy" bit.'

'Then I'll meet him after lunch when he's mellow and maybe we can teach him a trick or two,' Seymour Steigler had said, his eyes hardening. He stifled a yawn. 'I've got to call New York before I hit the sack. Hey, I've got all the papers on the GXR merger an—'

'I'll take those, Seymour,' Casey said.

'And I bought the 200,000 block of Rothwell-Gornt at 23.50—what're they today?'

'21.'

'Jesus, Linc, you're down 300 grand,' Casey said, perturbed. 'Why not sell and buy back? If and when.'

'No. We'll hold the stock.' Bartlett was not worried about the Rothwell stock loss for he was well ahead on his share of Gornt's selling-short ploy. 'Why don't you quit for the night, Seymour? If you're up we'll have breakfast—the three of us—say about eight?'

'Good idea. Casey, you'll fix me with Dawson?'

'First thing. They'll see you in the morning sometime. The tai-pan . . . Ian Dunross's told them our deal's top priority.'

'It should be,' Steigler said. 'Our down payment gets Dunross off the hook.'

'If he survives,' Casey said.

'Here today, gone tomorrow so let's enjoy!'

It was one of Steigler's standard sayings and the phrase was still ringing in Bartlett's head. Here today, gone tomorrow . . . like the fire last night. That could've been bad. I could've bashed my head in the way that poor bastard Pennyworth did. You never know when it's your turn, your accident, your bullet or your act of God. From outside or inside. Like Dad! Jesus—bronzed and healthy, hardly sick a day in his life, then the doc says he's got the big C and in three months he's wasted away and stinking and dying in great pain.

Bartlett felt a sudden sweat on his forehead. It had been a bad time then, during his divorce, burying his father, his mother distraught and everything falling apart. Then finalizing the divorce. The settlement had been vicious but he had just managed to retain control of the companies, to pay her off without having to sell out. He was still paying even though she'd remarried—along with an escalating maintenance for his children as well as future settlements—every cent still hurting, not the money itself but the unfairness of California law, the attorney in for a third until death us do part, screwed by my attorney and hers. One day I'll have vengeance on them,

Bartlett grimly promised himself again. On them and all the other goddamn parasites.

With an effort he thrust them aside. For today.

Here today, gone tomorrow, so let's enjoy, he repeated as he sipped his beer, tied his tie and looked at himself in the mirror. Without vanity. He liked living within himself and he had made his peace with himself, knowing who he was and what he was about. The war had helped him do that. And surviving the divorce, surviving her, finding out about her and living with it—Casey the only decent thing that whole year.

Casey.

What about Casey?

Our rules are quite clear, always have been. She set them: If I have a date or she has a date, we have dates and no questions and no recriminations.

Then why is it I'm all uptight now that I've decided to see Orlanda without telling Casey?

He glanced at his watch. Almost time to go.

There was a half-hearted knock on the door and instantly it opened and Nighttime Song beamed at him. 'Missee,' the old man announced and stepped aside. Casey was approaching down the corridor, a sheaf of papers and a notebook in her hand.

'Oh hi, Casey,' Bartlett said. 'I was just going to phone you.'

'Hi, Linc,' she called out and then said, '*Doh jeh*,' in Cantonese to the old man as she passed. Her walk was happy as she came into the two-bedroom suite. 'Got some stuff for you.' She handed him a sheaf of telexes and letters and went to the cocktail bar to pour herself a dry martini. She wore casual, slim-fitting gray pants and flat gray shoes with a gray silk open-necked shirt. Her hair was tied back and a pencil left there was her only decoration. Tonight she was wearing glasses, not her usual contacts. 'The first couple deal with the GXR merger. It's all signed, sealed and delivered, and we take possession September 2. There's a board meeting confirmed at 3:00 P.M. in L.A.—that gives us plenty of time to get back. I've ask—'

'Turn down bed, Master?' Nighttime Song interrupted importantly from the door.

Bartlett started to say no, but Casey was already shaking her head. '*Um ho*,' she said pleasantly in Cantonese, pronouncing the words well and with care. '*Cha z'er, doh jeh.*' No thank you, please do it later.

Nighttime Song stared at her blankly. '*Wat?*'

Casey repeated it. The old man snorted, irritated that Golden Pubics had the bad manners to address him in his own language. 'Turn down bed, *heya?* Now *heya?*' he asked in bad English.

Casey repeated the Cantonese, again with no reaction, began again then stopped and said wearily in English, 'Oh never mind! Not now. You can do it later.'

Nighttime Song beamed, having made her lose face. 'Yes, Missee.' He closed the door with just enough of a slam to make his point.

'Asshole,' she muttered. 'He had to understand me, I know I said it right, Linc. Why is it they insist on not understanding? I tried it on my maid and all she said was "*wat*" too.' She laughed in spite of herself as she aped the coarse guttural, '*Wat you say, heya?*'

Bartlett laughed. 'They're just ornery. But where'd you learn Chinese?'

'It's Cantonese. I got a teacher—fitted in an hour this morning—thought I should at least be able to say, Hi, Good morning, Give me the bill please . . . ordinary things. Goddamn but it's complicated. All the tones. In Cantonese there are seven tones—seven ways of saying the same word. You ask for the check, it's *mai dan*, but if you say it just a little wrong, it means fried eggs, they're *mai dan* too, and one'll get you fifty the waiter'll bring you the fried eggs just to put you down.' She sipped her martini and added an extra olive. 'I needed that. You want another beer?'

Bartlett shook his head. 'This's fine.' He had read all the telexes.

Casey sat on the sofa and opened her notepad. 'Vincenzo Banastasio's secretary phoned and asked me to confirm his suite for Saturday an—'

'I didn't know he was due in Hong Kong. You?'

'I think I remember him saying something about going to Asia the last time we saw him . . . at the track last month—at Del Mar—the time John Chen was there. Terrible about John, isn't it?'

'I hope they get those Werewolves. Bastards to murder him and put that sign on him like that.'

'I wrote a condolence note for us to his father and to his wife Dianne—you remember we met her at Ian's and at Aberdeen—Jesus, that seems like a million years ago.'

'Yes.' Bartlett frowned. 'I still don't remember Vincenzo saying anything. He staying here?'

'No, he wants to be Hong Kong side. I confirmed the booking at the Hilton by phone and I'll do it in person tomorrow. He's on JAL's Saturday morning flight from Tokyo.' Casey peered at him over her glasses. 'You want me to schedule a meeting?'

'How long's he staying?'

'Over the weekend. A few days. You know how vague he is. How about Saturday after the races? We'll be Hong Kong side and it's an easy walk from Happy Valley if we can't get a ride.'

Bartlett was going to say, Let's make it Sunday, but then he remembered Taipei on Sunday. 'Sure, Saturday after the races.' Then he saw her look. 'What?'

'I was just wondering what Banastasio's about.'

'When he bought 4 percent of our Par-Con stock,' he said, 'we ran it through Seymour, the SEC and a few others and they're all satisfied his money was clean. He's never been arrested or charged, though there're a lot of rumors. He's never given us any trouble, never wanted in on any board, never turns up for any shareholder meetings, always gives me his proxy, and he came through with the money when we needed.' He stared at her. 'So?'

'So nothing, Linc. You know my opinion of him. I agree we can't take the stock back. He bought it free and clear and asked first, and we sure as hell needed his money and put it to great use.' She adjusted her glasses and made a note. 'I'll fix the meeting and be polite as always. Next: Our company account at the Victoria Bank's operating. I put in 25,000 and here's your checkbook. We've established a revolving fund and First Central's ready to transfer the initial 7 million to the account whenever we say so. There's a confirm telex there. I also opened a personal account for you at the same bank—here's your checkbook with another 25 grand—20 in an HK treasury bill on a daily rollover.' She grinned. 'That should buy a couple of bowls of chop suey and a good piece of jade though I hear the phonys are hard to tell from the real ones.'

'No jade.' Bartlett wanted to look at his watch but he did not, just sipped his beer. 'Next?'

'Next: Clive Bersky called and asked a favor.'

'You told him to blow it out of his muffler?'

She laughed. Clive Bersky was chief executive of their branch of the First Central of New York. He was very meticulous, pedantic and drove Bartlett crazy with his need for perfect documentation. 'He asks that if the Struan deal goes through, we put our funds through the . . .' She referred to her pad. '. . . the Royal Belgium and Far East Bank here.'

'Why them?'

'I don't know. I'm checking them out. We've a date for a drink with the local chief exec at eight. The First Central's just bought his bank—it's got branches here, Singapore, Tokyo.'

'You deal with him, Casey.'

'Sure. I can drink and run. You want to eat afterwards? We could go down to the Escoffier or up to the Seven Dragons or maybe walk up Nathan Road for some Chinese chow. Somewhere close—the weatherman says more rain's expected.'

'Thanks but not tonight. I'm going Hong Kong side.'

'Oh? Wh—' Casey stopped. 'Fine. When are you leaving?'

'About now. No hurry.' Bartlett saw the same easy smile on her face as her eyes went down the list but he was sure she had instantly realized where he was going and suddenly he was furious. He kept his voice calm. 'What else do you have?'

'Nothing that won't wait,' she said in the same nice voice. 'I've an early meeting with Captain Jannelli about your Taipei trip—Armstrong's office sent over the documentation temporarily lifting the impounding on the airplane. All you have to do is sign the form agreeing to come back to H.K. I put Tuesday on it. Is that right?'

'Sure. Tuesday's D Day.'

She got up. 'That's it for tonight, Linc. I'll deal with the banker and the rest of this stuff.' She finished her martini and put the glass back on the mirrored cabinet. 'Hey that tie, Linc! Your blue one'd go better. See you at breakfast.' She blew him her usual kiss and walked off as she usually did and closed the door with her usual, 'Sweet dreams, Linc!'

'Why the hell'm I so goddamn mad?' he muttered angrily, out

loud. 'Casey's done nothing. Son of a bitch!' Unaware, he had crushed his empty beer can. Son of a bitch! Now what? Do I forget it and go or what?

Casey was walking up the corridor toward her own room, seething. I'll bet my life he's going out with that goddamn tramp. I should've drowned her while I had the chance.

Then she noticed that Nighttime Song had opened her door for her and was holding it wide with a smile she read as a smirk.

'Andyoucanblowitoutofyourasstoo!' she snarled at him before she could stop herself, then slammed the door and threw her papers and pad on the bed and was about to cry. 'You're not to cry,' she ordered herself out loud, tears on the words. 'No goddamn man is going to get you down no way. No way!' She stared down at her fingers, which were trembling with the rage that possessed her.

'Oh shit on all men!'

49

'Excuse me, your Excellency, you're wanted on the phone.'

'Thank you, John.' Sir Geoffrey Allison turned back to Dunross and the others. 'If you'll excuse me a moment, gentlemen?'

They were in Government House, the governor's official residence above Central, the French doors open to the cool of the evening, the air fresh and washed, trees and shrubs dripping nicely, and the governor walked across the crowded anteroom where predinner cocktails and snacks were being served, very pleased with the way the evening had gone so far. Everyone seemed to be having a good time. There was banter and good conversation, some laughter and no friction yet between the Hong Kong tai-pans and the MPs. At his request, Dunross had gone out of his way to soothe Grey and Broadhurst, and even Grey seemed to have mellowed.

The aide closed the door of his study, leaving him alone with the telephone. The study was dark green and pleasing, with blue flock wallpaper, fine Persian carpets from his two-year sojourn in the Teheran embassy, cherished crystal and silver and more showcases with fine Chinese porcelains. 'Hello?'

'Sorry to bother you, sir,' Crosse said.

'Oh hello, Roger.' The governor felt his chest tighten. 'No bother,' he said.

'Two rather good pieces of information, sir. Somewhat important. I wonder if I might drop by?'

Sir Geoffrey glanced at the porcelain clock on the mantel over the fireplace. 'Dinner's served in fifteen minutes, Roger. Where are you now?'

'Just three minutes away from you, sir. I won't delay your dinner. But, if you prefer, I could make it afterwards.'

'Come now, I could use some good news. With this whole banking affair and the stock market . . . Use the garden door if you wish. John will meet you.'

'Thank you, sir.' The phone clicked off. By custom, the head of SI had a key to the iron garden gate which was set into the high surrounding walls.

In exactly three minutes Crosse was crossing the terrace, walking lightly. The ground was very wet. He dried his feet carefully before he came through the french windows. 'We've caught a rather big fish, sir, an enemy agent, caught him with his hands in the honey pot,' he said softly. 'He's a major, KGB, off the *Ivanov*, and her political commissar. We caught him in the middle of an espionage act with an American computer expert off the nuclear carrier.'

The governor's face had gone red. 'That blasted *Ivanov*! Good God, Roger, a major? Have you any idea of the diplomatic and political storm this will precipitate with the USSR, the U.S. and London?'

'Yes sir. That's why I thought I'd better consult at once.'

'What the devil was the fellow doing?'

Crosse gave him the broad facts. He ended, 'Both of them are sedated now and very safe.'

'What was on the film?'

'It was blank, sir, fogged. Wh—'

'What?'

'Yes. Of course both men denied any espionage was involved. The sailor denied there was a drop, denied everything, said he'd won the $2,000 U.S. we found on him playing poker. Childish to lie once you're caught, childish to make things difficult, we always get the truth eventually. I thought we'd either missed the real film or it was a microdot transfer. We re-searched their clothing and I ordered immediate emetics and stool examinations. Major . . . the KGB agent passed the real negative film an hour ago.' Crosse offered the big manila envelope. 'These're eight-by-ten prints, sir, frame by frame.'

The governor did not open the envelope. 'What are they of? In general?'

'One set shows part of the ship's radar guidance system

manual.' Crosse hesitated. 'The other set's a photocopy of a complete manifest of the carrier's arsenal, ammunition, missiles and warheads. Quantities, qualities, their numbers and where stored in the ship.'

'Jesus Christ! Including nuclear warheads? No, please don't answer that.' Sir Geoffrey stared at Crosse. After a pause he said, 'Well, Roger, it's marvelous that the information didn't get into enemy hands. You're to be congratulated. Our American friends will be equally relieved, and they'll owe you a number of very great favors. Good God, in expert hands that knowledge would lay bare the ship's entire strike capability!'

'Yes sir.' Crosse smiled thinly.

Sir Geoffrey studied him.

'But what to do about this major of yours?'

'I would send the major to London with a special escort by RAF transport at once. I think they should do the debriefing there even though we're better equipped, more practiced, and more efficient here. My worry is that his superiors will surely know within an hour or so and might attempt to rescue him or to render him useless. They might even use extreme diplomatic pressure to force us to release him to the *Ivanov*. Besides, when the PRC and Nationalists hear we've caught such an official, they might try to acquire him themselves.'

'What about the American sailor?'

'It might be politic to turn him over to the CIA at once, with the negative of the film and these—they're the only prints I made. I developed and made them myself for obvious security reasons. I suspect Rosemont would be the best person.'

'Ah yes, Rosemont. He's here now.'

'Yes sir.'

Sir Geoffrey's eyes hardened. 'You have copies of all my guest lists, Roger?'

'No sir. Half an hour ago I called the consulate to find out where he was. They told me.'

Sir Geoffrey looked back at him under his shaggy eyebrows, disbelieving him, sure that the chief of SI did know whom he invited and when. Never mind, he thought testily, that's his job. And I'll bet a golden guinea to a doughnut that these prints aren't the only copies Roger made, for he knows our Admiralty would love to see them too and it's his duty to provide them.

'Could this have any connection with the AMG business?'

'No. No not at all,' Crosse said and the governor thought he heard the momentary flutter in Crosse's voice. 'I don't think there's any connection.'

Sir Geoffrey got out of the tall chair and paced for a moment, his mind sifting possibilities. Roger's right. Chinese Intelligence on both sides of the bamboo fence are bound to find out quickly, as every one of our Chinese police has PRC or Nationalist sympathies. So it's far better to have the spy out of reach. Then no one will be tempted—at least, not here. 'I think I should chat with the minister at once.'

'Perhaps, in the circumstances, sir, you could *inform* the minister what I've done about the major—sending him to London under es—'

'He's already gone?'

'No sir. But it's well within my authority to expedite that—if you agree.'

Thoughtfully Sir Geoffrey glanced again at the clock. At length he said with a small smile, 'Very well. It's lunchtime now in London, I'll *inform* him in an hour or so. Is that sufficient time?'

'Oh yes, thank you, sir. Everything's arranged.'

'I presumed it was.'

'I'll breathe a lot easier when the fellow's en route home, sir. Thank you.'

'Yes. And the sailor?'

'Perhaps you could *ask* the minister to approve our handing him over to Rosemont, sir.'

There were a dozen questions Sir Geoffrey would like to have asked but he asked none of them. From long experience he knew he was not a good liar, so the less he knew the better. 'Very well. Now, what's the second piece of "good" news, I trust this will be better.'

'We've caught the mole, sir.'

'Ah! Good. Excellent! Very good. Who?'

'Senior Superintendent Kwok.'

'Impossible!'

Crosse kept the pleasure off his face. 'I agree, sir. Even so, Superintendent Kwok's a Communist mole and spy for the PRC.' Crosse related how Brian Kwok's cover had been penetrated. 'I suggest Superintendent Armstrong should get a commendation—also Spectacles Wu. I'm taking him into SI, sir.'

Sir Geoffrey was staring out of the window, stunned. 'Bless my soul! Young Brian! Why? He would have been an assistant commissioner in a year or two . . . I suppose there's no mistake?'

'No sir. As I said, the proof is irrefutable. Of course, we don't know the how or the why yet but we soon will.'

Sir Geoffrey heard the finality and he saw the thin, hard face and cold eyes and he felt very sorry for Brian Kwok, whom he had liked for many years. 'Keep me advised about him. Perhaps we can discover what makes a man like that do such a thing. Good God, such a charming chap and a first-class cricketer too. Yes, keep me advised.'

'Certainly, sir.' Crosse got up. 'Interesting. I could never understand why he was always so anti-American—it was his only flaw. Now it's obvious. I should have spotted that. Sorry sir, and sorry to interrupt your evening.'

'You're to be congratulated, Roger. If the Soviet agent's being sent to London perhaps Brian Kwok should go too? The same reasons would apply to him?'

'No sir. No I don't think so. We can deal with Kwok here much quicker and better. We're the ones who need to know what he knows—London wouldn't understand. Kwok's a threat to Hong Kong, not to Britain. He's a PRC asset—the other man's Soviet. The two don't parallel.'

Sir Geoffrey sighed heavily, knowing Crosse was right. 'I agree. This has really been a quite dreadful day, Roger. First the bank runs, then the stock market . . . the deaths last night, poor Sir Charles Pennyworth and Toxe's wife . . . and this morning the Aberdeen mud-slide deaths . . . the Noble House's tottering . . . it looks as though this storm front's developing into a blasted typhoon which will probably wreck Saturday's racing . . . and now all your news, an American sailor betrays his country and ship and honor for a paltry $2,000?'

Crosse smiled his thin smile again. 'Perhaps $2,000 wasn't paltry to him.'

We live in terrible times, Sir Geoffrey was going to say, but he knew it was not the times. It was merely that people were people, that greed pride lust avarice jealousy gluttony anger and the bigger lust for power or money ruled people and would rule them forever. Most of them.

'Thank you for coming, Roger. Again, you're to be congratulated. I will so inform the minister. Good night.'

He watched Crosse walk off, tall, confident and deadly. When the iron door in the high wall had been bolted behind him by his aide, Sir Geoffrey Allison allowed the real unasked question to surface once more.

Who's the mole in my police?

AMG's paper was quite clear. The traitor's a Soviet asset, not from the PRC. Brian Kwok has been flushed out by chance. Why didn't Roger point out the obvious?

Sir Geoffrey shuddered. If Brian could be a mole anyone could. Anyone.

50

Almost before he took his finger off the bell the door swung open.

'Oh, Linc,' Orlanda said breathlessly, her happiness spilling over, 'I'd given you up. Please come in!'

'Sorry to be late,' Bartlett said, taken aback by her beauty and marvelous warmth. 'The traffic's snarled to hell and the ferries jammed and I couldn't get to a phone.'

'You're here so you're not late, not at all. I was just afraid that . . .' Then she added in a rush, 'I was afraid you wouldn't come back tonight and then I'd've been shattered. There, I've said it and all my defenses are down but I'm so happy to see you I don't care.' She stood on tiptoe and kissed him a swift happy kiss, took his arm and shut the door behind them.

Her perfume was delicate and barely there but he felt it as a physical presence. The dress she wore was knee-length white chiffon that sighed as she moved, close at the wrists and neck. It showed but somehow didn't quite show her golden skin. 'I'm so happy you're here,' she said again and took his umbrella and put it into a rack.

'So am I.'

The room was prettier by night, mostly candlelit, the tall glass doors of the terrace open to the air. They were just below the overcast and the city sprawled down the mountain to the sea, the lights misting from time to time as whiskers of the low clouds passed by. Sea level was seven hundred feet below. Kowloon was dim and the harbor dim but he knew the ships were there and he could see the huge carrier at the wharf, her great angled deck floodlit, the needle-nosed jets floodlit, her battle-gray bridge reaching for the sky—the Stars and Stripes hanging damp and listless.

'Hey,' he said, leaning on the terrace railing, 'what a great night, Orlanda.'

'Oh yes, yes it is. Come and sit down.'

'I'd rather look at the view, if it's okay.'

'Of course, anything you want's fine, anything. That suit's great on you, Linc, and I love your tie.' She said it happily, wanting to compliment him even though she did not think the tie matched too well. Never mind, she thought, he's just not color conscious like Quillan, and needs helping. I'll do what Quillan taught me to do, not criticize but go out and buy one I like and give it to him. If he likes it, marvelous, if not never mind, for what does it matter—he's the one who's wearing it. Blue, blue would match Linc's eyes and go better with that shirt 'You dress very well.'

'Thanks, so do you.' He was remembering what Casey had said about his tie and how furious he had been with her tonight all the way across the ferry, all the time waiting for a cab, and the old woman who had trod on his foot shoving past to usurp his cab but he had foiled her and cursed her back.

It was only now that his rage-temperature had vanished. It was Orlanda's pleasure at seeing me that did it, he told himself. It's years since Casey lit up like a Christmas tree or said anything when I . . . the hell with that. I'm not going to worry about Casey tonight. 'The view's fantastic and you're as pretty as a picture!'

She laughed. 'So're you and . . . *oh your drink*, sorry . . .' She whirled away for the kitchen, her skirt flying. 'I don't know why but you make me feel like a schoolgirl,' she called out. In a moment she came back. On the tray was an earthenware pot of pâté and rounds of fresh toast and a bottle of iced beer. 'I hope this's right.'

It was Anweiser. 'How did you know my brand?'

'You told me this morning, don't you remember?' Her warmth flooded over again at his obvious pleasure. 'Also that you like drinking it out of the bottle.'

He took it and grinned at her. 'Is that going to be in the article too?'

'No. No, I've decided not to write about you.'

He saw her sudden seriousness. 'Why?'

She was pouring herself a glass of white wine. 'I decided I could never do you justice in an article so I won't write one. Besides, I don't think you'd like that hanging over you.' Her hand went to her heart. 'Cross my heart and hope to die, no article, everything private. No article, no journalism, I swear by the Madonna,' she added, meaning it.

'Hey, no need to be dramatic!'

She was leaning with her back against the railing, an eighty-foot drop to the concrete below. He saw the sincerity in her face and he believed her completely. He was relieved. The article had been the only flaw, the only danger point for him—that and her being a journalist. He leaned forward and kissed her lightly, deliberately lightly. 'Sealed with a kiss. Thanks.'

'Yes.'

They watched the view for a moment.

'Is the rain over for good?'

'I hope not, Linc. We need a good series of storms to fill the reservoirs. Keeping clean's so hard and we still only get water one day in four.' She smiled mischievously as a child would. 'Last night during the torrent I stripped and bathed here. It was fantastic. The rain was even heavy enough to wash my hair.'

The thought of her naked, here, in the night, touched him. 'You'd better be careful,' he said. 'The railing's not that high. I wouldn't want you to slip.'

'Strange, I'm frightened to death of the sea but heights don't bother me a bit. You certainly saved my life.'

'C'mon! You would have made it without me.'

'Perhaps, but you certainly saved my face. Without you there I would surely have disgraced myself. So thanks for my face.'

'And that's more important than life out here, isn't it?'

'Sometimes, yes, yes it is. Why do you say that?'

'I was just thinking about Dunross and Quillan Gornt. Those two're having at each other, mostly over face.'

'Yes. You're right, of course.' She added thoughtfully, 'They're both fine men, in one way, both devils in another.'

'How do you mean?'

'They're both ruthless, both very very strong, very hard, adept and . . . and well conversed with life.' As she talked she

844

heaped one of the rounds of toast with pâté and offered it to him, her nails long and perfect. 'The Chinese have a saying: "*Chan ts'ao, chu ken*"—when pulling weeds make sure you get rid of the roots. The roots of those two go deep in Asia, very deep, too deep. It would be hard to get rid of those roots.' She sipped her wine and smiled a little smile. 'And probably not a good idea, not for Hong Kong. Some more pâté?'

'Please. It's wonderful. You make it?'

'Yes. It's an old English recipe.'

'Why wouldn't it be good for Hong Kong?'

'Oh, perhaps because they balance each other. If one destroys the other—oh I don't mean just Quillan or Dunross, I mean the *hongs* themselves, the companies, Struan's and Rothwell-Gornt. If one eats up the other, perhaps the remaining one would be too strong, there would certainly be no competition, then perhaps *the* tai-pan would become too greedy, perhaps he'd decide to dump Hong Kong.' She smiled hesitantly. 'Sorry . . . I'm talking too much. It's just an idea. Another beer?'

'Sure, in a moment, thanks, but that's an interesting thought.' Yes, Bartlett was thinking, and one that hadn't occurred to me—or to Casey. Are those two necessary to each other?

And Casey and I? Are we necessary to each other?

He saw her watching him and he smiled back. 'Orlanda, it's no secret I'm thinking about making a deal with one of them. If you were me, which one would you go with?'

'Neither,' she said at once and laughed.

'Why?'

'You're not British, not one of the "old boys," not a hereditary member of any of the clubs, and however much your money and power here, it's the Old Boy network that will finally decide what is to be.' She took his empty bottle and went and brought another.

'You think I couldn't make a go of it?'

'Oh I didn't mean that, Linc. You asked me about Struan's or Rothwell-Gornt, about going into business with one of *them*. If you do, they'll be the winners in the end.'

'They're that smart?'

'No. But they're Asian, they belong here. Here the saying is, "*Tien hsia wu ya i pan hei*"—all crows under heaven are black—

meaning that all the tai-pans are the same and they'll all stick together to destroy the outsider.'

'So neither Ian nor Quillan would welcome a partner?'

She hesitated. 'I think I'm getting out of my depth, Linc. I don't know about business things. It's just that I've never heard of an American who's come here and made it big.'

'What about Biltzmann, Superfoods and their takeover of H.K. General Stores?'

'Biltzmann's a joke. Everyone hates him and hopes he'll fall on his face, even Pug . . . Pugmire. Quillan's sure he will. No, even Cooper and Tillman didn't make it. They were Yankee traders in the first days, Linc, opium traders—they were even under Dirk Struan's protection. They're even related, the Struan's and the Coopers. Hag Struan married her eldest daughter, Emma, to old Jeff Cooper, Old Hook Nose was his nickname when he was in his dotage, the story is that the marriage was payment for his helping her destroy Tyler Brock. Have you heard about them, Linc? The Brocks, Sir Morgan and his father Tyler, and the Hag?'

'Peter Marlowe told us some of the stories.'

'If you want to know about the real Hong Kong, you should talk to Auntie Bright Eyes—that's Sarah Chen, Phillip Chen's maiden aunt! She's a great character, Linc, and sharp as a needle. She says she's eighty-eight. I think she's older. Her father was Sir Gordon Chen, Dirk Struan's illegitimate son by his mistress Kai-Sung, and her mother was the famous beauty Karen Yuan.'

'Who's she?'

'Karen Yuan was Robb Struan's granddaughter. Robb was Dirk's half-brother and he had a mistress called Yau Ming Soo with whom he had a daughter Isobel. Isobel married John Yuan, an illegitimate son of Jeff Cooper. John Yuan became a well-known pirate and opium smuggler, and Isobel died quite notorious as an enormous gambler who had lost two of her husbands' fortunes playing mah-jong. So it was Isobel and John's daughter, Karen, who married Sir Gordon Chen— actually she was his second wife, more like a concubine really, though it was a perfectly legal marriage. Here, even today, if you're Chinese you can legally have as many wives as you like.'

'That's convenient!'

'For a man!' Orlanda smiled. 'So this tiny branch of the Yuans are Cooper descendants—the T'Chungs and Chens are from Dirk Struan, the Sungs, Tups and Tongs from Aristotle Quance the painter—here in Hong Kong it's the custom for the children to take the name of their mother, usually an insignificant girl who was sold to the pillow by her parents.'

'By the parents?'

'Almost always,' she told him casually. '"T'ung t'ien yu ming"—listen to heaven and follow fate. Particularly when you're starving.' She shrugged. 'There's no shame in that, Linc, no loss of face, not in Asia.'

'How come you know so much about the Struans and Coopers and mistresses and so on?'

'This is a small place and we all love secrets but there are no real secrets in Hong Kong. Insiders—true insiders—know almost everything about the others. As I said, our roots go deep here. And don't forget that the Chens, Yuans and Sungs are Eurasian. As I told you, Eurasians marry Eurasians, so we should know who we're from. We're not desired by British or Chinese as wives or husbands, only as mistresses or lovers.' She sipped her wine and he was awed by the delicacy of her movements, her grace. 'It's custom for Chinese families to have their genealogy written down in the village book, that's the only legality they have—that gives them continuity, they've never had birth certificates.' She smiled up at him. 'To go back to your question. Both Ian Dunross and Quillan would welcome your money and your inside track into the U.S. market. And with either one you'd make a profit here—if you were content to be a silent partner.'

Thoughtfully Bartlett let his eyes stray to the view.

She waited patiently, allowing him his thoughts, staying motionless. I'm very glad Quillan was such a good teacher and such a clever man, she thought. And oh so wise. He was right again.

This morning she had called him in tears on his private line to report what had happened and, 'Oh Quillan, I think I've ruined everything. . . .'

'What did you say and what did he say?'

She had told him exactly and he had reassured her. 'I don't think you've any need to worry, Orlanda. He'll come back. If not tonight, tomorrow.'

'Oh are you sure?' she had said so gratefully.

'Yes. Now dry those tears and listen.' Then he had told her what to do and what to wear and above all to be a woman.

Ah how happy I am to be a woman, she thought, and remembered with sadness now the old days when they were happy together, she and Quillan, she nineteen, already his mistress for two years and no longer shy or afraid—of the pillow or him or of herself—how sometimes they would go on his yacht for a midnight cruise, just the two of them and he would lecture her. 'You're a woman and Hong Kong *yan* so if you want to have a good life and pretty things, to be cherished and loved and pillowed and safe in this world be female.'

'How, my darling?'

'Think only of my satisfaction and pleasure. Give me passion when I need it, quiet when I need it, privacy when I need it, and happiness and discretion all the time. Cook as a gourmet, know great wine, be discreet always, protect my face always and never nag.'

'But Quillan, you make it sound all so one-sided.'

'Yes. It is, of course it is. In return I do my part with equal passion. But that's what I want from you, nothing less. You wanted to be my mistress. I put it to you before we began and you agreed.'

'I know I did and I love being your mistress but . . . but sometimes I'm worried about the future.'

'Ah, my pet, you have nothing to worry about. You know our rules were set in advance. We will renew our arrangement yearly, provided *you* want to until you're twenty-four, and then, if you choose to leave me I will give you the flat, money enough for reasonable needs and a handsome dowry for a suitable husband. We agreed and your parents approved. . . .'

Yes they did. Orlanda remembered how her mother and father had enthusiastically approved the liaison—had even suggested it to her when she had just come back from school in America when they told her that Quillan had asked if he might approach her, saying that he had fallen in love with her. 'He's a good man,' her father had said, 'and he's promised to provide well for you, if you agree. It's your choice, Orlanda. We think we would recommend it.'

'But Father, I won't be eighteen until next month, and besides I want to go back to the States to live. I'm sure I can get a Green Card to remain there.'

'Yes, you can go, child,' her mother had said, 'but you will be poor. We can give you nothing, no help. What job will you get? Who will support you? This way in a little while you can go with an income, with property here to support you.'

'But he's so old. He's . . .'

'A man doesn't wear age like a woman,' both had told her. 'He's strong and respected and he's been good to us for years. He's promised to cherish you and the financial arrangements are generous, however long you stay with him.'

'But I don't love him.'

'You talk nonsense in eight directions! Without the protection of the lips the teeth grow cold!' her mother had said angrily. 'This opportunity you are being offered is like the hair of the phoenix and the heart of the dragon! What do you have to do in return? Just be a woman and honor and obey a good man for a few years—renewable yearly—and even after that there's no end to the years if you choose and are faithful and clever. Who knows? His wife is an invalid and wasting. If you satisfy him and cherish him enough why wouldn't he marry you?'

'Marry a Eurasian? Quillan Gornt?' she had burst out.

'Why not? You're not just Eurasian, you're Portuguese. He has British sons and daughters already, *heya*? Times are changing, even here in Hong Kong. If you do your best, who knows? Bear him a son, in a year or two, with his permission, and who knows? Gods are gods and if they want they can make thunder from a clear sky. Don't be stupid! Love? What is that word to you?'

Orlanda Ramos was staring down at the city now, not seeing it. How stupid and naive I was then, she thought. Naive and very stupid. But now I know better. Quillan taught me very well.

She glanced up at Linc Bartlett, moving just her eyes, not wanting to disturb him.

Yes, I'm trained very well, she told herself. I'm trained to be the best wife any man could ever have, that Bartlett will ever have. No mistakes this time. Oh no, no mistakes. Quillan will guide me. He will help remove Casey. I will be Mrs. Linc

Bartlett. All gods and all devils bear witness; that is what must happen. . . .

Soon he took his eyes off the city, having thought through what she had said. She was watching him, wearing a little smile that he could not read. 'What is it?'

'I was thinking how lucky I was to meet you.'

'Do you always compliment a man?'

'No, just the ones who please me—and they're as rare as the hair of the phoenix or the heart of a dragon. Pâté?'

'Thanks.' He accepted it. 'You're not eating?'

'I'm saving for dinner. I have to watch my diet, I'm not like you.'

'I work out daily. Tennis when I can, golf. You?'

'I play a little tennis, I'm a good walker but I'm still taking golf lessons.' Yes, she thought, I try very hard to be the best at everything I do and I'm the best for you, Linc Bartlett, in the whole wide world. Her tennis was very good and golf quite good because Quillan had insisted she be adept at both—because he enjoyed them. 'Are you hungry?'

'Starving.'

'You said Chinese food. Is that what you really want?'

He shrugged. 'It doesn't matter to me. Whatever you want.'

'Are you sure?'

'Positive. Why, what would you like?'

'Come in a moment.'

He followed her. She opened the dining room door. The table was set exquisitely for two. Flowers, and a bottle of Verdicchio on ice. 'Linc, I haven't cooked for anyone for such a long time,' she said in her breathless rush that he found so pleasing. 'But I wanted to cook for you. If you'd like it, I have an Italian dinner all set to go. Fresh pasta *aglio e olio*—garlic and oil—veal *piccata*, a green salad, *zabaglione*, espresso, and brandy. How does that sound? It will only take me twenty minutes and you can read the paper while you wait. Then afterwards we can leave everything for when the *amah* comes back and go dancing or drive. What do you say?'

'Italian's my favorite food, Orlanda!' he told her enthusiastically. Then a vagrant memory surfaced, and for a moment he wondered whom he had told about Italian being his favorite. Was it Casey—or was it Orlanda this morning?

51

Brian Kwok jerked out of sleep. One moment he was in a nightmare, the next awake but somehow still in the deep dark pit of sleep, his heart pounding, his mind disordered and no change between sleep and awake. Panic swamped him. Then he realized he was naked and still in the same warm darkness of the cell and remembered who he was and where he was.

They must have drugged me, he thought. His mouth was parched, his head ached, and he lay back on the mattress that was slimy to his touch and tried to collect himself. Vaguely he remembered being in Armstrong's office and before that with Crosse discussing the 16/2 but after that not much, just waking in this darkness, groping for the walls to get his bearings, feeling them close by, biting back the terror of knowing he was betrayed and defenseless in the bowels of Central Police HQ within a box with no windows and a door somewhere. Then, exhaustedly sleeping and waking and angry voices—or did I dream that—and then sleeping again . . . no, eating first, didn't I eat first . . . yes, slop they called dinner and cold tea . . . Come on, think! It's important to think and to remember . . . Yes, I remember, it was bedraggled stew and cold tea then, later, breakfast. Eggs. Was it eggs first or the stew first and . . . yes the lights came on for a moment each time I ate, just enough time to eat . . . no, the lights went off and each time I finished in darkness. I remember finishing in darkness and hating to eat in darkness and then I peed in the pail in darkness, got back onto the mattress and lay down again.

How long have I been here? Must count the days.

Wearily he swung his legs off the cot and stumbled to a wall, his limbs aching to match his head. Got to exercise, he thought, got to help work the drugs out of my system and get my head clear and ready for the interrogation. Must get my mind ready for when they go at me, really begin—when they think I've softened up—then they'll keep me awake until they break me.

No, they won't break me. I'm strong and prepared and I know some of the pitfalls.

Who gave me away?

The effort to solve that was too much for him so he mustered his strength and did a few weak knee bends. Then he heard muffled footsteps approaching. Hastily he groped back for the cot and lay down, pretending sleep, his heart hurting in his chest as he held down his terror.

The footsteps stopped. A sudden bolt clanged back and a trapdoor opened. A shaft of light came into the cell and a half-seen hand put down a metal plate and a metal cup.

'Eat your breakfast and hurry up,' the voice said in Cantonese. 'You're due for more interrogation shortly.'

'Listen, I want . . .' Brian Kwok called out but the trapdoor had already clanged back and he was alone in the darkness with the echo of his own words.

Keep calm, he ordered himself. Calm yourself and think.

Abruptly the cell flooded with light. The light hurt his eyes. When he had adjusted he saw that the light came from fixtures in the ceiling high above, and he remembered seeing them before. The walls were dark, almost black, and seemed to be pressing inward on him. Don't worry about them, he thought. You've seen the dark cells before and though you've never been part of an in-depth interrogation you know the principles and some of the tricks.

A surge of nausea came into his mouth at the thought of the ordeal ahead.

The door was hardly discernible and the trapdoor equally hidden. He could feel eyes though he could see no spyholes. On the plate were two fried eggs and a thick piece of rough bread. The bread was a little toasted. The eggs were cold and greasy and unappetizing. In the cup was cold tea. There were no utensils.

He drank the tea thirstily, trying to make it last, but it was finished before he knew it and the small amount had not quenched his thirst. *Dew neh loh moh* what I wouldn't give for a toothbrush and a bottle of beer an—

The lights went out as suddenly as they had come on. It took him much time to adjust again to the darkness. Be calm, it's just darkness and light, light and darkness. It's just to confuse and disorient. Be calm. Take each day as it comes, each interrogation as it comes.

His terror returned. He knew he was not really prepared, not experienced enough, though he had had some survival training against capture, what to do if the enemy captured you, the PRC Communist enemy. But the PRC's not the enemy. The real enemy are the British and Canadians who've pretended to be friend and teacher, they're the real enemy.

Don't think about that, don't try to convince yourself, just try to convince them.

I have to hold fast. Have to pretend it's a mistake for as long as I can and then, then I tell the story I've woven over the years and confuse them. That's duty.

His thirst was overpowering. And his hunger.

Brian Kwok wanted to hurl the empty cup against the wall and the plate against the wall and shout and call for help but that would be a mistake. He knew he must have great control and keep every particle of strength he could muster to fight back.

Use your head. Use your training. Put theory into practice. Think about the survival course last year in England. Now what do I do?

He remembered that part of the survival theory was that you must eat and drink and sleep whenever you can for you never know when they will cut off food and drink and sleep from you. And to use your eyes and nose and touch and intelligence to keep track of time in the dark and remember that your captors will always make a mistake sometime, and if you can catch the mistake you can relate to time, and if you can relate to time then you can keep in balance and then you can twist them and not divulge that which must not be divulged—exact names and real contacts. Pit your mind against them was the rule. Keep active, force yourself to observe.

Have they made any mistakes? Have these devil barbarian British slipped yet? Only once, he thought excitedly. The eggs! The stupid British and their eggs for breakfast!

Feeling better now and wide awake, he eased off the cot and groped his way to the metal plate and put the cup down gently beside it. The eggs were cold and the grease congealed but he chewed them and finished the bread and felt a little better for the food. Eating with his fingers in darkness was strange and uncomfortable especially with nothing to wipe his fingers on except his own nakedness.

A shudder went through him. He felt abandoned and unclean. His bladder was uncomfortable and he felt his way to the pail that was attached to the wall. The pail stank.

With an index finger he deftly measured the level in the pail. It was partially full. He emptied himself into it and measured the new level. His mind calculated the difference. If they haven't added to it to confuse me, I've peed three or four times. Twice a day? Or four times a day?

He rubbed his soiled finger against his chest and that made him feel dirtier but it was important to use everything and anything to keep balanced and time related. He lay down again. Out of touch with light or dark or day or night was nauseating. A wave of sickness came from his stomach but he dominated it and forced himself to remember the Brian Kwok who they, the enemy, thought was Brian Kar-shun Kwok and not the other man, the almost forgotten man whose parentage was Wu, his generation name Pah and his adult name Chu-toy.

He remembered Ning-tok and his father and mother and being sent to school to Hong Kong on his sixth birthday, wanting to learn and to grow up to become a patriot like his parents and the uncle he had seen flogged to death in his village square for being a patriot. He had learned from his Hong Kong relations that patriot and Communist were the same and not enemies of the State. That the Kuomintang overlords were just as evil as the foreign devils who had forced the unequal treaties on China, and the only true patriot was he who followed the teachings of Mao Tse-tung. Being sworn into the first of many secret Brotherhoods, working to be the best for the cause of China and Mao which was the cause of China, learning from secret teachers, knowing he was part of the new great wave of revolution that would take back control of China from foreign devils and their lackeys, and sweep them into the sea forever.

Winning that scholarship! At twelve!

Oh how proud his secret teachers had been. Then going to barbarian lands, now perfect in their language and safe against their evil thoughts and ways, going to London, the capital of the greatest empire the world has ever seen, knowing it was going to be humbled and laid waste someday, but then in 1937, still in its last flowering.

Two years there. Hating the English school and the English boys . . . Chinkee Chinkee Chinaman sitting on his tail . . . but hiding it and hiding his tears, his new Brotherhood teachers helping him, guiding him, putting questions and answers into context, showing him the wonder of dialectic, of being part of the true real unquestioned revolution. Never questioning, never a need to question.

Then the German war and being evacuated with all the other school boys and girls to safety in Canada, all that wonderful time in Vancouver, British Columbia, on the Pacific shore, all that immensity, mountains and sea and a thriving Chinatown with good Ning-tok cooking—and a new branch of the world Brotherhood and more teachers, always someone wise to talk to, always someone ready to explain and advise . . . not accepted by his school-mates but still beating them scholastically, in the gym with gloves and at their sports, being a prefect, playing cricket well and tennis well—part of his training. 'Excel, Chu-toy, my son, excel and be patient for the glory of the Party, for the glory of Mao Tse-Tung who is China,' the last words his father had said to him, secret words engraved since he was six—and repeated on his deathbed.

Joining the Royal Canadian Mounted Police had been part of the plan. It was easy to excel in the RCMP, assigned to Chinatown and the wharves and the byways, speaking English and Mandarin and Cantonese—his Ning-tok dialect buried deep— easy to become a fine policeman in that sprawling beautiful city port. Soon he became unique, Vancouver's Chinese expert, trusted, excelling and implacably against the crimes that the triad gangsters of Chinatown fed off—opium, morphine, heroin, prostitution and the ever-constant illegal gambling.

His work had been commended by his superiors and by Brotherhood leaders alike—they equally against gang rule and drug traffic and crime, assisting him to arrest and uncover, their only secret interest the inner workings of the RCMP, how the

RCMP hire and fire and promote and collate and investigate and watch, and who controls what, where and how. Sent from Vancouver to Ottawa for six months, loaned by a grateful chief of police to assist in an undercover investigation of a Chinese drug ring there, making new important Canadian contacts and Brotherhood contacts, learning more and more and breaking the ring and getting promotion. Easy to control crime and get promotion if you work and if you have secret friends by the hundreds, with secret eyes everywhere.

Then the war ending and applying for a transfer for the Hong Kong Police—the final part of the plan.

But not wanting to go, not wanting to leave, loving Canada and loving her. Jeannette. Jeannette deBois. She was nineteen, French-Canadian from Montreal, speaking French and English, her parents French-Canadians of many generations and them liking him and not disapproving, not against him because he was the *Chinoise*, as they jokingly called him. He was twenty-one then, already known as commandant material with a great career ahead of him, marriage ahead, a year or so ahead . . .

Brian Kwok shifted on the mattress in misery. His skin felt clammy and the dark was pressing down. He closed his leaden eyelids and let his mind roam back to her and that time, that bad time in his life. He remembered how he had argued with the Brotherhood, the leader, saying he could serve better in Canada than in Hong Kong where he would be only one of many. Here in Canada he was unique. In a few years he would be in Vancouver's police hierarchy.

But all his arguments had failed. Sadly he knew that they were right. He knew that if he had stayed, eventually he would have gone over to the other side, would have broken with the Party. There were too many unanswered questions now, thanks to reading RCMP reports on the Soviets, the KGB, the *gulags*, too many friends, Canadian and Nationalist, now. Hong Kong and China were remote, his past remote. Jeannette was here, loving her and their life, his souped-up car and prestige among his peers, seeing them as equals, no longer barbarians.

The leader had reminded him of his past, that barbarians are only barbarians, that he was needed in Hong Kong where the battle was just beginning, where Mao was still not yet Chairman Mao, not yet victorious, still embattled with Chiang Kai-shek.

Bitterly he had obeyed, hating being forced, knowing he was in their power and obeying because of their power. But then the heady four years till 1949, and Mao's incredible, unbelievable total victory. Then burrowing deep again, using his brilliant skills to fight the crime that was anathema to him and a disgrace to Hong Kong and a blot on the face of China.

Life was very good again now. He was picked for high promotion, the British bound to him, respecting him because he was from a fine English public school with a fine upper-class English accent and an English sportsman like the elite of the Empire before him.

And now it's 1963 and I'm thirty-nine and tomorrow . . . no, not tomorrow, on Sunday, on Sunday it's the hill climb and on Saturday there are the races and Noble Star—will it be Noble Star or Gornt's Pilot Fish or Richard Kwok's, no Richard *Kwang's* Butterscotch Lass or John Chen's outsider, Golden Lady? I think I'd put my money on Golden Lady—every penny I have, yes, all my life's savings and I'm also gambling the Porsche as well even though that's stupid but I have to. I have to because Crosse said so and Robert agrees and they both said I've got to put up my life as well but Jesus Christ now Golden Lady's limping in the paddock but the gamble's settled and now they're off and running, come on Golden Lady, come on for the love of Mao, don't mind the storm clouds and the lightning come on, all my savings and my life's riding on your rotten lousy god-cursed oh Jesus Chairman don't fail me . . .

He was deep in dreams now, bad dreams, drug-assisted dreams, and Happy Valley was the Valley of Death. His eyes did not feel the lights come up gently nor the door swing open.

It was time to begin again.

Armstrong looked down at his friend, pitying him. The lights were carefully dimmed. Beside him was Senior Agent Malcolm Sun, an SI guard and the SI doctor. Dr. Dorn was a small, dapper, slightly bald specialist with an animated, birdlike intensity. He took Brian Kwok's pulse and measured his blood pressure and listened to his heartbeat.

'The client's in fine shape, Superintendent, physically,' he said with a faint smile. 'His blood pressure and heart beat're nicely up but that's to be expected.' He noted his readings on the chart, handed it to Armstrong, who glanced at his watch, wrote down the time and signed the chart also.

'You can carry on,' he said.

The doctor filled the syringe carefully. With great care he gave Brian Kwok the injection in the rump with a new needle. There was almost no mark, just a tiny spot of blood that he wiped away. 'Dinner time whenever you want,' he said with a smile.

Armstrong just nodded. The SI guard had added a measure of urine to the pail and that was noted on the chart as well. 'Very smart of him to measure the level, didn't think he'd do that,' Malcolm Sun commented. Infrared rays made it easy to monitor a client's most tiny movement from spyholes set into the ceiling lights. '*Dew neh loh moh*, who'd've imagined he'd be the mole? Smart, he always was so fornicating smart.'

'Let's hope the poor bugger's not too fornicating smart,' Armstrong told him sourly. 'The sooner he talks the better. The Old Man won't give up on him.'

The others looked at him. The young SI guard shivered.

Dr. Dorn broke the uneasy silence. 'Should we still maintain the two-hour cycle, sir?'

Armstrong glanced at his friend. The first drug in the beer had been about 1:30 this afternoon. Since then, Brian Kwok had been on a Classification Two—a chemical sleep-wake-sleep-wake schedule. Every two hours. Wake up injections just before 4:30 P.M., 6:30, 8:30, and this would continue until 6:30 A.M. when the first serious interrogation would begin. Within ten minutes of each injection the client would be artificially pulled out of sleep, his thirst and his hunger increased by the drugs. Food would be wolfed and the cold tea gulped and the drugs therein would quickly take effect. Deep sleep, very deep very quick assisted by another injection. Darkness and harsh light alternated, metallic voices and silence alternated. Then wake-up. Breakfast. And two hours later, dinner, and two hours later breakfast. To an increasingly disoriented mind twelve hours would become six days—more if the client could stand it, twelve days, every hour on the hour. No need for physical torture, just darkness and disorientation, enough to discover that which you wish to discover from the enemy client, or to make your enemy client sign what you want him to sign, soon believing your truth to be his truth.

Anyone.

Anyone after a week of sleep-wake-sleep followed by two or three days of no sleep.

Anyone.

Oh Christ almighty, Armstrong thought, you poor bloody bastard, you'll try to hold out and it won't do you a bit of good. None.

But then most of Armstrong's mind shouted back, but he's not your friend but an enemy agent, just a 'client' and enemy who has betrayed you and everything and everyone for years. It was probably him who shopped Fong-fong and his lads who're now in some lousy stinking cell having the same but without doctors and monitoring and care. Still, can you be proud of this type of treatment—can any civilized person?

No. Is it necessary to stuff lousy chemicals into a helpless body?

No . . . yes, yes it is, yes it is sometimes, and killing's necessary sometimes, mad dogs, people—oh yes some people are evil and mad dogs are evil. Yes. You've got to use these modern psychic techniques, developed by Pavlov and other Soviets, developed by Communists under a KGB regime. Ah but do you have to follow them?

Christ I don't know but I do know the KGB're trying to destroy us all and bring us all down to their level an—

Armstrong's eyes focused and he saw them all staring at him. 'What?'

'Shall we maintain the two-hour cycle, sir?' the doctor repeated, disquieted.

'Yes. Yes, and at 6:30 we'll begin the first interview.'

'Are you doing that yourself?'

'It's on the orders, for chrissake,' Armstrong snarled. 'Can't you bloody read?'

'Oh sorry,' the doctor replied at once. They all knew of Armstrong's friendship for the client and of Crosse's ordering him to do the interrogation. 'Would you like a sedative, old chap?' Dr. Dorn asked solicitously.

Armstrong cursed him obscenely and left, angry that he had allowed the doctor to needle him into losing his temper. He went to the top floor, to the officers' mess.

'Barman!'

'Coming up, sir!'

His usual tankard of beer came quickly but tonight the smooth dark liquid he loved, malt heavy and bitter, did not quench his thirst or cleanse his mouth. A thousand times he had worried what he would do if he was caught by *them* and put naked into such a cell, knowing most techniques and practices and being on guard. Better than poor bloody Brian, he thought grimly. Poor bugger knows so little. Yes, but does more knowledge help when you're the client?

His skin felt clammy with fear-sweat as he thought of what was ahead of Brian Kwok.

'Barman!'

'Yes sir, coming up!'

'Evening Robert, can I join you?' Chief Inspector Donald C. C. Smyth asked.

'Oh, hello. Yes . . . sit down,' he told the younger man unenthusiastically.

Smyth sat on the bar stool beside him and eased his arm that was in a sling more comfortably. 'How's it going?'

'Routine.' Armstrong saw Smyth nod and he thought how apt his nickname was. The Snake. Smyth was good-looking, smooth, sinuous like a snake with the same deadly quality of danger there, and the same habit of licking his lips from time to time with the tip of his tongue.

'Christ! It's still impossible to believe it's Brian.' Smyth was one of the few in the know about Brian. 'Shocking.'

'Yes.'

'Robert, I've been ordered by the DCID'—Director of Criminal Investigation, Armstrong's ultimate boss—'to take over the Werewolf case from you while you're occupied. And any others you might want me to cover.'

'Everything's in the files. Sergeant Major Tang-po's my Number Two . . . he's a good detective, very good in fact.' Armstrong quaffed some beer and added cynically, 'He's well connected.'

Smyth smiled with his mouth. 'Good, that's a help.'

'Just don't organize my bloody district.'

'Perish the thought, old chum. East Aberdeen takes all of my skill. Now, what about the Werewolves? Continue surveillance on Phillip Chen?'

'Yes. And his wife.'

'Interesting that before Dianne married that old miser she was Mai-wei T'Chung, eh? Interesting too that one of her cousins was Hummingbird Sung.'

Armstrong stared at him. 'You've been doing your homework.'

'All part of the service!' Smyth added grimly, 'I'd like to get those Werewolves right smartly. We've already had three panic calls in East Aberdeen from people who have had phone calls from the Werewolves demanding *h'eung yau*, "velly quicklee" or else a kidnapping. I hear it's the same all over the Colony. If three frightened citizens called us, you can bet three hundred haven't had the courage.' Smyth sipped his whiskey and soda. 'That's not good for business, not good at all. There's only so much fat on the cow. If we don't get the Werewolves quickly the buggers'll have their own mint—a few quick phone calls and money'll be in the mail, the poor bloody victims happy to pay off to escape their attention—and every other bloody villain here with a sense of larceny will have a field day too.'

'I agree.' Armstrong finished his beer. 'You want another?'

'Let me. Barman!'

Armstrong watched his beer being drawn. 'You think there's a connection between John Chen and Hummingbird Sung?' He remembered Sung, the wealthy shipping magnate with the oral reputation, kidnapped six years ago, and smiled wryly. 'Christ, I haven't thought about him in years.'

'Nor me. The cases don't parallel and we put his kidnappers into pokey for twenty years and they'll rot there but you never know. Perhaps there's a connection.' Smyth shrugged. 'Dianne Chen must have hated John Chen and I'm sure he hated her back, everyone knows that. Same with old Hummingbird.' He laughed. 'Hummingbird's other nickname, in the trade so to speak, is Nosy-nosy.'

Armstrong grunted. He rubbed the tiredness out of his eyes. 'Might be worth going to see John's wife, Barbara. I was going to do that tomorrow but . . . well, it might be worthwhile.'

'I've already got an appointment. And I'm going out to Sha Tin first thing. Maybe those local buggers missed something in the rain.'

'Good idea.' Uneasily Armstrong watched the Snake sipping

his whiskey. 'What's on your mind?' he asked, knowing there was something.

Smyth looked up at him directly. 'There's a lot of things I don't understand about this kidnapping. For instance, why was such a huge reward offered by the High Dragons for John's recapture, curiously, dead or alive?'

'Ask them.'

'I have. At least, I asked someone who knows one of them.' The Snake shrugged. 'Nothing. Nothing at all ' He hesitated. 'We'll have to go back into John's past.'

Armstrong felt a shaft of cold that he kept buried. 'Good idea.'

'Did you know Mary knew him? In the POW camp at Stanley?'

'Yes.' Armstrong drank some beer without tasting it.

'She might give us a lead—if John was, say, connected with black market in the camp.' His pale blue eyes held Armstrong's pale blue eyes. 'Might be worth asking.'

'I'll think about that. Yes, I'll think about that.' The big man bore the Snake no malice. If he had been the Snake he would have asked too. The Werewolves were very bad news and the first wave of terror had already rushed through Chinese society. How many more people know about Mary and John Chen? he asked himself. Or about the 40,000 that's still burning a hole in my desk, still burning a hole in my soul. 'It was a long time ago.'

'Yes.'

Armstrong lifted his beer. 'You've got your "friends" helping you?'

'Let's just say very substantial rewards and payments are being made—paid gratefully, I hasten to add, by our gambling fraternity.' The sardonic smile left Smyth's face. And the banter. 'We've got to get those sodding Werewolves very fast or they'll really upset our applecart.'

52

Four Finger Wu was on the tall poop of the motorized junk that was wallowing in the chop at the rendezvous well out to sea, all lights doused. 'Listen, Werewolf turd,' he hissed irritably at Smallpox Kin who lay quivering on the deck at his feet, mindless with pain, trussed with rope and heavy chain. 'I want to know who else is in your fornicating gang and where you got the coin from, the half-coin.' There was no answer. 'Wake the fornicator up!'

Obligingly Goodweather Poon poured another bucket of seawater over the prostrate youth. When this had no effect, he leaned down with his knife. At once Smallpox Kin screamed and came out of his stupor. 'What, what is it, Lord?' he shrieked. 'No more . . . what is it, what do you want?'

Four Finger Wu repeated what he had said. The youth shrieked again as Goodweather Poon probed. 'I've told you everything . . . everything . . .' Desperately, never believing that there could be so much pain in the universe, beyond caring, he babbled again who were the members of the gang, all their real names and addresses, even about the old *amah* in Aberdeen. '. . . my father gave me the coin . . . I don't know where . . . he gave it to me never saying wh . . . he got it I swearrrrr. . . .' His voice trailed away. Once more he fainted.

Four Fingers spat disgustedly. 'The youth of today have no fortitude!'

The night was dark and an ill-tempered wind gusted from time to time under a lowering overcast, the powerful and well-tuned engine purring nicely, making just enough way to lessen the junk's inevitable corkscrewing—the rolling pitch and toss.

They were a few miles southwest of Hong Kong, just out of the sea-lanes, PRC waters and the vast mouth of the Pearl River just to port, open sea to starboard. All sails were furled.

He lit a cigarette and coughed. 'All gods curse all fornicating triad turds!'

'Shall I wake him again?' Goodweather Poon asked.

'No. No, the fornicator's told the truth as much as he knows.' Wu's calloused fingers reached up and nervously touched the half-coin that he wore now around his neck under his ragged sweat shirt, making sure it was still there. A knot of anxiety welled at the thought that the coin might be genuine, might be Phillip Chen's missing treasure. 'You did very well, Good-weather Poon. Tonight you'll get a bonus.' His eyes went to the southeast, seeking the signal. It was overdue but he was not yet worried. Automatically his nosed sniffed the wind and his tongue tasted it, tangy and heavy with salt. His eyes ranged the sky and the sea and the horizon. 'More rain soon,' he muttered.

Poon lit another cigarette from his butt and ground the butt into the deck with his horny bare foot. 'Will it ruin the races on Saturday?'

The old man shrugged. 'If the gods will it. I think it will be piss heavy again tomorrow. Unless the wind veers. Unless the wind veers we could have the Devil Winds, the Supreme Winds, and those fornicators could scatter us to the Four Seas. Piss on the Supreme Winds!'

'I'll piss on them if there are no races. My nose tells me it's Banker Kwang's horse.'

'Huh! That stinky, mealy-mouth nephew of mine certainly needs a change of joss! The fool's lost his bank!'

Poon hawked and spat for luck. 'Thank all gods for Profitable Choy!'

Since Four Fingers and his captains and his people had all successfully extracted all their monies from the Ho-Pak, thanks to information from Paul Choy—and since he himself was still enjoying vast profits from his son's illicit manipulation of Struan stock, Wu had dubbed him Profitable Choy. Because of the profit, he had forgiven his son the transgression. But only in his heart. Being prudent, the old man had showed none of it outwardly except to his friend and confidant, Goodweather Poon.

'Bring him on deck.'

'What about this Werewolf fornicator?' Poon's horny toe stabbed Kin. 'Young Profitable didn't like him or this matter at all, *heya*?'

'Time he grew up, time he knew how to treat enemies, time he knew real values, not ill-omened, stink-wind, fatuous Golden Mountain values.' The old man spat on the deck. 'He's forgotten who he is and where his interests lie.'

'You said yourself you don't send a rabbit against a dragon. Or a minnow against a shark. You've your investment to consider and don't forget Profitable Choy's returned everything he cost you over fifteen years twenty times over. In the money market he's a High Dragon and only twenty-six. Leave him where he's best, best for you and best for him. *Heya*?'

'Tonight he's best here.'

The old seaman scratched his ear. 'I don't know about that, Four Fingers. That the gods will decide. Me, I'd have left him ashore.' Now Goodweather Poon was watching the southeast. His peripheral vision had caught something. 'You see it?'

After a moment Four Fingers shook his head. 'There's plenty of time, plenty of time.'

'Yes.' The old seaman glanced back at the body trussed with chains like a plucked chicken. His face split into a grin. 'Eeeee, but when Profitable Choy turned white like a jellyfish at this fornicator's first scream and first blood, I had to break wind to release my laughter to save his face!'

'The young today have no fortitude,' Wu repeated, then lit a new cigarette and nodded. 'But you're right. After tonight Profitable's going to be left where he belongs to become even more profitable.' He glanced down at Smallpox Kin. 'Is he dead?'

'Not yet. What a dirty motherless whore to hit Number One Son Noble House Chen with a shovel and then lie about it to us, *heya*? And to cut off Chen's ear and blame his father and brothers and lie about that too! And then taking the ransom even though they couldn't deliver the goods! Terrible!'

'Disgusting!' The old man guffawed. 'Even more terrible to get caught. But then you showed the fornicator the error of his rotten ways, Goodweather Poon.'

They both laughed, happy together.

'Shall I cut off his other ear, Four Fingers?'

'Not yet. Soon, yes, very soon.'

Again Poon scratched his head. 'One thing I don't understand. I don't understand why you told me to put their sign on Number One Son and leave him as they planned to leave him.' He frowed at Four Fingers. 'When this fornicator's dead that's all the Werewolves dead, *heya*? So what good is the sign?'

Four Fingers cackled. 'All comes clear to he who waits. Patience,' he said, very pleased with himself. The sign implied the Werewolves were very much alive. If only he and Poon knew that they were all dead, he could at any time resurrect them, or the threat of them. At his whim. Yes, he thought happily, kill one to terrify ten thousand! The 'Werewolves' can easily become a continuous source of extra revenue at very little cost. A few phone calls, a judicious kidnapping or two, perhaps another ear. 'Patience, Goodweather Poon. Soon you'll un—' He stopped. Both men had centered their eyes on the same spot in the darkness. A small, dimly lit freighter was just nosing into sight. In a moment two lights flashed at her masthead. At once Wu went to the conn and flashed an answering signal. The freighter flashed the confirm. 'Good,' Wu said happily, flashing his reconfirm. The deck crew had also seen the lights. One hurried below to fetch the rest of the seamen and the others went to their action stations. Wu's eyes fell on Smallpox Kin. 'First him,' he said malevolently. 'Fetch my son here.'

Weakly Paul Choy groped his way on deck. He gulped the fresh air gratefully, the stench from below decks overpowering. He climbed the gangway to the poop. When he saw the red mess on the deck and the partial person on the deck, his stomach revolted and once more he threw up over the side.

Four Finger Wu said, 'Give Goodweather Poon a hand.'

'What?'

'Are your ears filled with vomit?' the old man shouted. 'Give him a hand.'

Frightened, Paul Choy reeled over to the old seaman, the helmsman watching interestedly. 'What do you . . . you want me to do?'

'Take his legs!'

Paul Choy tried to dominate his nausea. He closed his eyes. His nostrils were filled with the smell of vomit and blood. He reached down, took the legs and part of the heavy chain and staggered, half falling, to the side. Goodweather Poon was carrying most of the weight and he could easily have carried it all and Paul Choy too if need be. Effortlessly he balanced Smallpox Kin on the gunnel.

'Hold him there!' By prearrangement with Four Fingers, the old seaman backed away, leaving Paul Choy on his own, the unconscious, mutilated face and body slumped precariously against him.

'Put him overboard!' Wu ordered.

'But Father . . . please . . . he's . . . he's not de . . . not dead yet. Pl—'

'*Put him over the side!*'

Beside himself with fear and loathing, Paul Choy tried to pull the body back aboard but the wind squalled and heeled the junk and the last of the Werewolves toppled into the sea and sank without a trace. Helplessly Paul Choy stared at the waves slopping against the teak. He saw that there was blood on his shirt and on his hands. Another wave of nausea racked him, tormenting him.

'Here!' Gruffly Wu handed his son a flask. It contained whiskey, good whiskey. Paul Choy choked a little but his stomach held the whiskey. Wu turned back to the conn, waved the helmsman toward the freighter, the throttle opened to full ahead. Paul Choy almost fell but managed to grab the gunnel and stay on his feet, unprepared for the suddenness of the deep-throated roar and burst of speed. When he had his sea legs he looked at his father. Now the old man was near the tiller, Goodweather Poon nearby, and both were peering into the darkness. He could see the small ship and his stomach reeled, and he hated his father afresh, hated being on board and being involved in what obviously was smuggling—on top of the horror of the Werewolf.

Whatever that poor son of a bitch did, he thought, enraged, it doesn't merit taking the law into your own hands. He should've been handed over to the police to be hanged or imprisoned or whatever.

Wu felt the eyes on him and he glanced back. His face did not change. 'Come here,' he ordered, his thumbless hand stabbing the gunnel in front of him. 'Stand here.'

Numbly Paul Choy obeyed. He was much taller than his

father and Goodweather Poon but he was a piece of chaff against either of them.

The junk sped through the darkness on an intercept course, the sea black and the night black with just a little moonlight sifting through the overcast. Soon they were just aft of the vessel and a little to starboard, closing fast. She was small, slow and quite old and she dipped uneasily in the gathering swell. 'She's a coastal freighter,' Goodweather Poon volunteered, 'a Thai trawler we call them. There's dozens of the fornicators in all Asian waters. They're the lice of the seas, Profitable Choy, crewed by scum, captained by scum, and they leak like lobster pots. Most ply the Bangkok, Singapore, Manila, Hong Kong route, and wherever else they've a cargo for. This one's out of Bangkok.' He hawked and spat, revolting the young man again. 'I wouldn't want to voyage on one of those stinking whores. Th—'

He stopped. There was another brief flashing signal. Wu answered it. Then all on deck saw the splash on her starboard side as something heavy went overboard. At once Four Fingers rang up 'all engines stop'. The sudden quiet was deafening. Bow lookouts peered into the darkness, the junk wallowing and swerving as she slowed.

Then one of the bow lookouts signaled with a flag. At once Wu gave a little engine and made the correction. Another silent signal and another change of direction and then a sharper, more exited movement of the flag.

Immediately Wu reversed engines. The props bit the sea heavily. Then he killed the thrust, the junk swerving closer to the line of bobbing buoys. The gnarled old man seemed to be part of the ship as Paul Choy watched him with his eyes fixed into the sea ahead. Nimbly Wu maneuvered the ponderous junk into the course of the buoys. In a few moments a seaman with a long, hooked boarding pole leaned out from the main deck and hooked the line. The rough cork buoys were brought aboard deftly, other seamen helping, and the line attached securely to a stanchion. With practiced skill the chief deckhand cut away the buoys and cast them overboard while more seamen made sure that the bales attached to the other end of the line below the surface were safe and secure. Paul Choy could see the bales clearly now. There were two of them, perhaps six foot by three foot by three foot, roped together heavily underwater, their sinking weight keeping the thick line taut. As soon as all was tight and safe, the cargo secure alongside though still five or six feet beneath the surface of the sea, the chief deckhand signaled. At once Four Fingers brought the junk to cruising speed and they sped away on a different tack.

The whole operation had been done in silence, effortlessly and in seconds. In moments the weak riding lights of the Thai trawler had vanished into the darkness and they were alone on the sea once more.

Wu and Goodweather Poon lit cigarettes. 'Very good,' Goodweather Poon said. Four Fingers did not reply, his ears listening to the pleasing note of the engines. No trouble there, he thought. His senses tested the wind. No trouble there. His eyes ranged the darkness. Nothing there either, he told himself. Then why are you uneasy? Is it Seventh Son?

He glanced at Paul Choy who was at the port side, his back toward him. No. No danger there either.

Paul Choy was watching the bales. They picked up a small wake. His curiosity peaked and he was feeling a little better, the whiskey warming and the salt smelling good now, that and the excitement of the rendezvous and being away and safe. 'Why don't you bring them aboard, Father? You could lose them.'

Wu motioned Poon to answer.

'Better to leave the harvest of the sea to the sea, Profitable Choy, until it's quite safe to bring it ashore. *Heya?*'

'My name's Paul, not Profitable.' The young man looked back at his father and shivered. 'There was no need to murder that fornicator!'

'The captain didn't,' Goodweather Poon said with a grin, answering for the old man. 'You did, Profitable Choy. You did, you threw him overboard. I saw it clearly. I was within half a pace of you.'

'Lies! I tried to pull him back! And anyway he ordered me to. He threatened me.'

The old seaman shrugged. 'Tell that to a fine, foreign devil judge, Profitable Choy, and that won't be fornicating profitable at all!'

'My name's not Pro—'

'The Captain of the Fleets has called you Profitable so by all the gods Profitable you are forever. *Heya?'* he added, grinning at Four Fingers.

The old man said nothing, just smiled and showed his few broken teeth and that made his grimace even more frightening. His bald head and weathered face nodded his agreement. Then he put his eyes on his son. Paul Choy shivered in spite of his resolve.

'Your secret's safe with me, my son. Never fear. No one aboard this boat saw anything. Did they, Goodweather Poon?'

'No, nothing. By all gods great and small! No one saw anything!'

Paul Choy stared back sullenly. 'You can't wrap paper in fire!'

Goodweather Poon guffawed. 'On this boat you can!'

'Yes,' Wu said, his voice a rasp. 'On this boat you can keep a secret forever.' He lit another cigarette, hawked and spat. 'Don't you want to know what's in those bales?'

'No.'

'It's opium. Delivered on shore this night's work will bring a $200,000 profit, just to me, with plenty in bonuses for my crew.'

'That profit's not worth the risk, *not to me*. I made you th—' Paul Choy stopped.

Four Finger Wu looked at him. He spat on the deck and passed the conn to Goodweather Poon and went to the great cushioned seats aft that ringed the poop. 'Come here, Profitable Choy,' he commanded.

Frightened, Paul Choy sat at the point indicated. Now they were more alone.

'Profit is profit,' Wu said, very angry. '10,000 is your profit. That's enough to buy an air ticket to Honolulu and back to Hong Kong and have ten days of holiday together.' He saw the momentary flash of joy wash across his son's face and he smiled inside.

'I'll never come back,' Paul Choy said bravely. 'Never.'

'Oh yes you will. You will now. You've fished in fornicating dangerous waters.'

'I'll never come back. I've a U.S. passport and a—'

'And a Jap whore, *heya?'*

Paul Choy stared at his father, aghast that his father knew, then rage possessed him and he sprang up and bunched his

870

fists. 'She's not a whore by all gods! She's great, she's a lady and her folks're th—'

'Quiet!' Wu bit back the expletive carefully. 'Very well, she's not a whore, even though to me all women are whores. She's not a whore but an empress. But she's still a fornicating devil from the Eastern Sea, one of those who raped China.'

'She's American, she's American like me,' Paul Choy flared, his fists clenched tighter, ready to spring. The helmsman and Goodweather Poon readied to interfere without seeming to. A knife slid into Poon's fist. 'I'm American, she's American nisei and her father was with the 442 in Italy an—'

'You're Haklo, you're one of the Seaborne Wu, the ship people, and you'll obey me! You will, Profitable Choy, oh yes you will obey! *Heya?*'

Paul Choy stood in front of him shaking with equal fury, trying to keep up his courage, for, in rage, the old man was formidable and he could feel Goodweather Poon and the other men behind his back. 'Don't call her names! Don't!'

'You dare bunch your fists at me? Me who's given you life, given you everything? Every chance, even the chance of meeting this . . . this Eastern Sea Empress? *Heya?*'

Paul Choy felt himself spun around as though by a great wind. Goodweather Poon was peering up at him. 'This is the Captain of the Fleets. You will respect him!' The seaman's iron hand shoved him back to the seats. 'The captain said sit. *Sit!*'

After a moment, Paul Choy said sullenly, 'How did you know about her?'

Exasperated, the old man sputtered, 'All gods bear witness to this country person I sired, this monkey with the brains and manners of a country person. Do you think I didn't have you watched? Guarded? Do I send a mole among snakes or a civilized whelp among foreign devils unprotected? You're the son of Wu Sang Fang, Head of the Seaborne Wu, and I protect my own against all enemies. You think we don't have enemies enough who would slit your Secret Sack and send me the contents just to spite me? *Heya?*'

'I don't know.'

'Well know it very well now, my son!' Four Finger Wu was aware this was a clash to the death and he had to be wise as a father must be when his son finally calls him. He was not afraid.

871

He had done this with many sons and only lost one. But he was grateful to the tai-pan who had given him the information about the girl and about her parentage. That's the key, he thought, the key to this impudent child from a Third Wife whose Golden Gulley was as sweet and as tender as fresh bonefish as long as she lived. Perhaps I'll let him bring the whore here. The poor fool needs a whore whatever he calls her. Lady? Ha! I've heard the Eastern Sea Devils have no pubics! Disgusting! Next month he can bring the strumpet here. If her parents let her come alone that proves she's a whore. If they don't, then that's the end of her. Meanwhile I'll find him a wife. Yes. Who? One of Tightfist's granddaughters? Or Lando Mata's or . . . Ah, wasn't that half-caste's youngest brat trained in the Golden Mountain too, at a school for girls, a famous school for girls? What's the difference to this fool, pure blood or not?

I have many sons, he thought, feeling nothing for him. I gave them life. Their duty is to me and when I'm dead, to the clan. Perhaps a good broadhipped, hard-footed Haklo boat-girl'd be the right one for him, he thought grimly. Yes, but eeeee, there's no need to cut your Stalk to spite a weakness in your bladder, however rude and ill-mannered the fornicating dumblehead is! 'In a month Black Beard will grant you a holiday,' he said with finality. 'I will see to it. With your 10,000 profit you can take a passage on a flying machine . . . No! Better to bring her here,' he added as though it were a fresh thought. 'You will bring her here. You should see Manila and Singapore and Bangkok and visit our captains there. Yes, bring her here in a month, your 10,000 will pay for the ticket and pay for everyth—'

'No. I won't. I won't do it. And I don't want drug money! I'll never take drug money and I counsel you to get out of the drug trade immed—'

The whole junk was suddenly floodlit. Everyone was momentarily blinded. The searchlight was to starboard.

'*Haul to!*' came the order in English over the loud-hailer, then repeated in Haklo, then in Cantonese.

Wu and Goodweather Poon were the first to react and in a split second they were in motion. Wu swung the tiller hard to port away from the Marine Police patrol boat and gunned both the engines to full ahead. Poon had leapt down the gangway to the main deck and now he sliced the cargo line and the wake of

872

bales vanished as the bales sank into the deep.

'*Haul to for boarding!*' The metallic words ripped through Paul Choy who stood paralyzed with fright. He watched his father reach into a nearby sea locker and bring out some crumpled PRC peaked soldiers' hats and shove one on. 'Quick,' he ordered, throwing one to him. Petrified, he obeyed and crammed it onto his head. Miraculously all the crew were now wearing the same kind of hat and a few were struggling into equally drab and crumpled army tunics.

His heart stopped. Others were reaching into sea lockers and bringing out PRC army rifles and submachine guns as still others went to the side nearest the police boat and began shouting obscenities. The boat was sleek and battle gray with a deck gun, two searchlights now and her riding lights on. She lay a hundred yards to starboard, her engines growling, keeping pace with them easily. They could see the neat, white-clad sailors and, on the bridge, the peaked British officers' caps.

Four Fingers had a loud-hailer horn now and he went to the side, his hat pulled well down, and he roared, 'Go fornicate yourselves, barbarians! Look at our colors!' His hand stabbed towards his masthead. The PRC marine flag fluttered there. Aft on the stern was a fake Canton PRC registration number. 'Leave a peaceful patrol alone . . . you're in our waters!'

Poon's face was split into a malevolent grin. A PRC automatic pistol was in his hands and he stood at the gunnel silhouetted in the light, the cap pulled well down to preclude identification by the binoculars he knew were raking the ship. His heart was racing too and there was a sick-sweet-sour bile in his mouth. They were in international waters. Safety and PRC waters were fifteen minutes away. He cocked the gun. Orders were quite clear. No one was boarding tonight.

'*Haul to! We're coming aboard!*'

They all saw the patrol boat slow and the cutter splash into the sea and many aboard lost their initial confidence. Four Fingers squeezed the throttle forward to get the last fraction of power. He cursed himself for not seeing the police boat or sensing their presence earlier but he knew that they had electronic devices to see in the dark whereas he had to rely on eyes and nose and the sixth sense that so far had kept him and most of his people alive.

It was rare to find a patrol boat so close to Chinese waters.

Even so, the boat was there and though his cargo was gone, there were guns aboard and so was Paul Choy. Joss! All gods defecate on that patrol boat! Goodweather Poon was partially right, he told himself. The gods will decide if it was wise or not to bring the youth aboard.

'Go fornicate yourselves! No foreign devil comes aboard a patrol boat of the People's Republic of China!' All the crew cheered enthusiastically, adding their obscenities to the din.

'*Haul to!*'

The old man paid no attention. The junk was headed toward the Pearl River estuary at maximum speed and he and all aboard prayed that there were no PRC patrols nearby. In the searchlight they could see the cutter with ten armed sailors on an intercept course but it was not fast enough to overtake them.

'*For the last time, haul tooooo!*'

'For the fornicating last time leave peaceful PRC patrol to their own waters. . . .'

Suddenly the patrol's sirens started *whoopwhoopwhooping* and she seemed to jump forward from the violent thrust of her engines, a high churning wake astern. The searchlight still kept them centered as she charged ahead and cut across the junk's bow and stayed there, her engines growling malevolently, barring the path to safety.

Paul Choy was still staring at the battle gray, sharp-nosed craft with its deck gun manned and machine guns manned, big, with four times the power they had, the gap closing fast with no room to maneuver. They could see the uniformed sailors on her deck and the officers on the bridge, radar aerials sweeping.

'Get your head down,' Wu warned Paul Choy who obeyed instantly. Then Wu ran forward to the bow, Goodweather Poon beside him. Both had automatic machine guns.

'Now!'

Carefully he and his friend sprayed the sea toward the patrol boat that was almost on them, taking extreme care that none of the bullets splashed the deck. Instantly the searchlight went out and at once, in the blinding darkness, the helmsman put the junk hard to starboard and prayed that Wu had chosen correctly. The junk slid around the other ship with a few yards leeway as the other craft gunned ahead to get out of the way of the bullets. The helmsman heaved her back on her course and her dash for safety.

'Good,' Wu muttered, knowing he had gained another hundred yards. His mind carried the chart of these waters. Now they were in the gray area between Hong Kong and PRC waters, a few hundred yards from real safety. In the darkness all on deck had kept their eyes tightly shut. The moment they felt the searchlight again, they opened their eyes and adjusted more quickly. The attacker was ahead and to port out of machine gun range but still ahead and still in the way. Wu smiled grimly. 'Big Nose Lee!' His chief deckhand came promptly, and he handed him the machine gun. 'Don't use it till I order it and don't hit one of those fornicators!'

Suddenly the darkness split and the *parrang* of the deck gun deafened them. A split second and a vast spout of water burst from the sea near their bow. Wu was shocked and he shook his fist at the ship. 'Fornicate you and all your mothers! Leave us alone or Chairman Mao will sink all Hong Kong!'

He hurried aft. 'I'll take the tiller!'

The helmsman was frightened. So was Paul Choy, but at the same time he was curiously excited and vastly impressed with the way his father commanded and the way everyone aboard reacted with discipline instead of as the motley ragtag bunch of pirates he had imagined them to be.

'Haul to!'

Again the gap began closing but the patrol boat kept out of machine gun range and the cutter kept out of range aft. Stoically Wu held his course. Another flash then another and *parrang parrannng*. Two shells straddled the junk rocking her.

'Fornicate all mothers,' Wu gasped, 'all gods keep those gunners accurate!' He knew that the shots were only to frighten. His friend the Snake had given him assurances that all patrols were ordered never to hit or sink a fleeing junk carrying PRC colors in case the colors were real, never to forcibly board unless one of their own seamen was killed or wounded. 'Give them a burst,' he called out.

Obediently but with great care, the two men on the bow sprayed the waters. The searchlight never wavered, but suddenly it went out.

Wu kept his course firm. Now what? he asked himself desperately. Where's that fornicator going? He searched the darkness, his eyes straining to see the patrol boat and the promontory he knew was nearby. Then he saw the silhouette to port aft. She was bearing down fast in a swirling rush to come up alongside with grappling hooks. Safety was a hundred yards ahead. If he turned from the new danger he would parallel safety and stay in international waters and then the ship would do the same again and shepherd him into open seas until his ammunition was gone or the dawn came and he was lost. He dare not make a real battle for he knew British law had a long arm and the killing of one of their seamen was punished with hanging, and no money or high friends would prevent it. If he held his course the ship could grapple him and he knew how adept and well trained these Cantonese seamen were and how they hated Haklos.

His face split into a grimace. He waited until the patrol boat was fifty yards astern, coming up very fast, the siren whooping deafeningly, then grimly he turned the tiller into her and prayed the captain was awake. For a moment the two ships hung in the balance. Then the patrol boat swung away to avoid the collision, the wash from her props spraying them. Wu wheeled starboard and slammed all throttles forward even though they were already as far forward as they could go. A few more yards were gained.

He saw the patrol boat recover quickly. She roared around in a circle and came back at them on a different tack. They were just within Chinese waters. Without hope Four Fingers left the tiller and picked up another submachine gun and sprayed the darkness, the barking *thwack thwack thwack* and the smell of cordite making his fear more intense. Abruptly the searchlight splashed him, its light vicious. He turned his head, blinded, and blinked, keeping his head and cap well down. When he could see again he pointed the automatic directly at the light and cursed obscenely, frightened that they would grapple him and tow him from safety. The hot barrel shook as he aimed for the light, his finger on the trigger. It would be death if he fired and prison if he didn't. Fear spread through him and throughout his ship.

But the light did not sweep down as he expected. It remained aft and now he saw her bow wave lessening and her wake waves lessening and his heart began to beat again. The patrol boat was letting him go. The Snake had been right!

Shakily he put down the gun. The loud-hailer was nearby. He brought it to his mouth.

'Victory to Chairman Mao!' he bellowed with all his might. 'Stay out of our waters, you fornicating foreign devillls!' The joy-filled words echoed across the waters. His crew jeered, shaking their fists at the light. Even Paul Choy was caught up in the excitement and shouted too as they all realized the patrol boat would not venture into Chinese waters.

The searchlight vanished. When their eyes had adjusted they saw the patrol broadside, making hardly any way, her riding lights on now.

'She'll have us on their radar,' Paul Choy muttered in English.

'*Wat?*'

He repeated it in Haklo, using the English word, *radar*, but explaining it as a magic eye. Both Poon and Four Fingers knew about radar in principle though they had never seen one. 'What does that matter?' Wu scoffed. 'Their magic screens or magic eyes won't help them now. We can lose them easily in the channels near Lan Tao. There's no evidence against us, no contraband aboard, no nothing!'

'What about the guns?'

'We can lose them overboard, or we can lose those mad dogs and keep our guns! Eeeee, Goodweather Poon, when those shells straddled us I thought my anus was jammed shut forever!'

'Yes,' Poon agreed happily, 'and when we fired into the darkness at the fornicators . . . all gods fornicate! I've always wanted to use those guns!'

Wu laughed too until the tears were running down his face. 'Yes, yes, Old Friend.' Then he explained to Paul Choy the strategy that the Snake had worked out for them. 'Good, *heya?*'

'Who's the Snake?' Paul Choy asked.

Wu hesitated, his small eyes glittering. 'An employee, a police employee you might say, Profitable Choy.'

'With the cargo gone the night's not profitable at all,' Poon said sourly.

'Yes,' Wu agreed, equally sourly. He had already promised Venus Poon a diamond ring that he had planned to pay for from tonight's transactions. Now he would have to dip into his savings, which was against all his principles. You pay for whores out of current earnings, never out of savings, so piss on that police boat! he thought. Without the diamond present . . . Eeeee, but her Beauteous Box is everything Richard Kwang claimed, and the wriggle of her rump everything rumor had promised. And tonight . . . tonight after the TV station closes, her Gorgeous Gate is due to open once more!

'Filthy joss, that sharp-nosed bandit finding us tonight,' he said, his manhood stirring at the thought of Venus Poon. 'All that money gone and our expenses heavy!'

'The cargo's lost?' Paul Choy asked, greatly surprised.

'Of course lost, gone to the bottom,' the old man said irritably.

'You haven't got a marker on it, or a bleeper?' Paul Choy used the English word. He explained it to them. 'I presumed it would have one—or a float that would release itself in a day or two, chemically—so you could recover it or send frogmen to fetch it when it was safe to do so.' The two men were gaping at him. 'What's the matter?'

'It is easy to find these "bleepers" or to arrange a delayed float for a day or two?' Wu asked.

'Or a week or two weeks if you want, Father.'

'Would you write all this down, how to do it? Or you could arrange it?'

'Of course. But why don't you also have a magic eye, like theirs?'

'What do we need with them—and who could work them?' The old man scoffed again. 'We have noses and ears and eyes.'

'But you got caught tonight.'

'Watch your tongue!' Wu said angrily. 'That was joss, joss, a joke of the gods. We're safe and that's all that matters!'

'I disagree, Captain,' Paul Choy said, without fear now as everything fell into place. 'It would be easy to equip this boat with a magic eye—then you can see them as soon or sooner than they can see you. They can't surprise you. So you can thumb your noses at them without fear and never lose a cargo. *Heya*?' He smiled inwardly, seeing them hooked. 'Never a mistake, not even a little one. And never danger. And never a lost cargo. And cargo with bleepers. You don't even need to be anywhere near

878

the drop. Only a week later, *heya?*'

'That would be perfect,' Poon said fervently. 'But if the gods are against you, Profitable Choy, even magic eyes won't help. It was close tonight. That whore wasn't supposed to be here.'

They all looked at the ship, just lying aft. Waiting. A few hundred yards aft. Wu set the engine to slow ahead. 'We don't want to go too deep into PRC waters,' he said uneasily. 'Those civilized fornicators are not so polite or so law-abiding.' A shiver went through him. 'We could use a magic eye, Goodweather Poon.'

'Why don't you own one of those patrol boats?' Paul Choy said, baiting the hook again. 'Or one a little faster. Then you could outrun them.'

'One of those? Are you mad?'

'Who would sell us one?' Wu asked impatiently.

'Japanese.'

'Fornicate all Eastern Sea Devils,' Poon said.

'Perhaps, but they'd build you something like that, radar equipped. They—'

He stopped as the police patrol boat cut in her deep growling engines, and, with her siren *whoopwhoopwhooping*, hurtled off into the night, her wake churning.

'Look at her go,' Paul Choy said admiringly in English. 'Classy son of a bitch!'

He repeated it in Haklo. 'I'll bet she's still got the Thai trawler in her magic eye. They can see everything, every junk, every ship and cove and promontory for miles—even a storm.'

Thoughtfully Four Finger Wu gave a new course to the helmsman that kept them just in PRC waters heading north for the islands and reefs around Lan Tao Island where he would be safe to make the next rendezvous. There they would transfer to another junk with real registrations—PRC and Hong Kong—to slide back into Aberdeen. Aberdeen! His fingers nervously touched the half-coin again. He had forgotten the coin in the excitement. Now his fingers trembled and his anxiety was re-kindled as he thought about his meeting with the tai-pan tonight. There was plenty of time. He would not be late. Even so he increased speed.

'Come,' he ordered, motioning Poon and Paul Choy to join him on the cushions aft where they would be more private.

'Perhaps we'd be wise to stay with our junks, and not get one of those whores, my son.' Wu's finger stabbed the darkness where the patrol boat had been. 'The foreign devils would become even madder if I had one of those in my fleet. But this magic eye of yours . . . you could install it and show us how to use it?'

'I could get experts to do that. People from the Eastern Sea—it would be better to use them—not British or German.'

Wu looked at his friend. '*Heya?*'

'I don't want one of those turds or their magic eyes on my ship. Soon we'd rely on the fornicators and we'd lose our treasures along with our heads,' the other man grumbled.

'But to see when others can't?' Wu puffed on his cigarette. 'Is there another seller, Profitable Choy?'

'They would be the best. And cheapest, Father.'

'Cheapest, *heya?* How much will this cost?'

'I don't know. 20,000 U.S., perhaps 40—'

The old man exploded. '40,000 U.S.? Am I made of gold? I have to work for my money! Am I Emperor Wu?'

Paul Choy let the old man rave. He was feeling nothing for him anymore, not after all the night's horror and killing and entrapment and cruelty and blackmail, and most of all because of his father's words against his girl. He would respect his father for his seamanship, for his courage and his command. And as Head of the House. Nothing more. And from now on he would treat him like any other man.

When he felt the old man had raved enough, he said, 'I can have the first magic eye installed and two men trained at no cost to you, if you want.'

Wu and Poon stared at him. Wu was instantly on guard. 'How at no cost?'

'I will pay for it for you.'

Poon started to guffaw but Wu hissed, 'Shut up, fool, and listen. Profitable Choy knows things you don't know!' His eyes were glittering even more. If a magic eye, why not a diamond too? And if a diamond, why not a mink coat and all the necessary plunder that that mealy-mouthed whore will require to sustain her enthusiastic cleft, hands and mouth.

'How will you pay for it, my son?'

'Out of profit.'

'Profit of what?'

'I want control, for one month, of your money in the Victoria.'

'Impossible!'

'We opened accounts for 22,423,000. Control for one month.'

'To do what with?'

'The stock market.'

'Ah, gamble? Gamble with my money? My hard-earned cash? Never.'

'One month. We split the profit, Father.'

'Oh, we split? It is my fornicating money but you want half. Half of what?'

'Perhaps another 20 million.' Paul Choy let the sum hang. He saw the avarice on his father's face and knew that though the negotiation would be heated, they would make a deal. It was only a matter of time.·

'*Ayeeyah*, that's impossible, out of the question!'

The old man felt an itch below and he scratched the itch. His manhood stirred. Instantly he thought of Venus Poon who had made him stand as he had not stood for years and of their coming bout tonight. 'Perhaps I shall just pay for this magic eye,' he said, testing the young man's resolve.

Paul Choy took his spirit completely into his own hands. 'Yes, yes you can, but then I'm leaving Hong Kong.'

Wu's tongue darted spitefully. 'You will leave when I tell you to leave.'

'But if I can't be profitable and put my expensive training to work, why should I stay? Did you pay all that money for me to be a pimp on one of your Pleasure Boats? A deckhand on a junk that can be raped at will by the nearest foreign devil cutter? No, better I leave! Better I become profitable to someone else so that I can begin to repay your investment in me. I will give Black Bear a month's notice and leave then.'

'You will leave when I tell you to leave!' Wu added malevolently. 'You have fished in dangerous waters.'

'Yes.' And so have you, Paul Choy wanted to add, unafraid. If you think you can blackmail me, that I'm on your hook, you're on mine and you've more to lose. Haven't you heard of Queen's evidence, turning Queen's evidence—or plea bargaining? But he kept this future ploy secret, to be used when necessary, and kept his face polite and bland. 'All waters are dangerous if the gods decide they're dangerous,' he said cryptically.

Wu took a long deep drag of his cigarette, feeling the smoke deep within him. He had noticed the change in this young man before him. He had seen many such changes in many men. In many sons and many daughters. The experience of his long years screamed caution. This whelp's dangerous, very dangerous, he thought. I think Goodweather Poon was right: it was a mistake to bring Profitable Choy aboard tonight. Now he knows too much about us.

Yes. But that's easy to rectify, when I need to, he reminded himself. Any day or any night.

53

'Well, what the devil are you going to do, Paul?' the governor asked Havergill. Johnjohn was with them and they were on the terrace of Government House after dinner, leaning against the low balustrade. 'Good God! If the Victoria runs out of money too, this whole Island's ruined, eh?'

Havergill looked around to make sure they were not being overheard, and dropped his voice. 'We've been in touch with the Bank of England, sir. By midnight tomorrow night, London time, there'll be an RAF transport at Heathrow stuffed full of five- and ten-pound notes.' His usual confidence returned. 'As I said, the Victoria is perfectly sound, completely liquid and our assets here and in England substantial enough to cover any eventuality, well almost any eventuality.'

'Meanwhile you may not have enough Hong Kong dollars to weather the run?'

'Not if the, er, the problem continues but I'm sure all will be well, sir.'

Sir Geoffrey stared at him. 'How the devil did we get into this mess?'

'Joss,' Johnjohn said wearily. 'Unfortunately the mint can't print enough Hong Kong dollar notes for us in time. It'd take weeks to print and to ship the amount we'd need, and it wouldn't be healthy to have all those extra notes in our economy. The British currency's stopgap, sir. We can just announce that the, er, that the mint is working overtime to supply our needs.'

'How much do we actually need?' The governor saw Paul Havergill and Johnjohn look at each other and his disquiet increased.

'We don't know, sir,' Johnjohn said. 'Colony-wide, apart from ourselves, every other bank will also need to pledge its securities—just as we've pledged ours temporarily to the Bank of England—to obtain the cash they need. If every depositor on the Colony wants every dollar back . . .' The sweat was beading the banker's face now. 'We've no way of knowing how extended the other banks are, or the amount of their deposits. No one knows.'

'Is one RAF transport enough?' Sir Geoffrey tried not to sound sarcastic. 'I mean, well, a billion pounds in fives and tens? How in the hell are they going to collect that number of notes?'

Havergill mopped his brow. 'We don't know, sir, but they've promised a first shipment will arrive Monday night at the latest.'

'Not till then?'

'No sir. It's impossible before then.'

'There's nothing else we can do?'

Johnjohn swallowed. 'We considered asking you to declare a bank holiday to stem the tide but, er, we concluded—and the Bank of England agreed—if you did that it might blow the top off the Island.'

'No need to worry, sir.' Havergill tried to sound convincing. 'By the end of next week it will all be forgotten.'

'I won't forget it, Paul. And I doubt if China will—or our friends the Labour MPs will. They may have a point about some form of bank controls.'

Both bankers bridled and Paul Havergill said deprecatingly, 'Those two berks don't know their rears from a hole in the wall! Everything's in control.'

Sir Geoffrey would have argued that point but he had just seen Rosemont, the CIA deputy director, and Ed Langan, the FBI man, wander out onto the terrace. 'Keep me advised. I want a full report at noon. Would you excuse me a moment? Please help yourselves to another drink.'

He went off to intercept Rosemont and Langan. 'How're you two?'

'Great, thank you, sir. Great evening.' Both Americans watched Havergill and Johnjohn going back inside. 'How're our banker friends?' Rosemont asked.

'Fine, perfectly fine.'

'That MP, the Socialist guy, Grey, was sure as hell getting under Havergill's skin!'

'And the tai-pan's,' Ed Langan added with a laugh.

'Oh I don't know,' the governor said lightly. 'A little opposition's a good thing, what? Isn't that democracy at its best?'

'How's the Vic, sir? How's the run?'

'No problems that can't be solved,' Sir Geoffrey replied with his easy charm. 'No need to worry. Would you give me a moment, Mr. Langan?'

'Certainly, sir.' The American smiled. 'I was just leaving.'

'Not my party, I trust! Just to replenish your drink?'

'Yes sir.'

Sir Geoffrey led the way into the garden, Rosemont beside him. The trees were still dripping and the night dark. He kept to a path that was puddled and muddy. 'We've a slight problem, Stanley. SI's just caught one of your sailors from the carrier passing secrets to a KGB fellow. Bo—'

Rosemont stopped aghast. 'Off the *Ivanov*?'

'Yes.'

'Was it Suslev? Captain Suslev?'

'No. No, it wasn't that name. May I suggest you get on to Roger at once. Both men are in custody, both have been charged under the Official Secrets Act but I've cleared it with the minister in London and he agrees you should take charge of your fellow at once . . . a little less embarrassing, what? He's, er, he's a computer chap I believe.'

'Son of a bitch!' Rosemont muttered, then wiped the sudden sweat off his face with his hand. 'What did he pass over?'

'I don't know exactly. Roger will be able to fill you in on the details.'

'Do we get to interrogate . . . to interview the KGB guy too?'

'Why not discuss that with Roger? The minister's in direct touch with him, too.' Sir Geoffrey hesitated. 'I, er, I'm sure you'll appreciate . . .'

'Yes, of course, sorry, sir. I'd . . . I'd better get going at once.' Rosemont's face was chalky and he went off quickly, collecting Ed Langan with him.

Sir Geoffrey sighed. Bloody spies, bloody banks, bloody moles and bloody Socialist idiots who know nothing about

Hong Kong. He glanced at his watch. Time to close the party down.

Johnjohn was walking into the anteroom. Dunross was near the bar. 'Ian?'

'Oh hello? One for the road?' Dunross said.

'No, thanks. Can I have a word in private?'

'Of course. It'll have to be quick, I was just leaving. I said I'd drop our friendly MPs at the ferry.'

'You're on a pink ticket too?'

Dunross smiled faintly. 'Actually, old boy, I have one whenever I want it, whether Penn's here or not.'

'Yes. You're lucky, you always did have your life well organized,' Johnjohn said gloomily.

'Joss.'

'I know.' Johnjohn led the way out of the room onto the balcony. 'Rotten about John Chen, what?'

'Yes. Phillip's taking it very badly. Where's Havergill?'

'He left a few minutes ago.'

'Ah, that's why you mentioned "pink ticket"! He's on the town?'

'I don't know.'

'How about Lily Su of Kowloon?'

Johnjohn stared at him.

'I hear Paul's quite enamored.'

'How do you do it, know so much?'

Dunross shrugged. He was feeling tired and uneasy and had been hard put not to lose his temper several times tonight when Grey was in the center of another heated argument with some of the tai-pans.

'By the way, Ian, I tried to get Paul to call a board meeting but it's not in my bailiwick.'

'Of course.' They were in a smaller anteroom. Good Chinese silk paintings and more fine Persian carpets and silver. Dunross noticed the paint was peeling in the corners of the room and off the fine moldings of the ceiling, and this offended him. This is the British raj and the paint shouldn't be peeling.

The silence hung. Dunross pretended to examine some of the exquisite snuff bottles that were on a shelf.

Ian . . .' Johnjohn stopped and changed his mind. He began again. 'This is off the record. You know Tiptop Toe quite well, don't you?'

Dunross stared at him. Tiptop Toe was their nickname for Tip Tok-toh, a middle-aged man from Hunan, Mao Tse-tung's home province, who had arrived during the exodus in 1950. No one seemed to know anything about him, he bothered no one, had a small office in Princes Building, and lived well. Over the years it was evident that he had very particular contacts within the Bank of China and it came to be presumed that he was an official unofficial contact of the bank. No one knew his position in the hierarchy but rumor had it that he was very high. The Bank of China was the only commercial arm of the PRC outside of China, so all of its appointments and contacts were tightly controlled by the ruling hierarchy in Peking.

'What about Tiptop?' Dunross asked, on guard, liking Tiptop—a charming, quiet-spoken man who enjoyed Cognac and spoke excellent English, though, following a usual pattern, nearly always he used an interpreter. His clothes were well cut, though most times he wore a Maoist jacket, looked a little like Chou En-lai and was just as clever. The last time Dunross had dealt with him was about some civilian aircraft the PRC had wanted. Tip Tok-toh had arranged the letters of credit and financing through various Swiss and foreign banks within twenty-four hours. 'Tiptop's canny, Ian,' Alastair Struan had said many times. 'You have to watch yourself but he's the man to deal with. I'd say he was very high up in the Party in Peking. Very.'

Dunross watched Johnjohn, curbing his impatience. The smaller man had picked up one of the snuff bottles. The bottles were tiny, ornate ceramic or jade or glass bottles—many of them beautifully painted *inside*, within the glass: landscapes, dancing girls, flowers, birds, seascapes, even poems in incredibly delicate calligraphy. 'How do they do that, Ian? Paint on the inside like that?'

'Oh they use a very fine brush. The stem of the brush's bent ninety degrees. In Mandarin they call it *li myan huai*, "inside face painting".' Dunross lifted up an elliptical one that had a landscape on one side, a spray of camellias on the other and tiny calligraphy on the paintings.

'Astonishing! What patience! What's the writing say?'

Dunross peered at the tiny column of characters. 'Ah, it's one of Mao's sayings: "Know yourself, know your enemy; a hundred battles, a hundred victories." Actually the Chairman took it out of Sun Tzu.'

Thoughtfully Johnjohn examined it. The windows beyond him were open. A small breeze twisted the neat curtains. 'Would you talk to Tiptop for us?'

'About what?'

'We want to borrow the Bank of China's cash.'

Dunross gaped at him. 'Eh?'

'Yes, for a week or so. They're full to the gills with Hong Kong dollars and there's no run on them. No Chinese'd dare line up outside the Bank of China. They carry Hong Kong dollars as part of their foreign exchange. We'd pay good interest for the loan and put up whatever collateral they'd need.'

'This is a formal request by the Victoria?'

'No. It can't be formal. This's my idea, I haven't even discussed it with Paul—only with you. Would you?'

Dunross's excitement crested. 'Do I get my 100 million loan tomorrow by 10:00 A.M.?'

'Sorry, I can't do that.'

'But Havergill can.'

'He can but he won't.'

'So why should I help you?'

'Ian, if the bank doesn't stand as solid as the Peak, the market'll crash, and so will the Noble House.'

'If I don't get some financing right smartly I'm in the shit anyway.'

'I'll do what I can but will you talk to Tiptop at once? Ask him. I can't approach him . . . no one can officially. You'd be doing the Colony a great service.'

'Guarantee my loan and I'll talk to him tonight. An eye for an eye and a loan for a loan.'

'If you can deliver his promise of a credit up to half a billion in cash by 2:00 P.M. tomorrow, I'll get you the backing you need.'

'How?'

'I don't know!'

'Give that to me in writing by 10:00 A.M. signed by you, Havergill and the majority of the board and I'll go and see him.'

'That's not possible.'

'Tough. An eye for an eye and a loan for a loan.' Dunross got up. 'Why should the Bank of China bale out the Victoria?'

'We're Hong Kong,' Johnjohn said with great confidence. '*We are*. We're the Victoria Bank of Hong Kong and China! We're old friends of China. Without us there's nothing—the Colony'd fall apart and so would Struan's and therefore so would most of Asia.'

'Don't bet on that!'

'Without banking, particularly us, China's in bad shape. We've been partners for years with China.'

'Then ask Tiptop yourself.'

'I can't.' Johnjohn's jaw was jutting. 'Did you know the Trade Bank of Moscow has again asked for a license to trade in Hong Kong?'

Dunross gasped. 'Once they're in we're all on the merry-go-round.'

'We've been offered, privately, substantial Hong Kong dollars immediately.'

'The board'll vote against it.'

'The point is, my dear chap, if you're no longer on the board, the new board can do what the hell it likes,' Johnjohn said simply. 'If the "new" board agrees, the governor and the Colonial Office can easily be persuaded. That'd be a small price to pay—to save our dollar. Once an official Soviet bank's here what other devilment could they get up to, eh?'

'You're worse than bloody Havergill!'

'No old chum, better!' The jesting left the banker's face. 'Any major change and we become the Noble House, like it or not. Many of our directors would prefer you gone, at any price. I'm just asking you to do Hong Kong and therefore yourself a favor. Don't forget, Ian, the Victoria won't go under, we'll be hurt but not ruined.' He touched a bead of sweat away. 'No threats, Ian, but I'm asking for a favor. One day I may be chairman and I won't forget.'

'Either way.'

'Of course, old chum,' Johnjohn said sweetly and went to the sideboard. 'How about one for the road now? Brandy?'

* * *

Robin Grey was seated in the back of Dunross's Rolls with Hugh Guthrie and Julian Broadhurst, Dunross in the front beside his uniformed chauffeur. The windows were fogged. Idly Grey streaked the mist away, enjoying the deep luxury of the sweet-smelling leather.

Soon I'm going to have one of these, he thought. A Rolls of my very own. With a chauffeur. And soon all these bastards'll be crawling, Ian bloody Dunross included. And Penn! Oh yes, my dear sweet sneering sister's going to see the mighty humbled.

'Is it going to rain again?' Broadhurst was asking.

'Yes,' Dunross replied. 'They think this storm's developing into a full-scale typhoon—at least that's what the Met Office said. This evening I got a report from *Eastern Cloud*, one of our inbound freighters just off Singapore. She said that the seas were heavy even that far south.'

'Will the typhoon hit here, tai-pan?' Guthrie, the Liberal MP asked.

'You never know for certain. They can head for you then veer off at the last minute. Or the reverse.'

'I remember reading about Wanda, Typhoon Wanda last year. That was a dilly, wasn't it?'

'The worst I've been in. Over two hundred dead, thousands injured, tens of thousands made homeless.' Dunross had his arm across the seat and he was half turned around. '*Tai-fun*, the Supreme Winds, were gusting to 170 mph at the Royal Observatory, 190 at Tate's Cairn. The eye of the storm came over us at high tide so our tides in places were twenty-three feet over normal.'

'Christ!'

'Yes. At Sha Tin in the New Territories these gusts blew the tidal surge up the channel and breached the storm shelter and shoved fishing boats half a mile inland onto the main street and drowned most of the village. A thousand known fishing boats vanished, eight freighters aground, millions of dollars in damage, most of our squatters' areas blown into the sea.' Dunross shrugged. 'Joss! But considering the enormity of the storm, the seaborne damage here was incredibly small.' His fingers touched the leather seat. Grey noticed the heavy gold and bloodstone signet ring with the Dunross crest. 'A real typhoon shows you how really insignificant you are,' Dunross said.

'Pity we don't have typhoons every day in that case,' Grey said before he could stop himself. 'We could use having the mighty in Whitehall humbled twice a day.'

'You really are a bore, Robin,' Guthrie said. 'Do you have to make a sour remark every time?'

Grey went back to his brooding and shut his ears to their conversation. To hell with all of them, he thought.

Soon the car pulled up outside the Mandarin. Dunross got out. 'The car'll take you home to the V and A. See you all Saturday if not before. Night.'

The car drove off. It circled the huge hotel then headed for the car ferry which was slightly east of the Golden Ferry Terminal along Connaught Road. At the terminal a haphazard line of cars and trucks waited. Grey got out. 'I think I'll stretch my legs, walk back to the Golden Ferry and go across in one of them,' he said with forced bonhomie. 'I need the exercise. Night.'

He walked along the Connaught Road waterfront, quickly, relieved that it had been so easy to get away from them. Bloody fools, he thought, his excitement rising. Well, it won't be long before they all get their comeuppance, Broadhurst particularly.

When he was sure he was clear he stopped under a street-lamp, creating an eddy in the massed stream of pedestrians hurrying both ways, and flagged a taxi. 'Here,' he said and gave the driver a typed address on a piece of paper.

The driver took it, stared at it and scratched his head sullenly.

'It's in Chinese. It's in Chinese on the back,' Grey said help-fully.

The driver paid him no attention, just stared blankly at the English address. Grey reached over and turned the characters toward him. 'Here!'

At once the driver insolently turned the paper back and glared at the English again. Then he belched, let in his clutch with a jerk and eased into the honking traffic.

Rude sod, Grey thought, suddenly enraged.

The cab ground its gears continually as it went into the city, doubling back down one-way streets and narrow alleys to get back into Connaught Road.

At length they stopped outside a dingy old apartment building on a dingy street. The pavement was broken and narrow and puddled, the traffic honking irritably at the parked cab. There was no number that Grey could see. He got out and told the driver to wait and walked back a little to what seemed to be a side door. An old man was sitting on a battered chair, smoking and reading a racing paper under a bare bulb.

'Is this 68 Kwan Yik Street in Kennedy Town?' Grey asked politely.

The old man stared at him as though he was a monster from outer space, then let out a stream of querulous Cantonese.

'68 Kwan Yik Street,' Grey repeated, slower and louder, 'Ken-ned-dy Town?'

Another flood of guttural Cantonese and an insolent wave toward a small door. The old man hawked and spat and went back to his paper with a yawn.

'Sodding bastard,' Grey muttered, his temperature soaring. He opened the door. Inside was a tiny, grimy foyer with peeling paint, a sorry row of mailboxes with names on the boxes. With great relief he saw the name he sought.

At the cab he took out his wallet and carefully looked at the amount of the meter twice before he paid the man.

The elevator was tiny, claustrophobic, filthy and it squeaked as it rose. At the fourth floor he got off and pressed the button of number 44. The door opened.

'Mr. Grey, sir, this's an honor! Molly, his nibs's arrived!' Sam Finn beamed at him. He was a big beefy Yorkshireman, florid, with pale blue eyes, an ex-coal miner and shop steward with important friends in the Labour Party and Trades Union Council. His face was deeply lined and pitted, the pores ingrained with specks of coal dust. 'By gum, 'tis a pleasure!'

'Thank you, Mr. Finn. I'm glad to meet you too. I've heard a lot about you.' Grey took off his raincoat and gratefully accepted a beer.

'Sit thee down.'

The apartment was small, spotlessly clean, the furniture inexpensive. It smelt of fried sausages and fried potatoes and fried bread. Molly Finn came out of the kitchen, her hands and arms red from years of scrubbing and washing up. She was short and rotund, from the same mining town as her husband, the same age, sixty-five, and just as strong. 'By Harry,' she said warmly, 'thee could've knocked us'n down with feather when we heard thee'd be a-visiting us'n.'

'Our mutual friends wanted to hear firsthand how you were doing.'

'Grand. We're doing grand,' Finn said. ''Course it's not like home in Yorkshire and we miss our friends and the Union Hall but we've a bed and a bit of board.' There was the sound of a toilet flushing. 'We've a friend we thought thee'd like to meet,' Finn said and smiled again.

'Oh?'

'Aye.' Finn said.

The toilet door opened. The big bearded man stuck out his hand warmly. 'Sam's told me a lot about you, Mr. Grey. I'm Captain Gregor Suslev of the Soviet Marine. My ship's the *Ivanov*—we're having a small refit in this capitalist haven.'

Grey shook his hand formally. 'Pleased to meet you.'

'We have some mutual friends, Mr. Grey.'

'Oh?'

'Yes, Zdenek Hanzolova of Prague.'

'Oh! Oh yes!' Grey smiled. 'I met him on a Parliamentary Trade Delegation to Czechoslovakia last year.'

'How did you like Prague?'

'Very interesting. Very. I didn't like the repression though . . . or the Soviet presence.'

Suslev laughed. 'We're invited there, by them. We like to look after our friends. But much goes on I don't approve of either. There, in Europe. Even in Mother Russia.'

Sam Finn said, 'Sit thee down, please sit thee down.'

They sat around the dining room table in the living room that now had a neat white tablecloth with a potted aspidistra on it.

'Of course, you know I'm not a Communist, and never have been one,' Grey said. 'I don't approve of a police state. I'm totally convinced our British democratic socialism's the way of the future—Parliament, elected officials and all that it stands for—though a lot of Marxist-Leninist ideas are very worthwhile.'

'Politics!' Gregor Suslev said deprecatingly. 'We should leave politics to politics.'

'Mr. Grey's one of our best spokesmen in Parliament,

Gregor.' Molly Finn turned to Grey. 'Gregor's a good lad too, Mr. Grey. He's not one of them nasties.' She sipped her tea. 'Gregor's a good lad.'

'That's right, lass,' Finn said.

'Not too good, I hope,' Grey said and they all laughed. 'What made you take up residence here, Sam?'

'When we retired, Mrs. Finn and me, we wanted to see bit of the world. We'd put a bit of brass aside and we cashed in a wee coop insurance policy we had, and got a berth on a freighter . . .'

'Oh, my, we did have a good time,' Molly Finn broke in. 'We went to so many foreign parts. It were proper lovely. But when we cum here Sam was a bit poorly, so we got off and were to pick up a freighter when she cum back.'

'That's right, lass,' Sam said. 'Then I met a right proper nice man and he offered me a job.' He beamed and rubbed the black pits in his face. 'I was to be consultant to some mines he was superintendent for, in some place called Formosa. We went there once but no need to stay so we cum back here. That's all there is to it, Mr. Grey. We make a little brass, the beer's good, so Mrs. Finn and me we thought we'd stay. The kids are all growed up. . . .' He beamed again, showing his obviously false teeth. 'We're Hong Kongers now.'

They chatted pleasantly. Grey would have been totally convinced by the Finns' cover story if he had not read his very private dossier before he left London. It was known only to very few that for years Finn had been a card-carrying member of the BCP, the British Communist Party. On his retirement he had been sent out to Hong Kong by one of their secret inner committees, his mission to be a fountain of information about anything to do with the Hong Kong bureaucracy and legislature.

In a few minutes Molly Finn stifled a yawn. 'My my, I'm that tired! If thee will excuse me I think I'll go to bed.'

Sam said, 'Off thee go, lass.'

They talked a little more about inconsequential affairs then he too yawned. 'If thee'll excuse me, I think I'll go too,' adding hastily, 'Now don't thee move, chat to thy heart's content. We'll see thee before thee leaves Hong Kong, Mr. Grey . . . Gregor.'

He shook hands with them and closed the bedroom door behind him. Suslev went over to the television and turned it on with a laugh. 'Have you seen Hong Kong TV? The commercials are very funny.'

He adjusted the sound high enough so they could talk yet not be overheard. 'One can't be too careful, eh?'

'I bring you fraternal greetings from London,' Grey said, his voice as soft. Since 1947 he had been an inner-core Communist, even more secretly than Finn, his identity only known to half a dozen people in England.

'And I send them back.' Suslev jerked his thumb at the closed door. 'How much do they know?'

'Only that I'm left-wing and potential Party material.'

'Excellent.' Suslev relaxed. Center had been very clever to arrange this private meeting so neatly. Roger Crosse, who knew nothing of his connection with Grey, had already told him there were no SI tails on the MPs. 'We're quite safe here. Sam's very good. We get copies of his reports too. And he asks no questions. You British are very close-mouthed and very efficient, Mr. Grey. I congratulate you.'

'Thank you.'

'How was your meeting in Peking?'

Grey took out a sheaf of papers. 'This's a copy of our private and public reports to Parliament. Read it before I go—you'll get the full report through channels. Briefly, I think the Chinese are totally hostile and revisionist. Madman Mao and his henchman Chou En-lai are implacable enemies to international communism. China is weak in everything except the will to fight, and they will fight to protect their land to the last. The longer you wait the harder it will be to contain them, but so long as they don't get nuclear weapons and long-range delivery systems they'll never be a threat.'

'Yes. What about trade? What did they want?'

'Heavy industries, oil cracking plants, oil rigs, chemical plants, steel mills.'

'How are they going to pay?'

'They said they've plenty of foreign exchange. Hong Kong supplies much of it.'

'Did they ask for arms?'

'No. Not directly. They're clever and we didn't always talk or meet as a group. They were well briefed about me and Broadhurst and we weren't liked—or trusted. Perhaps they talked privately to Pennyworth or one of the other Tories—though they won't've helped them. You heard he died?'

'Yes.'

'Good riddance. He was an enemy.' Grey sipped his beer. 'The PRC want arms, of that I'm sure. They're a secretive lot and rotten.'

'What's Julian Broadhurst like?'

'An intellectual who thinks he's a Socialist. He's the dregs but useful at the moment. Patrician, old school tie,' Grey said with a sneer. 'Because of that he'll be a power in the next Labour government.'

'Labour will get in next time, Mr. Grey?'

'No, I don't think so, even though we're working very hard to help Labour and the Liberals.'

Suslev frowned. 'Why support Liberals? They're capitalists.'

Grey laughed sardonically. 'You don't understand our British system, Captain Suslev. We're very lucky, we've a three-party vote with a two-party system. The Liberals split the vote in our favor. We have to encourage them.' Happily he finished his beer and got two more from the refrigerator. 'If it wasn't for the Liberals, Labour would have *never* got in, not ever! And never will again.'

'I don't understand.'

'At the best of times the vote for Labour's only about 45 percent of the population, a little under 45 percent. Tory—Conservatives—are about the same, usually a little more. Most of the other 10-odd percent vote Liberal. If there was no Liberal candidate the majority'd vote with the Conservatives. They're all fools,' he said smugly. 'The British are stupid, comrade, the Liberal Party's Labour's permanent passport to power—therefore ours. Soon the BCP'll control the TUC, and so Labour completely—secretly of course.' He drank deeply. 'The great British unwashed are stupid, the middle class stupid, the upper class stupid—it's almost no challenge anymore. They're all lemmings. Only a very few believe in democratic socialism. Even so,' he added with great satisfaction, 'we pulled down their rotten Empire and pissed all over them with Operation Lion.' Operation Lion was formulated as soon as the Bolsheviks had come to power. Its purpose, the destruction of the British Empire. 'In just eighteen years, since 1945, the greatest empire the world has ever seen's become nonexistent.

'Except for Hong Kong.'

'Soon that will go too.'

'I cannot tell you how important my superiors consider your work,' Suslev said with pretended open admiration. 'You and all our fraternal British brothers.' His orders were to be deferential to this man, to debrief him on his Chinese mission, to pass on instructions as requests. And to flatter him. He had read Grey's dossier and the Finns'. Robin Grey had a Beria-KGB classification 4/22/a: 'An important British traitor paying lip service to Marxist-Leninist ideals. He is to be used but never trusted, and, should the British Communist Party ever reach power, is subject to immediate liquidation.'

Suslev watched Grey. Neither Grey nor the Finns knew his real position, only that he was a minor member of the Vladivostok Communist Party—which was also on his SI dossier.

'You have some information for me?' Grey asked.

'Yes, *tovarich*, and also, with your permission, a few questions. I was told to ask about your implementation of Directive 72/Prague.' This highly secret directive put top priority on infiltrating covert, hard-core experts into positions as shop stewards, in every car-manufacturing plant throughout the U.S and the West—the motor industry, because of its countless allied industries, being the core of any capitalist society.

'We're full speed ahead,' Grey told him enthusiastically. 'Wildcat strikes are the way of the future. With wildcats we can get around union hierarchies without disrupting existing unionism. Our unions're fragmented. Deliberately. Fifty men can be a separate union and that union can dominate thousands—and so long as there's never a secret ballot, the few will always rule the many!' He laughed. 'We're ahead of schedule, and now we've fraternal brothers in Canada, New Zealand, Rhodesia, Australia—particularly Australia. Within a few years we'll have trained agitators in every key machine-shop union in the English-speaking world. A Brit will lead the workers wherever there's a strike—Sydney, Vancouver, Johannesberg, Wellington. It'll be a Brit!'

'And you're one of the leaders, *tovarich*! How marvelous!' Suslev let him continue, leading him on, disgusted that it was so easy to flatter him. How dreadful traitors are, he told himself.

'Soon you'll have the democratic paradise you seek and there'll be peace on earth.'

'It won't be long,' Grey said fervently. 'We've cut the armed services and we'll cut them even more next year. War's over forever. The bomb's done that. It's only the rotten Americans and their arms race who stand in the way but soon we'll force even them to lay down their arms and we'll all be equal.'

'Did you know America's secretly arming the Japanese?'

'Eh?' Grey stared at him.

'Oh, didn't you know?' Suslev was well aware of Grey's three and a half years in Japanese POW camps. 'Didn't you know the U.S. has a military mission there right now asking them if they'd accept nuclear weapons?'

'They'd never dare.'

'But they have, Mr. Grey,' Suslev said, the lie coming so easily. 'Of course it's all totally secret.'

'Can you give me details I could use in Parliament?'

'Well, I'll certainly ask my superiors to furnish that to you if you think it'd be of value.'

'Please, as soon as possible. Nuclear bombs . . . Christ!'

'Are your people, your trained experts, in British nuclear plants too?'

'Eh?' Grey concentrated with an effort, heaving his mind off Japan. 'Nuclear plants?'

'Yes. Are you getting your Brits?'

'Well, no, there's only one or two plants in the U.K. and they're unimportant. The Yanks're really arming the Japs?'

'Isn't Japan capitalist? Isn't Japan a U.S. protégé? Aren't they building nuclear plants too? If it wasn't for America . . .'

'Those American sods! Thank God you've the bombs too or we'd all have to kowtow!'

'Perhaps you should concentrate some effort on your nuclear plants, eh?' Suslev said smoothly, astounded that Grey could be so gullible.

'Why?'

'There's a new study out, by one of your countrymen. Philby.'

'Philby?' Grey remembered how shocked and frightened he had been at Philby's discovery and flight, then how relieved he was that Philby and the others had escaped without giving lists of the inner core of the BCP that they must have had. 'How is he?'

'I understand he's very well. He's working in Moscow. Did you know him?'

'No. He was Foreign Office, stratosphere. None of us knew he was one of us.'

'He points out in this study that a nuclear plant is self-sustaining, that one plant can generate fuel for itself and for others. Once a nuclear plant is operating, in effect it is almost perpetual, it requires only a few highly skilled, highly educated technicians to operate it, no workers, unlike oil or coal. At the moment all industry in the West's dependent on coal or oil. He suggests it should be our policy to encourage use of oil, not coal, and completely discourage nuclear power. Eh?'

'Ah, I see his point!' Grey's face hardened. 'I shall get myself on the parliamentary committee to study atomic energy.'

'Will that be easy?'

'Too easy, comrade! Brits are lazy, they want no problems, they just want to work as little as possible for as much money as possible, to go to the pub and football on Saturdays—and no unpaid work, no tedious committees after hours, no arguments. It's too easy—when we have a plan and they don't.'

Suslev sighed, very satisfied, his work almost done. 'Another beer? No, let me get it, it's my honour, Mr. Grey. Do you happen to know a writer who's here at the moment, a U.S. citizen, Peter Marlowe?'

Grey's head snapped up. 'Marlowe? I know him very well, didn't know he was a U.S. citizen though. Why?'

Suslev kept his interest hidden and shrugged. 'I was just asked to ask you, since you are English and he originally was English.'

'He's a rotten upper-class sod with the morals of a barrow boy. Hadn't seen him for years, not since '45, until he turned up here. He was in Changi too. I didn't know he was a writer until yesterday, or one of those film people. What's important about him?'

'He's a writer,' Suslev said at once. 'He makes films. With television, writers can reach millions. Center keeps track of Western writers as a matter of policy. Oh yes, we know about writers in Mother Russia, how important they are. Our writers have always pointed the way for us, Mr. Grey, they've formed our thinking and feeling, Tolstoy, Dostoevski, Chekhov, Bunin . . .' He added with pride, 'Writers with us are pathfinders. That's why nowadays we must guide them in their formation and control their work or bury it.' He looked at Grey. 'You should do the same.'

'We support friendly writers, Captain, and damn the other shower whichever way we can, publicly and privately. When I get home, I'll put Marlowe on our formal BCP media shit list. It'll be easy to do him some harm—we've lots of friends in our media.'

Suslev lit a cigarette. 'Have you read his book?'

'The one about Changi? No, no I haven't. I'd never heard of it until I got here. It probably wasn't published in England. Besides, I don't have much time to read fiction and if he did it, it's got to be upper-class shit and a penny-dreadful and . . . well Changi's Changi and best forgotten.' A shudder went through him that he did not notice. 'Yes, best forgotten.'

But I can't, he wanted to shout. I can't forget and it's still a never-ending nightmare, those days of the camp, year after year, the tens of thousands dying, trying to enforce the law, trying to protect the weak against black market filth feeding off the weak, everyone starving and no hope of ever getting out, my body rotting away and only twenty-one with no women and no laughter and no food and no drink, twenty-one when I was caught in Singapore in 1942 and twenty-four, almost twenty-five when the miracle happened and I survived and got back to England—home gone, parents gone, world gone and my only sister sold out to the enemy, now talking like the enemy, eating like them, living like them, married to one, ashamed of our past, wanting the past dead, me dead, nobody caring and oh Christ, *the change*. Coming back to life after the no-life of Changi, all the nightmares and the no sleeping in the night, terrified of life, unable to talk about it, weeping and not knowing why I was weeping, trying to adjust to what fools called normal. Adjusting at length. But at what cost, oh dear sweet Jesus at what a cost . . .

Stop it!

With an effort Grey pulled himself off the descending spiral of Changi.

Enough of Changi! Changi's dead. Let Changi stay dead. It's dead—Changi's got to stay dead. But Ch—

'What?' he said, jerked into the present again.

'I just said, your present government is completely vulnerable now.'

'Oh? Why?'

'You remember the Profumo scandal? Your minister of war?'

'Of course. Why?'

'Some months ago, MI-5 began a very secret, very searching investigation into the alleged connection between the now famous call girl, Christine Keeler, and Commander Yevgeny Ivanov, our naval attaché, and other London social figures.'

'Is it finished?' Grey asked, suddenly attentive.

'Yes. It documents conversations the woman had with Commander Ivanov. Ivanov had asked her to find out from Profumo when nuclear weapons would be delivered to Germany. It claims,' Suslev said, deliberately lying now to excite Grey, 'that Profumo had been given security warnings by MI-5 about Ivanov *some months before* the scandal broke—that Commander Ivanov was KGB and also her lover.'

'Oh Christ! Will Commander Ivanov substantiate it?'

'Oh no. Absolutely not. That would not be correct—or necessary. But MI-5's report tells the facts accurately,' Suslev lied smoothly. 'The report's true!'

Grey let out a shout of laughter. 'Oh Christ, this'll blow the government off the front bench and bring about a general election!'

'And Labour in!'

'Yes! For five wonderful years! Oh yes and once we're in . . . oh my God!' Grey let out another bellow of laughter. 'First he lied about Keeler! And now you say he *knew* about Ivanov all the time! Oh bloody Christ, yes, that'll cause the government to fall! This'll be worth all the years of taking the shit from those middle-class sods. You're sure?' he asked with sudden anxiety. 'It's really true?'

'Would I lie to you?'

Suslev laughed to himself.

'I'll use it. Oh God will I use it.' Grey was beside himself with joy. 'You're absolutely sure? But Ivanov. What happened to him?'

'Promotion of course for a brilliantly executed maneuver to discredit an enemy government. If his work helps to bring it down, he'll be decorated. He's presently in Moscow waiting for reassignment. By the way, at your press conference tomorrow, do you plan to mention your brother-in-law?'

Grey was suddenly on guard. 'How did you know about him?'

Suslev stared back calmly. 'My superiors know everything. I was told to suggest you might consider mentioning your connection at the press conference, Mr. Grey.'

'Why?'

'To enhance your position, Mr. Grey. Such a close association with the tai-pan of the Noble House would make your words have much greater impact here. Wouldn't they?'

'But if you know about him,' Grey said, his voice hard, 'you also know about my sister and me, that we've an agreement not to mention it. It's a family matter.'

'Matters to do with the State take preference over family matters, Mr. Grey.'

'Who are you?' Grey was suddenly suspicious. 'Who are you really?'

'Just a messenger, Mr. Grey, really.' Suslev put his great hands on Grey's shoulders and held him warmly. '*Tovarich*, you know how we must use everything in our power to push the cause. I'm sure my superiors were only thinking of your future. A close family connection with such a capitalist family would help you in Parliament. Wouldn't it? When you and your Labour Party get in next year they'll need well-connected men and women, eh? For cabinet rank you need connections, you said so yourself. You'll be the Hong Kong expert, with special connections. You can help us tremendously to contain China, put her back on the right track, and put Hong Kong and all Hong Kong people where they belong—in the sewer. Eh?'

Grey thought about that, his heart thumping. 'We could obliterate Hong Kong?'

'Oh yes.' Suslev smiled. The smile broadened. 'There is no need to worry, you wouldn't have to volunteer anything about the tai-pan or break your word to your sister. I can arrange for you to be asked a question. Eh?'

54

Dunross was waiting for Brian Kwok in the Quance Bar of the Mandarin, sipping a long brandy and Perrier. The bar was men only and almost empty. Brian Kwok had never been late before but he was late now.

Too easy to have an emergency in his job, Dunross thought, unperturbed. I'll give him a couple more minutes.

Tonight Dunross did not mind waiting. He had plenty of time to get to Aberdeen and Four Finger Wu and as Penn was safely en route to England, there was no pressure to get back.

The trip will be good for her, he told himself. London, the theater, and then Castle Avisyard. It will be grand there. Soon autumn and crisp mornings, your breath visible, the grouse season, and then Christmas. It will be grand to be home for Christmas in the snow. I wonder what this Christmas will bring and what I'll think when looking back to this time, this bad time. Too many problems now. The plan working but creaking already, everything bad and not in control, my control. Bartlett, Casey, Gornt, Four Fingers, Mata, Tightfist, Havergill, Johnjohn, Kirk, Crosse, Sinders, AMG, his Riko, all moths around the flame—and now a new one, Tiptop, and Hiro Toda arriving tomorrow instead of Saturday.

This afternoon he had talked at length to his Japanese friend and shipbuilding partner. Toda had asked about the stock market and about Struan's, not directly English style but obliquely, politely Japanese style. Even so, he had asked. Dunross had heard the gravity under the smooth, American-tinged voice—the product of two years postgraduate school at Harvard.

903

'Everything's going to be fine, Hiro,' Dunross had told him. 'It's a temporary attack. We take delivery of the ships as planned.'

Will we?

Yes. Some way or another. Linbar goes to Sydney tomorrow to try to resurrect the Woolara deal and renegotiate the charter. A long shot.

Inexorably his mind turned back to Jacques. Is Jacques truly a Communist traitor? And Jason Plumm and Tuke? And R. Is he Roger Crosse or Robert Armstrong? Surely neither of them and surely not Jacques! For God's sake I've known Jacques most of my life—I've known the deVilles for most of my life. It's true Jacques could have given Bartlett some of the information about our inner workings, but not all of it. Not the company part, that's tai-pan knowledge only. That means Alastair, Father, me or old Sir Ross. All unthinkable.

Yes.

But someone's a traitor and it isn't me. And then there's Sevrin.

Dunross looked around. The bar was still almost empty. It was a small, pleasing, comfortable room with dark-green leather chairs and old polished oak tables, the walls lined with Quance paintings. They were all prints. Many of the originals were in the long gallery in the Great House, most of the remainder in the corridors of the Victoria and Blacs banks. A few were privately owned elsewhere. He leaned back in the alcove, at ease, glad to be surrounded by so much of his own past, feeling protected by it. Just above his head was a portrait of a Haklo boat-girl with a fair-haired boy in her arms, his hair in a queue. Quance was supposed to have painted this as a birthday present for Dirk Struan from the girl in the picture, May-May T'Chung, the child in her arms supposed to be their son, Duncan.

His eyes went across the room to the portraits of Dirk and his half-brother Robb beside another painting of the American trader Jeff Cooper, and landscapes of the Peak and the praya in 1841. I wonder what Dirk would say if he could see his creation now. Thriving, building, reclaiming, still the center of the world, the Asian world which is the only world.

'Another, tai-pan?'

'No thanks, Feng,' he said to the Chinese barman. 'Just a Perrier, please.'

A phone was nearby. He dialed.

'Police headquarters,' the woman's voice said.

'Superintendent Kwok please.'

'Just a moment, sir.'

As Dunross waited he tried to decide about Jacques. Impossible, he thought achingly, not without help. Sending him to France to pick up Susanne and Avril isolates him for a week or so. Perhaps I'll talk to Sinders, perhaps they already know. Christ almighty, if AMG hadn't put the R down I'd've gone direct to Crosse. Is it possible that he could be Arthur?

Remember Philby of the Foreign Office, he told himself, revolted that an Englishman of that background and in such a high position of trust could be a traitor. And the other two equally, Burgess and Maclean. And Blake. How far to believe AMG? Poor bugger. How far to trust Jamie Kirk?

'Who's calling Superintendent Kwok please?' a man's voice asked on the phone.

'Mr. Dunross of Struan's.'

'Just a moment please.' A short wait then a man's voice that he recognized at once. 'Evening, tai-pan. Robert Armstrong . . . sorry but Brian's not available. Was it anything important?'

'No. We just had a date for a drink now and he's late.'

'Oh, he never mentioned it—he's usually spot on about something like that. When did you make the date?'

'This morning. He called to tell me about John Chen. Anything new on those bastards?'

'No. Sorry. Brian had to go out of town—a quick trip, you know how it is.'

'Oh of course. If you talk to him tell him I'll see him Sunday at the hill climb, if not before.'

'Do you still intend to go to Taiwan?'

'Yes. With Bartlett. Sunday, back Tuesday. I hear we can use his plane.'

'Yes. Please make sure he comes back on Tuesday.'

'If not before.'

'Nothing I can do for you?'

'No thank you, Robert.'

'Tai-pan, we've, we've had another rather disturbing encounter, here in Hong Kong. Not to worry you but take it easy until tomorrow with Sinders, eh?'

'Of course. Brian said the same. And Roger. Thanks, Robert. Night.' Dunross hung up. He had forgotten that he had an SI bodyguard following him. The fellow must be better than the others. I didn't notice him at all. Now what to do about him? He's certainly unwelcome with Four Fingers.

'I'll be back in a moment,' he said.

'Yes, tai-pan,' the barman said.

Dunross went out and strolled to the men's room, watching without watching. No one followed him. When he had finished he went into the noisy crowded mezzanine, across and down the main staircase to the newsstand in the foyer to buy an evening paper. There were crowds everywhere. Coming back, he zeroed in on a slight, bespectacled Chinese who was watching him over a magazine from a chair in the foyer. Dunross hesitated, went back to the foyer and saw the eyes following him. Satisfied, he went back up the crowded stairs. 'Oh hello, Marlowe,' he said, almost bumping into him.

'Oh hello, tai-pan.'

At once Dunross saw the great weariness in the other man's face. 'What's up?' he asked, instantly sensing trouble, stepping out of the way of the crowds.

'Oh nothing . . . nothing at all.'

'Something's up.' Dunross smiled gently.

Peter Marlowe hesitated. 'It's, it's Fleur.' He told him about her.

Dunross was greatly concerned. 'Old Tooley's a good doctor so that's one thing.' He related to Marlowe how Tooley had filled him, Bartlett and Casey full of antibiotics. 'Are you all right?'

'Yes. Just a touch of the runs. Nothing to worry about for a month or so.' Peter Marlowe told him what Tooley had said about hepatitis. 'That doesn't worry me, it's Fleur and the baby, that's the worry.'

'Do you have an *amah*?'

'Oh yes. And the hotel's marvelous, the room boys are all pitching in.'

'Have you time for a drink?'

'No, no thanks, I'd better be getting back. The *amah*'s not . . .

906

there's no room for her so she's just baby-sitting. I've got to drop by the nursing home on the way back, just to check.'

'Oh, then another time. Please give your wife my regards. How's the research going?'

'Fine, thank you.'

'How many more of our skeletons have you wheedled out of our Hong Kong *yan*?'

'Lots. But they're all good.' Peter Marlowe smiled faintly. 'Dirk Struan was one helluva man. Everyone says you are too and they all hope you'll best Gornt, that you'll win again.'

Dunross looked at him, liking him. 'Do you mind questions about Changi?' He saw the shadow pass across the rugged used face that was young-old.

'That depends.'

'Robin Grey said you were a black marketeer in the camp. With an American. A corporal.'

There was a long pause and Peter Marlowe's face did not change. 'I was a trader, Mr. Dunross, or actually, an interpreter for my friend who was a trader. He was an American corporal. He saved my life and the life of my friends. There were four of us, a major, a group captain, a rubber planter and me. He saved dozens of others too. His name was King and he was a king, King of Changi in a way.' Again the faint smile. 'Trading was against Japanese law—and camp law.'

'You said Japanese, not Jap. That's interesting,' Dunross said at once. 'After all those horrors at Changi, you don't detest them?'

After a pause Peter Marlowe shook his head. 'I don't detest anyone. Even Grey. It takes all of my mind and energy to appreciate that I'm alive. Night!' He turned to go.

'Oh, Marlowe, one last thing,' Dunross said quickly, making a decision. 'Would you like to go to the races Saturday? My box? There'll be a few interesting people . . . if you're researching Hong Kong you might as well do it in style, eh?'

'Thank you. Thank you very much but Donald McBride's invited me. I'd like to stop by for a drink though, if I may. Any luck on the book?'

'Sorry?'

'The book on the history of Struan's, the one you're going to let me read.'

'Oh yes, of course. I'm having it retyped,' Dunross said. 'It seems there's only one copy. If you'll bear with me?'

'Of course. Thanks.'

'Give my best to Fleur.' Dunross watched him go, glad that Marlowe understood the difference between trading and black marketeering. His eyes fell on the Chinese SI man who still watched him over the magazine. He walked slowly back to the bar as though lost in thought. When he was safe inside he said quickly, 'Feng, there's a bloody newsman downstairs I don't want to see.'

At once the barman opened the countertop. 'It's a pleasure, tai-pan,' he said, smiling, not believing the excuse at all. His customers frequently used the servants' exit behind the bar. As women were not allowed inside the bar, it was usual that it was a woman who was to be avoided outside. Now what whore would the tai-pan want to avoid? he asked himself, bemused, watching him leave a generous tip and hurry away through the exit.

Once on the street in the side alley Dunross walked quickly around the corner and got a taxi, hunching down into the back seat.

'Aberdeen,' he ordered and gave directions in Cantonese.

'*Ayeeyah*, like an arrow, tai-pan,' the driver said at once, brightening as he recognized him. 'May I·ask what are the chances for Saturday? Rain or no rain?'

'No rain, by all the gods.'

'Eeeee, and the winner of the fifth?'

'The gods haven't whispered it to me, nor the foul High Tigers who bribe jockeys or drug horses to cheat honest people out of an honest gamble. But Noble Star will be trying.'

'All the fornicators'll be trying,' the driver said sourly, 'but who's the one chosen by the gods and by the High Tiger of Happy Valley Racetrack? What about Pilot Fish?'

'The stallion's good.'

'Butterscotch Lass? Banker Kwang needs a change of luck.'

'Yes. The Lass's good too.'

'Will the market go down more, tai-pan?'

'Yes, but buy Noble House at a quarter to three on Friday.'

'At what price?'

'Use your head, Venerable Brother. Am I Old Blind Tung?'

Orlanda and Linc Bartlett were dancing very close in the semi-darkness of the nightclub, feeling the length of each other. The music was soft and sensual, the beat good, the band Filipino, and the great mirrored luxurious room was deftly pool lit, with private alcoves and low deep chaises around low tables and tuxedoed waiters with pencil flashlights like so many fireflies. Many girls in colorful evening dresses sat together chatting or watching the few dancers. From time to time singly or in pairs they would join a man or men at the tables to ply them with laughter and conversation and drinks and, after a quarter of an hour or so, move on, their movements delicately orchestrated by the ever-watchful mama-*san* and her helpers. The mama-*san* here was a lithe attractive Shanghainese woman in her fifties, well dressed and discreet. She spoke six languages and was responsible to the owner for the girls. On her depended the success or failure of the business. The girls obeyed her totally. So did the bouncers and waiters. She was the nucleus, the queen of her domain, and as such, fawned upon.

It was rare for a man to bring a date though it was not resented—providing the tip was generous and the drinks continuous. Dozens of these pleasure places of the night were spread about the Colony, a few private, most open, catering to men—tourists, visitors or Hong Kong *yan*. All were well stocked with dancing partners of all races. You paid them to sit with you, to chat or to laugh or to listen. Prices varied, quality varied with your choice of place, the purpose always the same. Pleasure for the guest. Money for the house.

Linc Bartlett and Orlanda were closer now, swaying more than dancing, her head soft against his chest. One of her hands was gently on his shoulder, the other held by his, cool to his touch. He had one arm almost around her, his hand resting on her waist. She felt his warmth deep in her loins and almost absently, her fingers caressed the nape of his neck and she eased a little closer, drawn by the music. Her feet followed his perfectly, so did her body. In a moment she felt his stirring and then his length.

How do I deal with him tonight? she asked herself dreamily, loving the night and how perfect it had been. Do I or don't I? Oh how I want . . .

Her body seemed to be moving of its own volition, now even

909

closer, her back slightly arched, loins forward. A wave of heat swept her.

Too much heat, she thought. With an effort she pulled herself back.

Bartlett sensed her leaving him. His hand stayed on her waist and he held her against him, feeling nothing but her body under his hand, no undergarment. So rare. Just flesh under the gossamer chiffon . . . and more warmth than flesh. Jesus!

'Let's sit for a moment,' she said throatily.

'When the dance ends,' he muttered.

'No, no, Linc, my legs feel weak.' With an effort she put both hands around his neck and leaned back a little, keeping herself against him but letting him take some of her weight. Her smile was vast. 'I may fall. You wouldn't want me to fall, would you?'

'You can't fall,' he said, smiling back. 'No way.'

'Please . . .'

'You wouldn't want me to fall would you?'

She laughed and her laugh thrilled him. Jesus, he thought, slow down, she's got you going.

For a moment they danced, but apart, and that cooled him a little. Then he turned her and followed her close and they sat down at their table, lounging on their sofa, still aware of their closeness. Their legs touched.

'The same, sir?' the dinner-jacketed waiter asked.

'Not for me, Linc,' she said, wanting to curse the waiter for his ineptness, their drinks not yet finished.

'Another crème de menthe?' Bartlett said.

'Not for me, truly thanks. But you have one.'

The waiter vanished. Bartlett would have preferred a beer but he didn't want that smell on his breath and, even more, he did not want to spoil the most perfect meal he had ever had. The pasta had been wonderful, the veal tender and juicy with a lemon and wine sauce that was mouth tingling, the salad perfect. Then *zabaglione*, mixed in front of him, eggs and Marsala and magic. And always her radiance, the touch of her perfume.

'This is the best evening I've had in years.'

She raised her glass with mock solemnity. 'Here's to many more,' she said. Yes, here's to many many more but after we're married, or at least engaged. You're too heady, Linc Bartlett, too tuned in to my psyche, too strong. 'I'm glad you've enjoyed it.

So have I. Oh yes, so have I!' She saw his eyes slide off her as a hostess brushed by, her gown low cut. The girl was lovely, barely twenty, and she joined a group of boisterous Japanese businessmen with many girls at a corner table. At once another girl got up and excused herself and went away. Orlanda watched him watching them, her mind now crystal clear.

'Are they all for hire?' he asked involuntarily.

'For pillowing?'

His heart missed a beat and he glanced back at her, all attention. 'Yes, I suppose that's what I meant,' he said cautiously.

'The answer's no, and yes.' She kept her smile gentle, her voice soft. 'That's like most things in Asia, Linc. Nothing's ever really no or yes. It's always maybe. It depends on the availability of a hostess. It depends on the man, the money and the amount she's in debt.' Her smile was mischievous. 'Perhaps I shall just point you in the right direction but then you'd be up to no good—because you fascinate all pretty ladies, big strong man like you *heya?*'

'Come on, Orlanda!' he said with a laugh as she aped a coolie accent.

'I saw you notice her. I don't blame you, she's lovely,' she said, envying the girl her youth but not her life.

'What did you mean about debts?'

'When a girl first comes to work here she has to look pretty. Clothes are expensive, hairdressing expensive, stockings, makeup, everything expensive, so the mama-*san*—that's the woman who looks after the girls—or the night-club owner will advance the girl enough to buy all the things she needs. Of course in the beginning all the girls are young and frivolous, fresh like a first rose of summer, so they buy and buy and then they have to pay back. Most have nothing when they begin, just themselves—unless they've been a hostess in another club and have a following. Girls change nightclubs, Linc, naturally, once they're out of debt. Sometimes an owner will pay the debts of a girl to acquire her and her followers—many girls are very popular and sought after. For a girl it can be well paying, if you can dance, converse and speak several languages.'

'Their debts're heavy then?'

'Perpetual. The longer they stay the harder it is to look pretty so the more the cost. Interest on the debt is 20 percent at the very least. In the first months the girl can earn much to pay back much but never enough.' A shadow passed over her face. 'Interest builds up, the debt builds up. Not all patrons are patient. So the girl has to seek other forms of financing. Sometimes she has to borrow from loan sharks to pay back the patron. Inevitably she seeks help. Then one night the mama-*san* points out a man. "He wants to buy you out," she'll say. An—'

'What does that mean, to buy a girl out?'

'Oh that's just a nightclub custom here. All the girls have to be here promptly, say eight, when the club opens, neat and groomed. They have to stay till 1:00 P.M. or they'll be fined—and fined also if they are absent or if they're late or not neat and not groomed and not pleasant to customers. If a man wants to take a girl out by himself, for dinner or whatever, and many customers just take the girls for dinner—many even take a couple of girls for dinner, mostly to impress their friends—he buys the girl out of the club, he pays the club a fee, the amount depends on the time left before closing. I don't know how much she gets of the fee, I think it's 30 percent, but what she makes outside is all hers, unless the mama-*san* negotiates for her before she leaves. Then the house gets a fee.'

'Always a fee?'

'It's a matter of face, Linc. In this place, which is one of the best, to buy a girl out it would cost you about 80 HK an hour, about $16 U.S.'

'That's not much,' he said absently.

'Not much to a millionaire, my dear. But for thousands here, 80 HK has to last a family for a week.'

Bartlett was watching her, wondering about her, wanting her, so glad that he didn't have to buy her out. Shit, that'd be terrible. Or would it? he asked himself. At least that way it'd be a few bucks, then in the sack and move on again. Is that what I want?

'What?' she asked.

'I was just thinking what a rotten life these girls have.'

'Oh not rotten, not rotten at all,' she said with the immense innocence he found shattering. 'This is probably the best time in their lives, certainly the first time in their lives they've ever worn anything pretty, been flattered and sought after. What other kind of job can they get if you're a girl without a great education?

912

Secretarial if you're lucky, or else in a factory, twelve to fourteen hours a day for 10 HK a day. You should go to one, Linc, see the conditions. I'll take you. Please? You must see how people work, then you'll understand about us here. I'd love to be your guide. Now that you're staying you should know everything, Linc, experience everything. Oh no, they think themselves lucky. At least for a short time in their lives they live well and eat well and laugh a lot.'

'No tears?'

'Always tears. But tears is a way of life for a girl.'

'Not for you.'

She sighed and put her hand on his arm. 'I've had my share. But you make me forget all the tears I've ever had.' A sudden burst of laughter made them look up. The four Japanese businessmen were hunched down with six girls, their table loaded with drinks and more arriving. 'I'm so happy I don't have to . . . have to serve the Japanese,' she said simply, 'I bless my joss for that. But they are the biggest spenders, Linc, much more than any other tourists. They spend even more than the Shanghainese, so they get the best service even though they're hated and they know they're hated. They don't seem to care that their spending buys them nothing except falsehoods. Perhaps they know it, they're clever, very clever. Certainly they have a different attitude to pillowing and to Ladies of the Night, different from other people.' Another burst of laughter. 'Chinese call them *lang syin gou fei* in Mandarin, literally "wolf's heart, dog's lungs", meaning men without conscience.'

He frowned. 'That doesn't make sense.'

'Oh but it does! You see Chinese cook and eat every part of fish, fowl or animal except for a wolf's heart and a dog's lungs. They're the only two things that you cannot flavor—they always stink whatever you do to them.' She looked back at the other table. 'To Chinese, Japanese men're *lang syin gou fei*. So is money. Money has no conscience either.' She smiled a strange smile and sipped her liqueur. 'Nowadays many mama-*sans* or owners will advance money to a girl to help her learn Japanese. To entertain, of course you have to communicate, no?'

Another bevy of girls went past and she saw them look at Bartlett and then at her speculatively and look away again. Orlanda knew they despised her because she was Eurasian and with a *quai loh* customer. They joined another table. The club was filling up.

'Which one do you want?' she asked.

'What?'

She laughed at his shock. 'Oh come now, Linc Bartlett, I saw your wandering eye. Is—'

'Stop it, Orlanda!' he said uncomfortably, a sudden edge to his voice. 'In this place it's impossible not to notice.'

'Of course, that's why I suggested it,' she said immediately, forcing her smile steady, her reactions very fast and again she touched him, her hand tender on his knee. 'I picked this place for you so you could feast your eyes.' She snapped her fingers. Instantly the maître d' was there, kneeling politely beside their low table. 'Give me your card,' she said imperiously in Shanghainese, almost sick with an apprehension that she hid perfectly.

At once the man produced what looked like a playbill. 'Leave me your flashlight. I'll call you when I need you.'

The man went away. Like a conspirator she moved closer. Now their legs were touching. Linc put his arm around her. She directed the pencil light at the playbill. There were photographs, portraits of twenty or thirty girls. Underneath each were rows of Chinese characters. 'Not all these girls will be here tonight, but if you see one you like we'll bring her over.'

He stared at her. 'Are you serious?'

'Very serious, Linc. You don't have to worry, I'll negotiate for you, if you like her, after you've met her and talked to her.'

'I don't want one of these, I want you.'

'Yes. Yes I know, my darling, and . . . but for tonight, bear with me, please. Play a little game, let me design your night.'

'Jesus, you're something else!'

'And you're the most marvelous man I've ever known and I want to make your night perfect. I can't give you me now, much as I want to, so we'll find a temporary substitute. What do you say?'

Bartlett was still staring at her. He finished his drink and did not taste it. Another appeared out of nowhere. He drank half of it.

Orlanda knew the chance she was taking but felt that either way she would draw him tighter to her. If he accepted he would

914

be beholden to her for an exciting night, a night that Casey or any *quai loh* woman would never in a thousand years have offered to him. If he refused, then he would still be grateful for her generosity. 'Linc, this is Asia. Here sex is not Anglo-Saxon mumbo-jumbo and guilt-ridden. It's a pleasure to be sought like great food or great wine. What's the value of one night to a man, a real man, with one of these Pleasure Ladies? A moment of pleasure. A memory. Nothing more. What has that to do with love, real love? Nothing. I'm not for *one* night or for hire. I felt your yang. . . . No please, Linc,' she added quickly as she saw him bridle. 'About yang and yin things we cannot lie or tell falsehoods, that would destroy us. I felt you and I was filled with joy. Didn't you feel me? You're strong and a man, yang, and I'm a woman, yin, and when the music is soft and . . . Oh, Linc.' She put her hand around his and looked up at him beseechingly. 'I beg you, don't be bound by Anglo-American nonsense. This is Asia and I—I want to be everything a woman could be for you.'

'Jesus, you really mean it?'

'Of course. By the Madonna, I would like to be everything that you could desire in a woman,' she said. 'Everything. And I also swear that when I'm old or you no longer desire me I will help arrange *that* part of your life to be joyous, openly, freely. All that I would ask is to be *tai-tai*, to be part of your life.' Orlanda kissed him lightly. And then she saw the sudden change in him. She saw the awe and his defenselessness and she knew she had won. Her glee almost swamped her. Oh Quillan, you're a genius, she wanted to shout. I never believed, truly believed, that your suggestion would be so perfect, I never believed that you were so wise, oh thank you thank you.

But her face showed none of this and she waited patiently, motionless.

'What does *tai-tai* mean?' he asked throatily.

Tai-tai meant 'supreme of the supreme', wife. By ancient Chinese custom, in the home the wife was supreme, all powerful. 'To be part of your life,' she said softly, her whole being shouting caution.

Again she waited. Bartlett leaned down and she felt his lips brush hers. But his kiss was different and she knew that from now on their relationship would be on a different plane. Her excitement soared. She broke the spell. 'Now,' she said as though to a naughty child, 'now, Mr. Linc Bartlett, which one do you choose?'

'You.'

'And I choose you, but meanwhile we have to decide which one you're going to consider. If these aren't to your liking we'll go to another club.' Deliberately she kept her voice matter-of-fact. 'Now what about her?' The girl was lovely, the one he had looked at. Orlanda had already decided against her and had chosen the one that she would prefer but, she thought contentedly, very sure of herself, the poor boy's entitled to an opinion. Oh I'm going to be such a perfect wife for you! 'Her résumé says she's Lily Tee—all the girls have working names they choose themselves. She's twenty, from Shanghai, speaks Shanghainese and Cantonese and her hobbies are dancing, boating and . . .' Orlanda peered at the tiny characters and he saw the lovely curve of her neck. '. . . and hiking. What about her?'

His eyes went to the picture. 'Listen, Orlanda, I haven't been with a whore for years, not since I was in the army. I've never been much on them.'

'I understand completely and you're right,' she told him patiently, 'but these aren't whores, not in the American sense. There's nothing vulgar or secret about them or what I propose. These are Pleasure Ladies who *may* offer you their youth *which has great value*, in exchange for some of your money which has almost none. It's a fair exchange, given and received with face on both sides. For instance, you should *know* in advance how much she should receive and you must never give her the money direct, you must only put it into her handbag. That's important, and it's very important to me that your first encounter be perfect. I've got to protect your face too, an—'

'Come on, Orlan—'

'But I'm serious, Linc. This choosing, this gift from me to you has nothing to do with you and me, nothing. What happens with us is joss. It's just important to me for you to enjoy life, to know what Asia is, really is, not what Americans think it is. Please?'

Bartlett was floundering now, all his well-tested signposts and guides shattered and useless against this woman who fascinated and astounded him.

He was drunk with her warmth and tenderness. All of him believed her.

Then, suddenly, he remembered and his inner self screamed caution. His euphoria fled. He had just remembered to whom he had mentioned how much he loved Italian food. Gornt. Gornt, a couple of days ago. Talking about the best meal he had ever had. Italian food with beer. Gornt. Jesus are these two in cahoots? Can't be, just can't be! Maybe I told her about the same meal. Did I?

He searched his mind but could not remember exactly, all of him rocked but his eyes kept seeing her waiting there, smiling at him, loving him. Gornt and Orlanda? They can't be in cahoots! No way! Even so, be cautious. You know almost nothing about her, so watch out for chrissake, you're in a web, her web. Is it a Gornt web too?

Test her, the devil in him shouted. Test her. If she means what she says then that's something else and she's from outer space and just as rare and you'll have to decide about her—you'll only have her on her terms.

Test her while you've the chance—you've nothing to lose.

'What?' she asked, sensing a change.

'I was just thinking about what you said, Orlanda. Shall I choose now?'

55

Suslev was sitting in the half-dark of their safe house at 32 Sinclair Towers. Because of his meeting with Grey he had changed the rendezvous with Arthur to be here.

He sipped his drink in the dark. Beside him on the side table was a bottle of vodka, two glasses and the telephone. His heart thumped heavily as it always did when he was waiting for a clandestine meeting. Will I never get used to them? he asked himself. No. Tonight I'm tired though everything has gone beautifully. Grey's programmed now. That poor fool, driven by hatred and envy and jealousy! Center must further caution the leadership of the BCP about him—the trend's too vulnerable. And Travkin, once a prince, now nothing, and Jacques deVille—that impetuous incompetent—and all the others.

Never mind! Everything goes excellently. Everything's prepared against tomorrow and the arrival of the man Sinders. An involuntary shudder went through Suslev. I wouldn't want to be trapped by them. MI-6 are dangerous, committed and fanatic against us, like the CIA, but much worse. If the CIA and MI-6 plan, code name Anubis, to join Japan, China, England, Canada and America together ever comes to pass, Mother Russia will be ruined forever. Ah my country my country! How I miss Georgia, so beautiful and gentle and verdant.

The songs of his childhood, the folk songs of Georgia, welled up and took him back. He wiped away a small tear at the thought of so much beauty, so far away. Never mind, my leave's due soon. Then I'll be home. And my son will be home on leave at the same time from Washington with his young wife and their infant son, born so wisely in America. No trouble about a passport for him. He'll be our fourth generation to serve. We advance.

The darkness was pressing down on him. At Arthur's request, for further safety he had drawn the curtains and kept the windows closed though there was no possibility they could be seen. The apartment had air conditioning but again for safety he had been asked to leave it off, as well as the lights. It had been wise to leave the Finns' apartment before Grey in case there had been a change of plan and there was an SI tail on him. Crosse had told him there would be none tonight, though tomorrow another man would be assigned to him.

He had caught a taxi and stopped at Golden Ferry for the evening papers, pretending to lurch drunkenly in case he was being observed, then went to Rose Court and Clinker's and down the tunnel and then here. There was an SI man stationed outside Rose Court. The man was still outside and would stay there or not stay there. It made no difference.

The phone jangled. The sound made him jump even though the bell was carefully muted. Three rings, then silence. His heart picked up a beat. Arthur would be here shortly.

He touched the automatic that was secreted behind one of the cushions. Orders from Center. It was one of many orders he disapproved of. Suslev did not like guns, handguns. Guns could make mistakes, poison never. His fingers touched the tiny phial that was buried in his lapel close enough for his mouth to reach it. What would it be like to live *without* instant death so close?

Deliberately he relaxed and concentrated his senses like radar, wanting to sense Arthur's presence before it was actually there. Would Arthur use the front door or the back?

From where he was sitting he could see both doors. His ears searched carefully, mouth slightly open to increase their sensitivity. The whine of the elevator. His eyes went to the front door but the whine ceased floors below. He waited. The back door opened before he sensed anything. His insides fell over as he failed to recognize the dark shape. For a moment he was paralyzed. Then the shape straightened one shoulder and the slight stoop vanished.

'*Kristos!*' Suslev muttered. 'You gave me a fright.'

'All part of the service, old boy.' The soft, clipped words were mixed with the dry, hacking, put-on cough. 'Are you alone?'

'Of course!'

The shape moved noiselessly into the living room. Suslev saw the automatic being put away and he relaxed the hold on his but left it ready in hiding. He got up and stretched out his hand warmly. 'You're on time for once.'

They shook hands. Jason Plumm did not remove his gloves. 'I very nearly didn't arrive,' he said in his normal voice, the smile on the surface of his face only.

'What's wrong?' the Russian asked, reading the quality of the smile. 'And why all the "pull the curtains and keep the windows closed"?'

'I think this place may be under surveillance.'

'Eh?' Suslev's disquiet soared. 'Why didn't you mention it before?'

'I said, I *think* it may be. I'm not sure. We've gone to a lot of trouble to make this a safe house and I don't want it blown for any reason.' The tall Englishman's voice had a raw edge to it. 'Listen, comrade, all hell's broken loose. SI's caught a fellow called Metkin off your ship. He—'

'What?' Suslev stared at him with pretended shock.

'Metkin. He's supposed to be political comm—'

'But that's impossible,' Suslev said shakily, his acting consummate, hiding his delight that Metkin had fallen into his trap. 'Metkin would never make a pickup himself!'

'Even so, SI have him! Armstrong got him and an American off the carrier. They caught them in the act. Does Metkin know about Sevrin?'

'No, absolutely not.'

'You're sure?'

'Yes. Even I didn't know until a few days ago when Center told me to take over from Voranski,' Suslev said, the twisted truth coming easily.

'You're sure? Roger almost hit the roof! Metkin's supposed to be your political commissar, and a major, KGB. Is he?'

'Yes, but it's ridic—'

'Why the devil didn't he or you or someone tell us you've an operation going so we could have been prepared in case of a foul-up! I'm head of Sevrin and now you're operating here without liaising or keeping me advised. It was always agreed.

Voranski always told us in advance.'

'But, comrade,' Suslev said placatingly, 'I didn't know any-thing about a pickup. Metkin does what he wants. He's the chief, the senior man on the ship. I'm not party to everything—you know that!' Suslev was suitably apologetic and irritable, keeping up his perpetual cover that he was not the real arbiter of Sevrin. 'I can't think what possessed Metkin to have made a pickup himself. Stupid! He must've been mad! Thank God he's a dedicated man and his lapel's poisoned so there's no n—'

'They got him intact.'

Suslev gasped, now in real shock. He'd expected Metkin to be long since dead. 'You're sure?'

'They got him intact. They got his real name, rank and serial number and right now he's on an RAF transport under heavy guard heading for London.'

Suslev's mind blanked out for a moment. He had cunningly set up Metkin to take over from the agent who should have made the pickup. For months now he had found Metkin in-creasingly critical of him and nosy and therefore dangerous. Three times in the last year he had intercepted private reports to Center, written by his number two, criticizing the easy way he ran his ship and his job, and his liaison with Ginny Fu. Suslev was sure Metkin was preparing a trap for him, maybe even trying to guarantee his retirement to the Crimea—a plum post-ing—by pulling off some coup, like, for example, whispering to Center that he suspected there was a security leak aboard the *Ivanov* and that it must be Suslev.

Suslev shuddered. Neither Metkin, nor Center nor any of the others would need proof, just suspicion would damn him.

'It's definite Metkin's alive?' he asked, thinking through this new problem.

'Yes. You're absolutely sure he knows nothing about Sevrin?'

'Yes. Yes, I've already told you.' Suslev sharpened his voice. 'You're the only one who knows all the members of Sevrin, eh? Even Crosse doesn't know them all, does he?'

'No.' Plumm went to the refrigerator and took out the bottle of water. Suslev poured himself a vodka, delighted that Sevrin had so many important safety valves within it: Plumm not aware that Roger Crosse was a KGB informer on the side . . . Crosse alone knowing Suslev's own real position in Asia but neither Crosse nor Plumm knowing his longtime connection with deVille . . . none of the other members knowing each other . . . and none of them aware of Banastasio and the guns or of the real extent of the Soviet thrust into the Far East.

Wheels within wheels within wheels and now Metkin, one of the faulty wheels, gone forever. It had been so easy to drop the honey to Metkin that safe acquisition of the carrier's armament manifest would guarantee promotion for the agent involved. 'I'm surprised they caught him alive,' he said, meaning it.

'Roger told me they had the poor bugger pinioned and a neck collar on him before he could get his teeth into the lapel.'

'Did they find the evidence on him?'

'Roger didn't say. He had to work so damned fast. We thought the best thing to do was to whisk Metkin out of Hong Kong as quickly as possible. We were petrified he knew about us, being so senior. It'll be easier to deal with him in London.' Plumm's voice was grave.

'Crosse will resolve Metkin.'

'Perhaps.' Uneasily Plumm drank some more water.

'How did SI get to know about the pickup?' Suslev asked, wanting to find out how much Plumm knew. 'There must be a traitor aboard my ship.'

'No. Roger said the leak came through an informer MI-6 has aboard the carrier. Even the CIA didn't know.'

'*Kristos!* Why the hell did Roger have to be so efficient?'

'It was Armstrong. SI has checks and balances. But so long as Metkin knows nothing there's no harm!'

Suslev felt the Englishman's scrutiny. He kept his face guileless. Plumm was no fool. The man was strong, cunning, ruthless, a secret protégé and selectee of Philby's. 'I'm certain Metkin knows nothing that could damage us. Even so, Center should be informed at once. They can deal with it.'

'I've already done that. I asked for Priority One help.'

'Good,' Suslev said. 'You've done very well, comrade. You and Crosse. Acquiring Crosse for the cause was a brilliant coup. I must congratulate you again.' Suslev meant the compliment. Roger Crosse was a professional and not an amateur like this man and all the others of Sevrin.

'Perhaps I acquired him, perhaps he acquired me. I'm not sure sometimes,' Plumm said thoughtfully. 'Or about you, comrade. Voranski I knew. We'd done business over the years but you, you're a new, untried quantity.'

'Yes. It must be difficult for you.'

'You don't seem too upset about the loss of your superior.'

'I'm not. I must confess I'm not. Metkin was mad to put himself in such danger. That was totally against orders. To be frank . . . I think there have been security leaks from the *Ivanov*. Metkin was the only long-term member of the crew, apart from Voranski, who had access ashore. He was considered to be beyond reproach but you never know. Perhaps he made other mistakes, a loose tongue in a bar, eh?'

'Christ protect us from fools and traitors. Where did AMG get his information?'

'We don't know. As soon as we do, that leak will be plugged.'

'Are you going to be Voranski's permanent replacement?'

'I don't know. I have not been told.'

'I don't like change. Change is dangerous. Who killed him?'

'Ask Crosse. I want to know too.' Suslev watched Plumm back. He saw him nod, apparently satisfied. 'What about Sinders and the AMG papers?' he asked.

'Roger's covered everything. No need to worry. He's sure we'll get to look at them. You'll have your copy tomorrow.' Again Plumm watched him. 'What if we're named in the reports?'

'Impossible! Dunross would have told Roger at once—or one of his friends in the police, probably Chop Suey Kwok,' Suslev said with a sneer. 'If not him, the governor. Automatically it would get back to Roger. You're all safe.'

'Perhaps, perhaps not.' Plumm went to the window and looked at the brooding sky. 'Nothing's ever safe. Take Jacques. He's a risk now. He'll never make tai-pan.'

Suslev let himself frown and then, as though it was a sudden idea, he said, 'Why not guide him out of Hong Kong? Suggest to Jacques he ask to be posted to . . . say Struan's in Canada. He could use his recent tragedy as an excuse. In Canada he'll be in a backwater and he'll die on the vine there. Eh?'

'Very good idea. Yes, that should be easy. He has a number of good contacts there which might be useful.' Plumm nodded. 'I'll be a lot happier when we've read those files, and even happier when you find out how the hell AMG discovered us.'

'He discovered Sevrin, not you. Listen, comrade, I assure you you're safe to continue your vital work. Please continue to do everything you can to agitate the banking crisis and the stock market crash.'

'No need to worry. We all want that to happen.'

The phone came to life. Both men stared at it. It only sounded once. One ring. The code, *danger*, leaped into their heads. Aghast Suslev grabbed the hidden gun, remembering his fingerprints were on it as he hurtled through the kitchen for the back door, Plumm close behind him. He ripped open the door, letting Plumm through first onto the exit landing. At that moment there was the pounding of approaching feet and a crash against the front door behind them which held but buckled slightly. Suslev closed the back door silently, easing a bar into place. Another crash. He peered through a crack. Another crash. The front locks shattered. For an instant he saw the silhouettes of four men against the hall light, then he fled. Plumm was already down the stairs, covering him from the next landing, automatic out, and Suslev went down the steps three at a time past him to the next landing, then turned to cover in his turn. Above him the back door buckled nauseatingly. Silently Plumm ran past him and again covered him as they fled downward to the next landing. Then Plumm pulled away some camouflaging crates from the false door exit that branched off the main one. Footsteps noisily raced up toward them from downstairs. Another crash against the back door above. Suslev guarded as Plumm squeezed through the opening into the dark and he followed, pulling the partial door closed after him. Already Plumm had found the flashlight that was waiting in a clip. Footsteps raced closer. Cautiously Plumm led the way downward, both men moving well and silently. The footsteps passed with the sound of muffled voices. Both men stopped momentarily, trying to hear what was being said. But the sound was too indistinct and muted and they could not even tell if it was English or Chinese.

Plumm turned again and led the way downward. They hurried but with great caution, not wanting to make any unnecessary noise. Soon they were near the secret exit. Without hesitation the two men lifted the false floor and went below into the cool wet of the culvert. Once they were there and safe, they stopped for breath, their hearts pounding with the suddenness of it all.

When he could talk, Suslev whispered, 'Kuomintang?'

Plumm just shrugged. He wiped the sweat off. A car rumbled overhead. He directed his light to the dripping ceiling. There were many cracks and another avalanche of stones and mud cascaded. The floor was awash with half a foot of water that covered their shoes.

'Best we part, old chap,' Plumm said softly and Suslev noticed that though the man was sweating, his voice was icy calm and the light never wavered. 'I'll get Roger to deal with whatever shower that was at once. Very bloody boring.'

Suslev's heart was slowing. He still found it difficult to speak. 'Where do we meet tomorrow?'

'I'll let you know.' The Englishman's face was stark. 'First Voranski, then Metkin and now this. Too many leaks.' He jerked a thumb upward. 'That was too close. Maybe your Metkin knew more than you think he did.'

'No. I tell you he knew nothing about Sevrin, nothing, or about that apartment or Clinker or any of it. Only Voranski and me, we're the only ones who knew. There's no leak from our side.'

'I hope you're right.' Plumm added grimly, 'We'll find out, Roger'll find out one way or another, one day, and then God help the traitor!'

'Good. I want him too.'

After a pause Plumm said, 'Call me every half an hour from various phone booths, from 7:30 P.M. tomorrow.'

'All right. If for any reason there's a problem I'll be at Ginny's from eleven onwards. One last thing. If we don't get to look at the AMG papers, what's your opinion about Dunross?'

'His memory's incredible.'

'Then we isolate him for a chemical interrogation?'

'Why not?'

'Good, *tovarich*. I'll make all the preparations.'

'No. We'll snatch him and we'll deliver him. To the *Ivanov*?'

Suslev nodded and told him Metkin's suggestion of blaming the Werewolves, not saying it was Metkin's idea. 'Eh?'

Plumm smiled. 'Clever! See you tomorrow.' He handed Suslev the flashlight, took out a pencil light and turned, going down the culvert, his feet still under water. Suslev watched until the tall man had turned the corner and vanished. He had never followed the culvert below. Plumm had told him not to, that it was dangerous and subject to rockfalls.

He took a deep breath, now over his fright. Another car rumbled heavily overhead. That's probably a truck, he thought absently. More mud and a piece of the concrete fell with a splash, startling him. Suslev waited, then began to pick his way carefully up the slope. Another tiny avalanche. Suddenly Suslev hated the subterranean tube. It made him feel insecure and doom ridden.

56

Dunross was looking at the sad hulk of the burned-out *Floating Dragon* restaurant that lay on her side in twenty feet of Aberdeen water. The other multistoried eating palaces that floated nearby were still blazing with lights, gaudy and noisy, filled to capacity, their new, hastily erected, temporary kitchens on barges beside their mother ships, cauldrons smoking, fires under the cauldrons, and a mass of cooks and helpers like so many bees. Waiters hurried up and down precarious gangways with trays and dishes. Sampans sailed nearby, tourists staring, Hong Kong *yan* gaping, the hulk a great attraction.

Part of the hulk's superstructure jutted out of the water. Salvage crews were already working on her under floodlights, salvaging her, readying to float what remained of her. On her part of the wharf and parking lot temporary roofing and kitchens were set up. Vendors were busily selling photographs of the blaze, souvenirs, foods of a hundred kinds, and a huge floodlit sign in Chinese and English proudly proclaimed that the new, ONLY TOTALLY MODERN AND *FIREPROOF* FLOATING RESTAURANT, THE FLOATING DRAGON would soon be in business, bigger than ever, better than ever . . . meanwhile sample the foods of our famous chefs. It was business as usual except that temporarily the restaurant was on land and not on the sea.

Dunross walked along the wharf toward one of the sea steps. There were clusters of sampans nearby, big and small. Most of these were for hire, each small craft with one sculler, a man, woman or child of any age, each craft with a hooped canvas covering that sheltered half of the boat from sun or rain or prying eyes. Some of the sampans were more elaborate. Those were the nighttime Pleasure Boats. Inside were reclining pillows and low tables, the better craft luxurious with plenty of room for two to eat and drink and then to pillow, the single oarsman discreetly not part of the cabin. You could hire one for an hour or a night and the boat would lazily float the byways. Other sampans would come with all manner of drinks and foods, fresh foods served piping hot, served delicately, and you and your lady could dream the night away in perfect privacy.

You could go alone if you wished. Then, out near one of the vast islands of boats, your sampan would rendezvous with Ladies of the Night and you could choose and barter and then drift. In the harbor you could satisfy any wish, any thirst, any desire—at little cost, the price fair whoever you were—if you could pay and were a man. Opium, cocaine, heroin, whatever you wanted.

Sometimes the food was bad or the singsong girl bad, but this was just joss, a regretted mistake and not deliberate. Sometimes you could lose your wallet but then only a simpleton would come among such prideful poverty to flaunt his wealth.

Dunross smiled, seeing a heavyset tourist nervously ease himself into one of the craft, helped by a *cheong-sam*ed girl. You're in good hands, he thought, very glad with the hustle and bustle of business all around him, buying, selling, bartering. Yes, he told himself, Chinese are the real capitalists of the world.

What about Tiptop and Johnjohn's request? What about Lando Mata and Tightfist and Par-Con? And Gornt? And AMG and Riko Anjin and Sinders and . . .

Don't think about them now. Get your wits about you! Four Finger Wu hasn't summoned you to discuss the weather.

He passed the first sea steps and headed along the wharf to the main ones, the light from the streetlamps casting strong shadows. At once all the sampans there began to jostle for position, their owners calling out, beckoning. When he got to the top of the steps the commotion stopped.

'Tai-pan!'

A well-set Pleasure Boat with a Silver Lotus flag aft eased directly through them. The boatman was short, squat with many gold teeth. He wore torn khaki pants and a sweat shirt.

Dunross whistled to himself, recognizing Four Finger Wu's eldest son, the *loh-pan*, the head of Wu's fleet of Pleasure Boats. No wonder the other boats gave him leeway, he thought, impressed that Goldtooth Wu met him personally. Nimbly he went aboard, greeting him. Goldtooth sculled swiftly away.

'Make yourself at home, tai-pan,' Goldtooth said easily in perfect English-accented English. He had a B.Sc. from London University and had wanted to remain in England. But Four Fingers had ordered him home. He was a gentle, quiet, kind man whom Dunross liked.

'Thank you.'

On the lacquered table was fresh tea and whiskey and glasses, brandy and bottled water. Dunross looked around carefully. The cabin was neat and lit with little lights, clean, soft and expansive. A small radio played good music. This must be Goldtooth's flagship, he thought, amused and very much on guard.

There was no need to ask where Goldtooth was taking him. He poured himself a little brandy, adding soda water. There was no ice. In Asia he never used ice.

'Christ,' he muttered suddenly, remembering what Peter Marlowe had said about the possibility of infectious hepatitis. Fifty or sixty people have that hanging over their heads now, if they know it or not. Gornt's one of them too. Yes, but that sod's got the constitution of a meat ax. The bugger hasn't even had a touch of the runs. What to do about him? What's his permanent solution?

It was cool and pleasant in the cabin, half open to the breeze, the sky dark. A huge junk moved past, chugging throatily, and he lay back enjoying the tensions he felt, the anticipation. His heart was steady. He sipped the brandy, drifting, being patient.

The side of the sampan scraped another. His ears focused. Bare feet padded aboard. Two sets of feet, one nimble the other not. 'Halloa, tai-pan!' Four Fingers said, grinning toothlessly. He ducked under the canopy and sat down. 'How you okay?' he said in dreadful English.

'Fine and you?' Dunross stared at him, trying to hide his astonishment. Four Finger Wu was dressed in a good suit with a clean white shirt and gaudy tie and carried shoes and socks. The last time Dunross had seen him like this was the night of the fire and before that, the only other time years ago, at Shitee T'Chung's immense wedding.

More feet approached. Awkwardly Paul Choy sat down. 'Evening, sir. I'm Paul Choy.'

'Are you all right?' he asked, sensing great discomfort, and fear.

'Sure, yes, thank you, sir.'

Dunross frowned. 'Well this's a pleasure,' he said, letting it pass. 'You're working for your uncle now?' he asked, knowing all about Paul Choy, keeping up the pretense he and Four Fingers had agreed to, and very impressed with the young man. He had heard of his stock market coup through his old friend Soorjani.

'No sir. I'm with Rothwell-Gornt's. I just started a couple of days ago. I'm here to interpret . . . if you need me.' Paul Choy turned to his father and explained what had been said.

Four Fingers nodded. 'Blandeee?'

'It's fine, thank you.' Dunross raised his glass. 'Good you see, *heya*,' he continued in English, waiting for the old man to begin in Haklo. It was a matter of face and, with the presence of Paul Choy, Dunross's latent caution had increased a thousand-fold.

The old seaman chatted inconsequentially for a while, drinking whiskey. Paul Choy was not offered a drink, nor did he take one. He sat in the shadows, listening, frightened, not knowing what to expect. His father had sworn him to perpetual secrecy with hair-raising blood oaths.

Finally Wu gave up waiting the tai-pan out and started in Haklo. 'Our families have been Old Friends for many years,' he said, speaking slowly and carefully, aware that Dunross's Haklo was not perfect. 'Very many years.'

'Yes. Seaborne Wu and Struan's like brothers,' the tai-pan replied cautiously.

Four Fingers grunted. 'The present is like the past and the past the present. *Heya?*'

'Old Blind Tung says past and present same. *Heya?*'

'What does the name Wu Kwok mean to the tai-pan of the Noble House?'

Dunross's stomach twisted. 'He your great-grandfather, *heya?* Your illustrious forebear. Son and chief admiral of even more illustrious sea warlord, Wu Fang Choi, whose flag, the Silver Lotus, flew all four seas.'

'The very one!' Four Fingers leaned closer and Dunross's caution doubled. 'What was the connection between Green-Eyed Devil . . . between the first tai-pan of the Noble House and the illustrious Wu Kwok?'

'They meet at sea. They meet in Pearl River Estuary off Wh—'

'It was near here, off Pok Liu Chau, between Pok Liu Chau and Aplichau.' The old man's eyes were slits in his face.

'Then they meet off Hong Kong. The tai-pan went aboard Wu Kwok's flagship. He went alone and . . .' Dunross searched for the word. '. . . and he negotiate a, a bargain with him.'

'Was the bargain written onto paper and chopped?'

'No.'

'Was the bargain honored?'

'It is fornicating ill-mannered to ask such question from Old Friend when Old Friend opposite knows answer!'

Paul Choy jerked involuntarily at the sudden venom and slashing cut of the words. Neither man paid any attention to him.

'True, true, tai-pan,' the old man said, as unafraid as Dunross. 'Yes, the bargain was honored, though twisted, part was twisted. Do you know the bargain?'

'No, not all,' Dunross said truthfully. 'Why?'

'The bargain was that on each of your twenty clippers we put one man to train as a captain—my grandfather was one of these. Next, Green-Eyed Devil agreed to take three of Wu Kwok's boys and send them to his land to train them as foreign devils in the best schools, everything like his own sons would be trained. Next the tai—'

Dunross's eyes widened. 'What? Who? Who are these boys? Who did they become?'

Four Finger Wu just smiled crookedly. 'Next, Green-Eyed Devil agreed to get for the illustrious Wu Fang Choi a foreign devil clipper ship, armed and rigged and beautiful. Wu Fang Choi paid for her but the tai-pan arranged for her and called her *Lotus Cloud*. But when Culum the Weak delivered her, almost two years later, your fornicating chief admiral, Stride Orlov, the Hunchback, came out of the east like an assassin in the night and murdered our ship and Wu Kwok with her.'

931

Dunross sipped his brandy, waiting outwardly at ease, inwardly his brain shocked. Who could those boys be? Was that truly part of the bargain? There's nothing in Dirk's diary or testament about Wu Kwok's sons. Nothing. Who co—

'Heya?'

'I know about *Lotus Cloud*. Yes. And about men, captains. I think it was nineteen and not twenty clippers. But I know nothing about three boys. About *Lotus Cloud*, did my ancestor promise not to fight ship after he had give ship?'

'No. Oh no, tai-pan, no he did not promise that. Green-Eyed Devil was clever, very clever. Wu Kwok's death? Joss. We must all die. Joss. No, Green-Eyed Devil kept his bargain. Culum the Weak kept the bargain too. Will you keep his bargain?' Four Finger Wu opened his fist.

In it was the half-coin.

Dunross took it carefully, his heart grinding. They watched him like snakes, both of them, and he felt the strength of their eyes. His fingers shook imperceptibly. It was like the other half-coins that were still in Dirk's Bible, in the safe in the Great House, two still left, two gone, already redeemed, Wu Kwok's one of them. Fighting to control the trembling of his fingers, he handed the coin back. Wu took it, careless that his hand shook.

'Perhaps real,' Dunross said, his voice sounding strange. 'Must check. Where get it?'

'It's genuine, of course it's fornicating genuine. You acknowledge it as genuine?'

'No. Where get it?'

Four Fingers lit a cigarette and coughed. He cleared his throat and spat. 'How many coins were there at first? How many did the illustrious Mandarin Jin-qua give Green-Eyed Devil?'

'I not sure.'

'Four. There were four.'

'Ah, one to your illustrious ancestor, Wu Kwok, paid and honored. Why would great Jin-qua give him two? Not possible —so this stolen. From whom?'

The old man flushed and Dunross wondered if he had gone too far.

'Stolen or not,' the old man spat, 'you grant favor. Heya?' Dunross just stared at him. 'Heya? Or is the face of Green-Eyed Devil no longer the face of the Noble House?'

932

'Where get it?'

Wu stared at him. He stubbed out the cigarette on the carpet. 'Why should Green-Eyed Devil agree to four coins? Why? And why would he swear by his gods that he and all his heirs would honor his word, *heya*?'

'For another favor.'

'Ah, tai-pan, yes for a favor. Do you know what favor?'

Dunross stared back at him. 'Honorable Jin-qua loaned *the tai-pan*, my great-great-grandfather, forty lacs of silver.'

'Forty lac—$4 million. One hundred twenty years ago.' The old man sighed. His eyes slitted even more. Paul Choy was breathless, motionless. 'Was a paper asked for? A debt paper chopped by your illustrious forebear—on the chop of the Noble House?'

'No.'

'Forty lacs of silver. No paper no chop just trust! The bargain was just a bargain between Old Friends, no chop, just trust, *heya*?'

'Yes.'

The old man's thumbless hand snaked out palm upward and held the half-coin under Dunross's face. 'One coin, grant favor. Whoever asks. I ask.'

Dunross sighed. At length he broke the silence. 'First I fit half to half. Next make sure metal here same metal there. Then you say favor.' He went to pick up the half-coin but the fist snapped closed and withdrew and Four Fingers jerked his good thumb at Paul Choy. 'Explain,' he said.

'Excuse me, tai-pan,' Paul Choy said in English, very uneasily, hating the closeness of the cabin and the devil-borne currents in the cabin, all because of a promise given twelve decades ago by one pirate to another, both murdering cutthroats if half the stories were true, he thought. 'My uncle wants me to explain how he wants to do this.' He tried to keep his voice level. 'Of course he understands you'll have reservations and want to be a thousand percent sure. At the same time he doesn't want to give up possession, just at this time. Until he's sure, one way or the other, he'd pr—'

'You're saying he doesn't trust me?'

Paul Choy flinched at the viciousness of the words. 'Oh no, sir,' he said quickly and translated what Dunross had said.

'Of course I trust you,' Wu said. His smile was crooked. 'But do you trust me?'

'Oh yes, Old Friend. I trust very much. Give me coin. If real, I tai-pan of Noble House will grant your ask—if possible.'

'Whatever ask, whatever, is granted!' the old man flared.

'*If possible*. Yes. If real coin I grant favor, if not real, I give back the coin. Finish.'

'Not finish.' Wu waved his hand at Paul Choy. 'You finish, quickly!'

'My . . . my uncle suggests the following compromise. You take this.' The young man brought out a flat piece of beeswax. Three separate imprints of the half-coin had been pressed into it. 'You'll be able to fit the other half to these, sir. The edges're sharp enough for you to be sure, almost sure. This's step one. If you're reasonably satisfied, step two's we go together to a government assayer or the curator of a museum and get him to test both coins in front of us. Then we'll both know at the same time.' Paul Choy was dripping with sweat. 'That's what my uncle says.'

'One side could easily bribe the assayist.'

'Sure. But before we see him we mix up the two halves. We'd know ours, you'd know yours—but he wouldn't, huh?'

'He could be got at.'

'Sure. But if we . . . if we do this tomorrow and if Wu Sang gives you his word and you give him your word not to try a setup, it'd work.' The young man wiped the sweat off his face. 'Jesus, it's close in here!'

Dunross thought a moment. Then he turned his cold eyes on Four Fingers. 'Yesterday I ask favor, you said no.'

'That favor was different, tai-pan,' the old man replied at once, his tongue darting like a snake's. 'That was not the same as an ancient promise collecting an ancient debt.'

'You ask your friends concerning my ask, *heya*?'

Wu lit another cigarette. His voice sharpened. 'Yes. My friends are worried about the Noble House.'

'If no Noble House, no noble favor, *heya*?'

The silence thickened. Dunross saw the cunning old eyes dart at Paul Choy and then back to him again. He knew he was entrapped by the coin. He would have to pay. If it was genuine he would have to pay, whether stolen or not. Stolen from whom, his mind was shouting. Who here would have had one? Dirk Struan never knew who the others had been given to. In his testament he had written that he suspected one went to his mistress May-may but there was no reason for such a gift by Jin-qua. If to May-may, Dunross reasoned, then it would have passed down to Shitee T'Chung, who was presently the head of the T'Chung line, May-may's line. Maybe it was stolen from him.

Who else in Hong Kong?

If *the tai-pan* or the Hag couldn't answer that one, I can't. There's no family connection back to Jin-qua!

In the heavy silence Dunross watched and waited. Another bead of sweat dropped off Paul Choy's chin as he looked at his father, then back at the table again. Dunross sensed the hate and that interested him. Then he saw Wu sizing up Paul Choy strangely. Instantly his mind leaped forward. 'I'm the arbiter of Hong Kong,' he said in English. 'Support me and within a week huge profits can be made.'

'Heya?'

Dunross had been watching Paul Choy. He had seen him look up, startled. 'Please translate, Mr. Choy,' he said.

Paul Choy obeyed. Dunross sighed, satisfied. Paul Choy had not translated 'I'm the arbiter of Hong Kong.' Again a silence. He relaxed, more at ease now, sensing both men had taken the bait.

'Tai-pan, my suggestion, about the coin, you agree?' the old man said.

'About my ask, my ask for money support, you agree?'

Wu said angrily, 'The two are not interwoven like rain in a fornicating storm. Yes or no on the coin?'

'I agree on the coin. But not tomorrow. Next week. Fifth day.'

'Tomorrow.'

Paul Choy carefully interjected, 'Honored Uncle, perhaps you could ask your friends again tomorrow. Tomorrow morning. Perhaps they could help the tai-pan.' His shrewd eyes turned to Dunross. 'Tomorrow's Friday,' he said in English, 'how about Monday at . . . at 4:00 P.M. for the coin?' He repeated it in Haklo.

'Why that time?' Wu asked irritably.

'The foreign devil money market closes at the third hour of

935

the afternoon, Honored Uncle. By that time the Noble House will be noble or not.'

'We will always be the Noble House, Mr. Choy,' Dunross said politely in English, impressed with the man's skill—and shrewdness to take an oblique hint. 'I agree.'

'*Heya?*'

When Paul Choy had finished the old man grunted. 'First I will check the Heaven-Earth currents to see if that is an auspicious day. If it is, then I agree.' He jerked his thumb at Paul Choy. 'Go aboard the other boat.'

Paul Choy got up. 'Thank you, tai-pan. Good night.'

'See you soon, Mr. Choy,' Dunross replied, expecting him the next day.

When they were quite alone, the old man said softly, 'Thank you, Old Friend. Soon we'll do much closer business.'

'Remember, Old Friend, what my forebears say,' Dunross said ominously. 'Both Green-Eyed Devil and her of Evil Eye and Dragon's Teeth—how they put a great curse and Evil Eye on White Powders and those who profit from White Powders.'

The gnarled old seaman in the nice clothes shrugged nervously. 'What's that to me? I know nothing of White Powders. Fornicate all White Powders. I know nothing of them.'

Then he was gone.

Shakily Dunross poured a long drink. He felt the new motion of the sampan being sculled again. His fingers brought out the waxen imprints. A thousand to one the coin's genuine. Christ almighty, what will that devil ask? Drugs, I'll bet it's something to do with drugs! That about the curse and the Evil Eye was made up—not part of Dirk's bargain at all. Even so, I won't agree to drugs.

But he was ill-at-ease. He could see Dirk Struan's writing in the Bible that he had signed and endorsed, agreeing before God 'to grant to whomsoever shall present one of the half-coins, whatsoever he shall ask, if it is in the tai-pan's power to give. . . .'

His ears sensed the alien presence before the sound arrived. Another boat scraped his gently. The pad of feet. He readied, not knowing the danger.

The girl was young, beautiful and joyous. 'My name is Snow Jade, tai-pan, I'm eighteen years and Honorable Wu Sang's personal gift for the night!' Lilting Cantonese, neat *cheong-sam*, high collar, long stockinged legs and high heels. She smiled, showing her lovely white teeth. 'He thought you might be in need of sustenance.'

'Is that so?' he muttered, trying to collect himself.

She laughed and sat down. 'Oh yes, that's what he said and I'd like your sustenance also—I'm starving, aren't you? Honorable Goldtooth has ordered a morsel or two to whet your appetite: quick fried prawns with peapods, shredded beef in black bean sauce, some deep-fried dumplings Shanghai style, quick fried vegetables spiced with Szechuan cabbage and tangy Ch'iang Pao chicken.' She beamed. 'I'm dessert!'

FRIDAY

57

Irritably, Banker Kwang stabbed the doorbell again and again. The door swung open and Venus Poon screeched in Cantonese, 'How dare you come here at this time of night without an invitation!' Her chin jutted and she stood with one hand on the door, the other imperiously on her hip, her low-cut evening dress devastating.

'Quiet, you mealy-mouthed whore!' Banker Kwang shouted back at her and shoved past into her apartment. 'Who's paying the rent? Who bought all this furniture? Who paid for that dress? Why aren't you ready for bed? Wh—'

'*Quiet!*' Her voice was piercing and easily drowned out his. 'You *were* paying the rent, but today's the day when the rent was due and where is it, *heyaheyaheyaheya?*'

'Here!' Banker Kwang ripped the check out of his pocket and waved it under her nose. 'Do I forget my fornicating promises— *no!* Do you forget your fornicating promises—*yes!*'

Venus Poon blinked. Her rage disappeared, her face changed, her voice became laden with honey. 'Oh did Father remember? Oh I was told you'd forsaken your poor lonely Daughter and gone back to the whores of 1 Blore Street.'

'Lies!' Banker Kwang gasped, almost apoplectic even though it was the truth. 'Why aren't you dressed for bed? Why are you wear—'

'But I was called by three different people who said you'd been there this afternoon at 4:15. Oh how terrible people are,' she said crooningly, knowing that he was there though he only went to introduce Banker Ching from whom he was trying to borrow funds. 'Oh poor Father, how dreadful people are.' As

941

she talked placatingly, she moved closer. Suddenly her hand snaked out and she snatched the check before he could withdraw it though her voice continued to be sweet. 'Oh thank you, Father, from the bottom of my heart . . . *oh ko!*' Her eyes crossed, her voice hardened and the screech returned. 'The check is not signed, you dirty old dogmeat! It's another of your banker tricks! Oh oh oh I think I shall kill myself on your doorstep . . . no, better I shall do it in front of the TV camera, telling all Hong Kong how you . . . Oh oh oh. . . .'

Her *amah* was in the living room now, joining in, wailing and caterwauling, both women swamping him in a swelter of invective, challenges and accusations.

Impotently he cursed them both back but that only made them increase their volume. He stood his ground for a moment, then, vanquished, pulled out a fountain pen with a flourish, grabbed the check and signed it. The noise ceased. Venus Poon took it and examined it carefully. Very very carefully. It vanished into her purse.

'Oh thank you, Honorable Father,' she said meekly and abruptly whirled on her *amah*. 'How dare you interfere in a discussion between the love of my life and your mistress, you lump of festering dogmeat. It's all your fault for spreading other people's cruel lies about Father's infidelity! Out! Fetch tea and food! Out! Father needs a brandy . . . fetch a brandy, *hurry!*'

The old woman pretended to buckle under the assumed rage and scuttled out in pretended tears. Venus Poon cooed and bustled and her hands were soft on Richard Kwang's neck.

At length, under their magic, he allowed himself to be mollified and helped to drink, groaning aloud all the time at his ill joss and how his subordinates, friends, allies and debtors had maliciously forsaken him, after he alone in the whole Ho-Pak empire had worked his fingers to their tendons, his feet to the flesh, worrying over all of them.

'Oh you poor man,' Venus Poon said soothingly, her mind darting while her fingers were tender and deft. She had barely half an hour to reach her rendezvous with Four Finger Wu, and while she knew it would be wise to keep him waiting, she did not want to keep him waiting too long in case his ardor lagged. Their last encounter had excited him so much he had promised her a diamond if the performance was repeated.

'I guarantee it, Lord,' she had gasped weakly, her skin clammy with sweat from two hours of concentrated labor, feeling herself afloat with the immensity of his at long last explosion.

Her eyes crossed as she remembered Four Finger Wu's prodigious efforts, his size, conformity and undoubted technique. *Ayeeyah*, she thought, still massaging the neck of her former lover, I will need every tael of energy and every measure of juice the yin can muster to dominate that old reprobate's yowling yang. 'How is your neck, my dearest love?' she crooned.

'Better, better,' Richard Kwang said reluctantly. His head had cleared and he was well aware that her fingers were as skilled as her mouth and her peerless parts.

He pulled her down onto his knee and confidently slipped his hand into the low-cut black silk evening dress that he had bought for her last week and fondled her breasts. When she did not resist, he slipped one strap off and complimented her on the size, texture, taste and shape of the whole. Her warmth shafted him and he stirred. At once his other hand went for the yin but before he knew it she had neatly squirmed out of his grasp. 'Oh no, Father! Honorable Red's visiting me and as much as I wa—'

'Eh?' Banker Kwang said suspiciously. 'Honorable Red? Honorable Red's not due till the day after tomorrow!'

'Oh no, he arrived with storm th—'

'Eh? He's due the day after tomorrow. I know. I looked at my calendar and made sure before I came here! Am I a fool? Do I fish for a tiger in a stream? We have a long-standing date tonight, all night. Why else am I supposed to be in Taiwan? You're never early and ne—'

'Oh no it was this morning—the shock of the fire and the greater shock that you had forsaken me, br—'

'Come here, you little baggage,—'

'Oh no, Father, Honorable R—'

Before she could avoid him, his hands darted out and he sat her back on his knees and began to lift her dress but Venus Poon was an old stager in this kind of warfare and champion of a hundred jousts, even though she was only nineteen. She fought him not, just pressed closer, twisted and got one hand on him, caressingly, and whispered throatily, 'Oh but Father, it's very bad joss to interfere with Honorable Red and as much as I desire your immensity within, we both know there are other ways for the yin to titillate the vital vortex.'

'But first I wan—'

'First? First?' Pleased with herself, she felt him strengthening. 'Ah, how strong you are! It's easy to see why all the weevilmouthed baggages want my old Father, *ayeeyah*, such a strong, violent, marvelous man.'

Deftly she revealed the yang. Deftly she dominated it and left him gasping. 'Bed, dearest love,' he croaked. 'First a brandy then a little sleep an—'

'Quite right, but not here oh no!' she said firmly, helping him up.

'Eh? But I'm supposed to be in Tai—'

'Yes, so you'd better go to your club!'

'But I—'

'Oh but you've exhausted your poor Daughter.' She feigned weakness as she tidied him and had him up and at the door before he really knew what was happening. There, she kissed him passionately, swore eternal love, promised that she would see him tomorrow and closed the door behind him.

Shakily he stared at the door, his knees gone, his skin clammy, wanting to hammer on it to demand rest in the bed he had paid for. But he didn't. He had no strength and tottered to the elevator.

Going down, he suddenly beamed, delighted with himself. The check he had given her was for one month's rent only. She had forgotten he had agreed the month before to increase the amount by $500 a month. Eeeee, Little Marvelous Mouth, he chortled, the yang outsmarted the yin after all! Oh what a good drubbing I gave you tonight, and oh that Clouds and the Rain! Tonight it was truly the Small Death and the Great Birth and certainly cheap at twice one month's rent even with the increase!

Venus Poon finished brushing her teeth and began to repair her makeup. She spotted her *amah* in the bathroom mirror. 'Ah Poo,' she called shrilly, 'fetch my raincoat, the old black one, and phone for a taxi . . . and hurry or I'll pinch both your cheeks!'

The old woman scurried to obey, delighted that her mistress was out of her foul mood. 'I've already phoned for a taxi,' she wheezed. 'He'll be downstairs, waiting at the side entrance as soon as Mother gets there but you'd better give Father a few minutes in case he suspects something!'

'Huh, that old Turtle Top's good for nothing now! All he has strength for is to fall into the back of his car and be driven to his club!'

Venus Poon put the finishing touches to her lips and smiled at herself in the mirror, admiring herself greatly.

Now for the diamond, she thought excitedly.

'When see again, Paw'll?' Lily Su asked.

'Soon. Next week.' Havergill finished dressing and reluctantly picked up his raincoat. The room they were in was small but clean and pleasant, and had a bathroom with hot and cold running water that the hotel management had had installed privately, at great cost, with the clandestine help of some experts in the water board. 'I'll call you, as usual.'

'Why sad, Paw'll?'

He turned and looked at her. He had not told her that soon he would be leaving Hong Kong. From the bed, she watched him back, her skin shiny and youth-filled. She had been his friend for almost four months now, not his exclusive friend since he did not pay her rent or other expenses. She was a hostess in the Happy Hostess Dance Hall that was his favorite nighttime meeting place, Kowloon side. The owner there, One Eye Pok, was an old and valued client of the bank over many years, and the mama-*san* a clever woman who appreciated his custom. He had had many Happy Hostess friends over the years, most for a few hours, some for a month, very few for longer, and only one bad experience in fifteen years—a girl had tried blackmail. At once he had seen the mama-*san*. The girl had left that very night. Neither she nor her triad pimp was ever seen again.

'Why sad, *heya?*'

Because I'm leaving Hong Kong soon, he wanted to tell her. Because I want an exclusivity I can't have, mustn't have, dare not have—and have never wanted with any before. Dear God in Heaven how I want you.

'Not sad, Lily. Just tired,' he said instead, the bank troubles adding to the weight upon him.

'Everything be all good,' she said reassuringly. 'Call soon, *heya?*'

'Yes. Yes I will.' His arrangement with her was simple: a phone call. If he could not reach her direct he would call the mama-*san* and that night he would come to the dance hall, alone or with some friends, and he and Lily would dance a few dances for face and drink some drinks and then she would leave. After half an hour he would pay his bill and come here—everything paid for in advance. They did not walk together to this private and exclusive meeting place because she did not wish to be seen on the streets or by neighbors with a foreign devil. It would be disastrous for a girl's reputation to be seen alone with a barbarian. In public. Outside of her place of work. Any girl of beddable age would at once be presumed to be the lowest type of harlot, a foreign devil's harlot and despised as such, sneered at openly, and her value diminished.

Havergill knew this. It did not bother him. In Hong Kong it was a fact of life. *'Doh jeh,'* he said, thank you—loving her, wanting to stay, or to take her with him. *'Doh jeh,'* he just said and left.

Once alone she allowed the yawn that had almost possessed her many times this evening to overwhelm her and she lay back on the bed and stretched luxuriously. The bed was rumpled but a thousand times better than the cot in the room she rented in Tai-ping Shan.

A soft knock. 'Honored Lady?'

'Ah Chun?'

'Yes.' The door opened and the old woman padded in. She brought clean towels. 'How long will you be here?'

Lily Su hesitated. By custom the client in this place of assignation paid for the room for the whole night. Also by custom, if the room was vacated early, the management returned part of the fee to the girl. 'All night,' she said wanting to enjoy the luxury, not knowing when she would have the opportunity again. Perhaps this client will have lost his bank and everything by next week.

'Joss,' she said, then, 'please put on the bath.'

Grumbling the old woman did as she was told then went away. Again Lily Su yawned, happily listening to the water gurgling. She was tired too. The day had been exhausting. And tonight her client had talked more than usual as she had rested against him, trying to sleep, not listening, understanding only a word here and there but quite content for him to talk. She knew from long experience that this was a form of release, particularly for an old barbarian. Very odd, she thought, all that work and noise and tears and money to achieve nothing but more pain, more talk and more tears. 'Never mind if the yang is weak or if they talk or mumble or mutter their foul-sounding language or weep in your arms. Barbarians do that,' her mama-*san* had explained. 'Close your ears. And close your nostrils to the foreign devil smell and the old man smell and help this one enjoy a moment of pleasure. He's Hong Kong *yan*, an old friend, also he pays well, promptly, he's getting you quickly out of debt, and it's good face to have such a pillow patron. So be enthusiastic, pretend that he's virile and give value for his money.'

Lily Su knew she gave value for money received. Yes, my joss is very good and oh so much better than my poor sister and her patron. Poor Fragrant Flower and Noble House Chen Number One Son. What tragedy! What cruelty!

She shivered. Oh those terrible Werewolves! Terrible to cut off his ear, terrible to murder him and threaten all Hong Kong, terrible for my poor elder sister to be crushed to death by those smelly rotten dogmeat fishermen at Aberdeen. Oh what joss!

It was only this morning that she had seen a newspaper that had printed a copy of John Chen's love letter, recognizing it at once. For weeks they had laughed over it, she and Fragrant Flower, that and the other two letters that Fragrant Flower had left with her for safekeeping. 'Such a funny man, with almost no yang at all and almost never even a little upstanding,' her elder sister had told her. 'He pays me just to lie there for him to kiss, sometimes to dance without clothes, and always promise to tell others how strong he is! Eeeee, he gives me money like water! For eleven weeks I have been his "own true love"! If this continues for another eleven weeks . . . perhaps an apartment bought and paid for!'

This afternoon, fearfully, she had gone with her father to East Aberdeen Police Station to identify the body. They said nothing about knowing who the patron was. Wisely her father had said to keep that secret. 'Noble House Chen will surely prefer that secret. His face is involved too—and the face of the new heir, what's his name, the young one with the foreign devil name. In a day or two I'll phone Noble House Chen and sound him out. We must wait a little. After today's news of what the Werewolves've done to Number One Son, no father'd want to negotiate.'

Yes, Father's smart, she thought. It isn't for nothing that his fellow workers call him Nine Carat Chu. Thank all gods I have those other two letters.

After they had identified her sister's body, they had filled out forms with their real names and real family name Chu to claim her money, 4,360 HK in the name of Wisteria Su, 3,000 HK under Fragrant Flower Tak, all money earned outside the Good Luck Dance Hall. But the police sergeant had been inflexible. 'Sorry, but now that we know her real name we have to announce it so that all her debtors can claim against her estate.' Even a very generous offer of 25 percent of the money for immediate possession could not get through his rough manner. So they had left.

The rotten dogmeat foreign devil slave, she thought disgustedly. Nothing will be left after the dance hall collects its debts. Nothing. *Ayeeyah!*

But never mind, she told herself as she lay down in the bath with glorious contentment. Never mind, the secret of the letters will be worth a fortune to Noble House Chen.

And Noble House Chen has more red notes than a cat has hairs.

Casey was curled up in the window of her bedroom, the lights out except for a small reading lamp over the bed. She was staring gloomily down at the street five stories below. Even this late, almost 1:30 A.M., the street was still snarled with traffic. The sky was low and misty, no moon, making the lights from the huge neon signs and columns of Chinese characters more dazzling, reds and blues and greens that reflected in the puddles and turned ugliness into fairyland. The window was open, the air cool and she could see couples darting between buses and trucks and taxis. Many of the couples were heading for the foyer of the new Royal Netherlands Hotel and a late-night snack at the European coffee shop where she had had a nightcap coffee with Captain Jannelli, their pilot.

Everyone eats so much here, she thought idly. Jesus, and so many people here, so much work to provide, so few jobs, so few at the top, one at the top of each pile, always a man, everyone struggling to get there, to stay there . . . but for what? The new car the new house the new ensemble the new refrigerator the new gimmick or whatever.

Life's one long bill. Never enough of the green stuff to cope with the everyday bills let alone a private yacht or private condo on the shores of Acapulco or the Côte d'Azur, and the means to get there—even tourist.

I hate going tourist. First's worth it, worth it to me. Private jet's better, much better but I won't think about Linc. . . .

She had taken Seymour Steigler to dinner upstairs and they had settled all the business problems, most of them legal problems he kept bringing up.

'We gotta make it watertight. Can't be too cautious with foreigners, Casey,' he kept on saying. 'They don't play the game according to good old Yankee rules.'

As soon as dinner was finished she had feigned a load of work and left him. Her work was all done so she curled up in a chair and began to read, speed-read. *Fortune, Business Week, The Wall Street Journal* and several specialized business magazines. Then she had studied another Cantonese lesson, leaving the book till last. The book was Peter Marlowe's novel, *Changi*. She had found the dog-eared paperback in one of the dozens of street bookstalls in an alley just north of the hotel yesterday morning. It had given her great pleasure bargaining for it. The first asking price was 22 HK. Casey had bargained her down to 7.55 HK, barely $1.50 U.S. Delighted with herself and with her find she had continued window-shopping. Nearby was a modern bookshop, the windows stuffed with picture books on Hong Kong and China. Inside on a rack were three more paperbacks of *Changi*. New, they cost 5.75 HK.

At once Casey had cursed the old woman street seller for cheating her. But then the old hag wasn't cheating you at all, she had reminded herself. She outtraded you. After all, only a moment ago you were chortling because you'd trimmed her profit to nothing and God knows these people need profit.

Casey watched the street and the traffic on Nathan Road below. This morning she had walked up Nathan Road to Boundary Road, a mile and a half or so. It was on her list of things to see. It was a road like any other, snarled, busy, gaudy with street signs, except that everything north of Boundary Road to the border would revert to China in 1997. Everything. In 1898 the British had taken a ninety-nine-year lease on the land that extended from Boundary Road to the Sham Chun River where the new border was to be, along with a number of nearby islands. 'Wasn't that stupid, Peter?' she had asked Marlowe, meeting him by chance in the hotel foyer at teatime.

'Now it is,' he said thoughtfully. 'Then? Well, who knows? It must have been sensible then or they wouldn't have done it.'

'Yes, but God, Peter, ninety-nine years is so short. What possessed them to make it so short? Their heads must've been . . . must've been elsewhere!'

'Yes. You'd think so. Now. But in those days when all the British prime minister had to do was belch to send a shock wave around the world? World power makes the difference. In those days the British Lion was still the Lion. What's a small piece of land to the owners of a quarter of the earth?' She remembered how he had smiled. 'Even so, in the New Territories there was armed opposition from the locals. Of course it fizzled. The then governor, Sir Henry Blake, took care of it. He didn't war on them, just talked to them. Eventually the village elders agreed to turn the other cheek, provided their laws and customs remained in effect, provided they could be tried under Chinese law if they wished and that Kowloon City remained Chinese.'

'The locals here are still tried under Chinese law?'

'Yes, historic law—not PRC law—so you have to have British magistrates skilled in Confucian law. It's really quite different. For instance, Chinese law presumes that all witnesses will naturally lie, that it's their duty to lie and cover up, and it's up to the magistrate to find out the truth. He has to be a sort of legal Charlie Chan. Civilized people don't go in for swearing to tell the truth, all that sort of barbarism—they consider us mad to do that, and I'm not sure they're wrong. They've all kinds of crazy or sensible customs, depending how you look at it. Did you know it's quite legal here, throughout the Colony, to have more than one wife—if you're Chinese.'

'Bully for them!'

'Having more than one wife really does have certain advantages.'

'Now listen, Peter,' she had begun hotly, then realized he was merely teasing her. 'You don't need more than one. You've got Fleur. How are you both doing? How's the research? Would she like lunch tomorrow if you're busy?'

'Sorry to say but she's in hospital.'

'Oh God, what's the matter?'

He had told her about this morning and Doc Tooley. 'I've just seen her. She's . . . she's not too good.'

'Oh I am sorry. Is there anything I can do?'

'No thanks. I don't think so.'

'Just ask if there is. Okay?'

'Thanks.'

'Linc was right to jump into the water with her, Peter. Honestly.'

'Oh of course, Casey. Please don't think for a moment . . . Linc did what I . . . he did it better than I could. You too. And I think you both saved that other girl from lots of trouble. Orlanda, Orlanda Ramos.'

'Yes.'

'She should thank you forever. Both of you. She was panicked—I've seen too much of it not to know. Smashing-looking bird, isn't she?'

'Yes. How's the research coming?'

'Fine, thanks.'

'Sometime I'd like to swap impressions. Hey, by the way, I found your book—I bought it—haven't read it yet but it's on top of the pile.'

'Oh!' Casey remembered how he had tried to sound offhand. 'Oh. I hope you like it. Well, I've got to be off, it's the kids' teatime too.'

'Remember, Peter, if there's anything, just call me. Thanks for tea, and say hi to Fleur. . . .'

Casey stretched, an ache now in her back. She got off her perch and went back to bed. Her room was small and did not have the elegance of their suite—*his* suite now. He had decided to keep the second bedroom. 'We can always use it as an office,' he had said to her, 'or keep it as a spare. Don't worry, Casey, it's all tax deductible and you never know when we might need a spare.'

Orlanda? No, she wouldn't need that bed!

Casey, she ordered herself, don't be bitchy, or stupid. Or jealous. You've never been jealous, *so* jealous before. You set the rules. Yes, but I'm glad I moved out. That other night was tough, tough on Linc and tough on me, worse for him. Orlanda will be good for him . . . oh shit on Orlanda.

Her mouth felt dry. She went to the refrigerator and got a bottle of iced Perrier and the nice tang of it made her feel better. I wonder how the earth makes those bubbles, she thought idly, getting onto the bed. Earlier, she had tried to sleep but her mind was jumbled and would not stop working, too much of the new—new foods, new smells, air, mores, threats, people, customs, cultures. Dunross. Gornt. Dunross and Gornt. Dunross and Gornt and Linc. A new Linc. A new you, frightened of a pretty piece of ass . . . yes, ass if you want to be vulgar and that's new for you too. Before you came here you were assured, dynamic, in charge of your world, and now you're not. All over her, not just over her, over that bitch Lady Joanna too with her so upper-class English accent, 'Don't you remember, dear, it's our Over Thirty Club Lunch today. I mentioned it at the tai-pan's dinner. . . .'

Goddamn old bitch. Over thirty! I'm not even twenty-seven!

That's right, Casey. But you are all riled up like a mashed cat and it's not just her or Orlanda, it's also Linc and the hundreds of available girls you've already seen and you haven't even looked in the dance halls and bars and houses where they specialize. Didn't Jannelli wind you up too?

'Jesus, Casey,' he had said with a great beam, 'it's like being back on R and R in my Korean days. It's still only 20 bucks and you're the top banana!'

That evening around ten, Jannelli had called to ask if she'd like to join him and the rest of the crew at the Royal Netherlands for a night snack. Her heart had turned over when the phone rang, thinking it was Linc, and when she had found it wasn't she had pretended that she still had lots to do but had gratefully allowed herself to be persuaded. Once there she had had a double order of scrambled eggs and bacon and toast and coffee that she knew she did not want.

As a protest. A protest against Asia, Hong Kong, Joanna and Orlanda, and oh Jesus I wish I'd never got interested in Asia, never suggested to Linc we should go international.

Why did you?

Because it's the only way for U.S. business to go—the only way—the only way for Par-Con. Export. Multinational but export. And Asia's the biggest, most teaming untapped marketplace on earth and this is the century for Asia. Yes. And the Dunrosses and Gornts've got it made—if they go with us—'cause we've the greatest market in the world to back us, all the cash, technology, growth and expertise to do it.

But why did you go for Hong Kong so hot and heavy?

To get my drop dead money and to fill the time between now and my birthday—the end of the seventh year.

The rate you're going, she told herself, soon you'll have no job, no future, no Linc to say yes or no to. A sigh took her. Earlier, she had gone to the master suite and had left Bartlett a batch of telexes and letters to sign with a 'hope you had a good time' note. When she had come back from her night snack she had gone there again and taken back everything she had left him. 'It's Orlanda that's really got you going. Don't fool yourself,' she said out loud.

Never mind, tomorrow's another day. You can dump Orlanda easy, she told herself grimly, and now, having zeroed in on her enemy she felt better.

Peter Marlowe's dog-eared paperback caught her eye. She picked it up, plumped the pillows more comfortably and began to read. The pages slid by. Abruptly the phone went. She had been so engrossed she jumped and a sudden, vast happiness flooded her. 'Hi, Linc, did you have a good time?'

'Casey, it's me, Peter Marlowe, I'm terribly sorry to call so late but I checked and your room boy said your light was still on. . . . I hope I didn't wake you?'

'Oh, oh no Peter.' Casey felt sick with disappointment. 'What's up?'

'Sorry to call so late but there's a slight emergency, I've got to go to the hospital and I've . . . you said to call. I ho—'

'What is it?' Casey was completely zeroed in now.

'I don't know. They just asked if I'd come at once. The reason I called was about the kids. There'll be a room boy looking in

953

every so often but I wanted to leave a note for them with your number in case they wake up, just in case they wake up, a friendly face to call so to speak. When we all met yesterday in the foyer, they both thought you a smasher. They probably won't wake but just in case. Could they call you? I'm sor—'

'Of course. Even better, why don't I come right over?'

'Oh no, I wouldn't think of it. If you j—'

'I'm not sleepy and you are right next door. It's no problem, Peter, I'm on my way. So you just go ahead to the hospital.'

It took her only a minute to dress in pants and blouse and cashmere sweater. Before she even pressed the elevator button, Nighttime Song was there, wide-eyed and inquisitive. She volunteered nothing.

Downstairs, she crossed the foyer and went out onto Nathan Road, across the side road and into the foyer of the Annex. Peter Marlowe was waiting for her. 'This's Miss Tcholok,' he said hurriedly to the night porter. 'She'll be with the kids till I return.'

'Yes sir,' the Eurasian said, equally wide-eyed. 'The boy'll show you up, miss.'

'Hope everything's okay, Peter. . . .' She stopped. He was out the swinging doors, trying to hail a cab.

The apartment was small, on the sixth floor, the front door ajar. The floor boy, Nighttime Po, shrugged and went off muttering, cursing barbarians . . . as if he couldn't look after two sleeping children who played hide and seek with him every evening.

Casey closed the door and peeked into the tiny second bedroom. Both children were fast asleep in the bunk, Jane, the little one, in the upper berth and Alexandra sprawled in the lower one. Her heart went out to them. Blond, tousled, angelic, with teddy bears clutched in their arms. Oh how I'd love to have children, she thought. Linc's children.

Would you? All the diapers, always locked in, sleepless nights and no freedom.

I don't know. I think so. Oh yes, for two like these, oh yes.

Casey didn't know whether to tuck them up or not. The air was warm so she decided to do nothing lest she wake them. In the refrigerator she found bottled water and this refreshed her and settled her racing heart. Then she sat in the easy chair. After a moment she took Peter's book out of her handbag and, once more, began to read.

Two hours later he returned. She had not noticed the time pass.

'Oh,' she said, seeing his face. 'She lost the baby?'

He nodded, dulled. 'Sorry to be so long. Would you like a cup of tea?'

'Sure, hey, Peter, let me d—'

'No. No thank you. I know where everything is. I'm sorry to put you to all this trouble.'

'It's no trouble. She's all right though? Fleur?'

'They, they think so. It was the stomach cramps that did it, and the touch of enteric. Too soon to tell but there's no real danger there, that's what they said. The, the miscarriage, they said it's always a bit rough, physically and emotionally.'

'I am so sorry.'

He glanced back at her and she saw the strong, bent, lived-in face. 'Not to worry, Casey. Fleur's all right,' he said, holding his voice firm. 'The, the Japanese believe that nothing's set until after birth, until after thirty days, thirty days for a boy and thirty-one for a girl, nothing's set, there's no soul, no personality, no person . . . up to that time there's no person.' He turned back in the tiny kitchen and set the kettle to boil, trying to sound convincing. 'It's, it's best to believe that, eh? How could it be anything but . . . but an it. There's no person till then, thirty-odd days after birth, so that doesn't make it so bad. It's still ghastly for the mother but not so bad. Sorry, I'm not making much sense.'

'Oh you are. I hope she'll be all right now,' Casey said, wanting to touch him, not knowing whether to or not. He looked so dignified in his misery, trying to sound so calm, yet just a little boy to her.

'Chinese and Japanese are really very sensible, Casey. Their . . . their superstitions make life easier. I suppose their infant mortality rate was so awful in olden days that that made some wise father invent that wisdom to save a mother's grief.' He sighed. 'Or more likely, some wiser mother invented it to succor a broken father. Eh?'

'Probably,' she said, out of her depth, watching his hands make the tea. First boiling water into the teapot, the pot rinsed carefully, then the water thrown away. Three spoons of tea and one for the pot, the boiling water brought to the pot. 'Sorry we've no tea bags, I can't get used to them though Fleur says they're just as good and cleaner. Sorry, tea's all we've got.' He brought the tea tray into the living room and set it on the dining table. 'Milk and sugar?' he asked.

'Fine,' she said, never having had it that way.

It tasted strange. But strong and life-giving. They drank in silence. He smiled faintly. 'Christ, without a cuppa, eh?'

'It's great.'

His eyes saw his half-opened book. 'Oh!'

'I like what I've read so far, Peter. How true is it?'

Absently he poured himself another cup. 'As true as any telling about any happening fifteen years after the event. As best as I can remember the incidents are accurate. The people in the book didn't live, though people like them did and said those sort of things and did those deeds.'

'It's unbelievable. Unbelievable that people, youths could survive that. How old were you then?'

'Changi began when I was just eighteen and ended when I was twenty-one—twenty-one and a bit.'

'Who're you in the book?'

'Perhaps I'm not there at all.'

Casey decided to let that pass. For the time being. Until she had finished. 'I'd better go. You must be exhausted.'

'No, I'm not. Actually, I'm not tired. I've got some notes to write up—I'll sleep after the kids're off to school. But you, you must be. I can't thank you enough, Casey. I owe you a favor.'

She smiled and shook her head. After a pause she said, 'Peter, you know so much about this place, who would you go with, Dunross or Gornt?'

'In business, Gornt. For the future, Dunross, if he can weather this storm. From what I hear, though, that's not likely.'

'Why Dunross for the future?'

'Face. Gornt hasn't the style to be *the* tai-pan—or the necessary background.'

'Is that so important?'

'Totally, here. *If* Par-Con wants a hundred years of growth, Dunross. If you're in just for a killing, a quick in-and-out raid, go with Gornt.'

She finished her tea thoughtfully. 'What do you know about Orlanda?'

'Lots,' he said at once. 'But knowing scandal or gossip about a living person isn't the same as knowing legends or gossip about ancient times. Is it?'

She watched him back. 'Even for a favor?'

'That's different.' His eyes narrowed slightly. 'Are you asking for a favor?'

She set her teacup down and shook her head. 'No, Peter, not now. I might later but not now.' She saw his frown deepen. 'What?' she asked.

'I was wondering why Orlanda was a threat to you. Why tonight? Obviously, that leads to Linc. That leads inevitably to: she's out with him now, which explains why you sounded so ghastly when I called.'

'Did I?'

'Yes. Oh, of course, I'd noticed Linc looking at her at Aberdeen and you looking at him and her looking at you.' He sipped some tea, his face hardening. 'That was quite a party. Lots of beginnings at that party, great tensions, big drama. Fascinating, if you can disassociate yourself from it. But you can't, can you?'

'Do you always watch and listen?'

'I try to train myself as an observer. I try to use my ears and eyes and other senses, properly, as they should be used. You're the same. Not much escapes you.'

'Maybe, maybe not.'

'Orlanda's Hong Kong-trained and Gornt-trained and if you plan a clash with her over Linc you'd better be prepared for a battle royal—if she's decided to try to grab him, which I don't know yet.'

'Would Gornt be using her?'

After a pause, he said, 'I'd imagine Orlanda's Orlanda's keeper. Aren't most ladies?'

'Most ladies gear their lives to a man, whether they want to or not.'

'From what I know about you, you can take care of any opposition.'

'What *do* you know about me?'

'Lots.' Again the faint, easy, gentle smile. 'Amongst them, that you're smart, brave and have great face.'

'I'm so tired of face, Peter. In the future . . .' Her smile was equally warm. 'From here on in, in my book, a person's going to gain ass—or arse as you call it—or lose it.'

He laughed with her. 'The way you say it sounds more ladylike.'

'I'm no lady.'

'Oh but you are.' He added more gently, 'I saw the way Linc looked at you at Dunross's party too. He loves you. And he'd be a fool to swap you for her.'

'Thank you, Peter.' She got up and kissed him and left, at peace. When she got out of the elevator on her floor, Nighttime Song was there. He padded ahead of her and opened her door with a flourish. He saw her eyes go to the door at the end of the corridor.

'Master not home,' he volunteered grandly. 'Not yet come back.'

Casey sighed. 'You've just lost more ass, old friend.'

'Eh?'

She shut the door, feeling pleased with herself. In bed, she began to read again. With the dawn she finished the book. Then she slept.

58

9:25 A.M.:

Dunross came around the corner in his Jaguar fast, climbing the winding road easily, then turned into a driveway and stopped an inch from the tall gates. The gates were set into high walls. In a moment a Chinese porter peered through the side door. When he recognized the tai-pan he opened the gates wide and waved him through.

The driveway curled and stopped outside an ornate Chinese mansion. Dunross got out. Another servant greeted him silently. The grounds were well kept and down a slope was a tennis court where four Chinese, two men and two women, were playing mixed doubles. They paid no attention to him and Dunross did not recognize any of them.

'Please follow me, tai-pan,' the servant said.

Dunross hid his curiosity as he was shown into an anteroom. This was the first time he or anyone that he knew had ever been invited into Tiptop's home. The interior was clean and busy with the strange, careless but usual Chinese mixture of good lacquer antiques and ugly modern bric-à-brac. Walls were paneled and ornate with a few bad prints hanging on them. He sat down. Another servant brought tea and poured.

Dunross could feel that he was being observed but this too was usual. Most of these old houses had spyholes in the walls and doors—there were many even in the Great House.

When he had got back to the Great House this morning near 4:00 A.M. he had gone straight to his study and opened the safe. There was no doubt, with even a cursory glance, that one of the two remaining coins fitted the imprints that were in Four Finger Wu's beeswax matrix. No doubt at all. His fingers were trembling when he broke the half-coin from its restraining sealing wax in Dirk Struan's Bible and cleaned it. It fitted the indentations perfectly.

'Christ,' he had muttered. 'Now what?' Then he had put the matrix and the coin back into the safe. His eyes saw the loaded automatic and the empty space where AMG's files had been. Uneasily he had relocked the safe and went to bed. There was a message on his pillow: 'Father dear: Will you wake me when you leave? We want to watch the tryouts. Love, Adryon. P.S. Can I invite Martin to the races Saturday please please please? P.P.S. I think he's super. P.P.P.S. You're super too. P.P.P.P.S. You're out late, aren't you? Now it's 3:16!!!!'

He had tiptoed to her room and opened her door but she was fast asleep. When he had left this morning he had had to knock twice to awaken her. 'Adryon! It's 6:30.'

'Oh! Is it raining?' she said sleepily.

'No. Soon will be. Shall I open the blinds?'

'No, Father dear, thank you . . . doesn't matter, Martin won't . . . won't mind.' She had stifled a yawn. Her eyes had closed and, almost instantly, she was deep asleep again.

Amused, he had shaken her lightly but she had not come out of sleep. 'Doesn't matter, Father. Martin won't . . .' And now, remembering how lovely she was and what his wife had said about the pill, he decided to make a very serious check on Martin Haply. Just in case.

'Ah, tai-pan, sorry to keep you waiting.'

Dunross got up and shook the outstretched hand. 'It's good of you to see me, Mr. Tip. Sorry to hear about your cold.'

Tip Tok-toh was in his sixties, graying, with a round nice face. He wore a dressing gown and his eyes were red and his nose stuffed, his voice a little hoarse. 'It's this rotten climate. Last weekend I went sailing with Shitee T'Chung and I must've caught a chill.' His English accent was slightly American, perhaps Canadian. Neither Dunross nor Alastair Struan had ever been able to draw him out about his past, nor had Johnjohn or the other bankers any knowledge of him in banking circles in Nationalist China days, pre-1949. Even Shitee T'Chung and Phillip Chen who entertained him lavishly could not pry anything out of him. The Chinese had nicknamed him the Oyster.

960

'The weather has been bad,' Dunross agreed pleasantly. 'Thank God for the rain.'

Tiptop motioned to the man beside him. 'This is an associate, Mr. L'eung.'

The man was nondescript. He wore a drab Maoist jacket and drab trousers. His face was set and cold and guarded. He nodded. Dunross nodded back. 'Associate' could cover a multitude of positions, from boss to interpreter, from commissar to guard.

'Would you like coffee?'

'Thank you. Have you tried vitamin C to cure your cold?' Patiently Dunross began the formal chitchat that would precede the real reason for the meeting. Last night while he was waiting for Brian Kwok in the Quance Bar he had thought Johnjohn's proposal was worth a try so he had phoned Phillip Chen then and asked him to request an appointment early today. It would have been just as easy to have called Tiptop direct but that was not correct Chinese protocol. The civilized way was to go through a mutually friendly intermediary. Then, if the request was refused, you would not lose face, nor would the other person, nor would the intermediary.

He was listening to Tiptop with only half his head, making polite conversation, surprised they were still speaking English, because of L'eung. This could only mean the man's English was also perfect, and, possibly, that he did not understand either Cantonese or Shanghainese which Tiptop spoke and Dunross was fluent in. He fenced with Tiptop, waiting for the opening that at length the banker would give him. Then it came.

'This stock market crash on your stock must be very worrying for you, tai-pan.'

'Yes, yes it is, but it's not a crash, Mr. Tip, just a readjustment. The market ebbs and flows.'

'And Mr. Gornt?'

'Quillan Gornt is Quillan Gornt and always snapping at our heels. All crows under heaven are black.' Dunross kept his voice matter-of-fact, wondering how much the man knew.

'And the Ho-Pak mess? That's a readjustment too?'

'No, no that's bad. I'm afraid the Ho-Pak's out of luck.'

'Yes, Mr. Dunross, but luck hasn't much to do with it. It's the capitalistic system, that and ineptness by Banker Kwang.'

Dunross said nothing. His eyes flicked momentarily to L'eung who sat stiffly, immobile and very attentive. His ears were concentrated and so was his mind, seeking the oblique currents under what was said. 'I'm not party to Mr. Kwang's business, Mr. Tip. Unfortunately the run on the Ho-Pak's spilling over to other banks and that's very bad for Hong Kong and also, I think, bad for the People's Republic of China.'

'Not bad for the People's Republic of China. How can it be bad for us?'

'China is China, the Middle Kingdom. We of the Noble House have always considered China to be the mother and father of our house. Now our base in Hong Kong's under siege, a siege that's actually meaningless—just a temporary lack of confidence and a week or so of cash. Our banks have all the reserves and all of the wealth and strength they need to perform . . . for old friends, old customers and ourselves.'

'Then why don't they print more money if the currency's so strong?'

'It's a matter of time, Mr. Tip. It's not possible for the mint to print enough Hong Kong money.' Even more patiently, Dunross answered the questions, knowing now that most were for the benefit of L'eung, which suggested L'eung was senior to Tiptop, a more senior Party member, a nonbanker. 'Our interim solution would be to bring in, at once, a few aircraft loads of pounds sterling to cover withdrawals.' He saw both men's eyes narrow slightly.

'That would hardly support the Hong Kong dollar.'

'Yes, yes our bankers know that. But Blacs, the Victoria and Bank of England decided this would be best in the interim. We just don't have enough Hong Kong cash to satisfy every depositor.'

The silence thickened. Dunross waited. Johnjohn had told him he believed the Bank of China did not have substantial reserves of pounds because of the currency restrictions on their movement in and out of Britain but had very substantial amounts of Hong Kong dollars for which there were no export restrictions.

'It would not be at all good for the Hong Kong dollar to be weakened,' Tip Tok-toh said. He blew his nose noisily. 'Not good for Hong Kong.'

'Yes.'

Tip Tok-toh's eyes hardened and he leaned forward. 'Is it true, tai-pan, that the Orlin Merchant Bank won't renew your revolving fund?'

Dunross's heart picked up a beat. 'Yes.'

'And true that your fine bank will not cover this loan or advance you enough to stave off the Rothwell-Gornt attack on your stock?'

'Yes.' Dunross was very pleased to hear the calm quality of his voice.

'And true that many old friends have refused credit to you?'

'Yes.'

'And true that the . . . the person Hiro Toda arrives this afternoon and requires payment for ships ordered from his Japanese shipyards shortly?'

'Yes.'

'And true that Mata and Tung and their Great Good Luck Company of Macao have tripled their normal order for gold bullion but will not help you direct?'

'Yes.' Dunross's already fine-tuned concentration increased.

'And true that the running-dog Soviet hegemonists have once more, impudently, very very impudently, applied for a banking charter in Hong Kong?'

'I believe so. Johnjohn told me they had. I'm not sure. I would presume he would not tell me a falsehood.'

'What did he tell you?'

Dunross repeated it verbatim, ending, 'Certainly the application would be opposed by me, the boards of all British banks, all the tai-pans and the governor. Johnjohn also said the hegemonists had the temerity to offer immediate and substantial amounts of HK dollars to assist them in their present trouble.'

Tip Tok-toh finished his coffee. 'Would you like some more?'

'Thank you.' Dunross noted that L'eung poured and he felt he had achieved a great step forward. Last night he had delicately mentioned the Moscow bank to Phillip Chen, knowing that Phillip would know how to pass the information on, which would of course indicate to such an astute man as Tiptop the real reason for the urgent meeting and so give him the necessary time to contact the decision-maker who would assess its importance and ways to acquiesce or not. Dunross could feel a sheen of sweat on his forehead and prayed that neither of the men opposite him noticed it. His anxiety would push the price up—if a deal was to be made.

'Terrible, terrible,' Tiptop said thoughtfully. 'Terrible times! Old Friends forsaking Old Friends, enemies being welcomed to the hearth . . . terrible. Oh by the way, tai-pan, one of our old friends asks if you could get him a shipment of goods. Thorium oxide I think it was.'

With a great effort Dunross kept his face clean. Thorium oxide was a rare earth, the essential ingredient for old-fashioned gas mantles: it made the mantle emit its brilliant white light. Last year he had happened to hear that Hong Kong had recently become the greatest user after the United States. His curiosity had peaked as Struan's were not in what must clearly be a profitable trade. Quickly he had found out that access to the material was relatively easy and that the trade was prodigious, quite secret, with many small importers, all of them very vague about their business. In nature, thorium occurred in various radioactive isotopes. Some of these were easily converted into fissionable uranium 235, and thorium 232 itself was an enormously valuable breeder material for an atomic pile. Of course, these and many other thorium derivatives were restricted strategic materials but he had been astounded to discover the oxide and nitrate, chemically easily convertible, were not.

He could never find out where the thorium oxides actually went. Of course into China. For a long time, he and others had suspected the PRC of having a crash atomic program, though everyone believed it had to be formulative and at least ten years from fruition. The idea of China nuclear armed filled him with mixed feelings. On the one hand, any nuclear proliferation was dangerous; on the other, as a nuclear power China would instantly become a formidable rival to Soviet Russia, even an equal to Soviet Russia, even a threat, certainly unconquerable —particularly if it also had the means to deliver a retaliatory strike.

Dunross saw both men looking at him. The small vein in L'eung's forehead was pulsing though his face was impassive. 'That might be possible, Mr. Tip. How much would be needed and when?'

'I believe immediately, as much as can be obtained. As you

know, the PRC is attempting to modernize but much of our lighting is still by gas.'

'Of course.'

'Where would you obtain the oxides or nitrates?'

'Australia would probably be the quickest, though I've no idea at this moment about quality. Outside of the United States,' he added delicately, 'it's only found in Tasmania, Brazil, India, South Africa, Rhodesia and the Urals . . . big deposits there.' Neither man smiled. 'I imagine Rhodesia and Tasmania'd be best. Is there anyone Phillip or I should deal with?'

'A Mr. Vee Cee Ng, in Princes Building.'

Dunross bit back a whistle as another piece of the puzzle fell into place. Mr. Vee Cee Ng, Photographer Ng, was a great friend of Tsu-yan, the missing Tsu-yan, his old friend and associate who had mysteriously fled into China over the Macao border. Tsu-yan had been one of the thorium importers. Up to now, the connection had been meaningless. 'I know Mr. Ng. By the way, how is my old friend, Tsu-yan?'

L'eung was plainly startled. Bull's-eye, Dunross thought grimly, shocked that he had never once suspected Tsu-yan of being Communist or having Communist leanings.

'Tsu-yan?' Tiptop frowned. 'I haven't seen him for a week or more. Why?'

'I heard he was visiting Peking by way of Macao.'

'Curious! That's very curious. I wonder why he'd want to do that—an arch-capitalist? Well, wonders will never cease. If you'd be kind enough to contact Mr. Ng direct, I'm sure he will give you the details.'

'I'll do that this morning. As soon as I get back to the office.'

Dunross waited. There would be other concessions before they would grant what he sought, if it was to be granted. His mind was racing with the implication of their first request, how to get thorium oxides, whether to get them, wanting to know how far along the PRC was with its atomic program, knowing they would never tell him that. L'eung took out a pack of cigarettes and offered it.

'No thanks,' he said.

Both men lit up. Tiptop coughed and blew his nose. 'It's curious, tai-pan,' he said, 'very curious that you go out of your way to help the Victoria and Blacs and all your capitalist banks

965

while the strong rumor is that they'll not help you in your need.'

'Perhaps they'll see the error of their ways,' Dunross said. 'Sometimes it's necessary to forget present advantages for the common good. It would be bad for the Middle Kingdom for Hong Kong to falter.' He noted the scorn on L'eung's face but it did not bother him. 'It's ancient Chinese doctrine not to forget Old Friends, trusted ones, and as long as I'm tai-pan of the Noble House and have power, Mr. Tip, I and those like me—Mr. Johnjohn for one, our governor for another—will give eternal friendship to the Middle Kingdom and will never permit hegemonists to thrive on our barren rock.'

Tiptop said sharply, 'It is *our* barren rock, Mr. Dunross, that is presently administered by the British, is it not?'

'Hong Kong is and always was earth of the Middle Kingdom.'

'I will let your definition pass for the moment but everything in Kowloon and the New Territories north of Boundary Road reverts to us in thirty-five-odd years doesn't it—even if you accept the Unequal Treaties forced on our forebears which we don't.'

'My forebears have always found their Old Friends wise, very wise, and never men to cut off their Stalks to spite a Jade Gate.'

Tiptop laughed. L'eung continued to be set-faced and hostile. 'What do you forecast will happen in 1997, Mr. Dunross?'

'I am not Old Blind Tung, nor a soothsayer, Mr. Tip.' Dunross shrugged. '1997 can take care of 1997. Old friends will still need old friends. *Heya?*'

After a pause Tiptop said, 'If your bank will not help the Noble House, nor Old Friends, nor Orlin, how will you remain the Noble House?'

'My forebear, Green-Eyed Devil, was asked the same question by the Great and Honorable Jin-qua when he was beset by his enemies, Tyler Brock and his scum, and he just laughed and said, "*Neng che to lao*"—an able man has many burdens. As I'm abler than most I have to sweat more than most.'

Tip Tok-toh smiled with him. 'And you are sweating, Mr. Dunross?'

'Well, let me put it this way,' Dunross told him cheerfully, 'I'm trying to avoid the eighty-fourth. As you know, Buddha said that all men have eighty-three burdens. If we succeed in eliminating one we automatically acquire another. The secret of life is to adjust to eighty-three and avoid at all costs acquiring the eighty-fourth.'

The older man smiled. 'Have you considered selling part of your company, perhaps even 51 percent?'

'No, Mr. Tip. Old Green-Eyed Devil forbade that.' The lines around Dunross's eyes crinkled. 'He wanted us to sweat.'

'Let us hope you don't have to sweat too much. Yes.' Tiptop stubbed out his cigarette. 'In troubled times it would be good for the Bank of China to have a closer liaison with your banking system. Then these crises would not be so continuous.'

Instantly Dunross's mind leaped forward. 'I wonder if the Bank of China would consider having a permanent contact stationed within the Vic and an equivalent one in yours?' He saw the fleeting smile and he knew he had guessed correctly. 'That would ensure monitoring of any crisis, and assist you should you ever need international assistance.'

'Chairman Mao advises self-help and that's what we are doing. But your suggestion might be worthwhile. I will be glad to pass it on.'

'I'm sure the bank would be grateful if you would recommend someone to be their contact with the great Bank of China.'

'I would be glad to pass that on too. Do you think Blacs or the Victoria would advance the necessary foreign exchange for Mr. Ng's imports?'

'I'm sure they'd be delighted to be of service, the Victoria certainly. After all, the Victoria has had a century and more of association with China. Wasn't it instrumental in making most of your foreign loans, railway loans, aircraft loans?'

'To great profit,' Tiptop said dryly. His eyes darted at L'eung who was staring intently at Dunross. 'Capitalist profit,' he added thinly.

'Quite,' Dunross said. 'You must excuse us capitalists, Mr. Tip. Perhaps our only defense is that many of us are Old Friends of the Middle Kingdom.'

L'eung spoke to Tiptop briefly in a dialect Dunross did not understand. Tiptop answered him affirmatively. Both men looked back at him. 'I'm sorry but you must excuse me now, Mr. Dunross, I really must get some medication. Perhaps you'd phone me here after lunch, say around 2:30.'

Dunross got up and stretched out his hand, not sure if he had succeeded but very sure he had better do something about the thorium very quickly, certainly before 2:30. 'Thank you for seeing me.'

'What about our fifth race?' The older man peered up at him, walking with him to the door.

'Noble Star's worth a bet. Each way.'

'Ah! Butterscotch Lass?'

'Same.'

'And Pilot Fish?'

Dunross laughed. 'The stallion's good but not in the same class, unless there's an act of God, or the Devil.'

They were at the front door now and a servant had opened it wide. Again L'eung spoke in the dialect Dunross did not recognize. Again Tiptop answered affirmatively and led the way outside. At once L'eung walked off down toward the tennis court.

'I'd like you to meet a friend, a new friend, Mr. Dunross,' Tiptop said. 'He could, perhaps, be doing a lot of business with you in the future. If you wish.'

Dunross saw the flinty eyes and his good humor vanished.

The Chinese coming back with L'eung was well formed, fit and in his forties. His hair was blue-black and tousled from his game, his tennis clothes modern, smart and American. On the court behind him, the other three waited and watched. All were fit and well dressed.

'May I introduce Dr. Joseph Yu from California? Mr. Ian Dunross.'

'Hi, Mr. Dunross,' Joseph Yu said with easy American familiarity. 'Mr. Tip's filled me in on you and Struan's—happy to meet you. Mr. Tip thought we should meet before I leave— we're going into China tomorrow, Betty 'n' I, my wife and I.' He waved a vague hand toward one of the women on the tennis court. 'We're not expecting to come back for some time so I'd like to make a date to meet in Canton in a month or so.' He glanced back at Tiptop. 'No trouble about Mr. Dunross's visa, anything like that?'

'No, Dr. Yu. Oh no. None at all.'

'Great. If I give you a call, Mr. Dunross, or Mr. Tip does, can we arrange something at a couple days' notice?'

'Certainly, if all the paper work's done.' Dunross kept the smile on his face, noticing the assured hardness in Yu. 'What had you in mind?'

'If you'll excuse us,' Tiptop said, 'we'll leave you two together.' He nodded politely and went back inside with L'eung.

'I'm from the States,' Yu continued cheerfully, 'American born, Sacramento. I'm third-generation California though I was educated, in part, in Canton. My Ph.D. is from Stanford, aerospace engineering, my speciality rocketry and rocket fuels. NASA's where I've spent my best years, best since college.' Yu was no longer smiling. 'The equipment I'll be ordering will be all manner of sophisticated metallurgy and aerospace hardware. Mr. Tip said you'd be our best bet as the importer. The British, then the French and German, maybe Japanese will be the manufacturers. You interested?'

Dunross listened with growing concern that he did not bother to hide.

'If it's not strategic and not restricted,' he said.

'It'll be mostly strategic and mostly restricted. You interested?'

'Why're you telling me all this, Dr. Yu?'

Yu's mouth smiled. 'I'm going to reorganize China's space program.' His eyes slitted even more as he watched Dunross carefully. 'You find that surprising?'

'Yes.'

'So do I.' Yu glanced at his wife, then back to Dunross. 'Mr. Tip says you're to be trusted. He feels you're fair and since you owe him one or two, you'll pass on a message for me.' Yu's voice hardened. 'I'm telling you so that when you read about my demise or kidnapping or some "while his mind was disturbed" crap, you'll know it's all lies and as a favor will pass back that message to the CIA and from them up the line. The truth!' He took a deep breath. 'I'm leaving of my own free will. We both are. For three generations our folk and my people who're the best goddamn immigrants there are, have been kicked around in the States by Americans. My old man was in the First World War and I helped make the Big Bang, but the last goddamn straw was two months ago. June 16. Betty 'n' I wanted a house in Beverly Hills. Are you familiar with Beverly Hills in Los Angeles?'

'Yes.'

'We were turned down because we were Chinese. The son of a bitch came out and said it. "I'm not selling to goddamn Chinese." That wasn't the first time, hell no, but the son of a bitch said it in front of Betty and that that was it. That was the big one!' Yu's lips twisted with anger. 'Can you imagine the stupidity of that bastard? I'm the best there is in my field and that red-neck horse's ass says "I'm not selling to Chinese."' He spun his racket in his hands. 'You'll tell them?'

'Do you want me to pass this information on privately or publicly? I will quote you verbatim if you wish.'

'Privately to the CIA, but not before next Monday at 6:00 P.M. Okay? Then next month, after our Canton meeting, it's public. Okay, Mr. Dunross?'

'Very well. Can you give me the name of the house seller, the date, any details?'

Yu took out a typed slip of paper.

Dunross glanced at it. 'Thank you.' There were two names and addresses and phone numbers in Beverly Hills. 'Both the same refusal?'

'Yes.'

'I'll take care of it for you, Dr. Yu.'

'You think that's petty, huh?'

'No, I don't think so at all. I'm just sorry that it happened and happens everywhere—to all sorts of people. It's greatly saddening.' Dunross hesitated. 'It happens in China, Japan, here all over the world. Chinese and Japanese, Vietnamese, all manner of people, Dr. Yu, are sometimes equally intolerant and bigoted. Most times very much more so. Aren't we all called *quai loh*?'

'It shouldn't happen Stateside—not Americans to Americans. That's my bitch.'

'Do you think once you're inside China, you'll be allowed to go in and out freely?'

'No. But I don't give a damn about that. I'm going freely. I'm not just being tempted by money or being blackmailed to go. I'm just going.'

'What about NASA? I'm surprised they allowed such nonsense to happen in the first place.'

'Oh we had a fine house on offer, but it wasn't where we

970

wanted to live. Betty wanted that goddamn house and we had the money and position to pay for it, but we couldn't get in. It wasn't just that son of a bitch, it was the neighborhood too.' Yu wiped a thread of hair out of his eyes. 'They didn't want us so I'm going where I am wanted. What about China having a nuclear retaliatory strike force of its own? Like the French, eh? What do you think of that?'

'The idea of anyone having A- or H-bomb tipped rockets fills me with horror.'

'They're just the weapons of the day, Mr. Dunross, just the weapons of the day.'

'Jesus Christ!' Johnjohn said, aghast.

Havergill was equally shocked. 'Dr. Joseph Yu's really top bracket, Ian?'

'Absolutely. I phoned a friend in Washington. Yu's one of two or three in the world—rockets and rocket fuel.' It was after lunch. Dunross had just told them what had transpired this morning. 'It's also true no one knows he's going over the border, even that he's left Hawaii where he's supposed to be on vacation—he told me he traveled here quite openly.'

'Christ,' Johnjohn said again. 'If China gets experts like him . . .' He twisted the paper knife that was on Havergill's desk. 'Ian, have you considered telling Roger Crosse, or Rosemont to prevent that?'

'Of course, but I can't do that. I absolutely can't.'

'Of course Ian can't! Have you considered what's at stake?' Havergill jerked an angry thumb at the window. Fourteen floors below he could see an impatient, angry mob of people trying to get into the bank, the police stretched very thin now. 'Let's not delude ourselves, the run is on, we're getting down to the bottom of the barrel. We barely have enough cash to last the day, barely enough to pay government employees. Thank God it's Saturday tomorrow! If Ian says there's a chance we could get China's cash, of course he can't risk giving away such a confidence! Ian, did you hear the Ho-Pak's closed its doors?'

'No. I've been chasing around like a blue-arsed fly since I left Tiptop.'

'The Ching Prosperity closed too, the Far East and India's

971

tottering, Blacs is eking out its reserves and like us, praying they can last the next half an hour to closing.' He shoved the phone across his pristine desk. 'Ian, please call Tiptop now, it's just 2:30.'

Dunross kept his face stony and his voice level. 'There're a couple of things to settle first, Paul. What about the thorium imports?' He had told them he had contacted Photographer Ng who had happily given him an immediate firm order for as much of the rare earth as he could obtain. 'Will you provide the foreign exchange?'

'Yes, provided the trade is not restricted.'

'I'll need that in writing.'

'You'll have it before closing tonight. Please call him now.'

'In ten minutes. It's a matter of face. You'll agree to having a permanent Bank of China contact in the building?'

'Yes. I'm sure they'll never let one of our people inside their building, but no matter.' Havergill glanced at his watch again, then looked at Johnjohn. 'The fellow'd have to be monitored and we might have to change a few procedures for security, eh?'

Johnjohn nodded. 'Yes, but that shouldn't cause any problem, Paul. If it was Tiptop himself, that would be perfect. Ian, do you think there's a chance?'

'I don't know. Now, what about the Yu trade?'

Havergill said, 'We can't finance any smuggling. You would of necessity be on your own.'

'Who said anything about smuggling?'

'Quite. Then let me say we'll have to take a careful look at the Yu trade when and if you are asked to assist them.'

'Come on, Paul, you know damn well it's part of the deal—if there's a deal. Why else would they have wanted me to meet him?'

Johnjohn interjected, 'Why not table that one, Ian? We'll bend every which way to assist you when the time comes. You told Yu the same thing—that you'd wait and see but no actual commitment, eh?'

'But you agree to help in every way to assist me?'

'Yes, on this and the thorium.'

'Then what about my loan?'

Paul Havergill said, 'I'm not permitted to grant it, Ian. We've already been through that.'

'Then call a board meeting right now.'

'I'll consider it. Let's see how things're going, eh?' Paul Havergill pressed a button and spoke into the small speaker. 'Stock Exchange, please.'

In a moment a voice came over the speaker. Behind the voice they could hear pandemonium. 'Yes, Mr. Havergill?'

'Charles, what's the latest?'

'The whole market's off 28 points . . .' Both bankers blanched. The small vein in Dunross's forehead was pulsing. '. . . and it looks like the beginning of a panic. The bank's off 7 points, Struan's is down to 11.50 . . .'

'Christ!' Johnjohn muttered.

'. . . Rothwell-Gornt off 7, Hong Kong Power off 5, Asian Land 11 . . . everything's skidding. All bank stocks are tumbling. The Ho-Pak's frozen at 12 and when it gets unfrozen it'll go to a dollar. The Far East and India is only paying out maximum 1,000 a customer.'

Havergill's nervousness increased. Far East was one of the biggest in the Colony.

'I hate to be a pessimist but it looks like New York in '29! I th—' The voice was drowned out by a surge of shouting. 'Sorry, there's another huge sell offering up on Struan's. 200,000 shares. . . .'

'Christ, where the hell's all the stock coming from?' Johnjohn asked.

'From every Tom, Dick and Harry in Hong Kong,' Dunross said coldly. 'Including the Victoria.'

'We had to protect our investors,' Havergill said, then added into the mike, 'Thank you, Charles. Call me back at a quarter to three.' He clicked the speaker off. 'There's your answer, Ian. I cannot in all conscience recommend to the board we bail you out with another unsecured 100 million loan.'

'Are you going to call a board meeting right now or not?'

'Your stock's plunging. You've no assets to pledge to support the run on your stock, your bank holdings are already pledged, the stock in your treasury gets more valueless every minute. On Monday or Tuesday, Gornt will buy back in and then he'll control Struan's.'

Dunross watched him. 'You'll let Gornt take us over? I don't believe you. You'll buy in before he does. Or have you already

973

made a deal to split up Struan's between you?'

'No deal. Not yet. But if you'll resign from Struan's right now, agree in writing to sell us as much of your treasury stock as we want at market price at Monday's closing, agree to appoint a new tai-pan of our board's choosing, we'll announce that we're supporting Struan's totally.'

'When would you make the announcement?'

'Monday at 3:10.'

'In other words you'll give me nothing.'

'You've always said the best thing about Hong Kong was that it was a free marketplace, where the strong survive and the weak perish. Why didn't you persuade Sir Luis to withdraw your stock from trading?'

'He suggested it. I refused.'

'Why?'

'Struan's is as strong as ever.'

'Wasn't the real reason face—and your foolish pride? Sorry, there's nothing I can do to prevent the inevitable.'

'Balls!' Dunross said and Havergill flushed. 'You can call a meeting. You can c—'

'No meeting!'

'Ian.' Johnjohn tried to soften the open hostility between the two men. 'Listen, Paul, how about a compromise: If, through Ian, we get China's cash, you will call a meeting of the board at once, an extraordinary meeting, today. You could do that— there are enough directors in town, and it's fair. Eh?'

Havergill hesitated. 'I'll consider it.'

'That's not good enough,' Dunross said hotly.

'I'll consider it. Kindly call Tipt—'

'When's the meeting? If?'

'Next week.'

'No. Today as Johnjohn suggests.'

'I said I'll consider it,' Havergill said, flaring. 'Now please call Tiptop.'

'If you'll guarantee to call the board no later than tomorrow at ten!'

Havergill's voice harshened. 'I will not be blackmailed as I was the last time. If you don't want to call Tiptop, I will. I can now. If they want to lend us their money, they'll lend it to us whoever the hell calls. You've agreed to the thorium deal,

974

you've agreed to meet Yu next month, we agree to support that deal whoever controls the Noble House. I am not empowered to grant you any further loans. So take it or leave it. I will consider calling a board meeting before Monday's market opens. That's all I promise.'

The silence was heavy and electric.

Dunross shrugged. He picked up the phone and dialed.

'*Weyyyyy?*' The woman's voice was arrogant.

'The Honorable Tip Tok-toh please,' he said in Cantonese. 'This is the tai-pan.'

'Ah, the tai-pan. Ah, please wait a moment.' Dunross waited. A bead of sweat gathered on the bottom of Johnjohn's chin. '*Weyyyy?* Tai-pan, the doctor's with him, he's very sick. Please call back later!' The phone clicked off before Dunross could say anything. He redialed.

'This's the tai-pan, I wan—'

'This phone is terrible.' The *amah* doubled her volume. 'He's sick,' she shouted. 'Call back later.'

Dunross called in ten minutes. Now the line was busy. He kept on trying with no luck.

There was a knock and the harassed chief cashier hurried in. 'Sorry, sir, but there's no let up in the queues, we've a quarter of an hour to go. I suggest we limit withdrawals now, say a thou—'

'No,' Havergill said at once.

'But sir, we're almost empty. Don't y—'

'No. The Victoria must keep going. We must. No. Keep honoring every penny.'

The man hesitated, then went out. Havergill mopped his brow. Johnjohn too. Dunross dialed again. Still busy. Just before three he tried a last time, then dialed the phone company asking them to check the line. 'It's temporarily out of order, sir,' the operator said.

Dunross put the phone down. 'Twenty to a brass farthing it's deliberately off the hook.' His watch read 3:01. 'Let's find out about the market.'

Havergill wiped the palms of his hands. Before he could dial, the phone rang. 'Chief cashier, sir. We've . . . we're all right now. Last customer has been paid. The doors've closed. Blacs just made it too, sir.'

'Good. Check the remaining currency in the vault and call me back.'

'Thank God it's Friday,' Johnjohn said.

Havergill dialed. 'Charles? What's the latest?'

'The market finished off 37 points. Our stock's off 8 points.'

'Christ,' Johnjohn said. The bank had never fallen so much before, even during the '56 riots.

'Struan's?'

'9.50.'

Both bankers looked at Dunross. His face was impassive. He redialed Tiptop as the stockbroker continued to reel off the closing prices. Again a busy signal. 'I'll call again from the office,' he said. 'The moment I get him I'll call you. If no China money, what are you going to do?'

'There are only two solutions. We wait for the pounds, the governor declaring Monday a bank holiday or as long as we need. Or we accept the Moscow trade-bank offer.'

'Tiptop was bloody clear that'll backfire. That'll throw a monkey wrench in Hong Kong forever.'

'Those are the only solutions.'

Dunross got up. 'There's only one. By the way, did the governor phone you?'

'Yes,' Havergill said. 'He wants us to open the vaults at 6:00 P.M. for him, you, Roger Crosse and some fellow called Sinders. What's all that about?'

'Didn't he tell you?'

'No. Just that it was something covered by the Official Secrets Act.'

'See you at six.' Dunross walked out.

Havergill wiped more sweat off with a handkerchief. 'The only good thing about all this is that that arrogant sod's in worse trouble,' he muttered angrily. He dialed Tiptop's number. And again. The interoffice phone rang. Johnjohn picked it up for Havergill. 'Yes?'

'This is the chief cashier, sir. There's only 716,027 HK in the vault.' The man's voice trembled. 'We're . . . that's all we've left, sir.'

'Thank you.' Johnjohn put the phone down and told Havergill. The deputy chairman did not answer, just redialed Tiptop's number. It was still busy. 'You'd better open a dialogue with the Soviet contact.'

Johnjohn went red. 'But that's impossible—'

'*Do it!* Do it now!' Havergill, equally choleric, redialed Tiptop. Still busy.

Dunross went into his office.

'Mr. Toda's here with the usual entourage, tai-pan.' Claudia did not hide her distaste or nervousness.

'Show them in please.'

'Mr. Alastair called twice—asked that you call him back the moment you come in. And your father.'

'I'll call them later.'

'Yes sir. Here's the telex for Nelson Trading from Switzerland confirming that they've purchased triple the regular order of gold for the Great Good Luck Company of Macao.'

'Good. Send a copy to Lando at once and request the funds.'

'This telex is from Orlin Merchant Bank confirming they regret they cannot renew the loan and require payment.'

'Telex them, "Thank you."'

'I checked with Mrs. Dunross and they arrived safely.'

'Good. Get Kathy's specialist's home number so I can call him over the weekend.'

Claudia made another note. 'Master Duncan called from Sydney to say he had a great evening and he's on the Monday Qantas flight. Here's a list of your other calls.'

He glanced at the long list, wondering fleetingly if his son was no longer a virgin, or was not even before the lovely Sheila. Thinking of a lovely sheila reminded him again of the exquisite Snow Jade. Curious her name was Snow Jade—she reminded me so much of Elegant Jade who's somewhere in Taipei in charge of a House of Many Pleasures. Perhaps the time's come to find Elegant Jade and thank her. Once more he remembered old Chen-chen's admonition when he was dying. 'Listen, my son,' old Chen-chen had whispered, his voice failing, 'never try to find her. You will take away her face and take away beauty, both from her and from you. Now she'll be old, her Jade Gate withered and her pleasures will come from good food and good brandy. Children of the Pleasure World do not age well, nor do

977

their tempers. Leave her to her joss and to her memories. Be kind. Always be kind to those who give you their youth and their yin to succor your yang. Eeeee, how I wish I was as young as you again. . . .'

Dunross sighed. His evening with Snow Jade had been impeccable. And filled with laughter.

'I don't eat dessert,' he had replied at once. 'I'm on a diet.

'*Oh ko*, not you, tai-pan. I help you lose weight never mind.'

'Thank you but no dessert and never in Hong Kong.'

'Ah! Four Fingers said you'd say that, tai-pan, and for me not to be shamed.' She had beamed and poured him a whiskey. 'I'm to say, Have passport can travel.'

They had laughed together. 'What else did Four Fingers say?'

The tip of her tongue touched her lips. 'Only that foreign devils are mighty very peculiar in some things. Like saying no dessert! As if it mattered.' She watched him. 'I've never been with a barbarian before.'

'Oh? Some of us are really quite civilized.'

Dunross smiled to himself, remembering how tempted he was, their banter and the great meal, everything good-humored and satisfying. Yes. But that doesn't forgive that old bastard Four Fingers, nor the half-coin, nor the theft of the half-coin, he thought grimly, nor the trap that he thinks he has me in. But all that comes later. First things come first. Concentrate, there's a lot to do before you sleep tonight!

The list Claudia had given him was long, most of the calls urgent, and two hours of work were ahead of him. Tiptop wasn't on the list, nor Lando Mata, Tightfist Tung, Four Fingers or Paul Choy. Casey and Bartlett were there. Travkin, Robert Armstrong. Jacques deVille, Gavallan, Phillip Chen, Dianne Chen, Alan Holdbrook—Struan's in-house stockbroker—Sir Luis, and dozens of others spread throughout the world. 'We'll get to them after Hiro Toda, Claudia.'

'Yes sir.'

'After Toda, I want to see Jacques—then Phillip Chen. Anything on Mrs. Riko Gresserhoff?'

'Her plane's due in at 7:00 P.M. She's booked into the V and A and she'll be met. Flowers are in her room.'

'Thank you.' Dunross went into his office and stared out of the window. For the time being he had done everything he could for the Noble House and for Hong Kong. Now it was up to joss. And the next problem. The ships. His excitement picked up.

'Hello, tai-pan.'

'Hello, Hiro.' Dunross shook the outstretched hand warmly.

Hiro Toda, managing director of Toda Shipping Industries was of an age with Dunross, trim, hard, and much shorter, with wise eyes and a ready smile, his accent slightly American from two years of postgraduate work at UCLA in the late forties. 'May I introduce my associates: Mr. Kazunari, Mr. Ebe, Mr. Kasigi.'

The three younger men bowed and Dunross bowed back. They were all dressed in dark suits, well cut, with white shirts and subdued ties.

'Please sit down.' Airily Dunross waved to the chairs around the small conference table. The door opened and his Japanese interpreter and assistant, Akiko, came in. She brought a tray with green tea, introduced herself, poured the tea delicately, then took her seat near Dunross. Though his Japanese was easily good enough for a business meeting she was necessary for face.

Partially in Japanese, partially in English, he began the polite conversation about inconsequential matters, that by Japanese custom preceded serious discussion. It was also Japanese custom that business meetings were shared by many executives, the more senior the executive, usually the more people who came with him.

Dunross waited patiently. He liked the other man. Hiro Toda was titular head of the great shipping conglomerate that had been founded by his great-grandfather almost a hundred years before. His forebears were *daimyos*, feudal lords, until feudalism and the samurai class was abolished in 1870 and modern Japan began. His authority in Toda Shipping was outwardly all-powerful, but as frequently happened in Japan, all real power was centered in the hands of his seventy-three-year-old father who, ostensibly, was retired.

At length Toda came to the point. 'This stock market collapse must be very worrying, tai-pan.'

'A temporary loss of confidence. I'm sure everything will work itself out over the weekend.'

979

'Ah yes. I hope so too.'

'How long are you staying, Hiro?'

'Till Sunday. Yes Sunday. Then on to Singapore and Sydney. I shall be back for the closing of our business with you next week. I'm glad to tell you your ships are ahead of schedule.' Toda put a sheaf of papers on the table. 'Here's a detailed report.'

'Excellent!' Dunross swung to the attack, blessing the gods and AMG and Kirk. Coming home last night he had suddenly realized the enormity of the key AMG and Kirk had given him to a plan he had been working on for almost a year. 'Would you like to bring forward your payment schedule?'

'Ah!' The other man covered his surprise. 'Perhaps I could discuss that with my colleagues later but I'm glad to hear that everything is in control then, and the takeover bid contained.'

'Didn't Sun Tzu say, "He who exercises no forethought but makes light of his opponents is sure to be captured by them." Gornt is certainly snapping at our heels, of course the run on our banks is serious, but the worst is over. Everything's just fine. Don't you think we should expand the amount of business we're doing together?'

Toda smiled. 'Two ships, tai-pan? Giants by present standards. In one year? That's not a minor connection.'

'It could perhaps be twenty-two ships,' he said, outwardly nonchalant, his whole being concentrated. 'I have a proposal for you, in fact for all Japanese shipbuilding industrial complexes. At the moment you just build ships and sell them, either to *gai-jin*—outsiders—to ourselves for example, or to Japanese shippers. If to Japanese shippers, your operating costs with the high cost of Japanese crews—which by your law you have to carry—are already becoming noncompetitive, like American ships with American crews. Soon you won't be able to compete with the Greeks, with others and with us, because our costs will be so much lower.'

Dunross saw them all concentrating on Akiko who was translating almost simultaneously and he thought with glee of another Sun Tzu saying: 'In all fighting, the direct method may be used for joining battle but indirect methods will be needed to secure victory.' Then he continued, 'Second point: Japan has to import everything it needs to support its rising economy and standard of living and its industrial complex, and certainly the 95 percent of all energy it needs to sustain it. Oil's the key to your future. Oil has to come to you seaborne, so do all your bulk raw materials—always carried by bulk cargo ships. *Always* seaborne. You're building the great ships very efficiently, but as shipowners your operating costs and your own internal tax structure are going to drive you out of the marketplace. My proposal for you is simple: You stop trying to own your own uneconomic merchant fleets. You sell your ships abroad on a lease-back basis.'

'What?'

Dunross saw them staring at him, astounded. He waited a moment, then continued, 'A ship's life is, say fifteen years. You sell your bulk carrier say to us, but as part of the deal lease it back for fifteen years. We supply the captain and crew and operate her. Prior to delivery, you charter the ship to Mitsubishi or another of your own great companies for bulk supplies over fifteen years—coal, iron ore, rice, wheat, oil, whatever you want. This system guarantees Japan a continuous supply of raw material, set up at your whim and controlled by Japanese. Japan Inc. can increase its financing to you, because you yourselves, in effect, are the carriers of your own vital raw materials.

'Your industries can plan ahead. Japan Inc. can afford to assist financially selected buyers of your ships, because the purchase price is easily covered by the fifteen years' charter. And since the ships are on long-term charter, our bankers, like Blacs and the Victoria, will also be happy to finance the rest. Everyone gains. You gain most because you ensure a long-term supply line under your control. And I haven't yet mentioned the tax advantages to you, to Toda Industries particularly!'

Dunross got up in a dead silence, the others staring at him, and went to his desk. He brought back some stapled reports. 'Here's a tax study done by our people in Japan with specific examples, including methods to depreciate the ships' cost for added profit. Here's a suggested plan for bulk carriers. This one documents various ways Struan's could assist you in charters, should we be one of the foreign shippers chosen. For example, Woolara Mines of Australia are prepared, at our direction, to enter into a contract with Toda Industries to supply 95 percent of their coal output for one hundred years.'

Toda gasped. So did the others when Akiko had translated. Woolara Mines was a huge, highly efficient and productive mine.

'We could assist you in Australia which is the treasury of Asia—supplying all the copper, wheat, foodstuffs, fruit, iron ore you need. I'm told privately there are new, immense deposits of high-grade iron ore just discovered in Western Australia within easy access of Perth. There's oil, uranium, thorium, and other precious materials you require. Wool. Rice. With my scheme *you* control your own flow of materials, the foreign shippers get ships and a steady cash flow to finance and order more ships, to lease back, to carry more and more raw materials and more cars, more television sets, more electronic goods, and more goods outward bound to the States—and heavy industry plants and machines to the rest of the world. Last, back to your most vital import of all: oil. Here's a suggested pattern for a new fleet of bulk oil carriers, half a million to a million tons dead weight each.'

Toda gasped and abruptly finished the translation himself. Astounded, they all sucked in their breath when he mentioned the half a million to a million tons.

Dunross sat back enjoying the tension. He watched them glance at one another, then at Toda, waiting for him to react.

'I . . . I think we had better study your proposals, tai-pan,' Toda said, trying to keep his voice level. 'Obviously they are far-reaching. May we get back to you later?'

'Yes. You're coming to the races tomorrow? Lunch'll be 12:45.'

'Thank you, yes, if it's not too much trouble,' Toda said with sudden nervousness, 'but it would be impossible for us to have an answer by that time.'

'Of course. You got your invitations and badges?'

'Yes, thank you. I, er, I hope everything turns out well for you. Your proposal certainly sounds far-reaching.'

They left. For a moment Dunross allowed himself to enjoy the excitement. I've got them, he thought. Christ, in a year we can have the biggest fleet in Asia, all totally financed, with no risks to financier, builder, operator or supplier, with oil tankers, huge tankers as its nucleus—if we can weather this typhoon.

All I need's some luck. Somehow I've got to stave off the

crash till Tuesday when we sign with Par-Con. Par-Con pays for our ships, but what about Orlin and what about Gornt?'

'Mr. Jacques's on his way up, tai-pan. Mr. Phillip's in his office and'll come up whenever you're ready. Roger Crosse called, your appointment's at 7:00 P.M. instead of 6:00. He said Mr. Sinders's plane was late. He's informed the governor and everyone connected.'

'Thank you, Claudia.' He glanced at his list of calls. He dialed the V and A and asked for Bartlett. He was out. 'Miss Tcholok please.'

'Hello?'

'Hello! Ian Dunross returning your call and Linc Bartlett's call. How're things?'

There was a slight pause. 'Interesting. Tai-pan, can I drop by?'

'Of course. How about cocktails at 6:15 at the Mandarin? That'd give me half an hour-odd before my next appointment. Eh?' A twinge of anxiety went through him at the thought of Crosse, Sinders and AMG's admonition about never giving up the files.

'Is it possible for me to come by the office? I could leave now and be there in half to three quarters of an hour? I have something to talk over with you. I'll make it as short as possible.'

'All right. I may have to keep you waiting a moment or two but come on over.' He put the phone down, frowning. What's up there?

The door opened. Jacques deVille came in. He looked careworn and tired. 'You wanted me, tai-pan?'

'Yes, sit down, Jacques. I understood you were going to be on the plane last night.'

'We talked, Susanne and I, and she thought it best for Avril if I waited a day or two. . . .'

Dunross listened with fascination as they began to talk, still astounded that Jacques could be a Communist plant. But now he had thought through the possibility. It was easily possible for Jacques, being young, an idealist and in the Maquis during the hated and terrible Nazi occupation of France to have had his idealistic nationalism and anti-Nazi feelings channeled into communism—Christ, wasn't Russia our ally in those days? Wasn't communism fashionable everywhere in those days even in America? Didn't Marx and Lenin seem so sensible then? *Then*. Before we knew the truth about Stalin, about *gulags* and KGB and police state and mass murders and mass conquests and never freedom.

But how could all that Communist nonsense last for someone like Jacques? How could someone like Jacques retain such convictions and keep them buried for so long—if indeed he is the Sevrin plant AMG claimed?

'What did you think of Grey?' Dunross asked.

'A total *crétin*, tai-pan. He's far too left-wing for me. Even Broadhurst's a little too left for my taste. As I'm . . . I'm staying now, can I take over Bartlett and Casey again?'

'No, for the time being I'll deal with them, but you take care of the contract.'

'It's being drawn up now. I've already been on to our solicitors. One slight problem. Dawson met with Bartlett's lawyer, Mr. Steigler, this morning. Mr. Steigler wants to renegotiate the payment schedule and put off signing till next weekend.'

A wave of fury rushed through Dunross. He tried to keep it off his face. That's got to be the reason for Casey wanting a meeting, he thought. 'I'll deal with that,' he said, putting the problem aside for the more pressing one: Jacques deVille, who should be innocent until proven guilty.

He looked at him, liking the craggy, chunky man, remembering all the fine times they had had in Avisyard and in France. He, Penelope, Jacques and Susanne, their children along for Christmas or summer holidays, good food and good wine and good laughter and great plans for the future. Jacques certainly the wisest, the most close-mouthed, and until the AMG accusation, possibly the next in line. But now you're not, not until you've proved yourself and I'm certain. Sorry my friend, but you must be tested.

'I'm making some organizational changes,' he said. 'Linbar went to Sydney today as you know. I'm going to leave him there for a month to try to get the Woolara merger fixed. I don't hope for much. I want you to take over Australia.' He saw Jacques's eyes widen momentarily but could not read if it was concern or happiness. 'I've pushed the button on our Toda plan and I w—'

'How did he take it?'

'Hook, line and bait.'

984

'*Merde*, but that is great.' Dunross saw Jacques beam and read no guile in him. The man had been one of the main planners for the shipping scheme, working out the intricacies of the financing. 'What a shame poor John's not alive to know,' Jacques said.

'Yes.' John Chen had been working closely with Jacques deVille. 'Have you seen Phillip?'

'I had dinner with him last night. Poor fellow, he's aged twenty years.'

'So have you.'

A Gallic shrug. 'Life, *mon ami!* But yes, yes I am sad about poor Avril and poor Borge. Please excuse me, I interrupted you.'

'I'd like you to take over Australasia—effective today—and be responsible for putting into effect all our Australian and New Zealand plans. Keep this to yourself for the month—I'll tell Andrew only—but get yourself organized and be prepared to leave then.'

'Very well.' Jacques hesitated.

'What? Susanne never did like Hong Kong—you'll have no problem there, will you?'

'Oh no, tai-pan. Since the accident . . . frankly I was going to ask you if I could move for a while. Susanne's not been happy here and . . . But I was going to ask if I could take over Canada for a year or so.'

Dunross was startled at the new thought. 'Oh?'

'Yes. I thought that perhaps I could be useful there. My contacts among French-Canadians are good, very good. Perhaps we could shift Struan's Canadian office from Toronto to Montreal or to Ottawa. I could help very much from there. If our Japanese connection goes through, we'll need wood pulp, woods, copper, wheat, coal and a dozen other Canadian raw materials.' He smiled wanly, then rushed onward. 'We both know how Cousin David's been chomping to get back out here and I thought, if I moved there, he could return. Actually he's better equipped to be here, to deal with Australasia, *non*? He speaks Cantonese, a little Japanese and reads and writes Chinese which I don't. But whatever you say, tai-pan. I'll take Australasia if you wish. It is true I would like a change.'

Dunross let his mind range. He had decided to isolate Jacques from Hong Kong while he found out the truth. It would be too

985

easy to tell Crosse or Sinders secretly and ask them to use their sources to investigate, to watch and to probe. But Jacques was a member of the Inner Court. As such he was party to all sorts of skeletons and private information which would be put to risk. No, Dunross thought, much better to deal with our own. Perhaps it will take longer but I will find out the truth if he is or isn't. One way or another, I'll know about Jacques deVille.

But Canada?

Logically Jacques'd be better there. So would Struan's—I should have thought of that myself—there's never been any reason to question his business loyalty, or acumen. Good old David's certainly been screaming for two years to come back. The switch would be easier. Jacques's right. David's better equipped to do Australasia, and Australia and New Zealand are far more important to us than Canada, far more important— they're vital and the treasure house of all Asia. If Jacques's innocent he can help us in Canada. If he's not, he can harm us less there. 'I'll think about that,' he said, having already decided to make the change. 'Keep this all to yourself and we'll finalize it Sunday.'

Jacques got up and stuck out his hand. 'Thanks, *mon ami*.'

Dunross shook the hand. But in his heart he wondered whether it was the hand of his friend—or his Judas.

Alone once more, the weight of his burdens swamped him. The phone rang and he dealt with that problem, then another and another—Tiptop's phone still engaged—and he asked for Phillip to come up, and all the time it seemed as though he were sinking into a pit. Then his eyes caught the eye of Dirk Struan on the wall, looking out of the oil painting at him, half-smiling, supremely confident, arrogant, master of clipper ships—the loveliest craft ever built by man. As always, he was comforted.

He got up and stood before *the* tai-pan. 'Christ, I don't know what I'd do without you,' he said out loud, remembering that Dirk Struan had been beset by far greater burdens and had conquered them. Only to have the tempest, the wrath of nature, kill him at the zenith of his life, just forty-three, undisputed warlord of Hong Kong and Asia.

Is it always 'those whom the gods love die young'? he asked himself. Dirk was just my age when the Devil Winds of the Great Typhoon tore our brand-new three-story residence in

Happy Valley to pieces and buried him in the rubble. Is that old or young? I don't feel old. Was that the only way for Dirk to die? Violently? In storm? Young? Killed by nature? Or does the expression mean, those whom the gods love die young in heart?

'Never mind,' he said to his mentor and friend. 'I wish I'd lived to know you. I tell you openly, tai-pan, I hope to God there is a life after death so that in some eon of time, I can thank you personally.'

Confident again, he went back to his desk. In his top drawer was Four Finger Wu's matrix. His fingers touched it, caressing it. How do I squeeze out of this one? he asked himself grimly.

There was a knock. Phillip Chen came in. He had aged in the last few days. 'Good God, tai-pan, what are we going to do? 9.50!' he said in a rush, a nervous screech in his voice. 'I could tear my hair out! *Dew neh loh moh* because of the boom, you remember I bought in at 28.90, every penny of spare cash and a lot more and Dianne bought at 28.80 and sold at 16.80 and demands I make up the difference. *Oh ko* what're we going to do?'

'Pray—and do what we can,' Dunross said. 'Have you got hold of Tiptop?'

'Eh . . . no, no, tai-pan. I've been trying every few minutes but the phone's still out of order. The phone company says the phone's been left off the hook. I had my cousin in the phone company check it personally. Both lines into his house are off the hook.'

'What do you advise?'

'Advise? I don't know, I think we should send a messenger but I didn't want to until I'd consulted with you . . . what with our stock crash and the bank run and poor John and the reporters pestering . . . all my stocks are down, all of them!' The old man went into a paroxysm of Cantonese obscenities and curses on Gornt, his ancestors and all his future generations. 'If the Vic goes, what are we going to do, tai-pan?'

'The Vic won't go. The governor will certainly declare Monday a bank holiday if Tiptop fails us.' Dunross had already apprised his compradore of his conversations with Tiptop, Yu, Johnjohn and Havergill. 'Come on, Phillip, think!' he added with pretended anger, deliberately sharpening his voice to help the old man. 'I can't just send a god-cursed messenger there to say "you've deliberately left your bloody phone off the hook"!'

Phillip Chen sat down, the rare anger pulling him together a little. 'Sorry, yes, sorry but everything . . . and John, poor John . . .'

'When's the funeral?'

'Tomorrow, tomorrow at ten, the Christian one, Monday's the Chinese one. I was . . . I was wondering if you'd say a few words, tomorrow.'

'Of course, of course I will. Now, what about Tiptop?'

Phillip Chen concentrated, the effort hard for him. At length he said, 'Invite him to the races. To your box. He's never been and that would be great face. That's the way. You could say . . . No, sorry, I'm not thinking clearly. Better, much better, tai-pan, I will write. I'll write the note asking him for you. I'll say you wanted to ask personally but unfortunately his phone is out of order—then if he wants to come, or is forbidden by his superiors, his face is saved and so is yours. I could add that "by the way, the Noble House has already telexed firm orders to Sydney for the thoriums . . ."' Phillip Chen brightened a little. 'That will be a very good trade for us, tai-pan, the price offered. . . . I've checked prices and we can supply all their needs easily and get very competitive bids from Tasmania, South Africa and Rhodesia. Ah! Why not send young George Trussler from Singapore to Johannesburg and Salisbury on an exploratory mission for thoriums . . .' Phillip Chen hesitated. '. . . and er, certain other vital aerospace metals and materials. I did some quick checking, tai-pan. I was astounded to discover that, outside Russia, almost 90 percent of all the Free World's supply of vanadium, chrome, platinums, manganese, titanium —all vital and essential in aerospace and rocketry—come from the southern part of Rhodesia and South Africa. Think of that! 90 percent outside Russia. I never realized how vastly important that area is to the Free World, with all the gold, diamonds, uranium, thorium and God knows what other essential raw materials. Perhaps Trussler could also investigate the possibility of opening an office there. He's a sharp young man and due for promotion.' Now that his mind was fully occupied, the old man was breathing easier. 'Yes. This trade and, er, Mr. Yu's, could

988

be immense for us, tai-pan. I'm sure it can be handled delicately.' He looked up at Dunross. 'I'd also mention to Tiptop about Trussler, that we were sending an executive, one of the family, in preparation.'

'Excellent. Do it immediately.' Dunross clicked on the intercom. 'Claudia, get George Trussler please.' He glanced back at Phillip. 'Why would Tiptop cut himself off?'

'To bargain, to increase the pressure on us, to get more concessions.'

'Should we keep on calling him?'

'No. After the hand-delivered note, he will call us. He knows we're not fools.'

'When will he call?'

'When he has permission, tai-pan. Not before. Sometime before Monday at 10:00 A.M. when the banks are due to open. I suggest you tell that lump of dogmeat Havergill and Johnjohn not to call—they'll muddy already dark waters. You don't use a tadpole to catch a shark.'

'Good. Don't worry, Phillip,' he said compassionately, 'we're going to get out of this mess.'

'I don't know, tai-pan. I hope so.' Phillip Chen rubbed his red-rimmed eyes tiredly. 'Dianne . . . those damned shares! I see no way out of the morass. Th—'

Claudia interrupted on the intercom. 'Master Trussler on line two.'

'Thank you, Claudia.' He stabbed line two. 'Hello, George, how's Singapore?'

'Afternoon, sir. Fine, sir, hot and rainy,' the breezy, enthusiastic voice said. 'This's a pleasant surprise, what can I do for you?'

'I want you to get on the next plane to Johannesburg. Leave at once. Telex me your flight and hotel and call me as soon as you arrive at the hotel in Johannesburg. Got it?'

There was a slight hesitation and slightly less breeziness. 'Johannesburg, South Africa, tai-pan?'

'Yes. The next plane out.'

'I'm on my way. Anything else?'

'No.'

'Right you are, tai-pan. I'm on my way. 'Bye!'

Dunross put the phone down. Power's a marvelous device,

989

he thought with great satisfaction, but being tai-pan's better.

Phillip got up. 'I'll deal with that letter at once.'

'Just a minute, Phillip. I've another problem that I need your advice on.' He opened the desk and brought out the matrix. Apart from himself and previous tai-pans who were still alive, only Phillip Chen in all the world knew the secret of the four coins. 'Here. This was giv—'

Dunross stopped, paralyzed, totally unprepared for the effect the matrix had on his compradore. Phillip Chen was staring at it, his eyes almost popped from their sockets, his lips stretched back from his teeth. As though in a dream, everything in slow motion, Phillip Chen reached out and took the matrix, his fingers trembling, and peered at it closely, mouthing soundlessly.

Then Dunross's brain detonated and he realized the half-coin must have belonged to Phillip Chen, that it had been stolen from *him*. *Of course*, Dunross wanted to shout. Sir Gordon Chen must have been given one of the four coins by Jin-qua! But why? What was the connection between the Chen family and a Co-hong Mandarin that would make Jin-qua give the Eurasian son of Dirk Struan so valuable a gift?

Still in slow motion, he saw the old man raise his head to squint up at him. Again the mouth moved. No sound. Then in a strangled gasp, 'Bar . . . Bartlett gave this . . . this to you already?'

'Bartlett?' Dunross echoed incredulously. 'What in the name of Christ's Bartlett got to d—' He stopped as another explosion seemed to shatter his head and more pieces of the jigsaw slammed into place. Bartlett's secret knowledge! Knowledge that could only come from one of seven men, all of them unthinkable, Phillip Chen the most unthinkable of all!

Phillip Chen's the traitor! Phillip Chen's working in conjunction with Bartlett and Casey . . . it's Phillip Chen who's sold us out and passed over our secrets and passed over the coin.

A blinding rage overcame him. It took all of his training to hold the fury bottled. He saw himself get up and stride to the window and stare out of it. He did not know how long he stood there. But when he turned, his mind was purged clean and the vast error in his logic now clear to him.

'Well?' His voice was chilling.

'Tai-pan . . . tai-pan . . .' the old man began brokenly, wringing his hands.

'Tell the truth, compradore. *Now!*' The word frightened Phillip.

'It . . . it was John,' he gasped, tears spilling. 'It wasn't me I sw—'

'I know that! Hurry up for chrissake!'

Phillip Chen spewed out everything, how he had taken his son's key and opened his son's safety deposit box and discovered the letters to and from Bartlett and the second key and how, at dinner the night of the tai-pan's party, he had suddenly had a premonition about his oh so secret safe buried in the garden and how, after digging it up, he had discovered the worst. He even told the tai-pan about his quarrel with Dianne and how they thought the coin might be on John Chen somehow, and how, when the Werewolf phoned, she suggested calling his cousin, Four Finger Wu, to get his street fighters to follow him, then to follow them. . . .

Dunross gasped but Phillip Chen did not notice it, rambling on in tears, telling how he had lied to the police and had paid over the ransom to the Werewolf youths he would never recognize again and how the street fighters of Four Fingers who were supposed to be guarding him had not intercepted the Werewolves or recaptured John or recaptured his money. 'That's the truth, tai-pan, all of it,' he whimpered, 'there's no more . . . nothing. Nothing until this morning and my poor son's body at Sha Tin with that filthy sign on his chest. . . .'

Helplessly Dunross was trying to collect his wits. He had not known that Four Fingers was Phillip's cousin, nor could he fathom how the old seaman could have got the coin—unless he was the chief Werewolf or in league with them, or in league with John Chen who had masterminded a supposed kidnapping to squeeze money out of the father he hated and then Four Fingers and John Chen had quarreled or . . . or what? 'How did John know our secrets, get all those secrets to pass them over to Bartlett—how the House's structured? Eh?'

'I don't know,' the old man lied.

'You must have told John—there's only you; Alastair, my father, Sir Ross, Gavallan, deVille or me who know, and of those, only the first four know the structure!'

'I didn't tell him—I swear I didn't.'

Dunross's blinding rage began to swell again but once more he held it into place.

Be logical, he told himself. Phillip's more Chinese than European. Deal with him as a Chinese! Where's the link? The missing part of the jigsaw?

While he was trying to work out the problem, his eyes bored into the old man. He waited, knowing that silence too was a vast weapon, in defence or attack. What's the answer? Phillip would never tell John anything that secret, therefore . . .

'Jesus Christ!' he burst out at the sudden thought. 'You've been keeping records! Private records! That's how John found out! From your safe! *Eh?*'

Petrified by the tai-pan's devil rage, Phillip blurted out before he could stop himself, 'Yes . . . yes . . . I had to agree . .' He stopped, fighting for control.

'Had to? Why? Come on goddamnit!'

'Because . . . because my father, before he . . . he passed the House over to me and the coin to me . . . made me swear to keep . . . to record the private dealings of . . . of the Noble House to protect the House of Chen. It was just that, tai-pan, never to use against you or the House, just a protection. . . .'

Dunross stared at him, hating him, hating John Chen for selling Struan's out, hating his mentor Chen-chen for the first time in his life, sick with rage at so many betrayals. Then he remembered one of Chen-chen's admonitions years ago when Dunross was almost weeping with anger at the unfair way his father and Alastair were treating him: 'Don't get angry, young Ian, get even. I told Culum the same thing, and the Hag when they were equally young—Culum never listened but the Hag did. That's the civilized way: Don't get angry, get even! So Bartlett has our structure, our balance sheets. What else's he got?'

Phillip Chen just shivered and stared back blankly.

'Come on for chrissake, Phillip, think! We've all got skeletons, a lot of skeletons! So've you, the Hag, Chen-chen. Shitee T'Chung, Dianne . . . for chrissake, how much more's documented that John could have passed over?' A wave of nausea went through him as he remembered his theory about the connection between Banastasio, Bartlett, Par-Con, the

Mafia and the guns. Christ, if our secrets get into the wrong hands! *'Eh?'*

'I don't know, I don't know . . . What, what did Bartlett ask? For the coin?' Then Phillip cried out, 'It's mine, it belongs to me!'

He saw the uncontrollable trembling of Phillip's hands and a sudden tinge of gray in his face. There was brandy and whiskey in decanters on the sideboard and Dunross fetched some brandy and gave it to him. Gratefully the old man drank, choking a little. 'Than . . . thank you.'

'Go home and fetch everything and th—' Dunross stopped and stabbed an intercom button. 'Andrew?'

'Yes, tai-pan?' Gavallan said.

'Would you come up a second? I want you to go home with Phillip, he's not feeling too well and there're some papers to bring back.'

'On my way.'

Dunross's eyes had never left Phillip's.

'Tai-pan, what did, did Bar—'

'Stay away from them on your life! And give Andrew everything—John's letters, Bartlett's letters, everything,' he said, his voice chilling.

'Tai-pan . . .'

'Everything.' His head ached, he had so much rage in him. He was going to add, I'll decide about you and the House of Chen over the weekend. But he did not say it. 'Don't get mad, get even' kept ringing in his ears.

Casey came in. Dunross met her halfway. She carried an umbrella and was again wearing her pale green dress that set off her hair and eyes perfectly. Dunross noticed the shadows behind her eyes. They made her somehow more desirable. 'Sorry to keep you waiting.' His smile was warm but he enjoyed none of its warmth. He was still appalled over Phillip Chen.

Casey's hand was cool and pleasant. 'Thanks for seeing me,' she said. 'I know you're busy so I'll come to the point.'

'First tea. Or would you like a drink?'

'No liquor thanks, but I don't want to put you to any trouble.'

'No trouble, I'm going to have tea anyway. 4:40's tea time.' As though by magic the door opened and a liveried houseboy brought in a silver tray with tea for two—with thin buttered toast and hot scones in a silver warmer. The man poured and left. The tea was dark brown and strong. 'It's Darjeeling, one of our House blends. We've been trading it since 1830,' he said sipping it gratefully, as always thanking the unknown genius Englishman who had invented afternoon tea, which, somehow, always seemed to settle the cares of the day and put the world into perspective. 'I hope you like it.'

'It's great, maybe a mite too strong for me. I had some around 2:00 A.M., and it certainly woke me up.'

'Oh? You still on jet lag?'

She shook her head and told him about Peter Marlowe.

'Oh! What bad joss!' He stabbed the intercom. 'Claudia, call the Nathan Nursing Home and see how Mrs. Marlowe is. And send some flowers. Thanks.'

Casey frowned. 'How'd you know she was at the Nathan?'

'Doc Tooley always uses that place in Kowloon.' He was watching her closely, astonished that she seemed so friendly when obviously Par-Con was trying to sabotage their deal. If she's been up most of the night, that accounts for the shadows, he thought. Well, shadows or not, watch out, young lady, we shook on the deal. 'Another cup?' he asked solicitously.

'No thanks, this's fine.'

'I recommend the scones. We eat them like this: a big dollop of Devonshire clotted cream on top, a teaspoon of home-made strawberry jam in the center of the cream and . . magic! Here!'

Reluctantly she took it. The scone was just bite-sized. It vanished. 'Fantastic,' she gasped, wiping a touch of the cream off her mouth. 'But all those calories! No, really, no more, thanks. I've done nothing but eat since I got here.'

'It doesn't show.'

'It will.' He saw her smile back at him. She was sitting in one of the deep high-backed leather chairs, the tea table between them. Again she crossed her legs and Dunross thought once more that Gavallan had been right about her—that her Achilles' heel was impatience. 'May I start now?' she asked.

'You're sure you don't want some more tea?' he asked, deliberately to throw her off balance again.

'No thanks.'

'Then tea's over. What's cooking?'

Casey took a deep breath. 'It seems that Struan's is way out on a limb and about to go under.'

'Please don't concern yourself about that. Struan's really is in very fine shape.'

'You may be, tai-pan, but it doesn't look that way to us. Or to outsiders. I've checked. Most everyone seems to think Gornt, and or the Victoria, will make the raid stick. It's almost a general thumbs down. Now our deal's—'

'We have a deal till Tuesday. That's what we agreed,' he said, his voice sharpening. 'Do I understand you want to renege or change it?'

'No. But in the present state you're in, it'd be crazy and bad business to proceed. So we've two alternatives: It's either Rothwell-Gornt, or we've to help you with some kind of bail-out operation.'

'Oh?'

'Yes. I've a plan, a partial plan for how you could maybe extricate yourself and make us all a fortune. Okay? You're the best for us—long-term.'

'Thank you,' he said, not believing her, all attention, well aware that any concession she offered was going to be prohibitively expensive.

'Try this on for size. Our bankers are the First Central New York—the hated bank here. They want back into Hong Kong so much it hurts, but they'll never get a new charter, right?'

Dunross's interest peaked at this new thought. 'So?'

'So recently they bought a small foreign bank with branches in Tokyo, Singapore, Bangkok and Hong Kong: the Royal Belgium and Far East Bank. It's a tiny, nothing bank and they paid 3 million for everything. First Central has asked us to put our funds through the Royal Belgium if our deal goes through. Last night I met with Dave Murtagh who's in charge of Royal Belgium and he was moaning and groaning how bad business was, how they're squeezed out of everything by the Establishment here and though they've got the huge dollar resources of First Central behind them, almost nobody'll open accounts and deposit Hong Kong dollars which they need to make loans. You know about the bank?'

'Yes,' he said, not understanding what she was leading

to, 'but I didn't realize the First Central was behind them. I don't think that's common knowledge. When was it bought out?'

'A couple of months ago. Now, what if the Royal Belgium would advance you Monday 120 percent of the purchase price of the two Toda ships?'

Dunross gaped at her, caught off guard. 'Secured by what?'

'The ships.'

'Impossible! No bank'd do that!'

'The 100 percent is for Toda, the 20 percent to cover all carrying charges, insurances and the first months of operation.'

'With no cash flow, no charterer set?' he asked incredulously.

'Could you charter them in sixty days to give you a cash flow to sustain a reasonable repayment schedule?'

'Easily.' Jesus Christ, if I can pay Toda at once I can slam my lease-back scheme into operation with the first two ships, without having to wait. He held onto his hope, wondering what the cost, the real cost would be. 'Is this a theory or will they really do it?'

'They might.'

'In return for what?'

'In return for Struan's depositing 50 percent of all foreign exchange for a five-year period; a promise you'd keep average cash deposits with them of between 5 and 7 million Hong Kong dollars—one and one half million U.S. dollars' worth; that you'd use the bank as your second Hong Kong bank and the First Central as your prime lending American bank outside of Hong Kong for a five-year period. What do you say?'

It took all his training not to bellow with joy. 'Is this a firm offer?'

'I think it is, tai-pan. I'm a bit out of my depth—I've never been into ships but 120 percent seemed fantastic and the other terms okay. I didn't know how far I should go negotiating terms but I told him he'd better make it all fair or he'd never get to first base.'

An ice shaft went into his guts. 'The local man would never have the authority to make such an offer.'

'That was Murtagh's next point, but he said we've the weekend and if you'll go for the scheme he'll get on the wire.'

Dunross sat back, nonplussed. He put aside three vital questions and said, 'Let's hold this for the moment. What's your part in all this?'

'In a minute. There's another wrinkle to his offer. I think he's bananas but Murtagh said he'd try to persuade the brass to put up a revolving $50 million U.S. against the value of the unissued shares you got in your treasury. So you're home free. If.'

Dunross felt the sweat break out on his back and on his forehead, well aware what a tremendous gamble that would be, however big the bank. With effort he put his brain to work. With the ships paid for and that revolving fund, he could fight off Gornt and smash his attack. And with Gornt bottled, Orlin'd come back meekly because he'd always been a good customer—and wasn't First Central part of the Orlin Merchant Bank consortium? 'What about our deal?'

'That stays as is. You announce at the best time for both of us, for you and for Par-Con as we agreed. If, and it's a big if, if First Central'll go for the gamble, you and we could make a killing, a real killing by buying Struan at 9.50 Monday morning—it has to go back up to 28, maybe to 30, doesn't it? The only part I can't figure is how to deal with the bank runs.'

Dunross took out his handkerchief and unashamedly wiped his forehead. Then he got up and poured two brandy and sodas. He gave her one and sat back in his chair again, his mind amok, one moment blank, the next crammed with happiness, instantly to be agitated and hurting with all the hope and fear, the questions, answers, plans and counterplans.

Christallbloodymighty, he thought, trying to calm himself.

The brandy tasted good. The warming bite was very good. He noticed she only sipped hers and then set it down and watched him. When his brain had cleared and he was ready, he looked at her. 'All this in return for what?'

'You'll have to set the parameters with the Royal Belgium—that's up to you. I don't know accurately enough your net cash flow. Interest charges'll be steep, but worth it to get out from under. You'll have to put up your personal guarantee for every cent.'

'Christ!'

'Yes. Plus face.' He heard her voice harden. 'It'll cost you face to be dealing with the "yellow bastards." Wasn't that what Lady Joanna called the First Central people with her big fat sneer and

997

"But what do you expect, they're . . ." I guess she meant Americans.' He saw Casey's eyes flatten and his danger signals came up. 'That's some old bitch, that one.'

'She's not really,' he said. 'She's a bit caustic, and rough, but all right usually. She is anti-American, sorry to say, paranoid I suppose. You see, her husband, Sir Richard, was killed at Monte Cassino in Italy by American bombs, their aircraft mistaking British troops for Nazis.'

'Oh,' Casey said. 'Oh I see.'

'What does Par-Con want? And what do you and Linc Bartlett want?'

She hesitated, then put Lady Joanna aside for a moment, concentrating again. 'Par-Con wants a long-term deal with Struan's—as "Old Friends".' He saw the strange smile 'I've discovered what *Old Friend* means, Chinese style, and that's what I want for Par-Con. Old Friend status as and from the moment the Royal Belgium delivers.'

'Next?'

'Is that a yes?'

'I'd like to know all the terms before I agree to one.'

She sipped the brandy. 'Linc wants nothing. He doesn't know about all this.'

'I beg your pardon?' Again Dunross was caught off balance.

'Linc doesn't know about the Royal Belgium yet,' she said, her voice ordinary. 'I brainstormed all this with Dave Murtagh today. I don't know if I'm doing you much of a favor because your . . . because you'll be on the line, you personally. But it could get Struan's off the hook. Then our deal can work.'

'Don't you think you should consult with your fearless leader?' Dunross said, trying to work out the implications of this unexpected tack.

'I'm executive director and Struan's is my deal. It costs us nothing but our influence to get you out of your trap and that's what influence's for. I want our deal to go through and I don't want Gornt the winner.'

'Why?'

'I told you. You're the best for us long-term.'

'And you, Ciranoush? What do you want? In return for using your influence?'

Her eyes seemed to flatten even more and become more

hazel, like a lioness's. 'Equality. I want to be treated as an equal, not patronized or scoffed at as a woman who's in business on the coat tails of a man. I want equality with the tai-pan of the Noble House. And I want you to help me get my drop dead money—apart from anything to do with Par-Con.'

'The second's easy, if you're prepared to gamble. As to the first, I've never patronized or sloughed you o—'

'Gavallan did, and the others.'

'. . . off, and I never will. As to the others, if they don't treat you as you like, then leave the conference table and leave the battleground. Don't force your presence on them. I can't make you equal. You're not and you never will be. You're a woman and like it or not this's a man's world. Particularly in Hong Kong. And while I'm alive I'm going to continue to treat it as it is and treat a woman as a woman whoever the hell she is.'

'Then screw you!'

'When?' He beamed.

Her sudden laugh joined his and the tension fled. 'I deserved that,' she said. Another laugh. 'I really deserved that. Sorry. Guess I lost ass.'

'I beg your pardon?'

She explained her version of face. He laughed again. 'You didn't. You gained arse.'

After a pause she said, 'So whatever I do, I can never have equality?'

'Not in business, not on masculine terms, not if you want to be of this world. As I said, like it or not, that's the way it is. And I think you're wrong to try to change it. The Hag was undisputedly more powerful than anyone in Asia. And she got there as a woman, not as a neuter.'

Her hand reached out and lifted her brandy and he saw the swell of her breast against the light silk blouse. 'How the hell can we treat someone as attractive and smart as you as a non-person? Be fair!'

'I'm not asking for fairness, tai-pan, just equality.'

'Be content you're a woman.'

'Oh I am. I really am.' Her voice became bitter. 'I just don't want to be classed as someone whose only real value is on her back.' She took a last sip and got up. 'So you'll take it from here? With the Royal Belgium? David Murtagh's expecting a call. It's a long shot, but it's worth a try, isn't it? Maybe you could go see him, instead of sending for him—face, huh? He'll need all the support you can give him.'

Dunross had not got up. 'Please sit down a second, if you've time. There're still a couple of things.'

'Of course. I didn't want to take any more of your time.'

'First, what's the problem with your Mr. Steigler?'

'What do you mean?'

He told her what Dawson had related.

'Son of a bitch!' she said, obviously irritated. 'I told him to get the papers drawn, that's all. I'll take care of him. Lawyers always think they've the right to negotiate, "to improve the deal" is the way they put it, trying to put you down, I guess. I've lost more deals because of them than you can imagine. Seymour's not as bad as some. Attorneys're the plague of the United States. Linc thinks so too.'

'What about Linc?' he asked, remembering the 2 million he had advanced to Gornt to attack their stock. 'Is he going to be 100 percent behind this new twist?'

'Yes,' she said after a pause. 'Yes.'

Dunross's mind reached out for the missing piece. 'So you'll take care of Steigler and everything stands as before?'

'You'll have to work out title to the ships as we agreed but that shouldn't be a problem.'

'No. I can handle that.'

'You'll personally guarantee everything?'

'Oh, yes,' Dunross said carelessly. 'Dirk did all the time. That's the tai-pan's privilege. Listen, Ciranoush, I—'

'Will you call me Casey, tai-pan? Ciranoush is for a different era.'

'All right. Casey, whether this works or not, you're an Old Friend and I owe you a thank you for your bravery, your personal bravery at the fire.'

'I'm not brave. It must have been glands.' She laughed. 'Don't forget we've still got the hepatitis over our heads.'

'Oh. You thought of that too.'

'Yes.'

Her eyes were watching him and he could not gauge her. 'I'll help you with drop dead money,' he said. 'How much do you need?'

'2 million, tax free.'

'Your tax laws are rigid and tough. Are you prepared to stretch laws?'

She hesitated. 'It's the right of every red-blooded American to avoid taxes, but not evade them.'

'Got it. So at your bracket you might need 4?'

'My bracket's low, though my capital's high.'

'$46,000 at the San Fernando Savings and Loan's not very much,' he said, grimly amused to see her blanch. '$8,700 in your checking account at the Los Angeles and California's not too much either.'

'You're a bastard.'

He smiled. 'I merely have friends in high places. Like you.' Casually he opened the trap. 'Will you and Linc Bartlett have dinner with me tonight?'

'Linc's busy,' she said.

'Will you have dinner then? Eight? Let's meet in the lobby of the Mandarin.' He heard the undercurrent and the giveaway and he could almost see her mind waves churning. So Linc's busy! he thought. And what would Linc Bartlett be busy with in that tone of voice? Orlanda Ramos? Has to be, he told himself, delighted he had flushed out the real reason—the real why of her help. Orlanda! Orlanda leading to Linc Bartlett leading to Gornt. Casey's petrified of Orlanda. Is she petrified that Gornt's behind Orlanda's onslaught on Bartlett—or is she just frantic with jealousy and ready to bring Bartlett atumbling down?

59

Casey joined the packed lines going through the turnstiles at Golden Ferry. People were shoving and pushing and hurrying along the corridor for the next ferry. As the warning bell sounded shrilly, those in front broke into a frantic run. Involuntarily her feet quickened. The noisy, heated crush of humanity carried her along onto the ferry. She found a seat and stared out at the harbor gloomily, wondering if she had pulled off her side of the deal.

'Jesus, Casey,' Murtagh had burst out, 'head office'll never go for it in a million years!'

'If they don't they'll miss the greatest opportunity of their lives. And so will you. This is your big chance—grab it! If you help Struan's now think how much face everyone gets. When Dunross comes to see you th—'

'If he comes!'

'He'll come. I'll get him to come see you! And when he does, tell him this's all your idea, not mine, and that y—'

'But, Casey, don—'

'No. It's got to be your idea. I'll back you a thousand percent with New York. And when Dunross comes to you, tell him you want Old Friend status too.'

'Jesus, Casey, I've got enough troubles without having to explain to those meatheads back home about Old Friend and "face"!'

'So don't explain that part to them. You pull this off and you'll be the most important American banker in Asia.'

Yes, Casey told herself, sick with hope, and I'll have extricated Linc from Gornt's trap. I know I'm right about Gornt.

'The hell you are, Casey!' Bartlett had said angrily this morning, the first time in their life together he had ever flared at her.

'It's obvious, Linc,' she had slammed back. 'I'm not trying to interfere i—'

'The hell you're not!'

'You brought Orlanda up, I didn't! You're going overboard about—about her great cooking and great dancing and great outfit and great company! All I said was, did you have a nice time?'

'Sure, but you said it with a real crappy harpy jealous tone and I know you meant: I hope you had a lousy time!'

Linc was right, Casey thought in misery. If he wants to be out all night that's up to him. I should have buttoned up like the other times and not made a big deal of it. But this isn't like the other times. He's in danger and won't see it!

'For chrissake, Linc, that woman's after your money and power and that's all! How long have you known her? A couple of days. Where did you meet her? Gornt! She's got to be Gornt's puppet! That guy's as smart as they come! I've done some checking, Linc, her apartment's paid by him, her bills. Sh—'

'She told me all that and all about him and her and that's the past! You can forget Orlanda! Get it? Just don't bad-mouth her anymore. Understand?'

'Par-Con's got a lot riding on whether it's Struan's or Gornt and they'll both use any tactic to undermine you or lay you open to att—'

'And *lay*'s the operative word? C'mon, Casey, for chrissake! You've never been jealous before—admit you're fit to be tied. She's everything a man could want and you're . . .'

She remembered how he had stopped just before he'd said it. Tears filled her eyes. He's right, goddamnit! I'm not. I'm a goddamn business machine, not feminine like her, not an easy lay and not interested in being a housewife, at least not yet, and I could never do what she's done. Orlanda's soft, pliant, golden, a great cook, he says, feminine, great body great legs great taste, trained and beddable, Jesus, how beddable. And with no thought in her goddamn head but how to catch a rich husband. The Frenchwoman was right: Linc's a patsy for any no-account harpy, Asian gold digger, and Orlanda's the cream of the Hong Kong crop.

Shit!

But whatever Linc says, I'm still right about her and right about Gornt.

Or am I?

Let's face it, I've nothing to go on but a few rumors, and my own intuition. Orlanda's got me on the run, I'm running scared. I made a goddamn mistake letting myself go at Linc. Remember what he said before he left the suite. 'From here on in you stay the hell out of my private life!'

Oh God!

There was a fine wind blowing as the ferry skittered across the harbor, engines pounding, sampans and other boats moving nimbly out of the way, the sky brooding and overcast. Oblivious, she dabbed her tears away, took out her mirror and checked that her mascara was not running. A huge freighter sounded its horn, flags fluttering, and moved majestically past, but she did not see it, nor the immensity of the nuclear carrier tied up alongside the Admiralty Wharf, Hong Kong side. 'Get hold of yourself,' she muttered in misery to her mirror image. 'Jesus, you look forty.'

The cramped wooden benches were crowded and she shifted uncomfortably, jammed between other passengers, most of whom were Chinese, though here and there were camera-heavy tourists and other Europeans. There was not an inch of free space, all gangways clogged, seats clogged, and already blocks of passengers crowded the ramp exit on both decks. The Chinese beside her were awkwardly reading their newspapers as people would on any subway except that, from time to time, they would hawk noisily to clear their throats. One spat. On the bulkhead right in front of him was a large sign in Chinese and English: NO SPITTING—FINE TWENTY DOLLARS. He hawked again and Casey wanted to take his newspaper and thump him with it. The tai-pan's remark flooded her memory: 'We've been trying to change them for a hundred and twenty-odd years, but Chinese don't change easily.'

It's not just them, she thought, her head aching. It's everyone and everything in this man's world. The tai-pan's right.

So what am I going to do? About Linc? Change the rules or not?

I have already. I've gone over his head with the bail-out

scheme. That's a first. Am I going to tell him about it or not? Dunross won't give me away and Murtagh'll take all the credit, has to, if First Central'll buy it. I'll have to tell Linc sometime.

But whether the bail-out works or not, what about Linc and me?

Her eyes were fixed ahead, unseeing, as she tried to decide.

The ferry was nearing the Kowloon Terminal berth now. Two other ferries leaving for Hong Kong side swirled out of the way for the incomers. Everyone got up and began to jostle for position at the port exit ramp. The ship heeled slightly, unbalanced. Jesus, she thought uneasily, jerked out of her reverie, there must be five hundred of us on each deck. Then she winced as an impatient Chinese matron squeezed past, stomped carelessly on her foot and pushed on through the throng to the head of the line. Casey got up, her foot hurting, wanting to belt the woman with her umbrella.

'They're something else, eh?' the tall American behind her said with grim good humor.

'What? Oh yes, yes . . . something else, some of them.' People surrounded her, crowding her, pressing too close. Suddenly she felt claustrophobic and sickened. The man sensed it and used his bulk to force a little room. Those who were pushed aside gave way with ill humor. 'Thanks,' she said, relieved, the nausea gone. 'Yes, thanks.'

'I'm Rosemont, Stanley Rosemont. We met at the tai-pan's.'

Casey turned, startled. 'Oh, sorry, I guess . . . I guess I was a million miles away, I didn't . . . sorry. How's it going?' she asked, not remembering him.

'More of the same, Casey.' Rosemont looked down at her. 'Not so good with you, huh?' he asked kindly.

'Oh I'm fine. Sure, very fine.' She turned away, self-conscious that he'd noticed. Sailors were fore and aft and they tossed out guy lines which were instantly caught and dropped over stanchions. The thick ropes screeched under the tension, setting her teeth on edge. As the ferry eased perfectly into its berth, the drawbridge gate began to lower but before it was down completely the crowd was surging off the boat, Casey carried with it. After a few yards the pressure eased and she walked up the ramp at her own pace, other passengers flooding down the other ramp opposite to board for Hong Kong side.

Rosemont caught up with her. 'You at the V and A?'

'Yes,' she said. 'You?'

'Oh no! We've an apartment Hong Kong side—the consulate owns it.'

'Have you been here long?'

'Two years. It's interesting, Casey. After a month or so you feel locked in—no place to go, so many people, seeing the same friends day after day. But soon it's great. Soon you get to feel you're at the center of the action, the center of Asia where all the action is today. Sure, Hong Kong's the center of Asia— papers're good, you've great food, good golf, racing, boating and it's easy to go to Taipei, Bangkok or wherever. Hong Kong's okay—course it's nothing like Japan. Japan's something else. That's like out of Oz.'

'Is that good or bad?'

'Great—if you're a man. Tough for wives, very tough, and for kids. Your helplessness, your alienness is shoved back at you— you can't even read a street sign. I was there for a two-year tour. I liked it a lot. Athena, my wife, she got to hate it.' Rosemont laughed. 'She hates Hong Kong and wants to go back to In- dochina, to Vietnam or Cambodia. She was a nurse there some years back with the French Army.'

Through the fog of her own problems Casey heard an under- current and she began to listen. 'She's French?'

'American. Her father was ambassador for a tour during the French war.'

'You have kids?' she asked.

'Two. Both sons. Athena was married before.'

Another undercurrent. 'Your sons were from her first mar- riage?'

'One was. She was married to a Vietnamese. He was killed just before Dien Bien Phu, that was when the French ran the country or were getting run out. Poor guy was killed before young Vien was born. He's like my own son. Yes, both my boys are great. You staying long?'

'Depends on my boss and our deal. Guess you know we're hoping to tie in with Struan's.'

'It's the talk of the town—apart from the fire at Aberdeen, the flooding, all the mud slides, the storm, Struan's stock crash, the bank runs and the market falling apart—one thing about Hong

Kong: it's never dull. You think he'll make it?'

'The tai-pan? I've just left him. I hope so. He's confident, yes very confident. I like him.'

'Yes. I like Bartlett too. You been with him long?'

'Seven years, almost.'

They were out of the terminal now, the road just as crowded. On the right was the harbor and they chatted, heading east for the pedestrian underpass that would take them to the V and A. Rosemont pointed at a small shop, the Rice Bowl. 'Athena works there from time to time. It's a charity shop, run by Americans. All the profit goes to refugees. Lots of the wives put in a day or two there, keeps them busy. I guess you're busy all the time.'

'Only seven days a week.'

'I heard Linc say that you were taking off over the weekend for Taipei. Will that be your first visit?'

'Yes—but I'm not going, just Linc and the tai-pan.' Casey tried to stop the immediate thought welling but she could not: Is he going to take Orlanda? He's right, it's none of my affair. But Par-Con is. And since Linc's hooked, lined and sinkered by the enemy, the less he knows about the First Central ploy the better.

Pleased that she could come to the decision dispassionately, she continued to talk with Rosemont, answering his questions, not really concentrating, pleased to converse with a friendly soul who was as informative as he was interested. '. . . and Taipei's different, more easygoing, less hard-nosed, but a comer,' he was saying. 'We're popular in Taiwan which's a change. So you're really going to spread? On a big deal like this I guess you've a dozen execs on hand?'

'No. There's just the two of us at the moment, and Forrester— he's head of our foam division—and our attorney.' Mentioning him, Casey hardened. Damn him for trying to stymie us. 'Linc's got Par-Con organized very well. I handle the day-to-day and he fixes policy.'

'You're a public company?'

'Oh sure, but that's okay too. Linc has control and our directors and stockholders don't give us a hassle. Dividends're on the rise, and if the Struan deal goes through they'll sky-rocket.'

'We could use more U.S. firms in Asia. Trade is what made

the Empire great for the British. I wish you luck, Casey. Hey, that reminds me,' he added casually, 'you remember Ed, Ed Langan, my buddy, who was with me at the tai-pan's party? He knows one of your stockholders. A guy called Bestacio, some name like that.'

Casey was startled. 'Banastasio? Vincenzo Banastasio?'

'Yes, I think that was it,' he told her, lying easily, watching her, and at her look added, 'Did I say something?'

'No, it's just a coincidence. Banastasio arrives tomorrow. Tomorrow morning.'

'What?'

Casey saw him staring at her and she laughed. 'You can tell your friend he's staying at the Hilton.'

Rosemont's mind buzzed. 'Tomorrow? I'll be goddamned.'

Casey said carefully, 'He's a good friend of Langan's?'

'No, but he knows him. He says Banastasio's quite a guy. A gambler, isn't he?'

'Yes.'

'You don't like him?'

'I've only met him a couple of times. At the races. He's big at Del Mar. I'm not much on gamblers or gambling.'

They were weaving through the crowds. People jostled from behind and oncoming hordes jostled from the front. The underpass stank of mildew and bodies. She was very glad to get back into the air once more and looking forward to a shower and an aspirin and a rest before 8:00 P.M. Beyond the buildings ahead was the whole of the eastern harbor. A departing jet barreled into the overcast. Rosemont caught sight of the tall deck derricks of the *Sovetsky Ivanov* tied up alongside. Involuntarily he glanced Hong Kong side and saw how easy it would be for high-powered binoculars to rake the U.S. carrier and almost count her rivets.

'Makes you proud to be an American, doesn't it?' Casey said happily, following his look. 'If you're consulate, you'll get to go aboard her?'

'Sure. Guided tour!'

'Lucky you.'

'I was there yesterday. The captain had a shindig for locals. I tagged along.' Again Rosemont told the lie easily. He had gone aboard late last night and again this morning. His initial interview with the admiral, captain and security chief had been stormy. It was not until he produced photocopies of the secret manifest of the ship's armaments and the guidance systems manual that they had truly believed there had been a vast security leak. Now the traitor was under tight surveillance in the ship's brig, guarded by his own CIA people, twenty-four hours a day. Soon the man would break. Yes, Rosemont thought, and after that, jail for twenty years. If it was up to me I'd drop the bastard in the goddamn harbor. Shit, I've got nothing against the Metkins and the KGB. Those bastards're just doing their job for their side—however wrong they are. But our own Joes?

'Okay, fella, you're caught! First tell us why you did it.'

'Money.'

Jesus H. Christ! The sailor's dossier had shown that he had come from a small town in the Middle West, his work exemplary with nothing in his past or present to indicate a potential security risk. He was a quiet man, good at computer programming, liked by his compatriots and trusted by his superiors. No left-wing indications, no homosexuality, no problem of blackmail, no nothing. 'Then why?' he had asked him.

'This guy came up to me in San Diego and said he'd like to know all about the *Corregidor* and he'd pay.'

'But don't you understand about treason? About betraying your country?'

'Hell, all he wanted was a few facts and figures. So what? What's the difference? We can blast the hell outta the goddamn Commies anytime we like. The *Corregidor*'s the greatest carrier afloat! It was a caper and I wanted to see if I could do it and they paid on the dot. . . .'

Jesus, how we going to keep security when there are guys like him with their brains in their asses, Rosemont asked himself wearily.

He walked along, listening to himself chatting with Casey, probing her, trying to decide what sort of a risk she was and Bartlett was, with their tie-in to Banastasio. Soon they joined other people going up the wide steps to the hotel. A smiling pageboy opened the swing doors. The foyer was bustling. 'Casey, I'm early for my appointment. Can I buy you a drink?'

Casey hesitated, then smiled, liking him, enjoying chatting. 'Sure, thanks. First let me collect my messages, okay?' She went to the desk. There were a sheaf of telexes, and messages from Jannelli, Steigler and Forrester to please call. And a handwritten note from Bartlett. The note contained routine instructions about Par-Con, all of which she agreed to, and asked her to make sure that the airplane was ready to take off on Sunday. The note ended: 'Casey, we're going with Rothwell-Gornt. Let's meet for breakfast in the suite, 9:00 A.M. See you then.'

She went back to Rosemont. 'Can I take a raincheck?'

'Bad news?'

'Oh no, just a load of stuff to deal with.'

'Sure, but maybe you'd like dinner next week, you and Linc? I'd like Athena to meet you. She'll give you a call to fix the day, okay?'

'Thanks, I'd like that.' Casey left him, her whole being more than ever committed to the course she had decided upon.

Rosemont watched her go, then ordered a Cutty Sark and soda and began to wait, lost in thought. How much money's Banastasio got in Par-Con and what's he got in return? Jesus H. Christ, Par-Con's hot in defense and space and a lot of secret crap. What's that bum doing here? Thank God I took on Casey today and didn't leave her to one of the guys. He might've missed Banastasio. . . .

Robert Armstrong arrived.

'Jesus, Robert, you look terrible,' the American said. 'You better get yourself a vacation or a good night's rest or lay off the broads.'

'Get stuffed! You ready? We'd better leave.'

'You've time for a quick one. The bank date's been changed to seven, there's plenty of time.'

'Yes, but I don't want to be late as we're to meet the governor at his office.'

'Okay.'

Obediently Rosemont finished his drink, signed the bill and they walked back toward the ferry terminal.

'How's Dry Run?' Armstrong asked.

'They're still there with flags flying. Looks like the Azerbaijan revolt fizzled.' Rosemont noticed the heaviness on the Englishman. 'What's eating you, Robert?'

'Sometimes I don't like being a copper, that's all.' Armstrong took out a cigarette and lit it.

'I thought you gave up smoking.'

'I did. Listen, Stanley old friend, I'd better warn you: you're in the proverbial creek without a paddle. Crosse's so mad he's fit to be committed.'

'So what else's new? A lot of guys think he's a basket case anyway. Jesus, it was Ed Langan who tipped you off about the AMG files in the first place. We're allies for chrissake!'

'True,' Armstrong replied sourly, 'but that's no license to mount a totally unauthorized raid on a totally clean flat belonging to the totally clean telephone company!'

'Who me?' Rosemont looked pained. 'What flat?'

'Sinclair Towers, flat 32. You and your gorillas knocked down the door in the dead of the night. For what, may I ask?'

'How should I know?' Rosemont knew he had to bluff this one through, but he was still furious that whoever was in the apartment had escaped without identification. His rage over the carrier leak, Metkin's not being available for questioning, the whole Sevrin mess and Crosse's perfidy, had prompted him to order the raid. One of his Chinese informants had picked up a rumor that though the apartment was empty most of the time, sometimes it was used by Communist enemy agents—of gender unknown—and there was a meeting tonight. Connochie, one of his best agents, had led the raid and thought he caught a glimpse of two men going out the back but he wasn't sure, and though he searched diligently, they had vanished and he found nothing in the apartment to prove or disprove the rumor, just two half-empty glasses. The glasses were brought back and tested for fingreprints. One was clean, the other well marked. 'I've never been to 32 Sinclair Towers, for chrissake!'

'Maybe, but your Keystone Kops were there. Several tenants reported four tall, meaty Caucasians charging up and down the stairs.' Armstrong added even more sourly, 'All fat-arsed and fat-headed. Have to be yours.'

'Not mine. No sir.'

'Oh yes they were and that mistake's going to backfire. Crosse's already sent two pretty foul cables to London. The pity of it is you failed to catch anything and we catch hell because of your continual screw-ups!'

Rosemont sighed. 'Get off my back. I've got something for you.' He told Armstrong of his conversation with Casey about

Banastasio. 'Of course we knew his connection with Par-Con but I didn't know he was arriving tomorrow. What do you think?'

Armstrong had seen the arrival recorded on Photographer Ng's calendar. 'Interesting,' he said noncommittally. 'I'll tell the Old Man. But you'd better have a good explanation for him about Sinclair Towers and don't mention that I told you.' His fatigue was almost overwhelming him. This morning at 6:30 A.M. he had begun the first real probe of Brian Kwok.

It was an orchestrated set piece: while still drugged, Brian Kwok had been taken out of his clean white cell and put naked into a filthy dungeon with dank walls and a stinking thin mattress on the mildewed floor. Then, ten minutes after the wake-up drug had jerked him into parched, aching consciousness, the light had blazed on and Armstrong had ripped the door open and cursed the SI jailer. 'For chrissake, what're you doing to Superintendent Kwok? Have you gone mad? How dare you treat him like this!'

'Superintendent Crosse's orders, sir. This client's b—'

'There must be a mistake! I don't give a damn about Crosse!' He had thrown the man out and put his full, kind attention onto his friend. 'Here, old chum, do you want a cigarette?'

'Oh Christ. Thank . . . thanks.' Brian Kwok's fingers had trembled as he held the cigarette and drew the smoke deep. 'Robert, what . . . what the hell's going on?'

'I don't know. I've just heard, that's why I'm here. I was told you'd been on leave for a few days. Crosse's gone mad. He claims you're a Communist spy.'

'Me? For God's sake . . . what's the date today?'

'The thirtieth, Friday,' he had said at once, expecting the question, adding seven days.

'Who won the fifth race?'

'Butterscotch Lass,' he had said, caught off guard, astonished that Brian Kwok was still functioning so well and not at all certain if his own slight hesitation had been read for the lie it was. 'Why?'

'Just wondered . . . just . . . Listen, Robert, this's a mistake. You've got to help me. Don't you s—'

On cue Roger Crosse had come in like the wrath of God. 'Listen, spy, I want names and addresses of all your contacts

1012

right now. Who's your controller?'

Weakly Brian Kwok had stumbled to his feet. 'Sir, it's all a mistake. There's no controller and I'm no spy an—'

Crosse had suddenly shoved blowups of the photos in his face. 'Then explain how you were photographed in Ning-tok in front of your family pharmacy with your mother Fang-ling Wu. Explain how your real name's Chu-toy Wu, second son of these parents, Ting-top Wu and Fang-ling Wu . . .'

They had both seen the instant of shock on Brian Kwok's face.

'Lies,' he had mumbled, 'lies, I'm Brian Kar-shun Kwok and I'm—'

'You're a liar!' Crosse had shouted. 'We have witnesses! We have evidence! You are identified by your *gan sun*, Ah Tam!'

Another gasp, covered almost brilliantly, then 'I . . . I have no *gan sun* called Ah Tam. I h—'

'You'll spend the rest of your life in this cell unless you tell us everything. I'll see you in a week. You'd better answer everything truthfully or I'll put you in chains! Robert!' Crosse had whirled on him. 'You're forbidden to come here without permission!' Then he had stalked out of the cell.

In the silence Armstrong remembered how nauseated he had been, having seen the truth written on his friend's face. He was too well trained an observer to be mistaken. 'Christ, Brian,' he had said, continuing the game, hating his hypocrisy even so. 'What possessed you to do it?'

'Do what?' Brian Kwok had said defiantly. 'You can't cheat me—or trick me, Robert . . . It can't be seven days. I'm innocent.'

'And the photos?'

'Fake . . . they're fake, dreamed up by Crosse.' Brian Kwok had held onto his arm, a desperate light behind his eyes, and whispered hoarsely, 'I told you Crosse's the real mole. He's the mole, Robert . . . he's a homo—he's trying to frame me an—'

On cue, the brittle, officious SI jailer jerked the cell door open. 'Sorry, sir, but you've got to leave.'

'All right, but first give him some water.'

'No water's allowed!'

'Goddamn you, get him some water!'

Reluctantly the jailer obeyed. While they were momentarily alone, Armstrong had slipped the cigarettes under the mattress.

'Brian, I'll do what I can . . .' Then the jailer was back in the room with a battered cup.

'That's all you can have!' he said angrily. 'I want the cup back!'

Thankfully Brian Kwok had gulped it and with it the drug. Armstrong left. The door slammed and the bolts shoved home. Abruptly the lights went out, leaving Brian Kwok in darkness. Ten minutes later Armstrong had gone back in with Dr. Dorn. And Crosse. Brian Kwok was unconscious, deeply drugged again and dreaming fitfully. 'Robert, you did very well,' Crosse had said softly. 'Did you see the client's shock?'

'Yes sir.'

'Good. So did I. No mistake about that, or his guilt. Doctor, step up the sleep-wake-up every hour on the hour for the next twenty-four . . .'

'Christ,' Armstrong burst out, 'don't you th—'

'Every hour on the hour, Doctor, provided he checks out medically—I don't want him harmed, just pliable—for the next twenty-four. Robert, then you interrogate him again. If that doesn't work, we put him into the Red Room.'

Dr. Dorn had flinched and Armstrong recalled how his heart had missed a beat. 'No,' he said.

'For chrissake, the client's guilty, Robert,' Crosse snarled, no longer playacting. 'Guilty! The client shopped Fong-fong and our lads and has done us God knows what damage. We're under the gun. The orders came from London! Remember Metkin, our great commissar catch from the *Ivanov*? I've just heard the RAF transport's vanished. It refueled in Bombay then vanished somewhere over the Indian Ocean.'

60

6:58 P.M.:

The governor was in an Olympian rage. He got out of the car and stomped to the side door of the bank where Johnjohn was waiting for him.

'Have you read this?' The governor waved the evening edition of the *Guardian* in the night air. The huge headline read: MPs ACCUSE PRC. 'Bloody incompetent fools, what?'

'Yes sir.' Johnjohn was equally choleric. He led the way past the uniformed doorman into a large anteroom. 'Can't you hang both of them?'

At their afternoon press conference, Grey and Broadhurst had proclaimed publicly everything that he, Johnjohn, Dunross and the other tai-pans had, at length, patiently condemned as totally against Britain's, Hong Kong's and China's interest. Grey had gone on at length discussing his private and personal opinion that Red China was bent on world conquest and should be treated as the great enemy of world peace. 'I've already had one unofficial official scream.'

Johnjohn winced. 'Oh God, not from Tiptop?'

'Of course from Tiptop. He said, in that calm silky voice of his, "Your Excellency, when our peers in Peking read how important members of your great English Parliament view the Middle Kingdom, I think they will be really quite angry." I'd say our chances of getting the temporary use of their money now is nil.'

Another wave of anger went over Johnjohn.

'That damned man implied his views were the committee's views, which is totally untrue! Ridiculous to inflame China under any circumstances. Without China's benevolence our position here is totally untenable. Totally! Bloody fool! And we

1015

all went out of our way to explain!' The governor took out a handkerchief and blew his nose. 'Where are the others?'

'Superintendent Crosse and Mr. Sinders are using my office for a moment. Ian's on his way. What about Ian and Grey, sir, Grey being Ian's brother-in-law? Eh?'

'Extraordinary.' Since Grey had mentioned it in response to a question this afternoon he had had a dozen calls about it. 'Astonishing that Ian never mentioned it.'

'Or Penelope! Very odd. Do you th—' Johnjohn glanced up and stopped. Dunross was walking toward them.

'Evening, sir.'

'Hello, Ian. I put the time back to 7:00 P.M. to give me a chance to see Sinders and Stanley Rosemont.' The governor held up the paper. 'You've seen this?'

'Yes sir. The Chinese evening papers are so incensed, I'm surprised every edition's not on fire and all of Central with them.'

'I'd try them for treason,' Johnjohn said, his face sour. 'What the devil can we do, Ian?'

'Pray! I've already spoken to Guthrie, the Liberal MP, and some of the Tories. One of the *Guardian*'s top reporters is interviewing them right now and their opposite opinions will be the morning headlines refuting all this poppycock.' Dunross wiped his hands. He could feel the sweat on his back as well. The combination of Grey, Tiptop, Jacques, Phillip Chen, the coin and the AMG files were unnerving him. Christ Jesus, he thought, what next? His meeting with Murtagh of the Royal Belgium had been what Casey had forecast—a long shot but a good one. Coming out of that meeting someone had given him the afternoon papers and the bombshell that such ill-advised remarks was going to create had almost knocked him over. 'We'll have to just dismiss the whole thing publicly, and privately work like hell to make sure Grey's bill to bring Hong Kong down to Britain's level never gets to a vote, or is voted down, and Labour never gets elected.' He felt his bile rising. 'Broadhurst was just as bad if not worse.'

'Ian, have you talked to Tiptop?'

'No, Bruce. His line's still busy though I did send a message around.' He told them what he had arranged with Phillip Chen. Then the governor related Tiptop's complaint. Dunross was aghast. 'When did he call, sir?'

'Just before six.'

'He would have had our message by then.' Dunross felt his heart thumping. 'After this . . . this debacle, I'd lay heavy odds there's no chance for Chinese money.'

'I agree.'

Dunross was acutely aware they had not mentioned Grey's relationship to him. 'Robin Grey's worse than a fool,' he said, thinking he might just as well bring it out into the open. 'My god-cursed brother-in-law could not have done better for the Soviets if he was a member of the Politburo. Broadhurst as well. Stupid!'

After a pause the governor said, 'As the Chinese say, "The devil gives you your relations, thank all gods you can choose your friends."'

'You're so right. Fortunately, the committee's due to leave Sunday. With the races tomorrow and all the . . . all the other problems, perhaps it'll all get lost in the shuffle.' Dunross mopped his brow. 'It's close in here, isn't it?'

The governor nodded, then added testily, 'Is everything ready, Johnjohn?'

'Yes sir. The va—' In the hall the elevator opened and Roger Crosse and Edward Sinders, chief of MI-6, came out.

'Ah, Sinders,' the governor said as they both came into the anteroom, 'I'd like you to meet Mr. Dunross.'

'Pleased to meet you, sir.' Sinders shook hands with Dunross. He was a middle-aged, middle height, nondescript man with crumpled clothes. His face was thin and colorless, the stubble of his beard gray. 'Please excuse my rumpledness, sir, but I haven't been to the hotel yet.'

'Sorry about that,' Dunross replied. 'This could certainly have waited until tomorrow. Evening, Roger.'

'Evening, sir. Evening, Ian,' Crosse said crisply. 'As we're all here, perhaps we could proceed?'

Obediently Johnjohn began to lead the way but Dunross said, 'Just a moment. Sorry, Bruce, could you excuse us a moment?'

'Oh certainly.' Johnjohn covered his surprise, wondering what this was all about and who Sinders was, but much too wise to ask. He knew they would tell him if they wanted him to know. The door closed behind him.

1017

Dunross glanced at the governor. 'Do you attest, sir, formally, this is Edward Sinders, head of MI-6?'

'I do.' The governor handed him an envelope. 'I believe you wanted it in writing.'

'Thank you, sir.' To Sinders, Dunross said, 'Sorry, but you understand my reluctance.'

'Of course. Good, then that's settled. Shall we go, Mr. Dunross?'

'Who's Mary McFee?'

Sinders was shocked. Crosse and the governor stared at him, perplexed, then at Dunross. 'You have friends in high places, Mr. Dunross. May I ask who told you that?'

'Sorry.' Dunross kept his gaze on him. Alastair Struan had got the information from some VIP in the Bank of England who had approached someone high up in the government. 'All we want to do is to be sure Sinders is who he pretends to be.'

'Mary McFee's a friend,' Sinders said uneasily.

'Sorry, that's not good enough.'

'A girl friend.'

'Sorry, neither's that. What's her real name?'

Sinders hesitated, then, his face chalky, he took Dunross by the arm and guided him to the far end of the room. He put his lips very close to Dunross's ear. 'Anastasia Kekilova, First Secretary of the Czechoslovak Embassy in London,' he whispered, his back to Crosse and the governor.

Dunross nodded, satisfied, but Sinders held onto his arm with surprising strength and whispered even more softly, 'You'd better forget that name. If the KGB ever suspect you know they'll get it out of you. Then she's dead, I'm dead and so're you.'

Dunross nodded. 'Fair enough.'

Sinders took a deep breath, then turned and nodded at Crosse. 'Now let's have this done with, Roger. Your Excellency?'

Tensely they all followed him. Johnjohn was waiting at the elevator. Three floors below were the vaults. Two plainclothes guards waited in the small hallway in front of the heavy iron gates, one man CID, the other SI. Both saluted. Johnjohn unlocked the gates and let everyone through except the guards, then relocked them. 'Just a bank custom.'

'Have you ever had a break-in?' Sinders asked.

'No, though the Japanese did force the gates when the keys were, er, lost.'

'Were you here then, sir?'

'No. I was lucky.' After Hong Kong capitulated, at Christmas 1941, the two British banks, Blacs and the Victoria, became prime Japanese targets and were ordered to be liquidated. All the executives were separated and kept under guard and forced to assist the process. Over the months and years they were all subjected to extreme pressures. They were forced to issue bank notes illegally. And then the Kampeitai, the hated and feared Japanese secret police, had become involved. 'The Kampeitai executed several of our fellows and made the lives of the rest miserable,' Johnjohn said. 'The usual: no food, beatings, privation, shut up in cages. Some died of malnutrition— *starvation*'s the real word—and both Blacs and we lost our chief execs.' Johnjohn unlocked another grille. Beyond were rows and rows of safe deposit boxes in several interconnecting concrete, reinforced cellars. 'Ian?'

Dunross took out his passkey. 'It's 16.85.94.'

Johnjohn led the way. Very uncomfortable, he inserted his bank key in one lock. Dunross did the same with his. They turned both keys. The lock clicked open. Now all eyes were on the box. Johnjohn took out his key. 'I'll . . . I'll be waiting at the gate,' he said, glad it was over, and left.

Dunross hesitated. 'There are other things in here, private papers. Do you mind?'

Crosse did not move. 'Sorry but either Mr. Sinders or myself should ensure we get possession of all the files.'

Dunross noticed the sweat on both men. His own back was wet. 'Your Excellency, would you mind watching?'

'Not at all.'

Reluctantly the two other men retreated. Dunross waited until they were well away, then opened the box. It was large. Sir Geoffrey's eyes widened. The box was empty but for the blue covered files. Without comment he accepted them. There were eight. Dunross slammed the box closed and the lock clicked home.

Crosse came forward, his hand out. 'Shall I take them for you, sir?'

'No.'

Crosse stopped, startled, and bit back a curse. 'But, Exce—'

'The minister set up a procedure—approved by our American friends—which I agreed to,' Sir Geoffrey said. 'We will all go back to my office. We will all witness the photocopying. Two copies only. One for Mr. Sinders, one for Mr. Rosemont. Ian, I have been ordered direct by the Minister to give Mr. Rosemont copies.'

Dunross shrugged, desperately hoping that he still appeared unconcerned. 'If that's what the minister wants, that's perfectly all right. When you've photocopied the originals, sir, please burn them.' He saw them look at him but he was watching Crosse and he thought he saw an instant of pleasure. 'If the files're so special then it's better they shouldn't exist—except in the correct hands, MI-6 and the CIA. Certainly I shouldn't have a copy. If they're not special—then never mind. Most of poor old AMG was too farfetched and now that he's dead I must confess I don't consider the files special so long as they're in your hands. Please burn or shred them, Excellency.'

'Very well.' The governor turned his pale blue eyes on Roger Crosse. 'Yes, Roger?'

'Nothing, sir. Shall we go?'

Dunross said, 'I've got to get some corporate papers to check while I'm here. No need to wait for me.'

'Very well. Thank you, Ian,' Sir Geoffrey said and left with the other two men.

When he was quite alone Dunross went to another bank of boxes in the adjoining vault. He took out his key ring and selected two keys, grimly aware that Johnjohn would have a coronary if he knew he had a duplicate master key. The lock sprang back soundlessly. This box was one of dozens the Noble House possessed under different names. Inside were bundles of U.S. $100 notes, ancient deeds and papers. On top was a loaded automatic. As always, Dunross's psyche was unsettled, hating guns, hating Hag Struan, admiring her. In her 'Instructions to Tai-pans', written just before her death in 1917, that was part of her last will and testament and in the tai-pan's safe, she had laid down more rules and one of them was that there should always be substantial amounts of secret cash for the tai-pan's use, on hand, and another that there should be at least four loaded handguns perpetually available in secret places. She wrote: 'I abhor guns but I know them to be necessary. On Michaelmas Eve in 1916 when I was infirm and sick, my grandson Kelly O'Gorman, fourth tai-pan (in name only), believing I was on my deathbed, forced me from my bed to the safe in the Great House to fetch the seal-chop of the Noble House—to assign to him absolute power as tai-pan. Instead I took the gun that was secretly in the safe and shot him. He lingered two days then died. I am God-fearing and I abhor guns and some killing, but Kelly became a mad dog and it is the duty of the tai-pan to protect the succession. I regret his death not a jot or tittle. You who read this beware: kith or kin lust for power as others do. Do not be afraid to use *any* method to protect Dirk Struan's legacy . . .'

A bead of sweat trickled down his cheek. He remembered the hair on the nape of his neck rising when he had first read her instructions, the night he had taken over as tai-pan. He'd always believed that Cousin Kelly—eldest son of the Hag's last daughter Rose—had died of cholera in one of the great waves that perpetually washed Asia.

There were other monstrosities she had written about: 'In 1894, that most terrible of years, the second of Jin-qua's coins was brought to me. That was the year plague had come to Hong Kong, bubonic plague. Amongst our heathen Chinese, tens of thousands were dying. Our own population was equally savaged and the plague took high and low, Cousin Hannah and three children, two of Chen-chen's children, five grandchildren. Legend foretold that bubonic plague was wind-borne. Others thought it was the curse of God or a flux like malaria, the killing "bad air" or Happy Valley. Then the miracle! The Japanese research doctors Vitasato and Aoyama we brought to Hong Kong isolated the plague bacillus and proved the pest was flea-borne, and rat-borne, and that correct sanitation and the elimination of rats would cast out the curse forever. The eyesore hillside of Tai-ping Shan that Gordon owns—Gordon Chen, son of my beloved tai-pan—where most of our heathen always lived was a stinking, festering, overcrowded, rat-breeding cauldron for all pestilences, and as much as the authorities cajoled, ordered and insisted, the superstitious inhabitants there disbelieved everything and would do nothing to improve

1021

their lot, though the deaths continued and continued. Even Gordon, now a toothless old man, could do nothing—tearing his hair at his loss of rents, saving his energy for the four young women in his household.

'In the stench of late summer when it seemed the Colony was once more doomed, with deaths mounting daily, I had Tai-ping Shan put to the torch by night, the whole monstrous stenching mountainside. That some inhabitants were consumed is on my conscience, but without the cleansing fire the Colony was doomed and hundreds of thousands more doomed. I caused Tai-ping Shan to be fired but thereby I kept troth with Hong Kong. I kept troth with the Legacy. And I kept troth with the second of the half coins.

'On the twentieth of April a man called Chiang Wu-tah presented the half coin to my darling young cousin, Dirk Dunross, third tai-pan, who brought it to me, he not knowing the secret of the coins. I sent for the man Chiang who spoke English. The favor he asked was that the Noble House should grant immediate sanctuary and succor to a young, Western-educated Chinese revolutionary named Sun Yat-sen; that we should help this Sun Yat-sen with funds; and that we should help him as long as he lived, to the limits of our power in his fight to overthrow the alien Manchu Dynasty of China. Supporting any revolutionary against China's ruling dynasty with whom we had cordial relations and on whom depended much of our trade and revenues was against my principles, and seemingly against the interests of the House. I said no, I would not assist the overthrow of their emperor. But Chiang Wu-Tah said, "This is the favor required from the Noble House."

'And so it was done.

'At great risk I provided funds and protection. My darling Dirk Dunross spirited Dr. Sun out of Canton to the Colony and from there abroad to America. I wanted Dr. Sun to accompany young Dirk to England—he was leaving on the tide, Master of our steamer *Sunset Cloud*. That was the week I wanted to hand over to him as real tai-pan but he said, "No, not until I return." But he was never to return. He and all hands were lost at sea somewhere in the Indian Ocean. Oh how terrible my loss, our loss!

'But death is a part of life and we the living have our duty to be done. I do not yet know to whom I should hand over. It should have been Dirk Dunross, who was named for his grandfather. His sons are too young, none of the Coopers are adequate, or deVilles, Daglish is possible, none of the MacStruans are yet ready. Alastair Struan perhaps but there's a weakness there that comes down from Robb Struan.

'I don't mind admitting to you, future tai-pan, that I am weary unto death. But I am not yet ready to die. Pray God I am given the strength for a few more years. There is not one of my line or my beloved Dirk Struan's line worthy of his mantle. And now there is this Great War to see through, the House to rebuild, our merchant fleet to refurbish—so far German U-boats have sunk thirty of our ships, almost our whole fleet. Yes, and there is the favor of the second coin still to fulfill. This Dr. Sun Yat-sen must and will be supported until he dies and so retain our face in Asia. . . .'

And we did, Dunross thought. The Noble House supported him in all his troubles, even when he tried to join with Soviet Russia, until he died in 1925 and Chiang Kai-shek, his Soviet-trained lieutenant, assumed his mantle and launched China into the future—until his old ally but ancient enemy, Mao Tse-tung, took the future away from him to mount the Dragon Throne in Peking with bloody hands, first of a new dynasty.

Dunross took out a handkerchief and mopped his brow.

The air in the vault was dusty and dry and a little caught in his throat and he coughed. His hands were sweaty too and he could still feel the chill on his back. He rummaged carefully to the bottom of the deep metal box and found his corporate chop that he would need over the weekend in case the Royal Belgium-First Central deal came to pass. I certainly owe Casey more than one favor if the deal is made, he told himself.

His heart was thumping again and he could not resist making sure. With great care he lifted the secret false bottom of the safety deposit box a fraction. In the two-inch space beneath were eight blue-covered files. AMG's real files. Those that moments ago he had passed over to Sinders had been in the sealed package that Kirk and his wife had brought yesterday— those eight counterfeit files and a letter: 'Tai-pan: I am terribly worried that both you and I are betrayed and that information contained in previous files may fall into the wrong hands. The enclosed substitute files are safe and very similar. They drop vital names and vital information. You may pass these over if you are forced to do it, but only then. As to the originals, you should destroy them after you have seen Riko. Certain pages contain invisible writing. Riko will give you the key. Please excuse all these diversionary tactics but espionage is not for children; it deals in death, actual and in the future. Our lovely Britain is beset with traitors and evil walks the earth. Bluntly, freedom is under siege as never in history. I beg you to emulate your illustrious ancestor. He fought for freedom to trade, to live and to worship. Sorry, but I don't think he died in a storm. We'll never know the truth but I believe he was murdered, as I will be. Not to worry, my young friend. I've done very well in my life. I've put a lot of nails in the enemy coffin, more than my fair share—I ask you to do the same.'

The letter was signed, 'With great respect.'

Poor bugger, Dunross thought sadly.

Yesterday he had smuggled the counterfeit files into the vault, replacing the originals in the other box. He would have liked to have destroyed the originals then but there was no way to do that safely and anyway he had to wait for his meeting with the Japanese woman. Better and safer to leave them where they are for the moment, he said to himself. Plenty of ti—

Suddenly he felt eyes. His hand sneaked for the automatic. When his fingers had grasped it, he looked around. His stomach seemed to turn over. Crosse was watching him. And Johnjohn. They were at the entrance to the vault.

After a moment Crosse said, 'I just wanted to thank you for your cooperation, Ian. Mr. Sinders and I appreciate it.'

Relief poured through Dunross. 'That's all right. Glad to help.' Trying to be casual he relaxed his hold on the automatic and let it slide away. The false bottom fell silently into place. He saw Crosse's scrutiny but shrugged it off. From where the superintendent stood he did not think it possible for him to have seen the real files. Dunross blessed his joss that had prevented him from taking one of the files out to leaf through it. Carelessly he slammed the box shut and his breathing began again. 'It really is quite stuffy in here, isn't it?'

'Yes. Again, Ian, thank you.' Crosse left.

'How did you open that box?' Johnjohn asked coldly.

'With a key.'

'Two keys, Ian. That's against regulations.' Johnjohn held out his hand. 'May I have our property please.'

'Sorry, old chum,' Dunross said calmly, 'it's not your property.'

Johnjohn hesitated. 'We always suspected you had a duplicate master key. Paul is right about one thing: you've too much power, you consider this bank yours, our funds yours and the Colony yours.'

'We've had a long and happy association with both, and it's only in the last few years when Paul Havergill's had some measure of power that I've had a hard time, me personally, and my House personally. But worse than that, he's old-fashioned and I voted him out for that reason only. You're not, you're modern. You'll be fairer, far-seeing, less emotional and straighter.'

Johnjohn shook his head. 'I doubt it. If I ever become tai-pan of the bank I'm going to see it's wholly owned by its stockholders and controlled by directors appointed by them.'

'It is now. We just own 21 percent of the bank.'

'You used to own 21 percent. That stock's pledged against your revolving fund which you can't and probably never will repay. Besides, 21 percent is not control, thank God.'

'It very nearly is.'

'My whole point.' Johnjohn's voice was metallic. 'That's dangerous for the bank, very dangerous.'

'I don't think so.'

'I do. I want 11 percent back.'

'No sale, old lad.'

'When I'm tai-pan, old lad, I'll get it by hook or by crook.'

'We'll see.'

'When I'm tai-pan I'm going to make lots of changes. All these locks for example. No master keys, privately owned.'

'We'll see.' Dunross smiled.

On Kowloon side, Bartlett jumped from the wharf to the pitching boat, helped Orlanda aboard. Automatically she kicked off her high heels to protect the fine teak deck.

'Welcome aboard the *Sea Witch*, Mr. Bartlett. Evening,

Orlanda,' Gornt said with a smile. He was at the helm and at once he motioned to his deckhand who cast off from the wharf that was near the Kowloon ferry terminal. 'I'm delighted you accepted my invitation to dinner, Mr. Bartlett.'

'I didn't know I had one until Orlanda told me half an hour ago . . . hey, this's a great boat!'

Gornt jovially put the engines into slow astern. 'Until an hour ago I didn't know you two were going to dinner by yourselves. I presumed you'd never seen Hong Kong harbor by night so I thought it'd make a change for you. There were a couple of things I wanted to discuss privately so I asked Orlanda if she'd mind if I invited you aboard.'

'I hope it was no trouble to come Kowloon side.'

'No trouble, Mr. Bartlett. It's routine to pick up guests here.' Gornt smiled a secret smile, thinking about Orlanda and all the other guests he had fetched from this Kowloon wharf over the years. Deftly Gornt backed the motor cruiser away from the Kowloon dock near Golden Ferry where the waves slapped the quay dangerously. He put the engine levers into half ahead and swung the tiller starboard to get out into the roads and set a westerly course.

The boat was seventy feet, trim, elegant, sparkling and she handled like a speedboat. They were on the bridge deck, glass-sided, open to the air aft, awnings overhead tight and crackling in the breeze, the wake churning. Gornt wore rough, casual sea clothes, a light reefer jacket and a jaunty peaked cap sporting the Yacht Club emblem. The clothes and his trimmed black, grey-flecked beard suited him. He swayed easily with the motion of the boat, very much at home

Bartlett was watching him, at home too in sneakers and casual sweat shirt. Orlanda was beside him and he could feel her though they were not touching. She wore a dark evening pants suit and a shawl against the sea cold and she stood swaying easily, the wind in her hair, tiny without shoes.

He looked aft across the harbor at the ferries, junks, liners and the immense bulk of the battle-gray nuclear carrier, her decks floodlit, her flag fluttering bravely. A jet shrieked into the night sky from Kai Tak and incoming jets approaching Kowloon were stacked up.

He could not see the airport or his own airplane from this

angle but he knew where it was parked. This afternoon he had visited it with police permission to check and fetch some papers and provisions.

Orlanda, beside him, touched him casually and he looked at her. She smiled back and he was warmed.

'Great, isn't it?'

Happily she nodded. There was no need to answer. Both knew.

'It is,' Gornt said, thinking that Bartlett was talking to him and looked around at him. 'It's grand to be afloat at night, master of your own craft. We go west, then almost due south around Hong Kong—about three quarters of an hour.' He beckoned his captain who was nearby, a silent lithe Shanghainese wearing neat, starched white ducks.

'*Shey-shey*,' thank you, the man said taking the helm.

Gornt waved to the chairs aft around a table. 'Shall we?' He glanced at Orlanda. 'You're looking very pretty, Orlanda.'

'Thank you,' she said.

'You're not too cold?'

'Oh no, Quillan, thank you.'

A liveried steward came from below. On his tray were hot and cold canapés. In the ice bucket beside the table was an opened bottle of wine, four glasses, two cans of American beer and some soft drinks. 'What can I offer you, Mr. Bartlett?' Gornt asked. 'The wine's Frascati but I hear you prefer iced cold beer out of the can?'

'Tonight Frascati—beer later, if I may?'

'Orlanda?'

'Wine please, Quillan,' she said calmly, knowing that he knew she preferred Frascati to any other wine. I'll have to be very wise tonight, she thought, very strong and very wise and very clever. She had agreed to Gornt's suggestion at once for she, too, loved the water at night and the restaurant was a favorite though she would have preferred to have been alone with Linc Bartlett. But it was clearly an . . . No, she thought, correcting herself. It wasn't an order, it was a request. Quillan's on my side. And in this, my side and his side have the same aim in common: Linc. Oh how I enjoy Linc!

When she looked at him she saw he was watching Gornt. Her heart quickened. It was like once when Gornt had taken her to

Spain and she had seen a *mano a mano*. Yes, these two men are like matadors tonight. I know Quillan still desires me whatever he says. She smiled back at him, her excitement in place. 'Wine would be fine for me.'

It was dark on deck, the lighting comfortable and intimate. The steward poured, this wine as always very good, delicate, dry and enticing. Bartlett opened an air carry bag that he had brought with him. 'It's an old American custom to bring a gift the first time you go to a home—I guess this is a home.' He put the wine bottle on the table.

'Oh that's very kind of . . .' Gornt stopped. Delicately he picked up the bottle and stared at it, then got up and looked at it under the binnacle light. He sat down again. 'That's not a gift, Mr. Bartlett, that's bottled magic. I thought my eyes were deceiving me.' It was a Château Margaux, one of the great *premier cru* clarets from the Médoc in the province of Bordeaux. 'I've never had the '49. That was a dream year for clarets. Thank you. Thank you very much.'

'Orlanda said you liked red better than white but I guessed we might have some fish.' Casually he put the second bottle beside the first.

Gornt stared at it. It was a Château Haut-Brion. In good years Château Haut-Brion red compared with all the great Médocs, but the white—dry, delicate and little known because it was so scarce—was considered one of the finest of all the great Bordeaux whites. The year was '55.

Gornt sighed. 'If you know so much about wines, Mr. Bartlett, why do you drink beer?'

'I like beer with pasta, Mr. Gornt—and beer before lunch. But wine with food.' Bartlett grinned. 'Come Tuesday, we'll have beer with the pasta, then Frascati or Verdicchio or the Umbrian Casale with . . . with what?'

'*Piccata?*'

'Great,' Bartlett said, not wanting any *piccata* other than Orlanda's. 'That's just about my favorite.' He kept his attention on Gornt and did not glance at Orlanda but he knew she knew what he meant. I'm glad I tested her.

'Oh did you have a good time?' she had said when she had called for him this morning at the small hotel on Sunning Road. 'Oh I do hope so, Linc, darling.'

1028

The other girl had been beautiful but there had been no feeling other than lust, the satisfaction of the joining minimal. He had told her.

'Oh then that's my fault. We chose wrong,' she had said unhappily. 'Tonight we'll have dinner and we'll try somewhere else.'

Involuntarily he smiled and looked at her. The sea breeze was making her more beautiful. Then he noticed Gornt watching them. 'Are we eating fish tonight?'

'Oh yes. Orlanda, did you tell Mr. Bartlett about Pok Liu Chau?'

'No, Quillan, just that we've been invited for a sail.'

'Good. It won't be a banquet but the seafood there's excellent, Mr. Bartlett. You pi—'

'Why don't you call me Linc and let me call you Quillan? The "mister" bit gives me indigestion.'

They all laughed. Gornt said, 'Linc, with your permission we'll not open your gift tonight. Chinese food's not for these great wines, they wouldn't complement each other. I'll keep them, if I may, for our dinner Tuesday?'

'Of course.'

There was a small silence within the muted thunder of the diesel engines below. Immediately sensing Gornt wanted privacy, Orlanda got up with a smile. 'Excuse me a second, I just want to powder my nose.'

'Use the forward cabins, the forward gangway, Orlanda,' Gornt said, watching her.

'Thank you,' she said and walked off, in one way glad, in another hurt. The forward cabins were for guests. She would have automatically gone down this gangway to the main cabin, to the toilet off the master suite—the suite that once was theirs. Never mind. The past is the past and now there's Linc, she thought, going forward.

Bartlett sipped his wine, wondering why Orlanda had seemed to hesitate. He concentrated on Gornt. 'How many does this boat sleep?'

'Ten comfortably. There's a regular crew of four—captain-engineer, a deckhand, cook and steward. I'll show you around later if you like.' Gornt lit a cigarette. 'You don't smoke?'

'No, no thanks.'

'We can cruise for a week without refueling. If necessary. We still conclude our deal on Tuesday?'

'That's still D Day.'

'Have you changed your mind? About Struan's?'

'Monday'll still decide the battle. Monday at 3:00 P.M. When the market closes, you've got Ian or you haven't and it's a standoff again.'

'This time it won't be a standoff. He's ruined.'

'It sure as hell looks that way.'

'Are you still going to Taipei with him?'

'That's still the plan.'

Gornt took a deep drag of his cigarette. His eyes checked the lie of his ship. They were well out into the main channel. Gornt got up and stood beside the captain a moment but the captain had also seen the small unlit junk ahead and he skirted it without danger. 'Full ahead,' Gornt said and came back. He refilled the glasses, chose one of the deep-fried *dim sum* and looked at the American. 'Linc, may I be blunt?'

'Sure.'

'Orlanda.'

Bartlett's eyes narrowed. 'What about her?'

'As you probably know, she and I were very good friends once. Very good. Hong Kong's a very gossipy place and you'll hear all sorts of rumors, but we're still friends though we haven't been together for three years.' Gornt looked at him under his shaggy black-gray eyebrows. 'I just wanted to say that I wouldn't want her harmed.' His teeth glinted with his smile in the gimbaled light over the table. 'And she's as fine a person and companion as you could find.'

'I agree.'

'Sorry, don't want to belabor anything, just wanted to make three points, one man to another. That was the first. The second's that she's as closed-mouthed as any woman I've ever known. The third's that she's nothing to do with business—I'm not using her, she's not a prize, or bait or anything like that.'

Bartlett let the silence hang. Then he nodded. 'Sure.'

'You don't believe me?'

Bartlett laughed. It was a good laugh. 'Hell, Quillan, this's Hong Kong! I'm out of my depth in more ways than you can shake a stick at. I don't even know if Pok Liu Chau's the name of the restaurant, a part of Hong Kong or in Red China.' He drank the wine, enjoying it. 'As to Orlanda, she's great and you've no need to worry. I got the message.'

'I hope you don't mind my mentioning it.'

Bartlett shook his head. 'I'm glad you did.' He hesitated, then because the other man was open he decided to get everything into the open. 'She told me about the child.'

'Good.'

'Why the frown?'

'I'm just surprised she'd mention her now. Orlanda must like you very much.'

Bartlett felt the power of the eyes watching him and he tried to read if there was envy there. 'I hope she does. She said you'd been great to her since you split. And to her folks.'

'They're nice people. It's rough in Asia to raise five children, raise them well. It was always our company policy to help families where we could.' Gornt sipped his wine. 'The first time I saw Orlanda was when she was ten. It was a Saturday at the races in Shanghai. In those days everyone would dress up in their best clothes and stroll the paddocks. It was her first formal coming out. Her father was a manager in our shipping division —a good fellow, Eduardo Ramos, third-generation Macao, his wife pure Shanghainese. But Orlanda . . .' Gornt sighed. 'Orlanda was the prettiest girl I'd ever seen. Her dress was white . . . I don't remember seeing her after that until she came back from school. She was almost eighteen then and, well, I fell madly in love with her.' Gornt looked up from his glass. 'I can't tell you how lucky I felt all those years with her.' His eyes hardened. 'Did she tell you I broke the man who seduced her?'

'Yes.'

'Good. Then you know it all.' Gornt added with great dignity, 'I just wanted to mention my three points.'

Bartlett felt a sudden warmth toward the other man. 'I appreciate them.' He leaned forward to accept more wine. 'Why don't we leave it this way. Come Tuesday all debts and friendships are canceled and we start fresh. *All of us.*'

'Meanwhile, which side are you on?' Gornt asked, the front of his face a smile.

'For the raid, yours, one hundred percent!' Bartlett said at once. 'For Par-Con's probe into Asia? I'm in the middle. I wait

1031

for the winner. I lean toward you and I hope you're the winner, but I'm waiting.'

'The two aren't the same?'

'No. I set the ground rules of the raid way back. I said the raid was a onetime operation, a fool's mate.' Bartlett smiled. 'Sure, Quillan, I'm a hundred percent with you on the raid—didn't I put up the 2 million with no chop, no paper, just a handshake?'

After a pause, Gornt said, 'In Hong Kong, sometimes that's more valuable. I haven't the exact figures but on paper we're between 24 and 30 million HK ahead.'

Bartlett raised his glass. 'Hallelujah! But meanwhile how about the bank run? How will that affect us?'

Gornt frowned. 'I don't think it will. Our market's very volatile but Blacs and the Vic are solid, unbreakable, the government has to support both of them. There's a rumor the governor'll declare Monday a bank holiday and close the banks for as long as needed—it's just a matter of time before cash becomes available to stop the loss of confidence. Meanwhile, a lot will get burned and a lot of banks will go to the wall but that shouldn't affect our plan.'

'When do you buy back in?'

'That depends on when you dump Struan's.'

'How about noon Monday? That gives you plenty of time before closing for you and your secret nominees to buy after the news leaks and the shares go down some more.'

'Excellent. Chinese work on rumors, very much, so the market can swing from boom to bust or vice versa very easily. Noon is fine. You'll do that in Taipei?'

'Yes.'

'I'll need a telex confirmation.'

'Casey'll give it to you.'

'She knows? About the plan?'

'Yes. Now she does. How many shares do you need for control?'

'You should have that information.'

'That's the only piece missing.'

'When we buy in we'll have enough to give us at least three immediate seats on the board and Ian's through. Once we're on the board Struan's is in our power, and then, very soon, I merge Struan's with Rothwell-Gornt.'

'And you're tai-pan of the Noble House.'

'Yes.' Gornt's eyes glinted. He refilled the glasses. 'Health!'
'Health!'

They drank, content with their deal. But in their secret hearts
neither trusted the other, not even a little. Both were very glad
they had contingency plans—if need be.

Grim-faced, the three men came out of Government House and
got into Crosse's car. Crosse drove. Sinders sat in the front,
Rosemont in the back and both of them held on tightly to their
still unread copies of the AMG files. The night was dark, the sky
scudding and the traffic heavier than usual.

Rosemont, sitting in the back, said, 'You think the guv'll read
the originals before he shreds them?'

'I would,' Sinders replied without turning to look at him.

'Sir Geoffrey's much too clever to do that,' Crosse said. 'He
won't shred the originals until your copy's safely in the
minister's hands, just in case you don't arrive. Even so he's far
too shrewd to read something that could be an embarrassment
to Her Majesty's plenipotentiary and therefore Her Majesty's
Government.'

Again there was a silence.

Then, unable to hold back anymore, Rosemont said coldly
'What about Metkin? Eh? Where was the foul-up, Rog?'

'Bombay. The aircraft had to have been sabotaged there, if it
was sabotage.'

'For chrissake, Rog, gotta be. Of course someone was tipped.
Where was the leak? Your goddamn mole again?' He waited but
neither man answered him. 'What about the *Ivanov*, Rog? You
going to impound her and make a sudden search?'

'The governor checked with London and they thought it
unwise to create an incident.'

'What the hell do those meatheads know?' Rosemont said
angrily. 'She's a spy ship, for chrissake! Betcha fifty to a bent
hatpin we'd get current code books, a look at the best surveillance gear in the USSR and five or six KGB experts. Huh?'

'Of course, you're right, Mr. Rosemont,' Sinders said thinly.
'But we can't, not without the necessary approval.'

'Let me and my guys d—'

'Absolutely not!' Irritably Sinders took out his cigarettes. The pack was empty. Crosse offered his.

'So you're going to let 'em get away with it?'

'I'm going to invite the captain, Captain Suslev, to HQ tomorrow and ask him for an explanation,' Sinders said.

'I'd like to be party to that.'

'I'll consider it.'

'You'll have an official okay before 9:00 A.M.'

Sinders snapped, 'Sorry, Mr. Rosemont, but if I wish I can override any directives from your brass while I'm here.'

'We're allies for chrissake!'

Crosse said sharply, 'Then why did you raid 32 Sinclair Towers, uninvited?'

Rosemont sighed and told them.

Thoughtfully Sinders glanced at Crosse, then back to Rosemont. 'Who told you that it was an enemy safe house, Mr. Rosemont?'

'We've a wide network of informers here. It was part of a debriefing. I can't tell you who but I'll give you copies of the sets of fingerprints off the glass we got if you want them.'

Sinders said, 'That would be very useful. Thank you.'

'That still doesn't absolve you from a fatuous, unauthorized raid,' Crosse said coldly.

'I said I'm sorry, okay?' Rosemont flared and his chin jutted. 'We all make mistakes. Like Philby, Burgess and Maclean! London's so goddamn smart, eh? We've a hot tip you've a fourth guy—higher up, equally well placed and laughing at you.'

Crosse and Sinders were startled. They glanced at one another. Then Sinders craned around. 'Who?'

'If I knew, he'd be jumped. Philby got away with so much of our stuff it cost us millions to regroup and recode.'

Sinders said, 'Sorry about Philby. Yes, we all feel very bad about him.'

'We all make mistakes and the only sin's failure, right? If I'd caught a couple of enemy agents last night you'd be cheering. So I failed. I said I'm sorry, okay? I'll ask next time, okay?'

Crosse said, 'You won't but it would save us all a lot of grief if you did.'

'What have you heard about a fourth man?' Sinders asked,

his face pale, the stubble of his beard making him appear even more soiled than he was.

'Last month we busted another Commie ring, Stateside. Shit, they're like roaches. This cell was four people, two in New York, two in Washington. The guy in New York was Ivan Egorov, another officer in the UN Secretariat.' Rosemont added bitterly, 'Jesus, why don't our side wake up that the goddamn UN's riddled with plants, and the best Soviet weapon since they stole our goddamn bomb! We caught Ivan Egorov and his wife Alessandra passing industrial espionage secrets, computers. The guys in Washington, both'd taken American names of real people who were dead: a Roman Catholic priest and a woman from Connecticut. The four bastards were tied in with a joker from the Soviet Embassy, an attaché who was their controller. We pounced on him trying to recruit one of our CIA guys to spy for them. Sure. But before we ordered him out of the States, we frightened him enough to blow the cover on the other four. One of them tipped us that Philby wasn't kingpin, that there was a fourth man.'

Sinders coughed and lit another cigarette from the stub of the other. 'What did he say. Exactly?'

'Only that Philby's cell was four. The fourth's the guy who inducted the others, the controller of the cell and the main link to the Soviets. Rumor was he's up there. VVIP.'

'What sort? Political? Foreign Office? Gentry?'

Rosemont shrugged. 'Just VVIP.'

Sinders stared at him, then went back into his shell. Crosse swung into Sinclair Road, and stopped at his own apartment to let Sinders off, then drove to the consulate that was near Government House. Rosemont got a copy of the fingerprints then guided Crosse to his office. The office was large and well stocked with liquor. 'Scotch?'

'Vodka with a dash of Rose's lime juice,' Crosse said, eyeing the AMG files that Rosemont had put carelessly on his desk.

'Health.' They touched glasses. Rosemont drank his Scotch deeply. 'What's on your mind, Rog? You've been like a cat on a hot tin roof all day.'

Crosse nodded at the files. 'It's them. I want that mole. I want Sevrin smashed.'

Rosemont frowned. 'Okay,' he said after a pause, 'let's see what we got.'

He picked up the first file, put his feet on the desk and began reading. It took him barely a couple of minutes to finish, then he passed it over to Crosse who read equally fast. Quickly they went through the files one by one. Crosse closed the last page of the last one and handed it back. He lit a cigarette.

'Too much to comment on now,' Rosemont muttered absently.

Crosse caught an undercurrent in the American's voice and wondered if he was being tested. 'One thing jumps out,' he said, watching Rosemont. 'These don't compare in quality with the other one, the one we intercepted.'

Rosemont nodded. 'I got that too, Rog. How do you figure it?'

'These seem flat. All sorts of questions are unanswered. Sevrin's skirted, so's the mole.' Crosse toyed with his vodka then finished it. 'I'm disappointed.'

Rosemont broke the silence. 'So either the one we got was unique and different, written differently, or these're phonies or phonied up?'

'Yes.'

Rosemont exhaled. 'Which leads back to Ian Dunross. If these're phony, he's still got the real ones.'

'Either actually, or in his head.'

'What do you mean?'

'He's supposed to have a photographic memory. He could have destroyed the real ones and prepared these, but still remember the others.'

'Ah, so he could be debriefed if he . . . if he's cheated us.'

Crosse lit another cigarette. 'Yes. If the powers-that-be decided it was necessary.' He looked up at Rosemont. 'Of course, any such debriefing would be highly dangerous and would have to be ordered solely under the Official Secrets Act.'

Rosemont's used face became even grimmer. 'Should I take the ball and run?'

'No. First we have to be sure. That should be relatively easy.' Crosse glanced at the liquor cabinet. 'May I?'

'Sure. I'll take another shot of whiskey.'

Crosse handed him the refill. 'I'll make a deal with you: You really cooperate, completely, you don't do anything without

1036

telling me in advance, no secrets, no jumping the gun . . .'

'In return for?'

Crosse smiled his thin smile and took out some photocopies. 'How would you like to influence, perhaps even control, certain presidential hopefuls—perhaps even an election?'

'I don't follow you.'

Crosse passed over the letters of Thomas K. K. Lim that Armstrong and his team had acquired in the raid on Bucktooth Lo two days before. 'It seems that certain very rich, very well-connected U.S. families are in league with certain U.S. generals to build several large but unnecessary airfields in Vietnam, for personal gain. This documents the how, when and who.' Crosse told him where and how the papers had been found and added, 'Isn't Senator Wilf Tillman, the one that's here now, a presidential hopeful? I imagine he'd make you head of the CIA for these goodies—*if* you wanted to give them to him. These two're even juicier.' Crosse put them on the desk. 'These document how certain rather well-connected politicians and the same well-connected families have got congressional approval to channel millions into a totally fraudulent aid program in Vietnam. 8 millions have already been paid over.'

Rosemont read the letters. His face went chalky. He picked up the phone. 'Get me Ed Langan.' He waited a moment, then his face went suddenly purple. 'I don't give a goddamn!' he rasped. 'Get off your goddamn butt and get Ed here right now.' He slammed the phone back onto its hook, cursing obscenely, opened his desk, found a bottle of antacid pills and took three. 'I'll never make fifty at this rate,' he muttered. 'Rog, this joker, Thomas K. K. Lim, can we have him?'

'If you can find him, be my guest. He's somewhere in South America.' Crosse put down another paper. 'This's Anti-Corruption's confidential report. You shouldn't have any trouble tracking him.'

Rosemont read it. 'Jesus.' After a pause he said, 'Can we keep this between us? It's liable to blow the roof off a couple of our national monuments.'

'Of course. We have a deal? Nothing hidden on either side?'

'Okay.' Rosemont went to the safe and unlocked it. 'One good turn deserves another.' He found the file he was looking for, took out some papers, put the file back and relocked the safe. 'Here, these're photocopies. You can have 'em.'

The photocopies were headed 'Freedom Fighter' dated this month and last month. Crosse went through them quickly and whistled from time to time. They were espionage reports, their quality excellent. All the items dealt with Canton, happenings in and around that vital capital city of Kwantung Province: troop movements, promotions, appointments to the local presidiums and Communist Party, floods, food shortages, the military, numbers and types of East German and Czechoslovak goods available in the stores. 'Where'd you get these?' he asked.

'We've a cell operating in Canton. This's one of their reports, we get them monthly. Shall I give you a copy?'

'Yes. Yes thank you. I'll check it out through our sources for accuracy.'

'They're accurate, Rog. Of course top secret, yes? I don't want my guys blown like Fong-fong. We'll keep this between you'n me, okay?'

'All right.'

The American got up and put out his hand. 'And Rog, I'm sorry about the raid.'

'Yes.'

'Good. As to this joker, Lim, we'll find him.' Rosemont stretched wearily then went and poured himself another drink. 'Rog?'

'No thanks, I'll be off,' Crosse said.

Rosemont stabbed a blunt finger at the letters. 'About those, thanks. Yeah, thanks but . . .' He stopped a moment, near tears of rage. 'Sometimes I'm so sick to my stomach what our own guys'll do for goddamn dough even if it's a goddamn pile of goddamn gold I'd like to die. You know what I mean?'

'Oh yes!' Crosse kept his voice kind and gentle but he was thinking, How naive you are, Stanley!'

In a moment he left and went to police HQ and checked out the fingerprints in his private files, then got back into his car and headed haphazardly toward West Point. When he was sure that he was not being followed, he stopped at the next phone booth and dialed. In a moment the phone was picked up at the other end. No answer, just breathing. At once Crosse coughed Arthur's dry hacking cough and spoke in a perfect imitation of Arthur's voice. 'Mr. Lop-sing please.'

'There's no Mr. Lop-*ting* here. Sorry, you have a wrong number.'

Contentedly Crosse recognized Suslev. 'I want to leave a message,' he said continuing the code in the same voice that both he and Jason Plumm used on the telephone, both of them finding it very useful to be able to pretend to be Arthur whenever necessary, thus further covering each other and their real identities.

When the code was completed, Suslev said, 'And?'

Crosse smiled thinly, glad to be able to dupe Suslev. 'I've read the material. So has Our Friend.' Our friend was Arthur's code name for himself, Roger Crosse.

'Ah! And?'

'And we both agree it's excellent.' Excellent was a code word meaning counterfeit or false information.

A long pause. 'So?'

'Can our friend contact you, Saturday at four?' Can Roger Crosse contact you tonight at 10:00 P.M. at safe phones?

'Yes. Thank you for calling.' Yes. Message understood.

Crosse replaced the receiver.

He took out another coin and dialed again.

'Hello?'

'Hello, Jason, this's Roger Crosse,' he said affably.

'Oh hello, Superintendent, this's a pleasant surprise,' Plumm replied. 'Is our bridge game still on for tomorrow?' Did you make the intercept of the AMG files?

'Yes,' Crosse said, then added casually, 'But instead of six could we make it eight?' Yes, but we're safe, no names were mentioned.

There was a great sigh of relief. Then Plumm said, 'Shall I tell the others?' Do we meet tonight as arranged?

'No, no need to disturb them tonight, we can do that tomorrow.' No. We'll meet tomorrow.

'Fine. Thank you for calling.'

Crosse went back down the crowded street. Very pleased with himself, he got into his car and lit a cigarette. I wonder what Suslev—or his bosses—would think if they knew I was the real Arthur, not Jason Plumm. Secrets within secrets within secrets and Jason the only one who knows who Arthur really is!

He chuckled.

The KGB would be furious. They don't like secrets they're not party to. And they'd be even more furious if they knew it was I who inducted Plumm and formed Sevrin, not the other way around.

It had been easy to arrange. When Crosse was in Military Intelligence in Germany at the tail end of the war, information was whispered to him privately that Plumm, a signals expert, was operating a clandestine transmitter for the Soviets. Within a month he had got to know Plumm and had established the truth of this but almost immediately the war had ended. So he had docketed the information for future use—to barter with, or against a time he might want to switch sides. In espionage you never know when you're being set up, or betrayed, or being sold for something or someone more valuable. You always need secrets to barter with, the more important the secrets the safer you are, because you never know when you or an underling or overling will make the mistake that leaves you as naked and as helpless as a spiked butterfly. Like Voranski. Like Metkin. Like Dunross with his phony files. Like Rosemont with his naive idealism. Like Gregor Suslev, his fingerprints from the glass now on record with the CIA and so in a trap of my own choosing.

Crosse laughed aloud. He let in the clutch, easing out into the traffic. Switching sides and playing them all off against each other makes life exciting, he told himself. Yes, secrets really do make life very exciting indeed.

61

9:45 P.M.:

Pok Liu Chau was a small island southwest of Aberdeen, and dinner the best Chinese food Bartlett had ever had. They were on their eighth course, small bowls of rice. Traditionally rice was the last dish at a banquet.

'You're not really supposed to eat any, Linc!' Orlanda laughed. 'That sort of dramatizes to your host that you're full to bursting!'

'You can say that again, Orlanda! Quillan, it's been fantastic!'

'Yes, yes it was, Quillan,' she echoed. 'You chose beautifully.'

The restaurant was beside a small wharf near a fishing village —drab and lit with bare bulbs and furnished with oilcloth on the tables and bad chairs and broken tiles on the floor. Behind it was an alley of fish tanks where the daily catch of the island was kept for sale. Under the proprietor's direction they chose from what was swimming in the tanks: prawns, squid, shrimps, lobster, small crabs and fish of all kinds of shapes and sizes.

Gornt had argued with the proprietor over the menu, settling with what fish they could settle on. Both were experts and Gornt a valued customer. Later they had sat down at a table on the patio. It was cool and they drank beer, happy together, the three of them. All knew that at least during dinner there was a truce and no need for guards.

In moments the first dish had arrived—mounds of succulent quick-fried shrimps, sea-sweet and as delicious as any in the world. Then tiny octopus with garlic and ginger and chili and all the condiments of the East. Then some chicken wings deep fried which they ate with sea salt, then the great fish steamed with soy and slivers of fresh green onions and ginger and laid on a platter, the cheek, the delicacy of the fish, given to Bartlett as the honored guest. 'Jesus, when I saw this dump, sorry, this place, I figured you were putting me on.'

'Ah, my dear fellow,' Gornt said, 'you have to know the Chinese. They aren't concerned with the surroundings, just the food. They'd be very suspicious of any eating place that wasted money on decoration or tablecloths or candles. They want to see what they eat—hence the harsh light. Chinese are at their best eating. They're like Italians. They love to laugh and eat and drink and belch. . . .'

They all drank beer. 'That goes best with Chinese food though Chinese tea's better—it's more digestive and breaks down all the oil.'

'Why the smile, Linc?' Orlanda asked. She was sitting between them.

'No reason. It's just that you really know how to eat here. Say, what's this?'

She peered at the dish of fried rice mixed with various kinds of fish. 'Squid.'

'What?'

The others laughed and Gornt said, 'The Chinese say if its back faces heaven it's edible. Shall we go?'

As soon as they were back on board and out to sea, away from the wharf, there was coffee and brandy. Gornt said, 'Will you excuse me for a while? I've got some paper work to do. If you're cold, use the forward stateroom.' He went below.

Thoughtfully Bartlett sipped his brandy. Orlanda was across from him and they were lounging in the deck chairs on the aft deck. Suddenly he wished that this was his boat and they were alone. Her eyes were on him. Without being asked, she moved closer and put her hand on the back of his neck, kneading the muscles gently and expertly.

'That feels great,' he said, wanting her.

'Ah,' she replied, very pleased, 'I'm very good at massage, Linc. I took lessons from a Japanese. Do you have a regular massage?'

'No.'

'You should. It's very important for your body, very important to keep every muscle tuned. You tune your aircraft, don't you? So why not your body? Tomorrow I'll arrange it for

1042

you.' Her nails dug into his neck mischievously. 'She's a woman, but not to be touched, *heya!*'

'Come on, Orlanda!'

'I was teasing, silly,' she told him at once, brightly, taking away the sudden tension easily. 'This woman's blind. In olden days in China and even today in Taiwan, blind people are given a monopoly on the art and business of massage, their fingers being their eyes. Oh yes. Of course there are lots of quacks and charlatans who pretend to have knowledge but don't, not really. In Hong Kong you soon know who's real and who isn't. This is a very tiny village.' She leaned forward and brushed her lips against his neck. 'That's because you're beautiful.'

He laughed. 'I'm supposed to say that.' He put his arm around her, bewitched, and gave her a little hug, very conscious of the captain at the helm ten feet away.

'Would you like to go forward and see the rest of the ship?' she asked.

He stared at her. 'You a mind reader too?'

She laughed, her lovely face a mirror of joy. 'Isn't it the girl's part to notice if her . . . if her date's happy or sad or wanting to be alone or whatever? I was taught to use my eyes and senses, Linc. Certainly I try to read your mind but if I'm wrong you must tell me so that I can get better. But if I'm correct . . . doesn't that make it grander for you?' And so much easier to ensnare you beyond escape. To control you on a line you can so easily break if you wish, my art being to make the too thin line like a steel mesh.

Oh but that was not easy to learn! Quillan was a cruel teacher, oh so cruel. Much of my education was done in anger, Quillan cursing me, 'For chrissake can't you ever learn to use your bloody eyes? It should have been crystal clear when I came here that I was feeling rotten and had a rotten day! Why the hell didn't you get me a drink at once, touch me gently at once and then keep your bloody mouth shut for ten minutes while I recoup—just tender and understanding for ten bloody minutes and then I'd be fine again!'

'But Quillan,' she had whimpered through her tears, frightened by his rage, 'you came in so angrily you upset me and th—'

'I've told you fifty times not to be upset just because I'm bloody upset! It's your job to take the tension out of me! Use your bloody eyes and ears and sixth sense! All I need's ten minutes and I'm docile again and putty. For chrissake, don't I watch over you all the time? Don't I use my bloody eyes and try to defuse you? Every month at the same time you're always edgy, eh? Don't I take care to be as calm as possible then and keep you calmed? *Eh?*'

'Yes but d—'

'To hell with *but!* By God, now I'm in a worse temper than when I came in! It's your bloody fault because you're stupid, unwomanly, and you of all people should know better!'

Orlanda remembered how he had slammed out of the apartment and she had burst into tears, the birthday dinner she had cooked ruined and the evening wrecked. Later, he had come back, calm now, and had taken her into his arms and held her tenderly as she wept, sorry for the row that she agreed was unnecessary and her fault. 'Listen, Orlanda,' he had said so gently. 'I'm not the only man you'll have to control in this life, not the only one on whom you'll depend—it's a basic fact that women depend on some man, however rotten and evil and difficult. It's so easy for a woman to be in control. Oh so easy if you use your eyes, understand that men are children and, from time to time—most of the time—stupid, petulant and awful. But they supply the money and it's hard to do that, very hard. It's very hard to keep supplying the money day after day whoever you are. *Moh ching moh meng* . . . no money no life. In return the woman's got to supply the harmony—the man can't, not all the time. But the woman can *always* cheer her man if she wants to, can *always* take the poison out of him. *Always.* Just by being calm and loving and tender and understanding for such a short time. I'll teach you the game of life. You'll have a Ph.D. in survival, as a woman, but you've got to work . . .'

Oh how I worked, Orlanda thought grimly, remembering all her tears. But now I know. Now I can do instinctively what I forced myself to learn. 'Come on, let me show you the forward part of the ship.' She got up, conscious of the captain's eyes, and led the way confidently.

As they walked she slipped her arm momentarily in Linc's, then took the railing of the gangway and went below. The stateroom was big, with comfortable chaises and sofas and deep chairs fixed to the deck. The cocktail cabinet was well stocked.

'The galley's forward in the fo'c'sle with the crew quarters,' she said. 'They're cramped but good for Hong Kong.' A small corridor led forward. Four cabins, two with a double bunk, two with bunks one over the other. Neat and shipshape and inviting. 'Aft's Quillan's master stateroom and the master suite. It's luxurious.' She smiled thoughtfully. 'He enjoys the best.'

'Yes,' Bartlett said. He kissed her and she responded, fully responded. His desire made her limp and liquid and she let herself go into his desire, matching his passion, certain that he would stop and that she would not have to stop him.

The game had been planned that way.

She felt his strength. At once her loins pressed closer, moving slightly. His hands roved her and hers responded. It was glorious in his arms, better than she had ever known with Quillan who was always teacher, always in control, always unsharable. They were on the bunk when Bartlett backed off. Her body cried out for his, but still she exulted.

'Let's go back on deck,' she heard him say, his voice throaty.

Gornt crossed the fine stateroom and went into the master suite and locked the door behind him. The girl was sweetly asleep in the huge bed under the light blanket. He stood at the foot of the bed, enjoying the sight of her before he touched her. She came out of sleep slowly. '*Ayeeyah*, I slept so well, Honored Sir. Your bed is so inviting,' she said in Shanghainese with a smile and a yawn and stretched gloriously as a kitten would stretch. 'Did you eat well?'

'Excellently,' he replied in the same language. 'Was yours equally fine?'

'Oh yes, delicious!' she said politely. 'Boat Steward Cho brought the same dishes you had. I particularly liked the octopus with black bean and garlic sauce.' She sat up in the bed and leaned against the silk pillows, quite naked. 'Should I get dressed and come on deck now?'

'No, Little Kitten, not yet.' Gornt sat on the bed and reached out and touched her breasts and felt a little shiver run through her. Her Chinese hostess name was Beauty of the Snow and he had hired her for the evening from the Happy Hostess Night Club. He had considered bringing Mona Leung, his present girl

1045

friend instead, but she would be far too independent to remain below happily and only come on deck at his whim.

He had chosen Beauty of the Snow very carefully. Her beauty was extraordinary, in face and body and the texture of her skin. She was eighteen, and had been in Hong Kong barely a month. A friend in Taiwan had told him about her rarity and said that she was about to join the Happy Hostess Night Club from the sister club in Taiwan. Two weeks ago he had gone there and made an arrangement that had proved profitable to both of them. Tonight when Orlanda had told him she was dining with Bartlett and he had invited them aboard, at once he had called the Happy Hostess and bought Beauty of the Snow out of the club for the night and hurried her aboard.

'I'm playing a game on a friend tonight,' he had told her. 'I want you to stay here in this cabin, in this place, until I bring you on deck. It may be an hour or two but you are to stay here, quiet as a mouse, until I fetch you.'

'*Ayeeyah*, in this floating palace, I am prepared to stay a week without charge. Just my food and more of the champagne . . . though pillowing would be extra. May I sleep in the bed if I wish?'

'Certainly, but please shower first.'

'A shower? Bless all gods! Hot and cold water? That will be paradise—this water shortage is very unhygienic.'

Gornt had brought her tonight to taunt Orlanda if he decided he wanted to taunt her. Beauty of the Snow was much younger, prettier, and he knew that the sight of her wearing one of the elegant robes that once Orlanda had worn would send her into a spasm. All through dinner, he had chortled to himself, wondering when he should produce her for maximum effect: to excite Bartlett and to remind Orlanda that she was already old by Hong Kong standards, and that without his active help she would never get Bartlett, not the way she wanted.

Do I want her married to Bartlett? he asked himself, bemused.

No. And yet, if Orlanda were Bartlett's wife he would always be in my power because *she is and ever will be*. So far she hasn't forgotten that. So far she's been obedient and filial. And frightened.

He laughed. Oh revenge will be sweet when I lower the boom on you, my dear. As I will, one day. Oh yes, my dear, I haven't forgotten the snickers of all those smug bastards—Pug, Plumm, Havergill or Ian bloody Dunross—when they heard that you couldn't wait to leap into bed with a stud half my age.

Should I tell you now that you're my *mui jai?*

When Orlanda was thirteen her Shanghainese mother had come to see him. 'Times are very hard, Lord, our debts to the company are huge and your patience and kindess overwhelm us.'

'Times are bad for everyone,' he had told her.

'Unfortunately, since last week, my husband's department no longer exists. At the end of the month he is to leave, after seventeen years of service, and we cannot pay our debts to you.'

'Eduardo Ramos is a good man and will easily find a new and better position.'

'*Yin ksiao shih ta,*' she had said: We lose much because of a small thing.

'Joss,' he had said, hoping the trap was sprung and all the seeds he had sown would, at long last, bear fruit.

'Joss,' she had agreed. 'But there is Orlanda.'

'What about Orlanda?'

'Perhaps she could be a *mui jai.*' A *mui jai* was a daughter given by a debtor to a creditor forever, in settlement for debts that could not otherwise be paid—to be brought up as the creditor wished, or used or given away as the creditor wished. It was an ancient Chinese custom, and quite legal.

Gornt remembered the glow he had felt. The negotiations had taken several weeks. Gornt agreed to cancel Ramos's debts—the debts that Gornt had so carefully encouraged, agreed to reinstate Ramos, giving the man a modest guaranteed pension and help in setting up in Portugal, and to pay for Orlanda's schooling in America. In return the Ramoses guaranteed to provide Orlanda to him, virgin and suitably enamored, on or before her eighteenth birthday. There would be no refusal. 'This, by all the gods, will be a perpetual secret between us. I think, too, it would be equally better to keep it secret from her, Lord, forever. But we know and she will know where her rice bowl lies.'

Gornt beamed. The good years were worth all the patience and planning and the little money involved. Everyone gained, he told himself, and there is enjoyment yet to come.

Yes, he thought and concentrated on Beauty of the Snow. 'Life is very good,' he said, fondling her.

'I am happy you're happy, Honored Sir. I am happy too. Your shower was a gift of the gods. I washed my hair, everything.' She smiled. 'If you don't want me to play the prank yet on your friends, would you care to pillow?'

'Yes,' he said, delighted as always by the forthrightness of a Chinese pillow partner. His father had explained it early: 'You give them money, they give you their youth, the Clouds and the Rain and entertain you. In Asia it's a fair and honorable exchange. The more their youth, the more the laughter and gratification, the more you must pay. That's the bargain, but don't expect romance or real tears—that's not part of their commitment. Just temporary entertainment and pillowing. Don't abuse the fairness!'

Happily Gornt took off his clothes and lay beside her. She ran her hands over his chest, the hair dark, muscles sleek, and began. Soon she was making the small noises of passion, encouraging him. And though she had been told by the mama-*san* that this *quai loh* was different and there was no need to pretend, instinctively she was remembering the first rule of being a pillow partner to strangers: 'Never let you body become involved with a customer for then you cannot perform with taste or daring. Never forget, when with a *quai loh*, you must always pretend to enjoy him greatly, always pretend to achieve the Clouds and the Rain, otherwise he'll consider that somehow it's an affront to his masculinity. *Quai loh* are uncivilized and will never understand that the yin cannot be bought and that your gift of coupling is for the customer's enjoyment solely.'

When Gornt was finished and his heart had slowed, Beauty of the Snow got out of bed and went to the bathroom and showered again, singing happily. In euphoria he rested and put his hands under his head. Soon she came back with a towel. 'Thank you,' he said and dried himself and she slid in beside him once more.

'Oh I feel so clean and marvelous. Shall we pillow again?'

'Not now, Beauty of the Snow. Now you can rest and I will let my mind wander. You have settled the yang very favorably. I will inform the mama-*san*.'

'Thank you,' she said politely. 'I would like you as my special customer.'

He nodded, pleasured by her and her warmth and sensuousness. When would it be best for her to come on deck? he asked himself again, quite confident that Bartlett and Orlanda would be there now and not in bed as a civilized person would be.

A chuckle went through him.

There was a porthole beside the bed and he could see the lights of Kowloon in the distance, Kowloon and the dockyard of Kowloon. The engines throbbed sweetly, and in a moment he got out of bed and went to the cupboard. In it were some very expensive nightdresses and underthings and multicolored robes and rich lounging housecoats that he had bought for Orlanda. It amused him to keep them for others to wear.

'Make yourself very pretty and put this on.' He gave her a yellow silk, floor-length *cheong-sam* that had been one of Orlanda's favorites. 'Wear nothing underneath.'

'Yes, certainly. Oh, how beautiful it is!'

He began to dress. 'If my prank works you may keep it, as a bonus,' he said.

'Oh! Oh, then everything will be as you wish,' she said fervently, her open avarice making him laugh.

'We're going to drop my passengers Hong Kong side first.' He pointed out of the porthole. 'You see that big freighter, the one tied up at the wharf with the Hammer and Sickle flag?'

'Ah yes, Lord. The ship of ill-omen? I see it now!'

'When we are broadside please come on deck.'

'I understand. What should I say?'

'Nothing. Just smile sweetly at the man and the woman, then at me and come below again and wait for me here.'

Beauty of the Snow laughed. 'Is that all?'

'Yes, just be sweet and beautiful and smile—particularly at the woman.'

'Ah! Am I to like her or hate her?' she asked at once.

'Neither,' he said, impressed with her shrewdness, ecstatically aware that they would both loathe each other on sight.

In the privacy of his cabin aboard the *Sovetsky Ivanov*, Captain Gregor Suslev finished encoding the urgent message, then sipped some vodka, rechecking the cable. 'Ivanov to Center. Arthur reports the files may be counterfeit. His friend will supply me with copies tonight. Delighted to report Arthur's friend also intercepted the carrier information. Recommend he be given an immediate bonus. I have had extra copies sent by mail to Bangkok for the pouch, also London and Berlin for safety.'

Satisfied, he put the code books back into the safe and locked it, then picked up the phone. 'Send me the duty signalman. And the first officer.' He unbolted the cabin door then went back and stared out of the porthole at the carrier across the harbor, then saw the passing pleasure cruiser. He recognized the *Sea Witch*. Idly he picked up his binoculars and focused. He saw Gornt on the aft deck, a girl and another man with his back toward him sitting around a table. His high-powered lenses raked the ship and his envy soared. That bastard knows how to live, he thought. What a beauty! If only I could have one such as her on the Caspian, berthed at Baku!

Not so much to pray for, he told himself, watching the *Sea Witch* pass, not after so much service, so profitable to the cause. Many commissars do—senior ones.

Again his glasses centered the group. Another girl came up from below, an Asian beauty, and then there was a polite knock on his door.

'Evening, Comrade Captain,' the signalman said. He accepted the message and signed for it.

'Send it at once.'

'Yes sir.'

The first officer arrived. Vassili Boradinov was a tough, good-looking man in his thirties, captain, KGB, graduate of the espionage department of Vladivostok University with a master mariner's ticket. 'Yes, Comrade Captain?'

Suslev handed him a decoded cable from the pile on his desk. It read: 'First Officer Vassili Boradinov will assume Dimitri Metkin's duties as commissar of the *Ivanov* but Captain Suslev will be in complete command on all levels until alternate arrangements are made.'

'Congratulations,' he said.

Boradinov beamed. 'Yes sir. Thank you. What do you want me to do?'

1050

Suslev held up the key to the safe. 'If I fail to contact you or return by midnight tomorrow, open the safe. Instructions are in the package marked "Emergency One". They will tell you how to proceed. Next . . .' He handed him a sealed envelope. 'This gives two phone numbers where I can be reached. Open it only in an emergency.'

'Very well.' Sweat beaded the younger man's face.

'No need to worry. You're perfectly capable of taking command.'

'I hope that will not be necessary.'

Gregor Suslev laughed. 'So do I, my young friend. Please sit down.' He poured two vodkas. 'You deserve the promotion.'

'Thank you,' Boradinov hesitated. 'What happened to Metkin?'

'The first thing is he made a stupid and unnecessary mistake. Next, he was betrayed. Or he betrayed himself. Or the god-cursed SI tailed him and caught him. Or the CIA pegged him. Whatever happened, the poor fool should never have exceeded his authority and put himself into such danger. Stupid to risk himself, to say nothing of our whole security. Stupid!'

The first officer shifted nervously in his chair. 'What's our plan?'

'To deny everything. And to do nothing for the moment. We're due to sail on Tuesday at midnight; we can keep to that plan.'

Boradinov looked out of the porthole at the carrier, his face tight. 'Pity. That material could have jumped us forward a quantum.'

'What material?' Suslev asked, his eyes narrowing.

'Didn't you know, sir? Before Dimitri left, the poor fellow whispered he'd heard that this time we were to get some incredible information—a copy of the guidance system and a copy of their armament manifest, including atomics—that's why he was going himself. It was too important to trust to an ordinary courier. I must tell you I volunteered to go in his place.'

Suslev covered his shock that Metkin had confided to anyone. 'Where did he hear that?'

The other man shrugged. 'He didn't say. I presume the American sailor told him when Dimitri took the call at the phone box to arrange the drop.' He wiped a bead of sweat away.

'They'll break him, won't they?'

'Oh yes,' Suslev said thinly, wanting his subordinate suitably indoctrinated. 'They can break anyone. That's why we have to be prepared.' He fingered the slight bulge of the poison capsule in the point of his lapel and Boradinov shuddered. 'Better to have it quickly.'

'Bastards! They must have been tipped to capture him before he did it. Terrible. They're all animals.'

'Did . . . did Dimitri say anything else? Before he left?'

'No, just that he hoped we'd all get a few weeks' leave—he wanted to visit his family in his beloved Crimea.'

Satisfied that he was covered, Suslev shrugged. 'A great pity. I liked him very much.'

'Yes. Such a shame when he was due to retire so soon. He was a good man even though he made such a mistake. What will they do to him?'

Suslev considered showing Boradinov one of the other decoded cables on his desk that said in part: '. . . Advise Arthur that, following his request for a Priority One on the traitor Metkin, an immediate intercept was ordered for Bombay.' No need to give away that information, he thought. The less Boradinov knows the better. 'He'll just vanish—until we catch a bigger fish of theirs to use as an exchange. The KGB look after their own,' he added piously, not believing it, knowing that the younger man did not believe it either, but the saying of it was obligatory and policy.

They'd have to exchange me, he thought, very satisfied. Yes, and very quickly. I know too many secrets. They're my only protection. If it wasn't for what I know they'd order a Priority One on me as fast as they did on Metkin. So would I if I was them. Would I have bit my lapel as that stupid turd should have done?

A shudder went through him. I don't know.

He sipped his vodka. It tasted very good to him. I don't want to die. This life is too good.

'You're going ashore again, Comrade Captain?'

'Yes.' Suslev concentrated. He handed the younger man a note he had typed and signed. 'You're in command now. Here's your authority—post it on the bridge.'

'Thank you. Tomorr—' Boradinov stopped as the ship's intercom came on and the urgent voice said rapidly: 'This's the bridge! There's two police cars converging on the main gangway filled with police . . .' Both Suslev and Boradinov blanched. '. . . about a dozen of them. What should we do? Stop them, repel them, what do we do?'

Suslev jerked the sending switch on. 'Do nothing!' He hesitated then switched on the ship's intercom. 'All hands: Emergency, Red One . . .' This order meant: 'Hostile visitors are coming aboard. Radio and radar rooms: arm destructs on all secret equipment.' He switched the sender off and hissed at Boradinov, 'Go on deck, down the gangway, greet them, delay for five minutes then *invite* the leaders aboard, only them if you can. *Go on!*'

'Surely they daren't come aboard to sear—'

'Intercept them—*now!*'

Boradinov rushed out. Once alone Suslev armed the secret destruct on his safe. If anyone but him tried to open it now its incendiary napalm would obliterate everything.

He tried to put his panicked mind at ease. Think! Is everything covered against a sudden search? Yes. Yes we've done the Red One drill a dozen times. But God curse Roger Crosse and Arthur! Why the devil didn't we get a warning? Was Arthur caught? Or Roger? *Kristos*, let it not be Roger! What ab—'

His eyes caught the pile of coded and decoded cables. Frantically he scooped them into an ashtray, cursing himself for not doing it earlier, not knowing if there was enough time now. He found his lighter. His fingers were trembling. The lighter flamed as the intercom crackled on: 'Two men're coming aboard with Boradinov, two men, the rest're staying below.'

'All right, but delay them. I'll come on deck.' Suslev doused the flame with a curse and stuffed the cables in his pocket. He grabbed a half-empty vodka bottle, took a deep breath, put a broad beam on his face and went on deck. 'Ah, welcome aboard! What's the trouble, eh?' he said, a slight slur now in his voice, keeping up his well-known cover. 'One of our sailors has himself in trouble, Superintendent Armstrong?'

'This is Mr. Sun. May we have a word with you?' Armstrong said.

'Of course, of course!' Suslev said with a forced joviality he did not feel. He had never seen the Chinese before. He

1053

examined the cold-eyed, sallow, hate-filled face. 'Follow me please,' he said, then added in Russian to Boradinov who spoke perfect English, 'You too,' then again to Armstrong with continuing forced good humor. 'Who's going to win the fifth race, Superintendent?'

'I wish I knew, sir.'

Suslev led the way to the small wardroom that adjoined his cabin. 'Sit down, sit down. Can I offer you tea or vodka? Orderly, bring tea and vodka!'

They came quickly. Expansively Suslev poured vodka even though the two policemen refused politely. '*Prosit*,' he said and laughed jovially. 'Now what's the trouble?'

'It seems that one of your crew is engaged in espionage against Her Majesty's Government,' Armstrong said politely.

'Impossible, *tovarich!* Why joke with me, eh?'

'We've caught one. Her Majesty's Government is really quite upset.'

'This is a peaceful freighter, trading. You've known us for years. Your Superintendent Crosse has watched us for years. We don't deal in espionage.'

'How many of your crew are ashore, sir?'

'Six. Now listen, I don't want any trouble. I've had enough cursed trouble this voyage already with one of my innocent seamen murdered by unkn—'

'Ah yes, the late Major Yuri Bakyan of the KGB. Very unfortunate.'

Suslev pretended sullen anger. 'His name was Voranski. I know nothing of this major you talk about. I know nothing about that, nothing.'

'Of course. Now, sir, when are your sailors back from shore leave?'

'Tomorrow, at dusk.'

'Where are they staying?'

Suslev laughed. 'They're ashore, on leave. Where else should they be but with a girl or in a bar? With a girl, eh, happily, eh?'

'Not all of them are,' Armstrong said coldly. 'At least one is very miserable right now.'

Suslev watched him, glad that he knew Metkin was gone forever and they could not bluff him. 'Come now, Superintendent, I know nothing about any espionage.'

Armstrong put the eight-by-ten photos on the table. They showed Metkin going into the restaurant, then under guard, then being hustled into the Black Maria, then a mug shot of him, terror in the face.

'*Kristos!*' Suslev gasped, a consummate actor. 'Dimitri? It's impossible! It's another false arrest! I will have my gov—'

'It's already been reported to your government in London. Major Nicoli Leonov admitted espionage.'

Now Suslev's shock was real. He had never expected Metkin to break so quickly. 'Who? Who did you say?'

Armstrong sighed. 'Major Nicoli Leonov of your KGB. That's his real name and rank. He was also political commissar on this ship.'

'Yes . . . yes that is true but his . . . his name is Metkin, Dimitri Metkin.'

'Oh? You have no objection if we search this ship?' Armstrong began to get up. Suslev was aghast, Boradinov equally.

'Oh yes I object,' Suslev stuttered. 'Yes, Superintendent, so sorry but I formally object, and I mu—'

'If your ship is not engaged in espionage and is a peaceful freighter why should you object?'

'We have international protections. Unless you have a formal search warrant th—'

Armstrong's hand went into his pocket and Suslev's stomach turned over. He would have to comply with a formal warrant and then he would be ruined because they would find more evidence than even they could ever hope for. That god-cursed son of a whore bitch Metkin must've told them something vital. He wanted to shout in rage, the decoded and coded messages in his pocket suddenly lethal. His face had gone white. Boradinov was paralyzed. Armstrong's hand came out of his pocket with only a pack of cigarettes. Suslev's heart began again though his nausea still almost overwhelmed him. '*Matyeryebyets!*' he muttered.

'Sir?' Armstrong asked innocently. 'Is anything the matter?'

'No, no, nothing.'

'Would you care for an English cigarette?'

Suslev fought for control, wanting to smash the other man for tricking him. Sweat was on his back and on his face. He took the cigarette shakily. 'These things are . . . are terrible, eh? Espionage and searches and threats of searches.'

'Yes. Perhaps you'd be kind enough to leave tomorrow, not Tuesday.'

'Impossible! Are we being hounded like rats?' Suslev blustered, not knowing how far he dare go. 'I will have to inform my government and th—'

'Please do. Please tell them we have intercepted Major Leonov of the KGB, caught him in an espionage act, and that he has been charged under the Official Secrets Act.'

Suslev wiped the sweat off his face, trying to stay calm. Only the knowledge that Metkin was probably dead now kept him in one piece. But what else did he tell them, he was shrieking in his head, what else? He looked at Boradinov who was standing beside him, white-faced.

'Who're you?' Armstrong asked sharply, following his glance.

'First Officer Boradinov,' the younger man said, his voice strangled.

'Who's the new commissar, Captain Suslev? Who took over from your Mr. Leonov? Who's the senior Party man aboard?'

Boradinov went ashen and Suslev was thankful that some of the pressure was turned off him.

'Well?'

Suslev said, 'He is. First Officer Boradinov.'

At once Armstrong put his icy eyes on the younger man. 'Your full name please?'

'Vassili Boradinov, first officer,' the man stuttered.

'Very well, Mr. Boradinov, you're responsible for getting this ship under way by midnight Sunday at the latest. You are formally warned we have reason to believe there might be an attack on you by triads—by Chinese bandits. The rumor is the attack's planned for the early hours of Monday—just after midnight Sunday. It's a very strong rumor. Very. There are lots of Chinese bandits in Hong Kong, and Russians have stolen lots of Chinese land. We are concerned for your safety and health. I suggest it politic . . . eh?'

Boradinov was ashen. 'Yes, yes, I understand.'

'But my . . . my repairs,' Suslev began. 'If my repai—'

'Please see they're completed, Captain. If you need extra help or a tow outside Hong Kong waters, just ask. Oh yes, and would you be kind enough to appear at police headquarters at 10:00 A.M. Sunday—sorry about the weekend.'

Suslev blanched. 'Eh?'

'Here's your formal invitation.' Armstrong handed him an official letter. Suslev accepted it, began to read as Armstrong took out a second copy, wrote in Boradinov's name. 'Here's yours, Commissar Boradinov.' He shoved it into his hand. 'I suggest you confine the rest of your crew aboard—with the exception of yourselves of course—and bring your shore party back right smartly. I'm sure you'll have lots to do. Good night!' he added with startling suddenness, got up and went out of the wardroom, closing the door behind him.

There was a stunned silence. Suslev saw Malcolm Sun get up and leisurely head for the door. He got up to follow but stopped as the Chinese whirled on them.

'We'll get you, all of you!' Sun said malevolently.

'For what? We've done nothing,' Boradinov gasped. 'We've d—'

'Espionage. Spying? You KGB think you're so clever, *matyeryebyets!*'

'You get the hell off my ship,' Suslev snarled.

'We'll get you all—I don't mean us police . . .' Abruptly Malcolm Sun switched to fluent Russian. 'Get out of our lands, hegemonists! China's on the march! We can lose fifty million soldiers, a hundred and still have double that left. Get out while you've time!'

'We'll blast you off the earth!' Suslev bellowed. 'We'll atomize all China. We'll—' He stopped. Malcolm Sun was laughing at him.

'Your mother's tit in your atomics! We've our own atomics now! You start we finish. Atomics, fists, ploughshares!' Malcolm Sun's voice dropped. 'Get out of China while you've the chance. We're coming out of the East like Genghis Khan, all of us, Mao Tse-tung, Chiang Kai-shek, me, my grandsons, their grandsons, we're coming and we'll clean you off the earth and take back all our lands, *all of them!*'

'*Get off my ship!*' Suslev felt his chest hurting. Almost blind with rage, he readied to hurl himself at his tormentor, Boradinov as well.

Unafraid, Malcolm Sun came back a pace. '*Yeb tvoyu mat*' Turdhead!' Then in English, 'Hit me and I'll arrest you for assault and impound your ship!'

With a great effort the two men stopped. Choked with rage, Suslev stuffed his fists into his pockets. 'Please, you will . . . you will leave. Please.'

'*Dew neh loh moh* on you, your mother, your father and the whole of your turd-eating Soviet hegemonists!'

'You—will—leave—now.'

Equally enraged, Sun cursed them in Russian and shouted back, 'We're coming out of the East like locusts. . . .' Then there was a sudden noisy altercation outside on deck and a slight dull boom. At once he turned and went for the door, the other two rushing after him.

Appalled, Suslev saw that now Armstrong was standing at the doorway of the radio room which was next to his cabin. The door was burst open, the two frightened operators staring at the Englishman, aghast, paralyzed deckhand guards nearby. Already the beginning of smoke was welling from the innards of the radio equipment. Red One ordered the senior radio man to trigger the destruct on the secret scrambling device the instant a hostile opened the door or tried to break the lock.

Armstrong turned to face Suslev. 'Ah, Captain, so sorry, I stumbled. So sorry,' he said innocently. 'I thought this was the loo.'

'What?'

'The toilet. I stumbled and the door burst open. So sorry.' The policeman glanced back into the radio room. 'Good God! It seems there's a fire. I'll call the fire brigade at once. Malcolm, get th—'

'No . . . no!' Suslev said, then snarled in Russian to Boradinov and the deck crew, 'Get the fire out!' He jerked a fist out of his pocket and shoved Boradinov into motion. Unnoticed by him his cuff caught one of his decoded cables and it fell onto the deck. Smoke was pouring out from behind one of the complex radio panels. Already one of the deckhands had a fire extinguisher.

'Dear oh dear! What could have happened? You're sure you don't want assistance?' Armstrong asked.

'No, no thank you.' Suslev said, his face mottled with rage,

1058

'thank you, Superintendent. I'll . . . I'll see you Sunday.'

'Good night, sir. Come along, Malcolm.' In the growing confusion Armstrong headed for the gangway but stooped and before Suslev realized what was happening picked up the piece of paper and was halfway down the gangway, Malcolm Sun following him.

Appalled, Suslev's hand went to his pocket. Forgetting the fire he rushed into his cabin to check which cable was missing.

Below on the wharf, uniformed police had long since fanned out, covering both gangways. Armstrong was getting into the back of the car beside Sinders. The eyes of the chief of MI-6 were dark-rimmed and his suit a little rumpled but he was icily alert. 'Well done, you two! Yes. I imagine that'll interrupt their communications for a day or so.'

'Yes sir.' Armstrong began rummaging in his pocket for his lighter, his heart pounding. Sinders watched Malcolm Sun get into the driver's seat.

'What's the matter?' he asked thoughtfully, seeing his face.

'Nothing, nothing really, sir.' Malcolm Sun craned around, the sweat on his back, his heart hurting and the sick-sweet excitement rage-fear taste still in his mouth. 'When . . . when I was conducting delaying tactics for the superintendent I . . . they got me going, those two bastards.'

'Oh? How?'

'Just . . . they started cursing, so I . . . I just cursed them back.' Sun faced the front, settled himself, not wanting Sinder's penetrating eyes on his. 'Just cursing,' he added, trying to sound light.

'Pity one of them didn't hit you.'

'Yes, yes I was ready.'

Sinders glanced at Armstrong briefly as the big man clicked the lighter on, lit a cigarette and, under the light of the flame, peered at the paper. Sinders glanced up at the ship above. Once more Suslev was standing at the head of the gangway staring down at them. 'He looks very angry indeed. Good.' The flicker of a smile went over him. 'Very good.' With Sir Geoffrey's approval he had ordered the sudden arrival and attempt to disrupt the *Ivanov*'s communications—and complacency—to

1059

put pressure on Arthur and the Sevrin moles, hoping to flush them out. 'And our police mole,' Sir Geoffrey had added grimly. 'It's impossible that Brian Kwok's the spy mentioned in the AMG papers. Eh?'

'I agree,' he had said.

Armstrong clicked the lighter off. In the semidarkness of the car he hesitated. 'You'd better get the detail organized, Malcolm. No need to waste any more time here. All right, Mr. Sinders?'

'Yes. Yes we can go now.'

Obediently Malcolm Sun left. Armstrong was watching Suslev on the deck. 'You, er, you read Russian, don't you sir?'

'Yes, yes I do. Why?'

Carefully Armstrong passed over the paper, holding it by the edges. 'This fell out of Suslev's pocket.'

Equally carefully Sinders took the paper but his eyes never left Armstrong's. 'You don't trust senior agent, Sun?' he asked softly.

'Yes. Oh yes. But Chinese are Chinese and it's in Russian. I don't read Russian.'

Sinders frowned. After a moment he nodded. Armstrong lit the flame for him. The older man scanned the paper twice and sighed. 'It's a weather report, Robert. Sorry. Unless it's in code, it's just a meteorological report.' Carefully he folded the paper in its original creases. 'The fingerprints might be valuable. Perhaps it's code. Just for safety I'll pass it on to our cipher fellows.'

Sinders settled back more comfortably in the car. The paper read: 'Advise Arthur that following his request for a Priority One on the traitor Metkin, an immediate intercept was ordered for Bombay. Second, the meeting with the American is brought forward to Sunday. Third and final, the AMG files continue to be Priority One. Maximum effort must be made by Sevrin to achieve success. Center.'

Now which American? Sinders asked himself patiently, and is it Arthur's meeting or whose? Captain Suslev? Is he as innocent as he appears? Which American? Bartlett, Tcholok, Banastasio or who? Peter Marlowe—Anglo-American-Know-all writer with his curious theories?

Did Bartlett or Tcholok make contact with Center in June in Moscow when they were there, with or without Peter Marlowe,

1060

who also happened to be there when a highly secret meeting of foreign agents was taking place?

Or is the American not a visitor at all but someone who lives here in Hong Kong?

Is it Rosemont? Or Langan? Both would be perfect.

So much to wonder about.

Like who's the fourth man? Who's the VVIP above Philby? Where will those threads lead? Into *Burke's Peerage?* Perhaps to some castle, or even a palace?

Who's this mysterious Mrs. Gresserhoff who took Kiernan's second call and then vanished like a smoke ring?

And what about those bloody files? What about bloody AMG and bloody Dunross trying to be so bloody clever. . . .

It was getting toward midnight and Dunross and Casey were sitting happily side-by-side in the glassed-in forward section of one of the Golden Ferries, which swerved confidently toward its berth Kowloon side. It was a good night though the clouds still scudded low. Canvas storm panels still closed in and protected the open part of the decks, but here where they were, the view was good and a fine sea-salt breeze came through one of the open windows.

'It is going to rain again?' she asked, breaking their comfortable silence.

'Oh yes. But I certainly hope the heavy stuff stays away till late tomorrow afternoon.'

'You and your races! Are they that important?'

'To all Hong Kong *yan*, oh yes. To me, yes and no.'

'I'll put my entire fortune on your Noble Star.'

'I wouldn't do that,' he said. 'You should always hedge a bet.'

Casey glanced across at him. 'Some bets you don't hedge.'

'Some bets you can't hedge,' he said, correcting her with a smile. Casually he lifted her arm and linked his with hers and settled his hand back in his lap. The contact pleased both of them. It was their first real touch. All during their stroll from the Mandarin Hotel to the ferry Casey had wanted to take his arm. But she had fought back the impulse and now she pretended not to notice their interlinking though, instinctively, she had moved a fraction closer.

'Casey, you never finished your story of George Toffer—did you fire him?'

'No, no I never did, not as I thought I would. When we'd won control I went to his boardroom. Of course he was fit to be tied but by that time I'd found out he wasn't the hero he claimed to be and a few other things. He just waved one of my letters about the money he owed me in my face and shouted that I'd never get that back, never.' She shrugged. 'I never did, but I got his company.'

'What happened to him?'

'He's still around, still cheating someone. Say, can we stop talking about him, it gives me indigestion.'

He laughed. 'Perish that thought! Terrific night, isn't it?'

'Yes.' They had dined impeccably in the Dragon Room atop the skyscraper hotel. Chatcaubriand, a few thread-thin French fries, salad and *crème brûlée*. The wine was Château Lafite.

'Celebration?' she had asked.

'Just a thank you for the First Central New York.'

'Oh, Ian! They agreed?'

'Murtagh agreed to try.'

It had taken just a few seconds to fix the terms based on the bank's agreeing to the financing that Casey had laid out as possible: 120 percent of the cost of both ships, a 50 million revolving fund. 'Everything covered by your personal guarantee?' Murtagh had asked.

'Yes,' he had said, committing his future and his family's future.

'We, er, I figure with Struan's great management you'll make a profit so our money's secure and . . . but Mr. Dunross, sir, we gotta keep this secret as hell. Meanwhile, I'll give it the old college try.' Murtagh was trying to hide his nervousness.

'Please do, Mr. Murtagh. The very best old college try you can. How about joining me for the races tomorrow? Sorry, I can't invite you to lunch, I'm crammed to the gills and over-booked, but here, here's a pass if you're free to join us from 2:30 on.'

'Oh Jesus, tai-pan, you mean it?'

Dunross smiled to himself. In Hong Kong an invitation to a steward's box was like being presented at court, and just as useful.

1062

'Why the smile, tai-pan?' Casey asked, shifting slightly, feeling his warmth.

'Because all's well, at the moment, in the world. At least all the various problems are in their compartments.' Going ashore and out of the ferry terminal he explained his theory that the only way to deal with problems was the Asian way: to put them into individual compartments and take them up only when ready for them.

'That's good, if you can do it,' she said, walking close beside him but not touching now.

'If you can't you'll go under—ulcers, heart attack, old before your time, your health broken.'

'A woman cries, that's her safety valve. She cries and then she feels better. . . .' Casey had wept earlier, before leaving the V and A to meet him. Because of Linc Bartlett. Part rage, part frustration, part longing, and part need—physical need. It was six months since she had had one of her rare, very casual and very short affairs. When the need became too strong she would go away for a few days, skiing or sunning and she would choose whom she would allow into her bed. Then, as quickly, she would forget him.

'But oh, isn't it very bad, Ciran-Chek,' her mother had once said, 'to be so callous?'

'Oh no, Mama darling,' she had told her. 'It's a fair exchange. I enjoy sex—I mean I enjoy it when I'm in the mood, though I try to keep the mood as infrequent as possible. I love Linc and no one else. But I th—'

'How can you love him and go to bed with someone else?'

'It's, it's not easy, in fact, it's awful. But Mama, I work hard for Linc all hours, weekends and Sundays, I work hard for all of us, for you and Uncle Tashjian and Marian and the kids, I'm the wage earner now that Marian's on her own and I love it, truly I enjoy it, you know I do. But sometimes it all gets too much so I just go away. And that's when I choose a partner. Honestly, Mama, it's just biological, there's no difference that way between us and men, and now that we've the God-blessed pill *we* can choose. It's not like in your day, thank God, my darling . . .'

Casey stepped aside to avoid a phalanx of oncoming pedestrians and bumped Dunross slightly. Automatically she took his arm. He did not withdraw.

Since she had asked him for equality this afternoon and had been turned down . . . No, that's not fair, Casey, she told herself. Ian didn't turn me down, he just gave me the truth from his point of view. From mine? I don't know. I'm not sure. But the one thing I'm not is a fool and so tonight I dressed carefully, a little differently, and put on perfume and made my makeup more definite and tonight I bit my tongue three to thirty times and held back, not giving measure for measure, playing it more conventionally, saying sweetly, 'That's interesting!'

And most times it was. He was attentive, entertaining and receptive and I felt marvelous. Ian's certainly one helluva man. Dangerous and oh so tempting.

The wide marble steps up to the V and A were ahead. Discreetly she let go of his arm and felt nearer to him because of her understanding. 'Ian, you're a wise man. Do you think it's fair to make love to someone—if you don't love them?'

'Eh?' He was startled out of the pleasantness. Then he said lightly, '*Love* is a Western word, lady. Me, I'm *China*-man!'

'Seriously.'

He laughed. 'I don't think it's time to be serious.'

'But do you have an opinion?'

'Always.'

They went up the stairs into the foyer, crowded even this late. At once he felt many eyes and recognition which was why he had not left her on the steps. Every little helps, he thought. I must seem calm and confident. The Noble House is inviolate! I will not and cannot allow myself the luxury of normal fear—it would spill over and wreck others and do untold damage.

'Would you like a nightcap?' she asked. 'I'm not sleepy. Maybe Linc'll join us if he's in.'

'Good idea. Tea with lemon would be fine.' The smiling headwaiter appeared miraculously. And an empty table. 'Evening, tai-pan.'

'Evening, Nighttime Gup.'

'Tea and lemon's fine with me too,' she said. A waiter scurried away. 'I'll just check my messages.'

'Of course.' Dunross watched her walk away. Tonight, from the first moment in the Mandarin foyer, he had noticed how much more feminine she had seemed, nothing discernible just a subtle change. Interesting woman. A sexuality that's waiting to explode. How the devil can I help her to get her drop dead money quickly?

Nighttime Gup was bustling around and he said quietly in Cantonese, 'Tai-pan, we certainly hope you can deal with the stock market and Second Great House.'

'Thank you.' Dunross chatted awhile, exuding confidence, then his eyes strayed back to Casey at the front desk.

Nighttime Gup's shrewd old eyes twinkled. 'The gun-runner's not in the hotel, tai-pan.'

'Eh?'

'No. He left early with a girl. Around 7:00 P.M., I'd just come on duty,' the neat old man said airily. 'The gun-runner was dressed very casually. For a sail I imagine. A girl was with him.'

Dunross concentrated now. 'There are many girls in Hong Kong, Nighttime Gup.'

'Not like this one, tai-pai.' The old man guffawed carefully. 'Once she was the mistress of Black Beard.'

'Eeeee, old man, you have sharp eyes and a long memory. Are you sure?'

'Oh very sure!' Nighttime Gup was delighted with the way his news was received. 'Yes,' he added loftily, 'since we hear the Americans may be joining the Noble House if you can extricate yourself from all those other fornicators it might be good for you to know that. Also that Golden Pubics has moved her ro—'

'Who?'

Nighttime Gup explained the reason for the nickname. 'Can you imagine, tai-pan?'

Dunross sighed, astounded as always at how fast gossip traveled. 'She's changed her room?'

'Oh yes, it's along the corridor, 276, on the same floor. Eeeee, tai-pan, I heard she was weeping in the night, two nights ago, and again this evening before she left. Yes. Third Toiletmaid Fung saw her crying tonight.'

'They had a row? She and the gun-runner?'

'Oh no, not a row, no shoutings. But, *oh ko*, if Golden Pubics knows about the Orlanda flower that's cause enough for dragons to belch.' Nighttime Gup smiled toothily at Casey as she came back, a sheaf of cables and messages in her hand. Dunross noticed that now there was a shadow in her eyes. No message from Linc Bartlett, he surmised, getting up. Nighttime

1065

Gup solicitously pulled a chair away for her, poured her tea, continuing in his gutter Cantonese, 'Never mind, tai-pan, Golden Pubics or not it's all the same in the dark, *heya?*' The old man chuckled and left.

Dunross glanced at her papers. 'Trouble?'

'Oh no, just more of the same.' She looked at him direct, 'I've got them all compartmentalized for tomorrow. Tonight's mine. Linc's not back yet.' She sipped her tea, enjoying it. 'So I can monopolize you.'

'I thought I was doing the monopolizing. Isn't—' He stopped as he noticed Robert Armstrong and Sinders come in through the swing doors. The two men stood at the entrance, looking for a table.

'Your police work overtime,' Casey said, and, as the men's gaze fell on them, waved back half-heartedly. The two men hesitated, then went to a vacant table at the other end of the room. 'I like Armstrong,' she said. 'Is the other man police?'

'I imagine so. Where did you meet Robert?'

She told him. 'Still nothing on the smuggled guns. Where they came from or whatever.'

'Rotten business.'

'Would you like a brandy?'

'Why not? One for the road, then I must be going. Waiter!' He ordered the drinks. 'The car'll be here tomorrow at twelve sharp to pick you up.'

'Thank you. Ian, the invitation read, "Ladies Hats and Gloves". Do you really mean that?'

'Of course.' He frowned. 'Ladies have always worn hats and gloves at the races. Why?'

'I'll have to buy a hat. I haven't worn one in years.'

'Actually, I like ladies in hats.' Dunross glanced around the room. Armstrong and Sinders were watching him covertly. Is it a coincidence they're here? he wondered.

'You feel the eyes too, tai-pan? Everyone here seems to know you.'

'It's not me, it's just the Noble House and what I represent.'

The brandy came. 'Health!' They touched glasses.

'Will you answer my question now?'

'The answer's yes.' He swirled the brandy in the glass and inhaled it.

'Yes what?'

Abruptly he grinned. 'Yes nothing, yes it's not fair but yes it happens all the time and I'm not going to get into one of those lovely self-analyzing "Have you stopped beating your wife recently?" things, though I do hear that most ladies like being beaten occasionally but with great care, with or without hats!'

She laughed and most of her shadows vanished. 'It depends, does it?'

'It depends!' He watched her, his calm, easy smile on his face and he was thinking and she was thinking it depends on who and when and where and timing, circumstance and need, and right now it would be grand.

He reached out with his glass and touched hers. 'Health,' he said. 'And here's to Tuesday.'

She smiled back and lifted her glass, her heart quickening. 'Yes.'

'Everything can wait till then. Can't it?'

'Yes. Yes, I hope so, Ian.'

'Well, I'll be on my way.'

'I had a lovely time.'

'So did I.'

'Thanks for inviting me. Tomorr—' She stopped as Nighttime Gup bustled up to them.'

'Excuse me, tai-pan, telephone.'

'Oh, thank you. I'll be right there.' Dunross sighed. 'No peace for the wicked! Casey, shall we?'

'Sure, sure, tai-pan.' She got up too, her heart beating strongly, a sad sweet ache possessing her. 'I'll take care of the check!'

'Thanks, but that's already done. They'll just send it on to the office.' Dunross left a tip and guided her toward the elevator, both of them conscious of the eyes following them. For a second he was tempted to go upstairs with her just to set the tongues wagging. But that'd really be tempting the Devil and I've enough devils surrounding me already, he thought. 'Good night, Casey, see you tomorrow and don't forget cocktails 7:30 to 9:00 P.M. Give my best to Linc!' He waved cheerily and walked toward the front desk.

She watched him go, tall, immaculate and confident. The elevator doors closed. If this wasn't Hong Kong you wouldn't escape, not tonight, Ian Dunross. Oh no, tonight we'd make love. Oh yes, yes we would.

Dunross stopped at the front desk and picked up the phone. 'Hello, this is Dunross.'

'Tai-pan?'

'Oh hello, Lim,' he said, recognizing his majordomo's voice. 'What's up?'

'Mr. Tip Tok-toh just phoned, sir.' Dunross's heart picked up tempo. 'He asked me to try to reach you and would you please call him back. He said you could call him any time before two o'clock or after 7:00 A.M.'

'Thank you. Anything else?'

'Miss Claudia called at eight and said she's settled your guest . . .' There was a rustle of paper. '. . . Mrs. Gresserhoff at the hotel and that your appointment in your office at 11:00 A.M.'s confirmed.'

'Good. Next?'

'Missee called from London—everything fine there—and a Dr. Samson from London.'

'Ah!' Kathy's specialist. 'Did he leave a number?' Lim gave it to him and he scribbled it down. 'Anything else?'

'No, tai-pan.'

'Is Number One Daughter back yet?'

'No, tai-pan. Number One Daughter came in about 7:00 P.M. for a few minutes with a young man and then they left.'

'Was it Martin Haply?'

'Yes, yes it was.'

'Thanks, Lim. I'll call Tiptop then get a ferry home.'

He hung up. Wanting more privacy, he went to the phone booth that was near the stationer's. He dialed.

'Weyyyy?'

He recognized Tiptop's voice. 'Good evening, this's Ian Dunross.'

'Ah, tai-pan! Just a minute.' There was the sound of a hand being put over the mouthpiece and muffled voices. He waited. 'Ah, sorry to keep you waiting. I've had some very disquieting news.'

'Oh?'

'Yes. It seems your police once again are like dog's lungs and wolf's heart. They have falsely arrested a very good friend of

1068

yours, Superintendent Brian Kwok. He—'

'*Brian Kwok?*' Dunross gasped. 'But why?'

'I understand he's been falsely accused of being a spy for the PRC, an—'

'Impossible!'

'I agree. Ridiculous! Chairman Mao has no need of capitalist spies. He should be released at once, at once—and if he wishes to leave Hong Kong he should be permitted to do so and go wherever he wishes to go . . . at once!'

Dunross tried to get his mind working. If Tiptop said the man called Brian Kwok was to be released at once and permitted to leave Hong Kong if he wished, then Brian *was* a PRC spy, one of their spies, and that was impossible impossible impossible. 'I . . . I don't know what to say,' he said, giving Tiptop the opening he required.

'I must point out Old Friends could hardly be expected to consider assisting Old Friends when their police are so errored. *Heya*?'

'I agree,' he heard himself saying with the right amount of concern, his mind shouting, Christ almighty, they want to trade Brian for the money! 'I'll . . . I'll talk to the authorities first thing tom—'

'Perhaps you could do something tonight.'

'It's too late to call the governor now but . . .' Then Dunross remembered Sinders and Armstrong and his heart leaped. 'I'll try. At once. I'm sure there's some mistake. Mr. Tip. Yes. It must be a mistake. In any event I'm sure the governor will be helpful. And the police. Surely such a . . . a mistake could be handled satisfactorily—like the Victoria's request for the temporary use of the illustrious bank's cash?'

There was a long silence. 'It's possible that could be done. It's possible. Old Friends should assist Old Friends, and help correct mistakes. Yes, it could be possible.'

Dunross heard the unsaid *when* left hanging and automatically continued the negotiation, most of his mind still upset by what he had been told. 'Did you happen to get my note, Mr Tip? I've taken care of everything else. By the way, the Victoria will certainly assist the financing of the thorium.' He added delicately, 'Also most other further requests—at advantageous terms.'

1069

'Ah yes, thank you. Yes, I received your note and your very kind invitation. So sorry that I was unwell. Thank you, tai-pan. How long would your government require the cash loan, if it was possible?'

'I imagine thirty days would be more than enough, perhaps even two weeks. But it's the Victoria, Blacs and the other banks and not the Hong Kong Government. I could tell you that tomorrow. Do we have the privilege of seeing you at the races for lunch?'

'I regret not for lunch but perhaps after lunch, if that's possible.'

Dunross smiled grimly. The perfect compromise. 'Of course.'

'Thank you for calling. By the way, Mr. Yu was most impressed with you, tai-pan.'

'Please give him my regards. I look forward to seeing him soon. In Canton.'

'I was astonished to read your brother-in-law's comments about the Middle Kingdom.'

'Yes. So was I. My wife and her brother have been estranged for years. His views are alien, enemy and totally misguided.' Dunross hesitated. 'I hope to neutralize him.'

'Yes. Yes I agree. Thank you. Good night.' The phone went dead.

Dunross hung up. Christ! Brian Kwok! And I'd almost given him the AMG papers. Christ!

Collecting his wits with a great effort, he went back to the foyer. Armstrong and Sinders were still there. 'Evening, may I join you a moment?'

'Of course, Mr. Dunross. This is a pleasant surprise. May I offer you a drink?'

'Tea, Chinese tea. Thanks.'

Their table was away from others and when it was safe Dunross leaned forward. 'Robert, I hear you've arrested Brian Kwok,' he said still hoping it wasn't true. The two men stared at him.

'Who told you that?' Armstrong asked.

Dunross recounted his conversation. Both men listened noncommittally though from time to time he saw them glance at one another. 'Obviously it's a trade,' he told them. 'Him for cash.'

1070

Sinders sipped his hot chocolate. 'How important's the money?'

'Completely important, urgent and the sooner the better.' Dunross mopped his brow. 'The cash will completely stop the bank runs, Mr. Sinders. We've got t—' He stopped, aghast.

'What is it?' Sinders asked.

'I—I suddenly remembered what AMG wrote in the intercepted report. That the '. . . police mole may or may not be part of Sevrin.'' Is he?'

'Who?'

'For chrissake, don't play with me,' Dunross said angrily, 'this's serious. You think I'm a bloody fool? There's a Sevrin plant in Struan's. If Brian's part of Sevrin I've a right to know.'

'I quite agree,' Sinders said calmly though his eyes had become very flinty. 'The moment the traitor's uncovered you may rest assured you'll be informed. Have you any idea who it could be yet?'

Dunross shook his head, controlling his anger.

Sinders watched him. 'You were saying? "We've got to . . ." Got to what, Mr. Dunross?'

'We've got to get that cash at once. What's Brian done?'

After a moment Sinders said, 'Banks don't open till Monday. So Monday's D Day?'

'I imagine the banks will have to get the money before then— to open and have the money in the tills. What the devil's Brian done?'

Sinders lit a cigarette for himself and for Armstrong. 'If this person Brian actually has been arrested I don't think that's really a very discreet question, Mr. Dunross.'

'I'd've bet anything,' the tai-pan said helplessly, 'anything, but Tiptop'd never suggest a trade unless it was true. Never. Brian must be bloody important but Christ, what's the world coming to? Will you handle the trade or will Mr. Crosse—I suppose the governor's approval will be needed.'

Thoughtfully the chief of MI-6 blew the tip of his cigarette. 'I doubt if there will be a trade, Mr. Dunross.'

'Why not? The money's more impor—'

'That's a matter of opinion, Mr. Dunross, if this Brian Kwok actually is under arrest. In any event, Her Majesty's Government could hardly be subject to blackmail. Very poor taste.'

'Quite. But Sir Geoffrey will agree at once.'

'I doubt it. He impressed me as being much too clever to do that. As to trading, Mr. Dunross, I thought you were going to give us the AMG files.'

Dunross felt an ice pick in his stomach. 'I did, this evening.'

'For chrissake, don't play with me, this's serious! You think I'm a bloody fool?' Sinders said in exactly the same tone that Dunross had used. Abruptly he laughed dryly and continued with the same chilling calm, 'You certainly gave us a version of them but unfortunately they just don't compare in quality with the one intercepted.' The rumpled man's eyes became even more flinty and curiously menacing though his face did not change. 'Mr. Dunross, your subterfuge was deft, commendable but unnecessary. We really do want those files, the originals.'

'If those don't satisfy you, why not go through AMG's papers?'

'I did.' Sinders smiled without humor. 'Well, it's like the old highwayman saying, "The money or your life." Possession of those files may be lethal to you. You agree, Robert?'

'Yes sir.'

Sinders puffed his cigarette. 'So, Mr. Dunross, your Mr. Tiptop wants to trade, eh? Everyone in Hong Kong wants to trade. It's in the air. Eh? But to trade you have to get value for money. I imagine if you want concessions to get concessions from the *enemy* . . . well, all's fair in love and war, they say. Isn't it?'

Dunross kept his face guileless. 'So they say. I'll talk to the governor first thing. Let's keep this strictly confidential for the moment until I've talked to him. Night.'

They watched him walk through the swing doors and disappear.

'What do you think, Robert? Did Dunross switch the files on us?'

Armstrong sighed. 'I don't know. His face said nothing. I was watching closely. Nothing. But he's as sharp as a tack.'

'Yes.' Sinders pondered a moment. 'So the enemy want a trade, eh? I'd say we have possession of this particular client for twenty-four hours at the most. When do you do his next interrogation?'

'6:30 A.M.'

'Oh! Well if you've an early start we'd better be going.' Sinders called for the check. 'I'll consult with Mr. Crosse but I know what he'll say—what in fact London has ordered.'

'Sir?'

'They're very concerned because the client's been party to too many secrets, the General Staff Course, the Royal Canadian Mounted Police.' Sinders hesitated again. 'On second thoughts, now Robert, irrespective of what Mr. Dunross does our only course is to step up the debriefing. Yes. We'll cancel the 6:30 interrogation, continue with the hourly schedule, provided he's medically fit, and into the Red Room.'

Armstrong blanched. 'But si . . .'

'I'm sorry,' Sinders said, his voice gentle. 'I know he's a friend, was a friend, but now your Mr. Tiptop and your Mr. Dunross have taken away our time.'

SATURDAY

62

9:32 A.M.:

The JAL jet from Tokyo came in low over the sea and touched down perfectly at Kai Tak with a puff of smoke from its wheels. At once its engines went into reverse thrust and it howled toward the airport complex, decelerating.

Passengers, aircrew and visitors were milling in the busy terminal, Customs and Immigration and waiting areas. Outward-bound was easy. Incoming was mostly easy. Except for Japanese nationals. Chinese have long memories. The years of the Japanese war occupation of China and Hong Kong were too near, too strong, too vicious to forget. Or to forgive. So Japanese nationals were checked more thoroughly. Even members of the JAL crew now going through, even the pert, pretty, polite air hostesses, some of whom were hardly alive when the occupation had ended, they too were given back their travel documents with a frigid stare.

Next to them in line was an American. ''Morning,' he said handing his passport to the official.

''Morning.' The young Chinese flipped the book open and glanced at the photograph and at the man and leafed through to find the visa. Unnoticed, his foot touched a hidden switch. This alerted Crosse and Sinders who were in a nearby observation office. They went to the one-way mirror and looked at the man waiting at Immigration in front of one of the six crowded lines of passengers.

The passport, a year old, said, 'Vincenzo Banastasio, male, born New York City, August 16, 1910. Hair gray, eyes brown.' Casually the official checked the other visas and stamps: England, Spain, Italy, Holland, Mexico, Venezuela, Japan. He stamped the dull gray book, handed it back noncommittally.

Banastasio walked through the Customs, an expensive crocodile briefcase under his arm, carrying duty-free liquor in a gaudy plastic carrier, camera swinging off his shoulder.

'Good-looking fellow,' Sinders said. 'He takes care of himself.' They saw him disappear into the crowds. Crosse clicked on the portable CB. 'Do you have him covered?' he asked into it.

'Yes sir,' came the instant answer.

'I'll keep monitoring this frequency. Keep me advised.'

'Yes sir.'

To Sinders, Crosse said, 'We'll have no problem tailing him.'

'No. Glad I've seen him. I always like to see an enemy in the flesh.'

'Is he? Enemy?'

'Mr. Rosemont thinks so. Don't you?'

'I meant our enemy. I'm sure he's a crook—I meant I'm not sure he's tied into Intelligence.'

Sinders sighed. 'You've checked the bugs?'

'Yes.' Late last night a team of SI experts had secretly put bugs into the bedroom Banastasio had booked at the Hilton. Also the office and private suite of Photographer Ng, Vee Cee Ng.

They waited patiently. On the table the CB hissed and crackled slightly.

After a pause Sinders said absently, 'What about our other client?'

'Who? Kwok?'

'Yes. How long do you think it'll take?'

'Not long.' Crosse smiled to himself.

'When do you put him into the Red Room?'

'I thought noon might be rather apt. Before if he's ready '

'Armstrong'll do the interrogation?'

'Yes.'

'Armstrong's a good man. He handled himself very well at the *Ivanov*.'

'Next time would you mind keeping me advised? After all, this is my area.'

'Certainly, Roger. It was a sudden decision by London.'

'What's the idea? About the Sunday summons.'

'The minister is sending special instructions.' Sinders frowned. 'Brian Kwok's records say he's strong. We don't have too much time. He'll've been well indoctrinated to be hidden so deep, so long.'

'Oh yes. But I'm quite confident. Since I had the room built I've experimented on myself three times. The most I've ever stayed was five minutes and each time I was sick as a dog—and that was without any disorientation scheduling. I'm confident we'll have no problem.' Crosse stubbed out his cigarette. 'It's very effective—an exact pattern of the KGB prototype.'

After a moment Sinders said, 'Pity these methods have to be used. Very dicey. Disgusting really. I preferred it when . . . well, even then, I suppose our profession was never really clean.'

'You mean during the war?'

'Yes. I must say I preferred it then. Then there was no hypocrisy on the part of some of our leaders—or the media. Everyone understood we were at war. But today when our very survival's threatened we—' Sinders stopped, then pointed. 'Look, Roger, isn't that Rosemont?' The American was standing with another man by the exit door.

'Yes, yes it is. That's Langan with him. The FBI man,' Crosse said. 'Last night I agreed to a joint effort with him on Banastasio though I do wish those bloody CIA'd leave us alone to do our job.'

'Yes. They really are becoming quite difficult.'

Crosse picked up the CB and led the way outside. 'Stanley, we've got him well covered. We agreed last night that on this operation we handle this part, you handle the hotel. Right?'

'Sure, sure, Rog. 'Morning, Mr. Sinders.' Grim-faced, Rosemont introduced Langan who was equally taut. 'We're not interfering, Rog, though that bum is one of our nationals. That's not the reason we're here. I'm just seeing Ed off.'

'Oh?'

'Yes,' Langan said. He was as tired and gaunt as Rosemont. 'It's those photocopies, Rog. Thomas K. K. Lim's papers. I've got to deliver them personally. To the Bureau. I read part to my chief and his pots blew and he began to come apart at the seams.'

'I can imagine.'

'There's a request on your desk to let us have the originals and th—'

'No chance,' Sinders said for Crosse.

Langan shrugged. 'There's a request on your desk, Rog. Guess your brass'll send orders from heaven if ours really need them. I'd better get on board. Listen, Rog, we can't thank you enough. We—I owe you one. Those bastards . . . yeah we owe you one.' They shook hands and he hurried off onto the tarmac.

'Which piece of information blew the seams, Mr. Rosemont?'

'They're all lethal, Mr. Sinders. It's a coup for us, for us and the Bureau, mostly the Bureau. Ed said his folk went into hysterics. The political implications for Democrats and Republicans are immense. You were right. If Senator Tillman—the presidential hopeful who's in town right now—if he got hold of those papers, there's no telling what he'd do.' Rosemont was no longer his usual good-humored self. 'My brass telexed our South American contacts to put an all-points on Thomas K. K. Lim so we'll be interviewing him pretty damn soon—you'll get a copy don't worry. Rog, was there anything else?'

'I beg your pardon?'

'With these choice pieces, were there others we could use?'

Crosse smiled without humor. 'Of course. How about a blueprint for financing a private revolution in Indonesia?'

'Oh Jesus . . .'

'Yes. How about photostats of arrangements for payments into a French bank account of a very important Vietnamese lady and gentleman—for specific favors granted?'

Rosemont had gone chalky. 'What else?'

'Isn't that enough?'

'Is there more?'

'For chrissake, Stanley, of course there's more, you know it, we know it. There'll always be more.'

'Can we have them now?'

Sinders said, 'What can you do for us?'

Rosemont stared at them. 'Over lunch we'll ta—'

The CB crackled into life. 'The target's got his bags now and he's walking out of Customs, heading for the taxi rank . . . Now he's . . . Now he's . . . ah, someone's meeting him, a Chinese, good-looking man, expensive clothes, don't recognize him. . . . They're going over to a Rolls, registration HK. . . . ah, that's the hotel limousine. Both men're getting in.'

Into the sender Crosse said, 'Stay on this frequency.' He

switched frequences. Static and muffled traffic and noise.

Rosemont brightened. 'You bugged the limo?' Crosse nodded. 'Great, Rog. I'd've missed that!'

They listened, then clearly, '. . . good of you to meet me, Vee Cee,' Banastasio was saying. 'Hell you shouldn't've come all this wa—'

'Oh it's my pleasure,' the cultured voice replied. 'We can chat in the car, perhaps that'll save you coming to the office and then in Ma—'

'Sure . . . sure,' the American voice overrode the other man. 'Listen, I got something for you, Vee Cee . . .' Muffled sounds then a sudden high-pitched whine that totally dominated the airwave, completely obliterating the clarity and voices. At once Crosse switched frequencies but the others were operating perfectly.

'Shit, he's using a portable shaver to block us,' Rosemont said disgustedly. 'That bastard's a pro! Fifty to a blown cent they block all the bugs we got, hundred says when they come back on this channel it'll all be goddamn chitchat. I told you Banastasio was cream.'

63

'Tai-pan, Dr. Samson calling from London. He's on line three.'

'Oh thank you, Claudia.' Dunross punched the button. 'Hello, Doctor. You're up late.'

'I've just come back from the hospital—sorry not to call before. You were calling about your sister, Mrs. Gavallan?'

'Yes. How is she?'

'Well, sir, we've begun another stringent series of tests. Mentally, I must say she's in very good shape. I'm afraid physically not so good. . . .'

Dunross listened with a sinking heart as the doctor went into detail about multiple sclerosis, how no one really knew much about it, that there was no known cure and that the disease went in descending plateaus—once some deterioration of the nerve structure had taken place it was not possible with present medications to climb back to the previous level. 'I've taken the liberty of calling in Professor Klienberg from the clinc at UCLA in Los Angeles for a consultation—he's the world expert on the disease. Please rest assured we will do everything we can for Mrs. Gavallan.'

'It doesn't sound as if you can do anything at all.'

'Well, it's not quite as bad as that, sir. If Mrs. Gavallan takes care, rests, and is sensible, she can have a normal life for many years.'

'How long is many years?' Dunross heard the long hesitation. Oh Kathy, poor Kathy!

'I don't know. Many times this sort of problem's in the hands of God, Mr. Dunross. Patients do not follow the same time

1082

patterns. In Mrs. Gavallan's case I could answer you better in six months, perhaps by Christmas. Meanwhile, I have taken her on as a National Health patient so then—'

'No. She should be a private patient, Dr. Samson. Please send all bills to my office.'

'Mr. Dunross, there's no difference in the quality of service I give to her. She just has to wait a little while in my waiting room and be in a ward, not a private room at the hospital.'

'Please make her a private patient. I would prefer it, so would her husband.'

Dunross heard the sigh and hated it. 'Very well,' the doctor was saying. 'I have all your numbers and I'll call you the instant Professor Klienberg has made his examination and the tests are concluded.'

Dunross thanked him and replaced the phone. Oh Kathy, poor dear Kathy.

Earlier when he had got up at dawn he had talked to her and to Penelope. Kathy had said how much better she felt and how Samson was most encouraging. Penn had told him later that Kathy was looking very tired. 'It doesn't seem very good, Ian. Is there any chance you could come here for a week or two before October 10?'

'Not at the moment, Penn, but you never know.'

'I'm going to take Kathy to Avisyard as soon as she gets out of the hospital. Next week at the latest. She'll be better there. The land will make her better, don't worry, Ian.'

'Penn, when you get to Avisyard, would you go out to the Shrieking Tree for me?'

'What's the matter?'

He heard the concern in her voice. 'Nothing, darling,' he told her, thinking about Jacques and Phillip Chen—how can I explain about them? 'Nothing particular, just more of the same. I just wanted you to say hello to our real Shrieking Tree.'

'Our Jacaranda there's no good?'

'Oh yes, she's fine, but not the same. Perhaps you should bring a cutting back to Hong Kong.'

'No. Better we leave it where it is. Then you have to come home, don't you, Ian?'

'Can I make a bet for you this afternoon?'

Again a pause. 'Ten dollars on the horse you choose. I'll back your choice. I'll always back your choice. Call me tomorrow. Love you . . . 'bye.'

He remembered the first time she had said, I love you, and then, later, when he had asked her to marry him, all the refusals and then eventually, through shattering tears, the real reason: 'Oh Christ, Ian, I'm not good enough for you. You're upper class, I'm not. The way I talk now, I acquired. It was because I was evacuated at the beginning of the war to the country—my God I'd only been outside London twice in my whole life till then, just to the seaside. I was evacuated to a wonderful old manor house in Hampshire where all the other girls were from one of your fine upper class schools, Byculla was its name. There was a mix-up, Ian, my whole school went somewhere else, just me to Byculla, and it was only then that I found I talked different, differently—there, you see I still forget sometimes! Oh God, you've no idea how awful it was to find out so young . . . that I was common and talked common and that there are such limitless differences in England, the way we talk—the way we talk so important!

'Oh how I worked to imitate the others. They helped me and there was one teacher who was so wonderful to me. I hurled myself into the new life, theirs, and I swore to better myself and never go back, never, never, never, and I won't. But I can't marry you, my darling—let's just stay lovers—I'll never be good enough.'

But in time, her time, they had married. Granny Dunross had persuaded her. Penelope had agreed but only after going out to the Shrieking Tree, alone. She had never told him what she had said.

I'm lucky, Dunross thought. She's the best wife a man could have.

Since coming back from the track at dawn he had worked steadily. Half a hundred cables. Dozens of international phone calls. Countless locals. At 9:30 he had called the governor about Tiptop's proposal. 'I'll have to consult the minister,' Sir Geoffrey had said. 'The earliest I could call him would be four this afternoon. This must be kept entirely secret, Ian. Dear oh dear, Brian Kwok must be very important to them!'

'Or perhaps just another convenient concession for the money.'

'Ian, I don't think the minister will agree to trade.'

'Why?'

'Her Majesty's Government might consider it a precedent, a bad one. I would.'

'The money's vital.'

'The money's a temporary problem. Precedents unfortunately last forever. You were at the track?'

'Yes sir.'

'How's the form?'

'They all looked in fine fettle. Alexi Travkin says Pilot Fish's our main opposition and the going will be soft. Noble Star's grand though she's never raced in the wet.'

'Will it rain?'

'Yes. But perhaps we'll be lucky, sir.'

'Let's hope so. Terrible times, Ian. Still, these things are sent to try us, eh? Are you going to John's funeral?'

'Yes sir.'

'So am I. Poor fellow . . .'

At the funeral this morning Dunross had said kind words about John Chen for the face of the House of Chen and for all the Chen forebears who had served the Noble House so long and hard.

'Thank you, tai-pan,' Phillip Chen had said simply. 'Again, I'm sorry.'

Later he had said to Phillip Chen privately, 'Sorry is sorry but that still doesn't help us extricate ourselves from the trap your son, and you, put us into. Or solve bloody Four Fingers and the third coin.'

'I know, I know!' Phillip Chen had said, wringing his hands. 'I know, and unless we can get the stock back up we're ruined, we're all ruined! *Oh ko*, after you'd announced the boom I bought and bought and now we're ruined.'

Dunross had said sharply, 'We've got the weekend, Phillip. Now listen to me, dammit! You will claim every favor you're owed. I want Lando Mata and Tightfist Tung's backing by Sunday midnight. At least 20 million.'

'But, tai-pan, don—'

'If I don't get that by Sunday midnight, have your resignation on my desk by 9:00 A.M., you're no longer compradore, your son Kevin's out and all your branch is out forever and I'll choose a new compradore from another branch.'

Now he exhaled heavily, hating that Phillip Chen and John Chen—and probably Jacques deVille—had betrayed their trust. He went to the coffee tray and poured himself some coffee. Today it did not taste good to him. The phones had been incessant, most of the calls about the looming collapse of the market, the banking system. Havergill, Johnjohn, Richard Kwang. Nothing from Tightfist or Lando Mata or Murtagh. The only bright spot had been his call to David MacStruan in Toronto: 'David, I want you here for a conference on Monday. Can you g—' He had been swamped by the bellow of joy.

'Tai-pan, I'm on my way to the airport. Goo—'

'Hang on, David!' He had explained his plan about transferring Jacques to Canada.

'Och, laddie, if you do that I'm your slave forever!'

'I'm going to need more than slaves, David,' he had said carefully.

There was a long pause and the voice on the other end hardened. 'Anything you want, tai-pan, you've got. Anything.'

Dunross smiled, warmed by the thought of his distant cousin. He let his eyes drift out of the windows. The harbor was misted, the sky low and dark but no rain yet. Good, he thought, so long as it doesn't rain till after the fifth race. After four o'clock it can rain. I want to smash Gornt and Pilot Fish and oh God let First Central come up with my money, or Lando Mata or Tightfist or Par-Con! Your bet's covered, he told himself stoically, every way you can. And Casey? Is she setting me up like Bartlett? And like Gornt? What about . . .

The intercom clicked on. 'Tai-pan, your eleven o'clock appointment's here.'

'Claudia, come in a second.' He took an envelope out of his drawer with the $1,000 in it and gave it her. 'Betting money, as promised.'

'Oh thank you, tai-pan.' There were care lines in her jolly face and shadows under the smile.

'You're in Phillip's box?'

'Oh yes. Yes, Uncle Phillip invited me. He . . . he seems very upset,' she said.

'It's John.' Dunross wasn't sure if she knew. She probably

does, he thought, or soon will. There're no secrets in Hong Kong. 'What do you fancy?'

'Winner's Delight in the first, Buccaneer in the second.'

'Two outsiders?' He stared at her. 'You've inside info?'

'Oh no, tai-pan.' A little of her normal good humor came back. 'It's just the form.'

'And in the fifth?'

'I'm not betting the fifth, but all my hopes're on Noble Star.' Claudia added worriedly, 'Is there anything I can do to help, tai-pan? Anything? The stock market and . . . we have to slaughter Gornt somehow.'

'I'm rather fond of Gornt—he's such a *fang-pi*.' The Canton obscenity was picturesque and she laughed. 'Now show in Mrs. Gresserhoff.'

'Yes, yes tai-pan,' Claudia said. 'And thanks for the *h'eung yau!*'

In a moment, Dunross got up to greet his guest. She was the most beautiful woman he had ever seen. '*Ikaga desu ka?*' he asked in shock, his Japanese fluent—How are you?—astounded that she could have been married to Alan Medford Grant whose name, God help us, was also supposed to be Hans Gresserhoff.

'*Genki*, tai-pan. *Domo. Genki desu! Anatawa?*' Fine, tai-pan, thank you. And you?

'*Genki.*' He bowed slightly in return and did not shake hands though he noticed her hands and feet were tiny and her legs long. They chatted for a moment then she switched to English with a smile. 'Your Japanese is oh very good, tai-pan. My husband, he did not tell me you were so tall.'

'Would you care for coffee?'

'Thank you . . . but oh please let me get it for you too.' Before he could stop her she had gone to the coffee tray. He watched her pour delicately. She offered him the first cup with a little bow. 'Please.' Riko Gresserhoff—Riko Anjin—was barely five feet, perfectly proportioned with short hair and lovely smile and she weighed about ninety pounds. Her blouse and skirt were auburn silk, well cut and French. 'Thank you for the expense money Miss Claudia gave me.'

'It's nothing. We owe your, your husband's estate about 8,000 pounds. I'll have a cashier's check for you tomorrow.'

'Thank you.'

1087

'You have me at a disadvantage, Mrs. Gresserhoff. You kn—'

'Please call me Riko, tai-pan.'

'Very well, Riko-*san*. You know me but I know nothing about you.'

'Yes. My husband said I was to tell you whatever you wanted to know. He told me that, that once I had made sure you were the tai-pan, then I was to give you an envelope I have brought from him to you. May I bring it later?' Again the little interrogative smile. 'Please?'

'I'll come back with you now and collect it.'

'Oh no, that would be too much trouble. Perhaps I can bring it to you after luncheon. Please.'

'How big is it? The envelope?'

Her tiny hands measured the air. 'It is an ordinary envelope but not so thick. You could put it easily into your pocket.' Again the smile.

'Perhaps you'd like to . . . I tell you what,' he said, charmed by her presence. 'In a minute or two I'll send you back by car. You can fetch the envelope and come right back.' Then he added, knowing it would ruin the seating arrangements but not caring, 'Would you join us for lunch at the races?'

'Oh but . . . but I would have to change and . . . oh thank you but no, it would be too much trouble for you. Perhaps I could deliver the letter later, or tomorrow? My husband said I was only to put it into your hands.'

'No need to change, Riko-*san*. You look lovely. Oh! Do you have a hat?'

Perplexed she stared at him. 'Please?'

'Yes, it's, er, it's our custom that ladies wear hats and gloves to the races. Silly custom but do you? Have a hat?'

'Oh yes. Every lady has a hat. Of course.'

A wave of relief went through him. 'Good, then that's settled.'

'Oh! Then if you say so.' She got up. 'Shall I go now?'

'No, if you've time, please sit down. How long were you married?'

'Four years. Hans . . .' She hesitated. Then she said firmly, 'Hans told me to tell you, but you alone, if ever he was to die and I was to come as I have come, to tell you that our marriage was of convenience.'

'What?'

She reddened a little as she continued. 'Please excuse me but I was to tell you. It was a convenience to both of us. I obtained a Swiss citizenship and passport and he obtained someone to care for him when he came to Switzerland. I . . . I did not wish to marry but he asked me many times and he . . . and he stressed that it would protect me when he died.'

Dunross was startled. 'He knew he was going to die?'

'I think so. He said the marriage contract was for five years only but that we should have no children. He took me to an advocate in Zurich who drew up a contract for five years.' She opened her purse, her fingers trembling but not her voice, and pulled out an envelope. 'Hans told me to give you these. They're copies of the contract, my birth and marriage certificate, his will and birth certificate.' She took out a tissue and pressed it against her nose. 'Please excuse me.' Carefully she untied the string around the envelope and took out a letter.

Dunross accepted it. He recognized AMG's handwriting. 'Tai-pan: This will confirm my wife, Riko Gresserhoff—Riko Anjin—is who she says she is. I love her with all my heart. She merits and merited far better than me. If she needs help . . . please please please.' It was signed Hans Gresserhoff.

'I do not merit better, tai-pan,' she said with a sad, small, confident voice. 'My husband was good to me, very good. And I'm sorry he is dead.'

Dunross watched her. 'Was he ill? Did he know he was going to die from an illness?'

'I don't know. He never told me. One of his asks before I . . . before I married him was that I would not question him or question where he went, why, or when he was to return. I was just to accept him as he was.' A small shiver went through her. 'It was very hard living thus.'

'Why did you agree to live like that? Why? Surely it wasn't necessary?'

Again Riko hesitated. 'I was born in Japan in 1939 and went as an infant with my parents to Berne—my father was a minor official in the Japanese Embassy there. In 1943 he went back to Japan but left us in Geneva. Our family is—our family comes from Nagasaki. In 1945 my father was lost and all our family was lost. There was nothing to go back to and my mother wanted to stay in Switzerland, so we went to live in Zurich with a good man who died four years ago. He . . . they paid for my education and kept me and we had a happy family. For many years I knew they were not married though they pretended and I pretended. When he died there was no money, or just a little money. Hans Gresserhoff was an acquaintance of this man, my, my stepfather. His name was Simeon Tzerak. He was a displaced person, tai-pan, a stateless person from Hungary who had taken up residence in Switzerland. Before the war he was an accountant, he said, in Budapest. My mother arranged my marriage to Hans Gresserhoff.' Now she looked up from the carpet at him. 'It was . . . it was a good marriage, tai-pan, at least I tried very hard to be whatever my husband wanted and my mother wanted. My *giri*, my duty was to obey my mother, *neh?*'

'Yes,' he said kindly, understanding duty and *giri*, that most Japanese of words, most important of words that sums up a heritage and a way of life. 'You have performed your *giri* perfectly, I'm sure. What does your mother say is your *giri* now?'

'My mother is dead, tai-pan. When my stepfather died she did not wish to live. The moment I was married she went up the mountain and skied into a crevasse.'

'Terrible.'

'Oh no, tai-pan, very good. She died as she wished to die, at a time and place of her choosing. Her man was dead, I was safe, what more was there for her to do?'

'Nothing,' he told her, hearing the softness of her voice, the sincerity, and the calm. The Japanese word *wa* came to his mind: harmony. That's what this girl has, he thought. Harmony. Perhaps that's what's so beautiful about her. *Ayeeyah* that I could acqure such *wa!*

One of his phones sounded. 'Yes, Claudia?'

'It's Alexi Travkin, tai-pan. Sorry, he said it was important.'

'Thank you.' To the girl he said, 'Excuse me a moment. Yes, Alexi?'

'Sorry to interrupt, tai-pan, but Johnny Moore's sick and he won't be able to ride.' Johnny Moore was their chief jockey.

Dunross's voice sharpened. 'He seemed all right this morning.'

1090

'He's running 103-degree temperature, the doctor said it might be food poisoning.'

'You mean he's been tampered with, Alexi?'

'I don't know, tai-pan. I only know he's no good for us today.'

Dunross hesitated. He knew he was better than the rest of his jockeys though the extra weight Noble Star would have to carry would load the deck against the horse. Should I or shouldn't I? 'Alexi, schedule Tom Wong. We'll decide before the race.'

'Yes. Thank you.'

Dunross replaced the phone. 'Anjin's a curious name,' he said. 'It means pilot, just pilot, or navigator, doesn't it?'

'The legend in my family is that one of our forebears was an Englishman who became a samurai and advisor to the Shōgun Yoshi Toranaga, oh very many years ago, long long ago. We have many stories but they say first he had a fief in Hemi, near Yokohama, then went with his family to Nagasaki as inspector general of all foreigners.' Again the smile and the shrug and the tip of her tongue moistened her lips. 'It is just legend, tai-pan. He is supposed to have married a highborn lady called Riko.' Her chuckle filled the room. 'You know Japanese! A *gai-jin*, a foreigner, marrying a highborn lady—how could that be possible? But anyway, it is a pleasing story and an explanation of a name, *neh?*' She got up and he got up. 'I should go now. Yes?'

The black Daimler pulled up outside the V and A, the Struan arms discreetly on the doors. Casey and Bartlett waited at the top of the stairs, Casey wearing a green dress, self-conscious in a pert green pillbox hat and white gloves, Bartlett broad-shouldered, wearing a blue tie to match his well-cut suit. Both were set-faced.

The chauffeur approached them. 'Mr. Bartlett?'

'Yes.' They came down the steps to meet him. 'You our limo?'

'Yes sir. Excuse me sir, but do you both have your badge tickets, and the invitation card?'

'Yes, here they are,' Casey said.

'Ah, good. Sorry but without them . . . My name's Lim. The, er, the custom is for the gentlemen to tie both badges through the hole in their lapels and the ladies usually have a pin.'

'Whatever you say,' Bartlett said. Casey got in the back and he followed. They sat far apart. Silently they began to fix the small, individually numbered badges.

Blandly Lim closed the door, noticing the frigidity, and chortled inwardly. He closed the electric glass partition window and switched on his intercom mike. 'If you want to talk to me, sir, just use the microphone above you.' Through his rear mirror he saw Bartlett use the switch momentarily.

'Sure, thank you, Lim.'

Once Lim was in the traffic he reached under the dash and touched a hidden switch. At once Bartlett's voice came through the speaker.

'. . . going to rain?'

'I don't know, Linc. The radio said it would but everyone's praying.' A hesitation, then coldly, 'I still think you're wrong.'

Lim settled back happily. His trusted old brother Lim Chu, majordomo to the tai-pans of the Noble House, had arranged for another younger brother, an expert radio mechanic, to install this bypass switch so that he could overhear his passengers. It had been done at great cost to protect the tai-pan and older brother Lim had ordered that it was never to be used when the tai-pan was in the car. Never never never. It never had been. Yet. Lim felt queasy at the thought of being caught but their wish to know—of course to protect—overcame their anxiety. Oh oh oh, he chortled. Golden Pubics is certainly in a rage!

Casey was seething.

'Let's quit this, Linc, huh?' she said. 'Since our breakfast meeting you've been like a bear with a sore ass!'

'And what about you?' Bartlett glared at her. 'We're going with Gornt—the way I want it.'

'This's my deal, you've said that fifty times, you promised, you've always listened before. Jesus, we're on the same side. I'm only trying to protect you. I know you're wrong.'

'You *think* I'm wrong. And it's all because of Orlanda!'

'That's a crock! I went through my reasons fifty times. If Ian gets out of the trap then we're better off to go with him than Gornt.'

Bartlett's face was cold. 'We've never had a bust before, Casey, but if you want to vote your shares, I'll vote mine and your ass'll be in a vise before you can count to ten!'

Casey's heart was thumping. Ever since their breakfast meeting with Seymour Steigler, the day had been heavy going. Bartlett was adamant that their best course lay with Gornt and nothing she could say would dissuade him. After an hour of trying she had closed the meeting and gone off to deal with a pile of overnight telexes, then, remembering suddenly at the last moment, had rushed out in a panic and bought a hat.

When she had met Bartlett in the foyer with great trepidation, wanting the hat to please him, she had begun to make peace but he had interrupted her. 'Forget it,' he had said. 'So we disagree. So what?'

She had waited and waited but he hadn't even noticed. 'What do you think?'

'I told you. Gornt's best for us.'

'I mean my hat.'

She had seen his blank stare.

'Oh that's what's different! Hey, it's okay.'

She had felt like tearing it off and hurling it at him. 'It's Parisian,' she had said half-heartedly. 'It says hats and gloves on the invitation, remember? It's a crock but Ian said that la—'

'What makes you think he can get out of the trap?'

'He's clever. And *the* tai-pan.'

'Gornt's got him on the run.'

'It looks that way. So let's forget it for now. Maybe we'd better wait outside. The car's coming at noon promptly.'

'Just a minute, Casey. What have you got cooking?'

'What do you mean?'

'I know you better than anyone. What do you have on the burner?'

Casey hesitated, unsure of herself, wondering if she could reveal the First Central ploy. But there's no reason to, she reassured herself. If Ian gets the credit and squeezes out, I'll be the first to know. Ian promised. Then Linc can cover his 2 million with Gornt and they can buy back in to cover their selling short and make a huge profit. At the same time Ian, Linc and I get in at the bottom of the market and make our own killing. I'll be the first to know after Murtagh and Ian. Ian promised. Yes, yes he did. But can I trust him?

A wave of nausea went through her. Can you trust anyone in business here, or anywhere? Man or woman?

1093

At dinner last night she had trusted him. Influenced by the wine and food she had told him about her relationship with Linc, and about the bargain they had made.

'That's a bit rough, isn't it? On both of you?'

'Yes, yes and no. We were both over twenty-one, Ian, and I wanted so much more than being just Mrs. Linc Bartlett, a mother-mistress-servant-dishwasher-diaperwasher-slave and a left-at-home. That's the thing that kills off any woman. You're always left. At home. So home becomes prison in the end, and it drives you mad, being trapped until death do us part! I've seen it too many times.'

'Someone has to look after the home and the children. It's the man's job to make the money. It's the wife's j—'

'Yes. Most times. But not for me. *I'm* not prepared to accept that and I don't think it's wrong to want a different sort of life. I'm the wage earner for my family. My sister's husband died so there's my sister and her kids, and my Ma and uncle are getting on. I'm educated and good and better than most in business. The world's changing, everything's changing, Ian.'

'I said before, not here thank God!'

Casey remembered how she had readied to return measure for measure, but had bitten back the old Casey and said instead, 'Ian, what about the Hag? How did she do it? What was her secret? How did she become more equal than anyone?'

'She kept her hands on the purse strings. Absolutely. Oh she conceded outward position and face to Culum and following tai-pans but she kept the books, she hired and fired through him—she was the strength of that family. When Culum was dying, it was easy to persuade him to make her tai-pan. He gave her the Struan chop, family chop and all the reins and all the secrets. But, wisely, she kept it all very secret and after Culum she only appointed those she could control, and never once gave any one of them the purse strings, or real power, not until she herself was dying.'

'But ruling through others, is that enough?'

'Power is power and I don't think it matters so long as you rule. For a woman—after a certain age—power only comes with control of the purse. But you're right about drop dead money. Hong Kong's the only place on earth you can get it to keep it. With money, real money, you can be more equal than anyone. Even Linc Bartlett. I like him, by the way. I like him very much.'

'I love him. Our partnership's worked, Ian. I think it's been good for Linc—oh how I hope so. He's our tai-pan and I'm not trying to become one. I just want to succeed as a woman. He's helped me tremendously, of course he has. Without him I'd never have made it. So we're in business together, until my birthday. November 25 this year. That's D Day. That's when we both decide.'

'And?'

'I don't know. I honestly don't know. Oh I love Linc, more than ever, but we're not lovers.'

Later, coming back on the ferry, she had been sorely tempted to ask him about Orlanda. She had decided not to. 'Perhaps I should have,' she muttered out loud.

'Eh?'

'Oh!' She came out of her reverie, finding herself in the limo on the car ferry en route to Hong Kong. 'Sorry, Linc, I was daydreaming.'

She looked at him and saw that he was as handome as ever, even though now he stared back coldly. You're more attractive to me than either Ian or Quillan, she thought. And yet, right now, I'd prefer to pillow with either of them than with you. Because you're a bastard.

'Do you want to have at it?' he said. 'You want to vote your shares against mine?'

Casey stared back at him, enraged. Tell him to go screw, the devil half of her screamed, he needs you more than you need him, you've got the reins of Par-Con, you know where the bodies are buried, you can take apart what you helped to create. But the other half of her urged caution. She remembered what the tai-pan had said about this man's world, and about power. And about the Hag.

So she dropped her gaze a moment and allowed tears to seep. At once she saw the change in him.

'Jesus, Casey, don't cry, I'm sorry . . .' he was saying and his arms reached out for her. 'Jesus, you've never cried before . . . Listen, we've been through the mill a dozen times, hell, fifty times, there's no need to get so uptight. We've got Struan's and Gornt locked into battle. There's no difference in the end. We'll

1095

still be the Noble House, but up front, up front Gornt's better, I know I'm right.'

Oh no, you're not, she thought contentedly, warm in his embrace.

64

Brian Kwok was screaming and beyond terror. He knew he was in prison and in hell and it had gone on forever. His whole insane world was an instant of never-ending blinding light, everything blood-colored, the cell walls floor ceiling blood-colored, no doors or windows, and the floor awash with blood, but everything twisted and all upside down for somehow he was lying on the ceiling, his whole being in torment, frantically trying to claw his way down to normality, each time falling back into the mess of his own vomit, then the next instant once more in the blackness, grinding pulsating voices laughing, drowning out his friend, drowning out Robert who pleaded with the devils to stop stop for the love of God stop, then once more the eye-tearing head-exploding bloodlight, seeing the blood waters that would not fall, groping desperately, stretching down for the chairs and table that sat in the blood water but falling back, always falling back, floor meeting ceiling everything wrong upside sideways madness madness the Devil's invention . . .

Bloodlight and darkness and laughter and stench and blood again, on and on and on . . .

He knew he had begun raving years ago, begging them to stop, begging them to let him go, swearing he would do anything but let him go, that he was not the one they sought, not due for hell . . . It's a mistake, it's all a mistake, no it's not a mistake I was the enemy who was the enemy what enemy? Oh please let the world turn right side up and let me lie where I should be lying up there, down there, where oh Jesus Christ Robert Christ help, help meeeeee . . .

'All right, Brian. I'm here. I'm putting everything right. I am. I'm putting everything right!' He heard the compassionate words come soaring out of the maelstrom, drowning the laughter. The enveloping blood went away. He felt his friend's hand, cool and gentle, and he clutched it, terrified lest it was another dream within a dream within a dream, oh Christ Robert don't leave me. . . .

Oh Jesus it's impossible! Look there! The ceiling's there where it should be and I'm here, I'm lying on the bed where I should be and the room's dim but soft where it should be, everything's clean, flowers, blinds drawn but flowers and the water properly in the vase and I'm right side up, I'm right side up. 'Oh Christ, Robert . . .'

'Hello, chum,' Robert Armstrong said gently.

'Oh Jesus Robert thank you thank you, I'm right side up oh thank you thank you . . .'

It was hard to talk and he felt weak, his strength gone, but it was glorious just to be here, out of the nightmare, his friend's face misted but real. And smoking, am I smoking? Oh yes. Yes I think I remember Robert left me a packet of cigarettes though those devils came and found them and took them away last week . . . thank God for smoke . . . When was it, last month, last week, when? I remember yes but Robert came back again and gave me a secret drag last month, was it last month? 'Oh that tastes so good, so good and the peace, no nightmare, Robert, not seeing blood up there, the ceiling awash, not lying up there but down here not in hell oh thank you thank you . . .'

'I must go now.'

'Oh Christ don't go they may come back no don't go sit and stay please stay. Look, we'll talk, yes, that's it, talk, you wanted to talk . . . don't leave. Please talk . . .'

'All right, old friend, then talk. I won't go while we talk. What do you want to tell me, eh? Certainly I'll stay while you talk. Tell me about Ning-tok and your father. Didn't you go back to see him?'

'Oh yes, I went back to see him once, yes, just before he died, my friends helped me, they helped me it only took a day, my friends helped me . . . that, that was so long ago. . . .'

'Did Ian go with you?'

'Ian? No it . . . was it Ian? I can't remember . . . Ian, the tai-pan? Someone went with me. Was it you, Robert? Ah, with me in Ning-tok? No it wasn't you or Ian it was John Chancellor from Ottawa. He hates the Soviets too, Robert, they're the great enemy. Even in school, and devil Chiang Kai-shek and his assassins Fong-fong and . . . and . . . Oh I'm so tired and so pleased to see you. . . .'

'Tell me about Fong-fong.'

'Oh him. He was a bad man, Robert, him and all his spy group they were against us, the PRC, and pro-Chiang, I know; don't worry as soon as I read the . . . What are you asking me, eh? What?'

'It was that rotten Grant, eh?'

'Yes, yes it was and I almost fainted when he knew I was . . . I . . . where was I oh yes but I stopped Fong-fong at once. . . . Oh yes.'

'Who did you tell?'

'Tsu-yan. I whispered it to Tsu-yan. He's back in Peking now . . . Oh he was very high up, though he didn't know who I really was, Robert, I was all very hush-hush. . . . Yes then it was in school, my father sent me after old Sh'in was murdered . . . thugs came and flogged him to death in the village square because he was one of us, one of the people, one of Chairman Mao's people, and when I was in Hong Kong I stayed with . . . with Uncle . . . I went to school . . . and he schooled me at night . . . Can I sleep now?'

'Who was your uncle, Kar-shun, and where did he live?'

'I don't . . . don't remember. . . .'

'Then I must go. Next week I'll come ba—'

'No wait, Robert, wait, it was Wu Tsa-fing, on . . . on Fourth Alley in Aberdeen . . . number 8, lucky 8, fifth floor. There, I can remember! Don't go!'

'Very good, old chum. Very good. Were you at school long in Hong Kong?' Robert Armstrong kept his voice soft and kind and his heart went out to his friend that once was. He was astonished that Brian had broken so easily, so quickly.

The client's mind was open now, ready for him to take apart. He kept his eyes on the shell of the man who lay on the bed, encouraging him to remember so that the others who listened secretly could record all the facts and figures and names and places, the undercover truths and half-truths that were spilling out and would continue to spill out until Brian Kar-shun Kwok was a husk. And he knew that he would continue to probe, to cajole or threaten or become impatient or angry or pretend to want to leave or curse the jailer away who would interrupt, if necessary. With Crosse and Sinders monitoring the in-depth debriefing, he was just a tool like Brian Kwok had been a tool for others who had used his mind and talents for their own purposes. His job was just to be the medium, to keep the client talking, to bring him back when he rambled or became incoherent, to be his sole friend and his sole prop in this unreal universe, the one who brought the truth forth—like John Chancellor of Ottawa, who's he? Where does he fit? I don't know yet.

We'll get everything the client has now, he thought. We'll get all his contacts, his mentors, enemies and friends. Poor old Fong-fong and the lads. We'll never see them again—unless they turn up as agents of the other side. What a rotten filthy business this is, selling out your friends, working with the enemy who, everyone knows, wants you enslaved.

'. . . in Vancouver it was wonderful, wonderful, Robert. There was a girl there who . . . Yes and I almost married her but Sensible Tok, Sensible was my 489, he lived . . . he lived on . . . oh yes it was Pedder Street in Chinatown and he owned the Hoho-tok Restaurant . . . yes Sensible Tok said I should honor Chairman Mao before any *quai loh*. . . . Oh how I loved her but he said it was the *quai lohs* who raped China for centuries. . . . You know that's true that's true. . . .'

'Yes that's true,' he said, humoring him. 'Sensible Tok was your only friend in Canada?'

'Oh no Robert I have dozens. . . .'

Armstrong listened, astounded by the wealth of information about the inner workings of the Canadian Mounted Police, and the extent of Chinese Communist infiltration throughout the Americas and Europe and particularly on the Western seaboard —Vancouver, Seattle, San Francisco, Los Angeles, San Diego— wherever a Chinese restaurant or shop or business existed there was the potential of pressure, of funds and most of all of knowledge. '. . . and the Wo Tuk on Gerrard Street in London's the Center where I . . . when I was . . . Oh my head aches I'm so thirsty. . . .'

Armstrong gave him the water that contained stimulant. When he or Crosse considered the moment correct, the client would be given the thirst-quenching, delicately flavored Chinese tea that was his favorite. This contained the soporific.

Then it was up to Crosse and Sinders what happened, whether it was more of the same, more of the Red Room or the end of the exercise and then, carefully, the gradual bringing back of the client to reality, with great care, so that no permanent damage was done.

It's up to them, he thought. Sinders was right to put on the pressure while we've time. The client knows too much. He's too well trained, and if we'd had to give him back without knowing what he knows, well that would have been irresponsible. We've got to keep ahead.

Armstrong lit two cigarettes and inhaled his own deeply. I'll give up smoking for Christmas. I can't now, not with all this horror. It was Brian Kwok's wailing screams so soon, barely twenty minutes after being put into the room for the second time that had shattered him. He had been watching through spyholes with Crosse and Sinders, watching the insanity of trying to reach the ceiling that was the floor that was the ceiling, astonished that someone so strong, so well trained as Brian Kowk would break so quickly. 'It's impossible,' he had muttered.

'He may be faking,' Sinders said.

'No,' Crosse had said. 'No. It's real, for him. I know.'

'I don't believe he'd break so easily.'

'You will, Robert.' And then when Brian Kwok had been carried out to be brought to this room, clean and nice and all the Red Room had been mopped clean, Roger Crosse had said, 'All right, Robert, try it, then you'll see.'

'No, no thanks. It's like something out of *The Cabinet of Dr. Caligari*,' he had muttered, 'No thanks!'

'Please try it, just for a minute. It's an important experience for you. You may be caught by them, the other side, one day. You should be prepared. One minute might save your sanity. Test it, for your own safety.'

So he had agreed. They had closed the door. The room was totally scarlet, small but everything tilted, the lines all wrong, angles all wrong, the floor meeting the ceiling in one corner, perspectives all wrong, no angles ordinary. The tilted ceiling far

1101

above was a sheer sheet of scarlet glass. Above the glass, water washed down to be recycled and come down again. Attached to this tilted glass ceiling surface were scarlet chairs and a table and pens and paper casually on the table, scarlet cushions on the chairs, making it seem the floor, a false door nearby, almost ajar . . .

Sudden blackness. Then the blinding strobe and the stunning impact of the scarlet. Blackness, scarlet, blackness, scarlet. Involuntarily he groped for the reality of the table and chairs and the floor and door and stumbled and fell, unable to get his bearings, water above, the glass vanished, just insane scarlet water on the floor above. Blackness and now voices pounding and again blood-colored hell. His stomach told him that he was upside down though his mind said it was just a trick and to close your eyes it's a trick it's a trick it's a trick . . .

After an eternity, when at length normal lights came on and the real door opened, he was lying on the real floor, retching. 'You bastard,' he had snarled at Crosse, barely able to talk. 'You said a minute, you lying bastard!' His chest heaved and he fought to his feet, reeling, barely able to stand or to stop vomiting.

'Sorry, but it was only a minute, Robert,' Crosse said.

'I don't believe it. . . .'

'Honestly, it was,' Sinders said. 'I timed it myself. Really! Extraordinary. Most effective.'

Again Armstrong felt his chest heave at the thought of the water above and the tables and chairs. He put those thoughts away and concentrated on Brian Kwok, feeling that he had let the client ramble enough and it was now time to bring him back. 'You were saying? You passed over our dossiers to your friend Bucktooth Lo?'

'Well no, it wasn't . . . I'm tired, Robert, tired . . . what ar—'

'If you're tired I'll leave!' He got up and saw the client blanch. 'Next month I'll se—'

'No . . . no . . . please don't go . . . they . . . no, don't go. Pleasssssssse!'

So he sat back, continuing the game, knowing it to be unfair, and that with the client so totally disoriented he could be made to sign anything, say anything at whim. 'I'll stay while you talk, old friend. You were saying about Bucktooth Lo—the man in Princes Building? He was the go-between?'

'No . . . not . . . yes in a way . . . Dr. Meng . . . Dr. Meng would pick up any package that I left . . . Meng never knew that I . . . that it was me . . . the arrangements were by phone or by letter . . . he would take them to Lo who was paid . . . Bucktooth Lo was paid to give them to another man, I don't know who . . . I don't know . . .'

'Oh I think you do, Brian, I don't believe you want me to stay.'

'Oh Christ I do . . . I swear it . . . Bucktooth . . . Bucktooth would know . . . or perhaps Ng, Vee Cee Ng, Photographer Ng, he's on our side, he's on our side Robert . . . Ask him, he'll know . . . he was with Tsu-yan importing thoriums . . .'

'What're thoriums?'

'Rare earths for . . . for atomics, for our atomics . . . oh yes we'll have our own A-bombs and H-bombs in a few months. . . .' Brian Kwok went into a paroxysm of laughter. 'The first in a few weeks . . . our first explosion in just a few weeks now oh of course not perfect but the first and soon an H-bomb, dozens, Robert, soon we'll have ours to defend against those hegemonists who threaten to wipe us out, in a few weeks! Christ, Robert, think of that! Chairman Mao's done it, he has, he's done it . . . yes and then next year H-bombs and then Joe, yes we'll get back our lands, oh yes, with atomics we cancel out theirs . . . we will, Joe's going to help, Joe Yu's going to . . . Oh we'll stop them now, stop them we'll stop them and take our lands back.' His hand reached out and he held Robert Armstrong's arm but his grip was weak. 'Listen, we're at war already, us and the Soviets, Chung Li told me, he's my emergency . . . em, em contact . . . there's a war, a shooting war going on right now. In the north, divisions, not patrols near the Amur they're they're killing more Chinese and stealing more land but . . . but not for long.' He lay back weakly and began to mumble, his mind wandering.

'Atomics? Next year? I don't believe it,' Armstrong said, pretending to scoff, his mind blown as he listened to the continued outpouring that was giving chapter and verse and names. Christ, A-bombs in a few months? A few months? The world's been told that's ten years away. China with A- and H-bombs?

Carefully he let Brian Kwok peter out and then he said casually, 'Who's Joe? Joe Yu?'

1103

'Who?'

He saw Brian Kwok turn and stare at him, eyes strange, different, boring into him. Instantly he was on guard and he prepared. 'Joe Yu,' he said even more offhand.

'Who? I don't know any Joe Yu . . . no . . . What, what . . . what am I doing here? What is this place? What's happening? Yu? Why . . . why should I know him? Who?'

'No reason,' Armstrong said, calming him. 'Here, here's some tea, you must be very thirsty, old chum.'

'Oh yes . . . yes I am . . . where . . . yes . . . Christ what's happ . . . happening?'

Armstrong helped him drink. Then he gave him another cigarette and further calmed him. In a few moments Brian Kwok was again deeply asleep. Armstrong wiped his palms and his forehead, exhausted too.

The door opened. Sinders and Crosse came in.

'Very good, Robert,' Sinders said excitedly, 'very good indeed!'

'Yes,' Crosse said. 'I felt he was coming back too. Your timing was perfect.'

Armstrong said nothing, feeling soiled.

'My God,' Sinders chortled, 'this client's gold. The minister will be delighted. Atomics in a few months and a shooting war going on right now! No wonder our Parliamentary Trade Commission made such marvelous progress! Excellent, Robert, just excellent!'

'You believe the client, sir?' Crosse said.

'Absolutely, don't you?'

'I believe he was telling what he knew. Whether it's fact, that's another matter. Joe Yu? Does Joe or Joseph Yu mean anything to you?' The others shook their heads. 'John Chancellor?'

'No.'

'Chung Li?'

Armstrong said, 'There's a Chung Li who's a friend of Br—the client's, a car enthusiast—Shanghainese, big industrialist—could be him.'

'Good. But Joe Yu, that triggered something in him. Could be important.' Crosse glanced at Sinders. 'Proceed?'

'Of course.'

65

1:45 P.M.:

A roar of excitement went up from fifty thousand throats as the seven entries for the first race, jockeys up, came up the ramp out from under the stands to prance and skitter to the owners' paddock where trainers and owners waited. The owners and their wives were dressed in their very best, many of the wives laden and over-minked, Mai-ling Kwang and Dianne Chen among them, conscious of the envious stares of the multitude craning to see the horses—and them.

Either side of the soggy grass paddock and winner's circle, the packed mass of the crowds went down to the white sparkling rails and the perfectly kept turf of the encircling track. The winning post was opposite and beside it, on the other side of the track, was the huge Totalisator that would carry the names of the horses and jockeys and odds, race by race. The Totalisator was owned and operated by the Turf Club, as was the course. There were no legal bookmakers here or outside or any legal off-course betting places. This was the only legal form of betting in the Colony.

The sky was dark and forbidding. Earlier there had been a few sprinkles but now the air was clear.

Behind the paddock and winner's circle, on this level, were the jockeys' changing rooms and the offices of the officials, food concessions and the first banks of betting windows. Above them were the stands, four terraced tiers, each cantilevered floor with its own bank of betting windows. The first tier was for nonvoting members, next for voting members, and the two top floors set aside for the private boxes and radio room. Each box had its own private kitchen. Each of the ten annually elected stewards had a box and then there were some permannent ones: first his Excellency the governor, patron of the club; then the commander-in-chief; one each for Blacs and the Victoria. And last, Struan's. Struan's was in the best position, exactly opposite the winning post.

'Why's that, tai-pan?' Casey asked.

'Because Dirk Struan began the Turf Club, set the rules, brought out a famous racing expert, Sir Roger Blore, to be the first secretary of the club. He put up all the money for the first meeting, money for the stands, money to import the first batch of horses from India and helped persuade the first pleni-potentiary, Sir William Longstaff, to deed the land to the Turf Club in perpetuity.'

'Come now, tai-pan,' Donald McBride, the track steward for this meeting, said jovially, 'tell it as it happened, eh? You say Dirk "helped persuade"? Didn't Dirk just "order" Longstaff to do it?'

Dunross laughed with the others still seated at the table he had hosted, Casey, Hiro Toda and McBride, who had just arrived to visit. There was a bar and three round tables in the box, each seating twelve comfortably. 'I prefer my version,' he said. 'In any event, Casey, the legend is that Dirk was voted this position by popular acclaim when the first stands were built.'

'That's not true either, Casey,' Willie Tusk called out from the next table. 'Didn't old Tyler Brock demand the position as the right of Brock and Sons? Didn't he challenge Dirk to put up the position on a race, man to man, at the first meeting?'

'No, that's just a story.'

'Did those two race, tai-pan?' Casey asked.

'They were going to. But the typhoon came too soon, so they say. In any event Culum refused to budge so here we are. This's ours while the course exists.'

'And quite right too,' McBride said, with his happy smile. 'The Noble House deserves the best. Since the very first stewards were elected, Miss Casey, the tai-pan of Struan's has always been a steward. Always. By popular acclaim. Well, I must be off.' He glanced at his watch, smiled at Dunross. With great formality he said, 'Permission to start the first race, tai-pan?'

Dunross grinned back at him. 'Permission granted.' McBride hurried off.

Casey stared at Dunross. 'They have to ask your permission to begin?'

'It's just a custom.' Dunross shrugged. 'I suppose it's a good idea for someone to say, "All right, let's begin," isn't it? I'm afraid that unlike Sir Geoffrey, the governors of Hong Kong in the past haven't been known for their punctuality. Besides, tradition is not a bad thing at all—gives you a sense of continuity, of belonging—and protection.' He finished his coffee. 'If you'll excuse me a moment, I must do a few things.'

'Have fun!' She watched him go, liking him even more than last night. Just then Peter Marlowe came in and Dunross stopped a moment. 'Oh hello, Peter, good to see you. How's Fleur?'

'Getting better, thank you, tai-pan.'

'Come on in! Help yourself to a drink—I'll be back in a moment. Put your money on number five, Excellent Day, in the first! See you later.'

'Thanks, tai-pan.'

Casey beckoned to Peter Marlowe but he did not see her. His eyes had fixed on Grey who was with Julian Broadhurst out on the balcony, haranguing some of the others. She saw his face close and her heart leaped, remembering their hostility, so she called out, 'Peter! Hi, come and sit down.'

His eyes unglazed. 'Oh! Oh hello,' he said.

'Come sit down. Fleur's going to be fine.'

'She certainly appreciated your going to see her.'

'It was a pleasure. Are the kids okay?'

'Oh yes. You?'

'Fantastic. This is the only way to go to a race!' Lunch in the Struan box for the thirty-six guests had been a lavish buffet of hot Chinese foods or, if they preferred, hot steak-and-kidney pie and vegetables, with plates of smoked salmon, hors d'oeuvres and cold cuts, cheeses and pastries of all kinds and as a topper, a meringue sculpture of the Struan Building—all prepared in their own kitchen. Champagne, the best red and white wines, liqueurs. 'I'm gonna have to diet for fifty years.'

'Not you. How goes it?'

She felt his probing eyes. 'Fine. Why?'

'Nothing.' He glanced off at Grey again, then turned his attention to the others.

1107

'May I introduce Peter Marlowe? Hiro Toda of Toda Shipping Industries of Yokohama. Peter's a novelist-screenwriter from Hollywood.' Then all at once his book rushed into her mind and Changi and three and a half years as a prisoner of war and she waited for the explosion. There was a hesitation between both men. Toda politely offered his business card and Peter Marlowe gave his in return, equally politely. He hesitated a moment then put out his hand. 'How're you?'

The Japanese shook it. 'This's an honor, Mr. Marlowe.'

'Oh?'

'It's not often one meets a famous author.'

'I'm not, no, not at all.'

'You're too modest. I liked your book very much. Yes.'

'You've read it?' Peter Marlowe stared at him. 'Really?' He sat and looked at Toda, who was much shorter than he, lithe and well built, more handsome and well dressed in a blue suit, a camera hanging on his chair, his eyes equally level, the two men of an age. 'Where did you find it?'

'In Tokyo. We have many English bookshops. Please excuse me, I read the paperback, not the hardback. There was no hardback on sale. Your novel was very illuminating.'

'Oh?' Peter Marlowe took out his cigarettes and offered them. Toda took one.

Casey said, 'Smoking's not good for you, you both know that!'

They smiled at her. 'We'll give them up for Lent,' Peter Marlowe said.

'Sure.'

Peter Marlowe looked back at Toda. 'You were army?'

'No, Mr. Marlowe. Navy. Destroyers. I was at the Battle of the Coral Sea in '42, then at Midway, sub-lieutenant, later at Guadalcanal. I was sunk twice but lucky. Yes, I was lucky, apparently more lucky than you.'

'We're both alive, both in one piece, more or less.'

'More or less, Mr. Marlowe. I agree. War is a curious way of life.' Toda puffed his cigarette. 'Sometime, if it would please you and not hurt, I would like to talk about your Changi, about its lessons and our wars. Please?'

'Sure.'

'I'm here for a few days,' Toda said. 'At the Mandarin, back

1108

next week. A lunch, or dinner perhaps?'

'Thank you. I'll call. If not this time perhaps next. One day I'll be in Tokyo.'

After a pause the Japanese said, 'We need not discuss your Changi, if you wish. I would like to know you better. England and Japan have much in common. Now if you'll excuse me, I think I should place my bet.' He bowed politely and walked off. Casey sipped her coffee.

'Was that very hard for you? Being polite?'

'Oh no, Casey. No, it wasn't, not at all. Now we're equal, he and I, any Japanese. The Japanese—and Koreans—I hated were the ones with bayonets and bullets when I had none.' She saw him wipe the sweat off, noticing his twisted smile. ''*Mahlu*, I wasn't ready to meet one here.'

'*Mahlu?* What's that, Cantonese?'

''Malayan. It means "ashamed".' He smiled to himself. It was a contraction of *puki mahlu*. *Mahlu* ashamed, *puki* a Golden Gulley. Malays grant feelings to that part of a woman: hunger, sadness, kindness, rapaciousness, hesitancy, shame, anger— anything and everything.

'No need to be ashamed, Peter,' she said, not understanding. 'I'm astonished you'd talk to any of them after all that POW horror. Oh I really liked the book. Isn't it marvelous that he'd read it too?'

'Yes. That threw me.'

'May I ask you one question?'

'What?'

'You said Changi was genesis. What did you mean?'

He sighed. 'Changi changed everyone, changed values permanently. For instance, it gave you a dullness about death—we saw too much of it for it to have the same sort of meaning as for outsiders, normal people. We're a generation of dinosaurs, we the few who survived. I suppose anyone who goes to war, any war, sees life with different eyes if they end up in one piece.'

'What do you see?'

'A lot of bull that's worshipped as the be-all and end-all of existence. So much of "normal, civilized" life is bull that you can't imagine it. For us ex-Changi-ites—we're lucky, we're cleansed, we know what life is really all about. What frightens you, doesn't frighten me, what frightens me, you'd laugh at.'

1109

'Like what?'

He grinned at her. 'That's enough about me and my karma. I've a hot tip for th—' He stopped and stared off. 'Good sweet Christ who's that?'

Casey laughed. 'Riko Gresserhoff. She's Japanese.'

'Which one's Mr. Gresserhoff?'

'She's a widow.'

'Hallelujah!' They watched her go across the room, out onto the terrace.

'Don't you dare, Peter!'

His voice became Olympian. 'I'm a writer! It's a matter of research!'

'Baloney!'

'You're right.'

'Peter, they say all first novels are autobiographical. Who were you in the book?'

'The hero of course.'

'The King? The American trader?'

'Oh no. Not him. And that's quite enough of my past. Let's talk about you. You sure you're all right?' His eyes held hers, willing the truth out of her.

'What?'

'There was a rumor that you were in tears last night.'

'Nonsense.'

'Sure?'

She looked back at him, knowing he saw inside of her. 'Of course. I'm fine.' A hesitation. 'Sometime, sometime I might need a favor.'

'Oh?' He frowned. 'I'm in McBride's box, two down the hall. It's quite okay to visit if you want.' He glanced off at Riko. His pleasure faded. Now she was talking to Robin Grey and Julian Broadhurst, the Labour MPs. 'Guess it's not my day,' he muttered. 'I'll be back later, got to bet. See you, Casey.'

'What's your hot tip?'

'Number seven, Winner's Delight.'

Winner's Delight, an outsider, won handily by half a length over the favorite, Excellent Day. Hugely pleased with herself, Casey joined the line in front of the winner's pay window clutching her winning tickets, well aware of the envious stares of others who walked along the corridor outside the boxes.

Agonized betters were already putting down their money at other windows for the second race that was the first leg of the double quinella. To win a quinella they had to forecast the first and second runners in any order. The double quinella put the second race together with the fifth that was today's big race. The double quinella payout would be huge, the odds against forecasting four horses immense. The minimum bet was 5 HK. There was no maximum. 'Why's that, Linc?' she had asked just before the race, craning over the balcony watching the horses in the gate, all Hong Kong *yan* with their binoculars focused.

'Look at the Tote.' The electronic numbers were flashing and changing as money went onto different horses, narrowing the odds, to freeze just before the off. 'Look at the total money invested on this race, Casey! It's better than three and a half million Hong Kong. That's almost a dollar for every man woman and child in Hong Kong and it's only the first race. This's gotta be the richest track in the world! These guys are gambling crazy.'

A vast roar went up as the starters' gate opened. She had looked at him and smiled. 'You okay?'

'Sure. You?'

'Oh yes.'

Yes I am, she thought again, waiting her turn to collect her money. I'm a winner! She laughed out loud.

'Oh hello, Casey! Ah, you won too?'

'Oh! Oh hello, Quillan, yes I did.' She moved out of her place back to Gornt, the others in the line all strangers to her. 'I only had 10 on her but yes I won.'

'The amount doesn't matter, it's the winning.' Gornt smiled. 'I like your hat.'

'Thank you.' Curious, she thought, both Quillan and Ian had mentioned it immediately. Damn Linc!

'It's very lucky to pick the first winner, first time at the track.'

'Oh I didn't. It was a tip. Peter gave it to me. Peter Marlowe.'

'Ah yes. Marlowe.' She saw his eyes change slightly. 'You're still on for tomorrow?'

'Oh. Oh yes. Is it weather permitting?'

'Even if it's raining. Lunch anyway.'

'Great. The dock at ten sharp. Which's your box?' She noticed an instant change which he tried to hide.

1111

'I don't have one. I'm not a steward. Yet. I'm a fairly permanent guest at the Blacs box and from time to time I borrow the whole place for a party. It's down the corridor. Would you care to come by? Blacs is an excellent bank an—'

'Ah but not as good as the Vic,' Johnjohn called out good-naturedly as he passed. 'Don't believe a word he says, Casey. Congratulations! Good joss to get the first. See you both later.'

Casey watched him thoughtfully. Then she said. 'What about all the bank runs, Quillan? No one seems to care—it's as though they're not happening, the stock market's not crashing, and there's no pending doom.'

Gornt laughed, conscious of the ears that were tuned to their conversation. 'Today is race day, a rarity, and tomorrow will take care of tomorrow. Joss! The stock market opens 10:00 A.M. Monday and next week will decide a lot of fates. Meanwhile every Chinese who could get his money out, has it in his fist, here today. Casey, it's your turn.'

She collected her money. 15 to one. 150 HK. 'Hallelujah!' Gornt collected a vast bundle of red notes, 15,000. 'Hey, fantastic!'

'Worst race I've ever seen,' a sour American voice said. 'Hell, it was fantastic they didn't bust the jockey and disallow the win.'

'Oh hello, Mr. Biltzmann, Mr. Pugmire.' Casey remembered them from the night of the fire. 'Bust who?'

Biltzmann stood in the place line. 'Stateside there'd be an objection a mile wide. Coming into the straight out of the last bend you could see Excellent Day's jockey pull the bejesus out of her. It was a fix—he wasn't trying.'

Those in the know, the very few, smiled to themselves. The whisper in the jockeys' rooms and trainers' rooms had been that Excellent Day wasn't to win but Winner's Delight would.

'Come now, Mr. Biltzmann,' Dunross said. Unnoticed, he'd heard the exchange as he was passing and had stopped. 'If the jockey wasn't trying, or if there was any tampering, the stewards would be on to it at once.'

'Maybe it's okay for amateurs, Ian, and this little track but on any professional track at home, Excellent Day's jockey'd be banned for the rest of his life. I had my glasses on him all the time.' Biltzmann sourly collected his place winnings and stomped off.

Dunross said quietly, 'Pug, did you see the jockey do anything untoward? I didn't watch the race myself.'

'No, no I didn't.'

'Anyone?' Those nearby shook their heads.

'Seemed all right to me,' someone said. 'Nothing out of the ordinary.'

'None of the stewards queried anything.' Then Dunross noticed the large roll of notes in Gornt's hand. He looked up at him. 'Quillan?'

'No. But I must tell you frankly I find that berk's manner appalling. I hardly think he'd be a proper addition to the Turf Club.' Just then he saw Robin Grey go past to place a bet and smiled at a sudden thought. 'Excuse me, will you?' He nodded politely and walked off. Casey saw Dunross watching the roll of notes that Gornt put into a pocket and was inwardly aghast at the momentary look on his face.

'Could Biltzmann . . . could he've been correct?' she asked nervously.

'Of course.' Dunross put his full attention on her. 'Fixing happens everywhere. That's really not the point. There's been no objection from any of the stewards or jockeys or trainers.' His eyes were slate gray. The small vein in his forehead was pulsating. 'That's not the real point at issue.' No, he was thinking. It's a matter of bloody manners. Even so, calm yourself. You have to be very cool and very calm and very collected this weekend.

All day he had had nothing but trouble. The only bright moment had been Riko Anjin Gresserhoff. But then AMG's last letter had once more filled him with gloom. It was still in his pocket and it had told him that if by chance he had not destroyed the original files, to heat a dozen specified pages that were spread throughout the secret information written in invisible ink on these pages to be passed privately to the prime minister or the current head of MI-6, Edward Sinders, personally—and a copy given to Riko Anjin in a sealed envelope.

If I do that then I have to admit the files I gave him were false, he thought, weary of AMG, espionage and his instructions. Goddamnit, Murtagh doesn't arrive till later, Sir Geoffrey can't call London till 4:00 P.M. about Tiptop and Brian Kwok and, Christ Jesus, now some rude bastard calls us all amateurs . . which we are. I'll bet a hundred to a bent hatpin Quillan knew before the race.

At a sudden thought he said casually, 'How did you pick the winner, Casey? With the proverbial pin?'

'Peter gave it to me. Peter Marlowe.' Her face changed. 'Oh! Do you think he heard it was fixed?'

'If I thought that for a moment, the race would have been set aside. There's nothing I can do now. Biltzmann . . .' Suddenly he gasped as the idea hit him in all its glory.

'What's the matter?'

Dunross took her arm and led her aside. 'To get your drop dead money are you prepared to gamble?' he asked softly.

'Sure, sure, Ian, if it's legal. But gamble what?' she asked, her innate caution uppermost.

'Everything you've got in the bank, your house in Laurel Canyon, your stock in Par-Con against 2 to 4 million within thirty days. How about it?'

Her heart was thumping, his obvious excitement sweeping her. 'Okay,' she said and then wished she hadn't said it, her stomach fluttering. 'Jesus!'

'Good. Stay here a second. I'll go and find Bartlett.'

'Wait. Is he part of this? What is this, Ian?'

He beamed. 'A modest business opportunity. Yes, Bartlett's essential. Does that make you change your mind?'

'No,' she told him uneasily, 'but I said I wanted to get my . . . my stake outside of Par-Con.'

'I haven't forgotten. Wait here.' Dunross hurried back into his box, found Bartlett and brought him back, led the way down the bustling corridor to the Struan kitchen, greeting people here and there. The kitchen was small, busy and sparkling. The staff paid no attention to them. A door opened into a tiny private room, carefully soundproofed. Four chairs, a table and phone. 'My father had this constructed during his tenure—lots of business is done at the races. Sit down please. Now'—he looked at Bartlett—'I've a business proposal for you, for you and Casey as individuals, outside of our Par-Con deal, nothing to do with the Par-Con-Struan proposal. Are you interested?'

'Sure. This a Hong Kong scam?'

'Do you mind?' Dunross beamed. 'It's an honest-to-God Hong Kong business proposal.'

'Okay, let's have it.'

'Before I lay it out there are ground rules: It's my game, you two're bystanders but you're in for 49 percent of the profits, to be shared equally between you two. Okay?'

'What's the full game plan, Ian?' Bartlett asked cautiously.

'Next: You put up $2 million U.S. by Monday 9:00 A.M. into a Swiss bank of my choosing.'

Bartlett's eyes narrowed. 'Against what?'

'Against 49 percent of the profit.'

'What profit?'

'You put up $2 million for Gornt, no paper, no chop, no nothing except against potential profit.'

Bartlett grinned. 'How long have you known about that?'

Dunross smiled back. 'I told you, there're no secrets here. Are you in?' Dunross saw Bartlett glance at Casey and he held his breath.

'Casey, you know what this's all about?'

'No, Linc.' Casey turned to Dunross. 'What *is* the scam, Ian?'

'First I want to know if I get the 2 million advance free and clear—*if* you go for this scheme.'

'What's the profit potential?' Casey asked.

'$4 to $12 million. Tax free.'

Casey blanched. 'Tax free?'

'Free of any Hong Kong taxes and we can help you avoid States taxes if you want.'

'What's . . . what's the payout period?' Bartlett asked.

'The profit'll be set in thirty days. The payout will take five to six months.'

'The $4 to $12 million's the total, or our share only?'

'Your share.'

'That's a lot of profit for something completely, twenty-four-carat legal.'

There was a great silence. Dunross waited, willing them onward.

'$2 million cash?' Bartlett said. 'No security, no nothing?'

'No. But after I've laid it out you can put up or pass.'

'What's Gornt to do with this?'

1115

'Absolutely nothing. This venture has nothing to do with Gornt, Rothwell-Gornt, Par-Con, your interest in them or us or the Par-Con deal. This is totally outside, whatever happens—my word on that. And my word before God, that I'll never tell him you've put up this $2 million, that you two are my partners and in for a piece—or, by the way, that I know about the three of you selling me short.' He smiled. 'That was a very good idea by the way.'

'The deal's swung by my $2 million?'

'No. Greased. I haven't $2 million U.S. cash as you know, otherwise you wouldn't be invited in.'

'Why us, Ian? You could raise 2 mill from one of your friends here, easy, if it's so good.'

'Yes. But I choose to sweeten the lure to you two. By the way, you are held to Tuesday at midnight.' Dunross said it flat. Then his voice changed and the others felt the glee. 'But with this—this business venture—I can dramatize how much superior we are to Rothwell-Gornt, how much more exciting it'll be being associated with us than him. You're a gambler, so am I. Raider Bartlett they call you and I'm tai-pan of the Noble House. You gambled a paltry $2 million with Gornt, with no chop, why not with me?'

Bartlett glanced at Casey. She gave him neither a yes or a no though he knew the lure had her in spades.

'Since you're setting the rules, Ian, answer me this: I put up the $2 million. Why should we share equally, Casey and I?'

'I remember what you said over dinner about drop dead money. You've got yours, she hasn't. This could be a device to get her hers.'

'Why're you so concerned over Casey? You trying to divide and rule?'

'If that's possible then you shouldn't be in a very special partnership and business relationship. She's your right arm, you told me. She's clearly very important to you and to Par-Con so she's entitled to share.'

'What does she risk?'

'She'll put up her house, her savings, her Par-Con stock—that's everything she has—alongside yours. She'll sign it all over for half a share. Right?'

Casey nodded, numb. 'Sure.'

Sharply Bartlett glanced at Casey. 'I thought you said you knew nothing about this?'

She looked at him. 'Couple of minutes ago, Ian asked if I'd gamble my all to get some drop dead money, big money.' She gulped and added, 'I said okay and already wish I hadn't.'

Bartlett though a moment. 'Casey, blunt: You want in or you want out?'

'In.'

'Okay.' Then Bartlett beamed. 'Okay, tai-pan, now who do we have to kill?'

Nine Carat Chu, who was a sometime gold coolie for the Victoria Bank and also the father of two sons and two daughters—Lily Su who was Havergill's occasional friend and Wisteria who was John Chen's mistress, whose joss was to be trampled to death outside the Ho-Pak at Aberdeen—waited his turn at the betting window.

'Yes, old man?' the impatient teller said.

He pulled out a roll of money. It was all the money he had and all the money he could borrow, leaving only enough for three inhalations of the White Powder that he would need to see him through his night shift tonight. 'The double quinella, by all the gods! Eight and five in the second race, seven and one in the fifth.'

The teller methodically counted out the crumpled bills. 728 HK. He pressed the buttons of those numbers and checked the first ticket. It was correct: five and eight—second race; seven and one—fifth race. Carefully he counted 145 tickets, each of 5 HK, the minimum bet, and gave them to him with 3 HK change. 'Hurry up, by all the gods,' the next in line called out. 'Are your fingers in your Black Hole?'

'Be patient!' the old man muttered, feeling faint, 'this is serious business!' Carefully he checked his tickets. The first, three random ones and the last were correct, and the number of tickets correct, so he gave up his place and pushed his way out of the press into the air. Once in the air he felt a little better, still nauseated but better. He had walked all the way from his night shift of work at the construction site of the new high rise up above Kotewall Road in Mid Levels to save the fare.

Again he checked his tickets. Eight and five in this race and seven and one in the fifth, the big race. Good, he thought, putting them carefully into his pocket. I've done the best I can. Now it is up to the gods.

His chest was hurting him very much so he fought through the crowd to the toilet and there he lit a match and inhaled the smoke from the bubbling White Powder. In time he felt better and went outside again. The second race was already on. Beside himself with anxiety he pushed and shoved his way to the rails, careless of the curses that followed him. The horses were rounding the far bend, galloping toward him into the last straight for the winning post, now past in a thundering blur as he strained his rheumy old eyes to find his numbers.

'Who's leading?' he gasped but no one paid any attention to him, just shouted their own choice on to victory in a growing seething roar that was all possessing, then vanished as the winner won.

'Who won?' Nine Carat Chu gasped, his head exploding.

'Who cares!' someone said with a stream of curses. 'It wasn't mine! All gods piss on that jockey forever!'

'I can't read the tote, who won?'

'It was a photo finish, old fool, can't you see! There were three horses bunched together. Fornicate all photo finishes! We must wait.'

'But the numbers. . . . what are the numbers?'

'Five and eight and four, Lucky Court, my horse! Come on you son of a whore's left tit! Four and eight for the quinella by all the gods!'

They waited. And waited. The old man thought he would faint so he put his mind on to better things, like his conversation with Noble House Chen this morning. Three times he had called and each time a servant had answered and hung up. It was only when he had said 'Werewolf' that Noble House Chen himself had come to the phone.

'Please excuse me for mentioning the terrible slayers of your son,' he had said. 'It wasn't me, Honored Sir, oh no. I am just the father of your late honorable son's mistress, Wisteria Su, to whom he has written his undying love in the letter that was printed in all newspapers.'

'Eh? Liar! All lies. Do you think I'm a fool to be squeezed

by any dogmeat caller? Who are you?'

'My name is Hsi-men Su,' he had said, the lie coming easily. There are two more letters, Honorable Chen. I thought you might wish to have them back even though they're all we have from my poor dead daughter and your poor dead son who I considered like my own son over all the months that he an—'

'More lies! The mealy-mouthed strumpet never had any letters from my son! Our deadly police put forgers in jail, oh yes! Am I a peasant-headed monkey from the Outer Provinces? Beware! Now I suppose you'll produce an infant that you'll claim my son sired? Eh? *Eh?*'

Nine Carat Chu almost dropped the phone. He had discussed and arranged that very ploy with his wife and his sons and Lily. It had been easy to find a relation who would lend a babe in arms for a fee.

'Eh,' he spluttered in shock, 'am I a liar? Me who fairly, for modest cash, gave his only virgin daughter to be your son's whore and *only love*.' He used the English words carefully, his daughter Lily having coached him for hours so that he could say it properly. 'By all the gods we've protected your great name at no charge! When we went to claim my poor daughter's body we did not tell the deadly police who desire, *oh ko*, yes, who desire to find out who the writer was to trap the Werewolves! All gods curse those evil sons of whores! Haven't four Chinese papers already offered rewards for the name of the writer, *heya?* It is only fair I offer the letters to you before collecting the news-papers' reward, *heya?*'

Patiently he had listened to the stream of invective that had begun the negotiation. Several times both sides had pretended they were going to put the phone down, but neither side broke off the bargaining. At length it was left that if a photocopy of one of the other letters was sent to Noble House Chen as proof that it and the others were no forgery, then 'it might be, Honorable Su, the other letters—and this one—might be worth a very modest amount of Fragrant Grease.'

Nine Carat Chu chortled to himself now. Oh yes, he thought contentedly, Noble House Chen will pay handsomely, particularly when he reads the parts about himself. Oh if those were printed surely it would hold him up to ridicule before all Hong

Kong and take his face away forever. Now, how much should I settle f—

A sudden roar surrounded him and he almost fell over. His heart began pounding, his breath short. He held on to the rails and peered at the distant tote. 'Who . . . what are the numbers?' he asked, then screeched over the noise and tugged at his neighbors. 'The numbers, tell me the numbers!'

'The winner's eight, Buccaneer, the gelding of the Noble House. *Ayeeyah*, can't you see the tai-pan leading him into the winner's circle now? Buccaneer's paying 7 to 1.'

'The second? Who was the second horse?'

'Number five, Winsome Lady, 3 to 1 for a place. . . . What's wrong, old man, have you a palsy?'

'No . . . no . . .' Weakly Nine Carat Chu groped away. At length he found a small empty patch of concrete and spread his racing form on the wet concrete and sat down, his head on his knees and arms, his mind sweeping him into the ecstasy of winning the first leg. Oh oh oh! And nothing to do now but wait, and if the time of waiting is too long I will use one more of the White Powders, yes, and that will leave me the last to see me through tonight's work. Now, all gods concentrate! The first leg was won by my own shrewdness. Please concentrate on the fifth! Seven and one! All gods concentrate. . . .

Over by the winner's circle the stewards and owners and officials clustered. Dunross had intercepted his horse and congratulated the jockey. Buccaneer had run a fine race and now as he led the gelding into the winner's circle amid another burst of cheering and congratulations he kept his exuberance deliberately open. He wanted to let the world see his pleasure and confidence, very aware that winning this race was an immense omen, over and above the fact of winning. The omen would be doubled and tripled if he won with Noble Star. Two horses in the double quinella would absolutely set Gornt and his allies back on their heels. And if Murtagh works his magic or if Tiptop keeps his bargain to swap the money for Brian Kwok or if Tightfist or Lando or Four Fingers . . .

'Hey, Mr. Dunross, sir, congratulations!'

Dunross glanced at the crowd on the rails. 'Oh hello, Mr.

Choy,' he said, recognizing Four Finger Wu's Seventh Son and supposed nephew. He went closer and shook hands. 'Did you have the winner?'

'Yes sir, sure, I'm with the Noble House all the way! We're on the double quinella, my uncle and me. We just won the first leg five and eight, and we've seven and eight in the fifth. He's got 10,000 riding, me, my whole week's salary!'

'Then let's hope we win, Mr. Choy.'

'You can say that again, tai-pan,' the young man said with his easy American familiarity.

Dunross smiled and walked over to Travkin. 'Are you sure Johnny Moore can't ride Noble Star? I don't want Tom Wong.'

'I told you, tai-pan, Johnny's sicker than a drunken cossack.'

'I need the win. Noble Star is to win.'

Travkin saw Dunross look at Buccaneer speculatively. 'No, tai-pan, please don't ride Noble Star. The going's bad, very bad and very dangerous and it'll get worse as they hack up the turf, *Kristos!* I suppose that'll only make you want to ride her more.'

'My future could ride on that race—and the face of the Noble House.'

'I know.' Angrily the gnarled old Russian slapped the switch he carried perpetually against his ancient jodhpurs, shiny with use. 'And I know you're better than all the other jockeys but that turf's danger—'

'I don't trust anyone in this, Alexi. I can't afford a mistake.' Dunross dropped his voice. 'Was the first race fixed?'

Travkin stared back levelly. 'They weren't doped, tai-pan. Not to my knowledge. The police doctor has put the fear of God into those who might be tempted.'

'Good. But was it fixed?'

'It wasn't my race, tai-pan. I'm only interested in my horses and my races. I didn't watch that race.'

'That's convenient, Alexi. Seems that none of the other trainers did either.'

'Listen, tai-pan. I have a jockey for you. Me. I'll ride Noble Star.'

Dunross's eyes narrowed. He glanced at the sky. It was darker than before. There'll be rain soon, he thought and there's much to do before the rain. Me or Alexi? Alexi's legs are good, his hands the best, his experience immense. But he thinks more

1121

of the horse than of winning. 'I'll consider it,' he said. 'After the fourth race I'll decide.'

'I'll win,' the older man said, desperate for the chance to extricate himself from his agreement with Suslev. 'I'll win even if I have to kill Noble Star.'

'No need to do that, Alexi. I'm rather fond of that horse.'

'Tai-pan, listen, perhaps a favor? I've a problem. Can I see you tonight or Sunday, Sunday or Monday late, say at Sinclair Towers?'

'Why there?'

'We made our deal there, I'd like to talk there. But if it's not all right the day after.'

'You're going to leave us?'

'Oh no, no it's not that. If you've time. Please.'

'All right but it can't be tonight, or Sunday or Monday, I'm going to Taipei. I could see you Tuesday at 10:00 P.M. How's that?'

'Fine, Tuesday's fine yes, thank you.'

'I'll be down after the next race.'

Alexi watched the tai-pan walk for the elevators. He was near tears, an overwhelming affection for Dunross possessing him.

His eyes went to Suslev who was in the general stands nearby. Trying to appear casual he held up the prearranged number of fingers: one for tonight, two for Sunday, three Monday, four Tuesday. His eyes were very good and he saw Suslev acknowledge the signal. *Matyeryebyets*, he thought. Betrayer of Mother Russia and all us Russians, you and all your KGB brethren! I curse you in the name of God, for me and *all* Russians if the truth be known.

Never mind that! I'm going to ride Noble Star, he told himself grimly, one way or another.

Dunross got into the elevator amid more congratulations and much envy. At the top floor Gavallan and Jacques were waiting for him. 'Is everything ready?' he asked.

'Yes,' Gavallan replied. 'Gornt's there, and the others you wanted. What's cooking?'

'Come along and you'll see. By the way, Andrew, I'm switching Jacques and David MacStruan. Jacques will take over Canada for a year, David—'

Jacques's face lit up. 'Oh thank you tai-pan. Yes, thanks very much. I'll make Canada very profitable, I promise.'

'What about the changeover?' Gavallan asked. 'Do you want Jacques to go there first or will David come here?'

'He arrives Monday. Jacques, you hand over everything to David, then next week you can both go back together for a couple of weeks. You go via France, eh? Pick up Susanne and Avril, she should be well enough by then. There's nothing urgent in Canada at the moment—it's more urgent here.'

'Oh yes, *ma foi!* Yes, yes thank you, tai-pan.'

Gavallan said thoughtfully, 'It'll be good to see old David.' He liked David MacStruan very much but he was still wondering why the change, and did this mean that Jacques was out of the running to inherit the tai-pan's mantle and David in and his own position changed, changing or threatened?—if there was anything left to inherit after Monday. And what about Kathy?

Joss, he told himself. What is to be will be. Oh goddamn everything!

'You two go on ahead,' Dunross said. 'I'll get Phillip.' He turned into the Chen box. By ancient custom the compradore of the Noble House was automatically a steward. Perhaps for the last year, Dunross thought grimly. If Phillip doesn't deliver help in the form of Four Finger Wu, Lando Mata, Tightfist or something tangible by Sunday at midnight he's blackballed.

'Hello, Phillip,' he said, his voice friendly, greeting the other guests in the packed box. 'You ready?'

'Oh yes, yes, tai-pan.' Phillip Chen was looking older. 'Congratulations on the win.'

'Yes, tai-pan, a marvelous omen—we're all praying for the fifth!' Dianne Chen called out, trying equally hard to hide her apprehension, Kevin beside her, echoing her.

'Thank you,' Dunross said, sure that Phillip Chen had told her about their meeting. She wore a hat with birds of paradise feathers, and too many jewels.

'Champagne, tai-pan?'

'No thanks, later perhaps. Sorry, Dianne, have to borrow Phillip for a moment or two. Won't be long.'

Outside in the corridor he stopped a moment. 'Any luck, Phillip?'

'I've . . . I've talked to all the . . . all of them. They're meeting tomorrow morning.'

'Where? Macao?'

'No, here.' Phillip Chen dropped his voice even more. 'I'm sorry about . . . about all the mess my son's caused . . . yes, very sorry,' he said, meaning it.

'I accept your apology. If it hadn't been for your carelessness and treachery, we'd never have become that vulnerable. Christ Jesus, if Gornt gets our balance sheets for the last few years and our interlocking corporate structures, we're up the creek without a paddle.'

'I . . . I had a thought, tai-pan, how to extract our—how to extract the House. After the races, could I . . . a little time, please?'

'You're coming for drinks tonight? With Dianne?'

'Yes, if . . . yes please. May I bring Kevin?'

Dunross smiled fleetingly to himself. The heir apparent, officially and so soon. Karma. 'Yes. Come along.'

'What's this all about, tai-pan?'

'You'll see. Please say nothing, do nothing, just accept—with great confidence—that you're part of the package, and when I leave follow me, spread the word and good cheer. If we fail, the House of Chen fails first, come hell, high water or typhoon!' He turned into the McBride box. There were more immediate congratulations and many said it was great joss.

'Good God, tai-pan,' McBride said, 'if Noble Star wins the fifth, wouldn't it be marvelous!'

'Pilot Fish will beat Noble Star,' Gornt said confidently. He was at the bar with Jason Plumm getting a drink. '10,000 says he'll finish ahead of your filly.'

'Taken,' Dunross said at once. There were cheers and hoots of derision from the thirty-odd guests and once more Bartlett and Casey, who had by arrangement with Dunross ostensibly just wandered in a few minutes ago to visit Peter Marlowe, were inwardly staggered at the festive air and Dunross's high-flying confidence.

'How're you doing, Dunstan?' Dunross asked. He paid Casey and Bartlett no attention, concentrating on the big florid man who was more florid than usual, a double brandy in his hand.

'Very well, thank you, Ian. Got the first, and Buccaneer— made a bundle on Buccaneer, but blew my damned quinella. Lucky Court let me down.'

The room was the same size as the Struan box but not as well decorated, though equally well filled with many of the Hong Kong elite, some invited here a moment ago by Gavallan and McBride for Dunross. Lando Mata, Holdbrook—Struan's in-house stockbroker—Sir Luis Basilio—head of the stock exchange—Johnjohn, Havergill, Southerby—chairman of Blacs—Richard Kwang, Pugmire, Biltzmann, Sir Dunstan Barre, young Martin Haply of the *China Guardian*. And Gornt. Dunross looked at him. 'Did you get the winner of the last race too?'

'No. I didn't fancy any runner. What's all this about, Ian?' Gornt said, and everyone's attention soared. 'You want to make an announcement?'

'Yes, as a courtesy I thought you should know, along with other VIPs.' Dunross turned to Pugmire. 'Pug, the Noble House is formally contesting the American Superfoods takeover of your H.K. General Stores.'

There was a vast silence and everyone stared at him. Pugmire had gone white. 'What?'

'We're offering $5 a share more than Superfoods, we'll further improve their bid by making it 30 percent cash and 70 percent stock, everything done within thirty days!'

'You've gone mad,' Pugmire burst out. Didn't I sound everyone out first, he wanted to shout, including you? Didn't you and everyone approve or at least not disapprove? Isn't that the way it's done here for God's sake—private chats at the Club, here at the races, over a private dinner or wherever? 'You can't do that,' he muttered.

'I already have,' Dunross said.

Gornt said harshly, 'All you've done, Ian, is to make an announcement. How are you going to pay? In thirty or three hundred days?'

Dunross just looked at him. 'The bid's public. We complete in thirty days. Pug, you'll get the official papers by 9:30 A.M. Monday, with a cash down payment to cement the tender.'

Momentarily he was drowned out as others began talking, asking questions, everyone immediately concerned how this astonishing development would affect them personally. No one had ever contested a prearranged takeover before. Johnjohn and Havergill were furious that this had been done without consultation, and the other banker, Southerby of Blacs, who

1125

was merchant-banking the Superfoods takeover, was equally upset that he had been caught off balance. But all the bankers, even Richard Kwang, were counting possibilities, for if the stock market was normal and Struan's stock at its normal level, the Struan bid could be very good for both sides. Everyone knew that Struan's management could revitalize the rich but stagnant *hong*, and the acquisition would strengthen the Noble House immeasurably, put their end-of-year gross up at least 20 percent and of course increase their dividends. On top of all that, the takeover would keep all the profits in Hong Kong, and not have them trickle away to an outsider. Particularly Biltzmann.

Oh my God, Barre was thinking with vast admiration and not a little envy, for Ian to make the tender here, in public, on a Saturday, with never the breath of a rumor that he was contemplating the unthinkable, with nothing to give you an inkling so that you could have bought in quietly last week at bottom to make a fortune with one phone call, was brilliant. Of course Pug's General Stores shares will soar first thing on Monday. But how in the hell did Ian and Havergill keep it quiet? Christ I could've made a bundle if I'd known, perhaps I still can! The rumors about the Victoria not supporting Struan's is obviously a lot of cobblers. . . .

Wait a minute, Sir Luis Basilio was thinking, didn't we buy a huge block of General Stores last week for a nominee buyer? Good God, has the tai-pan outsmarted all of us? But Madonna, wait a minute, what about the run on his stock, what about the market crashing, what about the cash he'll have to put up to fix the tender, what about . . .

Even Gornt was counting, his mind flooded with fury that he had not thought of the ploy first. He knew the bid was good, perfect in fact, that he could not top it, not at the moment. But then, Ian can't complete. There's no wa—

'Can we go to press on this, tai-pan?' Martin Haply's incisive Canadian voice cut through the excited uproar.

'Certainly, Mr. Haply.'

'May I ask a few questions?'

'It depends what they are,' Dunross said easily. Looking at the penetrating brown eyes, he was grimly amused. We could use a right rotten young bastard in the family—if he could be trusted with Adryon. 'What had you in mind?'

'This's the first time a takeover's even been contested. May I ask why you're doing it at this time?'

'Struan's have always been innovative. As to timing, we considered it perfect.'

'Do you consider this Sat—'

Biltzmann interrupted harshly, 'We have a deal. It's set. Dickie?' He whirled on Pugmire. 'Eh?'

'It was all set, Mr. Biltzmann,' Dunross said crisply. 'But we're contesting your tender, just as it's done in the States, according to American rules. I presume you don't mind a contest? Of course we are amateurs here but we enjoy trying to learn from our peers. Until the stockholders' meeting nothing's final, that's the law isn't it?'

'Yes, but . . . but it was set!' The tall gray-haired man turned to Pugmire, hardly able to speak he was so angry. 'You said it was all agreed.'

'Well, the directors had agreed,' Pugmire said uneasily, conscious of everyone listening, particularly Haply, one half of him ecstatic with the vastly improved offer, the other furious that he, too, had had no advance warning so he could have bought in heavily. 'But, er, but of course it has to be ratified by the stockholders at the Friday meeting. We had no idea there'd be a . . . Er, Ian, er, Chuck, don't you think this is hardly the place to dis—'

'I agree,' the tai-pan said. 'But at the moment there's little to discuss. The offer's made. By the way, Pug, your own deal stands, except that it's extended from five to seven years, with a seat on Struan's board for the same period.'

Pugmire's mouth dropped open. 'That's part of the tender?'

'We'd need your expertise, of course,' Dunross said airily, and everyone knew Pugmire was hooked and landed. 'The rest of the package as negotiated by you and Superfoods stands. The papers will be on your desk by 9:30. Perhaps you'll put our tender to your stockholders on Friday.' He went over to Biltzmann and put out his hand. 'Good luck. I presume you'll be coming back with a counteroffer at once.'

'Well, er, I have to check with head office, Mr., er, tai-pan.' Blitzmann and flushed and angry. 'We . . . we put our best foot forward and . . . That's a mighty fine offer you made.

1127

Yes. But with the run on your stock, the run on the banks and the market going down, that's going to be kinda hard to close, isn't it?'

'Not at all, Mr. Biltzmann,' Dunross said, gambling everything that Bartlett would not renege on the promise of cash, that he would close with Par-Con, extricate himself from Gornt and put his stock back into its rightful place by next weekend. 'We can close with no trouble at all.'

Biltzmann's voice sharpened. 'Dickie, I think you'd better consider our bid carefully. It's good till Tuesday,' he said, confident that by Tuesday Struan's would be in a shambles. 'Now I'll make me a bet on the next race.' He stalked out. Tension in the box went up several decibels.

Everyone began talking but Haply called out, 'Tai-pan, may I ask a question?'

Again attention zeroed. 'What is it?'

'I understand it's customary in takeovers for there to be a down payment, in cash, a measure of good faith. May I ask how much Struan's is putting up?'

Everyone waited breathlessly, watching Dunross. He held the pause as his eyes raked the faces, enjoying the excitement, knowing everyone wanted him humbled, almost everyone, except . . . except who? Casey for one, even though she's in the know. Bartlett? I don't know, not for certain. Claudia? Oh yes, Claudia was staring at him, white-faced. Donald McBride, Gavallan, even Jacques.

His eyes stopped on Martin Haply. 'Perhaps Mr. Pugmire would prefer to have that detail in private,' he said, leading them on. 'Eh, Pug?'

Gornt interrupted Pugmire and said, as a challenge, 'Ian, since you've decided to be unorthodox, why not make it all public? How much you put down measures the value of your tender. Doesn't it?'

'No. Not really,' Dunross said. He heard the distant muted roar of the off for the third race and was sure, watching the faces, that no one heard it except him. 'Oh, very well,' he said, matter-of-fact. 'Pug, how about $2 million, U.S., with the papers at 9:30 Monday? In good faith.'

A gasp went through the room. Havergill, Johnjohn, Southerby, Gornt, were aghast. Phillip Chen almost fainted.

Involuntarily Havergill began, 'Ian, don't you think we, er, th—'

Dunross wheeled on him. 'Oh, don't you consider it enough, Paul?'

'Oh yes, yes of course, more than enough, but, er . . .' Havergill's words trailed off under Dunross's gaze.

'Oh for a moment . . .' Dunross stopped, pretending to have a sudden thought, 'Oh, you needn't worry, Paul, I haven't committed you without your approval of course. I have alternate financing for this deal, external financing,' he continued with his easy charm. 'As you know, Japanese banks and many others are anxious to expand into Asia. I thought it better—to keep everything secret and prevent the usual leaks—to finance this externally until I was ready to announce. Fortunately the Noble House has friends all over the world! See you all later!'

He turned and left. Phillip Chen followed. Martin Haply started for the phone and then everyone was talking and saying I don't believe it, Christ if Ian's got that sort of external funds . . .

In the hubbub Havergill asked Johnjohn, 'Which Japanese bank?'

'I wish I knew. If Ian's got finance for this . . . my God, $2 million U.S.'s twice as much as he needed to offer.'

Southerby, who was alongside them, wiped his palms. 'If Ian pulls this off it'll be worth $10 million U.S. the first year at least.' He smiled sardonically. 'Well, Paul, now it looks as though we're both out of this particular pie.'

'Yes, yes it does, but I just don't see how Ian could . . . and to keep it so quiet!'

Southerby bent closer. 'Meanwhile,' he asked softly, 'more important, what about Tiptop?'

'Nothing, nothing yet. He hasn't returned my calls, or Johnjohn's.' Havergill's eyes fell on Gornt who was now talking privately with Plumm. He turned his back on him. 'What will Quillan do now?'

'Buy first thing Monday morning. He has to. Has to now, too dangerous to hold on,' Southerby said.

'I agree,' Sir Luis Basilio added, joining them. 'If Ian can toss that sort of cash around, those who've been selling him short better watch out. Come to think of it, we've been buying

General Stores for nominees this last week. Probably Ian, eh? He has to have taken a position, lucky devil!'

'Yes,' Johnjohn muttered. 'For the life of me I can't figure . . . Good sweet Christ, and now if he wins with Noble Star! With joss like that he could turn his whole mess about, you know what Chinese're like!'

'Yes,' Gornt said, butting in, startling them. 'But thank God we're not all Chinese. We've yet to see the cash.'

'He must have it—must have it,' Johnjohn said. 'Matter of face.'

'Ah, face.' Gornt was sardonic. '9:30 A.M., eh? If he'd really been smart he would have said noon, or 3:00 P.M., then we wouldn't know all day and he could've manipulated us all day. As it is now . . .' Gornt shrugged. 'I win either way, millions, if not control.' He glanced across the noisy box, nodded non-committally to Bartlett and Casey, then turned away.

Bartlett took Casey's arm and led her on to the balcony. 'What do you think?' he asked softly.

'About Gornt?'

'About Dunross.'

'Fantastic! He's fantastic. "Japanese bank"—that was a stunning red herring,' she said excitedly. 'He's put this whole goup into a tailspin, you could see that, and if this group, the whole of Hong Kong. You heard what Southerby said?'

'Sure. It looks like we've all got it made—if he can squeeze out of Gornt's trap.'

'Let's hope.' Then she noticed his smile. 'What?'

'You know what we just did, Casey? We just bought the Noble House for the promise of 2 million bucks.'

'How?'

'Ian's gambling I will put up the 2.'

'That's no gamble, Linc, that was the deal.'

'Sure. But say I don't. His whole pack of cards collapses. If he doesn't get the 2 he's finished. Yesterday I told Gornt I might jerk the rug Monday morning. Say I withdraw Ian's 2 before the market opens. Ian's down the tube.'

She stared at him, appalled. 'You wouldn't?'

'We came here to raid and become the Noble House. Look what Ian did to Biltzmann, what they all did to him. That poor bastard didn't know what hit him. Pugmire made a deal but

1130

reneged to take Ian's better offer. Right?'

'That's different.' She looked at him searchingly. 'You're going to renege after making a deal?'

Bartlett smiled a strange smile, looked down at the packed crowds and at the tote. 'Maybe. Maybe that depends on who does what to whom over the weekend. Gornt or Dunross, it's all the same.'

'I don't agree.'

'Sure, Casey, I know,' he said calmly. 'But it's my $2 million and my game.'

'Yes, and your word and your face! You shook on the deal.'

'Casey, these guys here would eat us for breakfast if they got the chance. You think Dunross wouldn't sell us out if he had to choose between him and us?'

After a pause she said, 'You're saying a deal's never a deal, no matter what?'

'You want $4 million tax free?'

'You know the answer to that.'

'Say you're in for 49 percent of the new Par-Con-Gornt company, free and clear. It's got to be worth that.'

'More,' she said, afraid of this line of talk and for the first time in her life suddenly not sure of Bartlett.

'You want that 49 percent?'

'In return for what, Linc?'

'In return for getting in back of Gornt-Par-Con 100 percent.'

Her stomach felt weak and she looked at him searchingly, trying to read his mind. Normally she could, but not since Orlanda. 'Are you offering that?'

He shook his head, his smile the same, his voice the same. 'No. Not yet.'

She shivered, afraid she would take the deal if it were really offered. 'I'm glad,' Raider. I guess, yes, I'm glad.'

'The point's straight and simple, Casey: Dunross and Gornt play the game to win but for different stakes. Why this box would mean more to both of them than $2 or $4 million. We came here, you and I, to profit and to win.'

They both glanced at the sky as a few raindrops spattered. But it was from the roof overhang and not a new shower. She began to say something, stopped.

'What, Casey?'

1131

'Nothing.'

'I'm going to circulate, see what the reaction is. See you back in our box.'

'What about the fifth?' she asked.

'Wait for the odds. I'll be back before the start.'

'Have fun!' She followed him with her eyes, out of the door, then turned and leaned on the balcony to hide from him and everyone. She had almost blurted out, Are you going to pull the rug and renege?

Jesus, before Orlanda—before Hong Kong—I'd never have needed to ask that question. Linc would never go back on a deal before. But now, now I'm not sure.

Again she shivered. What about my tears? I've never pulled that one before, and what about Murtagh? Should I tell Linc about Murtagh now—or later—because he must be told, certainly before 9:30 Monday. Oh God, I wish we'd never come here.

The patter of rain splashed the stadium and someone said, 'Christ, I hope it doesn't get any worse!' The track was already scarred and muddy and very slippery. Outside the main entrance the road was slicked, puddled, traffic heavy and many late-coming people still hurried through the turnstiles.

Roger Crosse, Sinders and Robert Armstrong got out of the police car and went through the barriers and the checkpoints to the members' elevator, their blue lapel badges fluttering. Crosse had been a voting member for five years, Armstrong for one. Crosse was also a steward this year. Every year the commissioner of police suggested to the stewards that the police should have their own box and each year the stewards agreed enthusiastically and nothing happened.

In the members' stand Armstrong lit a cigarette. His face was lined, his eyes tired. The huge, crowded room went half the length of the stands. They went to the bar and ordered drinks, greeting other members. 'Who's that?' Sinders asked.

Armstrong followed his glance. 'That's a little of our local color, Mr. Sinders.' His voice was sardonic. 'Her name's Venus Poon and she's our top TV starlet.'

Venus Poon was wearing a full-length mink and surrounded

by an admiring group of Chinese. 'The fellow on her left's Charles Wang—he's a film producer, multimillionaire, cinemas, dance halls, nightclubs, bars, girls and a couple of banks in Thailand. The small old man who looks like a bamboo and's just as tough is Four Finger Wu, one of our local pirates— smuggling's his life's work and he's very good.'

'Yes,' Crosse said. 'We almost caught him a couple of days ago. We think he's into heroin now—of course gold.'

'Who's the nervous one in the gray suit? The fellow on the outside?'

'That's Richard Kwang of the Ho-Pak disaster,' Armstrong said. 'The banker. He's her current, or was her current—what's the word—*patron?*'

'Interesting.' Sinders concentrated on Venus Poon. Her dress was low-cut and saucy. 'Yes, very. And who's that? Over there—the one with the European.'

'Where? Oh. That's Orlanda Ramos, Portuguese which usually means Eurasian here. Once she was Quillan Gornt's mistress. Now, now I don't know. The man's Linc Bartlett, the "gun-runner".'

'Ah! She unattached?'

'Perhaps.'

'She looks expensive.' Sinders sipped his drink and sighed. 'Delectable, but expensive.'

'I'd say very,' Crosse told him distastefully. Orlanda Ramos was with several middle-aged women, all couturier dressed, around Bartlett. 'Rather overdone for my taste.'

Sinders glanced at him, surprised. 'I haven't seen so many smashers in years—or so many jewels. Have you ever had a raid here?'

Crosse's eyes soared. 'In the Turf Club? Good God, surely no one'd dare.'

Armstrong smiled his hard smile. 'Every copper who does duty here, from the high to the low, spends most of the time trying to work out the perfect heist. The final day's take must be 15 million at least. It's baffled us all. Security's too tight, too clever—Mr. Crosse set it up.'

'Ah!'

Crosse smiled. 'Would you like a snack, Edward? Perhaps a sandwich?'

'Good idea. Thank you.'

'Robert?'

'No thank you, sir. If you don't mind I'll study the form and see you later.' Armstrong was achingly aware that after the seventh race, they were due to return to HQ where Brian Kwok was scheduled for another session.

'Robert's a serious punter, Edward. Robert, do me a favor, show Mr. Sinders the ropes, where to bet, and order him a sandwich. I'd better see if the governor's free for a moment—I'll be back in a few minutes.'

'Glad to,' Armstrong said, hating the idea, the envelope with 40,000 *h'eung yau* dollars that he had taken from his desk on an impulse now a never-ending fire in his pocket. Christ, do I or don't I? he asked himself over and over, grimly trying to decide and all the while trying to push away the horror of his friend Brian and the next session—no, no longer his friend but a committed, highly trained foreign asset and enormously valuable catch that they had by a miracle uncovered.

'Robert,' Crosse said, keeping his voice deliberately kind, 'you've done a very good job today. Very good.'

'Yes,' Sinders agreed. 'I'll see the minister's aware of your help, and of course the CP.'

Crosse went for the elevator. Wherever he went nervous Chinese eyes followed him. On the top floor he bypassed the governor's box and went into Plumm's.

'Hello, Roger!' Plumm greeted him affably. 'Drink?'

'Coffee would be fine. How're things?'

'Lost my shirt so far, though a number of us have the first leg of the quinella. You?'

'I've just arrived.'

'Oh, then you missed the drama!' Plumm told Crosse about Dunross's takeover bid. 'Ian's thrown a monkey wrench into Pug.'

'Or given him a great offer,' someone volunteered.

'True, true.'

Plumm's box was as packed as all the others. Lots of chatter and laughter, drinks and good food. 'Tea'll be up in half an hour. I'm just going along to the stewards' committee room, Roger. Would you like to stroll with me?'

The committee room was at the end of the corridor, through

1134

guarded swing doors. It was small with a table and twelve chairs, a phone, good windows over the track and a tiny balcony. And empty. At once Plumm's easygoing facade vanished. 'I talked to Suslev.'

'Oh?'

'He's furious about the raid on the *Ivanov* last night.'

'I can imagine. That was ordered by London. I wasn't even told till this morning. Bloody Sinders!'

Plumm became even grimmer. 'They couldn't be on to you, could they?'

'Oh no. It's routine. Just Special Branch, MI-6 and Sinders flexing their wings. They're a secretive lot and quite right, nothing to do with SI. Go on.'

'He said if you came that he'd be by a phone booth.' Plumm handed him a slip of paper. 'Here's the number. He'll be there exactly at the off of the next three races. Please call him—he said it was urgent. What the hell was the raid for?'

'Just to frighten all the KGB aboard, to frighten them enough to flush out Sevrin. Pressure. Same as the order for Suslev and the new commissar to appear at HQ on Sunday. It was just to frighten.'

'Suslev's frightened all right.' A sardonic smile flickered over Plumm's handsome face. 'His sphincter's out of joint for ten years at least. They'll all have some explaining to do. When Armstrong "happened" to bust open the radio room, Red One operated and they dutifully and unnecessarily wrecked all their scramble and decoding equipment, along with their classified radar scanners.'

Crosse shrugged. 'The *Ivanov*'s leaving and they've got plenty to replace them with. It wasn't Suslev's fault, or ours. We can send a report telling Center what happened. If we want.'

Plumm's eyes narrowed. 'If?'

'Rosemont and his CIA thugs picked up a glass in their raid on Sinclair Towers. Suslev's prints are all over it.'

Plumm went white. 'Christ! Now he's on file?'

'Has to be. He's in our files as you know, not as KGB, and I think I've the only copies of his fingerprints existing. I removed them from his dossier years ago. I'd say it's only a matter of time before the CIA are on to him, so the sooner he leaves Hong Kong the better.'

'You think we should tell Center?' Plumm asked uneasily. 'They'll throw their book at him for being so careless.'

'We can decide over the weekend. We knew Voranski over a number of years, knew he was to be trusted. But this man?' Crosse left the word hanging, keeping up the pretense that his contact with Suslev was recent, the same as Plumm's. 'After all, isn't he only a minor KGB officer, a jumped-up courier. He's not even Voranski's official replacement and we've ourselves to think of.'

'True!' Plumm hardened. 'Maybe he's a real berk. I know I wasn't followed to Sinclair Towers. And as to the decoded cable—God stone the crows!'

'What?'

'The decoded cable—the one he dropped and Armstrong picked off the *Ivanov*'s deck. We've got to decide about that.'

Crosse turned away to hide his shock and fought for control, appalled that neither Armstrong nor Sinders had mentioned any cable. He pretended to stifle a yawn to cover. 'Sorry, I was up most of the night,' he said, making a major effort to keep his voice matter-of-fact. 'Did he tell you what was in it?'

'Of course. I insisted.'

Crosse saw Plumm watching him. 'Exactly what did he tell you was in it?'

'Oh? You mean he might be lying?' Plumm's anxiety showed. 'It went something like: "Inform Arthur that following his request for a Priority One on the traitor Metkin an immediate intercept was ordered for Bombay. Second, the meeting with the American is brought forward to Sunday. Third and final: The AMG files continue to be Priority One. Maximum effort must be made by Sevrin to achieve success. Center."' Plumm licked his lips. 'Is it correct?'

'Yes,' Crosse said, gambling, almost wet with relief. He began weighing odds on Armstrong and Sinders. Now why, deliberately, why didn't they tell me that?

'Terrible, eh?' Plumm said.

'Yes, but not serious.'

'I don't agree,' Plumm said irritably. 'It absolutely ties the KGB to Sevrin, absolutely confirms Arthur's existence and Sevrin's existence.'

'Yes, but the AMG files have already done that. Calm down, Jason, we're quite safe.'

'Are we? There've been too many leaks for my liking. Far too many. Perhaps we should close down for a time.'

'We are closed down. It's only those bloody AMG files that are causing us any grief.'

'Yes. At least that bugger Grant wasn't completely accurate.'

'You mean about Banastasio?'

'Yes. I still wonder where the hell he fits in.'

'Yes.' In AMG's intercepted file Banastasio had been named erroneously as Sevrin's American connection. It was only after the file that Crosse had learned from Rosemont who Banastasio actually was.

'The fellow who met him was Vee Cee Ng,' Crosse said.

Plumm's eyebrows soared. 'Photographer Ng? How does he connect?'

'I don't know. Shipping, ships, smuggling. He's into all kinds of shady deals.' Crosse shrugged.

'Could that writer fellow's theory work? What's his name? Marlowe. Could the KGB be doing an op in our territory without telling us?'

'Possible. Or it could be an utterly different department, perhaps GRU, instigated in America by the KGB or GRU there. Or just a coincidence.' Crosse was back in control now, the fright of the cable wearing off. He was thinking much more clearly. 'What's Suslev want that's so urgent?'

'Our cooperation. Koronski arrives by the afternoon plane.'

Crosse whistled. 'Center?'

'Yes. There was a message this morning. Now that the *Ivanov's* equipment is wrecked I'm the go-between.'

'Good. What's his cover name?'

'Hans Meikker, West German. He's to stay at the Seven Dragons.' Plumm's anxiety increased. 'Listen, Suslev said Center's ordered us to prepare to snatch Ian an—'

'They've gone mad!' Crosse exploded.

'I agree but Suslev says it's the only way to find out quickly if the files are counterfeit or not, and if so, where they're hidden. He claims Koronski can do it. In a chemical debriefing, well, Ian's memory can be . . . can be emptied.'

'That's madness,' Crosse said. 'We're not even sure if the files

1137

are counterfeit. That's a complete supposition for God's sake!'

'Suslev says Center told him we can blame it on the Were-wolves—those buggers snatched John Chen so why wouldn't they go after the big money, the tai-pan?'

'No. Too dangerous.'

Plumm wiped his hands. 'To snatch Ian now'd put the tai-pans and Hong Kong into a furor. It could be a perfect time, Roger.'

'Why?'

'The Noble House would be in total disarray and with all the bank runs and the stock market disaster, Hong Kong'd be down the sewer and that'd send all China into shock. We'd jump the Cause forward ten years and immeasurably assist international communism and the workers of the world. Christ, Roger, aren't you sick of just sitting and being a messenger? Now we can fulfill Sevrin with hardly any risk. Then we close everything down for a time.'

Crosse lit a cigarette. He had heard the tension in Plumm's voice. 'I'll think about it,' he said at length. 'Leave it for the moment. I'll call you tonight. Did Suslev say who the American in the cable was?'

'No. He just said it wasn't anything to do with us.'

Crosse's voice hardened. 'Everything here's to do with us.'

'I agree.' Plumm watched him. 'It could also be a code word, a code for anyone.'

'Possible.'

'I have a wild one for you. Banastasio.'

'Why him?' Crosse asked, having jumped to the same con-clusion.

'I don't know why, but I'll bet that whole scam, if it is a scam, has to be KGB inspired, or assisted. It's classic Sun Tzu: using the enemy's strength against himself—both enemies, the U.S. and China. A strong unified Vietnam's guaranteed militantly anti-Chinese. Eh?'

'Possible. Yes, it all fits,' Crosse agreed. Except one thing, he thought: Vee Cee Ng. Until Brian Kwok had blurted out, 'Vee Cee's one of us,' he had had no inkling that the man was anything other than a swinging photographer and trader-shipping capitalist. 'If Banastasio's the American, we'll know.' He finished his cigarette. 'Was there anything else?'

'No. Roger, consider Dunross. Please. The Werewolves make it possible.'

'It's considered.'

'This weekend would be perfect, Roger.'

'I know.'

Orlanda was watching the horses through her high-powered binoculars as they broke out of the starting gate for the fourth race. She stood in a corner of the members' balcony, Bartlett happily beside her, everyone watching the horses except him. He was watching her, the curve of her breasts under the silk, the angle of her cheekbones and the intensity of her excitement. 'Come on, Crossfire,' she muttered, 'come on! He's lying fifth, Linc, oh come on, you beauty, come on . . .'

He chuckled, Orlanda oblivious. They had arranged to meet here between the third and fourth race. 'Are you a voting member?' he had asked her last night.

'Oh no, my darling, I'm just going with friends. Old friends of my family. Another drink?'

'No, no thanks—I'd better go.'

They had kissed and again he had felt her overpowering welcome. It had kept him unsettled and on edge all the way back across the harbor home and most of the night. Much as he tried, he found the wanting of her difficult to contain and to keep in perspective.

You're hooked, old buddy, he told himself, watching her, the tip of her tongue touching her lips, her eyes concentrating, everything forgotten but her $50 on the nose of the big gray, the favorite.

'Come on . . . come . . . oh he's moving up, Linc . . . oh he's second. . . .'

Bartlett looked at the pack galloping now into the last stretch: Crossfire, the big gray well placed to Western Scot, a brown gelding who was slightly in the lead, the going very slow—one horse had fallen in the third race. Now a contender made his dash, Winwell Stag, a gelding belonging to Havergill that Peter Marlowe had tipped to win, and he was coming up strong on the outside with Crossfire and Western Scot neck and neck just ahead, all whips out now in the gathering roar.

'Oh come on come on come on Crossfire . . . oh he's won, he's won!'

Bartlett laughted in the pandemonium as Orlanda's glee burst out and she hugged him. 'Oh Linc, how wonderful!'

In a moment there was another roar as the winning numbers were flashed upon the tote board, confirming their order. Now everyone waited for the final odds. Another great cheer. Crossfire paid 5 to 2.

'That's not much,' he said.

'Oh but it is it is it is!' Orlanda had never looked prettier to him, her hat cute, much better than Casey's—he'd noticed it at once and complimented her on it. She moved forward and leaned on the railing and looked down at the winner's circle. 'There's the owner, Vee Cee Ng, he's one of our Shanghainese trader-shipping millionaires. My father knew him quite well.' She gave him the glasses.

Bartlett focused. The man leading the garlanded horse into the winner's circle was expensively dressed, a beaming, well-set Chinese in his fifties. Then Bartlett recognized Havergill leading in his Winwell Stag, second, defeated by a nose. In the paddock he saw Gornt, Plumm, Pugmire and many of the stewards. Dunross was near the rails talking to a smaller man. The governor was walking from group to group with his wife and aide. Bartlett watched them, envying them a little, the owners standing there with their caps and raincoats and shooting sticks and expensive women and girl friends, greeting one another, all members of the inner club, the powerhouse of Hong Kong, there and in the boxes above. All very British, he thought, all very clever. Will I fit in better than Biltzmann? Sure. Unless they want me out as much as they wanted him out. I'll be a voting member easy. Ian said as much. Would Orlanda fit there? Of course. As wife or girl friend, it's all the same.

'Who's that?' he asked. 'The man talking to Ian?'

'Oh that's Alexi Travkin, he's the tai-pan's trainer. . . .' She stopped as Robert Armstrong came up to them.

'Afternoon, Mr. Bartlett,' he said politely. 'Did you back the winner too?'

'No, no I lost this one. May I introduce Miss Ramos, Orlanda Ramos, Superintendent Robert Armstrong, CID.'

'Hello.' She smiled back at Armstrong, and he saw her immediate caution. Why are they all frightened of us, the innocent as well as the guilty? he asked himself, when all we do is try to enforce *their* laws, try to protect them from villains and the ungodly. It's because everyone breaks some law, even a little one, every day, most days, because a lot of laws are stupid—like our betting laws here. So everyone's guilty, even you, pretty lady with the oh so sensual walk and oh so promising smile. For Bartlett. What crime have you committed today, to snare this poor innocent? Sardonically he smiled to himself. Not so innocent in most things. But against someone trained by Quillan Gornt? A beautiful, hungry Eurasian girl with no place to go but down? *Ayeeyah!* But oh how I'd like to swap places! Yes, with your guns, money, birds like Casey and this one and meetings with the offal of the world like Banastasio, oh yes—I'd give ten years of my life, more, because today I swear to God I loathe what I have to do, what only I can do for good old England.

'Did you back the favorite too?' she was asking.

'No, no unfortunately.'

'This's her second winner,' Bartlett said proudly.

'Ah, if you're on a winning streak, who do you fancy in the fifth?'

'I've been trying to decide, Superintendent. I've no tips—it's wide open. What's yours?'

'Winning Billy's tipped, I hear. I can't make up my mind either. Well, good luck.' Armstrong left them, heading for the betting windows. He had put 500 on the third-place horse, covering his other bets. He always chose a main bet and then hedged it with others, hoping to come out ahead. Most times he did. This afternoon he was a little behind, but he still hadn't touched the 40,000.

In the corridor he hesitated. The Snake, Chief Inspector Donald C. C. Smyth, was turning away from one of the crowded winning windows, a roll of money in his hand. 'Hello, Robert. How're you doing?'

'So-so. You're in the big time again?'

'I try.' The Snake bent closer. 'How is everything?'

'Proceeding.' Once more Armstrong felt nauseated at the thought of more of the Red Room, then sitting there, letting Brian Kwok's mind spill out his most secret secrets, working against the clock that was ticking away—all of them aware that the governor was asking London for permission to trade.

'You're not looking so good, Robert.'

'I don't feel so good. Who's going to win the fifth?'

'I leaned on your friend Clubfoot at the Para. The word is Pilot Fish. He did tip Buccaneer in the first, though with this going anything could happen.'

'Yes. Anything on the Werewolves?'

'Nothing. It's a dead end. I'm having the whole area combed but with this rain it's almost hopeless. I did interview Dianne Chen this morning—and John Chen's wife Barbara. They gave me sweet talk. I'd lay a fiver to a bent hatpin they know more than they're telling. I had a brief talk with Phillip Chen but he was equally uncooperative. Poor bugger's pretty shook.' The Snake looked up at him. 'By chance did Mary have any clue about John?'

Armstrong looked back at him. 'I haven't had a chance to ask her. Tonight—if they give me any peace.'

'They won't.' Smyth's face crinkled with a twisted smile. 'Put your 40 on Pilot Fish.'

'What 40?'

'A dickie bird twittered that a certain golden nest egg has flown your coop—to mix metaphors.' The smaller man shrugged. 'Don't worry, Robert, have a flutter. There's plenty more where that came from. Good luck.' He went away. Armstrong stared after him, hating him.

The bugger's right though, he thought, his chest hurting. There's plenty more but once you take the first, what about the second and though you give nothing, admit nothing, guarantee nothing, there will come a time. As sure as God made little apples there's always a return payment.

Mary. She needs that holiday, needs it so much and there's the stockbroker's bill and all the other bills and oh Christ, with this market gone crazy I'm almost wiped out. God curse money—or the lack of it.

40 on a winning quinella'd solve everything. Or do I put it all on Pilot Fish? All or half or none. If it's all, there's plenty of time to place bets at other windows.

His feet took him to one of the betting lines. Many recognized him and those who did, feeling their instant internal fear, wished the police had their own box and own windows and did not mix with honest citizens. Four Finger Wu was one of these. Hastily he put 50,000 on a quinella of Pilot Fish and Butterscotch Lass and fled back to the members' room, gratefully to sip his brandy and soda. Dirty dogmeat police to frighten honest citizens, he thought, waiting for Venus Poon to return. Eeeee, he chortled, her Golden Gulley's worth every carat of the diamond I promised her last night. Two Clouds and Rain before dawn and a promise of another bout on Sunday when the yang recovers his ju—

A sudden roar from outside diverted his mind. At once he shoved his way through the crowds packing the balcony. The names of the fifth racehorses and their jockeys were coming up on the board, one by one. Pilot Fish, number one, got a full-bellied cheer; then Street Vendor, an outsider, two; Golden Lady, three and a ripple of excitement went through her many backers. When Noble Star, seven, flashed up there was a great roar and when the last, number eight, the favorite, Butterscotch Lass, there was an even greater roar.

Down by the rail Dunross and Travkin were grimly inspecting the turf. It was torn and slippery. The nearer the rail, the worse it was. Above, the sky was blacker and lowering. A sprinkle started and a nervous groan slipped from fifty thousand throats.

'It's rotten, tai-pan,' Travkin said, 'the going's rotten.'

'It's the same for everyone.' Dunross let his mind reestimate the odds a last time. If I ride and win, the omen will be immense. If I ride and lose, the omen will be very bad. To be beaten by Pilot Fish would be even worse. I could be hurt easily. I can't afford . . . the Noble House can't afford to be headless today, tomorrow or Monday. If Travkin rides and loses or finishes behind Pilot Fish that would be bad but not as bad. That would be joss.

But I won't get hurt. I'll win. I want this race more than anything in the world. I won't fail. I'm not sure about Alexi. I can win—if the gods are with me. Yes but how much are you prepared to gamble on the gods?

'Eeee, young Ian,' Old Chen-chen had told him many times, 'beware of expecting help from the gods, however much you petition them with gold or promises. Gods are gods and gods go out to lunch and sleep and get bored and turn their eyes away.

Gods are the same as people: good and bad, lazy and strong, sweet and sour, stupid and wise! Why else are they gods, *heya?*'

Dunross could feel his heart thumping and could smell the warm, acrid, sweet-sour horse sweat, could sense the mind-blinding, spirit-curdling motioning, hands gripping the whip, bunched in the corner, now into the far straight, now into the last corner, the aching, grand sweet terror of speed, wielding the whip, jamming your heels in, outstretched now, carefully bumping Pilot Fish into the rails, putting him off his stride, and now into the straight, ripping into the straight, Pilot Fish behind, winning post ahead . . . come on come on . . . winning. . . .

'We have to decide, tai-pan. It's time.'

Dunross came back slowly, bile in his mouth. 'Yes. You ride,' he said, putting the House before himself.

And now that he had said it he put the rest aside and clapped Travkin warmly on the shoulders. 'Win, Alexi, win by God.'

The older man, gnarled and leathery, peered up at him. He nodded once, then walked off to change. As he went he noticed Suslev in the stands watching him through binoculars. A tremor went through him. Suslev had promised that this Christmas Nestorova would come to Hong Kong, she would be allowed to join him in Hong Kong—and stay in Hong Kong—at Christmas. If he cooperated. If he cooperated and did what was asked.

Do you believe that? No. No, not at all, those *matyeryebyets* are liars and betrayers but maybe this time . . . Christ Jesus why should I be ordered to meet Dunross at Sinclair Towers by night, late at night? Why? Christ Jesus, what should I do? Don't think, old man. You're old and soon you'll be dead but your first duty is to win. If you win, the tai-pan will do your bidding. If you lose? If you win or lose, how can you live with the shame of betraying the man who befriended you and trusts you?

He went into the jockeys' room.

Behind him Dunross had turned to glance at the tote. The odds had shortened, the total amount at risk already two and a half million. Butterscotch Lass was 3 to 1, Noble Star 7 to 1, still no jockey listed, Pilot Fish 5 to 1, Golden Lady 7 to 1. Early yet, he thought, and so much time left to gamble. Travkin will shorten the odds. A cold shaft took him. I wonder if there's a deal going on right now, a deal among the trainers and jockeys? Christ, we'd all better be watching this one very carefully indeed.

'Ah Ian!'

'Oh hello, sir.' Dunross smiled at Sir Geoffrey who came up to him then looked at Havergill who was with the governor. 'Pity about Winwell Stag, Paul, I thought he ran a grand race.'

'Joss,' Havergill said politely. 'Who's riding Noble Star?'

'Travkin.'

The governor's face lit up. 'Ah, very good choice. Yes, he'll make a good race of it. For a moment, Ian, I was afraid you might be tempted.'

'I was. Still am, sir.' Dunross smiled faintly. 'If Alexi gets hit by a bus between now and then, I'm riding her.'

'Well, for the sake of all of us and the Noble House, let's hope that doesn't happen. We can't afford to have you hurt. The going looks terrible.' Another swirl of rain came and passed by. 'We've been very lucky so far. No bad accidents. If the rain starts in earnest, it might be worthwhile considering abandoning.'

'We've already discussed it, sir. We're running a little late. The race'll be delayed ten minutes. So long as the weather holds for this race most people will be satisfied.'

Sir Geoffrey watched him. 'Oh by the way, Ian, I tried the minister a few minutes ago but I'm afraid he was already in meetings. I left word and he'll call back the moment he can. It seems the ramifications of this damned Profumo scandal are once more tearing at the very roots of the Conservative government. The press are screaming, quite rightly, in case there have been breaches of security. Until the Commission of Enquiry comes out next month, settling once and for all security aspects and rumors that others in the government are implicated or not, there'll be no peace.'

'Yes,' Havergill said. 'But surely the worst's over, sir. As to the report, certainly it won't be adverse.'

'Adverse or not, this scandal will wreck the Conservatives,' Dunross said soberly, remembering AMG's forecast in the last report.

'Good God, I hope not.' Havergill was aghast. 'Those two twits, Grey and Broadhurst, in power amongst all the other Socialist shower? If their press conference was any indication,

1145

we might as well all go home.'

'We are home, and it all comes home to roost. Eventually,' Sir Geoffrey said sadly. 'Anyway, Ian made the correct decision not to ride.' He glanced at Havergill and his gaze sharpened. 'As I said, Paul, it's important to make correct decisions. It would be a very poor show if the Ho-Pak's depositors were wiped out, perhaps just because of poor judgment by Richard Kwang and the lack of a benevolent decision by those who could avoid such a disaster if they wished—perhaps to great profit. Eh?'

'Yes sir.'

Sir Geoffrey nodded and left them.

Dunross said, 'What was that about?'

'The governor thinks we should rescue the Ho-Pak,' Havergill said off-handedly.

'Why don't you?'

'Let's talk about the General Stores takeover.'

'First let's finish the Ho-Pak. The governor's right, it would benefit all of us, Hong Kong—and the bank.'

'You'd be in favor?'

'Yes, of course.'

'You'll approve, you and your block will approve making the takeover?'

'I don't have a block but certainly I'll support a reasonable takeover.'

Paul Havergill smiled thinly. 'I was thinking of 20 cents on the dollar on Richard's holdings.'

Dunross whistled. 'That's not much.'

'By Monday night he'll have zero. He'll probably settle for that—his holdings would give the bank control. We could easily stand surety for 100 percent of his depositors.'

'He's got that amount of securities?'

'No, but with the normalization of the market and our judicious management, over a year or two it's true the acquisition of the Ho-Pak could greatly benefit us. Oh yes. And there's a desperate need to restore confidence. Such a takeover would help immeasurably.'

'This afternoon would be a perfect announcement time.'

'I agree. Anything on Tiptop?'

Dunross studied him. 'Why the sudden change around, Paul? And why discuss it with me?'

'There's no change around. I've considered the Ho-Pak very carefully. The acquisition would be good bank policy.' Havergill watched him. 'We'll give him face and offer him a seat on our board.'

'So the rumors about the Big Bank are true?'

'Not to my knowledge,' the banker said coldly. 'As to why discuss it with you? Because you're a director of the bank, presently the most important one, with substantial influence on the board. That's a sensible thing to do, isn't it?'

'Yes, but.'

Havergill's eyes became colder. 'The interests of the bank have nothing to do with my distaste for you, or your methods. But you were right about Superfoods. You made a good offer at a perfect time and sent a wave of confidence soaring through everyone here. It's bound to spread over all Hong Kong. It was brilliant timing and now if we follow it up and announce we've assumed all the Ho-Pak responsibilities to its depositors, that's another immense vote of confidence. All we need to do is get back confidence. If Tiptop comes to our assistance with his cash, Monday is boom day for Hong Kong. So first thing on Monday morning, Ian, we buy Struan's heavily. By Monday evening we'll assume control. However I'll make you a deal right now: we'll put up the 2 million for General Foods in return for half your bank stock.'

'No thanks.'

'We'll have it all by next weekend. We'll guarantee that 2 million in any event to cover the takeover and guarantee the overall offer you made to Pug—if you fail to avoid your own takeover.'

'I won't.'

'Of course. But you don't mind if I mention it to him and to that nosy little cretin Haply?'

'You're a bastard, aren't you?'

Havergill's thin lips twisted with his smile. 'This is business— I want your block of bank stock. Your forebears bought it for nothing, practically stole it from the Brocks after smashing them. I want to do the same. And I want control of the Noble House. Of course. Like a great number of others. Probably even your American friend Bartlett if the truth were known. Where's the 2 million coming from?'

1147

'It's manna from heaven.'

'We'll find out sooner or later. We're your bankers and you owe us rather a lot of money! Will Tiptop bail us out?'

'I can't be sure but I talked to him last night. He was encouraging. He agreed to come here after lunch but he hasn't arrived yet. That's ominous.'

'Yes.' Havergill brushed some drizzle off his nose. 'We've had a very positive response from the Trade Bank of Moscow.'

'Even you're not that fat-headed!'

'It's a last resort, Ian. A serious last resort.'

'You'll call an immediate board meeting to discuss the Ho-Pak takeover?'

'Good Lord, no.' Havergill was sardonic. 'You think I'm that much of a fool? If we did that you could table the other directors about an extension of your loan. No, Ian, I propose to ask them individually, like you. With your agreement I have a majority already, the others of course fall into line. I do have your agreement?'

'At 20 cents on the dollar and full payout of investors, yes.'

'I might need leeway to go to 30 cents. Agreed?'

'Yes.'

'Your word?'

'Oh yes, you have my word.'

'Thank you.'

'But you'll call a board meeting before Monday's opening?'

'I agreed to consider it. Only. I've considered it and the answer now is *no*. Hong Kong's a freebooting society where the weak fail and the strong keep the fruits of their labors.' Havergill smiled and he glanced at the tote. The odds had shortened. 2 to 1 on Butterscotch Lass, well known for liking the wet. Pilot Fish now 3 to 1. While they watched, Travkin's name flashed up alongside Noble Star and a huge roar accompanied it. 'I think the governor was wrong, Ian. You should have ridden. Then I'd've put my modest bet on you. Yes. You'd have gone out in a blaze of glory. Yes, you would have won. I'm not sure about Travkin. Good afternoon.' He raised his hat and headed for Richard Kwang who stood with his wife and trainer to one side. 'Ah Richard! Can I have a word wi—' He was drowned by a huge roar from the crowd as the first of eight runners for the fifth race began to trickle out from under the stands.

Pilot Fish led the pack, the slight drizzle making his black coat shimmer.

'Yes, Paul?' Richard Kwang asked, following him into an empty space. 'I wanted to talk to you but didn't want to interrupt you with the governor and the tai-pan. Now,' he said with forced joviality, 'I've a plan. Let's lump all the Ho-Pak's securities together and if you'll lend me 50 mill—'

'No thank you, Richard,' Havergill said crisply. 'But we do have a proposal that's good till five o'clock today. We'll bail out the Ho-Pak and guarantee all your despositors. In return we'll buy your personal holdings at par an—'

'Par? That's a fiftieth of their value!' Richard Kwang screeched. 'That's a fiftieth of their worth—'

'Actually it's 5 cents on the dollar which is about all their value. Is it a deal?'

'No of course not, *Dew neh loh moh*, am I a dogmeat madman?' Richard Kwang's heart was almost bursting. A moment ago he had thought, impossibly, that Havergill was granting him a reprieve from the disaster that by now he was convinced was absolute, however much he pretended otherwise, however much it was not his fault but the work of rumormongers and malicious fools who had led him into inept banking deals. But now he was in the vise. *Oh ko!* Now he would be squeezed and whatever he did he could not escape the tai-pans. Oh oh oh! Disaster on disaster and now that ungrateful strumpet Venus Poon making me lose face in front of Uncle Four Fingers, Charlie Wang and even Photographer Ng and that even after I delivered to her personally the new mink coat that she trails in the mud so carelessly.

'New?' she had flared this morning. 'You claim this miserable second-hand coat is new?'

'Of course!' he had shouted. 'Do you think I am a monkey? Of course it's new. It cost 50,000 cash *oh ko!*' The 50,000 was an exaggeration but the cash wasn't and they both were well aware that it would be uncivilized not to exaggerate. The coat had cost him 14,000, through an intermediary, after much bargaining from a *quai loh* who had fallen on hard times and another 2,000 to the furrier who had overnight shortened and altered it enough to fit and not to be recognized, with a guarantee that the furrier would swear by all the gods that he had sold it under price at 42 even though it was actually worth 63,500.

'Paul,' Richard Kwang said importantly. 'The Ho-Pak's in better shape th—'

'Kindly shut up and listen,' Havergill said overriding him. 'The time has come to make a serious decision—for you, not us. You can go under on Monday with nothing. . . . I understand trading's opening on your stock first thing.'

'But Sir Luis assured me th—'

'I heard it was open for trading, so by Monday night you'll have no bank, no stock, no horses, no dollymoney to pay for mink coats for Venus P—'

'Eh?' Richard Kwang blanched, aware his wife was standing not twenty paces away, lugubriously watching them. 'What mink coat?'

Havergill sighed. 'All right, if you're not interested.' He turned away but the banker caught him by the arm.

'5 cents is ridiculous. 80 is nearer what I can get on the open mar—'

'Perhaps I can go to 7.'

'7?' The banker began cursing, more to give himself time to think than anything. 'I'll agree to a merger. A seat on the bank's board for ten years at a salary of f—'

'For five years, provided you give me your notorized resignation, undated, in advance, that you always vote exactly as *I* wish and at a salary equal to other directors.'

'No resignation in adv—'

'Then so sorry no deal.'

'I agree to that clause,' Richard Kwang said grandly. 'Now as to money. I th—'

'No. As to money, so sorry, Richard, I don't want to enter into a protracted negotiation. The governor, the tai-pan and I agree we should rescue the Ho-Pak. It is decided. I will see you retain face. We guarantee to keep the takeover price secret and are quite prepared to call it a merger—oh by the way, I want to make the announcement at 5:00 P.M., just after the seventh race. *Or not at all.*' Havergill's face was grim, but inside he was filled with glee. If it hadn't been for Dunross's announcement and the way it was being received he would have never considered doing the same. That bugger's quite right! It is time to be innovative and who better than us? It'll stop Southerby in his tracks and make us equal to Blacs at long last. With Struan's in our pocket next week, by next year . . .

'57 cents and that's a steal,' Kwang said.

'I'll go to 10 cents.'

Richard Kwang wheedled and twisted and almost wept and inside he was ecstatic with the chance of the bail-out. *Dew neh loh moh*, he wanted to shout, a few minutes ago I wouldn't be able to pay for Butterscotch Lass's feed next week let alone the diamond ring and now I'm worth at least $3½ million U.S. and with judicious manipulation much more. '30 by all the gods!'

'11.'

'I'll have to commit suicide,' he wailed. 'My wife will commit suicide, my children will . . .'

'Your pardon, Lord,' his Chinese trainer said in Cantonese, coming up to him. 'The race's put back ten minutes. Are there any instructions you wa—'

'Can't you see I'm busy, toad-belly! Go away!' Richard Kwang hissed in Cantonese with more obscenities, then said to Havergill, a final abject plea. '30, Mr. Havergill, and you'll have saved a poor man and his fam—'

'18 and that's final!'

'25 and it's a deal.'

'My dear fellow, so sorry but I must place a bet. 18. Yes or no?'

Richard Kwang kept up a pathetic patter but he was estimating his chances. He had seen the flash of irritation on his opponent's face. Dirty lump of dogmeat! Is now the time to close? Between now and five o'clock this leper dung could change his mind. If the tai-pan's got all this new financing perhaps I could . . . No, no chance. 18's three times as good as the opening bid! It's clear you are a clever fellow and a good negotiator, he chortled to himself. Has the time come to close?

He thought of Venus Poon, how she had abused his expensive gift and deliberately brushed her exquisite breasts against Four Finger's arm, and tears of rage welled from his eyes.

'Oh oh oh,' he said in an abject whisper, delighted that his stratagem to produce real tears had worked so well. '20, by all the gods, and I'm your slave forever.'

'Good,' Havergill said, very contentedly. 'Come to my box at quarter to five. I'll have a provisional letter of agreement ready for signature—and your undated resignation. At five we'll announce the merger, and Richard, until that time not a whisper! If the news leaks, the deal is off.'

'Of course.'

Havergill nodded and left and Richard Kwang walked back to his wife.

'What's going on?'

'Quiet!' he hissed. 'I've agreed to a merger with the Victoria.'

'At what price for our holdings?'

He lowered his voice even more. '20 cents on the, er, official book value.'

Glee lit her eyes. '*Ayeeyah!*' she said and quickly dropped her gaze for safety. 'You did very well.'

'Of course. And a directorship for five years an—'

'Eeee, our face will be huge!'

'Yes. Now listen, we've got until five today to make some private deals on Ho-Pak stock. We must buy in today—at fire-sale prices before every dogmeat gambler steals our rightful profit from us. We can't do it ourselves or others'll instantly suspect. Who can we use?'

She thought for a moment. Again her eyes gleamed. 'Profitable Choy. Give him 7 percent of anything he makes for us.'

'I'll offer 5 to begin with, perhaps I can settle for 6½ per cent! Excellent! And I'll also use Smiler Ching, he's a pauper now. He lost everything. Between the two of them . . . I'll meet you back at the box.' Importantly he turned away and went to his trainer and carefully kicked him in the shin. 'Oh so sorry,' he said for the benefit of those nearby who might have seen him, then hissed, 'Don't interrupt me when I'm busy, you cheating lump of dogmeat turd! And if you cheat me like you cheated Big Belly Tok I'll—'

'But I told you about that, Lord,' the man said sourly. 'He knew about it too! Wasn't it his idea? Didn't you both make a fortune?'

'*Oh ko*, if my horse doesn't win this race I'll ask my Uncle Four Fingers to send his street fighters and mash your Heavenly Orbs!'

A sprinkle of rain swept the paddock and they all looked anxiously at the sky. In the stands and on the balconies above, everyone was equally anxious. The shower turned into a slight

1152

drizzle and on the members' balcony Orlanda quivered, tense with excitement.

'Oh Linc, I'm going to bet now.'

'You're sure?' he asked with a laugh for she had been agonizing over her decision all afternoon, first Pilot Fish then Noble Star, then a hot tip, the outsider Winning Billy, and back to Butterscotch Lass again. The odds were even on Butterscotch Lass, 3 to 1 on both Pilot Fish and Noble Star—the moment Travkin was announced the money started pouring on—6 to 1 on Golden Lady, the rest hardly in the running. The total amount so far at risk was a staggering 4,700,000 HK. 'How much are you going to bet?'

She shut her eyes and said in a rush. 'All my winnings and an extra . . . an extra 100! Won't be a moment, Linc!'

'Good luck. I'll see you after the race.'

'Oh yes, sorry, in the excitement I forgot. Have fun!' She gave him a glorious smile and rushed off before he could ask her what she was betting on. He had already bet. This race was a quinella, as well as the second leg of the double quinella. 10,000 HK on any combination of Pilot Fish and Butterscotch Lass. That should do it, he thought, his own excitement growing.

He left the balcony and weaved through the tables heading for the elevators that would take him back upstairs. Many people watched him, some greeted him, most envious of the little badges fluttering in his lapel.

'Hi, Linc!'

'Oh hello,' he said to Biltzmann who had intercepted him. 'How's it going?'

'You heard about the foulup? Of course, you were there!' Biltzmann said. 'Say, Linc, you got a moment?'

'Sure.' Bartlett followed him down the corridor, conscious of the curious gazes of passersby.

'Listen,' Biltzmann said when they reached a quiet corner, 'you'd better watch yourself with these limey bastards. We sure as hell had a deal with General Stores.'

'You going to rebid?' Bartlett asked.

'That's up to head office, but me, hell, me I'd let this whole goddamn Island drown.'

Bartlett did not reply, aware of glances in their direction.

'Say, Linc!' Biltzmann dropped his voice and bent closer with

1153

a twisted grin. 'You got something special going with that girl?'

'What are you talking about?'

'The broad. The Eurasian. Orlanda, the one you were talking to.'

Bartlett felt the blood rush into his face but Biltzmann continued, 'Mind if I put my two cents in?' He winked. 'Make a date. Ask her for a date?'

'It's . . . it's a free country,' Bartlett said, suddenly hating him.

'Thanks. She's got a great ass.' Biltzmann beamed and came even closer. 'How much does she charge?'

Bartlett gasped, totally unprepared. 'She's not a hooker, for chrissake!'

'Didn't you know? Hey it's all over town. But Dickie said she was lousy in bed. That a fact?' Biltzmann misread the look on Bartlett's face. 'Oh, you haven't got there yet? Hell, Linc, all you gotta do's flash a little of the green st—'

'Listen you son of a bitch,' Bartlett hissed, almost blind with rage, 'she's no hooker and if you talk to her or go near her I'll stick my fist down your throat. Got it?'

'Listen, take it easy,' the other man gasped. 'I didn'—'

'You get the message?'

'Sure sure, no need to . . .' Biltzmann backed off. 'Take it easy. I asked, didn't I? Dickie . . .' He stopped, frightened, as Bartlett came closer. 'For chrissake it's not my fault—take it easy, huh?'

'Shut up!' Bartlett contained his rage with an effort, knowing this was not the time or the place to smash Biltzmann. He glanced around but Orlanda had already disappeared. 'Get lost, you son of a bitch,' he grated, 'and don't go near her or else!'

'Sure, sure take it easy, okay?' Biltzmann backed off another pace, then turned and fled thankfully. Bartlett hesitated, then went into the men's room and splashed a little water on his face to calm himself. The tap water, specially connected for the races, was brackish and seemed unclean. In a moment he found his elevator and walked to Dunross's box. It was tea time. The guests were being served little sandwiches, cakes, cheese and great pots of Indian tea with milk and sugar but he did not notice any of it, numb.

Donald McBride, bustling past, stopped briefly on his way

back to his box. 'Ah, Mr. Bartlett, I must tell you how happy we all are that you and Casey are going to be in business here. Pity about Biltzmann but all's fair in business. Your Casey's such a charming person. Sorry, got to dash.'

He hurried off. Bartlett hesitated in the doorway.

'Hey, Linc,' Casey called out joyously from the balcony. 'You want tea?' As they met halfway her smile faded. 'What's the matter?'

'Nothing, nothing, Casey.' Bartlett forced a smile. 'They at the starting gate?'

'Not yet but any moment now. You sure you're okay?'

'Of course. What did you bet on?'

'Noble Star, what else? Peter's tipping Doc Tooley's outsider, Winning Billy, for a place so I put 50 on him. You don't look well, Linc. Not your stomach, is it?'

He shook his head, warmed by her concern. 'No. I'm fine. You okay?'

'Sure. I've been having a wonderful time. Peter's in great form and Old Tooley's a gas.' Casey hesitated. 'I'm glad it's not your stomach. Doc Tooley says we should be safe from those lousy Aberdeen bugs, since we haven't gotten the trots yet. Of course we won't know for sure for twenty days.'

'Jesus,' Bartlett muttered, trying to force his mind off what Biltzmann had said. 'I'd almost forgotten about Aberdeen and the fire and that whole mess. The fire seems a million years ago.'

'To me too. Where did the time go?'

Gavallan was nearby. 'It's Hong Kong,' he said absently.

'How do you mean?'

'It's a Hong Kong characteristic. If you live here there's never enough time, whatever your work. Always too much to do. People are always arriving, leaving, friends, business people. There's always a crisis—flood, fire, mud slide, boom, scandal, business opportunity, funeral, banquet or cocktail party for visiting VIPs—or some disaster.' Gavallan shook off his anxieties. 'This's a small place and you soon get to know most people in your own circle. Then we're the crossroads of Asia and even if you're not in Struan's you're always on the move, planning, making money, risking money to make more, or you're off to Taiwan, Bangkok, Singapore, Sydney, Tokyo, London or wherever. It's the magic of Asia. Look what happened to you both since you got here: poor John Chen was kidnapped and murdered, guns were found on your aircraft, then there was the fire, the stock market mess, the run on our stock, Gornt after us and we after him. And now the banks may close on Monday or if Ian's right, Monday will be boom time. And we're in business together. . . .' He smiled wearily. 'What do you think of our tender?'

Casey held back her immediate comment and watched Bartlett.

'Great,' Bartlett said, thinking about Orlanda. 'You think Ian will be able to turn things around?'

'If anyone can, he can.' Gavallan sighed heavily. 'Well, let's hope, that's all we can do. Have you put your money on the winner yet?'

Bartlett smiled and Casey felt easier. 'Who you backing, Andrew?'

'Noble Star and Winning Billy for the quinella. See you later.' He left them.

'Curious what he was saying about Hong Kong. He's right. It makes the U.S. seem a million miles away.'

'Yes, but it isn't, not truly.'

'You want to stay here, Casey?'

She looked at him, wondering what was under the question, what he was really asking. 'That's up to you, Linc.'

He nodded slowly. 'Think I'll get me some tea.'

'Hey, I'll do that for you,' she said, then he saw Murtagh standing nervously at the doorway and her heart missed a beat. 'You haven't met our banker, Linc. Let me bring him over.'

She went through the throng. 'Hi, Dave.'

'Hi, Casey, have you seen the tai-pan?'

'He's busy till after the race. Is it yes or no?' she whispered urgently, keeping her back to Bartlett.

'It's a maybe.' Nervously Murtagh wiped his brow and took off his wet raincoat, his eyes red rimmed. 'Couldn't get a god-damn cab for an hour! Jesus!'

'Maybe what?'

'Maybe maybe. I gave them the plan and they told me to haul ass back home because I'd clearly gone mad. Then, after they calmed down, they said they'd get back to me. Those knuckle-heads called me at 4:00 A.M., asked me to repeat the whole scheme then S.J. himself came on.' His eyes rolled. 'S.J. said I was full of sh—I was loco and hung up on me.'

'But you said "maybe." What happened next?'

'I called them back and I've been on the phone five hours in the last ten trying to explain my brilliance to them since your harebrained scheme blew my mind.' Murtagh suddenly grinned. 'Hey, I'll tell you one thing, Casey. Now S.J. sure as hell knows who Dave Murtagh III is!'

She laughed. 'Listen, don't mention it to anyone here. Anyone. Except the tai-pan, okay?'

He looked at her, pained. 'You think I'm about to tell everybody my ass's chewed to hamburger?'

There was a burst of cheering and someone in the balcony called out, 'They're approaching the gate!'

'Quick,' Casey said, 'go put your bundle on the quinella. One and seven. Quick while you've time.'

'Which are they?'

'Never mind. You've no time.' She gave him a little shove and he rushed off. She collected herself, picked up a cup of tea and joined Bartlett and all the others crowding the balcony.

'Here's your tea, Linc.'

'Thanks. What did you tell him to bet?'

'One and seven.'

'I did one and eight.'

Another huge roar distracted them. The horses were cantering past and beginning to mill around the gate. They saw Pilot Fish skeetering and weaving, his jockey well up, knees tight, holding on firmly, guiding him to his post position. But the stallion wasn't ready yet and tossed his mane and neighed. At once the mare and the two fillies, Golden Lady and Noble Star, shivered, nostrils flaring and whinnied back. Pilot Fish brayed stridently, reared and pawed the air and everyone gasped. His jockey, Bluey White, cursed softly, dug his steel-strong hands into his mane, hanging on. 'C'mon, sport,' he called out with a curse, gentling him. 'Let the sheilas have a look at your dingle-dangle!'

Travkin on Noble Star was nearby. The filly had got the stallion's scent and it had unsettled her. Before Travkin could prevent it she twisted and backed and shoved her rump carelessly into Pilot Fish who swerved, startled, to bump the outsider Winning Billy, a bay gelding moving up to his gate. The gelding skeetered, shook his head angrily and whirled away for a few paces, almost trampling Lochinvar, another brown gelding.

'Get that bugger under control, Alexi, for chrissake!'

'Just stay out of my way, *ublyudok*,' Travkin muttered, his knees conscious of the untoward tremors racing through Noble Star. He sat very high, part of his mount, stirrups short, and he wondered, cursing, if Pilot Fish's trainer had smeared some of the stallion's musk onto his chest and flanks to agitate the mare and fillies. It's an old trick, he thought, very old.

'Come on!' the starter called out, his voice stentorian. 'Gentlemen, get your mounts into their stalls!'

Several were already there, Butterscotch Lass, the brown mare still heavily the favorite, was pawing the ground, nostrils flared, excitement of the coming race and the nearness of the stallion sending shiver after shiver through her. She had stall eight from the rails, Pilot Fish now entering the stall in post position one. Winning Billy had stall three between Street Vendor and Golden Lady, and the smell of them and the stallion's brazen challenge tore the gelding's mind. Before the gate could close behind him he backed out and, once free, fought the bit and reins, shaking his head violently from side to side, twirling like a dancer and on the slippery turf, almost colliding with Noble Star who swerved deftly out of the way.

'Alexi, come along!' the starter called out. 'Hurry it up!'

'Yes, certainly,' Travkin called back but he was not hurried. He knew Noble Star and he walked the trembling, big brown filly well away from the stallion, letting her prance, the wind under her tail. 'Gently, my darling,' he crooned in Russian, wanting to delay, wanting to keep the others off balance, now the only one not in the gate. A flash of lightning lit the eastern sky but he paid it no attention, or the ominous roll of thunder. The drizzle became stronger.

His whole being was concentrated. Just after the weigh-in, one of the other jockeys had sidled up to him. 'Mr. Travkin,' he had said softly, 'you're not to win.'

'Oh? Who says?'

The jockey shrugged.

'Who's the winner?'

Again the jockey shrugged.

'If the trainers and jockeys have a fix then let them know I'm not part of it. I never have been, not in Hong Kong.'

'You'n the tai-pan won with Buccaneer, that should satisfy you.'

'It satisfies me but in this race I'm a trier.'

'Fair enough, sport. I'll tell them.'

'Who's them?'

The jockey had gone away, the crowded changing room noisy and sweat-filled. Travkin was well aware who the ring was, some of them, who fixed races now and then, but he had never been a participant. He knew it was not because he was more honest than the others. Or less dishonest. It was only that his needs were few, a sure thing did not excite him and the touch of money did not please him.

The starter was becoming impatient. 'Come along, Alexi! Hurry it up!'

Obediently he jabbed the spurs and walked Noble Star forward into her stall. The gate clanged behind her. A moment's hush. Now the racers were under starter's orders.

66

4:00 P.M.:

In their stalls, jockeys dug their fingers into the horses' manes, all of them nervous, those in the know ready to crowd Noble Star. Then the doors flew open and in a mad instant the eight runners were galloping, packed together along a short part of the straight, now past the winning post, now racing into the first bend. The riders were all crouched high up, side by side, almost touching, some touching, the horses getting their pace, hurtling through the first part of the bend that would take them a quarter of the course into the far straight. Already Pilot Fish was half a length ahead on the rails, Butterscotch Lass in fine position not flat out yet, Winning Billy alongside, back a little from Noble Star on the outside, crowding the others for a better place in the pack, all jockeys knowing that all binoculars were trained on them so any pulling or interference better be clever and cautious. They had all been warned that millions would be won or lost and it would cost each one of them their future to foul up.

They pounded through the turn, mud splattering those behind, the going bad. As they came out of the turn into the straight still together, shoving for position, they lengthened their strides, the sweat-smell and the speed exciting horses and riders alike. Winning Billy took the bit and closed up alongside Butterscotch Lass, now half a length behind Pilot Fish, going well, the rest bunched, all waiting to make their run. Now Butterscotch Lass felt the spurs and she leapt forward and passed Pilot Fish, fell back a little and passed him again, Pilot Fish still hugging the rails carefully.

Travkin was holding the filly well, lying back in the pack, still

1160

outside, then he gave her the spurs and she increased speed and he cut closer to the leaders, herding the others, almost bumping Lochinvar. The rain increased. The sting of it was in his eyes, his knees and legs tight and already hurting. There was not a length between them as they galloped out of the stretch into the corner. Going into the far turn they were all packed close to take advantage of the corner when a whip came from nowhere and lashed across Travkin's wrists. The suddenness and pain unlocked his grip an instant and almost unbalanced him. A split second later he was in control again. Where the blow came from he did not know, or care, for they were well into the corner, the going dreadful. Abruptly, the gray outsider Kingplay on the rails just behind Pilot Fish slipped and stumbled, his jockey felt the earth twist and they went down smashing into the rails, pulling two horses with them. Everyone in the stadium was on their feet.

'Christ who's down . . .'

'Is it . . . it's Noble Star . . .'

'No, no it isn't . . . Winning Bill—'

'No he's lying third . . .'

'Come on for Christ's sweet sake . . .'

In the uproar in the stewards' room Dunross, whose binoculars were rock steady, called out, 'It was Kingplay who fell . . . Kingplay, Street Vendor and Golden Lady . . . Golden Lady's on her feet but Christ the jockey's hurt . . . Kingplay won't get up . . . he's hurt . . .'

'What's the order, what's the order?'

'Butterscotch Lass by a nose, then Pilot Fish on the rails, Winning Billy, Noble Star, nothing to choose amongst them. Now they're going into the last turn, the Lass's ahead by a neck, the others hacking at her . . .' Dunross watched the horses, his heart almost stopped, excitement possessing him. 'Come on, Alexi . . .' His shout added to those of others, Casey as excited, but Bartlett watching, uninvolved, his mind below.

Gornt in the Blacs box had his glasses focused as steadily as the tai-pan, his excitement as controlled. 'Come on,' he muttered, watching Bluey White give Pilot Fish the whip in the turn, Noble Star well placed on the outside, Winning Billy alongside the Lass who was a neck in front, the angle of the turn making it difficult to see.

Again Travkin felt the lash on his hands but he dismissed it and eased a little closer in the bend, the remaining five horses inches apart, Butterscotch Lass crowding the rails.

Bluey White on Pilot Fish knew it would soon be time to make his dash. Ten yards, five, four three two *now!* They were coming out of the turn and he gave Pilot Fish the whip. The stallion shot forward, inches from the rails, flat out now as Butterscotch Lass got the spurs and whip an instant later, for all the jockeys knew it was now or never.

Travkin, stretched out parallel to Noble Star's neck, leaned forward and let out a cossack scream near Noble Star's ear and the filly took the primeval call and lengthened her stride, nostrils flared, foam on her mouth. Now the five runners were pounding the stretch, Noble Star on the outside, Winning Billy inching ahead of the Lass, all their withers sweat-foamed, now the Lass, now Pilot Fish ahead and now the dappled gelding Lochinvar made his bid to conquer and he took the lead from Pilot Fish, taking the post position, all whips out and spurs in and only the winning post ahead.

One hundred yards to go.

In the stands and on the balconies and in the boxes, there was but one voice. Even the governor was pounding the balcony rail—'Come on come on Butterscotch Lasssss!'—and down by the winning post Nine Carat Chu was almost crushed against the rails by the press of the crowd craning forward.

Ninety yards, eighty . . . mud scattering, all runners flat out, all caught by the excitement and the crescendoing roar.

'The Lass's pulling away . . .'

'No, look at Pilot F—'

'Christ it's Lochinvarrrrr . . .'

'Winning Billy . . .'

'Come on come on come on . . .'

Travkin saw the winning post bearing down on them. There was another flash of lightning. Out of the corner of his eyes he saw Lochinvar ahead by a neck, then the Lass, now Winning Billy, now Pilot Fish easing forward taking the lead, now Winning Billy, Lochinvar crowding him.

Then Bluey White saw the opening he's been promised and he gave the stallion the final whip. Like an arrow he darted for the opening and swung up alongside Butterscotch Lass, then

1162

passed her. He was ahead by a neck. He saw the Lass's jockey, not in the know, give the mare the whip, shouting her onward. Travkin screamed exultantly and Noble Star put out her final effort. The five horses came down the final yards neck and neck, now Pilot Fish ahead, now Winning Billy, Noble Star closing, just a neck behind, just a nose, just a nostril, the crowd a single, mindless raving lunatic, all the runners bunched, Noble Star on the outside, Winning Billy inching away, the Lass closing, Pilot Fish closing, now ahead by a nose.

Forty . . . thirty . . . twenty . . . fifteen . . .

Noble Star was ahead by a nostril, then Pilot Fish, then the Lass then Noble Star . . . Winning Billy . . . and now they were past the winning post not one of them sure who had won—only Travkin sure he had lost. Abruptly he sawed the bit a vicious two inches and held it left in an iron hand, the movement imperceptible but enough to throw her off her stride and she shied. With a shriek she barreled down into the mud and threw her rider at the rails, the Lass almost falling but holding, the other three safe. Travkin felt himself sailing, then there was an impossible chest-tearing, head-splitting blackness.

The crowd gasped, the race momentarily forgotten. Another binding flash of lightning, pandemonium swooped over them, the downpour increased, mixing nicely with the thunder above.

'Pilot Fish by a nose . . .'

'Balls, it was Noble Star by a hair . . .'

'You're wrong, old boy, it was Pilot Fish . . .'

Dew neh loh moh . . .

'Christ what a race . . .'

'Oh Christ! Look! There's the steward's objection flag . . .'

'Where? Oh my God! Who fouled . . .'

'I didn't see anything, did you . . .'

'No. Difficult in this rain, even with glasses . . .'

'Christ, now what? Those bloody stewards, if they take victory from my winner by Christ . . .'

Dunross had rushed for the elevator the moment he saw Noble Star fall and throw Travkin. He had not seen the cause. Travkin was too clever.

Others were excitedly crowding the corridors waiting for the elevator, everyone talking, no one listening. 'We won by a nostril . . .'

'What's the objection for chrissake? Noble St—'

'What's the objection, tai-pan?'

'That's up to the stewards to announce.' In the uproar Dunross stabbed the button again.

Gornt hurried up as the doors opened, everyone packing in, Dunross wanting to bellow with rage at the slowness. 'It was Pilot Fish by a nose, Ian,' Gornt shouted above the uproar, his face flushed.

'What a race!' someone shouted. 'Anyone know what the objection is?'

'Do you, Ian?' Gornt asked.

'Yes,' he replied.

'It's against my Pilot Fish?'

'You know the procedure. First the stewards investigate, then they make an announcement.' He saw Gornt's flat brown eyes and he knew his enemy was suddenly blind with rage that he wasn't a steward. And you won't become one, you bastard, Dunross thought, enraged. I'll blackball you till I'm dead.

'Is it against Pilot Fish, tai-pan?' someone shouted.

'Good God,' he called back. 'You know the procedure.'

The elevator stopped at every level. More owners and friends crammed in. More shouts about what a great race but what the hell's the objection? At last they reached ground level. Dunross rushed out onto the track where a group of *ma-foo* and officials surrounded Travkin who lay there crumpled and inert. Noble Star had fought to her feet, unhurt, and was now on the far side galloping riderless around the course, stable hands scattered and waiting to intercept her. Up the track on the last bend, the vet was kneeling beside the agonized roan gelding, Kingplay, his back leg broken, the bone jutting through. The sound of the shot did not penetrate the roars and counter roars of the impatient onlookers, their eyes fixed on the Tote, waiting for the stewards' judgment.

Dunross knelt beside Travkin, one of the *ma-foo* holding an umbrella over the unconscious man. 'How is he, Doctor?'

'He didn't slam into the rails, missed them by a miracle. He's not dead, at least not yet, tai-pan,' Dr. Meng, the police pathologist, said nervously, used to dead bodies, not live patients. 'I can't tell, not until he comes around. There's no apparent hemorrhaging externally. His neck . . . and his back seem all right . . . I can't tell yet . . .'

Two St. John ambulance men hurried up with a stretcher. 'Where should we take him, sir?'

Dunross looked around. 'Sammy,' he said to one of his stableboys, 'go and fetch Doc Tooley. He should be in our box.' To the ambulance men he said, 'Keep Mr. Travkin in the ambulance till Doc Tooley gets here. What about the other three jockeys?'

'Two are just shook up, sir. One, Captain Pettikin, has a broken leg but he's already in a splint.'

Very carefully the men put Travkin on the stretcher. McBride joined them, then Gornt and others. 'How is he, Ian?'

'We don't know. Yet. He seems all right.' Gently Dunross lifted one of Travkin's hands, examining it. He had thought he had seen a blow in the far turn and Travkin falter. A heavy red weal disfigured the back of his right hand. And the other one. 'What could have caused this, Dr. Meng?'

'Oh!' More confidently the little man said, 'The reins perhaps. Perhaps a whip, could be a blow . . . perhaps in falling.'

Gornt said nothing, just watched, inwardly seething that Bluey White could have been so inept when everything had been so neatly set up beforehand with a word here, a promise there. Half the bloody stadium must have seen him, he thought.

Dunross examined Travkin's ashen face. No marks other than inevitable bruising. A little blood seeped out of the nose.

'It's already coagulating. That's a good sign,' Dr. Meng volunteered.

The governor hurried up. 'How is he?'

Dunross repeated what the doctor had said.

'Damned bad luck, Noble Star shying like that.'

'Yes.'

'What's the stewards' objection, Ian?'

'We're just going to discuss that, sir. Would you care to join us?'

'Oh, no, no thank you. I'll just wait and be patient. I wanted to make sure Travkin was all right.' The governor felt the rain running down his back. He looked up at the sky. 'Blasted weather—looks like it's here to stay. Are you going to continue the meet?'

'I'm going to recommend we cancel, or postpone.'

1165

'Good idea.'

'Yes,' McBride said. 'I agree. We can't afford another accident.'

'When you have a moment, Ian,' Sir Geoffrey said, 'I'll be in my box.'

Dunross's attention focused. 'Did you talk to the minister, sir?' he asked, trying to sound matter-of-fact.

'Yes.' Sir Geoffrey was equally casual. 'Yes, he called on the private line.'

Abruptly the tai-pan was conscious of Gornt and the others. 'I'll walk you back, sir.' To McBride he said, 'I'll follow you at once,' then turned away and the two of them walked for the elevator.

Once alone Sir Geoffrey muttered, 'Hardly the place for a private conversation, what?'

'We could examine the course, sir.' Dunross led the way to the rail, praying. 'The turf's terrible, isn't it?' he said, pointing.

'Very.' Sir Geoffrey also kept his back to the eyes. 'The minister was very perturbed. He left the decision about Brian to me, provided Mr. Sinders and Mr. Crosse first agree to the release, pro—'

'Surely they'll agree with you, sir?' Uneasily Dunross recalled his conversation with them last night.

'I can only advise. I will advise them it is necessary provided you assure me it is. You personally.'

'Of course,' Dunross said slowly. 'But surely Havergill, Southerby or the other bankers would carry more weight.'

'In banking matters, Ian, yes. But I think I require your personal assurance and cooperation also.'

'Sir?'

'This matter will have to be handled very delicately, by you, not by them. Then there's the problem of those files. The AMG files.'

'What about them, sir?'

'That's for you to answer. Mr. Sinders told me of his conversation with you last night.' Sir Geoffrey lit his pipe, his hands cupping the flame, protecting it from the rain. After the tai-pan's call to him this morning he had at once sent for Crosse and Sinders to discuss the matter of the exchange prior to asking the minister. Sinders had reiterated his concern that the files

1166

might have been doctored. He said he might agree to release Kwok if he was sure of those files. Crosse had suggested trading Kwok for Fong-fong and the others.

Now Sir Geoffrey looked at Dunross searchingly. 'Well, Ian?'

'Tiptop's due, or was due this afternoon. May I assume that I can say yes to his proposal?'

'Yes, provided you first get Mr. Sinders's agreement. And Mr. Crosse's.'

'Can't you give that to me, sir?'

'No. The minister was quite clear. If you want to ask them now, they are in the members' stands.'

'They know the result of your call?'

'Yes. Sorry but the minister made it very clear.' Sir Geoffrey was gentle. 'It seems the reputation for fairness and honesty of the present tai-pan of the Noble House is known in those hallowed places. Both the minister and I bank on it.' A burst of cheering distracted them. Noble Star had broken through the cordon of *ma-foo* trying to recapture her, and galloped past them, officials and stableboys scattering. 'Perhaps you'd better deal with the race objection first. I'll be in my box. Join me for tea or a cocktail if you wish.'

Dunross thanked him then hurried for the stewards' room, his mind in turmoil.

'Ah, Ian,' Shitee T'Chung, the nominal chairman called out anxiously as he came in, all the stewards now present. 'We really have to decide quickly.'

'That's hard without Travkin's evidence,' Dunross said. 'How many of you saw Bluey White slash at him?'

Only McBride put up his hand.

'That's only two of us out of twelve.' Dunross saw Crosse watching him. 'I'm certain. And there was a weal across both his hands. Dr. Meng said it could have been made by a whip or the reins in falling. Pug, what's your opinion?'

Pugmire broke an uncomfortable silence. 'I saw nothing malicious, personally. I was watching like hell because I was on Noble Star, 1,000 on the nose. Whether there was a blow or not it didn't seem to make much difference. I didn't see her falter, or any of the pack, other than Kingplay. Noble Star was well in the running till the post and everyone had their whips out.' He tossed over one of the copies of the photo finish.

Dunross picked it up. The photo was as he had seen it: Pilot Fish by a nose from Noble Star, by a nostril from Butterscotch Lass, by a nose from Winning Billy.

'They've all got their whips out,' Pugmire continued, 'and they had in the turn, quite rightly. It could easily have been accidental—if there was a blow.'

'Shitee?'

'I must confess, old boy, I was watching my Street Vendor and cursing Kingplay. I thought your filly'd pipped Pilot Fish. We, er, we've polled the other trainers and there's, er, no formal complaint. I agree with Pug.'

'Roger?'

'I saw nothing untoward.'

'Jason?'

To his surprise Plumm shook his head and disagreed and Dunross wondered again about AMG and his astonishing accusation of Plumm and Sevrin. 'We all know Bluey White's cunning,' Plumm was saying. 'We've had to warn him before. If the tai-pan and Donald say they saw it I vote we debar him and disqualify Pilot Fish when it comes to a vote.'

Dunross polled the other stewards, the rest wavering.

'Let's call in the jockeys, White last.'

They did. All the jockeys muttered permutations of the same thing: they were too busy with their own mounts to notice anything.

Now the stewards looked at Dunross, waiting. He stared back, well aware that if he said, I vote we unanimously debar Bluey White for interference and disqualify Pilot Fish, all in favor say aye! that they would concede and vote as he wished.

I saw him do it, he told himself, so did Donald, and others, and it shook Alexi for that necessary split second. Even so, in all honesty I don't think that cost Noble Star the race. I blew the race myself. Alexi was the wrong choice for this race. He should have shoved Pilot Fish into the rails on the second corner when he had the chance, or put his whip across Bluey White's face, not his hands as I'd have done, oh yes, without hesitation. And there are other considerations.

'There's no doubt in my mind there was interference,' he said. 'But whether by accident or design I doubt if even Alexi will know I agree it didn't cost Noble Star the race so I suggest we

1168

just caution Bluey and let the result stand.'

'Excellent.' Shitee T'Chung exhaled and beamed and they all relaxed, none of them, least of all Pugmire, wanting a confrontation with the tai-pan. 'Anyone against? Good! Let's release the photo finish to the papers and make the announcement over the loudspeakers. Will you do that, tai-pan?'

'Certainly. But what about the rest of the program? Look at the rain.' It was pelting down now. 'Listen, I've an idea.' He told it to them.

A whoop of excitement and they all laughed. 'Very good, oh very good!'

'Grand!' Dunstan Barre exploded.

'That'll give the buggers something to think about!' Pugmire said.

'Great idea, tai-pan!' McBride beamed. 'Oh very good.'

'I'll go to the control center—perhaps you'd get Bluey back and give him what for, scare him, eh?'

Pugmire said, 'A word, Ian?'

'Can we make it later?'

'Of course. Roger, can I have a word?'

'Of course. I'll be down in the members' stand with Sinders.'

'Oh, not in your box?'

'No, I let the commissioner have it for a private party.'

'Ian?'

'Yes, Jason?'

'Do you think they'll hold the hill climb tomorrow?'

'If this keeps up, no. That whole area'll be a quagmire. Why?'

'Nothing. I was planning a cocktail party early Sunday evening to celebrate your Superfoods coup!'

Shitee T'Chung chortled. 'Jolly good idea! Congratulations, Ian! Did you see Biltzmann's face?'

'Ian, would you be free? I won't invite Biltzmann,' Plumm added to much laughter. 'It'll be at our company flat in Sinclair Towers.'

'Sorry, I'm going to Taipei early afternoon, sorry, at least that's my present plan. Th—'

Pugmire interrupted with sudden concern, 'You won't be here Monday? What about our papers, and everything?'

'No problem, Pug. 9:30 we close.' To Plumm Dunross said, 'Jason if I cancel or postpone Taipei, I'll accept.'

'Good. 7:30 to 9:30 casual.'

Dunross walked off, his frown deepening, surprised that Plumm was so friendly. Ordinarily he was the opposition on all the boards they shared, siding with Gornt and Havergill against him, particularly on the Victoria's board.

Outside the stewards' room there were milling clusters of anxious reporters, owners, trainers and bystanders. Dunross brushed aside the barrage of questions all the way to the control room. It was on the top floor.

'Hello, sir,' the announcer said, everyone tense in the small glass booth that had the best view of the course. 'Marvelous race, pity about . . . Do you have the decision? It's Bluey, isn't it, we all saw the whip. . . .'

'May I use the mike?'

'Oh of course.' The man hastily moved and Dunross sat in his place. He clicked on the switch. 'This is Ian Dunross, the stewards have asked me to make two announcements. . . .'

The silence was vast as his words echoed and re-echoed over the stadium. The fifty thousand held their breaths, careless of the rain, in the stands and on every soaring level. 'First, the result of the fifth race.' Dead silence but for the sound of the rain. Dunross took a deep breath. 'Pilot Fish by a nose from Noble Star by a whisker from Butterscotch Lass. . . .' but the last was drowned by the cheers and counter cheers, happiness and disgust, and everyone throughout the stadium was shouting, arguing, cheering, cursing and, down in the paddock, Gornt was astonished, having been convinced that his jockey had been seen as he had seen him, had been caught and carpeted and the result would be set aside. In the pandemonium the winning numbers flashed on to the tote: one, seven, eight.

Dunross waited a moment and breezily repeated the result in Cantonese, the crowd more docile, their pent-up anxieties allayed, for the stewards' decision was final. 'Second, the stewards have decided, due to the weather and bad conditions, to cancel the rest of the meet . . .' A vast groan went over the crowd. '. . . actually to postpone until next Saturday for another special meet.' A sudden great roar and excitement picked up. 'We will have a meet of eight races and the fifth will be the same as today, with the same runners, Pilot Fish, Butterscotch Lass, Winning Billy, Street Vendor, Golden Lady, Lochinvar and

1170

Noble Star. A special return challenge with double stakes, 30,000 added. . . .'

Cheers and more cheers, applause and roars and someone in the booth said, 'Christ what a great idea, tai-pan! Noble Star'll take that black bastard!'

'Oh no he won't! Butterscotch . . .'

'Great idea, tai-pan.'

Into the mike Dunross said, 'The stewards appreciate your continued support.' He repeated it in Cantonese, adding, 'There will be a further special announcement in a few minutes. Thank you!' in both languages.

Another huge cheer and those in the rain scurried for cover or for the winning windows, everyone chattering, groaning, cursing the gods or blessing them, choking the exits, long lines of men, women and children seeking the long way home, a wonderful new happiness possessing them. Only those who possessed the winning double quinella numbers, eight and five in the second, one and seven in the fifth, stood paralyzed, staring at the tote, waiting for the winning odds to be declared.

'Another announcement, tai-pan?' the announcer asked anxiously.

'Yes,' Dunross said. 'Around five.' Havergill had told him that the deal with Richard Kwang had been struck and had asked him to go to the Victoria box as soon as possible. He reached the exit door and went down the steps three at a time to the next level, very pleased with himself. Giving the race to Pilot Fish's got to throw Gornt, he thought. Gornt knew and I knew it was a carve-up and that Alexi was set up whatever he did—which is the major reason I didn't ride. They'd've tried it on me and I would have killed someone. But next Saturday . . . ah, next Saturday I'll ride and Bluey White won't dare, nor will the other trainers, next Saturday'll be fair game and they'll be on notice by God. His excitement picked up a beat. Then ahead in the crowded corridor he saw Murtagh waiting for him.

'Oh tai-pan, can I se—'

'Of course.' Dunross led him through the kitchen into his private room.

'That was a great race. I won a bundle,' the young man said excitedly, 'and great about Saturday.'

'Good.' Then Dunross noticed the sweat on the man's forehead. Oh Christ, he thought. 'Are we in business, Mr. Murtagh?'

'Please call me Dave, the brass said, er, they said maybe. They've scheduled a board meeting for tomorrow, 9:00 A.M. their time. Our time that's . . .'

'10:00 P.M this evening. Yes. Excellent, Mr. Murtagh, then call me on this number.' Dunross wrote it down. 'Please don't lose it and don't give it to anyone else.'

'Oh, of course, tai-pan, I'll call the very moment . . . How late can I call?'

'The moment you put the phone down to them. Keep calling till you get me.' Dunross got up. 'Sorry but there's rather a lot to do.'

'Oh sure, sure!' Murtagh added uneasily, 'Say, tai-pan, I just heard about the 2 million down on the General Stores tender. 2 million from us by 9:30 Monday's gotta be kinda pushing it.'

'I rather expected it would be—for your group. Fortunately, Mr. Murtagh, I never planned on that modest amount of cash being your money. I know First Central is inclined to be like the mills of God—they grind slowly—unless they wish to remove themselves from the arena,' he added, remembering many friends who had been hurt by their precipitous withdrawal years back. 'Not to worry, my *new* external source of credit's more th—'

'What?' Murtagh blanched.

'My new external source of finance reacts at once to any sudden business opportunities, Mr. Murtagh. This took them just eight minutes. They seem to have more confidence than your principals.'

'Hell, tai-pan, please call me Dave, it's not lack of confidence but, well, they've no idea of Asia. I've got to convince them the General Stores takeover's got to double your gross in three years.'

'In one,' Dunross interrupted firmly, enjoying himself. 'So sorry your group won't share in our huge profits from that minor section of our immense expansion plans. Do have some tea in the box, sorry, I just have to make a phone call.' He took Murtagh's elbow and firmly led him out of the door shutting it after him.

In the kitchen Murtagh was staring at the closed door, the happy clatter of plates and Cantonese obscenities from the twenty cooks and helpers a vast din. 'Jesus,' he muttered in near panic, 'eight minutes? Shit, are the goddamn Swiss horning in on our client?' He tottered away.

Inside the room Dunross was on his private phone, listening to the ringing tone. *'Weyyyyy?'*

'Mr. Tip please,' he said carefully in Cantonese. 'This is Mr. Dunross calling.'

He heard the phone put down with a clatter and the *amah* shriek, 'It's the phone! For you, Father!'

'Who is it?'

'A foreign devil.'

Dunross smiled.

'Hello?'

'Ian Dunross, Mr. Tip. I was just concerned that your illness wasn't worse.'

'Ah, ah, yes, so sorry I could not arrive. Yes. I, I had some pressing business, you understand? Yes. Very pressing. Oh by the way, that was bad joss about Noble Star. I just heard on the wireless that Pilot Fish won by a nose after an objection. What was the objection?'

Patiently Dunross explained and answered questions about his General Stores takeover bid, delighted that that news had already reached him. If Tiptop, then all newspapers. Good, he thought, waiting Tiptop out but Tiptop outsmarted him. 'Well, thank you for calling, tai-pan.'

At once Dunross said, 'It was my pleasure, oh by the way, confidentially, I understand it may well be possible that the police have discovered one of their underlings has made a mistake.'

'Ah. I presume the mistake will be corrected immediately?'

'I would presume very soon, if the person concerned wishes to resign and take advantage of permission to travel abroad.'

'How soon might very soon be, tai-pan?'

Dunross was picking his words carefully, deliberately vague though formal now. 'There are certain formalities, but it is possible that it could be quickly achieved. Unfortunately VIPs have to be consulted elsewhere. I'm sure you understand.'

'Certainly. But the mighty dragon is no match for the native serpent, *heya?* I understand there is one of your VVIPs already in Hong Kong. A Mr. Sinders?'

Dunross blinked at the extent of Tiptop's knowledge. 'I have certain approvals already,' he said, disquieted.

'I would have thought very few approvals were necessary. True gold fears no fire.'

'Yes. Is there somewhere I could call you this evening—to report progress?'

'This number will find me. Please call me at 9:00 P.M.' Tiptop's voice became even drier. 'I understand it might well be possible that your last suggestion about banking might be serviced. Of course any bank would need proper documentation to secure an immediate half billion Hong Kong dollars in cash, but I hear that the Victoria's chop, the governor's chop and yours would be all that's required to secure the loan for thirty days. This . . . minor amount of cash is ready, for a limited time, whenever the correct procedures are entered into. Until that time this matter is confidential, very strictly confidential.'

'Of course.'

'Thank you for calling.'

Dunross put the phone down and wiped his palms. 'For a limited time' was branded on his mind. He knew, and he knew Tiptop knew he understood that the two 'procedures' were absolutely interlinked but not necessarily. Christ Jesus I love Asia, he thought happily as he rushed off.

The corridors were filled, many people already crowding the elevators to go home. He peered into his box, caught Gavallan's eye. 'Andrew, go down to the members' stand and get hold of Roger Crosse—he's there with a fellow called Sinders. Ask them if they've a moment to join me in my box! Hurry!'

Gavallan took off. Dunross hurried along the corridor past the betting windows.

'Tai-pan!' Casey called out. 'Sorry about Noble Star! Did y—'

'Be back in a minute, Casey. Sorry, can't stop!' Dunross called back on the run. He noticed Gornt at the winning window but it did not take away his happiness. First things first, he thought. 'How do you want the 10,000? Our bet?'

'Cash will do very nicely, thank you,' Gornt said.

'I'll send it around later.'

'Monday will do just as well.'

'Later tonight. Monday I'll be busy.' Dunross walked off with a polite nod.

In the packed Victoria box the uproar was the same as everywhere. Drinks, laughter, excitement and some cursing about Pilot Fish but already wagers were being placed on next Saturday's race. As Dunross came in there were more cheers, condolences and another volley of questions. He fielded them all casually and one from Martin Haply who was jammed beside the door with Adryon.

'Oh, Father, what rotten luck about Noble Star. I lost my shirt and my month's allowance!'

Dunross grinned. 'Young ladies shouldn't bet! Hello, Haply!'

'Can I ask ab—'

'Later. Adryon darling, don't forget cocktails. You're hostess.'

'Oh yes, we'll be there. Father, can you advance me my next mon—'

'Certainly,' Dunross said to her astonishment, gave her a hug and pushed his way over to Havergill, Richard Kwang nearby.

'Hello, Ian,' Havergill said. 'Bad luck, but clearly Pilot Fish had the edge.'

'Yes, yes he did. Hello, Richard.' Dunross gave him the copy of the photo finish. 'Damned bad luck for both of us.' Others crowded to see it.

'Good God, by a whisker . . .'

'I thought Noble Star . . .'

Taking advantage of the diversion Dunross bent closer to Havergill. 'Is everything signed?'

'Yes. 20 cents on the dollar. He agreed to and signed the provisional papers. Formal papers by the end of the week. Of course the rotter tried to wheedle but it's all signed.'

'Marvelous. You did a terrific deal.'

Havergill nodded. 'Yes. Yes, I know.'

Richard Kwang turned around. 'Ah, tai-pan.' He dropped his voice and whispered, 'Has Paul told you about the merger?'

'Of course. May I offer congratulations.'

'Congratulations?' Southerby echoed, coming up to them. 'Damned bad luck if you ask me! I had my bundle on Butterscotch Lass!'

The tempo of the room picked up as the governor came in.

1175

Havergill went to meet him, Dunross following. 'Ah, Paul, Ian. Damned bad luck but an excellent decision! Both of them.' His face hardened nicely. 'Next Saturday will certainly be a needle match.'

'Yes sir.'

'Paul, you wanted to make a formal announcement?'

'Yes sir.' Havergill raised his voice. 'May I have your attention please . . .' No one took any notice until Dunross took a spoon and banged it against a teapot. Gradually there was silence. 'Your Excellency, ladies and gentlemen, I have the honor to announce, on behalf of the directors of the Victoria Bank of Hong Kong and China, that an immediate merger has been arranged with the great Ho-Pak Bank of Hong Kong . . .' Martin Haply dropped his glass. '. . . and that the Victoria totally guarantees 100 percent of all Ho-Pak depositors and . . .'

The rest was drowned out with a great cheer. Guests in the nearby boxes craned over the balconies to see what was happening. The news was shouted across as others came in from the corridors and soon there were more cheers.

Havergill was besieged with questions and he held up his hand, delighted with the effect of his announcement. In the silence Sir Geoffrey said quickly, 'I must say, on behalf of Her Majesty's Government, that this is marvelous news, Paul, good for Hong Kong, good for the bank, good for you, Richard, and the Ho-Pak!'

'Oh yes, Sir Geoffrey,' Richard Kwang said, jovial and loud, sure that now he was a giant step nearer his knighthood. 'I decided—of course with our directors—I decided it would be good for the Victoria to have a major foothold in the Chinese community an—'

Hastily Havergill interrupted and overrode him. 'Richard, perhaps I'd better finish the formal announcement and leave the details to our press conference.' He glanced at Martin Haply. 'We have scheduled a formal press conference for Monday at noon but all details of the, er, merger have been agreed. Isn't that so, Richard?'

Richard Kwang began to make another variation but quickly changed his mind, seeing both Dunross's and Havergill's look. 'Er, yes, yes,' he said but could not resist adding, 'I'm delighted to be partners with the Victoria.'

Haply called out quickly, 'Excuse me, Mr. Havergill, may I ask a question?'

'Of course,' Havergill said affably, well aware of what he would be asked. This bastard Haply has to go, he thought, one way or another.

'May I ask, Mr. Havergill, how you propose to pay out all the Ho-Pak customers and yours, Blacs and all the other banks when there's a run on all of them and not enough cash in the till?'

'Rumors, rumors, Mr. Haply,' Havergill replied airily and added to laughter, 'Remember: A swarm of mosquitoes can create a noise like thunder! Hong Kong's economy has never been stronger. As to the so-called run on the Ho-Pak, that's over. The Victoria guarantees the Ho-Pak's depositors, guarantees the Struan-General Stores takeover and guarantees to be in business for the next hundred and twenty years.'

'But Mr. Havergill, would you ans—'

'Not to worry, Mr. Haply. Let's leave the details of our . . . our benevolent umbrella for the Ho-Pak till our press conference on Monday.' At once he turned to the governor. 'If you'll excuse me, sir, I'll make it public.' There were more cheers as he started through the crush toward the door.

Someone began singing, 'For he's a jolly good fellow . . .' Everyone joined in. The noise became deafening. Dunross said to Richard Kwang in Cantonese, quoting an old expression, '"When it is enough, stop." Heya?'

'Ah, ah yes. Yes, tai-pan. Yes indeed.' The banker smiled a sickly smile, understanding the threat, reminding himself of his good fortune, that Venus Poon would certainly kowtow now that he was an important director on the board of the Victoria. His smile broadened. 'You're right, tai-pan. "Inside the red doors there is much waste of meat and wine!" My expertise will greatly benefit our bank, heya?' He went off importantly.

'My God, what a day!' Johnjohn muttered.

'Yes, yes, marvelous! Johnjohn, old fellow,' McBride said, 'you must be very proud of Paul.'

'Yes, of course.' Johnjohn was watching Havergill leave.

'Are you feeling all right?'

'Oh yes, I was just working late.' Johnjohn had been up most of the night estimating how they could safely effect the takeover, safely for the bank and for the Ho-Pak depositors. He had been the architect and this morning he had spent more wearisome hours trying to convince Havergill that now was the time to be innovative. 'We can do it, Paul, and create such a resurgence of confid—'

'And a very dangerous precedent! I don't think your idea's as important as you imagine!'

It was only when Havergill had seen the enormous and immediate gain in confidence after Dunross's dramatic announcement that he had reconsidered. Never mind, Johnjohn thought wearily, we're all gainers. The bank, Hong Kong, the Ho-Pak. Certainly we'll do very well for their investors, stockholders and backers, far better than Richard! When I'm tai-pan I'll use the Ho-Pak as a pattern for future bail-outs. With our new management the Ho-Pak will be a marvelous asset. Like any one of a dozen enterprises. Even like Struan's!

Johnjohn's tiredness vanished. His smile broadened. Oh hurry up, Monday—when the market opens!

In the Struan box Peter Marlowe was gloomily leaning on the rail, watching the crowds below. Rain cascaded off the jutting overhang protecting the boxes. The three cantilever balconies of the members and nonvoting members were not so protected. Bedraggled horses were being led down the ramps, bedraggled grooms joining the bedraggled thousands streaming away.

'What's up, Peter?' Casey asked.

'Oh nothing.'

'Not Fleur, no problem there I hope?'

'No.'

'Was it Grey? I saw you both having at it.'

'No, no it wasn't Grey, though he's a pain, ill-mannered and stridently anti-everything of value.' Marlowe smiled curiously. 'We were just discussing the weather.'

'Sure. You were looking depressed as hell just then. You lost the fifth?'

'Yes, but it wasn't that. I'm ahead, well ahead on the day.' The tall man hesitated then motioned at the boxes and all around. 'It's just that I was thinking that there're fifty thousand-odd Chinese here and another three or four million out there,

1178

and each one's got a vast heritage, marvelous secrets, and fantastic stories to tell, to say nothing of the twenty-odd thousand Europeans, high and low, the tai-pans, the pirates, freebooters, accountants, shopkeepers, government people here—why did they choose Hong Kong too? And I know that however much I try, however much I read or listen or ask, I'll never really know very much about Hong Kong Chinese or about Hong Kong. Never. I'll only ever scratch the surface.'

She laughed. 'It's the same everywhere.'

'Oh no, no it isn't. This's the potpourri of Asia. Take that guy—the one in the third box over—the rotund Chinese. He's a millionaire many times over. His wife's a kleptomaniac so whenever she goes out he has his people follow her secretly and every time she steals something, his fellows pay for it. All the stores know her and him and it's all very civilized—where else in the world would you do that? His father was a coolie and his father a highwayman and *his* a Mandarin and *his* a peasant. One of the men near him's another multimillionaire, opium and illegal stuff into China, and his wife's . . . ah well, that's another story.'

'What story?'

He laughed. 'Some wives have stories just as fascinating as their husbands, sometimes more so. One of the wives you met today, she's a nympho an—'

'Oh come on, Peter! It's like Fleur says, you're making it all up.'

'Perhaps. Oh yes, but some Chinese ladies are just as . . . just as predatory as any ladies on earth, on the quiet.'

'Chauvinist! You're sure?'

'Rumor has it . . .' They laughed together. 'Actually they're so much smarter than we are, the Chinese. I'm told the few Chinese married ladies here who have a wandering eye usually prefer a European for a lover, for safety—Chinese adore gossip, love scandal, and it'd be rare to find a Chinese swinger who'd be able to keep such a secret or protect a lady's honor. Rightly, the lady would be afraid. To be caught would be very bad, very bad indeed. Chinese law's quite strict.' He took out a cigarette. 'Maybe that makes it all the more exciting.'

'To have a lover?'

He watched her, pondering what she would say if he told her

her nickname—whispered gleefully to him by four separate Chinese friends. 'Oh yes, ladies here get around, some of them. Look over there, in that box—the fellow holding forth wearing a blazer. He wears a green hat—that's a Chinese expression meaning he's a cuckold, that his wife's got a lover, actually in her case it was a Chinese friend of his.'

'Green hat?'

'Yes. Chinese are marvelous! They have such a terrific sense of humor. That fellow took out an ad in one of the Chinese papers some months ago that said, 'I know I wear a green hat but the wife of the man who gave it to me had two of his sons by other men!'''

Casey stared at him. 'You mean he signed his name to it?'

'Oh yes. It was a pun on one of his names, but everyone of importance knew who it was.'

'Was it true?'

Peter Marlowe shrugged. 'It doesn't matter. The other fellow's nose was neatly out of joint and his wife got hell.'

'That's not fair, not fair at all.'

'In her case it was.'

'What did she do?'

'Had two sons by anoth—'

'Oh come on, Mr. Storyteller!'

'Hey look, there's Doc Tooley!'

She searched the course below, then saw him. 'He doesn't look happy at all.'

'I hope Travkin's all right. I heard Tooley went to examine him.'

'That was some spill.'

'Yes. Terrible.'

Both had been subjected to Tooley's searching questions about their health, knowing the specter of typhus, perhaps cholera, and certainly hepatitis still hung over them.

'Joss!' Peter Marlowe had said firmly.

'Joss!' she had echoed, trying not to be worried about Linc. It's worse for a man, she thought, remembering what Tooley had said: Hepatitis can mess up your liver—and your life, forever, if you're a man.

After a moment she said, 'People here do seem to be more exciting, Peter. Is that because of Asia?'

1180

'Probably. The mores are so different. And here in Hong Kong we collect the cream. I think Asia's the center of the world and Hong Kong the nucleus.' Peter Marlowe waved to someone in another box who waved at Casey. 'There's another admirer of yours.'

'Lando? He is a fascinating man.'

Casey had spent time with him between races.

'You must come to Macao, Miss Tcholok perhaps we could have dinner tomorrow. Would 7:30 be convenient?' Mata had said with his marvelous old world charm and Casey had got the message very quickly.

During lunch Dunross had warned her a little about him. 'He's a good fellow, Casey,' the tai-pan had said delicately. 'But here, for a *quai loh* stranger, particularly someone as beautiful as you, on a first trip to Asia, well it's sometimes better to remember that being over eighteen isn't always enough.'

'Got you, tai-pan,' she had told him with a laugh. But this afternoon she had allowed herself to be mesmerized by Mata, in the safety of the tai-pan's box. Alone, her defenses would be up as she knew they would be tomorrow evening: 'It depends, Lando,' she had said, 'dinner would be fine. It depends what time I get back from the boat trip—I don't know if it's weather permitting or not.'

'With whom are you going? The tai-pan?'

'Just friends.'

'Ah. Well, if not Sunday, my dear, perhaps we could make it Monday. There are a number of business opportunities for you, here or in Macao, for you and Mr. Bartlett if you wish, and Par-Con. May I call you at seven tomorrow to see if you are free?'

I can deal with him, one way or another, she reassured herself, the thought warming her, though I'll watch the wine and maybe even the water in case of the old Mickey Finn.

'Peter, the men here, the ones on the make—are they into Mickey Finns?'

His eyes narrowed. 'You mean Mata?'

'No, just generally.'

'I doubt if a Chinese or Eurasian would give one to a *quai loh* if that's what you're asking.' A frown creased him. 'I'd say you'd have to be fairly circumspect though, with them and with

Europeans. Of course, to be blunt, you'd be high on their list. You have what it takes to send most of them into an orgiastic faint.'

'Thanks much!' She leaned on the balcony, enjoying the compliment. I wish Linc were here. Be patient. 'Who's that?' she asked. 'The old man leering at the young girl? Down on the first balcony. Look, he's got his hand on her butt!'

'Ah, that's one of our local pirates—Four Finger Wu. The girl's Venus Poon, a local TV star. The youth talking to them is his nephew. Actually the rumor is that he's a son. The fellow's got a Harvard business degree and a U.S. passport and he's as smart as a whip. Old Four Fingers is another multimillionaire, rumored to be a smuggler, gold and anything, with one official wife, three concs of various ages and now he's after Venus Poon. She was Richard Kwang's current. Was. But perhaps now with the Victoria takeover she'll dump Four Fingers and go back to him. Four Fingers lives on a rotten old Aberdeen junk and hoards his enormous wealth. Ah, look there! The wrinkled old man and woman the tai-pan's talking to.'

She followed his glance to the next box but one.

'That's Shitee T'Chung's box,' he said. 'Shitee's a direct descendant of May-may and Dirk through their son Duncan. Did the tai-pan ever show you Dirk's portraits?'

'Yes.' A small shiver touched her as she remembered the Hag's knife jammed through the portrait of her father, Tyler Brock. She considered telling him about it but decided not to. 'There's a great likeness,' she said.

'There certainly is! Wish I could see the Long Gallery. Anyway, that old couple he's talking to live in a tenement, a two-room, sixth-floor walk-up over in Glessing's Point. They own a huge block of Struan stock. Every year before each annual board meeting, the tai-pan, whoever he is, has to go cap in hand to ask for the right to vote the stock. It's always granted, that was part of the original agreement, but he still has to go personally.'

'Why's that?'

'Face. And because of the Hag.' A flicker of a smile. 'She was a great lady, Casey. Oh how I would like to have met her! During the Boxer revolt in 1899–1900, when China was in another of her conflagrations, the Noble House had all its possessions in

Peking, Tiensin, Foochow and Canton wiped out by the Boxer terrorists who were more or less sponsored and certainly encouraged by Tz'u Hsi, the old dowager empress. They called themselves the Righteous Harmonious Fists and their battle cry was "Protect the Ch'ing and kill all foreign devils!" Let's face it, the European powers and Japan had pretty much partitioned China. Anyway, the Boxers fell on all foreign business houses, settlements, the unprotected areas, and obliterated them. The Noble House was in terrible straits. At that time the nominal tai-pan was again old Sir Lochlin Struan—he was Robb Struan's last son, born with a withered arm. He was tai-pan after Culum. The Hag had appointed him when he was eighteen, just after Culum died—then again after Dirk Dunross—and she'd kept him tied to her apron strings till he died in 1915 at the age of seventy-two.'

'Where do you get all this information, Peter?'

'I make it up,' he said grandly. 'In any event, the Hag needed a lot of money fast. Gornt's grandfather had bought up a lot of Struan's paper and he had lowered the boom. There was no normal source of finance, nowhere she could borrow, for all Asia—all the *hongs*—were equally in turmoil. But that fellow's father, the father of the one the tai-pan's talking to, was the King of the Beggars in Hong Kong. Begging used to be a huge business here. Anyway, this man came to see her, so the story goes. "I come to buy a fifth part of the Noble House," this man said with great dignity, "is it for sale? I offer 200,000 taels of silver," which was exactly the amount she needed to redeem her paper. For face they haggled and he settled for a tenth, 10 percent—an incredibly fair deal—both knowing that he could have had 30 or 40 percent for the same amount because by that time the Hag was desperate. He required no contract other than her chop and her promise that once a year she, or the tai-pan, would come to him or his descendants wherever he or they lived, to ask for the vote of the stock. "So long as the tai-pan asks—the voting power is given."

'"But why, Honorable King of the Beggars? Why save me from my enemies?" she asked.

'"Because your grandfather, old Green-Eyed Devil, once saved my grandfather's face and helped him become the first King of the Beggars of Hong Kong."'

Casey sighed. 'Do you believe that, Peter?'

'Oh yes.' He looked out at Happy Valley. 'Once this was all a malarial swamp. Dirk cleaned that up too.' He puffed his cigarette. 'One day I'll write about Hong Kong.'

'If you continue to smoke you'll never write anything.'

'Point well taken. Okay, I'll stop. Now. For today. Because you're pretty.' He stubbed the cigarette out. Another smile, different. 'Eeeee, but I could tell some stories about lots of the people you met today. I won't, that's not fair, not right. I can never tell the real stories, though I know lots!' She laughed with him, letting her eyes wander from the strange old couple down to the other stands. Involuntarily she gasped. Sitting in the lee of the members' balcony she saw Orlanda. Linc was with her. He was very close. Both were very happy together, that was easy to see, even from this distance.

'What's th—' Peter Marlowe began, then he saw them too. 'Oh! Not to worry.'

After a pause she took her eyes away. 'Peter, that favor. May I ask for that favor, now?'

'What do you want as a favor?'

'I want to know about Orlanda.'

'To destroy her?'

'For protection. Protection for Linc against her.'

'Perhaps he doesn't want to be protected, Casey.'

'I swear I'll never use it unless I honest to God feel it's necessary.'

The tall man sighed. 'Sorry,' he said with great compassion, 'but nothing I could tell you about her would give you or Linc protection. Nothing to destroy her or make her lose face. Even if I could I wouldn't, Casey. That really wouldn't be cricket. Would it?'

'No, but I'm still asking.' She stared back at him, forcing the issue. 'You said a favor. I came when you needed a hand. I need a hand now. Please.'

He watched her a long time. 'What do you know about her?'

She told him what she had learned—about Gornt supporting Orlanda, Macao, about the child.

'Then you know everything I know, except perhaps that you should be sorry for her.'

'Why?'

'Because she's Eurasian, alone, Gornt her only support and that's as precarious as anything in the world. She's living on a knife edge. She's young, beautiful and deserves a future. Here there's none for her.'

'Except Linc?'

'Except Linc or someone like him.' Peter Marlowe's eyes were slate color. 'Perhaps that wouldn't be so bad from his point of view.'

'Because she's Asian and I'm not?'

Again the curious smile. 'Because she's a woman and so are you but you hold all the cards, and the only real thing you have to decide is if you really want that war.'

'Level with me, Peter, please. I'm asking. What's your advice? I'm running scared—there, I'll admit it to you. Please?'

'All right, but this isn't the favor I owe you,' he said. 'Rumor has it you and Linc are not lovers though you obviously love him. Rumor has it you've been together for six or seven years in close proximity but with no . . . no formal contact. He's a terrific fellow, you're a terrific lady and you'd make a great couple. The key word is *couple*, Casey. Maybe you want money and power and Par-Con more than you do him. That's your problem. I don't think you can have both.'

'Why not?'

'It seems to me you choose Par-Con and power and riches and no Bartlett, other than as a friend—or you become Mrs. Linc Bartlett and behave and *love* and be the kind of woman there's no doubt in hell Orlanda would be. Either way you have to be a hundred percent—you and Linc are both too strong and probably have tested each other too many times to be fooled. He's been divorced once, so he's on guard. You're over the age of a Juliet blindness so you're equally on guard.'

'Are you a psychiatrist too?'

He laughed. 'No, nor a father-confessor, though I like to know about people and like to listen but not to lecture and never to give advice—that's the most thankless task in the world.'

'So there's no compromise?'

'I don't think so, but then I'm not you. You have your own karma. Irrespective of Orlanda—if it's not her it'll be another woman, better or worse, prettier though maybe not, because win, lose or draw, Orlanda's quality and has what it takes to

1185

make a man content, happy, alive as a *man*. Sorry, I don't mean
to be chauvinistic, but since you asked, I'd advise you to make
up your mind quickly.'

Gavallan hurried into Shitee T'Chung's box and joined the
tai-pan. 'Afternoon,' he said politely to the old couple. 'Sorry,
tai-pan, Crosse and the other fellow you wanted had already
left.'

'Blast!' Dunross thought a second, then excused himself and
walked out with Gavallan. 'You're coming to the cocktail party?'

'Yes, if you want me there—afraid I'm not very good company.'

'Let's go in here a second.' Dunross led the way into his
private room. Tea was laid out and a bottle of Dom Pérignon in
an ice bucket.

'Celebration?' Gavallan asked.

'Yes. Three things: the General Stores takeover, the Ho-Pak
rescue and the dawn of the new era.'

'Oh?'

'Yes.' Dunross began to open the bottle. 'For instance you: I
want you to leave for London Monday evening with the
children.' Gavallan's eyes widened but he said nothing. 'I want
you to check on Kathy, see her specialist, then take her and the
kids to Castle Avisyard. I want you to take over Avisyard for six
months, perhaps a year or two. Six months certain—take over
the whole of the east wing.' Gavallan gasped. 'You're going to
head up a new division, very secret, secret from Alastair, my
father, every member of the family including David. Secret from
everyone except me.'

'What division?' Gavallan's excitement and happiness
showed.

'There's a fellow I want you to get close to tonight, Andrew
Jamie Kirk. His wife's a bit of a bore but invite them to Avisyard.
I want you to slide into Scotland, particularly Aberdeen. I want
you to buy property, but very quietly: factory areas, wharfage,
potential airfields, heliports near the docks. Are there docks
there?'

'Christ, tai-pan, I don't know. I've never been there.'

'Nor have I.'

'Eh?'

Dunross laughed at the look on Gavallan's face. 'Not to worry. Your initial budget is a million pounds sterling.'

'Christ, where the hell's a million coming fr—'

'Never mind!' Dunross twisted the cork and held it, deadening the explosion neatly. He poured the pale, oh so dry wine. 'You've a million sterling to commit in the next six months. A further 5 million sterling over the next two years.'

Gavallan was gaping at him openly.

'In that time I want the Noble House, oh so quietly, to become the power in Aberdeen, with the best land, best influence on the town councils. I want you laird of Aberdeen—and as far west as Inverness and south to Dundee. In two years. All right?'

'Yes but . . .' Gavallan stopped helplessly. All his life he had wanted to quit Asia. Kathy and the children too, but it had never been possible or even considered. Now Dunross had given him Utopia and he could not take it all in. 'But why?'

'Talk to Kirk, beguile his wife, and remember, laddie, a closed mouth.' Dunross gave him a glass and took one for himself. 'Here's to Scotland, the new era and our new fief.' Then he added in his most secret heart, And here's to the North Sea! All gods bear witness: The Noble House is implementing Contingency Plan One.

67

5:50 P.M.:

The stands were empty now but for the cleaners, most of the boxes dark. Rain cascaded from the sky, a solid sheet of water. It was near twilight. Traffic was snarled all around the racecourse. The thousands plodded homeward, sodden but light of heart. Next Saturday was another race day and another fifth race and oh oh oh, another challenge and this time the tai-pan will surely ride Noble Star and perhaps Black Beard will ride Pilot Fish and those two devil *quai loh* will kill themselves for our amusement.

A Rolls going out of the members' entrance splashed some of the pedestrians and they shouted a barrage of obscenities but none of the Chinese really minded. One day I'll have one of those, everyone thought. All I need's just a little fornicating joss. Just a little joss next Saturday and I'll have enough to buy some land or an apartment to rent out, to barter against a piece of a high rise, to mortgage against an acre of Central. Eee, how I'll enjoy riding in my Rolls with a lucky number plate like that one! Did you see who it was? Taximan Tok who seven years ago drove a *bo-pi*, an illegal taxi, and found 10,000 HK on his back-seat one day and hid it for five years till the statute of limitations had passed, then invested it in the stock market in the boom of three years ago to immense profit then took the profit and bought apartments. Eeee, the boom! Remember what Old Blind Tung wrote in his column about the coming boom! But what about the stock market crash and all the bank runs?

Ayeeyah, that's all over! Didn't you hear the astounding news? Great Bank is taking over the Ho-Pak and standing good for all Banker Kwang's debts. Did you hear about the Noble House buying General Stores? Both such good pieces of news announced on race day. That's never happened before! It's odd!

Very odd! You don't think . . . Fornicate all gods! It is all a foul ploy of those dirty foreign devils to manipulate the market to steal our rightful profits? Oh oh oh, I agree! Yes, it must be a foul plot! It's too much fornicating coincidence! Oh those cunning awful barbarians! Thank all gods I realized it so I can prepare! Now what should I do . . .

As they all headed for home their minds were consumed with growing excitement. Most were poorer than when they came to the track, but a few were much richer. Spectacles Wu, the police constable from the East Aberdeen Police station, was one of those. Crosse had allowed him to go to the races though he had to be back by 6:15 P.M. when the client was due to be interviewed again, Spectacles Wu there as interpreter for the Ningtok dialect. The young man shivered and his Secret Sack chilled at the thought of how quickly the great Brian Kwok had babbled his innermost secrets.

Ayeeyah, he thought, filled with superstitious dread. These pink barbarians are truly devils who can twist us civilized people as they wish to send us mad. But if I become SI that'll protect me and give me some of their secrets, and with those secrets and other foreign devil secrets I will become an ancestor!

He began to beam. His joss had changed ever since he had caught that old *amah*. Today the gods had favored him greatly. He had forecast one quinella, the daily double and three place horses, each time reinvesting all his winnings and now he was 5,753 HK richer. His plan for the money was already settled. He would finance Fifth Uncle to buy a used plastic molding machine to begin a plastic flower factory in return for 51 percent, another 1,000 would pay for the construction of two dwellings in the resettlement to be rented and the last 1,000 would be for next Saturday!

A Mercedes sounded its horn deafeningly, making him jump. Spectacles Wu recognized one of the men in the back: the man Rosemont, the CIA barbarian with limitless funds to spend. So naive, they are, the Americans, he thought. Last year when his relations had poured over the border in the exodus, he had sent them all down to the consulate on a roster basis, every month a different name and different story, to join the constant and evergrowing band of rice Christians or, to be more exact, rice non-Communists. It was easy to get free meals and handouts

1189

from the U.S. Consulate. All you had to do was to pretend to be frightened and say, nervously, that you had just come over the border, that you were staunchly against Chairman Mao and that in your village the Communists did such and such a terrible thing. The Americans would be happy to hear about PRC troop movements, real or imagined. Oh how quickly they would write it all down and ask for more. Any information, any stupid piece of information you could pick up if you could read a newspaper was to them—if whispered with rolling eyes—very valuable.

Three months ago Spectacles Wu had had a brainstorm. Now, with four members of his clan, one of whom was originally a journalist on a Communist newspaper in Canton, Spectacles Wu had offered—but through trusted intermediaries so he and his relations could not be traced—to supply Rosemont with a monthly undercover report, an intelligence pamphlet, code name 'Freedom Fighter', on conditions across the Bamboo Curtain in and around Canton. To prove the espionage quality Spectacles Wu had offered to supply the first two editions free—to catch a mighty tiger it is good business to sacrifice a stolen lamb. If these were considered acceptable to the CIA, the fee would be 1,000 HK each for the next three, and if these were equally valuable, then a new contract would be negotiated for a year of reports.

The first two had been so highly praised that an immediate deal was struck for five reports at 2,000 HK each. Next week they were to get their first fee. Oh how they had congratulated themselves. The content of the reports was culled from thirty Canton newspapers that came down on the daily Canton train that also brought pigs and poultry and foods of all kinds and could be purchased without effort in Wanchai paper shops. All they had had to do was to read them meticulously and copy the articles, after removing the Communist dialectic: articles about crops, building, economics, Party appointments, births, deaths, sentences, extortions and local color—anything they considered of interest. Spectacles Wu translated the stories the others picked.

He felt a huge wave of pleasure. Freedom Fighter had enormous potential. Their costs were almost nil. 'But sometimes we must be careful to make a few mistakes,' Spectacles Wu had told

1190

them, 'and occasionally we must miss a month—"we regret our agent in Canton was assassinated for giving away State secrets . . ."' Oh yes. And soon, when I'm a full member of SI and a trained espionage agent, I'll know better how to present the press information to the CIA. Perhaps we'll expand and experiment with a report from Peking, another from Shanghai. We can get day-old Peking and Shanghai papers equally with no trouble and very little investment. Thank all gods for American curiosity!

A taxi honked as it splashed past. He stopped a moment to allow it to pass, then shoved through, careless of the cursing, honking and noise alongside the tall fence that skirted the stadium. He glanced at his watch. He had plenty of time. Headquarters was not far away.

The rain became heavier but he did not feel it, the warmth of winnings in his pocket lightening his footsteps. He squared his shoulders. Be strong, be wise, he ordered himself. Tonight I must be alert. Perhaps they will ask my opinion. I know the Communist Superintendent Brian Kwok is a liar here and there and exaggerating. And as to atomics, what's so important about that? Of course the Middle Kingdom has its own atomics. Any fool knows what's been going on for years in Sinkiang near the shores of Lake Bos-teng-hu. And of course, soon we'll have our own rockets and satellites. Of course! Are we not civilized? Did we not invent gunpowder and rockets but discard them millennia ago as barbaric?

Throughout the stadium on the other side of the fence, women cleaners raked up the sodden leavings of the thousands, patiently sifting the rubbish carefully for a lost coin or ring, fountain pen or bottles that were worth a single copper cash. Crouched beside a pile of garbage cans in the lee of the rain was a man.

'Come on, old fellow, you can't sleep there,' a woman cleaner said, not unkindly, shaking him. 'It's time to go home!' The old man's eyes fluttered open for an instant, he began to get up but stopped, gave out a great sigh and subsided like a rag doll.

'*Ayeeyah*,' One Tooth Yang muttered. She had seen enough of death throughout her seventy years to recognize its finality.

1191

'Hey, Younger Sister,' she called out politely to her friend and second member of her team. 'Come over here! This old man's dead.'

Her friend was sixty-four, bent and lined but equally strong and also Shanghainese. She came out of the rain and peered down. 'He looks like a beggar.'

'Yes. We'd better tell the foreman.' One Tooth Yang knelt and carefully went through his ragged pockets. There were 3 HK in change, nothing else. 'That's not much,' she said. 'Never mind.' She divided the coins equally. Over the years they had always divided what they found.

'What's that in his left hand?' the other woman asked. One Tooth bent the clawlike hand open. 'Just some tickets.' She peered at them, then held them close to her eyes and flicked through them. 'It's the double quinella . . .' she began, then suddenly cackled, 'Eeee, the poor fool got the first leg and lost the second . . . he chose Butterscotch Lass!' Both women laughed hysterically at the mischief of the gods.

'That must have sent the poor old ancient into the seizure—it would me! *Ayeeyah*, to be so close and yet so far, Elder Sister.'

'Joss.' One Tooth Yang cackled again and tossed the tickets into the garbage can. 'Gods are gods and men are men but eee, I can imagine the old fellow dying. I would have too!' The two old women laughed again, the bad joss hurting them and the older one rubbed her chest to ease the pain. '*Ayeeyah*, I must get a physic. Go and tell the foreman about him. Younger Sister, eeee, but I'm tired tonight. Such bad joss, he was close to being a millionaire but now? Joss! Go tell the foreman. I'm tired tonight,' she said again, leaning on her rake, her voice wavering.

The other woman went off marveling at the gods and how quickly they can give or take away—if they exist at all, she thought in passing. Ah joss!

Wearily One Tooth Yang continued her work, her head aching, but the moment she was sure she was alone and unobserved she darted for the garbage can and frantically retrieved the tickets, her heart pounding like never in her whole life. Frantically she checked that her eyes had not deceived her and the numbers were correct. But there was no mistake. Each ticket was a winning ticket. Equally frantically she stuffed them in her pocket then made absolutely sure she had not left one carelessly in the rubbish. Quickly she piled more rubbish on top and lifted this can and dumped it into another, all the time her mind shrieking, Tomorrow I can redeem the tickets, I have three days to redeem them! Oh bless all gods, I'm rich I'm rich I'm rich! There must be a hundred or two hundred tickets and each a 5 HK ticket, each ticket pays 265 HK . . . if there's a hundred tickets that's 26,500 HK, if two hundred tickets 53,000 HK. . . .

Feeling faint, she squatted beside the corpse, leaning against the wall, not noticing it. She knew she dare not count the tickets now, there was no time. Every second was vital. She had to prepare. 'Be cautious, old fool,' she muttered aloud, then once more almost went into panic. Stop talking aloud! Be careful, you old fool, or Younger Sister will suspect . . . Oh oh oh is she now telling the foreman what she suspects? Oh what shall I do? The joss is mine, I found the old man . . . *ayeeyah*, what shall I do? Perhaps they'll search me. If they see me in this state they're bound to suspect. . . .

Her head was pounding terribly and a wave of nausea went through her. Nearby were some toilets. She groped to her feet and hobbled over to them. Behind her, other cleaners were sifting and tidying up. Tomorrow they would all come again for there would still be plenty to do. Her own shift was due back at nine in the morning. In the empty toilet room she took out the tickets, her fingers trembling, wrapped them in a piece of rag and found a loose brick in the wall and put them behind the brick.

Once safely outside she began to breathe. When the foreman came back with the other old woman he peered down at the man, went through his pockets with great care and found a twist of silver paper they had missed. Within it was a pinch of White Powder. 'It will bring 2 HK,' he said, knowing it was worth 6.04 HK. 'We will split it, 70 for me and 30 for you two.' For face, One Tooth argued and they settled that he would try to get 3.10 HK for it, and would split it 60 to him and 40 to them. Satisfied, he went away.

When they were alone again the younger woman began to sift the garbage.

'What're you doing?' One Tooth asked.

'I just wanted to check those tickets, Elder Sister. Your eyes are not so good.'

'Please yourself,' One Tooth said with a shrug. 'I've picked this lot clean. I'm going over there.' Her gnarled finger pointed at an unnoticed new source of virgin rubbish under a row of seats. The other woman hesitated then followed and now One Tooth almost chortled with glee, knowing she was safe. *Tomorrow I'll come back complaining of stomach sickness. I can retrieve my fortune and go home. Now what shall I do with my wealth?*

First the down payment on two quai loh *dancing dresses for Third Granddaughter in return for half her earnings in the first year. She'll make a fine whore in the Good Luck Dance Hall. Next, Second Son will stop being a coolie on the construction site up on Kotewall Road. He and Fifth Nephew and Second Grandson will become builders, and within the week we will put a down payment on a plot of land and begin to build a building . . .*

'You seem very happy, Elder Sister.'

'Oh yes I am, Younger Sister. My bones ache, the ague is with me as ever, my stomach is upset, but I am alive and that old man is dead. It is a lesson from the gods. All gods bear witness, when I first saw him, the first time, I thought it was my husband who died in our flight from Shanghai fifteen years ago. I thought I was seeing a ghost! My spirit almost left me for that old man was like his twin!'

'*Ayeeyah*, how horrible! How terrible! Ghosts! All gods protect us from ghosts!'

Oh yes, the old woman thought, ghosts're terrible. Now, where was I? Oh yes . . . 1,000 will go on the quinella next Saturday. And out of those winnings I will buy . . . I will buy myself a set of false teeth! Eeeee, how wonderful that will be, she wanted to cry out, almost fainting with suppressed pleasure. *All her life, all her life since she was fourteen when a Manchu rifle butt had smashed out her teeth in one of the constant revolutions against the foreign Ch'ing Dynasty, she had been nicknamed One Tooth. Always she had hated her nickname. But now . . . oh gods bear witness! I will buy a set of teeth from my winnings next Saturday—and also I will buy and light two candles in the nearest temple in return for such good joss.*

'I feel faint, Younger Sister,' she said, really faint with near

1194

ecstasy. 'Could you get me some water?'

The other woman went off grumbling. One Tooth sat down a moment and allowed herself a huge grin, her tongue feeling her gums. Eeeee, when I win, if I win heavily enough, I will have one gold tooth, right in the center, to remind me. Gold Tooth Yang, that has a nice sound to it, she thought, far too clever to mutter it aloud, even though she was completely alone. Yes, Honorable Gold Tooth Yang, of the Yang Constructions empire . . .

68

6:15 P.M.:

Suslev was hunched uncomfortably in the front of the small car
belonging to Ernie Clinker and they were grinding up the hill.
All the windows were steamed up, the rain even heavier. Mud
and stones washing down from the steep hillsides made the
road surface dangerous. Already they had passed two minor
accidents

'Cor, stone the crows, perhaps you'd better spend the night,
old chum,' Clinker said, driving with difficulty.

'No, not tonight,' Suslev said irritably. 'I already told you I
promised Ginny and tonight's my last night.' Ever since the
raid, Suslev had been in a blinding rage, his rage fed by unac-
customed fear—fear of the summons to police HQ in the morning; fear of catastrophic repercussions from the intercepted
decoded cable, fear of Center's probable displeasure over the
loss of Voranski, being ordered out of Hong Kong, the destruction of their radio equipment, the Metkin affair and now
Koronski's arrival and the possible kidnapping of Dunross. Too
many things have gone wrong this trip, he thought, chilled—
too long in the game to have any illusions. Even his phone
conversation during the fifth race with Crosse had not mollified
him.

'Not to worry, it's a routine request to appear, Gregor. Just a
few questions about Voranski, Metkin and so on,' Crosse had
said in a disguised voice.

'*Kristos*, what's the "and so on"?'

'I don't know. Sinders ordered it, not me.'

'You'd better cover me, Roger.'

1196

'You're covered. Listen, about this possible kidnapping, it's a very bad idea.'

'They want it set up, so help Arthur make the arrangements, eh, please? Unless you can delay my departure, we *will* implement it when it is ordered.'

'I recommend against it. This is my bailiwick and I rec—'

'Center approves and we will do it if it is ordered!' Suslev wanted to order Roger Crosse to shut up or else, but he was careful not to offend their best asset in Asia. 'Can we meet tonight?'

'No, but I'll call you. How about four? At 10:30?' Four was their present code for 32 Sinclair Towers. 10:30 meant 9:30 P.M.

'Is that wise?'

He had heard that dry confident laugh. 'Very wise. Would those fools come again? Of course it is wise. And I guarantee it!'

'All right. Arthur will be there. We should cement the plan.'

Clinker swerved to avoid a taxi cutting in and he cursed, then ground the gears, peering through the windshield ahead, getting into motion again. On his side Suslev rubbed the condensation away. 'God-cursed weather,' he said, his mind elsewhere. What about Travkin? Stupid motherless turd to fall off after passing the winning post. I thought he'd won. Decadent fool! No real cossack'd ever get caught like that. So he's out now, him and his crippled old crone princess with the broken bones.

Now how do we entice Dunross to the apartment tomorrow instead of Tuesday as Travkin had signaled. It has to be tonight or tomorrow. At the latest it must be tomorrow night. Arthur must arrange it or Roger. They are the keys to the Dunross plan.

And I must get those files—or Dunross—before I leave. One or the other. They're my only real protection against Center.

Bartlett and Casey got out of the Struan limo at the Hilton, the resplendent, turbaned Sikh doorman holding an unnecessary umbrella—the vast overhang already protecting them from the sheets of water.

'I'll be here, sir, whenever you're ready,' Chauffeur Lim said.

'Great. Thanks,' Bartlett replied. They went up the steps to the ground floor and took the escalator to the foyer.

'You're very quiet, Casey,' he said. All the way from the racetrack they had hardly said a word to each other, both locked into their own thoughts.

'So're you, Linc. I thought you didn't want to talk. You seemed distracted.' She smiled tentatively. 'Maybe it was all the excitement.'

'It was a great day.'

'You think the tai-pan's going to pull it off? The General Stores takeover?'

'Monday will tell.' Bartlett went to the reception desk. 'Mr. Banastasio please?'

The handsome Eurasian assistant manager said, 'Just a moment please. Oh yes, he changed his room again. Now it's 832.' He handed him a house phone. Bartlett dialed.

'Yeah?'

'Vincenzo? Linc, I'm downstairs.'

'Hey, Linc, good to hear your voice. Casey with you?'

'Sure.'

'You want to come up?'

'On our way.' Bartlett went back to Casey.

'You sure you want me along?'

'He asked for you.' Bartlett led the way to the elevator, thinking of Orlanda and their date later, thinking of Biltzmann and Gornt and Taipei tomorrow and whether or not he should ask Dunross if he could take her. Shit, life's complicated suddenly. 'It'll only be a few minutes,' he said, 'then it's cocktails with the tai-pan. The weekend's going to be interesting. And next week.'

'You out for dinner tonight?'

'Yes. We should have breakfast though. Seymour needs straightening out and as I'm off for a couple of days we'd better have our signals straight.'

They crowded into the elevator. Casey casually avoided being trampled on and ground her heel into her assailant's instep. 'Oh so sorry,' she said sweetly, then muttered *Dew neh loh moh* which Peter Marlowe had taught her this afternoon, just loud enough for the woman to hear. She saw the sudden flush. Hastily the woman shoved her way out at the mezzanine floor and Casey knew she had won a great victory. Amused, she glanced at Bartlett but he was lost in thought, staring into space, and she wondered very much what the real problem was. Orlanda?

On the eighth floor they got out. She followed Bartlett down the corridor. 'You know what this's all about, Linc? What Banastasio wants?'

'He said he just wanted to say hi and pass the time of day.' Bartlett pressed the button. The door opened.

Banastasio was a good-looking man with iron-gray hair and very dark eyes. He welcomed them cordially. 'Hey, Casey, you've lost weight—you're looking great. Drink?' He waved a hand at the bar. It was stocked with everything. Casey fixed herself a martini after opening a can of beer for Bartlett, lost in thought. *Peter Marlowe's right. So's the tai-pan. So's Linc. All I have to do is decide. By when? Very soon. Today, tomorrow? By Tuesday dinner for sure. Absolutely one hundred percent for sure and meanwhile maybe I'd better begin a few diversionary raids.*

'How's it going?' Banastasio was saying.

'Fine. With you?'

'Great.' Banastasio sipped a Coke then reached forward and turned on a small tape recorder. Out of it came a confusing mishmash of voices, the sort of background heard at any busy cocktail party.

'Just a habit, Linc, Casey, when I want to talk private,' Banastasio said quietly.

Bartlett stared at him. 'You think this place's bugged?'

'Maybe, maybe not. You never know who could be listening, huh?'

Bartlett glanced at Casey then back at Banastasio. 'What's on your mind, Vincenzo?'

Banastasio smiled. 'How's Par-Con?' the man asked.

'Same as ever—great,' Bartlett said. 'Our growth rate will be better'n forecast.'

'By 7 percent,' Casey added, all her senses equally sharpened.

'You going to deal with Struan's or Rothwell-Gornt?'

'We're working on it.' Bartlett covered his surprise. 'Isn't this new for you, Vincenzo? Asking about deals before they happen?'

'You going to deal with Struan's or Rothwell-Gornt?'

Bartlett watched the cold eyes and the strangely menacing

1199

smile. Casey was equally shocked. 'When the deal's done I'll tell you. The same time I tell the other stockholders.'

The smile did not change. The eyes got colder. 'The boys and I'd like to get invol—'

'What boys?'

Banastasio sighed. 'We've got a good piece of change in Par-Con, Linc, and now we'd like to figure in some of the up-front decisions. We figure I should have a seat on the board. And on the Finance Committee and the New Acquisitions Committee.'

Bartlett and Casey stared at him openly. 'That was never part of the stock deal,' Bartlett told him. 'Up front you said it was just an investment.'

'That's right,' Casey added, her voice sounding thin to her. 'You wrote us you were just an investor an—'

'Times've changed, little lady. Now we want in. Got it?' The man's voice was harsh. 'Just one seat, Linc. That much stock in General Motors and I'd have two seats.'

'We're not General Motors.'

'Sure. Sure, we know But what we want isn't out of line. We want Par-Con to grow faster. Maybe I ca—'

'It's growing just fine. Don't you think it'd be bet—' Again Banastasio turned his bleak gaze on her. Casey stopped. Bartlett's fists began to clench but he held them still. Carefully.

Banastasio said, 'It's settled.' The smile came back. 'I'm on the board from today, right?'

'Wrong. Directors get elected by the stockholders at the annual general meeting,' Bartlett said, his voice raw. 'Not before. There's no vacancy.'

Banastasio laughed. 'Maybe there will be.'

'Do you want to say that again?'

Abruptly Banastasio hardened. 'Listen, Linc, that's not a threat, just a possibility. I can be good on the board. I've got connections. And I want to put in my two cents' worth here and there.'

'About what?'

'Deals. For instance, Par-Con goes with Gornt.'

'And if I don't agree?'

'A little nudge from us and Dunross'll be on the street. Gornt's our boy, Linc. We checked and he's better.'

1200

Bartlett got up. Casey followed, her knees very weak. Banastasio didn't move. 'I'll think about all this,' Bartlett said. 'As of right now it's a toss-up if we make a deal with either one.'

Banastasio's eyes narrowed. 'What?'

'I'm not convinced that either's good for us. Right, Casey?'

'Yes, Linc.'

'My vote says Gornt. Got it?'

'Go screw.' Bartlett turned to go.

'Just a minute!' Banastasio stood up and came closer. 'No one wants trouble, not me, not the boys, n—'

'What boys?'

Again the other man sighed. 'C'mon, Linc, you're over twenty-one. You've had a good ride. We don't want to make waves, just money.'

'We have that in common. We'll buy back your stock and give you a profit of si—'

'No deal. It's not for sale.' Another sigh. 'We bought in when you needed dough. We paid a fair price and you used our cash to expand. Now, we want a piece of the exec action. Got it?'

'I'll put it to the stockholders at the annual gen—'

'Goddamnit, now!'

'Goddamnit no!' Bartlett was ready and very dangerous. 'Got it?'

Banastasio looked at Casey, his eyes flat like a reptile's. 'That your vote too, Miss Executive Vice-President and Treasurer?'

'Yes,' she said, surprised that her voice sounded firm. 'No seat on the board, Mr. Banastasio. If it comes to a vote, my stock's against you and totally against Gornt.'

'When we get control, you're fired.'

'When you get control, I'll already have left.' Casey walked toward the door, astonished that her legs worked.

Bartlett stood in front of the other man, on guard. 'See you around,' he said.

'You'd better change your mind!'

'You'd better stay the hell out of Par-Con.' Bartlett turned and followed Casey out of the room.

At the elevator he said, 'Jesus!'

'Yes,' she muttered as helplessly.

'We'd . . . we'd better talk.'

'Sure. I think I need a drink. Jesus, Linc, that man petrified

1201

me. I've never been so frightened in my whole life.' She shook her head, as though trying to clear it. 'That was like a goddamn nightmare.'

In the bar on the top floor she ordered a martini and he a beer and when the drinks had been silently consumed, he ordered another round. All the while their minds had been sifting, pitting facts against theories, changing the theories.

Bartlett shifted in his chair. She looked across at him. 'Ready for what I think?' she asked.

'Sure, sure, Casey. Go ahead.'

'There's always been a rumor he's Mafia or connected with Mafia and after our little talk I'd say that's a good bet. Mafia jumps us to narcotics and all sorts of evil. Theory: maybe it also jumps us somehow to the guns?'

The tiny lines beside Bartlett's eyes crinkled. 'I reached that too. Next?'

'Fact: if Banastasio's scared of being bugged that jumps us to surveillance. That means FBI.'

'Or CIA.'

'Or CIA. Fact: if he's Mafia and if the CIA or FBI're involved, we're in a game we've no right to be in, with nowhere to go but down. Now, as to what he wan—' Casey stopped. She gasped.

'What?'

'I just . . . I just remembered Rosemont, you remember him from the party, Stanley Rosemont, the tall, good-looking, gray-haired man from the consulate? We met on the ferry yesterday, yesterday afternoon. By chance. Maybe it's a coincidence, maybe not, but now that I think of it he brought up Banastasio, said his friend Ed someone, also at the consulate, knew him slightly—and when I said he was arriving today he was knocked for a loop.' She recapped her conversation. 'I never thought much about it at the time . . . but the consulate and what he said adds up: CIA.'

'Got to be. Sure. And if . . .' He stopped too. 'Come to think of it, Ian brought up Banastasio out of the blue too. Tuesday, in the lobby when you were at the phone, just before we went to the gold vaults.'

After a pause she said, 'Maybe we're in real deep shit! Fact: we got a murder, kidnapping, guns, Banastasio, Mafia, John Chen. Come to think of it, John Chen and Tsu-yan were very friendly with that bum.' Her eyes widened. 'Banastasio and John Chen's killing. Does that tie? From what the papers've said, the Were-wolves don't sound like Chinese—the ear bit. That's, that's brutal.'

Bartlett sipped his beer, lost in thought. 'Gornt? What about Gornt? Why did Banastasio go for him and not Struan's?'

'I don't know.'

'Try this for size, Casey. Say Banastasio's end play is guns, or narcotics, or both guns and narcotics. Both companies would be good for him. Struan's have ships and a huge complex at the airport that dominates inward and outward cargoes, great for smuggling. Gornt has ships and wharfing too. And Gornt's got All Asia Airways. An in with Asia's major feeder airline would give him—them—what they need. The airline goes to Bangkok, India, Vietnam, Cambodia, Japan—wherever!'

'And connects here with Pan-Am, TWA, JAL and all places east, west, north and south! And if we help Gornt to smash Struan's, the two companies together give them everything.'

'So, back to the sixty-four-dollar question: what do we do?' Bartlett asked.

'Couldn't we play a waiting game? The Struan-Gornt contest will be solved next week at the latest.'

'For this skirmish, we need information—and the right counterforces. Different guns, big guns, guns we don't have.' He sipped his beer, even more thoughtful. 'We'd better get some top-level advice. And help. Fast. It's Armstrong and the English cops—or Rosemont and the CIA.'

'Or both?'

'Or both.'

Dunross got out of the Daimler and hurried into police head-quarters. 'Evening, sir,' the young Australian duty inspector on the desk said. 'Sorry you lost the fifth—I heard Bluey White was carpeted for interference. Can't trust a bloody Aussie, eh?'

Dunross smiled. 'He won, Inspector. The stewards ruled the race was won fair and square. I've an appointment with Mr. Crosse.'

'Yes sir, square but not fair dinkum. Top floor, third on the left. Good luck next Saturday, sir.'

Crosse met him on the top floor. 'Evening. Come on in. Drink?'

'No thanks. Good of you to see me at once. Evening, Mr. Sinders.' They shook hands. Dunross had never been in Crosse's office before. The walls seemed as drab as the man and when the door was shut on the three of them the atmosphere seemed to close in even more.

'Please sit down,' Crosse said. 'Pity about Noble Star—we were both on her.'

'She'll be worth another flutter on Saturday.'

'You're going to ride her?'

'Wouldn't you?'

Both men smiled.

'What can we do for you?' Crosse asked.

Dunross put his full attention on Sinders. 'I can't give you new files—the impossible I can't do. But I can give you something—I don't know what, yet, but I've just received a package from AMG.'

Both men were startled. Sinders said, 'Hand-delivered?'

Dunross hesitated. 'Hand-delivered. Now, please, no more questions till I've finished.'

Sinders lit his pipe and chuckled. 'Just like AMG to have a bolt-hole, Roger. He always was clever, damn him. Sorry, please go on.'

'The message from AMG said the information was of very special importance and to be passed on to the prime minister personally or the current head of MI-6, Edward Sinders, at my convenience—*and if I considered it politic.*' In the dead silence, Dunross took a deep breath. 'Since you understand barter, I'll trade you—you direct, in secret, in the presence of the governor alone—whatever the hell "it" is. In return Brian Kwok is allowed out and over the border, if he wants to go, so we can deal with Tiptop.'

The silence deepened. Sinders puffed his pipe. He glanced at Crosse. 'Roger?'

Roger Crosse was thinking about *it*—and what information was so special that it was for Sinders or the P.M. only. 'I think you could consider Ian's proposal,' he said smoothly. 'At leisure.'

'No leisure,' Dunross said sharply. 'The money's urgent, and

1204

the release is clearly considered urgent. We can't delay past Monday at 10:00 A.M. when the ban—'

'Perhaps Tiptop and money don't come into the equation at all,' Sinders interrupted, his voice deliberately brittle. 'It doesn't matter a jot or a tittle to SI or MI-6 if all Hong Kong rots. Have you any idea the sort of value a senior superintendent in SI—especially a man with Brian Kwok's qualifications and experience—could have to the enemy, if in fact Brian Kwok is under arrest as you think and this Tiptop claims? Have you also considered that such an enemy traitor's information to us about his contacts and *them* could be of great importance to the whole realm? Eh?'

'Is that your answer?'

'Did Mrs. Gresserhoff hand-deliver the package?'

'Are you prepared to barter?'

Crosse said irritably, 'Who's Gresserhoff?'

'I don't know,' Sinders told him. 'Other than that she's the vanished recipient of the second phone call from AMG's assistant, Kiernan. We're tracing her with the help of the Swiss police.' His mouth smiled at Dunross. 'Mrs. Gresserhoff delivered the package to you?'

'No,' Dunross said. That's not a real lie, he assured himself. It was Riko Anjin.

'Who did?'

'I'm prepared to tell you that after we have concluded our deal.'

'No deal,' Crosse said.

Dunross began to get up.

'Just a moment, Roger,' Sinders said and Dunross sat back. The MI-6 man tapped the pipe stem against his tobacco-discolored teeth. Dunross kept his face guileless, knowing he was in the hands of experts.

At length Sinders said, 'Mr. Dunross, are you prepared to swear formally under the perjury conditions of the Official Secrets Act that you do not have possession of the original AMG files?'

'Yes,' Dunross said at once, quite prepared to twist the truth now—AMG had always had the originals, he had always been sent the top copy. If and when it came to a formal moment under oath, that would be another matter entirely. 'Next?'

1205

'Monday would be impossible.'

Dunross kept his eyes on Sinders. 'Impossible because Brian's being interrogated?'

'Any captured enemy asset would immediately be questioned, of course.'

'And Brian will be a very hard nut to take apart.'

'*If* he's the asset, you'd know that better than us. You've been friends a long time.'

'Yes, and I swear to God I still think it's impossible. Never once has Brian been anything other than an upright, staunch British policeman. How is it possible?'

'How were Philby, Klaus Fuchs, Sorge, Rudolf Abel, Blake and all the others possible?'

'How long would you need?'

Sinders shrugged, watching him.

Dunross watched him back. The silence became aching.

'You destroyed the originals?'

'No, and I must tell you I also noticed the difference between all the copies I gave you and the one you intercepted. I'd planned to call AMG to ask him why the difference.'

'How often were you in contact with him?'

'Once or twice a year.'

'What did you know about him? Who suggested him to you?'

'Mr. Sinders, I'm quite prepared to answer your questions, I realize it's my duty to answer them, but the time's not appropriate tonight be—'

'Perhaps it is, Mr. Dunross. We're in no rush.'

'Ah, I agree. But unfortunately I've got guests waiting and my association with AMG has nothing to do with my proposal. My proposal requires a simple yes or no.'

'Or a maybe.'

Dunross studied him. 'Or a maybe.'

'I'll consider what you've said.'

Dunross smiled to himself, liking the cat-and-mouse of the negotiation, aware he was dealing with masters. Again he let the silence hang until exactly the right moment. 'Very well. AMG said *at my discretion*. At the moment I don't know what "it" is. I realize I'm quite out of my depth and should not be involved in SI or MI-6 matters. It's not of my choosing. You intercepted my private mail. My understanding with AMG was quite clear: I had his assurance in writing that he was allowed to be in my employ and that he would clear everything with the government in advance. I'll give you copies of our correspondence if you wish, through the correct channels, with the correct secrecy provisions. My enthusiasm for my offer diminishes, minute by minute.' He hardened his voice. 'Perhaps it doesn't matter to SI or MI-6 if all Hong Kong rots but it does to me, so I'm making the offer a last time.' He got up. 'The offer's good to 8:30 P.M.'

Neither of the other men moved. 'Why 8:30, Mr. Dunross? Why not midnight or midday tomorrow?' Sinders asked, unperturbed. He continued to puff his pipe but Dunross noticed that the tempo had been interrupted the moment he laid down the challenge. That's a good sign, he thought.

'I have to call Tiptop then. Thanks for seeing me.' Dunross turned for the door.

Crosse, sitting behind the desk, glanced at Sinders. The older man nodded. Obediently Crosse touched the switch. The bolts sneaked back silently. Dunross jerked to a stop, startled, but recovered quickly, opened the door and went out without a comment, closing it after him.

'Cool bugger,' Crosse said, admiring him.

'Too cool.'

'Not too cool. He's tai-pan of the Noble House.'

'And a liar, but a clever one and quite prepared to finesse us. Would he obliterate "it"?'

'Yes. But I don't know if H hour's 8:30 P.M.' Crosse lit a cigarette. 'I'm inclined to think it is. They'd put immense pressure on him—they have to presume we'd thrust the client into interrogation. They've had plenty of time to study Soviet techniques and they've got a few twists of their own. They must presume we're fairly efficient too.'

'I'm inclined to think he hasn't got any more files and "it" is genuine. If "it" comes from AMG it must have special value. What's your counsel?'

'I repeat what I said to the governor: If we have possession of the client until Monday at noon we'll have everything of importance out of him.'

'But what about *them*? What can he tell them about us when he recovers?'

'We know most of that now. Concerning Hong Kong, we can certainly cover every security problem from today. It's standard SI policy never to let any one person know master plans an—'

'Except you.'

Crosse smiled. 'Except me. And you in the UK of course. The client knows a lot, but not everything. We can cover everything here, change codes and so on. Don't forget, most of what he passed on's routine. His real danger's over. He's uncovered, fortunately in time. Sure as God made little apples, he'd've been the first Chinese commissioner, and probably head of SI en route. That would have been catastrophic. We can't recover the private dossiers, Fong-fong and others, or the riot and counter-insurrection plans. A riot is a riot and there are only so many contingency plans. As to Sevrin, he knows no more than we knew before we caught him. Perhaps the "it" could provide keys, possibly keys to questions we should put to him.'

'That occurred to me instantly too. As I said, Mr. Dunross is too bloody cool.' Sinders lit another match, smoked the match a moment, then tamped the used-up tobacco. 'You believe him?'

'About the files, I don't know. I certainly believe he has an "it" and that AMG came back from the dead. Sorry I never met him. Yes. The "it" could easily be more important than this client—after Monday at noon. He's mostly a husk now.'

Since they had returned, the interrogation of Brian Kwok had continued, most of it rambling and incoherent but details here and there of value. More about atomics and names and addresses of contacts in Hong Kong and Canton, security risks here and patterns of information about the Royal Mounted Police, along with an immensely interesting reiteration of vast Soviet infiltration into Canada.

'Why Canada, Brian?' Armstrong had asked.

'Northern border, Robert . . . the weakest fence in the world, there isn't any. Such great riches in Canada . . . ah I wish . . . there was this girl I almost married, they said my duty . . . if Soviets can disrupt Canadians . . . they're so gullible, and wonderful up there. . . . Can I have a cigarette . . . oh thanks . . . Can I have a drink my . . . So we have counter-espionage cells everywhere to disrupt Soviet cells and find out . . . then there's Mexico . . . The Soviets are making a big push there too . . . Yes they have plants everywhere . . . did you know Philby . . .'

An hour had been enough.

'Curious he should break so quickly,' Sinders said.

Crosse was shocked. 'I guarantee that he's not controlled, not lying, that he's telling absolutely everything he believes, what has happened and will continue to do so un—'

'Yes of course,' Sinders said somewhat testily. 'I meant curious that a man of his quality should crumble so soon. I'd say he'd been wavering for years, that his dedication was now nonexistent or very small and he was probably ready to come over to us but somehow couldn't extract himself. Pity. He could have been very valuable to us.' The older man sighed and lit another match. 'After a time it always happens to their deep-cover moles in our societies. There's always some kindness, or girl or man friend or freedom or happiness that turns their whole world upside down, poor buggers. That's why we'll win, in the end. Even in Russia the tables'll be turned and the KGB'll get their comeuppance—from Russians—that's why the pressure now. No Soviet on earth can survive without dictatorship, secret police, injustice and terror.' He tapped out his pipe into the ashtray. The dottle was wet at the base. 'Don't you agree, Roger?'

Crosse nodded and stared back at the intense, pale blue eyes, wondering what was behind them. 'You'll phone the minister for instructions?'

'No. I can take the responsibility for this one. We'll decide at 8:30.' Sinders glanced at his watch. 'Let's get back to Robert. It's almost time to begin again. Good fellow that, very good. Did you hear that he was a big winner?'

69

'Ian? Sorry to interrupt,' Bartlett said.

'Oh hello!' Dunross turned back from the other guests he was chatting with. Bartlett was alone. 'You two aren't leaving, I hope—this'll go on till at least 9:30.'

'Casey's staying awhile. I've a date.'

Dunross grinned. 'I hope she's suitably pretty.'

'She is, but that comes later. First a business meeting. Do you have a minute?'

'Certainly, of course. Excuse me a moment,' Dunross said to the others and led the way out of the crowded anteroom to one of the terraces. The rain had lessened in strength but continued implacably. 'The General Stores takeover's almost certain at our figure, without any overbid from Superfoods. We really will make the proverbial bundle—if I can stop Gornt.'

'Yes. Monday will tell.'

Dunross looked at him keenly. 'I'm very confident.'

Bartlett smiled, tiredness and concern behind the smile. 'I noticed. But I wanted to ask, are we still on for Taipei tomorrow?'

'I was going to suggest we should postpone it till next week, next weekend? Tomorrow and Monday are rather important for both of us. Is that all right?'

Bartlett nodded, hiding his relief. 'Fine with me.' And that solves my problem about Orlanda, he thought. 'Well then, I think I'll be off.'

'Take the car. Just send Lim back when you're through with him. You're going to the hill climb if it's on? That's at 10:00 A.M. till about noon.'

'Where is it?'

'New Territories. I'll send the car for you, weather permitting. Casey too if she wants.'

'Thanks.'

'Don't worry about Casey tonight—I'll see she gets back safely. Is she free afterwards?'

'I think so.'

'Good, then I'll ask her to join us—a few of us are going for a Chinese supper.' Dunross studied him. 'No problem?'

'No. Nothing that can't be handled.' Bartlett grinned and walked away, girding himself for the next onslaught—Armstrong. He had cornered Rosemont a few moments ago and told him about the meeting with Banastasio.

'Best leave it with us, Linc,' Rosemont had said. 'As far as you're concerned we're informed officially. The consulate. I'll pass it on to whomever. Leave it all lie—tell Casey, okay? If Banastasio calls either of you, stall him, call us and we'll work out a scam. Here's my card—it's good twenty-four hours a day.'

Bartlett was outside the front door now and he joined the others waiting impatiently for their cars.

'Oh hi, Linc,' Murtagh said, hurriedly getting out of a cab, almost knocking him over. 'Sorry! Party still going on?'

'Sure it is, Dave. What's the rush?'

'Got to see the tai-pan!' Murtagh dropped his voice, his excitement showing. 'There's a chance that head office'll go for it, if Ian'll concede a little! Casey still here?'

'Sure,' Bartlett said at once and all his senses focused, everything else forgotten. 'What concessions?' he asked warily.

'Double the foreign exchange period and he's to deal direct with First Central, giving us first option on all future loans for five years.'

'That's not much,' Bartlett said, hiding his perplexity. 'What's the whole deal now?'

'Can't stop, Linc, gotta get the tai-pan's okay. They're waiting, but it's just as Casey and me laid it out. Hell, if we pull this off the tai-pan'll owe us favors till hell freezes!' Murtagh rushed off.

Bartlett stared after him blankly. His feet began to take him back into the house but he stopped and returned to his place in

1211

the line. There's plenty of time, he told himself. No need to ask her yet. Think it out.

Casey had told him about the Royal Belgium's connection with First Central, and Murtagh had elaborated this afternoon, adding how hard it was to get an in here with the Establishment but that was all. Bartlett had noted the Texan's nervousness and Casey's nervousness. At the time he'd put it down to the races.

But now? he asked himself suspiciously. Casey and Murtagh and the tai-pan! 'First Central'll go for the deal if' and 'the tai-pan'll owe us favors till hell freezes. . . .' and 'just as Casey and me laid it out'. She's the go-between? Casey'd run rings around that joker and she's no messenger. Hell, Casey has to lead him by the nose. He's no match for her. So probably she put him up to—to what? What does the tai-pan need most?

Credit, fast, in millions by Monday.

Jesus, First Central's going to back him! That's got to be it. If. If he makes concessions, and he's got to make some to get out from under . . .

'You want the car, sir?'

'Oh. Yes, Lim, sure. Police headquarters in Wanchai. Thanks.' He got into the back, his mind buzzing.

So Casey's got a private game going. It must've been in the works a day or so but she hasn't told me. Why? If I'm right and the scam succeeds, Ian's got the wherewithal to fight off Gornt, even cream him. She's gone out of her way to help him against Gornt. Without my okay. Why? And in return for what?

Drop dead money! Is the 50–50 a payoff—my 2 mill but she shares 50–50?

Sure. That's one possibility—one that I know about now. What're the others? Jesus! Casey independent, maybe going with the enemy? They're still both enemy, Ian and Gornt.

His excitement increased.

What to do?

The money at risk with Gornt is covered every which way. The 2 mill with Struan's is covered too, and stays. I'd never planned to jerk it—that was just testing Casey. The Struan deal's good either way. The Gornt deal's good, either way. So my plan's still good—I can still jump either way, though the timing's critical.

But now there's Orlanda.

If it's Orlanda, it's the States or somewhere else but not here. It's quite clear she'd never be welcome in Happy Valley's winner's circle. Or in the cliques and clubs. She'd never be freely invited into the great houses, except maybe by Ian. And Gornt, but that'd be to taunt, to jerk the reins, to remind her of the past—like last night when that other girl came on deck. I saw Orlanda's face. Oh she covered, better than anyone could have covered except maybe Casey. She hated that the other girl had been below, in the master suite that was once hers.

Maybe Gornt didn't do that deliberately? Maybe the girl came up on her own. She went back below almost at once. Maybe she wasn't supposed to come up at all. Maybe.

Shit! There's too much going on I can't figure: like the General Stores and the Ho-Pak rescue—too much agreed by a couple of guys on a Saturday—a couple of whiskeys here and a phone call there. It's all dynamite if you're in the club but Jesus watch out if you're not. Here you've got to be British or Chinese to belong.

I'm just as much an outsider as Orlanda.

Still, I could be happy here, for a time. And I could even handle it here with Orlanda, for a short time, on visits. I could handle the Pacific Rim and having Par-Con as a Noble House but for it to be accepted as *the* Noble House by British and Chinese, it'll still have to be Struan-Par-Con with our name in small letters, or Rothwell-Gornt-Par-Con the same.

Casey?

With Casey, Par-Con could be a Noble House, easily. But is Casey still to be trusted? Why didn't she tell me? Is she sucked in by Hong Kong and beginning to play her own game for Number One?

You'd better choose, old buddy, while you're still tai-pan.

'Yes, Phillip?'

They were in the study under the portrait of Dirk Struan, and Dunross had chosen the place deliberately. Phillip Chen sat opposite him. Very formal, very correct and very weary. 'How is Alexi?'

'Still unconscious. Doc Tooley says he'll be all right if he comes out of it in a couple of hours.'

'Tiptop?'

1213

'I'm to call him at 9:00 P.M.'

'Still no approval of his offer from . . . from the authorities?'

Dunross's eyes narrowed. 'You know the arrangement he suggested?'

'Oh yes, tai-pan. I . . . I was asked. I still find it hard to believe . . . Brian Kwok? God help us, but yes . . . my opinion was asked before the suggestion was put to you.'

'Why the devil didn't you tell me?' Dunross snapped.

'Rightly you no longer consider me compradore of the Noble House and favor me with your trust.'

'You consider yourself trustworthy?'

'Yes. I've proved it in the past many times, so did my father—and his. Even so, if I were you and sitting where you are sitting, I would not be having this meeting, I would not have you in my house and I would already have decided the ways and means of your destruction.'

'Perhaps I have.'

'Not you.' Phillip Chen pointed at the portrait. 'He would have, but not you, Ian Struan Dunross.'

'Don't bet on it.'

'I do.'

Dunross said nothing, just waited.

'First the coin: Wait until the favor is asked. I will endeavor to find out what it is in advance. If it is too much th—'

'It will be too much.'

'What will he ask for?'

'Something to do with narcotics. There's a strong rumor Four Fingers, Smuggler Yuen and White Powder Lee are in partnership, smuggling heroin.'

'It's under consideration. They're not actually partners yet,' Phillip Chen said.

'Again, why didn't you tell me? It's your duty as compradore to keep me informed, not to write down intimate details of our secrets and then lose them to enemies.'

'Again, I ask forgiveness. But now is the time to talk.'

'Because you're finished?'

'Because I might be finished—if once more I cannot prove my worth.' The old man looked at Dunross bleakly, seeing the face of many tai-pans in the face of the man opposite him, not liking the face or that of the man above the fireplace whose eyes bored

1214

into him—the foreign devil pirate who had forsaken his great-grandfather because of mixed blood, half of which was his own.

Ayeeyah, he thought, curbing his anger. These barbarians and their intolerance! Five generations of tai-pans we've served and now this one threatens to change Dirk's legacy for one mistake?

'About the ask: even if it's connected with heroin or narcotics, it will concern some future performance or action. Agree to it, tai-pan, and I promise I will deal with Four Fingers long before the ask has to be granted.'

'How?'

'This is China. I will deal with it in Chinese fashion. I swear it by the blood of my ancestors.' Phillip Chen pointed at the portrait. 'I will continue to protect the Noble House as I have sworn to do.'

'What other trickeries did you have in your safe? I've been through all the documents and balance sheets you gave Andrew. With that information in the wrong hands we're naked.'

'Yes, but only in front of Bartlett and Par-Con, provided he keeps them to himself and doesn't pass them over to Gornt or another enemy here. Tai-pan, Bartlett doesn't strike me as a malicious person. Perhaps we can deal with him to get what he has back and ask him to agree to keep the information secret.'

'To do that you have to barter with a secret he doesn't want let out. Do you have one?'

'Not yet. As partners to us he should protect us.'

'Yes. But he's already dealing with Gornt and advanced $2 million U.S. to cover Gornt selling us short.'

Phillip Chen whitened. 'Eeeee, I didn't know that.' He thought a moment. 'So Bartlett will withdraw from us on Monday and go over to the enemy?'

'I don't know. At the moment I think he's fence-sitting. I would if I was him.'

Phillip Chen shifted in his chair. 'He's very fond of Orlanda, tai-pan.'

'Yes, she could be a key. Gornt's got to have arranged that, or pushed her toward Bartlett.'

'Are you going to tell him?'

'No, not unless there's a reason. He's over twenty-one.' Dunross hardened even more. 'What do you propose?'

1215

'Are you agreeing to the new concessions First Central wants?'

'So you know about that too?'

'You must have wanted everyone to know that you're seeking support from them, tai-pan. Why else invite Murtagh to your box at the races, why else invite him here? It was easy to put two and two together, even if one hasn't copies of his telexes y—'

'Have you?'

'Some of them.' Phillip Chen took out a handkerchief and wiped his hands. 'Will you concede?'

'No. I told him I'd think about it—he's waiting downstairs for my answer but it's got to be no. I can't guarantee to give them first option on all future loans. I can't because the Victoria has so much power here and so much of our paper and they'd squeeze us to death. In any event I can't replace them with an American bank that's already proved to be politically unreliable. They're fine as a backup and fantastic if they'll get us out of this mess but I'm not sure about them long-term. They have to prove themselves.'

'They must be ready to compromise too. After all, giving us 2 million to cement the General Stores takeover's a great vote of confidence, *heya*?'

Dunross let that pass. 'What had you in mind?'

'May I suggest you counter by making a specific offer: all Canadian, U.S., Australian and South American loans for five years—that covers our expansion in those territories—plus the immediate loan for two giant oil tankers to be purchased through Toda, on the lease-back scheme, and, for an associate, firm orders for a further seven.'

'Christ Jesus, who's got that type of operation?' Dunross exploded.

'Vee Cee Ng.'

'Photographer Ng? Impossible.'

'Within twenty years Vee Cee will have a fleet bigger than Onassis.'

'Impossible.'

'Very probably, tai-pan.'

'How do you know?'

'I've been asked to help finance and arrange a huge extension to his fleet. If we put the first seven tankers into our package

1216

with the promise of more, and I can, *I can*, that should satisfy First Central.' Phillip Chen wiped the perspiration off his forehead. '*Heya?*'

'Christ, that'd satisfy the Chase Manhattan and the Bank of America jointly! Vee Cee?' Then Dunross's boggled mind jerked into top efficiency. 'Ah! Vee Cee plus thoriums plus Old Friends plus all sorts of delicate hardware plus oil plus Old Friends. Eh?'

Phillip smiled tentatively. 'All crows under heaven are black.'

'Yes.' After a pause, he said, 'First Central might go for it. But what about Bartlett?'

'With First Central you don't need Par-Con. First Central will be happy to help us get an alternate backer or partner in the States. It'd take a little time, but with Jacques in Canada, David MacStruan here, Andrew in Scotland . . . Tai-pan, I don't know what's in your mind about Andrew and this man Kirk but the theories he's been sporting strike me as farfetched, very farfetched.'

'You were saying about Bartlett?'

'I suggest we pray that First Central takes the bait, that Tiptop gives us the money, that I can cover First Central with a syndicate of Mata, Tightfist and Four Fingers. Then you, David MacStruan and I can easily find an alternate to Par-Con. I suggest we open an immediate office in New York. Put David in charge for three months with . . . perhaps Kevin as his assistant.' Phillip Chen let that set a moment in the air and rushed on. 'Within three months we should know if young Kevin has any value—I think you'll be very impressed, tai-pan, in fact I guarantee it. In three months we'll know what young George Trussler feels about Rhodesia and South Africa. When he has that office set up we could send him to New York. Or we could perhaps tempt your other cousin, the Virginian, Mason Kern, out of Cooper-Tillman and put him in charge of our New York office. After six months Kevin should go to Salisbury and Johannesburg—I have a great feeling that the thorium and precious metal trade will go from strength to strength.'

'Meanwhile, we still have our immediate problems. Bartlett, Gornt and the run on our stock?'

'To ensure Bartlett's silence we have to split him totally from Gornt and make him an ally, a complete ally.'

'How do you do that, Phillip?'

1217

'Leave that with me. There are . . . there are possibilities.'

Dunross kept his eyes on Phillip Chen but the old man did not look up from the desk. What possibilities? Orlanda? Has to be. 'All right,' he said. 'Next?'

'About the market. With the Bank of China supporting us, the bank runs are over. With the General Stores takeover and massive financial backing, the run on our stock has to cease. Everyone will rush to buy and the boom will be on. Now,' Phillip Chen said, 'I know you didn't want to before, but say we can get Sir Luis to withdraw our stock from trading till Monday at noon we ca—'

'What?'

'Yes. Say no one can trade Struan's officially until noon, say we set the price where it was on Wednesday last— 28.80. Gornt is trapped. He has to buy at whatever price he can to cover. If no one offers enough stock below that figure all his profits go out of the window, he might even be mauled.'

Dunross felt weak. The idea of jerking the stock now had not occurred to him. 'Christ, but Sir Luis'd never go for it.'

Phillip Chen was very pale, beads of sweat on his forehead. 'If the stock exchange committee agreed that it was necessary "to stabilize the market" . . . and if the great broking firms of Joseph Stern and Arjan Soorjani also agree not to offer any stock, any bulk stock below 28.80, what can Gornt do?' He wiped his forehead shakily. 'That's my plan.'

'Why should Sir Luis cooperate?'

'I think . . . I think he will, and Stern and Soorjani owe us many favors.' The old man's fingers were twitching nervously. 'Between Sir Luis, Stern, Soorjani, you and me, we control most of the major blocks of stock Gornt sold short.'

'Stern is Gornt's broker.'

'True, but he's Hong Kong yan and he needs goodwill more than one client.' Phillip Chen shifted more into the light. Dunross noticed the pallor and was greatly concerned. He got up and went to the liquor cabinet and fetched two brandy and sodas. 'Here.'

'Thank you.' Phillip Chen drank his quickly. 'Thank God for brandy.'

'You think we can line them all up by Monday's opening? By the way, I've canceled my trip to Taipei.'

'Good, yes that's wise. Will you be going to Jason Plumm's cocktail party now?'

'Yes. Yes, I said I would.'

'Good, we can talk more then. About Sir Luis. There's a good chance, tai-pan. Even if the stock isn't withdrawn, the price has to skyrocket, it must—if we get the support we need.'

That's obvious to anyone, Dunross thought sourly. If. He glanced at his watch. It was 8:35. Sinders was to call by 8:30. He had given him half an hour leeway before his call to Tiptop. His stomach seemed to fall apart but he dominated it. Christ, I can't call him, he thought irritably. 'What?' he asked, not having heard Phillip Chen.

'The deadline you gave me to have my resignation on your desk—Sunday midnight if Mata and Tightfist or—may I ask that it be extended a week?'

Dunross picked up Phillip Chen's glass to replenish it, liking the Asian subtlety of the request, to extend it to a time when it would have no value, for, in a week's time, the crisis would be long resolved. The way the request was put saved face on both sides. Yes, but he has to make a major effort. Can his health stand it? That's my only real consideration. As he poured the brandy he thought about Phillip Chen, Kevin Chen, Claudia Chen and old Chen-chen and what he would do without them. I need cooperation and service and no more betrayal or treachery. 'I'll consider that, Phillip. Let's discuss it just after Prayers on Monday.' Then he added carefully, 'Perhaps extensions would be justified.'

Gratefully Phillip Chen accepted the brandy and took a big swallow, his color better. He had heard the deft plural and was greatly relieved. All I have to do is deliver. That's all. He got up to go. 'Thank y—'

The phone jangled irritatingly and he almost jumped. So did Dunross.

'Hello? Oh hello, Mr. Sinders.' Dunross could hear the beating of his heart over the rain. 'What's new?'

'Very little I'm afraid. I've discussed your suggestion with the governor. If "it" is in my possession by noon tomorrow, I have reason to believe your friend could be delivered to the Lo Wu border terminal by sunset Monday. I cannot guarantee, of course, that he will wish to cross the border into Red China.'

Dunross got his voice going. 'There's a lot of "reason to believe" and "could be" in that, Mr. Sinders.'

'That's the best I can do, officially.'

'What guarantees do I have?'

'None, I'm afraid, from Mr. Crosse or myself. It would seem there has to be trust on both sides.'

Bastards, Dunross thought furiously, they know I'm trapped. 'Thank you, I'll consider what you've said. Noon tomorrow? I'm in the hill climb tomorrow if it's on—ten to noon. I'll come to police headquarters as soon as I can afterwards.'

'No need to worry, Mr. Dunross. If it's on, I'll be there too. Noon can be a deadline here or there. All right?'

'All right. Good night,' Grimly Dunross put the phone down. 'It's a maybe, Phillip. Maybe, by Monday sunset.'

Phillip Chen sat down, aghast. His pallor increased. 'That's too late.'

'We'll find out.' He picked up the phone and dialed again. 'Hello, good evening. Is the governor there, please? Ian Dunross.' He sipped his brandy. 'Sorry to disturb you, sir, but Mr. Sinders just called. He said, in effect: perhaps. Perhaps by sunset Monday. May I ask, could you guarantee that?'

'No, Ian, no I can't. I don't have jurisdiction over this matter. Sorry. You have to make any arrangements direct. Sinders struck me as a reasonable man though. Didn't you think so?'

'He seemed very unreasonable,' Dunross said with a hard smile. 'Thanks. Never mind. Sorry to disturb you, sir. Oh, by the way if this can be resolved, Tiptop said your chop would be required, with the bank's and mine. Would you be available tomorrow, if need be?'

'Of course. And Ian, good luck.'

Dunross replaced the phone. After a moment, he said, 'Would they agree, the money tomorrow for the fellow Monday sunset?'

'I wouldn't,' Phillip Chen said helplessly. 'Tiptop was clear. "Whenever the correct procedures are entered into." The exchange would be simultaneous.'

Dunross sat back in the high chair, sipped his brandy and let his mind roam.

At 9:00 P.M. he dialed Tiptop, and chatted inconsequentially until the moment had come. 'I hear the police underling will

1220

surely be fired for making such a mistake and that the wronged party could be at Lo Wu at noon Tuesday.'

There was a great silence. The voice was colder than ever. 'I hardly think that's immediate.'

'I agree. Perhaps I might be able to persuade them to bring it forward to Monday. Perhaps your friends could be a little patient. I would consider it a very great *favor*.' He used the word deliberately and let it hang.

'I will pass your message on. Thank you, tai-pan. Please call me at seven o'clock tomorrow evening. Good night.'

'Night.'

Phillip Chen broke the silence, very concerned. 'That's an expensive word, tai-pan.'

'I know. But I have no option,' he said, his voice hard. 'Certainly there'll be a return favor asked in payment someday.' Dunross brushed his hair away from his eyes and added, 'Perhaps it'll be with Joseph Yu, who knows? But I had to say it.'

'Yes. You're very wise. Wise beyond your years, much wiser than Alastair and your father, not as wise as the Hag.' A small shiver went through him. 'You were wise to barter the time, and wise not to mention the money, the bank money, very wise. He's much too smart not to know we need that tomorrow—I'd imagine by evening at the latest.'

'Somehow we'll get it. That'll take the Victoria pressure off us. Paul's got to call a board meeting soon,' Dunross added darkly. 'With Richard on the board, well, Richard owes us many favors. The new board will vote to increase our revolving fund, then we won't need Bartlett, First Central or Mata's god-cursed syndicate.'

Phillip Chen hesitated, then he blurted out, 'I hate to be the bearer of more bad tidings but I've heard that part of Richard Kwang's arrangement with Havergill included his signed, undated resignation from the Victoria board and a promise to vote exactly as Havergill wishes.'

Dunross sighed. Everything fell into place. If Richard Kwang voted with the opposition it would neutralize his dominating position. 'Now all we have to do is lose one more supporter and Paul and his opposition will squeeze us to death.' He looked up at Phillip Chen. 'You'd better nobble Richard.'

'I . . . I'll try, but he's nobbled already. What about P. B.

White? Do you think he'd help?'

'Not against Havergill, or the bank. With Tiptop he might,' Dunross said heavily. 'He's next—and last—on the list.'

70

10:55 P.M.:

The six people piled out of the two taxis at the private entrance of the Victoria Bank building on the side street. Casey, Riko Gresserhoff, Gavallan, Peter Marlowe, Dunross and P. B. White, a spare, sprightly Englishman of seventy-five. The rain had stopped, though the poorly lit street was heavily puddled.

'Sure you won't join us for a nightcap, Peter?' P. B. White asked.

'No thanks, P. B., I'd better be getting home. Night and thanks for supper, tai-pan!'

He walked off into the night, heading for the ferry terminal that was just across the square. Neither he nor the others noticed the car pull up and stop down the street. In it was Malcolm Sun, senior agent, SI, and Povitz, the CIA man. Sun was driving.

'This the only way in and out?' Povitz asked.

'Yes.'

They watched P. B. White press the door button. 'Lucky bastards. Those two broads are the best I've ever seen.'

'Casey's okay but the other? There are prettier girls in any dance hall. . . .' Sun stopped. A taxi went past.

'Another tail?'

'No, no I don't think so, but if we're watching the tai-pan you can bet others are.'

'Yes.'

They saw P. B. White press the button again. The door opened and the sleepy Sikh night guard greeted him, 'Evening, sahs, memsahs,' then went to the elevator, pressed the button and closed the front door.

1223

'The elevator's rather slow. Antiquated, like me. Sorry,' P. B. White said.

'How long have you lived here, P. B.?' Casey asked, knowing there was nothing ancient about him, given the dance in his step or the twinkle in his eyes.

'About five years, my dear,' he replied taking her arm. 'I'm very lucky.'

Sure, she thought, and you've got to be very important to the bank and powerful, must be to have one of the only three apartments in the whole vast building. He had told them one of the others belonged to the chief manager who was presently on sick leave. The last one was staffed but kept vacant. 'It's for visiting HRHs, the governor of the Bank of England, prime ministers, those sort of luminaries,' P. B. White had said grandly during the light spicy Szechuan food. 'I'm rather like a janitor, an unpaid caretaker. They let me in to look after the place.'

'I'll bet!'

'Oh it's true! Fortunately there's no connection between this part of the building and the bank proper, otherwise I'd have my hand in the till!'

Casey was feeling very happy, replete with good food and good wine and fine, witty conversation and much attention from the four men, particularly Dunross—and very content that she had held her own with Riko—everything in her life seemingly in place again, Linc so much more her Linc once more, even though he was out with the enemy. How to deal with her? she asked herself for the billionth time.

The elevator door opened. They went into it, crowding into the small area. P. B. White pressed the lowest of three buttons. 'God lives on the top floor,' he chuckled. 'When he's in town.'

Dunross said, 'When's he due back?'

'In three weeks, Ian, but it's just as well he's out of touch with Hong Kong—he'd be back on the next plane. Casey, our chief manager's a marvelous fellow. Unfortunately he's been quite sick for almost a year and now he's retiring in three months. I persuaded him to take some leave and go to Kashmir, to a little place I know on the banks of the Jehlum River, north of Srinagar. The floor of the valley's about six thousand feet up, and there amongst the greatest mountains on earth, it's paradise. They have houseboats on the rivers and lakes and you drift, no phones, no mail, just you and the Infinite, wonderful people, wonderful air, wonderful food, stupendous mountains.' His eyes twinkled. 'You have to go there very sick, or with someone you love very much.'

They laughed. 'Is that what you did, P. B.?' Gavallan asked.

'Of course, my dear fellow. It was in 1915, that was the first time I was there. I was twenty-seven, on leave from the Third Bengal Lancers.' He sighed, parodying a lovesick youth. 'She was Georgian, a princess.'

They chuckled with him. 'What were you really in Kashmir for?' Dunross asked.

'I'd been seconded for two years from the Indian General Staff. That whole area, the Hindu Kush, Afghanistan and what's now called Pakistan, on the borders of Russia and China's always been dicey, always will be. Then I was sent up to Moscow— that was late in '17.' His face tightened a little. 'I was there during the *putsch* when the real government of Kerenski was tossed out by Lenin, Trotsky and their Bolsheviks. . . .' The elevator stopped. They got out. The front door of his apartment was open, his Number One Boy Shu waiting.

'Come on in and make yourself at home,' P.B. said jovially. 'The ladies' bathroom's on the left, gentlemen on the right, champagne in the anteroom . . . I'll show you all around in a moment. Oh, Ian, you wanted to phone?'

'Yes.'

'Come along, you can use my study.' He led the way down a corridor lined with fine oils and a rare collection of icons. The apartment was spacious, four bedrooms, three anterooms, a dining room to seat twenty. His study was at the far end. Books lined three walls. Old leather, smell of good cigars, a fireplace. Brandy, whiskey and vodka in cut-glass decanters. And port. Once the door closed his concern deepened.

'How long will you be?' he asked.

'As quick as I can.'

'Don't worry, I'll entertain them—if you're not back in time I'll make your excuses. Is there anything else I can do?'

'Lean on Tiptop.' Dunross had told him earlier about the possible deal to exchange Brian Kwok, though nothing about

1225

the AMG papers and his problems with Sinders.

'Tomorrow I'll call some friends in Peking and some more in Shanghai. Perhaps they would see the value in helping us.'

Dunross had been acquainted with P. B. White for many years though, along with everyone else, he knew very little about his real past, his family, whether he had been married and had children, where his money came from or his real involvement with the Victoria. 'I'm just a sort of legal advisor though I retired years ago,' he would say vaguely and leave it at that. But Dunross knew him as a man of great charm with many equally discreet lady friends. 'Casey's quite a woman, P.B.,' he said with a grin. 'I think you're smitten.'

'I think so too. Yes. Ah, if I was only thirty years younger! And as for Riko!' P.B.'s eyebrows soared. 'Delectable. Are you certain she's a widow?'

'Pretty sure.'

'I would like three of those please, tai-pan.' He chuckled and went over to the bookcase and pressed a switch. Part of the bookcase swung open. A staircase led upward. Dunross had used it before to have private talks with the chief manager. As far as he knew he was the only outsider privy to the secret access—another of the many secrets that he could pass on only to his succeeding tai-pan. 'The Hag arranged it,' Alastair Struan had told him the night he took over. 'Along with this.' He had handed him the master passkey to the safety deposit boxes in the vaults. 'It's bank policy that Ch'ung Lien Loh Locksmiths Ltd. change locks. Only our tai-pans know we own that company.'

Dunross smiled back at P.B., praying that he could be so young when he was so old. 'Thanks.'

'Take your time, Ian.' P. B. White handed him a key.

Dunross ran up the stairs softly to the chief manager's landing. He unlocked a door which led to an elevator. The same key unlocked the elevator. There was only one button. He relocked the outside door and pressed the button. The machinery was well oiled and silent. At length it stopped and the inner door slid open. He pushed the outer door. He was in the chief manager's office. Johnjohn got up wearily. 'Now what the hell is all this about, Ian?'

Dunross shut the false door that fitted perfectly into the

bookcase. 'Didn't P.B. tell you?' he asked, his voice mild, none of his tension showing.

'He said you had to get to the vaults tonight to fetch some papers, that I should please let you in and there was no need to bother Havergill. But why the cloak-and-dagger bit? Why not use the front door?'

'Now give over, Bruce. We both know you've got the necessary authority to open the vault for me.'

Johnjohn began to say something but changed his mind. The chief manager had said before he left, 'Be kind enough to react favorably to whatever P.B. suggests, eh?' P.B. was on first-name terms with the governor, most of the visiting VVIPs and shared the chief manager's direct line to their skeleton staff in the bank offices still operating in Shanghai and Peking.

'All right,' he said.

Their footsteps echoed on the vast, dimly lit main floor of the bank. Johnjohn nodded to one of the night watchmen making his rounds, then pressed the button for the elevator to the vaults, stifling a nervous yawn. 'Christ, I'm bushed.'

'You architected the Ho-Pak takeover, didn't you?'

'Yes, yes I did, but if it hadn't been for your smashing coup with General Stores, I don't think Paul'd . . . well, that certainly helped. Smashing coup, Ian, if you can pull it off.'

'It's in the bag.'

'What Japenese bank's backing you with the 2 million?'

'Why did you force Richard Kwang's advance resignation?'

'Eh?' Johnjohn stared at him blankly. The elevator arrived. They got into it. 'What?'

Dunross explained what Phillip Chen had told him. 'That's not exactly cricket. A director of the Victoria being made to sign an undated resignation like a two-cent operation? Eh?'

Johnjohn shook his head slowly. 'No, that wasn't part of my plan.' His tiredness had vanished. 'I can see why you'd be concerned.'

'*Pissed off* would be the correct words.'

'Paul must have planned just a holding situation till the chief comes back. This whole operation's precedent-setting so you c—'

'If I get Tiptop's money for you, I want that torn up and a free vote guaranteed to Richard Kwang.'

After a pause, Johnjohn said, 'I'll support you on everything reasonable—till the chief comes back. Then he can decide.'

'Fair enough.'

'How much is the Royal Belgium-First Central backing you for?'

'I thought you said a Japanese bank?'

'Oh come on, old chum, everyone knows. How much?'

'Enough, enough for everything.'

'We still own most of your paper, Ian.'

Dunross shrugged. 'It makes no difference. We still have a major say in the Victoria.'

'If we don't get China's money, First Central won't save you from a crash.'

Again Dunross shrugged.

The elevator doors opened. Dim lights in the vaults cast hard shadows. The huge grille in front of them seemed like a cell door to Dunross. Johnjohn unlocked it.

'I'll be about ten minutes,' Dunross said, a sheen to his forehead. 'I've got to find a particular paper.'

'All right. I'll unlock your box for y—' Johnjohn stopped, his face etched in the overhead light. 'Oh, I forgot, you've your own master key.'

'I'll be as quick as I can. Thanks.' Dunross walked into the gloom, turned the corner and went unerringly to the far bank of boxes. Once there he made sure he was not being followed. All his senses were honed now. He put the two keys into their locks. The locks clicked back.

His fingers reached into his pocket and he took out AMG's letter that gave the numbers of the special pages spread throughout the files, then a flashlight, scissors and a butane Dunhill cigarette lighter that Penelope had given him when he still smoked. Quickly he lifted the false bottom of the box away and slid out the files.

I wish to Christ there was some way I could destroy them now and have done with it, he thought. I know everything that's in them, everything important, but I have to be patient and wait. Sometime soon, they—whoever they are, along with SI, the CIA and the PRC—they won't be following me. Then I can safely fetch the files and destroy them.

Following AMG's instructions with great care, he flicked the

1228

lighter and waved it back and forth just under the bottom right quadrant of the first special page. In a moment, a meaningless jumble of symbols, letters and numbers began to appear. As the heat brought them forth, the type in this quadrant began to vanish. Soon all the lettering had gone, leaving just the code. With the scissors he cut off this quarter neatly and put that file aside. AMG had written: 'The paper cannot be traced to the files, tai-pan, nor I believe, the information read by any but the highest in the land.'

A slight noise startled him and he looked off. His heart was thumping in his ears. A rat scurried around a wall of boxes and vanished. He waited but there was no more danger.

In a moment he was calm again. Now the next file. Again ciphers appeared and the lettering vanished.

Dunross worked steadily and efficiently. When the flame began to fade he was prepared. He refilled the lighter and continued. Now the last file. He cut out the quarter carefully and pocketed the eleven pieces of paper, then slid the files back into their hiding place.

Before he relocked the box he took out a deed for camouflage and laid it beside AMG's letter. Another hesitation, then, shielding AMG's letter with his body, he put the flame to it. The paper twisted as it flared and burned.

'What're you doing?'

Dunross jerked around and stared at the silhouette. 'Oh, it's you.' He began breathing again. 'Nothing, Bruce. Actually it's just an ancient love letter that shouldn't have been kept.' The flame died and Dunross pounded the ash to dust and scattered the remains.

'Ian, are you in trouble? Bad trouble?' Johnjohn asked gently.

'No, old chum. It's just the Tiptop mess.'

'You're sure?'

'Oh yes.' Wearily Dunross smiled back and took out a handkerchief to wipe his forehead and hands. 'Sorry to put you to all this trouble.'

He walked off firmly, Johnjohn following. The gate clanged after them. In a moment the elevator sighed open and sighed closed and now there was silence but for the scurry of the rats and the slight hiss of the air conditioner. A shadow moved. Silently Roger Crosse came from behind a tall bank of boxes and stood in front of the tai-pan's section. Unhurried, he took out a tiny Minox camera, a flashlight and a bunch of skeleton keys. In a moment, Dunross's box was open. His long fingers reached into it, found the false compartment and brought out the files. Very satisfied he put them in a tidy pile, clipped the flashlight into its socket and, with practiced skill, began to photograph the files, page by page. When he came to one of the special pages he peered at it and the missing section. A grim smile flickered over him. Then he continued, making no sound.

SUNDAY

71

Koronski came out of the foyer of the Nine Dragons Hotel and hailed a taxi, giving the driver directions in passable Cantonese. He lit a cigarette and slouched back in the seat, keeping a professional watch behind him in the unlikely chance that he was being followed. There was no real risk. His papers as Hans Meikker were flawless, his cover as a sporadic foreign journalist for a West German magazine syndicate real, and he visited Hong Kong frequently as a routine. His eyes reassured him, then he turned to watch the multitudes, wondering who was to be chemically debriefed, and where. He was a short, well-fed, nondescript man, his glasses rimless.

Behind him, fifty yards or so, ducking in and out of the traffic was a small, battered Mini. Tom Connochie, the senior CIA agent was in the back, one of his assistants, Roy Wong, driving.

'He's going left.'

'Sure. I see him. Relax, Tom, you're making me nervous for chrissake.' Roy Wong was third-generation American, a B.A. Lit., and CIA for four years, assigned to Hong Kong. He drove expertly, Connochie watching carefully—crumpled and very tired. He had been up most of the night with Rosemont trying to sort out the flood of top-secret instructions, requests and orders that the intercepted Thomas K. K. Lim's letters had generated. Just after midnight they'd been tipped by one of their hotel informants that Hans Meikker had just checked in for two days from Bangkok. He had been on their list for years as a possible security risk.

'Son of a bitch!' Roy Wong said as a traffic jam blossomed in the narrow, screeching street near the bustling intersections of Mong Kok.

Connochie craned out of the side window. 'He's screwed too, Roy. About twenty cars ahead.'

In a moment the jam began to ease, then closed in again as an overladen truck stalled. By the time it had cranked up again, their prey had vanished.

'Shit!'

'Cruise. Maybe we'll get lucky and pick him up.'

Two blocks ahead, Koronski got out of the taxi and went down a swarming alley, heading for another swarming road and another alley and Ginny Fu's tenement. He went up the soiled stairs to the top floor. He knocked three times on a drab door. Suslev beckoned him in and locked the door behind him. 'Welcome,' he said quietly in Russian. 'Good trip?'

'Yes, Comrade Captain, very good,' Koronski replied, also keeping his voice down by habit.

'Come and sit down.' Suslev waved at the table that had coffee and two cups. The room was drab with little furniture. Dirty blinds covered the windows.

'Coffee's good,' Koronski said politely, thinking it was hideous, nothing to compare with the French-style coffee of exquisite Bangkok, Saigon and Phnom Penh.

'It's the whiskey,' Suslev said, his face hard.

'Center said I was to put myself at your disposal, Comrade Captain. What is it you want me to do?'

'A man here has a photographic memory. We need to know what's in it.'

'Where is the client to be interrogated? Here?'

Suslev shook his head. 'Aboard my ship.'

'How much time do we have?'

'All the time you need. We will take him with us to Vladivostok.'

'How important is it to get quality information?'

'Very.'

'In that case I would prefer to do the investigation in Vladivostok—I can give you special sedatives and instructions that will keep the client docile during the voyage there and begin the softening-up process.'

Suslev rethought the problem. He needed Dunross's in-

1234

formation before he arrived in Vladivostok. 'Can't you come with me on my ship? We leave at midnight, on the tide.'

Koronski hesitated. 'My orders from Center are to assist you, so long as I do not jeopardize my cover. Going on your ship would certainly do that—the ship's sure to be under surveillance. If I vanish from the hotel, eh?'

Suslev nodded. 'I agree.' Never mind, he thought. I'm as well trained an interrogator as Koronski though I've never done an in-depth chemical. 'How do you conduct a chemical debriefing?'

'It's quite simple. Intravenous injections of a chemical agent we call Pentothal-V6, twice a day for ten days at twelve-hour intervals—once the client has been put into a suitably frightened, disoriented frame of mind, by the usual sleep-wake method, followed by four days of sleeplessness.'

'We've a doctor on the ship. Could he make the injections?'

'Oh yes, yes of course. May I suggest I write down the procedure and supply you with all the necessary chemicals. You will do the investigation?'

'Yes.'

'If you follow the procedure you should have no trouble. The only serious thing to remember is that once the Pentothal-V6 is administered the client's mind is like a wet sponge. It requires great tenderness and even greater care to extract just the right amount of water, the information, at just the right tempo or the mind will be permanently damaged and all other information lost forever.' Koronski puffed at a cigarette. 'It's easy to lose a client.'

'It's always easy to lose a client,' Suslev said. 'How effective is this Pentothal-V6?'

'We've had great success, and some failures, Comrade Captain,' Koronski replied with care. 'If the client is well prepared and initially healthy I'm sure you will be successful.'

Suslev did not answer, just let his mind reexamine the plan presented so enthusiastically by Plumm late last night, and agreed to reluctantly by Crosse. 'It's a cinch, Gregor, everything's falling into place. Now that Dunross's not going to Taipei he's coming to my party. I'll give him a doctored drink that'll make him as sick as a dog—it'll be easy to get him to lie down in one of the bedrooms—the same drug'll put him to sleep. Once the others have left—and I'm keeping the party short and sweet, six to eight—I'll put him in a trunk and have the trunk brought to the car through the side entrance. When he's reported missing I'll say I just left him there sleeping and have no idea what time he left. Now, how are we going to get the trunk aboard?'

'That's no trouble,' he had said. 'Have it delivered to go-down 7 in the Kowloon Dockyard. We're taking on all kinds of bulk supplies and stores, since our departure's been speeded up, and outward bound there's hardly any check.' Suslev had added with grim amusement, 'There is even a coffin if we need it. Voranski's body is coming from the morgue at 11:00 P.M., a special delivery. Bastards! Why hasn't our friend caught the bastards who murdered him?'

'He's doing what he can. He is, Gregor. I promise you. He'll catch them soon—but more important, this plan *will* work!'

Suslev nodded to himself. Yes, it's workable. And if the tai-pan's intercepted and discovered? I know nothing, Boradinov knows nothing, though he's responsible and I shall just sail away, leaving Boradinov to blame, if necessary. Roger will cover everything. Oh yes, he told himself grimly, this time it's Roger's neck on the British block if I'm not covered. Plumm's right. The Werewolf kidnapping of the tai-pan will help to create complete chaos for a time, certainly for almost no risk— enough time to cover the Metkin disaster and the intercept of the guns.

He had called Banastasio tonight to make sure the Par-Con ploy was in operation and was shocked to hear of Bartlett's response. 'But, Mr. Banastasio, you guaranteed you'd be in control. What do you intend to do?'

'Pressure, Mr. Marshall,' Banastasio had told him placatingly, using the alias by which Banastasio knew him. 'Pressure all the way. I'll do my part, you do yours.'

'Good. Then proceed with your meeting in Macao. I guarantee a substitute shipment will be in Saigon within a week.'

'But these jokers here have already said they won't deal without a shipment in their hands.'

'It'll be delivered direct to our Viet Cong friends in Saigon. Just you make whatever arrangements you want for payment.'

'Sure sure, Mr. Marshall. Where you staying in Macao?

Where do I get in touch?'

'I'll be at the same hotel,' he had told him, having no intention to make contact. In Macao another controller with the same alias would monitor that end of the operation.

He smiled to himself. Just before he had left Vladivostok, Center had ordered him to be the controller of this independent operation, code name King Kong, that had been mounted by one of the Washington KGB cells. All he knew of the plan was that they were sending highly classified advance-arms delivery schedules to the V.C. in Saigon through diplomatic pouch. In exchange and payment for the information, opium would be delivered FOB Hong Kong—the quantity depending on the numbers of arms hijacked. 'Whoever thought of this one deserves immediate promotion,' he had told Center delightedly, and had chosen the alias Marshall after General Marshall and his plan that they all knew had ruined the immediate and total Soviet takeover of Europe in the late forties. This is revenge, our Marshall Plan in reverse, he thought.

Abruptly he laughed out loud. Koronski waited attentively, far too practiced to ask what had been so amusing. But without thinking he had analyzed the laugh. There was fear in it. Fear was infectious. Frightened people make mistakes. Mistakes ensnare innocents.

Yes, he thought uneasily, this man smells of cowardice. I shall mention this in my next report, but delicately, in case he's important.

He looked up and saw Suslev watching him and queasily wondered if the man had read his thoughts. 'Yes, Comrade Captain?'

'How long will the instructions take to write?'

'A few minutes. I can do it all now if you wish, but I will have to go back to the hotel for the chemicals.'

'How many different chemicals are to be used?'

'Three: one for sleep, one for wake-up and the last, the Pentothal-V6. By the way, it should be kept cool until used.'

'Only the last intravenously?'

'Yes.'

'Good, then write it all down. Now. You have paper?'

Koronski nodded and pulled out a small notebook from his hip pocket. 'Would you prefer Russian, English or shorthand?'

'Russian. There's no need to describe the wake-sleep-wake pattern. I've used that many times. Just the last phase and don't name Pentothal-V6, just call it medicine. Understand?'

'Perfectly.'

'Good. When it's written, put it there.' He pointed to a small pile of used newspapers on the moth-eaten sofa. 'Put it in the second one from the top. I'll collect it later. As to the chemicals there's a men's room on the ground floor of the Nine Dragons Hotel. Tape them to the underside of the lid, the last booth on the right—and please be in your room at nine o'clock tonight in case I need some clarification. Everything clear?'

'Certainly.'

Suslev got up. At once Koronski did the same, offered his hand. 'Good luck, Comrade Captain.'

Suslev nodded politely as to an inferior and walked out. He went to the end of the corridor and through a bent door up a staircase to the roof. He felt better in the air on the roof. The room smell and Koronski's smell had displeased him. The sea beckoned him, the wide clean ocean and salt-kelp smell. It will be good to be at sea again, away from the land. The sea and the ocean and the ship keep you sane.

Like most roofs in Hong Kong this one was packed with a polyglot of makeshift dwellings, the space rented—the only alternative to the crude, packed mud slopes of the squatter settlements that were far in the New Territories or in the hills of Kowloon or Hong Kong. Every inch of space in the city had long since been taken by the vast influx of immigrants. Most squatters' areas were illegal, like all roof dwellings, and as much as the authorities forbade it and deplored it, wisely they ignored these transgressions for where else were these unfortunates to go? There was no sanitation, no water, not even simple hygiene, but it was still better than on the streets. From the rooftops, the method of disposal was just to hurl it below. Hong Kong *yan* always walked in the center of the street and never on the sidewalk, even if there was one.

Suslev ducked under clotheslines, stepped over the flotsam and jetsam of lifetimes, oblivious of the automatic obscenities that followed him, amused by the urchins who ran before him shrieking, '*Quai loh . . . quai loh!*', laughing together, holding out their hands. He was too Hong Kong *yan* to give them any money though he was touched by them, their poverty and good humor, so he just cursed them genially and tousled a few crew-cut heads.

On the far side of the roof the entrance to Ginny Fu's tenement jutted like an ancient funnel. The door was ajar. He went down.

'Halloa, Gregy,' Ginny Fu said, breathlessly opening her front door for him. She was dressed as he had ordered in a drab coolie outfit with a big straw conical hat hanging down her back, her face and hands dirtied. 'How I look? Like film star, *heya?*'

'Greta Garbo herself,' he said with a laugh as she ran into his arms and gave him a great hug.

'You want jig-jig more 'fore go, *heya?*'

'*Nyet.* Plenty of time in the next weeks. Plenty, *heya?*' He set her down. He had pillowed with her at dawn, more to prove his manhood than out of desire. That's the problem, he thought. No desire. She's boring. 'Now, you understand plan, *heya?*'

'Oh yes,' she said grandly. 'I find go-down 7 and join coolies, carry bales to ship. Once on ship I go door opposite stairway, go in and give paper.' She pulled it out of her pocket to show that she had it safely. On the paper was written in Russian, 'Cabin 3.' Boradinov would be expecting her. 'In 3 cabin, can use bath, change to clothes you buy and wait.' Another big smile. '*Heya?*'

'Excellent.' The clothes had cost little and the buying saved any baggage. Much more simple without baggage. Baggage would be noticed. Nothing about her should be noticed.

'Sure no need bring anything, Gregy?' she asked anxiously.

'No, only makeup things, woman things. Everything in pocket, understand?'

'Of course,' she said haughtily. 'Am I fool?'

'Good. Then off you go.'

Once more she embraced him. 'Oh thanks holiday, Gregy—I be bestest ever.' She left.

The meeting with Koronski had made him hungry. He went to the battered refrigerator and found the chocolates he sought. He munched on one, then lit the gas stove and began to fry some eggs. His anxiety began to return. Don't worry, he ordered himself. The plan will work, you will get possession of the tai-pan and it will be routine at police headquarters.

Put those things aside. Think of Ginny. Perhaps at sea she

won't be boring. She'll divert the nights, some of the nights, the tai-pan the days until we dock. By then he'll be empty and she'll vanish into a new life and that danger will be gone forever and I'll go to my *dacha* where the Zergeyev hellcat'll be waiting and we'll fight, she calling me every obscenity until I lose my temper and tear her clothes off, maybe use the whip again and she'll fight back and fight back until I fight into her and explode, explode taking her with me sometimes, *Kristos* how I wish it was every time. Then sleeping, never knowing when she'll kill me in my sleep. But she's been warned. If anything happens to me my men will give her to lepers on the east side of Vladivostok with the rest of her family.

The radio announced the seven o'clock news in English. 'Good morning. This is Radio Hong Kong. More heavy rain is expected. The Victoria Bank has confirmed officially that it will assume all depositor debts of the Ho-Pak and asks depositors to line up peacefully if they require their money on Monday.

'During the night there were numerous land and mud slides throughout the Colony. Worst hit were the squatters' settlement area above Aberdeen, Sau Ming Ping, and Sui Fai Terrace in Wanchai where six major landslips affected buildings in the area. In all, thirty-three persons are known to have lost their lives and many are feared still buried in the slides.

'There are no new developments in the foul murder and kidnapping of Mr. John Chen by the Werewolf gang. Rewards of $100,000 for information leading to their capture have been posted.

'Reports from London confirm that this year's harvest in the USSR has again failed. . . .'

Suslev didn't hear the rest of the broadcast. He knew the report from London was true. Top-secret KGB forecasts had predicted the harvest would once more be below even that necessary for subsistence.

Kristos, why the hell can't we feed ourselves? he wanted to shout, knowing famine, knowing the bloatedness and pains in his own lifetime let alone the ghastly tales his father and mother would tell.

So there's to be famine once more, tightening the belt once more, having to buy wheat from abroad, using up our hard-earned foreign currency, our future in danger, terrible danger, food our Achilles' heel. Never enough. Never enough skill or tractors or fertilizers or wealth, all the real wealth going for arms and armies and airplanes and ships first, far more important to become strong enough to protect ourselves from capitalist swine and revisionist Chinese swine and carry the war to them and smash them before they smash us, but never enough food for us and our buffer lands—the Balkans, Hungary, Czechoslovakia, Poland, East Germany, the Baltic lands. Why is it those bastards could feed themselves most times? Why is it they falsify their harvests and cheat us and lie and steal from us? We protect them and what do they do? Brood and hate us and yet without our armies and the KGB to keep the filthy scum revisionist dissidents in thrall, they'll foment rebellion—like East Germany and Hungary—and turn the stupid masses against us.

But famine causes revolution. Always. Famine will always make the masses rise up against their government. So what can we do? Keep them chained—all of them—until we smash America and Canada and take their wheatlands for ourselves. Then our system will double their harvest.

Don't fool yourself, he thought, agonized. Our agricultural system doesn't work. It never has. One day it will. Meanwhile we cannot feed ourselves. Those motherless turd farmers should . . .

'Stop it,' Suslev muttered aloud, 'you're not responsible, it's not your problem. Deal with your own problems, have faith in the Party and Marxist-Leninism!'

The eggs were done now and he made toast. Rain spattered the open windows. An hour ago the all-night torrent had ceased, but across the street and above the opposite tenement there were the dark clouds. More rain there, he thought, lots more. It's either god-cursed drought or god-cursed flood in this cesspit! A gust caught one of the sodden, cardboard makeshift lean-tos on the roof and collapsed it. At once stoic repairs began, children barely old enough to walk helping.

With deft hands, liking neatness, he laid himself a place at the table, humming in time with the radio music. Everything's fine, he reassured himself. Dunross will go to the party, Koronski will supply the means, Plumm the client, Roger the protection, and all I have to do is go to police headquarters for an hour or so, then leisurely board my ship. On the midnight tide I kiss my arse to Hong Kong, leaving the Werewolves to bury the dead. . . .

The hackles of his neck rose as he heard the screech of an approaching police siren. He stood, paralyzed. But the siren whined past and went away. Stoically he sat and began to eat. Then the secret phone rang.

72

The small Bell helicopter swung in over the city, just below the overcast, and continued climbing the slopes to ease past the Peak funicular and the multiple high rises that dotted the steepness. Now the chopper was almost in the bottom layer of cloud.

Warily the pilot climbed another hundred feet, slowed and hovered, then saw the misted helipad in the grounds of the Great House near a great jacaranda tree. Immediately he swooped to the landing. Dunross was already waiting there. He ducked low to avoid the swirling blades, got into the left side of the bubble and buckled on his safety belts and headphones. 'Morning, Duncan,' he said into the mouth mike. 'Didn't think you'd make it.'

'Nor me,' the older man said, and Dunross adjusted the headphone volume to hear better. 'Doubt if we'll be able to get back, tai-pan. The overcast's dropping too fast again. Best leave if we're leaving. You have control.'

'Here we go.'

Gently Dunross's left hand twisted the throttle grip and increased the revs smoothly and eased the lever up, while his right hand moved the control stick right, left, forward, back, inching it in a gentle tiny circle, seeking and feeling for the air cushion that was building nicely—his left hand controlling speed, climbing or descending, his right hand direction, his feet on the rudder pedals keeping the whole unstable aircraft straight, preventing torque. Dunross loved to fly choppers. It was so much more of a challenge than fixed-wing flying. It required so much concentration and skill that he forgot his

1243

problems, the flying cleansing him. But he rarely flew alone. The sky was for professionals or for those who flew daily, so he would always have a pilot-instructor along with him, the presence of the other man not detracting from his pleasure.

His hands felt the cushion building and then the craft was an inch airborne. Instantly he corrected the slight slide to the right as a wind gusted. He checked his instruments, feeling for dangers, eyes outside, ears tuned to the music of the engine. When all was stable, he increased revs as he raised the left lever, eased the stick forward and left an inch, feet compensating, and went into a skidding left turn, gaining altitude and speed to drop away down the mountainside.

Once he was steady he pushed the transmit button on the stick, reporting in to Air Traffic Control at Kai Tak.

'Watch your revs,' Mac said.

'Got it. Sorry.' Dunross corrected just a fraction too hastily and cursed himself, then got the helicopter trimmed nicely, cruising sweetly, everything in the green, a thousand feet above sea level heading out across the harbor toward Kowloon, the New Territories and the hill-climb area.

'You really going to do the hill climb, tai-pan?'

'Doubt it, Duncan,' he said through the mike. 'But I wanted our ride anyway. I've been looking forward to it all week.' Duncan MacIver ran this small helicopter business from the airport. Most of his business was local, most from government for surveys. The police hired him sometimes, the fire department, Customs. He was a short man, ex-RAF, with a lined face, very wide, sharp eyes that raked constantly.

Once Dunross was settled and trimmed, MacIver leaned forward and put circles of cardboard over the instruments to force Dunross to fly by feel and sound only, to listen to the pitch and tone; slowing meant the engine was working harder so they were climbing—watch for stalling—and faster, that was diving, losing altitude.

'Tai-pan, look down there.' MacIver pointed at the scar on one of the mountainsides just outside Kowloon; it scored a path through one of the vast squatter hovel slums. 'There're mud slides all over. Did you hear the seven o'clock news?'

'Yes, yes I did.'

'Let me take her a minute.' Dunross took his hands and feet

off the controls. MacIver went into a lovely diving turn to swoop nearer the settlement to examine the damage. The damage was great. Perhaps two hundred of the hovels were scattered and buried. Others near the slide were now even more precarious than before. Smoke from the fires that came with every slide still hung like a pall.

'Christ! It looks terrible.'

'I was up at dawn this morning. The fire department asked me to help them on Hill Three, over above Aberdeen. They had a slide there a couple of days ago, a child almost got buried. Last night there was another slip in the same area. Very dicey. The slip's about two hundred feet by fifty. Two or three hundred hovels gone but only ten dead—bloody lucky!' MacIver circled for a moment, made a note on a pad, then gunned the ship back to altitude and to course. Once she was steady, level and trimmed he said, 'She's all yours.' Dunross took control.

Sha Tin was coming up on their right-side horizon. When they were close, MacIver took off the cardboard instrument covers. 'Good,' he said checking the readings. 'Spot on.'

'Had any interesting jobs recently?'

'Just more of the same. Got a charter for Macao, weather permitting, tomorrow morning.'

'Lando Mata?'

'No, some American called Banastasio. Watch your revs! Oh, there's your landfall.'

The fishing village at Sha Tin was near tracks that led back into the hills where the hill climb was to be held. The course consisted of a crude dirt road bulldozed out of the mountainside. At the foot of the slopes were a few cars, some on trailers and trailer rigs, but almost no spectators. Normally there would be hundreds, Europeans mostly. It was the only car-racing event in the Colony. British law forbade using any part of the public road system for racing, and this was the reason that the annual amateur Grand Prix race at Macao had been organized under the joint banner of the Sportscar and Rally Club of Hong Kong and the Portuguese Municipal Council. Last year Guillo Rodriguez of the Hong Kong Police had won the sixty-lap race in three hours twenty-six minutes at an average speed of 72 mph, and Dunross, driving a Lotus, and Brian Kwok in a borrowed E-Type Jag had been neck and neck for second place until Dunross blew a tire, flat out, going into Fisherman's Bend and nearly killed himself at the same spot where his engine blew in '59, the year before he became tai-pan.

Dunross was concentrating on his landing now, knowing that they would be watched.

The chopper was lined up, revs correct for descent, wind ahead and to the right, swirling a little as they came closer to the ground. Dunross held her meticulously. At the exact spot, he corrected and stopped, hovering, in total control, then, keeping everything coordinated, eased off the throttle oh so gently, raising the left lever to change the pitch of the blades to cushion the landing. The landing skids touched the earth. Dunross took off the remaining throttle and smoothly lowered the lever to bottom. The landing was as good as he had ever done.

MacIver said nothing, paying him a fine compliment by pretending to take it for granted, and watched while Dunross began the shutdown drill. 'Tai-pan, why don't you let me finish it for you,' he said. 'Those fellows look somewhat anxious.'

'Thanks.'

Dunross kept his head down and went to the rain-coated group, his feet squelching in the mud. 'Morning.'

'It's bloody awful, tai-pan,' George T'Chung, Shitee T'Chung's eldest son, said. 'I tried my bus out and she stuck on the first bend.' He pointed at the track. The E-Type was bogged down with one of its fenders bent. 'I'll have to get a tractor.' A spatter of rain washed them.

'Bloody waste of time,' Don Nikklin said sourly. He was a short, bellicose man in his late twenties. 'We should have canceled it yesterday.'

Quite true, Dunross thought contentedly, but then I wouldn't have had the excuse to fly, and the extreme pleasure of seeing you here, your morning wasted. 'The consensus was to try for today. Everyone agreed it was a long shot,' Dunross said sweetly. 'You were there. So was your father. Eh?'

McBride said hastily, 'I formally suggest we postpone.'

'Approved.' Nikklin went off back to his brand-new four-wheel-drive truck with its souped-up Porsche under a neat tarp.

'Friendly fellow,' someone said.

They watched as Nikklin got his rig into motion and swirled away with great skill on the treacherous dirt road, past the chopper, its engine dying and the rotors slowing down.

'Pity he's such a shit,' someone else said. 'He's an awfully good driver.'

'Roll on Macao, eh, tai-pan?' George T'Chung said with a laugh, his voice patrician and English public school.

'Yes,' Dunross said, his voice sharpening, looking forward to November, to beating Nikklin again. He had beaten him three out of six tries but he had never won the Grand Prix, his cars never strong enough to sustain his heavy right foot. 'This time I'll win, by God.'

'Oh no you won't, tai-pan. This's my year! I've a Lotus 22, the works, my old man sprung for the lot. You'll see my tail for all sixty laps!'

'Not on your nelly! My new E-Type'll . . .' Dunross stopped. A police car was skidding and slipping in the quagmire, approaching him. Why's Sinders here so early? he asked himself, his stomach tightening. He had said noon. Involuntarily his hand moved to check that the envelope was safe in his buttoned-down hip pocket. His fingers reassured him.

Last night when he had returned to P. B. White's study he had taken out the eleven pieces of paper and examined them again under the light. The ciphers were meaningless. I'm glad, he had thought. Then he had gone to the photocopier that was beside the leather-topped desk and made two copies of each page. He put each set into a separate envelope and sealed them. One he marked: 'P. B. White—please hand this to the tai-pan of Struan's unopened.' That one he put into a book that he chose at random from the bookshelves, replacing it with equal care. Following AMG's instructions, he marked the second with a G for Riko Gresserhoff and pocketed it. The originals he sealed in a last envelope and pocketed that too. With a final check that the secret door was back in place, he unlocked the door and went out. In a few minutes he and Gavallan had left with Casey and Riko and though there was plenty of opportunity to give Riko her set privately, he had decided it was better to wait until the originals were delivered.

Should I give Sinders the originals now or at noon? he asked himself, watching the police car. The car stopped. Chief Inspector Donald C. C. Smyth got out. Neither Sinders nor Crosse was with him.

1247

'Morning,' Smyth said politely, touching his peaked cap with his swagger stick, his other arm still in a sling. 'Excuse me, Mr. Dunross, is the chopper your charter?'

'Yes, yes it is, Chief Inspector,' Dunross said. 'What's up?'

'I've a small show on down the road and saw you coming in. Wonder if we could borrow MacIver and the bird for an hour—or if you're going back at once, perhaps we could take her on after?'

'Certainly. I'll be off in a second. The hill climb's canceled.'

Smyth glanced at the mountain track and the sky and grunted. 'I'd say that was wise, sir. Someone would've been hurt, sure as shooting. If it's all right, I'll talk to MacIver?'

'Of course. Nothing serious I hope?'

'No, no, not at all. Interesting though. The rain's uncovered a couple of bodies that'd been buried in the same area where John Chen's body was found.'

The others came closer. 'The Werewolves?' George T'Chung asked, shocked. 'More kidnap victims?'

'We presume so. They were both young. One had his head bashed in and the other poor bugger half his head cut off, looks like with a spade. Both were Chinese.'

'Christ!' Young George T'Chung had gone white.

Smyth nodded sourly. 'You haven't heard of any rich sons being kidnapped, have you?'

Everyone shook their heads.

'Not surprised,' Smyth said. 'Stupid for the families of victims to deal with kidnappers and keep quiet about it. Unfortunately the bodies were discovered by locals so it'll be headlines by tonight from here to Peking!'

'You want to fly the bodies back?'

'Oh no, tai-pan. The hurry's to get some CID experts here to search the area before the rain comes again. We need to try to identify the poor buggers. Can you leave at once?'

'Yes, certainly.'

'Thanks. Sorry to bother you. Sorry about Noble Star, but my bundle'll be on you on Saturday.' Smyth nodded politely and walked off.

George T'Chung was openly upset. 'We're all targets for those bastards, the Werewolves. You, me, my old man, anyone! Christ, how can we protect ourselves against them?'

No one answered him.

Then Dunross said with a laugh, 'No need to worry, old chap, we're inviolate, we're all inviolate.'

73

The phone rang in the semidarkness of the bedroom. Bartlett scrambled out of sleep. 'Hello?'

'Good morning, Mr. Bartlett, this is Claudia Chen. The tai-pan asked if you'd need the car today anyway?'

'No, no thanks.' Bartlett glanced at his watch. 'Jesus,' he muttered aloud, astounded he had slept so long. 'Er, thanks, thanks, Claudia.'

'The Taipei trip's rescheduled for next Friday, Friday back Monday noon. Is that convenient?'

'Yes, er yes, sure.'

'Thank you.'

Bartlett hung up and lay back a moment, collecting his wits. He stretched luxuriously, glad that there was no rush for anything, enjoying the rare pleasantness of being just a little lazy.

It had been four o'clock this morning when he had hung up a 'do not disturb', cut off the phones till 10:00 A.M. and had gone to bed. Last night Orlanda had taken him to Aberdeen where she had hired a Pleasure Boat. They had drifted the channels, the rain making the hooped cabin more cozy, the brazier warming, the food hot and spicy.

'In Shanghai we cook with garlic and chilies and peppers and all manner of spices,' she had told him, serving him, her chopsticks a delicate extension of her fingers. 'The farther north you go the hotter the food, the less rice is eaten, more breads and noodles. The north's wheat-eating, only the southern part of China's rice-eating, Linc. More?'

He had eaten well and drunk the beer she had brought with

her. The night had been happy for him, the time going unnoticed as she regaled him with stories of Asia and Shanghai, her mind deft and darting. Then, afterward, the rain pattering on the canvas, the dishes taken away and they reclining side-by-side on the cushions, fingers entwined, she had said, 'Linc, I'm sorry, but I love you.'

It had taken him by surprise.

'No need to be sorry,' he had said, not ready yet to reply in kind.

'Oh but I am. It complicates things, oh yes, it complicates things very much.'

Yes, he thought. It's so easy for a woman to say I love you, so hard for a man, unwise for a man, for then you're stuck. Is that the right word? Again the answer did not present itself.

As he lay now in bed, his head cradled in his arms, he rethought the night. Touching and leaving alone, then hands searching, his and hers, but not finalizing. Not that she prevented him or stopped him. He just held back. Finally.

'You've never done that before,' he muttered out loud. 'Once you had a girl going, you went all the way,' and he wished he had, remembering how heavy the desire had been upon them. 'I'm not a one-night stand or Eurasian tramp' had rung in his ears.

In the taxi to her home they had not spoken, just held hands. That's the goddamnedest part, he thought, feeling foolish, childish, just holding hands. If anyone had told me a month ago, a week ago that I'd settle for that. I'd've said he was a meathead and bet big money.

Money. I have more than enough for Orlanda and me. But what about Casey? And Par-Con? First things first. Let's see if Casey tells me about Murtagh and why she's been sitting on that hot potato. Gornt? Gornt or Dunross? Dunross has style and if Banastasio's against him that's one great vote of confidence.

After he had told Armstrong their theory about Banastasio, Armstrong had said, 'We'll see what we can come up with, though Mr. Gornt's credentials are as impeccable as any in the Colony. You can rest assured Vincenzo Banastasio will be high up on our shit list, but isn't his real threat in the States?'

'Oh yes. But I told Rosemont an—'

'Ah, good! That was wise. He's a good man. Did you see Ed Langan?'

'No. Is he CIA too?'

'I don't even know, officially, if Rosemont is, Mr. Bartlett. Leave it with me. Did he have any suggestion about the guns?'

'No.'

'Well, never mind. I'll pass on your information and liaise with him—he's very good by the way.'

A small tremor went through Bartlett. He'll have to be very good to clobber Mafia, if Banastasio really is Mafia.

He reached over and dialed Casey's room number. No answer, so he called down for his messages. The receptionist told him everything was already under his door. 'Would you like your cables and telexes sent up?'

'Sure, thanks. Any message from Casey Tcholok?'

'No sir.'

'Thanks.'

He jumped out of bed and went to the door. Among the phone messages was an envelope. He recognized her writing. The messages were all business calls except one: 'Mr. Banastasio called. Please return his call.' Bartlett put that aside. He opened Casey's envelope. The note was timed 9:45 A.M. and read: 'Hi, Linc! Didn't want to disturb your beauty sleep—back sixish. Have fun!'

Where's she off to? he asked himself absently.

He picked up the phone to call Rosemont but changed his mind and dialed Orlanda. No answer. He redialed the number. The calling tone droned on and on.

'Shit!' He pushed away his discontent.

You've a date for lunch so what's so tough? Sunday brunch here atop the V and A and lots of time, Sunday brunch where 'all the best people go for lunch, Linc. Oh it's super, the hot and cold buffet's the talk of Asia. The very best!'

'Jesus, all this food, by next week I'll weigh a ton!'

'Not you, never never never. If you like, we'll go for a long walk or when the rain stops we'll play tennis. Whatever you want we'll do! Oh Linc, I love you so. . . .'

*   *   *

1252

Casey was leaning on the balustrade at the Kowloon wharf among the crowds. She wore khaki pants and a yellow silk shirt that showed her figure without flaunting it, a matching cashmere sweater tied casually around her neck, sneakers, and in her big handbag was a swimsuit—not that I'll need it today, she told herself, the Peak shrouded to Mid Levels with cloud, blackdark sky to the east and a heavy line of rain squall already touching the Island. A small helicopter putt-putted overhead to go out across the harbor on course for Central. She saw it land on one of the buildings. Isn't that the Struan building? Sure, sure it is. Wonder if Ian's in it?

Wonder if the hill climb's back on again? Last night he had said it was off but that some of them might do it anyway.

Then her eyes saw the approaching motor cruiser. It was big, expensive, the lines sleek, a Red Ensign aft, a colorful pennant on the stubby mast. She picked out Gornt at the helm. He was dressed casually, shirt-sleeves rolled up, canvas pants, his black hair ruffled by the sea breeze. He waved and she waved back. There were others on the bridge main deck: Jason Plumm she had met at the races, Sir Dunstan Barre at the tai-pan's—he was wearing a smart blue blazer and white pants, Pugmire was equally nautical.

Gornt put the cumbersome craft alongside skillfully, fenders out, two deckhands with hooked fending poles. She headed along the quay toward the wet slippery steps. Five Chinese girls were already waiting on the landing, gaily dressed in boating clothes, laughing and chattering and waving. As she watched, they jumped awkwardly aboard helped by a deckhand, kicked their high heels off. One went to Barre, another to Pugmire, another to Plumm as old friends would and the other two went cheerfully below.

I'll be goddamned, she thought disgustedly. It's one of those parties. She began to turn to leave but she saw Gornt leaning over the side, watching her. 'Hello, Casey, sorry about the rain, come aboard!'

The craft was dipping and twisting in the swell, waves slapping the steps and the hull. 'Come aboard, it's quite safe,' he called out. Reacting at once to what she interpreted as a taunt, she came down the steps quickly, refused the proffered help of the deckhand, waited for the correct moment and jumped. 'You did that as though you've been aboard a yacht before,' Gornt said with admiration, coming to meet her. 'Welcome aboard the *Sea Witch*.'

'I like sailing, Quillan, though I think maybe I'm out of my depth here.'

'Oh?' Gornt frowned and she could read no taunt or challenge there. 'You mean the girls?'

'Yes.'

'They're just guests of my guests.' His eyes bored into her. 'I understood you wanted to be treated with equality.'

'What?'

'I thought you wanted to be treated equally in a masculine world, in business and pleasure? To be accepted, eh?'

'I do,' she said coldly.

His warmth did not change. 'Are you upset because the others are married and you've met some of their wives?'

'Yes, I suppose I am.'

'Isn't that rather unfair?'

'No, I don't think it is,' she said uncomfortably.

'*You're* my guest, *my* guest, the others are my guests' guests. If you want equality, perhaps you should be prepared to accept equality.'

'This isn't equality.'

'I'm certainly putting you in a position of trust. As an equal. I must tell you the others didn't think you as trustworthy as I consider you.' The smile hardened. 'I told them they could leave or stay. I do what I like on my ship and I stood surety for your discretion and good manners. This is Hong Kong, our customs are different. This isn't a puritan society though we have very serious rules. You're alone. Unmarried. Very attractive and very welcome. As an equal. If you were married to Linc, you would not have been asked, together or by yourself, though he might have been and what he told you when he came back would be his own affair.'

'You're saying this is regular Hong Kong custom—the boys out with the girls bit on a Sunday afternoon?'

'No, not at all. I'm saying my guests asked if they could invite some guests who'd brighten what might otherwise be a dull luncheon for them.' Gornt's eyes were level.

The *Sea Witch* heeled under another wave and Barre and his

girl friend stumbled and almost lost their footing. She dropped her glass of champagne. Gornt had not moved. Nor did Casey. She didn't even need to hold on.

'You've done lots of sailing?' he said with admiration.

'I've an eighteen-footer, fibreglass, Olympic class, sloop-rigged, on a trailer. I sail some weekends.'

'Alone?'

'Mostly. Sometimes Linc comes along.'

'He's at the hill climb?'

'No. I heard it was canceled.'

'He's going to Taipei this afternoon?'

'No. I heard that was canceled too.'

Gornt nodded. 'Wise. A lot to do tomorrow.' His eyes were kindly. 'I'm sorry you're offended. I thought you different from the usual. I'm sorry the others came now.'

Casey heard the strange gentleness. 'Yes, I'm sorry too.'

'Would you still like to stay? I hope so, though I will expect your discretion—I did guarantee it.'

'I'll stay,' she said simply. 'Thanks for trusting me.'

'Come on the bridge. There's champagne and I think lunch'll please you.'

Having chosen, Casey put away her reservations and decided to enjoy the day. 'Where're we going?'

'Up by Sha Tin. The sea'll be calm there.'

'Say, Quillan, this is a wonderful boat.'

'I'll show you around in a moment.' There was a spatter of rain and they moved into the lee of the overhanging deck. Gornt glanced at the clock tower. It was 10:10. He was about to order their castoff when Peter Marlowe hurried down the steps and came aboard. His eyes widened as he noticed Casey.

'Sorry I'm late, Mr. Gornt.'

'That's all right, Mr. Marlowe. I was going to give you a couple of minutes—I know how it is with young children. Excuse me a second, I believe you know each other. Oh, Casey's *my* guest—her discretion's guaranteed.' He smiled at her 'Isn't it?'

'Of course.'

He turned and left them, going to the bridge to take the conn. They watched a moment, both embarrassed, the sea breeze freshening the rain that slanted down.

'I didn't expect to see you, Peter,' she said.

'I didn't expect to see you either.'

She studied him, her hazel eyes level. 'Is one of the, the others yours? Give it to me straight.'

His smile was curious. 'Even if one was I'd say it wasn't any of your business. Discretion and all that. By the way, are you Gornt's girl friend?'

She stared at him. 'No. No, of course not!'

'Then why're you here?'

'I don't know. He . . . he just said I was invited as an equal.'

'Oh. Oh I see.' Peter Marlowe was equally relieved. 'He's got a strange sense of humor. Well, I did warn you. To answer your question, at least eight are part of the Marlowe harem!' She laughed with him and he added more seriously, 'You don't have to worry about Fleur. She's very wise.'

'I wish I was, Peter. This's all rather new to me. Sorry about . . yes, sorry.'

'It's new to me too. I've never been on a Sunday cruise before. Why did y—' His smile vanished. She followed his glance. Robin Grey had come up from below and was pouring himself a glass of champagne, one of the girls holding out her glass too. Casey turned and stared at Gornt, watching him glance from man to man, then at her.

'Come aloft,' Gornt called out. 'There's wine, champagne, Bloody Marys or, if you prefer, coffee.' He kept his face expressionless but inside he was vastly amused.

74

'I repeat, Mr. Sinders, I know nothing of any cable, any Arthur, any files, any American and I know no Major Yuri Bakyan—the man was Igor Voranski, seaman first class.' Suslev kept a firm hold on his temper. Sinders sat opposite him, behind the desk in the drab interview room at police headquarters. Suslev had expected Roger Crosse to be there, to help. But he had not seen him since he arrived.

Be careful, he cautioned himself, you're on your own. You'll get no help from Roger. Rightly. That spy has to be protected. And as to Boradinov, he's no help either. He glanced at his first officer who sat beside him, stiff, upright in his chair and greatly ill-at-ease.

'And you still insist this spy Dimitri Metkin's name was not Leonov—Nicoli Leonov—also a major in the KGB?'

'It's nonsense, all nonsense. I shall report this whole incident to my government, I sh—'

'Are your repairs completed?'

'Yes, at least they will be by midnight. We bring good money into Hong Kong and pay our bi—'

'Yes and create nothing but curious troubles. Like Major Leonov, like Bakyan?'

'You mean Metkin?' Suslev glared at Boradinov to take off some of the heat. 'Did you know any Leonov?'

'No, Comrade Captain,' Boradinov stuttered. 'We didn't know anything.'

'What a lot of cobblers!' Sinders sighed. 'Fortunately Leonov

1257

told us quite a lot about you and the *Ivanov* before you murdered him. Yes, your Major Leonov was very cooperative.' Suddenly his voice became a whiplash. 'First Officer Boradinov, please wait outside!'

The younger man was on his feet before he knew it, white-faced. He opened the door. Outside a hostile Chinese SI agent motioned him to a chair, closing the door once more.

Sinders put his pipe aside, took out a package of cigarettes and leisurely lit one. Rain battered the windows. Suslev waited, his heart grinding. He watched his enemy from under his bushy eyebrows, wondering what Roger Crosse had for him that was so urgent. This morning when the secret phone had rung it was Arthur asking if Suslev would meet Roger Crosse around eight o'clock tonight at Sinclair Towers. 'What's so urgent? I should be on my ship and mak—'

'I don't know. Roger said it was urgent. There was no time to discuss anything. Did you see Koronski?'

'Yes. Everything's arranged. Can you deliver?'

'Oh yes. Long before midnight.'

'Don't fail, Center's counting on you now,' he had added, lying. 'Tell our friend it's ordered.'

'Excellent. We won't fail.'

Suslev had heard the excitement. Some of his dread had left him. Now it was returning. He did not like being here, so near to staying permanently. Sinders's reputation was well known in the KGB: dedicated, smart and given to great leaps of insight. 'I'm very tired of these questions, Mr. Sinders,' he said, astonished that the head of MI-6 had personally come to Hong Kong and could appear to be so unimportant. He stood up, testing him. 'I'm leaving.'

'Tell me about Sevrin.'

'Sevrin? What is Sevrin? I do not have to stay to answer your questions, I do n—'

'I agree, Comrade Captain, normally, but one of your men has been caught spying and our American friends really want possession of you.'

'Eh?'

'Oh yes and I'm afraid they're not as patient as we are.'

Suslev's dread swooped back. 'More threats! Why threaten me?' he flustered. 'We are law-abiding. I'm not responsible for

1258

troubles! I demand to be allowed to go back to my ship! Now!'

Sinders just looked at him. 'All right. Please leave,' he said quietly.

'I can go?'

'Yes, yes of course. Good morning.'

Astonished, Suslev stared at him a moment, then turned and went for the door.

'Of course we will certainly leak it to your superiors that you gave us Leonov.'

Suslev stopped, ashen. 'What, what did you say?'

'Leonov told us, among other things, that you encouraged him to make the intercept. Then you leaked the exchange.'

'Lies . . . lies,' he said, suddenly aghast that perhaps Roger Crosse had been caught as Metkin was caught.

'Didn't you also leak to North Korean agents about Bakyan?'

'No, no I did not,' Suslev stuttered, enormously relieved to discover Sinders was kiting him, probably without any real information. Some of his confidence returned. 'That's more nonsense. I know no North Koreans.'

'I believe you, but I'm sure the First Directorate won't. Good morning.'

'What do you mean?'

'Tell me about the cable.'

'I know nothing about it. Your superintendent was mistaken. I did not drop it.'

'Oh but you did. What American?'

'I know nothing about an American.'

'Tell me about Sevrin.'

'I know nothing of this Sevrin. What is it, who is it?'

'I'm sure you know your superiors in the KGB are impatient with leaks and very untrusting. If you manage to sail, I suggest you, your first officer, your ship and your entire crew do not come back into these waters again—'

'You threaten me again? This will become an international incident. I will inform my government and yours an—'

'Yes, and so will we, officially and privately. Very privately.' Sinders's eyes were freezing though his lips wore a smile.

'I . . . I can go now?'

'Yes. For information.'

'What?'

1259

'Who is the American, and who is "Arthur"?'

'I don't know any Arthur. Arthur who?'

'I will wait till midnight. If you sail without telling me, when I return to London I will make sure information gets to the ears of your naval attaché in London that you leaked Leonov whom you call Metkin, and you leaked Bakyan whom you call Voranski in return for SI favors.'

'That's lies, all lies, you know it's lies.'

'Five hundred people saw you at the racetrack with Superintendent Crosse. That's when you gave him Metkin.'

'All lies.' Suslev tried to hide his terror.

Sinders chuckled. 'We'll see, won't we? Your new naval attaché in London will clutch at any straws to ingratiate himself with his superiors. Eh?'

'I don't understand,' Suslev said, understanding very well. He was trapped.

Sinders leaned forward to tap out his pipe. 'Listen to me clearly,' he said with absolute finality. 'I'll swap you your life for the American and Arthur.'

'I don't know any Arthur.'

'This will be a secret between you and me only. I'll tell no one. I give you my word.'

'I know no Arthur.'

'You pinpoint him and you're safe. You and I are professionals, we understand barter—and safety—and an occasional private, very secret deal. You're caught, this time, so you have to deliver. If you sail without telling me who Arthur is, as sure as God made little apples and the KGB exists, I will shop you.' The eyes bored into him. 'Good morning, Comrade Captain.'

Suslev got up and left. When he and Boradinov were in the air once more, in the reality of Hong Kong, both began to breathe. Silently Suslev led the way across the street to the nearest bar. He ordered two double vodkas.

Suslev's mind was ripped. *Kristos*, he wanted to shout, I'm dead if I do and dead if I don't. That goddamned cable! If I finger Banastasio and Arthur, I admit I know Sevrin and I'm in their power forever. And if I don't, my life will surely be finished. One way or another it will be dangerous to return home now, and equally dangerous to come back. One way or another now I need those AMG files or Dunross, or both, for protection. One way or an—

'Comrade Cap—'

He whirled on Boradinov and cursed him in Russian The younger man whitened and stopped, petrified.

'Vodka! Two more,' he called. 'Please.'

The bar girl brought them. 'My name Sally, what you, *heya?*'

'Piss off,' Boradinov snarled.

'*Dew neh loh moh* on your piss off, *heya?* You Mr. Pissoff? I no like your face Mr. Pissoff so piss off without swearings.' She picked up the vodka bottle and prepared to carry the battle forward.

'Apologize to her,' Suslev snapped, wanting no trouble, not sure that she wasn't a plant, the bar being so close to police headquarters.

Boradinov was shocked. 'What?'

'Apologize to her, you motherless turd!'

'Sorry,' Boradinov muttered, his face flushed.

The girl laughed. 'Hey, big man, you want jig-jig?'

'No,' Suslev said. 'Just more vodka.'

Crosse got out of the police car and hurried through the light rain into the Struan Building. Behind him the streets were crowded with umbrellas and snarled traffic, the sidewalks massed, people going to and from work, Sunday not a general holiday. On the twentieth floor he got out.

'Good morning, Superintendent Crosse. I'm Sandra Yi, Mr. Dunross's secretary. This way please.'

Crosse followed her down the corridor, his eyes noticing her *cheong-sam*ed rump. She opened a door for him. He went in.

'Hello, Edward,' he said to Sinders.

'You're early too, as usual.' Sinders was sipping a beer. 'Old army habit, eh, five minutes early's on time?' Behind him in the lavish boardroom was a well-stocked bar. And coffee.

'Would you care for something, sir? Bloody Marys are mixed,' Sandra Yi said.

'Thank you, just coffee. Black.'

She served him and went out.

'How did it go?' Crosse asked.

'Our visitors? Fine, just fine. I'd say his sphincter's out of whack.' Sinders smiled. 'I taped the session. You can listen to it after lunch. Ah, yes, lunch. Roger, can you get fish and chips in Hong Kong?'

'Certainly. Fish and chips it is.' Crosse stifled a yawn. He had been up most of the night developing and printing the roll of film he had taken in the vault. This morning he had read and reread AMG's real pages with enormous interest, privately agreeing with Dunross that the tai-pan had been perfectly correct to be so circumspect. AMG gave value for money whatever he cost, he thought. There's no doubt these files're worth a fortune.

The gimbaled clock struck the hour nicely. Noon. The door opened and Dunross strode in. ''Morning. Thanks for coming here.'

Politely the other two got up and shook hands.

'More coffee?'

'No thank you, Mr. Dunross.'

As Crosse watched closely Dunross took a sealed envelope out of his pocket and offered it to Sinders. The older man took it, weighing it in his hand. Crosse noticed his fingers were trembling slightly. 'Of course you've read the contents, Mr. Dunross?'

'Yes, Mr. Sinders.'

'And?'

'And nothing. See for yourself.'

Sinders opened the envelope. He stared at the first page, then leafed through all eleven sheets. From where Crosse stood he could not see what was on the pieces of paper. Silently Sinders handed him the top one. The letters and numbers and symbols of the code were meaningless. 'Looks like they've been cut from something.' Crosse looked at Dunross. 'Eh?'

'What about Brian?'

'Where did you get them, Ian?' Crosse saw Dunross's eyes change a little.

'I've kept my side of the trade, are you going to keep yours?'

Sinders sat down. 'I did not agree to a trade, Mr. Dunross. I only agreed that it was possible that your request might be complied with.'

'Then you won't release Brian Kwok?'

'It's possible that he will be where you want him, when you want him.'

'It has to be left like that?'

'Sorry.'

There was a long silence. The tick of the clock filled the room. Except for the rain. Another squall came and went. Rain had been falling sporadically since this morning. Weather reports forecast that the storm would be over soon and that the reservoirs, for all the rain, were hardly touched.

Dunross said, 'Will you give me the odds? Accurately. Please?'

'First three questions: Did you cut these out of something yourself?'

'Yes.'

'From what and how?'

'AMG had written instructions. I was to use a cigarette lighter under the bottom right quadrant of some pages he'd sent—it was an innocuous typed report. When I heated the pages the type disappeared and what you see was left. When I'd finished, again following his instructions, I cut out the pertinent pieces and destroyed the remainder. And his letter.'

'Have you kept a copy?'

'Of the eleven pieces? Yes.'

'I must ask you for them.'

'You mav have them when you complete the bargain,' Dunross said, his voice pleasant. 'Now, what are the odds?'

'Please give me the copies.'

'I will, when you complete. Monday at sunset.'

Sinders's eyes were even colder. 'The copies, now, if you please.'

'When you complete. That's a decision. Now, odds please.'

'50-50,' Sinders said, testing him.

'Good. Thank you. I've arranged that on Tuesday morning all eleven pages will be published in the *China Guardian* and two Chinese papers, one Nationalist and one Communist.'

'Then you do so at your peril. Her Majesty's Government does not enjoy coercion.'

'Have I threatened you? No, not at all. Those letters and figures are a meaningless mumbo-jumbo, except perhaps—

perhaps to some code cipher expert. Perhaps. Perhaps this's all a joke from a dead man.'

'I can stop it under the Official Secrets Act.'

'You can certainly try.' Dunross nodded. 'But come hell or the Official Secrets Act, if I choose, those pages will be published somewhere on earth this week. That's a decision too. The matter was left to my discretion by AMG. Was there anything else, Mr. Sinders?'

Sinders hesitated. 'No. No, thank you, Mr. Dunross.'

Equally politely Dunross turned and opened the door. 'Sorry, I've got to get back to work. Thank you for coming.'

Crosse let Sinders go first and followed him to the elevator. Sandra Yi, at the reception desk, had already pressed the button for them.

'Oh excuse me, sir,' she said to Crosse, 'do you know when Superintendent Kwok will be back in the Colony?'

Crosse stared at her. 'I'm not sure. I could inquire if you like. Why?'

'We were going to have dinner Friday evening and neither his housekeeper nor his office seems to know.'

'I'd be glad to inquire.'

The phone buzzer on the switchboard went. 'Oh, thank you, sir. Hello, Struan's.' she said into the phone. 'Just a moment.' She began to make the connection. Crosse offered a cigarette to Sinders as they waited, watching the elevator numbers approaching. 'Your call to Mr. Alastair, tai-pan,' Sandra Yi said into the phone. Again the buzzer on the switchboard went.

'Hello,' Sandra Yi said. 'Just a moment, madam, I'll check.' She referred to a typed appointment list as the elevator doors opened. Sinders went in and Crosse began to follow.

'It's for 1:00 P.M., Mrs. Gresserhoff.'

At once Crosse stopped and bent down as though to tie his shoelace and Sinders, as efficiently and as casually, held the door.

'Oh that's all right, madam, it's easy to mistake a time. The table's booked in the tai-pan's name. The Skyline at the Mandarin at 1:00 P.M.'

Crosse got up.

'All right?' Sinders asked.

'Oh yes.' The doors closed on them. Both smiled.

'Everything comes to him who waits,' Crosse said.

'Yes. We'll have fish and chips for dinner instead.'

'No. You can have them for lunch. We shouldn't eat at the Mandarin. I suggest we just peg her secretly ourselves. Meanwhile, I'll assign surveillance to find out where she's staying, eh?'

'Excellent.' Sinders's face hardened. 'Gresserhoff, eh? Hans Gresserhoff was the cover name of an East German spy we've been trying to catch for years.'

'Oh?' Crosse kept his interest off his face.

'Yes. He was partners with another right rotten bastard, a trained assassin. One of his names was Viktor Grunwald, another Simeon Tzerak. Gresserhoff, eh?' Sinders was silent a moment. 'Roger, that publishing business, Dunross's threat. That could be very dicey.'

'Can you read the code?'

'Good God, no.'

'What could it be?'

'Anything. The pages are for me or the P.M. so they're probably names and addresses of contacts.' Sinders added gravely, 'I daren't trust them to cables, however coded. I think I'd better return to London at once.'

'Today?'

'Tomorrow. I should finish this business first and I'd very much like to identify this Mrs. Gresserhoff. Will Dunross do what he said?'

'Absolutely.'

Sinders pulled at his eyebrows, his washed-out blue eyes even more colorless than usual. 'What about the client?'

'I'd say . . .' The elevator door opened. They got out and walked across the foyer. The uniformed doorman opened the door of Crosse's car for him.

Crosse cut into the snarled traffic, the harbor misted and the rain stopped for a moment. 'I'd say one more session, then Armstrong can begin rebuilding. Monday sunset is too fast but . . .' He shrugged. 'I wouldn't suggest any more of the Red Room.'

'No. I agree, Roger. Thank God the fellow's got a strong constitution.'

'Yes.'

'I think Armstrong's ready to crack, poor fellow.'

'He can conduct one more. Safely.'

'I hope so. My God we've been very lucky. Unbelievable!' The session, at 6:00 this morning, had brought forth nothing. But just as they were about to quit, Armstrong's probing produced gold: at long last, the who and the why and the what of Professor Joseph Yu. Of Cal Tech, Princeton, Stanford. Rocket expert par excellence and NASA consultant.

'When's he due in Hong Kong, Brian?' Armstrong had asked, the whole SI team in the control room breathless.

'I . . . I don't . . . let me think, let me think . . . ah, I can't remember . . . ah yes, it, it's in a we . . . at the end of . . . of this month . . . what is this month? I can't rem . . . remember . . . which day it is. He was to arrive . . . and then go on.'

'Where from and where to?'

'Oh I don't know, oh no they didn't tell me . . . except . . . except someone said he . . . he was sailing in Guam on holiday from Hawaii and due here ten days . . . I think it's ten days after . . . after Race Day.'

And when Crosse had called in Rosemont and told him— though not where the information came from—the American was speechless and in panic. At once he had ordered the Guam area scoured to prevent defection.

'I wonder if they'll catch him,' Crosse muttered.

'Who?'

'Joseph Yu.'

'I jolly well hope so,' Sinders said. 'Why the devil do these scientists defect? Damnable! The only good point is he'll launch China's rocketry into the stratosphere and send shivers of horror down all Soviet spines. Bloody good if you ask me. If those two fall out it could help us immensely.' He eased more comfortably in the seat of the car, his back aching. 'Roger, I can't risk Dunross publishing those ciphers or keeping a copy.'

'Yes.'

'He's too damned clever for his own boots is your tai-pan. If it leaks that AMG sent us a ciphered message and if Dunross has the memory he's supposed to have, he's a marked man. Eh?'

'Yes.'

They reached the Skyline penthouse restaurant in good time.

Crosse was instantly recognized and at once a discreet table was empty at the bar. As Sinders ordered a drink and more coffee Crosse phoned for two agents, one British and one Chinese. They arrived very fast.

At a few minutes to one o'clock Dunross walked in and they watched him go to the best table, maître d' in advance, waiters in tow, champagne already in a silver bucket.

'The buggers's got everyone well trained, eh?'

'Wouldn't you?' Crosse said. His eyes ranged the room, then stopped. 'There's Rosemont! Is that a coincidence?'

'What do you think?'

'Ah, look over there. In the far corner. That's Vincenzo Banastasio. The Chinese he's with is Vee Cee Ng. Perhaps that's who they're watching.'

'Perhaps.'

'Rosemont's clever,' Crosse said. 'Bartlett went to see him too. It could be Banastasio they're watching.' Armstrong had reported Bartlett's conversation about Banastasio to them. Surveillance on the man had been increased. 'By the way. I heard he's chartered a helicopter for Macao on Monday.'

'We should cancel that.'

'It's already done. Engine trouble.'

'Good. I suppose Bartlett reporting Banastasio rather clears him, what?'

'Perhaps.'

'I still think I'd better go Monday. Yes. Interesting, ah, that Dunross's receptionist had a date with the client. Good God, there's a smasher,' Sinders said.

The girl was following the maître d'. Both men were taken by surprise when she stopped at the tai-pan's table, smiled, bowed and sat down. 'Christ! Mrs. Gresserhoff's Chinese?' Sinders gasped.

Crosse was concentrating on their lips. 'No Chinese'd bow like that. She's Japanese.'

'How in the hell does she fit?'

'Perhaps there's more than one guest. Per—oh Christ!'

'What?'

'They're not speaking English. Must be Japanese.'

'Dunross speaks Jap?'

Crosse looked at him. 'Yes *Japanese*. And German, French,

1267

three dialects of Chinese and passable Italian.'

Sinders stared back. 'You needn't be so disapproving, Roger. I lost a son on *HMS Prince of Wales*, my brother starved to death on the Burma Road, so don't give me any sanctimonious bullshit, though I still think she's a smasher.'

'At least that shows a certain amount of tolerance.' Crosse turned back to study Dunross and the girl.

'Your war was in Europe, eh?'

'My war, Edward, is never ending.' Crosse smiled, liking the sound of that. 'World War Two's ancient history. Sorry about your kin but now Japan's not the enemy, they're our allies, the only real ones we've got in Asia.'

For half an hour they waited. He could not read their lips at all.

'She must be Gresserhoff,' Sinders said.

Crosse nodded. 'Then shall we go? No point in waiting. Shall we fish and chip?'

They went out. The British and Chinese SI agents stayed, waiting patiently, unable to overhear what was being said, envying Dunross, as many did in the room—because he was the tai-pan and because of her.

'*Gehen Sie?*' she asked in German. Are you going?

'To Japan, Riko-*san*? Oh yes,' he answered in the same language, 'the week after next. We take delivery of a new supercargo ship from Toda Shipping. Did you chat with Hiro Toda yesterday?'

'Yes, yes I had that honor. The Toda family is famous in Japan. Before the Restoration when the samurai class was abolished, my family served the Toda.'

'Your family was samurai?'

'Yes, but of low degree. I, I did not mention about my family to him. Those were ancient days. I would not like him to know.'

'As you wish,' he said, his curiosity piqued. 'Hiro Toda's an interesting man,' he added, leading her on.

'Toda-*sama* is very wise, very strong, very famous.' The waiter brought their salad and when he had left she said, 'Struan's are famous in Japan, too.'

'Not really.'

'Oh yes. We remember Prince Yoshi.'

'Ah. I didn't know you knew.'

In 1854 when Perry forced the Shōgun Yoshimitsu Toranaga to open up Japan to trade, the Hag had sailed north from Hong Kong, her father and enemy, Tyler Brock, in pursuit. Thanks to her, Struan's was the first into Japan, first to buy land for a trading post and the first outsider to trade. Over the years and many voyages, she made Japan a cornerstone of Struan policy.

During the early years she met a young prince, Prince Yoshi, a relation of the Emperor and cousin to the Shōgun—without whose permission nothing happened in Japan. At her suggestion and with her help, this prince went to England on a Struan clipper to learn about the might of the British Empire. When he returned home a few years later, it was in another Struan ship, and that year some of the feudal barons—*daimyo*—hating the incursion of foreigners, revolted against the Shōgun whose family, the Toranaga, had exclusively ruled Japan for two and a half centuries in an unbroken line back to the great general Yoshi Toranaga. The revolt of the *daimyo* succeeded and power was restored to the Emperor but the land was riven. 'Without Prince Yoshi, who became one of the Emperor's chief ministers,' she said, unconsciously turning to English, 'Japan would still be trembling and torn apart in civil war.'

'Why so?' he asked, wanting to keep her talking, her lilting accent pleasing him.

'Without his help, the Emperor could not have succeeded, could not have abolished the Shōgunate, abolished feudal law, the *daimyo*, the whole samurai class, and forced them to accept a modern constitution. It was Prince Yoshi who negotiated a peace among the *daimyo*, and then invited English experts to Japan to build our navy, our banks and our civil service, and help us into the modern world.' A small shadow went across her face. 'My father told me much about those times, tai-pan, not yet a hundred years ago. Transition from samurai rule to democracy was often bloody. But the Emperor had decreed an ending so there was an ending and all the *daimyo* and samurai dragged themselves painfully into a new life.' She toyed with her glass, watching the bubbles. 'The Toda were Lords of Izu and Sagami where Yokohama is. For centuries they had had shipyards. It was easy for them and their allies, the Kasigi, to come into this modern age. For us . . .' She stopped. 'Oh, but you already know this, so sorry.'

'Only about Prince Yoshi. What happened to your family?'

'My great-grandfather became a very minor member of Prince Yoshi's staff, as a civil servant. He was sent to Nagasaki where my family have lived since. He found it difficult not to wear the two swords. My grandfather was also a civil servant, like my father, but only very tiny.' She looked up and smiled at him. 'The wine is too good. It makes my tongue run away.'

'No, not at all,' he said, then conscious of the eyes watching them, he added in Japanese, 'Let us talk Japanese for a while.'

'It is my honor, tai-pan-*san*.'

Later, over coffee he said, 'Where should I deposit the money owing to you, Riko-*san*?'

'If you could give me a cashier's check or bank draft'—she used the English words for there was no Japanese equivalent—'before I leave that would be perfect.'

'On Monday morning I will have it sent to you. There's £10,625, and a further £8,500 payable in January, and the same the following year,' he told her, knowing her good manners would not permit to ask outright. He saw the flash of relief and was glad he had decided to give her two extra years of salary—AMG's information about oil alone was more than worth it. 'Would eleven o'clock be convenient for the "sight draft"?' Again Dunross used the English word.

'Whatever pleases you. I do not wish to put you to any trouble.'

Dunross noticed how she was speaking slowly and distinctly to help him. 'What will be your travel plans?'

'On Monday I think I will go to Japan, then . . . then I don't know. Perhaps back to Switzerland though I have no real reason to return. I have no relations there, the house was a rented house and the garden not mine. My Gresserhoff life ended with his death. Now I think I should be Riko Anjin again. Karma is karma.'

'Yes,' he told her, 'karma is karma.' He reached into his pocket and brought out a gift-wrapped package. 'This is a present from the Noble House to thank you for taking so much trouble and such a tiring trip on our behalf.'

'Oh. Oh thank you, but it was my honor and pleasure.' She bowed. 'Thank you. May I open it now?'

'Perhaps later. It is just a simple jade pendant but the box also contains a confidential envelope that your husband wanted you to have, for your eyes only and not for the eyes that surround us.'

'Ah. I understand. Of course.' She bowed again. 'So sorry please excuse my stupidity.'

Dunross smiled back at her. 'No stupidity, never, only beauty.'

Color came into her face and she sipped coffee to cover. 'The envelope is sealed, tai-pan-*san*?'

'Yes, as he instructed. Do you know what's in it?'

'No. Only that . . . only that Mr. Gresserhoff said that you would give me a sealed envelope.'

'Did he say why? Or what you were supposed to do with it?'

'One day someone would come to claim it.'

'By name?'

'Yes, but my husband told me I was never to divulge the name, not even to you. Never. Everything else I could tell you but not the . . . the name. So sorry, please excuse me.'

Dunross frowned. 'You're just to give it to him?'

'Or her,' she said pleasantly. 'Yes, when I am asked, not before. After it has been digested, Mr. Gresserhoff said the person would repay a debt. Thank you for the gift, tai-pan-*san*. I will cherish it.'

The waiter came and poured the last of the champagne for him then went away again. 'How do I reach you in the future, Riko-*san*?'

'I will give you three addresses and phone numbers that will find me, one in Switzerland, two in Japan.'

After a pause he said, 'Will you be in Japan the week after next?'

Riko looked up at him and his spirit twisted at such beauty. 'Yes. If you wish it,' she said.

'I wish it.'

1271

75

2:30 P.M.:

The *Sea Witch* was tied just offshore beside Sha Tin boat harbor where they had moored for lunch. As soon as they had arrived, the cook, Casey and Peter Marlowe had gone ashore with Gornt in command to select the prawns and shrimps and fish that were still swimming in sea tanks, then on to the bustling market for morning-fresh vegetables. Lunch had been quick-fried prawns with crunchy broccoli, then fish rubbed with garlic and pan-fried, served with mixed Chinese greens, again *al dente.*

The lunch had been laughter filled, the Chinese girls entertaining and happy, all of them speaking varying degrees of salty English, Dunstan Barre choleric and outrageously funny, the others joining in, and Casey thought how different the men were. How much more unrestrained and boyish, and she thought that sad. The talk had turned to business, and in the few short hours she had learned more about Hong Kong techniques than through all the reading she had done. More and more it was clear that unless you were on the inside, real power and real riches would escape you.

'Oh, you'll do very well here, Casey, you and Bartlett,' Barre had said. 'If you play the game according to Hong Kong rules, Hong Kong tax structures and not U.S. rules, right, Quillan?'

'Up to a point. If you go with Dunross and Struan's—if Struan's and Dunross exist as an entity by next Friday—you'll get some milk but none of the cream.'

'With you we'll do better?' she had asked.

Barre had laughed. 'Very much better, Casey, but it'll still be milk and very little cream!'

'Let's say, Casey, with us the milk'll be homogenized,' Gornt had said amiably.

Now the wonderful smell of freshly roasted coffee, freshly ground, was wafting up from the galley. Conversation was general around the table, banter back and forth, mostly for her benefit, about trading in Asia, supply and demand and the Asian attitude to smuggling, the Chinese girls chattering among themselves.

Abruptly, Grey's voice, a biting rasp to it, cut through. 'You'd better ask Marlowe about that, Mr. Gornt. He knows everything about smuggling and blackmailing from our Changi days.'

'Come on, Grey,' Peter Marlowe said in the sudden silence. 'Give over!'

'I thought you were proud of it, you and your Yankee blackmailer mate. Weren't you?'

'Let's leave it, Grey,' Marlowe said, his face set.

'Whatever you say, old lad.' Grey turned to Casey. 'Ask him.'

Gornt said, 'This is hardly the time to rehash old quarrels, Mr. Grey.' He kept his voice calm and the enjoyment off his face, outwardly the perfect host.

'Oh, I wasn't, Mr. Gornt. You were talking about smuggling and black marketeering. Marlowe's an expert, that's all.'

'Shall we have coffee on deck?' Gornt got up.

'Good idea. A cuppa coffee's ever so good after grub.' Grey used the word deliberately, knowing it would offend them, not caring now, suddenly tired of the banter, hating them and what they represented, hating being the odd-man out here, wanting one of the girls, any one. 'Marlowe and his Yankee friend used to roast beans in the camp when the rest of us were starving,' he said, his face stark. 'Used to drive us mad.' He looked at Peter Marlowe, his hate open now. 'Didn't you?'

After a pause, Peter Marlowe said, 'Everyone had coffee some of the time. Everyone roasted coffee beans.'

'Not like you two.' Grey turned to Casey. 'They had coffee every day, him and his Yankee friend. Me, I was provost marshal and I had it once a month if I was lucky.' He glanced back. 'How did you get coffee and food while the rest of us starved?'

1273

Casey noticed the vein in Peter Marlowe's forehead knotting and she realized, aghast, that no answer was also an answer. 'Robin . . .' she began, but Grey overrode her, his voice taunting.

'Why don't you answer, Marlowe?'

In the silence they all looked from Grey to Peter Marlowe, staring at each other, even the girls tense and on guard, feeling the sudden violence in the cabin.

'My dear fellow,' Gornt interrupted, deliberately using that slight nuance of accent he knew would goad Grey, 'surely those are ancient times and rather unimportant now. It is Sunday afternoon and we're all friends.'

'I think 'em *rather* important, Sunday afternoon or not and Marlowe and I aren't friends, never have been! He's a toff, I'm not.' Grey aped the long *a* he loathed and broadened his accent. 'Yes. But the war changed everything and us workers'll never forget!'

'You consider yourself a worker and me not?' Peter Marlowe asked, his voice grating.

'We're the exploited, you're the exploiters. Like in Changi.'

'Get off that old broken record, Grey! Changi was another world, another place, and other time, an—'

· 'It was the same as everywhere. There was bosses and the bossed, workers and them that fed off the workers. Like you and the King.'

'Stuff and nonsense!'

Casey was near to Grey and she reached out and took his arm. 'Let's have coffee, okay?'

'Of course,' Grey said. 'But first ask him, Casey.' Grimly Grey stood his ground, well aware he had, at long last, brought his enemy to bay in front of his peers. 'Mr. Gornt, ask him, eh? Any of you . . .'

They all stood there in silence, embarrassed for Peter Marlowe and shocked with the implied accusations—Gornt and Plumm privately amused and fascinated. Then one of the girls turned for the gangway and left quietly, the others following. Casey would have liked to have gone too but she did not.

'Now is not the time, Mr. Grey,' she heard Gornt say gently and she was glad he was there to break it up. 'Would you kindly leave this matter alone. Please?'

Grey looked at them all, his eyes ending up on his adversary. 'You see, Casey, not one's got the guts to ask—they're all his class, so-called upper class and they look after their own.'

Barre flushed. 'I say, old chap, don't you th—'

Peter Marlowe said, his voice flat, 'It's easy to stop this nonsense. You can't equate Changi—or Dachau or Buchenwald—with normality. You just can't. There were different rules, different patterns. We were soldiers, war prisoners, teen-agers most of us. Changi was genesis, everything new, upside down, ev—'

'Were you a black marketeer?'

'No. I was an interpreter in Malay for a friend who was a trader and there's a lot of difference between trading and black marketing an—'

'But it was against camp rules, camp law, and that makes it black marketing, right?'

'Trading with the guards was against *enemy* rules, Japanese rules.'

'And tell them how the King'd buy some poor bugger's watch or ring or fountain pen for a pittance, the last bloody thing he had in the world, and sell it high and never tell and cheat on the price, cheat, always cheat. Eh?'

Peter Marlowe stared back. 'Read my book. In it th—'

'Book?' Again Grey laughed, goading him. 'Tell 'em on your honor as a gent, your father's honor and your family's honor you're so bloody proud of—did the King cheat or didn't he? On your honor! Eh?'

Almost paralyzed, Casey saw Peter Marlowe make a fist. 'If we weren't guests here,' he hissed, 'I'd tell them what a shower you really were!'

'You can rot in hell. . . .'

'Now that's enough,' Gornt said as a command and Casey began to breathe again. 'For the last time, kindly leave this all alone!'

Grey tore his eyes off Marlowe. 'I will. Now, can I get a taxi in the village? I think I'd *rather* get home meself by meself if you don't mind.'

'Of course,' Gornt said, his face suitably grave, delighted that Grey had asked so that he did not have to finesse the suggestion in the open. 'But surely,' he added, delivering the coup de grâce, 'surely you and Marlowe could shake hands like gentlemen and forget about th—'

'Gentlemen? Ta, but no. No, I've had gentlemen like Marlowe forever. Gentlemen? Thank God England's changing and soon'll be in proper hands again—and the very British Oxford accent won't be a permanent passport to gentry and power, not ever again. We'll reform the Lords and if I have my way . . .'

'Let's hope you don't!' Pugmire said.

Gornt said firmly, 'Pug! It's coffee and port time!' Affably he took Grey's arm. 'If you'll excuse Mr. Grey and myself a moment . . .'

They went on deck. The chatter of the Chinese girls stopped a moment. Secretly very pleased with himself, Gornt led the way to the gangway and went ashore onto the wharf. Everything was turning out far better than he had thought.

'Sorry about that, Mr. Grey,' he said. 'I had no idea that Marlowe . . . Disgusting! Well, you never know, do you?'

'He's a bastard, always was, always will be—him and his filthy Yank friend. Hate Yanks too! About time we broke up with that shower!'

Gornt found a taxi easily.

'Are you sure, Mr. Grey, you won't change your mind?'

'Ta, but no thanks.'

'Sorry about Marlowe. Clearly you were provoked. When are you and your trade commission off?'

'In the morning, early.'

'If there's anything I can do for you here, just let me know.'

'Ta. When you come home give me a tinkle.'

'Thank you. I will, and thanks for coming.' He paid the fare in advance and waved politely as the taxi drove off. Grey did not look around.

Gornt smiled. That revolting bastard's going to be a useful ally in the years to come, he chortled as he walked back.

Most of the others were on deck, drinking coffee and liqueurs, Casey and Peter Marlowe to one side.

'What a bloody berk!' Gornt called out to general agreement. 'Frightfully sorry about that, Marlowe, the bugger pr—'

'No, it was my fault,' Peter Marlowe said, clearly very upset. 'Sorry. I feel terrible that he left.'

'No need to apologize. I should never have invited him—thanks for being such a gentleman about it, he clearly provoked you.'

'Quite right,' Pugmire said to more agreement. 'If I'd been you I'd've given him one. Whatever happened is in the past.'

'Oh yes,' Casey said quickly, 'what an awful man! If you hadn't stopped it, Quillan, Grey wou—'

'Enough of that berk,' Gornt said warmly, wanting the specter laid to rest. 'Let's forget him, let's not allow him to spoil a wonderful afternoon.' He put his arm around Casey and gave her a hug. 'Eh?' He saw the admiration in her eyes and he knew, gleefully, he was getting there fast. 'It's too cold for a swim. Shall we just cruise leisurely home?'

'Good idea!' Dunstan Barre said. 'I think I'm going to have a siesta.'

'Smashing idea!' someone said to laughter. The girls joined in but the laughter was forced. Everyone was still unsettled and Gornt felt it strongly. 'First some brandy! Marlowe?'

'No thank you, Mr. Gornt.'

Gornt studied him. 'Listen to me, Marlowe,' he said with real compassion and everyone fell silent. 'We've all seen too much of life, too much of Asia, not to know that whatever you did, you did for good and not evil. What you said was right. Changi was special with special problems. Pug was locked up in Stanley Prison—that's on Hong Kong Island, Casey—for three and a half years. I got out of Shanghai barely with my skin, and blood on my hands. Jason was grabbed by the Nazis after Dunkirk and had a couple of dicey years with them. Dunstan operated in China—Dunstan's been in Asia forever and he knows too. Eh?'

'Oh yes,' Dunstan Barre said sadly. 'Casey, in war to survive you have to stretch things a bit sometimes. As to trading, Marlowe, I agree, most times you have to equate the problem to the time and place. I thank God I was never caught. Don't think I'd've survived, know I wouldn't.' He refilled his port from the decanter, embarrassed to be speaking real truths.

'What was Changi really like, Peter?' Casey asked for all of them.

'It's hard to talk about,' he said. 'It was the nearest to no-life that you could get. We were issued a quarter of a pound of dry rice a day, some vegetables, one egg a week. Sometimes meat was . . . was waved over the soup. It was different, that's all I can say about it. Most of us had never seen a jungle before, let alone Chinese and Japanese and to lose a war . . . I was just eighteen when Changi began.'

'Christ, I can't stand Japs, just can't!' Pugmire said and the others nodded.

'But that's not fair, really. They were just playing the game according to their rules,' Peter Marlowe said. 'That was fair from the Japanese point of view. Look what wonderful soldiers they were, look how they fought and almost never allowed themselves to be captured. We were dishonored according to their standards by surrendering.' Peter Marlowe shivered. 'I felt dishonored, still feel dishonored.'

'That's not right, Marlowe,' Gornt said. 'There's no dishonor in that. None.'

Casey, standing beside Gornt, put her hand on his arm lightly. 'Oh yes. He's right, Peter. He really is.'

'Yes.' Dunstan Barre said. 'But Grey, what the devil got Grey all teed off? Eh?'

'Nothing and everything. He became fanatical about enforcing camp rules—which were Japanese rules—stupidly, a lot of us thought. As I said, Changi was different, officers and men were locked up together, no letters from home, no food, two thousand miles of enemy-occupied territory in every direction, malaria, dysentery, and the death rate terrible. He hated this American friend of mine, the King. It was true the King was a cunning businessman and he ate well when others didn't and drank coffee and smoked tailor-made cigarettes. But he kept a lot of us alive with his skill. Even Grey. He even kept Grey alive. Grey's hatred kept him alive, I'm sure. The King fed almost the whole American contingent—there were about thirty of them, officers and men. Oh they worked for it, American style, but even so, without him they would have died. I would have. I know.' Peter Marlowe shuddered. 'Joss. Karma. Life. I think I'll have that brandy now, Mr. Gornt.'

Gornt poured. 'Whatever happened to this man, this fellow you call the King? After the war?'

Pugmire interrupted with a laugh, 'One of the buggers in our camp who was a trader became a bloody millionaire afterwards. Is it the same with this King?'

'I don't know,' Peter Marlowe said.

'You never saw him again, Peter?' Casey asked, surprised. 'You didn't see him back in the States?'

'No, no I never did. I tried to find him but never could.'

'That's often the rule, Casey,' Gornt said casually. 'When you leave a regiment all debts and friendships are canceled.' He was very content. Everything's perfect, he told himself, thinking of the double bed in his cabin, and smiled at her across the deck. She smiled back.

Riko Anjin Gresserhoff went into the foyer of the V and A. It was crowded with those having early-afternoon tea or late lunches. As she walked to the elevator a tremor went through her, the eyes bothering her—not the usual lusting eyes of European men or the dislike in the eyes of their women—but Chinese and Eurasian eyes. She had never experienced so much general hatred. It was a strange feeling. This was her first time outside of Switzerland, other than school trips to Germany and two journeys to Rome with her mother. Her husband had taken her abroad only once, to Vienna for a week.

I don't like Asia, she thought, suppressing another shudder. But then it's not Asia, it's Hong Kong, surely it's just here, the people here. And surely, there is right on their side to be antagonistic. I wonder if I'll like Japan? Will I be alien, even there?

The elevator came and she went to her suite on the sixth floor, the room boy not opening her door for her. Alone and with the door bolted, she felt better. The red message light on the phone was blinking but she paid it no attention, quickly taking off her shoes, hat, gloves and coat, putting them at once in a vast closet, the clothes already there neat and organized, like her three pairs of shoes. The suite was small but delicate, a living room, bedroom and bath. Flowers from Struan's were on the table and a bowl of fruit from the hotel.

Her fingers slid the gift wrapping away neatly. Inside was a rectangular black plush box and she opened it. Warmth went through her. The pendant was on a thin gold chain, the jade green with flecks of lighter green, carved like a cornucopia. Light shimmered off the polished surface. At once she put it on,

1279

studying it in the mirror, admiring the stone as it lay against her breast. She had never been given jade before.

Underneath the black, plush-covered cardboard was the envelope. It was a plain envelope, not Struan's, the seal equally plain, made of ordinary red sealing wax. With great care she slid a paper knife under the seal and studied the pages, one by one, a small frown on her forehead. Just a jumble of numbers and letters and an occasional symbol. A tiny, satisfied smile touched her lips. She found the hotel letter-writing folder and, settling herself comfortably at the desk, began to copy the pages, one by one.

When she had finished she checked them again. She put the copies into a hotel envelope and sealed it, the originals in another envelope, a plain one she took out of her bag. Next she found the new stick of sealing wax, lit a match and daubed the melting wax on both envelopes, sealing them, making sure the seal on the envelope of the originals was a pattern of the one Dunross had made. The phone rang, startling her. She watched it, her heart thumping, until it stopped. Once more at ease, she went back to her labor, ensuring there was no telltale indentations left on the pad that she had used, examining it under the light. As soon as she was satisfied, she stamped the envelope containing the copies, addressed it to: R. Anjin, Box 154, General Post Office, Sydney, Australia. This and the other envelope with the originals she put into her handbag.

Carefully she rechecked that nothing had been missed, then went to a small refrigerator near the stocked bar and took out a bottle of sparkling mineral water and drank some.

Again the phone rang. She watched it, sipping the soda water, her mind checking and rechecking, thinking about her lunch with Dunross, wondering if she had been wise to accept his invitation to cocktails tonight and, later, to dinner with him and his friends. I wonder if there will be friends or if we will be alone. Would I like to be alone with that man?

Her thoughts went back to the small, untidy, slightly balding Hans Gresserhoff, and the four years of life that she had led with him, weeks alone, sleeping alone, waking alone, walking alone, no real friends, rarely going out, her husband strangely secretive, cautioning her about making friends, wanting her to be alone and always safe and calm and patient. That was the hardest part to bear, she thought. Patience. Patience alone, patience together, asleep or awake. Patience and outwardly calm. When all the time she was like a volcano, desperate to erupt.

That he loved her was beyond doubt. All she felt for him was *giri*, duty. He gave her money and her life was smooth, neither rich nor poor—even, like the country of their choice. His arrivals and departures had no pattern. When he was with her he always wanted her, wanted to be near her. Their pillowing satisfied him but not her, though she pretended, for his pleasure. But then, she told herself, you have had no other man to judge by.

He was a good man and it was as I told the tai-pan. I tried to be a good wife to him, to obey him in everything, to honor my mother's wish, to fulfill my *giri* to her, and to him. And now?

She looked down at her wedding ring and twisted it on her finger. For the first time since she had married she took it off and looked at it closely in the palm of her hand. Small, empty and uninteresting. So many lonely nights, tears in the nights, waiting waiting waiting. Waiting for what? Children forbidden, friends forbidden, travel forbidden. Not forbidden as a Japanese would: *Kin jiru!* But, 'Don't you think, my dear,' he would say, 'don't you think it would be better if you didn't go to Paris while I'm away? We can go the next time I'm here . . .' both of them knowing they would never go.

The time in Vienna had been terrible. It was the first year. They went for a week. 'I have to go out tonight,' he had told her the first night. 'Please stay in the room, eat in the room till I get back.' Two days passed and when he came back he was sallow-faced and drawn, frightened, and then at once, in the darkest part of the night, they had got into the hired car and fled back to Switzerland, going the long way, the wrong way, up through the Tyrolean mountains, his eyes constantly on the rear mirrors in case they were being followed, not talking to her until they were safe across the border once more.

'But why, why, Hans?'

'Because nothing! Please. You're not to ask questions, Riko. That was your agreement . . . our agreement. I'm sorry about the holiday. We'll go to Wengen or Biarritz, it will be grand, it will be grand there. Please remember your *giri* and that I love you with all my heart.'

Love!

I do not understand that word, she thought, standing there at the window, looking at the harbor, sullen clouds, the light bad. Strange that in Japanese we do not have such a word. Only duty and shades of duty, affection and shades of affection. Not *lieben*. *Ai? Ai* really means respect though some use it for *lieben*.

Riko caught herself thinking in German and she smiled. Most times she thought in German though today, with the tai-pan, she had thought in Japanese. It's such a long time since I spoke my own language. What is my own language? Japanese? That's the language my parents and I spoke. German? That's the language of our part of Switzerland. English? That's the language of my husband even though he claimed that German was his first tongue.

Was he English?

She had asked herself that question many times. It was not that his German was not fluent, it was just attitudes. His attitudes were not German, like mine are not Japanese. Or are they?

I don't know. But now, now I can find out.

He had never told her what his work was and she had never asked. After Vienna it had been very easy to predict that it was clandestine and connected somehow to international crime or espionage. Hans was not the type to be in crime.

So from then on she had been even more cautious. Once or twice she had thought that they were under surveillance in Zurich and when they went skiing, but he had dismissed it and told her not to worry about him. 'But be prepared in case of accidents. Keep all your valuables and private papers, passport and birth certificate in your traveling bag, *Ri-chan*,' he had said, using her nickname. 'Just in case, just in case.'

With the death of her husband and his instructions almost all carried out, the money and the tai-pan's phone call and summons, everything had become new. Now she could start again. She was twenty-four. The past was past and karma was karma. The tai-pan's money would be more than enough for her needs for years.

On their wedding night, her husband had told her, 'If anything happens to me, you will get a call from a man called Kiernan. Cut the phone wires as I will show you and leave Zurich instantly. Leave everything except the clothes you wear and your travel bag. Drive to Geneva. Here is a key. This key will open a safety deposit box in the Swiss Bank of Geneva on Rue Charles. In it there's money and some letters. Follow the instructions exactly, my darling, oh how I love you. Leave everything. Do exactly as I've said. . . .'

And she had. Exactly. It was her *giri*.

She had cut the phone wires with the wire snips as he had shown her, just behind the box that was attached to the wall so that the cut was hardly noticeable. In Geneva in the bank there had been a letter of instructions, $10,000 U.S. in cash in the safety deposit box, a new Swiss passport, stamped, with her photograph but a new name and new birthday and new birth certificate that documented she was born in the city of Berne twenty-three years ago. She had liked the new name he had chosen for her and she remembered how, in the safety of her hotel room overlooking the lovely lake, she had wept for him.

Also in the safety deposit box had been a savings book in her new name for $20,000 U.S. in this same bank, and a key, an address and a deed. The deed was for a small chalet on the lake, private and furnished and paid for, with a caretaker who knew her only by her new name and that she was a widow who had been abroad—the deed registered in her new name though purchased four years before, a few days prior to her marriage.

'Ah, mistress, I am so happy you have come home at long last. Traveling in all those foreign places must be very tiring,' the pleasant, though simple old lady had said in greeting. 'Oh, for the last year or so, your home has been rented to such a charming, quiet Englishman. He paid promptly every month, here are the accounts. Perhaps he will come back this year, he said, perhaps not. Your agent is on Avenue Firmet. . . .'

Later, wandering around the lovely house, the lake vast and clean in the bowl of the mountains, the house clean like the mountains, pictures on the walls, flowers in vases, three bed-rooms and a living room and verandas, tiny but perfect for her, the garden cherished, she had gone into the main bedroom. Among a kaleidoscope of small pictures of various shapes and sizes on one of the walls was what seemed to be part of an old

1283

letter in a glass-covered frame, the paper already yellowing. She recognized his writing. It was in English. 'So many happy hours in your arms, *Ri-chan*, so many happy days in your company, how do I say that I love you? Forget me, I will never forget you. How do I beg God to grant you ten thousand days for every one of mine, my darling, my darling, my darling.'

The huge double bed was almost convex with its thick eiderdown quilt, multicolored, the windows opened to the tender air, late summer perfumes within it, snow dusting the mountaintops. She had wept again, the chalet taking her to itself.

Within a few hours of being there Dunross had called and she had boarded the first jet and now she was here, most of her work completed, never a need to return, the past obliterated—if she wished it. The new passport was genuine as far as she could tell, and the birth certificate. No reason ever to return to Switzerland—except for the chalet. And the picture.

She had left it on the wall undisturbed. And she had resolved, as long as she owned the house, the picture would stay where he had placed it. Always.

76

5:10 P.M.:

Orlanda was driving her small car, Bartlett beside her, his hand resting lightly across her shoulders. They had just come over the pass from Aberdeen and now, still in cloud, were heading down the mountainside in Mid Levels toward her home in Rose Court. They were happy together, aware and filled with expectation. After lunch they had crossed to Hong Kong and she had driven to Shek-O on the southeastern tip of the Island to show him where some of the tai-pans had weekend houses. The countryside was rolling and sparsely populated, hills, ravines, the sea always near, sheer cliffs and rocks.

From Shek-O they had slid along the southern road that curled and twisted until they got to Repulse Bay where she had stopped at the wonderful hotel for tea and cakes on the veranda, looking out at the sea, then on again, past Deepwater Cove to Discovery Bay where she stopped again at a lookout. 'Look over there, Linc, that's Castle Tok!' Castle Tok was a vast, incongruous house that looked like a Norman castle and was perched on the cliffside high over the water. 'During the war the Canadians—Canadian soldiers—were defending this part of the Island against the invading Japanese and they all retreated to Castle Tok for a last stand. When they were overwhelmed and surrendered there were about two hundred and fifty of them left alive. The Japanese herded them all onto the terrace of Castle Tok and drove them by bayonet over the terrace wall to the rocks below.'

'Jesus.' The drop was a hundred feet or more.

'Everyone. The wounded, the . . . the others, everyone.' He had seen her shiver and at once had reached out to touch her.

1285

'Don't, Orlanda, that's such a long time ago.'

'It's not, no, not at all. I'm afraid history and war's still very much with us, Linc. It always will be. Ghosts walk those terraces by night.'

'You believe that?'

'Yes. Oh yes.'

He remembered looking back at the brooding house, the surf crashing against the rocks below, her perfume surrounding him as she leaned back against him, feeling her heat, glad to be alive and not one of those soliders. 'Your Castle Tok looks like something out of the movies. You ever been inside?'

'No. But they say there are suits of armor and dungeons and it's a copy of a real castle in France. The owner was old Sir Cha-sen Tok, Builder Tok. He was a multimillionaire who made his money in tin. They say that when he was fifty a soothsayer told him to begin building a "big mansion" or he would die. So he began to build and he built dozens of places, all mansions, three in Hong Kong, one near Sha Tin and many in Malaya. Castle Tok was the last one he built. He was eighty-nine but hale and hearty and like a middle-aged man. But after Castle Tok the story is he said enough, and quit building. Within a month he was dead and the soothsayer's prophecy came true.'

'You're making it all up, Orlanda!'

'Oh no, Linc, I wouldn't, not without telling. But what's true and what's false? Who really knows, eh, my darling?'

'I know I'm mad about you.'

'Oh Linc, you must know I feel the same.'

They had driven on past Aberdeen, warm and together, his hand on her shoulder, her hair brushing his hand. From time to time she would point out houses and places and the hours went by imperceptibly, delightfully for both of them. Now, as they came down from the pass through the clouds and broke out of them, they could see most of the city below. Lights were not on yet, though here and there the huge colored neon signs down by the water's edge were beginning to brighten.

The traffic was heavy and on the steep mountain roads water still ran in the gutters with piles of fresh mud and rocks and vegetation here and there. She drove deftly, without taking chances, and he felt safe with her though driving on the wrong side of the road had been hair-raising on the bends.

'But we're on the correct side,' she said. '*You* drive on the wrong side!'

'The hell we do. It's only the English who drive on the left. You're as American as I am, Orlanda.'

'I wish I were, Linc, oh so very much.'

'You are. You sound American and you dress American.'

'Ah, but I know what I am, my darling.'

He let himself just watch her. I've never enjoyed watching anyone so much, he thought. Not Casey, not anyone in my whole life. Then his mind took him again to Biltzmann and he wished he had that man's neck in his hands.

Put him away, old buddy, away with the shit of the world. That's what he is—he and Banastasio. Bartlett felt another twinge go through him. He had had a phone call just before lunch, and an apology that was really an added threat.

'Let's break bread, baby, you'n me? Hell, Linc, it's shitsville with you'n me hollerin'. How about steaks tonight? There's a great steak house off Nathan Road, the San Francisco.'

'No thanks. I've got a date,' he had said coldly. 'Anyway, you made your point yesterday. Let's leave it at that, okay? We'll get together at the annual board meeting, if you attend.'

'Hey Linc, this is me, your old buddy. Remember we came through for you when you needed the cash. Didn't we give you cash up front?'

'Cash up front in return for shares which have been the best investment—the best regular investment you ever had. You've doubled your money in five years.'

'Sure we have. Now we want a little of the say-so, that's only fair, isn't it?'

'No. Not after yesterday. What about the guns?' he had asked on a sudden hunch.

There was a pause. 'What guns?'

'The ones aboard my airplane. The hijacked M14s and grenades.'

'It's news to me, baby.'

'My name's Linc. Baby. Got it?'

Another pause. The voice grated now. 'I got it. About our deal. You gonna change your mind?'

'No. No way.'

'Not now, not later?'

'No.'

There had been the silence on the other end of the line and then a click and the endless dial tone began. At once he had called Rosemont.

'Don't worry, Linc. Banastasio's a top target of ours and we have lots of help in these parts.'

'Anything on the guns?'

'You're in the clear. The Hong Kong brass here've withdrawn the lien on you. You'll hear that officially tomorrow.'

'They found something?'

'No. We did. We checked out your hangar in L.A. One of the night watchmen remembered seeing a couple of jokers fiddling around in your landing bay. He thought nothing about it till we asked.'

'Jesus. You catch anybody?'

'No. Maybe never will. No sweat. About Banastasio, he'll be off your back soon enough. Don't worry.'

Now, thinking about it, Bartlett felt chilled again.

'What's the matter, darling?' Orlanda asked. 'What is it?'

'Nothing.'

'Tell me.'

'I was just thinking that fear's lousy and can destroy you if you don't watch out.'

'Oh yes I know, I know so very well.' She took her eyes off the road a second and smiled hesitantly and put her hand on his knee. 'But you're strong, my darling. You're afraid of nothing.'

He laughed. 'I wish that were true.'

'Oh but it is. I *know*.' She slowed to go around a pile of slush, the road steeper here, water swirling in a minor flood in and out of the gutters. The car was hugging the tall retaining wall as she turned down into Kotewall Road and around the corner to Rose Court. When she came alongside he held his breath as she hesitated a moment, then firmly bypassed the foyer and turned into the steep down-path that led to the garage. 'It's cocktail time,' she said.

'Great,' he said, his voice throaty. He did not look at her. When they stopped he got out and went to her side and opened the door. She locked the car and they went to the elevator. Bartlett felt the pulse in his neck throbbing.

Two Chinese caterers carrying trays of canapés got in with

them and asked for the Asian Properties flat. 'It's on the fifth floor,' she said, and after the caterers had got out Bartlett said, 'Asian Properties're the landlords here?'

'Yes,' she said. 'They're also the original builders.' She hesitated. 'Jason Plumm and Quillan are good friends. Quillan still owns the penthouse though he sublet it when we broke up.'

Bartlett put his arm around her. 'I'm glad you did.'

'So'm I.' Her smile was tender and her wide-eyed innocence tore at him. 'Now I am.'

They reached the eighth floor and he noticed her fingers tremble slightly as she put the key into her lock. 'Come in, Linc. Tea, coffee, beer or a cocktail?' She slipped off her shoes and looked up at him. His heart was pounding and his senses reached out to feel whether the apartment was empty. 'We're alone,' she said simply.

'How do you know what I'm thinking?'

She shrugged a little shrug. 'It's only some things.'

He put his hands on her waist. 'Orlanda . . .'

'I know, my darling.'

Her voice was husky and it sent a tremor through him. When he kissed her, her lips welcomed him, her loins soft and unresisting. His hands traced her. He felt her nipples harden and the throb of her heart equal to his. Then her hands left his neck and pressed against his chest but this time he held her against him, his kiss more urgent. The pressure of hands ceased and once more the hands slid around his neck, her loins closer now. They broke from the kiss but held each other.

'I love you, Linc.'

'I love you, Orlanda,' he replied, and the sudden truth of it consumed him. Again they kissed, her hands tender but strong, his own hands wandering and in their wake, fire. For him and for her. More of her weight rested on his arms as her knees weakened and he lifted her easily and carried her through the open door into the bedroom. The gossamer curtains that hung from the ceiling to form the four-poster moved gently in the cool sweet breeze from the open windows.

The coverlet was soft and down-filled.

'Be kind to me, my darling,' she whispered huskily. 'Oh how I love you.'

From the stern of the *Sea Witch*, Casey waved good-bye to Dunstan Barre, Plumm and Pugmire who stood on the wharf, Hong Kong side, where they had just been dropped, the late afternoon pleasant but still overcast. The boat was heading back across the harbor again—Peter Marlowe and the girls had already been dropped off at Kowloon—Gornt having persuaded her to stay on board for the extra trip. 'I've got to come back to Kowloon again,' he had told her. 'I've an appointment at the Nine Dragons. Keep me company. Please?'

'Why not?' she had agreed happily, in no hurry, still in plenty of time to change for the cocktail party to which Plumm had invited her this afternoon. She had decided to postpone her dinner with Lando Mata for one day next week.

On the way back from Sha Tin this afternoon she had dozed part of the time, wrapped up warm against a stiff breeze, curled up on the wide, comfortable cushions that circled the stern, the other guests scattered, sometimes Gornt there at the conn, tall, strong and captain of the ship, Peter Marlowe alone in a deck chair dozing at the bow. Later they had had tea and cakes, he and Casey and Barre. During tea, Pugmire and Plumm had appeared, tousled and content, their girls in tow.

'Sleep well?' Gornt had asked with a smile.

'Very,' Plumm had said.

I'll bet, she had thought, watching him and his girl, liking her—big, dark eyes, svelte, a happy soul called Wei-wei who stayed with him like his shadow.

Earlier, when she and Gornt had been alone on deck, he had told her that none of these were casual friends, all of them special.

'Does everyone here have a mistress?'

'Good lord no. But, well, sorry, but men and women age differently and after a certain age it's difficult. Bluntly, pillowing and love and marriage aren't the same.'

'There's no such thing as faithfulness?'

'Of course. Absolutely. For a woman it means one thing, for a man another.'

Casey had sighed. 'That's terrible. Terrible and so unfair.'

'Yes. But only if you wish it to be.'

'That's not right! Think of the millions of women who work and slave all their lives, looking after the man, scrubbing and

1290

cleaning and nowadays helping to support their children, to be shoved aside just because they're old.'

'You can't blame men, that's the way society is.'

'And who runs society? Men! Jesus, Quillan, you've got to admit men are responsible!'

'I already agree it's unfair, but it's unfair on men too. What about the millions of men who work themselves to death to *provide*—that jolly word—to provide the money for others to spend, mostly women. Face it, Ciranoush, men have to go on working until they are dead, to support others, and more than frequently at the end of their lives, a hacking, shrewish wife— look at Pug's wife for God's sake! I could point out fifty who are unnecessarily fat, ugly and stink—literally. Then there's the other neat little female trick of the women who use their sex to trap, get pregnant to ensnare, then cry havoc and scream for a highly paid divorce. What about Linc Bartlett, eh? What sort of a wringer did that wonderful wife of his put him through, eh?'

'You know about that?'

'Of course. You ran a tape on me, I ran one on both of you. Are your divorce laws fair? Fifty percent of everything and then the poor bloody American male has to go to court to decide what proportion of his fifty percent he can retain.'

'It's true Linc's wife and her attorney almost put him away. But not every wife's like that. But God, we're not chattel and most women need protection. Women throughout the world still get a raw deal.'

'I've never known a real woman to get a raw deal,' he said. 'I mean a woman like you or Orlanda who understands what femininity means.' Suddenly he had beamed at her. 'Of course, en route she has to give us poor weak bastards what we want to stay healthy.'

She had laughed with him, also wanting to change the subject—too difficult to solve now.

'Ah, Quillan, you're one of the bad ones all right.'

'Oh?'

'Yes.'

He had turned away to search the sky ahead. She watched him and he looked fine to her, standing there, swaying slightly, the wind ruffling the hairs on his strong forearms, his sea cap jaunty. I'm glad he trusts me and considers me a woman, she

1291

had thought, lulled by the wine and the food and by his desire. Ever since she had come aboard she had felt it strongly and she had wondered again how she would deal with it when it manifested itself, as it would, inevitably. Would it be yes or no? Or maybe? Or maybe next week?

Will there be a next week?

'What's going to happen tomorrow, Quillan? At the stock market?'

'Tomorrow can take care of tomorrow,' he had said, the wind whipping him.

'Seriously?'

'I will win or I will not win.' Gornt shrugged. 'Either way I'm covered. Tomorrow I buy. With joss I have him by the shorts.'

'And then?'

He had laughed. 'Have you any doubt? I take him over, lock, stock and box at the races.'

'Ah, you really want that, don't you?'

'Oh yes. Oh yes, that represents victory. He and his forebears have kept me and mine out. Of course I want that.'

I wonder if I could make a deal with Ian, she had thought absently. Wonder if I could get the tai-pan to allow Quillan a box, his own box, and help make him a steward. Crazy for these two to be like bulls in a china shop—there's more than enough room for both. Ian owes me a favor if Murtagh delivers.

Her heart fluttered and she wondered what had happened with Murtagh and the bank, and if the answer was yes, what Quillan would do.

And where is Linc? Is he with Orlanda, in her arms, dreaming the afternoon away?

She curled up again on the stern and closed her eyes. The salt air and the throb of the engines and the motion through the sea put her to sleep. Her sleep was dreamless, womblike, and in a few minutes she awoke refreshed. Gornt was sitting opposite her now, watching her. They were alone again, the Cantonese captain at the wheel.

'You have a nice sleeping face,' he said.

'Thank you.' She moved and rested on one elbow. 'You're a strange man. Part devil, part prince, compassionate one minute, ruthless the next. That was a wonderful thing you did for Peter.'

1292

He just smiled and waited, his eyes strangely and pleasantly challenging.

'Linc's . . . I think Linc's smitten with Orlanda,' she said without thinking and saw a shadow go over him.

'Oh?'

'Yes.' She waited but he said nothing, just watched her. Pushed by the silence, she added involuntarily, 'I think she's smitten with him.' Again a long silence. 'Quillan, is that part of a plan?'

He laughed softly and she felt his dominance. 'Ah, Ciranoush, you're the strange one. I don—'

'Will you call me Casey? Please? Ciranoush is not right.'

'But I don't like Casey. May I use Kamalian?'

'Casey.'

'What about Ciranoush today, Casey tomorrow, Kamalian for Tuesday dinner? That's when we close the deal. Eh?'

Her guards came up without thinking. 'That's up to Linc.'

'You're not tai-pan of Par-Con?'

'No. No, I'll never be that.'

He laughed. Then he said, 'Then let's make it Ciranoush today, Casey tomorrow and the hell with Tuesday?'

'All right!' she said, warmed by him.

'Good. Now as to Orlanda and Linc,' he said, his voice gentle. 'That's up to them and I never discuss the affairs of others with others, even a lady. Never. That's not playing the game. If you're asking if I've some devious plot, using her against Linc or you and Par-Con, that's ridiculous.' Again he smiled. 'I've always noticed that ladies manipulate men, not the other way around.'

'Dreamer!'

'One question deserves another: Are you and Linc lovers?'

'No. Not in the conventional sense, but yes I love him.'

'Ah, then are you going to marry?'

'Perhaps.' Again she shifted and she saw his eyes move over her. Her hands pulled the blanket closer around her, her heart beating nicely, very conscious of him as she knew he was conscious of her. 'But I don't discuss my affairs with another man,' she said with a smile. 'That's not playing the game either.'

Gornt reached out and touched her lightly. 'I agree, Ciranoush.'

1293

The *Sea Witch* came out of the breakwater into the harbor waves, Kowloon ahead. She sat up and turned to watch the Island and the Peak, most of it cloud covered. 'It's so beautiful.'

'The south coast of Hong Kong's grand around Shek-O, Repulse Bay. I've a place at Shek-O. Would you like to see the boat now?'

'Yes, yes I'd like that.'

He took her forward first. The cabins were neat, no sign of having been used. Each had shower stalls and a toilet. A small general cabin served them all. 'We're rather popular with ladies at the moment because they can shower to their hearts' content. The water shortage does have advantages.'

'I'll bet,' she said, carried along by his joviality.

Aft, separate from the rest of the boat, was the master cabin. Big double bed. Neat, tidy and inviting.

Her heart was sounding loud in her ears now, and when he casually closed the cabin door and put his hand on her waist she did not back off. He came closer. She had never kissed a man with a beard before. Gornt's body was hard against hers and it felt good to her, her breath picking up tempo, his lips firm and cigar tasting. Most of her whispered: Go, let go, and most of her said, No, don't, and all of her felt sensual in his arms, too good.

What about Linc?

The question barreled into her mind like never before and all at once her mind cleared and, carried along by his sensuality, she knew for the first time with absolute clarity that it was Linc she wanted, not Par-Con or power if that had to be the choice. Yes, it's Linc, just Linc, and tonight I'll cancel our deal. Tonight I'll offer to cancel.

'Now's not the time,' she whispered, her voice throaty.

'What?'

'No, not now. We can't, sorry.' She reached up and kissed him lightly on the lips, talking through the kisses. 'Not now, my dear, sorry, but we can't, not now. Tuesday, perhaps Tuesday . . .'

He held her away from him and she saw his dark eyes searching her. She held her gaze as long as she could, then buried her head against his chest and held him tenderly, still enjoying the

1294

closeness, sure that she was safe now, and that he was convinced. That was a close one, she thought weakly, her knees feeling strange, all of her pulsating. I was almost gone then and that wouldn't have been good, good for me or Linc or him.

It would have been good for him, she thought strangely.

Her heart was pounding as she rested against him, waiting, recouping, confident in a moment—with warmth and gentleness and the promise of next week—he would say, 'Let's go back on deck.'

Then all at once she felt his arms tighten around her and before she knew what was happening she was on the bed, his kisses strong and his hands wandering. She began to fight back but he caught her hands expertly and stretched her out with his great strength and lay across her, his loins pinioning her, making her helpless. At leisure he kissed her and his passion and her heat mingled with her fury and fear and want. As much as she struggled, she could not move.

The heat grew. In a moment he shifted his grip. Instantly she swept to the attack, wanting more though now she was preparing to fight seriously. Again his grip on her hands tightened. She felt herself swamped, wanting to be overpowered, not wanting it, his passion strong, loins hard, the bed soft. And then, as abruptly as he had begun, he released her and rolled away with a laugh.

'Let's have a drink!' he said without rancor.

She was gasping for breath. 'You bastard!'

'I'm not actually. I'm very legitimate.' Gornt propped himself on an elbow, his eyes crinkling. 'But you, Ciranoush, you're a liar.'

'Go to hell!'

His voice was calm and genially taunting. 'I will, soon enough. Far be it from me to ask a lady to prove such a thing.'

She threw herself at him, her nails hacking for his face, furious that he was so controlled when she was not. Easily he caught her hands and held her. 'Gently gently catchee monkeeee,' he said even more genially. 'Calm down, Ciranoush. Remember, we're both over twenty-one. I've already seen you almost naked, and if I really wanted to rape you I'm afraid it wouldn't be much of a contest. You could scream bloody murder and my crew wouldn't hear a thing.'

'You're a goddamn lou—'

'Stop!' Gornt kept his smile but she stopped, sensing danger. 'The tumble was not to frighten, just to amuse,' he said gently. 'A prank, nothing more. Truly.' He released her and she scrambled off the bed, her breathing still heavy.

Angrily she walked over to the mirror and pushed her hair back into place, then saw him in the mirror, still lying casually on the bed watching her, and she whirled, 'You're a black-eyed bastard!'

Gornt let out a bellow of laughter, infectious, belly-shaking, and, all at once, seeing the foolishness of it all, she began to laugh too. In a moment they were both aching with laughter, he spread out on the bed and Casey leaning against the sea chest.

On deck, as good friends, they drank some champagne that was already opened in a silver bucket, the silent, obsequious steward serving them, then going away.

At the dock in Kowloon, she kissed him again. 'Thanks for a lovely time. Tuesday, if not before!' She went ashore and waved the ship good-bye a long time, then hurried home.

Spectacles Wu was also hurrying home. He was tired and anxious and filled with dread. The way up through the maze of dwellings and hovels in the resettlement area high above Aberdeen was difficult, slippery and dangerous, mud and mess everywhere, and he was breathing hard from the climb. The runoff in the concrete storm drain had overflowed its banks many times in many places, the flood shoving structures aside and spreading more havoc. Smoke hung over many of the wrecked dwellings, some still smoldering from the fires that had spread so quickly when the slides began. He skirted the deep slide where Fifth Niece had almost perished the day before yesterday, a hundred or more hovels wrecked by new slides in the same area.

The candy shop had vanished and the old woman with it. 'Where is she?' he asked.

The scavenger shrugged and continued to sift through wreckage, seeking good wood or good cardboard or corrugated iron.

'How is it above?' he asked.

'As below,' the man said in halting Cantonese. 'Some good, some bad. Joss.'

Wu thanked him. He was barefoot, carrying his shoes to protect them and now he left the storm drain and forced his way over some of the debris wreckage to find the path that meandered upward. From where he was he could not see his area though it seemed there were no slides there. Armstrong had allowed him to come home to check when the radio news had again reported bad slides in this part of the resettlement area. 'But be back as quickly as you can. Another interrogation's scheduled for seven o'clock.'

'Oh yes, I'll be back,' he muttered out loud.

The sessions had been very tiring but for him good, with much praise from Armstrong and the chief of SI, his place in SI assured now, transfer and training to begin next week. He had had little sleep, partially because the session hours bore no relationship to day or night, and partially because of his wish to succeed. The client was shifting from English to Ning-tok dialect to Cantonese and back again and it had been hard to follow all the ramblings. It was only when his fingers had touched the wonderful, rare roll of bills in his pocket, his winnings at the races, that a lightness had taken hold and carried him through the difficult hours. Again he touched them to reassure himself, blessing his joss, as he climbed the narrow pathway, the path at times a rickety bridge over small ravines, climbing steadily. People passed by, going down, and others were following going up, the noise of hammers and rebuilding, reroofing all over the mountainside.

His area was a hundred yards ahead now, around this corner, and he turned it and stopped. His area was no more, just a deep scar in the earth, the piled-up avalanche of mud and debris two hundred feet below. No dwellings where there had been hundreds.

Numbly he climbed, skirting the treacherous slide, and went to the nearest hovel, banging on the door. An old woman opened it suspiciously.

'Excuse me, Honored Lady, I'm Wu Cho-tam's son from Ning-tok. . . .'

The woman, One Tooth Yang, stared at him blankly, then

started speaking but Wu did not understand her language so he thanked her and went off, remembering that this was one of the areas settled by the Yang, some of the northern foreigners who came from Shanghai.

Closer to the top of the slide he stopped and knocked on another door.

'Excuse me, Honored Sir, but what happened? I'm Wu Cho-tam's son from Ning-tok and my family were there.' He pointed at the scar.

'It happened in the night, Honorable Wu,' the man told him, speaking a Cantonese dialect he could understand. 'It was like the sound of the old Canton express train and then a rumbling from the earth, then screams then some fires came. It happened the same last year over there. Ah yes, the fires began quickly but the rains doused them. *Dew neh loh moh* but the night was very bad.' The neighbor was an old man with no teeth and his mouth split into a grimace. 'Bless all gods you weren't sleeping there, *heya?*' He shut the door.

Wu looked back at the scar, then picked his way down the hill. At length he found one of the elders of his area who was also from Ning-tok.

'Ah, Spectacles Wu, Policeman Wu! Several of your family are there.' His gnarled old finger pointed above. 'There, in the house of your cousin, Wu Wam-pak.'

'How many were lost, Honorable Sir?'

'Fornicate all mud slides how do I know? Am I keeper of the mountainside? There are dozens missing.'

Spectacles Wu thanked him. When he found the hut, Ninth Uncle was there, Grandmother, Sixth Uncle's wife and their four children, Third Uncle's wife and baby. Fifth Uncle had a broken arm, now in a crude splint.

'And the rest of us?' he asked. Seven were missing.

'In the earth,' grandmother said. 'Here's tea, Spectacles Wu.'

'Thank you, Honored Grandmother. And Grandfather?'

'He went to the Void before the slide. He went to the Void in the night, before the slide.'

'Joss. And Fifth Niece?'

'Gone. Vanished, somewhere.'

'Could she still be alive?'

'Perhaps. Sixth Uncle's searching for her now, below, and the others, even though she's a useless mouth. But what about my sons, and their sons, and theirs?'

'Joss,' Wu said sadly, not cursing the gods or blessing them. Gods make mistakes. 'We will light joss sticks for them that they may be reborn safely, if there is rebirth. Joss.' He sat down on a broken crate. 'Ninth Uncle, our factory, was the factory damaged?'

'No, thank all gods.' The man was numbed. He had lost his wife and three children, somehow scrambling out of the sea of mud that had swallowed them all. 'The factory is undamaged.'

'Good.' All the papers and research materials for Freedom Fighter were there—along with the old typewriter and ancient Gestetner copying machine. 'Very good. Now, Fifth Uncle, tomorrow you will buy a plastic-making machine. From now on we'll make our own flowers. Sixth Uncle will help you and we will begin again.'

The man spat disgustedly, 'How can we pay, eh? How can we start? How can we . . .' He stopped and stared. They all gasped. Spectacles Wu had brought out the roll of bills. '*Ayeeyah*, Honored Younger Brother, I can see that at long last you have seen the wisdom of joining the Snake!'

'How wise!' the others chorused proudly. 'All gods bless Younger Brother!'

The young man said nothing. He knew they would not believe him if he said otherwise, so he let them believe. 'Tomorrow begin looking for a good secondhand machine. You can pay only $900,' he told the older man, knowing that 1,500 was available if necessary. Then he went outside and arranged with their cousin, the owner of this hut, to lease them a corner until they could rebuild, haggling over the price until it was correct. Satisfied that he had done what he could for the Wu clan, he left them and plodded downhill back to headquarters, his heart weeping, his whole soul wanting to shriek at the gods for their unfairness, or carelessness, for taking so many of them away, taking Fifth Niece who but a day or so ago was given back her life in another slide.

Don't be a fool, he ordered himself. Joss is joss. You have wealth in your pocket, a vast future with SI, Freedom Fighter to manufacture, and the time of dying is up to the gods.

Poor little Fifth Niece. So pretty, so sweet.

'Gods are gods,' he muttered wearily, echoing the last words he remembered her ever saying, then put her out of his mind.

77

6:30 P.M.:

Ah Tat hobbled up the wide staircase in the Great House, her old joints creaking, muttering to herself, and went along the Long Gallery, hating the gallery and the faces that seemed ever to be watching her. Too many ghosts here, she thought with superstitious dread, knowing too many of the faces in life, growing up in this house, born in this house eighty-five years ago. Uncivilized to hold their spirits in thrall by hanging their likenesses on the wall. Better to act civilized and cast them into memory where spirits belong.

As always when she saw the Hag's knife stuck through the heart of her father's portrait a shudder went through her. *Dew neh loh moh*, she thought, now there was a wild one, her with the unquenchable demon in her Jade Gate, ever secretly bemoaning the loss of *the tai-pan*, her husband's father, bemoaning her fate that she had married the weakling son and not the father, never to be bedded by the father, her Jade Gate unquenchable because of that.

Ayeeyah, and all the strangers that climbed these stairs over the years to enter her bed, barbarians of all nations, of all ages, shapes and sizes, to be cast aside like so much chaff once their essence had been taken and used up, the fire never touched.

Ah Tat shuddered again. All gods bear witness! The Jade Gate and the One-Eyed Monk are truly yin and yang, truly everlasting, truly godlike, both insatiable however much one consumes the other. Thank all gods my parents allowed me to take the vow of chastity, to devote my life to bringing up children, never to be split by a Steaming Stalk, never to be the same ever after. Thank all gods all women do not need men to elevate them to be one with the gods. Thank all gods some women wisely prefer women to cuddle and touch and kiss and enjoy. The Hag had had women too, many, when she was old, finding in their youth-filled arms pleasure but never satisfaction, not like me. Curious she would pillow with a civilized girl but not a civilized man who would surely have put out her fire, one way or another, with pillow tools or without. All gods bear witness, how many times did I tell her? Me the only one she would talk to about such things!

Poor fool, her with her twisted dreams of power, twisted dreams of lust, just like the old dowager empress—nightmares of a lifetime that no shaft could allay.

Ah Tat pulled her eyes off the knife and plodded onward. The House will never be whole until someone pulls out the knife and casts it into the sea—curse or no curse.

The old woman did not knock on the bedroom door but went in noiselessly so as not to wake him and stood over the vast double bed and looked down. This was the time she enjoyed most, when her man-child was still sleeping, alone, and she could see his sleeping face and study it and not have to worry about Chief Wife's spleen and ill-temper over her comings and goings.

Silly woman, she thought gravely, seeing the lines in his face. Why doesn't she do her duty as Chief Wife and provide my son with another wife, young, child bearing, a civilized person, like old Green-Eyed Devil had. Then this house would be bright again. Yes, the house needs more sons—stupid to risk posterity on the shoulders of one son. And stupid to leave this bull alone, stupid to leave his bed empty, stupid to leave him to be tempted by some mealy-mouthed whore to waste his essence in alien pastures. Why doesn't she realize we have the house to protect! Barbarians.

She saw his eyes open and focus and then he stretched luxuriously. 'Time to get up, my son,' she said, trying to sound harsh and commanding. 'You have to bathe and get dressed and make more phone calls, *heya*, and leave your poor old Mother with more chores and more work, *heya?*'

'Yes, Mother,' Dunross mumbled through a yawn in Cantonese, then shook himself like a dog, stretched once more and got out of bed and strode naked for the bathroom.

She studied his tall body critically, the crinkled, savage scars of the old burns from his airplane crash covering most of his legs. But the legs were strong, the flanks strong and the yang resolute and healthy. Good, she thought. I'm glad to see all's well. Even so, she was concerned at his perpetual leanness, with no substantial belly that his wealth and position merited. 'You're not eating enough, my son!'

'More than enough!'

'There's hot water in the bucket. Don't forget to wash your teeth.'

Contentedly she began to remake the bed. 'He needed that rest,' she muttered, not realizing she was talking aloud. 'He's been like a man possessed for the last week, working all hours, fear in his face and over him. Such fear can kill.' When she had finished the bed she called out, 'Now don't stay out late tonight. You must take care of yourself and if you go with a whore bring her here like a sensible person, *heya?*'

She heard him laugh and she was glad for it. There hasn't been enough laughter from him the last few days, she thought. 'A man needs laughter and youthful yin to nourish the yang. Eh what, what did you say?'

'I said, where's Number One Daughter?'

'In, out, always out, out with that barbarian,' she said going to the bathroom door and peering at him as he doused water over himself. 'The one with long hair and crumpled clothes who works for the *China Guardian*. I don't approve of him, my son. No, not at all!'

'Where are they "out", Ah Tat?'

The old woman shrugged, chomping her gums. 'The sooner Number One Daughter's married the better. Better for her to be another man's problem than yours. Or you should give her a good whip to her rump.' He laughed again and she wondered why he laughed this time. 'He's getting simple in the head,' she muttered, then turned away. At the far door, remembering, she called out, 'There's a small chow for you before you leave.'

'Don't worry about food . . .' Dunross stopped, knowing it was a waste of time. He heard her go off mumbling, closing the door after her.

He was standing in the bath and bailed more cold water over himself. Christ, I wish this bloody water shortage'd cease, he thought. I could use a really long hot shower, his mind inexorably zeroing in on Adryon. At once he heard Penelope's admonition, 'Do grow up, Ian! It really is her own life, do grow up!'

'I'm trying,' he muttered, toweling himself vigorously. Just before he had slept he had called Penelope. She was already at Castle Avisyard, Kathy still in the London clinic for more tests. 'She'll be coming up next week. I do so hope everything will be all right.'

'I'm in touch with the doctors, Penn.' He told her about sending Gavallan to Scotland. 'He's always wanted to be there, Kathy too, it'll be better for both of them, eh?'

'Oh, that's marvelous, Ian. That'll be a marvelous tonic.'

'They can take over the whole east wing.'

'Oh yes. Ian, the weather's wonderful today, wonderful, and the house so lovely. No chance you can come for a few days I suppose?'

'I'm up to my nose in it, Penn! You heard about the market?'

He had heard the momentary silence and he could see her face change and within her head hear her impotent raging against the market and Hong Kong and business, as much as she tried to cast it away.

'Yes. It must be terrible,' she had said, still a thread in her voice. 'Poor you. Alastair was carrying on a bit last night. It'll be all right, won't it?'

'Oh yes,' he said with great confidence, wondering what she would say if he told her that he would have to guarantee personally the Murtagh loan if it came through. Oh Christ let it come through. He gave her all the news, then told her that AMG had sent him a very interesting message that he would tell her about when he saw her, adding that the messenger was a Japanese-Swiss woman. 'She's quite a bird!'

'I hope not too much!'

'Oh no! How's Glenna and how're you?'

'Just fine. Have you heard from Duncan?'

'Yes. He arrives tomorrow—I'll get him to phone you the moment he's home. That's about it, Penn, love you!'

'I love you too and wish you were here. Oh, how's Adryon?'

'More of the same. She and that Haply fellow seem to be inseparable!'

'Do remember she's very grown up, darling, and don't worry about her. Just try to grow up yourself.'

He finished drying himself and looked at his reflection in the mirror, wondering if he was old for his years or young, not feeling any different from when he was nineteen—at university or at war. After a moment, he said, 'You're lucky to be alive, old chum. You're oh so lucky.' His sleep had been heavy and he had been dreaming about Tiptop and, just at waking, someone had said in his dream, 'What're you going to do?' I don't know, he thought. How far do I trust that bugger Sinders? Not far. But I got under his guard with my threat . . . no, my promise to publish the eleven pieces of paper. And I will, by God!

I'd better call Tiptop before I leave for Plumm's. I'd better . . .

His ears heard the bedroom door swing open again and Ah Tat padded back across the room to stand at the bathroom. 'Ah, my son, I forgot to tell you, there's a barbarian waiting for you downstairs.'

'Oh? Who?'

She shrugged. 'A barbarian. Not as tall as you. He has a strange name, and he's more ugly than usual with hair of straw!' She searched in her pocket and found the card. 'Here.'

The card read, Dave Murtagh III, Royal Belgium and Far East Bank. Dunross's stomach twisted. 'How long's he been waiting?'

'An hour, perhaps more.'

'*What?* Fornicate all gods. Why didn't you wake me?'

'Eh? Why didn't I wake you?' she asked caustically. 'Why? Why do you think? Am I a fool? A foreign devil? *Ayeeyah*, what is more important, him waiting or your rest? *Ayeeyah!*' she added disdainfully and stalked off, grumbling, 'As if I didn't know what was best for you.'

Dunross dressed hurriedly and rushed downstairs. Murtagh was sprawled out in an easy chair. He awoke with a start as the door opened. 'Oh, hi!'

'I'm terribly sorry, I was having a kip and didn't know you were here.'

'That's all right, tai-pan.' Dave Murtagh was haggard. 'The old biddy threatened the hell out of me if I so much as murmured but it didn't matter, I dropped off.' He stretched wearily, stifling a yawn and shook his head to try to clear it. 'Jesus, sorry to come uninvited but it's better than on the phone.'

Dunross held his aching disappointment off his face. It must be turndown, he thought. 'Whiskey?'

'Sure, with soda. Thanks. Jesus I'm tired.'

Dunross went to the decanter and poured, and a brandy and soda for himself. 'Health,' he said, resisting the urge to ask.

They touched glasses.

'Health. And you got your deal!' The young man's face cracked into an enormous grin. 'We did it!' he almost shouted. 'They screamed and they hollered but an hour ago they agreed. We got everything! 120 percent of the ships and a $50 million U.S. revolving fund, cash's up Wednesday, but you can commit Monday at 10:00 A.M., the offer of the tanker deals was the clincher. Jesus, we did it for chrissake!'

It took all of Dunross's training to hold in his bellow of triumph and keep the joy off his face and say calmly, 'Oh, jolly good,' and take another sip of his brandy. 'What's the matter?' he asked, seeing the shock on the younger man's face.

Murtagh shook his head and slumped down exhaustedly. 'You limeys're something else! I'll never understand you. I give you a hundred percent parole with the sweetest deal God ever gave man and all you say is "Oh jolly good".'

Dunross laughed. It was a great bellow of laughter and all his happiness spilled out. He pummeled Murtagh's hand and thanked him. 'How's that?' he asked, beaming.

'That's better!' He grabbed his briefcase and opened it and pulled out a sheaf of contracts and papers. 'These're just as we agreed. I was up all night drafting them. Here's the main loan agreement, this's your personal guarantee, these're for the corporate seal, ten copies of everything.'

'I'll initial one set now which you keep, you initial one which I'll keep and then we'll sign formally tomorrow morning. Can you meet me in my office tomorrow morning, say at 7:30? We'll chop all the documents an—'

The young man let out an involuntary moan. 'How 'bout 8:00, tai-pan, or 8:30? I just gotta catch up on some sleep.'

'7:30. You can sleep all day.' Dunross added at a sudden thought, 'Tomorrow night your evening's reserved.'

'It is?'

'Yes. You best get all the rest you can, your evening will be busy.'

'Doing what?'

'You're not married, you're not attached, so an entertaining evening wouldn't be bad. Eh?'

'Gee.' Murtagh brightened perceptibly. 'It'd be terrific.'

'Good. I'll send you to a friend of mine at Aberdeen. Gold-tooth Wu.'

'Who?'

'An old friend of the family. Perfectly safe. While I think of it, lunch at the races next week?'

'Oh Jesus, thanks. Yesterday Casey gave me a hot tip and I won a bundle. The rumor is you're going to ride Noble Star Saturday. Are you?'

'Perhaps.' Dunross kept his eyes on him. 'The deal's really through? No chance of a foul-up?'

'Cross my heart and hope to die! Oh here I forgot.' He handed him the confirming telex. 'It's as we agreed.' Murtagh glanced at his watch. 'It's 6:00 A.M. New York time now but you're to call S. J. Beverly, our chairman of the board, in an hour—he's expecting your call. Here's his number.' The young man beamed. 'They made me VP in charge of all Asia.'

'Congratulations.'

Dunross saw the time. He would have to leave soon or he would be late and he did not want to keep Riko waiting. His heart picked up a beat. 'Let's initial now, shall we?'

Murtagh was already sorting the papers. 'Just one thing, tai-pan, S.J. said we got to keep this secret.'

'That's going to be difficult. Who typed these?'

'My secretary—but she's American, she's as tight as a clam.'

Dunross nodded but inside he was unconvinced. The telex operator—didn't Phillip Chen say he had already had copies of some of the telexes?—or cleaners, or phone operators, it would be impossible to gauge who but the news would be common knowledge soon, whatever he or Murtagh did. Now, how to use everything to the best advantage while it's still secret? he was asking himself, hard put not to dance with joy, the fact of the deal unprecedented and almost impossible to believe. He began to initial his set of papers, Murtagh another. He stopped as he heard the front door open and slam. Adryon shrieked, '*Ah*

Tat!' and followed up with a flood of *amah* Cantonese ending, '. . . and did you iron my new blouse by all the gods?'

'Blouse? What blouse, Young Miss with the piercing voice and no patience? The red one? The red one belonging to Chief Wife and who told y—'

'Oh, it's mine now, Ah Tat! I told you very seriously to iron it.'

Murtagh had stopped too, listening to the stream of screeching Cantonese from both of them. 'Jesus,' he said tiredly, 'I'll never get used to the way the servants go on, no matter what you tell 'em!'

Dunross laughed and beckoned him, opening the door softly, Murtagh gasped. Adryon had her hands on her hips and she was going at Ah Tat who gave it back to her, both of them raucous, both talking over the other and neither listening.

'*Quiet!'* Dunross said. Both stopped. 'Thank you. You really do go on a bit, Adryon!' he said mildly.

She beamed. 'Oh hello, Father. Do you th—' She stopped, seeing Murtagh. Dunross noticed the instant change. A warning shaft soared through him.

'Oh, Adryon, may I introduce Dave Murtagh, Vice-President for Asia of the Royal Belgium and Far East Bank?' He looked at Murtagh and saw the stunned expression on his face. 'This is my daughter, Adryon.'

'You, er, speak Chinese, Miss, er, Dunross?'

'Oh yes, yes of course, Cantonese. Of course. You're new in Hong Kong?'

'Oh no, ma'am, no, I've, er, I've been here half a year or more.'

Dunross was watching both of them with growing amusement, knowing that for the moment he was totally forgotten. Ah, boy meets girl, girl meets boy and maybe this one'd be the perfect foil to throw into Haply's works. 'Would you like to join us for a drink, Adryon?' he asked casually, the moment their conversation lapsed and she prepared to leave.

'Oh. Oh thank you, Father, but I don't want to disturb you.'

'We're just finishing. Come along. How're things?'

'Oh fine, fine.' Adryon turned back to Ah Tat who still stood there solidly—she too had noticed the instant mutual attraction.

'You'll iron my blouse! Please,' she said imperiously in Cantonese. 'I have to leave in fifteen minutes.'

'*Ayeeyah* on your fifteen minutes, Young Empress.' Ah Tat huffed, and went back into the kitchen, grumbling.

Adryon focused on Murtagh who blossomed noticeably, his fatigue vanished. 'What part of the States are you from?'

'Texas, ma'am, though I've spent time in Los Angeles, New York and New Orleans. You play tennis?'

'Oh, yes, I do.'

'We've some good courts at the American Club. You, maybe you'd like a game next week?'

'I'd love that. I've played there before. Are you good?'

'Oh no, ma'am, er, Miss Dunross, just college class.'

'College class could mean very good. Why don't you call me Adryon?'

Dunross gave her the glass of sherry he had poured and she thanked him with a smile though still concentrating on Murtagh. You'd better be top of your class, young fellow, he thought, knowing how competitive she was, or you're in for a drubbing. Carefully keeping his amusement private, he went back to the papers. When he finished initialing his set, he watched the two of them critically, his daughter sitting casually on the edge of the sofa, beautiful and so assured, very much a woman, and Murtagh tall and well mannered, a little shy, but holding his own very well.

Could I stand a banker in the family? I'd better check up on him! God help us, an American? Well he's Texan, and that's not the same, is it? I wish Penn were back here.

'. . . oh no, Adryon,' Murtagh was saying. 'I've a company apartment over at West Point. It's a little bitty place but great.'

'That makes such a difference, doesn't it? I live here but I'm going to have my own apartment soon.' She added pointedly, 'Aren't I, Father?'

'Of course.' Dunross added at once, 'After university! Here's my set, Mr. Murtagh, do you think you could sign yours?'

'Oh yes . . . oh sorry!' Murtagh almost ran over, hurriedly initialed his set with a flourish. 'Here you are, sir. You, er, you said 7:30 at your office tomorrow morning, huh?'

Adryon arched an eyebrow. 'You'd better be punctual, Dave, the tai-pan's uncomfortably ornery at unpunctuality.'

1309

'Rubbish,' Dunross said.

'I love you, Father, but that's not rubbish!'

They chatted for a minute then Dunross glanced at his watch, pretending to be concerned. 'Damn! I've got to make a phone call then rush.' At once Murtagh picked up his briefcase but Dunross added blandly, 'Adryon, you said you were leaving in a few minutes. I wonder, would you have time to drop Mr. Murtagh?'

The young man said at once, 'Oh, I can get a cab, there's no need to trouble yoursel—'

'Oh it's no trouble,' she said happily, 'no trouble at all. West Point's on my way.'

Dunross said good night and left them. They hardly noticed his going. He went to his study and closed the door and with the closing of the door, shut out everything else but Tiptop. From the fireplace Dirk Struan watched him. Dunross stared back a moment.

'I've plan A, B or C,' he said aloud. 'They all add up to disaster if Sinders doesn't perform.'

The eyes just smiled in their curious way.

'It was easy for you,' Dunross muttered. 'When someone got in your way you could kill them, even the Hag.'

Earlier he had discussed the plans with Phillip Chen. 'They're all fraught with danger,' his compradore had said, very concerned.

'Which do you advise?'

'The choice must be yours, tai-pan. You will have to make personal guarantees. It's face too, though I'd support you in everything, and you did ask for a *favor* as an Old Friend.'

'What about Sir Luis?'

'I've arranged to see him tonight, tai-pan. I hope for co-operation.' Phillip Chen had seemed grayer and older than ever. 'It's a pity there's nothing we can give Tiptop in case Sinders reneges.'

'What about bartering the tanker fleet? Can we lean on Vee Cee? What about thoriums—or Joseph Yu?'

'Tiptop needs something to barter with, not a threat, tai-pan. Did P.B. say he'd help?'

'He promised to phone Tiptop this afternoon—he said he'd also try one of his friends in Peking.'

At exactly seven o'clock Dunross dialed. 'Mr. Tip, please. Ian Dunross.'

'Good evening, tai-pan. How are you? I hear you may be riding Noble Star next Saturday?'

'That's possible.' They talked about inconsequential matters, then Tiptop said, 'And that unfortunate person? At the latest, when is he going to be released?'

'Dunross held on to himself, then committed his future. 'Sunset tomorrow, at Lo Wu.'

'Do you personally guarantee he will be there?'

'I personally guarantee I've done everything in my power to persuade the authorities to release him.'

'That's not the same as saying the man will be there. Is it?'

'No. But he'll be there. I'm . . .' Dunross stopped. He was going to say, 'almost certain' and then he knew he would surely fail—not daring to guarantee it because a failure to perform would take away his face, his credulity, forever—but he remembered something Phillip Chen had said about Tiptop having something to barter with and all at once he had an opening. 'Listen, Mr. Tip,' he began, his sudden excitement almost nauseating. 'These are foul times. Old Friends need Old Friends like never before. Privately, very privately, I hear that our Special Branch in the last two days discovered there's a major Soviet spy ring here, a deep-cover ring, the code name of the operation Sevrin. The purpose of Sevrin's the destruction of the Middle Kingdom's link with the rest of the world.'

'That's nothing new, tai-pan. Hegemonists will always be hegemonists, Tsarist Russia or Soviet Russia, there's no difference. For four hundred years it's been that way. Four hundred years since their first incursions and theft of our lands. But please go on.'

'It's my belief Hong Kong and the Middle Kingdom are equal targets. We're your only window on the world. Old Green-Eyed Devil was the first to see that and it's true. Any interruption here and only the hegemonists will gain. Some documentation, part of the Special Branch documentation has come into my hands.' With complete accuracy Dunross began to quote verbatim from the stolen head documents in AMG's report, his mind seeming to read from the pages that effortlessly appeared from his memory. He gave Tiptop all the pertinent

1311

details of Sevrin, the spies, and about the police mole.

There was a shocked silence. 'What's the date on the Sevrin head document, tai-pan?'

'It was approved by an "L.B." on March 14, 1950.'

A long sigh. Very long. 'Lavrenti Beria?'

'I don't know.' The more Dunross thought about this new ploy the more excited he became, certain now that this information and proof positive in the right Peking hands would cause a tidal wave in Soviet-Chinese relations.

'Is it possible to see this document?'

'Yes. Yes it would be possible,' Dunross said, sweat on his back, thanking his foresight in photocopying the Sevrin sections of AMG's report.

'And the Czechoslovak STB document you referred to?'

'Yes. The part I have.'

'When was that dated?'

'April 6, 1959.'

'So our so-called allies were always wolf's heart and dog's lungs?'

'I'm afraid so.'

'Why is it Europe and those capitalists in America don't understand who the real enemy in the world is? *Heya?*'

'It's difficult to understand,' Dunross said, playing a waiting game now.

After a pause, controlled once more, Tiptop said, 'I'm sure my friends would like a copy of this, this Sevrin paper, and any supporting documents.'

Dunross wiped the sweat off his forehead but kept his voice calm. 'As an Old Friend, it's my privilege to assist in any way I can.'

Another silence. 'A mutual friend called to offer his support to your request for the Bank of China's cash and a few minutes ago I was told that a very important person called from Peking to suggest any help that could be given in your need would be merited.' Another silence and Dunross could almost feel Tiptop and the others who were probably listening on the phone weighing, nodding or shaking their heads. 'Could you excuse me a moment, tai-pan, there's someone at the door.'

'Would you like me to call you back?' he said at once to give them time to consider.

'No, that won't be necessary—if you don't mind waiting a moment.'

Dunross heard the phone put down. A radio was playing in the background. Indeterminate sounds that might be muffled voices. His heart was racing. The waiting seemed to go on forever. Then the phone was picked up again.

'Sorry, tai-pan. Please send those copies early—would after your morning meeting be convenient?'

'Yes, yes certainly.'

'Please give Mr. David MacStruan my best wishes when he arrives.'

Dunross almost dropped the phone but recovered in time. 'I'm sure he would wish me to return them. How is Mr. Yu?' he asked, stabbing in the dark, wanting to scream down the phone 'What about the money?' But he was heavily engaged in a Chinese negotiation. His caution increased.

Another silence. 'Fine,' Tiptop said but Dunross had heard a different tone. 'Oh, that reminds me,' Tiptop was saying, 'Mr. Yu phoned from Canton this afternoon. He would like to bring the date of your meeting forward, if that's possible. To two weeks tomorrow, Monday.'

Dunross thought a moment. That was the week he would be in Japan with Toda Shipping negotiating his whole buy-lease-back scheme that, now that First Central was backing him, would have an enormous chance of success. 'That Monday's difficult. The following one would be better for me. Could I confirm to you by Friday?'

'Yes, certainly. Well, I won't keep you anymore, tai-pan.'

Dunross 's tension became almost unbearable now that the final stage had been reached. His listened intently to the pleasant, friendly voice.

'Thank you for your information. I presume that that poor fellow will be at Lo Wu border by sunset. Oh, by the way, if the necessary bank papers are brought in person by Mr. Havergill, yourself and the governor at 9:00 A.M. tomorrow, a half a billion dollars of cash can be transferred to the Victoria immediately.'

Instantly Dunross saw through the ploy. 'Thank you,' he said easily, avoiding the trap. 'Mr. Havergill and I will be there. Unfortunately I understand the governor has been ordered by the prime minister's office to remain at Government House until noon, for consultations. But I will bring his authority and chop, guaranteeing the loan,' he added, for of course, it would be impossible for the governor to go personally, cap in hand, like a common debtor and so create an unacceptable precedent. 'I presume that will be satisfactory.'

Tiptop's voice was almost a purr. 'I'm sure the bank would be prepared to delay until noon to accommodate the governor's duty.'

'Before and after noon he will be on the streets with the riot police, Mr. Tip, and the army, directing possible procedures against misguided riots stirred up by hegemonists. He is of course commander-in-chief, Hong Kong.'

Tiptop's voice sharpened. 'Surely even a commander-in-chief can take a few precious moments for what is obviously such an important matter?'

'It would be his pleasure, I'm sure,' Dunross said, unafraid, knowing the art of Asian negotiation, prepared for rage, honey and everything in between. 'But the protection of the Middle Kingdom's interest as well as that of the Colony would be uppermost in his mind. I'm sure, regretfully, he would have to refuse until the emergency was over.'

There was a hostile silence. 'Then what would you suggest?'

Again Dunross sidestepped the trap, leaping to the next level, 'Oh, by the way, his aide-de-camp asked me to mention that his Excellency is having a party for a few of our most important Chinese citizens at the races next Saturday and he wondered if you would happen to be in the Colony so he could send you an invitation?' He held on to his hope. Putting it that way gave Tiptop the option of accepting or refusing without loss of face—and, at the same time, protected the face of the governor who would thus avoid sending such a politically important invitation that might be refused. Dunross smiled to himself, since the governor knew nothing yet about this important party he would be giving.

Another silence while Tiptop considered the political implications. 'Please thank him for his consideration. I believe I will be here. May I confirm it Tuesday?'

'I will be glad to pass your message on.' Dunross considered mentioning Brian Kwok but decided to leave that in limbo. 'Will you be at the bank at 9:00 A.M., Mr. Tip?'

1314

'Oh no. It is really nothing to do with me. I'm merely an interested bystander.' Another silence. 'Your representatives should see the chief manager.'

Dunross sighed, all his senses honed. No mention of the governor's physical presence. Have I won? 'I wonder if someone could confirm to Radio Hong Kong, in time for tonight's nine o'clock news, that the Bank of China is extending the Colony an immediate credit of one half a billion dollars of cash.'

Another silence. 'Oh I'm sure that's not necessary, Mr. Dunross,' Tiptop said and now, for the first time, there was a chuckle in his voice. 'Surely the word of the tai-pan of the Noble House is sufficient for a simple capitalist radio station. Good night.'

Dunross put down the phone. His fingers were trembling. There was an ache in his back and his heart was pounding. 'Half a billion dollars!' he muttered, his mind blown. 'No paper, no chop, no handshake, a few phone calls, a little negotiation and one half a billion dollars *will be* available for transfer by truck at 9:00 A.M.!'

We've won! Murtagh's money and now China's! Yes. But how to use this knowledge to the best advantage? How? he asked himself helplessly. No point in going to Plumm's now. What to do? What to do?

His knees felt weak, his mind was buzzing with plan and counterplan. Then his pent-up excitement erupted in a huge bellow that richocheted off his study walls, and he jumped up and down and let out another war cry that melted into a laugh. He went into the bathroom to splash water on his face. He ripped off his soaking shirt, not bothering about the buttons and threw it into a trash can. The study door whirled open. Adryon rushed in, white-faced and anxious. 'Father!'

'Good God what's up?' Dunross said, aghast.

'What's up with you? I heard you shout like a mad bull. Are you all right?'

'Oh, oh yes I'm, I, er, I just stubbed my toe!' Dunross's happiness exploded again and he caught her up, lifting her easily. 'Thank you, my darling, everything's fine! Oh very fine!'

'Oh, thank God,' she said and at once added, 'Then I can have my own flat starting next month?'

'Ye—' He caught himself just in time. 'Oh no you don't, Miss

Smarty Pants. Just because I'm happy th—'

'But Father, do—'

'No. Thank you, Adryon, but no. Off you go!'

She glared at him then burst out laughing. 'I almost caught you that time!'

'Yes, yes you did! Don't forget Duncan's in tomorrow on the Qantas noon flight.'

'I won't, don't worry. I'll meet him. It'll be fun to have Dunc back, haven't had a good game of billiards since he left. Where're you off to now?'

'I was going to Plumm's at Rose Court to celebrate the General Foods takeover but I don't th—'

'Martin thought that was a wonderful coup! If the stock market doesn't crash. I told the silly man you were bound to arrange everything.'

All at once Dunross realized that Plumm's party would be the ideal place. Gornt would be there, Phillip Chen and all the others. Gornt! Now I can put that bugger away for all time, he told himself, his heart racing. 'Is Murtagh still downstairs?'

'Oh yes. We were just leaving. He's dreamy.'

Dunross turned away to hide a smile and grabbed a clean silk shirt. 'Could you hang on a second? I've got some rather good news for him.'

'All right.' She came over to him, big blue eyes. 'My own flat for a Christmas present, pretty please?'

'After university, if you qualify, off you go!'

'Christmas. I'll love you forever.'

He sighed, remembering how upset and frightened she had been seeing Gornt in the billiards room. Perhaps I can give you a present of his head tomorrow, he thought. 'Not this Christmas, next!'

She hurled her arms around his neck. 'Oh thank you Daddy darling but this Christmas, please please please.'

'No, because yo—'

'Please please please!'

'All right. But don't tell your mother I agreed for God's sake! She'll skin me alive!'

78

7:15 P.M.:

The curtains around Orlanda's bed moved gently, touched by the night breeze, the air clean and salt tasting. She was in his arms as they slept, a pervading warmth between them, and then, as her hand moved, Bartlett awoke. For a moment he wondered where he was and who he was, and then everything came back and his heart picked up a beat. Their lovemaking had been wonderful. He remembered how she had responded, cresting again and again, lifting him to heights he had never experienced before. And then the after. She had got out of bed and walked to the kitchen and warmed water and brought back a hot, wet towel and toweled the sweat off him. 'I'm so sorry there's no bath or shower, my darling, that's such a shame, but if you're patient I can make everything nice.'

A new clean towel and feeling grand, never before knowing the wonder of a real afterward—her gentle ministrations, tender, loving, unself-conscious, the tiny crucifix around her neck her only adornment. He had noticed it glinting in the half-light. Its implications had begun to seep into his brain but somehow, all at once, she was caressing the alien thoughts away with magic hands and touch and lips until, in time, they had both become one with the gods again and, through their generosity, slid into euphoria—and thence into sleep again.

Idly he watched the curtains that fell from the ceiling waver in the air currents, their surrounding embrace making the bed more intimate, the patterns against the light of the window pleasing, everything pleasing. He lay still, not wishing to move to awaken her, not wanting to break the spell, her breath soft against his chest, her sleep face blemishless.

1317

What to do, what to do, what to do?

Nothing, for the moment, he answered himself. The airplane's free, you're free, she's unbelievable and no woman's ever pleased you more. Never. But can it last, could it last—and then there's Casey.

Bartlett sighed. Orlanda moved again in her sleep. He waited but she did not waken.

His eyes were mesmerized by the patterns, his spirit at rest. It was neither hot nor cold in the room; everything was perfect, her weight imperceptible. What is it about her? he asked himself. What causes the spell, because sure as death and taxes you're under a spell, enchanted. We've pillowed, that's all. I've made no promises and yet . . . You're enchanted, old buddy.

Yes. And it's wonderful.

He closed his eyes and drifted into sleep.

When Orlanda awoke she was careful not to move. She did not want to awaken him, both for his pleasure and for hers. And she wanted time to think. Sometimes she would do that in Gornt's arms but she knew it was not the same, would never be the same. Always she had been afraid of Quillan, on guard, desperately wanting to please, wondering if she had forgotten anything. No, she thought in ecstasy, this pillowing was better than I ever remember it with Quillan, oh so much better. Linc's so clean and no smoke taste, just clean and wonderful and I promise by the Madonna I will make him a perfect wife, I'll be the best that ever was. I will use my mind and hands and lips and body to please and to satisfy and there will be nothing he needs that I will not do. Nothing. Everything that Quillan taught me I will do for Linc, even the things I did not enjoy, I will enjoy now with Linc. My body and soul will be an instrument for his pleasure, and for mine, when he's learned.

She smiled to herself, curled up in his arms. Linc's technique is nothing in comparison with Quillan's but what my darling lacks in skill he more than makes up with strength and vigor. And tenderness. He has magic hands and lips for me. Never never never before was it ever like this.

'Pillowing's just the beginning of sex, Orlanda,' Gornt had said. 'You can become an enchantress. You can fill a man with such an unquenchable longing that, through you, he will

1318

understand all life.' But to reach ecstasy you have to seek it and work for it.

Oh I will seek it for Linc. By the Madonna I will put my mind and my heart and my soul to his life. When he's angry I will turn it into calm. Didn't I stop Quillan's anger a thousand times by being gentle? Isn't it wonderful to have so much power, and oh so easy once I had learned, so very easy and perfect and satisfying.

I will read all the best papers and train my mind, and after the Clouds and the Rain I will not speak, just caress, not to arouse but just for pleasure and I'll never say, 'Tell me you love me!' but say only, 'Linc I love you.' And long before the bloom is off my skin I will have sons to excite him and daughters to delight him and then, long before I'm no longer exciting to him, I will very carefully arrange another for his pleasure, a dullard with beautiful breasts and tight rump and I will be suitably amused and benign—and compassionate when he fails, for by then he will be much older and less virile and my hands will control the money and I will be ever more essential. And when he tires of the first I will find another, and we will live out our lives, yang and yin, the yin ever dominating the yang!

Yes. I will be *tai-tai*.

And one day he will ask to go to Portugal to see my daughter and I will refuse the first time and the second and third time and then we will go—if I have our son in my arms. Then he will see *her* and love *her* too, and that specter will be laid to rest forever.

Orlanda sighed, feeling wonderful, weightless, with his head resting comfortably against her chest. Pillowing without precautions is so much more glorious, she thought. Ecstasy. Oh so wonderful to feel the surge, knowing you're young and fertile and ready, giving yourself totally, deliberately, praying to create a new life—his life and yours joined forever. Oh yes.

Yes but have you been wise? Have you? Say he leaves you? The only other time in your life you deliberately left yourself free was that single month with Quillan. But that was with permission. This time you have none.

Say Linc leaves you. Perhaps he'll be furious and tell you to stop the child!

He won't, she told herself with complete confidence. Linc's not Quillan. There's nothing to worry about. Nothing.

Madonna, please help me! All gods help me! Let his seed grow, oh please please please, I beg you with all my heart.

Bartlett stirred and half awoke. 'Orlanda?'

'Yes, my darling, I'm here. Oh how wonderful you are!' She cradled him happily, so glad that she had given her *amah* the day and the night away. 'Go back to sleep, we've all the time in the world, sleep.'

'Yes but . . .'

'Sleep. In a little while I'm going to fetch some Chinese food an—'

'Maybe you'd like t—'

'Sleep, my darling. Everything's arranged.'

79

7:30 P.M.:

Three stories below on the other side of the building, facing the mountainside, Four Finger Wu was watching television. He was in Venus Poon's apartment, in front of her set, his shoes off, his tie loose, sprawled in the easy chair. The old *amah* was sitting on a stiff chair beside him and they both guffawed at the antics of Laurel and Hardy.

'Eeeeee, the Fat One's going to catch his fornicating foot in the scaffolding,' he chortled, 'and the—'

'And the Thin One's going to hit him with the plank! Eeeeee.'

They both laughed at the routine they had seen a hundred times in a hundred re-re-reruns of the old black-and-white movies. Then the film ended and Venus Poon reappeared to announce the next program and he sighed. She was looking directly at him from the box and he—along with every other male viewer—was certain that her smile was for him alone, and though he did not understand her English, he understood her very well. His eyes were glued to her breasts that had fascinated him for hours, examining them closely, never seeing or feeling a sign of the surgical interference that all Hong Kong whispered about.

'I attest your tits are blemishless, certainly the biggest and best I've ever touched,' he had volunteered importantly, still mounted, the night before last.

'You're just saying that to please your poor impoverished Daughter oh oh oh!'

'Impoverished? Ha! Didn't Banker Kwang give you that miserable fur yesterday and I hear he added an extra 1,000 to his monthly check! And *me*, didn't I supply the winner of the first, third and the runner-up in the fifth? 30,000 those brought you

1321

minus 15 percent for my informant—for less effort than it takes me to fart!'

'P'shaw! That 25,800 HK's not worth talking about, I have to buy my own wardrobe, a new costume every day! My public demands it, I have my public to think of.'

They had argued back and forth until, feeling the moment of truth approaching, he had asked her to move her buttocks more vigorously. She had obliged with such enthusiasm that he was left a husk. When at length he had miraculously recovered his spirit from the Void he choked out, '*Ayeeyah*, Little Strumpet, if you can do that one more time I'll give you a diamond ring the—no, no, not now by all the gods! Am I a god? Not now, Little Mealy Mouth, no, not now and not tomorrow but the next day. . . .'

And now it was the next day. Elated and filled with anticipation he watched her on television, all smiles and dimples as she said good night and the new program began. Tonight was her early night and in his mind he could almost see her hurry out of the TV station to his waiting Rolls, sure that she would be just as anxious. He had sent Paul Choy with the Rolls to escort her to the station tonight, to talk English with her, to ensure she arrived safely and returned quickly. And then, after their new bout, the Rolls would take them to the barbarian eating palace in the barbarian hotel with its foul barbarian food and foul smells but one of the places where all the tai-pans go, and all important, civilized persons go with their wives—and, when their wives were busy, with their whores—so he could show off his mistress and how rich he was to all Hong Kong, and she could show off the diamond.

'*Ayeeyah*,' he chortled out loud.

'Eh, Honored Lord?' the *amah* asked suspiciously. 'What's amiss?'

'Nothing, nothing. Please give me some brandy.'

'My mistress doesn't like the brandy smell!'

'Huh, old woman, give me brandy. Am I a fool? Am I a barbarian from the Outer Provinces? Of course I have fragrant tea leaves to chew before our bout. Brandy!'

She went off grumbling but he paid her no attention—she was trying to protect her mistress's interests and that was perfectly correct.

1322

His fingers touched the small box in his pocket. He had purchased the ring this morning, wholesale, from a first cousin who owed him a favor. The stone was worth 48,000 at least though the real cost was barely half that amount, the quality blue-white and excellent, the carats substantial.

Another bout like the last one will be well worth it, he thought ecstatically, though a little uneasily. Oh yes. Eeee, that last time I thought my spirit was truly gone forever into the Void, taken by the gods at the height of all life! Eeee, how lucky I would be to go thence, at the exact moment! Yes, but more wonderful to come back to storm the Jade Gate again and again and once more!

He laughed out loud, daring the gods, very content. Today had been excellent for him. He had met secretly with Smuggler Yuen and White Powder Lee and they had elected him chief of their new Brotherhood, which was only right, he thought. Hadn't he supplied the link to the marketplace through the foreign devil Ban—whatever his name was—because he had lent money to Number One Son Chen who, in return for such favors, had proposed the gun into opium scheme to him but had had the stupidity to be kidnapped and now murdered? Oh yes. And wasn't he meeting with the same foreign devil in Macao next week to arrange finances, payments, to set into motion the whole vast operation? Of course he should be High Tiger, of course he should have the most profit! With their combined expertise—and Profitable Choy's modern techniques—he could revolutionize the smuggling of the opium into Hong Kong, and once here, revolutionize the conversion of the raw narcotic into the immensely profitable White Powders, and finally, the means of export to the markets of the world. Now that Paul Choy was already in the shipping and air freighting department of Second Big Company and two grandsons of Yuen, also American trained, in their customs broking operation—and another four English university-trained relations of White Powder Lee placed within Noble House's Kai Tak go-down operations and All Asia Air's loading and unloading division, imports and exports would be ever safer, easier and ever more profitable.

They had discussed who they would co-opt in the police, particularly Marine.

'None of the barbarians, never one of those fornicators,' White Powder Lee had said hotly. 'They won't support us, never. Not in drugs. We must use only the Dragons.'

'Agreed. All the Dragons have all been approached and all will cooperate. All except Tang-po of Kowloon.'

'We must have Kowloon, he's senior and Marine operates from there. Is he holding out for a better deal personally? Or is he against us?'

'I don't know. At the moment.' Four Fingers had shrugged. 'Tang-po is up to the High Dragon to solve. The High Dragon has agreed, so it is agreed.'

Yes, Four Fingers thought, I outsmarted them to make me High Tiger and I outsmarted Profitable Choy on my money. I didn't give the young fornicator control of my fortune to gamble with as he thought I would. Oh no! I'm not that much of a fool! I only let him have 2 million and promised him 17 percent of all profit—let's see what he can do with that. Yes. Let's see what he can do with that!

The old man's heart picked up and he scratched himself. I'll bet the cunning young man'll triple it within the week, he told himself gleefully, not a little awed—the diamond paid for by his son's wits from the first profit on the stock sale, and a year of Venus Poon already allocated from the same source and not a copper cash of his own capital to lay out! Eeeee! And the cunning schemes Profitable comes up with! Like the one to deal with the tai-pan tomorrow when we meet.

Anxiously his fingers reached up and touched the half-coin that was on the heavy thong around his neck under his shirt, a coin like that his illustrious ancestor, Wu Fang Choi, had called upon to claim a clipper ship to rival the finest in Dirk Struan's fleet. But Wu Fang Choi, he thought grimly, had been the fool—he had never demanded safe passage for the ship as part of his favor and so had been outsmarted by the Green-Eyed Devil, the tai-pan.

Yes, by all the gods, it was Wu Fang Choi's own fault he lost. But he didn't lose everything. He hunted down that hunchback called Stride Orlov who ruled the ships of the Noble House for Culum the Weak. His men caught Orlov ashore in Singapore and brought him in chains to Taiwan where his headquarters were. There he tied him to a post, just at high-water mark, and drowned him very slowly.

I won't be foolish like Wu Fang Choi. No. I will make sure my ask from this tai-pan is watertight.

Tomorrow, the tai-pan will agree to open his ships to my cargoes—secretly of course; will agree to open some of the Noble House accounts for me to hide in—secretly of course, though to his great profit; will agree, equally secretly, to finance with me the vast new pharmaceutical plant that, *oh ko*, Profitable Choy says will be the perfect, legitimate undetectable narcotic smoke screen for me and mine forever; and last, the tai-pan will intercede with the half-person, Lando Mata, and choose my name and my suggested syndicate to replace the existing Macao gold and gambling syndicate of Tightfist Tung and the Chin, and he, the tai-pan, he will promise to be part of it.

Four Finger Wu was filled with ecstasy. The tai-pan will have to agree to everything. Everything. And everything is within his fief.

'Here's the brandy.'

Four Finger Wu took it from the *amah* and sipped it dreamily, with vast enjoyment. All gods bear witness: For seventy-six years, I, Four Finger Wu, Head of the Seaborne Wu, have lived life to the full and if you gods will take my spirit during the Clouds and the Rain, I will sing your praises in heaven—if there is a heaven—forever more. And if you don't . . .

The old man shrugged to himself and beamed and curled his toes. He yawned and closed his eyes, warm and toasty and very happy. Gods are gods and gods sleep and make mistakes but as sure as the great storms will come this year and next, Little Strumpet will earn her diamond tonight. Now which way should it be, he asked himself, going to sleep.

The taxi stopped at the foyer below. Suslev got out drunkenly and paid the man, then, reeling slightly, stepped over the rainwater swirling in the gutters and went in.

There was a crowd of people chattering and waiting at the elevator and he recognized Casey and Jacques deVille among them. Unsteadily he belched his way down the stairs to the lower level, crossed the garage and banged on Clinker's door.

'Hello, matey,' Clinker said.

'*Tovarich!*' Suslev gave him a bear hug.

'Vodka's up! Beer's up. Mabel, say hello to the captain!' The sleepy old bulldog just opened one eye, chomped her gums and farted loudly.

Clinker sighed and shut the door. 'Poor old Mabel! Wish to Christ she wouldn't do that, the place gets proper niffy! Here.' He handed Suslev a full glass of water with a wink. 'It's your favorite, old mate. 120 proof.'

Suslev winked back and slurped the water loudly. 'Thanks, old shipmate. Another of these'n I'll sail away from this capitalist paradise happily!'

'Another of those,' Clinker guffawed, keeping up the pretense, 'an' you'll slip out'uv Hong Kong harbor on your knees!' He refilled the glass. 'How long you staying tonight?'

'Just had to have some last drinks with you, eh? So long as I leave here by ten I'm fine. Drink up!' he roared with forced bonhomie. 'Let's have some music, eh?'

Happily Clinker turned on the tape recorder, loud. The sad Russian ballad filled the room.

Suslev put his lips close to Clinker's ear. 'Thanks, Ernie. I'll be back in good time.'

'All right,' Clinker winked, still believing Suslev's cover that he had an assignation with a married woman in Sinclair Towers. 'Who is she, eh?' He had never asked before.

'No names, no pack drill,' Suslev whispered with a broad grin. 'But her husband's a nob, a capitalist swine and on the legislature!'

Clinker beamed. 'Smashing! Give her one for me, eh?'

Suslev went down the trapdoor and found the flashlight. Water dripped from the cracked concrete roof of the tunnel, the cracks bigger than before. Small avalanches of rubble made the floor precarious and slippery. His nervousness increased, not liking the closeness, nor the necessity to go to meet Crosse, wanting to be far away, safe on his ship with a complete alibi when Dunross was drugged and snatched. But Crosse had been adamant.

'Goddamn it, Gregor, you have to be there! I've got to see you in person and I'm certainly not going aboard the *Ivanov*. It's perfectly safe, I guarantee it!'

1326

Guarantee? Suslev thought angrily again. How can one guarantee anything? He took out the snub-nosed automatic with the silencer, checked it and clicked off the safety catch. Then he continued again, picking his way carefully, and climbed the ladder to the false cupboard. Once on the stairs, he stopped and listened, holding his breath, all his concentration seeking danger. Finding none, he began to breathe easier, went up the stairs silently and into the apartment. Light from the high rise just below and from the city came through the windows and illuminated everything well enough for him to see. He checked the apartment thoroughly. When he had finished he went to the refrigerator and opened a bottle of beer. Absently he stared out of the windows. From where he was he could not see his ship but he knew where she would be and that thought gave him another good feeling. I'll be glad to leave, he thought. And sorry. I want to come back—Hong Kong's too good—but can I?

What about Sinders? Dare I trust him?

Suslev's heart hurt in his chest. Without a doubt, his future was in the balance. It would be easy for his own KGB people to prove he had fingered Metkin. Center could get that out of Roger Crosse by a simple phone call—if they hadn't already come to the same conclusion themselves.

May Sinders rot in hell! I know he'll shop me—I would if I was him. Will Roger know the secret deal Sinders put to me? No. Sinders would keep that secret, secret even from Roger. It doesn't matter. Once I've passed *anything* over to the other side I'm in his power forever.

The minutes ticked by. There was the sound of an elevator. At once he went into a defensive position. His finger slid the safety catch off: a key turned in the lock. The door opened and closed quickly.

'Hello, Gregor,' Crosse said softly. 'I wish you wouldn't point that bloody thing at me.'

Suslev put the safety catch on. 'What's so important? What about that turd Sinders? What'd he—'

'Calm down and listen.' Crosse took out a roll of microfilm, his pale blue eyes unusually excited. 'Here's a gift. It's expensive but all the real AMG files're on that film.'

'Eh?' Suslev stared at him. 'But how?' He listened as Crosse told him about the vault, ending, 'and after Dunross left I photographed the files and put them back.'

'Is the film developed?'

'Oh yes. I made one print which I read and at once destroyed. That's safer than giving it to you and risk your being stopped and searched—Sinders is on the warpath. What the devil happened between you and him?'

'First tell me about the files, Roger.'

'Sorry, but they're the same as the other ones, word for word. No difference.'

'What?'

'Yes. Dunross was telling us the truth. The copies he gave us are exact patterns.'

Suslev was shocked. 'But we were sure, you were sure!'

Crosse shrugged and passed over the film. 'Here's your proof.'

Suslev swore obscenely.

Crosse watched him and kept his face grave, hiding his amusement. The real files are far too valuable to pass over—yet—he told himself again. Oh yes. Now's not the time. In due course, Gregor old chap, parts will bring a very great price. And all that knowledge will have to be sifted and offered very carefully indeed. And as to the eleven pieces of code—whatever the devil they mean—they should be worth a fortune, in due course. 'I'm afraid this time we've drawn a blank, Gregor.'

'But what about Dunross?' Suslev was ashen. He looked at his watch. 'Perhaps he's already in the crate?' He saw Crosse shrug, the lean face etched in the half-light.

'There's no need to interrupt that plan,' Crosse said. 'I've considered that whole operation very carefully. I agree with Jason it'll be good to shake up Hong Kong. Dunross's kidnapping will create all sorts of waves. With the bank runs and the stock market crash—yes it would help us very much. I'm rather worried. Sinders is sniffing around too closely and asking me all sorts of wrong questions. Then there's the Metkin affair, Voranski, the AMG papers, you—too many mistakes. Pressure needs to be taken off Sevrin. Dunross'll do that admirably.'

'You're sure?' Suslev asked, needing reassurance.

'Yes. Oh yes, Dunross will do very nicely thank you. He's the decoy. I'll need all the help I can get. You're going to shop Arthur. Aren't you?'

Suslev saw the eyes boring into him and his heart almost stopped but he kept his shock off his face. Just. 'I'm glad Sinders told you about our meeting. That saves me the trouble. How can I get out of this trap?'

'How're *you* going to avoid it?'

'I don't know, Roger. Will Sinders do what he threatened?'

Crosse snapped, 'Come on, for God's sake! Wouldn't you?'

'What can I do?'

'It's your neck or Arthur's. If it's Arthur's, then the next neck could be mine.' There was a long, violent pause and Suslev felt the hair on the nape of his neck twist. 'So long as it's not mine—and I know what's going on in advance—I don't care.'

Suslev looked back at him. 'You want a drink?'

'You know I don't drink.'

'I meant water—or soda.' The big man went to the refrigerator and took out the vodka bottle and drank from the bottle. 'I'm glad Sinders told you.'

'For chrissake, Gregor, where've your brains gone? Of course he didn't tell me—the fool still thinks it was a secret, private deal, just you and him, of course he does! Good sweet Christ, this's my bailiwick! I maneuvered him into a room that I'd bugged. Am I a simpleton?' The eyes hardened even more and Suslev felt his chest tighten unbearably. 'So it's a simple choice, Gregor. It's you or Arthur. If you shop him I'm in danger and so's everyone else. If you don't concede to Sinders you're finished. Of the two choices I'd prefer you dead—and me, Arthur and Sevrin safe.'

'The best solution's that I betray Arthur,' Suslev said. 'But that before they catch him he flees. He can come aboard the *Ivanov*. Eh?'

'Sinders'll be ahead of you and he'll stop you in Hong Kong waters.'

'That's possible. Not probable. I'd resist a boarding at sea.' Suslev watched him, the bile in his mouth. 'It's that or Arthur commits suicide—or is eliminated.'

Crosse stared at him. 'You must be joking! You want me to send Jason into the Great Hereafter?'

'You said yourself, it's someone's neck. Listen, at the moment we're just examining possibilities. But it's a fact you're not expendable. Arthur is. The others. I am,' Suslev said, meaning it. 'So whatever happens it mustn't be you—and preferably not me. I never did like the idea of dying.' He took another swig of the vodka and felt the lovely, stomach-warming sensation, then turned his eyes back on his ally. 'You are an ally, aren't you?'

'Yes. Oh yes. So long as the money keeps up and I enjoy the game.'

'If you *believed*, you would live a longer and better life, *tovarich*.'

'The only thing that keeps me alive is that I don't. You and your KGB friends can try and take over the world, infiltrate capitalism and any other ism you like, for whatever purpose you admit, or enjoy, and meanwhile, I shall jolly you along.'

'What does that mean?'

'It's an old English expression that means to help,' Crosse said dryly. 'So you're going to shop Arthur?'

'I don't know. Could you lay a false trail to the airport to give us time to escape Hong Kong waters?'

'Yes, but Sinders has already doubled surveillance there.'

'What about Macao?'

'I could do that. I don't like it. What about the others of Sevrin?'

'Let them burrow deeper, we close everything down. You take over Sevrin and we activate again once the storm subsides. Could deVille become tai-pan after Dunross?'

'I don't know. I think it'll be Gavallan. Incidentally, two more Werewolf victims were discovered out at Sha Tin this morning.'

Suslev's hope quickened and some of his dread left him. 'What happened?'

Crosse told him how they were found. 'We're still trying to identify the poor buggers. Gregor, shopping Arthur's dicey, whatever happens. It might spill back to me. Perhaps with the stock market crashing, the banks all messed up and Dunross vanishing, it might be cover enough. It might.'

Suslev nodded. His nausea increased. The decision had to be made. 'Roger, I'm going to do nothing. I'm just going to leave and take the chance. I'll, I'll make a private report to forestall Sinders and tell Center what happened. Whatever Sinders does, well, that's up to the future. I've got friends in high places too. Perhaps the Hong Kong disaster and having Dunross—I'll do the chemical debrief myself anyway, just in case he's cheating us and is as clever as you say he is . . . what is it?'

'Nothing. What about Koronski?'

'He left this morning after I got all the chemicals. I rescheduled the debrief to be on the *Ivanov*, not ashore. Why?'

'Nothing. Go on.'

'Perhaps the Hong Kong debacle'll placate my superiors.' Now that Suslev had made the decision he felt a little better. 'Send an urgent report to Center through the usual channels to Berlin. Get Arthur to do the same by radio tonight. Make the report very pro-me, eh? Blame the Metkin affair on the CIA here, the carrier leak, Voranski. Eh? Blame the CIA and the Kuomintang.'

'Certainly. For a double fee. By the way, Gregor, if I were you I'd clean my prints off that bottle.'

'Eh?'

'Sardonically Crosse told him about Rosemont filching the glass in the raid and how, months ago, to protect Suslev he had extracted his prints from his dossier.

The Russian was white. 'The CIA have my prints on file?'

'Only if they've a better dossier than ours. I doubt that.'

'Roger, I expect you to cover my back.'

'Don't worry, I'll make the report so lily-white they'll promote you. In return you recommend my bonus's 100,000 dol—'

'That's too much!'

'That's the fee! I'm getting you out of one helluva mess.' The mouth smiled, the eyes did not. 'It's fortunate we're professionals. Isn't it?'

'I'll—I'll try.'

'Good. Wait here. Clinker's phone's bugged. I'll phone from Jason's flat the moment I know about Dunross.' Crosse put out his hand. 'Good luck, I'll do what I can with Sinders.'

'Thanks.' Suslev gave him a bear hug. 'Good luck to you too, Roger. Don't fail me on Dunross.'

'We won't fail.'

'And keep up the good work, eh?'

'Tell your friends to keep up the money. Eh?'

'Yes.' Suslev closed the door behind Crosse, then wiped the palms of his hands on his trousers and took out the roll of film.

Quietly he cursed it and Dunross and Hong Kong and Sinders, the specter of the KGB questioning him about Metkin swamping him. Somehow I've got to avoid that, he told himself, the cold sweat running down his back. Perhaps I should shop Arthur after all. How to do it, and keep Roger in the clear? There must be a way.

Outside on the landing, Roger Crosse got into the elevator and pressed the ground-floor button. Alone now he leaned exhaustedly against the rickety walls and shook his head to try to get the fear out. 'Stop it!' he muttered. With an effort he dominated himself and lit a cigarette, noticing his fingers were trembling. If that bugger chemically debriefs Dunross, he told himself, I'm up the creek. And I'll bet fifty dollars to a pile of dung Suslev still hasn't ruled out the possibility of shopping Plumm. And if he does that, Christ my whole pack of cards can come tumbling down about my ears. One mistake, one tiny slip and I'm finished.

The elevator stopped. Some Chinese got in noisily but he did not notice them.

On the ground floor, Rosemont was waiting.

'And?'

'Nothing, Stanley.'

'You and your hunches, Rog.'

'You never know, Stanley, there might have been something,' Crosse said, trying to get his mind working. He had invented the hunch and invited Rosemont along—to wait below—the ruse just to throw off Rosemont's CIA men he knew were still watching the foyer.

'You all right, Rog?'

'Oh yes. Yes, thanks. Why?'

Rosemont shrugged. 'You want a coffee or a beer?' They walked out into the night. Rosemont's car was waiting outside.

'No thanks. I'm going there.' Crosse pointed to Rose Court, the high rise that loomed over them on the road above. 'It's a cocktail party obligation.' He felt his fear welling again. What the hell do I do now?

'What's up, Rog?'

'Nothing.'

'Rose Court, huh? Maybe I should get me an apartment there. Rosemont of Rose Court.'

'Yes.' Crosse mustered his strength. 'Do you want to come down to the dock to see the *Ivanov* off?'

'Sure, why not? I'm glad you sent that mother packing.' Rosemont stifled a yawn. 'We broke that computer bastard tonight. Seems he had all sorts of secrets stacked away.'

'What?'

'Bits and pieces about the *Corregidor*, her top speed, where her nukes come from, their arming codes, things like that. I'll give you a rundown tonight. You pick me up at midnight, okay?'

'Yes, yes all right.' Crosse turned and hurried off. Rosemont frowned after him, then looked up at Rose Court. Lights blazed from all of the twelve floors. Again the American put his eyes back on Crosse, a small figure now in the dark as he turned the corner, climbing the steep curling roadway.

What's with Rog? he asked himself thoughtfully. Something's wrong.

80

8:10 P.M.:

Roger Crosse got out of the elevator on the fifth floor, his face taut, and went through the open door into the Asian Properties apartment. The large room was crowded and noisy. He stood at the doorway, his eyes ranging the guests, seeking Plumm or Dunross. At once he noticed that there was little happiness here, an air of gloom over most of the guests, and this added to his disquiet. Few wives were present—the few that were stood uneasily grouped together at the far end. Everywhere conversation was heated and about the coming debacle of the stock market crash and bank runs.

'Oh come on for chrissake, it's all very well for the Victoria to announce a multimillion takeover of the Ho-Pak but where's the cash to keep us all afloat?'

'It was a merger, not a takeover, Dunstan,' Richard Kwang began, 'the Ho-Pak's n—'

Barre's face was suddenly choleric. 'For chrissake, Richard, we're all friends here and we all know there's more in it than a bail-out, for God's sake. Are we children? My point,' Barre said, raising his voice louder to drown Richard Kwang and Johnjohn out, 'my point, old boy, is that merger or not, we the business-men of Hong Kong can't stay afloat if all you bloody banks have stupidly run out of cash. Eh?'

'It's not our fault, for God's sake,' Johnjohn rapped. 'It's just a temporary loss of confidence.'

'Bloody mismanagement if you ask me,' Barre replied sourly to general agreement, then noticed Crosse trying to pass. 'Oh, oh hello, Roger!' he said with a pasty smile.

Roger Crosse saw the immediate caution that was normal whenever he caught anyone unawares. 'Is Ian here?'

'No. No, not yet,' Johnjohn said and Crosse exhaled, wet with relief. 'You're sure?'

'Oh yes. Soon as he arrives I'm leaving,' Dunstan said sourly. 'Bloody banks! If it wasn't—'

Johnjohn interrupted. 'What about those bloody Werewolves, Roger?' The discovery of the two bodies had been the lead item of Radio Hong Kong and all Chinese newspapers—there being no afternoon English Sunday papers.

'I know nothing more than you do,' Crosse told them. 'We're still trying to identify the victims.' His eyes zeroed in on Richard Kwang, who quailed. 'You don't know of any sons or nephews, missing or kidnapped, do you, Richard?'

'No, no sorry, Roger, no.'

'If you'll excuse me, I'd better see our host.' Crosse pushed his way through the crush. 'Hello, Christian,' he said, easing past the tall, thin editor of the *Guardian*. He saw the desolation the man desperately tried to hide. 'Sorry about your wife.'

'Joss,' Christian Toxe said, attempting to sound calm, and stood in his way. 'Joss, Roger. She, well, she'd . . . life has to go on, doesn't it?' His forced smile was almost grotesque. 'The *Guardian* has to do its work, eh?'

'Yes.'

'Can I have a word later?'

'Certainly—off the record, as always?'

'Of course.'

He went on, passing Pugmire and Sir Luis deep in conversation about the General Stores-Struan takeover and noticed Casey in the center of a group on the wide balcony overlooking the harbor, deVille among them, Gornt also part of the group, looking benign, which Crosse found strange. 'Hello, Jason,' he said coming up behind Plumm who was talking with Joseph Stern and Phillip Chen. 'Thanks for inviting me.'

'Oh. Oh hello, Roger. Glad you could come.'

'Evening,' he said to the others. 'Jason, where's your guest of honor?'

'Ian phoned to. say he'd been delayed but was on his way. He'll be here any moment.' Plumm's tension was evident. 'The, er, the champagne's ready, and my little speech. Everything's

1335

ready,' he said, watching him. 'Come along, Roger, let me get you a drink. It's Perrier, isn't it? I've got some on ice.'

Crosse followed him, equally glad for the opportunity to talk privately but just as they reached the kitchen door there was a momentary hush. Dunross was at the door with Riko, Gavallan beside them. All three were beaming.

'Listen, Jason, I—' Crosse stopped. Plumm had already turned back to the bar and if he hadn't been watching very carefully he would never have seen Plumm's left hand deftly break the tiny vial over one of the filled champagne glasses, then palm the shreds back into his pocket, pick up the tray with four glasses on it and head for the door. Fascinated, he watched Plumm come up to Dunross and offer the champagne.

Dunross let Riko take a glass, then Gavallan. Without any apparent prompting Dunross took the doctored glass. Plumm took the last, giving the tray to an embarrassed waiter. 'Welcome, Ian, and congratulations on the coup,' Plumm said, casually toasting him, not making a big thing of it. Those nearby politely followed suit. Dunross of course did not drink his own toast.

'Now, perhaps you should toast Richard Kwang and John-john and their merger?' Plumm said, his voice sounding strange.

'Why not?' Dunross replied with a laugh and glanced across the room at Johnjohn. 'Bruce,' he called out, raising his glass, and there was a small hole in the general level of noise. 'Here's to the Victoria!' His voice picked up power and cut through neatly. Others glanced over and stopped in midsentence. 'Perhaps everyone should share the toast. I've just heard the Bank of China's agreed to lend you and the other banks half a billion in cash in good time for Monday's opening.'

There was a sudden vast silence. Those on the balcony came into the room, Gornt to the fore. 'What?'

'I've just heard the Bank of China's lending Hong Kong— lending the Vic to lend to other banks—half a billion in cash and as much more as you want. All bank runs're over!' Dunross raised his glass. 'To the Victoria!'

As pandemonium broke out and everyone started asking questions, Crosse got his feet into motion and the moment before Dunross could drink, appeared to stumble and collided with him, knocking the glass out of his hand. It shattered as it hit the parquet flooring. 'Oh Christ, I'm sorry,' he said apologetically.

Plumm stared at him appalled. 'For chrissa—'

'Ah, Jason, I'm so sorry,' Crosse overrode him, adding more quickly as a waiter hastily retrieved the pieces, 'Perhaps you'd get Ian another glass.'

'Eh, yes, but . . .' Numbly Plumm went to obey but stopped as Riko said, 'Oh, here, tai-pan, please to take mine.' Then Johnjohn shouted over the uproar, 'Quiet, quiet a moment!' and pushed over to Dunross. 'Ian,' he said in the utter silence, 'You're sure? Sure about the cash?'

'Oh yes,' Dunross replied leisurely, sipping Riko's drink, enjoying the moment. 'Tiptop called me personally. It'll be on the nine o'clock news.'

There was a sudden great cheer and more questions and answers and Dunross saw Gornt staring at him from across the room. His smile hardened and he raised his glass, paying no attention to the barrage of questions. 'Your health, Quillan!' he called out, mocking him. Quickly the conversation died again. Everyone's attention zeroed on them.

Gornt toasted him back, equally mocking. 'Your health, Ian. We've really got China's money?'

'Yes, and by the way, I've just arranged a new revolving fund of 50 million U.S. Now the Noble House's the soundest *hong* in the Colony.'

'Secured by what?' Gornt's voice slashed through the abrupt silence.

'The honor of the Noble House!' With a nonchalance he did not feel, Dunross turned to Johnjohn. 'The loan's from the Royal Belgium, a subsidiary of First Central of New York and backed by them.' Deliberately he did not look back at Gornt as he repeated, enjoying greatly the sound, '50 million U.S. Oh by the way, Bruce, tomorrow I'm retiring your loans on both my ships. I no longer need the Vic loan—Royal Belgium's given me better terms.'

Johnjohn just stared at him.

'You're joking?'

'No. I've just talked to Paul.' Momentarily Dunross glanced at Plumm. 'Sorry, Jason, that was why I was late. Naturally I had to see him. Bruce, old fellow, Paul's already down at the bank making arrangements for the transfer of China's cash in time for opening—he asked if you'd go there, at once.'

'Eh?'

'At once. Sorry.'

Johnjohn stared at him blankly, started to talk, stopped, then erupted with a cheer that everyone took up, and rushed out, cheers following him.

'Christ, tai-pan, but did you . . .'

'Tiptop? That means it's real! Don't you think . . .'

'First Central of New York? Aren't they the berks who . . .'

'Christ, I've been selling short . . .'

'Me too! Shit, I'd better buy first thing or . . .'

'Or I'll be wiped out and . . .'

Dunross saw that Sir Luis, Joseph Stern and Phillip Chen had their heads together, Gornt still staring at him, his face frozen. Then he saw Casey smiling at him so happily and he raised his glass and toasted her. She toasted him back. Gornt saw this and he went over to her and those nearby shivered and fell silent. 'First Central's Par-Con's bank. Isn't it?'

'Yes, yes it is, Quillan,' she said, her voice sounding small but it went through the room and once more all attention surrounded them.

'You and Bartlett, you did this?' Gornt asked, towering over her.

Dunross said quickly, 'I arrange our loans.'

Gornt paid no attention to him, just watched her. 'You and Bartlett. You helped him?'

She looked back at him, her heart thumping. 'I've no control over that bank, Quillan.'

'Ah but your fingers're in that pie somewhere,' Gornt said coldly. 'Aren't they?'

'Murtagh asked *me* if I thought Struan's a good risk,' she said, her voice controlled. 'I told him, yes, that Struan's was an admirable risk.'

'Struan's is on the rocks,' Gornt said.

Dunross came up to them. 'The whole point is, we're not. By the way, Quillan, Sir Luis has agreed to withdraw Struan's from trading until noon.'

All eyes went to Sir Luis who stood stoically, Phillip Chen

1338

beside him, then went back to Dunross and Gornt again.

'Why?'

'To give the market time to adjust to the boom.'

'What boom?'

'The boom we all deserve, the boom Old Blind Tung forecast.'
A wave of electricity went through everyone, even Casey. 'Also
to adjust our stock value,' Dunross's voice rasped. 'We open at
30.'

'Impossible,' someone gasped, and Gornt snarled, 'You
can't! You closed at 9:50 by God! Your stock closed at at 9.50!'

'So we offer stock at 30 by God!' Dunross snarled back.

Gornt whirled on Sir Luis. 'You're going along with this
highway robbery?'

'There isn't any, Quillan,' Sir Luis said calmly. 'I've agreed,
with the committee's unanimous approval, that it's the best for
all, for the safety of all investors, that there should be a
quiescent period—so that everyone could prepare for the boom.
Till noon seemed fair.'

'Fair eh?' Gornt grated. 'You've got lots of stock I've sold
short. Now I buy it all back. What price?'

Sir Luis shrugged. 'I'll deal at noon tomorrow, on the floor,
not away from the market.'

'I'll deal with you right now, Quillan,' Dunross said harshly.
'How many shares've you sold short? 700,000? 8? I'll let you buy
back in at 18 if you will sell the controlling interest in All Asia Air
at 15.'

'All Asia Air's not for sale,' Gornt said, enraged, his mind
shouting that at 30 he would be wiped out.

'The offer's good till opening tomorrow.'

'The pox on you, tomorrow, and your 30!' Gornt whirled on
Joseph Stern. 'Buy Struan's! Now, in the morning or at noon!
You're responsible!'

'At, at what price, Mr. Gornt?'

'Just buy!' Gornt's face closed and he turned on Casey.
'Thanks,' he said to her and stomped off, slamming the door
behind him. Then conversation exploded, and Dunross was
surrounded, people pounding him on the back, swamping him
with questions. She stayed alone at the doorway of the veranda,
shocked by the violence that had been. Absently, in turmoil, she
saw Plumm hurry off, Roger Crosse following, but she paid

them little attention, just watched Dunross, Riko now beside him.

In the small back bedroom Plumm reached into the drawer of a bureau that was near the big iron-bound sea trunk. The door swung open and he spun around and when he saw it was Roger Crosse his face twisted. 'What the shit're you doing? You deliberately f—'

With catlike speed Crosse was across the room and he belted the man open-handed before Plumm knew what was happening. Plumm gasped and blindly readied to leap at Crosse but again Crosse belted him and Plumm stumbled backward against the bed and fell onto it. 'What the f—'

'*Shut up and listen!*' Crosse hissed. 'Suslev's going to shop you!'

Plumm gaped at him, the weal from the blows scarlet. At once his anger vanished. 'What?'

'Suslev's going to shop you to Sinders, and that means all of us.' Crosse's eyes narrowed. 'You all right now? For chrissake keep your voice down.'

'What? Yes . . . yes. I . . . yes.'

'Sorry, Jason, it was the only thing to do.'

'That's, that's all right. What the hell's going on, Roger?' Plumm scrambled off the bed, rubbing his face, a thin trickle of blood at the corner of his mouth, now totally controlled. Outside was the rise and fall of indistinct conversation.

'We've got to make a plan,' Crosse said grimly and recapped his conversation with Suslev. 'I think I've got him convinced, but that bugger's slippery and there's no telling what he'll do. Sinders'll shop him, I'm sure of that, if Suslev doesn't finger Arthur—and if Sinders shops him, Suslev won't come back to Hong Kong. They'll keep him and break him. Then wh—'

'But what about Dunross?' Plumm asked helplessly. 'Surely Dunross could've got him out of the mess. Now Gregor's bound to talk. Why stop me?'

'I had to. There was no time to tell you. Listen, after I left Suslev I checked with HQ. They told me Tiptop'd helped those bastards squeeze out of the trap with China's money. Earlier I'd heard that Ian'd arranged his loan,' Crosse added, lying. 'So the

1340

runs're over, the stock market's got to boom, Dunross or not. But worse than that, Jason, I got a whisper from an informant in Special Branch that Sinders has tripled security on Kai Tak, the same on the *Ivanov* wharf, and that, right now, they're opening every crate, every bag, searching every piece of equipment, checking every coolie that goes aboard. If they'd intercepted Dunross, and they would—SI's too smart—we'd be trapped.'

Plumm's nervousness increased. A tremor went through him. 'What, what about . . . Say we give Sinders Gregor?' he burst out. 'What if we gi—'

'Keep your voice down! You're not thinking clearly, for God's sake! Gregor knows all of us. Sinders'd shove him on a sleep-wake-sleep regimen and into the Red Room and he'd tell everything! That'd wreck us, wreck Sevrin and put the Soviets back ten years in Asia.'

Plumm shivered and wiped his face. 'Then what're we going to do?'

'Let Gregor go aboard and out of Hong Kong, and hope to God he convinces his bosses. Even if he leaks your name to Sinders I think we're buried so deep we can squeeze out of that. You're British, not a foreign national. Thank God we've laws to protect us—even under the Official Secrets Act. Don't worry, nothing'll happen without me knowing and if anything happens I'll know at once. There'll always be time enough for Plan Three.' Plan Three was an elaborate escape that Plumm had erected against such an eventuality—with false passports, valid air tickets, ready luggage, clothes, disguises and covers, even including passkeys to airplane waiting areas without going through Emigration—that had a ninety-five percent chance of success given an hour's notice.

'Christ!' Plumm looked down at the waiting trunk. 'Christ,' he said again, then went to the mirror to look at his face. The redness was going. He doused some water on it.

Crosse watched him, wondering if Plumm was convinced. It was the best he could do in the circumstances. He hated improvisation, but in this case he had little option. What a life we lead! Every one expendable except yourself: Suslev, Plumm, Sinders, Kwok, Armstrong, even the governor.

'What?' Plumm asked, looking at him in the mirror

'I was just thinking we're in a rough business.'

'The Cause makes it worthwhile. That's the only part that counts.'

Crosse hid his contempt. *I really think you've outlived your usefulness, Jason old fellow,* he thought, then went over to the phone. There were no extensions on this line and he knew it was not bugged. He dialed.

'Yes?' He recognized Suslev and coughed Arthur's dry cough. 'Mr. Lop-sing please,' continuing the code in a perfect imitation of Plumm's voice, then said urgently, 'There's been a foul-up. The target did not appear. Be careful at the dock. Surveillance is tripled. We cannot deliver the trunk. Good luck.' He hung up. The silence gathered.

'That's his death knell, isn't it?' Plumm said sadly.

Crosse hesitated. He smiled thinly. 'Better his death than yours. Eh?'

81

8:25 P.M.:

In the noise-filled living room at the other end of the hall, Casey finished her drink and set it down. She was feeling unsettled and very strange. Part of her was joyous at Dunross's reprieve and the other part sad that Gornt was now entrapped. It was quite clear to her with the wheeling and dealing now going on around her that Struan's opening price would be very high. Poor Quillan, she thought. If he doesn't cover his position he'll be in shitsville—and let's face it, I put him there. Didn't I?

Sure, but I had to bail out Dunross because, without him, Gornt would have squeezed us dry—and maybe everyone else. And don't forget, I didn't start the raid on Struan's. That was Linc's raid, not mine. Hasn't Linc always said business and pleasure should never mix? Haven't we both always gone along with that?

Linc. Always back to Linc.

Casey had not seen him all day, nor even heard from him. They were supposed to have met for breakfast but there was a 'do not disturb' on his door and a 'do not disturb' on his phone so she left him and pushed away the thought of Orlanda—was Orlanda there too? And tonight, when she had returned from the day's sailing, there was a message: 'Hi, have fun.' So she had showered and changed and bottled her impatience and had come here tonight. It had been no fun in the beginning, everyone gloom and doom-filled, then after the news and Gornt slamming out, no fun again. Shortly afterward Dunross had forced his way over and thanked her again but almost at once he had been surrounded by excited men discussing deals and chances. She watched them, feeling very lonely. Perhaps Linc's back at the hotel now, she thought. I wish . . . never mind, but it is time to go home. No one noticed her slip out.

Roger Crosse was standing at the elevator. He held the door for her then pressed the *down* button.

'Thanks. Nice party, wasn't it?' she said.

'Yes, yes it was,' he replied absently.

On the ground floor Crosse let her get out first then strode off out the front door and down the hill. What's his hurry? she asked herself, heading for the group that waited for taxis, glad that it was not raining again. She jerked to a stop. Orlanda Ramos, with packages in her arms, was coming into the foyer. Each woman saw the other at the same instant. Orlanda was the first to recover. 'Evening, Casey,' she said with her best smile. 'How pretty you look.'

'So do you,' Casey replied. Her enemy did. The pale blue skirt and blouse were perfectly matched.

Orlanda poured a stream of impatient Cantonese over the crumpled concierge who was lounging nearby. At once he took her packages, mumbling.

'Sorry, Casey,' she said nicely, a thread of nervousness to her voice, 'but there's been a small landslide just down the hill and I had to leave my car there. You're, you're visiting here?'

'No, just leaving. You live here?'

'Yes. Yes I do.'

Another silence between them, both readying. Then Casey nodded a polite good night and began to leave.

'Perhaps we should talk,' Orlanda said and Casey stopped.

'Certainly, Orlanda, whenever you wish.'

'Do you have time now?'

'I think so.'

'Would you like to walk with me back to my car? I've got to get the rest of my packages. You won't be able to get a taxi here anyway, below will be easy.'

'Sure.'

The two women went out. The night was cool but Casey was burning and so was Orlanda, each knowing what was coming, each fearful of the other. Their feet picked a way carefully. The street was wet from the water that rushed downward. There was a promise of more rain soon from the heavy nimbus overcast. Ahead, fifty yards away, Casey could see where the em-

1344

bankment had partially given way, sending a mess of earth and rocks and shrubs and rubble across the road. There was no sidewalk. On the other side of the slip, a line of cars were stopped, impatiently maneuvering to turn around. A few pedestrians scrambled over the embankment.

'Have you lived in Rose Court long?' Casey asked.

'A few years. It's very pleasant. I th—— Oh! Were you at Jason Plumm's party, the Asian Properties party?'

'Yes.' Casey saw the relief on Orlanda's face and it angered her but she contained the anger and stopped and said quietly, 'Orlanda, there's nothing really for us to talk about, is there? Let's say good night.'

Orlanda looked up at her. 'Linc's with me. He's with me in my apartment. At the moment.'

'I presumed that.'

'That doesn't bother you?'

'It bothers me very much. But that's up to Linc. We're not married, as you know, not even engaged, as you know—you have your way, I have mine, so th—'

'What do you mean by that?' Orlanda asked.

'I mean that I've known Linc for seven years, you haven't known him for seven days.'

'That doesn't matter,' Orlanda said defiantly. 'I love him and he loves me.'

'That's y—' Casey was almost shoved aside by some Chinese who barreled past, chattering noisily. Others were approaching up the incline. Then some of the party guests walked around them, heading down the slope. One of the women was Lady Joanna, and she eyed them curiously but went on.

When they were alone again, Casey said, 'That's yet to be proved. Good night, Orlanda,' she said, wanting to scream at her, You make your money on your back, I work for mine, and all the love you protest is spelled *money*. Men are such jerks.

'Curiously I don't blame Linc,' she muttered out loud seeing the firm jaw, the flashing determined eyes, the perfect, voluptuous yet trim body. 'Good night.'

She walked on. Now my plan has to change, she was thinking, all her being concentrated. Tonight I was going to love Linc properly, but now everything has to change. If he's in her bed he's under her spell. Jesus, I'm glad I found that out. God, if I'd offered he would have had to say no and then. . . . Now I can. . . . what should I do?

Shit on the Orlandas of the world! It's so easy for them. They have a game plan from day one. But the rest of us?

What do I do? Stick to November 25 and gamble Orlanda will bore the hell out of him by that time?

Not that lady. That one's dynamite and she knows Linc's her passport to eternity.

Her heart picked up a beat. I'm a match for her, she told herself confidently. Maybe not in bed or in the kitchen, but I can learn.

She stepped up and over a boulder, cursing the mud that fouled her shoes, and jumped down the other side of the earth barrier. Dunross's Rolls and his chauffeur were at the head of the line.

'Excuse, Missee, is the tai-pan still there?'

'Yes, yes he is.'

'Ah, thank you.' The driver locked the car and hurried over the roadblock back up the hill. Casey turned and watched him. Her eyes centered on Orlanda who was approaching and she looked at her, wanting to shove her into the mud. The thought amused her and she stood there letting her enemy approach, letting her wonder what she would do. She saw the eyes harden and there was no fear on Orlanda's face, just a very confident half-smile. Orlanda passed her fearlessly, and a tremor of apprehension went through Casey that she managed to dominate. Maybe you're just as afraid of me and my power as I am of yours, she thought, her eyes now on Rose Court, a brilliant tower of light, wondering which light surrounded Linc or which darkened window. . . .

When Orlanda had first seen Casey, she had immediately jumped to the conclusion that Casey had been to her apartment and confronted Bartlett—that's what I would have done, she told herself. And, even though she knew now where Casey had been, fear again swept through her at the sight of her rival. Has she power over him through Par-Con? she asked herself, trembling. Can she control Linc through stocks or shares? If Linc's first wife nearly destroyed him financially and Casey saved him as many times as he said, she's bound to have him tied up. I would if I were she, of course I would.

Involuntarily Orlanda glanced back. Casey was still watching Rose Court. Beyond her, Dunross and others—Riko, Toxe, Phillip and Dianne Chen among them—came out of the foyer and started down the hill. She dismissed them and everything except the question of how to deal with Linc when she returned. Should she tell him about meeting Casey or not? Numbly she took the remainder of her packages from her car. I know one thing, she told herself over and over again. Linc's mine, and Casey or no Casey I'll marry him, whatever the cost.

Casey had seen Dunross come out of the foyer and she watched him, enjoying the sight of him, tall, debonair, ten years younger than when she first saw him, and it pleased her very much that she had helped him. Then, just as she turned away, she heard him call out, 'Casey! Casey! Hang on a moment!' She glanced back. 'How about joining us for dinner?' he called out to her.

She shook her head, not in the mood, and called out, 'Thanks but I've a date! See you tomorr—'

At that moment the earth fell away.

82

8:56 P.M.:

The landslide had begun further up the mountain on the other side of Po Shan Road, and it swept across the road, smashing into a two-story garage, its mass and velocity so vast that the garage building rotated and toppled off the garden terrace, slid down for a short distance, then fell over. The slide gathered momentum and rushed past a darkened high rise, crossed Conduit Road and smashed into Richard Kwang's two-story house, obliterating it. Then, together with these buildings, the slip, now nine hundred feet long and two hundred feet wide— fifty thousand tons of earth and rock—continued on its downward path across Kotewall Road and struck Rose Court.

The landslide had taken seven seconds.

When Rose Court was struck, it appeared to shudder, and then the building came away from its foundations and moved forward in the direction of the harbor, toppled over and broke up near the middle like a man kneeling then falling.

As it fell, the upper stories struck and ripped off a corner of the upper stories of Sinclair Towers below, then crumpled and disintegrated into rubble. Part of the slide and the demolished building continued on and fell into a construction site farther down the mountain, then stopped. The lights went out as the building collapsed in a cloud of dust. And now over all Mid Levels there was a stunned, vast silence.

Then the screams began. . . .

In the tunnel under Sinclair Road, Suslev was choking, half-buried in rubble. Part of the tunnel roof was torn off, water gushing in now from fractured mains and drains, the tunnel filling rapidly. He scrambled and fought up into the open, his confused mind helpless, not knowing what was happening, what had happened, only that somehow he must have been captured and drugged and now he was in a wake-sleep nightmare from the Red Room. He looked around, panic-stricken. All buildings were dark, power gone, a monstrous pile of shrieking, shifting wreckage surrounding him. Then his glands overpowered him and he fled pell-mell down Sinclair Road. . . .

Far above on Kotewall Road, those on the other side of the barrage were safe though paralyzed with shock. The few still on their feet, Casey among them, could not believe what they had witnessed. The vast slide had torn away all of the roadway as far as they could see. Most of the mountainside that a moment ago was terraced was now an undulating, ugly mud-earth-rock slope—roads vanished, buildings gone, and Dunross and his party carried away somewhere down the slope.

Casey tried to scream but she had no voice. Then, *'Oh Jesus Christ! Linc!'* tore from her mouth and her feet moved and before she knew what was happening she was scrambling, falling, groping her way toward the wreckage. The darkness was awful now, the screams awful, voices beginning, shouts for help from everywhere, the unbelievable twisted pile of debris still moving here and there, bits still falling and being crushed. All at once the night was lit by power lines exploding, sending cascades of fireballs into the air among the wreckage.

Frantically she rushed to where the foyer once had been. Extended below, far below, the darkness obscuring almost everything, was the twisted mass of rubble, concrete blocks, girders, shoes, toys, pots pans sofas chairs beds radios TVs clothes limbs books, three cars that had been parked outside, and more screams. Then in the light of the exploding power lines she saw the mashed wreckage that was once the elevator down the slope, broken arms and legs jutting from its carcass.

'Linc!' she shrieked at the top of her voice, again and again, not knowing she was crying, the tears streaming down her face.

But there was no answer. Desperately she clambered and half fell and groped her way into and over the dangerous rubble. Around her, men and women were shouting, screaming. Then she heard a faint wail of terror nearby and part of the rubble moved. She was on her knees now, stockings torn, dress torn, knees bruised and she pulled away some bricks and found a small cavity, and there was a Chinese child of three or four, beyond terror, coughing, almost choking, trapped under a vast, groaning pile of debris in the rubble dust.

'Oh Jesus you poor darling.' Casey looked around frantically but there was no one to help. Part of the rubble shifted, screaming and groaning, a big chunk of concrete with its imbedded, reinforcing iron almost hanging loose. Careless of her safety, Casey fought the debris away, fingers bleeding. Again the wreckage twisted over her as some of it slid farther down the slope. Desperately she clawed a crawlspace and grabbed the child's arm, helping her to squeeze out, then caught her in her arms and darted back to safety as this part of the wreckage collapsed and she stood alone, the trembling child safe and unhurt in her arms, clutching her tightly. . . .

When the avalanche toppled the high rise and tore up most of the roadway and parapet, Dunross and the others on its edge were hurtled down the steep slope, head over heels, brush and vegetation breaking part of their fall. The tai-pan picked himself up in the semidarkness, felt himself blankly, dazed, astonished to find he could stand and was unhurt. From near him came whimpers of agony. The slope was steep and everywhere muddy and sodden as he groped up to Dianne Chen. She was semiconscious, groaning, one leg twisted brutally underneath her. Part of her shinbone jutted through the skin but as far as he could see, no arteries were severed and there was no dangerous bleeding. As carefully as he could he straightened her and her limb, but she let out a howl of pain and fainted. He felt someone nearby and glanced up. Riko was standing there, her dress ripped, her shoes gone, her hair akimbo, a small trickle of blood from her nose.

'Christ, you all right?'

'Yes . . . yes,' she said shakily. 'It's . . . was it an earthquake?'

At that moment there was another crackling explosion of power cables short-circuiting, and momentarily fireballs lit up the area. 'Oh my God!' he gasped. 'It's like London in the blitz.' Then he caught sight of Phillip Chen in an inert heap around a sapling, sprawled headfirst down the slope. 'Stay here with Dianne,' he ordered and scrambled down the slope. Hanging on to his dread, he turned Phillip over. His compradore was still breathing. Dunross shook with relief. He settled him as best he could and looked around in the gloom. Others were picking themselves up. Nearby, Christian Toxe was shaking his head, trying to clear it.

'Bloody sodding Christ,' he was muttering over and over. 'There must be a couple of hundred people living there.' He reeled to his feet then slipped in the mud and cursed again. 'I've . . . I've got to get to a phone. Give me, give me a hand will you?' Toxe swore as he slipped again. 'It's my ankle, the bloody thing's twisted a bit.'

Dunross helped him stand and then, with Riko on Toxe's other side, they climbed awkwardly back to the remains of the roadway. People were still standing paralyzed, others clambering over the first slide to see if they could help, a few of the tenants frantic and moaning. One mother was being held back, her husband already running falling clambering toward the wreckage, their three children and *amah* somewhere there.

The moment they were on level ground, Toxe hobbled off down Kotewall Road and Dunross rushed for his car to fetch his flashlight and emergency medical pack.

Lim was nowhere to be seen. Then Dunross remembered his chauffeur had been with them when the avalanche hit. As he found the keys to unlock the trunk he searched his memory. Who was with us? Toxe, Riko, Jacques—no, Jacques had left— Phillip and Dianne Chen, Barre . . . no we left Barre at the party. Jesus Christ! The party! I'd forgotten the party! Who was still there? Richard Kwang and his wife, Plumm, Johnjohn, no he'd gone earlier, Roger Crosse, no wait a minute, didn't he leave?

Dunross jerked open the trunk and found two flashlights and the medical kit, a length of rope. He ran back to Riko, his back hurting him now. 'Will you go back and look after Dianne and

Phillip till I can get help?' His voice was deliberately firm. 'Here.' He gave her a flashlight, some bandages and a bottle of aspirin. 'Off you go. Dianne's broken her leg. I don't know about Phillip. Do what you can and stay with them till an ambulance comes or I come back. All right?'

'Yes, yes, all right.' Her eyes flickered with fear as she looked above. 'Will there . . . is there any danger from another slide?'

'No. You'll be quite safe. Go quickly!' His will took away her fear and she started down the slope with the flashlight, picking her way carefully. It was only then he noticed that she was barefoot. Then he remembered Dianne had been barefoot too and Phillip. He stretched to ease his back. His clothes were ripped, but he paid them no attention and rushed for the barrier. In the distance he heard police sirens. His relief became almost nauseating as he broke into a run.

Then he noticed Orlanda at the head of the line of cars. She was staring fixedly at where Rose Court had been, her mouth moving, tiny spasms trembling her face and body, and he remembered the night of the fire when she had been equally petrified and near snapping. Quickly he went to her and shook her hard, hoping to jerk her out of the panic breakdown that he had witnessed so many times during the war. 'Orlanda!'

She came out of her almost trance. 'Oh . . . oh . . . what, what . . .'

Greatly relieved, he saw her eyes were normal now and the agony normal, the spilling tears normal. 'You're all right. Nothing to worry about. Get hold now, you're all right, Orlanda!' he said, his voice kind though very firm, and leaned her against the hood of a car and left her.

Her eyes focused. 'Oh my God! Linc!' Then she shrieked after him through her tears, 'Linc . . . Linc's there!'

He jerked to a stop, turned back. 'Where? Where was he?'

'He's . . . in my, my apartment. It's on the eighth floor . . . it's on the eighth floor!'

Dunross ran off again, his flashlight the only moving speck of light on the morass.

Here and there people were groping blindly, ankle-deep in the soaking earth, their hands cupped around matches, heading for the ruins. As he came near the catastrophe, his heart twisted. He could smell gas. Every second the smell became stronger.

'*Put out the matches, for chrissake!*' he roared. *You'll blow us all to helllll!*'

Then he saw Casey .

The police car following the fire truck roared up the hill, sirens howling, the traffic heavy here and no one getting out of the way. Inside the car Armstrong was monitoring the radio calls: 'All police units and fire trucks converge on Kotewall Road. Emergency, emergency emergency! There's a new landslip in the vicinity of Po Shan and Sinclair Road! Callers say Rose Court and two other twelve-story buildings've collapsed.'

'Bloody ridiculous!' Armstrong muttered, then, 'Watch out for chrissake!' he shouted at the driver who had cut across the road to the wrong side, narrowly missing a truck. 'Turn right here, then cut up Castle into Robinson and into Sinclair that way,' he ordered. He had been going home from another re-build session with Brian Kwok, his head aching and exhausted, when he had heard the emergency call. Remembering that Crosse lived on Sinclair Road and that he'd said he would be going to Jason Plumm's party after he'd followed a lead with Rosemont, he had decided to check it out. Christ, he thought grimly, if he's been clobbered who'll take over SI? And do we still let Brian go or hold him or what?

A new voice came on, firm, unhurried, the static on the radio heavy. 'This is Deputy Fire Chief Soames. Emergency One!' Armstrong and the driver gasped. 'I'm at the junction of Sinclair, Robinson and Kotewall Road where I have set up a command post. Emergency One repeat One! Inform the commissioner and the governor at once, this is a disaster of very great proportions. Inform all hospitals on the Island to be on standby. Order every ambulance and all paramedics to the area. We will require immediate and heavy army assistance. All power is out so we require generators, cables and lights. . . .'

'Jesus Christ,' Armstrong muttered. Then sharply, 'Get the lead out for chrissake, and hurry it up!'

The police car increased speed. . . .

'Oh, Ian,' Casey said beyond tears, the petrified child still in her arms. 'Linc's somewhere down there.'

'Yes, yes I know,' he said above the insane bedlam of screams and cries for help that came through the ominous grinding of the wreckage as it still settled. People wandered around blindly, not knowing where to look, where to start, how to help. 'You all right?'

'Oh yes but . . . but Linc. I don—' She stopped. Just ahead, down the slope near the remains of the elevator, a vast pile of twisted beams and shattered fragments of concrete subsided deafeningly, starting a chain reaction all down the slope and as he focused his flashlight on it they saw a loosened mass of debris smash against the elevator, claw it loose and send it reeling, leaving bodies in its wake.

'Oh Jesus,' she whimpered. The child clutched her in panic.

'Go back to the car, you'll be saf—' At that moment a man crazed with anxiety rushed up to them, peered at the child in her arms, then grabbed her, clutching her to him, mumbling his thanks to God and to her. 'Where, where did you find her?'

Casey pointed numbly.

The man peered at the spot blankly then went off into the night, weeping openly with relief.

'Stay here, Casey,' Dunross said urgently, sirens approaching from every direction. 'I'll take a quick look.'

'Do be careful. Jesus, do you smell gas?'

'Yes, lots of it.' Using the flashlight he began to thread his way over and under and through the wreckage, slipping and sliding. It was treacherous, the whole mass uneasy and creaking. The first crumpled body was a Chinese woman he did not know. Ten yards below was a European man, his head mashed and almost obliterated. Quickly he scoured the way ahead with his light but could not see Bartlett among the other dead. Farther below were two broken bodies, both Chinese. Swallowing his nausea, he worked his way under a dangerous overhang toward the European, then, holding the flashlight carefully, reached into the dead man's pockets. The driver's license said: Richard Pugmire.

'Christ!' Dunross muttered. The smell of gas was heavy. His stomach turned over as, far below, more power lines gushed sparks. We'll all go to kingdom come if those bloody sparks reach up here, he thought. Carefully he eased out of the debris and stood at his full height, breathing easier now. A last look at Pugmire's body and he started down the slope again. A few steps later he heard a faint moan. It took a little time to find the source but he centered on it and climbed down, his heart beating heavily. With great care he squirmed into the depths under a monstrous overhang of beams and rubble. His fingers took hold. Using all his strength he tilted the broken concrete and shoved it aside. A man's head was below. 'Help,' Clinker said weakly. 'God love you, mate. . . .'

'Hang on a second.' Dunross could see the man was wedged down by a huge rafter but the rafter was also keeping the debris above from crushing him. With the flashlight he searched until he found a broken piece of pipe. With this as a lever he tried to raise the rafter. A pyramid of rubble shifted ominously. 'Can you move?' he gasped.

'It's . . . it's me legs, I hurt proper bad, but I can try.' Clinker reached out and gripped an imbedded piece of iron. 'Ready when you are.'

'What's your name?'

'Clinker, Ernie Clinker. Wot's yorn?'

'Dunross. Ian Dunross.'

'Oh!' Clinker moved his head painfully and peered upward, his face and head bleeding, hair matted and lips raw. 'Thanks, tai-pan,' he said. 'Ready, ready when you are.'

Dunross put his weight and strength onto his makeshift lever. The beam raised an inch. Clinker squirmed but could not dislodge himself. 'Bit more, mate,' he gasped, in great pain. Again Dunross bore down. He felt the sinews of his arms and legs cry out under the strain, The beam came up a fraction. A trickle of rubble cascaded into the cavity. Higher still. 'Now!' he said urgently. 'I can't hold it. . . .'

The old man's grip on the iron tightened and he dragged himself out inch by inch. More rubble moved as he shifted his grip. Now he was halfway out. Once his trunk was free, Dunross let the rafter settle back, oh so gently, and when it was completely at rest he grabbed the old man and wrenched him free. It was then that he saw the trail of blood, the left foot missing. 'Don't move, old fellow,' he said compassionately as Clinker lay panting, half unconscious, trying to stop the whimpers of pain. Dunross tore open a bandage, tying a rough tourniquet just under the knee.

Then he stood up in the small space and looked at the vicious overhang above him, trying to decide what to do next. Next I get the poor bugger out, he thought, loathing the closeness. Then he heard the rumble and shriek of shifting debris. The earth lurched and he ducked, his arms protecting his head. A new avalanche began. . . .

83

It was just sixteen minutes since Rose Court was struck, but all over the vast area of destruction people were moving. Some had fought themselves out of the rubble. Others were rescuers and down below, near the command post set up at the junction, police cars, four fire trucks and rescue units were there, their mobile lights washing the slope, firemen and police frantically working their way through the wreckage. A small fire flickered and it was quickly doused, everyone aware of the gas danger. An ambulance with wounded or dying had already been dispatched, more were converging.

It was chaotic in the darkness, all streetlighting failed, the rain beginning again. The senior divisional fire officer had arrived a moment ago and had sent for gas company engineers and organized other experts to inspect the foundations of the other high rises and buildings nearby in case they should be evacuated—the whole three tiers of Kotewall, Conduit and Po Shan Roads suspect. 'Christ,' he muttered, appalled, 'this's going to take weeks to dig out and clean up.' But he stood in the open, an outward picture of calm. Another patrol car whined to a halt. 'Oh hello, Robert,' he said as Armstrong joined him. 'Yes,' he said, seeing his shock, 'Christ knows how many're buried th—'

'Look out!' someone shouted and everyone ran for cover as a huge lump of reinforced concrete came crashing down from the mutilated top stories of Sinclair Towers. One of the police cars turned its light upward. Now they could see the shreds of rooms open to the skies. A tiny figure was teetering on the brink. 'Get someone up there and see what the hell's going on!'

A fireman took to his heels. . . .

In the darkness at the roadblock up on Kotewall Road, on-lookers from nearby buildings had been collecting, everyone petrified that there would be another slide, tenants frantic, not knowing whether to evacuate or not. Orlanda was still leaning numbly against the car, the rain on her face mixing with her tears. Another group of police reinforcements poured over the barrier onto the morass and fanned out with heavy-duty flashlights searching the terrain. One heard a call for help from below and directed his light into the brush, then changed direction quickly as he saw Riko waving and shouting, two figures inert beside her.

Down Kotewall Road at the fork, Gornt's car skidded to a halt. Brushing aside orders from the harassed policeman there, he pressed the keys into his hand and rushed off up the hill. When he got near to the barrier and saw the extent of the disaster he was stunned. Only moments ago he had been there, drinking and flirting with Casey, everything settled, Orlanda settled, then his whole victory upside down and raging at Dunross, but some miracle had sent him away in time and now perhaps all the others were dead and buried and gone forever. Christ! Dunross Orlanda Casey Jason Bar—

'Keep out of the way!' the policeman shouted. More ambulance bearers hurried past, fireman with axes following, up and over the mess of mud and boulders and trees toward the ruins. 'Sorry, but you can't stay there, sir.'

Gornt moved aside, breathing heavily from his run. 'Did anyone get out?'

'Oh yes, of course, I'm sure th—'

'Have you seen Dunross, Ian Dunross?'

'Who?'

'The tai-pan, Dunross?'

'No, no sorry I haven't.' The policeman turned away to intercept and calm some disheveled parents.

Gornt's eyes went back to the disaster, still appalled by its immensity.

'Jesus,' an American voice muttered.

Gornt turned. Paul Choy and Venus Poon were crammed in a new group who were straggling up. Everyone stared, dumbfounded, into the darkness. 'Jesus!'

'What're you doing here, Paul?'

1358

'Oh hello, Mr. Gornt! My . . . my uncle's in there,' Paul Choy said, hardly able to talk. 'Jesus Christ, lookit!'

'Four Fingers?'

'Yes. He . . .'

Venus Poon overrode him grandly. 'Mr. Wu's waiting for me to discuss a movie contract. He's going to be a film producer.'

Gornt dismissed the patent fabrication as his mind raced. If he could save Four Fingers, perhaps the old man would help extricate him from the looming stock market debacle. 'What floor was he on?'

'The fifth,' Venus Poon said.

'Paul, cut around to Sinclair and work your way up this side of the slope. I'll work down to meet you! Off you go!'

The young man raced off before Venus Poon could stop him. The policeman was still distracted. Without hesitation Gornt darted for the barrier. He knew Plumm's fifth-floor apartment well—Four Fingers should be nearby. In the darkness he did not notice Orlanda on the other side of the road.

Once over the barrier he moved as fast as he could, his feet sinking into the earth. From time to time he stumbled. '*Heya*, Honored Sir!' he called out in Cantonese to a nearby stretcher bearer. 'Do you have a spare flashlight?'

'Yes, yes, here you are!' the man said. 'But beware, the path is treacherous. There are many ghosts here.'

Gornt thanked him and hurried off, making better time. Nearing where the foyer would have been he stopped. Up the mountainside as far as he could see was the ugly sloping gash of the slide, a hundred yards wide. On the edges of all three tiers were other buildings and high rises, one under construction, and the thought of being caught in one of those nauseated him. All of Conduit Road had gone, trees torn up, parapets gone. When he looked below he shuddered. 'It's impossible,' he muttered, remembering the size and strength of the high rise and the joy of Rose Court over the years. Then he saw the lights skeetering over the top of Sinclair Towers, the building that he had always hated—had hated Dunross even more for financing and owning—for destroying his wonderful view. When he noticed the upper corner missing, a flash of pleasure went through him, but it quickly turned to bile as he remembered his own penthouse apartment that had been on the twelfth floor of

Rose Court, and all the good times he had had with Orlanda, there on the eighth floor, now rubble and death filled. 'Christ,' he said out loud, blessing his joss. Then he went onward. . . .

Casey was sitting on a pile of rubble, waiting and in misery. Rescuers were all over the slope working in semidarkness, picking their way over the dangerous surfaces, alternatively calling and listening for calls from those who were trapped. Here and there a few were digging desperately, moving rubble away as another unfortunate was found.

Nervously she got up and peered down the slope, seeking Dunross. He had quickly disappeared from her line of sight into the wreckage, but from time to time she had caught a glint from his flashlight. Now for some minutes she had seen nothing. Her anxiety increased, the minutes hanging, and whenever the wreck settled more fear had whipped her. Linc, Linc's somewhere there, was pounding on her brain. I've got to do something, I can't just sit, better to sit and wait and pray and wait, wait for Ian to come back. He'll find him . . .

In a sudden fright she leapt to her feet. A great section halfway down the slope had broken free, scattering rescuers who ran for their lives. In a moment the chain reaction ceased and it was quiet again but her heart kept up its pounding. There was no moving glint of Dunross's light to reassure her. 'Oh Jesus let him be all right!'

'Casey? Casey, is that you?' Gornt came out of the darkness and scrambled up to her.

'Oh Quillan,' she began pathetically and he held her in his arms, his strength giving her strength. 'Please help Lin—'

'I came as soon as I heard,' he told her quickly, overriding her. 'It was on the wireless. Christ, I was petrified you were . . . I never expected . . . Hold on, Casey!'

'I'm . . . I'm all right. Linc's in . . . he's in there somewhere, Quillan.'

'What? But how? Did he an—'

'He was in Or . . . Orlanda's apartment and Ia—'

'Perhaps you're wrong, Casey. Lis—'

'No. Orlanda told me.'

'Eh? She got out too?' Gornt gasped. 'Orlanda got out?'

1360

'Yes. She was with me, near me, back there, I saw it all happen, Quillan, I saw the whole terrible avalanche and the whole building collapse and then I ran here, Ian came to help and Linc's d—'

'Dunross? He got out too?' he asked, bile in his mouth.

'Oh yes. Yes, he's down there now. Some of the building shifted and the elevator, the elevator was full of bodies. He's down there somewhere, looking . . . looking in case . . .' Her voice died away.

She saw Gornt shift his attention to the slope. 'Who else got out?'

'Jacques, the Chens, that newspaperman, I don't know . . .' She could not see his face so she could not read him. 'You're sorry that . . . that Ian's alive?'

'No. On the contrary. Where did he go?'

'Down there.' She took his flashlight and directed it. 'There, where that outcrop is. He, I haven't seen him for a while but just there. You see the remains of the elevator? Near there.' Now she could see his face better, dark eyes, the bearded chiseled face, but it told her nothing.

'Stay here,' he said. 'You're safe here.' He took the flashlight and moved into the wreckage, soon to be swallowed by it.

The rain was heavier now, warm like the night was warm, and Gornt spat the bile out of his mouth, glad that his enemy was alive, hating that he was alive, but wanting him alive more.

It was very slippery as he worked his way down. A slab teetered and gave way. He stumbled, barked his shin and cursed, then moved onward, his flashlight seeking safety where he knew there was none. So Ian bloody tai-pan Dunross got out before it collapsed, he was thinking. That bugger's got a charmed life! Christ! But don't forget, the gods were on your side too. Don't forget th—

He stopped. Faint calls for help from somewhere near. Intently he listened again but he could not identify the direction. He called out, 'Where are you, where are you?' listening again. Nothing. Hesitating, he reexamined the way ahead. This whole god-cursed mess can slide down a hundred feet or more at the drop of a hat, he thought. 'Where are you?' Still nothing, so cautiously he went on, the gas smell heavy.

When he got nearer to the remains of the elevator he looked at the bodies, not recognizing any of them, went on and eased around a corner, ducking under an overhang. Suddenly a flashlight blinded him.

'What the hell're you doing here, Quillan?' Dunross asked.

'Looking for you,' Gornt said grimly, putting the light on him. 'Casey told me you were playing hide and seek.'

Dunross was resting on some rubble, catching his breath, his arms ripped and bloody, clothes in tatters. When this part of the wreckage had shifted, the way in had shrieked closed. As he had darted for safety the flashlight had been knocked out of his hand and when the avalanche subsided he was trapped with Clinker. It had taken him all his will not to panic in the darkness. Patiently he worked the area, his fingers groping, seeking the flashlight. Inch by inch. And when he was almost ready to give up, his fingers locked on it. In the light once more, fear had left him. The light had pointed a new way out. He stared back at Gornt, then smiled with the skin of his face. 'Sorry I'm not dead?'

Gornt shrugged and smiled the same rotten smile. 'Yes. Joss. But it'll happen soon enough.' The overhang creaked and shifted slightly and his light swung upward. Both men held their breath. It settled back with a sigh. 'Sooner if we don't get the hell out of here.'

Dunross got up, grunted as a stab of pain went up his back.

'You're not hurt, I hope?' Gornt asked.

Dunross laughed and felt better, the fright of entombment wearing off. 'No. Give me a hand will you?'

'What?'

Dunross pointed into the wreckage with his light. Now Gornt could see the old man. 'I got trapped down there trying to get him out.' At once Gornt moved to help, squatting down, moving what rubble they could to increase the crawlspace.

'His name's Clinker. His legs're a mess and he's lost a foot.'

'Christ! Here, let me do that.' Gornt got a better grip on the slab, shifted it away, then jumped down into the cavity. In a moment he turned back and peered up at Dunross. 'Sorry, the bugger's dead.'

'Oh Christ! You're sure?'

Gornt lifted the old man like a doll and they put him into the open.

1362

'Poor bugger.'

'Joss. Did he say where he was in the building? What floor? Was anyone with him?'

'He muttered something about caretaker, and being underneath the building, and something about, I think he said Mabel.'

Gornt put the flash all around. 'Did you hear anything or anyone?'

'No.'

'Let's get him out of here,' Gornt said with finality.

They picked him up. When they were in the open and relatively safe they stopped to get their breath Some stretcher bearers were nearby. Dunross beckoned them. 'We will take him away, Honored Lord,' one said. They bundled the body onto a stretcher and hurried off.

'Quillan, before we get back to Casey. She sai—'

'About Bartlett? Yes, she told me he was in Orlanda's place.' Gornt watched him. 'Her flat was on the eighth floor.'

Dunross looked down the slope. There were more lights than before. 'Where would that have ended up?'

'He's got to be dead. The *eighth* floor?'

'Yes. But whereabouts?'

Gornt searched the hillside. 'I can't see from here. I might recognize something, but I doubt it. It'd be, it'd be down there, almost at Sinclair Road.'

'He could be alive, in a pocket. Let's go and look.'

Gornt's face twisted with a curious smile. 'You need him and his deal, don't you?'

'No, no not now.'

'Bullshit.' Gornt clambered onto an outcrop. 'Casey!' he shouted, cupping his hands around his mouth. 'We're going below! Go back to the barrier and wait there!'

They heard her call back faintly, 'Okay, be careful!' Then Gornt said sourly, 'All right, Gunga Din, if we're going to play hero, we'd better do it right. I lead.' He moved off.

Equally sourly, but needing him, Dunross followed, his anger gathering. The two men worked their way out. Once clear, they scrambled down the slope. From time to time they would see a body or a part body but no one they recognized. They passed a few frantic survivors or relatives of those missing, pathetically digging or trying to dig with their hands, a broken piece of wood—anything they could find.

Down at the bottom of the slope Gornt stopped, his flashlight examining the wreckage carefully.

'Anything?' Dunross asked.

'No.' Gornt caught sight of some bedraggled curtains that might have been Orlanda's but it had been almost two years since he was in her apartment. His light hesitated.

'What is it?'

'Nothing.' Gornt began climbing, seeking clues to her apartment or to the Asian Properties apartment on the fifth floor. 'That could be part of Plumm's furniture,' he said. The sofa was torn in half, the springs akimbo.

'Help! Help in the name of all gods!' The faint Cantonese cry came from somewhere in the middle of this section. At once Gornt scrambled toward the sound, thinking he recognized Four Fingers, Dunross close behind, up and over and under. In the center of a mass of debris was an old Chinese man, bedraggled, covered with rubble dust. He was sitting in the wreckage, looking around perplexed, seemingly unhurt. When Gornt and Dunross came up to him he grimaced at them, squinting in their light.

At once they recognized him and now he recognized them. It was Smiler Ching, the banker. 'What happened, Honored Sirs?' he asked, his Cantonese heavy-accented, his teeth protruding.

Gornt told him briefly and the man gasped. 'By all the gods, that's impossible! Am I alive? Truly alive?'

'Yes. What floor were you on, Smiler Ching?'

'The twelfth—I was in my living room. I was watching television.' Smiler Ching searched his memory and his lips opened into another grimace. 'I'd just seen Little Mealy Mouth, Venus Poon, and then . . . then there was a thunderous noise from the direction of Conduit Road. The next thing I remember is waking up here, just a few minutes ago, waking up here.'

'Who was in the flat with you?'

'My *amah*. First Wife is out playing mah-jong!' The small old man got up cautiously, felt all his limbs and let out a cackle. '*Ayeeyah*, by all the gods, it's a fornicating miracle, tai-pan and second tai-pan! Obviously the gods favor me, obviously I shall recover my bank and become rich again and a steward at the

Turf Club! *Ayeeyah!* What joss!' Again he tested his feet and legs then clambered off, heading for safety.

'If this mess was part of the twelfth floor, the eighth should be back there,' Dunross said, his light pointing.

Gornt nodded, his face taut.

'If that old bastard can survive, so could Bartlett.'

'Perhaps. Let's look.'

84

11:05 P.M.:

An army truck swirled up in the heavy rain, spattering mud, and stopped near the command posts. Irish guardsmen in fatigues and raincoats, some with fire axes, jumped down. An officer was waiting for them. 'Go up there, Sergeant! Work alongside R.S.M. O'Connor!' He was a young man and he pointed with a swagger stick to the right of the slide, his uniform raincoat, boots and trousers mud filthy. 'No smoking, there's still a bloody gas leak, and get the lead out!'

'Where's Alpha Company, sir?'

'Up at Po Shan. Delta's halfway. We've an aid station on Kotewall. I'm monitoring Channel 4. Off you go!'

The men stared at the devastation. 'Glory be to God,' someone muttered. They charged off, following their sergeant. The officer went back to his command post and picked up the field telephone. 'Delta Company, this is Command. Give me a report.'

'We've recovered four bodies, sir, and two injured up here. We're halfway across the slope now. One's a Chinese woman called Kwang, multiple fractures but all right, and her husband, he's just shook up a bit.'

'What part of the building were they in?'

'Fifth floor. We think the heavy-duty girders protected them. Both casualties're on their way to our aid station at Kotewall. We can hear someone buried deep but, glory be, sir, we can't get at him—the firemen can't use their oxy-acetylene cutters. The gas's too heavy. Nothing else in our area, sir.'

'Keep it up.' The officer turned around and snapped at an orderly, 'Go and chase up those gas board fellows and see what

1366

the hell's holding them up! Tell'em to get their fingers out!'

'Yes sir.'

He switched channels. 'Kotewall Aid Station, this is Command. What's the score?'

'Fourteen bodies so far, Captain, and nineteen injured, some very bad. We're getting their names as quick as we can. Sir Dunstan Barre, we dug him out, he just has a broken wrist.'

'Keep up the good work! The police've set up a missing persons station on Channel 16. Get them all the names, dead, injured, everyone, quick as you can. We've some pretty anxious people down here.'

'Yes sir. The rumor's we're going to evacuate the whole area.'

'The governor, commissioner and the fire chief're deciding that right now.' The officer rubbed his face tiredly, then rushed out to intercept another incoming truck with Gurkhas from the Engineers Corps, passing the governor, commissioner and senior fire officer who stood at the central command post under the foyer overhang of Sinclair Towers. A white-haired engineer-surveyor from the Public Works Department got out of a car and hurried over to them.

'Evening, sir,' he said anxiously. 'We've been all through all the buildings now, from Po Shan down to here. I recommend we evacuate nineteen buildings.'

'Good God,' Sir Geoffrey exploded. 'You mean the whole bloody mountainside's going to collapse?'

'No sir. But if this rain keeps up another slip could start. This whole area's got a history of them.' He pointed into the darkness. 'In '41 and '50 it was along Bonham, '59 was the major disaster on Robertson, Lytton Road, the list's endless, sir. I recommend evacuation.'

'Which buildings?'

The man handed the governor a list then waved into the dark at the three levels. 'I'm afraid it'll affect more than two thousand people.'

Everyone gasped. All eyes went to the governor. He read the list, glanced up at the hillside. The slide dominated everything, the mass of the mountain looming above. Then he said, 'Very well, do it. But for God's sake tell your fellows to make it an orderly withdrawal, we don't want a panic.'

'Yes sir.' The man hurried away.

'Can't we get more men and equipment, Donald?'

'Sorry, not at the moment, sir,' the police commissioner replied. He was a strong-faced man in his fifties. 'We're spread rather thinly, I'm afraid. There's the massive slip over in Kowloon, another at Kwun Tong—eighty squatters huts've been swamped, we've already forty-four dead in that one so far, twenty children.'

Sir Geoffrey stared out at the hillside. 'Christ!' he muttered. 'With Dunross getting us Tiptop's cooperation I thought our troubles were over, at least for tonight.'

The fire chief shook his head, his face drawn. 'I'm afraid they're just beginning, sir. Our estimates suggest there may be a hundred or more still buried in that mess.' He added heavily, 'It'll take us weeks to sift through that lot, if ever.'

'Yes.' Again the governor hesitated, then he said firmly, 'I'm going to go up to Kotewall. I'll monitor Channel 5.' He went to his car. His aide opened the door but Sir Geoffrey stopped. Roger Crosse and Sinders were coming back from the great gash across Sinclair Road where the roof of the tunnel culvert had been ripped off. 'Any luck?'

'No sir. We managed to get into the culvert but it's collapsed fifty yards in. We could never get into Rose Court that way,' Crosse said.

When Rose Court had collapsed and had torn the side from the top four stories of Sinclair Towers, Crosse had been near his own apartment block, seventy yards away. Once he had recovered his wits, his first thought had been for Plumm, the second Suslev. Suslev was closer. By the time he had got to the darkened Sinclair Towers foyer, terrified tenants were already pouring out. Shoving them aside he had pushed and cursed his way up the stairs to the top floor, lighting his way with a pencil flashlight. Apartment 32 had almost vanished, the adjoining back staircase carried away for three stories. As Crosse gaped down into the darkness, it was obvious that if Suslev had been caught here, or caught with Clinker, he was dead—the only possible escape place was the tunnel-culvert.

Back on the ground floor once more, he had gone around the back and slipped into the secret tunnel entrance. The water was a boiling torrent below. Quickly he had hurried to the roadway where the roof of the tunnel had been carried away. The gash was overflowing. More than a little satisfied, for he was certain now that Suslev was dead, he had gone to the nearest phone, called in the alarm, then asked for Sinders.

'Yes? Oh hello, Roger.'

He had told Sinders where he was and what had happened, adding, 'Suslev was with Clinker. My people know he hasn't come out, so he's buried. Both of them must be buried. No chance they could be alive.'

'Damn!' A long pause. 'I'll come right away.'

Crosse had gone outside again and begun to organize the evacuation of Sinclair Towers and rescue attempts. Three families had been lost when the corner top stories went. By the time uniformed police and fire chiefs had arrived, the dead count was seven including two children and four others dying. When the governor and Sinders had arrived, they had gone back to open part of the tunnel to see if they could obtain access.

'There's no way we can get in from there, Sir Geoffrey. The whole culvert's collapsed, I'd say gone forever, sir.' Crosse was suitably grave, though inwardly delighted with the divine solution that had presented itself.

Sinders was very sour. 'Great pity! Yes, very bad luck indeed. We've lost a valuable asset.'

'Do you really think he'd've told you who this devil Arthur is?' Sir Geoffrey asked.

'Oh yes.' Sinders was very confident. 'Don't you agree, Roger?'

'Yes.' Crosse was hard put not to smile. 'Yes, I'm sure of it.'

Sir Geoffrey sighed. 'There'll be the devil to pay on a diplomatic level when he doesn't return to the *Ivanov*.'

'Not our fault, sir,' Sinders said. 'That's an act of God.'

'I agree, but you know how xenophobic the Soviets are. I'll bet any money they'll believe we have him locked up and under investigation. We'd better find him or his body rather quickly.'

'Yes sir.' Sinders turned his collar higher against the rain. 'What about the departure of the *Ivanov*?'

'What do you suggest?'

'Roger?'

'I suggest we call them at once, sir, tell Boradinov what's happened and that we'll postpone their departure if they wish.

I'll send a car for him and whoever he wants to bring to help in the search.'

'Good. I'll be up at Kotewall for a while.'

They watched Sir Geoffrey go, then went to the lee of the building. Sinders stared at the organized confusion. 'No chance he'd still be alive, is there?'

'None.'

A harassed policeman hurried up. 'Here's the latest list, sir, dead and rescued.' The young man gave Crosse the paper and added quickly, 'Radio Hong Kong's got Venus Poon coming on any moment, sir. She's up at Kotewall.'

'All right, thank you.' Rapidly Crosse scanned the list. 'Christ!'

'They found Suslev?'

'No. Just a lot of old acquaintances're dead.' He handed him the list. 'I'll take care of Boradinov then I'm going back to the Clinker area.'

Sinders nodded, looking at the paper. Twenty-eight rescued, seventeen dead, the names meaningless to him. Among the dead was Jason Plumm. . . .

At the wharf in Kowloon where the *Ivanov* was tied up, coolies were trudging up and down the gangplanks, laden with last-minute cargo and equipment. Because of the emergency, police surveillance had been cut to a minimum and now there were only two police on each gangway. Suslev, disguised under a huge coolie hat and wearing a coolie smock and trousers, barefoot like the others, went past them unnoticed and up on deck. When Boradinov saw him, he hastily guided the way to Suslev's cabin. Once the cabin door was shut, he burst out, '*Kristos*, Comrade Captain, I'd almost given you up for lost. We're due to le—'

'Shut up and listen.' Suslev was panting, still very shaken. He tipped the vodka bottle and gulped the spirit, choking a little. 'Is our radio equipment repaired?'

'Yes some of it, yes it is, except the top-security scrambler.'

'Good.' Shakily he related what had happened. 'I don't know how I got out, but the next thing I remember was I was halfway down the hill. I found a taxi and made my way here.' He took another swallow, the liquor helping him, the wonder of his escape from death and from Sinders enveloping him. 'Listen, as far as everyone else is concerned, I'm still there, at Rose Court! I'm dead or missing presumed dead,' he said, the plan leaping into his head.

Boradinov stared at him. 'But Com—'

'Get on to police headquarters and say that I've not returned —ask if you can delay departure. If they say no, good, we leave. If they say yes we can stay, we'll stay for a token day, then regretfully leave. Understand?'

'Yes, Comrade Captain, but why?'

'Later. Meanwhile make sure *everyone* else aboard thinks I'm missing. Understand?'

'Yes.'

'No one is to come into this cabin until we're safe in international waters. The girl's aboard?'

'Yes, in the other cabin as you ordered.'

'Good.' Suslev considered her. He could put her back ashore, as he was 'missing' and would stay missing. Or keep with his plan. 'We stay with that plan. Safer. When the police report I'm missing—I had my usual SI followers so they'll know I'm with Clinker—just tell her our departure's delayed, to stay in the cabin "until I arrive". Off you go.'

Suslev locked the door, his relief almost overpowering, and switched on the radio. Now he could vanish. Sinders could never betray a dead man. Now he could easily persuade Center to allow him to pass over his duties in Asia to another and assume a different identity to get a different assignment. He could say that the various European security leaks documented in the AMG papers made it necessary for someone new to begin with Crosse and Plumm—if either of them is still alive, he thought. Better they're both dead. No, not Roger. Roger's too valuable.

Happier and more confident than he had been in years he went into the bathroom, found a razor and shaving brush, humming a Beatles tune along with the radio. Perhaps I should request a posting to Canada. Isn't Canada one of our most vital and important posts—on a par with Mexico in importance?

He beamed at himself in the mirror. New places to go to, new assignments to achieve, with a new name and promotion, where a few hours ago there was only disaster ahead. Perhaps I'll take Vertinskaya with me to Ottawa.

He began shaving. When Boradinov returned with police permission to delay their departure, he hardly recognized Gregor Suslev without his mustache and beard.

85

Bartlett was twenty feet down under a cat's cradle of girders that kept the wreckage from crushing him. When the avalanche had hit almost three hours ago he had been standing in the kitchen doorway sipping an ice-cold beer, staring out at the city. He was bathed, dressed and feeling wonderful, waiting for Orlanda to return. Then he was falling, the whole world wrong, unearthly, the floor coming up, the stars below, the city above. There had been a blinding, monstrous, soundless explosion and all air had rushed out of him and he had fallen into the upward pit forever.

Coming back to consciousness was a long process for him. It was dark within his tomb and he hurt everywhere. He could not grasp what had happened or where he was. When he truly awoke, he stared around trying to see where he was, his hands touching things he could not understand. The closed darkness nauseated him and he reeled in panic to his feet, smashing his head against a jutting chunk of concrete that was once part of the outside wall and fell back stunned, his fall protected by the debris of an easy chair. In a little while his mind cleared, but his head ached, arms ached, body ached. The phosphorescent figures on his watch attracted his attention. He peered at them. The time was 11:41.

I remember . . . what do I remember?

'Come on for chrissake,' he muttered, 'get with it! Get yourself together. Where the hell was I?' His eyes traced the darkness with growing horror. Vague shapes of girders, broken concrete and the remains of a room. He could see little and recognized nothing. Light from somewhere glistened off a shiny surface. It was a wrecked oven. All at once his memory flooded back.

'I was standing in the kitchen,' he gasped out loud. 'That's it, and Orlanda had just left, about an hour, no less'n that, half an hour. That'd make it around nine when . . . when whatever happened happened. Was it an earthquake? What?'

Carefully he felt his limbs and face, a stab of pain from his right shoulder every time he moved. 'Shit,' he muttered, knowing it was dislocated. His face and nose were burning and bruised. It was hard to breathe. Everything else seemed to be working, though every joint felt as though he had been racked and his head ached terribly. 'You're okay, you can breathe, you can see, you can . . .'

He stopped, then groped around and found a small piece of rubble, carefully raised his hand, then dropped it. He heard the sound the rubble made and his heart picked up. 'And you can hear. Now, what the hell happened? Jesus, it's like that time on Iwo Jima.'

He lay back to conserve his strength. 'That's the thing to do,' the old top sergeant had told them, 'you lay back and use your goddamn loaf if you're caught in an excavation or buried by a bomb. First make sure you can breathe safe. Then burrow a hole, do anything, but breathe any way you can, that's first, then test your limbs and hearing, you'll sure as hell know you can see but then lay back and get your goddamn head together and *don't panic*. Panic'll kill you. I've dug out guys after four days'n they've been like a pig in shit. So long's you can breathe and see and hear, you can live a week easy. Shit, four days's a piece of cake. But other guys we got to within'n hour'd drowned themselves in mud or crap or their own fear vomit or beaten their goddamn heads unconscious against a goddamn piece of iron when we was within a few feet of the knuckleheads an' if they'd just been lying there like I told you, nice'n easy, quiet like, they'd've heard us and they could've shouted. Shit! Any you bastards panic when you're buried you'd better believe you're dead men. Sure. Me I been buried fifty times. No panic!'

'No panic. No sir,' Bartlett said aloud and felt better, blessing that man. Once during the bad time on Iwo Jima, the hangar he had been building was bombed and blown up and he had been buried. When he had dug the earth out of his eyes and mouth and ears, panic had taken him and he had hurled himself at the tomb and then he had remembered, *Don't panic*, and forced

1374

himself to stop. He had discovered himself shivering like a cowed dog under the threat of a lash but he had dominated the terror. Once over the terror and whole, he had looked around carefully. The bombing had been during the day so he could see well enough and noticed the beginning of a way out. But he had waited, cautiously, remembering instructions. Very soon he heard voices. He called out, conserving his voice.

'That's another goddamn obvious thing, conserve your voice, huh? You don't shout yourself hoarse the first time you hear help near. Be patient. Shit, some guys I know shouted themselves so goddamn hoarse they was goddamn dumb when we was within easy distance and we lost 'em. Get it through your goddamn heads, we gotta have help to find you. Don't panic! If you can't shout, tap, use anything, make a noise somehow, but give us a sign and we'll get you out, so long's you can breathe— a week's easy, no sweat. You bastards should go on a diet anyways . . .'

Now Bartlett was using all his faculties. He could hear the wreckage shifting. Water was dripping nearby but no sounds of humans. Then, faintly, a police siren which died away. Reassured that help was on the way, he waited. His heart was controlled. He lay back and blessed that old top sergeant. His name was Spurgeon, Spurgeon Roach, and he was black.

It must've been an earthquake, he thought. Has the whole building collapsed or was it just our floor and the next above? Maybe an airplane crashed into . . . Hell, no, I'd've heard the incoming noise. Impossible for a building to collapse, not with building regs, but hey, this's Hong Kong and we heard some contractors don't always obey regulations, cheat a little, don't use first-grade steel or concrete. Jesus if I get, no, *when* I get out . . .

That was another inviolate rule of the old man. 'Never forget, so long's you can breathe, you will get out, *you will*. . . .'

Sure. When I get out I'm going to find old Spurgeon and thank him properly and I'm going to sue the ass out of someone. Casey's sure to . . . ah Casey, I'm sure as hell glad she's not in this shit, nor Orlanda. They're both . . . Jesus, could Orlanda have been caught wh—

The wreckage began to settle again. He waited, his heart pounding. Now he could see just a little better. Above him was a twisted mass of steel beams, and pipes half imbedded in broken jagged concrete, pots and pans and broken furniture. The floor he was lying on was equally broken. His tomb was small, barely enough space to stand. Reaching up above with his good arm he could not touch the makeshift ceiling. On his knees now he reached again, then stood, feeling his way, the tiny space claustrophobic. 'Don't panic,' he said out loud. Groping and bumping into outcrops he circumnavigated the space he was in. 'About six feet by five feet,' he said out loud, the sound of his voice encouraging. 'Don't be afraid to talk out loud,' Spurgeon Roach had said.

Again the light glinting off the oven attracted him. If I'm near that, I'm still in the kitchen. Now where was the oven in relation to anything else? He sat down and tried to reconstruct the apartment in his mind. The oven had been set into a wall opposite the big cutting table, opposite the window, near the door, and the big refrigerator was beside the door and across the w—

Shit, if I'm in the kitchen there's food and beer and I can last out the week easy! Jesus, if I could only get some light. Was there a flash? Matches? Matches and a candle? Hey, wait a minute, sure, there was a flash on the wall near the refrigerator! She said they were always blowing fuses and sometimes the power failed and . . . and sure, there were matches in the kitchen drawer, lots of them, when she lit the gas. Gas.

Bartlett stopped and sniffed the air. His nose was bruised and stuffed and he tried to clear it. Again he sniffed. No smell of gas. Good, good he thought, reassured. Getting his bearings from the oven he groped around, inch by inch. He found nothing. After another half an hour his fingers touched some cans of food, then some beer. Soon he had four cans. They were still chilled. Opening one, he felt oh so much better, sipping it, conserving it—knowing that he might have to wait days, finding it eerie down there in the dark, the building creaking, not knowing exactly where he was, rubble falling from time to time, sirens from time to time, water dripping, strange chilling sounds everywhere. Abruptly a nearby tie-beam shrieked, tormented by the thousands of tons above. It settled an inch. Bartlett held his breath. Movement stopped. He sipped his beer again.

Now do I wait or try to get out? he asked himself uneasily. Remember how old Spurgeon'd always duck that one. 'It depends, man. It depends,' he'd always say.

More creaking above. Panic began to well but he shoved it back. 'Let's recap,' he said aloud to reassure himself. 'I got provisions now for two, three days easy. I'm in good shape an' I can last three, four days easy but you, you bastard,' he said to the wreckage above, 'what're you going to do?'

The tomb did not answer him.

Another spine-chilling screech. Then a faint voice, far overhead and to the right. He lay back and cupped his hands around his mouth. 'Helllp!' he shouted carefully and listened. The voices were still there. 'Helllp!'

He waited but now there was a vast emptiness. He waited. Nothing. His disappointment began to engulf him. 'Stop it and wait!' The minutes dragged heavily. There was more water dripping, much more than before. Must be raining again, he thought. Jesus! I'll bet there was a landslide. Sure, don't you remember the cracks in the roads? Goddamn son of a bitching landslide! Wonder who all else got caught? Jesus what a goddamn mess!

He tore off a strip of his shirt and tied a knot in it. Now he could tell the days. One knot for each day. His watch had read 10:16 when his head had first cleared, now it was 11:58.

Again all his attention zeroed. Faint voices, but nearer now. Chinese voices.

'Helllp!'

The voices stopped. Then, 'Where you arrrr, *heya?*' came back faintly.

'Down here! Can you hear meeeeee?'

Silence, then more faintly, 'Where youuuuuarrrrre?'

Bartlett cursed and picked up the empty beer can and began to bang it against a girder. Again he stopped and listened. Nothing.

He sat back. 'Maybe they've gone for help.' His fingers reached out and touched another can of beer. He dominated his overpowering urge to break it open. 'Don't panic and be patient. Help's near. The best I can do's wait an—' At that moment the whole earth twisted and rose up under the strain with an ear-dulling cacophony of noise, the protective girders above grinding out of safety, rubble avalanching down. Protecting his head with his arms, he cowered back, covering himself as best he could. The shrieking movement seemed to go on for an eternity. Then it ceased. More or less. His heart was thumping heavily now, his chest tight and dust bile in his mouth. He spat it out and sought a beer can. They had vanished. And all the other cans. He cursed, then, cautiously, raised his head and almost banged it against the shifted ceiling of the tomb. Now he could touch the ceiling and the walls without moving. Easily.

Then he heard the hissing sound. His stomach twisted. His hand reached out and he felt the slight draft. Now he could smell the gas. 'You'd better get the hell out of here, old buddy,' he muttered, aghast.

Getting his bearings as best he could, he eased out of the space. Now that he was on the move, in action, he felt better.

The dark was oppressive and it was very hard to make progress upward. There was no straight line. Sometimes he had to make a diversion and go down again, left then right, up a little, down again under the remains of a bathtub, over a body or part of a body, moans and one time voices far away. 'Whereareyouuuu?' he shouted and waited then crawled on, inch by inch, being patient, not panicking. After a while he came into a space where he could stand. But he did not stand, just lay there for a moment, panting, exhausted. There was more light here. When his breathing had slowed he looked at his watch. He gathered his strength and continued but again his upward path was blocked. Another way but still blocked. He slid under a broken pier and, once through, began to squirm onward. Another impasse. With difficulty he retreated and tried another way. And another, never enough space to stand, his bearings lost now, not knowing if he was going deeper into the wreckage. Then he stopped to rest and lay in the wet of his tomb, his chest pounding, head pounding, fingers bleeding, shins bleeding, elbows bleeding.

'No sweat, old buddy,' he said out loud. 'You rest, then you start again . . .'

MONDAY

86

Gurkha soldiers with flashlights were patiently picking their way over this part of the dangerous, sloping, broken surface calling out, 'Anyone there?' then listening. Beyond and all around, up and down the slope, soldiers, police, firemen and distraught people were doing the same.

It was very dark, the arcs set up below not touching this area halfway up the wreckage.

'Anyone there?' a soldier called, listened again, then moved on a few feet. Over to the left of the line one of them stumbled and fell into a crevice. This soldier was very tired but he laughed to himself and lay there a moment, then called down into the earth, 'Anyone there?' He began to get up then froze, listening. Once more he lay down and shouted into the wreckage, 'Can you hear me?' and listened intently.

'Yesss . . .' came back faintly, very faintly.

Excitedly the soldier scrambled up. 'Sergeant! Sergeant Sah!'

Fifty yards away, on the edge of the wreckage, Gornt was with the young lieutenant who had been directing rescue operations in this section. They were listening to a news broadcast on a small transistor: '. . . slips all over the Colony. And now here is another report direct from Kotewall Road.' There was a short silence then the well-known voice came on and the young man smiled to himself. 'Good evening. This is Venus Poon reporting live on the single worst disaster to hit the Colony.' There was a wonderful throb to her voice, and, remembering the brave, harrowing way she had described the Aberdeen fire disaster that she also had been involved in, his excitement quickened. 'Rose Court on Kotewall Road is no

1381

more. The great twelve-story tower of light that all Hong Kong could see as a landmark has vanished into an awesome pyre of rubble. My home is no more. Tonight, the finger of the Almighty struck down the tower and those who lived there, amongst them my devoted *gan sun* who raised me from birth. . . .'

'Sir,' the sergeant called from the middle of the slip, 'there's one over here!'

At once the officer and Gornt began hurrying towards him. 'Is it a man or woman?'

'Man, sah! I think he said his name was Barter or something like that. . . .'

Up at the Kotewall Road barrier Venus Poon was enjoying herself, the center of all attention in the lights of mobile radio and television teams. She continued to read the script that had been thrust into her hand, changing it here and there, dropping her voice a little, raising it, letting the tears flow—though not enough to spoil her makeup—describing the holocaust so that all her listeners felt they were there with her on the slope, felt chills of horror, and thanked their joss that death had passed them by this time, and that they and theirs were safe.

'The rain is still falling,' she whispered into the microphone. 'Where Rose Court tore away part of the upper stories of Sinclair Towers, seven dead already counted, four children, three Chinese, one English, more still buried. . . .' The tears were seeping out of her eyes now. She stopped and those watching caught their breath too.

In the beginning she had almost torn her hair out at the thought of her apartment gone and all her clothes and all her jewelry and her new mink. But then she had remembered that all her real jewelry was safely in the jewelers being reset—a present of her old suitor, Banker Kwang—and her mink was being altered at the tailor's. And as to her clothes, pshaw, Four Fingers will be happy to replace them!

Four Fingers! Oh oh I hope that old goat got out and will be saved like Smiler Ching, she had prayed fervently. Eeeee, what a miracle! If one, why not another? And surely no building falling can kill old Ah Poo. She'll survive! Of course she will!

1382

And Banker Kwang saved! Didn't I weep with happiness that he was saved? Oh lucky lucky day! And now Profitable Choy, such a smart, good-looking interesting fellow. Now if he had money, real money, he would be the one for me. No more of these old bags of fart with their putty yangs for delectable yin, the most delectable . . .

The producer could not wait anymore. He leaped for the mike and said urgently, 'We will continue the report as soon as Miss Ven—'

Instantly she came out of her reverie. 'No, no,' she said bravely, 'the show must go on!' Dramatically she wiped her tears away and continued reading and improvising, 'Down the slope members of our glorious Gurkha and Irish Guards, heroically risking their lives, are digging out our Brothers and Sisters. . . .'

'My God,' an Englishman muttered. 'What courage! She deserves a medal, don't you think so, old boy?' He turned to his neighbor and was embarrassed to see the man was Chinese. 'Oh, ah sorry.'

Paul Choy hardly heard him, his attention on the stretchers that were coming back from the wreckage, the bearers slipping and sliding under the arc lamps that had been erected a few minutes ago. He had just come back from the aid station that was set up at the fork of Kotewall Road under a makeshift overhang where frantic relations like himself were trying to identify the dead or injured or report the names of those who were missing and believed still buried. All evening he had been going back and forth in case Four Fingers had been found somewhere else and was coming in from another direction. Half an hour ago one of the firemen had broken through a mass of wreckage to reach into the area of the collapsed fifth floor. That was when Richard and Mai-ling Kwang had been pulled out, then Jason Plumm with half his head missing, then others, more dead than living.

Paul Choy counted the stretchers. Four of them. Three had blankets covering the bodies, two very small. He shuddered, thinking how fleeting life was, wondering again what would now happen at the stock exchange tomorrow. Would they keep it closed as a mark of respect? Jesus, if they keep it closed all Monday, Struan's is sure to be at 30 by Tuesday opening— gotta be! His stomach churned and he felt faint. Friday, just before closing, he had gambled five times every penny that Four Fingers had reluctantly loaned him, buying on margin. Five times 2 million HK. He had bought Struan's, Blacs, Victoria Bank and the Ho-Pak, gambling that somehow this weekend the tai-pan would turn disaster into victory, that the rumors of China being approached for cash were true, and Blacs or the Victoria had a scam going. Ever since the meeting with Gornt at Aberdeen when he had put his theory of a bail-out by Blacs or the Victoria of the Ho-Pak to Gornt and had seen a flicker behind those cunning eyes, he had wondered if he had sniffed out a scam of the Big Boys. Oh sure, they're Big Boys all right. They've got Hong Kong by the shorts, Jesus, have they got an inside track! And Jesus, oh Jesus when at the races Richard Kwang asked him to buy Ho-Pak and, almost at once, Havergill had announced his takeover, he had gone to the men's room and vomited. 10 million in Ho-Pak, Blacs, Victoria and Struan's, bought at the bottom of the market. And then, tonight, when the nine o'clock news announced that China was advancing half a billion cash so all bank runs were finished, he knew he was a multimillionaire, a multi-multimillionaire.

The young man could not hold his stomach together and rushed off to the bushes by the side of the road and retched till he thought he would die.

The English bystander turned his back on him and said quietly to a friend, 'These Chinese fellows really don't have much of a stiff upper lip, do they, old boy?'

Paul Choy wiped his mouth, feeling terrible, the thought of all his maybe money, so near now, too much for him.

The stretchers were passing. Numbly he followed them to the aid station. In the background under the makeshift overhang, Dr. Meng was doing emergency surgery. Paul Choy watched Dr. Tooley turn back the blankets. A European woman. Her eyes were open and staring. Dr. Tooley sighed and closed them. The next was an English boy of ten. Dead too. Then a Chinese child. The last stretcher was a Chinese man, bleeding and in pain. Quickly the doctor gave him a morphia injection.

·Paul Choy turned aside and was sick again. When he came back Dr. Tooley said kindly, 'Nothing you can do here, Mr. Choy. Here, this'll settle your stomach.' He gave him two aspirins and some water. 'Why don't you wait in one of the cars? We'll tell you the instant we hear anything about your uncle.'

'Yes, thanks.'

More stretchers were arriving. An ambulance pulled up. Stretcher bearers got the tagged injured aboard and the ambulance took off into the drizzle. Outside, away from the stench of blood and death, the young man felt better.

'Hello, Paul, how're things going?'

'Oh. Oh hello, tai-pan. Fine, thanks.' He had encountered the tai-pan earlier and told him about Four Fingers. Dunross had been shocked and very concerned.

'Nothing yet, Paul?'

'No sir.'

Dunross hesitated. 'No news is good news perhaps. If Smiler Ching could survive, let's hope for the best, eh?'

'Yes sir.' Paul Choy had watched Dunross hurry off up the road toward the barrier, his mind rehashing all the permutations he had worked out. With the tai-pan's fantastic takeover of General Stores—that was so smart, oh so smart—and now sliding out of Gornt's trap, his stock's gotta go to 30. And with Ho-Pak pegged at 12.50, the moment that's back on the board it's gotta go back to 20. Now, figure it, 17.5 percent of 10 million times 50 is—

'Mr. Choy! Mr. Choy!'

It was Dr. Tooley beckoning him from the aid station. His heart stopped. He ran back as fast as he could.

'I'm not sure but follow me, please.'

There was no mistake. It was Four Finger Wu. He was dead, seemingly unharmed. On his face was a wonderful calmness and a strange, seraphic smile.

Tears spilled down Paul Choy's cheeks. He squatted beside the stretcher, his grief possessing him. Compassionately Dr. Tooley left him and hurried over to the other stretchers, someone screaming now, another distraught mother clutching the broken body of a child in her arms.

Paul Choy stared at the face, a good face in death, hardly seeing it.

Now what? he asked himself, wiping away his tears, not really feeling he had lost a father but rather the head of the family, which in Chinese families is worse than losing your own father. Jesus, now what? I'm not the eldest son so I don't have to make the arrangements. But even so, what do I do now?

Sobbing distracted him. It was an old man sobbing over an old woman, lying on a nearby stretcher. So much death here, too much, Paul Choy thought. Yes. But the dead must bury the dead, the living must go on. I'm no longer bound to him. And I'm American.

He lifted the blankets as though to cover Four Finger Wu's face and deftly slipped off the thong necklace with its half-coin and pocketed it. Again making sure no one was watching, he went through the pockets. Money in a billfold, a bunch of keys, the personal pocket chop. And the diamond ring in its little box.

He got up and went to Dr. Tooley. 'Excuse me, Doc. Would you, would you please leave the old man there? I'll be back with a car. The family, we'd . . . Is that okay?'

'Of course. Inform the police before you take him away, their Missing Persons is set up at the roadblock. I'll sign the death certificate tomorrow. Sorry there's no ti—' Again the kind man was distracted and he went over to Dr. Meng. 'Here, let me help. It's like Korea, eh?'

Paul Choy walked down the hill, careless of the drizzle, his heart light, stomach settled, future settled. The coin's mine now, he told himself, certain that Four Fingers would have told no one else, keeping to his usual pattern of secrecy, only trusting those he had to.

Now that I've possession of his personal chop I can chop whatever I like, do whatever I like, but I'm not going to do that. That's cheating. Why should I cheat when I'm ahead? I'm smarter than any of his other sons. They know it, I know it and that's not being crazy. I *am* better. It's only fair I keep the coin and all the profits on the 2 mill. I'll set the family up, modernize everything, equip the ships, anything they want. But with my profit I'm going to start my own empire. Sure. But first I'm going to Hawaii. . . .

At the head of the line of cars near the first slip Dunross stopped beside his car and opened the door to the backseat. Casey jerked out of a reverie and the color drained out of her face. 'Linc?'

'No, nothing yet. Quillan's fairly sure he's pinpointed the

area. Gurkhas are combing that part right now. I'm going back to relieve him.' Dunross tried to sound confident. 'The experts say there's a very good chance he'll be okay. Not to worry. You all right?'

'Yes. Yes thanks.'

When he had returned from their first search, he had sent Lim for coffee, sandwiches and a bottle of brandy, knowing the night would be very long. He had wanted Casey to leave with Riko but she had refused. So Riko had gone back to her hotel in the other car with Lim.

'You want a brandy, Ian?' Casey said.

'Thanks.' He watched her pour for him, noticing her fingers were steady. The brandy tasted good. 'I'll take Quillan a sandwich. Why not put a good slug of brandy into the coffee, eh? I'll take that.'

'Sure,' she said, glad for something to do. 'Have any others been rescued?'

'Donald McBride—he's all right, just shaken. Both he and his wife.'

'Oh good. Any, any bodies?'

'None that I know of,' he said, deciding not to tell her about Plumm or his old friend Southerby, chairman of Blacs. At that moment Adryon and Martin Haply hurtled up and Adryon threw her arms around him, sobbing with relief. 'Oh, Father we just heard, oh, Father, I was petrified.'

'There, there,' he said, gentling her. 'I'm fine. Good God, Adryon, no bloody landslip will ever touch the tai-pan of the Noble Ho—'

'Oh don't say that,' she begged him with a shiver of superstitious dread. 'Don't ever say that! This's China, gods listen, don't say that!'

'All right, my love!' Dunross hugged her and smiled at Martin Haply who was also wet with relief. 'Everything all right?'

'Oh yes sir, we were over in Kowloon, I was covering the other slide when we heard the news.' The youth was so relieved. 'Goddamn I'm pleased to see you, tai-pan. We . . . afraid we bashed up the car a little getting up here.'

'Never mind.' Dunross held Adryon away from him. 'All right, pet?'

Again she hugged him. 'Oh yes.' Then she saw Casey. 'Oh.

Oh hello, Casey I was, er, so—'

'Oh don't be silly. Come on out of the rain. Both of you.'

Adryon obeyed. Martin Haply hesitated then said to Dunross, 'If you don't mind, sir, I'll just look around.'

'Christian got out,' Dunross said quickly. 'He ph—'

'Yes sir. I called the office. Thanks. Won't be long, honey,' he said to Adryon and went off toward the barrier. Dunross watched him go, young, tough and very assured, then caught sight of Gornt hurrying down the hill. Gornt stopped, well away from the car and beckoned him anxiously.

Dunross glanced at Casey, his heart thumping uneasily. From where she was she could not see Gornt. 'I'll be back soon as I can.'

'Take care!'

Dunross came up to Gornt. The older man was filthy, clothes torn, beard matted and his face set.

'We've pegged him,' Gornt said. 'Bartlett.'

'He's dead?'

'No. We've found him but we can't get at him.' Gornt motioned at the thermos. 'Is that tea?'

'Coffee with brandy.'

Gornt took it, drank gratefully. 'Casey's still in the car?'

'Yes. How deep is he?'

'We don't know. Deep. Perhaps it's best not to say anything about him to her, not yet.'

Dunross hesitated.

'Better to leave it,' the other man said again. 'It looks dicey.'

'All right.' Dunross was weary of all the death and suffering. 'All right.'

Rain made the night more filthy and the morass even more dangerous. Ahead, past the slide area, Kotewall Road ran almost straight for seventy yards, climbing steeply, then curled up and away around the mountainside. Already tenants were streaming out of buildings, evacuating.

'There's no mistake about Tiptop and the money?' Gornt said, picking his way carefully with the flashlight.

'None. The bank runs're over.'

'Good. What did you have to barter?'

Dunross did not answer him, just shrugged. 'We'll open at 30.'

1388

'That remains to be seen.' Gornt added sardonically, 'Even at 30 I'm safe.'

'Oh?'

'I'll be about $2 million U.S. down. That's what Bartlett advanced.'

Dunross felt a glow. That'll teach Bartlett to try a heist on me, he thought. 'I knew about that. It was a good idea—but at 30 you'll be down about $4 million, Quillan, his 2 and 2 of yours. But I'll settle for All Asia Air.'

'Never.' Gornt stopped and faced him. 'Never. My airline's still not for sale.'

'Please yourself. The deal's on offer until the market opens.'

'The pox on your deals.'

They plodded onward on the top of the slope, now nearing the foyer area. They passed a stretcher returning. The injured woman was no one either of them knew. If Dunross were on one of those, Gornt thought grimly, it'd solve all my problems neatly . . .

87

1:20 A.M.:

The Gurkha sergeant had his flashlight directed downward. Around him were other soldiers, the young lieutenant, firemen hurrying up with one of the fire chiefs.

'Where is he?' Fire Chief Harry Hooks asked.

'There, somewhere down there. His name's Bartlett, Linc Bartlett.' Hooks saw the light seep down a few feet then stop, blocked by the maze. He lay down on the ground. Close to the ground the gas smell was heavier. 'Down there, Mr. Bartlett! Can you hear me?' he shouted into the wreckage.

They all listened intently. 'Yes,' came back faintly.

'Are you hurt?'

'No!'

'Can you see our light?'

'No!'

Hooks cursed, then shouted, 'Stay where you are for the moment!'

'All right, but the gas is heavy!'

He got up. The officer said, 'A Mr. Gornt was here and he's gone to get more help.'

'Good. Everyone spread out, see if you can find a passage down to him, or where we can get closer.' They did as he ordered. In a moment one of the Gurkhas let out a shout. 'Over here!'

It was a small space between ugly broken slabs of concrete, broken timbers and joists and some steel H-beams, perhaps enough for a man to crawl down into. Hooks hesitated then took off his heavy equipment. 'No,' the officer said. 'We'd better try.' He looked at his men. 'Eh?'

At once they grinned and all moved for the hole. 'No,' the officer ordered. 'Sangri, you're the smallest.'

'Thank you, sah,' the little man said with a great beam, his teeth white in his dark face. They all watched him squirm underground headfirst like an eel.

Twenty-odd feet below, Bartlett was craning around in the darkness. He was in a small crawlspace, his way up blocked by a big slab of flooring, the smell of gas strong. Then his eyes caught a flicker of light ahead off to one side and he got a quick look at his surroundings. He could hear nothing except the drip of water and the creaking wreckage. With great care he squirmed off toward where he had seen the light. A small avalanche began as he shoved some boards aside. Soon it stopped. Above was another small space. He wormed his way up and along this space and reached a dead end. Another way, dead end. Above he felt some loosened boards in the crumpled flooring. He lay on his back and fought the boards away, coughing and choking in the dust. Abruptly light doused him. Not much, very little, but when his eyes adjusted it was enough for him to see a few yards. His elation vanished as he realized the extent of the tomb. In every direction he was blocked.

'Hello above!'

Faintly, 'We hear youuuuu!'

'I'm in the light now!'

After a moment, 'Which light?'

'How the hell do I know for chrissake?' Bartlett said. *Don't panic, think and wait*, he almost heard Spurgeon say. Holding on, he waited, then the light he was in moved a little. 'That one!' he shouted.

Instantly the light stopped.

'We have you positioned! Stay where you are!'

Bartlett looked around, quartering the area very carefully. A second time with still the same result: there was no way out.

None.

'They'll have to dig me out,' he muttered, his fear gathering . . .

Sangri, the young Gurkha, was down about ten feet under the surface but well away to the right from Bartlett. He could go no farther. His way was blocked. He squirmed around and got a purchase on a jagged concrete slab and moved it slightly. At once this part of the wreckage began to shift. He froze, let the slab rest again. But there was no other way to go, so, gritting his teeth and praying that everything would not collapse on him and whoever was below, he pulled the slab aside. The wreckage held. Panting, he put his flash into the cavity, then his head, peering around

Another dead end Impossible to go farther. Reluctantly, he pulled back. 'Sergeant,' he shouted in Nepalese, 'I can go no farther.'

'Are you sure?'

'Oh yes sah, very sure!'

'Come back!'

Before he left he shouted down into the darkness, 'Hello down there!'

'I hear you!' Bartlett called back.

'We're not far away! We'll get you out, sah! Don't worry!'

'Okay!'

With great difficulty Sangri began to back out, retracing his way painfully. A small avalanche pelted him with rubble. Grimly he continued climbing.

Dunross and Gornt clambered over the wreckage to join the clusters of men, who were in a chain, removing rubble and beams where they could.

'Evening, tai-pan, Mr. Gornt. We've pegged him but we're not close.' Hooks pointed at the man who was holding the flash steady. 'That's his direction.'

'How far down is he?'

'By the sound of his voice about twenty feet.'

'Christ!'

'Aye, Christ it is. The poor bugger's in a pickle. Look't those!' Heavy steel H-beams were blocking the way down. 'We daren't use cutters, too much gas.'

'There must be another way? From the side?' Dunross asked.

'We're looking. Best we can do's get more men and clear what we can away.' Hooks glanced off at an encouraging shout. They all hurried toward the excited soldiers. Below a mess of torn-up flooring that the men had taken away was a rough passageway that seemed to lead downward, twisting out of sight. They saw one of the small men jump into the cavity, then vanish. Others watched, shouting encouragement. The way was easy for six feet, very hard for the next ten feet, twisting and turning, then he was blocked. 'Hello down there, sah, can you see my light?'

'Yes!' Bartlett's voice was louder. There was almost no need to shout.

'I'm going to move the light around, sah. Please if it gets near, please give me right or left, up or down, sah.'

'Okay.' Bartlett could see a tiny particle of light up and to his right through a mass of the beams, girders and joists and broken rooms. Directly above him was an impenetrable mess of flooring and girders. Once he lost the light beam but soon picked it up again. 'Right a bit,' he called, his voice already a little hoarse. Obediently the light moved. 'Down! Stop there! Now up a fraction.' It seemed to take an age but the light centered on him. 'That's it!'

The soldier held the flash steady, made a cradle for it with rubble, then took his hand away. 'All right, sah?' he shouted.

'Yesss! You're on the money!'

'I'm going back for more help.'

'All right.'

The soldier retreated. In ten minutes he had guided Hooks back. The fire chief gauged the path of the beam and meticulously examined the obstacle course ahead. 'Stone the crows, it'll take a month of Sundays,' he muttered. Then, containing his dread, he took out his compass and measured the angle carefully.

'Don't you worry, mate,' he called down. 'We'll get you out nice and easy. Can you get closer to the light?'

'No. I don't think so.'

'Just stay where you are and rest. Are you hurt?'

'No, no but I can smell gas.'

'Don't worry, lad, we're not far away.' Hooks clambered out of the passage. On the surface again, he measured the line on the compass and then paced out over the tilted surface. 'He's below this spot, tai-pan, Mr. Gornt, within five feet or so, about twenty feet down.' They were two-thirds of the way down the slope, closer to Sinclair Road than to Kotewall. There was no way in from the sides that they could see, mud and earth of the slide heavier to the right than to the left.

'The only thing we can do's dig,' he said with finality. 'We can't get a crane here, so it's elbow grease. We'll try here first.' Hooks indicated an area that seemed promising, ten feet away, close to the hole the soldiers had discovered.

'Why there?'

'Safer, tai-pan, in case we start the whole mess a-shifting. Come on, mates, lend a hand. But take care!'

So they began to dig and to carry away everything removable. It was very hard work. All surfaces were wet and treacherous, the wreckage itself unbalanced. Beams, joists, flooring, planks, concrete, plaster, pots, radios, TV sets, bureaus, clothes, all in an untidy impossible jumble. Work stopped as they uncovered another body.

'Get a medic up here!' Hooks shouted.

'She's alive?'

'In a manner of speaking.' The woman was old, her once white smock and black trousers tattered and mud-colored, her long hair tied in a ratty queue. It was Ah Poo.

'Someone's *gan sun*,' Dunross said.

Gornt was staring incredulously at the place she had been found, a tiny hole within an ugly, almost solid, jagged mess of broken and reinforced concrete. 'How the hell do people survive?'

Hooks's face split with his grin, his broken teeth brown and tobacco stained. 'Joss, Mr. Gornt. There's always hope so long as a body can breathe. Joss.' Then he bellowed below. 'Send a stretcher up here, Charlie! On the double!'

It came quickly. The stretcher bearers carried her away. Work continued. The pit deepened. An hour later, four or five feet lower they were blocked by tons of steel beams. 'We'll have to detour,' Hooks said. Patiently they began again. A few feet later again blocked. 'Detour over there.'

'Can't we saw through this mess?'

'Oh yes, tai-pan, but one spark and we're all bloody angels. Come on, lads. Here. Let's try here.'

Men rushed to obey . . .

88

4:10 A.M.:

Bartlett could hear them loudly now. From time to time dust and dirt would cascade, sodden rubble in its wake, as timbers and beams and mess above were removed. His rescuers seemed to be about ten yards away as far as he could judge, still five or six feet above him, the trickle of light making the waiting easier. His own escape was blocked all around. Earlier he had considered going back, down under this flooring, then down again to try to find another route and seek better safety that way.

'Better wait, Mr. Bartlett!' Hooks had shouted to him. 'We knows where you be!'

So he had stayed. He was rain soaked, lying on some boards, not too uncomfortably and well protected by heavy beams. Most of his line of sight was blocked a few feet away. Above was more twisted flooring. There was just enough room to lie down or, with care, to sit up. The smell of gas was strong but he had no headache yet and felt he was safe enough, the air good enough to last forever. He was tired, very tired. Even so, he forced himself to stay awake. From his vantage point he knew it would take them the rest of the night, perhaps part of the day, to work a shaft to him. That did not worry him at all. They were there. And he had made contact An hour ago he had heard Dunross nearby. 'Linc? Linc, it's Ian!'

'What the hell're you doing here?' he had called back happily.

'Looking for you. Don't worry, we're not far away.'

'Sure. Say, Ian,' he had begun, his anxiety almost over-whelming, 'Orlanda, Orlanda Ramos, you know her? I was wai—'

'Yes. Yes I saw her just after the slip hit the building. She's fine. She's waiting up at Kotewall. She's fine. How about you?'

'Hell, no sweat,' he had said, almost light-headed now, knowing she was safe. And when Dunross had told him about his own miraculous escape and that Casey had seen the whole catastrophe happen, he was appalled at the thought of how close the others had all been to disaster. 'Jesus! A couple of minutes either way and you'd all've been clobbered.'

'Joss!'

They had chatted for a while then Dunross had moved out of the way so the rescue could continue.

Thinking about Orlanda now, another tremor shook him and again he thanked God that she was safe and Casey was safe. Orlanda'd never make it underground, he thought. Casey maybe, but not Orlanda. Never. But that's no loss of face either.

He eased himself more comfortably, his soaking clothes making his skin crawl, the shouts and noises of the approaching rescue comforting. To pass the time, he continued his reverie about the two women. I've never known a body like Orlanda's or a woman like her. It's almost as though I've known her for years, not a couple of days. That's a fact. She's exciting, unknown, female, wonderfully dangerous. Casey's no danger. She'd make a great wife, a great partner but she's not female like Orlanda is. Sure Orlanda likes pretty clothes, expensive presents, and if what people here say is true she'll spend money like there's no tomorrow. But isn't that what most of it's for? My ex's taken care of, so're the kids. Shouldn't I have some fun? And be able to protect her from the Blitzmanns of the world?

Sure. But I still don't know what it is about her—or Hong Kong—that's got to me. It's the best place I've ever been and I feel more at home here than back home. 'Maybe, Linc, you've been here in a previous lifetime,' Orlanda had said.

'You believe in reincarnation?'

'Oh yes.'

Wouldn't that be wonderful, he thought in his reverie, not noticing the gas or that now the gas was touching him a little. To have more than one lifetime would be the best luck in all the world an—

'Linc!'

'Hey! Hi, Ian, what's cooking?' Bartlett's happiness picked up. Dunross's voice was quite close. Very close.

'Nothing. We're just going to take a short break. It's heavy going. We've got to detour again but we're only a few yards away. Thought I'd chat. As far as we can judge we're about five feet above you, coming in from the west. Can you see us yet?'

'No. There's a floor above me, all busted up, and beams, but I'm okay. I can last out easy. Hey, you know something?'

'What?'

'Tonight's the first time you called me Linc.'

'Oh? I hadn't noticed.'

Bullshit, Bartlett thought and grinned to himself. 'What y—' A sudden chill took both men as the wreckage began groaning, twisting here and there. In a moment the noise ceased, most of it. Bartlett began to breathe easier. 'What you going to do tomorrow?'

'What about?'

'The stock market. How are you going to beat Gornt?' He listened with growing awe as Dunross told him about the Bank of China's money, Plumm's party and his challenge to Gornt, backed by his new 50 million revolving fund.

'Fantastic! Who's supporting you, Ian?'

'Father Christmas!'

Bartlett laughed. 'So Murtagh came through, huh?' He heard the silence and smiled again.

'Casey told you?'

'No. No, I had that figured. I told you Casey's as smart as a whip. So you're home free. Congratulations,' he said with a grin, meaning it. 'I thought I had you, Ian.' Bartlett laughed. 'You really think your stock'll open at 30?'

'I'm hoping.'

'If you're hoping, that means you and your pals have fixed it. But Gornt's smart. You won't get him.'

'Oh yes I will.'

'No you won't! How about our deal?'

'Par-Con? That stands of course. I thought that was all arranged?'

Bartlett heard the dry innocence. 'Quillan must be fit to be tied.'

'He is! He's just above. He's helping too.'

Bartlett was surprised. 'Why?'

There was a pause. 'Quillan's a first-class, twenty-four-carat berk but . . . I don't know. Maybe he likes you!'

'Screw you too!' Bartlett was equally good-natured. 'What're you going to do about Quillan?'

'I've made him a proposal.' Dunross told it to him.

Bartlett grunted. 'So my 2 mill's down the sewer?'

'Of course. That 2 million is. But your share of the General Stores takeover'll bring you 5, perhaps more, our Struan-Par-Con deal much more.'

'You really figure 5?'

'Yes. You 5, Casey 5.'

'Great! I always wanted her to get her drop dead money.' I wonder what she'll do now? he asked himself. 'She's always wanted to be independent and now she is. Great! What?' he asked, missing what Dunross had said.

'I just said, would you like to talk to her? It's dicey but safe enough.'

'No,' Bartlett said firmly. 'Just say hi, I can say it better when I'm out.'

'Casey's said she's not moving till you are.' There was a slight pause. 'Orlanda too. How about her? You want to say hello or anything?'

'No thanks. Plenty of time later. Tell them both to go home.'

'They won't. I'm afraid you're rather popular.'

Bartlett laughed and sat up and bumped his head. A pain snaked down his back and he grunted, then moved more comfortably, his head almost touching the roof.

Dunross was cramped in a small space not far away at the bottom of the twisting passage, hating the closeness, his claustrophobia nauseating, a chill cold sweat soaking him because of it. He could see no sign of Bartlett but he had noted his voice sounded strong and confident. Hooks had asked him to keep Bartlett talking while they rested, in case the gas was enveloping him. 'You never know, tai-pan, gas can sneak up on you. We need him alert. We'll be needing his help soon now.'

The tai-pan squirmed around uneasily, sensing danger. Someone was climbing down, rubble cascading with him. It was Hooks. He stopped a few feet above.

'All right, tai-pan. Best come out now, we'll get some of my lads back in.'

'Right away. Linc! Stay awake. We're starting again.'

'Okay, no sweat. Say, Ian, would you consider being a best man?'

'Certainly,' he said at once, his brain shouting. Which one? 'It'd be an honor.'

'Thanks,' he heard Bartlett say and as much as he wanted to know, he knew he could never ask. He was sure Bartlett would volunteer the who. But all Bartlett said was, 'Thanks. Yes, thanks very much.' He smiled, surprised. Linc's learning, he told himself. It'll be good to have him as a partner—and a voting member of the Turf Club. Casey too—'We'll have you out in a jiffy!'

Just as he was leaving he heard: 'Wouldn't it be great if they could be friends? Guess that's too much to hope for?'

Dunross was not sure if it had been meant for him. 'What?' he called out.

'Nothing,' Bartlett replied. 'Say, Ian, we've got lots to do this week! Hey, I'm glad you won over Gornt!' Yes, he told himself happily. It'll be good maneuvering with you, watching you carefully, building *our* Noble House.

About eight yards away, a few feet up, Dunross turned awkwardly and began to climb back.

Sixteen feet above him, Gornt and the others were waiting beside the greatly widened mouth of the pit. Dawn was lightening the east, a patch of sky now among the enveloping clouds. All over the slope tired men were still digging, searching, calling and listening. Wearily Hooks clambered out of the deepening pit. At that moment there was a tremendous noise from up near Po Shan Road. All heads jerked around. Then far above and to the left they saw part of the slope moving. The noise increased, then a wall of water and mud surged from behind the curve of the hillside up Kotewall Road and gathering speed, rushed at them. Men began to flee as the sludge crest swept down to where the foyer had been and poured over the slope and wreckage, inundating it, the enormous mass of the sludge pressing the crest forward and down. Gornt saw it coming and hung on to an H-beam, the others hanging on as best they could. The foul, stinking murk swept up to them and passed, Gornt buried to his knees but his grip firm against the suction. The wave surged onward leaving inches of slush over everything, Hooks and the others pulling themselves out, everything else momentarily forgotten.

Gornt had not forgotten.

From where he was he could see down into the pit. He saw Dunross's hands and head appear out of the sludge. The hands grabbed a hold. More sludge was sweeping downward into the pit, finding a level, filling it. Dunross's grip slipped and he was sucked under but he fought out again and hung on precariously.

Gornt watched. And waited. And did not move. The mud poured down. The level rose more.

Dunross felt himself falling, the suction very great. He was choking in the slime, but his fingers held, he forced his toes into a crevice and began to climb. Somehow he tore himself out of the suction and now he was safe, hugging the side, half out of the mud, his chest heaving, heart pounding, retching. Still half in shock, his knees trembling, he wiped the mud from his eyes and mouth and stared around blankly. Then he saw Gornt ten feet above, watching him, resting easily against an outcrop . . .

For an instant his whole being concentrated, seeing the sardonic twisted smile, the hate open and disappointment vast, and he knew that if he had been above and Gornt trapped as he had been trapped, he would have watched and waited too.

Would I?

I'd've watched and waited equally and never never a helping hand. Not for Gornt. And then, at long last, Dirk Struan's curse would be ended, be laid to rest, and those who follow me never bedeviled again.

Then the instant was over. His head cleared. He remembered Bartlett and he stared downward in horror. Where the crawl-space had been was now only a slimy pool.

'Oh Christ! Helllp!' he cried out. Then there was sudden pandemonium and others were in the pit, Hooks and firemen and soldiers, and they hurled themselves impotently at the slime with shovels and with hands.

Dunross pulled himself out. Shakily he stood on the edge. In anguish. Gornt had already gone. In a little while all attempts ceased. The puddle remained.

TUESDAY

89

Dunross stood at the bay window of his penthouse atop the
Struan Building, watching the harbor. The sunset was wonderful, visibly unlimited, the sky clear except for a few tinged
cumuli westward over Mainland China, reddish there, darkness touching the eastern horizon. Below, the harbor was busy
as usual, ordinary as usual, Kowloon glowing in the falling sun.

Claudia knocked and opened the door. Casey came in. Her
face was stark, her tawny hair like the sunset. Her grief made
her ethereal.

'Hello, Casey.'

'Hello, Ian.'

There was no need to say any more. Everything about Bartlett
had been said already. It had taken until late last night to get his
body out. Casey had waited on the slope for him. Then she had
gone back to the hotel. This morning she had called and now
she was here.

'Drink? Tea? Coffee? There's wine. I made martinis.'

'A martini. Thanks, Ian,' she said, her voice flat, the hurt in it
tearing him. 'Yes, I'd like that.'

She sat on the sofa. He poured and put in an olive. 'Everything can wait, Casey,' he said compassionately. 'There's no
hurry.'

'Yes, yes I know. But we agreed. Thanks.' She accepted the
chilled glass and raised it. 'Joss.'

'Joss.'

She sipped the ice-cold liquor, all her movements studied,
almost apart from herself, then opened her briefcase and put a

manila envelope on his desk. 'This contains all the John Chen papers about Struan's and everything he offered or told us. These're all the copies I have here. The ones in the States I'll shred.' Casey hesitated. 'You're sure to have made changes by now but, well, it's all there.'

'Thanks. Did Linc give anything to Gornt?'

'No, I don't think so.' Again the hesitation. 'For safety I'd consider part of the information leaked.'

'Yes.'

'Next, our Par-Con-Struan deal.' The sheaf of documents she gave him was quite thick. 'All six copies are signed and sealed with the corporate seal. I've the executive power to sign.' She hesitated. 'We had a deal, Linc and I. I willed him voting power of all my stock for ten years, he did the same for me. So I'm head of Par-Con.'

Dunross's eyes widened slightly. 'For ten years?'

'Yes,' she said without emotion, feeling nothing, wanting nothing except to weep and to die.

Later I can be weak, she thought. Now I must be strong and wise. 'For ten years. Linc . . . Linc had voting control. I'll send you a formal verification when it's official.'

Dunross nodded. From the lacquer desk he brought back an equivalent set of papers. 'These are the same. I've chopped them formally. This'—he put an envelope onto the pile—'this's our private agreement giving Par-Con title to my ships as collateral.'

'Thanks. But with your revolving fund that's not necessary.'

'Even so, it was part of our agreement.' Dunross watched her, admiring her courage. There had been no tears at the new beginning on the slope, just a numbed nod and, 'I'll wait. I'll wait until . . . I'll wait.' Orlanda had broken at once. He had sent her to a hotel and, later, a doctor to succor her. 'It was part of our deal.'

'All right. Thanks. But it's not necessary.'

'Next: Here is the letter of agreement on our deal on General Stores. I'll get you the formal documents within ten days. I'll nee—'

'But Linc never put up the 2 million.'

'Oh but he did. He did it by cable Saturday night. My Swiss bank confirmed the transaction yesterday and the money was

1406

duly passed over to the board of General Stores. They accepted so that deal's accomplished now.'

'Even though Pug's dead?'

'Yes. His widow agreed to the board's recommendation. It's a very good deal by the way. Far better than the Superfoods tender.'

'I don't want that, any part of that.'

'When I was down in the pit, chatting with Linc, he said how happy he was that the General Stores deal was going through. His exact words were, "Great! 5 mill? I always wanted her to get her drop dead money. She always wanted to be independent, and now, she is. Great!"'

'But at what a cost,' she told him, her misery welling. 'Linc always warned me that drop dead money costs more than you're prepared to pay. It has. I don't want it.'

'Money is money. You're not thinking clearly. It was his to give and he gave it to you. Freely.'

'You gave it to me.'

'You're wrong, he did. I just helped you as you helped me.' He sipped his drink. 'I'll need to know where to send his profits. You'll remember there were no voting rights included. Who's his trustee?'

'It's a bank. First Central. I'm his executor, along with a man from the bank.' She hesitated. 'I guess his mother's his heir. She's the only one named in his will—Linc, Linc was open about that, to me. His ex-wife and their kids are well taken care of and specifically excluded from his will. There's just the voting control to me and the rest goes, the rest to his ma.'

'Then she'll be very rich.'

'That won't help her.' Casey was trying very hard to keep her voice level and the tears away. 'I talked to her last night and she broke up, poor lady. She's . . . she's in her sixties, nice woman, Linc's her only son.' A tear seeped in spite of her resolve. 'She, she asked me to bring him back. His will says he's to be cremated.'

'Look, Casey,' Dunross said quickly, 'perhaps I could make the arr—'

'No. Oh no, thanks, Ian. Everything's done. I've done it. I wanted to do it. The airplane's cleared and all the paper work done.'

1407

'When do you leave?'

'At ten tonight.'

'Oh.' Dunross was surprised. 'I'll be there to see you off.'

'No, no thanks. The car's fine but there's no ne—'

'I insist.'

'No. Please?' She looked at him, begging him.

After a moment he said, 'What's your plan?'

'Nothing very much. I'm going to . . . I'm going to make sure all his wishes are taken care of, papers, his will, and wind up his affairs. Then I'll reorganize Par-Con—I'll try to reorganize it as he'd want, and then, then I don't know. All that'll take me thirty days. Maybe I'll be back in thirty days to begin, maybe I'll send Forrester or someone else. I don't know. I'll let you know in thirty days. Everything's covered till then. You've got my numbers. Please call me anytime if there's a problem.' She started to get up but he stopped her.

'Before you go there's something I should tell you. I didn't last night because the time wasn't right. Perhaps now is, I'm not sure, but just before I left Linc he asked me if I'd consider being a best man.' He saw Casey go white and rushed on. 'I told him it would be an honor.'

'He said me? He wanted to marry *me*?' she asked incredulously.

'We'd been talking about you. Doesn't that follow?'

'He never mentioned Orlanda?'

'Not at that time. No. Earlier on he'd been very concerned about her because he was in her flat and didn't know what had happened to her.' Dunross watched her. 'When I told him she was safe he was very relieved, naturally. When I told him you'd almost been caught in the landslide he almost had a heart attack. Then, just as I was leaving I heard him say softly, "Guess it'd be too much to hope for those two to be friends." I wasn't sure if I was meant to hear that—while we were digging he'd been talking to himself a lot.' He finished his drink. 'I'm sure he meant you, Casey.'

She shook her head. 'It's a good try, Ian. I'll bet it was Orlanda.'

'I think you're wrong.'

Again a silence. 'Maybe. Friends?' She looked at him. 'Are you going to be friends with Quillan?'

'No. Never. But that's not the same. Orlanda's a nice person. Truly.'

'I'm sure.' Casey stared at her drink, sipped but did not taste it. 'What about Quillan? What happened today? I'm afraid I didn't hear. What did you do about him? I saw you closed at 30.01 but I . . . I really didn't notice much else.'

Dunross felt a sudden glow. Because of the Kotewall catastrophe the governor had ordered the stock market to remain closed all Monday. And the banks, as a sign of mourning. By ten this morning, the Bank of China's cash was on hand in every branch of every bank, throughout the Colony. The bank runs fizzled. By three o'clock many customers were lined up returning to deposit their cash once more.

Just before the market opened at ten o'clock this morning Gornt had called him.

'I accept,' he had said.

'You don't want to bargain?'

'I want no quarter from you, just as you expect none from me. The papers are on their way.' The phone had gone dead.

'What about Quillan?' she asked again.

'We made a deal. We opened at 28 but I let him buy back in at 18.'

She gaped at him. Without thinking she made the quick calculation. 'That'd cost him just about 2 million. But that's Linc's 2 million. So Quillan's off the hook!'

'I told Linc the deal and that it'd cost him the 2 million and he laughed. I did point out that with General Stores and the Par-Con deal, his capital loss of 2 is set off against a capital gain of 20 or more.' Dunross watched her, gauging her. 'I think it's fair that the 2 was forfeit.'

'You're not telling me you let Gornt off the hook for nothing?'

'No. I've got my airline back. The control of All Asia Air.'

'Ah.' Casey shivered remembering the story of that Christmas night when Gornt and his father went unexpectedly to the Great House. Her sadness was brimming. 'Do me a favor?'

'Of course. Provided it's not for Quillan.'

She had been going to ask Dunross to let Gornt in as a steward, to let him have a box. But now she did not. She knew it would have been a waste of time.

'What favor?'

'Nothing. Nothing now. I'll be off, Ian.' Weary, so weary, she got up. Her knees were trembling. All of her was aching monstrously. She held out her hand. He took it and kissed it with the same grace-filled gesture she remembered from the night of the party, the first night in the Long Gallery when, frightened, she had seen the knife buried in the heart of the portrait. All at once her agony crested and she wanted to scream out her hatred of Hong Kong and the people of Hong Kong who had somehow caused the death of her Linc. But she did not.

Later, she ordered herself, holding on to the limit of her strength. Don't break. Don't let go. Be self-contained. You have to, now. Linc's gone forever.

'See you soon, Casey.'

''Bye, Ian,' she said and left.

He stared at the closed door a long time, then sighed and pressed a buzzer.

In a moment Claudia came in. 'Evening, tai-pan,' she said with her enormous warmth. 'There're a few calls that should be dealt with—most important, Master Duncan wants to borrow 1,000 HK.'

'What the devil for?'

'It seems he wants to buy a diamond ring for a "lady". I tried to pry her name out of him but he wouldn't tell.'

Oh God, the sheila, Dunross thought as the memory rushed back of what his son had said about his 'girl.' Sheila Scragger, the nurse from England, on holiday with Duncan at the Australian station called Paldoon. 'Well, he's not going to buy much for 1,000. Tell him he has to ask me. No, wait!' He thought a moment. 'Give him 1,000 out of petty cash—offer it to him at 3 percent interest per month against his written guarantee that you can stop it from his pocket money at the rate of 100 a month. If he falls for that it'll teach him a fine lesson. If he doesn't I'll give him the 1,000, but not till next Easter.'

She nodded, then added sadly, 'Poor Miss Casey. She's dying inside.'

'Yes.'

'Here are your calls, tai-pan. Master Linbar called from Sydney, please call him back when you have a moment. He thinks he's got Woolara back in line.'

Dunross stared at her. 'I'll be damned!'

'Mr. Alastair called with congratulations, and your father, and most members of the family. Please call Master Trussler in Jo'burg, it's about thoriums.' She sniffed. 'Mrs. Gresserhoff called to say good-bye.'

'When's she off?' Dunross asked noncommittally, knowing the flight.

'Tomorrow, JAL's early flight. Isn't it awful about Travkin? Oh I'm so sad about him.'

'Yes.' Travkin had died in the night. Dunross had visited him at the Matilda Hospital several times but his trainer had never recovered consciousness since the Saturday accident. 'Have we tracked down any next of kin?'

'No. He had no special girl friend or, or anyone. Master Jacques has made the burial arrangements.'

'Good. Yes. That's the least we can do for him.'

'Are you going to ride Saturday?'

'I don't know.' Dunross hesitated. 'Remind me to talk to the stewards about making the fifth the Travkin Stakes—a way of thanking him.'

'Yes. Oh, that would be wonderful. I did so like him, yes that would be wonderful.'

Dunross glanced at his watch. 'Is my next appointment downstairs yet?'

'Yes.'

'Good,' the tai-pan said, his face closing.

He went down to the next floor, to his office. 'Afternoon, Mr. Choy, what can I do for you?' He had already sent condolences about Four Finger Wu.

When the door was shut, Paul Choy wiped his hands without noticing it. 'I've come about step one, sir. Sorry we had to put it off from yesterday, but, er, the wax impressions—they fitted one of your two remaining half-coins?'

'First I would ask who has the other half, now that Four Fingers is an ancestor.'

'The family Wu, sir.'

'Who in the family Wu?' Dunross asked harshly, deliberately rough. 'The coin was given to an individual who would pass it on to an individual. *Who?*'

'Me. Sir.' Paul Choy stared back at the tai-pan, unafraid, even though his heart was beating faster than it had ever beaten—

even more than when he was on the junk a lifetime ago—the young Werewolf's blood on his hands, the half-dead, mutilated body leaning against him, and his father shouting at him to throw the man overboard.

'You'll have to prove Four Fingers gave it to you.'

'Sorry, tai-pan, I don't have to prove anything,' Paul Choy replied confidently. 'I just have to present the coin and ask the favor. In secret. Everything secret, that's the deal. If it's the real coin your honor and the face of the Noble House is at stake and the fa—'

'I know what I have at stake.' Dunross made his voice grate. '*Do you?*'

'Sir?'

'This is China. Lots of curious things happen in China. You think I'm a fool to be bamboozled by an ancient legend?'

The young man shook his head, his throat tight. 'No. You're absolutely no fool, tai-pan. But if I present the coin, you *will* grant the favor.'

'What's your favor?'

'First I guess I'd like to know if you're . . . if you're satisfied it's *one* of the four. I'm satisfied.'

'Are you now?'

'Yes sir.'

'You know this coin was stolen from Phillip Chen?'

Paul Choy stared at him, then recovered quickly. 'This coin's from Four Finger Wu. I know of no theft. It came from my father, that's all I know. It was my father's.'

'You should give it back to Phillip Chen.'

'Did you ever see it, this particular one, in his possession, sir?'

Dunross had already talked to Phillip Chen about the coin. 'Is there no way to prove it's yours, Phillip?' he had asked him.

'None, tai-pan. None,' the old man had said, wringing his hands.

Dunross kept his eyes boring into the youth. 'It's Phillip Chen's.'

Paul Choy shifted uneasily. 'There were four coins, tai-pan. Mr. Chen's coin must be one of the others. This one belongs, belonged to my father. You remember what he said at Aberdeen?'

Dunross stared at him silently, trying to shake him, dealing

1412

with him Western style. Paul Choy wavered but held his gaze steady. Interesting, Dunross thought. You're a tough little bastard and good. Now, are you an emissary of Goldtooth Wu, the eldest son, or a thief and here on your own account? He left the silence hanging, using it to undermine his opponent while he rethought his position. The moment Paul Choy had called yesterday to ask for an appointment he had known the reason. But how to handle it? Four Fingers barely dead and now I've a new enemy, he thought, strong, well trained with lots of balls. Even so, he's got weak links like anyone. Like you have. Gornt's one of them. Riko could be another. Ah, Riko! What is it about her that moves you so much?

Forget that! How do you recover the half-coin before the favor?

'I presume you have your half with you. Let's go to the assayist right now.' He got up, testing Paul Choy.

'No sir, sorry but no.' Paul Choy felt his heart about to burst, the thong around his neck suddenly a noose, the half-coin burning into his flesh. 'Sorry, but I don't think that's a good idea.'

'I think it's a very good idea,' Dunross continued brusquely, pressuring him. 'We'll go and fetch it. Come along!'

'No. No thanks, tai-pan.' Paul Choy said it with a polite firmness Dunross recognized. 'Could we please do it next week? Say a week Friday? There's no hurry now.'

'I won't be in Hong Kong on Friday.'

'Yes sir. You'll be in Japan. Could you put aside an hour during your stay there? Anytime to suit you. To go visit an assayist?'

Dunross's eyes narrowed. 'You seem to know a lot, Mr. Choy.'

'It's easy to find out anything here, sir. Japan would be better for both of us. Less chance of a, a foul-up and in Japan we're both equal.'

'You're suggesting you won't be here?'

'No, no, tai-pan. But as you said, this is China, strange things happen in China. Four Fingers and his group're well connected too. The coin's a one shot—person to person—and should be handled that way. That's the way I figure it.'

Paul Choy was sweating now, thanking God that part of the

'favor' was that everything was to be secret. Ever since he had brought back the body of Four Fingers he had been maneuvering for power in the family. At length he had achieved exactly what he wanted, the very special position—in Mafia terms—of *consigliere*, chief advisor to Goldtooth Wu, the eldest son, now titular head of the Seaborne Wu. That's what we are, he thought, his fear rising again. We're Chinese mafioso. Isn't there blood on me too? I was aboard with the opium. What does Goldtooth know that I don't?

'You can trust me implicitly, Goldtooth,' he had said to his brother, fighting for his future.

'I'm afraid I have little choice. I'm in uncharted waters. I need all the help I can get. Your expertise will be very valuable,' Goldtooth had said in his clipped English when they were in the final stages of negotiation.

'I figure we can work together.'

'Let's be blunt, Brother. We're both university trained, the rest aren't. We need each other and the Seaborne Wu must be modernized. I can't do it. I need serious help—my years running his Pleasure Boats hardly fit me for command. I kept asking but, well, you know our father. Good God, I couldn't even change a girl's hourly rate without getting his approval. His four fingers were on every ship, in every transaction in the fleet.'

'Sure, but now if his captains'll go along with change, in a year you'll have the best-run Chinese operation in Asia.'

That's exactly what I want. Exactly.'

'What about opium?'

'The Seaborne Wu have always carried that cargo.'

'What about guns?'

'What guns?'

'I heard whispers Four Fingers was going into gun-running.'

'I know nothing about guns.'

'Let's get rid of the opium-heroin racket. Let's stay to hell out of narcotics. Isn't it true he was joining up with those two jokers, Smuggler Yuen and White Powder Lee?'

'Rumors. I'll consider what you suggest. But let me say I'm captain of the fleets and head of the Seaborne Wu now. My decision is final. We'll consult. You'll be *consigliere* with all that means, but if I make a decision it's final. For instance, I heard about the coup, the stock market coup, that you pulled off without his permission. It was brilliant, yes, but there's to be no more of that—I must be consulted and must know in advance.'

'Agreed. But from here on in, I'm also in business on my own account. I've resigned from Gornt's. Next, any private dealings I began with Four Fingers are mine to continue.'

'What are they?'

'Friday he advanced me 2 million to play the market. My deal was 17.5 percent of the profits. I want all the profits.'

'50 percent.'

'90. As of right now, there's nothing to keep me in Hong Kong. Even at 50 percent, if I sell the present holdings—and only I know what they are by the way—I'm worth around 3 million U.S.'

They had haggled and settled at 70 percent, Goldtooth's 30 percent to be deposited in a Swiss bank, a numbered account.

'I figure the market'll be on the come for two more days, then I off-load. My decision, okay?'

'Yes. *Profitable* suits you, Younger Brother, better than Paul. I'd like to stay with Profitable. What else were you doing with Four Fingers?'

'There was one last scam. He swore me to secrecy, forever. Forever, with blood oaths. I have to honor his wish.'

Reluctantly Goldtooth Wu had agreed and now, waiting for the tai-pan to answer him about Japan, the young man's confidence was brimming. I'm rich. I've got all Goldtooth's power if I need it, and I've a U.S. passport and I'm going to Hawaii. In Japan there's a chance I can outsmart Dunross—no, not outsmart him, he's far too good for that, but maybe there I can get a safe, fair shake to prove, once and for all, *my* coin's real.

'Would Japan suit you, tai-pan?' he repeated.

'I hear you made a killing on the market?'

The youth beamed, not expecting the nonsequitur. 'Yes sir. I'm about 5.5 million U.S. ahead.'

Dunross whistled. 'That's not bad for a couple of weeks' work, Profitable Choy. At 15 percent tax,' he added innocently.

The youth winced and fell into the trap. 'Hell, I'm a U.S. citizen, so subject to U.S. taxes every which way.' He hesitated. 'I've a couple of ideas that'd . . . say, tai-pan, we might make a deal that'd be good for you and good for me.'

Dunross saw Paul Choy's eyes flatten and his caution increase.

'My Old Man trusted you,' the youth said. 'You and he were Old Friends. Maybe I could inherit that—be worth that, one day.'

'Return the coin freely and I'll grant all sorts of favors.'

'First things first, tai-pan. First we find out if my coin's real. Japan, okay?'

'No. Here, or not at all!' Dunross snapped, deciding to gamble.

Paul Choy's eyes slitted even more. Abruptly he decided too and reached under his shirt and took out the coin and laid it on the desk. 'I ask a favor in Jin-qua's name from the tai-pan of the Noble House.'

In the silence Dunross stared at the coin. 'Well?'

'First, I want Old Friend status, equal to Four Fingers with all that that implies. Second: I want to be appointed a director of Struan's for a four-year period at a salary equal to other directors—for face I'll buy a block of shares at market bringing my holdings to 100,000 shares.' He felt a bead of sweat drop off his chin in the silence. 'Next: I want to joint venture, 50-50 partners, a pharmaceutical plant with Struan's, capitalized at 6 million U.S.—I put up half within 30 days.'

Dunross stared at him, perplexed. 'To do what?'

'The market for pharmaceuticals throughout Asia is vast. We could make a bundle, given your expertise in manufacturing, mine in marketing. Agreed?'

'Is that all? All the favor?'

'Three more things. Th—'

'Only three?' Dunross asked witheringly.

'Three. First, next year I'm going to start another stock exchange. I'll—'

'You'll what?' Dunross gaped at him, thrown.

Profitable Choy grinned and wiped the sweat off his face. 'Sure. A stock exchange for Chinese, run by Chinese.'

Dunross laughed suddenly, 'You've got balls, Profitable Choy. Oh yes. Incidentally, that's not a bad idea at all. What about it, the new exchange?'

'Just your benevolent Old Friend assistance to get started, to stop the big guys from blocking me.'

'For 50 percent.'

'For very favorable inside terms. Very favorable, guaranteed. Next,' the youth held on to his hope, 'I want you to introduce me to Lando Mata and tell him you're backing me as part of my father's group to bid for the gambling and gold syndicate monopoly. All right?'

'You said three things. What's last?'

'In three years a stewardship of the Turf Club. In that time I'll guarantee to donate a million U.S. to any charity or charities you name, I'll back all worthy causes and swear by God I'll make it as easy for you as I can.' The young man wiped the sweat off. 'I'm finished.'

Dunross hesitated. 'If the coin's real I'll agree to everything except the part about Lando Mata.'

'No. That's part of the deal.'

'I don't agree.'

'I've asked for nothing illegal, nothing you can't gr—'

'Lando Mata's out!'

The young man sighed. He took the coin off the desk, stared at it. 'If that's out, then the whole deal's off and I'll put Four Finger Wu's ask in place. It's still the same coin,' he said, readying to play his last card.

'And?'

'And that'll make you party to narcotics, guns and everything you detest *but will have to honor.* Sorry, tai-pan, but I'm bucking to be an ancestor.' He tossed the coin back on the table. 'You choose.'

Dunross was suddenly perturbed. The favor was cleverly couched. Nothing illegal, nothing extravagant. Paul Choy had done very well against him. Too well. Four Fingers was a known quantity. But this one, this devil's spawn? I can't risk narcotics —he knows that.

To give himself time Dunross reached into his pocket and found the little silk pouch and put his coin on the table. He moved his half into the other. The fit was perfect.

Without knowing it both men exhaled, staring at the now-joined coin that would lock them immutably together. Dunross knew it was a waste of time but he would go to the assayist anyway. For a moment he held the two halves in his hand. What to do about this cocky young bugger, he asked himself. Ah,

1417

now there's a good thought! Phillip Chen should be given the problem!

'All right, Profitable Choy,' he said putting him very high on his private Suspected Persons list. 'I'll agree to grant your favor—if your half's real—except I'll *ask* Lando, I can't *tell* him anything. All right?'

'Thank you, tai-pan, You won't regret it.' Wet with relief Profitable Choy took out a list of names. 'Here's all the expert assayists in Hong Kong. You like to choose one? I, er, I checked and they're all open to seven o'clock.'

Dunross smiled faintly. 'You're very sure of yourself, Profitable Choy.'

'Just try to keep ahead of the game, sir.'

Casey came out of the Struan Building and went to the waiting Rolls. At once Lim opened the door for her. She sank back into the deep cushions feeling nothing, knowing nothing except that her anguish was consuming her and any moment she would break, not even noticing Lim ease the car into the heavy traffic to head for the vehicular ferry.

Tears were very near. So much time before we leave, she thought. Everything packed and sent to the airplane. I'm checked out, all bills paid, but so much time still left.

For a moment she considered just stopping the car and walking off but that would have been worse, no privacy, no protection and she felt so terrible. Yet I've got to get out, be by myself. I've got to. Oh Jesus, Linc poor Linc. 'Lim,' she said on an impulse, 'go to the Peak.'

'Missee?'

'Just drive to the top of the Peak, to the lookout. Please?' she said, desperately trying to keep her voice ordinary. 'I've, I haven't been there. I want to see it before I go. Please.'

'Yes, Missee.'

Casey leaned back and closed her eyes against the tears that poured out silently.

90

6:45 P.M.:

It was almost sunset.

Up at Lo Wu, the central border village between the Colony and China, the usual crowds of Chinese were crossing the bridge in both directions. The bridge was barely fifty yards long and spanned a trickling muddy stream and yet those fifty yards, for some, were a million miles. At both ends were guard posts and immigration checkpoints and customs, and in the middle, a small removable barrier. Two Hong Kong police stood there and two PRC soldiers. Two train tracks went across the bridge.

In the old days trains came from Canton to Hong Kong and back again, nonstop, but now passenger trains stopped on either side and passengers crossed on foot. And the trains themselves went back the way they came. Freight trains from China went through without problem. Most days.

Each day hundreds of locals crossed the border as they would cross any road. Their fields or work was on both sides of the border and had been so for generations. These border people were a hardy, suspicious lot, hating change, hating interference, hating uniforms, hating police particularly and foreigners of every kind. A foreigner to them, as to most Chinese, was anyone not of their village. To them there was no border, could never be a border.

The Lo Wu bridge was one of the most sensitive single spots in all China—it and the other two crossing points. Of these, one was at Mau Kam Toh where cattle and vegetables came daily over a rickety bridge across this same stream that marked most of the border. The last, at the very eastern tip of the border, was at the fishing village of Tau Kok. Here the border was not

1419

marked but, by common consent, was said to run down the middle of the single village street.

These were China's only contact points with the West. Everything was meticulously controlled and monitored—by both sides. The tension and manner of the guards was a barometer.

Today the guards on the PRC side of Lo Wu had been jittery. Because of that, the Hong Kong side was nervous too, not knowing what to expect—perhaps a sudden closure, perhaps a sudden invasion like last year, the Colony existing at the whim of China. 'And that's a fact of life,' Chief Inspector Smyth muttered. Today he had been assigned here for special duty and he was standing uneasily near the police station that was discreetly set back a hundred yards from the real border so as not to offend or create waves. Christ, he thought, waves? One fart in London could start millions of refugees marching here—if the powers across the border decided that that tiny piece of wind was an affront to the dignity of China.

'Come on, for chrissake,' he said impatiently, his khaki shirt sticking to his back, his eyes on the road back to Hong Kong. The road was puddled. It curled away. Then, in the distance, he saw the police car approaching. Greatly relieved, he went to meet it. Armstrong got out. Then Brian Kwok. Smyth saluted Robert Armstrong with his swagger stick to cover his shock. Brian Kwok was in civilian clothes. There was a curious, vacant, petrified look in his eyes. 'Hello, Robert,' Smyth said.

'Hello. Sorry to be late,' Armstrong said.

'It's only a couple of minutes. Actually I was told sunset.' Smyth squinted westward. The sun was not yet down. He turned his attention back to Brian Kwok. It was hard to keep the contempt out of his face.

The tall, handsome Chinese took out a pack of cigarettes. His fingers trembled as he offered it to Smyth.

'No thanks,' Smyth said coldly. Armstrong took one. 'I thought you'd given up smoking?'

'I did. I started again.'

Brian Kwok laughed nervously. 'Afraid it's me. Robert's been trying to keep . . . to keep Crosse and his angels off my back.'

Neither man laughed.

'Is anyone coming? Anyone else?' Smyth asked.

'I don't think so. Not officially.' Armstrong looked around.

There were the usual gaping bystanders but they appeared haphazard. 'They're here though. Somewhere.' Both men felt the hackles on their necks rising. 'You can get on with it.'

Smyth took out a formal document. 'Wu Chu-toy, alias Brian Kar-shun Kwok, you are formally charged with espionage against Her Majesty's Government on behalf of a foreign power. Under the authority of the Deportation Order of Hong Kong you are formally ordered out of the Crown Colony. If you return you are formally warned you do so at your peril and are liable for arraignment and ·imprisonment at Her Majesty's pleasure.' Grimly Smyth handed him the paper.

Brian Kwok took it. It seemed to take him time to see and to hear, his senses dulled. 'Now . . . now what happens?'

Smyth said, 'You walk over that bloody bridge and go back to your pals.'

'Eh? You think I'm a fool? You think I believe you're, you're letting me go?' Brian Kwok spun on Armstrong. 'Robert, I keep telling you they're playing with me, with you, they'll never let me go free! You know that!'

'You're free, Brian.'

'No . . . no, I know what's happening. The moment I, the moment I'm almost there they'll pull me back, the torture of hope, that's it, isn't it?' There was a shrillness creeping into his voice, a fleck of foam at the corner of his lips. 'Of course! The torture of hope.'

'For chrissake, I've told you you're free! You're free to go,' Armstrong said, his voice hard, wanting to end it. 'Go for chrissake! Don't ask me why they're letting you go but they are. Go!'

Filled with disbelief, Brian Kwok wiped his mouth, started to speak, stopped. 'You're . . . it's a . . . it's a lie, has to be!'

'Go!'

'All right, I'll . . .' Brian Kwok went off a pace then stopped. They had not moved. 'You're, you really mean it?'

'Yes.'

Shakily Brian Kwok put out his hand to Smyth. Smyth looked at it, then into his face. 'If it was up to me I'd have you shot.'

A flash of hatred went over Kwok's face. 'What about you and graft? What about you selling police pro—'

'Don't let's go into that! H'eung yau's part of China!' Smyth snarled and Armstrong nodded uneasily, remembering the first 40,000 gambled on Saturday.

'A little feathering's an old Chinese custom,' Smyth continued, shaking with rage. 'Treason isn't. Fong-fong was one of my lads before he went to SI. Go get stuffed and get the hell across the bridge or I'll whip you across it!'

Brian Kwok began to speak, stopped. Bleakly he offered his hand to Armstrong. Armstrong shook it without friendship. 'That's just for old times' sake, for the Brian I used to know. I don't approve of traitors either.'

'I, I know I was drugged but thanks.' Brian Kwok backed away, still suspecting a trick, then turned. Every few seconds he looked back, petrified that they were coming after him. When his halting feet reached the bridge he broke into a frantic run. Tension skyrocketed. Police at the barrier did not stop him. Neither did the soldiers. Both sides, forewarned, pretended not to notice him. The crowds streaming across either side of the tracks, bicycles, pedestrians, carts, mostly laden, paid him no attention at all. At the other side of the barrier, Brian Kwok skidded to a stop and turned back.

'We'll win, we'll, we'll win you know,' he called back to them, his chest heaving. 'We will!' Then still suspecting a trick, he hunched down and fled into China. Near the train they saw a nondescript group of people intercept him but now it was too far away to see clearly. Tension on the bridge subsided. The sun began to set.

In the small observation tower atop the police station, Roger Crosse watched with high-powered binoculars. He was well concealed. Beside him was an SI operator with a telescopic camera, equally concealed. His face closed. One of the men meeting Brian Kwok was Tsu-yan, the missing millionaire.

The sun was almost under the western seas. Casey was at the Peak lookout, all Hong Kong spread below, lights on the gloaming, part of the city and Kowloon blood-colored, part already dark with deep shadows and blazing highlights. The sun vanished and night, true night began.

But she saw none of the beauty of it. Her face was wet with the tears that still coursed. She was leaning on the railing at the far

1422

corner, oblivious. The other sightseers and people waiting at the nearby bus stops left her alone—too interested in their own affairs.

'By all the gods I made a fortune today. . . .'

'I bought in first thing and doubled my fornicating money. . . .'

'*Ayeeyah* so did I, and I spent most of the day negotiating a loan from Best Bank against my portfolio. . . .'

'Thank all gods the Middle Kingdom bailed out those stupid foreign devils . . .'

'I bought Noble House at 20. . . .' .

'Did you hear they dug out two more bodies at Kotewall and now the count's sixty-seven dead. . . .'

'Joss! Isn't it wonderful about the market! Old Blind Tung's prediction came true again. . . .'

'Did you hear about my sister, Third Toiletmaid Fung from Great Hotel? She and her syndicate bought at the darkest time and now she's a millionaire. . . .'

Casey heard nothing, saw nothing, misery overwhelming her. People came and went, a few lovers. The only Europeans were tourists with their cameras. Casey hid from them as best she could.

'Say, can I help?' one of them said.

'No, no thank you,' she replied, her voice flat, not looking at him, helpless to stop the tears.

I have to stop, she thought. I have to stop. I have to begin again. I have to begin again and be strong and live, for me and for Linc. I've got to guard him and his, I've got to be strong, be strong.

But how?

'I won't let go,' she told herself aloud. I won't. I have to think.

I have to think about what the tai-pan said. Not about marriage, oh Linc, not about that. I have to think about Orlanda.

'Is it too much to hope they'd be friends?' Did he really say that?

What to do about her?

Bury her. She took Linc away from me. Yes. But that was within my rules, the rules I set down. Ian's right. She's not like Quillan and it was Linc—he fell for her, he went out with her. She's not like Quillan Gornt.

Quillan. What about him? He had come to the hotel this afternoon, again offering her whatever help she needed. She had thanked him and refused. 'I'm okay, Quillan. I have to work this out myself. No, please don't see me off. Please. I'll be back in thirty days, maybe. Then I'll be more sensible.'

'You're signing with Struan's?'

'Yes. Yes, that's what I want to do. Sorry.'

'No need to be sorry. You've been warned. But that doesn't preclude dinner the first night you're back. Yes?'

'Yes.'

Oh Quillan, what to do about you?

Nothing for thirty days. Linc must have the next thirty days. Totally. I have to protect him against the vultures.

Seymour Steigler for one. This morning he had come to her suite. 'Hey Casey, I'll get the coffin arranged and—'

'It's done, everything's done.'

'That a fact? Great. Listen, I'm all packed. Jannelli can take my bags and I'll be at the airplane in good time so we c—'

'No. I'm taking Linc home alone.'

'But hell, Casey, we've got a lot to talk about. There's his will, there's the Par-Con deal, we got time now to figure it good. We can delay and maybe get us a few extra points. We—'

'It can all wait. I'll see you back in L.A. Take off a couple of days, Seymour. Be back next Monday.'

'Monday? For chrissake there's a million things to do! Linc's affairs'll take a year to untangle. We gotta get counsel fast. Sure, the best in town. I'll do that first thing, the best. Don't forget there's his widow and his kids. She'll sue on their behalf, of course she'll sue—and then there's you! For chrissake you're entitled to a fat share. We'll sue too, haven't you been like a wife to him for seven ye—'

'Seymour, you're fired! Get your ass out of here an—'

'What the hell's with you? I'm only thinking of your legal rights an—'

'Don't you hear, Seymour? You're fired!'

'You can't fire me. I've got rights. I got a contract!'

'You're a son of a bitch. You'll get top dollar to settle your contract but if you take after me or Linc or Linc's affairs I'll see to it you get nothing. Nothing. Now get the hell out of here!'

Casey wiped away her tears, remembering her exploding

rage. Well he is a son of a bitch. I was never sure before but I am now. I'm glad I fired him. I'll bet any money he'll come sniffing around like a hyena. Sure. I'll bet he'll go see the ex-Mrs. Bartlett if he hasn't already called her and work her into a frenzy, to represent her brood to attack Par-Con and Linc. Sure, I'll bet any money I'll see him in court, one way or another.

Well, God help me, I swear he won't beat me. I'll protect Linc whatever.

Forget that bastard, Casey. Forget the battles you're going to fight, concentrate on the now. What about Orlanda? Linc, Linc liked her—loved her maybe. Did he? I don't know for sure. And never will, not now.

Orlanda.

Should I go see her?

91

Orlanda was sitting in the dark of her room at the Mandarin Hotel staring out at the night. Her grief was spent.

Joss about Linc, she told herself for the ten thousandth time. Joss. Now everything's as before. Everything has to start again. The gods laughed at me again. Perhaps there'll be another chance—of course there'll be another chance. There are other men . . . Oh God! Don't worry, everything will be as it was. Quillan said not to worry, my allowance would contin—

The phone jangled, startling her. 'Hello?'

'Orlanda? It's Casey.' Orlanda sat bolt upright, astonished. 'I'm leaving tonight but I wanted to see you before I go. Is that possible? I'm downstairs.'

Her enemy calling her? Why? To gloat? But they'd both lost. 'Yes, Casey,' she said hesitantly. 'Would you like to come up? It's more private here. 363.'

'Sure. 363.'

Orlanda switched on a light and hurried to the bathroom to check her face. She saw sadness and recent tears—but no age. Not yet. But age is coming, she thought, a shiver of apprehension taking her. A comb to her hair and a little makeup on her eyes. Nothing else needed. Not yet.

Stop it! Age is inevitable. Be Asian! Be aware.

She slipped on her shoes. The waiting seemed long. Her heart was grinding. The bell rang. The door opened. Each saw the desolation of the other.

'Come in, Casey.'

'Thanks.'

The room was small. Casey noticed two small cases standing

1426

neatly beside the bed. 'You leaving too?' Her voice sounded far away to her.

'Yes. Yes I'm moving in with friends of my parents. The hotel's a, it's a bit expensive. My friends said I could stay with them until I can find another apartment. Please sit down.'

'But you're covered by insurance?'

Orlanda blinked. 'Insurance? No, no I don't think so. I never . . . no, I don't think so.'

Casey sighed. 'So you've lost everything?'

'Joss.' Orlanda half-shrugged. 'It doesn't matter. I have a little money in the bank and . . . I'm fine.' She saw the misery in Casey's face, and her compassion reached out. 'Casey,' she said quickly, 'about Linc. I wasn't trying to trap him, not for anything bad. Oh yes, I loved him and yes, I'd've done anything to marry him, but that's only fair, and honestly I believe I'd've been a wonderful wife for him, I'd've tried so very hard to be the best, honestly. I did love him and . . .' Again Orlanda shrugged her tiny shrug. 'You know. Sorry.'

'Yes, yes I know. No need to be sorry.'

'The first time I met you at Aberdeen, the night of the fire,' Orlanda said, rushing on, 'I thought how foolish Linc was, perhaps you were for not . . .' She sighed. 'Perhaps it's as you said, Casey, there's nothing to talk about. Now most of all.' The tears began again. And her tears, the reality of them, brought tears from Casey.

For a moment they sat there, the two women. Then Casey found a tissue, dried her eyes, feeling awful, nothing resolved, wanting now to finish quickly what she had begun. She took out an envelope. 'Here's a check. It's for $10,000 U.S. I th—'

Orlanda gasped. 'I don't want your money! I don't want anything fr—'

'It's not from me. It's Linc's. Listen a moment.' Casey told her what Dunross had said about Bartlett. All of it. The repeating of it tearing her anew. 'That's what Linc said. I think it was you he wanted to marry. Maybe I'm wrong. I don't know. Even so, he'd want you to have some drop . . . some protection.'

Orlanda felt her heart about to burst at the irony of it all. 'Linc said "best man"? Truly?'

'Yes.'

'And to be friends? He wanted us to be friends?'

'Yes,' Casey told her, not knowing if she was doing the right thing, what Linc would have wanted. But sitting here now, seeing the tender youthful beauty, the wide eyes, exquisite skin that needed no makeup, perfect figure, again she could not blame her or blame Linc. It was my fault, not his and not hers. And I know Linc wouldn't have left her destitute. So I can't. For him. He wanted us to be friends. Maybe we can be. 'Why don't we try?' she said. 'Listen, Hong Kong's no place for you. Why not try some other place?'

'I can't. I'm locked in here, Casey. I've no training. I'm nothing. My B.S. means nothing.' The tears began again. 'I'm just . . . I'd go mad punching a clock.'

On a sudden impulse Casey said, 'Why not try the States? Maybe I could help you find a job.'

'What?'

'Yes. Perhaps in fashion—I don't know what exactly but I'll try.'

Orlanda was staring at her incredulously. 'You'd help me, really help me?'

'Yes.' Casey put the envelope and her card on the table and got up, her whole body aching. 'I'll try.'

Orlanda went to her and put her arms around her. 'Oh thank you, Casey, thank you.'

Casey hugged her back, their tears mixing.

The night was dark now with little light from the small moon that came through the high clouds from time to time. Roger Crosse walked silently up to the half-hidden gate in the tall walls that surrounded Government House and used his key. He locked the gate behind him, walked quickly along the path, keeping to the shadows. Near the house he detoured and went to the east side, down some steps to a basement door and took out another key.

This door swung open, equally quietly. The armed sentry, a Gurkha, held his rifle ready. 'Password, sir!'

Crosse gave it. The sentry saluted and stepped aside. At the far end of the corridor Crosse knocked. The door was opened by the governor's aide. 'Evening, Superintendent.'

'I hope I haven't kept you waiting?'

'No, not at all.' This man led the way through communicating cellars to a thick iron door set into a concrete box that was crudely constructed in the middle of the big main cellar, wine racks nearby. He took out the single key and unlocked it. The door was very heavy. Crosse went inside alone and closed the door after him. Once inside, the door barred, he relaxed. Now he was totally safe from prying eyes and prying ears. This was the Holy of Holies, a conference room for very private conversations, the concrete room and communications center laboriously built by trusted SI officers, British only, to ensure against enemy listening devices being inserted into the walls— the whole structure tested weekly by Special Branch experts—in case some were somehow infiltrated.

In one corner was the complicated, highly sophisticated transmitter that fed signals into the unbreachable code scrambler, thence to the complex of antenna atop Government House, thence to the stratosphere, and thence to Whitehall.

Crosse switched it on. There was a comforting hum. 'The minister, please. This is Asian One.' It gave him great pleasure to use his inner code name.

'Yes, Asian One?'

'Tsu-yan was one of the persons meeting the spy, Brian Kwok.'

'Ah! So we can strike him off the list.'

'Both of them, sir. They're isolated now. On Saturday, the defector Joseph Yu was seen crossing the border.'

'Damn! You'd better have a team assigned to monitor him. Do we have fellows at their atomic center at Siankiang?'

'No sir. However there's a rumor Dunross is going to meet Mr. Yu in Canton in a month.'

'Ah, what about Dunross?'

'He's loyal—but he'll never work for us.'

'What about Sinders?'

'He performed well. I do not consider him a security risk.'

'Good. What about the *Ivanov*?'

'She sailed at noon. We haven't found Suslev's body—it'll take weeks to sift and dig out that wreckage. I'm afraid we may never find him in one piece. With Plumm gone too we'll have to rethink Sevrin.'

'It's too good a ploy not to have in existence, Roger.'

'Yes, sir. The other side will think so too. When Suslev's replacement arrives I'll see what they have in mind, then we can formulate a plan.'

'Good. What about deVille?'

'He is to be transferred to Toronto. Please inform the RCMP. Next, about the nuclear carrier: Her complement is 5,500 officers and men, 83,350 tons, eight reactors, top speed sixty-two knots, forty-two F-4 Phantom IIs each with nuclear capability, two Hawks Mark V. Curiously her only defense against an attack is one bank of SAMs on her starboard side . . .'

Crosse continued to give his report, very pleased with himself, loving his work, loving being on both sides, on three, he reminded himself. Yes, triple agent, with money to spare, both sides not trusting him completely yet needing him, praying he was on their side—*not theirs*.

Sometimes I almost wonder myself, he thought with a smile.

In the terminal building at Kai Tak, Armstrong was leaning heavily against the information counter, watching the door, feeling rotten. Crowds were milling as usual. To his surprise, he saw Peter Marlowe come in with Fleur Marlowe and their two children, dolls and small suitcases in their hands. Fleur was pale and drawn. Marlowe too. He was laden with suitcases.

'Hello, Peter,' Armstrong said.

'Hello, Robert. You're working late.'

'No, I've, er, I've just seen Mary off. She's off on a vacation to England for a month. Evening, Mrs. Marlowe. I was sorry to hear.'

'Oh, thank you, Superintendent. I'm qu—'

'We're going to Binkok,' the four-year-old interrupted gravely. 'That's in Minland.'

'Oh come along, silly,' her sister said. 'It's Bunkok in Mainland. That's China,' she added importantly to Armstrong. 'We're on vacation too. Mummy's been sick.'

Peter Marlowe smiled tiredly, his face creased. 'Bangkok for a week, Robert. A holiday for Fleur. Old Doc Tooley said it was important for her to get a rest.' He stopped as the two children began to squabble. 'Quiet, you two! Darling,' he said to his wife, 'you check us in. I'll catch you up.'

Of course. Come along. Oh do behave, both of you!' She walked off, the two children skittering ahead.

'Won't be much of a holiday for her, I'm afraid,' Peter Marlowe said. Then he dropped his voice. 'One of my friends told me to pass on that the meeting in Macao of the narcotics villains is this Thursday.'

'Do you know where?'

'No. But White Powder Lee's supposed to be one of them. And an American. Banastasio. That's the rumor.'

'Thanks. And?'

'That's all.'

'Thanks, Peter. Have a good trip. Listen, there's a fellow in the Bangkok police you should look up. Inspector Samanthajal —tell him I said so.'

'Thanks. Rotten about Linc Bartlett and the others, wasn't it? Christ, I was invited to that party too.'

'Joss.'

'Yes. But that doesn't help him or them, does it? Poor buggers! See you next week.'

Armstrong watched the tall man walk away, then went back to the information counter and leaned against it, continuing to wait, sick at heart.

His mind inexorably turned to Mary. Last night they had had a grinding row, mostly over John Chen, but more because of his last few days, Brian and the Red Room and borrowing the money, betting it all on Pilot Fish, waiting in agony, then winning and putting all the $40,000 back in his desk drawer— never a need to touch another penny—paying off his debts and buying her a ticket home but another row tonight and her saying, 'You forgot our anniversary! That's not much to remember is it? Oh I hate this bloody place and bloody Werewolves and bloody everything. Don't expect me back!'

Dully he lit a cigarette, loathing the taste yet liking it. The air was humid again, sour. Then he saw Casey come in. He stubbed out his cigarette and went to intercept her, the heaviness in her walk saddening him. 'Evening,' he said, feeling very tired.

'Oh, oh hello, Superintendent. How, how're things?'

'Fine. I'll see you through.'

'Oh that's kind of you.'

'I was damned sorry to hear about Mr. Bartlett.'

'Yes. Yes, thank you.'

They walked on. He knew better than to talk. What was there to say? Pity, he thought, liking her, admiring her courage, proved at the fire, proved on the slope, proved now, keeping her voice firm when all of her is torn up.

There were no customs outwardbound. The Emigration officer stamped her passport and handed it back with untoward politeness. 'Please have a safe journey and return soon.' The death of Bartlett had been headlines, among the sixty-seven.

Along corridors to the VIP lounge. Armstrong opened the door for her. To his surprise and her astonishment Dunross was there. The glass door to Gate 16 and the tarmac was open, *Yankee 2* just beyond.

'Oh. Oh hello, Ian,' she said. 'But I didn't want you to s—'

'Had to, Casey. Sorry. I've a little unfinished business with you and I had to meet a plane. My cousin's coming back from Taiwan—he went to fix the factory sites pending your approval.' Dunross glanced at Armstrong. 'Evening, Robert. How're things?'

'Same, same as usual.' Armstrong put out his hand to Casey and smiled wearily. 'I'll leave you now. Have a safe trip. Everything's cleared as soon as you're aboard.'

'Thank you, Superintendent. I wish . . . thank you.'

Armstrong nodded to Dunross and began to leave.

'Robert, did that consignment get delivered to Lo Wu?'

He pretended to think. 'Yes, yes I believe it did.' He saw the relief.

'Thanks. Can you hang on a moment? I'd like to hear about it.'

'Certainly,' Armstrong replied. 'I'll be outside.'

When they were alone Dunross handed her a thin envelope. 'This is a cashier's check for $750,000 U.S. I bought Struan's for you at 9.50 and sold at 28.'

'What?'

'Well I, er, I bought in for us first thing—at 9.50 as I promised I would. Your part of the deal was three quarters of a million. Struan's made millions. I made millions, so did Phillip and Dianne, I let them in early too.'

She could not take it in. 'Sorry, I don't understand.'

He smiled and repeated what he had said, then added,

'There's also another check—for a quarter of a million dollars U.S. against your share of the General Stores takeover.'

She gasped. 'I don't believe you.'

A smile went over him fleetingly. 'Yes. In thirty days another three quarters of a million will be on call. In sixty days we could advance another half million if need be.'

Behind her, in the cockpit of *Yankee 2*, Jannelli fired the first jet engine. It shrieked into life.

'Is that enough to tide you over?' he asked.

Her mouth worked but no sound came out, then, 'A quarter million?'

'Yes. Actually it comes to a million—these two checks. By the way, don't forget you're tai-pan of Par-Con now. That's Linc's real gift to you. *Tai-pan*. The money's unimportant.' He grinned at her and gave her a brusque hug. 'Good luck, Casey. See you in thirty days. Eh?' The second engine shrieked into life.

'A million U.S.?'

'Yes. I'll get Dawson to send you some tax advice. As your profit is Hong Kong money I'm sure there are legitimate ways to avoid—not evade—taxes.' Another engine howled awake.

She was staring at him, speechless. The door of the VIP lounge opened and a tall man came in breezily. 'Hello, Ian! They told me I could find you here.'

'Hello, David. Casey, this is David MacStruan, my cousin.'

Blankly Casey looked at him, half-smiled, but did not really notice him. 'Hello. But, Ian, you mean that—you mean what you said?'

'Of course.' The last engine exploded into life. 'You'd better go aboard! See you next month.'

'What? Oh. Oh, but I, yes, see you!' Dazed, she put the envelope in her bag, turned around and left.

They watched her go up the gangway. 'So that's the famous Casey,' David MacStruan said thoughtfully. He was as tall as Dunross but a few years younger, redheaded, with curious slanting, almost Asian eyes, though green, his face very used, most of the three smaller fingers of his left hand missing where the shrouds of his parachute had mashed them.

'Yes. Yes, that's Kamalian Ciranoush Tcholok.'

'Smasher!'

'More than that. Think of her as the Hag.'

MacStruan whistled. 'Is she that good?'

'She could be, with the right training.'

Aboard the airplane Svensen closed the cabin door, locked it. 'You want anything, Casey?' he asked kindly, very concerned for her.

'No,' she said helplessly. 'Just leave me, Sven. I'll, I'll call if I need anything. Okay?'

'Sure.' He closed the door.

Now she was alone. Numbly she buckled on her seat belt and looked out of a porthole. Through her tears she saw Dunross and the other man whose name she did not remember wave. She waved back but they did not see her.

Clouds went over the moon. The engines picked up tempo, the airplane taxied away, lined up and shrieked into the black sky, climbing steeply. Casey noticed none of it, Dunross's words still pounding in her brain, over and over, taking her apart and putting her back together again.

Tai-pan. That's Linc's real gift to you, he had said. Tai-pan, the money's unimportant.

Yes, yes that's true but . . .

But . . .

What was it Linc said that time, that first day at the stock market? Wasn't it: 'If Gornt wins, we win. If Dunross wins, we win. Either way we become the Noble House—which's why we're here.'

The darkness lifted off her. Her mind cleared. The tears stopped.

That's what he wanted, truly wanted, she thought, her excitement growing. He wanted us to be the Noble House. Sure. Maybe that's what I can do for him in return, make that his epitaph—*the Noble House*.

'Oh Linc,' she said joyously. 'It's worth a try. Isn't it?'

The jetliner barreled into the high clouds, continuing its faultless departure. The night was warm and very dark, the moon crescent, the wind kind.

Below was the Island.

Dunross came out on to the Peak Road fast, heading for home, the traffic light and the engine sounding sweet. On a sudden impulse he changed direction and pulled up at the Peak lookout and stood at the rail, alone.

Hong Kong was a sea of lights. Over in Kowloon another jet took off from the floodlit runway. A few stars came through the high clouds.

'Christ, it's so good to be alive,' he said.

JAMES CLAVELL

KING RAT

During the Second World War the key British bastion in Asia was Singapore. The fall of the city meant the loss of the East Indies – and of the Allied armies. Nearly 150,000 young men were captured and only one in fifteen was to survive the three and a half long years to VJ day.

Set in Changi, the most notorious POW camp in Asia, KING RAT is an heroic story of survival. This fictionalised account comes from a master story-teller who lived through those years as a young soldier. KING RAT shows how only one man in fifteen had the strength, luck or cleverness that meant survival, why only one man was King . . . and why he was an American.

'James Clavell is a brilliant observer . . . he is also a spellbinding story-teller . . . one of the best five books of fiction this year'

New York Times

'Terrifyingly exciting suspense'

Ian Fleming

CORONET BOOKS

JAMES CLAVELL

TAI-PAN

Dirk Struan was the ruler – the Tai-pan – of the most powerful trading company in the Far East. He was also a pirate, an opium smuggler, a master manipulator of men, a ruthless intriguer and a mighty lover.

Set in the turbulent days of the founding of Hong Kong in the 1840's, Tai-pan is the exciting story of a man and an island. For Dirk Struan was determined to transform the barren island called Hong Kong into the brightest jewel of the British Empire. And the opium run was the surest and most dangerous way for him to achieve riches beyond imagination . . .

'Packed with action . . . gaudy and flamboyant with blood and sin, treachery and conspiracy, sex and murder . . . Grand entertainment'

New York Times

'Intensely readable and exciting'

Sunday Telegraph

'The most stirring and exciting historical novel I have ever read'

Robin Moore,
author of *The French Connection*

CORONET BOOKS

JAMES CLAVELL

SHŌGUN

Here from the world's master story teller is a magnificent saga of feudal Japan, a stunningly dramatic re-creation of an exotic and alien world.

JOHN BLACKTHORNE, whose dream is to be the first Englishman to circumnavigate the globe, to wrest control of the trade between Japan and China from the Portuguese, and to return home a man of wealth and position.

TORANAGA, the most powerful feudal lord in Japan, who strives and schemes to seize ultimate power by becoming Shōgun – supreme military dictator – and to unite the warring samurai fiefdoms under his own masterful and farsighted leadership.

LADY MARIKO, a Catholic convert whose conflicting loyalties to the Church and her country are compounded when she falls in love with Blackthorne, the barbarian intruder.

'An extraordinary performance . . . one of the major works of fiction this year'

Publishers Weekly

'SHŌGUN does for Japan what *Gone With the Wind* did for the South'

Time

CORONET BOOKS

JAMES CLAVELL

NOBLE HOUSE is the fourth novel in the Asian saga that so far consists of:

1600 A.D.	....	Shōgun
1841 A.D.	....	Tai-Pan
1945 A.D.	....	King Rat
1963 A.D.	....	Noble House